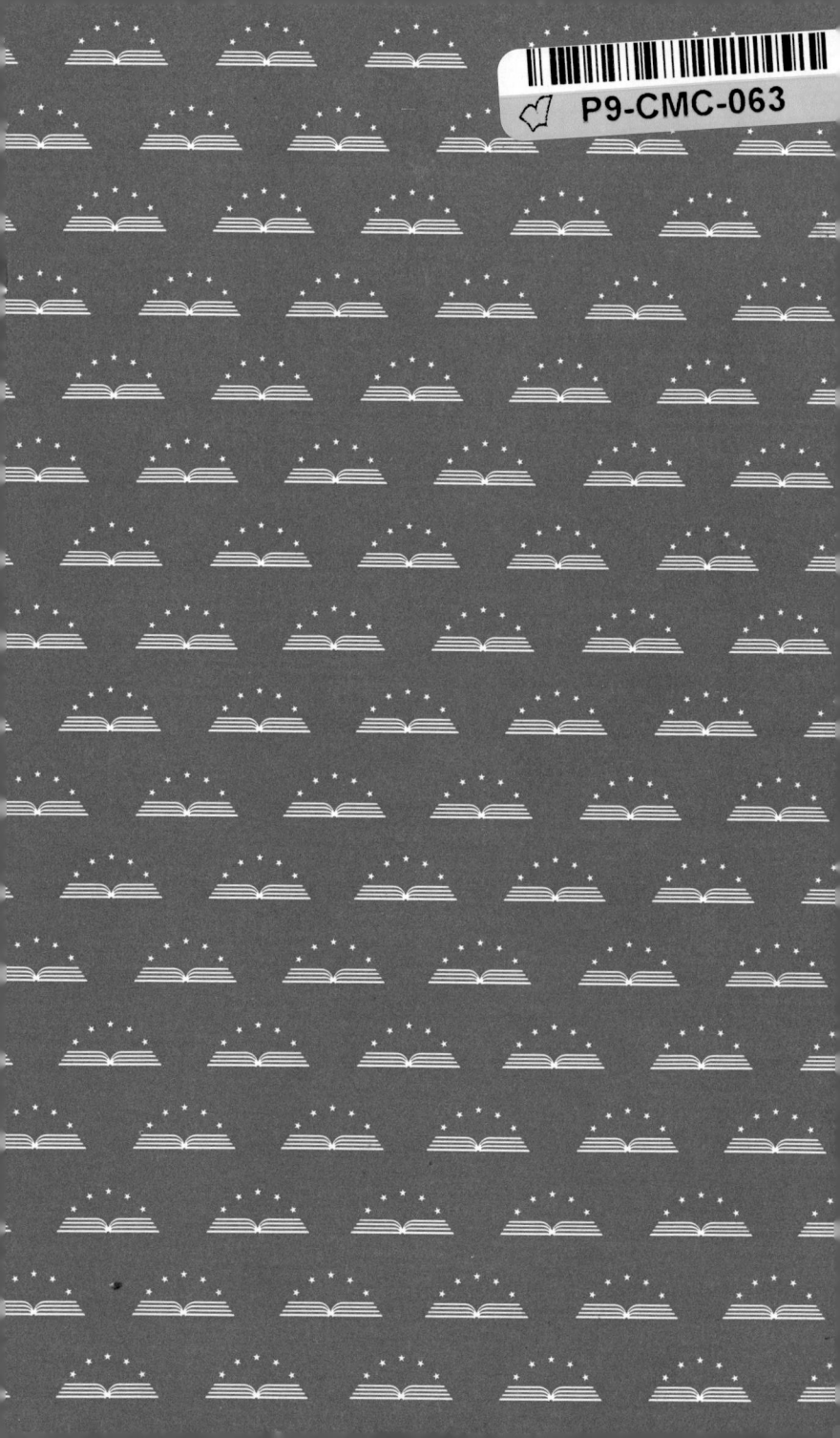

FLANNERY O'CONNOR

FLANNERY O'CONNOR

COLLECTED WORKS

Wise Blood
A Good Man Is Hard to Find
The Violent Bear It Away
Everything That Rises Must Converge
Stories and Occasional Prose
Letters

R O 3 4 0 9 8

THE LIBRARY OF AMERICA

813.54
O

Second Printing
The Library of America—39
Manufactured in the United States of America

*Grateful acknowledgment is made to the
National Endowment for the Humanities, the Ford Foundation,
and the Andrew W. Mellon Foundation for their
generous financial support of this series.*

*The publishers wish to thank
Robert Giroux, the Estate of Flannery O'Connor, and
the Ina Dillard Russell Library of Georgia College for
the use of Flannery O'Connor materials.*

Contents

WISE BLOOD

FOR REGINA

Chapter 1

HAZEL MOTES sat at a forward angle on the green plush train seat, looking one minute at the window as if he might want to jump out of it, and the next down the aisle at the other end of the car. The train was racing through tree tops that fell away at intervals and showed the sun standing, very red, on the edge of the farthest woods. Nearer, the plowed fields curved and faded and the few hogs nosing in the furrows looked like large spotted stones. Mrs. Wally Bee Hitchcock, who was facing Motes in the section, said that she thought the early evening like this was the prettiest time of day and she asked him if he didn't think so too. She was a fat woman with pink collars and cuffs and pear-shaped legs that slanted off the train seat and didn't reach the floor.

He looked at her a second and, without answering, leaned forward and stared down the length of the car again. She turned to see what was back there but all she saw was a child peering around one of the sections and, farther up at the end of the car, the porter opening the closet where the sheets were kept.

"I guess you're going home," she said, turning back to him again. He didn't look, to her, much over twenty, but he had a stiff black broad-brimmed hat on his lap, a hat that an elderly country preacher would wear. His suit was a glaring blue and the price tag was still stapled on the sleeve of it.

He didn't answer her or move his eyes from whatever he was looking at. The sack at his feet was an army duffel bag and she decided that he had been in the army and had been released and that now he was going home. She wanted to get close enough to see what the suit had cost him but she found herself squinting instead at his eyes, trying almost to look into them. They were the color of pecan shells and set in deep sockets. The outline of a skull under his skin was plain and insistent.

She felt irked and wrenched her attention loose and squinted at the price tag. The suit had cost him $11.98. She felt that that placed him and looked at his face again as if she were fortified against it now. He had a nose like a shrike's bill

3

and a long vertical crease on either side of his mouth; his hair looked as if it had been permanently flattened under the heavy hat, but his eyes were what held her attention longest. Their settings were so deep that they seemed, to her, almost like passages leading somewhere and she leaned halfway across the space that separated the two seats, trying to see into them. He turned toward the window suddenly and then almost as quickly turned back again to where his stare had been fixed.

What he was looking at was the porter. When he had first got on the train, the porter had been standing between the two cars—a thick-figured man with a round yellow bald head. Haze had stopped and the porter's eyes had turned toward him and away, indicating which car he was to go into. When he didn't go, the porter said, "To the left," irritably, "to the left," and Haze had moved on.

"Well," Mrs. Hitchcock said, "there's no place like home."

He gave her a glance and saw the flat of her face, reddish under a cap of fox-colored hair. She had got on two stops back. He had never seen her before that. "I got to go see the porter," he said. He got up and went toward the end of the car where the porter had begun making up a berth. He stopped beside him and leaned on a seat arm, but the porter didn't look at him. He was pulling a wall of the section farther out.

"How long does it take you to make one up?"

"Seven minutes," the porter said, not looking at him.

Haze sat down on the seat arm. He said, "I'm from Eastrod."

"That isn't on this line," the porter said. "You on the wrong train."

"Going to the city," Haze said. "I said I was raised in Eastrod."

The porter didn't say anything.

"Eastrod," Haze said, louder.

The porter jerked the shade down. "You want your berth made up now, or what you standing there for?" he asked.

"Eastrod," Haze said. "Near Melsy."

The porter wrenched one side of the seat flat. "I'm from Chicago," he said. He wrenched the other side down. When he bent over, the back of his neck came out in three bulges.

"Yeah, I bet you are," Haze said with a leer.

"Your feet in the middle of the aisle. Somebody going to want to get by you," the porter said, turning suddenly and brushing past.

Haze got up and hung there a few seconds. He looked as if he were held by a rope caught in the middle of his back and attached to the train ceiling. He watched the porter move in a fine controlled lurch down the aisle and disappear at the other end of the car. He knew him to be a Parrum nigger from Eastrod. He went back to his section and folded into a slouched position and settled one foot on a pipe that ran under the window. Eastrod filled his head and then went out beyond and filled the space that stretched from the train across the empty darkening fields. He saw the two houses and the rust-colored road and the few Negro shacks and the one barn and the stall with the red and white CCC snuff ad peeling across the side of it.

"Are you going home?" Mrs. Hitchcock asked.

He looked at her sourly and gripped the black hat by the brim. "No, I ain't," he said in a sharp high nasal Tennessee voice.

Mrs. Hitchcock said neither was she. She told him she had been a Miss Weatherman before she married and that she was going to Florida to visit her married daughter, Sarah Lucile. She said it seemed like she had never had time to take a trip that far off. The way things happened, one thing after another, it seemed like time went by so fast you couldn't tell if you were young or old.

He thought he could tell her she was old if she asked him. He stopped listening to her after a while. The porter passed back up the aisle and didn't look at him. Mrs. Hitchcock lost her train of talk. "I guess you're on your way to visit somebody?" she asked.

"Going to Taulkinham," he said and ground himself into the seat and looked at the window. "Don't know nobody there, but I'm going to do some things.

"I'm going to do some things I never have done before," he said and gave her a sidelong glance and curled his mouth slightly.

She said she knew an Albert Sparks from Taulkinham. She said he was her sister-in-law's brother-in-law and that he . . .

"I ain't from Taulkinham," he said. "I said I'm going there, that's all." Mrs. Hitchcock began to talk again but he cut her short and said, "That porter was raised in the same place where I was raised but he says he's from Chicago."

Mrs. Hitchcock said she knew a man who lived in Chi . . .

"You might as well go one place as another," he said. "That's all I know."

Mrs. Hitchcock said well that time flies. She said she hadn't seen her sister's children in five years and she didn't know if she'd know them if she saw them. There were three of them, Roy, Bubber, and John Wesley. John Wesley was six years old and he had written her a letter, dear Mammadoll. They called her Mammadoll and her husband Papadoll . . .

"I reckon you think you been redeemed," he said.

Mrs. Hitchcock snatched at her collar.

"I reckon you think you been redeemed," he repeated.

She blushed. After a second she said yes, life was an inspiration and then she said she was hungry and asked him if he didn't want to go into the diner. He put on the fierce black hat and followed her out of the car.

The dining car was full and people were waiting to get in it. He and Mrs. Hitchcock stood in line for a half-hour, rocking in the narrow passageway and every few minutes flattening themselves against the side to let a trickle of people through. Mrs. Hitchcock talked to the woman on the side of her. Hazel Motes looked at the wall. Mrs. Hitchcock told the woman about her sister's husband who was with the City Water Works in Toolafalls, Alabama, and the lady told about a cousin who had cancer of the throat. Finally they got almost up to the entrance of the diner and could see inside it. There was a steward beckoning people to places and handing out menus. He was a white man with greased black hair and a greased black look to his suit. He moved like a crow, darting from table to table. He motioned for two people and the line moved up so that Haze and Mrs. Hitchcock and the lady she was talking to were ready to go next. In a minute two more people left. The steward beckoned and Mrs. Hitchcock and the woman walked in and Haze followed them. The man stopped him and said, "Only two," and pushed him back to the doorway.

Haze's face turned an ugly red. He tried to get behind the next person and then he tried to get through the line to go back to the car he had come from but there were too many people bunched in the opening. He had to stand there while everyone around looked at him. No one left for a while. Finally a woman at the far end of the car got up and the steward jerked his hand. Haze hesitated and saw the hand jerk again. He lurched up the aisle, falling against two tables on the way and getting his hand wet in somebody's coffee. The steward placed him with three youngish women dressed like parrots.

Their hands were resting on the table, red-speared at the tips. He sat down and wiped his hand on the tablecloth. He didn't take off his hat. The women had finished eating and were smoking cigarettes. They stopped talking when he sat down. He pointed to the first thing on the menu and the steward, standing over him, said, "Write it down, sonny," and winked at one of the women; she made a noise in her nose. He wrote it down and the steward went away with it. He sat and looked in front of him, glum and intense, at the neck of the woman across from him. At intervals her hand holding the cigarette would pass the spot on her neck; it would go out of his sight and then it would pass again, going back down to the table; in a second a straight line of smoke would blow in his face. After it had blown at him three or four times, he looked at her. She had a bold game-hen expression and small eyes pointed directly on him.

"If you've been redeemed," he said, "I wouldn't want to be." Then he turned his head to the window. He saw his pale reflection with the dark empty space outside coming through it. A boxcar roared past, chopping the empty space in two, and one of the women laughed.

"Do you think I believe in Jesus?" he said, leaning toward her and speaking almost as if he were breathless. "Well I wouldn't even if He existed. Even if He was on this train."

"Who said you had to?" she asked in a poisonous Eastern voice.

He drew back.

The waiter brought his dinner. He began eating slowly at first, then faster as the women concentrated on watching the muscles that stood out on his jaw when he chewed. He was eating something spotted with eggs and livers. He finished that and drank his coffee and then pulled his money out. The steward saw him but he wouldn't come total the bill. Every time he passed the table, he would wink at the women and stare at Haze. Mrs. Hitchcock and the lady had already finished and gone. Finally the man came and added up the bill. Haze shoved the money at him and then pushed past him out of the car.

For a while he stood between two train cars where there was fresh air of a sort and made a cigarette. Then the porter passed between the two cars. "Hey you Parrum," he called.

The porter didn't stop.

Haze followed him into the car. All the berths were made up. The man in the station in Melsy had sold him a berth because he said he would have to sit up all night in the coaches; he had sold him an upper one. Haze went to it and pulled his sack down and went into the men's room and got ready for the night. He was too full and he wanted to hurry and get in the berth and lie down. He thought he would lie there and look out the window and watch how the country went by a train at night. A sign said to get the porter to let you into the uppers. He stuck his sack up into his berth and then went to look for the porter. He didn't find him at one end of the car and he started back to the other. Going around the corner he ran into something heavy and pink; it gasped and muttered, "Clumsy!" It was Mrs. Hitchcock in a pink wrapper, with her hair in knots around her head. She looked at him with her eyes squinted nearly shut. The knobs framed her face like dark toadstools. She tried to get past him and he tried to let her but they were both moving the same way each time. Her face became purplish except for little white marks over it that didn't heat up. She drew herself stiff and stopped and said, "What IS the matter with you?" He slipped past her and dashed down the aisle and ran into the porter so that the porter fell down.

"You got to let me into the berth, Parrum," he said.

The porter picked himself up and went lurching down the aisle and after a minute he came lurching back again, stone-faced, with the ladder. Haze stood watching him while he put the ladder up; then he started up it. Halfway up, he turned and said, "I remember you. Your father was a nigger named Cash Parrum. You can't go back there neither, nor anybody else, not if they wanted to."

"I'm from Chicago," the porter said in an irritated voice. "My name is not Parrum."

"Cash is dead," Haze said. "He got the cholera from a pig."

The porter's mouth jerked down and he said, "My father was a railroad man."

Haze laughed. The porter jerked the ladder off suddenly with a wrench of his arm that sent the boy clutching at the blanket into the berth. He lay on his stomach for a few minutes and didn't move. After a while he turned and found the light and looked around him. There was no window. He was closed up in the thing except for a little space over the curtain. The top of the berth was low and curved over. He lay down and noticed that the curved top looked as if it were not quite closed; it looked as if it were closing. He lay there for a while, not moving. There was something in his throat like a sponge with an egg taste; he didn't want to turn over for fear it would move. He wanted the light off. He reached up without turning and felt for the button and snapped it and the darkness sank down on him and then faded a little with light from the aisle that came in through the foot of space not closed. He wanted it all dark, he didn't want it diluted. He heard the porter's footsteps coming down the aisle, soft into the rug, coming steadily down, brushing against the green curtains and fading up the other way out of hearing. Then after a while when he was almost asleep, he thought he heard them again coming back. His curtains stirred and the footsteps faded.

In his half-sleep he thought where he was lying was like a coffin. The first coffin he had seen with someone in it was his grandfather's. They had left it propped open with a stick of kindling the night it had sat in the house with the old man in it, and Haze had watched from a distance, thinking: he ain't going to let them shut it on him; when the time comes, his elbow is going to shoot into the crack. His grandfather had been a circuit preacher, a waspish old man who had ridden over three counties with Jesus hidden in his head like a stinger. When it was time to bury him, they shut the top of his box down and he didn't make a move.

Haze had had two younger brothers; one died in infancy and was put in a small box. The other fell in front of a mowing machine when he was seven. His box was about half the size of an ordinary one, and when they shut it, Haze ran and opened it up again. They said it was because he was heartbroken to part with his brother, but it was not; it was because he had thought, what if he had been in it and they had shut it on him.

He was asleep now and he dreamed he was at his father's burying again. He saw him humped over on his hands and knees in his coffin, being carried that way to the graveyard. "If I keep my can in the air," he heard the old man say, "nobody can shut nothing on me," but when they got his box to the hole, they let it drop down with a thud and his father flattened out like anybody else. The train jolted and stirred him half awake again and he thought, there must have been twenty-five people in Eastrod then, three Motes. Now there were no more Motes, no more Ashfields, no more Blasengames, Feys, Jacksons . . . or Parrums—even niggers wouldn't have it. Turning in the road, he saw in the dark the store boarded and the barn leaning and the smaller house half carted away, the porch gone and no floor in the hall.

It had not been that way when he was eighteen years old and had left it. Then there had been ten people there and he had not noticed that it had got smaller from his father's time. He had left it when he was eighteen years old because the army had called him. He had thought at first he would shoot his foot and not go. He was going to be a preacher like his grandfather and a preacher can always do without a foot. A preacher's power is in his neck and tongue and arm. His grandfather had traveled three counties in a Ford automobile. Every fourth Saturday he had driven into Eastrod as if he were just in time to save them all from Hell, and he was shouting before he had the car door open. People gathered around his Ford because he seemed to dare them to. He would climb up on the nose of it and preach from there and sometimes he would climb onto the top of it and shout down at them. They were like stones! he would shout. But Jesus had died to redeem them! Jesus was so soul-hungry that He had died, one death for all, but He would have died every soul's death for one! Did they understand that? Did they understand that for each stone soul, He would have died ten million deaths, had His arms and legs stretched on the cross and nailed ten million times for one of them? (The old man would point to his grandson, Haze. He had a particular disrespect for him because his own face was repeated almost exactly in the child's and seemed to mock him.) Did they know that even for that boy there, for that mean sinful unthinking boy standing there with his dirty hands clenching and unclenching at his sides, Jesus would die ten million deaths before He would let him lose his soul? He would chase him over the waters of sin! Did they doubt Jesus could walk on the waters of sin? That boy had been redeemed and Jesus wasn't going to leave him ever. Jesus would never let him forget he was redeemed. What did the sinner think there was to be gained? Jesus would have him in the end!

The boy didn't need to hear it. There was already a deep black wordless conviction in him that the way to avoid Jesus was to avoid sin. He knew by the time he was twelve years old that he was going to be a preacher. Later he saw Jesus move from tree to tree in the back of his mind, a wild ragged figure motioning him to turn around and come off into the dark where he was not sure of his footing, where he might be walking on the water and not know it and then suddenly know it and drown. Where he wanted to stay was in Eastrod with his two eyes open, and his hands always handling the familiar thing, his feet on the known track, and his tongue not too loose. When he was eighteen and the army called him, he saw the war as a trick to lead him into temptation, and he would have shot his foot except that he trusted himself to get back in a few months, uncorrupted. He had a strong confidence in his power to resist evil; it was something he had inherited, like his face, from his grandfather. He thought that if the government wasn't through with him in four months, he would leave anyway. He had thought, then when he was eighteen years old, that he would give them exactly four months of his time. He was gone four years; he didn't get back, even for a visit.

The only things from Eastrod he took into the army with him were a black Bible and a pair of silver-rimmed spectacles that had belonged to his mother. He had gone to a country school where he had learned to read and write but that it was wiser not to; the Bible was the only book he read. He didn't read it often but when he did he wore his mother's glasses. They tired his eyes so that after a short time he was always obliged to stop. He meant to tell anyone in the army who invited him to sin that he was from Eastrod, Tennessee, and that he meant to get back there and stay back there, that he was going to be a preacher of the gospel and that he wasn't going to have his soul damned by the government or by any foreign place it sent him to.

After a few weeks in the camp, when he had some friends—they were not actually friends but he had to live with them—he was offered the chance he had been waiting for; the invitation. He took his mother's glasses out of his pocket and put them on. Then he told them he wouldn't go with them for a million dollars and a feather bed to lie on; he said he was from Eastrod, Tennessee, and that he was not going to have his soul damned by the government or any foreign place they . . . but his voice cracked and he didn't finish. He only stared at them, trying to steel his face. His friends told him that nobody was interested in his goddam soul unless it was the priest and he managed to answer that no priest taking orders from no pope was going to tamper with his soul. They told him he didn't have any soul and left for their brothel.

He took a long time to believe them because he wanted to believe them. All he wanted was to believe them and get rid of it once and for all, and he saw the opportunity here to get rid of it without corruption, to be converted to nothing instead of to evil. The army sent him halfway around the world and forgot him. He was wounded and they remembered him long enough to take the shrapnel out of his chest—they said they took it out but they never showed it to him and he felt it still in there, rusted, and poisoning him—and then they sent him to another desert and forgot him again. He had all the time he could want to study his soul in and assure himself that it was not there. When he was thoroughly convinced, he saw that this was something that he had always known. The misery he had was a longing for home; it had nothing to do with Jesus. When the army finally let him go, he was pleased to think that he was still uncorrupted. All he wanted was to get back to Eastrod, Tennessee. The black Bible and his mother's glasses were still in the bottom of his duffel bag. He didn't read any book now but he kept the Bible because it had come from home. He kept the glasses in case his vision should ever become dim.

When the army had released him two days before in a city about three hundred miles north of where he wanted to be, he had gone immediately to the railroad station there and bought a ticket to Melsy, the nearest railroad stop to Eastrod. Then since he had to wait four hours for the train, he went into a dark dry-goods store near the station. It was a thin cardboard-smelling store that got darker as it got deeper. He went deep into it and was sold a blue suit and a dark hat. He had his army suit put in a paper sack and he stuffed it into a trashbox on the corner. Once outside in the light, the new suit turned glare-blue and the lines of the hat seemed to stiffen fiercely.

He was in Melsy at five o'clock in the afternoon and he caught a ride on a cotton-seed truck that took him more than half the distance to Eastrod. He walked the rest of the way and got there at nine o'clock at night, when it had just got dark. The house was as dark as the night and open to it and though he saw that the fence around it had partly fallen and that weeds were growing through the porch floor, he didn't realize all at once that it was only a shell, that there was nothing here but the skeleton of a house. He twisted an envelope and struck a match to it and went through all the empty rooms, upstairs and down. When the envelope burnt out, he lit another one and went through them all again. That night he slept on the floor in the kitchen, and a board fell on his head out of the roof and cut his face.

There was nothing left in the house but the chifforobe in the kitchen. His mother had always slept in the kitchen and had her walnut chifforobe in there. She had given thirty dollars for it and hadn't bought herself anything else big again. Whoever had got everything else, had left that. He opened all the drawers. There were two lengths of wrapping cord in the top one and nothing in the others. He was surprised nobody had come and stolen a chifforobe like that. He took the wrapping cord and tied it around the legs and through the floor boards and left a piece of paper in each of the drawers: THIS SHIFFER-ROBE BELONGS TO HAZEL MOTES. DO NOT STEAL IT OR YOU WILL BE HUNTED DOWN AND KILLED.

He thought about the chifforobe in his half-sleep and decided his mother would rest easier in her grave, knowing it was guarded. If she came looking any time at night, she would see. He wondered if she walked at night and came there ever. She would come with that look on her face, unrested and looking; the same look he had seen through the crack of her coffin. He had seen her face through the crack when they were shutting the top on her. He was sixteen then. He had seen the shadow that came down over her face and pulled her mouth down as if she wasn't any more satisfied dead than alive, as if she were going to spring up and shove the lid back and fly out and satisfy herself: but they shut it. She might have been going to fly out of there, she might have been going to spring. He saw her in his sleep, terrible, like a huge bat, dart from the closing, fly out of there, but it was falling dark on top of her, closing down all the time. From inside he saw it closing, coming closer closer down and cutting off the light and the room. He opened his eyes and saw it closing and he sprang up between the crack and wedged his head and shoulders through it and hung there, dizzy, with the dim light of the train slowly showing the rug below. He hung there over the top of the berth curtain and saw the porter at the other end of the car, a white shape in the darkness, standing there watching him and not moving.

"I'm sick!" he called. "I can't be closed up in this thing. Get me out!"

The porter stood watching him and didn't move.

"Jesus," Haze said, "Jesus."

The porter didn't move. "Jesus been a long time gone," he said in a sour triumphant voice.

Chapter 2

HE DIDN'T get to the city until six the next evening. That morning he had got off the train at a junction stop to get some air and while he had been looking the other way, the train had slid off. He had run after it but his hat had blown away and he had had to run in the other direction to save the hat. Fortunately, he had carried his duffel bag out with him lest someone should steal something out of it. He had to wait six hours at the junction stop until the right train came.

When he got to Taulkinham, as soon as he stepped off the train, he began to see signs and lights. PEANUTS, WESTERN UNION, AJAX, TAXI, HOTEL, CANDY. Most of them were electric and moved up and down or blinked frantically. He walked very slowly, carrying his duffel bag by the neck. His head turned to one side and then the other, first toward one sign and then another. He walked the length of the station and then he walked back as if he might be going to get on the train again. His face was stern and determined under the heavy hat. No one observing him would have known that he had no place to go. He walked up and down the crowded waiting room two or three times, but he did not want to sit on the benches there. He wanted a private place to go to.

Finally he pushed open a door at one end of the station where a plain black and white sign said, MEN'S TOILET. WHITE. He went into a narrow room lined on one side with washbasins and on the other with a row of wooden stalls. The walls of this room had once been a bright cheerful yellow but now they were more nearly green and were decorated with handwriting and with various detailed drawings of the parts of the body of both men and women. Some of the stalls had doors on them and on one of the doors, written with what must have been a crayon, was the large word, WELCOME, followed by three exclamation points and something that looked like a snake. Haze entered this one.

He had been sitting in the narrow box for some time, studying the inscriptions on the sides and door, before he noticed one that was to the left over the toilet paper. It was written in a drunken-looking hand. It said,

> Mrs. Leora Watts!
> 60 Buckley Road
> The friendliest bed in town!
>   Brother.

After a while he took a pencil out of his pocket and wrote down the address on the back of an envelope.

Outside he got in a yellow taxi and told the driver where he wanted to go. The driver was a small man with a big leather cap on his head and the tip of a cigar coming out from the center of his mouth. They had driven a few blocks before Haze noticed him squinting at him through the rear-view mirror. "You ain't no friend of hers, are you?" the driver asked.

"I never saw her before," Haze said.

"Where'd you hear about her? She don't usually have no preachers for company." He did not disturb the position of the cigar when he spoke; he was able to speak on either side of it.

"I ain't any preacher," Haze said, frowning. "I only seen her name in the toilet."

"You look like a preacher," the driver said. "That hat looks like a preacher's hat."

"It ain't," Haze said, and leaned forward and gripped the back of the front seat. "It's just a hat."

They stopped in front of a small one-story house between a filling station and a vacant lot. Haze got out and paid his fare through the window.

"It ain't only the hat," the driver said. "It's a look in your face somewheres."

"Listen," Haze said, tilting the hat over one eye, "I'm not a preacher."

"I understand," the driver said. "It ain't anybody perfect on this green earth of God's, preachers nor nobody else. And you can tell people better how terrible sin is if you know from your own personal experience."

Haze put his head in at the window, knocking the hat accidentally straight again. He seemed to have knocked his face straight too for it became completely expressionless. "Listen," he said, "get this: I don't believe in anything."

The driver took the stump of cigar out of his mouth. "Not in nothing at all?" he asked, leaving his mouth open after the question.

"I don't have to say it but once to nobody," Haze said.

The driver closed his mouth and after a second he returned the piece of cigar to it. "That's the trouble with you preachers," he said. "You've all got too good to believe in anything," and he drove off with a look of disgust and righteousness.

Haze turned and looked at the house he was going into. It was little more than a shack but there was a warm glow in one front window. He went up on the front porch and put his eye to a convenient crack in the shade, and found himself looking directly at a large white knee. After some time he moved away from the crack and tried the front door. It was not locked and he went into a small dark hall with a door on either side of it. The door to the left was cracked and let out a narrow shaft of light. He moved into the light and looked through the crack.

Mrs. Watts was sitting alone in a white iron bed, cutting her toenails with a large pair of scissors. She was a big woman with very yellow hair and white skin that glistened with a greasy preparation. She had on a pink nightgown that would better have fit a smaller figure.

Haze made a noise with the doorknob and she looked up and observed him standing behind the crack. She had a bold steady penetrating stare. After a minute, she turned it away from him and began cutting her toenails again.

He went in and stood looking around him. There was nothing much in the room but the bed and a bureau and a rocking chair full of dirty clothes. He went to the bureau and fingered a nail file and then an empty jelly glass while he looked into the yellowish mirror and watched Mrs. Watts, slightly distorted, grinning at him. His senses were stirred to the limit. He turned quickly and went to her bed and sat down on the far corner of it. He drew a long draught of air through one side of his nose and began to run his hand carefully along the sheet.

The pink tip of Mrs. Watts's tongue appeared and moistened her lower lip. She seemed just as glad to see him as if he had been an old friend but she didn't say anything.

He picked up her foot, which was heavy but not cold, and moved it about an inch to one side, and kept his hand on it.

Mrs. Watts's mouth split in a wide full grin that showed her teeth. They were small and pointed and speckled with green and there was a wide space between each one. She reached out and gripped Haze's arm just above the elbow. "You huntin' something?" she drawled.

If she had not had him so firmly by the arm, he might have leaped out the window. Involuntarily his lips formed the words, "Yes, mam," but no sound came through them.

"Something on your mind?" Mrs. Watts asked, pulling his rigid figure a little closer.

"Listen," he said, keeping his voice tightly under control, "I come for the usual business."

Mrs. Watts's mouth became more round, as if she were perplexed at this waste of words. "Make yourself at home," she said simply.

They stared at each other for almost a minute and neither moved. Then he said in a voice that was higher than his usual voice, "What I mean to have you know is: I'm no goddam preacher."

Mrs. Watts eyed him steadily with only a slight smirk. Then she put her other hand under his face and tickled it in a motherly way. "That's okay, son," she said. "Momma don't mind if you ain't a preacher."

Chapter 3

HﾠIS SECOND NIGHT in Taulkinham, Hazel Motes walked along down town close to the store fronts but not looking in them. The black sky was underpinned with long silver streaks that looked like scaffolding and depth on depth behind it were thousands of stars that all seemed to be moving very slowly as if they were about some vast construction work that involved the whole order of the universe and would take all time to complete. No one was paying any attention to the sky. The stores in Taulkinham stayed open on Thursday nights so that people could have an extra opportunity to see what was for sale. Haze's shadow was now behind him and now before him and now and then broken up by other people's shadows, but when it was by itself, stretching behind him, it was a thin nervous shadow walking backwards. His neck was thrust forward as if he were trying to smell something that was always being drawn away. The glary light from the store windows made his blue suit look purple.

After a while he stopped where a lean-faced man had a card table set up in front of a department store and was demonstrating a potato peeler. The man had on a small canvas hat and a shirt patterned with bunches of upside-down pheasants and quail and bronze turkeys. He was pitching his voice under the street noises so that it reached every ear distinctly as if in a private conversation. A few people gathered around. There were two buckets on the card table, one empty and the other full of potatoes. Between the two buckets there was a pyramid of green cardboard boxes and, on top of the stack, one peeler was open for demonstration. The man stood in front of this altar, pointing over it at various people. "How about you?" he said, pointing at a damp-haired pimpled boy. "You ain't gonna let one of these go by?" He stuck a brown potato in one side of the open machine. The machine was a square tin box with a red handle, and as he turned the handle, the potato went into the box and then in a second, backed out the other side, white. "You ain't gonna let one of these go by!" he said.

The boy guffawed and looked at the other people gathered around. He had yellow hair and a fox-shaped face.

"What's yer name?" the peeler man asked.

"Name Enoch Emery," the boy said and snuffled.

"Boy with a pretty name like that ought to have one of these," the man said, rolling his eyes, trying to warm up the others. Nobody laughed but the boy. Then a man standing across from Hazel Motes laughed, not a pleasant laugh but one that had a sharp edge. He was a tall cadaverous man with a black suit and a black hat on. He had on dark glasses and his cheeks were streaked with lines that looked as if they had been painted on and had faded. They gave him the expression of a grinning mandrill. As soon as he laughed, he began to move forward in a deliberate way, jiggling a tin cup in one hand and tapping a white cane in front of him with the other. Just behind him there came a child, handing out leaflets. She had on a black dress and a black knitted cap pulled down low on her forehead; there was a fringe of brown hair sticking out from it on either side; she had a long face and a short sharp nose. The man selling peelers was irritated when he saw the people looking at this pair instead of him. "How about you, you there," he said, pointing at Haze. "You'll never be able to get a bargain like this in any store."

Haze was looking at the blind man and the child. "Hey!" Enoch Emery said, reaching across a woman and punching his arm. "He's talking to you! He's talking to you!" Enoch had to punch him again before he looked at the peeler man.

"Whyn't you take one of these home to yer wife?" the peeler man was saying.

"Don't have one," Haze muttered, looking back at the blind man again.

"Well, you got a dear old mother, ain't you?"

"No."

"Well pshaw," the man said, with his hand cupped to the people, "he needs one theseyer just to keep him company."

Enoch Emery thought that was so funny that he doubled over and slapped his knee, but Hazel Motes didn't look as if he had heard it yet. "I'm going to give away a half a dozen peeled potatoes to the first person purchasing one theseyer machines," the man said. "Who's gonna step up first? Only a dollar and a half for a machine'd cost you three dollars in any store!" Enoch Emery began fumbling in his pockets. "You'll thank the day you ever stopped here," the man said, "you'll never forget it. Ever' one of you people purchasing one theseyer machines'll never forget it!"

The blind man was moving forward slowly, saying in a kind of garbled mutter, "Help a blind preacher. If you won't repent, give up a nickel. I can use it as good as you. Help a blind unemployed preacher. Wouldn't you rather have me beg than preach? Come on and give a nickel if you won't repent."

There were not many people gathered around but the ones who were began to move off. When the machine-seller saw this, he learned, glaring over the card table. "Hey you!" he yelled at the blind man. "What you think you doing? Who you think you are, running people off from here?" The blind man didn't pay any attention to him. He kept on rattling the cup and the child kept on handing out the pamphlets. He passed Enoch Emery and came on toward Haze, hitting the white cane out at an angle from his leg. Haze leaned forward and saw that the lines on his face were not painted on; they were scars.

"What the hell you think you doing?" the man selling peelers yelled. "I got these people together, how you think you can horn in?"

The child held one of the pamphlets out to Haze and he grabbed it. The words on the outside of it said, "Jesus Calls You."

"I'd like to know who the hell you think you are!" the man with the peelers was yelling. The child went back to where he was and handed him a tract. He looked at it for an instant with his lip curled and then he charged around the card table, upsetting the bucket of potatoes. "These damn Jesus fanatics," he yelled, glaring around, trying to find the blind man. New people gathered, hoping to see a disturbance. "These goddam Communist foreigners!" the peeler man screamed. "I got this crowd together!" He stopped, realizing there was a crowd.

"Listen folks," he said, "one at a time, there's plenty to go around, just don't push, a half a dozen peeled potatoes to the first person stepping up to buy." He got back behind the card table quietly and started holding up the peeler boxes. "Step on up, plenty to go around," he said, "no need to crowd."

Haze didn't open his tract. He looked at the outside of it and then he tore it across. He put the two pieces together and tore them across again. He kept re-stacking the pieces and tearing them again until he had a little handful of confetti. He turned his hand over and let the shredded leaflet sprinkle to the ground. Then he looked up and saw the blind man's child not three feet away, watching him. Her mouth was open and her eyes glittered on him like two chips of green bottle glass. She had a white gunny sack hung over her shoulder. Haze scowled and began rubbing his sticky hands on his pants.

"I seen you," she said. Then she moved quickly over to where the blind man was standing now, beside the card table, and turned her head and looked at Haze from there. Most of the people had moved off.

The peeler man leaned over the card table and said, "Hey!" to the blind man. "I reckon that showed you. Trying to horn in."

"Lookerhere," Enoch Emery said, "I ain't got but a dollar sixteen cent but I . . ."

"Yah," the man said, "I reckon that'll show you you can't muscle in on me. Sold eight peelers, sold . . ."

"Give me one of them," the blind man's child said, pointing to the peelers.

"Hanh," he said.

She was untying a handkerchief. She untied two fifty-cent pieces out of the knotted corner of it. "Give me one of them," she said, holding out the money.

The man eyed it with his mouth hiked to one side. "A buck fifty, sister," he said.

She pulled her hand in quickly and all at once glared at Hazel Motes as if he had made a noise at her. The blind man was moving on. She stood a second glaring at Haze, and then she turned and followed the blind man. Haze started.

"Listen," Enoch Emery said, "I ain't got but a dollar sixteen cent and I want me one of them . . ."

"You can keep it," the man said, taking the bucket off the card table. "This ain't no cut-rate joint."

Haze could see the blind man moving down the street some distance away. He stood staring after him, jerking his hands in and out of his pockets as if he were trying to move forward and backward at the same time. Then suddenly he thrust two dollars at the man selling peelers and snatched a box off the card table and started running down the street. In a second Enoch Emery was panting at his elbow. "My, I reckon you got a heap of money," Enoch Emery said.

Haze saw the child catch up with the blind man and take him by the elbow. They were about a block ahead of him. He slowed down some and saw Enoch Emery there. Enoch had on a yellowish white suit and a pinkish white shirt and his tie was the color of green peas. He was smiling. He looked like a friendly hound dog with light mange. "How long you been here?" he inquired.

"Two days," Haze muttered.

"I been here two months," Enoch said. "I work for the city. Where you work?"

"Not working," Haze said.

"That's too bad," Enoch said. "I work for the city." He skipped a step to get in line with Haze, then he said, "I'm eighteen year old and I ain't been here but two months and I already work for the city."

"That's fine," Haze said. He pulled his hat down farther on the side Enoch Emery was on and walked very fast. The blind man up ahead began to make mock bows to the right and left.

"I didn't ketch your name good," Enoch said.

Haze said his name.

"You look like you might be follerin' them hicks," Enoch remarked. "You go in for a lot of Jesus business?"

"No," Haze said.

"No, me neither, not much," Enoch agreed. "I went to thisyer Rodemill Boys' Bible Academy for four weeks. This-yer woman that traded me from my daddy she sent me. She was a Welfare woman. Jesus, four weeks and I thought I was going to be sanctified crazy."

Haze walked to the end of the block and Enoch stayed at

his elbow, panting and talking. When Haze started across the street, Enoch yelled, "Don't you see theter light! That means you got to wait!" A cop blew a whistle and a car blasted its horn and stopped short. Haze went on across, keeping his eyes on the blind man in the middle of the block. The policeman kept on blowing his whistle. He crossed the street to where Haze was and stopped him. He had a thin face and oval-shaped yellow eyes.

"You know what that little thing hanging up there is for?" he asked, pointing to the traffic light over the intersection.

"I didn't see it," Haze said.

The policeman looked at him without saying anything. A few people stopped. He rolled his eyes at them. "Maybe you thought the red ones was for white folks and the green ones for niggers," he said.

"Yeah I thought that," Haze said. "Take your hand off me."

The policeman took his hand off and put it on his hip. He backed one step away and said, "You tell all your friends about these lights. Red is to stop, green is to go—men and women, white folks and niggers, all go on the same light. You tell all your friends so when they come to town, they'll know." The people laughed.

"I'll look after him," Enoch Emery said, pushing in by the policeman. "He ain't been here but only two days. I'll look after him."

"How long you been here?" the cop asked.

"I was born and raised here," Enoch said. "This is my ol' home town. I'll take care of him for you. Hey wait!" he yelled at Haze. "Wait on me!" He pushed out of the crowd and caught up with him. "I reckon I saved you that time," he said.

"I'm obliged," Haze said.

"It wasn't nothing," Enoch said. "Whyn't we go in Walgreen's and get us a soda? Ain't no night clubs open this early."

"I don't like drug stores," Haze said. "Good-by."

"That's all right," Enoch said. "I reckon I'll go along and keep you company for a while." He looked up ahead at the blind man and the child and said, "I sho wouldn't want to get messed up with no hicks this time of night, particularly

the Jesus kind. I done had enough of them myself. Thisyer
Welfare woman that traded me from my daddy didn't do
nothing but pray. Me and daddy we moved around with a
sawmill where we worked and it set up outside Boonville one
summer and here come thisyer woman." He caught hold of
Haze's coat. "Only objection I got to Taulkinham is there's
too many people on the streets," he said confidentially. "Look
like all they want to do is knock you down—well here she
come and I reckon she took a fancy to me. I was twelve year
old and I could sing some hymns good I learnt off a nigger.
So here she comes taking a fancy to me and traded me off my
daddy and took me to Boonville to live with her. She had a
brick house but it was Jesus all day long." A little man lost in
a pair of faded overalls jostled him. "Whyn't you look wher
you going?" Enoch growled.

The little man stopped and raised his arm in a vicious gesture and a nasty-dog look came on his face. "Who you tellin'
what?" he snarled.

"You see," Enoch said, jumping to catch up with Haze, "all
they want to do is knock you down. I ain't never been to such
a unfriendly place before. Even with that woman. I stayed
with her for two months in that house of hers," he went on,
"and then come fall she sent me to the Rodemill Boys' Bible
Academy and I thought that sho was going to be some relief.
This woman was hard to get along with—she wasn't old, I
reckon she was forty year old—but she sho was ugly. She had
theseyer brown glasses and her hair was so thin it looked like
ham gravy trickling over her skull. I thought it was going to
be some certain relief to get to theter Academy. I had run
away oncet on her and she got me back and come to find out
she had papers on me and she could send me to the penitentiary if I didn't stay with her so I sho was glad to get to theter
Academy. You ever been to a academy?"

Haze didn't seem to hear the question.

"Well, it won't no relief," Enoch said. "Good Jesus, it won't
no relief. I run away from there after four weeks and durn if
she didn't get me back and brought me to that house of hers
again. I got out though." He waited a minute. "You want to
know how?"

After a second he said, "I scared hell out of that woman,

that's how. I studied on it and studied on it. I even prayed. I said, 'Jesus, show me the way to get out of here without killing thisyer woman and getting sent to the penitentiary,' and durn if He didn't. I got up one morning at just daylight and I went in her room without my pants on and pulled the sheet off her and giver a heart attact. Then I went back to my daddy and we ain't seen hide of her since.

"Your jaw just crawls," he observed, watching the side of Haze's face. "You don't never laugh. I wouldn't be surprised if you wasn't a real wealthy man."

Haze turned down a side street. The blind man and the girl were on the corner a block ahead. "Well, I reckon we going to ketch up with them after all," Enoch said. "You know many people here?"

"No," Haze said.

"You ain't gonna know none neither. This is one more hard place to make friends in. I been here two months and I don't know nobody. Look like all they want to do is knock you down. I reckon you got a right heap of money," he said. "I ain't got none. Had, I'd sho know what to do with it." The blind man and his child stopped on the corner and turned up the left side of the street. "We ketchin' up," he said. "I bet we'll be at some meeting singing hymns with her and her daddy if we don't watch out."

Up in the next block there was a large building with columns and a dome. The blind man and the girl were going toward it. There was a car parked in every space around the building and on the other side of the street and up and down the streets near it. "That ain't no picture show," Enoch said. The blind man and the girl turned up the steps to the building. The steps went all the way across the front, and on either side there were stone lions sitting on pedestals. "Ain't no church," Enoch said. Haze stopped at the steps. He looked as if he were trying to settle his face into an expression. He pulled the black hat forward at a sharp angle and started toward the two, who had sat down in the corner by one of the lions. He came up to where the blind man was without saying anything and stood leaning forward in front of him as if he were trying to see through the black glasses. The child stared at him.

The blind man's mouth thinned slightly. "I can smell the sin on your breath," he said.

Haze drew back.

"What'd you follow me for?"

"I never followed you," Haze said.

"She said you were following," the blind man said, jerking his thumb in the direction of the child.

"I ain't followed you," Haze said. He felt the peeler box in his hand and looked at the girl. Her black knitted cap made a straight line across her forehead. She grinned suddenly and then quickly drew her expression back together as if she smelled something bad. "I ain't followed you nowhere," Haze said. "I followed her." He stuck the peeler out at her.

At first she looked as if she were going to grab it, but she didn't. "I don't want that thing," she said. "What you think I want with that thing? Take it. It ain't mine. I don't want it!"

"You take it," the blind man said. "You put it in your sack and shut up before I hit you."

Haze thrust the peeler at her again.

"I won't have it," she muttered.

"You take it like I told you," the blind man said. "He never followed you."

She took it and shoved it in the sack where the tracts were. "It ain't mine," she said. "I got it but it ain't mine."

"I followed her to say I ain't beholden for none of her fast eye like she gave me back there," Haze said, looking at the blind man.

"What you mean?" she shouted. "I never looked at you with no fast eye. I only watched you tearing up that tract. He tore it up in little pieces," she said, pushing the blind man's shoulder. "He tore it up and sprinkled it all over the ground like salt and wiped his hands on his pants."

"He followed me," the blind man said. "Nobody would follow you. I can hear the urge for Jesus in his voice."

"Jesus," Haze muttered. "My Jesus." He sat down by the girl's leg and set his hand on the step next to her foot. She had on sneakers and black cotton stockings.

"Listen at him cursing," she said in a low tone. "He never followed you, Papa."

The blind man gave his edgy laugh. "Listen boy," he said, "you can't run away from Jesus. Jesus is a fact."

"I know a whole heap about Jesus," Enoch said. "I attended thisyer Rodemill Boys' Bible Academy that a woman sent me to. If it's anything you want to know about Jesus, just ast me." He had got up on the lion's back and he was sitting there sideways, cross-legged.

"I come a long way," Haze said, "since I would believe anything. I come halfway around the world."

"Me too," Enoch Emery said.

"You ain't come so far that you could keep from following me," the blind man said. He reached out suddenly and his hands covered Haze's face. For a second Haze didn't move or make any sound. Then he knocked the hands off.

"Quit it," he said in a faint voice. "You don't know anything about me."

"My daddy looks just like Jesus," Enoch remarked from the lion's back. "His hair hangs to his shoulders. Only difference is he's got a scar acrost his chin. I ain't never seen who my mother is."

"Some preacher has left his mark on you," the blind man said with a kind of snicker. "Did you follow for me to take it off or give you another one?"

"Listen here, there's nothing for your pain but Jesus," the child said suddenly. She tapped Haze on the shoulder. He sat there with his black hat tilted forward over his face. "Listen," she said in a louder voice, "this here man and woman killed this little baby. It was her own child but it was ugly and she never give it any love. This child had Jesus and this woman didn't have nothing but good looks and a man she was living in sin with. She sent the child away and it come back and she sent it away again and it come back again and ever' time she sent it away, it come back to where her and this man was living in sin. They strangled it with a silk stocking and hung it up in the chimney. It didn't give her any peace after that, though. Everything she looked at was that child. Jesus made it beautiful to haunt her. She couldn't lie with that man without she saw it, staring through the chimney at her, shining through the brick in the middle of the night."

"My Jesus," Haze muttered.

"She didn't have nothing but good looks," she said in the loud fast voice. "That ain't enough. No sirree."

"I hear them scraping their feet inside there," the blind man said. "Get out the tracts, they're fixing to come out."

"It ain't enough," she repeated.

"What we gonna do?" Enoch asked. "What's inside theter building?"

"A program letting out," the blind man said. "My congregation."

The child took the tracts out of the gunny sack and gave him two bunches of them, tied with a string. "You and the other boy go over on that side and give out," he said to her. "Me and the one that followed me'll stay over here."

"He don't have no business touching them," she said. "He don't want to do anything but shred them up."

"Go like I told you," the blind man said.

She stood there a second, scowling. Then she said, "You come on if you're coming," to Enoch Emery and Enoch jumped off the lion and followed her over to the other side.

Haze ducked down a step but the blind man's hand shot out and clamped him around the arm. He said in a fast whisper, "Repent! Go to the head of the stairs and renounce your sins and distribute these tracts to the people!" and he thrust a stack of pamphlets into Haze's hand.

Haze jerked his arm away but he only pulled the blind man nearer. "Listen," he said, "I'm as clean as you are."

"Fornication and blasphemy and what else?" the blind man said.

"They ain't nothing but words," Haze said. "If I was in sin I was in it before I ever committed any. There's no change come in me." He was trying to pry the fingers off from around his arm but the blind man kept wrapping them tighter. "I don't believe in sin," Haze said, "take your hand off me."

"Jesus loves you," the blind man said in a flat mocking voice, "Jesus loves you, Jesus loves you . . ."

"Nothing matters but that Jesus don't exist," Haze said, pulling his arm free.

"Go to the head of the stairs and distribute these tracts and . . ."

"I'll take them up there and throw them over into the bushes!" Haze shouted. "You be watching and see can you see."

"I can see more than you!" the blind man yelled, laughing. "You got eyes and see not, ears and hear not, but you'll have to see some time."

"You be watching if you can see!" Haze said, and started running up the steps. A crowd of people were already coming out the auditorium doors and some were halfway down the steps. He pushed through them with his elbows out like sharp wings and when he got to the top, a new surge of them pushed him back almost to where he had started up. He fought through them again until somebody shouted, "Make room for this idiot!" and people got out of his way. He rushed to the top and pushed his way over to the side and stood there, glaring and panting.

"I never followed him," he said aloud. "I wouldn't follow a blind fool like that. My Jesus." He stood against the building, holding the stack of leaflets by the string. A fat man stopped near him to light a cigar and Haze pushed his shoulder. "Look down yonder," he said. "See that blind man down there? He's giving out tracts and begging. Jesus. You ought to see him and he's got this here ugly child dressed up in woman's clothes, giving them out too. My Jesus."

"There's always fanatics," the fat man said, moving on.

"My Jesus," Haze said. He leaned forward near an old woman with blue hair and a collar of red wooden beads. "You better get on the other side, lady," he said. "There's a fool down there giving out tracts." The crowd behind the old woman pushed her on, but she looked at him for an instant with two bright flea eyes. He started toward her through the people but she was already too far away and he pushed back to where he had been standing against the wall. "Sweet Jesus Christ Crucified," he said, "I want to tell you people something. Maybe you think you're not clean because you don't believe. Well you are clean, let me tell you that. Every one of you people are clean and let me tell you why if you think it's because of Jesus Christ Crucified you're wrong. I don't say he wasn't crucified but I say it wasn't for you. Listenhere, I'm a preacher myself and I preach the truth." The crowd was moving fast. It was like a large spread raveling and the separate threads disappeared down the dark streets. "Don't I know what exists and what don't?" he cried. "Don't I have eyes in my head? Am I a blind man? Listenhere," he called, "I'm going to preach a new church—the church of truth without Jesus Christ Crucified. It won't cost you nothing to join my church. It's not started yet but it's going to be." The few people who were left glanced at him once or twice. There were tracts scattered below over the sidewalk and out on the street. The blind man was sitting on the bottom step. Enoch Emery was on the other side, standing on the lion's head, trying to balance himself, and the child was standing near him, watching Haze. "I don't need Jesus," Haze said. "What do I need with Jesus? I got Leora Watts."

He went down the stairs quietly to where the blind man was and stopped. He stood there a second and the blind man laughed. Haze moved away, and started across the street. He was on the other side before the voice pierced after him. He turned and saw the blind man standing in the middle of the street, shouting, "Hawks, Hawks, my name is Asa Hawks when you try to follow me again!" A car had to swerve to the side to keep from hitting him. "Repent!" he shouted and laughed and ran forward a little way, pretending he was going to come after Haze and grab him.

Haze drew his head down nearer his hunched shoulders and went on quickly. He didn't look back until he heard other footsteps coming behind him.

"Now that we got shut of them," Enoch Emery panted, "whyn't we go somewher and have us some fun?"

"Listen," Haze said roughly, "I got business of my own. I seen all of you I want." He began walking very fast.

Enoch kept skipping steps to keep up. "I been here two months," he said, "and I don't know nobody. People ain't friendly here. I got me a room and there ain't never nobody in it but me. My daddy said I had to come. I wouldn't never have come but he made me. I think I seen you sommers before. You ain't from Stockwell, are you?"

"No."

"Melsy?"

"No."

"Sawmill set up there oncet," Enoch said. "Look like you had a kind of familer face."

They walked on without saying anything until they got on the main street again. It was almost deserted. "Good-by," Haze said.

"I'm going thisaway too," Enoch said in a sullen voice. On the left there was a movie house where the electric bill was being changed. "We hadn't got tied up with them hicks we could have gone to a show," he muttered. He strode along at Haze's elbow, talking in a half mumble, half whine. Once he caught at his sleeve to slow him down and Haze jerked it away. "My daddy made me come," he said in a cracked voice. Haze looked at him and saw he was crying, his face seamed and wet and a purple-pink color. "I ain't but eighteen year old," he cried, "an' he made me come and I don't know nobody, nobody here'll have nothing to do with nobody else. They ain't friendly. He done gone off with a woman and made me come but she ain't going to stay for long, he'll beat hell out of her before she gets herself stuck to a chair. You the first familer face I seen in two months. I seen you sommers before. I know I seen you sommers before."

Haze looked straight ahead with his face set and Enoch kept up the half mumble, half blubber. They passed a church and a hotel and an antique shop and turned up Mrs. Watts's street.

"If you want you a woman you don't have to be follering nothing looked like that kid you give a peeler to," Enoch said. "I heard about where there's a house where we could have us some fun. I could pay you back next week."

"Look," Haze said, "I'm going where I'm going—two doors from here. I got a woman. I got a woman, see? And that's where I'm going—to visit her. I don't need to go with you."

"I could pay you back next week," Enoch said. "I work at the city zoo. I guard a gate and I get paid ever' week."

"Get away from me," Haze said.

"People ain't friendly here. You ain't from here but you ain't friendly neither."

Haze didn't answer him. He went on with his neck drawn close to his shoulder blades as if he were cold.

"You don't know nobody neither," Enoch said. "You ain't got no woman nor nothing to do. I knew when I first seen you you didn't have nobody nor nothing but Jesus. I seen you and I knew it."

"This is where I'm going in at," Haze said, and he turned up the walk without looking back at Enoch.

Enoch stopped. "Yeah," he cried, "oh yeah," and he ran his sleeve under his nose to stop the snivel. "Yeah," he cried, "go on where you goin' but lookerhere." He slapped at his pocket and ran up and caught Haze's sleeve and rattled the peeler box at him. "She give me this. She give it to me and there ain't nothing you can do about it. She told me where they lived and ast me to visit them and bring you—not you bring me, me bring you—and it was you follerin' them." His eyes glinted through his tears and his face stretched in an evil crooked grin. "You act like you think you got wiser blood than anybody else," he said, "but you ain't! I'm the one has it. Not you. *Me.*"

Haze didn't say anything. He stood there for an instant, small in the middle of the steps, and then he raised his arm and hurled the stack of tracts he had been carrying. It hit Enoch in the chest and knocked his mouth open. He stood looking, with his mouth hanging open, at where it had hit his front, and then he turned and tore off down the street; and Haze went into the house.

Since the night before was the first time he had slept with any woman, he had not been very successful with Mrs. Watts. When he finished, he was like something washed ashore on her, and she had made obscene comments about him, which he remembered off and on during the day. He was uneasy in the thought of going to her again. He didn't know what she would say when he opened the door and she saw him there.

When he opened the door and she saw him there, she said, "Ha ha."

The black hat sat on his head squarely. He came in with it on and when it knocked the electric light bulb that hung down from the middle of the ceiling, he took it off. Mrs. Watts was in bed, applying a grease to her face. She rested her chin on her hand and watched him. He began to move around the room, examining this and that. His throat got dryer and his heart began to grip him like a little ape clutching the bars of its cage. He sat down on the edge of her bed, with his hat in his hand.

Mrs. Watts's grin was as curved and sharp as the blade of a sickle. It was plain that she was so well-adjusted that she didn't have to think any more. Her eyes took everything in whole, like quicksand. "That Jesus-seeing hat!" she said. She sat up and pulled her nightgown from under her and took it off. She reached for his hat and put it on her head and sat with her hands on her hips, walling her eyes in a comical way. Haze stared for a minute, then he made three quick noises that were laughs. He jumped for the electric light cord and took off his clothes in the dark.

Once when he was small, his father took him to a carnival that stopped in Melsy. There was one tent that cost more money a little off to one side. A dried-up man with a horn voice was barking it. He didn't say what was inside. He said it was so SINsational that it would cost any man that wanted to see it thirty-five cents, and it was so EXclusive, only fifteen could get in at a time. His father sent him to a tent where two monkeys danced, and then he made for it, moving close to the walls of things like he moved. Haze left the monkeys and followed him, but he didn't have thirty-five cents. He asked the barker what was inside.

"Beat it," the man said. "There ain't no pop and there ain't no monkeys."

"I already seen them," he said.

"That's fine," the man said, "beat it."

"I got fifteen cents," he said. "Whyn't you lemme in and I could see half of it?" It's something about a privy, he was thinking. It's some men in a privy. Then he thought, maybe it's a man and a woman in a privy. She wouldn't want me in there. "I got fifteen cents," he said.

"It's more than half over," the man said, fanning with his straw hat. "You run along."

"That'll be fifteen cents worth then," Haze said.

"Scram," the man said.

"Is it a nigger?" Haze asked. "Are they doing something to a nigger?"

The man leaned off his platform and his dried-up face drew into a glare. "Where'd you get that idear?" he said.

"I don't know," Haze said.

"How old are you?" the man asked.

"Twelve," Haze said. He was ten.

"Gimme that fifteen cents," the man said, "and get in there."

He slid the money on the platform and scrambled to get in before it was over. He went through the flap of the tent and inside there was another tent and he went through that. All he could see were the backs of the men. He climbed up on a bench and looked over their heads. They were looking down into a lowered place where something white was lying, squirming a little, in a box lined with black cloth. For a second he thought it was a skinned animal and then he saw it was a woman. She was fat and she had a face like an ordinary woman except there was a mole on the corner of her lip, that moved when she grinned, and one on her side.

"Had one of themther built into ever' casket," his father, up toward the front, said, "be a heap ready to go sooner."

Haze recognized the voice without looking. He slid down off the bench and scrambled out of the tent. He crawled out under the side of the outside one because he didn't want to pass the barker. He got in the back of a truck and sat down in the far corner of it. The carnival was making a tin roar outside.

His mother was standing by the washpot in the yard, looking at him, when he got home. She wore black all the time and her dresses were longer than other women's. She was standing there straight, looking at him. He moved behind a tree and got out of her view, but in a few minutes, he could feel her watching him through the tree. He saw the lowered place and the casket again and a thin woman in the casket who was too long for it. Her head stuck up at one end and her knees were raised to make her fit. She had a cross-shaped face and hair pulled close to her head. He stood flat against the tree, waiting. She left the washpot and came toward him with a stick. She said, "What you seen?

"What you seen?" she said.

"What you seen," she said, using the same tone of voice all the time. She hit him across the legs with the stick, but he was like part of the tree. "Jesus died to redeem you," she said.

"I never ast him," he muttered.

She didn't hit him again but she stood looking at him, shut-mouthed, and he forgot the guilt of the tent for the nameless unplaced guilt that was in him. In a minute she threw the stick away from her and went back to the washpot, still shut-mouthed.

The next day he took his shoes in secret out into the woods. He didn't wear them except for revivals and in the winter. He took them out of the box and filled the bottoms of them with stones and small rocks and then he put them on. He laced them up tight and walked in them through the woods for what he knew to be a mile, until he came to a creek, and then he sat down and took them off and eased his feet in the wet sand. He thought, that ought to satisfy Him. Nothing happened. If a stone had fallen he would have taken it as a sign. After a while he drew his feet out of the sand and let them dry, and then he put the shoes on again with the rocks still in them and he walked a half-mile back before he took them off.

Chapter 4

H E GOT OUT of Mrs. Watts's bed early in the morning before any light came in the room. When he woke up, her arm was flung across him. He leaned up and lifted it off and eased it down by her side, but he didn't look at her. There was only one thought in his mind: he was going to buy a car. The thought was full grown in his head when he woke up, and he didn't think of anything else. He had never thought before of buying a car; he had never even wanted one before. He had driven one only a little in his life and he didn't have any license. He had only fifty dollars but he thought he could buy a car for that. He got stealthily out the bed, without disturbing Mrs. Watts, and put his clothes on silently. By six-thirty, he was down town, looking for used-car lots.

Used-car lots were scattered among the blocks of old buildings that separated the business section from the railroad yards. He wandered around in a few of them before they were open. He could tell from the outside of the lot if it would have a fifty-dollar car in it. When they began to be open for business, he went through them quickly, paying no attention to anyone who tried to show him the stock. His black hat sat on his head with a careful, placed expression and his face had a fragile look as if it might have been broken and stuck together again, or like a gun no one knows is loaded.

It was a wet glary day. The sky was like a piece of thin polished silver with a dark sour-looking sun in one corner of it. By ten o'clock he had canvassed all the better lots and was nearing the railroad yards. Even here, the lots were full of cars that cost more than fifty dollars. Finally he came to one between two deserted warehouses. A sign over the entrance said: SLADE'S FOR THE LATEST.

There was a gravel road going down the middle of the lot and over to one side near the front, a tin shack with the word, OFFICE, painted on the door. The rest of the lot was full of old cars and broken machinery. A white boy was sitting on a gasoline can in front of the office. He had the look of being there to keep people out. He wore a black raincoat and his face was partly hidden under a leather cap. There was a cigarette hanging out of one corner of his mouth and the ash on it was about an inch long.

Haze started off toward the back of the lot where he saw a particular car. "Hey!" the boy yelled. "You don't just walk in here like that. I'll show you what I got to show," but Haze didn't pay any attention to him. He went on toward the back of the lot where he saw the car. The boy came huffing behind him, cursing. The car he saw was on the last row of cars. It was a high rat-colored machine with large thin wheels and bulging headlights. When he got up to it, he saw that one door was tied on with a rope and that it had an oval window in the back. This was the car he was going to buy.

"Lemme see Slade," he said.

"What you want to see him for?" the boy asked in a testy voice. He had a wide mouth and when he talked he used one side only of it.

"I want to see him about this car," Haze said.

"I'm him," the boy said. His face under the cap was like a thin picked eagle's. He sat down on the running board of a car across the gravel road and kept on cursing.

Haze walked around the car. Then he looked through the window at the inside of it. Inside it was a dull greenish dust-color. The back seat was missing but it had a two-by-four stretched across the seat frame to sit on. There were dark green fringed window shades on the two side-back windows. He looked through the two front windows and he saw the boy sitting on the running board of the car across the gravel road. He had one trouser leg hitched up and he was scratching his ankle that stuck up out of a pulp of yellow sock. He cursed far down in his throat as if he were trying to get up phlegm. The two window glasses made him a yellow color and distorted his shape. Haze moved quickly from the far side of the car and came around in front. "How much is it?" he asked.

"Jesus on the cross," the boy said, "Christ nailed."

"How much is it?" Haze growled, paling a little.

"How much do you think it's worth?" the boy said. "Give us a estimit."

"It ain't worth what it would take to cart it off. I wouldn't have it."

The boy gave all his attention to his ankle where there was a scab. Haze looked up and saw a man coming from between two cars over on the boy's side. As he came closer, he saw that the man looked exactly like the boy except that he was two heads taller and he had on a sweat-stained brown felt hat. He was coming up behind the boy, between a row of cars. When he got just behind him, he stopped and waited a second. Then he said in a sort of controlled roar, "Get your butt off that running board!"

The boy snarled and disappeared, scrambling between two cars.

The man stood looking at Haze. "What you want?" he asked.

"This car here," Haze said.

"Seventy-fi' dollars," the man said.

On either side of the lot there were two old buildings, reddish with black empty windows, and behind there was another without any windows. "I'm obliged," Haze said, and he started back toward the office.

When he got to the entrance, he glanced back and saw the man about four feet behind him. "We might argue it some," he said.

Haze followed him back to where the car was.

"You won't find a car like that ever' day," the man said. He sat down on the running board that the boy had been sitting on. Haze didn't see the boy but he was there, sitting up on the hood of a car two cars over. He was sitting huddled up as if he were freezing but his face had a sour composed look. "All new tires," the man said.

"They were new when it was built," Haze said.

"They was better cars built a few years ago," the man said. "They don't make no more good cars."

"What you want for it?" Haze asked again.

The man stared off, thinking. After a while he said, "I might could let you have it for sixty-fi'."

Haze leaned against the car and started to roll a cigarette but he couldn't get it rolled. He kept spilling the tobacco and then the papers.

"Well, what you want to pay for it?" the man asked. "I wouldn't trade me a Chrysler for a Essex like that. That car yonder ain't been built by a bunch of niggers.

"All the niggers are living in Detroit now, putting cars together," he said, making conversation. "I was up there a while myself and I seen. I come home."

"I wouldn't pay over thirty dollars for it," Haze said.

"They got one nigger up there," the man said, "is almost as light as you or me." He took off his hat and ran his finger around the sweat band inside it. He had a little bit of carrot-colored hair.

"We'll drive it around," the man said, "or would you like to get under and look up it?"

"No," Haze said.

The man gave him a half look. "You pay when you leave," he said easily. "You don't find what you looking for in one there's others for the same price obliged to have it." Two cars over the boy began to curse again. It was like a hacking cough. Haze turned suddenly and kicked his foot into the front tire. "I done tole you them tires won't bust," the man said.

"How much?" Haze said.

"I might could make it fifty dollar," the man offered.

Before Haze bought the car, the man put some gas in it and drove him around a few blocks to prove it would run. The boy sat hunched up in the back on the two-by-four, cursing. "Something's wrong with him howcome he curses so much," the man said. "Just don't listen at him." The car rode with a high growling noise. The man put on the brakes to show how well they worked and the boy was thrown off the two-by-four at their heads. "Goddam you," the man roared, "quit jumping at us thataway. Keep your butt on the board." The boy didn't say anything. He didn't even curse. Haze looked back and he was sitting huddled up in the black raincoat with the black leather cap pulled down almost to his eyes. The only thing different was that the ash had been knocked off his cigarette.

He bought the car for forty dollars and then he paid the man extra for five gallons of gasoline. The man had the boy go in the office and bring out a five-gallon can of gas to fill up the tank with. The boy came cursing and lugging the yellow gas can, bent over almost double. "Give it here," Haze said, "I'll do it myself." He was in a terrible hurry to get away in the car. The boy jerked the can away from him and straightened up. It was only half full but he held it over the tank until five gallons would have spilled out slowly. All the time he kept saying, "Sweet Jesus, sweet Jesus, sweet Jesus."

"Why don't he shut up?" Haze said suddenly. "What's he keep talking like that for?"

"I don't never know what ails him," the man said and shrugged.

When the car was ready the man and the boy stood by to watch him drive it off. He didn't want anybody watching him because he hadn't driven a car in four or five years. The man and the boy didn't say anything while he tried to start it. They only stood there, looking in at him. "I wanted this car mostly to be a house for me," he said to the man. "I ain't got any place to be."

"You ain't took the brake off yet," the man said.

He took off the brake and the car shot backward because the man had left it in reverse. In a second he got it going forward and he drove off crookedly, past the man and the boy still standing there watching. He kept going forward, thinking nothing and sweating. For a long time he stayed on the street he was on. He had a hard time holding the car in the road. He went past railroad yards for about a half-mile and then warehouses. When he tried to slow the car down, it stopped altogether and then he had to start it again. He went past long blocks of gray houses and then blocks of better, yellow houses. It began to drizzle rain and he turned on the windshield wipers; they made a great clatter like two idiots clapping in church. He went past blocks of white houses, each sitting with an ugly dog face on a square of grass. Finally he went over a viaduct and found the highway.

He began going very fast.

The highway was ragged with filling stations and trailer camps and roadhouses. After a while there were stretches where red gulleys dropped off on either side of the road and behind them there were patches of field buttoned together with 666 posts. The sky leaked over all of it and then it began to leak into the car. The head of a string of pigs appeared snout-up over the ditch and he had to screech to a stop and watch the rear of the last pig disappear shaking into the ditch on the other side. He started the car again and went on. He had the feeling that everything he saw was a broken-off piece of some giant blank thing that he had forgotten had happened to him. A black pick-up truck turned off a side road in front of him. On the back of it an iron bed and a chair and table were tied, and on top of them, a crate of barred-rock chickens. The truck went very slowly, with a rumbling sound, and in the middle of the road. Haze started pounding his horn and he had hit it three times before he realized it didn't make any sound. The crate was stuffed so full of wet barred-rock chickens that the ones facing him had their heads outside the bars. The truck didn't go any faster and he was forced to drive slowly. The fields stretched sodden on either side until they hit the scrub pines.

The road turned and went down hill and a high embankment appeared on one side with pines standing on it, facing a gray boulder that jutted out of the opposite gulley wall. White letters on the boulder said, WOE TO THE BLASPHEMER AND WHOREMONGER! WILL HELL SWALLOW YOU UP? The pick-up truck slowed even more as if it were reading the sign and Haze pounded his empty horn. He beat on it and beat on it but it didn't make any sound. The pick-up truck went on, bumping the glum barred-rock chickens over the edge of the next hill. Haze's car was stopped and his eyes were turned toward the two words at the bottom of the sign. They said in smaller letters, "Jesus Saves."

He sat looking at the sign and he didn't hear the horn. An oil truck as long as a railroad car was behind him. In a second a red square face was at his car window. It watched the back of his neck and hat for a minute and then a hand came in and sat on his shoulder. "What you doing parked in the middle of the road?" the truck driver asked.

Haze turned his fragile placed-looking face toward him. "Take your hand off me," he said. "I'm reading the sign."

The driver's expression and his hand stayed exactly the way they were, as if he didn't hear very well.

"There's no person a whoremonger, who wasn't something worse first," Haze said. "That's not the sin, nor blasphemy. The sin came before them."

The truck driver's face remained exactly the same.

"Jesus is a trick on niggers," Haze said.

The driver put both his hands on the window and gripped it. He looked as if he intended to pick up the car. "Will you get your goddam outhouse off the middle of the road?" he said.

"I don't have to run from anything because I don't believe in anything," Haze said. He and the driver looked at each other for about a minute. Haze's look was the more distant; another plan was forming in his mind. "Which direction is the zoo in?" he asked.

"Back around the other way," the driver said. "Did you exscape from there?"

"I got to see a boy that works in it," Haze said. He started the car up and left the driver standing there, in front of the letters painted on the boulder.

Chapter 5

THAT MORNING Enoch Emery knew when he woke up that today the person he could show it to was going to come. He knew by his blood. He had wise blood like his daddy.

At two o'clock that afternoon, he greeted the second-shift gate guard. "You ain't but only fifteen minutes late," he said irritably. "But I stayed. I could of went on but I stayed." He wore a green uniform with yellow piping on the neck and sleeves and a yellow stripe down the outside of each leg. The second-shift guard, a boy with a jutting shale-textured face and a toothpick in his mouth, wore the same. The gate they were standing by was made of iron bars and the concrete arch that held it was fashioned to look like two trees; branches curved to form the top of it where twisted letters said, CITY FOREST PARK. The second-shift guard leaned against one of the trunks and began prodding between his teeth with the pick.

"Ever' day," Enoch complained; "look like ever' day I lose fifteen good minutes standing here waiting for you."

Every day when he got off duty, he went into the park, and every day when he went in, he did the same things. He went first to the swimming pool. He was afraid of the water but he liked to sit up on the bank above it if there were any women in the pool, and watch them. There was one woman who came every Monday who wore a bathing suit that was split on each hip. At first he thought she didn't know it, and instead of watching openly on the bank, he had crawled into some bushes, snickering to himself, and had watched from there. There had been no one else in the pool—the crowds didn't come until four o'clock—to tell her about the splits and she had splashed around in the water and then lain up on the edge of the pool asleep for almost an hour, all the time without suspecting there was somebody in the bushes looking at her. Then on another day when he stayed a little later, he saw three women, all with their suits split, the pool full of people, and nobody paying them any mind. That was how the city was—always surprising him. He visited a whore when he felt like it but he was always being shocked by the looseness he saw in the open. He crawled into the bushes out

44

of a sense of propriety. Very often the women would pull the suit straps down off their shoulders and lie stretched out.

The park was the heart of the city. He had come to the city and—with a knowing in his blood—he had established himself at the heart of it. Every day he looked at the heart of it; every day; and he was so stunned and awed and overwhelmed that just to think about it made him sweat. There was something, in the center of the park, that he had discovered. It was a mystery, although it was right there in a glass case for everybody to see and there was a typewritten card over it telling all about it. But there was something the card couldn't say and what it couldn't say was inside him, a terrible knowledge without any words to it, a terrible knowledge like a big nerve growing inside him. He could not show the mystery to just anybody; but he had to show it to somebody. Who he had to show it to was a special person. This person could not be from the city but he didn't know why. He knew he would know him when he saw him and he knew that he would have to see him soon or the nerve inside him would grow so big that he would be forced to steal a car or rob a bank or jump out of a dark alley onto a woman. His blood all morning had been saying the person would come today.

He left the second-shift guard and approached the pool from a discreet footpath that led behind the ladies' end of the bath house to a small clearing where the entire pool could be seen at once. There was nobody in it—the water was bottle-green and motionless—but he saw, coming up the other side and heading for the bath house, the woman with the two little boys. She came every other day or so and brought the two children. She would go in the water with them and swim down the pool and then she would lie up on the side in the sun. She had a stained white bathing suit that fit her like a sack, and Enoch had watched her with pleasure on several occasions. He moved from the clearing up a slope to some abelia bushes. There was a nice tunnel under them and he crawled into it until he came to a slightly wider place where he was accustomed to sit. He settled himself and adjusted the abelia so that he could see through it properly. His face was always very red in the bushes. Anyone who parted the abelia sprigs at just that place, would think he saw a devil and would fall down the slope and into the pool. The woman and the two little boys entered the bath house.

Enoch never went immediately to the dark secret center of the park. That was the peak of the afternoon. The other things he did built up to it. When he left the bushes, he would go to the FROSTY BOTTLE, a hotdog stand in the shape of an Orange Crush with frost painted in blue around the top of it. Here he would have a chocolate malted milkshake and would make some suggestive remarks to the waitress, whom he believed to be secretly in love with him. After that he would go to see the animals. They were in a long set of steel cages like Alcatraz Penitentiary in the movies. The cages were electrically heated in the winter and air-conditioned in the summer and there were six men hired to wait on the animals and feed them T-bone steaks. The animals didn't do anything but lie around. Enoch watched them every day, full of awe and hate. Then he went *there*.

The two little boys ran out the bath house and dived into the water, and simultaneously a grating noise issued from the driveway on the other side of the pool. Enoch's head pierced out of the bushes. He saw a high rat-colored car passing, which sounded as if its motor were dragging out the back. The car passed and he could hear it rattle around the turn in the drive and on away. He listened carefully, trying to hear if it would stop. The noise receded and then gradually grew louder. The car passed again. Enoch saw this time that there was only one person in it, a man. The sound of it died away again and then grew louder. The car came around a third time and stopped almost directly opposite Enoch across the pool. The man in the car looked out the window and down the grass slope to the water where the two little boys were splashing and screaming. Enoch's head was as far out of the bushes as it would come and he was squinting. The door by the man was tied on with a rope. The man got out the other door and walked in front of the car and came halfway down the slope to the pool. He stood there a minute as if he were looking for somebody and then he sat down stiffly on the grass. He had on a blue suit and a black hat. He sat with his knees drawn up. "Well, I'll be dog," Enoch said. "Well, I'll be dog."

He began crawling out of the bushes immediately, his heart

moving so fast it was like one of those motorcycles at fairs that the fellow drives around the walls of a pit. He even remembered the man's name—Mr. Hazel Motes. In a second he appeared on all fours at the end of the abelia and looked across the pool. The blue figure was still sitting there in the same position. He had the look of being held there, as if by an invisible hand, as if, if the hand lifted up, the figure would spring across the pool in one leap without the expression on his face changing once.

The woman came out of the bath house and went to the diving board. She spread her arms out and began to bounce, making a big flapping sound with the board. Then suddenly she swirled backward and disappeared below the water. Mr. Hazel Motes's head turned very slowly, following her down the pool.

Enoch got up and went down the path behind the bath house. He came stealthily out on the other side and started walking toward Haze. He stayed on the top of the slope, moving softly in the grass just off the sidewalk, and making no noise. When he was directly behind him, he sat down on the edge of the sidewalk. If his arms had been ten feet long, he could have put his hands on Haze's shoulders. He studied him quietly.

The woman was climbing out of the pool, chinning herself up on the side. First her face appeared, long and cadaverous, with a bandage-like bathing cap coming down almost to her eyes, and sharp teeth protruding from her mouth. Then she rose on her hands until a large foot and leg came up from behind her and another on the other side and she was out, squatting there, panting. She stood up loosely and shook herself, and stamped in the water dripping off her. She was facing them and she grinned. Enoch could see part of Hazel Motes's face watching the woman. It didn't grin in return but it kept on watching her as she padded over to a spot of sun almost directly under where they were sitting. Enoch had to move a little closer to see.

The woman sat down in the spot of sun and took off her bathing cap. Her hair was short and matted and all colors, from deep rust to a greenish yellow. She shook her head and then she looked up at Hazel Motes again, grinning through her pointed teeth. She stretched herself out in the spot of sun, raising her knees and settling her backbone down against the concrete. The two little boys, at the other end of the water, were knocking each other's heads against the side of the pool. She settled herself until she was flat against the concrete and then she reached up and pulled the bathing suit straps off her shoulders.

"King Jesus!" Enoch whispered and before he could get his eyes off the woman, Hazel Motes had sprung up and was almost to his car. The woman was sitting straight up with the suit half off her in front, and Enoch was looking both ways at once.

He wrenched his attention loose from the woman and darted after Hazel Motes. "Wait on me!" he shouted and waved his arms in front of the car which was already rattling and starting to go. Hazel Motes cut off the motor. His face behind the windshield was sour and frog-like; it looked as if it had a shout closed up in it; it looked like one of those closet doors in gangster pictures where someone is tied to a chair behind it with a towel in his mouth.

"Well," Enoch said, "I declare if it ain't Hazel Motes. How are you, Hazel?"

"The guard said I'd find you at the swimming pool," Hazel Motes said. "He said you hid in the bushes and watched the swimming."

Enoch blushed. "I allus have admired swimming," he said. Then he stuck his head farther through the window. "You were looking for me?" he exclaimed.

"That blind man," Haze said, "that blind man named Hawks—did his child tell you where they lived?"

Enoch didn't seem to hear. "You came out here special to see me?" he said.

"Asa Hawks. His child gave you the peeler. Did she tell you where they lived?"

Enoch eased his head out of the car. He opened the door and climbed in beside Haze. For a minute he only looked at him, wetting his lips. Then he whispered, "I got to show you something."

"I'm looking for those people," Haze said. "I got to see that man. Did she tell you where they lived?"

"I got to show you this thing," Enoch said. "I got to show it to you, here, this afternoon. I got to." He gripped Hazel Motes's arm and Haze shook him off.

"Did she tell you where they live?" he said again.

Enoch kept wetting his lips. They were pale except for his fever blister, which was purple. "Cert'nly," he said. "Ain't she invited me to come to see her and bring my mouth organ? I got to show you this thing, then I'll tell you."

"What thing?" Haze muttered.

"This thing I got to show you," Enoch said. "Drive straight on ahead and I'll tell you where to stop."

"I don't want to see anything of yours," Haze Motes said. "I want that address."

Enoch didn't look at Hazel Motes. He looked out the window. "I won't be able to remember it unless you come," he said. In a minute the car started. Enoch's blood was beating fast. He knew he had to go to the FROSTY BOTTLE and the zoo before there, and he foresaw a terrible struggle with Hazel Motes. He would have to get him there, even if he had to hit him over the head with a rock and carry him on his back up to it.

Enoch's brain was divided into two parts. The part in communication with his blood did the figuring but it never said anything in words. The other part was stocked up with all kinds of words and phrases. While the first part was figuring how to get Hazel Motes through the FROSTY BOTTLE and the zoo, the second inquired, "Where'd you git thisyer fine car? You ought to paint you some signs on the outside it, like 'Step-in, baby'—I seen one with that on it, then I seen another, said . . ."

Hazel Motes's face might have been cut out of the side of a rock.

"My daddy once owned a yeller Ford automobile he won on a ticket," Enoch murmured. "It had a roll-top and two aerials and a squirrel tail all come with it. He swapped it off. Stop here! Stop here!" he yelled—they were passing the FROSTY BOTTLE.

"Where is it?" Hazel Motes said as soon as they were inside. They were in a dark room with a counter across the back of it and brown stools like toad stools in front of the counter.

On the wall facing the door there was a large advertisement for ice cream, showing a cow dressed up like a housewife.

"It ain't here," Enoch said. "We have to stop here on the way and get something to eat. What you want?"

"Nothing," Haze said. He stood stiffly in the middle of the room with his hands in his pockets.

"Well, sit down," Enoch said. "I have to have a little drink."

Something stirred behind the counter and a woman with bobbed hair like a man's got up from a chair where she had been reading the newspaper, and came forward. She looked sourly at Enoch. She had on a once-white uniform clotted with brown stains. "What you want?" she said in a loud voice, leaning close to his ear. She had a man's face and big muscled arms.

"I want a chocolate malted milkshake, baby girl," Enoch said softly. "I want a lot of ice cream in it."

She turned fiercely from him and glared at Haze.

"He says he don't want nothing but to sit down and look at you for a while," Enoch said. "He ain't hungry but for just to see you."

Haze looked woodenly at the woman and she turned her back on him and began mixing the milkshake. He sat down on the last stool in the row and started cracking his knuckles.

Enoch watched him carefully. "I reckon you done changed some," he said after a few minutes.

Haze got up. "Give me those people's address. Right now," he said.

It came to Enoch in an instant—the police. His face was suddenly suffused with secret knowledge. "I reckon you ain't as uppity as you was last night," he said. "I reckon maybe," he said, "you ain't got so much cause now as you had then." Stole theter automobile, he thought.

Hazel Motes sat back down.

"Howcome you jumped up so fast down yonder by the pool?" Enoch asked. The woman turned around to him with the malted milk in her hand. "Of course," he said evilly, "I wouldn't have had no truck with a ugly dish like that neither."

The woman thumped the malted milk on the counter in front of him. "Fifteen cents," she roared.

"You're worth more than that, baby girl," Enoch said. He snickered and began gassing his malted milk through the straw.

The woman strode over to where Haze was. "What you come in here with a son of a bitch like that for?" she shouted. "A nice quiet boy like you to come in here with a son of a bitch. You ought to mind the company you keep." Her name was Maude and she drank whisky all day from a fruit jar under the counter. "Jesus," she said, wiping her hand under her nose. She sat down in a straight chair in front of Haze but facing Enoch, and folded her arms across her chest. "Ever' day," she said to Haze, looking at Enoch, "ever' day that son of a bitch comes in here."

Enoch was thinking about the animals. They had to go next to see the animals. He hated them; just thinking about them made his face turn a chocolate purple color as if the malted milk were rising in his head.

"You're a nice boy," she said. "I can see, you got a clean nose, well keep it clean, don't go messin' with a son a bitch like that yonder. I always know a clean boy when I see one." She was shouting at Enoch, but Enoch watched Hazel Motes. It was as if something inside Hazel Motes was winding up, although he didn't move on the outside. He only looked pressed down in that blue suit, as if inside it, the thing winding was getting tighter and tighter. Enoch's blood told him to hurry. He raced the milkshake up the straw.

"Yes sir," she said, "there ain't anything sweeter than a clean boy. God for my witness. And I know a clean one when I see him and I know a son a bitch when I see him and there's a heap of difference and that pus-marked bastard zlurping through that straw is a goddamned son a bitch and you a clean boy had better mind how you keep him company. I know a clean boy when I see one."

Enoch screeched in the bottom of his glass. He fished fifteen cents from his pocket and laid it on the counter and got up. But Hazel Motes was already up; he was leaning over the counter toward the woman. She didn't see him right away because she was looking at Enoch. He leaned on his hands over the counter until his face was just a foot from hers. She turned around and stared at him.

"Come on," Enoch started, "we don't have no time to be sassing around with her. I got to show you this right away, I got . . ."

"I AM clean," Haze said.

It was not until he said it again that Enoch caught the words.

"I AM clean," he said again, without any expression on his face or in his voice, just looking at the woman as if he were looking at a wall. "If Jesus existed, I wouldn't be clean," he said.

She stared at him, startled and then outraged. "What do you think I care!" she yelled. "Why should I give a goddam what you are!"

"Come on," Enoch whined, "come on or I won't tell you where them people live." He caught Haze's arm and pulled him back from the counter and toward the door.

"You bastard!" the woman screamed, "what do you think I care about any of you filthy boys?"

Hazel Motes pushed the door open quickly and went out. He got back in his car and Enoch climbed in behind him. "Okay," Enoch said, "drive straight on ahead down this road."

"What you want for telling me?" Haze said. "I'm not staying here. I have to go. I can't stay here any longer."

Enoch shuddered. He began wetting his lips. "I got to show it to you," he said hoarsely. "I can't show it to nobody but you. I had a sign it was you when I seen you drive up at the pool. I knew all morning somebody was going to come and then when I saw you at the pool, I had thisyer sign."

"I don't care about your signs," Haze said.

"I go to see it ever' day," Enoch said. "I go ever' day but I ain't ever been able to take nobody else with me. I had to wait on the sign. I'll tell you them people's address just as soon as you see it. You got to see it," he said. "When you see it, something's going to happen."

"Nothing's going to happen," Haze said.

He started the car again and Enoch sat forward on the seat. "Them animals," he muttered. "We got to walk by them first. It won't take long for that. It won't take a minute." He saw the animals waiting evil-eyed for him, ready to throw him off time. He thought what if the police were screaming out here now with sirens and squad cars and they got Hazel Motes just before he showed it to him.

"I got to see those people," Haze said.

"Stop here! Stop here!" Enoch yelled.

There was a long shining row of steel cages over to the left and behind the bars, black shapes were sitting or pacing. "Get out," Enoch said. "This won't take one second."

Haze got out. Then he stopped. "I got to see those people," he said.

"Okay, okay, come on," Enoch whined.

"I don't believe you know the address."

"I do! I do!" Enoch cried. "It begins with a three, now come on!" He pulled Haze toward the cages. Two black bears sat in the first one, facing each other like two matrons having tea, their faces polite and self-absorbed. "They don't do nothing but sit there all day and stink," Enoch said. "A man comes and washes them cages out ever' morning with a hose and it stinks just as much as if he'd left it." He went past two more cages of bears, not looking at them, and then he stopped at the next cage where there were two yellow-eyed wolves nosing around the edges of the concrete. "Hyenas," he said. "I ain't got no use for hyenas." He leaned closer and spit into the cage, hitting one of the wolves on the leg. It shuttled to the side, giving him a slanted evil look. For a second he forgot Hazel Motes. Then he looked back quickly to make sure he was still there. He was right behind him. He was not looking at the animals. Thinking about them police, Enoch thought. He said, "Come on, we don't have time to look at all theseyer monkeys that come next." Usually he stopped at every cage and made an obscene comment aloud to himself, but today the animals were only a form he had to get through. He hurried past the cages of monkeys, looking back two or three times to make sure Hazel Motes was behind him. At the last of the monkey cages, he stopped as if he couldn't help himself.

"Look at that ape," he said, glaring. The animal had its back to him, gray except for a small pink seat. "If I had a ass like that," he said prudishly, "I'd sit on it. I wouldn't be exposing it to all these people come to this park. Come on, we don't have to look at theseyer birds that come next." He ran past the cages of birds and then he was at the end of the zoo. "Now we don't need the car," he said, going on ahead, "we'll go right down that hill yonder through them trees." Haze had stopped at the last cage for birds. "Oh Jesus," Enoch groaned. He stood and waved his arms wildly and shouted, "Come on!" but Haze didn't move from where he was looking into the cage.

Enoch ran back to him and grabbed him by the arm but Haze pushed him off and kept on looking in the cage. It was empty. Enoch stared. "It's empty!" he shouted. "What you have to look in that ole empty cage for? You come on!" He stood there, sweating and purple. "It's empty!" he shouted. And then he saw it wasn't empty. Over in one corner on the floor of the cage, there was an eye. The eye was in the middle of something that looked like a piece of mop sitting on an old rag. He squinted close to the wire and saw that the piece of mop was an owl with one eye open. It was looking directly at Hazel Motes. "That ain't nothing but a ole hoot owl," he moaned. "You seen them things before."

"I AM clean," Haze said to the eye. He said it just the way he said it to the woman in the FROSTY BOTTLE. The eye shut softly and the owl turned its face to the wall.

He's done murdered somebody, Enoch thought. "Oh sweet Jesus, come on!" he wailed. "I got to show you this right now." He pulled him away but a few feet from the cage, Haze stopped again, looking at something in the distance. Enoch's eyesight was very poor. He squinted and made out a figure far down the road behind them. There were two smaller figures jumping on either side of it.

Hazel Motes turned back to him suddenly and said, "Where's this thing? Let's see it right now and get it over with. Come on."

"Ain't that where I been trying to take you?" Enoch said. He felt the perspiration drying on him and stinging and his skin was pin-pointed, even in his scalp. "We got to cross this road and go down this hill. We got to go on foot," he said.

"Why?" Haze muttered.

"I don't know," Enoch said. He knew something was going to happen to him. His blood stopped beating. All the time it had been beating like drum noises and now it had stopped. They started down the hill. It was a steep hill, full of trees painted white from the ground up four feet. They looked as if they had on ankle-socks. He gripped Hazel Motes's arm. "It gets damp as you go down," he said, looking around vaguely. Hazel Motes shook him off. In a second, Enoch gripped his arm again and stopped him. He pointed down through the trees. "Muvseevum," he said. The strange word made him shiver. That was the first time he had ever said it aloud. A piece of gray building was showing where he pointed. It grew larger as they went down the hill, then as they came to the end of the wood and stepped out on the gravel driveway, it seemed to shrink suddenly. It was round and soot-colored. There were columns at the front of it and in between each column there was an eyeless stone woman holding a pot on her head. A concrete band was over the columns and the letters, MVSEVM, were cut into it. Enoch was afraid to pronounce the word again.

"We got to go up the steps and through the front door," he whispered. There were ten steps up to the porch. The door was wide and black. Enoch pushed it in cautiously and inserted his head in the crack. In a minute he brought it out again and said, "All right, go on in and walk easy. I don't want to wake up theter ole guard. He ain't very friendly with me." They went into a dark hall. It was heavy with the odor of linoleum and creosote and another odor behind these two. The third one was an undersmell and Enoch couldn't name it as anything he had ever smelled before. There was nothing in the hall but two urns and an old man asleep in a straight chair against the wall. He had on the same kind of uniform as Enoch and he looked like a dried-up spider stuck there. Enoch looked at Hazel Motes to see if he was smelling the undersmell. He looked as if he were. Enoch's blood began to beat again, urging him forward. He gripped Haze's arm and tiptoed through the hall to another black door at the end of it. He cracked it a little and inserted his head in the crack. Then in a second he drew it out and crooked his finger in a gesture for Haze to follow him. They went into another hall, like the last one, but running crosswise. "It's in that first door yonder," Enoch said in a small voice. They went into a dark room full of glass cases. The glass cases covered the walls and there were three coffin-like ones in the middle of the floor. The ones on the walls were full of birds tilted on varnished sticks and looking down with dried piquant expressions.

"Come on," Enoch whispered. He went past the two cases in the middle of the floor and toward the third one. He went to the farthest end of it and stopped. He stood looking down with his neck thrust forward and his hands clutched together; Hazel Motes moved up beside him.

The two of them stood there, Enoch rigid and Hazel Motes bent slightly forward. There were three bowls and a row of blunt weapons and a man in the case. It was the man Enoch was looking at. He was about three feet long. He was naked and a dried yellow color and his eyes were drawn almost shut as if a giant block of steel were falling down on top of him.

"See theter notice," Enoch said in a church whisper, pointing to a typewritten card at the man's foot, "it says he was once as tall as you or me. Some A-rabs did it to him in six months." He turned his head cautiously to see Hazel Motes.

All he could tell was that Hazel Motes's eyes were on the shrunken man. He was bent forward so that his face was reflected on the glass top of the case. The reflection was pale and the eyes were like two clean bullet holes. Enoch waited, rigid. He heard footsteps in the hall. Oh Jesus Jesus, he prayed, let him hurry up and do whatever he's going to do! The woman with the two little boys came in the door. She had one by each hand, and she was grinning. Hazel Motes had not raised his eyes once from the shrunken man. The woman came toward them. She stopped on the other side of the case and looked down into it and the reflection of her face appeared grinning on the glass, over Hazel Motes's.

She snickered and put two fingers in front of her teeth. The little boys' faces were like pans set on either side to catch the grins that overflowed from her. When Haze saw her face on the glass, his neck jerked back and he made a noise. It might have come from the man inside the case. In a second Enoch knew it had. "Wait!" he screamed, and tore out of the room after Hazel Motes.

He overtook him halfway up the hill. He caught him by

the arm and swung him around and then he stood there, suddenly weak and light as a balloon, and stared. Hazel Motes grabbed him by the shoulders and shook him. "What is that address!" he shouted. "Give me that address!"

Even if Enoch had been sure what the address was, he couldn't have thought of it then. He could not even stand up. As soon as Hazel Motes let him go, he fell backward and landed against one of the white-socked trees. He rolled over and lay stretched out on the ground, with an exalted look on his face. He thought he was floating. A long way off he saw the blue figure spring and pick up a rock, and he saw the wild face turn, and the rock hurtle toward him; he shut his eyes tight and the rock hit him on the forehead.

When he came to again, Hazel Motes was gone. He lay there a minute. He put his fingers to his forehead and then held them in front of his eyes. They were streaked with red. He turned his head and saw a drop of blood on the ground and as he looked at it, he thought it widened like a little spring. He sat straight up, frozen-skinned, and put his finger in it, and very faintly he could hear his blood beating, his secret blood, in the center of the city.

Then he knew that whatever was expected of him was only just beginning.

Chapter 6

THAT EVENING Haze drove his car around the streets until he found the blind man and the child again. They were standing on a corner, waiting for the light to change. He drove the Essex at some distance behind them for about four blocks up the main street and then turned it after them down a side street. He followed them on into a dark section past the railroad yards and watched them go up on the porch of a box-like two-story house. When the blind man opened the door a shaft of light fell on him and Haze craned his neck to see him better. The child turned her head, slowly, as if it worked on a screw, and watched his car pass. His face was so close to the glass that it looked like a paper face pasted there. He noted the number of the house and a sign on it that said, ROOMS FOR RENT.

Then he drove back down town and parked the Essex in front of a movie house where he could catch the drain of people coming out from the picture show. The lights around the marquee were so bright that the moon, moving overhead with a small procession of clouds behind it, looked pale and insignificant. Haze got out of the Essex and climbed up on the nose of it.

A thin little man with a long upper lip was at the glass ticket box, buying tickets for three portly women who were behind him. "Gotta get these girls some refreshments too," he said to the woman in the ticket box. "Can't have 'em starve right before my eyes."

"Ain't he a card?" one of the women hollered. "He keeps me in stitches!"

Three boys in red satin lumberjackets came out of the foyer. Haze raised his arms. "Where has the blood you think you been redeemed by touched you?" he cried.

The women all turned around at once and stared at him.

"A wise guy," the little thin man said, and glared as if someone were about to insult him.

The three boys moved up, pushing each other's shoulders.

Haze waited a second and then he cried again, "Where has the blood you think you been redeemed by touched you?"

"Rabble rouser," the little man said. "One thing I can't stand it's a rabble rouser."

"What church you belong to, you boy there?" Haze asked, pointing at the tallest boy in the red satin lumberjacket.

The boy giggled.

"You then," he said impatiently, pointing at the next one. "What church you belong to?"

"Church of Christ," the boy said in a falsetto to hide the truth.

"Church of Christ!" Haze repeated. "Well, I preach the Church Without Christ. I'm member and preacher to that church where the blind don't see and the lame don't walk and what's dead stays that way. Ask me about that church and I'll tell you it's the church that the blood of Jesus don't foul with redemption."

"He's a preacher," one of the women said. "Let's go."

"Listen, you people, I'm going to take the truth with me wherever I go," Haze called. "I'm going to preach it to whoever'll listen at whatever place. I'm going to preach there was no Fall because there was nothing to fall from and no Redemption because there was no Fall and no Judgment because there wasn't the first two. Nothing matters but that Jesus was a liar."

The little man herded his girls into the picture show quickly and the three boys left but more people came out and he began over and said the same thing again. They left and some more came and he said it a third time. Then they left and no one else came out; there was no one there but the woman in the glass box. She had been glaring at him all the time but he had not noticed her. She wore glasses with rhinestones in the bows and she had white hair stacked in sausages around her head. She stuck her mouth to a hole in the glass and shouted, "Listen, if you don't have a church to do it in, you don't have to do it in front of this show."

"My church is the Church Without Christ, lady," he said. "If there's no Christ, there's no reason to have a set place to do it in."

"Listen," she said, "if you don't get from in front of this show, I'll call the police."

"There's plenty of shows," he said and got down and got

back in the Essex and drove off. That night he preached in front of three other picture shows before he went to Mrs. Watts.

In the morning he drove back to the house where the blind man and the child had gone in the night before. It was yellow clapboard, the second one in a block of them, all alike. He went up to the front door and rang the bell. After a few minutes a woman with a mop opened it. He said he wanted to rent a room.

"What you do?" she asked. She was a tall bony woman, resembling the mop she carried upside-down.

He said he was a preacher.

The woman looked at him thoroughly and then she looked behind him at his car. "What church?" she asked.

He said the Church Without Christ.

"Protestant?" she asked suspiciously, "or something foreign?"

He said no mam, it was Protestant.

After a minute she said, "Well, you can look at it," and he followed her into a white plastered hall and up some steps at the side of it. She opened a door into a back room that was a little larger than his car, with a cot and a chest of drawers and a table and straight chair in it. There were two nails on the wall to hang clothes on. "Three dollars a week in advance," she said. There was one window and another door opposite the door they had come in by. Haze opened the extra door, expecting it to be a closet. It opened out onto a drop of about thirty feet and looked down into a narrow bare back yard where the garbage was collected. There was a plank nailed across the door frame at knee level to keep anyone from falling out. "A man named Hawks lives here, don't he?" Haze asked quickly.

"Downstairs in the front room," she said, "him and his child." She was looking down into the drop too. "It used to be a fire-escape there," she said, "but I don't know what happened to it."

He paid her three dollars and took possession of the room, and as soon as she was out of the way, he went down the stairs and knocked on the Hawkses' door.

The blind man's child opened it a crack and stood looking

at him. She seemed at once to have to balance her face so that her expression would be the same on both sides. "It's that boy, Papa," she said in a low tone. "The one that keeps following me." She held the door close to her head so he couldn't see in past her. The blind man came to the door but he didn't open it any wider. His look was not the same as it had been two nights before; it was sour and unfriendly, and he didn't speak, he only stood there.

Haze had got what he had to say in mind before he left his room. "I live here," he said. "I thought if your girl wanted to give me so much eye, I might return her some of it." He wasn't looking at the girl; he was staring at the black glasses and the curious scars that started somewhere behind them and ran down the blind man's cheeks.

"What I give you the other night," she said, "was a looker indignation for what I seen you do. It was you give me the eye. You should have seen him, Papa," she said, "looked me up and down."

"I've started my own church," Haze said. "The Church Without Christ. I preach on the street."

"You can't let me alone, can you?" Hawks said. His voice was flat, nothing like it had been the other time. "I didn't ask you to come here and I ain't asking you to hang around," he said.

Haze had expected a secret welcome. He waited, trying to think of something to say. "What kind of a preacher are you?" he heard himself murmur, "not to see if you can save my soul?" The blind man pushed the door shut in his face. Haze stood there a second facing the blank door, and then he ran his sleeve across his mouth and went out.

Inside, Hawks took off his dark glasses and, from a hole in the window shade, watched him get in his car and drive off. The eye he put to the hole was slightly rounder and smaller than his other one, but it was obvious he could see out of both of them. The child watched from a lower crack. "Howcome you don't like him, Papa?" she asked, "—because he's after me?"

"If he was after you, that would be enough to make me welcome him," he said.

"I like his eyes," she observed. "They don't look like they see what he's looking at but they keep on looking."

Their room was the same size as Haze's but there were two
cots and an oil cooking stove and a wash basin in it and a
trunk that they used for a table. Hawks sat down on one of
the cots and put a cigarette in his mouth. "Goddam Jesus-
hog," he muttered.

"Well, look what you used to be," she said. "Look what
you tried to do. You got over it and so will he."

"I don't want him hanging around," he said. "He makes
me nervous."

"Listen here," she said, sitting down on the cot with him,
"you help me to get him and then you go away and do what
you please and I can live with him."

"He don't even know you exist," Hawks said.

"Even if he don't," she said, "that's all right. That's howcome I can get him easy. I want him and you ought to help
and then you could go on off like you want to."

He lay down on the cot and finished the cigarette; his face
was thoughtful and evil. Once while he was lying there, he
laughed and then his expression constricted again. "Well, that
might be fine," he said after a while. "That might be the oil
on Aaron's beard."

"Listen here," she said, "it would be the nuts! I'm just crazy
about him. I never seen a boy that I liked the looks of any
better. Don't run him off. Tell him how you blinded yourself
for Jesus and show him that clipping you got."

"Yeah, the clipping," he said.

Haze had gone out in his car to think and he had decided
that he would seduce Hawks's child. He thought that when
the blind preacher saw his daughter ruined, he would realize
that he was in earnest when he said he preached The Church
Without Christ. Besides this reason, there was another: he
didn't want to go back to Mrs. Watts. The night before, after
he was asleep, she had got up and cut the top of his hat out
in an obscene shape. He felt that he should have a woman,
not for the sake of the pleasure in her, but to prove that he
didn't believe in sin since he practiced what was called it; but
he had had enough of her. He wanted someone he could
teach something to and he took it for granted that the blind
man's child, since she was so homely, would also be innocent.

Before he went back to his room, he went to a dry-goods

store to buy a new hat. He wanted one that was completely opposite to the old one. This time he was sold a white panama with a red and green and yellow band around it. The man said they were really the thing and particularly if he was going to Florida.

"I ain't going to Florida," he said. "This hat is opposite from the one I used to have is all."

"You can use it anywheres," the man said; "it's new."

"I know that," Haze said. He went outside and took the red and green and yellow band off it and thumped out the crease in the top and turned down the brim. When he put it on, it looked just as fierce as the other one had.

He didn't go back to the Hawkses' door until late in the afternoon, when he thought they would be eating their supper. It opened almost at once and the child's head appeared in the crack. He pushed the door out of her hand and went in without looking at her directly. Hawks was sitting at the trunk. The remains of his supper were in front of him but he wasn't eating. He had barely got the black glasses on in time.

"If Jesus cured blind men, howcome you don't get Him to cure you?" Haze asked. He had prepared this sentence in his room.

"He blinded Paul," Hawks said.

Haze sat down on the edge of one of the cots. He looked around him and then back at Hawks. He crossed and uncrossed his knees and then he crossed them again. "Where'd you get them scars?" he asked.

The fake blind man leaned forward and smiled. "You still have a chance to save yourself if you repent," he said. "I can't save you but you can save yourself."

"That's what I've already done," Haze said. "Without the repenting. I preach how I done it every night on the . . ."

"Look at this," Hawks said. He took a yellow newspaper clipping from his pocket and handed it to him, and his mouth twisted out of the smile. "This is how I got the scars," he muttered. The child made a sign to him from the door to smile and not look sour. As he waited for Haze to finish reading, the smile slowly returned.

The headline on the clipping said, EVANGELIST PROMISES TO BLIND SELF. The rest of it said that Asa Hawks, an evangelist of the Free Church of Christ, had promised to blind himself to justify his belief that Christ Jesus had redeemed him. It said he would do it at a revival on Saturday night at eight o'clock, the fourth of October. The date on it was more than ten years before. Over the headline was a picture of Hawks, a scarless, straight-mouthed man of about thirty, with one eye a little smaller and rounder than the other. The mouth had a look that might have been either holy or calculating, but there was a wildness in the eyes that suggested terror.

Haze sat staring at the clipping after he had read it. He read it three times. He took his hat off and put it on again and got up and stood looking around the room as if he were trying to remember where the door was.

"He did it with lime," the child said, "and there was hundreds converted. Anybody that blinded himself for justification ought to be able to save you—or even somebody of his blood," she added, inspired.

"Nobody with a good car needs to be justified," Haze murmured. He scowled at her and hurried out the door, but as soon as it was shut behind him, he remembered something. He turned around and opened it and handed her a piece of paper, folded up several times into a small pellet shape; then he hurried out to his car.

Hawks took the note away from her and opened it up. It said, BABE, I NEVER SAW ANYBODY THAT LOOKED AS GOOD AS YOU BEFORE IS WHY I CAME HERE. She read it over his arm, coloring pleasantly.

"Now you got the written proof for it, Papa," she said.

"That bastard got away with my clipping," Hawks muttered.

"Well you got another clipping, ain't you?" she asked, with a little smirk.

"Shut your mouth," he said and flung himself down on the cot. The other clipping was one that said, EVANGELIST'S NERVE FAILS.

"I can get it for you," she offered, standing close to the door so that she could run if she disturbed him too much, but he had turned toward the wall as if he were going to sleep.

Ten years ago at a revival he had intended to blind himself and two hundred people or more were there, waiting for him to do it. He had preached for an hour on the blindness of Paul, working himself up until he saw himself struck blind by a Divine flash of lightning and, with courage enough then, he had thrust his hands into the bucket of wet lime and streaked them down his face; but he hadn't been able to let any of it get into his eyes. He had been possessed of as many devils as were necessary to do it, but at that instant, they disappeared, and he saw himself standing there as he was. He fancied Jesus, Who had expelled them, was standing there too, beckoning to him; and he had fled out of the tent into the alley and disappeared.

"Okay, Pa," she said, "I'll go out for a while and leave you in peace."

Haze had driven his car immediately to the nearest garage where a man with black bangs and a short expressionless face had come out to wait on him. He told the man he wanted the horn made to blow and the leaks taken out of the gas tank, the starter made to work smoother and the windshield wipers tightened.

The man lifted the hood and glanced inside and then shut it again. Then he walked around the car, stopping to lean on it here and there, and thumping it in one place and another. Haze asked him how long it would take to put it in the best order.

"It can't be done," the man said.

"This is a good car," Haze said. "I knew when I first saw it that it was the car for me, and since I've had it, I've had a place to be that I can always get away in."

"Was you going some place in this?" the man asked.

"To another garage," Haze said, and he got in the Essex and drove off. At the other garage he went to, there was a man who said he could put the car in the best shape overnight, because it was such a good car to begin with, so well put together and with such good materials in it, and because, he added, he was the best mechanic in town, working in the best-equipped shop. Haze left it with him, certain that it was in honest hands.

Chapter 7

THE NEXT AFTERNOON when he got his car back, he drove it out into the country to see how well it worked on the open road. The sky was just a little lighter blue than his suit, clear and even, with only one cloud in it, a large blinding white one with curls and a beard. He had gone about a mile out of town when he heard a throat cleared behind him. He slowed down and turned his head and saw Hawks's child getting up off the floor onto the two-by-four that stretched across the seat frame. "I been here all the time," she said, "and you never known it." She had a bunch of dandelions in her hair and a wide red mouth on her pale face.

"What do you want to hide in my car for?" he said angrily. "I got business before me. I don't have time for foolishness." Then he checked his ugly tone and stretched his mouth a little, remembering that he was going to seduce her. "Yeah sure," he said, "glad to see you."

She swung one thin black-stockinged leg over the back of the front seat and then let the rest of herself over. "Did you mean 'good to look at' in that note, or only 'good'?" she asked.

"The both," he said stiffly.

"My name is Sabbath," she said. "Sabbath Lily Hawks. My mother named me that just after I was born because I was born on the Sabbath and then she turned over in her bed and died and I never seen her."

"Unh," Haze said. His jaw tightened and he entrenched himself behind it and drove on. He had not wanted any company. His sense of pleasure in the car and in the afternoon was gone.

"Him and her wasn't married," she continued, "and that makes me a bastard, but I can't help it. It was what he done to me and not what I done to myself."

"A bastard?" he murmured. He couldn't see how a preacher who had blinded himself for Jesus could have a bastard. He turned his head and looked at her with interest for the first time.

She nodded and the corners of her mouth turned up. "A real bastard," she said, catching his elbow, "and do you know

66

what? A bastard shall not enter the kingdom of heaven!" she said.

Haze was driving his car toward the ditch while he stared at her. "How could you be . . . ," he started and saw the red embankment in front of him and pulled the car back on the road.

"Do you read the papers?" she asked.

"No," he said.

"Well, there's this woman in it named Mary Brittle that tells you what to do when you don't know. I wrote her a letter and ast her what I was to do."

"How could you be a bastard when he blinded him . . . ," he started again.

"I says, 'Dear Mary, I am a bastard and a bastard shall not enter the kingdom of heaven as we all know, but I have this personality that makes boys follow me. Do you think I should neck or not? I shall not enter the kingdom of heaven anyway so I don't see what difference it makes.' "

"Listen here," Haze said, "if he blinded himself how . . ."

"Then she answered my letter in the paper. She said, 'Dear Sabbath, Light necking is acceptable, but I think your real problem is one of adjustment to the modern world. Perhaps you ought to re-examine your religious values to see if they meet your needs in Life. A religious experience can be a beautiful addition to living if you put it in the proper prespective and do not let it warp you. Read some books on Ethical Culture.' "

"You couldn't be a bastard," Haze said, getting very pale. "You must be mixed up. Your daddy blinded himself."

"Then I wrote her another letter," she said, scratching his ankle with the toe of her sneaker, and smiling, "I says, 'Dear Mary, What I really want to know is should I go the whole hog or not? That's my real problem. I'm adjusted okay to the modern world.' "

"Your daddy blinded himself," Haze repeated.

"He wasn't always as good as he is now," she said. "She never answered my second letter."

"You mean in his youth he didn't believe but he came to?" he asked. "Is that what you mean or ain't it?" and he kicked her foot roughly away from his.

"That's right," she said. Then she drew herself up a little. "Quit that feeling my leg with yours," she said.

The blinding white cloud was a little ahead of them, moving to the left. "Why don't you turn down that dirt road?" she asked. The highway forked off onto a clay road and he turned onto it. It was hilly and shady and the country showed to advantage on either side. One side was dense honeysuckle and the other was open and slanted down to a telescoped view of the city. The white cloud was directly in front of them.

"How did he come to believe?" Haze asked. "What changed him into a preacher for Jesus?"

"I do like a dirt road," she said, "particularly when it's hilly like this one here. Why don't we get out and sit under a tree where we could get better acquainted?"

After a few hundred feet Haze stopped the car and they got out. "Was he a very evil-seeming man before he came to believe," he asked, "or just part way evil-seeming?"

"All the way evil," she said, going under the barbed wire fence on the side of the road. Once under it she sat down and began to take off her shoes and stockings. "How I like to walk in a field is barefooted," she said with gusto.

"Listenhere," Haze muttered, "I got to be going back to town. I don't have time to walk in any field," but he went under the fence and on the other side he said, "I suppose before he came to believe he didn't believe at all."

"Let's us go over that hill yonder and sit under the trees," she said.

They climbed the hill and went down the other side of it, she a little ahead of Haze. He saw that sitting under a tree with her might help him to seduce her, but he was in no hurry to get on with it, considering her innocence. He felt it was too hard a job to be done in an afternoon. She sat down under a large pine and patted the ground close beside her for him to sit on, but he sat about five feet away from her on a rock. He rested his chin on his knees and looked straight ahead.

"I can save you," she said. "I got a church in my heart where Jesus is King."

He leaned in her direction, glaring. "I believe in a new kind of jesus," he said, "one that can't waste his blood redeeming people with it, because he's all man and ain't got any God in him. My church is the Church Without Christ!"

She moved up closer to him. "Can a bastard be saved in it?" she asked.

"There's no such thing as a bastard in the Church Without Christ," he said. "Everything is all one. A bastard wouldn't be any different from anybody else."

"That's good," she said.

He looked at her irritably, for something in his mind was already contradicting him and saying that a bastard couldn't, that there was only one truth—that Jesus was a liar—and that her case was hopeless. She pulled open her collar and lay down on the ground full length. "Ain't my feet white, though?" she asked raising them slightly.

Haze didn't look at her feet. The thing in his mind said that the truth didn't contradict itself and that a bastard couldn't be saved in the Church Without Christ. He decided he would forget it, that it was not important.

"There was this child once," she said, turning over on her stomach, "that nobody cared if it lived or died. Its kin sent it around from one to another of them and finally to its grandmother who was a very evil woman and she couldn't stand to have it around because the least good thing made her break out in these welps. She would get all itching and swoll. Even her eyes would itch her and swell up and there wasn't nothing she could do but run up and down the road, shaking her hands and cursing and it was twicet as bad when this child was there so she kept the child locked up in a chicken crate. It seen its granny in hell-fire, swoll and burning, and it told her everything it seen and she got so swoll until finally she went to the well and wrapped the well rope around her neck and let down the bucket and broke her neck.

"Would you guess me to be fifteen years old?" she asked.

"There wouldn't be any sense to the word, bastard, in the Church Without Christ," Haze said.

"Why don't you lie down and rest yourself?" she inquired.

Haze moved a few feet away and lay down. He put his hat over his face and folded his arms across his chest. She lifted herself up on her hands and knees and crawled over to him and gazed at the top of his hat. Then she lifted it off like a lid and peered into his eyes. They stared straight upward. "It don't make any difference to me," she said softly, "how much you like me."

He trained his eyes into her neck. Gradually she lowered her head until the tips of their noses almost touched but still he didn't look at her. "I see you," she said in a playful voice.

"Git away!" he said, jumping violently.

She scrambled up and ran around behind the tree. Haze put his hat back on and stood up, shaken. He wanted to get back in the Essex. He realized suddenly that it was parked on a country road, unlocked, and that the first person passing would drive off in it.

"I see you," a voice said from behind the tree.

He walked off quickly in the opposite direction toward the car. The jubilant expression on the face that looked from around the tree, flattened.

He got in his car and went through the motions of starting it but it only made a noise like water lost somewhere in the pipes. A panic took him and he began to pound the starter. There were two instruments on the dashboard with needles that pointed dizzily in first one direction and then another, but they worked on a private system, independent of the whole car. He couldn't tell if it was out of gas or not. Sabbath Hawks came running up to the fence. She got down on the ground and rolled under the barbed wire and then stood at the window of the car, looking in at him. He turned his head at her fiercely and said, "What did you do to my car?" Then he got out and started walking down the road, without waiting for her to answer. After a second, she followed him, keeping her distance.

Where the highway had forked off onto the dirt road, there had been a store with a gas pump in front of it. It was about a half-mile back; Haze kept up a steady fast pace until he reached it. It had a deserted look, but after a few minutes a man appeared from out of the woods behind it, and Haze told him what he wanted. While the man got out his pick-up truck to drive them back to the Essex, Sabbath Hawks arrived and went over to a cage about six feet high that was at the side of the shack. Haze had not noticed it until she came up.

He saw that there was something alive in it, and went near enough to read a sign that said, Two DEADLY ENEMIES. HAVE A LOOK FREE.

There was a black bear about four feet long and very thin, resting on the floor of the cage; his back was spotted with bird lime that had been shot down on him by a small chicken hawk that was sitting on a perch in the upper part of the same apartment. Most of the hawk's tail was gone; the bear had only one eye.

"Come on here if you don't want to get left," Haze said roughly, grabbing her by the arm. The man had his truck ready and the three of them drove back in it to the Essex. On the way Haze told him about the Church Without Christ; he explained its principles and said there was no such thing as a bastard in it. The man didn't comment. When they got out at the Essex, he put a can of gas in the tank and Haze got in and tried to start it but nothing happened. The man opened up the hood and studied the inside for a while. He was a one-armed man with two sandy-colored teeth and eyes that were slate-blue and thoughtful. He had not spoken more than two words yet. He looked for a long time under the hood while Haze stood by, but he didn't touch anything. After a while he shut it and blew his nose.

"What's wrong in there?" Haze asked in an agitated voice. "It's a good car, ain't it?"

The man didn't answer him. He sat down on the ground and eased under the Essex. He wore hightop shoes and gray socks. He stayed under the car a long time. Haze got down on his hands and knees and looked under to see what he was doing but he wasn't doing anything. He was just lying there, looking up, as if he were contemplating; his good arm was folded on his chest. After a while, he eased himself out and wiped his face and neck with a piece of flannel rag he had in his pocket.

"Listenhere," Haze said, "that's a good car. You just give me a push, that's all. That car'll get me anywhere I want to go."

The man didn't say anything but he got back in the truck and Haze and Sabbath Hawks got in the Essex and he pushed them. After a few hundred yards the Essex began to belch and gasp and jiggle. Haze stuck his head out the window and motioned for the truck to come alongside. "Ha!" he said. "I told you, didn't I? This car'll get me anywhere I want to go. It may stop here and there but it won't stop permanent. What do I owe you?"

"Nothing," the man said, "not a thing."

"But the gas," Haze said, "how much for the gas?"

"Nothing," the man said with the same level look. "Not a thing."

"All right, I thank you," Haze said and drove on. "I don't need no favors from him," he said.

"It's a grand auto," Sabbath Hawks said. "It goes as smooth as honey."

"It ain't been built by a bunch of foreigners or niggers or one-arm men," Haze said. "It was built by people with their eyes open that knew where they were at."

When they came to the end of the dirt road and were facing the paved one, the pick-up truck pulled alongside again and while the two cars paused side by side, Haze and the slate-eyed man looked at each other out of their two windows. "I told you this car would get me anywhere I wanted to go," Haze said sourly.

"Some things," the man said, " 'll get some folks somewheres," and he turned the truck up the highway.

Haze drove on. The blinding white cloud had turned into a bird with long thin wings and was disappearing in the opposite direction.

Chapter 8

Enoch Emery knew now that his life would never be the same again, because the thing that was going to happen to him had started to happen. He had always known that something was going to happen but he hadn't known what. If he had been much given to thought, he might have thought that now was the time for him to justify his daddy's blood, but he didn't think in broad sweeps like that, he thought what he would do next. Sometimes he didn't think, he only wondered; then before long he would find himself doing this or that, like a bird finds itself building a nest when it hasn't actually been planning to.

What was going to happen to him had started to happen when he showed what was in the glass case to Haze Motes. That was a mystery beyond his understanding, but he knew that what was going to be expected of him was something awful. His blood was more sensitive than any other part of him; it wrote doom all through him, except possibly in his brain, and the result was that his tongue, which edged out every few minutes to test his fever blister, knew more than he did.

The first thing that he found himself doing that was not normal was saving his pay. He was saving all of it, except what his landlady came to collect every week and what he had to use to buy something to eat with. Then to his surprise, he found he wasn't eating very much and he was saving that money too. He had a fondness for Supermarkets; it was his custom to spend an hour or so in one every afternoon after he left the city park, browsing around among the canned goods and reading the cereal stories. Lately he had been compelled to pick up a few things here and there that would not be bulky in his pockets, and he wondered if this could be the reason he was saving so much money on food. It could have been, but he had the suspicion that saving the money was connected with some larger thing. He had always been given to stealing but he had never saved before.

At the same time, he began cleaning up his room. It was a little green room, or it had once been green, in the attic of an elderly rooming house. There was a mummified look and feel

73

to this residence, but Enoch had never thought before of brightening the part (corresponding to the head) that he lived in. Then he simply found himself doing it.

First, he removed the rug from the floor and hung it out the window. This was a mistake because when he went to pull it back in, there were only a few long strings left with a carpet tack caught in one of them. He imagined that it must have been a very old rug and he decided to handle the rest of the furniture with more care. He washed the bed frame with soap and water and found that under the second layer of dirt, it was pure gold, and this affected him so strongly that he washed the chair. It was a low round chair that bulged around the legs so that it seemed to be in the act of squatting. The gold began to appear with the first touch of water but it disappeared with the second and with a little more, the chair sat down as if this were the end of long years of inner struggle. Enoch didn't know if it was for him or against him. He had a nasty impulse to kick it to pieces, but he let it stay there, exactly in the position it had sat down in, because for the time anyway, he was not a foolhardy boy who took chances on the meanings of things. For the time, he knew that what he didn't know was what mattered.

The only other piece of furniture in the room was a washstand. This was built in three parts and stood on bird legs six inches high. The legs had clawed feet that were each one gripped around a small cannon ball. The lowest part was a tabernacle-like cabinet which was meant to contain a slop-jar. Enoch didn't own a slop-jar but he had a certain reverence for the purpose of things and since he didn't have the right thing to put in it, he left it empty. Directly over this place for the treasure, there was a gray marble slab and coming up from behind it was a wooden trellis-work of hearts, scrolls and flowers, extending into a hunched eagle wing on either side, and containing in the middle, just at the level of Enoch's face when he stood in front of it, a small oval mirror. The wooden frame continued again over the mirror and ended in a crowned, horned headpiece, showing that the artist had not lost faith in his work.

As far as Enoch was concerned, this piece had always been the center of the room and the one that most connected him with what he didn't know. More than once after a big supper, he had dreamed of unlocking the cabinet and getting in it and then proceeding to certain rites and mysteries that he had a very vague idea about in the morning. In his cleaning up, his mind was on the washstand from the first, but as was usual with him, he began with the least important thing and worked around and in toward the center where the meaning was. So before he tackled the washstand, he took care of the pictures in the room.

These were three, one belonging to his landlady (who was almost totally blind but moved about by an acute sense of smell) and two of his own. Hers was a brown portrait of a moose standing in a small lake. The look of superiority on this animal's face was so insufferable to Enoch that, if he hadn't been afraid of him, he would have done something about it a long time ago. As it was, he couldn't do anything in his room but what the smug face was watching, not shocked because nothing better could be expected and not amused because nothing was funny. If he had looked all over for one, he couldn't have found a roommate that irritated him more. He kept up a constant stream of inner comment, un-complimentary to the moose, though when he said anything aloud, he was more guarded. The moose was in a heavy brown frame with leaf designs on it and this added to his weight and his self-satisfied look. Enoch knew the time had come when something had to be done; he didn't know what was going to happen in his room, but when it happened, he didn't want to have the feeling that the moose was running it. The answer came to him fully prepared: he realized with a sudden intuition that taking the frame off him would be equal to taking the clothes off him (although he didn't have on any) and he was right because when he had done it, the animal looked so reduced that Enoch could only snicker and look at him out the corner of his eye.

After this success he turned his attention to the other two pictures. They were over calendars and had been sent him by the Hilltop Funeral Home and the American Rubber Tire Company. One showed a small boy in a pair of blue Doctor Denton sleepers, kneeling at his bed, saying, "And bless daddy," while the moon looked in at the window. This was

Enoch's favorite painting and it hung directly over his bed. The other pictured a lady wearing a rubber tire and it hung directly across from the moose on the opposite wall. He left it where it was, pretty certain that the moose only pretended not to see it. Immediately after he finished with the pictures, he went out and bought chintz curtains, a bottle of gilt, and a paint brush with all the money he had saved.

This was a disappointment to him because he had hoped that the money would be for some new clothes for him, and here he saw it going into a set of drapes. He didn't know what the gilt was for until he got home with it; when he got home with it, he sat down in front of the slop-jar cabinet in the washstand, unlocked it, and painted the inside of it with the gilt. Then he realized that the cabinet was to be used FOR something.

Enoch never nagged his blood to tell him a thing until it was ready. He wasn't the kind of a boy who grabs at any possibility and runs off, proposing this or that preposterous thing. In a large matter like this, he was always willing to wait for a certainty, and he waited for this one, certain at least that he would know in a few days. Then for about a week his blood was in secret conference with itself every day, only stopping now and then to shout some order at him.

On the following Monday, he was certain when he woke up that today was the day he was going to know on. His blood was rushing around like a woman who cleans up the house after the company has come, and he was surly and rebellious. When he realized that today was the day, he decided not to get up. He didn't want to justify his daddy's blood, he didn't want to be always having to do something that something else wanted him to do, that he didn't know what it was and that was always dangerous.

Naturally, his blood was not going to put up with any attitude like this. He was at the zoo by nine-thirty, only a half-hour later than he was supposed to be. All morning his mind was not on the gate he was supposed to guard but was chasing around after his blood, like a boy with a mop and a bucket, beating something here and sloshing down something there, without a second's rest. As soon as the second-shift guard came, Enoch headed toward town.

Town was the last place he wanted to be because anything could happen there. All the time his mind had been chasing around it had been thinking how as soon as he got off duty he was going to sneak off home and go to bed.

By the time he got into the center of the business district he was exhausted and he had to lean against Walgreen's window and cool off. Sweat crept down his back and provoked him to itch so that in just a few minutes he appeared to be working his way across the glass by his muscles, against a background of alarm clocks, toilet waters, candies, sanitary pads, fountain pens, and pocket flashlights, displayed in all colors to twice his height. He appeared to be working his way to a rumbling noise which came from the center of a small alcove that formed the entrance to the drug store. Here was a yellow and blue, glass and steel machine, belching popcorn into a cauldron of butter and salt. Enoch approached, already with his purse out, sorting his money. His purse was a long gray leather pouch, tied at the top with a drawstring. It was one he had stolen from his daddy and he treasured it because it was the only thing he owned now that his daddy had touched (besides himself). He sorted out two nickels and handed them to a pasty boy in a white apron who was there to serve the machine. The boy felt around in its vitals and filled a white paper bag with the corn, not taking his eye off Enoch's purse the while. On any other day Enoch would have tried to make friends with him but today he was too preoccupied even to see him. He took the bag and began stuffing the pouch back where it had come from. The youth's eye followed to the very edge of the pocket. "That thang looks like a hawg bladder," he observed enviously.

"I got to go now," Enoch murmured and hurried into the drug store. Inside, he walked abstractedly to the back of the store, and then up to the front again by the other aisle as if he wanted any person who might be looking for him to see he was there. He paused in front of the soda fountain to see if he would sit down and have something to eat. The fountain counter was pink and green marble linoleum and behind it there was a red-headed waitress in a lime-colored uniform and a pink apron. She had green eyes set in pink and they resembled a picture behind her of a Lime-Cherry Surprise, a special that day for ten cents. She confronted Enoch while he studied the information over her head. After a minute she laid her chest on the counter and surrounded it by her folded arms, to wait. Enoch couldn't decide which of several concoctions was the one for him to have until she ended it by moving one arm under the counter and bringing out a Lime-Cherry Surprise. "It's okay," she said, "I fixed it this morning after breakfast."

"Something's going to happen to me today," Enoch said.

"I told you it was okay," she said. "I fixed it today."

"I seen it this morning when I woke up," he said, with the look of a visionary.

"God," she said, and jerked it from under his face. She turned around and began slapping things together; in a second she slammed another—exactly like it, but fresh—in front of him.

"I got to go now," Enoch said, and hurried out. An eye caught at his pocket as he passed the popcorn machine but he didn't stop. I don't want to do it, he was saying to himself. Whatever it is, I don't want to do it. I'm going home. It'll be something I don't want to do. It'll be something I ain't got no business doing. And he thought of how he had had to spend all his money on drapes and gilt when he could have bought him a shirt and a phosphorescent tie. It'll be something against the law, he said. It's always something against the law. I ain't going to do it, he said, and stopped. He had stopped in front of a movie house where there was a large illustration of a monster stuffing a young woman into an incinerator.

I ain't going in no picture show like that, he said, giving it a nervous look. I'm going home. I ain't going to wait around in no picture show. I ain't got the money to buy a ticket, he said, taking out his purse again. I ain't even going to count thisyer change.

It ain't but forty-three cent here, he said, that ain't enough. A sign said the price of a ticket for adults was forty-five cents, balcony, thirty-five. I ain't going to sit in no balcony, he said, buying a thirty-five cent ticket.

I ain't going in, he said.

Two doors flew open and he found himself moving down

a long red foyer and then up a darker tunnel and then up a
higher, still darker tunnel. In a few minutes he was up in a
high part of the maw, feeling around, like Jonah, for a seat. I
ain't going to look at it, he said furiously. He didn't like any
picture shows but colored musical ones.

The first picture was about a scientist named The Eye who
performed operations by remote control. You would wake up
in the morning and find a slit in your chest or head or stomach and something you couldn't do without would be gone.
Enoch pulled his hat down very low and drew his knees up
in front of his face; only his eyes looked at the screen. That
picture lasted an hour.

The second picture was about life at Devil's Island Penitentiary. After a while, Enoch had to grip the two arms of his
seat to keep himself from falling over the rail in front of him.

The third picture was called, "Lonnie Comes Home
Again." It was about a baboon named Lonnie who rescued
attractive children from a burning orphanage. Enoch kept
hoping Lonnie would get burned up but he didn't appear to
get even hot. In the end a nice-looking girl gave him a medal.
It was more than Enoch could stand. He made a dive for the
aisle, fell down the two higher tunnels, and raced out the red
foyer and into the street. He collapsed as soon as the air hit
him.

When he recovered himself, he was sitting against the wall
of the picture show building and he was not thinking any
more about escaping his duty. It was night and he had the
feeling that the knowledge he couldn't avoid was almost on
him. His resignation was perfect. He leaned against the wall
for about twenty minutes and then he got up and began to
walk down the street as if he were led by a silent melody or
by one of those whistles that only dogs hear. At the end of
two blocks he stopped, his attention directed across the street.
There, facing him under a street light, was a high rat-colored
car and up on the nose of it, a dark figure with a fierce white
hat on. The figure's arms were working up and down and
he had thin, gesticulating hands, almost as pale as the hat.
"Hazel Motes!" Enoch breathed, and his heart began to slam
from side to side like a wild bell clapper.

There were a few people standing on the sidewalk near the

car. Enoch didn't know that Hazel Motes had started the
Church Without Christ and was preaching it every night on
the street; he hadn't seen him since that day at the park when
he had showed him the shriveled man in the glass case.

"If you had been redeemed," Hazel Motes was shouting,
"you would care about redemption but you don't. Look inside yourselves and see if you hadn't rather it wasn't if it was.
There's no peace for the redeemed," he shouted, "and I
preach peace, I preach the Church Without Christ, the church
peaceful and satisfied!"

Two or three people who had stopped near the car started
walking off the other way. "Leave!" Hazel Motes cried. "Go
ahead and leave! The truth don't matter to you. Listen," he
said, pointing his finger at the rest of them, "the truth don't
matter to you. If Jesus had redeemed you, what difference
would it make to you? You wouldn't do nothing about it.
Your faces wouldn't move, neither this way nor that, and if it
was three crosses there and Him hung on the middle one,
that one wouldn't mean no more to you and me than the
other two. Listen here. What you need is something to take
the place of Jesus, something that would speak plain. The
Church Without Christ don't have a Jesus but it needs one!
It needs a new jesus! It needs one that's all man, without
blood to waste, and it needs one that don't look like any
other man so you'll look at him. Give me such a jesus, you
people. Give me such a new jesus and you'll see how far the
Church Without Christ can go!"

One of the people watching walked off so there were only
two left. Enoch was standing in the middle of the street,
paralyzed.

"Show me where this new jesus is," Hazel Motes cried,
"and I'll set him up in the Church Without Christ and then
you'll see the truth. Then you'll know once and for all that
you haven't been redeemed. Give me this new jesus, somebody, so we'll all be saved by the sight of him!"

Enoch began shouting without a sound. He shouted that
way for a full minute while Hazel Motes went on.

"Look at me!" Hazel Motes cried, with a tare in his throat,
"and you look at a peaceful man! Peaceful because my blood
has set me free. Take counsel from your blood and come into

the Church Without Christ and maybe somebody will bring us a new jesus and we'll all be saved by the sight of him!"

An unintelligible sound spluttered out of Enoch. He tried to bellow, but his blood held him back. He whispered, "Listenhere, I got him! I mean I can get him! You know! Him! Him I shown you to. You seen him yourself!"

His blood reminded him that the last time he had seen Haze Motes was when Haze Motes had hit him over the head with a rock. And he didn't even know yet how he would steal it out of the glass case. The only thing he knew was that he had a place in his room prepared to keep it in until Haze was ready to take it. His blood suggested he just let it come as a surprise to Haze Motes. He began to back away. He backed across the street and over a piece of sidewalk and out into the other street and a taxi had to stop short to keep from hitting him. The driver put his head out the window and asked him how he got around so well when God had made him by putting two backs together instead of a back and a front.

Enoch was too preoccupied to think about it. "I got to go now," he murmured, and hurried off.

Chapter 9

HAWKS KEPT his door bolted and whenever Haze knocked on it, which he did two or three times a day, the ex-evangelist sent his child out to him and bolted the door again behind her. It infuriated him to have Haze lurking in the house, thinking up some excuse to get in and look at his face; and he was often drunk and didn't want to be discovered that way.

Haze couldn't understand why the preacher didn't welcome him and act like a preacher should when he sees what he believes is a lost soul. He kept trying to get into the room again; the window he could have reached was kept locked and the shade pulled down. He wanted to see, if he could, *behind* the black glasses.

Every time he went to the door, the girl came out and the bolt shut inside; then he couldn't get rid of her. She followed him out to his car and climbed in and spoiled his rides or she followed him up to his room and sat. He abandoned the notion of seducing her and tried to protect himself. He hadn't been in the house a week before she appeared in his room one night after he had gone to bed. She was holding a candle burning in a jelly glass and wore, hanging onto her thin shoulders, a woman's nightgown that dragged on the floor behind her. Haze didn't wake up until she was almost up to his bed, and when he did, he sprang from under his cover into the middle of the room.

"What you want?" he said.

She didn't say anything and her grin widened in the candle light. He stood glowering at her for an instant and then he picked up the straight chair and raised it as if he were going to bring it down on her. She lingered only a fraction of a second. His door didn't bolt so he propped the chair under the knob before he went back to bed.

"Listen," she said when she got back to their room, "nothing works. He would have hit me with a chair."

"I'm leaving out of here in a couple of days," Hawks said, "you better make it work if you want to eat after I'm gone." He was drunk but he meant it.

Nothing was working the way Haze had expected it to. He had spent every evening preaching, but the membership of the Church Without Christ was still only one person: himself. He had wanted to have a large following quickly to impress the blind man with his powers, but no one had followed him. There had been a sort of follower but that had been a mistake. That had been a boy about sixteen years old who had wanted someone to go to a whorehouse with him because he had never been to one before. He knew where the place was but he didn't want to go without a person of experience, and when he heard Haze, he hung around until he stopped preaching and then asked him to go. But it was all a mistake because after they had gone and got out again and Haze had asked him to be a member of the Church Without Christ, or more than that, a disciple, an apostle, the boy said he was sorry but he couldn't be a member of that church because he was a Lapsed Catholic. He said that what they had just done was a mortal sin, and that should they die unrepentant of it they would suffer eternal punishment and never see God. Haze had not enjoyed the whorehouse anywhere near as much as the boy had and he had wasted half his evening. He shouted that there was no such thing as sin or judgment, but the boy only shook his head and asked him if he would like to go again the next night.

If Haze had believed in praying, he would have prayed for a disciple, but as it was all he could do was worry about it a lot. Then two nights after the boy, the disciple appeared.

That night he preached outside of four different picture shows and every time he looked up, he saw the same big face smiling at him. The man was plumpish, and he had curly blond hair that was cut with showy sideburns. He wore a black suit with a silver stripe in it and a wide-brimmed white hat pushed onto the back of his head, and he had on tight-fitting black pointed shoes and no socks. He looked like an ex-preacher turned cowboy, or an ex-cowboy turned mortician. He was not handsome but under his smile, there was an honest look that fitted into his face like a set of false teeth.

Every time Haze looked at him, the man winked.

At the last picture show he preached in front of, there were three people listening to him besides the man. "Do you people care anything about the truth?" he asked. "The only way to the truth is through blasphemy, but do you care? Are you going to pay any attention to what I've been saying or are you just going to walk off like everybody else?"

There were two men and a woman with a cat-faced baby sprawled over her shoulder. She had been looking at Haze as if he were in a booth at the fair. "Well, come on," she said, "he's finished. We got to be going." She turned away and the two men fell in behind her.

"Go ahead and go," Haze said, "but remember that the truth don't lurk around every street corner."

The man who had been following reached up quickly and pulled Haze's pantsleg and gave him a wink. "Come on back heah, you folks," he said. "I want to tell you all about *me*."

The woman turned around again and he smiled at her as if he had been struck all along with her good looks. She had a square red face and her hair was freshly set. "I wisht I had my gittarr here," the man said, " 'cause I just somehow can say sweet things to music bettern plain. And when you talk about Jesus you need a little music, don't you, friends?" He looked at the two men as if he were appealing to the good judgment that was impressed on their faces. They had on brown felt hats and black town suits, and they looked like older and younger brother. "Listen, friends," the disciple said confidentially, "two months ago before I met the Prophet here, you wouldn't know me for the same man. I didn't have a friend in the world. Do you know what it's like not to have a friend in the world?"

"It ain't no worsen havinum that would put a knife in your back when you wasn't looking," the older man said, barely parting his lips.

"Friend, you said a mouthful when you said that," the man said. "If we had time, I would have you repeat that just so ever'body could hear it like I did." The picture show was over and more people were coming up. "Friends," the man said, "I know you're all interested in the Prophet here," pointing to Haze on the nose of the car, "and if you'll just give me time I'm going to tell you what him and his idears've done for me. Don't crowd because I'm willing to stay here all night and tell you if it takes that long."

Haze stood where he was, motionless, with his head slightly forward, as if he weren't sure what he was hearing.

"Friends," the man said, "lemme innerduce myself. My name is Onnie Jay Holy and I'm telling it to you so you can check up and see I don't tell you any lie. I'm a preacher and I don't mind who knows it but I wouldn't have you believe nothing you can't feel in your own hearts. You people coming up on the edge push right on up in here where you can hear good," he said. "I'm not selling a thing, I'm giving something away!" A considerable number of people had stopped.

"Friends," he said, "two months ago you wouldn't know me for the same man. I didn't have a friend in the world. Do you know what it's like not to have a friend in the world?"

A loud voice said, "It ain't no worsen havinum that would put . . ."

"Why, friends," Onnie Jay Holy said, "not to have a friend in the world is just about the most miserable and lonesome thing that can happen to a man or woman! And that's the way it was with me. I was ready to hang myself or to despair completely. Not even my own dear old mother loved me, and it wasn't because I wasn't sweet inside, it was because I never known how to make the natural sweetness inside me show. Every person that comes onto this earth," he said, stretching out his arms, "is born sweet and full of love. A little child loves ever'body, friends, and its nature is sweetness—until something happens. Something happens, friends, I don't need to tell people like you that can think for theirselves. As that little child gets bigger, its sweetness don't show so much, cares and troubles come to perplext it, and all its sweetness is driven inside it. Then it gets miserable and lonesome and sick, friends. It says, 'Where is all my sweetness gone? where are all the friends that loved me?' and all the time, that little beat-up rose of its sweetness is inside, not a petal dropped, and on the outside is just a mean lonesomeness. It may want to take its own life or yours or mine, or to despair completely, friends." He said it in a sad nasal voice but he was smiling all the time so that they could tell he had been through what he was talking about and come out on top. "That was the way it was with me, friends. I know what of I speak," he said, and folded his hands in front of him. "But all the time that I was ready to hang myself or to despair completely, I was sweet inside, like ever'body else, and I only needed something to bring it out. I only needed a little help, friends.

"Then I met this Prophet here," he said, pointing at Haze on the nose of the car. "That was two months ago, folks, that I heard how he was out to help me, how he was preaching the Church of Christ Without Christ, the church that was going to get a new jesus to help me bring my sweet nature into the open where ever'body could enjoy it. That was two months ago, friends, and now you wouldn't know me for the same man. I love ever'one of you people and I want you to listen to him and me and join our church, the Holy Church of Christ Without Christ, the new church with the new jesus, and then you'll all be helped like me!"

Haze leaned forward. "This man is not true," he said. "I never saw him before tonight. I wasn't preaching this church two months ago and the name of it ain't the Holy Church of Christ Without Christ!"

The man ignored this and so did the people. There were ten or twelve gathered around. "Friends," Onnie Jay Holy said, "I'm mighty glad you're seeing me now instead of two months ago because then I couldn't have testified to this new church and this Prophet here. If I had my gittarr with me I could say all this better but I'll just have to do the best I can by myself." He had a winning smile and it was evident that he didn't think he was any better than anybody else even though he was.

"Now I just want to give you folks a few reasons why you can trust this church," he said. "In the first place, friends, you can rely on it that it's nothing foreign connected with it. You don't have to believe nothing you don't understand and approve of. If you don't understand it, it ain't true, and that's all there is to it. No jokers in the deck, friends."

Haze leaned forward. "Blasphemy is the way to the truth," he said, "and there's no other way whether you understand it or not!"

"Now, friends," Onnie Jay said, "I want to tell you a second reason why you can absolutely trust this church—it's based on the Bible. Yes sir! It's based on your own personal interpitation of the Bible, friends. You can sit at home and interpit your own Bible however you feel in your heart it ought to be interpited. That's right," he said, "just the way Jesus would have done it. Gee, I wisht I had my gittarr here," he complained.

"This man is a liar," Haze said. "I never saw him before tonight. I never . . ."

"That ought to be enough reasons, friends," Onnie Jay Holy said, "but I'm going to tell you one more, just to show I can. This church is up-to-date! When you're in this church you can know that there's nothing or nobody ahead of you, nobody knows nothing you don't know, all the cards are on the table, friends, and that's a fack!"

Haze's face under the white hat began to take on a look of fierceness. Just as he was about to open his mouth again, Onnie Jay Holy pointed in astonishment to the baby in the blue bonnet who was sprawled limp over the woman's shoulder. "Why yonder is a little babe," he said, "a little bundle of helpless sweetness. Why, I know you people aren't going to let that little thing grow up and have all his sweetness pushed inside him when it could be on the outside to win friends and make him loved. That's why I want ever' one of you people to join the Holy Church of Christ Without Christ. It'll cost you each a dollar but what is a dollar? A few dimes! Not too much to pay to unlock that little rose of sweetness inside you!"

"Listen!" Haze shouted. "It don't cost you any money to know the truth! You can't know it for money!"

"You hear what the Prophet says, friends," Onnie Jay Holy said, "a dollar is not too much to pay. No amount of money is too much to learn the truth! Now I want each of you people that are going to take advantage of this church to sign on this little pad I have in my pocket here and give me your dollar personally and let me shake your hand!"

Haze slid down from the nose of his car and got in it and slammed his foot on the starter.

"Hey wait! Wait!" Onnie Jay Holy shouted, "I ain't got any of these friends' names yet!"

The Essex had a tendency to develop a tic by nightfall. It would go forward about six inches and then back about four; it did that now a succession of times rapidly; otherwise Haze would have shot off in it and been gone. He had to grip the steering wheel with both hands to keep from being thrown either out the windshield or into the back. It stopped this after a few seconds and slid about twenty feet and then began it again.

Onnie Jay Holy's face showed a great strain; he put his hand to the side of it as if the only way he could keep his smile on was to hold it. "I got to go now, friends," he said quickly, "but I'll be at this same spot tomorrow night, I got to go catch the Prophet now," and he ran off just as the Essex began to slide again. He wouldn't have caught it, except that it stopped before it had gone ten feet farther. He jumped on the running board and got the door open and plumped in, panting, beside Haze. "Friend," he said, "we just lost ten dollars. What you in such a hurry for?" His face showed that he was in some kind of genuine pain even though he looked at Haze with a smile that revealed all his upper teeth and the tops of his lowers.

Haze turned his head and looked at him long enough to see the smile before it was thrown forward at the windshield. After that the Essex began running smoothly. Onnie Jay took out a lavender handkerchief and held it in front of his mouth for some time. When he removed it, the smile was back on his face. "Friend," he said, "you and me have to get together on this thing. I said when I first heard you open your mouth, 'Why, yonder is a great man with great idears.' "

Haze didn't turn his head.

Onnie Jay took in a long breath. "Why, do you know who you put me in mind of when I first saw you?" he asked. After a minute of waiting, he said in a soft voice, "Jesus Christ and Abraham Lincoln, friend."

Haze's face was suddenly swamped with outrage. All the expression on it was obliterated. "You ain't true," he said in a barely audible voice.

"Friend, how can you say that?" Onnie Jay said. "Why I was on the radio for three years with a program that give real religious experiences to the whole family. Didn't you ever listen to it—called, Soulsease, a quarter hour of Mood, Melody, and Mentality? I'm a real preacher, friend."

Haze stopped the Essex. "You get out," he said.

"Why friend!" Onnie Jay said. "You ought not to say such a thing! That's the absolute truth that I'm a preacher and a radio star."

"Get out," Haze said, reaching across and opening the door for him.

"I never thought you would treat a friend thisaway," Onnie Jay said. "All I wanted to ast you about was this new jesus."

"Get out," Haze said, and began to push him toward the door. He pushed him to the edge of the seat and gave him a shove and Onnie Jay fell out the door and into the road.

"I never thought a friend would treat me thisaway," he complained. Haze kicked his leg off the running board and shut the door again. He put his foot on the starter but nothing happened except a noise somewhere underneath him that sounded like a person gargling without water. Onnie Jay got up off the pavement and stood at the window. "If you would just tell me where this new jesus is you was mentioning," he began.

Haze put his foot on the starter a succession of times but nothing happened.

"Pull out the choke," Onnie Jay advised, getting up on the running board.

"There's no choke on it," Haze snarled.

"Maybe it's flooded," Onnie Jay said. "While we're waiting, you and me can talk about the Holy Church of Christ Without Christ."

"My church is the Church Without Christ," Haze said. "I've seen all of you I want to."

"It don't make any difference how many Christs you add to the name if you don't add none to the meaning, friend," Onnie Jay said in a hurt tone. "You ought to listen to me because I'm not just an amateur. I'm an artist-type. If you want to get anywheres in religion, you got to keep it sweet. You got good idears but what you need is an artist-type to work with you."

Haze rammed his foot on the gas and then on the starter and then on the starter and then on the gas. Nothing happened. The street was practically deserted. "Me and you could get behind it and push it over to the curb," Onnie Jay suggested.

"I ain't asked for your help," Haze said.

"You know, friend, I certainly would like to see this new jesus," Onnie Jay said. "I never heard a idear before that had more in it than that one. All it would need is a little promotion."

Haze tried to start the car by forcing his weight forward on the steering wheel, but that didn't work. He got out and got behind it and began to push it over to the curb. Onnie Jay got behind with him and added his weight. "I kind of have had that idear about a new jesus myself," he remarked. "I seen how a new one would be more up-to-date.

"Where you keeping him, friend?" he asked. "Is he somebody you see ever' day? I certainly would like to meet him and hear some of his idears."

They pushed the car into a parking space. There was no way to lock it and Haze was afraid that if he left it out all night so far away from where he lived someone would be able to steal it. There was nothing for him to do but sleep in it. He got in the back and began to pull down the fringed shades. Onnie Jay had his head in the front, however. "You needn't to be afraid that if I seen this new jesus I would cut you out of anything," he said. "Why friend, it would just mean a lot to me for the good of my spirit."

Haze moved the two-by-four off the seat frame to make more room to fix up his pallet. He kept a pillow and an army blanket back there and he had a sterno stove and a coffee pot up on the shelf under the back oval window. "Friend, I would even be glad to pay you a little something to see him," Onnie Jay suggested.

"Listen here," Haze said, "you get away from here. I've seen all of you I want to. There's no such thing as any new jesus. That ain't anything but a way to say something."

The smile more or less slithered off Onnie Jay's face. "What you mean by that?" he asked.

"That there's no such thing or person," Haze said. "It wasn't nothing but a way to say a thing." He put his hand on the door handle and began to close it in spite of Onnie Jay's head. "No such thing exists!" he shouted.

"That's the trouble with you innerleckchuls," Onnie Jay muttered, "you don't never have nothing to show for what you're saying."

"Get your head out my car door, Holy," Haze said.

"My name is Hoover Shoats," the man with his head in the door growled. "I known when I first seen you that you wasn't nothing but a crackpot."

Haze opened the door enough to be able to slam it. Hoover Shoats got his head out the way but not his thumb. A howl arose that would have rended almost any heart. Haze opened the door and released the thumb and then slammed the door again. He pulled down the front shades and lay down in the back of the car on the army blanket. Outside he could hear Hoover Shoats jumping around on the pavement and howling. When the howls died down, Haze heard a few steps up to the car and then an impassioned, breathless voice say through the tin, "You watch out, friend. I'm going to run you out of business. I can get my own new jesus and I can get Prophets for peanuts, you hear? Do you hear me, friend?" the hoarse voice said.

Haze didn't answer.

"Yeah and I'll be out there doing my own preaching tomorrow night. What you need is a little competition," the voice said. "Do you hear me, friend?"

Haze got up and leaned over the front seat and banged his hand down on the horn of the Essex. It made a sound like a goat's laugh cut off with a buzz saw. Hoover Shoats jumped back as if a charge of electricity had gone through him. "All right, friend," he said, standing about fifteen feet away, trembling, "you just wait, you ain't heard the last of me yet," and he turned and went off down the quiet street.

Haze stayed in his car about an hour and had a bad experience in it: he dreamed he was not dead but only buried. He was not waiting on the Judgment because there was no Judgment, he was waiting on nothing. Various eyes looked through the back oval window at his situation, some with considerable reverence, like the boy from the zoo, and some only to see what they could see. There were three women with paper sacks who looked at him critically as if he were something—a piece of fish—they might buy, but they passed on after a minute. A man in a canvas hat looked in and put his thumb to his nose and wiggled his fingers. Then a woman with two little boys on either side of her stopped and looked in, grinning. After a second, she pushed the boys out of view and indicated that she would climb in and keep him company for a while, but she couldn't get through the glass and finally she went off. All this time Haze was bent on getting out but since there was no use to try, he didn't make any move one way or the other. He kept expecting Hawks to appear at the oval window with a wrench, but the blind man didn't come.

Finally he shook off the dream and woke up. He thought it should be morning but it was only midnight. He pulled himself over into the front of the car and eased his foot on the starter and the Essex rolled off quietly as if nothing were the matter with it. He drove back to the house and let himself in but instead of going upstairs to his room, he stood in the hall, looking at the blind man's door. He went over to it and put his ear to the keyhole and heard the sound of snoring; he turned the knob gently but the door didn't move.

For the first time, the idea of picking the lock occurred to him. He felt in his pockets for an instrument and came on a small piece of wire that he sometimes used for a toothpick. There was only a dim light in the hall but it was enough for him to work by and he knelt down at the keyhole and inserted the wire into it carefully, trying not to make a noise.

After a while when he had tried the wire five or six different ways, there was a slight click in the lock. He stood up, trembling, and opened the door. His breath came short and his heart was palpitating as if he had run all the way here from a great distance. He stood just inside the room until his eyes got accustomed to the darkness and then he moved slowly over to the iron bed and stood there. Hawks was lying across it. His head was hanging over the edge. Haze squatted down by him and struck a match close to his face and he opened his eyes. The two sets of eyes looked at each other as long as the match lasted; Haze's expression seemed to open onto a deeper blankness and reflect something and then close again.

"Now you can get out," Hawks said in a short thick voice, "now you can leave me alone," and he made a jab at the face over him without touching it. It moved back, expressionless under the white hat, and was gone in a second.

Chapter 10

THE NEXT NIGHT, Haze parked the Essex in front of the Odeon Theater and climbed up on it and began to preach. "Let me tell you what I and this church stand for!" he called from the nose of the car. "Stop one minute to listen to the truth because you may never hear it again." He stood there with his neck thrust forward, moving one arm upward in a vague arc. Two women and a boy stopped.

"I preach there are all kinds of truth, your truth and somebody else's, but behind all of them, there's only one truth and that is that there's no truth," he called. "No truth behind all truths is what I and this church preach! Where you come from is gone, where you thought you were going to never was there, and where you are is no good unless you can get away from it. Where is there a place for you to be? No place.

"Nothing outside you can give you any place," he said. "You needn't to look at the sky because it's not going to open up and show no place behind it. You needn't to search for any hole in the ground to look through into somewhere else. You can't go neither forwards nor backwards into your daddy's time nor your children's if you have them. In yourself right now is all the place you've got. If there was any Fall, look there, if there was any Redemption, look there, and if you expect any Judgment, look there, because they all three will have to be in your time and your body and where in your time and your body can they be?

"Where in your time and your body has Jesus redeemed you?" he cried. "Show me where because I don't see the place. If there was a place where Jesus had redeemed you that would be the place for you to be, but which of you can find it?"

Another trickle of people came out of the Odeon and two stopped to look at him. "Who is that that says it's your conscience?" he cried, looking around with a constricted face as if he could smell the particular person who thought that. "Your conscience is a trick," he said, "it don't exist though you may think it does, and if you think it does, you had best get it out in the open and hunt it down and kill it, because it's no more than your face in the mirror is or your shadow behind you."

He was preaching with such concentration that he didn't notice a high rat-colored car that had been driven around the block three times already, while the two men in it hunted a place to park. He didn't see it when it pulled in two cars over from him in a space that another car had just pulled out of, and he didn't see Hoover Shoats and a man in a glare-blue suit and white hat get out of it, but after a few seconds, his head turned that way and he saw the man in the glare-blue suit and white hat up on the nose of it. He was so struck with how gaunt and thin he looked in the illusion that he stopped preaching. He had never pictured himself that way before. The man he saw was hollow-chested and carried his neck thrust forward and his arms down by his side; he stood there as if he were waiting for some signal he was afraid he might not catch.

Hoover Shoats was walking about on the sidewalk, striking a few chords on his guitar. "Friends," he called, "I want to innerduce you to the True Prophet here and I want you all to listen to his words because I think they're going to make you happy like they've made me!" If Haze had noticed Hoover he might have been impressed by how happy he looked, but his attention was fixed on the man on the nose of the car. He slid down from his own car and moved up closer, never taking his eyes from the bleak figure. Hoover Shoats raised his hand with two fingers pointed and the man suddenly cried out in a high nasal singsong voice. "The unredeemed are redeeming theirselves and the new jesus is at hand! Watch for this miracle! Help yourself to salvation in the Holy Church of Christ Without Christ!" He called it over again in exactly the same tone of voice, but faster. Then he began to cough. He had a loud consumptive cough that started somewhere deep in him and finished with a long wheeze. He expectorated a white fluid at the end of it.

Haze was standing next to a fat woman who after a minute turned her head and stared at him and then turned it again and stared at the True Prophet. Finally she touched his elbow with hers and grinned at him. "Him and you twins?" she asked.

"If you don't hunt it down and kill it, it'll hunt you down and kill you," Haze answered.

"Huh? Who?" she said.

He turned away and she stared at him as he got back in his car and drove off. Then she touched the elbow of a man on the other side of her. "He's nuts," she said. "I never seen no twins that hunted each other down."

When he got back to his room, Sabbath Hawks was in his bed. She was pushed over into one corner of it, sitting with one arm drawn around her knees and one hand holding onto the sheet as if she meant to hang on by it. Her face was sullen and apprehensive. Haze sat down on the bed but he barely glanced at her. "I don't care if you hit me with the table," she said. "I'm not going. There's no place for me to go. He's run off on me and it was you run him off. I was watching last night and I seen you come in and hold that match to his face. I thought anybody would have seen what he was before that without having to strike no match. He's just a crook. He ain't even a big crook, just a little one, and when he gets tired of that, he begs on the street."

Haze leaned down and began untying his shoes. They were old army shoes that he had painted black to get the government off. He untied them and eased his feet out and sat there looking down, while she watched him cautiously.

"Are you going to hit me or not?" she asked. "If you are, go ahead and do it right now because I'm not going. I ain't got any place to go." He didn't look as if he were going to hit anything; he looked as if he were going to sit there until he died. "Listen," she said, with a quick change of tone, "from the minute I set eyes on you I said to myself, that's what I got to have, just give me some of him! I said look at those pee-can eyes and go crazy, girl! That innocent look don't hide a thing, he's just pure filthy right down to the guts, like me. The only difference is I like being that way and he don't. Yes sir!" she said. "I like being that way, and I can teach you how to like it. Don't you want to learn how to like it?"

He turned his head slightly and just over his shoulder he saw a pinched homely little face with bright green eyes and a grin. "Yeah," he said with no change in his stony expression,

"I want to." He stood up and took off his coat and his trousers and his drawers and put them on the straight chair. Then he turned off the light and sat down on the cot again and pulled off his socks. His feet were big and white and damp to the floor and he sat there, looking at the two white shapes they made.

"Come on! Make haste," she said, knocking his back with her knee.

He unbuttoned his shirt and took it off and wiped his face with it and dropped it on the floor. Then he slid his legs under the cover by her and sat there as if he were waiting to remember one more thing.

She was breathing very quickly. "Take off your hat, king of the beasts," she said gruffly and her hand came up behind his head and snatched the hat off and sent it flying across the room in the dark.

Chapter II

THE NEXT MORNING toward noon a person in a long black raincoat, with a lightish hat pulled down low on his face and the brim of it turned down to meet the turned-up collar of the raincoat, was moving rapidly along certain back streets, close to the walls of the buildings. He was carrying something about the size of a baby, wrapped up in newspapers, and he carried a dark umbrella too, as the sky was an unpredictable surly gray like the back of an old goat. He had on a pair of dark glasses and a black beard which a keen observer would have said was not a natural growth but was pinned onto his hat on either side with safety pins. As he walked along, the umbrella kept slipping from under his arm and getting tangled in his feet, as if it meant to keep him from going anywhere.

He had not gone half a block before large putty-colored drops began to splatter on the pavement and there was an ugly growl in the sky behind him. He began to run, clutching the bundle in one arm and the umbrella in the other. In a second, the storm overtook him and he ducked between two show-windows into the blue and white tiled entrance of a drug store. He lowered his dark glasses a little. The pale eyes that looked over the rims belonged to Enoch Emery. Enoch was on his way to Hazel Motes's room.

He had never been to Hazel Motes's place before but the instinct that was guiding him was very sure of itself. What was in the bundle was what he had shown Hazel at the museum. He had stolen it the day before.

He had darkened his face and hands with brown shoe polish so that if he were seen in the act, he would be taken for a colored person; then he had sneaked into the museum while the guard was asleep and had broken the glass case with a wrench he'd borrowed from his landlady; then, shaking and sweating, he had lifted the shriveled man out and thrust him in a paper sack, and had crept out again past the guard, who was still asleep. He realized as soon as he got out of the museum that since no one had seen him to think he was a colored boy, he would be suspected immediately and would have to disguise himself. That was why he had on the black beard and dark glasses.

When he'd got back to his room, he had taken the new jesus out of the sack and, hardly daring to look at him, had laid him in the gilted cabinet; then he had sat down on the edge of his bed to wait. He was waiting for something to happen, he didn't know what. He knew something was going to happen and his entire system was waiting on it. He thought it was going to be one of the supreme moments in his life but apart from that, he didn't have the vaguest notion what it might be. He pictured himself, after it was over, as an entirely new man, with an even better personality than he had now. He sat there for about fifteen minutes and nothing happened.

He sat there for about five more.

Then he realized that he had to make the first move. He got up and tiptoed to the cabinet and squatted down at the door of it; in a second he opened it a crack and looked in. After a while, very slowly, he broadened the crack and inserted his head into the tabernacle.

Some time passed.

From directly behind him, only the soles of his shoes and the seat of his trousers were visible. The room was absolutely silent; there was no sound even from the street; the Universe might have been shut off; not a flea jumped. Then without any warning, a loud liquid noise burst from the cabinet and there was the thump of bone cracked once against a piece of wood. Enoch staggered backward, clutching his head and his face. He sat on the floor for a few minutes with a shocked expression on his whole figure. At the first instant, he had thought it was the shriveled man who had sneezed, but after a second, he perceived the condition of his own nose. He wiped it off with his sleeve and then he sat there on the floor for some time longer. His expression had showed that a deep unpleasant knowledge was breaking on him slowly. After a while he had kicked the ark door shut in the new jesus' face, and then he had got up and begun to eat a candy bar very rapidly. He had eaten it as if he had something against it.

The next morning he had not got up until ten o'clock—it was his day off—and he had not set out until nearly noon to

look for Hazel Motes. He remembered the address Sabbath
Hawks had given him and that was where his instinct was
leading him. He was very sullen and disgruntled at having to
spend his day off in such a way as this, and in bad weather,
but he wanted to get rid of the new jesus so that if the police
had to catch anybody for the robbery, they could catch Hazel
Motes instead of him. He couldn't understand at all why he
had let himself risk his skin for a dead shriveled-up part-
nigger dwarf that had never done anything but get himself embalmed and then lain stinking in a museum the rest
of his life. It was far beyond his understanding. He was very
sullen. So far as he was now concerned, one jesus was as
bad as another.

He had borrowed his landlady's umbrella and he discovered as he stood in the entrance of the drug store, trying to
open it, that it was at least as old as she was. When he finally
got it hoisted, he pushed his dark glasses back on his eyes and
re-entered the downpour.

The umbrella was one his landlady had stopped using fifteen years before (which was the only reason she had lent it
to him) and as soon as the rain touched the top of it, it came
down with a shriek and stabbed him in the back of the neck.
He ran a few feet with it over his head and then backed into
another store entrance and removed it. Then to get it up
again, he had to place the tip of it on the ground and ram it
open with his foot. He ran out again, holding his hand up
near the spokes to keep them open and this allowed the handle, which was carved to represent the head of a fox terrier,
to jab him every few seconds in the stomach. He proceeded
for another quarter of a block this way before the back half
of the silk stood up off the spokes and allowed the storm to
sweep down his collar. Then he ducked under the marquee
of a movie house. It was Saturday and there were a lot of
children standing more or less in a line in front of the ticket
box.

Enoch was not very fond of children but children always
seemed to like to look at him. The line turned and twenty or
thirty eyes began to observe him with a steady interest. The
umbrella had assumed an ugly position, half up and half
down, and the half that was up was about to come down and

spill more water under his collar. When this happened the children laughed and jumped up and down. Enoch glared at them and turned his back and lowered his dark glasses. He found himself facing a life-size four-color picture of a gorilla. Over the gorilla's head, written in red letters was, "GONGA! Giant Jungle Monarch and a Great Star! HERE IN PERSON!!!" At the level of the gorilla's knee, there was more that said, "Gonga will appear in person in front of this theater at 12 A.M. *TODAY!* A free pass to the first ten brave enough to step up and shake his hand!"

Enoch was usually thinking of something else at the moment that Fate began drawing back her leg to kick him. When he was four years old, his father had brought him home a tin box from the penitentiary. It was orange and had a picture of some peanut brittle on the outside of it and green letters that said, A NUTTY SURPRISE! When Enoch had opened it, a coiled piece of steel had sprung out at him and broken off the ends of his two front teeth. His life was full of so many happenings like that that it would seem he should have been more sensitive to his times of danger. He stood there and read the poster twice through carefully. To his mind, an opportunity to insult a successful ape came from the hand of Providence. He suddenly regained all his reverence for the new jesus. He saw that he was going to be rewarded after all and have the supreme moment he had expected.

He turned around and asked the nearest child what time it was. The child said it was twelve-ten and that Gonga was already ten minutes late. Another child said that maybe the rain had delayed him. Another said, no not the rain, his director was taking a plane from Hollywood. Enoch gritted his teeth. The first child said that if he wanted to shake the star's hand, he would have to get in line like the rest of them and wait his turn. Enoch got in line. A child asked him how old he was. Another observed that he had funny-looking teeth. He ignored all this as best he could and began to straighten out the umbrella.

In a few minutes a black truck turned around the corner and came slowly up the street in the heavy rain. Enoch pushed the umbrella under his arm and began to squint through his dark glasses. As the truck approached, a phonograph inside it began to play "Tarara Boom Di Aye," but the music was almost drowned out by the rain. There was a large illustration of a blonde on the outside of the truck, advertising some picture other than the gorilla's.

The children held their line carefully as the truck stopped in front of the movie house. The back door of it was constructed like a paddy wagon, with a grate, but the ape was not at it. Two men in raincoats got out of the cab part, cursing, and ran around to the back and opened the door. One of them stuck his head in and said, "Okay, make it snappy, willya?" The other jerked his thumb at the children and said, "Get back willya, willya get back?"

A voice on the record inside the truck said, "Here's Gonga, folks, Roaring Gonga and a Great Star! Give Gonga a big hand, folks!" The voice was barely a mumble in the rain.

The man who was waiting by the door of the truck stuck his head in again. "Okay willya get out?" he said.

There was a faint thump somewhere inside the van. After a second a dark furry arm emerged just enough for the rain to touch it and then drew back inside.

"Goddam," the man who was under the marquee said; he took off his raincoat and threw it to the man by the door, who threw it into the wagon. After two or three minutes more, the gorilla appeared at the door, with the raincoat buttoned up to his chin and the collar turned up. There was an iron chain hanging from around his neck; the man grabbed it and pulled him down and the two of them bounded under the marquee together. A motherly-looking woman was in the glass ticket box, getting the passes ready for the first ten children brave enough to step up and shake hands.

The gorilla ignored the children entirely and followed the man over to the other side of the entrance where there was a small platform raised about a foot off the ground. He stepped up on it and turned facing the children and began to growl. His growls were not so much loud as poisonous; they appeared to issue from a black heart. Enoch was terrified and if he had not been surrounded by the children, he would have run away.

"Who'll step up first?" the man said. "Come on come on, who'll step up first? A free pass to the first kid stepping up."

There was no movement from the group of children. The man glared at them. "What's the matter with you kids?" he barked. "You yellow? He won't hurt you as long as I got him by this chain." He tightened his grip on the chain and jangled it at them to show he was holding it securely.

After a minute a little girl separated herself from the group. She had long wood-shaving curls and a fierce triangular face. She moved up to within four feet of the star.

"Okay okay," the man said, rattling the chain, "make it snappy."

The ape reached out and gave her hand a quick shake. By this time there was another little girl ready and then two boys. The line re-formed and began to move up.

The gorilla kept his hand extended and turned his head away with a bored look at the rain. Enoch had got over his fear and was trying frantically to think of an obscene remark that would be suitable to insult him with. Usually he didn't have any trouble with this kind of composition but nothing came to him now. His brain, both parts, was completely empty. He couldn't think even of the insulting phrases he used every day.

There were only two children in front of him by now. The first one shook hands and stepped aside. Enoch's heart was beating violently. The child in front of him finished and stepped aside and left him facing the ape, who took his hand with an automatic motion.

It was the first hand that had been extended to Enoch since he had come to the city. It was warm and soft.

For a second he only stood there, clasping it. Then he began to stammer. "My name is Enoch Emery," he mumbled. "I attended the Rodemill Boys' Bible Academy. I work at the city zoo. I seen two of your pictures. I'm only eighteen year old but I already work for the city. My daddy made me com . . ." and his voice cracked.

The star leaned slightly forward and a change came in his eyes: an ugly pair of human ones moved closer and squinted at Enoch from behind the celluloid pair. "You go to hell," a surly voice inside the ape-suit said, low but distinctly, and the hand was jerked away.

Enoch's humiliation was so sharp and painful that he

turned around three times before he realized which direction he wanted to go in. Then he ran off into the rain as fast as he could.

By the time he reached Sabbath Hawks's house, he was soaked through and so was his bundle. He held it in a fierce grip but all he wanted was to get rid of it and never see it again. Haze's landlady was out on the porch, looking distrustfully into the storm. He found out from her where Haze's room was and went up to it. The door was ajar and he stuck his head in the crack. Haze was lying on his cot, with a washrag over his eyes; the exposed part of his face was ashen and set in a grimace, as if he were in some permanent pain. Sabbath Hawks was sitting at the table by the window, studying herself in a pocket mirror. Enoch scratched on the wall and she looked up. She put the mirror down and tiptoed out into the hall and shut the door behind her.

"My man is sick today and sleeping," she said, "because he didn't sleep none last night. What you want?"

"This is for him, it ain't for you," Enoch said, handing her the wet bundle. "A friend of his give it to me to give to him. I don't know what's in it."

"I'll take care of it," she said. "You needn't to worry none."

Enoch had an urgent need to insult somebody immediately; it was the only thing that could give his feelings even a temporary relief. "I never known he would have nothing to do with you," he remarked, giving her one of his special looks.

"He couldn't leave off following me," she said. "Sometimes it's thataway with them. You don't know what's in this package?"

"Lay-overs to catch meddlers," he said. "You just give it to him and he'll know what it is and you can tell him I'm glad to get shut of it." He started down the stairs and halfway he turned and gave her another special look. "I see why he has to put theter washrag over his eyes," he said.

"You keep your beeswax in your ears," she said. "Nobody asked you." When she heard the front door slam behind him, she turned the bundle over and began to examine it. There was no telling from the outside what was in it; it was too hard to be clothes and too soft to be a machine. She tore a hole in the paper at one end and saw what looked like five dried peas in a row but the hall was too dark for her to see clearly what they were. She decided to take the package to the bathroom, where there was a good light, and open it up before she gave it to Haze. If he was so sick as he said he was, he wouldn't want to be bothered with any bundle.

Early that morning he had claimed to have a terrible pain in his chest. He had begun to cough during the night—a hard hollow cough that sounded as if he were making it up as he went along. She was certain he was only trying to drive her off by letting her think he had a catching disease.

He's not really sick, she said to herself going down the hall, he just ain't used to me yet. She went in and sat down on the edge of a large green claw-footed tub and ripped the string off the package. "But he'll get used to me," she muttered. She pulled off the wet paper and let it fall on the floor; then she sat with a stunned look, staring at what was in her lap.

Two days out of the glass case had not improved the new jesus' condition. One side of his face had been partly mashed in and on the other side, his eyelid had split and a pale dust was seeping out of it. For a while her face had an empty look, as if she didn't know what she thought about him or didn't think anything. She might have sat there for ten minutes, without a thought, held by whatever it was that was familiar about him. She had never known anyone who looked like him before, but there was something in him of everyone she had ever known, as if they had all been rolled into one person and killed and shrunk and dried.

She held him up and began to examine him and after a minute her hands grew accustomed to the feel of his skin. Some of his hair had come undone and she brushed it back where it belonged, holding him in the crook of her arm and looking down into his squinched face. His mouth had been knocked a little to one side so that there was just a trace of a grin covering his terrified look. She began to rock him a little in her arm and a slight reflection of the same grin appeared on her own face. "Well I declare," she murmured, "you're right cute, ain't you?"

His head fitted exactly into the hollow of her shoulder. "Who's your momma and daddy?" she asked.

An answer came into her mind at once and she let out a short little bark and sat grinning, with a pleased expression in her eyes. "Well, let's go give him a jolt," she said after a while.

Haze had already been jolted awake when the front door slammed behind Enoch Emery. He had sat up and seeing she was not in the room, he had jumped up and begun to put on his clothes. He had one thought in mind and it had come to him, like his decision to buy a car, out of his sleep and without any indication of it beforehand: he was going to move immediately to some other city and preach the Church Without Christ where they had never heard of it. He would get another room there and another woman and make a new start with nothing on his mind. The entire possibility of this came from the advantage of having a car—of having something that moved fast, in privacy, to the place you wanted to be. He looked out the window at the Essex. It sat high and square in the pouring rain. He didn't notice the rain, only the car; if asked he would not have been able to say that it was raining. He was charged with energy and he left the window and finished putting on his clothes. Earlier that morning, when he had waked up for the first time, he had felt as if he were about to be caught by a complete consumption in his chest; it had seemed to be growing hollow all night and yawning underneath him, and he had kept hearing his coughs as if they came from a distance. After a while he had been sucked down into a strengthless sleep, but he had waked up with this plan, and with the energy to carry it out right away.

He snatched his duffel bag from under the table and began plunging his extra belongings into it. He didn't have much and a quarter of what he had was already in. His hand managed the packing so that it never touched the Bible that had sat like a rock in the bottom of the bag for the last few years, but as he rooted out a place for his second shoes, his fingers clutched around a small oblong object and he pulled it out. It was the case with his mother's glasses in it. He had forgotten that he had a pair of glasses. He put them on and the wall that he was facing moved up closer and wavered. There was a small white-framed mirror hung on the back of the door and he made his way to it and looked at himself. His blurred face was dark with excitement and the lines in it were deep and crooked. The little silver-rimmed glasses gave him a look of deflected sharpness, as if they were hiding some dishonest plan that would show in his naked eyes. His fingers began to snap nervously and he forgot what he had been going to do. He saw his mother's face in his, looking at the face in the mirror. He moved back quickly and raised his hand to take off the glasses but the door opened and two more faces floated into his line of vision; one of them said, "Call me Momma now."

The smaller dark one, just under the other, only squinted as if it were trying to identify an old friend who was going to kill it.

Haze stood motionless with one hand still on the bow of the glasses and the other arrested in the air at the level of his chest; his head was thrust forward as if he had to use his whole face to see with. He was about four feet from them but they seemed just under his eyes.

"Ask your daddy yonder where he was running off to—sick as he is?" Sabbath said. "Ask him isn't he going to take you and me with him?"

The hand that had been arrested in the air moved forward and plucked at the squinting face but without touching it; it reached again, slowly, and plucked at nothing and then it lunged and snatched the shriveled body and threw it against the wall. The head popped and the trash inside sprayed out in a little cloud of dust.

"You've broken him!" Sabbath shouted, "and he was mine!"

Haze snatched the skin off the floor. He opened the outside door where the landlady thought there had once been a fire-escape, and flung out what he had in his hand. The rain blew in his face and he jumped back and stood, with a cautious look, as if he were bracing himself for a blow.

"You didn't have to throw him out," she yelled. "I might have fixed him!"

He moved up closer and hung out the door, staring into the gray blur around him. The rain fell on his hat with loud splatters as if it were falling on tin.

"I knew when I first seen you you were mean and evil," a furious voice behind him said. "I seen you wouldn't let nobody have nothing. I seen you were mean enough to slam a baby against a wall. I seen you wouldn't never have no fun or let anybody else because you didn't want nothing but Jesus!"

He turned and raised his arm in a vicious gesture, almost losing his balance in the door. Drops of rain water were splattered over the front of the glasses and on his red face and here and there they hung sparkling from the brim of his hat. "I don't want nothing but the truth!" he shouted, "and what you see is the truth and I've seen it!"

"Preacher talk," she said. "Where were you going to run off to?"

"I've seen the only truth there is!" he shouted.

"Where were you going to run off to?"

"To some other city," he said in a loud hoarse voice, "to preach the truth. The Church Without Christ! And I got a car to get there in, I got . . ." but he was stopped by a cough. It was not much of a cough—it sounded like a little yell for help at the bottom of a canyon—but the color and the expression drained out of his face until it was as straight and blank as the rain falling down behind him.

"And when were you going?" she asked.

"After I get some more sleep," he said, and pulled off the glasses and threw them out the door.

"You ain't going to get none," she said.

Chapter 12

IN SPITE of himself, Enoch couldn't get over the expectation that the new jesus was going to do something for him in return for his services. This was the virtue of Hope, which was made up, in Enoch, of two parts suspicion and one part lust. It operated on him all the rest of the day after he left Sabbath Hawks. He had only a vague idea how he wanted to be rewarded, but he was not a boy without ambition: he wanted to become something. He wanted to better his condition until it was the best. He wanted to be THE young man of the future, like the ones in the insurance ads. He wanted, some day, to see a line of people waiting to shake his hand.

All afternoon, he fidgeted and fooled in his room, biting his nails and shredding what was left of the silk off the landlady's umbrella. Finally he denuded it entirely and broke off the spokes. What was left was a black stick with a sharp steel point at one end and a dog's head at the other. It might have been an instrument for some specialized kind of torture that had gone out of fashion. Enoch walked up and down his room with it under his arm and realized that it would distinguish him on the sidewalk.

About seven o'clock in the evening, he put on his coat and took the stick and headed for a little restaurant two blocks away. He had the sense that he was setting off to get some honor, but he was very nervous, as if he were afraid he might have to snatch it instead of receive it.

He never set out for anything without eating first. The restaurant was called the Paris Diner; it was a tunnel about six feet wide, located between a shoe shine parlor and a dry-cleaning establishment. Enoch slid in and climbed up on the far stool at the counter and said he would have a bowl of split-pea soup and a chocolate malted milkshake.

The waitress was a tall woman with a big yellow dental plate and the same color hair done up in a black hairnet. One hand never left her hip; she filled orders with the other one. Although Enoch came in every night, she had never learned to like him.

Instead of filling his order, she began to fry bacon; there

was only one other customer in the place and he had finished
his meal and was reading a newspaper; there was no one to
eat the bacon but her. Enoch reached over the counter and
prodded her hip with his stick. "Listenhere," he said, "I got
to go. I'm in a hurry."

"Go then," she said. Her jaw began to work and she stared
into the skillet with a fixed attention.

"Lemme just have a piece of theter cake yonder," he said,
pointing to a half of pink and yellow cake on a round glass
stand. "I think I got something to do. I got to be going. Set
it up there next to him," he said, indicating the customer
reading the newspaper. He slid over the stools and began
reading the outside sheet of the man's paper.

The man lowered the paper and looked at him. Enoch
smiled. The man raised the paper again. "Could I borrow
some part of your paper that you ain't studying?" Enoch
asked. The man lowered it again and stared at him; he had
muddy unflinching eyes. He leafed deliberately through the
paper and shook out the sheet with the comic strips and
handed it to Enoch. It was Enoch's favorite part. He read it
every evening like an office. While he ate the cake that the
waitress had torpedoed down the counter at him, he read and
felt himself surge with kindness and courage and strength.

When he finished one side, he turned the sheet over and
began to scan the advertisements for movies, that filled the
other side. His eye went over three columns without stopping; then it came to a box that advertised Gonga, Giant Jungle Monarch, and listed the theaters he would visit on his
tour and the hours he would be at each one. In thirty minutes
he would arrive at the Victory on 57th Street and that would
be his last appearance in the city.

If anyone had watched Enoch read this, he would have
seen a certain transformation in his countenance. It still shone
with the inspiration he had absorbed from the comic strips,
but something else had come over it: a look of awakening.

The waitress happened to turn around to see if he hadn't
gone. "What's the matter with you?" she said. "Did you swallow a seed?"

"I know what I want," Enoch murmured.

"I know what I want too," she said with a dark look.

Enoch felt for his stick and laid his change on the counter. "I got to be going."

"Don't let me keep you," she said.

"You may not see me again," he said, "—the way I am."

"Any way I don't see you will be all right with me," she said.

Enoch left. It was a pleasant damp evening. The puddles on the sidewalk shone and the store windows were steamy and bright with junk. He disappeared down a side street and made his way rapidly along the darker passages of the city, pausing only once or twice at the end of an alley to dart a glance in each direction before he ran on. The Victory was a small theater, suited to the needs of the family, in one of the closer subdivisions; he passed through a succession of lighted areas and then on through more alleys and back streets until he came to the business section that surrounded it. Then he slowed up. He saw it about a block away, glittering in its darker setting. He didn't cross the street to the side it was on but kept on the far side, moving forward with his squint fixed on the glary spot. He stopped when he was directly across from it and hid himself in a narrow stair cavity that divided a building.

The truck that carried Gonga was parked across the street and the star was standing under the marquee, shaking hands with an elderly woman. She moved aside and a gentleman in a polo shirt stepped up and shook hands vigorously, like a sportsman. He was followed by a boy of about three who wore a tall Western hat that nearly covered his face; he had to be pushed ahead by the line. Enoch watched for some time, his face working with envy. The small boy was followed by a lady in shorts, she by an old man who tried to draw extra attention to himself by dancing up instead of walking in a dignified way. Enoch suddenly darted across the street and slipped noiselessly into the open back door of the truck.

The handshaking went on until the feature picture was ready to begin. Then the star got back in the van and the people filed into the theater. The driver and the man who was master of ceremonies climbed in the cab part and the truck rumbled off. It crossed the city rapidly and continued on the highway, going very fast.

There came from the van certain thumping noises, not those of the normal gorilla, but they were drowned out by the drone of the motor and the steady sound of wheels against the road. The night was pale and quiet, with nothing to stir it but an occasional complaint from a hoot owl and the distant muted jarring of a freight train. The truck sped on until it slowed for a crossing, and as the van rattled over the tracks, a figure slipped from the door and almost fell, and then limped hurriedly off toward the woods.

Once in the darkness of a pine thicket, he laid down a pointed stick he had been clutching and something bulky and loose that he had been carrying under his arm, and began to undress. He folded each garment neatly after he had taken it off and then stacked it on top of the last thing he had removed. When all his clothes were in the pile, he took up the stick and began making a hole in the ground with it.

The darkness of the pine grove was broken by paler moonlit spots that moved over him now and again and showed him to be Enoch. His natural appearance was marred by a gash that ran from the corner of his lip to his collarbone and by a lump under his eye that gave him a dulled insensitive look. Nothing could have been more deceptive for he was burning with the intensest kind of happiness.

He dug rapidly until he had made a trench about a foot long and a foot deep. Then he placed the stack of clothes in it and stood aside to rest a second. Burying his clothes was not a symbol to him of burying his former self; he only knew he wouldn't need them any more. As soon as he got his breath, he pushed the displaced dirt over the hole and stamped it down with his foot. He discovered while he did this that he still had his shoes on, and when he finished, he removed them and threw them from him. Then he picked up the loose bulky object and shook it vigorously.

In the uncertain light, one of his lean white legs could be seen to disappear and then the other, one arm and then the other: a black heavier shaggier figure replaced his. For an instant, it had two heads, one light and one dark, but after a second, it pulled the dark back head over the other and corrected this. It busied itself with certain hidden fastenings and what appeared to be minor adjustments of its hide.

For a time after this, it stood very still and didn't do anything. Then it began to growl and beat its chest; it jumped up and down and flung its arms and thrust its head forward. The growls were thin and uncertain at first but they grew louder after a second. They became low and poisonous, louder again, low and poisonous again; they stopped altogether. The figure extended its hand, clutched nothing, and shook its arm vigorously; it withdrew the arm, extended it again, clutched nothing, and shook. It repeated this four or five times. Then it picked up the pointed stick and placed it at a cocky angle under its arm and left the woods for the highway. No gorilla in existence, whether in the jungles of Africa or California, or in New York City in the finest apartment in the world, was happier at that moment than this one, whose god had finally rewarded it.

A man and woman sitting close together on a rock just off the highway were looking across an open stretch of valley at a view of the city in the distance and they didn't see the shaggy figure approaching. The smokestacks and square tops of buildings made a black uneven wall against the lighter sky and here and there a steeple cut a sharp wedge out of a cloud. The young man turned his neck just in time to see the gorilla standing a few feet away, hideous and black, with its hand extended. He eased his arm from around the woman and disappeared silently into the woods. She, as soon as she turned her eyes, fled screaming down the highway. The gorilla stood as though surprised and presently its arm fell to its side. It sat down on the rock where they had been sitting and stared over the valley at the uneven skyline of the city.

Chapter 13

ON HIS SECOND night out, working with his hired Prophet and the Holy Church of Christ Without Christ, Hoover Shoats made fifteen dollars and thirty-five cents clear. The Prophet got three dollars an evening for his services and the use of his car. His name was Solace Layfield; he had consumption and a wife and six children and being a Prophet was as much work as he wanted to do. It never occurred to him that it might be a dangerous job. The second night out, he failed to observe a high rat-colored car parked about a half-block away and a white face inside it, watching him with the kind of intensity that means something is going to happen no matter what is done to keep it from happening.

The face watched him for almost an hour while he performed on the nose of his car every time Hoover Shoats raised his hand with two fingers pointed. When the last showing of the movie was over and there were no more people to attract, Hoover paid him and the two of them got in his car and drove off. They drove about ten blocks to where Hoover lived; the car stopped and Hoover jumped out, calling, "See you tomorrow night, friend"; then he went inside a dark doorway and Solace Layfield drove on. A half-block behind him the other rat-colored car was following steadily. The driver was Hazel Motes.

Both cars increased their speed and in a few minutes they were heading rapidly toward the outskirts of town. The first car cut off onto a lonesome road where the trees were hung over with moss and the only light came like stiff antennae from the two cars. Haze gradually shortened the distance between them and then, grinding his motor suddenly, he shot ahead and rammed the back end of the other car. Both cars came to a stop.

Haze backed the Essex a little way down the road, while the other Prophet got out of his car and stood squinting in the glare from Haze's lights. After a second, he came up to the window of the Essex and looked in. There was no sound but from crickets and tree frogs. "What you want?" he said in a nervous voice. Haze didn't answer, he only looked at

him, and in a second the man's jaw slackened and he seemed
to perceive the resemblance in their clothes and possibly in
their faces. "What you want?" he said in a higher voice. "I
ain't done nothing to you."

Haze ground the motor of the Essex again and shot forward. This time he rammed the other car at such an angle
that it rolled to the side of the road and over into the ditch.

The man got up off the ground where he had been thrown
and ran back to the window of the Essex. He stood about
four feet away, looking in.

"What you keep a thing like that on the road for?" Haze
said.

"It ain't nothing wrong with that car," the man said.
"Howcome you knockt it in the ditch?"

"Take off that hat," Haze said.

"Listenere," the man said, beginning to cough, "what you
want? Quit just looking at me. Say what you want."

"You ain't true," Haze said. "What do you get up on top
of a car and say you don't believe in what you do believe in
for?"

"Whatsit to you?" the man wheezed. "Whatsit to you what
I do?"

"What do you do it for?" Haze said. "That's what I asked
you."

"A man has to look out for hisself," the other Prophet said.

"You ain't true," Haze said. "You believe in Jesus."

"Whatsit to you?" the man said. "What you knockt my car
off the road for?"

"Take off that hat and that suit," Haze said.

"Listenere," the man said, "I ain't trying to mock you. He
bought me thisyer suit. I thrown my othern away."

Haze reached out and brushed the man's white hat off.
"And take off that suit," he said.

The man began to sidle off, out into the middle of the
road.

"Take off that suit," Haze shouted and started the car forward after him. Solace began to lope down the road, taking
off his coat as he went. "Take it all off," Haze yelled, with his
face close to the windshield.

The Prophet began to run in earnest. He tore off his shirt

and unbuckled his belt and ran out of his trousers. He began grabbing for his feet as if he would take off his shoes too, but before he could get at them, the Essex knocked him flat and ran over him. Haze drove about twenty feet and stopped the car and then began to back it. He backed it over the body and then stopped and got out. The Essex stood half over the other Prophet as if it were pleased to guard what it had finally brought down. The man didn't look so much like Haze, lying on the ground on his face without his hat or suit on. A lot of blood was coming out of him and forming a puddle around his head. He was motionless all but for one finger that moved up and down in front of his face as if he were marking time with it. Haze poked his toe in his side and he wheezed for a second and then was quiet. "Two things I can't stand," Haze said, "—a man that ain't true and one that mocks what is. You shouldn't ever have tampered with me if you didn't want what you got."

The man was trying to say something but he was only wheezing. Haze squatted down by his face to listen. "Give my mother a lot of trouble," he said through a kind of bubbling in his throat. "Never giver no rest. Stole theter car. Never told the truth to my daddy or give Henry what, never give him . . ."

"You shut up," Haze said, leaning his head closer to hear the confession.

"Told where his still was and got five dollars for it," the man gasped.

"You shut up now," Haze said.

"Jesus . . ." the man said.

"Shut up like I told you to now," Haze said.

"Jesus hep me," the man wheezed.

Haze gave him a hard slap on the back and he was quiet. He leaned down to hear if he was going to say anything else but he wasn't breathing any more. Haze turned around and examined the front of the Essex to see if there had been any damage done to it. The bumper had a few splurts of blood on it but that was all. Before he turned around and drove back to town, he wiped them off with a rag.

Early the next morning he got out of the back of the car and drove to a filling station to get the Essex filled up and checked for his trip. He hadn't gone back to his room but had spent the night parked in an alley, not sleeping but thinking about the life he was going to begin, preaching the Church Without Christ in the new city.

At the filling station a sleepy-looking white boy came out to wait on him and he said he wanted the tank filled up, the oil and water checked, and the tires tested for air, that he was going on a long trip. The boy asked him where he was going and he told him to another city. The boy asked him if he was going that far in this car here and he said yes he was. He tapped the boy on the front of his shirt. He said nobody with a good car needed to worry about anything, and he asked the boy if he understood that. The boy said yes he did, that that was his opinion too. Haze introduced himself and said that he was a preacher for the Church Without Christ and that he preached every night on the nose of this very car here. He explained that he was going to another city to preach. The boy filled up the gas tank and checked the water and oil and tested the tires, and while he was working, Haze followed him around, telling him what it was right to believe. He said it was not right to believe anything you couldn't see or hold in your hands or test with your teeth. He said he had only a few days ago believed in blasphemy as the way to salvation, but that you couldn't even believe in that because then you were believing in something to blaspheme. As for the Jesus who was reported to have been born at Bethlehem and crucified on Calvary for man's sins, Haze said, He was too foul a notion for a sane person to carry in his head, and he picked up the boy's water bucket and bammed it on the concrete pavement to emphasize what he was saying. He began to curse and blaspheme Jesus in a quiet intense way but with such conviction that the boy paused from his work to listen. When he had finished checking the Essex, he said that there was a leak in the gas tank and two in the radiator and that the rear tire would probably last twenty miles if he went slow.

"Listen," Haze said, "this car is just beginning its life. A lightening bolt couldn't stop it!"

"It ain't any use to put water in it," the boy said, "because it won't hold it."

"You put it in just the same," Haze said, and he stood there and watched while the boy put it in. Then he got a road map from him and drove off, leaving little bead-chains of water and oil and gas on the road.

He drove very fast out onto the highway, but once he had gone a few miles, he had the sense that he was not gaining ground. Shacks and filling stations and road camps and 666 signs passed him, and deserted barns with CCC snuff ads peeling across them, even a sign that said, "Jesus Died for YOU," which he saw and deliberately did not read. He had the sense that the road was really slipping back under him. He had known all along that there was no more country but he didn't know that there was not another city.

He had not gone five miles on the highway before he heard a siren behind him. He looked around and saw a black patrol car coming up. It drove alongside him and the patrolman in it motioned for him to pull over to the edge of the road. The patrolman had a red pleasant face and eyes the color of clear fresh ice.

"I wasn't speeding," Haze said.

"No," the patrolman agreed, "you wasn't."

"I was on the right side of the road."

"Yes you was, that's right," the cop said.

"What you want with me?"

"I just don't like your face," the patrolman said. "Where's your license?"

"I don't like your face either," Haze said, "and I don't have a license."

"Well," the patrolman said in a kindly voice, "I don't reckon *you* need one."

"Well I ain't got one if I do," Haze said.

"Listen," the patrolman said, taking another tone, "would you mind driving your car up to the top of the next hill? I want you to see the view from up there, puttiest view you ever did see."

Haze shrugged but he started the car up. He didn't mind fighting the patrolman if that was what he wanted. He drove to the top of the hill, with the patrol car following close behind him. "Now you turn it facing the embankment," the patrolman called. "You'll be able to see better thataway." Haze turned it facing the embankment. "Now maybe you

better had get out," the cop said. "I think you could see better
if you was out."

Haze got out and glanced at the view. The embankment
dropped down for about thirty feet, sheer washed-out red
clay, into a partly burnt pasture where there was one scrub
cow lying near a puddle. Over in the middle distance there
was a one-room shack with a buzzard standing hunch-shouldered on the roof.

The patrolman got behind the Essex and pushed it over the
embankment and the cow stumbled up and galloped across
the field and into the woods; the buzzard flapped off to a tree
at the edge of the clearing. The car landed on its top, with
the three wheels that stayed on, spinning. The motor
bounced out and rolled some distance away and various odd
pieces scattered this way and that.

"Them that don't have a car, don't need a license," the patrolman said, dusting his hands on his pants.

Haze stood for a few minutes, looking over at the scene.
His face seemed to reflect the entire distance across the clearing and on beyond, the entire distance that extended from his
eyes to the blank gray sky that went on, depth after depth,
into space. His knees bent under him and he sat down on the
edge of the embankment with his feet hanging over.

The patrolman stood staring at him. "Could I give you a
lift to where you was going?" he asked.

After a minute he came a little closer and said, "Where was
you going?"

He leaned on down with his hands on his knees and said
in an anxious voice, "Was you going anywheres?"

"No," Haze said.

The patrolman squatted down and put his hand on Haze's
shoulder. "You hadn't planned to go anywheres?" he asked
anxiously.

Haze shook his head. His face didn't change and he didn't
turn it toward the patrolman. It seemed to be concentrated
on space.

The patrolman got up and went back to his car and stood
at the door of it, staring at the back of Haze's hat and shoulder. Then he said, "Well, I'll be seeing you," and got in and
drove off.

After a while Haze got up and started walking back to town. It took him three hours to get inside the city again. He stopped at a supply store and bought a tin bucket and a sack of quicklime and then he went on to where he lived, carrying these. When he reached the house, he stopped outside on the sidewalk and opened the sack of lime and poured the bucket half full of it. Then he went to a water spigot by the front steps and filled up the rest of the bucket with water and started up the steps. His landlady was sitting on the porch, rocking a cat. "What you going to do with that, Mr. Motes?" she asked.

"Blind myself," he said and went on in the house.

The landlady sat there for a while longer. She was not a woman who felt more violence in one word than in another; she took every word at its face value but all the faces were the same. Still, instead of blinding herself, if she had felt that bad, she would have killed herself and she wondered why anybody wouldn't do that. She would simply have put her head in an oven or maybe have given herself too many painless sleeping pills and that would have been that. Perhaps Mr. Motes was only being ugly, for what possible reason could a person have for wanting to destroy their sight? A woman like her, who was so clear-sighted, could never stand to be blind. If she had to be blind she would rather be dead. It occurred to her suddenly that when she was dead she would be blind too. She stared in front of her intensely, facing this for the first time. She recalled the phrase, "eternal death," that preachers used, but she cleared it out of her mind immediately, with no more change of expression than the cat. She was not religious or morbid, for which every day she thanked her stars. She would credit a person who had that streak with anything, though, and Mr. Motes had it or he wouldn't be a preacher. He might put lime in his eyes and she wouldn't doubt it a bit, because they were all, if the truth was only known, a little bit off in their heads. What possible reason could a sane person have for wanting to not enjoy himself any more?

She certainly couldn't say.

Chapter 14

BUT SHE KEPT it in mind because after he had done it, he continued to live in her house and every day the sight of him presented her with the question. She first told him he couldn't stay because he wouldn't wear dark glasses and she didn't like to look at the mess he had made in his eye sockets. At least she didn't think she did. If she didn't keep her mind going on something else when he was near her, she would find herself leaning forward, staring into his face as if she expected to see something she hadn't seen before. This irritated her with him and gave her the sense that he was cheating her in some secret way. He sat on her porch a good part of every afternoon, but sitting out there with him was like sitting by yourself; he didn't talk except when it suited him. You asked him a question in the morning and he might answer it in the afternoon, or he might never. He offered to pay her extra to let him keep his room because he knew his way in and out, and she decided to let him stay, at least until she found out how she was being cheated.

He got money from the government every month for something the war had done to his insides and so he was not obliged to work. The landlady had always been impressed with the ability to pay. When she found a stream of wealth, she followed it to its source and before long, it was not distinguishable from her own. She felt that the money she paid out in taxes returned to all the worthless pockets in the world, that the government not only sent it to foreign niggers and a-rabs, but wasted it at home on blind fools and on every idiot who could sign his name on a card. She felt justified in getting any of it back that she could. She felt justified in getting anything at all back that she could, money or anything else, as if she had once owned the earth and been dispossessed of it. She couldn't look at anything steadily without wanting it, and what provoked her most was the thought that there might be something valuable hidden near her, something she couldn't see.

To her, the blind man had the look of seeing something. His face had a peculiar pushing look, as if it were going for-

ward after something it could just distinguish in the distance.
Even when he was sitting motionless in a chair, his face had
the look of straining toward something. But she knew he was
totally blind. She had satisfied herself of that as soon as he
took off the rag he used for a while as a bandage. She had
got one long good look and it had been enough to tell her
he had done what he'd said he was going to do. The other
boarders, after he had taken off the rag, would pass him
slowly in the hall, tiptoeing, and looking as long as they
could, but now they didn't pay any attention to him; some of
the new ones didn't know he had done it himself. The Hawks
girl had spread it over the house as soon as it happened. She
had watched him do it and then she had run to every room,
yelling what he had done, and all the boarders had come running. That girl was a harpy if one ever lived, the landlady felt.
She had hung around pestering him for a few days and then
she had gone on off; she said she hadn't counted on no hon-
est-to-Jesus blind man and she was homesick for her papa; he
had deserted her, gone off on a banana boat. The landlady
hoped he was at the bottom of the salt sea; he had been a
month behind in his rent. In two weeks, of course, she was back,
ready to start pestering him again. She had the disposition
of a yellow jacket and you could hear her a block away, shouting and screaming at him, and him never opening his mouth.

The landlady conducted an orderly house and she told him
so. She told him that when the girl lived with him, he would
have to pay double; she said there were things she didn't
mind and things she did. She left him to draw his own conclusions about what she meant by that, but she waited, with
her arms folded, until he had drawn them. He didn't say anything, he only counted out three more dollars and handed
them to her. "That girl, Mr. Motes," she said, "is only after
your money."

"If that was what she wanted she could have it," he said.
"I'd pay her to stay away."

The thought that her tax money would go to support such
trash was more than the landlady could bear. "Don't do that,"
she said quickly. "She's got no right to it." The next day she
called the Welfare people and made arrangements to have the
girl sent to a detention home; she was eligible.

She was curious to know how much he got every month from the government and with that set of eyes removed, she felt at liberty to find out. She steamed open the government envelope as soon as she found it in the mailbox the next time; in a few days she felt obliged to raise his rent. He had made arrangements with her to give him his meals and as the price of food went up, she was obliged to raise his board also; but she didn't get rid of the feeling that she was being cheated. Why had he destroyed his eyes and saved himself unless he had some plan, unless he saw something that he couldn't get without being blind to everything else? She meant to find out everything she could about him.

"Where were your people from, Mr. Motes?" she asked him one afternoon when they were sitting on the porch. "I don't suppose they're alive?"

She supposed she might suppose what she pleased; he didn't disturb his doing nothing to answer her. "None of my people's alive either," she said. "All Mr. Flood's people's alive but him." She was a Mrs. Flood. "They all come here when they want a hand-out," she said, "but Mr. Flood had money. He died in the crack-up of an airplane."

After a while he said, "My people are all dead."

"Mr. Flood," she said, "died in the crack-up of an airplane."

She began to enjoy sitting on the porch with him, but she could never tell if he knew she was there or not. Even when he answered her, she couldn't tell if he knew it was she. She herself. Mrs. Flood, the landlady. Not just anybody. They would sit, he only sit, and she sit rocking, for half an afternoon and not two words seemed to pass between them, though she might talk at length. If she didn't talk and keep her mind going, she would find herself sitting forward in her chair, looking at him with her mouth not closed. Anyone who saw her from the sidewalk would think she was being courted by a corpse.

She observed his habits carefully. He didn't eat much or seem to mind anything she gave him. If she had been blind, she would have sat by the radio all day, eating cake and ice cream, and soaking her feet. He ate anything and never knew the difference. He kept getting thinner and his cough deepened and he developed a limp. During the first cold months, he took the virus, but he walked out every day in spite of that. He walked about half of each day. He got up early in the morning and walked in his room—she could hear him below in hers, up and down, up and down—and then he went out and walked before breakfast and after breakfast, he went out again and walked until midday. He knew the four or five blocks around the house and he didn't go any farther than those. He could have kept on one for all she saw. He could have stayed in his room, in one spot, moving his feet up and down. He could have been dead and get all he got out of life but the exercise. He might as well be one of them monks, she thought, he might as well be in a monkery. She didn't understand it. She didn't like the thought that something was being put over her head. She liked the clear light of day. She liked to see things.

She could not make up her mind what would be inside his head and what out. She thought of her own head as a switch-box where she controlled from; but with him, she could only imagine the outside in, the whole black world in his head and his head bigger than the world, his head big enough to include the sky and planets and whatever was or had been or would be. How would he know if time was going backwards or forwards or if he was going with it? She imagined it was like you were walking in a tunnel and all you could see was a pin point of light. She had to imagine the pin point of light; she couldn't think of it at all without that. She saw it as some kind of a star, like the star on Christmas cards. She saw him going backwards to Bethlehem and she had to laugh.

She thought it would be a good thing if he had something to do with his hands, something to bring him out of himself and get him in connection with the real world again. She was certain he was out of connection with it; she was not certain at times that he even knew she existed. She suggested he get himself a guitar and learn to strum it; she had a picture of them sitting on the porch in the evening and him strumming it. She had bought two rubber plants to make where they sat more private from the street, and she thought that the sound of him strumming it from behind the rubber plant would take away the dead look he had. She suggested it but he never answered the suggestion.

After he paid his room and board every month, he had a good third of the government check left but that she could see, he never spent any money. He didn't use tobacco or drink whisky; there was nothing for him to do with all that money but lose it, since there was only himself. She thought of benefits that might accrue to his widow should he leave one. She had seen money drop out of his pocket and him not bother to reach down and feel for it. One day when she was cleaning his room, she found four dollar bills and some change in his trash can. He came in about that time from one of his walks. "Mr. Motes," she said, "here's a dollar bill and some change in this waste basket. You know where your waste basket is. How did you make that mistake?"

"It was left over," he said. "I didn't need it."

She dropped onto his straight chair. "Do you throw it away every month?" she asked after a time.

"Only when it's left over," he said.

"The poor and needy," she muttered. "The poor and needy. Don't you ever think about the poor and needy? If you don't want that money somebody else might."

"You can have it," he said.

"Mr. Motes," she said coldly, "I'm not charity yet!" She realized now that he was a mad man and that he ought to be under the control of a sensible person.

The landlady was past her middle years and her plate was too large but she had long race-horse legs and a nose that had been called Grecian by one boarder. She wore her hair clustered like grapes on her brow and over each ear and in the middle behind, but none of these advantages were any use to her in attracting his attention. She saw that the only way was to be interested in what he was interested in. "Mr. Motes," she said one afternoon when they were sitting on the porch, "why don't you preach any more? Being blind wouldn't be a hinderance. People would like to go see a blind preacher. It would be something different." She was used to going on without an answer. "You could get you one of those seeing dogs," she said, "and he and you could get up a good crowd. People'll always go to see a dog.

"For myself," she continued, "I don't have that streak. I believe that what's right today is wrong tomorrow and that the time to enjoy yourself is now so long as you let others do the same. I'm as good, Mr. Motes," she said, "not believing in Jesus as a many a one that does."

"You're better," he said, leaning forward suddenly. "If you believed in Jesus, you wouldn't be so good."

He had never paid her a compliment before! "Why Mr. Motes," she said, "I expect you're a fine preacher! You certainly ought to start it again. It would give you something to do. As it is, you don't have anything to do but walk. Why don't you start preaching again?"

"I can't preach any more," he muttered.

"Why?"

"I don't have time," he said, and got up and walked off the porch as if she had reminded him of some urgent business. He walked as if his feet hurt him but he had to go on.

Some time later she discovered why he limped. She was cleaning his room and happened to knock over his extra pair of shoes. She picked them up and looked into them as if she thought she might find something hidden there. The bottoms of them were lined with gravel and broken glass and pieces of small stone. She spilled this out and sifted it through her fingers, looking for a glitter that might mean something valuable, but she saw that what she had in her hand was trash that anybody could pick up in the alley. She stood for some time, holding the shoes, and finally she put them back under the cot. In a few days she examined them again and they were lined with fresh rocks. Who's he doing this for? she asked herself. What's he getting out of doing it? Every now and then she would have an intimation of something hidden near her but out of her reach. "Mr. Motes," she said that day, when he was in her kitchen eating his dinner, "what do you walk on rocks for?"

"To pay," he said in a harsh voice.

"Pay for what?"

"It don't make any difference for what," he said. "I'm paying."

"But what have you got to show that you're paying for?" she persisted.

"Mind your business," he said rudely. "You can't see."

The landlady continued to chew very slowly. "Do you

think, Mr. Motes," she said hoarsely, "that when you're dead, you're blind?"

"I hope so," he said after a minute.

"Why?" she asked, staring at him.

After a while he said, "If there's no bottom in your eyes, they hold more."

The landlady stared for a long time, seeing nothing at all.

She began to fasten all her attention on him, to the neglect of other things. She began to follow him in his walks, meeting him accidentally and accompanying him. He didn't seem to know she was there, except occasionally when he would slap at his face as if her voice bothered him, like the singing of a mosquito. He had a deep wheezing cough and she began to badger him about his health. "There's no one," she would say, "to look after you but me, Mr. Motes. No one that has your interest at heart but me. Nobody would care if I didn't." She began to make him tasty dishes and carry them to his room. He would eat what she brought, immediately, with a wry face, and hand back the plate without thanking her, as if all his attention were directed elsewhere and this was an interruption he had to suffer. One morning he told her abruptly that he was going to get his food somewhere else, and named the place, a diner around the corner, run by a foreigner. "And you'll rue the day!" she said. "You'll pick up an infection. No sane person eats there. A dark and filthy place. Encrusted! It's you that can't see, Mr. Motes.

"Crazy fool," she muttered when he had walked off. "Wait till winter comes. Where will you eat when winter comes, when the first wind blows the virus into you?"

She didn't have to wait long. He caught influenza before winter and for a while he was too weak to walk out and she had the satisfaction of bringing his meals to his room. She came earlier than usual one morning and found him asleep, breathing heavily. The old shirt he wore to sleep in was open down the front and showed three strands of barbed wire, wrapped around his chest. She retreated backwards to the door and then she dropped the tray. "Mr. Motes," she said in a thick voice, "what do you do these things for? It's not natural."

He pulled himself up.

"What's that wire around you for? It's not natural," she repeated.

After a second he began to button the shirt. "It's natural," he said.

"Well, it's not normal. It's like one of them gory stories, it's something that people have quit doing—like boiling in oil or being a saint or walling up cats," she said. "There's no reason for it. People have quit doing it."

"They ain't quit doing it as long as I'm doing it," he said.

"People have quit doing it," she repeated. "What do you do it for?"

"I'm not clean," he said.

She stood staring at him, unmindful of the broken dishes at her feet. "I know it," she said after a minute, "you got blood on that night shirt and on the bed. You ought to get you a washwoman . . ."

"That's not the kind of clean," he said.

"There's only one kind of clean, Mr. Motes," she muttered. She looked down and observed the dishes he had made her break and the mess she would have to get up and she left for the hall closet and returned in a minute with the dust pan and broom. "It's easier to bleed than sweat, Mr. Motes," she said in the voice of High Sarcasm. "You must believe in Jesus or you wouldn't do these foolish things. You must have been lying to me when you named your fine church. I wouldn't be surprised if you weren't some kind of a agent of the pope or got some connection with something funny."

"I ain't treatin' with you," he said and lay back down, coughing.

"You got nobody to take care of you but me," she reminded him.

Her first plan had been to marry him and then have him committed to the state institution for the insane, but gradually her plan had become to marry him and keep him. Watching his face had become a habit with her; she wanted to penetrate the darkness behind it and see for herself what was there. She had the sense that she had tarried long enough and that she must get him now while he was weak, or not at all. He was so weak from the influenza that he tottered when he walked; winter had already begun and the wind slashed at the house from every angle, making a sound like sharp knives swirling in the air.

"Nobody in their right mind would like to be out on a day like this," she said, putting her head suddenly into his room in the middle of the morning on one of the coldest days of the year. "Do you hear that wind, Mr. Motes? It's fortunate for you that you have this warm place to be and someone to take care of you." She made her voice more than usually soft. "Every blind and sick man is not so fortunate," she said, "as to have somebody that cares about him." She came in and sat down on the straight chair that was just at the door. She sat on the edge of it, leaning forward with her legs apart and her hands braced on her knees. "Let me tell you, Mr. Motes," she said, "few men are as fortunate as you but I can't keep climbing these stairs. It wears me out. I've been thinking what we could do about it."

He had been lying motionless on the bed but he sat up suddenly as if he were listening, almost as if he had been alarmed by the tone of her voice. "I know you wouldn't want to give up your room here," she said, and waited for the effect of this. He turned his face toward her; she could tell she had his attention. "I know you like it here and wouldn't want to leave and you're a sick man and need somebody to take care of you as well as being blind," she said and found herself breathless and her heart beginning to flutter. He reached to the foot of the bed and felt for his clothes that were rolled up there. He began to put them on hurriedly over his night shirt. "I been thinking how we could arrange it so you would have a home and somebody to take care of you and I wouldn't have to climb these stairs, what you dressing for today, Mr. Motes? You don't want to go out in this weather.

"I been thinking," she went on, watching him as he went on with what he was doing, "and I see there's only one thing for you and me to do. Get married. I wouldn't do it under any ordinary condition but I would do it for a blind man and a sick one. If we don't help each other, Mr. Motes, there's nobody to help us," she said. "Nobody. The world is a empty place."

The suit that had been glare-blue when it was bought was a softer shade now. The panama hat was wheat-colored. He kept it on the floor by his shoes when he was not wearing it.

He reached for it and put it on and then he began to put on his shoes that were still lined with rocks.

"Nobody ought to be without a place of their own to be," she said, "and I'm willing to give you a home here with me, a place where you can always stay, Mr. Motes, and never worry yourself about."

His cane was on the floor near where his shoes had been. He felt for it and then stood up and began to walk slowly toward her. "I got a place for you in my heart, Mr. Motes," she said and felt it shaking like a bird cage; she didn't know whether he was coming toward her to embrace her or not. He passed her, expressionless, out the door and into the hall. "Mr. Motes!" she said, turning sharply in the chair, "I can't allow you to stay here under no other circumstances. I can't climb these stairs. I don't want a thing," she said, "but to help you. You don't have anybody to look after you but me. Nobody to care if you live or die but me! No other place to be but mine!"

He was feeling for the first step with his cane.

"Or were you planning to find you another rooming house?" she asked in a voice getting higher. "Maybe you were planning to go to some other city!"

"That's not where I'm going," he said. "There's no other house nor no other city."

"There's nothing, Mr. Motes," she said, "and time goes forward, it don't go backward and unless you take what's offered you, you'll find yourself out in the cold pitch black and just how far do you think you'll get?"

He felt for each step with his cane before he put his foot on it. When he reached the bottom, she called down to him. "You needn't to return to a place you don't value, Mr. Motes. The door won't be open to you. You can come back and get your belongings and then go on to wherever you think you're going." She stood at the top of the stairs for a long time. "He'll be back," she muttered. "Let the wind cut into him a little."

That night a driving icy rain came up and lying in her bed, awake at midnight, Mrs. Flood, the landlady, began to weep. She wanted to run out into the rain and cold and hunt him and find him huddled in some half-sheltered place and bring him back and say, Mr. Motes, Mr. Motes, you can stay here forever, or the two of us will go where you're going, the two of us will go. She had had a hard life, without pain and without pleasure, and she thought that now that she was coming to the last part of it, she deserved a friend. If she was going to be blind when she was dead, who better to guide her than a blind man? Who better to lead the blind than the blind, who knew what it was like?

As soon as it was daylight, she went out in the rain and searched the five or six blocks he knew and went from door to door, asking for him, but no one had seen him. She came back and called the police and described him and asked for him to be picked up and brought back to her to pay his rent. She waited all day for them to bring him in the squad car, or for him to come back of his own accord, but he didn't come. The rain and wind continued and she thought he was probably drowned in some alley by now. She paced up and down in her room, walking faster and faster, thinking of his eyes without any bottom in them and of the blindness of death.

Two days later, two young policemen cruising in a squad car found him lying in a drainage ditch near an abandoned construction project. The driver drew the squad car up to the edge of the ditch and looked into it for some time. "Ain't we been looking for a blind one?" he asked.

The other consulted a pad. "Blind and got on a blue suit and ain't paid his rent," he said.

"Yonder he is," the first one said, and pointed into the ditch. The other moved up closer and looked out of the window too.

"His suit ain't blue," he said.

"Yes it is blue," the first one said. "Quit pushing up so close to me. Get out and I'll show you it's blue." They got out and walked around the car and squatted down on the edge of the ditch. They both had on tall new boots and new policemen's clothes; they both had yellow hair with sideburns, and they were both fat, but one was much fatter than the other.

"It might have uster been blue," the fatter one admitted.

"You reckon he's daid?" the first one asked.

"Ast him," the other said.

"No, he ain't daid. He's moving."

"Maybe he's just unconscious," the fatter one said, taking out his new billy. They watched him for a few seconds. His hand was moving along the edge of the ditch as if it were hunting something to grip. He asked them in a hoarse whisper where he was and if it was day or night.

"It's day," the thinner one said, looking at the sky. "We got to take you back to pay your rent."

"I want to go on where I'm going," the blind man said.

"You got to pay your rent first," the policeman said. "Ever' bit of it!"

The other, perceiving that he was conscious, hit him over the head with his new billy. "We don't want to have no trouble with him," he said. "You take his feet."

He died in the squad car but they didn't notice and took him on to the landlady's. She had them put him on her bed and when she had pushed them out the door, she locked it behind them and drew up a straight chair and sat down close to his face where she could talk to him. "Well, Mr. Motes," she said, "I see you've come home!"

His face was stern and tranquil. "I knew you'd come back," she said. "And I've been waiting for you. And you needn't to pay any more rent but have it free here, any way you like, upstairs or down. Just however you want it and with me to wait on you, or if you want to go on somewhere, we'll both go."

She had never observed his face more composed and she grabbed his hand and held it to her heart. It was resistless and dry. The outline of a skull was plain under his skin and the deep burned eye sockets seemed to lead into the dark tunnel where he had disappeared. She leaned closer and closer to his face, looking deep into them, trying to see how she had been cheated or what had cheated her, but she couldn't see anything. She shut her eyes and saw the pin point of light but so far away that she could not hold it steady in her mind. She felt as if she were blocked at the entrance of something. She sat staring with her eyes shut, into his eyes, and felt as if she had finally got to the beginning of something she couldn't begin, and she saw him moving farther and farther away, farther and farther into the darkness until he was the pin point of light.

A GOOD MAN
IS HARD TO FIND

and Other Stories

FOR SALLY AND ROBERT FITZGERALD

Contents

A Good Man Is Hard to Find

T HE GRANDMOTHER didn't want to go to Florida. She wanted to visit some of her connections in east Tennessee and she was seizing at every chance to change Bailey's mind. Bailey was the son she lived with, her only boy. He was sitting on the edge of his chair at the table, bent over the orange sports section of the *Journal*. "Now look here, Bailey," she said, "see here, read this," and she stood with one hand on her thin hip and the other rattling the newspaper at his bald head. "Here this fellow that calls himself The Misfit is aloose from the Federal Pen and headed toward Florida and you read here what it says he did to these people. Just you read it. I wouldn't take my children in any direction with a criminal like that aloose in it. I couldn't answer to my conscience if I did."

Bailey didn't look up from his reading so she wheeled around then and faced the children's mother, a young woman in slacks, whose face was as broad and innocent as a cabbage and was tied around with a green head-kerchief that had two points on the top like rabbit's ears. She was sitting on the sofa, feeding the baby his apricots out of a jar. "The children have been to Florida before," the old lady said. "You all ought to take them somewhere else for a change so they would see different parts of the world and be broad. They never have been to east Tennessee."

The children's mother didn't seem to hear her but the eight-year-old boy, John Wesley, a stocky child with glasses, said, "If you don't want to go to Florida, why dontcha stay at home?" He and the little girl, June Star, were reading the funny papers on the floor.

"She wouldn't stay at home to be queen for a day," June Star said without raising her yellow head.

"Yes and what would you do if this fellow, The Misfit, caught you?" the grandmother asked.

"I'd smack his face," John Wesley said.

"She wouldn't stay at home for a million bucks," June Star said. "Afraid she'd miss something. She has to go everywhere we go."

"All right, Miss," the grandmother said. "Just remember that the next time you want me to curl your hair."

June Star said her hair was naturally curly.

The next morning the grandmother was the first one in the car, ready to go. She had her big black valise that looked like the head of a hippopotamus in one corner, and underneath it she was hiding a basket with Pitty Sing, the cat, in it. She didn't intend for the cat to be left alone in the house for three days because he would miss her too much and she was afraid he might brush against one of the gas burners and accidentally asphyxiate himself. Her son, Bailey, didn't like to arrive at a motel with a cat.

She sat in the middle of the back seat with John Wesley and June Star on either side of her. Bailey and the children's mother and the baby sat in front and they left Atlanta at eight forty-five with the mileage on the car at 55890. The grandmother wrote this down because she thought it would be interesting to say how many miles they had been when they got back. It took them twenty minutes to reach the outskirts of the city.

The old lady settled herself comfortably, removing her white cotton gloves and putting them up with her purse on the shelf in front of the back window. The children's mother still had on slacks and still had her head tied up in a green kerchief, but the grandmother had on a navy blue straw sailor hat with a bunch of white violets on the brim and a navy blue dress with a small white dot in the print. Her collars and cuffs were white organdy trimmed with lace and at her neckline she had pinned a purple spray of cloth violets containing a sachet. In case of an accident, anyone seeing her dead on the highway would know at once that she was a lady.

She said she thought it was going to be a good day for driving, neither too hot nor too cold, and she cautioned Bailey that the speed limit was fifty-five miles an hour and that the patrolmen hid themselves behind billboards and small clumps of trees and sped out after you before you had a chance to slow down. She pointed out interesting details of the scenery: Stone Mountain; the blue granite that in some places came up to both sides of the highway; the brilliant red clay banks slightly streaked with purple; and the various crops that made rows of green lace-work on the ground. The trees were full of silver-white sunlight and the meanest of them sparkled. The children were reading comic magazines and their mother had gone back to sleep.

"Let's go through Georgia fast so we won't have to look at it much," John Wesley said.

"If I were a little boy," said the grandmother, "I wouldn't talk about my native state that way. Tennessee has the mountains and Georgia has the hills."

"Tennessee is just a hillbilly dumping ground," John Wesley said, "and Georgia is a lousy state too."

"You said it," June Star said.

"In my time," said the grandmother, folding her thin veined fingers, "children were more respectful of their native states and their parents and everything else. People did right then. Oh look at the cute little pickaninny!" she said and pointed to a Negro child standing in the door of a shack. "Wouldn't that make a picture, now?" she asked and they all turned and looked at the little Negro out of the back window. He waved.

"He didn't have any britches on," June Star said.

"He probably didn't have any," the grandmother explained. "Little niggers in the country don't have things like we do. If I could paint, I'd paint that picture," she said.

The children exchanged comic books.

The grandmother offered to hold the baby and the children's mother passed him over the front seat to her. She set him on her knee and bounced him and told him about the things they were passing. She rolled her eyes and screwed up her mouth and stuck her leathery thin face into his smooth bland one. Occasionally he gave her a faraway smile. They passed a large cotton field with five or six graves fenced in the middle of it, like a small island. "Look at the graveyard!" the grandmother said, pointing it out. "That was the old family burying ground. That belonged to the plantation."

"Where's the plantation?" John Wesley asked.

"Gone With the Wind," said the grandmother. "Ha. Ha."

When the children finished all the comic books they had brought, they opened the lunch and ate it. The grandmother ate a peanut butter sandwich and an olive and would not let the children throw the box and the paper napkins out the window. When there was nothing else to do they played a game by choosing a cloud and making the other two guess what shape it suggested. John Wesley took one the shape of a cow and June Star guessed a cow and John Wesley said, no, an automobile, and June Star said he didn't play fair, and they began to slap each other over the grandmother.

The grandmother said she would tell them a story if they would keep quiet. When she told a story, she rolled her eyes and waved her head and was very dramatic. She said once when she was a maiden lady she had been courted by a Mr. Edgar Atkins Teagarden from Jasper, Georgia. She said he was a very good-looking man and a gentleman and that he brought her a watermelon every Saturday afternoon with his initials cut in it, E. A. T. Well, one Saturday, she said, Mr. Teagarden brought the watermelon and there was nobody at home and he left it on the front porch and returned in his buggy to Jasper, but she never got the watermelon, she said, because a nigger boy ate it when he saw the initials, E. A. T.! This story tickled John Wesley's funny bone and he giggled and giggled but June Star didn't think it was any good. She said she wouldn't marry a man that just brought her a water-melon on Saturday. The grandmother said she would have done well to marry Mr. Teagarden because he was a gentle-man and had bought Coca-Cola stock when it first came out and that he had died only a few years ago, a very wealthy man.

They stopped at The Tower for barbecued sandwiches. The Tower was a part stucco and part wood filling station and dance hall set in a clearing outside of Timothy. A fat man named Red Sammy Butts ran it and there were signs stuck here and there on the building and for miles up and down the highway saying, TRY RED SAMMY'S FAMOUS BAR-BECUE. NONE LIKE FAMOUS RED SAMMY'S! RED SAM! THE FAT BOY WITH THE HAPPY LAUGH. A VETERAN! RED SAMMY'S YOUR MAN!

Red Sammy was lying on the bare ground outside The Tower with his head under a truck while a gray monkey about a foot high, chained to a small chinaberry tree, chattered nearby. The monkey sprang back into the tree and got on the highest limb as soon as he saw the children jump out of the car and run toward him.

Inside, The Tower was a long dark room with a counter at one end and tables at the other and dancing space in the middle. They all sat down at a board table next to the nickel-odeon and Red Sam's wife, a tall burnt-brown woman with hair and eyes lighter than her skin, came and took their order. The children's mother put a dime in the machine and played "The Tennessee Waltz," and the grandmother said that tune always made her want to dance. She asked Bailey if he would like to dance but he only glared at her. He didn't have a naturally sunny disposition like she did and trips made him nervous. The grandmother's brown eyes were very bright. She swayed her head from side to side and pretended she was dancing in her chair. June Star said play something she could tap to so the children's mother put in another dime and played a fast number and June Star stepped out onto the dance floor and did her tap routine.

"Ain't she cute?" Red Sam's wife said, leaning over the counter. "Would you like to come be my little girl?"

"No I certainly wouldn't," June Star said. "I wouldn't live in a broken-down place like this for a million bucks!" and she ran back to the table.

"Ain't she cute?" the woman repeated, stretching her mouth politely.

"Arn't you ashamed?" hissed the grandmother.

Red Sam came in and told his wife to quit lounging on the counter and hurry up with these people's order. His khaki trousers reached just to his hip bones and his stomach hung over them like a sack of meal swaying under his shirt. He came over and sat down at a table nearby and let out a combination sigh and yodel. "You can't win," he said. "You can't win," and he wiped his sweating red face off with a gray handkerchief. "These days you don't know who to trust," he said. "Ain't that the truth?"

"People are certainly not nice like they used to be," said the grandmother.

"Two fellers come in here last week," Red Sammy said, "driving a Chrysler. It was a old beat-up car but it was a good one and these boys looked all right to me. Said they worked at the mill and you know I let them fellers charge the gas they bought? Now why did I do that?"

"Because you're a good man!" the grandmother said at once.

"Yes'm, I suppose so," Red Sam said as if he were struck with this answer.

His wife brought the orders, carrying the five plates all at once without a tray, two in each hand and one balanced on her arm. "It isn't a soul in this green world of God's that you can trust," she said. "And I don't count nobody out of that, not nobody," she repeated, looking at Red Sammy.

"Did you read about that criminal, The Misfit, that's escaped?" asked the grandmother.

"I wouldn't be a bit surprised if he didn't attact this place right here," said the woman. "If he hears about it being here, I wouldn't be none surprised to see him. If he hears it's two cent in the cash register, I wouldn't be a tall surprised if he . . ."

"That'll do," Red Sam said. "Go bring these people their Co'-Colas," and the woman went off to get the rest of the order.

"A good man is hard to find," Red Sammy said. "Everything is getting terrible. I remember the day you could go off and leave your screen door unlatched. Not no more."

He and the grandmother discussed better times. The old lady said that in her opinion Europe was entirely to blame for the way things were now. She said the way Europe acted you would think we were made of money and Red Sam said it was no use talking about it, she was exactly right. The children ran outside into the white sunlight and looked at the monkey in the lacy chinaberry tree. He was busy catching fleas on himself and biting each one carefully between his teeth as if it were a delicacy.

They drove off again into the hot afternoon. The grandmother took cat naps and woke up every few minutes with her own snoring. Outside of Toombsboro she woke up and recalled an old plantation that she had visited in this neighborhood once when she was a young lady. She said the house had six white columns across the front and that there was an avenue of oaks leading up to it and two little wooden trellis arbors on either side in front where you sat down with your suitor after a stroll in the garden. She recalled exactly which road to turn off to get to it. She knew that Bailey would not be willing to lose any time looking at an old house, but the more she talked about it, the more she wanted to see it once again and find out if the little twin arbors were still standing. "There was a secret panel in this house," she said craftily, not telling the truth but wishing that she were, "and the story went that all the family silver was hidden in it when Sherman came through but it was never found . . ."

"Hey!" John Wesley said. "Let's go see it! We'll find it! We'll poke all the woodwork and find it! Who lives there? Where do you turn off at? Hey Pop, can't we turn off there?"

"We never have seen a house with a secret panel!" June Star shrieked. "Let's go to the house with the secret panel! Hey Pop, can't we go see the house with the secret panel!"

"It's not far from here, I know," the grandmother said. "It wouldn't take over twenty minutes."

Bailey was looking straight ahead. His jaw was as rigid as a horseshoe. "No," he said.

The children began to yell and scream that they wanted to see the house with the secret panel. John Wesley kicked the back of the front seat and June Star hung over her mother's shoulder and whined desperately into her ear that they never had any fun even on their vacation, that they could never do what THEY wanted to do. The baby began to scream and John Wesley kicked the back of the seat so hard that his father could feel the blows in his kidney.

"All right!" he shouted and drew the car to a stop at the side of the road. "Will you all shut up? Will you all just shut up for one second? If you don't shut up, we won't go any-where."

"It would be very educational for them," the grandmother murmured.

"All right," Bailey said, "but get this: this is the only time we're going to stop for anything like this. This is the one and only time."

"The dirt road that you have to turn down is about a mile back," the grandmother directed. "I marked it when we passed."

"A dirt road," Bailey groaned.

After they had turned around and were headed toward the dirt road, the grandmother recalled other points about the house, the beautiful glass over the front doorway and the candle-lamp in the hall. John Wesley said that the secret panel was probably in the fireplace.

"You can't go inside this house," Bailey said. "You don't know who lives there."

"While you all talk to the people in front, I'll run around behind and get in a window," John Wesley suggested.

"We'll all stay in the car," his mother said.

They turned onto the dirt road and the car raced roughly along in a swirl of pink dust. The grandmother recalled the times when there were no paved roads and thirty miles was a day's journey. The dirt road was hilly and there were sudden washes in it and sharp curves on dangerous embankments. All at once they would be on a hill, looking down over the blue tops of trees for miles around, then the next minute, they would be in a red depression with the dust-coated trees looking down on them.

"This place had better turn up in a minute," Bailey said, "or I'm going to turn around."

The road looked as if no one had traveled on it in months.

"It's not much farther," the grandmother said and just as she said it, a horrible thought came to her. The thought was so embarrassing that she turned red in the face and her eyes dilated and her feet jumped up, upsetting her valise in the corner. The instant the valise moved, the newspaper top she had over the basket under it rose with a snarl and Pitty Sing, the cat, sprang onto Bailey's shoulder.

The children were thrown to the floor and their mother, clutching the baby, was thrown out the door onto the ground; the old lady was thrown into the front seat. The car turned over once and landed right-side-up in a gulch off the side of the road. Bailey remained in the driver's seat with the cat—gray-striped with a broad white face and an orange nose—clinging to his neck like a caterpillar.

As soon as the children saw they could move their arms and legs, they scrambled out of the car, shouting, "We've had an ACCIDENT!" The grandmother was curled up under the dashboard, hoping she was injured so that Bailey's wrath would not come down on her all at once. The horrible thought she had had before the accident was that the house she had remembered so vividly was not in Georgia but in Tennessee.

Bailey removed the cat from his neck with both hands and flung it out the window against the side of a pine tree. Then he got out of the car and started looking for the children's mother. She was sitting against the side of the red gutted ditch, holding the screaming baby, but she only had a cut down her face and a broken shoulder. "We've had an ACCI-DENT!" the children screamed in a frenzy of delight.

"But nobody's killed," June Star said with disappointment as the grandmother limped out of the car, her hat still pinned to her head but the broken front brim standing up at a jaunty angle and the violet spray hanging off the side. They all sat down in the ditch, except the children, to recover from the shock. They were all shaking.

"Maybe a car will come along," said the children's mother hoarsely.

"I believe I have injured an organ," said the grandmother, pressing her side, but no one answered her. Bailey's teeth were clattering. He had on a yellow sport shirt with bright blue parrots designed in it and his face was as yellow as the shirt. The grandmother decided that she would not mention that the house was in Tennessee.

The road was about ten feet above and they could see only the tops of the trees on the other side of it. Behind the ditch they were sitting in there were more woods, tall and dark and deep. In a few minutes they saw a car some distance away on top of a hill, coming slowly as if the occupants were watching them. The grandmother stood up and waved both arms dramatically to attract their attention. The car continued to come on slowly, disappeared around a bend and appeared again, moving even slower, on top of the hill they had gone over. It was a big black battered hearse-like automobile. There were three men in it.

It came to a stop just over them and for some minutes, the driver looked down with a steady expressionless gaze to where they were sitting, and didn't speak. Then he turned his head and muttered something to the other two and they got out. One was a fat boy in black trousers and a red sweat shirt with a silver stallion embossed on the front of it. He moved around on the right side of them and stood staring, his mouth partly open in a kind of loose grin. The other had on khaki pants and a blue striped coat and a gray hat pulled down very low, hiding most of his face. He came around slowly on the left side. Neither spoke.

The driver got out of the car and stood by the side of it, looking down at them. He was an older man than the other two. His hair was just beginning to gray and he wore silver-rimmed spectacles that gave him a scholarly look. He had a long creased face and didn't have on any shirt or undershirt. He had on blue jeans that were too tight for him and was holding a black hat and a gun. The two boys also had guns.

"We've had an ACCIDENT!" the children screamed.

The grandmother had the peculiar feeling that the bespectacled man was someone she knew. His face was as familiar to her as if she had known him all her life but she could not recall who he was. He moved away from the car and began to come down the embankment, placing his feet carefully so that he wouldn't slip. He had on tan and white shoes and no socks, and his ankles were red and thin. "Good afternoon," he said. "I see you all had you a little spill."

"We turned over twice!" said the grandmother.

"Oncet," he corrected. "We seen it happen. Try their car and see will it run, Hiram," he said quietly to the boy with the gray hat.

"What you got that gun for?" John Wesley asked. "Whatcha gonna do with that gun?"

"Lady," the man said to the children's mother, "would you mind calling them children to sit down by you? Children make me nervous. I want all you all to sit down right together there where you're at."

"What are you telling US what to do for?" June Star asked.

Behind them the line of woods gaped like a dark open mouth. "Come here," said their mother.

"Look here now," Bailey began suddenly, "we're in a predicament! We're in . . ."

The grandmother shrieked. She scrambled to her feet and stood staring. "You're The Misfit!" she said. "I recognized you at once!"

"Yes'm," the man said, smiling slightly as if he were pleased in spite of himself to be known, "but it would have been better for all of you, lady, if you hadn't of reckernized me."

Bailey turned his head sharply and said something to his mother that shocked even the children. The old lady began to cry and The Misfit reddened.

"Lady," he said, "don't you get upset. Sometimes a man says things he don't mean. I don't reckon he meant to talk to you thataway."

"You wouldn't shoot a lady, would you?" the grandmother said and removed a clean handkerchief from her cuff and began to slap at her eyes with it.

The Misfit pointed the toe of his shoe into the ground and made a little hole and then covered it up again. "I would hate to have to," he said.

"Listen," the grandmother almost screamed, "I know you're a good man. You don't look a bit like you have common blood. I know you must come from nice people!"

"Yes mam," he said, "finest people in the world." When he smiled he showed a row of strong white teeth. "God never made a finer woman than my mother and my daddy's heart was pure gold," he said. The boy with the red sweat shirt had come around behind them and was standing with his gun at his hip. The Misfit squatted down on the ground. "Watch them children, Bobby Lee," he said. "You know they make me nervous." He looked at the six of them huddled together in front of him and he seemed to be embarrassed as if he couldn't think of anything to say. "Ain't a cloud in the sky," he remarked, looking up at it. "Don't see no sun but don't see no cloud neither."

"Yes, it's a beautiful day," said the grandmother. "Listen," she said, "you shouldn't call yourself The Misfit because I know you're a good man at heart. I can just look at you and tell."

"Hush!" Bailey yelled. "Hush! Everybody shut up and let me handle this!" He was squatting in the position of a runner about to sprint forward but he didn't move.

"I pre-chate that, lady," The Misfit said and drew a little circle in the ground with the butt of his gun.

"It'll take a half a hour to fix this here car," Hiram called, looking over the raised hood of it.

"Well, first you and Bobby Lee get him and that little boy to step over yonder with you," The Misfit said, pointing to Bailey and John Wesley. "The boys want to ast you something," he said to Bailey. "Would you mind stepping back in them woods there with them?"

"Listen," Bailey began, "we're in a terrible predicament! Nobody realizes what this is," and his voice cracked. His eyes were as blue and intense as the parrots in his shirt and he remained perfectly still.

The grandmother reached up to adjust her hat brim as if she were going to the woods with him but it came off in her hand. She stood staring at it and after a second she let it fall on the ground. Hiram pulled Bailey up by the arm as if he were assisting an old man. John Wesley caught hold of his father's hand and Bobby Lee followed. They went off toward the woods and just as they reached the dark edge, Bailey turned and supporting himself against a gray naked pine trunk, he shouted, "I'll be back in a minute, Mamma, wait on me!"

"Come back this instant!" his mother shrilled but they all disappeared into the woods.

"Bailey Boy!" the grandmother called in a tragic voice but she found she was looking at The Misfit squatting on the ground in front of her. "I just know you're a good man," she said desperately. "You're not a bit common!"

"Nome, I ain't a good man," The Misfit said after a second as if he had considered her statement carefully, "but I ain't the worst in the world neither. My daddy said I was a different breed of dog from my brothers and sisters. 'You know,' Daddy said, 'it's some that can live their whole life out without asking about it and it's others has to know why it is, and this boy is one of the latters. He's going to be into everything!'" He put on his black hat and looked up suddenly and then away deep into the woods as if he were embarrassed again. "I'm sorry I don't have on a shirt before you ladies," he said, hunching his shoulders slightly. "We buried our clothes that we had on when we escaped and we're just making do until we can get better. We borrowed these from some folks we met," he explained.

"That's perfectly all right," the grandmother said. "Maybe Bailey has an extra shirt in his suitcase."

"I'll look and see terrectly," The Misfit said.

"Where are they taking him?" the children's mother screamed.

"Daddy was a card himself," The Misfit said. "You couldn't put anything over on him. He never got in trouble with the Authorities though. Just had the knack of handling them."

"You could be honest too if you'd only try," said the grandmother. "Think how wonderful it would be to settle down and live a comfortable life and not have to think about somebody chasing you all the time."

The Misfit kept scratching in the ground with the butt of his gun as if he were thinking about it. "Yes'm, somebody is always after you," he murmured.

The grandmother noticed how thin his shoulder blades were just behind his hat because she was standing up looking down on him. "Do you ever pray?" she asked.

He shook his head. All she saw was the black hat wiggle between his shoulder blades. "Nome," he said.

There was a pistol shot from the woods, followed closely by another. Then silence. The old lady's head jerked around. She could hear the wind move through the tree tops like a long satisfied insuck of breath. "Bailey Boy!" she called.

"I was a gospel singer for a while," The Misfit said. "I been most everything. Been in the arm service, both land and sea, at home and abroad, been twict married, been an undertaker, been with the railroads, plowed Mother Earth, been in a tornado, seen a man burnt alive oncet," and he looked up at the children's mother and the little girl who were sitting close together, their faces white and their eyes glassy; "I even seen a woman flogged," he said.

"Pray, pray," the grandmother began, "pray, pray . . ."

"I never was a bad boy that I remember of," The Misfit said in an almost dreamy voice, "but somewhere along the line I done something wrong and got sent to the penitentiary. I was buried alive," and he looked up and held her attention to him by a steady stare.

"That's when you should have started to pray," she said. "What did you do to get sent to the penitentiary that first time?"

"Turn to the right, it was a wall," The Misfit said, looking up again at the cloudless sky. "Turn to the left, it was a wall. Look up it was a ceiling, look down it was a floor. I forget what I done, lady. I set there and set there, trying to remember what it was I done and I ain't recalled it to this day. Oncet in a while, I would think it was coming to me, but it never come."

"Maybe they put you in by mistake," the old lady said vaguely.

"Nome," he said. "It wasn't no mistake. They had the papers on me."

"You must have stolen something," she said.

The Misfit sneered slightly. "Nobody had nothing I wanted," he said. "It was a head-doctor at the penitentiary said what I had done was kill my daddy but I known that for a lie. My daddy died in nineteen ought nineteen of the epidemic flu and I never had a thing to do with it. He was buried in the Mount Hopewell Baptist churchyard and you can go there and see for yourself."

"If you would pray," the old lady said, "Jesus would help you."

"That's right," The Misfit said.

"Well then, why don't you pray?" she asked trembling with delight suddenly.

"I don't want no hep," he said. "I'm doing all right by myself."

Bobby Lee and Hiram came ambling back from the woods. Bobby Lee was dragging a yellow shirt with bright blue parrots in it.

"Thow me that shirt, Bobby Lee," The Misfit said. The shirt came flying at him and landed on his shoulder and he put it on. The grandmother couldn't name what the shirt reminded her of. "No, lady," The Misfit said while he was buttoning it up, "I found out the crime don't matter. You can do one thing or you can do another, kill a man or take a tire off his car, because sooner or later you're going to forget what it was you done and just be punished for it."

The children's mother had begun to make heaving noises as if she couldn't get her breath. "Lady," he asked, "would you and that little girl like to step off yonder with Bobby Lee and Hiram and join your husband?"

"Yes, thank you," the mother said faintly. Her left arm dangled helplessly and she was holding the baby, who had gone to sleep, in the other. "Hep that lady up, Hiram," The Misfit said as she struggled to climb out of the ditch, "and Bobby Lee, you hold onto that little girl's hand."

"I don't want to hold hands with him," June Star said. "He reminds me of a pig."

The fat boy blushed and laughed and caught her by the arm and pulled her off into the woods after Hiram and her mother.

Alone with The Misfit, the grandmother found that she had lost her voice. There was not a cloud in the sky nor any sun. There was nothing around her but woods. She wanted to tell him that he must pray. She opened and closed her mouth several times before anything came out. Finally she found herself saying, "Jesus. Jesus," meaning, Jesus will help you, but the way she was saying it, it sounded as if she might be cursing.

"Yes'm," The Misfit said as if he agreed. "Jesus thown everything off balance. It was the same case with Him as with me except He hadn't committed any crime and they could prove I had committed one because they had the papers on me. Of course," he said, "they never shown me my papers. That's why I sign myself now. I said long ago, you get you a signature and sign everything you do and keep a copy of it. Then you'll know what you done and you can hold up the crime to the punishment and see do they match and in the end you'll have something to prove you ain't been treated right. I call myself The Misfit," he said, "because I can't make what all I done wrong fit what all I gone through in punishment."

There was a piercing scream from the woods, followed closely by a pistol report. "Does it seem right to you, lady, that one is punished a heap and another ain't punished at all?"

"Jesus!" the old lady cried. "You've got good blood! I know you wouldn't shoot a lady! I know you come from nice people! Pray! Jesus, you ought not to shoot a lady. I'll give you all the money I've got!"

"Lady," The Misfit said, looking beyond her far into the woods, "there never was a body that give the undertaker a tip."

There were two more pistol reports and the grandmother raised her head like a parched old turkey hen crying for water and called, "Bailey Boy, Bailey Boy!" as if her heart would break.

"Jesus was the only One that ever raised the dead," The Misfit continued, "and He shouldn't have done it. He thown everything off balance. If He did what He said, then it's nothing for you to do but thow away everything and follow Him, and if He didn't, then it's nothing for you to do but enjoy the few minutes you got left the best way you can—by killing somebody or burning down his house or doing some other meanness to him. No pleasure but meanness," he said and his voice had become almost a snarl.

"Maybe He didn't raise the dead," the old lady mumbled, not knowing what she was saying and feeling so dizzy that she sank down in the ditch with her legs twisted under her.

"I wasn't there so I can't say He didn't," The Misfit said. "I wisht I had of been there," he said, hitting the ground with his fist. "It ain't right I wasn't there because if I had of been there I would of known. Listen lady," he said in a high voice, "if I had of been there I would of known and I wouldn't be like I am now." His voice seemed about to crack and the grandmother's head cleared for an instant. She saw the man's face twisted close to her own as if he were going to cry and she murmured, "Why you're one of my babies. You're one of my own children!" She reached out and touched him on the shoulder. The Misfit sprang back as if a snake had bitten him and shot her three times through the chest. Then he put his gun down on the ground and took off his glasses and began to clean them.

Hiram and Bobby Lee returned from the woods and stood over the ditch, looking down at the grandmother who half sat and half lay in a puddle of blood with her legs crossed under her like a child's and her face smiling up at the cloudless sky.

Without his glasses, The Misfit's eyes were red-rimmed and pale and defenseless-looking. "Take her off and thow her where you thown the others," he said, picking up the cat that was rubbing itself against his leg.

"She was a talker, wasn't she?" Bobby Lee said, sliding down the ditch with a yodel.

"She would of been a good woman," The Misfit said, "if it had been somebody there to shoot her every minute of her life."

"Some fun!" Bobby Lee said.

"Shut up, Bobby Lee," The Misfit said. "It's no real pleasure in life."

The River

THE CHILD stood glum and limp in the middle of the dark living room while his father pulled him into a plaid coat. His right arm was hung in the sleeve but the father buttoned the coat anyway and pushed him forward toward a pale spotted hand that stuck through the half-open door.

"He ain't fixed right," a loud voice said from the hall.

"Well then for Christ's sake fix him," the father muttered. "It's six o'clock in the morning." He was in his bathrobe and barefooted. When he got the child to the door and tried to shut it, he found her looming in it, a speckled skeleton in a long pea-green coat and felt helmet.

"And his and my carfare," she said. "It'll be twict we have to ride the car."

He went in the bedroom again to get the money and when he came back, she and the boy were both standing in the middle of the room. She was taking stock. "I couldn't smell those dead cigarette butts long if I was ever to come sit with you," she said, shaking him down in his coat.

"Here's the change," the father said. He went to the door and opened it wide and waited.

After she had counted the money she slipped it somewhere inside her coat and walked over to a watercolor hanging near the phonograph. "I know what time it is," she said, peering closely at the black lines crossing into broken planes of violent color. "I ought to. My shift goes on at 10 P.M. and don't get off till 5 and it takes me one hour to ride the Vine Street car."

"Oh, I see," he said; "well, we'll expect him back tonight, about eight or nine?"

"Maybe later," she said. "We're going to the river to a healing. This particular preacher don't get around this way often. I wouldn't have paid for that," she said, nodding at the painting, "I would have drew it myself."

"All right, Mrs. Connin, we'll see you then," he said, drumming on the door.

A toneless voice called from the bedroom, "Bring me an icepack."

"Too bad his mamma's sick," Mrs. Connin said. "What's her trouble?"

"We don't know," he muttered.

"We'll ask the preacher to pray for her. He's healed a lot of folks. The Reverend Bevel Summers. Maybe she ought to see him sometime."

"Maybe so," he said. "We'll see you tonight," and he disappeared into the bedroom and left them to go.

The little boy stared at her silently, his nose and eyes running. He was four or five. He had a long face and bulging chin and half-shut eyes set far apart. He seemed mute and patient, like an old sheep waiting to be let out.

"You'll like this preacher," she said. "The Reverend Bevel Summers. You ought to hear him sing."

The bedroom door opened suddenly and the father stuck his head out and said, "Good-by, old man. Have a good time."

"Good-by," the little boy said and jumped as if he had been shot.

Mrs. Connin gave the watercolor another look. Then they went out into the hall and rang for the elevator. "I wouldn't have drew it," she said.

Outside the gray morning was blocked off on either side by the unlit empty buildings. "It's going to fair up later," she said, "but this is the last time we'll be able to have any preaching at the river this year. Wipe your nose, Sugar Boy."

He began rubbing his sleeve across it but she stopped him. "That ain't nice," she said. "Where's your handkerchief?"

He put his hands in his pockets and pretended to look for it while she waited. "Some people don't care how they send one off," she murmured to her reflection in the coffee shop window. "You pervide." She took a red and blue flowered handkerchief out of her pocket and stooped down and began to work on his nose. "Now blow," she said and he blew. "You can borry it. Put it in your pocket."

He folded it up and put it in his pocket carefully and they walked on to the corner and leaned against the side of a closed drugstore to wait for the car. Mrs. Connin turned up her coat collar so that it met her hat in the back. Her eyelids began to droop and she looked as if she might go to sleep against the wall. The little boy put a slight pressure on her hand.

"What's your name?" she asked in a drowsy voice. "I don't know but only your last name. I should have found out your first name."

His name was Harry Ashfield and he had never thought at any time before of changing it. "Bevel," he said.

Mrs. Connin raised herself from the wall. "Why ain't that a coincident!" she said. "I told you that's the name of this preacher!"

"Bevel," he repeated.

She stood looking down at him as if he had become a marvel to her. "I'll have to see you meet him today," she said. "He's no ordinary preacher. He's a healer. He couldn't do nothing for Mr. Connin though. Mr. Connin didn't have the faith but he said he would try anything once. He had this griping in his gut."

The trolley appeared as a yellow spot at the end of the deserted street.

"He's gone to the government hospital now," she said, "and they taken one-third of his stomach. I tell him he better thank Jesus for what he's got left but he says he ain't thanking nobody. Well I declare," she murmured, "Bevel!"

They walked out to the tracks to wait. "Will he heal me?" Bevel asked.

"What you got?"

"I'm hungry," he decided finally.

"Didn't you have your breakfast?"

"I didn't have time to be hungry yet then," he said.

"Well when we get home we'll both have us something," she said. "I'm ready myself."

They got on the car and sat down a few seats behind the driver and Mrs. Connin took Bevel on her knees. "Now you be a good boy," she said, "and let me get some sleep. Just don't get off my lap." She lay her head back and as he watched, gradually her eyes closed and her mouth fell open to show a few long scattered teeth, some gold and some darker than her face; she began to whistle and blow like a musical skeleton. There was no one in the car but themselves and the driver and when he saw she was asleep, he took out the flowered handkerchief and unfolded it and examined it carefully. Then he folded it up again and unzipped a place in the innerlining of his coat and hid it in there and shortly he went to sleep himself.

Her house was a half-mile from the end of the car line, set back a little from the road. It was tan paper brick with a porch across the front of it and a tin top. On the porch there were three little boys of different sizes with identical speckled faces and one tall girl who had her hair up in so many aluminum curlers that it glared like the roof. The three boys followed them inside and closed in on Bevel. They looked at him silently, not smiling.

"That's Bevel," Mrs. Connin said, taking off her coat. "It's a coincident he's named the same as the preacher. These boys are J. C., Spivey, and Sinclair, and that's Sarah Mildred on the porch. Take off that coat and hang it on the bed post, Bevel."

The three boys watched him while he unbuttoned the coat and took it off. Then they watched him hang it on the bed post and then they stood, watching the coat. They turned abruptly and went out the door and had a conference on the porch.

Bevel stood looking around him at the room. It was part kitchen and part bedroom. The entire house was two rooms and two porches. Close to his foot the tail of a light-colored dog moved up and down between two floor boards as he scratched his back on the underside of the house. Bevel jumped on it but the hound was experienced and had already withdrawn when his feet hit the spot.

The walls were filled with pictures and calendars. There were two round photographs of an old man and woman with collapsed mouths and another picture of a man whose eyebrows dashed out of two bushes of hair and clashed in a heap on the bridge of his nose; the rest of his face stuck out like a bare cliff to fall from. "That's Mr. Connin," Mrs. Connin said, standing back from the stove for a second to admire the face with him, "but it don't favor him any more." Bevel turned from Mr. Connin to a colored picture over the bed of a man wearing a white sheet. He had long hair and a gold circle around his head and he was sawing on a board while some children stood watching him. He was going to ask who that was when the three boys came in again and motioned for him to follow them. He thought of crawling under the bed and hanging onto one of the legs but the three boys only stood there, speckled and silent, waiting, and after a second he followed them at a little distance out on the porch and around the corner of the house. They started off through a field of rough yellow weeds to the hog pen, a five-foot boarded square full of shoats, which they intended to ease him over into. When they reached it, they turned and waited silently, leaning against the side.

He was coming very slowly, deliberately bumping his feet together as if he had trouble walking. Once he had been beaten up in the park by some strange boys when his sitter forgot him, but he hadn't known anything was going to happen that time until it was over. He began to smell a strong odor of garbage and to hear the noises of a wild animal. He stopped a few feet from the pen and waited, pale but dogged.

The three boys didn't move. Something seemed to have happened to them. They stared over his head as if they saw something coming behind him but he was afraid to turn his own head and look. Their speckles were pale and their eyes were still and gray as glass. Only their ears twitched slightly. Nothing happened. Finally, the one in the middle said, "She'd kill us," and turned, dejected and hacked, and climbed up on the pen and hung over, staring in.

Bevel sat down on the ground, dazed with relief, and grinned up at them.

The one sitting on the pen glanced at him severely. "Hey you," he said after a second, "if you can't climb up and see these pigs you can lift that bottom board off and look in thataway." He appeared to offer this as a kindness.

Bevel had never seen a real pig but he had seen a pig in a book and knew they were small fat pink animals with curly tails and round grinning faces and bow ties. He leaned forward and pulled eagerly at the board.

"Pull harder," the littlest boy said. "It's nice and rotten. Just lift out thet nail."

He eased a long reddish nail out of the soft wood.

"Now you can lift up the board and put your face to the . . ." a quiet voice began.

He had already done it and another face, gray, wet and sour, was pushing into his, knocking him down and back as it scraped out under the plank. Something snorted over him and charged back again, rolling him over and pushing him up from behind and then sending him forward, screaming through the yellow field, while it bounded behind.

The three Connins watched from where they were. The one sitting on the pen held the loose board back with his dangling foot. Their stern faces didn't brighten any but they seemed to become less taut, as if some great need had been partly satisfied. "Maw ain't going to like him lettin out thet hawg," the smallest one said.

Mrs. Connin was on the back porch and caught Bevel up as he reached the steps. The hog ran under the house and subsided, panting, but the child screamed for five minutes. When she had finally calmed him down, she gave him his breakfast and let him sit on her lap while he ate it. The shoat climbed the two steps onto the back porch and stood outside the screen door, looking in with his head lowered sullenly. He was long-legged and hump-backed and part of one of his ears had been bitten off.

"Git away!" Mrs. Connin shouted. "That one yonder favors Mr. Paradise that has the gas station," she said. "You'll see him today at the healing. He's got the cancer over his ear. He always comes to show he ain't been healed."

The shoat stood squinting a few seconds longer and then moved off slowly. "I don't want to see him," Bevel said.

They walked to the river, Mrs. Connin in front with him and the three boys strung out behind and Sarah Mildred, the tall girl, at the end to holler if one of them ran out on the road. They looked like the skeleton of an old boat with two pointed ends, sailing slowly on the edge of the highway. The white Sunday sun followed at a little distance, climbing fast through a scum of gray cloud as if it meant to overtake them. Bevel walked on the outside edge, holding Mrs. Connin's hand and looking down into the orange and purple gulley that dropped off from the concrete.

It occurred to him that he was lucky this time that they had found Mrs. Connin who would take you away for the day instead of an ordinary sitter who only sat where you lived or went to the park. You found out more when you left where you lived. He had found out already this morning that he had been made by a carpenter named Jesus Christ. Before he had thought it had been a doctor named Slade-wall, a fat man with a yellow mustache who gave him shots and thought his name was Herbert, but this must have been a joke. They joked a lot where he lived. If he had thought about it before, he would have thought Jesus Christ was a word like "oh" or "damm" or "God," or maybe somebody who had cheated them out of something sometime. When he had asked Mrs. Connin who the man in the sheet in the picture over her bed was, she had looked at him a while with her mouth open. Then she had said, "That's Jesus," and she had kept on looking at him.

In a few minutes she had got up and got a book out of the other room. "See here," she said, turning over the cover, "this belonged to my great grandmamma. I wouldn't part with it for nothing on earth." She ran her finger under some brown writing on a spotted page. "Emma Stevens Oakley, 1832," she said. "Ain't that something to have? And every word of it the gospel truth." She turned the next page and read him the name: "The Life of Jesus Christ for Readers Under Twelve." Then she read him the book.

It was a small book, pale brown on the outside with gold edges and a smell like old putty. It was full of pictures, one of the carpenter driving a crowd of pigs out of a man. They were real pigs, gray and sour-looking, and Mrs. Connin said Jesus had driven them all out of this one man. When she finished reading, she let him sit on the floor and look at the pictures again.

Just before they left for the healing, he had managed to get the book inside his innerlining without her seeing him. Now it made his coat hang down a little farther on one side than the other. His mind was dreamy and serene as they walked along and when they turned off the highway onto a long red clay road winding between banks of honeysuckle, he began to make wild leaps and pull forward on her hand as if he wanted to dash off and snatch the sun which was rolling away ahead of them now.

They walked on the dirt road for a while and then they crossed a field stippled with purple weeds and entered the shadows of a wood where the ground was covered with thick pine needles. He had never been in woods before and he walked carefully, looking from side to side as if he were entering a strange country. They moved along a bridle path that twisted downhill through crackling red leaves, and once, catching at a branch to keep himself from slipping, he looked into two frozen green-gold eyes enclosed in the darkness of a tree hole. At the bottom of the hill, the woods opened suddenly onto a pasture dotted here and there with black and white cows and sloping down, tier after tier, to a broad orange stream where the reflection of the sun was set like a diamond.

There were people standing on the near bank in a group, singing. Long tables were set up behind them and a few cars and trucks were parked in a road that came up by the river. They crossed the pasture, hurrying, because Mrs. Connin, using her hand for a shed over her eyes, saw the preacher already standing out in the water. She dropped her basket on one of the tables and pushed the three boys in front of her into the knot of people so that they wouldn't linger by the food. She kept Bevel by the hand and eased her way up to the front.

The preacher was standing about ten feet out in the stream where the water came up to his knees. He was a tall youth in khaki trousers that he had rolled up higher than the water. He had on a blue shirt and a red scarf around his neck but no hat and his light-colored hair was cut in sideburns that curved into the hollows of his cheeks. His face was all bone and red light reflected from the river. He looked as if he might have been nineteen years old. He was singing in a high twangy voice, above the singing on the bank, and he kept his hands behind him and his head tilted back.

He ended the hymn on a high note and stood silent, looking down at the water and shifting his feet in it. Then he looked up at the people on the bank. They stood close together, waiting; their faces were solemn but expectant and every eye was on him. He shifted his feet again.

"Maybe I know why you come," he said in the twangy voice, "maybe I don't.

"If you ain't come for Jesus, you ain't come for me. If you just come to see can you leave your pain in the river, you ain't come for Jesus. You can't leave your pain in the river," he said. "I never told nobody that." He stopped and looked down at his knees.

"I seen you cure a woman oncet!" a sudden high voice shouted from the hump of people. "Seen that woman git up and walk out straight where she had limped in!"

The preacher lifted one foot and then the other. He seemed almost but not quite to smile. "You might as well go home if that's what you come for," he said.

Then he lifted his head and arms and shouted, "Listen to what I got to say, you people! There ain't but one river and that's the River of Life, made out of Jesus' Blood. That's the river you have to lay your pain in, in the River of Faith, in the River of Life, in the River of Love, in the rich red river of Jesus' Blood, you people!"

His voice grew soft and musical. "All the rivers come from that one River and go back to it like it was the ocean sea and if you believe, you can lay your pain in that River and get rid of it because that's the River that was made to carry sin. It's a River full of pain itself, pain itself, moving toward the Kingdom of Christ, to be washed away, slow, you people, slow as this here old red water river round my feet.

"Listen," he sang, "I read in Mark about an unclean man, I read in Luke about a blind man, I read in John about a dead man! Oh you people hear! The same blood that makes this River red, made that leper clean, made that blind man stare, made that dead man leap! You people with trouble," he cried, "lay it in that River of Blood, lay it in that River of Pain, and watch it move away toward the Kingdom of Christ."

While he preached, Bevel's eyes followed drowsily the slow circles of two silent birds revolving high in the air. Across the river there was a low red and gold grove of sassafras with hills of dark blue trees behind it and an occasional pine jutting over the skyline. Behind, in the distance, the city rose like a cluster of warts on the side of the mountain. The birds revolved downward and dropped lightly in the top of the highest pine and sat hunch-shouldered as if they were supporting the sky.

"If it's this River of Life you want to lay your pain in, then come up," the preacher said, "and lay your sorrow here. But don't be thinking this is the last of it because this old red river don't end here. This old red suffering stream goes on, you people, slow to the Kingdom of Christ. This old red river is good to Baptize in, good to lay your faith in, good to lay your pain in, but it ain't this muddy water here that saves you. I been all up and down this river this week," he said. "Tuesday I was in Fortune Lake, next day in Ideal, Friday me and my wife drove to Lulawillow to see a sick man there. Them people didn't see no healing," he said and his face burned redder for a second. "I never said they would."

While he was talking a fluttering figure had begun to move forward with a kind of butterfly movement—an old woman with flapping arms whose head wobbled as if it might fall off any second. She managed to lower herself at the edge of the bank and let her arms churn in the water. Then she bent farther and pushed her face down in it and raised herself up finally, streaming wet; and still flapping, she turned a time or two in a blind circle until someone reached out and pulled her back into the group.

"She's been that way for thirteen years," a rough voice shouted. "Pass the hat and give this kid his money. That's what he's here for." The shout, directed out to the boy in the river, came from a huge old man who sat like a humped stone on the bumper of a long ancient gray automobile. He had on a gray hat that was turned down over one ear and up over the other to expose a purple bulge on his left temple. He sat bent forward with his hands hanging between his knees and his small eyes half closed.

Bevel stared at him once and then moved into the folds of Mrs. Connin's coat and hid himself.

The boy in the river glanced at the old man quickly and raised his fist. "Believe Jesus or the devil!" he cried. "Testify to one or the other!"

"I know from my own self-experience," a woman's mysterious voice called from the knot of people, "I know from it that this preacher can heal. My eyes have been opened! I testify to Jesus!"

The preacher lifted his arms quickly and began to repeat all that he had said before about the River and the Kingdom of Christ and the old man sat on the bumper, fixing him with a narrow squint. From time to time Bevel stared at him again from around Mrs. Connin.

A man in overalls and a brown coat leaned forward and dipped his hand in the water quickly and shook it and leaned back, and a woman held a baby over the edge of the bank and splashed its feet with water. One man moved a little distance away and sat down on the bank and took off his shoes and waded out into the stream; he stood there for a few minutes with his face tilted as far back as it would go, then he waded back and put on his shoes. All this time, the preacher sang and did not appear to watch what went on.

As soon as he stopped singing, Mrs. Connin lifted Bevel up and said, "Listen here, preacher, I got a boy from town today that I'm keeping. His mamma's sick and he wants you to pray for her. And this is a coincident—his name is Bevel! Bevel," she said, turning to look at the people behind her, "same as his. Ain't that a coincident, though?"

There were some murmurs and Bevel turned and grinned over her shoulder at the faces looking at him. "Bevel," he said in a loud jaunty voice.

"Listen," Mrs. Connin said, "have you ever been Baptized, Bevel?"

He only grinned.

"I suspect he ain't ever been Baptized," Mrs. Connin said, raising her eyebrows at the preacher.

"Swang him over here," the preacher said and took a stride forward and caught him.

He held him in the crook of his arm and looked at the grinning face. Bevel rolled his eyes in a comical way and thrust his face forward, close to the preacher's. "My name is Bevvvuuuuul," he said in a loud deep voice and let the tip of his tongue slide across his mouth.

The preacher didn't smile. His bony face was rigid and his narrow gray eyes reflected the almost colorless sky. There was a loud laugh from the old man sitting on the car bumper and

Bevel grasped the back of the preacher's collar and held it tightly. The grin had already disappeared from his face. He had the sudden feeling that this was not a joke. Where he lived everything was a joke. From the preacher's face, he knew immediately that nothing the preacher said or did was a joke. "My mother named me that," he said quickly.

"Have you ever been Baptized?" the preacher asked.

"What's that?" he murmured.

"If I Baptize you," the preacher said, "you'll be able to go to the Kingdom of Christ. You'll be washed in the river of suffering, son, and you'll go by the deep river of life. Do you want that?"

"Yes," the child said, and thought, I won't go back to the apartment then, I'll go under the river.

"You won't be the same again," the preacher said. "You'll count." Then he turned his face to the people and began to preach and Bevel looked over his shoulder at the pieces of the white sun scattered in the river. Suddenly the preacher said, "All right, I'm going to Baptize you now," and without more warning, he tightened his hold and swung him upside down and plunged his head into the water. He held him under while he said the words of Baptism and then he jerked him up again and looked sternly at the gasping child. Bevel's eyes were dark and dilated. "You count now," the preacher said. "You didn't even count before."

The little boy was too shocked to cry. He spit out the muddy water and rubbed his wet sleeve into his eyes and over his face.

"Don't forget his mamma," Mrs. Connin called. "He wants you to pray for his mamma. She's sick."

"Lord," the preacher said, "we pray for somebody in affliction who isn't here to testify. Is your mother sick in the hospital?" he asked. "Is she in pain?"

The child stared at him. "She hasn't got up yet," he said in a high dazed voice. "She has a hangover." The air was so quiet he could hear the broken pieces of the sun knocking in the water.

The preacher looked angry and startled. The red drained out of his face and the sky appeared to darken in his eyes. There was a loud guffaw from the bank and Mr. Paradise shouted, "Haw! Cure the afflicted woman with the hang-over!" and began to beat his knee with his fist.

"He's had a long day," Mrs. Connin said, standing with him in the door of the apartment and looking sharply into the room where the party was going on. "I reckon it's past his regular bedtime." One of Bevel's eyes was closed and the other half closed; his nose was running and he kept his mouth open and breathed through it. The damp plaid coat dragged down on one side.

That would be her, Mrs. Connin decided, in the black britches—long black satin britches and barefoot sandals and red toenails. She was lying on half the sofa, with her knees crossed in the air and her head propped on the arm. She didn't get up.

"Hello Harry," she said. "Did you have a big day?" She had a long pale face, smooth and blank, and straight sweet-potato-colored hair, pulled back.

The father went off to get the money. There were two other couples. One of the men, blond with little violet-blue eyes, leaned out of his chair and said, "Well Harry, old man, have a big day?"

"His name ain't Harry. It's Bevel," Mrs. Connin said.

"His name is Harry," *she* said from the sofa. "Whoever heard of anybody named Bevel?"

The little boy had seemed to be going to sleep on his feet, his head drooping farther and farther forward; he pulled it back suddenly and opened one eye; the other was stuck.

"He told me this morning his name was Bevel," Mrs. Connin said in a shocked voice. "The same as our preacher. We been all day at a preaching and healing at the river. He said his name was Bevel, the same as the preacher's. That's what he told me."

"Bevel!" his mother said. "My God! what a name."

"This preacher is name Bevel and there's no better preacher around," Mrs. Connin said. "And furthermore," she added in a defiant tone, "he Baptized this child this morning!"

His mother sat straight up. "Well the nerve!" she muttered.

"Furthermore," Mrs. Connin said, "he's a healer and he prayed for you to be healed."

"Healed!" she almost shouted. "Healed of what for Christ's sake?"

"Of your affliction," Mrs. Connin said icily.

The father had returned with the money and was standing near Mrs. Connin waiting to give it to her. His eyes were lined with red threads. "Go on, go on," he said, "I want to hear more about her affliction. The exact nature of it has escaped . . ." He waved the bill and his voice trailed off. "Healing by prayer is mighty inexpensive," he murmured.

Mrs. Connin stood a second, staring into the room, with a skeleton's appearance of seeing everything. Then, without taking the money, she turned and shut the door behind her. The father swung around, smiling vaguely, and shrugged. The rest of them were looking at Harry. The little boy began to shamble toward the bedroom.

"Come here, Harry," his mother said. He automatically shifted his direction toward her without opening his eye any farther. "Tell me what happened today," she said when he reached her. She began to pull off his coat.

"I don't know," he muttered.

"Yes you do know," she said, feeling the coat heavier on one side. She unzipped the innerlining and caught the book and a dirty handkerchief as they fell out. "Where did you get these?"

"I don't know," he said and grabbed for them. "They're mine. She gave them to me."

She threw the handkerchief down and held the book too high for him to reach and began to read it, her face after a second assuming an exaggerated comical expression. The others moved around and looked at it over her shoulder. "My God," somebody said.

One of the men peered at it sharply from behind a thick pair of glasses. "That's valuable," he said. "That's a collector's item," and he took it away from the rest of them and retired to another chair.

"Don't let George go off with that," his girl said.

"I tell you it's valuable," George said. "1832."

Bevel shifted his direction again toward the room where he slept. He shut the door behind him and moved slowly in the darkness to the bed and sat down and took off his shoes and got under the cover. After a minute a shaft of light let in the tall silhouette of his mother. She tiptoed lightly across the room and sat down on the edge of his bed. "What did that dolt of a preacher say about me?" she whispered. "What lies have you been telling today, honey?"

He shut his eye and heard her voice from a long way away, as if he were under the river and she on top of it. She shook his shoulder. "Harry," she said, leaning down and putting her mouth to his ear, "tell me what he said." She pulled him into a sitting position and he felt as if he had been drawn up from under the river. "Tell me," she whispered and her bitter breath covered his face.

He saw the pale oval close to him in the dark. "He said I'm not the same now," he muttered. "I count."

After a second, she lowered him by his shirt front onto the pillow. She hung over him an instant and brushed her lips against his forehead. Then she got up and moved away, swaying her hips lightly through the shaft of light.

He didn't wake up early but the apartment was still dark and close when he did. For a while he lay there, picking his nose and eyes. Then he sat up in bed and looked out the window. The sun came in palely, stained gray by the glass. Across the street at the Empire Hotel, a colored cleaning woman was looking down from an upper window, resting her face on her folded arms. He got up and put on his shoes and went to the bathroom and then into the front room. He ate two crackers spread with anchovy paste, that he found on the coffee table, and drank some ginger ale left in a bottle and looked around for his book but it was not there.

The apartment was silent except for the faint humming of the refrigerator. He went into the kitchen and found some raisin bread heels and spread a half jar of peanut butter between them and climbed up on the tall kitchen stool and sat chewing the sandwich slowly, wiping his nose every now and then on his shoulder. When he finished he found some chocolate milk and drank that. He would rather have had the ginger ale he saw but they left the bottle openers where he couldn't reach them. He studied what was left in the refrigerator for a while—some shriveled vegetables that she had forgot were there and a lot of brown oranges that she bought and didn't squeeze; there were three or four kinds of cheese and something fishy in a paper bag; the rest was a pork bone. He left the refrigerator door open and wandered back into the dark living room and sat down on the sofa.

He decided they would be out cold until one o'clock and that they would all have to go to a restaurant for lunch. He wasn't high enough for the table yet and the waiter would bring a highchair and he was too big for a highchair. He sat in the middle of the sofa, kicking it with his heels. Then he got up and wandered around the room, looking into the ash-trays at the butts as if this might be a habit. In his own room he had picture books and blocks but they were for the most part torn up; he found the way to get new ones was to tear up the ones he had. There was very little to do at any time but eat; however, he was not a fat boy.

He decided he would empty a few of the ashtrays on the floor. If he only emptied a few, she would think they had fallen. He emptied two, rubbing the ashes carefully into the rug with his finger. Then he lay on the floor for a while, studying his feet which he held up in the air. His shoes were still damp and he began to think about the river.

Very slowly, his expression changed as if he were gradually seeing appear what he didn't know he'd been looking for. Then all of a sudden he knew what he wanted to do.

He got up and tiptoed into their bedroom and stood in the dim light there, looking for her pocketbook. His glance passed her long pale arm hanging off the edge of the bed down to the floor, and across the white mound his father made, and past the crowded bureau, until it rested on the pocketbook hung on the back of a chair. He took a car-token out of it and half a package of Life Savers. Then he left the apartment and caught the car at the corner. He hadn't taken a suitcase because there was nothing from there he wanted to keep.

He got off the car at the end of the line and started down the road he and Mrs. Connin had taken the day before. He knew there wouldn't be anybody at her house because the three boys and the girl went to school and Mrs. Connin had told him she went out to clean. He passed her yard and walked on the way they had gone to the river. The paper brick houses were far apart and after a while the dirt place to walk on ended and he had to walk on the edge of the highway. The sun was pale yellow and high and hot.

He passed a shack with an orange gas pump in front of it but he didn't see the old man looking out at nothing in particular from the doorway. Mr. Paradise was having an orange drink. He finished it slowly, squinting over the bottle at the small plaid-coated figure disappearing down the road. Then he set the empty bottle on a bench and, still squinting, wiped his sleeve over his mouth. He went in the shack and picked out a peppermint stick, a foot long and two inches thick, from the candy shelf, and stuck it in his hip pocket. Then he got in his car and drove slowly down the highway after the boy.

By the time Bevel came to the field speckled with purple weeds, he was dusty and sweating and he crossed it at a trot to get into the woods as fast as he could. Once inside, he wandered from tree to tree, trying to find the path they had taken yesterday. Finally he found a line worn in the pine needles and followed it until he saw the steep trail twisting down through the trees.

Mr. Paradise had left his automobile back some way on the road and had walked to the place where he was accustomed to sit almost every day, holding an unbaited fishline in the water while he stared at the river passing in front of him. Anyone looking at him from a distance would have seen an old boulder half hidden in the bushes.

Bevel didn't see him at all. He only saw the river, shimmering reddish yellow, and bounded into it with his shoes and his coat on and took a gulp. He swallowed some and spit the rest out and then he stood there in water up to his chest and looked around him. The sky was a clear pale blue, all in one piece—except for the hole the sun made—and fringed around the bottom with treetops. His coat floated to the surface and surrounded him like a strange gay lily pad and he stood grinning in the sun. He intended not to fool with preachers any more but to Baptize himself and to keep on going this time until he found the Kingdom of Christ in the river. He didn't mean to waste any more time. He put his head under the water at once and pushed forward.

In a second he began to gasp and sputter and his head reappeared on the surface; he started under again and the same thing happened. The river wouldn't have him. He tried again and came up, choking. This was the way it had been when the preacher held him under—he had had to fight with something that pushed him back in the face. He stopped and thought suddenly: it's another joke, it's just another joke! He thought how far he had come for nothing and he began to hit and splash and kick the filthy river. His feet were already treading on nothing. He gave one low cry of pain and indignation. Then he heard a shout and turned his head and saw something like a giant pig bounding after him, shaking a red and white club and shouting. He plunged under once and this time, the waiting current caught him like a long gentle hand and pulled him swiftly forward and down. For an instant he was overcome with surprise; then since he was moving quickly and knew that he was getting somewhere, all his fury and his fear left him.

Mr. Paradise's head appeared from time to time on the surface of the water. Finally, far downstream, the old man rose like some ancient water monster and stood empty-handed, staring with his dull eyes as far down the river line as he could see.

The Life You Save May Be Your Own

THE OLD WOMAN and her daughter were sitting on their porch when Mr. Shiftlet came up their road for the first time. The old woman slid to the edge of her chair and leaned forward, shading her eyes from the piercing sunset with her hand. The daughter could not see far in front of her and continued to play with her fingers. Although the old woman lived in this desolate spot with only her daughter and she had never seen Mr. Shiftlet before, she could tell, even from a distance, that he was a tramp and no one to be afraid of. His left coat sleeve was folded up to show there was only half an arm in it and his gaunt figure listed slightly to the side as if the breeze were pushing him. He had on a black town suit and a brown felt hat that was turned up in the front and down in the back and he carried a tin tool box by a handle. He came on, at an amble, up her road, his face turned toward the sun which appeared to be balancing itself on the peak of a small mountain.

The old woman didn't change her position until he was almost into her yard; then she rose with one hand fisted on her hip. The daughter, a large girl in a short blue organdy dress, saw him all at once and jumped up and began to stamp and point and make excited speechless sounds.

Mr. Shiftlet stopped just inside the yard and set his box on the ground and tipped his hat at her as if she were not in the least afflicted; then he turned toward the old woman and swung the hat all the way off. He had long black slick hair that hung flat from a part in the middle to beyond the tips of his ears on either side. His face descended in forehead for more than half its length and ended suddenly with his features just balanced over a jutting steel-trap jaw. He seemed to be a young man but he had a look of composed dissatisfaction as if he understood life thoroughly.

"Good evening," the old woman said. She was about the size of a cedar fence post and she had a man's gray hat pulled down low over her head.

The tramp stood looking at her and didn't answer. He turned his back and faced the sunset. He swung both his whole and his short arm up slowly so that they indicated an expanse of sky and his figure formed a crooked cross. The old woman watched him with her arms folded across her chest as if she were the owner of the sun, and the daughter watched, her head thrust forward and her fat helpless hands hanging at the wrists. She had long pink-gold hair and eyes as blue as a peacock's neck.

He held the pose for almost fifty seconds and then he picked up his box and came on to the porch and dropped down on the bottom step. "Lady," he said in a firm nasal voice, "I'd give a fortune to live where I could see me a sun do that every evening."

"Does it every evening," the old woman said and sat back down. The daughter sat down too and watched him with a cautious sly look as if he were a bird that had come up very close. He leaned to one side, rooting in his pants pocket, and in a second he brought out a package of chewing gum and offered her a piece. She took it and unpeeled it and began to chew without taking her eyes off him. He offered the old woman a piece but she only raised her upper lip to indicate she had no teeth.

Mr. Shiftlet's pale sharp glance had already passed over everything in the yard—the pump near the corner of the house and the big fig tree that three or four chickens were preparing to roost in—and had moved to a shed where he saw the square rusted back of an automobile. "You ladies drive?" he asked.

"That car ain't run in fifteen year," the old woman said. "The day my husband died, it quit running."

"Nothing is like it used to be, lady," he said. "The world is almost rotten."

"That's right," the old woman said. "You from around here?"

"Name Tom T. Shiftlet," he murmured, looking at the tires.

"I'm pleased to meet you," the old woman said. "Name Lucynell Crater and daughter Lucynell Crater. What you doing around here, Mr. Shiftlet?"

He judged the car to be about a 1928 or '29 Ford. "Lady," he said, and turned and gave her his full attention, "lemme tell you something. There's one of these doctors in Atlanta that's taken a knife and cut the human heart—the human heart," he repeated, leaning forward, "out of a man's chest and held it in his hand," and he held his hand out, palm up, as if it were slightly weighted with the human heart, "and studied it like it was a day-old chicken, and lady," he said, allowing a long significant pause in which his head slid forward and his clay-colored eyes brightened, "he don't know no more about it than you or me."

"That's right," the old woman said.

"Why, if he was to take that knife and cut into every corner of it, he still wouldn't know no more than you or me. What you want to bet?"

"Nothing," the old woman said wisely. "Where you come from, Mr. Shiftlet?"

He didn't answer. He reached into his pocket and brought out a sack of tobacco and a package of cigarette papers and rolled himself a cigarette, expertly with one hand, and attached it in a hanging position to his upper lip. Then he took a box of wooden matches from his pocket and struck one on his shoe. He held the burning match as if he were studying the mystery of flame while it traveled dangerously toward his skin. The daughter began to make loud noises and to point to his hand and shake her finger at him, but when the flame was just before touching him, he leaned down with his hand cupped over it as if he were going to set fire to his nose and lit the cigarette.

He flipped away the dead match and blew a stream of gray into the evening. A sly look came over his face. "Lady," he said, "nowadays, people'll do anything anyways. I can tell you my name is Tom T. Shiftlet and I come from Tarwater, Tennessee, but you never have seen me before: how you know I ain't lying? How you know my name ain't Aaron Sparks, lady, and I come from Singleberry, Georgia, or how you know it's not George Speeds and I come from Lucy, Alabama, or how you know I ain't Thompson Bright from Toolafalls, Mississippi?"

"I don't know nothing about you," the old woman muttered, irked.

"Lady," he said, "people don't care how they lie. Maybe

the best I can tell you is, I'm a man; but listen lady," he said and paused and made his tone more ominous still, "what is a man?"

The old woman began to gum a seed. "What you carry in that tin box, Mr. Shiftlet?" she asked.

"Tools," he said, put back. "I'm a carpenter."

"Well, if you come out here to work, I'll be able to feed you and give you a place to sleep but I can't pay. I'll tell you that before you begin," she said.

There was no answer at once and no particular expression on his face. He leaned back against the two-by-four that helped support the porch roof. "Lady," he said slowly, "there's some men that some things mean more to them than money." The old woman rocked without comment and the daughter watched the trigger that moved up and down in his neck. He told the old woman then that all most people were interested in was money, but he asked what a man was made for. He asked her if a man was made for money, or what. He asked her what she thought she was made for but she didn't answer, she only sat rocking and wondered if a one-armed man could put a new roof on her garden house. He asked a lot of questions that she didn't answer. He told her that he was twenty-eight years old and had lived a varied life. He had been a gospel singer, a foreman on the railroad, an assistant in an undertaking parlor, and he had come over the radio for three months with Uncle Roy and his Red Creek Wranglers. He said he had fought and bled in the Arm Service of his country and visited every foreign land and that everywhere he had seen people that didn't care if they did a thing one way or another. He said he hadn't been raised thataway.

A fat yellow moon appeared in the branches of the fig tree as if it were going to roost there with the chickens. He said that a man had to escape to the country to see the world whole and that he wished he lived in a desolate place like this where he could see the sun go down every evening like God made it to do.

"Are you married or are you single?" the old woman asked.

There was a long silence. "Lady," he asked finally, "where would you find you an innocent woman today? I wouldn't have any of this trash I could just pick up."

The daughter was leaning very far down, hanging her head almost between her knees, watching him through a triangular door she had made in her overturned hair; and she suddenly fell in a heap on the floor and began to whimper. Mr. Shiftlet straightened her out and helped her get back in the chair.

"Is she your baby girl?" he asked.

"My only," the old woman said, "and she's the sweetest girl in the world. I wouldn't give her up for nothing on earth. She's smart too. She can sweep the floor, cook, wash, feed the chickens, and hoe. I wouldn't give her up for a casket of jewels."

"No," he said kindly, "don't ever let any man take her away from you."

"Any man come after her," the old woman said, " 'll have to stay around the place."

Mr. Shiftlet's eye in the darkness was focused on a part of the automobile bumper that glittered in the distance. "Lady," he said, jerking his short arm up as if he could point with it to her house and yard and pump, "there ain't a broken thing on this plantation that I couldn't fix for you, one-arm jackleg or not. I'm a man," he said with a sullen dignity, "even if I ain't a whole one. I got," he said, tapping his knuckles on the floor to emphasize the immensity of what he was going to say, "a moral intelligence!" and his face pierced out of the darkness into a shaft of doorlight and he stared at her as if he were astonished himself at this impossible truth.

The old woman was not impressed with the phrase. "I told you you could hang around and work for food," she said, "if you don't mind sleeping in that car yonder."

"Why listen, Lady," he said with a grin of delight, "the monks of old slept in their coffins!"

"They wasn't as advanced as we are," the old woman said.

The next morning he began on the roof of the garden house while Lucynell, the daughter, sat on a rock and watched him work. He had not been around a week before the change he had made in the place was apparent. He had patched the front and back steps, built a new hog pen, restored a fence, and taught Lucynell, who was completely deaf and had never said a word in her life, to say the word "bird."

The big rosy-faced girl followed him everywhere, saying "Burrttddt ddbirrrttdt," and clapping her hands. The old woman watched from a distance, secretly pleased. She was ravenous for a son-in-law.

Mr. Shiftlet slept on the hard narrow back seat of the car with his feet out the side window. He had his razor and a can of water on a crate that served him as a bedside table and he put up a piece of mirror against the back glass and kept his coat neatly on a hanger that he hung over one of the windows.

In the evenings he sat on the steps and talked while the old woman and Lucynell rocked violently in their chairs on either side of him. The old woman's three mountains were black against the dark blue sky and were visited off and on by various planets and by the moon after it had left the chickens. Mr. Shiftlet pointed out that the reason he had improved this plantation was because he had taken a personal interest in it. He said he was even going to make the automobile run.

He had raised the hood and studied the mechanism and he said he could tell that the car had been built in the days when cars were really built. You take now, he said, one man puts in one bolt and another man puts in another bolt and another man puts in another bolt so that it's a man for a bolt. That's why you have to pay so much for a car: you're paying all those men. Now if you didn't have to pay but one man, you could get you a cheaper car and one that had had a personal interest taken in it, and it would be a better car. The old woman agreed with him that this was so.

Mr. Shiftlet said that the trouble with the world was that nobody cared, or stopped and took any trouble. He said he never would have been able to teach Lucynell to say a word if he hadn't cared and stopped long enough.

"Teach her to say something else," the old woman said.

"What you want her to say next?" Mr. Shiftlet asked.

The old woman's smile was broad and toothless and suggestive. "Teach her to say 'sugarpie,' " she said.

Mr. Shiftlet already knew what was on her mind.

The next day he began to tinker with the automobile and that evening he told her that if she would buy a fan belt, he would be able to make the car run.

The old woman said she would give him the money. "You see that girl yonder?" she asked, pointing to Lucynell who was sitting on the floor a foot away, watching him, her eyes blue even in the dark. "If it was ever a man wanted to take her away, I would say, 'No man on earth is going to take that sweet girl of mine away from me!' but if he was to say, 'Lady, I don't want to take her away, I want her right here,' I would say, 'Mister, I don't blame you none. I wouldn't pass up a chance to live in a permanent place and get the sweetest girl in the world myself. You ain't no fool,' I would say."

"How old is she?" Mr. Shiftlet asked casually.

"Fifteen, sixteen," the old woman said. The girl was nearly thirty but because of her innocence it was impossible to guess.

"It would be a good idea to paint it too," Mr. Shiftlet remarked. "You don't want it to rust out."

"We'll see about that later," the old woman said.

The next day he walked into town and returned with the parts he needed and a can of gasoline. Late in the afternoon, terrible noises issued from the shed and the old woman rushed out of the house, thinking Lucynell was somewhere having a fit. Lucynell was sitting on a chicken crate, stamping her feet and screaming, "Burrddttt! bddurrddtttt!" but her fuss was drowned out by the car. With a volley of blasts it emerged from the shed, moving in a fierce and stately way. Mr. Shiftlet was in the driver's seat, sitting very erect. He had an expression of serious modesty on his face as if he had just raised the dead.

That night, rocking on the porch, the old woman began her business at once. "You want you an innocent woman, don't you?" she asked sympathetically. "You don't want none of this trash."

"No'm, I don't," Mr. Shiftlet said.

"One that can't talk," she continued, "can't sass you back or use foul language. That's the kind for you to have. Right there," and she pointed to Lucynell sitting cross-legged in her chair, holding both feet in her hands.

"That's right," he admitted. "She wouldn't give me any trouble."

"Saturday," the old woman said, "you and her and me can drive into town and get married."

Mr. Shiftlet eased his position on the steps.

"I can't get married right now," he said. "Everything you want to do takes money and I ain't got any."

"What you need with money?" she asked.

"It takes money," he said. "Some people'll do anything anyhow these days, but the way I think, I wouldn't marry no woman that I couldn't take on a trip like she was somebody. I mean take her to a hotel and treat her. I wouldn't marry the Duchesser Windsor," he said firmly, "unless I could take her to a hotel and give her something good to eat.

"I was raised thataway and there ain't a thing I can do about it. My old mother taught me how to do."

"Lucynell don't even know what a hotel is," the old woman muttered. "Listen here, Mr. Shiftlet," she said, sliding forward in her chair, "you'd be getting a permanent house and a deep well and the most innocent girl in the world. You don't need no money. Lemme tell you something: there ain't any place in the world for a poor disabled friendless drifting man."

The ugly words settled in Mr. Shiftlet's head like a group of buzzards in the top of a tree. He didn't answer at once. He rolled himself a cigarette and lit it and then he said in an even voice, "Lady, a man is divided into two parts, body and spirit."

The old woman clamped her gums together.

"A body and a spirit," he repeated. "The body, lady, is like a house: it don't go anywhere; but the spirit, lady, is like a automobile: always on the move, always . . ."

"Listen, Mr. Shiftlet," she said, "my well never goes dry and my house is always warm in the winter and there's no mortgage on a thing about this place. You can go to the courthouse and see for yourself. And yonder under that shed is a fine automobile." She laid the bait carefully. "You can have it painted by Saturday. I'll pay for the paint."

In the darkness, Mr. Shiftlet's smile stretched like a weary snake waking up by a fire. After a second he recalled himself and said, "I'm only saying a man's spirit means more to him than anything else. I would have to take my wife off for the

week end without no regards at all for cost. I got to follow
where my spirit says to go."

"I'll give you fifteen dollars for a week-end trip," the old
woman said in a crabbed voice. "That's the best I can do."

"That wouldn't hardly pay for more than the gas and the
hotel," he said. "It wouldn't feed her."

"Seventeen-fifty," the old woman said. "That's all I got so
it isn't any use you trying to milk me. You can take a lunch."

Mr. Shiftlet was deeply hurt by the word "milk." He didn't
doubt that she had more money sewed up in her mattress but
he had already told her he was not interested in her money.
"I'll make that do," he said and rose and walked off without
treating with her further.

On Saturday the three of them drove into town in the car
that the paint had barely dried on and Mr. Shiftlet and Lucynell were married in the Ordinary's office while the old
woman witnessed. As they came out of the courthouse, Mr.
Shiftlet began twisting his neck in his collar. He looked morose and bitter as if he had been insulted while someone held
him. "That didn't satisfy me none," he said. "That was just
something a woman in an office did, nothing but paper work
and blood tests. What do they know about my blood? If they
was to take my heart and cut it out," he said, "they wouldn't
know a thing about me. It didn't satisfy me at all."

"It satisfied the law," the old woman said sharply.

"The law," Mr. Shiftlet said and spit. "It's the law that
don't satisfy me."

He had painted the car dark green with a yellow band
around it just under the windows. The three of them climbed
in the front seat and the old woman said, "Don't Lucynell
look pretty? Looks like a baby doll." Lucynell was dressed up
in a white dress that her mother had uprooted from a trunk
and there was a Panama hat on her head with a bunch of red
wooden cherries on the brim. Every now and then her placid
expression was changed by a sly isolated little thought like a
shoot of green in the desert. "You got a prize!" the old
woman said.

Mr. Shiftlet didn't even look at her.

They drove back to the house to let the old woman off and
pick up the lunch. When they were ready to leave, she stood

staring in the window of the car, with her fingers clenched around the glass. Tears began to seep sideways out of her eyes and run along the dirty creases in her face. "I ain't ever been parted with her for two days before," she said.

Mr. Shiftlet started the motor.

"And I wouldn't let no man have her but you because I seen you would do right. Good-by, Sugarbaby," she said, clutching at the sleeve of the white dress. Lucynell looked straight at her and didn't seem to see her there at all. Mr. Shiftlet eased the car forward so that she had to move her hands.

The early afternoon was clear and open and surrounded by pale blue sky. Although the car would go only thirty miles an hour, Mr. Shiftlet imagined a terrific climb and dip and swerve that went entirely to his head so that he forgot his morning bitterness. He had always wanted an automobile but he had never been able to afford one before. He drove very fast because he wanted to make Mobile by nightfall.

Occasionally he stopped his thoughts long enough to look at Lucynell in the seat beside him. She had eaten the lunch as soon as they were out of the yard and now she was pulling the cherries off the hat one by one and throwing them out the window. He became depressed in spite of the car. He had driven about a hundred miles when he decided that she must be hungry again and at the next small town they came to, he stopped in front of an aluminum-painted eating place called The Hot Spot and took her in and ordered her a plate of ham and grits. The ride had made her sleepy and as soon as she got up on the stool, she rested her head on the counter and shut her eyes. There was no one in The Hot Spot but Mr. Shiftlet and the boy behind the counter, a pale youth with a greasy rag hung over his shoulder. Before he could dish up the food, she was snoring gently.

"Give it to her when she wakes up," Mr. Shiftlet said. "I'll pay for it now."

The boy bent over her and stared at the long pink-gold hair and the half-shut sleeping eyes. Then he looked up and stared at Mr. Shiftlet. "She looks like an angel of Gawd," he murmured.

"Hitch-hiker," Mr. Shiftlet explained. "I can't wait. I got to make Tuscaloosa."

The boy bent over again and very carefully touched his finger to a strand of the golden hair and Mr. Shiftlet left.

He was more depressed than ever as he drove on by himself. The late afternoon had grown hot and sultry and the country had flattened out. Deep in the sky a storm was preparing very slowly and without thunder as if it meant to drain every drop of air from the earth before it broke. There were times when Mr. Shiftlet preferred not to be alone. He felt too that a man with a car had a responsibility to others and he kept his eye out for a hitch-hiker. Occasionally he saw a sign that warned: "Drive carefully. The life you save may be your own."

The narrow road dropped off on either side into dry fields and here and there a shack or a filling station stood in a clearing. The sun began to set directly in front of the automobile. It was a reddening ball that through his windshield was slightly flat on the bottom and top. He saw a boy in overalls and a gray hat standing on the edge of the road and he slowed the car down and stopped in front of him. The boy didn't have his hand raised to thumb the ride, he was only standing there, but he had a small cardboard suitcase and his hat was set on his head in a way to indicate that he had left somewhere for good. "Son," Mr. Shiftlet said, "I see you want a ride."

The boy didn't say he did or he didn't but he opened the door of the car and got in, and Mr. Shiftlet started driving again. The child held the suitcase on his lap and folded his arms on top of it. He turned his head and looked out the window away from Mr. Shiftlet. Mr. Shiftlet felt oppressed. "Son," he said after a minute, "I got the best old mother in the world so I reckon you only got the second best."

The boy gave him a quick dark glance and then turned his face back out the window.

"It's nothing so sweet," Mr. Shiftlet continued, "as a boy's mother. She taught him his first prayers at her knee, she give him love when no other would, she told him what was right and what wasn't, and she seen that he done the right thing. Son," he said, "I never rued a day in my life like the one I rued when I left that old mother of mine."

The boy shifted in his seat but he didn't look at Mr.

Shiftlet. He unfolded his arms and put one hand on the door handle.

"My mother was a angel of Gawd," Mr. Shiftlet said in a very strained voice. "He took her from heaven and giver to me and I left her." His eyes were instantly clouded over with a mist of tears. The car was barely moving.

The boy turned angrily in the seat. "You go to the devil!" he cried. "My old woman is a flea bag and yours is a stinking pole cat!" and with that he flung the door open and jumped out with his suitcase into the ditch.

Mr. Shiftlet was so shocked that for about a hundred feet he drove along slowly with the door still open. A cloud, the exact color of the boy's hat and shaped like a turnip, had descended over the sun, and another, worse looking, crouched behind the car. Mr. Shiftlet felt that the rottenness of the world was about to engulf him. He raised his arm and let it fall again to his breast. "Oh Lord!" he prayed. "Break forth and wash the slime from this earth!"

The turnip continued slowly to descend. After a few minutes there was a guffawing peal of thunder from behind and fantastic raindrops, like tin-can tops, crashed over the rear of Mr. Shiftlet's car. Very quickly he stepped on the gas and with his stump sticking out the window he raced the galloping shower into Mobile.

A Stroke of Good Fortune

R UBY CAME IN the front door of the apartment building
and lowered the paper sack with the four cans of number three beans in it onto the hall table. She was too tired to
take her arms from around it or to straighten up and she
hung there collapsed from the hips, her head balanced like a
big florid vegetable at the top of the sack. She gazed with
stony unrecognition at the face that confronted her in the
dark yellow-spotted mirror over the table. Against her right
cheek was a gritty collard leaf that had been stuck there half
the way home. She gave it a vicious swipe with her arm and
straightened up, muttering, "Collards, collards," in a voice of
sultry subdued wrath. Standing up straight, she was a short
woman, shaped nearly like a funeral urn. She had mulberry-
colored hair stacked in sausage rolls around her head but
some of these had come loose with the heat and the long walk
from the grocery store and pointed frantically in various directions. "Collard greens!" she said, spitting the word from
her mouth this time as if it were a poisonous seed.

She and Bill Hill hadn't eaten collard greens for five years
and she wasn't going to start cooking them now. She had
bought these on account of Rufus but she wasn't going to
buy them but once. You would have thought that after two
years in the armed forces Rufus would have come back ready
to eat like somebody from somewhere; but no. When she
asked him what he would like to have *special*, he had not had
the gumption to think of one civilized dish—he had said collard greens. She had expected Rufus to have turned out into
somebody with some get in him. Well, he had about as much
get as a floor mop.

Rufus was her baby brother who had just come back from
the European Theater. He had come to live with her because
Pitman where they were raised was not there any more. All
the people who had lived at Pitman had had the good sense
to leave it, either by dying or by moving to the city. She had
married Bill B. Hill, a Florida man who sold Miracle Products, and had come to live in the city. If Pitman had still been
there, Rufus would have been in Pitman. If one chicken had

been left to walk across the road in Pitman, Rufus would have been there too to keep him company. She didn't like to admit it about her own kin, least about her own brother, but there he was—good for absolutely nothing. "I seen it after five minutes of him," she had told Bill Hill and Bill Hill, with no expression whatsoever, had said, "It taken me three." It was mortifying to let that kind of a husband see you had that kind of a brother.

She supposed there was no help for it. Rufus was like the other children. She was the only one in her family who had been different, who had had any get. She took a stub of pencil from her pocketbook and wrote on the side of the sack: Bill you bring this upstairs. Then she braced herself at the bottom of the steps for the climb to the fourth floor.

The steps were a thin black rent in the middle of the house, covered with a mole-colored carpet that looked as if it grew from the floor. They stuck straight up like steeple steps, it seemed to her. They reared up. The minute she stood at the bottom of them, they reared up and got steeper for her benefit. As she gazed up them, her mouth widened and turned down in a look of complete disgust. She was in no condition to go up anything. She was sick. Madam Zoleeda had told her but not before she knew it herself.

Madam Zoleeda was the palmist on Highway 87. She had said, "A long illness," but she had added, whispering, with a very I-already-know-but-I-won't-tell look, "it will bring you a stroke of good fortune!" and then had sat back grinning, a stout woman with green eyes that moved in their sockets as if they had been oiled. Ruby didn't need to be told. She had already figured out the good fortune. Moving. For two months she had had a distinct feeling that they were going to move. Bill Hill couldn't hold off much longer. He couldn't kill her. Where she wanted to be was in a subdivision—she started up the steps, leaning forward and holding onto the banisters—where you had your drugstores and grocery and a picture show right in your own neighborhood. As it was now, living downtown, she had to walk eight blocks to the main business streets and farther than that to get to a supermarket. She hadn't made any complaints for five years much but now with her health at stake as young as she was what did he think she was going to do, kill herself? She had her eye on a place in Meadowcrest Heights, a duplex bungalow with yellow awnings. She stopped on the fifth step to blow. As young as she was—thirty-four—you wouldn't think five steps would stew her. You better take it easy, baby, she told herself, you're too young to bust your gears.

Thirty-four wasn't old, wasn't any age at all. She remembered her mother at thirty-four—she had looked like a puckered-up old yellow apple, sour, she had always looked sour, she had always looked like she wasn't satisfied with anything. She compared herself at thirty-four with her mother at that age. Her mother's hair had been gray—hers wouldn't be gray now even if she hadn't touched it up. All those children were what did her mother in—eight of them: two born dead, one died the first year, one crushed under a mowing machine. Her mother had got deader with every one of them. And all of it for what? Because she hadn't known any better. Pure ignorance. The purest of downright ignorance!

And there her two sisters were, both married four years with four children apiece. She didn't see how they stood it, always going to the doctor to be jabbed at with instruments. She remembered when her mother had had Rufus. She was the only one of the children who couldn't stand it and she had walked all the way in to Melsy, in the hot sun ten miles, to the picture show to get clear of the screaming, and had sat through two westerns and a horror picture and a serial and then had walked all the way back and found it was just beginning, and she had had to listen all night. All that misery for Rufus! And him turned out now to have no more charge than a dish rag. She saw him waiting out nowhere before he was born, just waiting, waiting to make his mother, only thirty-four, into an old woman. She gripped the banister rail fiercely and heaved herself up another step, shaking her head. Lord, she was disappointed in him! After she had told all her friends her brother was back from the European Theater, here he comes—sounding like he'd never been out of a hog lot.

He looked old too. He looked older than she did and he was fourteen years younger. She was extremely young looking for her age. Not that thirty-four is any age and anyway she was married. She had to smile, thinking about that, because she had done so much better than her sisters—they had married from around. "This breathlessness," she muttered, stopping again. She decided she would have to sit down.

There were twenty-eight steps in each flight—twenty-eight.

She sat down and jumped quickly, feeling something under her. She caught her breath and then pulled the thing out: it was Hartley Gilfeet's pistol. Nine inches of treacherous tin! He was a six-year-old boy who lived on the fifth floor. If he had been hers, she'd have worn him out so hard so many times he wouldn't know how to leave his mess on a public stair. She could have fallen down those stairs as easy as not and ruined herself! But his stupid mother wasn't going to do anything to him even if she told her. All she did was scream at him and tell people how smart he was. "Little Mister Good Fortune!" she called him. "All his poor daddy left me!" His daddy had said on his death bed, "There's nothing but him I ever given you," and she had said, "Rodman, you given me a fortune!" and so she called him Little Mister Good Fortune. "I'd wear the seat of his good fortune out!" Ruby muttered.

The steps were going up and down like a seesaw with her in the middle of it. She did not want to get nauseated. Not that again. Now no. No. She was not. She sat tightly to the steps with her eyes shut until the dizziness stopped a little and the nausea subsided. No, I'm not going to no doctor, she said. No. No. She was not. They would have to carry her there knocked out before she would go. She had done all right doctoring herself all these years—no bad sick spells, no teeth out, no children, all that by herself. She would have had five children right now if she hadn't been careful.

She had wondered more than once if this breathlessness could be heart trouble. Once in a while, going up the steps, there'd be a pain in her chest along with it. That was what she wanted it to be—heart trouble. They couldn't very well remove your heart. They'd have to knock her in the head before they'd get her near a hospital, they'd have to—suppose she would die if they didn't?

She wouldn't.

Suppose she would?

She made herself stop this gory thinking. She was only thirty-four. There was nothing permanent wrong with her. She was fat and her color was good. She thought of herself again in comparison with her mother at thirty-four and she pinched her arm and smiled. Seeing that her mother or father neither had been much to look at, she had done very well. They had been the dried-up type, dried up and Pitman dried into them, them and Pitman shrunk down into something all dried and puckered up. And she had come out of that! A somebody as alive as her! She got up, gripping the banister rail but smiling to herself. She was warm and fat and beautiful and not too fat because Bill Hill liked her that way. She had gained some weight but he hadn't noticed except that he was maybe more happy lately and didn't know why. She felt the wholeness of herself, a whole thing climbing the stairs. She was up the first flight now and she looked back, pleased. As soon as Bill Hill fell down those steps once, maybe they would move. But they would move before that! Madam Zoleeda had known. She laughed aloud and moved on down the hall. Mr. Jerger's door grated and startled her. Oh Lord, she thought, *him*. He was a second-floor resident who was peculiar.

He peered at her coming down the hall. "Good morning!" he said, bowing the upper part of his body out the door. "Good morning to you!" He looked like a goat. He had little raisin eyes and a string beard and his jacket was a green that was almost black or a black that was almost green.

"Morning," she said. "Hower you?"

"Well!" he screamed. "Well indeed on this glorious day!" He was seventy-eight years old and his face looked as if it had mildew on it. In the mornings he studied and in the afternoons, he walked up and down the sidewalks, stopping children and asking them questions. Whenever he heard anyone in the hall, he opened his door and looked out.

"Yeah, it's a nice day," she said languidly.

"Do you know what great birthday this is?" he asked.

"Uh-uh," Ruby said. He always had a question like that. A history question that nobody knew; he would ask it and then make a speech on it. He used to teach in a high school.

"Guess," he urged her.

"Abraham Lincoln," she muttered.

"Hah! You are not trying," he said. "Try."

"George Washington," she said, starting up the stairs.

"Shame on you!" he cried. "And your husband from there! Florida! Florida! Florida's birthday," he shouted. "Come in here." He disappeared into his room, beckoning a long finger at her.

She came down the two steps and said, "I gotta be going," and stuck her head inside the door. The room was the size of a large closet and the walls were completely covered with picture postcards of local buildings; this gave an illusion of space. A single transparent bulb hung down on Mr. Jerger and a small table.

"Now examine this," he said. He was bending over a book, running his finger under the lines: " 'On Easter Sunday, April 3, 1516, he arrived on the tip of this continent.' Do you know who this *he* was?" he demanded.

"Yeah, Christopher Columbus," Ruby said.

"Ponce de Leon!" he screamed. "Ponce de Leon! You should know something about Florida," he said. "Your husband is from Florida."

"Yeah, he was born in Miami," Ruby said. "He's not from Tennessee."

"Florida is not a noble state," Mr. Jerger said, "but it is an important one."

"It's important alrighto," Ruby said.

"Do you know who Ponce de Leon was?"

"He was the founder of Florida," Ruby said brightly.

"He was a Spaniard," Mr. Jerger said. "Do you know what he was looking for?"

"Florida," Ruby said.

"Ponce de Leon was looking for the fountain of youth," Mr. Jerger said, closing his eyes.

"Oh," Ruby muttered.

"A certain spring," Mr. Jerger went on, "whose water gave perpetual youth to those who drank it. In other words," he said, "he was trying to be young always."

"Did he find it?" Ruby asked.

Mr. Jerger paused with his eyes still closed. After a minute he said, "Do you think he found it? Do you think he found

it? Do you think nobody else would have got to it if he had
found it? Do you think there would be one person living on
this earth who hadn't drunk it?"

"I hadn't thought," Ruby said.

"Nobody thinks any more," Mr. Jerger complained.

"I got to be going."

"Yes, it's been found," Mr. Jerger said.

"Where at?" Ruby asked.

"I have drunk of it."

"Where'd you have to go to?" she asked. She leaned a little
closer and got a whiff of him that was like putting her nose
under a buzzard's wing.

"Into my heart," he said, placing his hand over it.

"Oh." Ruby moved back. "I gotta be going. I think my
brother's home." She got over the door sill.

"Ask your husband if he knows what great birthday this
is," Mr. Jerger said, looking at her coyly.

"Yeah, I will." She turned and waited until she heard his
door click. She looked back to see that it was shut and then
she blew out her breath and stood facing the dark remaining
steep of steps. "God Almighty," she commented. They got
darker and steeper as you went up.

By the time she had climbed five steps her breath was gone.
She continued up a few more, blowing. Then she stopped.
There was a pain in her stomach. It was a pain like a piece of
something pushing something else. She had felt it before, a
few days ago. It was the one that frightened her most. She
had thought the word *cancer* once and dropped it instantly
because no horror like that was coming to her because it
couldn't. The word came back to her immediately with the
pain but she slashed it in two with Madam Zoleeda. It will
end in good fortune. She slashed it twice through and then
again until there were only pieces of it that couldn't be recognized. She was going to stop on the next floor—God, if
she ever got up there—and talk to Laverne Watts. Laverne
Watts was a third-floor resident, the secretary to a chiropodist, and an especial friend of hers.

She got up there, gasping and feeling as if her knees were
full of fizz, and knocked on Laverne's door with the butt of
Hartley Gilfeet's gun. She leaned on the door frame to rest

and suddenly the floor around her dropped on both sides. The walls turned black and she felt herself reeling, without breath, in the middle of the air, terrified at the drop that was coming. She saw the door open a great distance away and Laverne, about four inches high, standing in it.

Laverne, a tall straw-haired girl, let out a great guffaw and slapped her side as if she had just opened the door on the most comical sight she had yet seen. "That gun!" she yelled. "That gun! That look!" She staggered back to the sofa and fell on it, her legs rising higher than her hips and falling down again helplessly with a thud.

The floor came up to where Ruby could see it and remained, dipping a little. With a terrible stare of concentration, she stepped down to get on it. She scrutinized a chair across the room and then headed for it, putting her feet carefully one before the other.

"You should be in a wild-west show!" Laverne Watts said. "You're a howl!"

Ruby reached the chair and then edged herself onto it. "Shut up," she said hoarsely.

Laverne sat forward, pointing at her, and then fell back on the sofa, shaking again.

"Quit that!" Ruby yelled. "Quit that! I'm sick."

Laverne got up and took two or three long strides across the room. She leaned down in front of Ruby and looked into her face with one eye shut as if she were squinting through a keyhole. "You are sort of purple," she said.

"I'm damm sick," Ruby glowered.

Laverne stood looking at her and after a second she folded her arms and very pointedly stuck her stomach out and began to sway back and forth. "Well, what'd you come in here with that gun for? Where'd you get it?" she asked.

"Sat on it," Ruby muttered.

Laverne stood there, swaying with her stomach stuck out, and a very wise expression growing on her face. Ruby sat sprawled in the chair, looking at her feet. The room was getting still. She sat up and glared at her ankles. They were swollen! I'm not going to no doctor, she started, I'm not going to one. I'm not going. "Not going," she began to mumble, "to no doctor, not . . ."

"How long you think you can hold off?" Laverne murmured and began to giggle.

"Are my ankles swollen?" Ruby asked.

"They look like they've always looked to me," Laverne said, throwing herself down on the sofa again. "Kind of fat." She lifted her own ankles up on the end pillow and turned them slightly. "How do you like these shoes?" she asked. They were a grasshopper green with very high thin heels.

"I think they're swollen," Ruby said. "When I was coming up that last flight of stairs I had the awfulest feeling, all over me like . . ."

"You ought to go on to the doctor."

"I don't need to go to no doctor," Ruby muttered. "I can take care of myself. I haven't done bad at it all this time."

"Is Rufus at home?"

"I don't know. I kept myself away from doctors all my life. I kept—why?"

"Why what?"

"Why, is Rufus at home?"

"Rufus is cute," Laverne said. "I thought I'd ask him how he liked my shoes."

Ruby sat up with a fierce look, very pink and purple. "Why Rufus?" she growled. "He ain't but a baby." Laverne was thirty years old. "He don't care about women's shoes."

Laverne sat up and took off one of the shoes and peered inside it. "Nine B," she said. "I bet he'd like what's in it."

"That Rufus ain't but an enfant!" Ruby said. "He don't have time to be looking at your feet. He ain't got that kind of time."

"Oh, he's got plenty of time," Laverne said.

"Yeah," Ruby muttered and saw him again, waiting, with plenty of time, out nowhere before he was born, just waiting to make his mother that much deader.

"I believe your ankles are swollen," Laverne said.

"Yeah," Ruby said, twisting them. "Yeah. They feel tight sort of. I had the awfulest feeling when I got up those steps, like sort of out of breath all over, sort of tight all over, sort of—awful."

"You ought to go on to the doctor."

"No."

"You ever been to one?"

"They carried me once when I was ten," Ruby said, "but I got away. Three of them holding me didn't do any good."

"What was it that time?"

"What you looking at me that way for?" Ruby muttered.

"What way?"

"That way," Ruby said, "—swagging out that stomach of yours that way."

"I just asked you what it was that time?"

"It was a boil. A nigger woman up the road told me what to do and I did it and it went away." She sat slumped on the edge of the chair, staring in front of her as if she were remembering an easier time.

Laverne began to do a kind of comic dance up and down the room. She took two or three slow steps in one direction with her knees bent and then she came back and kicked her leg slowly and painfully in the other. She began to sing in a loud guttural voice, rolling her eyes, "Put them all together, they spell MOTHER! MOTHER!" and stretching out her arms as if she were on the stage.

Ruby's mouth opened wordlessly and her fierce expression vanished. For a half-second she was motionless; then she sprang from the chair. "Not me!" she shouted. "Not me!"

Laverne stopped and only watched her with the wise look.

"Not me!" Ruby shouted. "Oh no not me! Bill Hill takes care of that. Bill Hill takes care of that! Bill Hill's been taking care of that for five years! That ain't going to happen to me!"

"Well old Bill Hill just slipped up about four or five months ago, my friend," Laverne said. "Just slipped up . . ."

"I don't reckon you know anything about it, you ain't even married, you ain't even . . ."

"I bet it's not one, I bet it's two," Laverne said. "You better go on to the doctor and find out how many it is."

"It is not!" Ruby shrilled. She thought she was so smart! She didn't know a sick woman when she saw one, all she could do was look at her feet and shoe em to Rufus, shoe em to Rufus and he was an enfant and she was thirty-four years old. "Rufus is an enfant!" she wailed.

"That will make two!" Laverne said.

"You shut up talking like that!" Ruby shouted. "You shut up this minute. I ain't going to have any baby!"

"Ha ha," Laverne said.

"I don't know how you think you know so much," Ruby said, "single as you are. If I was so single I wouldn't go around telling married people what their business is."

"Not just your ankles," Laverne said, "you're swollen all over."

"I ain't going to stay here and be insulted," Ruby said and walked carefully to the door, keeping herself erect and not looking down at her stomach the way she wanted to.

"Well I hope *all* of you feel better tomorrow," Laverne said.

"I think my heart will be better tomorrow," Ruby said. "But I hope we will be moving soon. I can't climb these steps with this heart trouble and," she added with a dignified glare, "Rufus don't care nothing about your big feet."

"You better put that gun up," Laverne said, "before you shoot somebody."

Ruby slammed the door shut and looked down at herself quickly. She was big there but she had always had a kind of big stomach. She did not stick out there different from the way she did any place else. It was natural when you took on some weight to take it on in the middle and Bill Hill didn't mind her being fat, he was just more happy and didn't know why. She saw Bill Hill's long happy face, grinning at her from the eyes downward in a way he had as if his look got happier as it neared his teeth. He would never slip up. She rubbed her hand across her skirt and felt the tightness of it but hadn't she felt that before? She had. It was the skirt—she had on the tight one that she didn't wear often, she had . . . she didn't have on the tight skirt. She had on the loose one. But it wasn't very loose. But that didn't make any difference, she was just fat.

She put her fingers on her stomach and pushed down and then took them off quickly. She began walking toward the stairs, slowly, as if the floor were going to move under her. She began the steps. The pain came back at once. It came back with the first step. "No," she whimpered, "no." It was just a little feeling, just a little feeling like a piece of her inside rolling over but it made her breath tighten in her throat. Nothing in her was supposed to roll over. "Just one step," she whispered, "just one step and it did it." It couldn't be cancer. Madam Zoleeda said it would end in good fortune. She began crying and saying, "Just one step and it did it," and going on up them absently as if she thought she were standing still. On the sixth one, she sat down suddenly, her hand slipping weakly down the banister spoke onto the floor.

"Noooo," she said and leaned her round red face between the two nearest poles. She looked down into the stairwell and gave a long hollow wail that widened and echoed as it went down. The stair cavern was dark green and mole-colored and the wail sounded at the very bottom like a voice answering her. She gasped and shut her eyes. No. No. It couldn't be any baby. She was not going to have something waiting in her to make her deader, she was not. Bill Hill couldn't have slipped up. He said it was guaranteed and it had worked all this time and it could not be that, it could not. She shuddered and held her hand tightly over her mouth. She felt her face drawn puckered: two born dead one died the first year and one run under like a dried yellow apple no she was only thirty-four years old, she was old. Madam Zoleeda said it would end in no drying up. Madam Zoleeda said oh but it will end in a stroke of good fortune! Moving. She had said it would end in a stroke of good moving.

She felt herself getting calmer. She felt herself, after a minute, getting almost calm and thought she got upset too easy; heck, it was gas. Madam Zoleeda hadn't been wrong about anything yet, she knew more than . . .

She jumped: there was a bang at the bottom of the stairwell and a rumble rattling up the steps, shaking them even up where she was. She looked through the banister poles and saw Hartley Gilfeet, with two pistols leveled, galloping up the stairs and heard a voice pierce down from the floor over her, "You Hartley, shut up that racket! You're shaking the house!" But he came on, thundering louder as he rounded the bend on the first floor and streaked up the hall. She saw Mr. Jerger's door fly open and him spring with clawed fingers and grasp a flying piece of shirt that whirled and shot off again with a high-pitched, "Leggo, you old goat teacher!" and came on nearer until the stairs rumbled directly under her and a charging chipmunk face crashed into her and rocketed through her head, smaller and smaller into a whirl of dark.

She sat on the step, clutching the banister spoke while the breath came back into her a thimbleful at a time and the stairs stopped seesawing. She opened her eyes and gazed down into the dark hole, down to the very bottom where she had started up so long ago. "Good Fortune," she said in a hollow voice that echoed along all the levels of the cavern, "Baby."

"Good Fortune, Baby," the three echoes leered.

Then she recognized the feeling again, a little roll. It was as if it were not in her stomach. It was as if it were out no-where in nothing, out nowhere, resting and waiting, with plenty of time.

A Temple of the Holy Ghost

ALL WEEK END the two girls were calling each other Temple One and Temple Two, shaking with laughter and getting so red and hot that they were positively ugly, particularly Joanne who had spots on her face anyway. They came in the brown convent uniforms they had to wear at Mount St. Scholastica but as soon as they opened their suitcases, they took off the uniforms and put on red skirts and loud blouses. They put on lipstick and their Sunday shoes and walked around in the high heels all over the house, always passing the long mirror in the hall slowly to get a look at their legs. None of their ways were lost on the child. If only one of them had come, that one would have played with her, but since there were two of them, she was out of it and watched them suspiciously from a distance.

They were fourteen—two years older than she was—but neither of them was bright, which was why they had been sent to the convent. If they had gone to a regular school, they wouldn't have done anything but think about boys; at the convent the sisters, her mother said, would keep a grip on their necks. The child decided, after observing them for a few hours, that they were practically morons and she was glad to think that they were only second cousins and she couldn't have inherited any of their stupidity. Susan called herself Su-zan. She was very skinny but she had a pretty pointed face and red hair. Joanne had yellow hair that was naturally curly but she talked through her nose and when she laughed, she turned purple in patches. Neither one of them could say an intelligent thing and all their sentences began, "You know this boy I know well one time he . . ."

They were to stay all week end and her mother said she didn't see how she would entertain them since she didn't know any boys their age. At this, the child, struck suddenly with genius, shouted, "There's Cheat! Get Cheat to come! Ask Miss Kirby to get Cheat to come show them around!" and she nearly choked on the food she had in her mouth. She doubled over laughing and hit the table with her fist and looked at the two bewildered girls while water started in her eyes and rolled down her fat cheeks and the braces she had in her mouth glared like tin. She had never thought of anything so funny before.

Her mother laughed in a guarded way and Miss Kirby blushed and carried her fork delicately to her mouth with one pea on it. She was a long-faced blonde schoolteacher who boarded with them and Mr. Cheatam was her admirer, a rich old farmer who arrived every Saturday afternoon in a fifteen-year-old baby-blue Pontiac powdered with red clay dust and black inside with Negroes that he charged ten cents apiece to bring into town on Saturday afternoons. After he dumped them he came to see Miss Kirby, always bringing a little gift—a bag of boiled peanuts or a watermelon or a stalk of sugar cane and once a wholesale box of Baby Ruth candy bars. He was bald-headed except for a little fringe of rust-colored hair and his face was nearly the same color as the unpaved roads and washed like them with ruts and gulleys. He wore a pale green shirt with a thin black stripe in it and blue galluses and his trousers cut across a protruding stomach that he pressed tenderly from time to time with his big flat thumb. All his teeth were backed with gold and he would roll his eyes at Miss Kirby in an impish way and say, "Haw haw," sitting in their porch swing with his legs spread apart and his hightopped shoes pointing in opposite directions on the floor.

"I don't think Cheat is going to be in town this week end," Miss Kirby said, not in the least understanding that this was a joke, and the child was convulsed afresh, threw herself backward in her chair, fell out of it, rolled on the floor and lay there heaving. Her mother told her if she didn't stop this foolishness she would have to leave the table.

Yesterday her mother had arranged with Alonzo Myers to drive them the forty-five miles to Mayville, where the convent was, to get the girls for the week end and Sunday afternoon he was hired to drive them back again. He was an eighteen-year-old boy who weighed two hundred and fifty pounds and worked for the taxi company and he was all you could get to drive you anywhere. He smoked or rather chewed a short black cigar and he had a round sweaty chest that showed through the yellow nylon shirt he wore. When he drove all the windows of the car had to be open.

"Well there's Alonzo!" the child roared from the floor. "Get Alonzo to show em around! Get Alonzo!"

The two girls, who had seen Alonzo, began to scream their indignation.

Her mother thought this was funny too but she said, "That'll be about enough out of you," and changed the subject. She asked them why they called each other Temple One and Temple Two and this sent them off into gales of giggles. Finally they managed to explain. Sister Perpetua, the oldest nun at the Sisters of Mercy in Mayville, had given them a lecture on what to do if a young man should—here they laughed so hard they were not able to go on without going back to the beginning—on what to do if a young man should—they put their heads in their laps—on what to do if—they finally managed to shout it out—if he should "behave in an ungentlemanly manner with them in the back of an automobile." Sister Perpetua said they were to say, "Stop sir! I am a Temple of the Holy Ghost!" and that would put an end to it. The child sat up off the floor with a blank face. She didn't see anything so funny in this. What was really funny was the idea of Mr. Cheatam or Alonzo Myers beauing them around. That killed her.

Her mother didn't laugh at what they had said. "I think you girls are pretty silly," she said. "After all, that's what you are—Temples of the Holy Ghost."

The two of them looked up at her, politely concealing their giggles, but with astonished faces as if they were beginning to realize that she was made of the same stuff as Sister Perpetua.

Miss Kirby preserved her set expression and the child thought, it's all over her head anyhow. I am a Temple of the Holy Ghost, she said to herself, and was pleased with the phrase. It made her feel as if somebody had given her a present.

After dinner, her mother collapsed on the bed and said, "Those girls are going to drive me crazy if I don't get some entertainment for them. They're awful."

"I bet I know who you could get," the child started.

"Now listen. I don't want to hear any more about Mr. Cheatam," her mother said. "You embarrass Miss Kirby. He's her only friend. Oh my Lord," and she sat up and looked mournfully out the window, "that poor soul is so lonesome she'll even ride in that car that smells like the last circle in hell."

And she's a Temple of the Holy Ghost too, the child reflected. "I wasn't thinking of him," she said. "I was thinking of those two Wilkinses, Wendell and Cory, that visit old lady Buchell out on her farm. They're her grandsons. They work for her."

"Now that's an idea," her mother murmured and gave her an appreciative look. But then she slumped again. "They're only farm boys. These girls would turn up their noses at them."

"Huh," the child said. "They wear pants. They're sixteen and they got a car. Somebody said they were both going to be Church of God preachers because you don't have to know nothing to be one."

"They would be perfectly safe with those boys all right," her mother said and in a minute she got up and called their grandmother on the telephone and after she had talked to the old woman a half an hour, it was arranged that Wendell and Cory would come to supper and afterwards take the girls to the fair.

Susan and Joanne were so pleased that they washed their hair and rolled it up on aluminum curlers. Hah, thought the child, sitting cross-legged on the bed to watch them undo the curlers, wait'll you get a load of Wendell and Cory! "You'll like these boys," she said. "Wendell is six feet tall ands got red hair. Cory is six feet six inches talls got black hair and wears a sport jacket and they gottem this car with a squirrel tail on the front."

"How does a child like you know so much about these men?" Susan asked and pushed her face up close to the mirror to watch the pupils in her eyes dilate.

The child lay back on the bed and began to count the narrow boards in the ceiling until she lost her place. I know them all right, she said to someone. We fought in the world war together. They were under me and I saved them five times from Japanese suicide divers and Wendell said I am going to marry that kid and the other said oh no you ain't I am and I said neither one of you is because I will court marshall you all before you can bat an eye. "I've seen them around is all," she said.

When they came the girls stared at them a second and then began to giggle and talk to each other about the convent. They sat in the swing together and Wendell and Cory sat on the banisters together. They sat like monkeys, their knees on a level with their shoulders and their arms hanging down between. They were short thin boys with red faces and high cheekbones and pale seed-like eyes. They had brought a harmonica and a guitar. One of them began to blow softly on the mouth organ, watching the girls over it, and the other started strumming the guitar and then began to sing, not watching them but keeping his head tilted upward as if he were only interested in hearing himself. He was singing a hillbilly song that sounded half like a love song and half like a hymn.

The child was standing on a barrel pushed into some bushes at the side of the house, her face on a level with the porch floor. The sun was going down and the sky was turning a bruised violet color that seemed to be connected with the sweet mournful sound of the music. Wendell began to smile as he sang and to look at the girls. He looked at Susan with a dog-like loving look and sang,

> "I've found a friend in Jesus,
> He's everything to me,
> He's the lily of the valley,
> He's the One who's set me free!"

Then he turned the same look on Joanne and sang,

> "A wall of fire about me,
> I've nothing now to fear,
> He's the lily of the valley,
> And I'll always have Him near!"

The girls looked at each other and held their lips stiff so as not to giggle but Susan let out one anyway and clapped her hand on her mouth. The singer frowned and for a few seconds only strummed the guitar. Then he began "The Old Rugged Cross" and they listened politely but when he had finished they said, "Let us sing one!" and before he could start another, they began to sing with their convent-trained voices,

> *"Tantum ergo Sacramentum*
> *Veneremur Cernui:*
> *Et antiquum documentum*
> *Novo cedat ritui:"*

The child watched the boys' solemn faces turn with perplexed frowning stares at each other as if they were uncertain whether they were being made fun of.

> *"Praestet fides supplementum*
> *Sensuum defectui.*
> *Genitori, Genitoque*
> *Laus et jubilatio*
>
> *Salus, honor, virtus quoque . . ."*

The boys' faces were dark red in the gray-purple light. They looked fierce and startled.

> *"Sit et benedictio;*
> *Procedenti ab utroque*
> *Compar sit laudatio.*
> *Amen."*

The girls dragged out the Amen and then there was a silence.

"That must be Jew singing," Wendell said and began to tune the guitar.

The girls giggled idiotically but the child stamped her foot on the barrel. "You big dumb ox!" she shouted. "You big dumb Church of God ox!" she roared and fell off the barrel and scrambled up and shot around the corner of the house as they jumped from the banister to see who was shouting.

Her mother had arranged for them to have supper in the back yard and she had a table laid out there under some Japanese lanterns that she pulled out for garden parties. "I ain't eating with them," the child said and snatched her plate off the table and carried it to the kitchen and sat down with the thin blue-gummed cook and ate her supper.

"Howcome you be so ugly sometime?" the cook asked.

"Those stupid idiots," the child said.

The lanterns gilded the leaves of the trees orange on the level where they hung and above them was black-green and below them were different dim muted colors that made the girls sitting at the table look prettier than they were. From time to time, the child turned her head and glared out the kitchen window at the scene below.

"God could strike you deaf dumb and blind," the cook said, "and then you wouldn't be as smart as you is."

"I would still be smarter than some," the child said.

After supper they left for the fair. She wanted to go to the fair but not with them so even if they had asked her she wouldn't have gone. She went upstairs and paced the long bedroom with her hands locked together behind her back and her head thrust forward and an expression, fierce and dreamy both, on her face. She didn't turn on the electric light but let the darkness collect and make the room smaller and more private. At regular intervals a light crossed the open window and threw shadows on the wall. She stopped and stood looking out over the dark slopes, past where the pond glinted silver, past the wall of woods to the speckled sky where a long finger of light was revolving up and around and away, searching the air as if it were hunting for the lost sun. It was the beacon light from the fair.

She could hear the distant sound of the calliope and she saw in her head all the tents raised up in a kind of gold saw-dust light and the diamond ring of the ferris wheel going around and around up in the air and down again and the screeking merry-go-round going around and around on the ground. A fair lasted five or six days and there was a special afternoon for school children and a special night for niggers. She had gone last year on the afternoon for school children and had seen the monkeys and the fat man and had ridden on the ferris wheel. Certain tents were closed then because they contained things that would be known only to grown people but she had looked with interest at the advertising on the closed tents, at the faded-looking pictures on the canvas of people in tights, with stiff stretched composed faces like the faces of the martyrs waiting to have their tongues cut out by the Roman soldier. She had imagined that what was inside these tents concerned medicine and she had made up her mind to be a doctor when she grew up.

She had since changed and decided to be an engineer but as she looked out the window and followed the revolving searchlight as it widened and shortened and wheeled in its arc, she felt that she would have to be much more than just a doctor or an engineer. She would have to be a saint because that was the occupation that included everything you could know; and yet she knew she would never be a saint. She did not steal or murder but she was a born liar and slothful and she sassed her mother and was deliberately ugly to almost everybody. She was eaten up also with the sin of Pride, the worst one. She made fun of the Baptist preacher who came to the school at commencement to give the devotional. She would pull down her mouth and hold her forehead as if she were in agony and groan, "Fawther, we thank Thee," exactly the way he did and she had been told many times not to do it. She could never be a saint, but she thought she could be a martyr if they killed her quick.

She could stand to be shot but not to be burned in oil. She didn't know if she could stand to be torn to pieces by lions or not. She began to prepare her martyrdom, seeing herself in a pair of tights in a great arena, lit by the early Christians hanging in cages of fire, making a gold dusty light that fell on her and the lions. The first lion charged forward and fell at her feet, converted. A whole series of lions did the same. The lions liked her so much she even slept with them and finally the Romans were obliged to burn her but to their astonishment she would not burn down and finding she was so hard to kill, they finally cut off her head very quickly with a sword and she went immediately to heaven. She rehearsed this several times, returning each time at the entrance of Paradise to the lions.

Finally she got up from the window and got ready for bed and got in without saying her prayers. There were two heavy double beds in the room. The girls were occupying the other one and she tried to think of something cold and clammy that she could hide in their bed but her thought was fruitless. She didn't have anything she could think of, like a chicken carcass or a piece of beef liver. The sound of the calliope coming through the window kept her awake and she remembered that she hadn't said her prayers and got up and knelt down and began them. She took a running start and went through to the other side of the Apostle's Creed and then hung by her chin on the side of the bed, empty-minded. Her prayers, when she remembered to say them, were usually perfunctory but sometimes when she had done something wrong or heard music or lost something, or sometimes for no reason at all, she would be moved to fervor and would think of Christ on the long journey to Calvary, crushed three times under the rough cross. Her mind would stay on this a while and then get empty and when something roused her, she would find that she was thinking of a different thing entirely, of some dog or some girl or something she was going to do some day. Tonight, remembering Wendell and Cory, she was filled with thanksgiving and almost weeping with delight, she said, "Lord, Lord, thank You that I'm not in the Church of God, thank You Lord, thank You!" and got back in bed and kept repeating it until she went to sleep.

The girls came in at a quarter to twelve and waked her up with their giggling. They turned on the small blue-shaded lamp to see to get undressed by and their skinny shadows climbed up the wall and broke and continued moving about softly on the ceiling. The child sat up to hear what all they had seen at the fair. Susan had a plastic pistol full of cheap candy and Joanne a pasteboard cat with red polka dots in it. "Did you see the monkeys dance?" the child asked. "Did you see that fat man and those midgets?"

"All kinds of freaks," Joanne said. And then she said to Susan, "I enjoyed it all but the you-know-what," and her face assumed a peculiar expression as if she had bit into something that she didn't know if she liked or not.

The other stood still and shook her head once and nodded slightly at the child. "Little pitchers," she said in a low voice but the child heard it and her heart began to beat very fast.

She got out of her bed and climbed onto the footboard of theirs. They turned off the light and got in but she didn't move. She sat there, looking hard at them until their faces were well defined in the dark. "I'm not as old as you all," she said, "but I'm about a million times smarter."

"There are some things," Susan said, "that a child of your age doesn't know," and they both began to giggle.

"Go back to your own bed," Joanne said.

The child didn't move. "One time," she said, her voice hollow-sounding in the dark, "I saw this rabbit have rabbits."

There was a silence. Then Susan said, "How?" in an indifferent tone and she knew that she had them. She said she wouldn't tell until they told about the you-know-what. Actually she had never seen a rabbit have rabbits but she forgot this as they began to tell what they had seen in the tent.

It had been a freak with a particular name but they couldn't remember the name. The tent where it was had been divided into two parts by a black curtain, one side for men and one for women. The freak went from one side to the other, talking first to the men and then to the women, but everyone could hear. The stage ran all the way across the front. The girls heard the freak say to the men, "I'm going to show you this and if you laugh, God may strike you the same way." The freak had a country voice, slow and nasal and neither high nor low, just flat. "God made me thisaway and if you laugh He may strike you the same way. This is the way He wanted me to be and I ain't disputing His way. I'm showing you because I got to make the best of it. I expect you to act like ladies and gentlemen. I never done it to myself nor had a thing to do with it but I'm making the best of it. I don't dispute hit." Then there was a long silence on the other side of the tent and finally the freak left the men and came over onto the women's side and said the same thing.

The child felt every muscle strained as if she were hearing the answer to a riddle that was more puzzling than the riddle itself. "You mean it had two heads?" she said.

"No," Susan said, "it was a man and woman both. It pulled up its dress and showed us. It had on a blue dress."

The child wanted to ask how it could be a man and woman both without two heads but she did not. She wanted to get back into her own bed and think it out and she began to climb down off the footboard.

"What about the rabbit?" Joanne asked.

The child stopped and only her face appeared over the foot-board, abstracted, absent. "It spit them out of its mouth," she said, "six of them."

She lay in bed trying to picture the tent with the freak walking from side to side but she was too sleepy to figure it out. She was better able to see the faces of the country people watching, the men more solemn than they were in church, and the women stern and polite, with painted-looking eyes, standing as if they were waiting for the first note of the piano to begin the hymn. She could hear the freak saying, "God made me thisaway and I don't dispute hit," and the people saying, "Amen. Amen."

"God done this to me and I praise Him."

"Amen. Amen."

"He could strike you thisaway."

"Amen. Amen."

"But he has not."

"Amen."

"Raise yourself up. A temple of the Holy Ghost. You! You are God's temple, don't you know? Don't you know? God's Spirit has a dwelling in you, don't you know?"

"Amen. Amen."

"If anybody desecrates the temple of God, God will bring him to ruin and if you laugh, He may strike you thisaway. A temple of God is a holy thing. Amen. Amen."

"I am a temple of the Holy Ghost."

"Amen."

The people began to slap their hands without making a loud noise and with a regular beat between the Amens, more and more softly, as if they knew there was a child near, half asleep.

The next afternoon the girls put on their brown convent uniforms again and the child and her mother took them back to Mount St. Scholastica. "Oh glory, oh Pete!" they said. "Back to the salt mines." Alonzo Myers drove them and the child sat in front with him and her mother sat in back between the two girls, telling them such things as how pleased she was to have had them and how they must come back again and then about the good times she and their mothers had had when they were girls at the convent. The child didn't listen to any of this twaddle but kept as close to the locked door as she could get and held her head out the window. They had thought Alonzo would smell better on Sunday but he did not. With her hair blowing over her face she could look directly into the ivory sun which was framed in the middle of the blue afternoon but when she pulled it away from her eyes she had to squint.

Mount St. Scholastica was a red brick house set back in a garden in the center of town. There was a filling station on one side of it and a firehouse on the other. It had a high black grillework fence around it and narrow bricked walks between old trees and japonica bushes that were heavy with blooms. A big moon-faced nun came bustling to the door to let them in and embraced her mother and would have done the same to her but that she stuck out her hand and preserved a frigid frown, looking just past the sister's shoes at the wainscoting. They had a tendency to kiss even homely children, but the nun shook her hand vigorously and even cracked her knuckles a little and said they must come to the chapel, that benediction was just beginning. You put your foot in their door and they got you praying, the child thought as they hurried down the polished corridor.

You'd think she had to catch a train, she continued in the same ugly vein as they entered the chapel where the sisters were kneeling on one side and the girls, all in brown uniforms, on the other. The chapel smelled of incense. It was light green and gold, a series of springing arches that ended with the one over the altar where the priest was kneeling in front of the monstrance, bowed low. A small boy in a surplice was standing behind him, swinging the censer. The child knelt down between her mother and the nun and they were well into the *"Tantum Ergo"* before her ugly thoughts stopped and she began to realize that she was in the presence of God. Hep me not to be so mean, she began mechanically. Hep me not to give her so much sass. Hep me not to talk like I do. Her mind began to get quiet and then empty but when the priest raised the monstrance with the Host shining ivory-colored in the center of it, she was thinking of the tent at the fair that had the freak in it. The freak was saying, "I don't dispute hit. This is the way He wanted me to be."

As they were leaving the convent door, the big nun swooped down on her mischievously and nearly smothered her in the black habit, mashing the side of her face into the crucifix hitched onto her belt and then holding her off and looking at her with little periwinkle eyes.

On the way home she and her mother sat in the back and Alonzo drove by himself in the front. The child observed three folds of fat in the back of his neck and noted that his ears were pointed almost like a pig's. Her mother, making conversation, asked him if he had gone to the fair.

"Gone," he said, "and never missed a thing and it was good I gone when I did because they ain't going to have it next week like they said they was."

"Why?" asked her mother.

"They shut it on down," he said. "Some of the preachers from town gone out and inspected it and got the police to shut it on down."

Her mother let the conversation drop and the child's round face was lost in thought. She turned it toward the window and looked out over a stretch of pasture land that rose and fell with a gathering greenness until it touched the dark woods. The sun was a huge red ball like an elevated Host drenched in blood and when it sank out of sight, it left a line in the sky like a red clay road hanging over the trees.

The Artificial Nigger

M R. HEAD AWAKENED to discover that the room was full of moonlight. He sat up and stared at the floor boards—the color of silver—and then at the ticking on his pillow, which might have been brocade, and after a second, he saw half of the moon five feet away in his shaving mirror, paused as if it were waiting for his permission to enter. It rolled forward and cast a dignifying light on everything. The straight chair against the wall looked stiff and attentive as if it were awaiting an order and Mr. Head's trousers, hanging to the back of it, had an almost noble air, like the garment some great man had just flung to his servant; but the face on the moon was a grave one. It gazed across the room and out the window where it floated over the horse stall and appeared to contemplate itself with the look of a young man who sees his old age before him.

Mr. Head could have said to it that age was a choice blessing and that only with years does a man enter into that calm understanding of life that makes him a suitable guide for the young. This, at least, had been his own experience.

He sat up and grasped the iron posts at the foot of his bed and raised himself until he could see the face on the alarm clock which sat on an overturned bucket beside the chair. The hour was two in the morning. The alarm on the clock did not work but he was not dependent on any mechanical means to awaken him. Sixty years had not dulled his responses; his physical reactions, like his moral ones, were guided by his will and strong character, and these could be seen plainly in his features. He had a long tube-like face with a long rounded open jaw and a long depressed nose. His eyes were alert but quiet, and in the miraculous moonlight they had a look of composure and of ancient wisdom as if they belonged to one of the great guides of men. He might have been Vergil summoned in the middle of the night to go to Dante, or better, Raphael, awakened by a blast of God's light to fly to the side of Tobias. The only dark spot in the room was Nelson's pallet, underneath the shadow of the window.

Nelson was hunched over on his side, his knees under his

chin and his heels under his bottom. His new suit and hat were in the boxes that they had been sent in and these were on the floor at the foot of the pallet where he could get his hands on them as soon as he woke up. The slop jar, out of the shadow and made snow-white in the moonlight, appeared to stand guard over him like a small personal angel. Mr. Head lay back down, feeling entirely confident that he could carry out the moral mission of the coming day. He meant to be up before Nelson and to have the breakfast cooking by the time he awakened. The boy was always irked when Mr. Head was the first up. They would have to leave the house at four to get to the railroad junction by five-thirty. The train was to stop for them at five forty-five and they had to be there on time for this train was stopping merely to accommodate them.

This would be the boy's first trip to the city though he claimed it would be his second because he had been born there. Mr. Head had tried to point out to him that when he was born he didn't have the intelligence to determine his whereabouts but this had made no impression on the child at all and he continued to insist that this was to be his second trip. It would be Mr. Head's third trip. Nelson had said, "I will've already been there twict and I ain't but ten."

Mr. Head had contradicted him.

"If you ain't been there in fifteen years, how you know you'll be able to find your way about?" Nelson had asked. "How you know it hasn't changed some?"

"Have you ever," Mr. Head had asked, "seen me lost?"

Nelson certainly had not but he was a child who was never satisfied until he had given an impudent answer and he replied, "It's nowhere around here to get lost at."

"The day is going to come," Mr. Head prophesied, "when you'll find you ain't as smart as you think you are." He had been thinking about this trip for several months but it was for the most part in moral terms that he conceived it. It was to be a lesson that the boy would never forget. He was to find out from it that he had no cause for pride merely because he had been born in a city. He was to find out that the city is not a great place. Mr. Head meant him to see everything there is to see in a city so that he would be content to stay at home for the rest of his life. He fell asleep thinking how the boy would at last find out that he was not as smart as he thought he was.

He was awakened at three-thirty by the smell of fatback frying and he leaped off his cot. The pallet was empty and the clothes boxes had been thrown open. He put on his trousers and ran into the other room. The boy had a corn pone on cooking and had fried the meat. He was sitting in the half-dark at the table, drinking cold coffee out of a can. He had on his new suit and his new gray hat pulled low over his eyes. It was too big for him but they had ordered it a size large because they expected his head to grow. He didn't say anything but his entire figure suggested satisfaction at having arisen before Mr. Head.

Mr. Head went to the stove and brought the meat to the table in the skillet. "It's no hurry," he said. "You'll get there soon enough and it's no guarantee you'll like it when you do neither," and he sat down across from the boy whose hat teetered back slowly to reveal a fiercely expressionless face, very much the same shape as the old man's. They were grandfather and grandson but they looked enough alike to be brothers and brothers not too far apart in age, for Mr. Head had a youthful expression by daylight, while the boy's look was ancient, as if he knew everything already and would be pleased to forget it.

Mr. Head had once had a wife and daughter and when the wife died, the daughter ran away and returned after an interval with Nelson. Then one morning, without getting out of bed, she died and left Mr. Head with sole care of the year-old child. He had made the mistake of telling Nelson that he had been born in Atlanta. If he hadn't told him that, Nelson couldn't have insisted that this was going to be his second trip.

"You may not like it a bit," Mr. Head continued. "It'll be full of niggers."

The boy made a face as if he could handle a nigger.

"All right," Mr. Head said. "You ain't ever seen a nigger."

"You wasn't up very early," Nelson said.

"You ain't ever seen a nigger," Mr. Head repeated. "There hasn't been a nigger in this county since we run that one out twelve years ago and that was before you were born." He looked at the boy as if he were daring him to say he had ever seen a Negro.

"How you know I never saw a nigger when I lived there before?" Nelson asked. "I probably saw a lot of niggers."

"If you seen one you didn't know what he was," Mr. Head said, completely exasperated. "A six-month-old child don't know a nigger from anybody else."

"I reckon I'll know a nigger if I see one," the boy said and got up and straightened his slick sharply creased gray hat and went outside to the privy.

They reached the junction some time before the train was due to arrive and stood about two feet from the first set of tracks. Mr. Head carried a paper sack with some biscuits and a can of sardines in it for their lunch. A coarse-looking orange-colored sun coming up behind the east range of mountains was making the sky a dull red behind them, but in front of them it was still gray and they faced a gray transparent moon, hardly stronger than a thumbprint and completely without light. A small tin switch box and a black fuel tank were all there was to mark the place as a junction; the tracks were double and did not converge again until they were hidden behind the bends at either end of the clearing. Trains passing appeared to emerge from a tunnel of trees and, hit for a second by the cold sky, vanish terrified into the woods again. Mr. Head had had to make special arrangements with the ticket agent to have this train stop and he was secretly afraid it would not, in which case, he knew Nelson would say, "I never thought no train was going to stop for you." Under the useless morning moon the tracks looked white and fragile. Both the old man and the child stared ahead as if they were awaiting an apparition.

Then suddenly, before Mr. Head could make up his mind to turn back, there was a deep warning bleat and the train appeared, gliding very slowly, almost silently around the bend of trees about two hundred yards down the track, with one yellow front light shining. Mr. Head was still not certain it would stop and he felt it would make an even bigger idiot of him if it went by slowly. Both he and Nelson, however, were prepared to ignore the train if it passed them.

The engine charged by, filling their noses with the smell of hot metal and then the second coach came to a stop exactly where they were standing. A conductor with the face of an ancient bloated bulldog was on the step as if he expected them, though he did not look as if it mattered one way or the other to him if they got on or not. "To the right," he said.

Their entry took only a fraction of a second and the train was already speeding on as they entered the quiet car. Most of the travelers were still sleeping, some with their heads hanging off the chair arms, some stretched across two seats, and some sprawled out with their feet in the aisle. Mr. Head saw two unoccupied seats and pushed Nelson toward them. "Get in there by the winder," he said in his normal voice which was very loud at this hour of the morning. "Nobody cares if you sit there because it's nobody in it. Sit right there."

"I heard you," the boy muttered. "It's no use in you yelling," and he sat down and turned his head to the glass. There he saw a pale ghost-like face scowling at him beneath the brim of a pale ghost-like hat. His grandfather, looking quickly too, saw a different ghost, pale but grinning, under a black hat.

Mr. Head sat down and settled himself and took out his ticket and started reading aloud everything that was printed on it. People began to stir. Several woke up and stared at him. "Take off your hat," he said to Nelson and took off his own and put it on his knee. He had a small amount of white hair that had turned tobacco-colored over the years and this lay flat across the back of his head. The front of his head was bald and creased. Nelson took off his hat and put it on his knee and they waited for the conductor to come ask for their tickets.

The man across the aisle from them was spread out over two seats, his feet propped on the window and his head jutting into the aisle. He had on a light blue suit and a yellow shirt unbuttoned at the neck. His eyes had just opened and Mr. Head was ready to introduce himself when the conductor came up from behind and growled, "Tickets."

When the conductor had gone, Mr. Head gave Nelson the return half of his ticket and said, "Now put that in your pocket and don't lose it or you'll have to stay in the city."

"Maybe I will," Nelson said as if this were a reasonable suggestion.

Mr. Head ignored him. "First time this boy has ever been on a train," he explained to the man across the aisle, who was sitting up now on the edge of his seat with both feet on the floor.

Nelson jerked his hat on again and turned angrily to the window.

"He's never seen anything before," Mr. Head continued. "Ignorant as the day he was born, but I mean for him to get his fill once and for all."

The boy leaned forward, across his grandfather and toward the stranger. "I was born in the city," he said. "I was born there. This is my second trip." He said it in a high positive voice but the man across the aisle didn't look as if he understood. There were heavy purple circles under his eyes.

Mr. Head reached across the aisle and tapped him on the arm. "The thing to do with a boy," he said sagely, "is to show him all it is to show. Don't hold nothing back."

"Yeah," the man said. He gazed down at his swollen feet and lifted the left one about ten inches from the floor. After a minute he put it down and lifted the other. All through the car people began to get up and move about and yawn and stretch. Separate voices could be heard here and there and then a general hum. Suddenly Mr. Head's serene expression changed. His mouth almost closed and a light, fierce and cautious both, came into his eyes. He was looking down the length of the car. Without turning, he caught Nelson by the arm and pulled him forward. "Look," he said.

A huge coffee-colored man was coming slowly forward. He had on a light suit and a yellow satin tie with a ruby pin in it. One of his hands rested on his stomach which rode majestically under his buttoned coat, and in the other he held the head of a black walking stick that he picked up and set down with a deliberate outward motion each time he took a step. He was proceeding very slowly, his large brown eyes gazing over the heads of the passengers. He had a small white mustache and white crinkly hair. Behind him there were two young women, both coffee-colored, one in a yellow dress and one in a green. Their progress was kept at the rate of his and they chatted in low throaty voices as they followed him.

Mr. Head's grip was tightening insistently on Nelson's arm. As the procession passed them, the light from a sapphire ring on the brown hand that picked up the cane reflected in Mr. Head's eye, but he did not look up nor did the tremendous man look at him. The group proceeded up the rest of the aisle and out of the car. Mr. Head's grip on Nelson's arm loosened. "What was that?" he asked.

"A man," the boy said and gave him an indignant look as if he were tired of having his intelligence insulted.

"What kind of a man?" Mr. Head persisted, his voice expressionless.

"A fat man," Nelson said. He was beginning to feel that he had better be cautious.

"You don't know what kind?" Mr. Head said in a final tone.

"An old man," the boy said and had a sudden foreboding that he was not going to enjoy the day.

"That was a nigger," Mr. Head said and sat back.

Nelson jumped up on the seat and stood looking backward to the end of the car but the Negro had gone.

"I'd of thought you'd know a nigger since you seen so many when you was in the city on your first visit," Mr. Head continued. "That's his first nigger," he said to the man across the aisle.

The boy slid down into the seat. "You said they were black," he said in an angry voice. "You never said they were tan. How do you expect me to know anything when you don't tell me right?"

"You're just ignorant is all," Mr. Head said and he got up and moved over in the vacant seat by the man across the aisle.

Nelson turned backward again and looked where the Negro had disappeared. He felt that the Negro had deliberately walked down the aisle in order to make a fool of him and he hated him with a fierce raw fresh hate; and also, he understood now why his grandfather disliked them. He looked toward the window and the face there seemed to suggest that he might be inadequate to the day's exactions. He wondered if he would even recognize the city when they came to it.

After he had told several stories, Mr. Head realized that the man he was talking to was asleep and he got up and suggested to Nelson that they walk over the train and see the parts of it. He particularly wanted the boy to see the toilet so they went first to the men's room and examined the plumbing. Mr. Head demonstrated the ice-water cooler as if he had invented it and showed Nelson the bowl with the single spigot where the travelers brushed their teeth. They went through several cars and came to the diner.

This was the most elegant car in the train. It was painted a rich egg-yellow and had a wine-colored carpet on the floor. There were wide windows over the tables and great spaces of the rolling view were caught in miniature in the sides of the coffee pots and in the glasses. Three very black Negroes in white suits and aprons were running up and down the aisle, swinging trays and bowing and bending over the travelers eating breakfast. One of them rushed up to Mr. Head and Nelson and said, holding up two fingers, "Space for two!" but Mr. Head replied in a loud voice, "We eaten before we left!"

The waiter wore large brown spectacles that increased the size of his eye whites. "Stan' aside then please," he said with an airy wave of the arm as if he were brushing aside flies.

Neither Nelson nor Mr. Head moved a fraction of an inch. "Look," Mr. Head said.

The near corner of the diner, containing two tables, was set off from the rest by a saffron-colored curtain. One table was set but empty but at the other, facing them, his back to the drape, sat the tremendous Negro. He was speaking in a soft voice to the two women while he buttered a muffin. He had a heavy sad face and his neck bulged over his white collar on either side. "They rope them off," Mr. Head explained. Then he said, "Let's go see the kitchen," and they walked the length of the diner but the black waiter was coming fast behind them.

"Passengers are not allowed in the kitchen!" he said in a haughty voice. "Passengers are NOT allowed in the kitchen!"

Mr. Head stopped where he was and turned. "And there's good reason for that," he shouted into the Negro's chest, "because the cockroaches would run the passengers out!"

All the travelers laughed and Mr. Head and Nelson walked out, grinning. Mr. Head was known at home for his quick wit and Nelson felt a sudden keen pride in him. He realized the old man would be his only support in the strange place they were approaching. He would be entirely alone in the world if he were ever lost from his grandfather. A terrible excitement shook him and he wanted to take hold of Mr. Head's coat and hold on like a child.

As they went back to their seats they could see through the passing windows that the countryside was becoming speckled with small houses and shacks and that a highway ran alongside the train. Cars sped by on it, very small and fast. Nelson felt that there was less breath in the air than there had been thirty minutes ago. The man across the aisle had left and there was no one near for Mr. Head to hold a conversation with so he looked out the window, through his own reflection, and read aloud the names of the buildings they were passing. "The Dixie Chemical Corp!" he announced. "Southern Maid Flour! Dixie Doors! Southern Belle Cotton Products! Patty's Peanut Butter! Southern Mammy Cane Syrup!"

"Hush up!" Nelson hissed.

All over the car people were beginning to get up and take their luggage off the overhead racks. Women were putting on their coats and hats. The conductor stuck his head in the car and snarled, "Firstopppppmry," and Nelson lunged out of his sitting position, trembling. Mr. Head pushed him down by the shoulder.

"Keep your seat," he said in dignified tones. "The first stop is on the edge of town. The second stop is at the main railroad station." He had come by this knowledge on his first trip when he had got off at the first stop and had had to pay a man fifteen cents to take him into the heart of town. Nelson sat back down, very pale. For the first time in his life, he understood that his grandfather was indispensable to him.

The train stopped and let off a few passengers and glided on as if it had never ceased moving. Outside, behind rows of brown rickety houses, a line of blue buildings stood up, and beyond them a pale rose-gray sky faded away to nothing. The train moved into the railroad yard. Looking down, Nelson saw lines and lines of silver tracks multiplying and crisscrossing. Then before he could start counting them, the face in the window started out at him, gray but distinct, and he looked the other way. The train was in the station. Both he and Mr. Head jumped up and ran to the door. Neither noticed that they had left the paper sack with the lunch in it on the seat.

They walked stiffly through the small station and came out of a heavy door into the squall of traffic. Crowds were hurrying to work. Nelson didn't know where to look. Mr. Head leaned against the side of the building and glared in front of him.

Finally Nelson said, "Well, how do you see what all it is to see?"

Mr. Head didn't answer. Then as if the sight of people passing had given him the clue, he said, "You walk," and started off down the street. Nelson followed, steadying his hat. So many sights and sounds were flooding in on him that for the first block he hardly knew what he was seeing. At the second corner, Mr. Head turned and looked behind him at the station they had left, a putty-colored terminal with a concrete dome on top. He thought that if he could keep the dome always in sight, he would be able to get back in the afternoon to catch the train again.

As they walked along, Nelson began to distinguish details and take note of the store windows, jammed with every kind of equipment—hardware, drygoods, chicken feed, liquor. They passed one that Mr. Head called his particular attention to where you walked in and sat on a chair with your feet upon two rests and let a Negro polish your shoes. They walked slowly and stopped and stood at the entrances so he could see what went on in each place but they did not go into any of them. Mr. Head was determined not to go into any city store because on his first trip here, he had got lost in a large one and had found his way out only after many people had insulted him.

They came in the middle of the next block to a store that had a weighing machine in front of it and they both in turn stepped up on it and put in a penny and received a ticket. Mr. Head's ticket said, "You weigh 120 pounds. You are upright and brave and all your friends admire you." He put the ticket in his pocket, surprised that the machine should have got his character correct but his weight wrong, for he had weighed on a grain scale not long before and knew he weighed 110. Nelson's ticket said, "You weigh 98 pounds. You have a great destiny ahead of you but beware of dark women." Nelson did not know any women and he weighed only 68 pounds but Mr. Head pointed out that the machine had probably printed the number upsidedown, meaning the 9 for a 6.

They walked on and at the end of five blocks the dome of the terminal sank out of sight and Mr. Head turned to the left. Nelson could have stood in front of every store window for an hour if there had not been another more interesting one next to it. Suddenly he said, "I was born here!" Mr. Head turned and looked at him with horror. There was a sweaty brightness about his face. "This is where I come from!" he said.

Mr. Head was appalled. He saw the moment had come for drastic action. "Lemme show you one thing you ain't seen yet," he said and took him to the corner where there was a sewer entrance. "Squat down," he said, "and stick your head in there," and he held the back of the boy's coat while he got down and put his head in the sewer. He drew it back quickly, hearing a gurgling in the depths under the sidewalk. Then Mr. Head explained the sewer system, how the entire city was underlined with it, how it contained all the drainage and was full of rats and how a man could slide into it and be sucked along down endless pitchblack tunnels. At any minute any man in the city might be sucked into the sewer and never heard from again. He described it so well that Nelson was for some seconds shaken. He connected the sewer passages with the entrance to hell and understood for the first time how the world was put together in its lower parts. He drew away from the curb.

Then he said, "Yes, but you can stay away from the holes," and his face took on that stubborn look that was so exasperating to his grandfather. "This is where I come from!" he said.

Mr. Head was dismayed but he only muttered, "You'll get your fill," and they walked on. At the end of two more blocks he turned to the left, feeling that he was circling the dome; and he was correct for in a half-hour they passed in front of the railroad station again. At first Nelson did not notice that he was seeing the same stores twice but when they passed the one where you put your feet on the rests while the Negro polished your shoes, he perceived that they were walking in a circle.

"We done been here!" he shouted. "I don't believe you know where you're at!"

"The direction just slipped my mind for a minute," Mr. Head said and they turned down a different street. He still did not intend to let the dome get too far away and after two blocks in their new direction, he turned to the left. This street contained two- and three-story wooden dwellings. Anyone passing on the sidewalk could see into the rooms and Mr. Head, glancing through one window, saw a woman lying on an iron bed, looking out, with a sheet pulled over her. Her knowing expression shook him. A fierce-looking boy on a bicycle came driving down out of nowhere and he had to jump to the side to keep from being hit. "It's nothing to them if they knock you down," he said. "You better keep closer to me."

They walked on for some time on streets like this before he remembered to turn again. The houses they were passing now were all unpainted and the wood in them looked rotten; the street between was narrower. Nelson saw a colored man. Then another. Then another. "Niggers live in these houses," he observed.

"Well come on and we'll go somewheres else," Mr. Head said. "We didn't come to look at niggers," and they turned down another street but they continued to see Negroes everywhere. Nelson's skin began to prickle and they stepped along at a faster pace in order to leave the neighborhood as soon as possible. There were colored men in their undershirts standing in the doors and colored women rocking on the sagging porches. Colored children played in the gutters and stopped what they were doing to look at them. Before long they began to pass rows of stores with colored customers in them but they didn't pause at the entrances of these. Black eyes in black faces were watching them from every direction. "Yes," Mr. Head said, "this is where you were born—right here with all these niggers."

Nelson scowled. "I think you done got us lost," he said.

Mr. Head swung around sharply and looked for the dome. It was nowhere in sight. "I ain't got us lost either," he said. "You're just tired of walking."

"I ain't tired, I'm hungry," Nelson said. "Give me a biscuit."

They discovered then that they had lost the lunch.

"You were the one holding the sack," Nelson said. "I would have kepaholt of it."

"If you want to direct this trip, I'll go on by myself and leave you right here," Mr. Head said and was pleased to see the boy turn white. However, he realized they were lost and drifting farther every minute from the station. He was hungry himself and beginning to be thirsty and since they had been in the colored neighborhood, they had both begun to sweat. Nelson had on his shoes and he was unaccustomed to them. The concrete sidewalks were very hard. They both wanted to find a place to sit down but this was impossible and they kept on walking, the boy muttering under his breath, "First you lost the sack and then you lost the way," and Mr. Head growling from time to time, "Anybody wants to be from this nigger heaven can be from it!"

By now the sun was well forward in the sky. The odor of dinners cooking drifted out to them. The Negroes were all at their doors to see them pass. "Whyn't you ast one of these niggers the way?" Nelson said. "You got us lost."

"This is where you were born," Mr. Head said. "You can ast one yourself if you want to."

Nelson was afraid of the colored men and he didn't want to be laughed at by the colored children. Up ahead he saw a large colored woman leaning in a doorway that opened onto the sidewalk. Her hair stood straight out from her head for about four inches all around and she was resting on bare brown feet that turned pink at the sides. She had on a pink dress that showed her exact shape. As they came abreast of her, she lazily lifted one hand to her head and her fingers disappeared into her hair.

Nelson stopped. He felt his breath drawn up by the woman's dark eyes. "How do you get back to town?" he said in a voice that did not sound like his own.

After a minute she said, "You in town now," in a rich low tone that made Nelson feel as if a cool spray had been turned on him.

"How do you get back to the train?" he said in the same reed-like voice.

"You can catch you a car," she said.

He understood she was making fun of him but he was too paralyzed even to scowl. He stood drinking in every detail of her. His eyes traveled up from her great knees to her forehead and then made a triangular path from the glistening sweat on her neck down and across her tremendous bosom and over her bare arm back to where her fingers lay hidden in her hair. He suddenly wanted her to reach down and pick him up and draw him against her and then he wanted to feel her breath on his face. He wanted to look down and down into her eyes while she held him tighter and tighter. He had never had such a feeling before. He felt as if he were reeling down through a pitchblack tunnel.

"You can go a block down yonder and catch you a car take you to the railroad station, Sugarpie," she said.

Nelson would have collapsed at her feet if Mr. Head had not pulled him roughly away. "You act like you don't have any sense!" the old man growled.

They hurried down the street and Nelson did not look back at the woman. He pushed his hat sharply forward over his face which was already burning with shame. The sneering ghost he had seen in the train window and all the foreboding feelings he had on the way returned to him and he remembered that his ticket from the scale had said to beware of dark women and that his grandfather's had said he was upright and brave. He took hold of the old man's hand, a sign of dependence that he seldom showed.

They headed down the street toward the car tracks where a long yellow rattling trolley was coming. Mr. Head had never boarded a streetcar and he let that one pass. Nelson was silent. From time to time his mouth trembled slightly but his grandfather, occupied with his own problems, paid him no attention. They stood on the corner and neither looked at the Negroes who were passing, going about their business just as if they had been white, except that most of them stopped and eyed Mr. Head and Nelson. It occurred to Mr. Head that since the streetcar ran on tracks, they could simply follow the tracks. He gave Nelson a slight push and explained that they would follow the tracks on into the railroad station, walking, and they set off.

Presently to their great relief they began to see white people again and Nelson sat down on the sidewalk against the wall of a building. "I got to rest myself some," he said. "You lost the sack and the direction. You can just wait on me to rest myself."

"There's the tracks in front of us," Mr. Head said. "All we got to do is keep them in sight and you could have remembered the sack as good as me. This is where you were born. This is your old home town. This is your second trip. You ought to know how to do," and he squatted down and continued in this vein but the boy, easing his burning feet out of his shoes, did not answer.

"And standing there grinning like a chim-pan-zee while a nigger woman gives you directions. Great Gawd!" Mr. Head said.

"I never said I was nothing but born here," the boy said in a shaky voice. "I never said I would or wouldn't like it. I never said I wanted to come. I only said I was born here and I never had nothing to do with that. I want to go home. I never wanted to come in the first place. It was all your big idea. How you know you ain't following the tracks in the wrong direction?"

This last had occurred to Mr. Head too. "All these people are white," he said.

"We ain't passed here before," Nelson said. This was a neighborhood of brick buildings that might have been lived in or might not. A few empty automobiles were parked along the curb and there was an occasional passerby. The heat of the pavement came up through Nelson's thin suit. His eyelids began to droop, and after a few minutes his head tilted forward. His shoulders twitched once or twice and then he fell over on his side and lay sprawled in an exhausted fit of sleep.

Mr. Head watched him silently. He was very tired himself but they could not both sleep at the same time and he could not have slept anyway because he did not know where he

was. In a few minutes Nelson would wake up, refreshed by
his sleep and very cocky, and would begin complaining that
he had lost the sack and the way. You'd have a mighty sorry
time if I wasn't here, Mr. Head thought; and then another
idea occurred to him. He looked at the sprawled figure for
several minutes; presently he stood up. He justified what he
was going to do on the grounds that it is sometimes necessary
to teach a child a lesson he won't forget, particularly when
the child is always reasserting his position with some new
impudence. He walked without a sound to the corner about
twenty feet away and sat down on a covered garbage can in
the alley where he could look out and watch Nelson wake up
alone.

The boy was dozing fitfully, half conscious of vague noises
and black forms moving up from some dark part of him into
the light. His face worked in his sleep and he had pulled his
knees up under his chin. The sun shed a dull dry light on the
narrow street; everything looked like exactly what it was.
After a while Mr. Head, hunched like an old monkey on the
garbage can lid, decided that if Nelson didn't wake up soon,
he would make a loud noise by bamming his foot against the
can. He looked at his watch and discovered that it was two
o'clock. Their train left at six and the possibility of missing it
was too awful for him to think of. He kicked his foot backwards on the can and a hollow boom reverberated in the
alley.

Nelson shot up onto his feet with a shout. He looked
where his grandfather should have been and stared. He
seemed to whirl several times and then, picking up his feet
and throwing his head back, he dashed down the street like a
wild maddened pony. Mr. Head jumped off the can and galloped after but the child was almost out of sight. He saw a
streak of gray disappearing diagonally a block ahead. He ran
as fast as he could, looking both ways down every intersection, but without sight of him again. Then as he passed the
third intersection, completely winded, he saw about half a
block down the street a scene that stopped him altogether. He
crouched behind a trash box to watch and get his bearings.

Nelson was sitting with both legs spread out and by his
side lay an elderly woman, screaming. Groceries were scat-

tered about the sidewalk. A crowd of women had already gathered to see justice done and Mr. Head distinctly heard the old woman on the pavement shout, "You've broken my ankle and your daddy'll pay for it! Every nickel! Police! Police!" Several of the women were plucking at Nelson's shoulder but the boy seemed too dazed to get up.

Something forced Mr. Head from behind the trash box and forward, but only at a creeping pace. He had never in his life been accosted by a policeman. The women were milling around Nelson as if they might suddenly all dive on him at once and tear him to pieces, and the old woman continued to scream that her ankle was broken and to call for an officer. Mr. Head came on so slowly that he could have been taking a backward step after each forward one, but when he was about ten feet away, Nelson saw him and sprang. The child caught him around the hips and clung panting against him.

The women all turned on Mr. Head. The injured one sat up and shouted, "You sir! You'll pay every penny of my doctor's bill that your boy has caused. He's a juve-nile delinquent! Where is an officer? Somebody take this man's name and address!"

Mr. Head was trying to detach Nelson's fingers from the flesh in the back of his legs. The old man's head had lowered itself into his collar like a turtle's; his eyes were glazed with fear and caution.

"Your boy has broken my ankle!" the old woman shouted. "Police!"

Mr. Head sensed the approach of the policeman from behind. He stared straight ahead at the women who were massed in their fury like a solid wall to block his escape. "This is not my boy," he said. "I never seen him before."

He felt Nelson's fingers fall out of his flesh.

The women dropped back, staring at him with horror, as if they were so repulsed by a man who would deny his own image and likeness that they could not bear to lay hands on him. Mr. Head walked on, through a space they silently cleared, and left Nelson behind. Ahead of him he saw nothing but a hollow tunnel that had once been the street.

The boy remained standing where he was, his neck craned forward and his hands hanging by his sides. His hat was jammed on his head so that there were no longer any creases in it. The injured woman got up and shook her fist at him and the others gave him pitying looks, but he didn't notice any of them. There was no policeman in sight.

In a minute he began to move mechanically, making no effort to catch up with his grandfather but merely following at about twenty paces. They walked on for five blocks in this way. Mr. Head's shoulders were sagging and his neck hung forward at such an angle that it was not visible from behind. He was afraid to turn his head. Finally he cut a short hopeful glance over his shoulder. Twenty feet behind him, he saw two small eyes piercing into his back like pitchfork prongs.

The boy was not of a forgiving nature but this was the first time he had ever had anything to forgive. Mr. Head had never disgraced himself before. After two more blocks, he turned and called over his shoulder in a high desperately gay voice, "Let's us go get us a Co' Cola somewheres!"

Nelson, with a dignity he had never shown before, turned and stood with his back to his grandfather.

Mr. Head began to feel the depth of his denial. His face as they walked on became all hollows and bare ridges. He saw nothing they were passing but he perceived that they had lost the car tracks. There was no dome to be seen anywhere and the afternoon was advancing. He knew that if dark overtook them in the city, they would be beaten and robbed. The speed of God's justice was only what he expected for himself, but he could not stand to think that his sins would be visited upon Nelson and that even now, he was leading the boy to his doom.

They continued to walk on block after block through an endless section of small brick houses until Mr. Head almost fell over a water spigot sticking up about six inches off the edge of a grass plot. He had not had a drink of water since early morning but he felt he did not deserve it now. Then he thought that Nelson would be thirsty and they would both drink and be brought together. He squatted down and put his mouth to the nozzle and turned a cold stream of water into his throat. Then he called out in the high desperate voice, "Come on and getcher some water!"

This time the child stared through him for nearly sixty

seconds. Mr. Head got up and walked on as if he had drunk poison. Nelson, though he had not had water since some he had drunk out of a paper cup on the train, passed by the spigot, disdaining to drink where his grandfather had. When Mr. Head realized this, he lost all hope. His face in the waning afternoon light looked ravaged and abandoned. He could feel the boy's steady hate, traveling at an even pace behind him and he knew that (if by some miracle they escaped being murdered in the city) it would continue just that way for the rest of his life. He knew that now he was wandering into a black strange place where nothing was like it had ever been before, a long old age without respect and an end that would be welcome because it would be the end.

As for Nelson, his mind had frozen around his grandfather's treachery as if he were trying to preserve it intact to present at the final judgment. He walked without looking to one side or the other, but every now and then his mouth would twitch and this was when he felt, from some remote place inside himself, a black mysterious form reach up as if it would melt his frozen vision in one hot grasp.

The sun dropped down behind a row of houses and hardly noticing, they passed into an elegant suburban section where mansions were set back from the road by lawns with bird-baths on them. Here everything was entirely deserted. For blocks they didn't pass even a dog. The big white houses were like partially submerged icebergs in the distance. There were no sidewalks, only drives, and these wound around and around in endless ridiculous circles. Nelson made no move to come nearer to Mr. Head. The old man felt that if he saw a sewer entrance he would drop down into it and let himself be carried away; and he could imagine the boy standing by, watching with only a slight interest, while he disappeared.

A loud bark jarred him to attention and he looked up to see a fat man approaching with two bulldogs. He waved both arms like someone shipwrecked on a desert island. "I'm lost!" he called. "I'm lost and can't find my way and me and this boy have got to catch this train and I can't find the station. Oh Gawd I'm lost! Oh hep me Gawd I'm lost!"

The man, who was bald-headed and had on golf knickers, asked him what train he was trying to catch and Mr. Head began to get out his tickets, trembling so violently he could hardly hold them. Nelson had come up to within fifteen feet and stood watching.

"Well," the fat man said, giving him back the tickets, "you won't have time to get back to town to make this but you can catch it at the suburb stop. That's three blocks from here," and he began explaining how to get there.

Mr. Head stared as if he were slowly returning from the dead and when the man had finished and gone off with the dogs jumping at his heels, he turned to Nelson and said breathlessly, "We're going to get home!"

The child was standing about ten feet away, his face bloodless under the gray hat. His eyes were triumphantly cold. There was no light in them, no feeling, no interest. He was merely there, a small figure, waiting. Home was nothing to him.

Mr. Head turned slowly. He felt he knew now what time would be like without seasons and what heat would be like without light and what man would be like without salvation. He didn't care if he never made the train and if it had not been for what suddenly caught his attention, like a cry out of the gathering dusk, he might have forgotten there was a station to go to.

He had not walked five hundred yards down the road when he saw, within reach of him, the plaster figure of a Negro sitting bent over on a low yellow brick fence that curved around a wide lawn. The Negro was about Nelson's size and he was pitched forward at an unsteady angle because the putty that held him to the wall had cracked. One of his eyes was entirely white and he held a piece of brown watermelon.

Mr. Head stood looking at him silently until Nelson stopped at a little distance. Then as the two of them stood there, Mr. Head breathed, "An artificial nigger!"

It was not possible to tell if the artificial Negro were meant to be young or old; he looked too miserable to be either. He was meant to look happy because his mouth was stretched up at the corners but the chipped eye and the angle he was cocked at gave him a wild look of misery instead.

"An artificial nigger!" Nelson repeated in Mr. Head's exact tone.

The two of them stood there with their necks forward at almost the same angle and their shoulders curved in almost exactly the same way and their hands trembling identically in their pockets. Mr. Head looked like an ancient child and Nelson like a miniature old man. They stood gazing at the artificial Negro as if they were faced with some great mystery, some monument to another's victory that brought them together in their common defeat. They could both feel it dissolving their differences like an action of mercy. Mr. Head had never known before what mercy felt like because he had been too good to deserve any, but he felt he knew now. He looked at Nelson and understood that he must say something to the child to show that he was still wise and in the look the boy returned he saw a hungry need for that assurance. Nelson's eyes seemed to implore him to explain once and for all the mystery of existence.

Mr. Head opened his lips to make a lofty statement and heard himself say, "They ain't got enough real ones here. They got to have an artificial one."

After a second, the boy nodded with a strange shivering about his mouth, and said, "Let's go home before we get ourselves lost again."

Their train glided into the suburb stop just as they reached the station and they boarded it together, and ten minutes before it was due to arrive at the junction, they went to the door and stood ready to jump off if it did not stop; but it did, just as the moon, restored to its full splendor, sprang from a cloud and flooded the clearing with light. As they stepped off, the sage grass was shivering gently in shades of silver and the clinkers under their feet glittered with a fresh black light. The treetops, fencing the junction like the protecting walls of a garden, were darker than the sky which was hung with gigantic white clouds illuminated like lanterns.

Mr. Head stood very still and felt the action of mercy touch him again but this time he knew that there were no words in the world that could name it. He understood that it grew out of agony, which is not denied to any man and which is given in strange ways to children. He understood it was all a man could carry into death to give his Maker and he suddenly burned with shame that he had so little of it to take with him.

He stood appalled, judging himself with the thoroughness of God, while the action of mercy covered his pride like a flame and consumed it. He had never thought himself a great sinner before but he saw now that his true depravity had been hidden from him lest it cause him despair. He realized that he was forgiven for sins from the beginning of time, when he had conceived in his own heart the sin of Adam, until the present, when he had denied poor Nelson. He saw that no sin was too monstrous for him to claim as his own, and since God loved in proportion as He forgave, he felt ready at that instant to enter Paradise.

Nelson, composing his expression under the shadow of his hat brim, watched him with a mixture of fatigue and suspicion, but as the train glided past them and disappeared like a frightened serpent into the woods, even his face lightened and he muttered, "I'm glad I've went once, but I'll never go back again!"

A Circle in the Fire

S OMETIMES the last line of trees was a solid gray blue wall a little darker than the sky but this afternoon it was almost black and behind it the sky was a livid glaring white. "You know that woman that had that baby in that iron lung?" Mrs. Pritchard said. She and the child's mother were underneath the window the child was looking down from. Mrs. Pritchard was leaning against the chimney, her arms folded on a shelf of stomach, one foot crossed and the toe pointed into the ground. She was a large woman with a small pointed face and steady ferreting eyes. Mrs. Cope was the opposite, very small and trim, with a large round face and black eyes that seemed to be enlarging all the time behind her glasses as if she were continually being astonished. She was squatting down pulling grass out of the border beds around the house. Both women had on sunhats that had once been identical but now Mrs. Pritchard's was faded and out of shape while Mrs. Cope's was still stiff and bright green.

"I read about her," she said.

"She was a Pritchard that married a Brookins and so's kin to me—about my seventh or eighth cousin by marriage."

"Well, well," Mrs. Cope muttered and threw a large clump of nut grass behind her. She worked at the weeds and nut grass as if they were an evil sent directly by the devil to destroy the place.

"Beinst she was kin to us, we gone to see the body," Mrs. Pritchard said. "Seen the little baby too."

Mrs. Cope didn't say anything. She was used to these calamitous stories; she said they wore her to a frazzle. Mrs. Pritchard would go thirty miles for the satisfaction of seeing anybody laid away. Mrs. Cope always changed the subject to something cheerful but the child had observed that this only put Mrs. Pritchard in a bad humor.

The child thought the blank sky looked as if it were pushing against the fortress wall, trying to break through. The trees across the near field were a patchwork of gray and yellow greens. Mrs. Cope was always worrying about fires in her woods. When the nights were very windy, she would say to the child, "Oh Lord, do pray there won't be any fires, it's so windy," and the child would grunt from behind her book or not answer at all because she heard it so often. In the evenings in the summer when they sat on the porch, Mrs. Cope would say to the child who was reading fast to catch the last light, "Get up and look at the sunset, it's gorgeous. You ought to get up and look at it," and the child would scowl and not answer or glare up once across the lawn and two front pastures to the gray-blue sentinel line of trees and then begin to read again with no change of expression, sometimes muttering for meanness, "It looks like a fire. You better get up and smell around and see if the woods ain't on fire."

"She had her arm around it in the coffin," Mrs. Pritchard went on, but her voice was drowned out by the sound of the tractor that the Negro, Culver, was driving up the road from the barn. The wagon was attached and another Negro was sitting in the back, bouncing, his feet jogging about a foot from the ground. The one on the tractor drove it past the gate that led into the field on the left.

Mrs. Cope turned her head and saw that he had not gone through the gate because he was too lazy to get off and open it. He was going the long way around at her expense. "Tell him to stop and come here!" she shouted.

Mrs. Pritchard heaved herself from the chimney and waved her arm in a fierce circle but he pretended not to hear. She stalked to the edge of the lawn and screamed, "Get off, I toljer! She wants you!"

He got off and started toward the chimney, pushing his head and shoulders forward at each step to give the appearance of hurrying. His head was thrust up to the top in a white cloth hat streaked with different shades of sweat. The brim was down and hid all but the lower parts of his reddish eyes.

Mrs. Cope was on her knees, pointing the trowel into the ground. "Why aren't you going through the gate there?" she asked and waited, her eyes shut and her mouth stretched flat as if she were prepared for any ridiculous answer.

"Got to raise the blade on the mower if we do," he said and his gaze bore just to the left of her. Her Negroes were as destructive and impersonal as the nut grass.

Her eyes, as she opened them, looked as if they would keep on enlarging until they turned her wrongsideout. "Raise it," she said and pointed across the road with the trowel.

He moved off.

"It's nothing to them," she said. "They don't have the responsibility. I thank the Lord all these things don't come at once. They'd destroy me."

"Yeah, they would," Mrs. Pritchard shouted against the sound of the tractor. He opened the gate and raised the blade and drove through and down into the field; the noise diminished as the wagon disappeared. "I don't see myself how she had it *in* it," she went on in her normal voice.

Mrs. Cope was bent over, digging fiercely at the nut grass again. "We have a lot to be thankful for," she said. "Every day you should say a prayer of thanksgiving. Do you do that?"

"Yes'm," Mrs. Pritchard said. "See she was in it four months before she even got thataway. Look like to me if I was in one of them, I would leave off . . . how you reckon they . . . ?"

"Every day I say a prayer of thanksgiving," Mrs. Cope said. "Think of all we have. Lord," she said and sighed, "we have everything," and she looked around at her rich pastures and hills heavy with timber and shook her head as if it might all be a burden she was trying to shake off her back.

Mrs. Pritchard studied the woods. "All I got is four abscess teeth," she remarked.

"Well, be thankful you don't have five," Mrs. Cope snapped and threw back a clump of grass. "We might all be destroyed by a hurricane. I can always find something to be thankful for."

Mrs. Pritchard took up a hoe resting against the side of the house and struck lightly at a weed that had come up between two bricks in the chimney. "I reckon *you* can," she said, her voice a little more nasal than usual with contempt.

"Why, think of all those poor Europeans," Mrs. Cope went on, "that they put in boxcars like cattle and rode them to Siberia. Lord," she said, "we ought to spend half our time on our knees."

"I know if I was in an iron lung there would be some

things I wouldn't do," Mrs. Pritchard said, scratching her bare ankle with the end of the hoe.

"Even that poor woman had plenty to be thankful for," Mrs. Cope said.

"She could be thankful she wasn't dead."

"Certainly," Mrs. Cope said, and then she pointed the trowel up at Mrs. Pritchard and said, "I have the best kept place in the county and do you know why? Because I work. I've had to work to save this place and work to keep it." She emphasized each word with the trowel. "I don't let anything get ahead of me and I'm not always looking for trouble. I take it as it comes."

"If it all come at oncet sometime," Mrs. Pritchard began.

"It doesn't all come at once," Mrs. Cope said sharply.

The child could see over to where the dirt road joined the highway. She saw a pick-up truck stop at the gate and let off three boys who started walking up the pink dirt road. They walked single file, the middle one bent to the side carrying a black pig-shaped valise.

"Well, if it ever did," Mrs. Pritchard said, "it wouldn't be nothing you could do but fling up your hands."

Mrs. Cope didn't even answer this. Mrs. Pritchard folded her arms and gazed down the road as if she could easily enough see all these fine hills flattened to nothing. She saw the three boys who had almost reached the front walk by now. "Lookit yonder," she said. "Who you reckon they are?"

Mrs. Cope leaned back and supported herself with one hand behind her and looked. The three came toward them but as if they were going to walk on through the side of the house. The one with the suitcase was in front now. Finally about four feet from her, he stopped and set it down. The three boys looked something alike except that the middle-sized one wore silver-rimmed spectacles and carried the suitcase. One of his eyes had a slight cast to it so that his gaze seemed to be coming from two directions at once as if it had them surrounded. He had on a sweat shirt with a faded destroyer printed on it but his chest was so hollow that the destroyer was broken in the middle and seemed on the point of going under. His hair was stuck to his forehead with sweat. He looked to be about thirteen. All three boys had white penetrating stares. "I don't reckon you remember me, Mrs. Cope," he said.

"Your face is certainly familiar," she murmured, scrutinizing him. "Now let's see . . ."

"My daddy used to work here," he hinted.

"Boyd?" she said. "Your father was Mr. Boyd and you're J. C.?"

"Nome, I'm Powell, the secont one, only I've growed some since then and my daddy he's daid now. Done died."

"Dead. Well I declare," Mrs. Cope said as if death were always an unusual thing. "What was Mr. Boyd's trouble?"

One of Powell's eyes seemed to be making a circle of the place, examining the house and the white water tower behind it and the chicken houses and the pastures that rolled away on either side until they met the first line of woods. The other eye looked at her. "Died in Florda," he said and began kicking the valise.

"Well I declare," she murmured. After a second she said, "And how is your mother?"

"Mah'd again." He kept watching his foot kick the suitcase. The other two boys stared at her impatiently.

"And where do you all live now?" she asked.

"Atlanta," he said. "You know, out to one of them developments."

"Well I see," she said, "I see." After a second she said it again. Finally she asked, "And who are these other boys?" and smiled at them.

"Garfield Smith him, and W. T. Harper him," he said, nodding his head backward first in the direction of the large boy and then the small one.

"How do you boys do?" Mrs. Cope said. "This is Mrs. Pritchard. Mr. and Mrs. Pritchard work here now."

They ignored Mrs. Pritchard who watched them with steady beady eyes. The three seemed to hang there, waiting, watching Mrs. Cope.

"Well well," she said, glancing at the suitcase, "it's nice of you to stop and see me. I think that was real sweet of you."

Powell's stare seemed to pinch her like a pair of tongs. "Come back to see how you was doing," he said hoarsely.

"Listen here," the smallest boy said, "all the time we been

knowing him he's been telling us about this here place. Said it was everything here. Said it was horses here. Said he had the best time of his entire life right here on this here place. Talks about it all the time."

"Never shuts his trap about this place," the big boy grunted, drawing his arm across his nose as if to muffle his words.

"Always talking about them horses he rid here," the small one continued, "and said he would let us ride them too. Said it was one name Gene."

Mrs. Cope was always afraid someone would get hurt on her place and sue her for everything she had. "They aren't shod," she said quickly. "There was one named Gene but he's dead now but I'm afraid you boys can't ride the horses because you might get hurt. They're dangerous," she said, speaking very fast.

The large boy sat down on the ground with a noise of disgust and began to finger rocks out of his tennis shoe. The small one darted looks here and there and Powell fixed her with his stare and didn't say anything.

After a minute the little boy said, "Say, lady, you know what he said one time? He said when he died he wanted to come here!"

For a second Mrs. Cope looked blank; then she blushed; then a peculiar look of pain came over her face as she realized that these children were hungry. They were staring because they were hungry! She almost gasped in their faces and then she asked them quickly if they would have something to eat. They said they would but their expressions, composed and unsatisfied, didn't lighten any. They looked as if they were used to being hungry and it was no business of hers.

The child upstairs had grown red in the face with excitement. She was kneeling down by the window so that only her eyes and forehead showed over the sill. Mrs. Cope told the boys to come around on the other side of the house where the lawn chairs were and she led the way and Mrs. Pritchard followed. The child moved from the right bedroom across the hall and over into the left bedroom and looked down on the other side of the house where there were three white lawn chairs and a red hammock strung between two hazelnut trees.

She was a pale fat girl of twelve with a frowning squint and a large mouth full of silver bands. She knelt down at the window.

The three boys came around the corner of the house and the large one threw himself into the hammock and lit a stub of cigarette. The small boy tumbled down on the grass next to the black suitcase and rested his head on it and Powell sat down on the edge of one of the chairs and looked as if he were trying to enclose the whole place in one encircling stare. The child heard her mother and Mrs. Pritchard in a muted conference in the kitchen. She got up and went out into the hall and leaned over the banisters.

Mrs. Cope's and Mrs. Pritchard's legs were facing each other in the back hall. "Those poor children are hungry," Mrs. Cope said in a dead voice.

"You seen that suitcase?" Mrs. Pritchard asked. "What if they intend to spend the night with you?"

Mrs. Cope gave a slight shriek. "I can't have three boys in here with only me and Sally Virginia," she said. "I'm sure they'll go when I feed them."

"I only know they got a suitcase," Mrs. Pritchard said.

The child hurried back to the window. The large boy was stretched out in the hammock with his wrists crossed under his head and the cigarette stub in the center of his mouth. He spit it out in an arc just as Mrs. Cope came around the corner of the house with a plate of crackers. She stopped instantly as if a snake had been slung in her path. "Ashfield!" she said. "Please pick that up. I'm afraid of fires."

"Gawfield!" the little boy shouted indignantly. "Gawfield!"

The large boy raised himself without a word and lumbered for the butt. He picked it up and put it in his pocket and stood with his back to her, examining a tattooed heart on his forearm. Mrs. Pritchard came up holding three Coca-Colas by the necks in one hand and gave one to each of them.

"I remember everything about this place," Powell said, looking down the opening of his bottle.

"Where did you all go when you left here?" Mrs. Cope asked and put the plate of crackers on the arm of his chair.

He looked at it but didn't take one. He said, "I remember

it was one name Gene and it was one name George. We gone to Florda and my daddy he, you know, died, and then we gone to my sister's and then my mother she, you know, mah'd, and we been there ever since."

"There are some crackers," Mrs. Cope said and sat down in the chair across from him.

"He don't like it in Atlanta," the little boy said, sitting up and reaching indifferently for a cracker. "He ain't ever satisfied with where he's at except this place here. Lemme tell you what he'll do, lady. We'll be playing ball, see, on this here place in this development we got to play ball on, see, and he'll quit playing and say, 'Goddam, it was a horse down there name Gene and if I had him here I'd bust this concrete to hell riding him!' "

"I'm sure Powell doesn't use words like that, do you, Powell?" Mrs. Cope said.

"No, mam," Powell said. His head was turned completely to the side as if he were listening for the horses in the field.

"I don't like them kind of crackers," the little boy said and returned his to the plate and got up.

Mrs. Cope shifted in her chair. "So you boys live in one of those nice new developments," she said.

"The only way you can tell your own is by smell," the small boy volunteered. "They're four stories high and there's ten of them, one behind the other. Let's go see them horses," he said.

Powell turned his pinching look on Mrs. Cope. "We thought we would just spend the night in your barn," he said. "My uncle brought us this far on his pick-up truck and he's going to stop for us again in the morning."

There was a moment in which she didn't say a thing and the child in the window thought: she's going to fly out of that chair and hit the tree.

"Well, I'm afraid you can't do that," she said, getting up suddenly. "The barn's full of hay and I'm afraid of fire from your cigarettes."

"We won't smoke," he said.

"I'm afraid you can't spend the night in there just the same," she repeated as if she were talking politely to a gangster.

"Well, we can camp out in the woods then," the little boy said. "We brought our own blankets anyways. That's what we got in thatere suitcase. Come on."

"In the woods!" she said. "Oh no! The woods are very dry now, I can't have people smoking in my woods. You'll have to camp out in the field, in this field here next to the house, where there aren't any trees."

"Where she can keep her eye on you," the child said under her breath.

"Her woods," the large boy muttered and got out of the hammock.

"We'll sleep in the field," Powell said but not particularly as if he were talking to her. "This afternoon I'm going to show them about this place." The other two were already walking away and he got up and bounded after them and the two women sat with the black suitcase between them.

"Not no thank you, not no nothing," Mrs. Pritchard remarked.

"They only played with what we gave them to eat," Mrs. Cope said in a hurt voice.

Mrs. Pritchard suggested that they might not like *soft* drinks.

"They certainly *looked* hungry," Mrs. Cope said.

About sunset they appeared out of the woods, dirty and sweating, and came to the back porch and asked for water. They did not ask for food but Mrs. Cope could tell that they wanted it. "All I have is some cold guinea," she said. "Would you boys like some guinea and some sandwiches?"

"I wouldn't eat nothing bald-headed like a guinea," the little boy said. "I would eat a chicken or a turkey but not no guinea."

"Dog wouldn't eat one of them," the large boy said. He had taken off his shirt and stuck it in the back of his trousers like a tail. Mrs. Cope carefully avoided looking at him. The little boy had a cut on his arm.

"You boys haven't been riding the horses when I asked you not to, have you?" she asked suspiciously and they all said, "No mam!" at once in loud enthusiastic voices like the Amens are said in country churches.

She went into the house and made them sandwiches and,

while she did it, she held a conversation with them from inside the kitchen, asking what their fathers did and how many brothers and sisters they had and where they went to school. They answered in short explosive sentences, pushing each other's shoulders and doubling up with laughter as if the questions had meanings she didn't know about. "And do you have men teachers or lady teachers at your school?" she asked.

"Some of both and some you can't tell which," the big boy hooted.

"And does your mother work, Powell?" she asked quickly.

"She ast you does your mother work!" the little boy yelled. "His mind's affected by them horses he only looked at," he said. "His mother she works at a factory and leaves him to mind the rest of them only he don't mind them much. Lemme tell you, lady, one time he locked his little brother in a box and set it on fire."

"I'm sure Powell wouldn't do a thing like that," she said, coming out with the plate of sandwiches and setting it down on the step. They emptied the plate at once and she picked it up and stood holding it, looking at the sun which was going down in front of them, almost on top of the tree line. It was swollen and flame-colored and hung in a net of ragged cloud as if it might burn through any second and fall into the woods. From the upstairs window the child saw her shiver and catch both arms to her sides. "We have so much to be thankful for," she said suddenly in a mournful marveling tone. "Do you boys thank God every night for all He's done for you? Do you thank Him for everything?"

This put an instant hush over them. They bit into the sandwiches as if they had lost all taste for food.

"Do you?" she persisted.

They were as silent as thieves hiding. They chewed without a sound.

"Well, I know I do," she said at length and turned and went back to the house and the child watched their shoulders drop. The large one stretched his legs out as if he were releasing himself from a trap. The sun burned so fast that it seemed to be trying to set everything in sight on fire. The white water tower was glazed pink and the grass was an unnatural green as if it were turning to glass. The child suddenly stuck her head far out the window and said, "Ugggghhrhh," in a loud voice, crossing her eyes and hanging her tongue out as far as possible as if she were going to vomit.

The large boy looked up and stared at her. "Jesus," he growled, "another woman."

She dropped back from the window and stood with her back against the wall, squinting fiercely as if she had been slapped in the face and couldn't see who had done it. As soon as they left the steps, she came down into the kitchen where Mrs. Cope was washing the dishes. "If I had that big boy down I'd beat the daylight out of him," she said.

"You keep away from those boys," Mrs. Cope said, turning sharply. "Ladies don't beat the daylight out of people. You keep out of their way. They'll be gone in the morning."

But in the morning they were not gone.

When she went out on the porch after breakfast, they were standing around the back door, kicking the steps. They were smelling the bacon she had had for her breakfast. "Why boys!" she said. "I thought you were going to meet your uncle." They had the same look of hardened hunger that had pained her yesterday but today she felt faintly provoked.

The big boy turned his back at once and the small one squatted down and began to scratch in the sand. "We ain't, though," Powell said.

The big boy turned his head just enough to take in a small section of her and said, "We ain't bothering nothing of yours."

He couldn't see the way her eyes enlarged but he could take note of the significant silence. After a minute she said in an altered voice, "Would you boys care for some breakfast?"

"We got plenty of our own food," the big boy said. "We don't want nothing of yours."

She kept her eyes on Powell. His thin white face seemed to confront but not actually to see her. "You boys know that I'm glad to have you," she said, "but I expect you to behave. I expect you to act like gentlemen."

They stood there, each looking in a different direction, as if they were waiting for her to leave. "After all," she said in a suddenly high voice, "this is my place."

The big boy made some ambiguous noise and they turned

and walked off toward the barn, leaving her there with a shocked look as if she had had a searchlight thrown on her in the middle of the night.

In a little while Mrs. Pritchard came over and stood in the kitchen door with her cheek against the edge of it. "I reckon you know they rode them horses all yesterday afternoon," she said. "Stole a bridle out the saddle room and rode bareback because Hollis seen them. He runnum out the barn at nine o'clock last night and then he runnum out the milk room this morning and there was milk all over their mouths like they had been drinking out the cans."

"I cannot have this," Mrs. Cope said and stood at the sink with both fists knotted at her sides. "I cannot have this," and her expression was the same as when she tore at the nut grass.

"There ain't a thing you can do about it," Mrs. Pritchard said. "What I expect is you'll have them for a week or so until school begins. They just figure to have themselves a vacation in the country and there ain't nothing you can do but fold your hands."

"I do not fold my hands," Mrs. Cope said. "Tell Mr. Pritchard to put the horses up in the stalls."

"He's already did that. You take a boy thirteen year old is equal in meanness to a man twict his age. It's no telling what he'll think up to do. You never know where he'll strike next. This morning Hollis seen them behind the bull pen and that big one ast if it wasn't some place they could wash at and Hollis said no it wasn't and that you didn't want no boys dropping cigarette butts in your woods and he said, 'She don't own them woods,' and Hollis said, 'She does too,' and that there little one he said, 'Man, Gawd owns them woods and her too,' and that there one with the glasses said, 'I reckon she owns the sky over this place too,' and that there littlest one says, 'Owns the sky and can't no airplane go over here without she says so,' and then the big one says, 'I never seen a place with so many damm women on it, how do you stand it here?' and Hollis said he had done had enough of their big talk by then and he turned and walked off without giving no reply one way or the other."

"I'm going out there and tell those boys they can get a ride

away from here on the milk truck," Mrs. Cope said and she
went out the back door, leaving Mrs. Pritchard and the child
together in the kitchen.

"Listen," the child said. "I could handle them quicker than
that."

"Yeah?" Mrs. Pritchard murmured, giving her a long leering look. "How'd you handle them?"

The child gripped both hands together and made a contorted face as if she were strangling someone.

"They'd handle you," Mrs. Pritchard said with satisfaction.

The child retired to the upstairs window to get out of her
way and looked down where her mother was walking off
from the three boys who were squatting under the water
tower, eating something out of a cracker box. She heard her
come in the kitchen door and say, "They say they'll go on the
milk truck, and no wonder they aren't hungry—they have
that suitcase half full of food."

"Likely stole every bit of it too," Mrs. Pritchard said.

When the milk truck came, the three boys were nowhere
in sight, but as soon as it left without them their three faces
appeared, looking out of the opening in the top of the calf
barn. "Can you beat this?" Mrs. Cope said, standing at one
of the upstairs windows with her hands at her hips. "It's not
that I wouldn't be glad to have them—it's their attitude."

"You never like nobody's attitude," the child said. "I'll go
tell them they got five minutes to leave here in."

"You are not to go anywhere near those boys, do you hear
me?" Mrs. Cope said.

"Why?" the child asked.

"I'm going out there and give them a piece of my mind,"
Mrs. Cope said.

The child took over the position in the window and in a
few minutes she saw the stiff green hat catching the glint of
the sun as her mother crossed the road toward the calf barn.
The three faces immediately disappeared from the opening,
and in a second the large boy dashed across the lot, followed
an instant later by the other two. Mrs. Pritchard came out
and the two women started for the grove of trees the boys
had vanished into. Presently the two sunhats disappeared in
the woods and the three boys came out at the left side of it

and ambled across the field and into another patch of woods. By the time Mrs. Cope and Mrs. Pritchard reached the field, it was empty and there was nothing for them to do but come home again.

Mrs. Cope had not been inside long before Mrs. Pritchard came running toward the house, shouting something. "They've let out the bull!" she hollered. "Let out the bull!" And in a second she was followed by the bull himself, ambling, black and leisurely, with four geese hissing at his heels. He was not mean until hurried and it took Mr. Pritchard and the two Negroes a half-hour to ease him back to his pen. While the men were engaged in this, the boys let the oil out of the three tractors and then disappeared again into the woods.

Two blue veins had come out on either side of Mrs. Cope's forehead and Mrs. Pritchard observed them with satisfaction. "Like I toljer," she said, "there ain't a thing you can do about it."

Mrs. Cope ate her dinner hastily, not conscious that she had her sunhat on. Every time she heard a noise, she jumped up. Mrs. Pritchard came over immediately after dinner and said, "Well, you want to know where they are now?" and smiled in an omniscient rewarded way.

"I want to know at once," Mrs. Cope said, coming to an almost military attention.

"Down to the road, throwing rocks at your mailbox," Mrs. Pritchard said, leaning comfortably in the door. "Done already about knocked it off its stand."

"Get in the car," Mrs. Cope said.

The child got in too and the three of them drove down the road to the gate. The boys were sitting on the embankment on the other side of the highway, aiming rocks across the road at the mailbox. Mrs. Cope stopped the car almost directly beneath them and looked up out of her window. The three of them stared at her as if they had never seen her before, the large boy with a sullen glare, the small one glint-eyed and unsmiling, and Powell with his two-sided glassed gaze hanging vacantly over the crippled destroyer on his shirt.

"Powell," she said, "I'm sure your mother would be ashamed of you," and she stopped and waited for this to make its effect. His face seemed to twist slightly but he continued to look through her at nothing in particular.

"Now I've put up with this as long as I can," she said. "I've tried to be nice to you boys. Haven't I been nice to you boys?"

They might have been three statues except that the big one, barely opening his mouth, said, "We're not even on your side the road, lady."

"There ain't a thing you can do about it," Mrs. Pritchard hissed loudly. The child was sitting on the back seat close to the side. She had a furious outraged look on her face but she kept her head drawn back from the window so that they couldn't see her.

Mrs. Cope spoke slowly, emphasizing every word. "I think I have been very nice to you boys. I've fed you twice. Now I'm going into town and if you're still here when I come back, I'll call the sheriff," and with this, she drove off. The child, turning quickly so that she could see out the back window, observed that they had not moved; they had not even turned their heads.

"You done angered them now," Mrs. Pritchard said, "and it ain't any telling what they'll do."

"They'll be gone when we get back," Mrs. Cope said.

Mrs. Pritchard could not stand an anticlimax. She required the taste of blood from time to time to keep her equilibrium. "I known a man oncet that his wife was poisoned by a child she had adopted out of pure kindness," she said. When they returned from town, the boys were not on the embankment and she said, "I would rather to see them than not to see them. When you see them you know what they're doing."

"Ridiculous," Mrs. Cope muttered. "I've scared them and they've gone and now we can forget them."

"I ain't forgetting them," Mrs. Pritchard said. "I wouldn't be none surprised if they didn't have a gun in that there suitcase."

Mrs. Cope prided herself on the way she handled the type of mind that Mrs. Pritchard had. When Mrs. Pritchard saw signs and omens, she exposed them calmly for the figments of imagination that they were, but this afternoon her nerves were taut and she said, "Now I've had about enough of this. Those boys are gone and that's that."

"Well, we'll wait and see," Mrs. Pritchard said.

Everything was quiet for the rest of the afternoon but at supper time, Mrs. Pritchard came over to say that she had heard a high vicious laugh pierce out of the bushes near the hog pen. It was an evil laugh, full of calculated meanness, and she had heard it come three times, herself, distinctly.

"I haven't heard a thing," Mrs. Cope said.

"I look for them to strike just after dark," Mrs. Pritchard said.

That night Mrs. Cope and the child sat on the porch until nearly ten o'clock and nothing happened. The only sounds came from tree frogs and from one whippoorwill who called faster and faster from the same spot of darkness. "They've gone," Mrs. Cope said, "poor things," and she began to tell the child how much they had to be thankful for, for she said they might have had to live in a development themselves or they might have been Negroes or they might have been in iron lungs or they might have been Europeans ridden in box-cars like cattle, and she began a litany of her blessings, in a stricken voice, that the child, straining her attention for a sudden shriek in the dark, didn't listen to.

There was no sign of them the next morning either. The fortress line of trees was a hard granite blue, the wind had risen overnight and the sun had come up a pale gold. The season was changing. Even a small change in the weather made Mrs. Cope thankful, but when the seasons changed she seemed almost frightened at her good fortune in escaping whatever it was that pursued her. As she sometimes did when one thing was finished and another about to begin, she turned her attention to the child who had put on a pair of overalls over her dress and had pulled a man's old felt hat down as far as it would go on her head and was arming herself with two pistols in a decorated holster that she had fastened around her waist. The hat was very tight and seemed to be squeezing the redness into her face. It came down almost to the tops of her glasses. Mrs. Cope watched her with a tragic look. "Why do you have to look like an idiot?" she asked. "Suppose company were to come? When are you going to grow up? What's going to become of you? I look at you and I want to cry! Sometimes you look like you might belong to Mrs. Pritchard!"

"Leave me be," the child said in a high irritated voice. "Leave me be. Just leave me be. I ain't you," and she went off to the woods as if she were stalking out an enemy, her head thrust forward and each hand gripped on a gun.

Mrs. Pritchard came over, sour-humored, because she didn't have anything calamitous to report. "I got the misery in my face today," she said, holding on to what she could salvage. "Theseyer teeth. They each one feel like an individual boil."

The child crashed through the woods, making the fallen leaves sound ominous under her feet. The sun had risen a little and was only a white hole like an opening for the wind to escape through in a sky a little darker than itself, and the tops of the trees were black against the glare. "I'm going to get you," she said. "I'm going to get you one by one and beat you black and blue. Line up. LINE UP!" she said and waved one of the pistols at a cluster of long bare-trunked pines, four times her height, as she passed them. She kept moving, muttering and growling to herself and occasionally hitting out with one of the guns at a branch that got in her way. From time to time she stopped to remove the thorn vine that caught in her shirt and she would say, "Leave me be, I told you. Leave me be," and give it a crack with the pistol and then stalk on.

Presently she sat down on a stump to cool off but she planted both feet carefully and firmly on the ground. She lifted them and put them down several times, grinding them fiercely into the dirt as if she were crushing something under her heels. Suddenly she heard a laugh.

She sat up, prickle-skinned. It came again. She heard the sound of splashing and she stood up, uncertain which way to run. She was not far from where this patch of woods ended and the back pasture began. She eased toward the pasture, careful not to make a sound, and coming suddenly to the edge of it, she saw the three boys, not twenty feet away, washing in the cow trough. Their clothes were piled against the black valise out of reach of the water that flowed over the side of the tank. The large boy was standing up and the small one was trying to climb onto his shoulders. Powell was sitting down looking straight ahead through glasses that were splashed with water. He was not paying any attention to the other two. The trees must have looked like green waterfalls through his wet glasses. The child stood partly hidden behind a pine trunk, the side of her face pressed into the bark.

"I wish I lived here!" the little boy shouted, balancing with his knees clutched around the big one's head.

"I'm goddam glad I don't," the big boy panted, and jumped up to dislodge him.

Powell sat without moving, without seeming to know that the other two were behind him, and looked straight ahead like a ghost sprung upright in his coffin. "If this place was not here any more," he said, "you would never have to think of it again."

"Listen," the big boy said, sitting down quietly in the water with the little one still moored to his shoulders, "it don't belong to nobody."

"It's ours," the little boy said.

The child behind the tree did not move.

Powell jumped out of the trough and began to run. He ran all the way around the field as if something were after him and as he passed the tank again, the other two jumped out and raced with him, the sun glinting on their long wet bodies. The big one ran the fastest and was the leader. They dashed around the field twice and finally dropped down by their clothes and lay there with their ribs moving up and down. After a while, the big one said hoarsely, "Do you know what I would do with this place if I had the chance?"

"No, what?" the little boy said and sat up to give him his full attention.

"I'd build a big parking lot on it, or something," he muttered.

They began to dress. The sun made two white spots on Powell's glasses and blotted out his eyes. "I know what let's do," he said. He took something small from his pocket and showed it to them. For almost a minute they sat looking at what he had in his hand. Then without any more discussion, Powell picked up the suitcase and they got up and moved past the child and entered the woods not ten feet from where she was standing, slightly away from the tree now, with the imprint of the bark embossed red and white on the side of her face.

She watched with a dazed stare as they stopped and collected all the matches they had between them and began to set the brush on fire. They began to whoop and holler and beat their hands over their mouths and in a few seconds there was a narrow line of fire widening between her and them. While she watched, it reached up from the brush, snatching and biting at the lowest branches of the trees. The wind carried rags of it higher and the boys disappeared shrieking behind it.

She turned and tried to run across the field but her legs were too heavy and she stood there, weighted down with some new unplaced misery that she had never felt before. But finally she began to run.

Mrs. Cope and Mrs. Pritchard were in the field behind the barn when Mrs. Cope saw smoke rising from the woods across the pasture. She shrieked and Mrs. Pritchard pointed up the road to where the child came loping heavily, screaming, "Mama, Mama, they're going to build a parking lot here!"

Mrs. Cope began to scream for the Negroes while Mrs. Pritchard, charged now, ran down the road shouting. Mr. Pritchard came out of the open end of the barn and the two Negroes stopped filling the manure spreader in the lot and started toward Mrs. Cope with their shovels. "Hurry, hurry!" she shouted. "Start throwing dirt on it!" They passed her almost without looking at her and headed off slowly across the field toward the smoke. She ran after them a little way, shrilling, "Hurry, hurry, don't you see it! Don't you see it!"

"It'll be there when we git there," Culver said and they thrust their shoulders forward a little and went on at the same pace.

The child came to a stop beside her mother and stared up at her face as if she had never seen it before. It was the face of the new misery she felt, but on her mother it looked old and it looked as if it might have belonged to anybody, a Negro or a European or to Powell himself. The child turned her head quickly, and past the Negroes' ambling figures she could see the column of smoke rising and widening unchecked inside the granite line of trees. She stood taut, listening, and could just catch in the distance a few wild high shrieks of joy as if the prophets were dancing in the fiery furnace, in the circle the angel had cleared for them.

A Late Encounter with the Enemy

GENERAL SASH was a hundred and four years old. He lived with his granddaughter, Sally Poker Sash, who was sixty-two years old and who prayed every night on her knees that he would live until her graduation from college. The General didn't give two slaps for her graduation but he never doubted he would live for it. Living had got to be such a habit with him that he couldn't conceive of any other condition. A graduation exercise was not exactly his idea of a good time, even if, as she said, he would be expected to sit on the stage in his uniform. She said there would be a long procession of teachers and students in their robes but that there wouldn't be anything to equal *him* in his uniform. He knew this well enough without her telling him, and as for the damm procession, it could march to hell and back and not cause him a quiver. He liked parades with floats full of Miss Americas and Miss Daytona Beaches and Miss Queen Cotton Products. He didn't have any use for processions and a procession full of schoolteachers was about as deadly as the River Styx to his way of thinking. However, he was willing to sit on the stage in his uniform so that they could see him.

Sally Poker was not as sure as he was that he would live until her graduation. There had not been any perceptible change in him for the last five years, but she had the sense that she might be cheated out of her triumph because she so often was. She had been going to summer school every year for the past twenty because when she started teaching, there were no such things as degrees. In those times, she said, everything was normal but nothing had been normal since she was sixteen, and for the past twenty summers, when she should have been resting, she had had to take a trunk in the burning heat to the state teachers' college; and though when she returned in the fall, she always taught in the exact way she had been taught not to teach, this was a mild revenge that didn't satisfy her sense of justice. She wanted the General at her graduation because she wanted to show what she stood for, or, as she said, "what all was behind her," and was not behind them. This *them* was not anybody in particular. It was just all the upstarts who had turned the world on its head and unsettled the ways of decent living.

She meant to stand on that platform in August with the General sitting in his wheel chair on the stage behind her and she meant to hold her head very high as if she were saying, "See him! See him! My kin, all you upstarts! Glorious upright old man standing for the old traditions! Dignity! Honor! Courage! See him!" One night in her sleep she screamed, "See him! See him!" and turned her head and found him sitting in his wheel chair behind her with a terrible expression on his face and with all his clothes off except the general's hat and she had waked up and had not dared to go back to sleep again that night.

For his part, the General would not have consented even to attend her graduation if she had not promised to see to it that he sit on the stage. He liked to sit on any stage. He considered that he was still a very handsome man. When he had been able to stand up, he had measured five feet four inches of pure game cock. He had white hair that reached to his shoulders behind and he would not wear teeth because he thought his profile was more striking without them. When he put on his full-dress general's uniform, he knew well enough that there was nothing to match him anywhere.

This was not the same uniform he had worn in the War between the States. He had not actually been a general in that war. He had probably been a foot soldier; he didn't remember what he had been; in fact, he didn't remember that war at all. It was like his feet, which hung down now shriveled at the very end of him, without feeling, covered with a blue-gray afghan that Sally Poker had crocheted when she was a little girl. He didn't remember the Spanish-American War in which he had lost a son; he didn't even remember the son. He didn't have any use for history because he never expected to meet it again. To his mind, history was connected with processions and life with parades and he liked parades. People were always asking him if he remembered this or that—a dreary black procession of questions about the past. There was only one event in the past that had any significance for him and that he cared to talk about: that was twelve years ago when he had received the general's uniform and had been in the premiere.

"I was in that preemy they had in Atlanta," he would tell visitors sitting on his front porch. "Surrounded by beautiful guls. It wasn't a thing local about it. It was nothing local about it. Listen here. It was a nashnul event and they had me in it—up onto the stage. There was no bob-tails at it. Every person at it had paid ten dollars to get in and had to wear his tuxseeder. I was in this uniform. A beautiful gul presented me with it that afternoon in a hotel room."

"It was in a suite in the hotel and I was in it too, Papa," Sally Poker would say, winking at the visitors. "You weren't alone with any young lady in a hotel room."

"Was, I'd a known what to do," the old General would say with a sharp look and the visitors would scream with laughter. "This was a Hollywood, California, gul," he'd continue. "She was from Hollywood, California, and didn't have any part in the pitcher. Out there they have so many beautiful guls that they don't need that they call them a extra and they don't use them for nothing but presenting people with things and having their pitchers taken. They took my pitcher with her. No, it was two of them. One on either side and me in the middle with my arms around each of them's waist and their waist ain't any bigger than a half a dollar."

Sally Poker would interrupt again. "It was Mr. Govisky that gave you the uniform, Papa, and he gave me the most exquisite corsage. Really, I wish you could have seen it. It was made with gladiola petals taken off and painted gold and put back together to look like a rose. It was exquisite. I wish you could have seen it, it was . . ."

"It was as big as her head," the General would snarl. "I was tellin it. They gimme this uniform and they gimme this so-ward and they say, 'Now General, we don't want you to start a war on us. All we want you to do is march right up on that stage when you're innerduced tonight and answer a few questions. Think you can do that?' 'Think I can do it!' I say. 'Listen here. I was doing things before you were born,' and they hollered."

"He was the hit of the show," Sally Poker would say, but she didn't much like to remember the premiere on account of what had happened to her feet at it. She had bought a new dress for the occasion—a long black crepe dinner dress with a rhinestone buckle and a bolero—and a pair of silver slippers to wear with it, because she was supposed to go up on the stage with him to keep him from falling. Everything was arranged for them. A real limousine came at ten minutes to eight and took them to the theater. It drew up under the marquee at exactly the right time, after the big stars and the director and the author and the governor and the mayor and some less important stars. The police kept traffic from jamming and there were ropes to keep the people off who couldn't go. All the people who couldn't go watched them step out of the limousine into the lights. Then they walked down the red and gold foyer and an usherette in a Confederate cap and little short skirt conducted them to their special seats. The audience was already there and a group of UDC members began to clap when they saw the General in his uniform and that started everybody to clap. A few more celebrities came after them and then the doors closed and the lights went down.

A young man with blond wavy hair who said he represented the motion-picture industry came out and began to introduce everybody and each one who was introduced walked up on the stage and said how really happy he was to be here for this great event. The General and his granddaughter were introduced sixteenth on the program. He was introduced as General Tennessee Flintrock Sash of the Confederacy, though Sally Poker had told Mr. Govisky that his name was George Poker Sash and that he had only been a major. She helped him up from his seat but her heart was beating so fast she didn't know whether she'd make it herself.

The old man walked up the aisle slowly with his fierce white head high and his hat held over his heart. The orchestra began to play the Confederate Battle Hymn very softly and the UDC members rose as a group and did not sit down again until the General was on the stage. When he reached the center of the stage with Sally Poker just behind him guiding his elbow, the orchestra burst out in a loud rendition of the Battle Hymn and the old man, with real stage presence, gave a vigorous trembling salute and stood at attention until the last blast had died away. Two of the usherettes in Confederate caps and short skirts held a Confederate and a Union flag crossed behind them.

The General stood in the exact center of the spotlight and it caught a weird moon-shaped slice of Sally Poker—the corsage, the rhinestone buckle and one hand clenched around a white glove and handkerchief. The young man with the blond wavy hair inserted himself into the circle of light and said he was *really* happy to have here tonight for this great event, one, he said, who had fought and bled in the battles they would soon see daringly re-acted on the screen, and "Tell me, General," he asked, "how old are you?"

"Niiiiiinnttty-two!" the General screamed.

The young man looked as if this were just about the most impressive thing that had been said all evening. "Ladies and gentlemen," he said, "let's give the General the biggest hand we've got!" and there was applause immediately and the young man indicated to Sally Poker with a motion of his thumb that she could take the old man back to his seat now so that the next person could be introduced; but the General had not finished. He stood immovable in the exact center of the spotlight, his neck thrust forward, his mouth slightly open, and his voracious gray eyes drinking in the glare and the applause. He elbowed his granddaughter roughly away. "How I keep so young," he screeched, "I kiss all the pretty guls!"

This was met with a great din of spontaneous applause and it was at just that instant that Sally Poker looked down at her feet and discovered that in the excitement of getting ready she had forgotten to change her shoes: two brown Girl Scout oxfords protruded from the bottom of her dress. She gave the General a yank and almost ran with him off the stage. He was very angry that he had not got to say how glad he was to be here for this event and on the way back to his seat, he kept saying as loud as he could, "I'm glad to be here at this preemy with all these beautiful guls!" but there was another celebrity going up the other aisle and nobody paid any attention to him. He slept through the picture, muttering fiercely every now and then in his sleep.

Since then, his life had not been very interesting. His feet were completely dead now, his knees worked like old hinges, his kidneys functioned when they would, but his heart persisted doggedly to beat. The past and the future were the same thing to him, one forgotten and the other not remembered; he had no more notion of dying than a cat. Every year on Confederate Memorial Day, he was bundled up and lent to the Capitol City Museum where he was displayed from one to four in a musty room full of old photographs, old uniforms, old artillery, and historic documents. All these were carefully preserved in glass cases so that children would not put their hands on them. He wore his general's uniform from the premiere and sat, with a fixed scowl, inside a small roped area. There was nothing about him to indicate that he was alive except an occasional movement in his milky gray eyes, but once when a bold child touched his sword, his arm shot forward and slapped the hand off in an instant. In the spring when the old homes were opened for pilgrimages, he was invited to wear his uniform and sit in some conspicuous spot and lend atmosphere to the scene. Some of these times he only snarled at the visitors but sometimes he told about the premiere and the beautiful girls.

If he had died before Sally Poker's graduation, she thought she would have died herself. At the beginning of the summer term, even before she knew if she would pass, she told the Dean that her grandfather, General Tennessee Flintrock Sash of the Confederacy, would attend her graduation and that he was a hundred and four years old and that his mind was still clear as a bell. Distinguished visitors were always welcome and could sit on the stage and be introduced. She made arrangements with her nephew, John Wesley Poker Sash, a Boy Scout, to come wheel the General's chair. She thought how sweet it would be to see the old man in his courageous gray and the young boy in his clean khaki—the old and the new, she thought appropriately—they would be behind her on the stage when she received her degree.

Everything went almost exactly as she had planned. In the summer while she was away at school, the General stayed with other relatives and they brought him and John Wesley, the Boy Scout, down to the graduation. A reporter came to the hotel where they stayed and took the General's picture with Sally Poker on one side of him and John Wesley on the other. The General, who had had his picture taken with beautiful girls, didn't think much of this. He had forgotten precisely what kind of event this was he was going to attend but he remembered that he was to wear his uniform and carry the sword.

On the morning of the graduation, Sally Poker had to line up in the academic procession with the B.S.'s in Elementary Education and she couldn't see to getting him on the stage herself—but John Wesley, a fat blond boy of ten with an executive expression, guaranteed to take care of everything. She came in her academic gown to the hotel and dressed the old man in his uniform. He was as frail as a dried spider. "Aren't you just thrilled, Papa?" she asked. "I'm just thrilled to death!"

"Put the soward acrost my lap, damm you," the old man said, "where it'll shine."

She put it there and then stood back looking at him. "You look just grand," she said.

"God damm it," the old man said in a slow monotonous certain tone as if he were saying it to the beating of his heart. "God damm every goddam thing to hell."

"Now, now," she said and left happily to join the procession.

The graduates were lined up behind the Science building and she found her place just as the line started to move. She had not slept much the night before and when she had, she had dreamed of the exercises, murmuring, "See him, see him?" in her sleep but waking up every time just before she turned her head to look at him behind her. The graduates had to walk three blocks in the hot sun in their black wool robes and as she plodded stolidly along she thought that if anyone considered this academic procession something impressive to behold, they need only wait until they saw that old General in his courageous gray and that clean young Boy Scout stoutly wheeling his chair across the stage with the sunlight catching the sword. She imagined that John Wesley had the old man ready now behind the stage.

The black procession wound its way up the two blocks and started on the main walk leading to the auditorium. The visitors stood on the grass, picking out their graduates. Men were pushing back their hats and wiping their foreheads and women were lifting their dresses slightly from the shoulders to keep them from sticking to their backs. The graduates in their heavy robes looked as if the last beads of ignorance were being sweated out of them. The sun blazed off the fenders of automobiles and beat from the columns of the buildings and pulled the eye from one spot of glare to another. It pulled Sally Poker's toward the big red Coca-Cola machine that had been set up by the side of the auditorium. Here she saw the General parked, scowling and hatless in his chair in the blazing sun while John Wesley, his blouse loose behind, his hip and cheek pressed to the red machine, was drinking a Coca-Cola. She broke from the line and galloped to them and snatched the bottle away. She shook the boy and thrust in his blouse and put the hat on the old man's head. "Now get him in there!" she said, pointing one rigid finger to the side door of the building.

For his part the General felt as if there were a little hole beginning to widen in the top of his head. The boy wheeled him rapidly down a walk and up a ramp and into a building and bumped him over the stage entrance and into position where he had been told and the General glared in front of him at heads that all seemed to flow together and eyes that moved from one face to another. Several figures in black robes came and picked up his hand and shook it. A black procession was flowing up each aisle and forming to stately music in a pool in front of him. The music seemed to be entering his head through the little hole and he thought for a second that the procession would try to enter it too.

He didn't know what procession this was but there was something familiar about it. It must be familiar to him since it had come to meet him, but he didn't like a black procession. Any procession that came to meet him, he thought irritably, ought to have floats with beautiful guls on them like the floats before the preemy. It must be something connected with history like they were always having. He had no use for any of it. What happened then wasn't anything to a man living now and he was living now.

When all the procession had flowed into the black pool, a

black figure began orating in front of it. The figure was telling something about history and the General made up his mind he wouldn't listen, but the words kept seeping in through the little hole in his head. He heard his own name mentioned and his chair was shuttled forward roughly and the Boy Scout took a big bow. They called his name and the fat brat bowed. Goddam you, the old man tried to say, get out of my way, I can stand up!—but he was jerked back again before he could get up and take the bow. He supposed the noise they made was for him. If he was over, he didn't intend to listen to any more of it. If it hadn't been for the little hole in the top of his head, none of the words would have got to him. He thought of putting his finger up there into the hole to block them but the hole was a little wider than his finger and it felt as if it were getting deeper.

Another black robe had taken the place of the first one and was talking now and he heard his name mentioned again but they were not talking about him, they were still talking about history. "If we forget our past," the speaker was saying, "we won't remember our future and it will be as well for we won't have one." The General heard some of these words gradually. He had forgotten history and he didn't intend to remember it again. He had forgotten the name and face of his wife and the names and faces of his children or even if he had a wife and children, and he had forgotten the names of places and the places themselves and what had happened at them.

He was considerably irked by the hole in his head. He had not expected to have a hole in his head at this event. It was the slow black music that had put it there and though most of the music had stopped outside, there was still a little of it in the hole, going deeper and moving around in his thoughts, letting the words he heard into the dark places of his brain. He heard the words, Chickamauga, Shiloh, Johnston, Lee, and he knew he was inspiring all these words that meant nothing to him. He wondered if he had been a general at Chickamauga or at Lee. Then he tried to see himself and the horse mounted in the middle of a float full of beautiful girls, being driven slowly through downtown Atlanta. Instead, the old words began to stir in his head as if they were trying to wrench themselves out of place and come to life.

The speaker was through with that war and had gone on to the next one and now he was approaching another and all his words, like the black procession, were vaguely familiar and irritating. There was a long finger of music in the General's head, probing various spots that were words, letting in a little light on the words and helping them to live. The words began to come toward him and he said, Dammit! I ain't going to have it! and he started edging backwards to get out of the way. Then he saw the figure in the black robe sit down and there was a noise and the black pool in front of him began to rumble and to flow toward him from either side to the black slow music, and he said, Stop dammit! I can't do but one thing at a time! He couldn't protect himself from the words and attend to the procession too and the words were coming at him fast. He felt that he was running backwards and the words were coming at him like musket fire, just escaping him but getting nearer and nearer. He turned around and began to run as fast as he could but he found himself running toward the words. He was running into a regular volley of them and meeting them with quick curses. As the music swelled toward him, the entire past opened up on him out of nowhere and he felt his body riddled in a hundred places with sharp stabs of pain and he fell down, returning a curse for every hit. He saw his wife's narrow face looking at him critically through her round gold-rimmed glasses; he saw one of his squinting bald-headed sons; and his mother ran toward him with an anxious look; then a succession of places— Chickamauga, Shiloh, Marthasville—rushed at him as if the past were the only future now and he had to endure it. Then suddenly he saw that the black procession was almost on him. He recognized it, for it had been dogging all his days. He made such a desperate effort to see over it and find out what comes after the past that his hand clenched the sword until the blade touched bone.

The graduates were crossing the stage in a long file to receive their scrolls and shake the president's hand. As Sally Poker, who was near the end, crossed, she glanced at the General and saw him sitting fixed and fierce, his eyes wide open, and she turned her head forward again and held it a perceptible degree higher and received her scroll. Once it was all over and she was out of the auditorium in the sun again, she located her kin and they waited together on a bench in the shade for John Wesley to wheel the old man out. That crafty scout had bumped him out the back way and rolled him at high speed down a flagstone path and was waiting now, with the corpse, in the long line at the Coca-Cola machine.

Good Country People

BESIDES the neutral expression that she wore when she
was alone, Mrs. Freeman had two others, forward and
reverse, that she used for all her human dealings. Her forward
expression was steady and driving like the advance of a heavy
truck. Her eyes never swerved to left or right but turned as
the story turned as if they followed a yellow line down the
center of it. She seldom used the other expression because it
was not often necessary for her to retract a statement, but
when she did, her face came to a complete stop, there was an
almost imperceptible movement of her black eyes, during
which they seemed to be receding, and then the observer
would see that Mrs. Freeman, though she might stand there
as real as several grain sacks thrown on top of each other, was
no longer there in spirit. As for getting anything across to her
when this was the case, Mrs. Hopewell had given it up. She
might talk her head off. Mrs. Freeman could never be
brought to admit herself wrong on any point. She would
stand there and if she could be brought to say anything, it
was something like, "Well, I wouldn't of said it was and I
wouldn't of said it wasn't," or letting her gaze range over the
top kitchen shelf where there was an assortment of dusty
bottles, she might remark, "I see you ain't ate many of them
figs you put up last summer."

They carried on their most important business in the
kitchen at breakfast. Every morning Mrs. Hopewell got up at
seven o'clock and lit her gas heater and Joy's. Joy was her
daughter, a large blonde girl who had an artificial leg. Mrs.
Hopewell thought of her as a child though she was thirty-
two years old and highly educated. Joy would get up while
her mother was eating and lumber into the bathroom and
slam the door, and before long, Mrs. Freeman would arrive
at the back door. Joy would hear her mother call, "Come on
in," and then they would talk for a while in low voices that
were indistinguishable in the bathroom. By the time Joy came
in, they had usually finished the weather report and were on
one or the other of Mrs. Freeman's daughters, Glynese or
Carramae. Joy called them Glycerin and Caramel. Glynese, a

redhead, was eighteen and had many admirers; Carramae, a blonde, was only fifteen but already married and pregnant. She could not keep anything on her stomach. Every morning Mrs. Freeman told Mrs. Hopewell how many times she had vomited since the last report.

Mrs. Hopewell liked to tell people that Glynese and Carramae were two of the finest girls she knew and that Mrs. Freeman was a *lady* and that she was never ashamed to take her anywhere or introduce her to anybody they might meet. Then she would tell how she had happened to hire the Freemans in the first place and how they were a godsend to her and how she had had them four years. The reason for her keeping them so long was that they were not trash. They were good country people. She had telephoned the man whose name they had given as a reference and he had told her that Mr. Freeman was a good farmer but that his wife was the nosiest woman ever to walk the earth. "She's got to be into everything," the man said. "If she don't get there before the dust settles, you can bet she's dead, that's all. She'll want to know all your business. I can stand him real good," he had said, "but me nor my wife neither could have stood that woman one more minute on this place." That had put Mrs. Hopewell off for a few days.

She had hired them in the end because there were no other applicants but she had made up her mind beforehand exactly how she would handle the woman. Since she was the type who had to be into everything, then, Mrs. Hopewell had decided, she would not only let her be into everything, she would *see to it* that she was into everything—she would give her the responsibility of everything, she would put her in charge. Mrs. Hopewell had no bad qualities of her own but she was able to use other people's in such a constructive way that she never felt the lack. She had hired the Freemans and she had kept them four years.

Nothing is perfect. This was one of Mrs. Hopewell's favorite sayings. Another was: that is life! And still another, the most important, was: well, other people have their opinions too. She would make these statements, usually at the table, in a tone of gentle insistence as if no one held them but her, and the large hulking Joy, whose constant outrage had obliterated every expression from her face, would stare just a little to the side of her, her eyes icy blue, with the look of someone who has achieved blindness by an act of will and means to keep it.

When Mrs. Hopewell said to Mrs. Freeman that life was like that, Mrs. Freeman would say, "I always said so myself." Nothing had been arrived at by anyone that had not first been arrived at by her. She was quicker than Mr. Freeman. When Mrs. Hopewell said to her after they had been on the place a while, "You know, you're the wheel behind the wheel," and winked, Mrs. Freeman had said, "I know it. I've always been quick. It's some that are quicker than others."

"Everybody is different," Mrs. Hopewell said.

"Yes, most people is," Mrs. Freeman said.

"It takes all kinds to make the world."

"I always said it did myself."

The girl was used to this kind of dialogue for breakfast and more of it for dinner; sometimes they had it for supper too. When they had no guest they ate in the kitchen because that was easier. Mrs. Freeman always managed to arrive at some point during the meal and to watch them finish it. She would stand in the doorway if it were summer but in the winter she would stand with one elbow on top of the refrigerator and look down on them, or she would stand by the gas heater, lifting the back of her skirt slightly. Occasionally she would stand against the wall and roll her head from side to side. At no time was she in any hurry to leave. All this was very trying on Mrs. Hopewell but she was a woman of great patience. She realized that nothing is perfect and that in the Freemans she had good country people and that if, in this day and age, you get good country people, you had better hang onto them.

She had had plenty of experience with trash. Before the Freemans she had averaged one tenant family a year. The wives of these farmers were not the kind you would want to be around you for very long. Mrs. Hopewell, who had divorced her husband long ago, needed someone to walk over the fields with her; and when Joy had to be impressed for these services, her remarks were usually so ugly and her face so glum that Mrs. Hopewell would say, "If you can't come pleasantly, I don't want you at all," to which the girl, standing square and rigid-shouldered with her neck thrust slightly forward, would reply, "If you want me, here I am—LIKE I AM."

Mrs. Hopewell excused this attitude because of the leg (which had been shot off in a hunting accident when Joy was ten). It was hard for Mrs. Hopewell to realize that her child was thirty-two now and that for more than twenty years she had had only one leg. She thought of her still as a child because it tore her heart to think instead of the poor stout girl in her thirties who had never danced a step or had any *normal* good times. Her name was really Joy but as soon as she was twenty-one and away from home, she had had it legally changed. Mrs. Hopewell was certain that she had thought and thought until she had hit upon the ugliest name in any language. Then she had gone and had the beautiful name, Joy, changed without telling her mother until after she had done it. Her legal name was Hulga.

When Mrs. Hopewell thought the name, Hulga, she thought of the broad blank hull of a battleship. She would not use it. She continued to call her Joy to which the girl responded but in a purely mechanical way.

Hulga had learned to tolerate Mrs. Freeman who saved her from taking walks with her mother. Even Glynese and Carramae were useful when they occupied attention that might otherwise have been directed at her. At first she had thought she could not stand Mrs. Freeman for she had found that it was not possible to be rude to her. Mrs. Freeman would take on strange resentments and for days together she would be sullen but the source of her displeasure was always obscure; a direct attack, a positive leer, blatant ugliness to her face—these never touched her. And without warning one day, she began calling her Hulga.

She did not call her that in front of Mrs. Hopewell who would have been incensed but when she and the girl happened to be out of the house together, she would say something and add the name Hulga to the end of it, and the big spectacled Joy-Hulga would scowl and redden as if her privacy had been intruded upon. She considered the name her personal affair. She had arrived at it first purely on the basis of its ugly sound and then the full genius of its fitness had struck her. She had a vision of the name working like the ugly sweating Vulcan who stayed in the furnace and to whom, presumably, the goddess had to come when called. She saw it as the name of her highest creative act. One of her major triumphs was that her mother had not been able to turn her dust into Joy, but the greater one was that she had been able to turn it herself into Hulga. However, Mrs. Freeman's relish for using the name only irritated her. It was as if Mrs. Freeman's beady steel-pointed eyes had penetrated far enough behind her face to reach some secret fact. Something about her seemed to fascinate Mrs. Freeman and then one day Hulga realized that it was the artificial leg. Mrs. Freeman had a special fondness for the details of secret infections, hidden deformities, assaults upon children. Of diseases, she preferred the lingering or incurable. Hulga had heard Mrs. Hopewell give her the details of the hunting accident, how the leg had been literally blasted off, how she had never lost consciousness. Mrs. Freeman could listen to it any time as if it had happened an hour ago.

When Hulga stumped into the kitchen in the morning (she could walk without making the awful noise but she made it—Mrs. Hopewell was certain—because it was ugly-sounding), she glanced at them and did not speak. Mrs. Hopewell would be in her red kimono with her hair tied around her head in rags. She would be sitting at the table, finishing her breakfast and Mrs. Freeman would be hanging by her elbow outward from the refrigerator, looking down at the table. Hulga always put her eggs on the stove to boil and then stood over them with her arms folded, and Mrs. Hopewell would look at her—a kind of indirect gaze divided between her and Mrs. Freeman—and would think that if she would only keep herself up a little, she wouldn't be so bad looking. There was nothing wrong with her face that a pleasant expression wouldn't help. Mrs. Hopewell said that people who looked on the bright side of things would be beautiful even if they were not.

Whenever she looked at Joy this way, she could not help but feel that it would have been better if the child had not taken the Ph.D. It had certainly not brought her out any and now that she had it, there was no more excuse for her to go to school again. Mrs. Hopewell thought it was nice for girls to go to school to have a good time but Joy had "gone through." Anyhow, she would not have been strong enough to go again. The doctors had told Mrs. Hopewell that with the best of care, Joy might see forty-five. She had a weak heart. Joy had made it plain that if it had not been for this condition, she would be far from these red hills and good country people. She would be in a university lecturing to people who knew what she was talking about. And Mrs. Hopewell could very well picture her there, looking like a scarecrow and lecturing to more of the same. Here she went about all day in a six-year-old skirt and a yellow sweat shirt with a faded cowboy on a horse embossed on it. She thought this was funny; Mrs. Hopewell thought it was idiotic and showed simply that she was still a child. She was brilliant but she didn't have a grain of sense. It seemed to Mrs. Hopewell that every year she grew less like other people and more like herself—bloated, rude, and squint-eyed. And she said such strange things! To her own mother she had said—without warning, without excuse, standing up in the middle of a meal with her face purple and her mouth half full—"Woman! do you ever look inside? Do you ever look inside and see what you are *not*? God!" she had cried sinking down again and staring at her plate, "Malebranche was right: we are not our own light. We are not our own light!" Mrs. Hopewell had no idea to this day what brought that on. She had only made the remark, hoping Joy would take it in, that a smile never hurt anyone.

The girl had taken the Ph.D. in philosophy and this left Mrs. Hopewell at a complete loss. You could say, "My daughter is a nurse," or "My daughter is a school teacher," or even, "My daughter is a chemical engineer." You could not say, "My daughter is a philosopher." That was something that had ended with the Greeks and Romans. All day Joy sat on her neck in a deep chair, reading. Sometimes she went for walks but she didn't like dogs or cats or birds or flowers or nature or nice young men. She looked at nice young men as if she could smell their stupidity.

One day Mrs. Hopewell had picked up one of the books the girl had just put down and opening it at random, she read, "Science, on the other hand, has to assert its soberness and seriousness afresh and declare that it is concerned solely with what-is. Nothing—how can it be for science anything but a horror and a phantasm? If science is right, then one thing stands firm: science wishes to know nothing of nothing. Such is after all the strictly scientific approach to Nothing. We know it by wishing to know nothing of Nothing." These words had been underlined with a blue pencil and they worked on Mrs. Hopewell like some evil incantation in gibberish. She shut the book quickly and went out of the room as if she were having a chill.

This morning when the girl came in, Mrs. Freeman was on Carramae. "She thrown up four times after supper," she said, "and was up twict in the night after three o'clock. Yesterday she didn't do nothing but ramble in the bureau drawer. All she did. Stand up there and see what she could run up on."

"She's got to eat," Mrs. Hopewell muttered, sipping her coffee, while she watched Joy's back at the stove. She was wondering what the child had said to the Bible salesman. She could not imagine what kind of a conversation she could possibly have had with him.

He was a tall gaunt hatless youth who had called yesterday to sell them a Bible. He had appeared at the door, carrying a large black suitcase that weighted him so heavily on one side that he had to brace himself against the door facing. He seemed on the point of collapse but he said in a cheerful voice, "Good morning, Mrs. Cedars!" and set the suitcase down on the mat. He was not a bad-looking young man though he had on a bright blue suit and yellow socks that were not pulled up far enough. He had prominent face bones and a streak of sticky-looking brown hair falling across his forehead.

"I'm Mrs. Hopewell," she said.

"Oh!" he said, pretending to look puzzled but with his eyes sparkling, "I saw it said 'The Cedars,' on the mailbox so I thought you was Mrs. Cedars!" and he burst out in a pleasant laugh. He picked up the satchel and under cover of a pant, he fell forward into her hall. It was rather as if the suitcase had moved first, jerking him after it. "Mrs. Hopewell!" he said and grabbed her hand. "I hope you are well!" and he laughed again and then all at once his face sobered completely. He paused and gave her a straight earnest look and said, "Lady, I've come to speak of serious things."

"Well, come in," she muttered, none too pleased because her dinner was almost ready. He came into the parlor and sat down on the edge of a straight chair and put the suitcase between his feet and glanced around the room as if he were sizing her up by it. Her silver gleamed on the two side-boards; she decided he had never been in a room as elegant as this.

"Mrs. Hopewell," he began, using her name in a way that sounded almost intimate, "I know you believe in Chrustian service."

"Well, yes," she murmured.

"I know," he said and paused, looking very wise with his head cocked on one side, "that you're a good woman. Friends have told me."

Mrs. Hopewell never liked to be taken for a fool. "What are you selling?" she asked.

"Bibles," the young man said and his eye raced around the room before he added, "I see you have no family Bible in your parlor, I see that is the one lack you got!"

Mrs. Hopewell could not say, "My daughter is an atheist and won't let me keep the Bible in the parlor." She said, stiffening slightly, "I keep my Bible by my bedside." This was not the truth. It was in the attic somewhere.

"Lady," he said, "the word of God ought to be in the parlor."

"Well, I think that's a matter of taste," she began. "I think . . ."

"Lady," he said, "for a Chrustian, the word of God ought to be in every room in the house besides in his heart. I know you're a Chrustian because I can see it in every line of your face."

She stood up and said, "Well, young man, I don't want to buy a Bible and I smell my dinner burning."

He didn't get up. He began to twist his hands and looking down at them, he said softly, "Well lady, I'll tell you the truth—not many people want to buy one nowadays and be-sides, I know I'm real simple. I don't know how to say a thing but to say it. I'm just a country boy." He glanced up into her unfriendly face. "People like you don't like to fool with country people like me!"

"Why!" she cried, "good country people are the salt of the earth! Besides, we all have different ways of doing, it takes all kinds to make the world go 'round. That's life!"

"You said a mouthful," he said.

"Why, I think there aren't enough good country people in the world!" she said, stirred. "I think that's what's wrong with it!"

His face had brightened. "I didn't inraduce myself," he said. "I'm Manley Pointer from out in the country around Willohobie, not even from a place, just from near a place."

"You wait a minute," she said. "I have to see about my dinner." She went out to the kitchen and found Joy standing near the door where she had been listening.

"Get rid of the salt of the earth," she said, "and let's eat."

Mrs. Hopewell gave her a pained look and turned the heat down under the vegetables. "*I* can't be rude to anybody," she murmured and went back into the parlor.

He had opened the suitcase and was sitting with a Bible on each knee.

"You might as well put those up," she told him. "I don't want one."

"I appreciate your honesty," he said. "You don't see any more real honest people unless you go way out in the country."

"I know," she said, "real genuine folks!" Through the crack in the door she heard a groan.

"I guess a lot of boys come telling you they're working their way through college," he said, "but I'm not going to tell you that. Somehow," he said, "I don't want to go to college. I want to devote my life to Chrustian service. See," he said, lowering his voice, "I got this heart condition. I may not live long. When you know it's something wrong with you and you may not live long, well then, lady . . ." He paused, with his mouth open, and stared at her.

He and Joy had the same condition! She knew that her eyes were filling with tears but she collected herself quickly and murmured, "Won't you stay for dinner? We'd love to have you!" and was sorry the instant she heard herself say it.

"Yes mam," he said in an abashed voice, "I would sher love to do that!"

Joy had given him one look on being introduced to him and then throughout the meal had not glanced at him again. He had addressed several remarks to her, which she had pretended not to hear. Mrs. Hopewell could not understand deliberate rudeness, although she lived with it, and she felt she had always to overflow with hospitality to make up for Joy's lack of courtesy. She urged him to talk about himself and he did. He said he was the seventh child of twelve and that his father had been crushed under a tree when he himself was eight year old. He had been crushed very badly, in fact, almost cut in two and was practically not recognizable. His mother had got along the best she could by hard working and she had always seen that her children went to Sunday School and that they read the Bible every evening. He was now nineteen year old and he had been selling Bibles for four months. In that time he had sold seventy-seven Bibles and had the promise of two more sales. He wanted to become a missionary because he thought that was the way you could do most for people. "He who losest his life shall find it," he said simply and he was so sincere, so genuine and earnest that Mrs. Hopewell would not for the world have smiled. He prevented his peas from sliding onto the table by blocking them with a piece of bread which he later cleaned his plate with. She could see Joy observing sidewise how he handled his knife and fork and she saw too that every few minutes, the boy would dart a keen appraising glance at the girl as if he were trying to attract her attention.

After dinner Joy cleared the dishes off the table and disappeared and Mrs. Hopewell was left to talk with him. He told her again about his childhood and his father's accident and about various things that had happened to him. Every five minutes or so she would stifle a yawn. He sat for two hours until finally she told him she must go because she had an appointment in town. He packed his Bibles and thanked her and prepared to leave, but in the doorway he stopped and wrung her hand and said that not on any of his trips had he met a lady as nice as her and he asked if he could come again. She had said she would always be happy to see him.

Joy had been standing in the road, apparently looking at something in the distance, when he came down the steps toward her, bent to the side with his heavy valise. He stopped where she was standing and confronted her directly. Mrs. Hopewell could not hear what he said but she trembled to think what Joy would say to him. She could see that after a minute Joy said something and that then the boy began to speak again, making an excited gesture with his free hand. After a minute Joy said something else at which the boy began to speak once more. Then to her amazement, Mrs. Hopewell saw the two of them walk off together, toward the gate. Joy had walked all the way to the gate with him and Mrs. Hopewell could not imagine what they had said to each other, and she had not yet dared to ask.

Mrs. Freeman was insisting upon her attention. She had moved from the refrigerator to the heater so that Mrs. Hopewell had to turn and face her in order to seem to be listening. "Glynese gone out with Harvey Hill again last night," she said. "She had this sty."

"Hill," Mrs. Hopewell said absently, "is that the one who works in the garage?"

"Nome, he's the one that goes to chiropracter school," Mrs. Freeman said. "She had this sty. Been had it two days. So she says when he brought her in the other night he says, 'Lemme get rid of that sty for you,' and she says, 'How?' and he says, 'You just lay yourself down acrost the seat of that car and I'll show you.' So she done it and he popped her neck. Kept on a-popping it several times until she made him quit. This morning," Mrs. Freeman said, "she ain't got no sty. She ain't got no traces of a sty."

"I never heard of that before," Mrs. Hopewell said.

"He ast her to marry him before the Ordinary," Mrs. Freeman went on, "and she told him she wasn't going to be married in no *office*."

"Well, Glynese is a fine girl," Mrs. Hopewell said. "Glynese and Carramae are both fine girls."

"Carramae said when her and Lyman was married Lyman said it sure felt sacred to him. She said he said he wouldn't take five hundred dollars for being married by a preacher."

"How much would he take?" the girl asked from the stove.

"He said he wouldn't take five hundred dollars," Mrs. Freeman repeated.

"Well we all have work to do," Mrs. Hopewell said.

"Lyman said it just felt more sacred to him," Mrs. Freeman said. "The doctor wants Carramae to eat prunes. Says instead of medicine. Says them cramps is coming from pressure. You know where I think it is?"

"She'll be better in a few weeks," Mrs. Hopewell said.

"In the tube," Mrs. Freeman said. "Else she wouldn't be as sick as she is."

Hulga had cracked her two eggs into a saucer and was bringing them to the table along with a cup of coffee that she had filled too full. She sat down carefully and began to eat, meaning to keep Mrs. Freeman there by questions if for any reason she showed an inclination to leave. She could perceive her mother's eye on her. The first roundabout question would be about the Bible salesman and she did not wish to bring it on. "How did he pop her neck?" she asked.

Mrs. Freeman went into a description of how he had popped her neck. She said he owned a '55 Mercury but that Glynese said she would rather marry a man with only a '36 Plymouth who would be married by a preacher. The girl asked what if he had a '32 Plymouth and Mrs. Freeman said what Glynese had said was a '36 Plymouth.

Mrs. Hopewell said there were not many girls with Glynese's common sense. She said what she admired in those girls was their common sense. She said that reminded her that they had had a nice visitor yesterday, a young man selling Bibles. "Lord," she said, "he bored me to death but he was so sincere and genuine I couldn't be rude to him. He was just good country people, you know," she said, "—just the salt of the earth."

"I seen him walk up," Mrs. Freeman said, "and then later— I seen him walk off," and Hulga could feel the slight shift in her voice, the slight insinuation, that he had not walked off alone, had he? Her face remained expressionless but the color rose into her neck and she seemed to swallow it down with the next spoonful of egg. Mrs. Freeman was looking at her as if they had a secret together.

"Well, it takes all kinds of people to make the world go

'round," Mrs. Hopewell said. "It's very good we aren't all alike."

"Some people are more alike than others," Mrs. Freeman said.

Hulga got up and stumped, with about twice the noise that was necessary, into her room and locked the door. She was to meet the Bible salesman at ten o'clock at the gate. She had thought about it half the night. She had started thinking of it as a great joke and then she had begun to see profound implications in it. She had lain in bed imagining dialogues for them that were insane on the surface but that reached below to depths that no Bible salesman would be aware of. Their conversation yesterday had been of this kind.

He had stopped in front of her and had simply stood there. His face was bony and sweaty and bright, with a little pointed nose in the center of it, and his look was different from what it had been at the dinner table. He was gazing at her with open curiosity, with fascination, like a child watching a new fantastic animal at the zoo, and he was breathing as if he had run a great distance to reach her. His gaze seemed somehow familiar but she could not think where she had been regarded with it before. For almost a minute he didn't say anything. Then on what seemed an insuck of breath, he whispered, "You ever ate a chicken that was two days old?"

The girl looked at him stonily. He might have just put this question up for consideration at the meeting of a philosophical association. "Yes," she presently replied as if she had considered it from all angles.

"It must have been mighty small!" he said triumphantly and shook all over with little nervous giggles, getting very red in the face, and subsiding finally into his gaze of complete admiration, while the girl's expression remained exactly the same.

"How old are you?" he asked softly.

She waited some time before she answered. Then in a flat voice she said, "Seventeen."

His smiles came in succession like waves breaking on the surface of a little lake. "I see you got a wooden leg," he said. "I think you're real brave. I think you're real sweet."

The girl stood blank and solid and silent.

"Walk to the gate with me," he said. "You're a brave sweet little thing and I liked you the minute I seen you walk in the door."

Hulga began to move forward.

"What's your name?" he asked, smiling down on the top of her head.

"Hulga," she said.

"Hulga," he murmured, "Hulga. Hulga. I never heard of anybody name Hulga before. You're shy, aren't you, Hulga?" he asked.

She nodded, watching his large red hand on the handle of the giant valise.

"I like girls that wear glasses," he said. "I think a lot. I'm not like these people that a serious thought don't ever enter their heads. It's because I may die."

"I may die too," she said suddenly and looked up at him. His eyes were very small and brown, glittering feverishly.

"Listen," he said, "don't you think some people was meant to meet on account of what all they got in common and all? Like they both think serious thoughts and all?" He shifted the valise to his other hand so that the hand nearest her was free. He caught hold of her elbow and shook it a little. "I don't work on Saturday," he said. "I like to walk in the woods and see what Mother Nature is wearing. O'er the hills and far away. Pic-nics and things. Couldn't we go on a pic-nic to-morrow? Say yes, Hulga," he said and gave her a dying look as if he felt his insides about to drop out of him. He had even seemed to sway slightly toward her.

During the night she had imagined that she seduced him. She imagined that the two of them walked on the place until they came to the storage barn beyond the two back fields and there, she imagined, that things came to such a pass that she very easily seduced him and that then, of course, she had to reckon with his remorse. True genius can get an idea across even to an inferior mind. She imagined that she took his remorse in hand and changed it into a deeper understanding of life. She took all his shame away and turned it into something useful.

She set off for the gate at exactly ten o'clock, escaping without drawing Mrs. Hopewell's attention. She didn't take anything to eat, forgetting that food is usually taken on a picnic. She wore a pair of slacks and a dirty white shirt, and as an afterthought, she had put some Vapex on the collar of it since she did not own any perfume. When she reached the gate no one was there.

She looked up and down the empty highway and had the furious feeling that she had been tricked, that he had only meant to make her walk to the gate after the idea of him. Then suddenly he stood up, very tall, from behind a bush on the opposite embankment. Smiling, he lifted his hat which was new and wide-brimmed. He had not worn it yesterday and she wondered if he had bought it for the occasion. It was toast-colored with a red and white band around it and was slightly too large for him. He stepped from behind the bush still carrying the black valise. He had on the same suit and the same yellow socks sucked down in his shoes from walking. He crossed the highway and said, "I knew you'd come!"

The girl wondered acidly how he had known this. She pointed to the valise and asked, "Why did you bring your Bibles?"

He took her elbow, smiling down on her as if he could not stop. "You can never tell when you'll need the word of God, Hulga," he said. She had a moment in which she doubted that this was actually happening and then they began to climb the embankment. They went down into the pasture toward the woods. The boy walked lightly by her side, bouncing on his toes. The valise did not seem to be heavy today; he even swung it. They crossed half the pasture without saying anything and then, putting his hand easily on the small of her back, he asked softly, "Where does your wooden leg join on?"

She turned an ugly red and glared at him and for an instant the boy looked abashed. "I didn't mean you no harm," he said. "I only meant you're so brave and all. I guess God takes care of you."

"No," she said, looking forward and walking fast, "I don't even believe in God."

At this he stopped and whistled. "No!" he exclaimed as if he were too astonished to say anything else.

She walked on and in a second he was bouncing at her side,

fanning with his hat. "That's very unusual for a girl," he remarked, watching her out of the corner of his eye. When they reached the edge of the wood, he put his hand on her back again and drew her against him without a word and kissed her heavily.

The kiss, which had more pressure than feeling behind it, produced that extra surge of adrenalin in the girl that enables one to carry a packed trunk out of a burning house, but in her, the power went at once to the brain. Even before he released her, her mind, clear and detached and ironic anyway, was regarding him from a great distance, with amusement but with pity. She had never been kissed before and she was pleased to discover that it was an unexceptional experience and all a matter of the mind's control. Some people might enjoy drain water if they were told it was vodka. When the boy, looking expectant but uncertain, pushed her gently away, she turned and walked on, saying nothing as if such business, for her, were common enough.

He came along panting at her side, trying to help her when he saw a root that she might trip over. He caught and held back the long swaying blades of thorn vine until she had passed beyond them. She led the way and he came breathing heavily behind her. Then they came out on a sunlit hillside, sloping softly into another one a little smaller. Beyond, they could see the rusted top of the old barn where the extra hay was stored.

The hill was sprinkled with small pink weeds. "Then you ain't saved?" he asked suddenly, stopping.

The girl smiled. It was the first time she had smiled at him at all. "In my economy," she said, "I'm saved and you are damned but I told you I didn't believe in God."

Nothing seemed to destroy the boy's look of admiration. He gazed at her now as if the fantastic animal at the zoo had put its paw through the bars and given him a loving poke. She thought he looked as if he wanted to kiss her again and she walked on before he had the chance.

"Ain't there somewheres we can sit down sometime?" he murmured, his voice softening toward the end of the sentence.

"In that barn," she said.

They made for it rapidly as if it might slide away like a train. It was a large two-story barn, cool and dark inside. The boy pointed up the ladder that led into the loft and said, "It's too bad we can't go up there."

"Why can't we?" she asked.

"Yer leg," he said reverently.

The girl gave him a contemptuous look and putting both hands on the ladder, she climbed it while he stood below, apparently awestruck. She pulled herself expertly through the opening and then looked down at him and said, "Well, come on if you're coming," and he began to climb the ladder, awkwardly bringing the suitcase with him.

"We won't need the Bible," she observed.

"You never can tell," he said, panting. After he had got into the loft, he was a few seconds catching his breath. She had sat down in a pile of straw. A wide sheath of sunlight, filled with dust particles, slanted over her. She lay back against a bale, her face turned away, looking out the front opening of the barn where hay was thrown from a wagon into the loft. The two pink-speckled hillsides lay back against a dark ridge of woods. The sky was cloudless and cold blue. The boy dropped down by her side and put one arm under her and the other over her and began methodically kissing her face, making little noises like a fish. He did not remove his hat but it was pushed far enough back not to interfere. When her glasses got in his way, he took them off of her and slipped them into his pocket.

The girl at first did not return any of the kisses but presently she began to and after she had put several on his cheek, she reached his lips and remained there, kissing him again and again as if she were trying to draw all the breath out of him. His breath was clear and sweet like a child's and the kisses were sticky like a child's. He mumbled about loving her and about knowing when he first seen her that he loved her, but the mumbling was like the sleepy fretting of a child being put to sleep by his mother. Her mind, throughout this, never stopped or lost itself for a second to her feelings. "You ain't said you loved me none," he whispered finally, pulling back from her. "You got to say that."

She looked away from him off into the hollow sky and then

down at a black ridge and then down farther into what appeared to be two green swelling lakes. She didn't realize he had taken her glasses but this landscape could not seem exceptional to her for she seldom paid any close attention to her surroundings.

"You got to say it," he repeated. "You got to say you love me."

She was always careful how she committed herself. "In a sense," she began, "if you use the word loosely, you might say that. But it's not a word I use. I don't have illusions. I'm one of those people who see *through* to nothing."

The boy was frowning. "You got to say it. I said it and you got to say it," he said.

The girl looked at him almost tenderly. "You poor baby," she murmured. "It's just as well you don't understand," and she pulled him by the neck, face-down, against her. "We are all damned," she said, "but some of us have taken off our blindfolds and see that there's nothing to see. It's a kind of salvation."

The boy's astonished eyes looked blankly through the ends of her hair. "Okay," he almost whined, "but do you love me or don'tcher?"

"Yes," she said and added, "in a sense. But I must tell you something. There mustn't be anything dishonest between us." She lifted his head and looked him in the eye. "I am thirty years old," she said. "I have a number of degrees."

The boy's look was irritated but dogged. "I don't care," he said. "I don't care a thing about what all you done. I just want to know if you love me or don'tcher?" and he caught her to him and wildly planted her face with kisses until she said, "Yes, yes."

"Okay then," he said, letting her go. "Prove it."

She smiled, looking dreamily out on the shifty landscape. She had seduced him without even making up her mind to try. "How?" she asked, feeling that he should be delayed a little.

He leaned over and put his lips to her ear. "Show me where your wooden leg joins on," he whispered.

The girl uttered a sharp little cry and her face instantly drained of color. The obscenity of the suggestion was not what shocked her. As a child she had sometimes been subject to feelings of shame but education had removed the last traces of that as a good surgeon scrapes for cancer; she would no more have felt it over what he was asking than she would have believed in his Bible. But she was as sensitive about the artificial leg as a peacock about his tail. No one ever touched it but her. She took care of it as someone else would his soul, in private and almost with her own eyes turned away. "No," she said.

"I known it," he muttered, sitting up. "You're just playing me for a sucker."

"Oh no no!" she cried. "It joins on at the knee. Only at the knee. Why do you want to see it?"

The boy gave her a long penetrating look. "Because," he said, "it's what makes you different. You ain't like anybody else."

She sat staring at him. There was nothing about her face or her round freezing-blue eyes to indicate that this had moved her; but she felt as if her heart had stopped and left her mind to pump her blood. She decided that for the first time in her life she was face to face with real innocence. This boy, with an instinct that came from beyond wisdom, had touched the truth about her. When after a minute, she said in a hoarse high voice, "All right," it was like surrendering to him completely. It was like losing her own life and finding it again, miraculously, in his.

Very gently he began to roll the slack leg up. The artificial limb, in a white sock and brown flat shoe, was bound in a heavy material like canvas and ended in an ugly jointure where it was attached to the stump. The boy's face and his voice were entirely reverent as he uncovered it and said, "Now show me how to take it off and on."

She took it off for him and put it back on again and then he took it off himself, handling it as tenderly as if it were a real one. "See!" he said with a delighted child's face. "Now I can do it myself!"

"Put it back on," she said. She was thinking that she would run away with him and that every night he would take the leg off and every morning put it back on again. "Put it back on," she said.

"Not yet," he murmured, setting it on its foot out of her reach. "Leave it off for a while. You got me instead."

She gave a little cry of alarm but he pushed her down and began to kiss her again. Without the leg she felt entirely dependent on him. Her brain seemed to have stopped thinking altogether and to be about some other function that it was not very good at. Different expressions raced back and forth over her face. Every now and then the boy, his eyes like two steel spikes, would glance behind him where the leg stood. Finally she pushed him off and said, "Put it back on me now."

"Wait," he said. He leaned the other way and pulled the valise toward him and opened it. It had a pale blue spotted lining and there were only two Bibles in it. He took one of these out and opened the cover of it. It was hollow and contained a pocket flask of whiskey, a pack of cards, and a small blue box with printing on it. He laid these out in front of her one at a time in an evenly-spaced row, like one presenting offerings at the shrine of a goddess. He put the blue box in her hand. THIS PRODUCT TO BE USED ONLY FOR THE PREVENTION OF DISEASE, she read, and dropped it. The boy was unscrewing the top of the flask. He stopped and pointed, with a smile, to the deck of cards. It was not an ordinary deck but one with an obscene picture on the back of each card. "Take a swig," he said, offering her the bottle first. He held it in front of her, but like one mesmerized, she did not move.

Her voice when she spoke had an almost pleading sound. "Aren't you," she murmured, "aren't you just good country people?"

The boy cocked his head. He looked as if he were just beginning to understand that she might be trying to insult him. "Yeah," he said, curling his lip slightly, "but it ain't held me back none. I'm as good as you any day in the week."

"Give me my leg," she said.

He pushed it farther away with his foot. "Come on now, let's begin to have us a good time," he said coaxingly. "We ain't got to know one another good yet."

"Give me my leg!" she screamed and tried to lunge for it but he pushed her down easily.

"What's the matter with you all of a sudden?" he asked, frowning as he screwed the top on the flask and put it quickly back inside the Bible. "You just a while ago said you didn't believe in nothing. I thought you was some girl!"

Her face was almost purple. "You're a Christian!" she hissed. "You're a fine Christian! You're just like them all— say one thing and do another. You're a perfect Christian, you're . . ."

The boy's mouth was set angrily. "I hope you don't think," he said in a lofty indignant tone, "that I believe in that crap! I may sell Bibles but I know which end is up and I wasn't born yesterday and I know where I'm going!"

"Give me my leg!" she screeched. He jumped up so quickly that she barely saw him sweep the cards and the blue box back into the Bible and throw the Bible into the valise. She saw him grab the leg and then she saw it for an instant slanted forlornly across the inside of the suitcase with a Bible at either side of its opposite ends. He slammed the lid shut and snatched up the valise and swung it down the hole and then stepped through himself.

When all of him had passed but his head, he turned and regarded her with a look that no longer had any admiration in it. "I've gotten a lot of interesting things," he said. "One time I got a woman's glass eye this way. And you needn't to think you'll catch me because Pointer ain't really my name. I use a different name at every house I call at and don't stay nowhere long. And I'll tell you another thing, Hulga," he said, using the name as if he didn't think much of it, "you ain't so smart. I been believing in nothing ever since I was born!" and then the toast-colored hat disappeared down the hole and the girl was left, sitting on the straw in the dusty sunlight. When she turned her churning face toward the opening, she saw his blue figure struggling successfully over the green speckled lake.

Mrs. Hopewell and Mrs. Freeman, who were in the back pasture, digging up onions, saw him emerge a little later from the woods and head across the meadow toward the highway. "Why, that looks like that nice dull young man that tried to sell me a Bible yesterday," Mrs. Hopewell said, squinting. "He must have been selling them to the Negroes back in there. He was so simple," she said, "but I guess the world would be better off if we were all that simple."

Mrs. Freeman's gaze drove forward and just touched him before he disappeared under the hill. Then she returned her attention to the evil-smelling onion shoot she was lifting from the ground. "Some can't be that simple," she said. "I know I never could."

The Displaced Person

THE PEACOCK was following Mrs. Shortley up the road to
the hill where she meant to stand. Moving one behind
the other, they looked like a complete procession. Her arms
were folded and as she mounted the prominence, she might
have been the giant wife of the countryside, come out at some
sign of danger to see what the trouble was. She stood on two
tremendous legs, with the grand self-confidence of a mountain, and rose, up narrowing bulges of granite, to two icy
blue points of light that pierced forward, surveying everything. She ignored the white afternoon sun which was creeping behind a ragged wall of cloud as if it pretended to be an
intruder and cast her gaze down the red clay road that turned
off from the highway.

The peacock stopped just behind her, his tail—glittering
green-gold and blue in the sunlight—lifted just enough so
that it would not touch the ground. It flowed out on either
side like a floating train and his head on the long blue reed-
like neck was drawn back as if his attention were fixed in the
distance on something no one else could see.

Mrs. Shortley was watching a black car turn through the
gate from the highway. Over by the toolshed, about fifteen
feet away, the two Negroes, Astor and Sulk, had stopped
work to watch. They were hidden by a mulberry tree but
Mrs. Shortley knew they were there.

Mrs. McIntyre was coming down the steps of her house to
meet the car. She had on her largest smile but Mrs. Shortley,
even from her distance, could detect a nervous slide in it.
These people who were coming were only hired help, like the
Shortleys themselves or the Negroes. Yet here was the owner
of the place out to welcome them. Here she was, wearing her
best clothes and a string of beads, and now bounding forward
with her mouth stretched.

The car stopped at the walk just as she did and the priest
was the first to get out. He was a long-legged black-suited
old man with a white hat on and a collar that he wore backwards, which, Mrs. Shortley knew, was what priests did who
wanted to be known as priests. It was this priest who had

arranged for these people to come here. He opened the back door of the car and out jumped two children, a boy and a girl, and then, stepping more slowly, a woman in brown, shaped like a peanut. Then the front door opened and out stepped the man, the Displaced Person. He was short and a little sway-backed and wore gold-rimmed spectacles.

Mrs. Shortley's vision narrowed on him and then widened to include the woman and the two children in a group picture. The first thing that struck her as very peculiar was that they looked like other people. Every time she had seen them in her imagination, the image she had got was of the three bears, walking single file, with wooden shoes on like Dutchmen and sailor hats and bright coats with a lot of buttons. But the woman had on a dress she might have worn herself and the children were dressed like anybody from around. The man had on khaki pants and a blue shirt. Suddenly, as Mrs. McIntyre held out her hand to him, he bobbed down from the waist and kissed it.

Mrs. Shortley jerked her own hand up toward her mouth and then after a second brought it down and rubbed it vigorously on her seat. If Mr. Shortley had tried to kiss her hand, Mrs. McIntyre would have knocked him into the middle of next week, but then Mr. Shortley wouldn't have kissed her hand anyway. He didn't have time to mess around.

She looked closer, squinting. The boy was in the center of the group, talking. He was supposed to speak the most English because he had learned some in Poland and so he was to listen to his father's Polish and say it in English and then listen to Mrs. McIntyre's English and say that in Polish. The priest had told Mrs. McIntyre his name was Rudolph and he was twelve and the girl's name was Sledgewig and she was nine. Sledgewig sounded to Mrs. Shortley like something you would name a bug, or vice versa, as if you named a boy Bollweevil. All of them's last name was something that only they themselves and the priest could pronounce. All she could make out of it was Gobblehook. She and Mrs. McIntyre had been calling them the Gobblehooks all week while they got ready for them.

There had been a great deal to do to get ready for them because they didn't have anything of their own, not a stick of furniture or a sheet or a dish, and everything had had to be scraped together out of things that Mrs. McIntyre couldn't use any more herself. They had collected a piece of odd furniture here and a piece there and they had taken some flowered chicken feed sacks and made curtains for the windows, two red and one green, because they had not had enough of the red sacks to go around. Mrs. McIntyre said she was not made of money and she could not afford to buy curtains. "They can't talk," Mrs. Shortley said. "You reckon they'll know what colors even is?" and Mrs. McIntyre had said that after what those people had been through, they should be grateful for anything they could get. She said to think how lucky they were to escape from over there and come to a place like this.

Mrs. Shortley recalled a newsreel she had seen once of a small room piled high with bodies of dead naked people all in a heap, their arms and legs tangled together, a head thrust in here, a head there, a foot, a knee, a part that should have been covered up sticking out, a hand raised clutching nothing. Before you could realize that it was real and take it into your head, the picture changed and a hollow-sounding voice was saying, "Time marches on!" This was the kind of thing that was happening every day in Europe where they had not advanced as in this country, and watching from her vantage point, Mrs. Shortley had the sudden intuition that the Gobblehooks, like rats with typhoid fleas, could have carried all those murderous ways over the water with them directly to this place. If they had come from where that kind of thing was done to them, who was to say they were not the kind that would also do it to others? The width and breadth of this question nearly shook her. Her stomach trembled as if there had been a slight quake in the heart of the mountain and automatically she moved down from her elevation and went forward to be introduced to them, as if she meant to find out at once what they were capable of.

She approached, stomach foremost, head back, arms folded, boots flopping gently against her large legs. About fifteen feet from the gesticulating group, she stopped and made her presence felt by training her gaze on the back of Mrs. McIntyre's neck. Mrs. McIntyre was a small woman of sixty with a round wrinkled face and red bangs that came almost down to two high orange-colored penciled eyebrows. She had a little doll's mouth and eyes that were a soft blue when she opened them wide but more like steel or granite when she narrowed them to inspect a milk can. She had buried one husband and divorced two and Mrs. Shortley respected her as a person nobody had put anything over on yet—except, ha, ha, perhaps the Shortleys. She held out her arm in Mrs. Shortley's direction and said to the Rudolph boy, "And this is Mrs. Shortley. Mr. Shortley is my dairyman. Where's Mr. Shortley?" she asked as his wife began to approach again, her arms still folded. "I want him to meet the Guizacs."

Now it was Guizac. She wasn't calling them Gobblehook to their face. "Chancey's at the barn," Mrs. Shortley said. "He don't have time to rest himself in the bushes like them niggers over there."

Her look first grazed the tops of the displaced people's heads and then revolved downwards slowly, the way a buzzard glides and drops in the air until it alights on the carcass. She stood far enough away so that the man would not be able to kiss her hand. He looked directly at her with little green eyes and gave her a broad grin that was toothless on one side. Mrs. Shortley, without smiling, turned her attention to the little girl who stood by the mother, swinging her shoulders from side to side. She had long braided hair in two looped pigtails and there was no denying she was a pretty child even if she did have a bug's name. She was better looking than either Annie Maude or Sarah Mae, Mrs. Shortley's two girls going on fifteen and seventeen but Annie Maude had never got her growth and Sarah Mae had a cast in her eye. She compared the foreign boy to her son, H. C., and H. C. came out far ahead. H. C. was twenty years old with her build and eyeglasses. He was going to Bible school now and when he finished he was going to start him a church. He had a strong sweet voice for hymns and could sell anything. Mrs. Shortley looked at the priest and was reminded that these people did not have an advanced religion. There was no telling what all they believed since none of the foolishness had been reformed out of it. Again she saw the room piled high with bodies.

The priest spoke in a foreign way himself, English but as if he had a throatful of hay. He had a big nose and a bald rectangular face and head. While she was observing him, his large mouth dropped open and with a stare behind her, he said, "Arrrrrrr!" and pointed.

Mrs. Shortley spun around. The peacock was standing a few feet behind her, with his head slightly cocked.

"What a beauti-ful birdrrrd!" the priest murmured.

"Another mouth to feed," Mrs. McIntyre said, glancing in the peafowl's direction.

"And when does he raise his splendid tail?" asked the priest.

"Just when it suits him," she said. "There used to be twenty or thirty of those things on the place but I've let them die off. I don't like to hear them scream in the middle of the night."

"So beauti-ful," the priest said. "A tail full of suns," and he crept forward on tiptoe and looked down on the bird's back where the polished gold and green design began. The peacock stood still as if he had just come down from some sun-drenched height to be a vision for them all. The priest's homely red face hung over him, glowing with pleasure.

Mrs. Shortley's mouth had drawn acidly to one side. "Nothing but a peachicken," she muttered.

Mrs. McIntyre raised her orange eyebrows and exchanged a look with her to indicate that the old man was in his second childhood. "Well, we must show the Guizacs their new home," she said impatiently and she herded them into the car again. The peacock stepped off toward the mulberry tree where the two Negroes were hiding and the priest turned his absorbed face away and got in the car and drove the displaced people down to the shack they were to occupy.

Mrs. Shortley waited until the car was out of sight and then she made her way circuitously to the mulberry tree and stood about ten feet behind the two Negroes, one an old man holding a bucket half full of calf feed and the other a yellowish boy with a short woodchuck-like head pushed into a rounded felt hat. "Well," she said slowly, "yawl have looked long enough. What you think about them?"

The old man, Astor, raised himself. "We been watching," he said as if this would be news to her. "Who they now?"

"They come from over the water," Mrs. Shortley said

with a wave of her arm. "They're what is called Displaced Persons."

"Displaced Persons," he said. "Well now. I declare. What do that mean?"

"It means they ain't where they were born at and there's nowhere for them to go—like if you was run out of here and wouldn't nobody have you."

"It seem like they here, though," the old man said in a reflective voice. "If they here, they somewhere."

"Sho is," the other agreed. "They here."

The illogic of Negro-thinking always irked Mrs. Shortley. "They ain't where they belong to be at," she said. "They belong to be back over yonder where everything is still like they been used to. Over here it's more advanced than where they come from. But yawl better look out now," she said and nodded her head. "There's about ten million billion more just like them and I know what Mrs. McIntyre said."

"Say what?" the young one asked.

"Places are not easy to get nowadays, for white or black, but I reckon I heard what she stated to me," she said in a sing-song voice.

"You liable to hear most anything," the old man remarked, leaning forward as if he were about to walk off but holding himself suspended.

"I heard her say, 'This is going to put the Fear of the Lord into those shiftless niggers!' " Mrs. Shortley said in a ringing voice.

The old man started off. "She say something like that every now and then," he said. "Ha. Ha. Yes indeed."

"You better get on in that barn and help Mr. Shortley," she said to the other one. "What you reckon she pays you for?"

"He the one sont me out," the Negro muttered. "He the one gimme something else to do."

"Well you better get to doing it then," she said and stood there until he moved off. Then she stood a while longer, reflecting, her unseeing eyes directly in front of the peacock's tail. He had jumped into the tree and his tail hung in front of her, full of fierce planets with eyes that were each ringed in green and set against a sun that was gold in one second's light and salmon-colored in the next. She might have been looking at a map of the universe but she didn't notice it any more than she did the spots of sky that cracked the dull green of the tree. She was having an inner vision instead. She was seeing the ten million billion of them pushing their way into new places over here and herself, a giant angel with wings as wide as a house, telling the Negroes that they would have to find another place. She turned herself in the direction of the barn, musing on this, her expression lofty and satisfied.

She approached the barn from an oblique angle that allowed her a look in the door before she could be seen herself. Mr. Chancey Shortley was adjusting the last milking machine on a large black and white spotted cow near the entrance, squatting at her heels. There was about a half-inch of cigarette adhering to the center of his lower lip. Mrs. Shortley observed it minutely for half a second. "If she seen or heard of you smoking in this barn, she would blow a fuse," she said.

Mr. Shortley raised a sharply rutted face containing a washout under each cheek and two long crevices eaten down both sides of his blistered mouth. "You gonter be the one to tell her?" he asked.

"She's got a nose of her own," Mrs. Shortley said.

Mr. Shortley, without appearing to give the feat any consideration, lifted the cigarette stub with the sharp end of his tongue, drew it into his mouth, closed his lips tightly, rose, stepped out, gave his wife a good round appreciative stare, and spit the smoldering butt into the grass.

"Aw Chancey," she said, "haw haw," and she dug a little hole for it with her toe and covered it up. This trick of Mr. Shortley's was actually his way of making love to her. When he had done his courting, he had not brought a guitar to strum or anything pretty for her to keep, but had sat on her porch steps, not saying a word, imitating a paralyzed man propped up to enjoy a cigarette. When the cigarette got the proper size, he would turn his eyes to her and open his mouth and draw in the butt and then sit there as if he had swallowed it, looking at her with the most loving look anybody could imagine. It nearly drove her wild and every time he did it, she wanted to pull his hat down over his eyes and hug him to death.

"Well," she said, going into the barn after him, "the

Gobblehooks have come and she wants you to meet them, says, 'Where's Mr. Shortley?' and I says, 'He don't have time . . .'"

"Tote up them weights," Mr. Shortley said, squatting to the cow again.

"You reckon he can drive a tractor when he don't know English?" she asked. "I don't think she's going to get her money's worth out of them. That boy can talk but he looks delicate. The one can work can't talk and the one can talk can't work. She ain't any better off than if she had more niggers."

"I rather have a nigger if it was me," Mr. Shortley said.

"She says it's ten million more like them, Displaced Persons, she says that there priest can get her all she wants."

"She better quit messin with that there priest," Mr. Shortley said.

"He don't look smart," Mrs. Shortley said, "—kind of foolish."

"I ain't going to have the Pope of Rome tell me how to run no dairy," Mr. Shortley said.

"They ain't Eye-talians, they're Poles," she said. "From Poland where all them bodies were stacked up at. You remember all them bodies?"

"I give them three weeks here," Mr. Shortley said.

Three weeks later Mrs. McIntyre and Mrs. Shortley drove to the cane bottom to see Mr. Guizac start to operate the silage cutter, a new machine that Mrs. McIntyre had just bought because she said, for the first time, she had somebody who could operate it. Mr. Guizac could drive a tractor, use the rotary hay-baler, the silage cutter, the combine, the letz mill, or any other machine she had on the place. He was an expert mechanic, a carpenter, and a mason. He was thrifty and energetic. Mrs. McIntyre said she figured he would save her twenty dollars a month on repair bills alone. She said getting him was the best day's work she had ever done in her life. He could work milking machines and he was scrupulously clean. He did not smoke.

She parked her car on the edge of the cane field and they got out. Sulk, the young Negro, was attaching the wagon to the cutter and Mr. Guizac was attaching the cutter to the tractor. He finished first and pushed the colored boy out of the way and attached the wagon to the cutter himself, gesticulating with a bright angry face when he wanted the hammer or the screwdriver. Nothing was done quick enough to suit him. The Negroes made him nervous.

The week before, he had come upon Sulk at the dinner hour, sneaking with a croker sack into the pen where the young turkeys were. He had watched him take a frying-size turkey from the lot and thrust it in the sack and put the sack under his coat. Then he had followed him around the barn, jumped on him, dragged him to Mrs. McIntyre's back door and had acted out the entire scene for her, while the Negro muttered and grumbled and said God might strike him dead if he had been stealing any turkey, he had only been taking it to put some black shoe polish on its head because it had the sorehead. God might strike him dead if that was not the truth before Jesus. Mrs. McIntyre told him to go put the turkey back and then she was a long time explaining to the Pole that all Negroes would steal. She finally had to call Rudolph and tell him in English and have him tell his father in Polish, and Mr. Guizac had gone off with a startled disappointed face.

Mrs. Shortley stood by hoping there would be trouble with the silage machine but there was none. All of Mr. Guizac's motions were quick and accurate. He jumped on the tractor like a monkey and maneuvered the big orange cutter into the cane; in a second the silage was spurting in a green jet out of the pipe into the wagon. He went jolting down the row until he disappeared from sight and the noise became remote.

Mrs. McIntyre sighed with pleasure. "At last," she said, "I've got somebody I can depend on. For years I've been fooling with sorry people. Sorry people. Poor white trash and niggers," she muttered. "They've drained me dry. Before you all came I had Ringfields and Collins and Jarrells and Perkins and Pinkins and Herrins and God knows what all else and not a one of them left without taking something off this place that didn't belong to them. Not a one!"

Mrs. Shortley could listen to this with composure because she knew that if Mrs. McIntyre had considered her trash, they couldn't have talked about trashy people together. Neither of them approved of trash. Mrs. McIntyre continued with the monologue that Mrs. Shortley had heard oftentimes before. "I've been running this place for thirty years," she said, looking with a deep frown out over the field, "and always just barely making it. People think you're made of money. I have the taxes to pay. I have the insurance to keep up. I have the repair bills. I have the feed bills." It all gathered up and she stood with her chest lifted and her small hands gripped around her elbows. "Ever since the Judge died," she said, "I've barely been making ends meet and they all take something when they leave. The niggers don't leave—they stay and steal. A nigger thinks anybody is rich he can steal from and that white trash thinks anybody is rich who can afford to hire people as sorry as they are. And all I've got is the dirt under my feet!"

You hire and fire, Mrs. Shortley thought, but she didn't always say what she thought. She stood by and let Mrs. McIntyre say it all out to the end but this time it didn't end as usual. "But at last I'm saved!" Mrs. McIntyre said. "One fellow's misery is the other fellow's gain. That man there," and she pointed where the Displaced Person had disappeared, "—he has to work! He wants to work!" She turned to Mrs. Shortley with her bright wrinkled face. "That man is my salvation!" she said.

Mrs. Shortley looked straight ahead as if her vision penetrated the cane and the hill and pierced through to the other side. "I would suspicion salvation got from the devil," she said in a slow detached way.

"Now what do you mean by that?" Mrs. McIntyre asked, looking at her sharply.

Mrs. Shortley wagged her head but would not say anything else. The fact was she had nothing else to say for this intuition had only at that instant come to her. She had never given much thought to the devil for she felt that religion was essentially for those people who didn't have the brains to avoid evil without it. For people like herself, for people of gumption, it was a social occasion providing the opportunity to sing; but if she had ever given it much thought, she would have considered the devil the head of it and God the hanger-on. With the coming of these displaced people, she was obliged to give new thought to a good many things.

"I know what Sledgewig told Annie Maude," she said, and when Mrs. McIntyre carefully did not ask her what but reached down and broke off a sprig of sassafras to chew, she continued in a way to indicate she was not telling all, "that they wouldn't be able to live long, the four of them, on seventy dollars a month."

"He's worth raising," Mrs. McIntyre said. "He saves me money."

This was as much as to say that Chancey had never saved her money. Chancey got up at four in the morning to milk her cows, in winter wind and summer heat, and he had been doing it for the last two years. They had been with her the longest she had ever had anybody. The gratitude they got was these hints that she hadn't been saved any money.

"Is Mr. Shortley feeling better today?" Mrs. McIntyre asked.

Mrs. Shortley thought it was about time she was asking that question. Mr. Shortley had been in bed two days with an attack. Mr. Guizac had taken his place in the dairy in addition to doing his own work. "No he ain't," she said. "That doctor said he was suffering from over-exhaustion."

"If Mr. Shortley is over-exhausted," Mrs. McIntyre said, "then he must have a second job on the side," and she looked at Mrs. Shortley with almost closed eyes as if she were examining the bottom of a milk can.

Mrs. Shortley did not say a word but her dark suspicion grew like a black thunder cloud. The fact was that Mr. Shortley did have a second job on the side and that, in a free country, this was none of Mrs. McIntyre's business. Mr. Shortley made whisky. He had a small still back in the farthest reaches of the place, on Mrs. McIntyre's land to be sure, but on land that she only owned and did not cultivate, on idle land that was not doing anybody any good. Mr. Shortley was not afraid of work. He got up at four in the morning and milked her cows and in the middle of the day when he was supposed to be resting, he was off attending to his still. Not every man would work like that. The Negroes knew about his still but he knew about theirs so there had never been any disagreeableness between them. But with foreigners on the place, with people who were all eyes and no understanding, who had come from a place continually fighting, where the religion had not been reformed—with this kind of people, you had to be on the lookout every minute. She thought there ought to be a law against them. There was no reason they couldn't stay over there and take the places of some of the people who had been killed in their wars and butcherings.

"What's furthermore," she said suddenly, "Sledgewig said as soon as her papa saved the money, he was going to buy him a used car. Once they get them a used car, they'll leave you."

"I can't pay him enough for him to save money," Mrs. McIntyre said. "I'm not worrying about that. Of course," she said then, "if Mr. Shortley got incapacitated, I would have to use Mr. Guizac in the dairy all the time and I would have to pay him more. He doesn't smoke," she said, and it was the fifth time within the week that she had pointed this out.

"It is no man," Mrs. Shortley said emphatically, "that works as hard as Chancey, or is as easy with a cow, or is more of a Christian," and she folded her arms and her gaze pierced the distance. The noise of the tractor and cutter increased and Mr. Guizac appeared coming around the other side of the cane row. "Which can not be said about everybody," she muttered. She wondered whether, if the Pole found Chancey's still, he would know what it was. The trouble with these people was, you couldn't tell what they knew. Every time Mr. Guizac smiled, Europe stretched out in Mrs. Shortley's imagination, mysterious and evil, the devil's experiment station.

The tractor, the cutter, the wagon passed, rattling and rumbling and grinding before them. "Think how long that would have taken with men and mules to do it," Mrs. McIntyre shouted. "We'll get this whole bottom cut within two days at this rate."

"Maybe," Mrs. Shortley muttered, "if don't no terrible accident occur." She thought how the tractor had made mules worthless. Nowadays you couldn't give away a mule. The next thing to go, she reminded herself, will be niggers.

In the afternoon she explained what was going to happen to them to Astor and Sulk who were in the cow lot, filling the manure spreader. She sat down next to the block of salt under a small shed, her stomach in her lap, her arms on top of it. "All you colored people better look out," she said. "You know how much you can get for a mule."

"Nothing, no indeed," the old man said, "not one thing."

"Before it was a tractor," she said, "it could be a mule. And before it was a Displaced Person, it could be a nigger. The time is going to come," she prophesied, "when it won't be no more occasion to speak of a nigger."

The old man laughed politely. "Yes indeed," he said. "Ha ha."

The young one didn't say anything. He only looked sullen but when she had gone in the house, he said, "Big Belly act like she know everything."

"Never mind," the old man said, "your place too low for anybody to dispute with you for it."

She didn't tell her fears about the still to Mr. Shortley until he was back on the job in the dairy. Then one night after they were in bed, she said, "That man prowls."

Mr. Shortley folded his hands on his bony chest and pretended he was a corpse.

"Prowls," she continued and gave him a sharp kick in the side with her knee. "Who's to say what they know and don't know? Who's to say if he found it he wouldn't go right to her and tell? How you know they don't make liquor in Europe? They drive tractors. They got them all kinds of machinery. Answer me."

"Don't worry me now," Mr. Shortley said. "I'm a dead man."

"It's them little eyes of his that's foreign," she muttered. "And that way he's got of shrugging." She drew her shoulders up and shrugged several times. "Howcome he's got anything to shrug about?" she asked.

"If everybody was as dead as I am, nobody would have no trouble," Mr. Shortley said.

"That priest," she muttered and was silent for a minute. Then she said, "In Europe they probably got some different way to make liquor but I reckon they know all the ways. They're full of crooked ways. They never have advanced or reformed. They got the same religion as a thousand years ago. It could only be the devil responsible for that. Always fighting amongst each other. Disputing. And then get us into it. Ain't they got us into it twict already and we ain't got no more

sense than to go over there and settle it for them and then
they come on back over here and snoop around and find your
still and go straight to her. And liable to kiss her hand any
minute. Do you hear me?"

"No," Mr. Shortley said.

"And I'll tell you another thing," she said. "I wouldn't be a
tall surprised if he don't know everything you say, whether it
be in English or not."

"I don't speak no other language," Mr. Shortley murmured.

"I suspect," she said, "that before long there won't be no
more niggers on this place. And I tell you what. I'd rather
have niggers than them Poles. And what's furthermore, I aim
to take up for the niggers when the time comes. When Gobblehook first come here, you recollect how he shook their
hands, like he didn't know the difference, like he might have
been as black as them, but when it come to finding out Sulk
was taking turkeys, he gone on and told her. I known he was
taking turkeys. I could have told her myself."

Mr. Shortley was breathing softly as if he were asleep.

"A nigger don't know when he has a friend," she said.
"And I'll tell you another thing. I get a heap out of Sledgewig. Sledgewig said that in Poland they lived in a brick house
and one night a man come and told them to get out of it
before daylight. Do you believe they ever lived in a brick
house?

"Airs," she said. "That's just airs. A wooden house is good
enough for me. Chancey," she said, "turn thisaway. I hate to
see niggers mistreated and run out. I have a heap of pity for
niggers and poor folks. Ain't I always had?" she asked. "I say
ain't I always been a friend to niggers and poor folks?

"When the time comes," she said, "I'll stand up for the
niggers and that's that. I ain't going to see that priest drive
out all the niggers."

Mrs. McIntyre bought a new drag harrow and a tractor
with a power lift because she said, for the first time, she had
someone who could handle machinery. She and Mrs. Shortley
had driven to the back field to inspect what he had harrowed
the day before. "That's been done beautifully!" Mrs. Mc-
Intyre said, looking out over the red undulating ground.

Mrs. McIntyre had changed since the Displaced Person had been working for her and Mrs. Shortley had observed the change very closely: she had begun to act like somebody who was getting rich secretly and she didn't confide in Mrs. Shortley the way she used to. Mrs. Shortley suspected that the priest was at the bottom of the change. They were very slick. First he would get her into his Church and then he would get his hand in her pocketbook. Well, Mrs. Shortley thought, the more fool she! Mrs. Shortley had a secret herself. She knew something the Displaced Person was doing that would floor Mrs. McIntyre. "I still say he ain't going to work forever for seventy dollars a month," she murmured. She intended to keep her secret to herself and Mr. Shortley.

"Well," Mrs. McIntyre said, "I may have to get rid of some of this other help so I can pay him more."

Mrs. Shortley nodded to indicate she had known this for some time. "I'm not saying those niggers ain't had it coming," she said. "But they do the best they know how. You can always tell a nigger what to do and stand by until he does it."

"That's what the Judge said," Mrs. McIntyre said and looked at her with approval. The Judge was her first husband, the one who had left her the place. Mrs. Shortley had heard that she had married him when she was thirty and he was seventy-five, thinking she would be rich as soon as he died, but the old man was a scoundrel and when his estate was settled, they found he didn't have a nickel. All he left her were the fifty acres and the house. But she always spoke of him in a reverent way and quoted his sayings, such as, "One fellow's misery is the other fellow's gain," and "The devil you know is better than the devil you don't."

"However," Mrs. Shortley remarked, "the devil you know is better than the devil you don't," and she had to turn away so that Mrs. McIntyre would not see her smile. She had found out what the Displaced Person was up to through the old man, Astor, and she had not told anybody but Mr. Shortley. Mr. Shortley had risen straight up in bed like Lazarus from the tomb.

"Shut your mouth!" he had said.

"Yes," she had said.

"Naw!" Mr. Shortley had said.

"Yes," she had said.

Mr. Shortley had fallen back flat.

"The Pole don't know any better," Mrs. Shortley had said. "I reckon that priest is putting him up to it is all. I blame the priest."

The priest came frequently to see the Guizacs and he would always stop in and visit Mrs. McIntyre too and they would walk around the place and she would point out her improvements and listen to his rattling talk. It suddenly came to Mrs. Shortley that he was trying to persuade her to bring another Polish family onto the place. With two of them here, there would be almost nothing spoken but Polish! The Negroes would be gone and there would be the two families against Mr. Shortley and herself! She began to imagine a war of words, to see the Polish words and the English words coming at each other, stalking forward, not sentences, just words, gabble gabble gabble, flung out high and shrill and stalking forward and then grappling with each other. She saw the Polish words, dirty and all-knowing and unreformed, flinging mud on the clean English words until everything was equally dirty. She saw them all piled up in a room, all the dead dirty words, theirs and hers too, piled up like the naked bodies in the newsreel. God save me! she cried silently, from the stinking power of Satan! And she started from that day to read her Bible with a new attention. She pored over the Apocalypse and began to quote from the Prophets and before long she had come to a deeper understanding of her existence. She saw plainly that the meaning of the world was a mystery that had been planned and she was not surprised to suspect that she had a special part in the plan because she was strong. She saw that the Lord God Almighty had created the strong people to do what had to be done and she felt that she would be ready when she was called. Right now she felt that her business was to watch the priest.

His visits irked her more and more. On the last one, he went about picking up feathers off the ground. He found two peacock feathers and four or five turkey feathers and an old brown hen feather and took them off with him like a bouquet. This foolish-acting did not deceive Mrs. Shortley any. Here he was: leading foreigners over in hoards to places that were not theirs, to cause disputes, to uproot niggers, to plant the Whore of Babylon in the midst of the righteous! Whenever he came on the place, she hid herself behind something and watched until he left.

It was on a Sunday afternoon that she had her vision. She had gone to drive in the cows for Mr. Shortley who had a pain in his knee and she was walking slowly through the pasture, her arms folded, her eyes on the distant low-lying clouds that looked like rows and rows of white fish washed up on a great blue beach. She paused after an incline to heave a sigh of exhaustion for she had an immense weight to carry around and she was not as young as she used to be. At times she could feel her heart, like a child's fist, clenching and unclenching inside her chest, and when the feeling came, it stopped her thought altogether and she would go about like a large hull of herself, moving for no reason; but she gained this incline without a tremor and stood at the top of it, pleased with herself. Suddenly while she watched, the sky folded back in two pieces like the curtain to a stage and a gigantic figure stood facing her. It was the color of the sun in the early afternoon, white-gold. It was of no definite shape but there were fiery wheels with fierce dark eyes in them, spinning rapidly all around it. She was not able to tell if the figure was going forward or backward because its magnificence was so great. She shut her eyes in order to look at it and it turned blood-red and the wheels turned white. A voice, very resonant, said the one word, "Prophesy!"

She stood there, tottering slightly but still upright, her eyes shut tight and her fists clenched and her straw sun hat low on her forehead. "The children of wicked nations will be butchered," she said in a loud voice. "Legs where arms should be, foot to face, ear in the palm of hand. Who will remain whole? Who will remain whole? Who?"

Presently she opened her eyes. The sky was full of white fish carried lazily on their sides by some invisible current and pieces of the sun, submerged some distance beyond them, appeared from time to time as if they were being washed in the opposite direction. Woodenly she planted one foot in front of the other until she had crossed the pasture and reached the lot. She walked through the barn like one in a daze and did not speak to Mr. Shortley. She continued up the road until she saw the priest's car parked in front of Mrs. McIntyre's house. "Here again," she muttered. "Come to destroy."

Mrs. McIntyre and the priest were walking in the yard. In order not to meet them face to face, she turned to the left and entered the feed house, a single-room shack piled on one side with flowered sacks of scratch feed. There were spilled oyster shells in one corner and a few old dirty calendars on the wall, advertising calf feed and various patent medicine remedies. One showed a bearded gentleman in a frock coat, holding up a bottle, and beneath his feet was the inscription, "I have been made regular by this marvelous discovery!" Mrs. Shortley had always felt close to this man as if he were some distinguished person she was acquainted with but now her mind was on nothing but the dangerous presence of the priest. She stationed herself at a crack between two boards where she could look out and see him and Mrs. McIntyre strolling toward the turkey brooder, which was placed just outside the feed house.

"Arrrr!" he said as they approached the brooder. "Look at the little biddies!" and he stooped and squinted through the wire.

Mrs. Shortley's mouth twisted.

"Do you think the Guizacs will want to leave me?" Mrs. McIntyre asked. "Do you think they'll go to Chicago or some place like that?"

"And why should they do that now?" asked the priest, wiggling his finger at a turkey, his big nose close to the wire.

"Money," Mrs. McIntyre said.

"Arrr, give them some morrre then," he said indifferently. "They have to get along."

"So do I," Mrs. McIntyre muttered. "It means I'm going to have to get rid of some of these others."

"And arrre the Shortleys satisfactory?" he inquired, paying more attention to the turkeys than to her.

"Five times in the last month I've found Mr. Shortley smoking in the barn," Mrs. McIntyre said. "Five times."

"And arrre the Negroes any better?"

"They lie and steal and have to be watched all the time," she said.

"Tsk, tsk," he said. "Which will you discharge?"

"I've decided to give Mr. Shortley his month's notice to-morrow," Mrs. McIntyre said.

The priest scarcely seemed to hear her he was so busy wiggling his finger inside the wire. Mrs. Shortley sat down on an open sack of laying mash with a dead thump that sent feed dust clouding up around her. She found herself looking straight ahead at the opposite wall where the gentleman on the calendar was holding up his marvelous discovery but she didn't see him. She looked ahead as if she saw nothing whatsoever. Then she rose and ran to her house. Her face was an almost volcanic red.

She opened all the drawers and dragged out boxes and old battered suitcases from under the bed. She began to unload the drawers into the boxes, all the time without pause, without taking off the sunhat she had on her head. She set the two girls to doing the same. When Mr. Shortley came in, she did not even look at him but merely pointed one arm at him while she packed with the other. "Bring the car around to the back door," she said. "You ain't waiting to be fired!"

Mr. Shortley had never in his life doubted her omniscience. He perceived the entire situation in half a second and, with only a sour scowl, retreated out the door and went to drive the automobile around to the back.

They tied the two iron beds to the top of the car and the two rocking chairs inside the beds and rolled the two mattresses up between the rocking chairs. On top of this they tied a crate of chickens. They loaded the inside of the car with the old suitcases and boxes, leaving a small space for Annie Maude and Sarah Mae. It took them the rest of the afternoon and half the night to do this but Mrs. Shortley was determined that they would leave before four o'clock in the morning, that Mr. Shortley should not adjust another milking machine on this place. All the time she had been working, her face was changing rapidly from red to white and back again.

Just before dawn, as it began to drizzle rain, they were ready to leave. They all got in the car and sat there cramped up between boxes and bundles and rolls of bedding. The square black automobile moved off with more than its customary grinding noises as if it were protesting the load. In the back, the two long bony yellow-haired girls were sitting on a pile of boxes and there was a beagle hound puppy and a cat with two kittens somewhere under the blankets. The car moved slowly, like some overfreighted leaking ark, away from their shack and past the white house where Mrs. McIntyre was sleeping soundly—hardly guessing that her cows would not be milked by Mr. Shortley that morning—and past the Pole's shack on top of the hill and on down the road to the gate where the two Negroes were walking, one behind the other, on their way to help with the milking. They looked straight at the car and its occupants but even as the dim yellow headlights lit up their faces, they politely did not seem to see anything, or anyhow, to attach significance to what was there. The loaded car might have been passing mist in the early morning half-light. They continued up the road at the same even pace without looking back.

A dark yellow sun was beginning to rise in a sky that was the same slick dark gray as the highway. The fields stretched away, stiff and weedy, on either side. "Where we goin?" Mr. Shortley asked for the first time.

Mrs. Shortley sat with one foot on a packing box so that her knee was pushed into her stomach. Mr. Shortley's elbow was almost under her nose and Sarah Mae's bare left foot was sticking over the front seat, touching her ear.

"Where we goin?" Mr. Shortley repeated and when she didn't answer again, he turned and looked at her.

Fierce heat seemed to be swelling slowly and fully into her face as if it were welling up now for a final assault. She was sitting in an erect way in spite of the fact that one leg was twisted under her and one knee was almost into her neck, but there was a peculiar lack of light in her icy blue eyes. All the vision in them might have been turned around, looking inside her. She suddenly grabbed Mr. Shortley's elbow and Sarah Mae's foot at the same time and began to tug and pull on them as if she were trying to fit the two extra limbs onto herself.

Mr. Shortley began to curse and quickly stopped the car and Sarah Mae yelled to quit but Mrs. Shortley apparently intended to rearrange the whole car at once. She thrashed forward and backward, clutching at everything she could get her hands on and hugging it to herself, Mr. Shortley's head,

Sarah Mae's leg, the cat, a wad of white bedding, her own big moon-like knee; then all at once her fierce expression faded into a look of astonishment and her grip on what she had loosened. One of her eyes drew near to the other and seemed to collapse quietly and she was still.

The two girls, who didn't know what had happened to her, began to say, "Where we goin, Ma? Where we goin?" They thought she was playing a joke and that their father, staring straight ahead at her, was imitating a dead man. They didn't know that she had had a great experience or ever been displaced in the world from all that belonged to her. They were frightened by the gray slick road before them and they kept repeating in higher and higher voices, "Where we goin, Ma? Where we goin?" while their mother, her huge body rolled back still against the seat and her eyes like blue-painted glass, seemed to contemplate for the first time the tremendous frontiers of her true country.

II

"Well," Mrs. McIntyre said to the old Negro, "we can get along without them. We've seen them come and seen them go—black and white." She was standing in the calf barn while he cleaned it and she held a rake in her hand and now and then pulled a corn cob from a corner or pointed to a soggy spot that he had missed. When she discovered the Shortleys were gone, she was delighted as it meant she wouldn't have to fire them. The people she hired always left her—because they were that kind of people. Of all the families she had had, the Shortleys were the best if she didn't count the Displaced Person. They had been not quite trash; Mrs. Shortley was a good woman, and she would miss her but as the Judge used to say, you couldn't have your pie and eat it too, and she was satisfied with the D. P. "We've seen them come and seen them go," she repeated with satisfaction.

"And me and you," the old man said, stooping to drag his hoe under a feed rack, "is still here."

She caught exactly what he meant her to catch in his tone. Bars of sunlight fell from the cracked ceiling across his back and cut him in three distinct parts. She watched his long hands clenched around the hoe and his crooked old profile pushed close to them. You might have been here *before* I was, she said to herself, but it's mighty likely I'll be here when you're gone. "I've spent half my life fooling with worthless people," she said in a severe voice, "but now I'm through."

"Black and white," he said, "is the same."

"I am through," she repeated and gave her dark smock that she had thrown over her shoulders like a cape a quick snatch at the neck. She had on a broad-brimmed black straw hat that had cost her twenty dollars twenty years ago and that she used now for a sunhat. "Money is the root of all evil," she said. "The Judge said so every day. He said he deplored money. He said the reason you niggers were so uppity was because there was so much money in circulation."

The old Negro had known the Judge. "Judge say he long for the day when he be too poor to pay a nigger to work," he said. "Say when that day come, the world be back on its feet."

She leaned forward, her hands on her hips and her neck stretched and said, "Well that day has almost come around here and I'm telling each and every one of you: you better look sharp. I don't have to put up with foolishness any more. I have somebody now who *has* to work!"

The old man knew when to answer and when not. At length he said, "We seen them come and we seen them go."

"However, the Shortleys were not the worst by far," she said. "I well remember those Garrits."

"They was before them Collinses," he said.

"No, before the Ringfields."

"Sweet Lord, them Ringfields!" he murmured.

"None of that kind *want* to work," she said.

"We seen them come and we seen them go," he said as if this were a refrain. "But we ain't never had one before," he said, bending himself up until he faced her, "like what we got now." He was cinnamon-colored with eyes that were so blurred with age that they seemed to be hung behind cobwebs.

She gave him an intense stare and held it until, lowering his hands on the hoe, he bent down again and dragged a pile of shavings alongside the wheelbarrow. She said stiffly, "He

can wash out that barn in the time it took Mr. Shortley to
make up his mind he had to do it."

"He from Pole," the old man muttered.

"From Poland."

"In Pole it ain't like it is here," he said. "They got different
ways of doing," and he began to mumble unintelligibly.

"What are you saying?" she said. "If you have anything to
say about him, say it and say it aloud."

He was silent, bending his knees precariously and edging
the rake along the underside of the trough.

"If you know anything he's done that he shouldn't, I expect
you to report it to me," she said.

"It warn't like it was what he should ought or oughtn't,"
he muttered. "It was like what nobody else don't do."

"You don't have anything against him," she said shortly,
"and he's here to stay."

"We ain't never had one like him before is all," he murmured and gave his polite laugh.

"Times are changing," she said. "Do you know what's happening to this world? It's swelling up. It's getting so full of
people that only the smart thrifty energetic ones are going to
survive," and she tapped the words, smart, thrifty, and energetic out on the palm of her hand. Through the far end of
the stall she could see down the road to where the Displaced
Person was standing in the open barn door with the green
hose in his hand. There was a certain stiffness about his figure
that seemed to make it necessary for her to approach him
slowly, even in her thoughts. She had decided this was because she couldn't hold an easy conversation with him. Whenever she said anything to him, she found herself shouting and
nodding extravagantly and she would be conscious that one of
the Negroes was leaning behind the nearest shed, watching.

"No indeed!" she said, sitting down on one of the feed
racks and folding her arms, "I've made up my mind that I've
had enough trashy people on this place to last me a lifetime
and I'm not going to spend my last years fooling with
Shortleys and Ringfields and Collins when the world is full
of people who *have* to work."

"Howcome they so many extra?" he asked.

"People are selfish," she said. "They have too many children. There's no sense in it any more."

He had picked up the wheelbarrow handles and was backing out the door and he paused, half in the sunlight and half out, and stood there chewing his gums as if he had forgotten which direction he wanted to move in.

"What you colored people don't realize," she said, "is that I'm the one around here who holds all the strings together. If you don't work, I don't make any money and I can't pay you. You're all dependent on me but you each and every one act like the shoe is on the other foot."

It was not possible to tell from his face if he heard her. Finally he backed out with the wheelbarrow. "Judge say the devil he know is better than the devil he don't," he said in a clear mutter and turned and trundled off.

She got up and followed him, a deep vertical pit appearing suddenly in the center of her forehead, just under the red bangs. "The Judge has long since ceased to pay the bills around here," she called in a piercing voice.

He was the only one of her Negroes who had known the Judge and he thought this gave him title. He had had a low opinion of Mr. Crooms and Mr. McIntyre, her other husbands, and in his veiled polite way, he had congratulated her after each of her divorces. When he thought it necessary, he would work under a window where he knew she was sitting and talk to himself, a careful roundabout discussion, question and answer and then refrain. Once she had got up silently and slammed the window down so hard that he had fallen backwards off his feet. Or occasionally he spoke with the peacock. The cock would follow him around the place, his steady eye on the ear of corn that stuck up from the old man's back pocket or he would sit near him and pick himself. Once from the open kitchen door, she had heard him say to the bird, "I remember when it was twenty of you walking about this place and now it's only you and two hens. Crooms it was twelve. McIntyre it was five. You and two hens now."

And that time she had stepped out of the door onto the porch and said, "MISTER Crooms and MISTER McIntyre! And I don't want to hear you call either of them anything else again. And you can understand this: when that pea-chicken dies there won't be any replacements."

She kept the peacock only out of a superstitious fear of annoying the Judge in his grave. He had liked to see them walking around the place for he said they made him feel rich. Of her three husbands, the Judge was the one most present to her although he was the only one she had buried. He was in the family graveyard, a little space fenced in the middle of the back cornfield, with his mother and father and grandfather and three great aunts and two infant cousins. Mr. Crooms, her second, was forty miles away in the state asylum and Mr. McIntyre, her last, was intoxicated, she supposed, in some hotel room in Florida. But the Judge, sunk in the cornfield with his family, was always at home.

She had married him when he was an old man and because of his money but there had been another reason that she would not admit then, even to herself: she had liked him. He was a dirty snuff-dipping Court House figure, famous all over the county for being rich, who wore hightop shoes, a string tie, a gray suit with a black stripe in it, and a yellowed panama hat, winter and summer. His teeth and hair were tobacco-colored and his face a clay pink pitted and tracked with mysterious prehistoric-looking marks as if he had been unearthed among fossils. There had been a peculiar odor about him of sweaty fondled bills but he never carried money on him or had a nickel to show. She was his secretary for a few months and the old man with his sharp eye had seen at once that here was a woman who admired him for himself. The three years that he lived after they married were the happiest and most prosperous of Mrs. McIntyre's life, but when he died his estate proved to be bankrupt. He left her a mortgaged house and fifty acres that he had managed to cut the timber off before he died. It was as if, as the final triumph of a successful life, he had been able to take everything with him.

But she had survived. She had survived a succession of tenant farmers and dairymen that the old man himself would have found hard to outdo, and she had been able to meet the constant drain of a tribe of moody unpredictable Negroes, and she had even managed to hold her own against the incidental bloodsuckers, the cattle dealers and lumber men and the buyers and sellers of anything who drove up in pieced-together trucks and honked in the yard.

She stood slightly reared back with her arms folded under her smock and a satisfied expression on her face as she watched the Displaced Person turn off the hose and disappear inside the barn. She was sorry that the poor man had been chased out of Poland and run across Europe and had had to take up in a tenant shack in a strange country, but she had not been responsible for any of this. She had had a hard time herself. She knew what it was to struggle. People ought to have to struggle. Mr. Guizac had probably had everything given to him all the way across Europe and over here. He had probably not had to struggle enough. She had given him a job. She didn't know if he was grateful or not. She didn't know anything about him except that he did the work. The truth was that he was not very real to her yet. He was a kind of miracle that she had seen happen and that she talked about but that she still didn't believe.

She watched as he came out of the barn and motioned to Sulk, who was coming around the back of the lot. He gesticulated and then took something out of his pocket and the two of them stood looking at it. She started down the lane toward them. The Negro's figure was slack and tall and he was craning his round head forward in his usual idiotic way. He was a little better than half-witted but when they were like that they were always good workers. The Judge had said always hire you a half-witted nigger because they don't have sense enough to stop working. The Pole was gesticulating rapidly. He left something with the colored boy and then walked off and before she rounded the turn in the lane, she heard the tractor crank up. He was on his way to the field. The Negro was still hanging there, gaping at whatever he had in his hand.

She entered the lot and walked through the barn, looking with approval at the wet spotless concrete floor. It was only nine-thirty and Mr. Shortley had never got anything washed until eleven. As she came out at the other end, she saw the Negro moving very slowly in a diagonal path across the road in front of her, his eyes still on what Mr. Guizac had given him. He didn't see her and he paused and dipped his knees and leaned over his hand, his tongue describing little circles. He had a photograph. He lifted one finger and traced it lightly over the surface of the picture. Then he looked up and saw her and seemed to freeze, his mouth in a half-grin, his finger lifted.

"Why haven't you gone to the field?" she asked.

He raised one foot and opened his mouth wider while the hand with the photograph edged toward his back pocket.

"What's that?" she said.

"It ain't nothin," he muttered and handed it to her automatically.

It was a photograph of a girl of about twelve in a white dress. She had blond hair with a wreath in it and she looked forward out of light eyes that were bland and composed. "Who is this child?" Mrs. McIntyre asked.

"She his cousin," the boy said in a high voice.

"Well what are you doing with it?" she asked.

"She going to mah me," he said in an even higher voice.

"Marry you!" she shrieked.

"I pays half to get her over here," he said. "I pays him three dollar a week. She bigger now. She his cousin. She don't care who she mah she so glad to get away from there." The high voice seemed to shoot up like a nervous jet of sound and then fall flat as he watched her face. Her eyes were the color of blue granite when the glare falls on it, but she was not looking at him. She was looking down the road where the distant sound of the tractor could be heard.

"I don't reckon she goin to come nohow," the boy murmured.

"I'll see that you get every cent of your money back," she said in a toneless voice and turned and walked off, holding the photograph bent in two. There was nothing about her small stiff figure to indicate that she was shaken.

As soon as she got in the house, she lay down on her bed and shut her eyes and pressed her hand over her heart as if she were trying to keep it in place. Her mouth opened and she made two or three dry little sounds. Then after a minute she sat up and said aloud, "They're all the same. It's always been like this," and she fell back flat again. "Twenty years of

being beaten and done in and they even robbed his grave!"
and remembering that, she began to cry quietly, wiping her
eyes every now and then with the hem of her smock.

What she had thought of was the angel over the Judge's
grave. This had been a naked granite cherub that the old man
had seen in the city one day in a tombstone store window. He
had been taken with it at once, partly because its face reminded him of his wife and partly because he wanted a genuine
work of art over his grave. He had come home with it sitting
on the green plush train seat beside him. Mrs. McIntyre
had never noticed the resemblance to herself. She had always
thought it hideous but when the Herrins stole it off the old
man's grave, she was shocked and outraged. Mrs. Herrin had
thought it very pretty and had walked to the graveyard frequently to see it, and when the Herrins left the angel left with
them, all but its toes, for the ax old man Herrin had used to
break it off with had struck slightly too high. Mrs. McIntyre
had never been able to afford to have it replaced.

When she had cried all she could, she got up and went into
the back hall, a closet-like space that was dark and quiet as a
chapel and sat down on the edge of the Judge's black mechanical chair with her elbow on his desk. This was a giant roll-
top piece of furniture pocked with pigeon holes full of dusty
papers. Old bankbooks and ledgers were stacked in the half-
open drawers and there was a small safe, empty but locked,
set like a tabernacle in the center of it. She had left this part
of the house unchanged since the old man's time. It was a
kind of memorial to him, sacred because he had conducted
his business here. With the slightest tilt one way or the other,
the chair gave a rusty skeletal groan that sounded something
like him when he had complained of his poverty. It had been
his first principle to talk as if he were the poorest man in the
world and she followed it, not only because he had but because it was true. When she sat with her intense constricted
face turned toward the empty safe, she knew there was nobody poorer in the world than she was.

She sat motionless at the desk for ten or fifteen minutes
and then as if she had gained some strength, she got up and
got in her car and drove to the cornfield.

The road ran through a shadowy pine thicket and ended

on top of a hill that rolled fan-wise down and up again in a broad expanse of tasseled green. Mr. Guizac was cutting from the outside of the field in a circular path to the center where the graveyard was all but hidden by the corn, and she could see him on the high far side of the slope, mounted on the tractor with the cutter and wagon behind him. From time to time, he had to get off the tractor and climb in the wagon to spread the silage because the Negro had not arrived. She watched impatiently, standing in front of her black coupe with her arms folded under her smock, while he progressed slowly around the rim of the field, gradually getting close enough for her to wave to him to get down. He stopped the machine and jumped off and came running forward, wiping his red jaw with a piece of grease rag.

"I want to talk to you," she said and beckoned him to the edge of the thicket where it was shady. He took off the cap and followed her, smiling, but his smile faded when she turned and faced him. Her eyebrows, thin and fierce as a spider's leg, had drawn together ominously and the deep vertical pit had plunged down from under the red bangs into the bridge of her nose. She removed the bent picture from her pocket and handed it to him silently. Then she stepped back and said, "Mr. Guizac! You would bring this poor innocent child over here and try to marry her to a half-witted thieving black stinking nigger! What kind of a monster are you!"

He took the photograph with a slowly returning smile. "My cousin," he said. "She twelve here. First Communion. Six-ten now."

Monster! she said to herself and looked at him as if she were seeing him for the first time. His forehead and skull were white where they had been protected by his cap but the rest of his face was red and bristled with short yellow hairs. His eyes were like two bright nails behind his gold-rimmed spectacles that had been mended over the nose with haywire. His whole face looked as if it might have been patched together out of several others. "Mr. Guizac," she said, beginning slowly and then speaking faster until she ended breathless in the middle of a word, "that nigger cannot have a white wife from Europe. You can't talk to a nigger that way. You'll excite him and besides it can't be done. Maybe it can be done in Poland but it can't be done here and you'll have to stop. It's all foolishness. That nigger don't have a grain of sense and you'll excite . . ."

"She in camp three year," he said.

"Your cousin," she said in a positive voice, "cannot come over here and marry one of my Negroes."

"She six-ten year," he said. "From Poland. Mamma die, pappa die. She wait in camp. Three camp." He pulled a wallet from his pocket and fingered through it and took out another picture of the same girl, a few years older, dressed in something dark and shapeless. She was standing against a wall with a short woman who apparently had no teeth. "She mamma," he said, pointing to the woman. "She die in two camp."

"Mr. Guizac," Mrs. McIntyre said, pushing the picture back at him, "I will not have my niggers upset. I cannot run this place without my niggers. I can run it without you but not without them and if you mention this girl to Sulk again, you won't have a job with me. Do you understand?"

His face showed no comprehension. He seemed to be piecing all these words together in his mind to make a thought.

Mrs. McIntyre remembered Mrs. Shortley's words: "He understands everything, he only pretends he don't so as to do exactly as he pleases," and her face regained the look of shocked wrath she had begun with. "I cannot understand how a man who calls himself a Christian," she said, "could bring a poor innocent girl over here and marry her to something like that. I cannot understand it. I cannot!" and she shook her head and looked into the distance with a pained blue gaze.

After a second he shrugged and let his arms drop as if he were tired. "She no care black," he said. "She in camp three year."

Mrs. McIntyre felt a peculiar weakness behind her knees. "Mr. Guizac," she said, "I don't want to have to speak to you about this again. If I do, you'll have to find another place yourself. Do you understand?"

The patched face did not say. She had the impression that he didn't see her there. "This is my place," she said. "I say who will come here and who won't."

"Ya," he said and put back on his cap.

"I am not responsible for the world's misery," she said as an afterthought.

"Ya," he said.

"You have a good job. You should be grateful to be here," she added, "but I'm not sure you are."

"Ya," he said and gave his little shrug and turned back to the tractor.

She watched him get on and maneuver the machine into the corn again. When he had passed her and rounded the turn, she climbed to the top of the slope and stood with her arms folded and looked out grimly over the field. "They're all the same," she muttered, "whether they come from Poland or Tennessee. I've handled Herrins and Ringfields and Short-leys and I can handle a Guizac," and she narrowed her gaze until it closed entirely around the diminishing figure on the tractor as if she were watching him through a gunsight. All her life she had been fighting the world's overflow and now she had it in the form of a Pole. "You're just like all the rest of them," she said, "—only smart and thrifty and energetic but so am I. And this is my place," and she stood there, a small black-hatted, black-smocked figure with an aging che-rubic face, and folded her arms as if she were equal to any-thing. But her heart was beating as if some interior violence had already been done to her. She opened her eyes to include the whole field so that the figure on the tractor was no larger than a grasshopper in her widened view.

She stood there for some time. There was a slight breeze and the corn trembled in great waves on both sides of the slope. The big cutter, with its monotonous roar, continued to shoot it pulverized into the wagon in a steady spurt of fodder. By nightfall, the Displaced Person would have worked his way around and around until there would be nothing on either side of the two hills but the stubble, and down in the center, risen like a little island, the graveyard where the Judge lay grinning under his desecrated monument.

III

The priest, with his long bland face supported on one finger, had been talking for ten minutes about Purgatory while Mrs. McIntyre squinted furiously at him from an opposite chair. They were drinking ginger ale on her front porch and she had kept rattling the ice in her glass, rattling her beads, rattling her bracelet like an impatient pony jingling its harness. There is no moral obligation to keep him, she was saying under her breath, there is absolutely no moral obligation. Suddenly she lurched up and her voice fell across his brogue like a drill into a mechanical saw. "Listen!" she said, "I'm not theological. I'm practical! I want to talk to you about something practical!"

"Arrrrrr," he groaned, grating to a halt.

She had put at least a finger of whisky in her own ginger ale so that she would be able to endure his full-length visit and she sat down awkwardly, finding the chair closer to her than she had expected. "Mr. Guizac is not satisfactory," she said.

The old man raised his eyebrows in mock wonder.

"He's extra," she said. "He doesn't fit in. I have to have somebody who fits in."

The priest carefully turned his hat on his knees. He had a little trick of waiting a second silently and then swinging the conversation back into his own paths. He was about eighty. She had never known a priest until she had gone to see this one on the business of getting her the Displaced Person. After he had got her the Pole, he had used the business introduction to try to convert her—just as she had supposed he would.

"Give him time," the old man said. "He'll learn to fit in. Where is that beautiful birrrrd of yours?" he asked and then said, "Arrrr, I see him!" and stood up and looked out over the lawn where the peacock and the two hens were stepping at a strained attention, their long necks ruffled, the cock's violent blue and the hens' silver-green, glinting in the late afternoon sun.

"Mr. Guizac," Mrs. McIntyre continued, bearing down with a flat steady voice, "is very efficient. I'll admit that. But he doesn't understand how to get on with my niggers and they don't like him. I can't have my niggers run off. And I don't like his attitude. He's not in the least grateful for being here."

The priest had his hand on the screen door and he opened it, ready to make his escape. "Arrrr, I must be off," he murmured.

"I tell you if I had a white man who understood the Negroes, I'd have to let Mr. Guizac go," she said and stood up again.

He turned then and looked her in the face. "He has nowhere to go," he said. Then he said, "Dear lady, I know you well enough to know you wouldn't turn him out for a trifle!" and without waiting for an answer, he raised his hand and gave her his blessing in a rumbling voice.

She smiled angrily and said, "I didn't create his situation, of course."

The priest let his eyes wander toward the birds. They had reached the middle of the lawn. The cock stopped suddenly and curving his neck backwards, he raised his tail and spread it with a shimmering timbrous noise. Tiers of small pregnant suns floated in a green-gold haze over his head. The priest stood transfixed, his jaw slack. Mrs. McIntyre wondered where she had ever seen such an idiotic old man. "Christ will come like that!" he said in a loud gay voice and wiped his hand over his mouth and stood there, gaping.

Mrs. McIntyre's face assumed a set puritanical expression and she reddened. Christ in the conversation embarrassed her the way sex had her mother. "It is not my responsibility that Mr. Guizac has nowhere to go," she said. "I don't find myself responsible for all the extra people in the world."

The old man didn't seem to hear her. His attention was fixed on the cock who was taking minute steps backward, his head against the spread tail. "The Transfiguration," he murmured.

She had no idea what he was talking about. "Mr. Guizac didn't have to come here in the first place," she said, giving him a hard look.

The cock lowered his tail and began to pick grass.

"He didn't have to come in the first place," she repeated, emphasizing each word.

The old man smiled absently. "He came to redeem us," he said and blandly reached for her hand and shook it and said he must go.

If Mr. Shortley had not returned a few weeks later, she would have gone out looking for a new man to hire. She had not wanted him back but when she saw the familiar black automobile drive up the road and stop by the side of the house, she had the feeling that she was the one returning, after a long miserable trip, to her own place. She realized all at once that it was Mrs. Shortley she had been missing. She had had no one to talk to since Mrs. Shortley left, and she ran to the door, expecting to see her heaving herself up the steps.

Mr. Shortley stood there alone. He had on a black felt hat and a shirt with red and blue palm trees designed in it but the hollows in his long bitten blistered face were deeper than they had been a month ago.

"Well!" she said. "Where is Mrs. Shortley?"

Mr. Shortley didn't say anything. The change in his face seemed to have come from the inside; he looked like a man who had gone for a long time without water. "She was God's own angel," he said in a loud voice. "She was the sweetest woman in the world."

"Where is she?" Mrs. McIntyre murmured.

"Daid," he said. "She had herself a stroke on the day she left out of here." There was a corpse-like composure about his face. "I figure that Pole killed her," he said. "She seen through him from the first. She known he come from the devil. She told me so."

It took Mrs. McIntyre three days to get over Mrs. Shortley's death. She told herself that anyone would have thought they were kin. She rehired Mr. Shortley to do farm work though actually she didn't want him without his wife. She told him she was going to give thirty days' notice to the Displaced Person at the end of the month and that then he could have his job back in the dairy. Mr. Shortley preferred the dairy job but he was willing to wait. He said it would give him some satisfaction to see the Pole leave the place, and Mrs. McIntyre said it would give her a great deal of satisfaction. She confessed that she should have been content with the help she had in the first place and not have been reaching into other parts of the world for it. Mr. Shortley said he never had cared for foreigners since he had been in the first world's war and seen what they were like. He said he had seen all kinds then but that none of them were like us. He said he recalled the face of one man who had thrown a hand-grenade at him and that the man had had little round eye-glasses exactly like Mr. Guizac's.

"But Mr. Guizac is a Pole, he's not a German," Mrs. McIntyre said.

"It ain't a great deal of difference in them two kinds," Mr. Shortley had explained.

The Negroes were pleased to see Mr. Shortley back. The Displaced Person had expected them to work as hard as he worked himself, whereas Mr. Shortley recognized their limitations. He had never been a very good worker himself with Mrs. Shortley to keep him in line, but without her, he was even more forgetful and slow. The Pole worked as fiercely as ever and seemed to have no inkling that he was about to be fired. Mrs. McIntyre saw jobs done in a short time that she had thought would never get done at all. Still she was resolved to get rid of him. The sight of his small stiff figure moving quickly here and there had come to be the most irritating sight on the place for her, and she felt she had been tricked by the old priest. He had said there was no legal obligation for her to keep the Displaced Person if he was not satisfactory, but then he had brought up the moral one.

She meant to tell him that *her* moral obligation was to her own people, to Mr. Shortley, who had fought in the world war for his country and not to Mr. Guizac who had merely arrived here to take advantage of whatever he could. She felt she must have this out with the priest before she fired the Displaced Person. When the first of the month came and the priest hadn't called, she put off giving the Pole notice for a little longer.

Mr. Shortley told himself that he should have known all along that no woman was going to do what she said she was when she said she was. He didn't know how long he could afford to put up with her shilly-shallying. He thought himself that she was going soft and was afraid to turn the Pole out for fear he would have a hard time getting another place. He could tell her the truth about this: that if she let him go, in three years he would own his own house and have a television aerial sitting on top of it. As a matter of policy, Mr. Shortley began to come to her back door every evening to put certain facts before her. "A white man sometimes don't get the consideration a nigger gets," he said, "but that don't matter because he's still white, but sometimes," and here he would pause and look off into the distance, "a man that's fought and bled and died in the service of his native land don't get the consideration of one of them like them he was fighting. I ast you: is that right?" When he asked her such questions he could watch her face and tell he was making an impression. She didn't look too well these days. He noticed lines around her eyes that hadn't been there when he and Mrs. Shortley had been the only white help on the place. Whenever he thought of Mrs. Shortley, he felt his heart go down like an old bucket into a dry well.

The old priest kept away as if he had been frightened by his last visit but finally, seeing that the Displaced Person had not been fired, he ventured to call again to take up giving Mrs. McIntyre instructions where he remembered leaving them off. She had not asked to be instructed but he instructed anyway, forcing a little definition of one of the sacraments or of some dogma into each conversation he had, no matter with whom. He sat on her porch, taking no notice of her partly mocking, partly outraged expression as she sat shaking her foot, waiting for an opportunity to drive a wedge into his talk. "For," he was saying, as if he spoke of something that had happened yesterday in town, "when God sent his Only Begotten Son, Jesus Christ Our Lord"—he slightly bowed his head—"as a Redeemer to mankind, He . . ."

"Father Flynn!" she said in a voice that made him jump. "I want to talk to you about something serious!"

The skin under the old man's right eye flinched.

"As far as I'm concerned," she said and glared at him fiercely, "Christ was just another D. P."

He raised his hands slightly and let them drop on his knees. "Arrrrrr," he murmured as if he were considering this.

"I'm going to let that man go," she said. "I don't have any obligation to him. My obligation is to the people who've done something for their country, not to the ones who've just come over to take advantage of what they can get," and she began to talk rapidly, remembering all her arguments. The priest's attention seemed to retire to some private oratory to wait until she got through. Once or twice his gaze roved out onto the lawn as if he were hunting some means of escape but she didn't stop. She told him how she had been hanging onto this place for thirty years, always just barely making it against people who came from nowhere and were going nowhere, who didn't want anything but an automobile. She said she had found out they were the same whether they came from Poland or Tennessee. When the Guizacs got ready, she said, they would not hesitate to leave her. She told him how the people who looked rich were the poorest of all because they had the most to keep up. She asked him how he thought she paid her feed bills. She told him she would like to have her house done over but she couldn't afford it. She couldn't even afford to have the monument restored over her husband's grave. She asked him if he would like to guess what her insurance amounted to for the year. Finally she asked him if he thought she was made of money and the old man suddenly let out a great ugly bellow as if this were a comical question.

When the visit was over, she felt let down, though she had clearly triumphed over him. She made up her mind now that on the first of the month, she would give the Displaced Person his thirty days' notice and she told Mr. Shortley so.

Mr. Shortley didn't say anything. His wife had been the only woman he was ever acquainted with who was never scared off from doing what she said. She said the Pole had been sent by the devil and the priest. Mr. Shortley had no doubt that the priest had got some peculiar control over Mrs. McIntyre and that before long she would start attending his Masses. She looked as if something was wearing her down from the inside. She was thinner and more fidgety and not as sharp as she used to be. She would look at a milk can now and not see how dirty it was and he had seen her lips move when she was not talking. The Pole never did anything the wrong way but all the same he was very irritating to her. Mr. Shortley himself did things as he pleased—not always her way—but she didn't seem to notice. She had noticed though that the Pole and all his family were getting fat; she pointed out to Mr. Shortley that the hollows had come out of their cheeks and that they saved every cent they made. "Yes'm, and one of these days he'll be able to buy and sell you out," Mr. Shortley had ventured to say, and he could tell that the statement had shaken her.

"I'm just waiting for the first," she had said.

Mr. Shortley waited too and the first came and went and she didn't fire him. He could have told anybody how it would be. He was not a violent man but he hated to see a woman done in by a foreigner. He felt that that was one thing a man couldn't stand by and see happen.

There was no reason Mrs. McIntyre should not fire Mr. Guizac at once but she put it off from day to day. She was worried about her bills and about her health. She didn't sleep at night or when she did she dreamed about the Displaced Person. She had never discharged any one before; they had all left her. One night she dreamed that Mr. Guizac and his family were moving into her house and that she was moving in with Mr. Shortley. This was too much for her and she woke up and didn't sleep again for several nights; and one night she dreamed that the priest came to call and droned on and on, saying, "Dear lady, I know your tender heart won't suffer you to turn the porrrrr man out. Think of the thousands of them, think of the ovens and the boxcars and the camps and the sick children and Christ Our Lord."

"He's extra and he's upset the balance around here," she said, "and I'm a logical practical woman and there are no ovens here and no camps and no Christ Our Lord and when he leaves, he'll make more money. He'll work at the mill and buy a car and don't talk to me—all they want is a car."

"The ovens and the boxcars and the sick children," droned the priest, "and our dear Lord."

"Just one too many," she said.

The next morning, she made up her mind while she was eating her breakfast that she would give him his notice at once, and she stood up and walked out of the kitchen and down the road with her table napkin still in her hand. Mr. Guizac was spraying the barn, standing in his sway-backed way with one hand on his hip. He turned off the hose and gave her an impatient kind of attention as if she were interfering with his work. She had not thought of what she would say to him, she had merely come. She stood in the barn door, looking severely at the wet spotless floor and the dripping stanchions. "Ya goot?" he said.

"Mr. Guizac," she said, "I can barely meet my obligations now." Then she said in a louder, stronger voice, emphasizing each word, "I have bills to pay."

"I too," Mr. Guizac said. "Much bills, little money," and he shrugged.

At the other end of the barn, she saw a long beak-nosed shadow glide like a snake halfway up the sunlit open door and stop; and somewhere behind her, she was aware of a silence where the sound of the Negroes shoveling had come a minute before. "This is my place," she said angrily. "All of you are extra. Each and every one of you are extra!"

"Ya," Mr. Guizac said and turned on the hose again.

She wiped her mouth with the napkin she had in her hand and walked off, as if she had accomplished what she came for.

Mr. Shortley's shadow withdrew from the door and he leaned against the side of the barn and lit half of a cigarette that he took out of his pocket. There was nothing for him to do now but wait on the hand of God to strike, but he knew one thing: he was not going to wait with his mouth shut.

Starting that morning, he began to complain and to state his side of the case to every person he saw, black or white. He complained in the grocery store and at the courthouse and on the street corner and directly to Mrs. McIntyre herself, for there was nothing underhanded about him. If the Pole could have understood what he had to say, he would have said it to him too. "All men was created free and equal," he said to Mrs. McIntyre, "and I risked my life and limb to prove it. Gone over there and fought and bled and died and come back on over here and find out who's got my job—just exactly who I been fighting. It was a hand-grenade come that near to killing me and I seen who throwed it—little man with eyeglasses just like his. Might have bought them at the same store. Small world," and he gave a bitter little laugh. Since he didn't have Mrs. Shortley to do the talking any more, he had started doing it himself and had found that he had a gift for it. He had the power of making other people see his logic. He talked a good deal to the Negroes.

"Whyn't you go back to Africa?" he asked Sulk one

morning as they were cleaning out the silo. "That's your country, ain't it?"

"I ain't goin there," the boy said. "They might eat me up."

"Well, if you behave yourself it isn't any reason you can't stay here," Mr. Shortley said kindly. "Because you didn't run away from nowhere. Your granddaddy was brought. He didn't have a thing to do with coming. It's the people that run away from where they come from that I ain't got any use for."

"I never felt no need to travel," the Negro said.

"Well," Mr. Shortley said, "if I was going to travel again, it would be to either China or Africa. You go to either of them two places and you can tell right away what the difference is between you and them. You go to these other places and the only way you can tell is if they say something. And then you can't always tell because about half of them know the English language. That's where we make our mistake," he said, "—letting all them people onto English. There'd be a heap less trouble if everybody only knew his own language. My wife said knowing two languages was like having eyes in the back of your head. You couldn't put nothing over on her."

"You sho couldn't," the boy muttered, and then he added, "She was fine. She was sho fine. I never known a finer white woman than her."

Mr. Shortley turned in the opposite direction and worked silently for a while. After a few minutes he leaned up and tapped the colored boy on the shoulder with the handle of his shovel. For a second he only looked at him while a great deal of meaning gathered in his wet eyes. Then he said softly, "Revenge is mine, saith the Lord."

Mrs. McIntyre found that everybody in town knew Mr. Shortley's version of her business and that everyone was critical of her conduct. She began to understand that she had a moral obligation to fire the Pole and that she was shirking it because she found it hard to do. She could not stand the increasing guilt any longer and on a cold Saturday morning, she started off after breakfast to fire him. She walked down to the machine shed where she heard him cranking up the tractor.

There was a heavy frost on the ground that made the fields look like the rough backs of sheep; the sun was almost silver

and the woods stuck up like dry bristles on the sky line. The
countryside seemed to be receding from the little circle of
noise around the shed. Mr. Guizac was squatting on the
ground beside the small tractor, putting in a part. Mrs. Mc-
Intyre hoped to get the fields turned over while he still had
thirty days to work for her. The colored boy was standing by
with some tools in his hand and Mr. Shortley was under the
shed about to get up on the large tractor and back it out. She
meant to wait until he and the Negro got out of the way
before she began her unpleasant duty.

She stood watching Mr. Guizac, stamping her feet on the
hard ground, for the cold was climbing like a paralysis up her
feet and legs. She had on a heavy black coat and a red head-
kerchief with her black hat pulled down on top of it to keep
the glare out of her eyes. Under the black brim her face had
an abstracted look and once or twice her lips moved silently.
Mr. Guizac shouted over the noise of the tractor for the Negro to hand him a screwdriver and when he got it, he turned
over on his back on the icy ground and reached up under the
machine. She could not see his face, only his feet and legs and
trunk sticking impudently out from the side of the tractor.
He had on rubber boots that were cracked and splashed with
mud. He raised one knee and then lowered it and turned himself slightly. Of all the things she resented about him, she
resented most that he hadn't left of his own accord.

Mr. Shortley had got on the large tractor and was backing
it out from under the shed. He seemed to be warmed by it as
if its heat and strength sent impulses up through him that he
obeyed instantly. He had headed it toward the small tractor
but he braked it on a slight incline and jumped off and turned
back toward the shed. Mrs. McIntyre was looking fixedly at
Mr. Guizac's legs lying flat on the ground now. She heard the
brake on the large tractor slip and, looking up, she saw it
move forward, calculating its own path. Later she remembered that she had seen the Negro jump silently out of the
way as if a spring in the earth had released him and that she
had seen Mr. Shortley turn his head with incredible slowness
and stare silently over his shoulder and that she had started
to shout to the Displaced Person but that she had not. She
had felt her eyes and Mr. Shortley's eyes and the Negro's eyes

come together in one look that froze them in collusion forever, and she had heard the little noise the Pole made as the
tractor wheel broke his backbone. The two men ran forward
to help and she fainted.

She remembered, when she came to, running somewhere,
perhaps into the house and out again but she could not remember what for or if she had fainted again when she got
there. When she finally came back to where the tractors were,
the ambulance had arrived. Mr. Guizac's body was covered
with the bent bodies of his wife and two children and by a
black one which hung over him, murmuring words she didn't
understand. At first she thought this must be the doctor but
then with a feeling of annoyance she recognized the priest,
who had come with the ambulance and was slipping something into the crushed man's mouth. After a minute he stood
up and she looked first at his bloody pants legs and then at
his face which was not averted from her but was as withdrawn and expressionless as the rest of the countryside. She
only stared at him for she was too shocked by her experience
to be quite herself. Her mind was not taking hold of all that
was happening. She felt she was in some foreign country
where the people bent over the body were natives, and she
watched like a stranger while the dead man was carried away
in the ambulance.

That evening Mr. Shortley left without notice to look for a
new position and the Negro, Sulk, was taken with a sudden
desire to see more of the world and set off for the southern
part of the state. The old man Astor could not work without
company. Mrs. McIntyre hardly noticed that she had no help
left for she came down with a nervous affliction and had to
go to the hospital. When she came back, she saw that the
place would be too much for her to run now and she turned
her cows over to a professional auctioneer (who sold them at
a loss) and retired to live on what she had, while she tried to
save her declining health. A numbness developed in one of
her legs and her hands and head began to jiggle and eventually she had to stay in bed all the time with only a colored
woman to wait on her. Her eyesight grew steadily worse and
she lost her voice altogether. Not many people remembered
to come out to the country to see her except the old priest.

He came regularly once a week with a bag of breadcrumbs and, after he had fed these to the peacock, he would come in and sit by the side of her bed and explain the doctrines of the Church.

THE VIOLENT BEAR IT AWAY

"From the days of John the Baptist until now, the kingdom of heaven suffereth violence, and the violent bear it away."
Matthew 11:12

For Edward Francis O'Connor

1896–1941

ONE

I

FRANCIS MARION TARWATER'S uncle had been dead for only half a day when the boy got too drunk to finish digging his grave and a Negro named Buford Munson, who had come to get a jug filled, had to finish it and drag the body from the breakfast table where it was still sitting and bury it in a decent and Christian way, with the sign of its Saviour at the head of the grave and enough dirt on top to keep the dogs from digging it up. Buford had come along about noon and when he left at sundown, the boy, Tarwater, had never returned from the still.

The old man had been Tarwater's great-uncle, or said he was, and they had always lived together so far as the child knew. His uncle had said he was seventy years of age at the time he had rescued and undertaken to bring him up; he was eighty-four when he died. Tarwater figured this made his own age fourteen. His uncle had taught him Figures, Reading, Writing, and History beginning with Adam expelled from the Garden and going on down through the presidents to Herbert Hoover and on in speculation toward the Second Coming and the Day of Judgment. Besides giving him a good education, he had rescued him from his only other connection, old Tarwater's nephew, a schoolteacher who had no child of his own at the time and wanted this one of his dead sister's to raise according to his own ideas.

The old man was in a position to know what his ideas were. He had lived for three months in the nephew's house on what he had thought at the time was Charity but what he said he had found out was not Charity or anything like it. All the time he had lived there, the nephew had secretly been making a study of him. The nephew, who had taken him in under the name of Charity, had at the same time been creeping into his soul by the back door, asking him questions that meant more than one thing, planting traps around the house and watching him fall into them, and finally coming up with a written study of him for a schoolteacher magazine. The stench of his behaviour had reached heaven and the Lord Himself had rescued the old man. He had sent him a rage of vision, had told him to fly with the orphan boy to the farthest part of the backwoods and raise him up to justify his Redemption. The Lord had assured him a long life and he had snatched the baby from under the schoolteacher's nose and taken him to live in the clearing, Powderhead, that he had a title to for his lifetime.

The old man, who said he was a prophet, had raised the boy to expect the Lord's call himself and to be prepared for the day he would hear it. He had schooled him in the evils that befall prophets; in those that come from the world, which are trifling, and those that come from the Lord and burn the prophet clean; for he himself had been burned clean and burned clean again. He had learned by fire.

He had been called in his early youth and had set out for the city to proclaim the destruction awaiting a world that had abandoned its Saviour. He proclaimed from the midst of his fury that the world would see the sun burst in blood and fire and while he raged and waited, it rose every morning, calm and contained in itself, as if not only the world, but the Lord Himself had failed to hear the prophet's message. It rose and set, rose and set on a world that turned from green to white and green to white and green to white again. It rose and set and he despaired of the Lord's listening. Then one morning he saw to his joy a finger of fire coming out of it and before he could turn, before he could shout, the finger had touched him and the destruction he had been waiting for had fallen in his own brain and his own body. His own blood had been burned dry and not the blood of the world.

Having learned much by his own mistakes, he was in a position to instruct Tarwater—when the boy chose to listen—in the hard facts of serving the Lord. The boy, who had ideas of his own, listened with an impatient conviction that he would not make any mistakes himself when the time came and the Lord called him.

That was not the last time the Lord had corrected the old man with fire, but it had not happened since he had taken Tarwater from the schoolteacher. That time his rage of vision had been clear. He had known what he was saving the boy from and it was saving and not destruction he was seeking. He had learned enough to hate the destruction that had to come and not all that was going to be destroyed.

Rayber, the schoolteacher, had shortly discovered where they were and had come out to the clearing to get the baby back. He had had to leave his car on the dirt road and walk a mile through the woods on a path that appeared and disappeared before he came to the corn patch with the gaunt two-story shack standing in the middle of it. The old man had been fond of recalling for Tarwater the red sweating bitten face of his nephew bobbing up and down through the corn and behind it the pink flowered hat of a welfare-woman he had brought along with him. The corn was planted up to four feet from the porch that year and as the nephew came out of it, the old man appeared in the door with his shotgun and shouted that he would shoot any foot that touched his step and the two stood facing each other while the welfare-woman bristled out of the corn, ruffled like a peahen upset on the nest. The old man said if it hadn't been for the welfare-woman, his nephew wouldn't have taken a step. Both their faces were scratched and bleeding from thorn bushes and a switch of blackberry bush hung from the sleeve of the welfare-woman's blouse.

She had only to let out her breath slowly as if she were releasing the last patience on earth and the nephew lifted his foot and planted it on the step and the old man shot him in the leg. He recalled for the boy's benefit the nephew's expression of outraged righteousness, a look that had so infuriated him that he had raised the gun slightly higher and shot him again, this time taking a wedge out of his right ear. The second shot flushed the righteousness off his face and left it blank and white, revealing that there was nothing underneath it, revealing, the old man sometimes admitted, his own failure as well, for he had tried and failed, long ago, to rescue the nephew. He had kidnapped him when the child was seven and had taken him to the backwoods and baptized him and instructed him in the facts of his Redemption, but the instruction had lasted only for a few years; in time the child had set himself a different course. There were moments when the thought that he might have helped the nephew on to his new course himself became so heavy in the old man that he would stop telling the story to Tarwater, stop and stare in front of him as if he were looking into a pit which had opened up before his feet.

At such times he would wander into the woods and leave Tarwater alone in the clearing, occasionally for days, while he thrashed out his peace with the Lord, and when he returned, bedraggled and hungry, he would look the way the boy thought a prophet ought to look. He would look as if he had been wrestling a wildcat, as if his head were still full of the visions he had seen in its eyes, wheels of light and strange beasts with giant wings of fire and four heads turned to the four points of the universe. These were the times that Tarwater knew that when he was called, he would say, "Here I am, Lord, ready!" At other times when there was no fire in his uncle's eye and he spoke only of the sweat and stink of the cross, of being born again to die, and of spending eternity eating the bread of life, the boy would let his mind wander off to other subjects.

The old man's thought did not always move at the same rate of speed through every point in his story. Sometimes, as if he did not want to think of it, he would speed over the part where he shot the nephew and race on, telling how the two of them, the nephew and the welfare-woman (whose very name was comical—Bernice Bishop) had scuttled off, making a disappearing rattle in the corn, and how the welfare-woman had screamed, "Why didn't you tell me? You knew he was crazy!" and how when they came out of the corn on the other side, he had noted from the upstairs window where he had run that she had her arm around the nephew and was holding him up while he hopped into the woods. Later he learned that he had married her though she was twice his age and he could only possibly get one child out of her. She had never let him come back again.

And the Lord, the old man said, had preserved the one child he had got out of her from being corrupted by such parents. He had preserved him in the only possible way: the child was dim-witted. The old man would pause here and let the weight of this mystery sink in on Tarwater. He had made,

since he learned of that child's existence, several trips into
town to try to kidnap him so that he could baptize him, but
each time he had come back unsuccessful. The schoolteacher
was on his guard and the old man was too fat and stiff now
to make an agile kidnapper.

"If by the time I die," he had said to Tarwater, "I haven't
got him baptized, it'll be up to you. It'll be the first mission
the Lord sends you."

The boy doubted very much that his first mission would be
to baptize a dim-witted child. "Oh no it won't be," he said.
"He don't mean for me to finish up your leavings. He has
other things in mind for me." And he thought of Moses who
struck water from a rock, of Joshua who made the sun stand
still, of Daniel who stared down lions in the pit.

"It's no part of your job to think for the Lord," his great-
uncle said. "Judgment may rack your bones."

The morning the old man died, he came down and
cooked the breakfast as usual and died before he got the first
spoonful to his mouth. The downstairs of their house was all
kitchen, large and dark, with a wood stove at one end of
it and a board table drawn up to the stove. Sacks of feed
and mash were stacked in the corners and scrapmetal, wood-
shavings, old rope, ladders, and other tinder were wherever
he or Tarwater had let them fall. They had slept in the kitchen
until a bobcat sprang in the window one night and frightened
his uncle into carrying the bed upstairs where there were
two empty rooms. The old man prophesied at the time that
the stairsteps would take ten years off his life. At the moment of his death, he sat down to his breakfast and lifted his
knife in one square red hand halfway to his mouth, and then
with a look of complete astonishment, he lowered it until
the hand rested on the edge of the plate and tilted it up off
the table.

He was a bull-like old man with a short head set directly
into his shoulders and silver protruding eyes that looked like
two fish straining to get out of a net of red threads. He had
on a putty-colored hat with the brim turned up all around
and over his undershirt a grey coat that had once been black.
Tarwater, sitting across the table from him, saw red ropes

appear in his face and a tremor pass over him. It was like the tremor of a quake that had begun at his heart and run outward and was just reaching the surface. His mouth twisted down sharply on one side and he remained exactly as he was, perfectly balanced, his back a good six inches from the chair back and his stomach caught just under the edge of the table. His eyes, dead silver, were focussed on the boy across from him.

Tarwater felt the tremor transfer itself and run lightly over him. He knew the old man was dead without touching him and he continued to sit across the table from the corpse, finishing his breakfast in a kind of sullen embarrassment as if he were in the presence of a new personality and couldn't think of anything to say. Finally he said in a querulous tone, "Just hold your horses. I already told you I would do it right." The voice sounded like a stranger's voice, as if the death had changed him instead of his great-uncle.

He got up and took his plate out the back door and set it down on the bottom step and two long-legged black game roosters tore across the yard and finished what was on it. He sat down on a long pine box on the back porch and his hands began absently to unravel a length of rope while his long face stared ahead beyond the clearing over the woods that ran in grey and purple folds until they touched the light blue fortress line of trees set against the empty morning sky.

Powderhead was not simply off the dirt road but off the wagon track and footpath, and the nearest neighbors, colored not white, still had to walk through the woods, pushing plum branches out of their way to get to it. Once there had been two houses; now there was only the one house with the dead owner inside and the living owner outside on the porch, waiting to bury him. The boy knew he would have to bury the old man before anything would begin. It was as if there would have to be dirt over him before he would be thoroughly dead. The thought seemed to give him respite from something that pressed on him.

A few weeks before, the old man had started an acre of corn to the left and had run it beyond the fenceline almost up to the house on one side. The two strands of barbed-wire ran through the middle of the patch. A line of fog, hump-shaped, was creeping toward it like a white hound dog ready to crouch under and crawl across the yard.

"I'm going to move that fence," Tarwater said. "I ain't going to have any fence I own in the middle of a patch." The voice was loud and strange and disagreeable. Inside his head it continued: you ain't the owner. The schoolteacher owns it.

I own it, Tarwater said, because I'm here and can't nobody get me off. If any schoolteacher comes to claim the property, I'll kill him.

The Lord may send you off, he thought. There was a complete stillness over everything and the boy felt his heart begin to swell. He held his breath as if he were about to hear a voice from on high. After a few moments he heard a hen scratching beneath him under the porch. He ran his arm fiercely under his nose and gradually his face paled again.

He had on a faded pair of overalls and a grey hat pulled down over his ears like a cap. He followed his uncle's custom of never taking off his hat except in bed. He had always followed his uncle's customs up to this date but: if I want to move that fence before I bury him, it wouldn't be a soul to hinder me, he thought; no voice will be uplifted.

Bury him first and get it over with, the loud stranger's disagreeable voice said. He got up and went to look for the shovel.

The pine box he had been sitting on was his uncle's coffin but he didn't intend to use it. The old man was too heavy for a thin boy to hoist over the side of a box and though old Tarwater had built it himself a few years before, he had said that if it wasn't feasible to get him into it when the time came, then just to put him in the hole as he was, only to be sure the hole was deep. He wanted it ten foot, he said, not just eight. He had worked on the box a long time and when he finished it, he had scratched on the lid, MASON TARWATER, WITH GOD, and had climbed into it where it stood on the back porch, and had lain there for some time, nothing showing but his stomach which rose over the top like over-leavened bread. The boy had stood at the side of the box, studying him. "This is the end of us all," the old man said with satisfaction, his gravel voice hearty in the coffin.

"It's too much of you for the box," Tarwater said. "I'll have to sit on the lid to press you down or wait until you rot a little."

"Don't wait," old Tarwater had said. "Listen. If it ain't feasible to use the box when the time comes, if you can't lift it or whatever, just get me in the hole but I want it deep. I want it ten foot, not just eight, ten. You can roll me to it if nothing else. I'll roll. Get two boards and set them down the steps and start me rolling and dig where I stop and don't let me roll over into it until it's deep enough. Prop me with some bricks so I won't roll into it and don't let the dogs nudge me over the edge before it's finished. You better pen up the dogs," he said.

"What if you die in bed?" the boy asked. "How'm I going to get you down the stairs?"

"I ain't going to die in bed," the old man said. "As soon as I hear the summons, I'm going to run downstairs. I'll get as close to the door as I can. If I should get stuck up there, you'll have to roll me down the stairs, that's all."

"My Lord," the child said.

The old man sat up in the box and brought his fist down on the edge of it. "Listen," he said. "I never asked much of you. I taken you and raised you and saved you from that ass in town and now all I'm asking in return is when I die to get me in the ground where the dead belong and set up a cross over me to show I'm there. That's all in the world I'm asking you to do. I ain't even asking you to go for the niggers and try to get me in the plot with my daddy. I could ask you that but I ain't. I'm doing everything to make it easy for you. All I'm asking you is to get me in the ground and set up a cross."

"I'll be doing good if I get you in the ground," Tarwater said. "I'll be too wore out to set up any cross. I ain't bothering with trifles."

"Trifles!" his uncle hissed. "You'll learn what a trifle is on the day those crosses are gathered! Burying the dead right may be the only honor you ever do yourself. I brought you out here to raise you a Christian, and more than a Christian, a prophet!" he hollered, "and the burden of it will be on you!"

"If I don't have the strength to do it," the child said, watching him with a careful detachment, "I'll notify my uncle in town and he can come out and take care of you. The school-teacher," he drawled, observing that the pockmarks in his uncle's face had already turned pale against the purple. "He'll tend to you."

The threads that restrained the old man's eyes thickened. He gripped both sides of the coffin and pushed forward as if he were going to drive it off the porch. "He'd burn me," he said hoarsely. "He'd have me cremated in an oven and scatter my ashes. 'Uncle,' he said to me, 'you're a type that's almost extinct!' He'd be willing to pay the undertaker to burn me to be able to scatter my ashes," he said. "He don't believe in the Resurrection. He don't believe in the Last Day. He don't believe in the bread of life . . . ."

"The dead don't bother with particulars," the boy interrupted.

The old man grabbed the front of his overalls and pulled him up against the side of the box and glared into his pale face. "The world was made for the dead. Think of all the dead there are," he said, and then as if he had conceived the answer for all the insolence in the world, he said, "There's a million times more dead than living and the dead are dead a million times longer than the living are alive," and he released him with a laugh.

The boy had shown only by a slight quiver that he was shaken by this, and after a minute he had said, "The school-teacher is my uncle. The only blood connection with good sense I'll have and a living man and if I wanted to go to him, I'd go; now."

The old man looked at him silently for what seemed a full minute. Then he slammed his hands flat on the sides of the box and roared, "Whom the plague beckons, to the plague! Whom the sword to the sword! Whom fire to fire!" And the child trembled visibly.

"I saved you to be free, your own self!" he had shouted, "and not a piece of information inside his head! If you were living with him, you'd be information right now, you'd be inside his head, and what's furthermore," he said, "you'd be going to school."

The boy grimaced. The old man had always impressed on him his good fortune in not being sent to school. The Lord had seen fit to guarantee the purity of his up-bringing, to preserve him from contamination, to preserve him as His elect servant, trained by a prophet for prophesy. While other children his age were herded together in a room to cut out paper pumpkins under the direction of a woman, he was left free for the pursuit of wisdom, the companions of his spirit Abel and Enoch and Noah and Job, Abraham and Moses, King David and Solomon, and all the prophets, from Elijah who escaped death, to John whose severed head struck terror from a dish. The boy knew that escaping school was the surest sign of his election.

The truant officer had come only once. The Lord had told the old man to expect it and what to do and old Tarwater had instructed the boy in his part against the day when, as the devil's emissary, the officer would appear. When the time came and they saw him cutting across the field, they were ready. The child got behind the house and the old man sat on the steps and waited. When the officer, a thin bald-headed man with red galluses, stepped out of the field onto the packed dirt of the yard, he greeted old Tarwater warily and commenced his business as if he had not come for it. He sat down on the steps and spoke of poor weather and poor health. Finally, gazing out over the field, he said, "You got a boy, don't you, that ought to be in school?"

"A fine boy," the old man said, "and I wouldn't stand in his way if anybody thought they could teach him. You boy!" he called. The boy didn't come at once. "Oh you boy!" the old man shouted.

In a few minutes Tarwater appeared from around the side of the house. His eyes were open but not well-focused. His head rolled uncontrollably on his slack shoulders and his tongue lolled in his open mouth.

"He ain't bright," the old man said, "but he's a mighty good boy. He knows to come when you call him."

"Yes," the truant officer said, "well yes, but it might be best to leave him in peace."

"I don't know, he might take to schooling," the old man said. "He ain't had a fit for going on two months."

"I speck he better stay at home," the officer said. "I wouldn't want to put a strain on him," and he commenced to speak of other things. Shortly he took his leave and the two of them watched with satisfaction as the diminishing figure moved back across the field and the red galluses were finally lost to view.

If the schoolteacher had got hold of him, right now he would have been in school, one among many, indistinguishable from the herd, and in the schoolteacher's head, he would be laid out in parts and numbers. "That's where he wanted me," the old man said, "and he thought once he had me in that schoolteacher magazine, I would be as good as in his head." The schoolteacher's house had had little in it but books and papers. The old man had not known when he went there to live that every living thing that passed through the nephew's eyes into his head was turned by his brain into a book or a paper or a chart. The schoolteacher had appeared to have a great interest in his being a prophet, chosen by the Lord, and had asked numerous questions, the answers to which he had sometimes scratched down on a pad, his little eyes lighting every now and then as if in some discovery.

The old man had fancied he was making progress in convincing the nephew again of his Redemption, for he at least listened though he did not *say* he believed. He seemed to delight to talk about the things that interested his uncle. He questioned him at length about his early life, which old Tarwater had practically forgotten. The old man had thought this interest in his forebears would bear fruit, but what it bore, what it bore, stench and shame, were dead words. What it bore was a dry and seedless fruit, incapable even of rotting, dead from the beginning. From time to time, the old man would spit out of his mouth, like gobbets of poison, some of the idiotic sentences from the schoolteacher's piece. Wrath had burned them on his memory, word for word. "His fixation of being called by the Lord had its origin in insecurity. He needed the assurance of a call, and so he called himself."

"Called myself!" the old man would hiss, "called myself!" This so enraged him that half the time he could do nothing but repeat it. "Called myself. I called myself. I, Mason Tarwater, called myself! Called myself to be beaten and tied up.

Called myself to be spit on and snickered at. Called myself to be struck down in my pride. Called myself to be torn by the Lord's eye. Listen boy," he would say and grab the child by the straps of his overalls and shake him slowly, "even the mercy of the Lord burns." He would let go the straps and allow the boy to fall back into the thorn bed of that thought, while he continued to hiss and groan.

"Where he wanted me was inside that schoolteacher magazine. He thought once he got me in there, I'd be as good as inside his head and done for and that would be that, that would be the end of it. Well, that wasn't the end of it! Here I sit. And there you sit. In freedom. Not inside anybody's head!" and his voice would run away from him as if it were the freest part of his free self and were straining ahead of his heavy body to be off. Something of his great-uncle's glee would take hold of Tarwater at that point and he would feel that he had escaped some mysterious prison. He even felt he could smell his freedom, pine-scented, coming out of the woods, until the old man would continue, "You were born into bondage and baptized into freedom, into the death of the Lord, into the death of the Lord Jesus Christ."

Then the child would feel a sullenness creeping over him, a slow warm rising resentment that this freedom had to be connected with Jesus and that Jesus had to be the Lord.

"Jesus is the bread of life," the old man said.

The boy, disconcerted, would look off into the distance over the dark blue treeline where the world stretched out, hidden and at its ease. In the darkest, most private part of his soul, hanging upsidedown like a sleeping bat, was the certain, undeniable knowledge that he was not hungry for the bread of life. Had the bush flamed for Moses, the sun stood still for Joshua, the lions turned aside before Daniel only to prophesy the bread of life? Jesus? He felt a terrible disappointment in that conclusion, a dread that it was true. The old man said that as soon as he died, he would hasten to the banks of the Lake of Galilee to eat the loaves and fishes that the Lord had multiplied.

"Forever?" the horrified boy asked.

"Forever," the old man said.

The boy sensed that this was the heart of his great-uncle's

madness, this hunger, and what he was secretly afraid of was that it might be passed down, might be hidden in the blood and might strike some day in him and then he would be torn by hunger like the old man, the bottom split out of his stomach so that nothing would heal or fill it but the bread of life.

He tried when possible to pass over these thoughts, to keep his vision located on an even level, to see no more than what was in front of his face and to let his eyes stop at the surface of that. It was as if he were afraid that if he let his eye rest for an instant longer than was needed to place something—a spade, a hoe, the mule's hind quarters before his plow, the red furrow under him—that the thing would suddenly stand before him, strange and terrifying, demanding that he name it and name it justly and be judged for the name he gave it. He did all he could to avoid this threatened intimacy of creation. When the Lord's call came, he wished it to be a voice from out of a clear and empty sky, the trumpet of the Lord God Almighty, untouched by any fleshly hand or breath. He expected to see wheels of fire in the eyes of unearthly beasts. He had expected this to happen as soon as his great-uncle died. He turned his mind off this quickly and went to get the shovel. The schoolteacher is a living man, he thought as he went, but he'd better not come out here and try to get me off this property because I'll kill him. Go to him and be damned, his uncle had said. I've saved you from him this far and if you go to him the minute I'm in the ground there's nothing I can do about it.

The shovel lay against the side of the hen house. "I'll never set my foot in the city again," the boy said to himself aloud. I'll never go to him. Him nor nobody else will ever get me off this place.

He decided to dig the grave under the fig tree because the old man would be good for the figs. The ground was sandy on top and solid brick underneath and the shovel made a clanging sound when he struck it in the sand. Two hundred pounds of dead mountain to bury, he thought, and stood with one foot on the shovel, leaning forward, studying the white sky through the leaves of the tree. It would take all day to get a hole big enough out of this rock and the schoolteacher would burn him in a minute.

Tarwater had seen the schoolteacher once from a distance of about twenty feet and he had seen the dim-witted child closer up. The little boy somewhat resembled old Tarwater except for his eyes which were grey like the old man's but clear, as if the other side of them went down and down into two pools of light. It was plain to look at him that he did not have any sense. The old man had been so shocked by the likeness and the unlikeness that the time he and Tarwater had gone there, he had only stood in the door, staring at the little boy and rolling his tongue around outside his mouth as if he had no sense himself. That had been the first time he had seen the child and he could not forget him. "Married her and got one child out of her and that without sense," he would murmur. "The Lord preserved him and now He means to see he's baptized."

"Well whyn't you get on with it then?" the boy asked, for he wanted something to happen, wanted to see the old man in action, wanted him to kidnap the child and have the schoolteacher have to come after him so that he could get a closer look at his other uncle. "What ails you?" he asked. "What makes you tarry so long? Why don't you make haste and steal him?"

"I take my directions from the Lord God," the old man said, "Who moves in His own time. I don't take them from you."

The white fog had eased through the yard and disappeared into the next bottom and the air was clear and blank. His mind continued to dwell on the schoolteacher's house. "Three months there," his great-uncle had said. "It shames me. Betrayed for three months in the house of my own kin and if when I'm dead you want to turn me over to my betrayer and see my body burned, go ahead! Go ahead, boy," he had shouted, sitting up splotch-faced in his box. "Go ahead and let him burn me but watch out for the Lord's lion after that. Remember the Lord's lion set in the path of the false prophet! I been leavened by the yeast he don't believe in," he had said, "and I won't be burned! And when I'm gone, you'll be better off in these woods by yourself with just as much light as the sun wants to let in than you'll be in the city with him."

He kept on digging but the grave did not get any deeper. "The dead are poor," he said in the voice of the stranger. You can't be any poorer than dead. He'll have to take what he gets. Nobody to bother me, he thought. Ever. No hand uplifted to hinder me from anything; except the Lord's and He ain't said anything. He ain't even noticed me yet.

A sand-colored hound beat its tail on the ground nearby and a few black chickens scratched in the raw clay he was turning up. The sun had slipped over the blue line of trees and circled by a haze of yellow was moving slowly across the sky. "Now I can do anything I want to," he said, softening the stranger's voice so that he could stand it. Could kill off all those chickens if I had a mind to, he thought, watching the worthless black game bantams that his uncle had been fond of keeping.

He favored a lot of foolishness, the stranger said. The truth is he was childish. Why, that schoolteacher never did him any harm. You take, all he did was to watch him and write down what he seen and heard and put it in a paper for school-teachers to read. Now what was wrong in that? Why nothing. Who cares what a schoolteacher reads? And the old fool acted like he had been killed in his very soul. Well he wasn't so near dead as he thought he was. Lived on fourteen years and raised up a boy to bury him, suitable to his own taste.

As Tarwater slashed at the ground with the shovel, the stranger's voice took on a kind of restrained fury and he kept repeating, you got to bury him whole and completely by hand and that schoolteacher would burn him in a minute.

After he had dug for an hour or more, the grave was only a foot deep, not as deep yet as the corpse. He sat down on the edge of it for a while. The sun was like a furious white blister in the sky.

The dead are a heap more trouble than the living, the stranger said. That schoolteacher wouldn't consider for a min-ute that on the last day all the bodies marked by crosses will be gathered. In the rest of the world they do things different than what you been taught.

"I been there once," Tarwater muttered. "Nobody has to tell me."

His uncle two or three years before had gone to call on the

lawyers to try to get the property unentailed so that it would skip the schoolteacher and go to Tarwater. Tarwater had sat at the lawyer's twelfth-story window and looked down into the pit of the street while his uncle transacted the business. On the way from the railroad station he had walked tall in the mass of moving metal and concrete speckled with the very small eyes of people. The glitter of his own eyes was shaded under the stiff roof-like brim of a new grey hat, balanced perfectly straight on his buttressing ears. Before coming he had read facts in the almanac and he knew that there were 75,000 people here who were seeing him for the first time. He wanted to stop and shake hands with each of them and say his name was F. M. Tarwater and that he was here only for the day to accompany his uncle on business at a lawyer's. His head jerked backwards after each passing figure until they began to pass too thickly and he observed that their eyes didn't grab at you like the eyes of country people. Several people bumped into him and this contact that should have made an acquaintance for life, made nothing because the hulks shoved on with ducked heads and muttered apologies that he would have accepted if they had waited.

Then he had realized, almost without warning, that this place was evil—the ducked heads, the muttered words, the hastening away. He saw in a burst of light that these people were hastening away from the Lord God Almighty. It was to the city that the prophets came and he was here in the midst of it. He was here enjoying what should have repelled him. His lids narrowed with caution and he looked at his uncle who was rolling on ahead of him, no more concerned with it all than a bear in the woods. "What kind of prophet are you?" the boy hissed.

His uncle paid him no attention, did not stop.

"Call yourself a prophet!" he continued in a high rasping carrying voice.

His uncle stopped and turned. "I'm here on bidnis," he said mildly.

"You always said you were a prophet," Tarwater said. "Now I see what kind of prophet you are. Elijah would think a heap of you."

His uncle thrust his head forward and his eyes began to

bulge. "I'm here on bidnis," he said. "If you been called by the Lord, then be about your own mission."

The boy paled slightly and his gaze shifted. "I ain't been called *yet*," he muttered. "It's you that's been called."

"And I know what times I'm called and what times I ain't," his uncle said and turned and paid him no more attention.

At the lawyer's window, he knelt down and let his face hang out upsidedown over the floating speckled street moving like a river of tin below and watched the glints on it from the sun which drifted pale in a pale sky, too far away to ignite anything. When he was called, on that day when he returned, he would set the city astir, he would return with fire in his eyes. You have to do something particular here to make them look at you, he thought. They ain't going to look at you just because you're here. He considered his uncle with renewed disgust. When I come for good, he said to himself, I'll do something to make every eye stick on me, and leaning forward, he saw his new hat drop down gently, lost and casual, dallied slightly by the breeze on its way to be smashed in the tin river below. He clutched at his bare head and fell back inside the room.

His uncle was in argument with the lawyer, both hitting the desk that separated them, bending their knees and hitting their fists at the same time. The lawyer, a tall dome-headed man with an eagle's nose, kept repeating in a restrained shriek, "But I didn't make the will. I didn't make the law," and his uncle's gravel voice grated, "I can't help it. My daddy wouldn't have seen a fool inherit his property. That's not how he intended it."

"My hat is gone," Tarwater said.

The lawyer threw himself backwards into his chair and screaked it toward Tarwater and saw him without interest from pale blue eyes and screaked it forward again and said to his uncle, "There's nothing I can do. You're wasting your time and mine. You might as well resign yourself to this will."

"Listen," old Tarwater said, "at one time I thought I was finished, old and sick and about to die and no money, nothing, and I accepted his hospitality because he was my closest blood connection and you could have called it his duty to take me, only I thought it was Charity, I thought . . . "

"I can't help what you thought or did or what your connection thought or did," the lawyer said and closed his eyes.

"My hat fell," Tarwater said.

"I'm only a lawyer," the lawyer said, letting his glance rove over the lines of clay-colored books of law that fortressed his office.

"A car is liable to have run over it by now."

"Listen," his uncle said, "all the time he was studying me for this paper. Taking secret tests on me, his own kin, crawling into my soul through the back door and then says to me, 'Uncle, you're a type that's almost extinct!' Almost extinct!" the old man piped, barely able to force a thread of sound from his throat. "You see how extinct I am!"

The lawyer closed his eyes again and smiled into one cheek.

"Other lawyers," the old man growled and they had left and visited three more, without stopping, and Tarwater had counted eleven men who might have had on his hat or might not. Finally when they came out of the fourth lawyer's office, they sat down on the window ledge of a bank building and his uncle felt in his pocket for some biscuits he had brought and handed one to Tarwater. The old man unbuttoned his coat and allowed his stomach to ease forward and rest on his lap while he ate. His face worked wrathfully; the skin between the pockmarks appeared to jump from one spot to another. Tarwater was very pale and his eyes glittered with a peculiar hollow depth. He had an old work kerchief tied around his head, knotted at the four corners. He didn't observe the passing people who observed him now. "Thank God we're finished and can go home," he muttered.

"We ain't finished here," the old man said and got up abruptly and started down the street.

"My Lord!" the boy groaned, jumping to catch up with him. "Can't we sit down for one minute? Ain't you got any sense? They all tell you the same thing. It's only one law and it's nothing you can do about it. I got sense enough to get that; why ain't you? What's the matter with you?"

The old man strode on with his head thrust forward as if he were smelling out an enemy.

"Where we going?" Tarwater asked after they had walked out of the business streets and were passing between rows of grey bulbous houses with sooty porches that overhung the sidewalks. "Listen," he said, hitting at his uncle's hip, "I never ast to come."

"You would have ast to come soon enough," the old man muttered. "Get your fill now."

"I never ast for no fill. I never ast to come at all. I'm here before I knew this here was here."

"Just remember," the old man said, "just remember that I told you to remember when you ast to come that you never liked it when you were here," and they kept on going, crossing one length of sidewalk after another, row after row of overhanging houses with half-open doors that let a little dried light fall on the stained passageways inside. Finally they came out into another section where the houses were clean and squat and almost identical and each had a square of grass in front of it. After a few blocks Tarwater dropped down on the sidewalk and said, "I ain't going no further. I don't even know where I'm going and I ain't going no further." His uncle didn't stop or look back. In a second he jumped up and followed him again in a panic lest he be left.

The old man kept straining forward as if his blood scent were leading him closer and closer to the place where his enemy was hiding. He suddenly turned up the short walk of a pale yellow brick house and moved rigidly to the white door, his heavy shoulders hunched as if he were going to crash through it. He struck the wood with his fist, ignoring a polished brass knocker. At that instant Tarwater realized that this was where the schoolteacher lived, and he stopped where he was and remained rigid, his eye on the door. He knew by some obscure instinct that the door was going to open and reveal his destiny. In his mind's eye, he saw the schoolteacher about to appear in it, lean and evil, waiting to engage whom the Lord would send to conquer him. The boy clamped his teeth together to keep them from chattering. The door opened.

A small pink-faced boy stood in it with his mouth hung in a silly smile. He had white hair and a knobby forehead. He wore steel-rimmed spectacles and had pale silver eyes like the old man's except that they were clear and empty. He was gnawing on a brown apple core.

The old man stared at him, his lips parting slowly until his mouth hung open. He looked as if he beheld an unspeakable mystery. The little boy made an unintelligible noise and pushed the door almost shut, hiding himself all but one spectacled eye.

Suddenly a tremendous indignation seized Tarwater. He eyed the small face peering from the crack. He searched his mind fiercely for the right word to hurl at it. Finally he said in a slow emphatic voice, "Before you was here, *I* was here."

The old man caught his shoulder and pulled him back. "He don't have good sense," he said. "Can't you see he don't have good sense? He don't know what you're talking about."

The boy grew more furious than ever. He swung around on his heel to leave.

"Wait," his uncle said and caught him. "Get behind that hedge yonder and hide yourself. I'm going in there and baptize him."

Tarwater's mouth was agape.

"Get behind there like I told you," he said and gave him a push toward the hedge. Then the old man braced himself. He turned and went back to the door. Just as he reached it, it was flung open and a lean young man with heavy black-rimmed spectacles stood in it, his head thrust forward, glaring at him.

Old Tarwater raised his fist. "The Lord Jesus Christ sent me to baptize that boy!" he shouted. "Stand aside. I mean to do it!"

Tarwater's head popped up from behind the hedge. Breathlessly he took the schoolteacher in—the narrow boney face slanting backwards from the jutting jaw, the hair that receded from the high forehead, the eyes encircled in glass. The white-haired child had caught hold of his father's leg and was hanging onto it. The schoolteacher pushed him back inside the house. Then he stepped outside and slammed the door behind him and continued to glare at the old man as if he dared him to take a step.

"That boy cries out for his baptism," the old man said. "Precious in the sight of the Lord even an idiot!"

"Get off my property," the nephew said in a tight voice as if he were keeping it calm by force. "If you don't, I'll have you put back in the asylum where you belong."

"You can't touch the servant of the Lord!" the old man hollered.

"You get away from here!" the nephew shouted, losing control of his voice. "Ask the Lord why He made him an idiot in the first place, uncle. Tell him I want to know why!"

The boy's heart was beating so fast he was afraid it was going to gallop out of his chest and disappear forever. He was head and shoulders out of the shrubbery.

"Yours not to ask!" the old man shouted. "Yours not to question the mind of the Lord God Almighty. Yours not to grind the Lord into your head and spit out a number!"

"Where's the boy?" the nephew asked, looking around suddenly as if he had just thought of it. "Where's the boy you were going to raise into a prophet to burn my eyes clean?" and he laughed.

Tarwater lowered his head into the bush again, instantly disliking the schoolteacher's laugh which seemed to reduce him to the least importance.

"His day is going to come," the old man said. "Either him or me is going to baptize that child. If not me in my day, him in his."

"You'll never lay a hand on him," the schoolteacher said. "You could slosh water on him for the rest of his life and he'd still be an idiot. Five years old for all eternity, useless forever. Listen," he said, and the boy heard his taut voice turn low with a kind of subdued intensity, a passion equal and opposite to the old man's, "he'll never be baptized—just as a matter of principle, nothing else. As a gesture of human dignity, he'll never be baptized."

"Time will discover the hand that baptizes him," the old man said.

"Time will discover it," the nephew said and opened the door behind him and stepped back inside and slammed it on himself.

The boy had risen from the shrubbery, his head swirling with excitement. He had never been back there again, never seen his cousin again, never seen the schoolteacher again, and he hoped to God, he told the stranger digging the grave along with him now that he would never see him again though he had nothing against him himself and he would dislike to have to kill him but if he came out here, messing in what was none of his business except by law, then he would be obliged to.

Listen, the stranger said, what would he want to come out here for—where there's nothing?

Tarwater didn't answer. He didn't search out the stranger's face but he knew by now that it was sharp and friendly and wise, shadowed under a stiff broad-brimmed panama hat that obscured the color of his eyes. He had lost his dislike for the thought of the voice. Only every now and then it sounded like a stranger's voice to him. He began to feel that he was only just now meeting himself, as if as long as his uncle had lived, he had been deprived of his own acquaintance. I ain't denying the old man was a good one, his new friend said, but like you said: you can't be any poorer than dead. They have to take what they can get. His soul is off this mortal earth now and his body is not going to feel the pinch, of fire or anything else.

"It was the last day he was thinking of," Tarwater murmured.

Well now, the stranger said, don't you think any cross you set up in the year 1952 would be rotted out by the year the Day of Judgment comes in? Rotted to as much dust as his ashes if you reduced him to ashes? And lemme ast you this: what's God going to do with sailors drowned at sea that the fish have et and the fish that et them et by other fish and they et by yet others? And what about people that get burned up naturally in house fires? Burnt up one way or another or lost in machines until they're pulp? And all those sojers blasted to nothing? What about all those that there's nothing left of to burn or bury?

If I burnt him, Tarwater said, it wouldn't be natural, it would be deliberate.

Oh I see, the stranger said. It ain't the Day of Judgment for him you're worried about. It's the Day of Judgment for you.

That's my bidnis, Tarwater said.

I ain't buttin into your bidnis, the stranger said. It don't mean a thing to me. You're left by yourself in this empty place. Forever by yourself in this empty place with just as much light as that dwarf sun wants to let in. You don't mean a thing to a soul as far as I can see.

"Redeemed," Tarwater muttered.

Do you smoke? the stranger asked.

Smoke if I want to and don't if I don't, Tarwater said. Bury if need be and don't if don't.

Go take a look at him and see if he's fell off his chair, his friend suggested.

Tarwater let the shovel drop in the grave and returned to the house. He opened the front door a crack and put his face to it. His uncle glared slightly to the side of him like a judge intent upon some terrible evidence. The boy shut the door quickly and went back to the grave, cold in spite of the sweat that stuck his shirt to his back. He began digging again.

The schoolteacher was too smart for him, that's all, the stranger said presently. You remember well enough how he said he kidnapped him when the schoolteacher was seven years of age. Gone to town and persuaded him out of his own backyard and brought him out here and baptized him. And what come of it? Nothing. The schoolteacher don't care now if he's baptized or if he ain't. It don't mean a thing to him one way or the other. Don't care if he's Redeemed or not neither. He only spent four days out here; you've spent fourteen years and now got to spend the rest of your life.

You see he was crazy all along, he continued. Wanted to make a prophet out of that schoolteacher too, but the schoolteacher was too smart for him. He got away.

He had somebody to come for him, Tarwater said. His daddy came and got him back. Nobody came and got me back.

The schoolteacher himself come after you, the stranger said, and got shot in the leg and the ear for his trouble.

I was not yet one year old, Tarwater said. A baby can't walk off and leave.

You ain't a baby now, his friend said.

The grave did not appear to get any deeper though he continued to dig. Look at the big prophet, the stranger jeered, and watched him from the shade of the speckled tree shadows. Lemme hear you prophesy something. The truth is the Lord ain't studying about you. You ain't entered His Head.

Tarwater turned around abruptly and worked from the other side and the voice continued from behind him. Anybody that's a prophet has got to have somebody to prophesy to. Unless you're just going to prophesy to yourself, he amended—or go baptize that dim-witted child, he added in a tone of high sarcasm.

The truth is, he said after a minute, the truth is that you're just as smart, if you ain't actually smarter, than the schoolteacher. Because he had somebody—his daddy and his mother—to tell him the old man was crazy, whereas you ain't had anybody and yet you've figured it out for yourself. Of course, it's taken you longer, but you've come to the right conclusion: you know he was a crazy man even when he wasn't in the asylum, even those last years.

Or if he wasn't actually crazy, he was the same thing in a different way: he didn't have but one thing on his mind. He was a one-notion man. Jesus. Jesus this and Jesus that. Ain't you in all your fourteen years of supporting his foolishness fed up and sick to the roof of your mouth with Jesus? My Lord and Saviour, the stranger sighed, I am if you ain't.

After a pause he continued. The way I see it, he said, you can do one of two things. One of them, not both. Nobody can do both of two things without straining themselves. You can do one thing or you can do the opposite.

Jesus or the devil, the boy said.

No no no, the stranger said, there ain't no such thing as a devil. I can tell you that from my own self-experience. I know that for a fact. It ain't Jesus or the devil. It's Jesus or *you*.

Jesus or me, Tarwater repeated. He put the shovel down for a rest and thought: he said the schoolteacher was glad to come. He said all he had to do was go out in the schoolteacher's back yard where he was playing and say, Let's you and me go to the country for a while—you have to be born again. The Lord Jesus Christ sent me to see to it. And the schoolteacher got up and took hold of his hand without a word and came with him and all the four days while he was out here he said the schoolteacher was hoping they wouldn't come for him.

Well that's all the sense a seven-year-old boy's got, the stranger said. You can't expect no more from a child. He learned better as soon as he got back to town; his daddy told him the old man was crazy and not to believe a word of what all he had learnt him.

That's not the way he told it, Tarwater said. He said that when the schoolteacher was seven years old, he had good sense but later it dried up. His daddy was an ass and not fit to raise him and his mother was a whore. She ran away from here when she was eighteen years old.

It took her that long? the stranger said in an incredulous tone. My, she was kind of a ass herself.

My great uncle said he hated to admit it that his own sister was a whore but he had to say it to say the truth, the boy said.

Shaw, you know yourself that it give him great satisfaction to admit she was a whore, the stranger said. He was always admitting somebody was an ass or a whore. That's all a prophet is good for—to admit somebody else is an ass or a whore. And anyway, he asked slyly, what do you know about whores? Where have you ever run up on one of them?

Certainly I know what one of them is, the boy said.

The Bible was full of them. He knew what they were and to what they were liable to come, and just as Jezebel was discovered by dogs, an arm here and a foot there, so said his great-uncle, it had almost been with his own mother and grandmother. The two of them, along with his grandfather, had been killed in an automobile crash, leaving only the schoolteacher alive in that family, and Tarwater himself, for his mother (unmarried and shameless) had lived just long enough after the crash for him to be born. He had been born at the scene of the wreck.

The boy was very proud that he had been born in a wreck. He had always felt that it set his existence apart from the ordinary one and he had understood from it that the plans of God for him were special, even though nothing of consequence had happened to him so far. Often when he walked in the woods and came upon some bush a little removed from the rest, his breath would catch in his throat and he would stop and wait for the bush to burst into flame. It had not done it yet.

His uncle had never seemed to be aware of the importance of

the way he had been born, only of how he had been born again.
He would often ask him why he thought the Lord had rescued
him out of the womb of a whore and let him see the light of day
at all, and then why, having done it once, He had gone and
done it again, allowing him to be baptized by his great-uncle
into the death of Christ, and then having done it twice, gone
on and done it a third time, allowing him to be rescued by
his great-uncle from the schoolteacher and brought to the
backwoods and given a chance to be brought up according
to the truth. It was because, his uncle said, the Lord meant
him to be trained for a prophet, even though he was a bastard,
and to take his great-uncle's place when he died. The old
man compared their situation to that of Elijah and Elisha.

All right, the stranger said, I suppose you know what one
of them is. But there's a heap else you don't know. You go
ahead and put your feet in his shoes. Elisha after Elijah like
he said. But just lemme ast you this: where is the voice of the
Lord? I haven't heard it. Who's called you this morning? Or
any morning? Have you been told what to do? You ain't even
heard the sound of natural thunder this morning. There ain't
a cloud in the sky. The trouble with you, I see, he concluded,
is that you ain't got but just enough sense to believe every
word he told you.

The sun was directly overhead, apparently dead still, holding its breath, waiting out the noontime. The grave was
about two feet deep. Ten foot now, remember, the stranger
said and laughed. Old men are selfish. You got to expect the
least of them. The least of everybody, he added and let out a
flat sigh that was like a gust of sand raised and dropped suddenly by the wind.

Tarwater looked up and saw two figures cutting across the
field, a colored man and woman, each dangling an empty
vinegar jug by a finger. The woman, tall and Indianlike, had
on a green sun hat. She stooped under the fence without
pausing and came on across the yard toward the grave; the
man held the wire down and swung his leg over and followed
at her elbow. They kept their eyes on the hole and stopped at
the edge of it, looking down into the raw ground with
shocked satisfied expressions. The man, Buford, had a crinkled face, darker than his hat. "Old man passed," he said.

The woman lifted her head and let out a slow sustained wail, piercing and formal. She set her jug down on the ground and crossed her arms and then lifted them in the air and wailed again.

"Tell her to shut up that," Tarwater said. "I'm in charge here now and I don't want no nigger-mourning."

"I seen his spirit for two nights," she said. "Seen him two nights and he was unrested."

"He ain't been dead but since this morning," Tarwater said. "If you all want your jugs filled, give them to me and dig while I'm gone."

"He'd been predicting his passing for many years," Buford said. "She seen him in her dream several nights and he wasn't rested. I known him well. I known him very well indeed."

"Poor sweet sugar boy," the woman said to Tarwater, "what you going to do here now by yourself in this lonesome place?"

"Mind my bidnis," the boy said, jerking the jug out of her hand. He started off so quickly that he almost fell. He stalked across the back field toward the rim of trees that surrounded the clearing.

The birds had gone into the deep woods to escape the noon sun and one thrush, hidden some distance ahead of him, called the same four notes again and again, stopping each time after them to make a silence. Tarwater began to walk faster, then he began to lope, and in a second he was running like something hunted, sliding down slopes waxed with pine needles and grasping the limbs of trees to pull himself, panting, up the slippery inclines. He crashed through a wall of honeysuckle and lept across a sandy near-dry stream bed and fell down against the high clay bank that formed the back wall of a cove where the old man kept his extra liquor hidden. He hid it in a hollow of the bank, covered with a large stone. Tarwater began to fight at the stone to pull it away, while the stranger stood over his shoulder panting, he was crazy! He was crazy! That's the long and short of it, he was crazy!

Tarwater got the stone away and pulled out a black jug and sat down against the bank with it. Crazy! the stranger hissed, collapsing by his side.

The sun appeared, a furious white, edging its way secretly behind the tops of the trees that rose over the hiding place.

A man, seventy years of age, to bring a baby out into the backwoods to raise him right! Suppose he had died when you were four years old instead of fourteen? Could you have toted mash to the still then and supported yourself? I never heard of no four-year-old running a still.

Never did I hear of that, he continued. You weren't anything to him but something that would grow big enough to bury him when the time came and now that he's dead, he's shut of you but you got two hundred and fifty pounds of him to put below the face of the earth. And don't think he wouldn't heat up like a coal stove to see you take a drop of liquor, he added. Though he had a weakness for it himself. When he couldn't stand the Lord one instant longer, he got drunk, prophet or no prophet. Hah. He might say it would hurt you but what he meant was you might get so much you wouldn't be in no fit condition to bury him. He said he brought you out here to raise you according to principle and that was the principle: that you should be fit when the time came to bury him so he would have a cross to mark where he was at.

A prophet with a still! He's the only prophet I ever heard of making liquor for a living.

After a minute he said in a softer tone as the boy took a long swallow from the black jug, well, a little won't interfere. Moderation never hurt no one.

A burning arm slid down Tarwater's throat as if the devil were already reaching inside him to finger his soul. He squinted at the angry sun creeping behind the topmost fringe of trees.

Take it easy, his friend said. Do you remember them nigger gospel singers you saw one time, all drunk, all singing, all dancing around that black Ford automobile? Jesus, they wouldn't have been near so glad they were Redeemed if they hadn't had that liquor in them. I wouldn't pay too much attention to my Redemption if I was you. Some people take everything too hard.

Tarwater drank more slowly. He had been drunk only one time before and that time his uncle had beat him with a piece of crate for it, saying liquor would dissolve a child's gut, another of his lies because his gut had not dissolved.

It should be clear to you, his kind friend said, how all your life you been tricked by that old man. You could have been a city slicker for the last fourteen years. Instead, you been deprived of any company but his, you been living in a two-story barn in the middle of this earth's bald patch, following behind a mule and plow since you were seven. And how do you know the education he give you is true to the facts? Maybe he taught you a system of figures nobody else uses? How do you know that two added to two makes four? Four added to four makes eight? Maybe other people don't think so. How do you know if there was an Adam or if Jesus eased your situation any when He redeemed you? Or how do you know if He actually done it? Nothing but that old man's word and it ought to be obvious to you by now that he was crazy. And as for Judgment Day, the stranger said, every day is Judgment Day.

Ain't you old enough to have learnt that yet for yourself? Don't everything you do, everything you have ever done, work itself out right or wrong before your eye and usually before the sun has set? Have you ever got by with anything? No you ain't nor ever thought you would. You might as well drink all that liquor since you've already drunk so much. Once you pass the moderation mark you've passed it, and that gyration you feel working down from the top of your brain, he said, that's the Hand of God laying a blessing on you. He has given you your release. That old man was the stone before your door and the Lord has rolled it away. He ain't rolled it quite far enough, of course. You got to finish up yourself but He's done the main part. Praise Him.

Tarwater had ceased to have any feeling in his legs. He dozed for a while, his head hanging to the side and his mouth open and the liquor trickling slowly down the side of his overalls where the jug had overturned in his lap. Eventually there was only a drip at the neck of the bottle, forming and filling and dropping, silent and measured and sun-colored. The bright even sky began to fade, coarsening with clouds until every shadow had gone in. He woke with a wrench forward, his eyes focussing and unfocussing on something that looked like a burnt rag hanging close to his face.

Buford said, "This ain't no way for you to act. Old man don't deserve this. There's no rest until the dead is buried." He was squatting on his heels, one hand gripped around Tarwater's arm. "I gone yonder to the door and seen him sitting there at the table, not even laid out on a cooling board. He ought to be laid out and have some salt on his bosom if you mean to keep him overnight."

The boy's lids pinched together to hold the image steady and in a second he made out two small red blistered eyes.

"He deserves to lie in a grave that fits him," Buford said. "He was deep in this life, he was deep in Jesus' misery."

"Nigger," the child said, working his strange swollen tongue, "take your hand off me."

Buford lifted his hand. "He needs to be rested," he said.

"He'll be rested all right when I get through with him," Tarwater said vaguely. "Go on and lea' me to my bidnis."

"Nobody going to bother you," Buford said, standing up. He waited a minute, bent, looking down at the limp figure sprawled against the bank. The boy's head was tilted backwards over a root that jutted out of the clay wall. His mouth hung open and his turned-up hat cut a straight line across his forehead, just over his half-open unseeing eyes. His cheekbones protruded, narrow and thin like the arms of a cross, and the hollows under them had an ancient look as if the child's skeleton beneath were as old as the world. "Nobody going to bother you," the Negro muttered, pushing through the wall of honeysuckle without looking back. "That going to be your trouble."

Tarwater closed his eyes again.

Some night bird complaining close by woke him up. It was not a screeching noise, only an intermittent hump-hump as if the bird had to recall his grievance each time before he repeated it. Clouds were moving convulsively across a black sky and there was a pink unsteady moon that appeared to be jerked up a foot or so and then dropped and jerked up again. This was because, as he observed in an instant, the sky was lowering, coming down fast to smother him. The bird screeched and flew off in time and Tarwater lurched into the middle of the stream bed and crouched on his hands and knees. The moon was reflected like pale fire in the few spots of water in the sand. He sprang at the wall of honeysuckle and began to tear through it, confusing the sweet familiar odor with the weight coming down on him. When he stood up on the other side, the black ground swung slowly and threw him down again. A flare of pink lightning lit the woods and he saw the black shapes of trees pierce out of the ground all around him. The night bird began to hump again from a thicket where he had settled.

He got up and began to move in the direction of the clearing, feeling his way from tree to tree, the trunks very cold and dry to his touch. There was distant thunder and a continuous flicker of pale lightning firing one section of woods and then another. Finally he saw the shack, standing gaunt-black and tall in the middle of the clearing, with the pink moon trembling directly over it. His eyes glittered like open pits of light as he moved across the sand, dragging his crushed shadow behind him. He didn't turn his head to that side of the yard where he had started the grave. He stopped at the far back corner of the house and squatted down on the ground and looked underneath at the litter there, chicken crates and barrels and old rags and boxes. He had a small box of wooden matches in his pocket.

He crawled under and began to set small fires, building one from another, and working his way out at the front porch, leaving the fire behind him eating greedily at the dry tinder and the floor boards of the house. He crossed the front side of the yard and went through the rutted field without looking back until he reached the edge of the opposite woods. Then he glanced over his shoulder and saw that the pink moon had dropped through the roof of the shack and was bursting and he began to run, forced on through the woods by two bulging silver eyes that grew in immense astonishment in the center of the fire behind him. He could hear it moving up through the black night like a whirling chariot.

Toward midnight he came out on the highway and caught a ride with a salesman who was a manufacturer's representative, selling copper flues throughout the Southeast, and who gave the silent boy what he said was the best advice he could give any young fellow setting out to find himself a place in the world. While they sped forward on the black untwisting highway, watched on either side by a dark wall of trees, the salesman said that it had been his personal experience that you couldn't sell a copper flue to a man you didn't love. He was a thin fellow with a narrow face that appeared to have been worn down to the sharpest possible depressions. He wore a broad-brimmed stiff grey hat of the kind used by businessmen who would like to look like cowboys. He said love was the only policy that worked 95% of the time. He said when he went to sell a man a flue, he asked first about that man's wife's health and how his children were. He said he had a book that he kept the names of his customers' families in and what was wrong with them. A man's wife had cancer, he put her name down in the book and wrote *cancer* after it and inquired about her every time he went to that man's hardware store until she died; then he scratched out the word *cancer* and wrote *dead* there. "And I say thank God when they're dead," the salesman said; "that's one less to remember."

"You don't owe the dead anything," Tarwater said in a loud voice, speaking for almost the first time since he had got in the car.

"Nor they you," said the stranger. "And that's the way it ought to be in this world—nobody owing nobody nothing."

"Look," Tarwater said suddenly, sitting forward, his face close to the windshield, "we're headed in the wrong direction. We're going back where we came from. There's the fire again. There's the fire we left!"

Ahead of them in the sky there was a faint glow, steady, and not made by lightning. "That's the same fire we came from!" the boy said in a high voice.

"Boy, you must be nuts," the salesman said. "That's the city we're coming to. That's the glow from the city lights. I reckon this is your first trip anywhere."

"You're turned around," the child said; "it's the same fire."

The stranger twisted his rutted face sharply. "I've never been turned around in my life," he said. "And I didn't come from any fire. I come from Mobile. And I know where I'm going. What's the matter with you?"

Tarwater sat staring at the glow in front of him. "I was asleep," he muttered. "I'm just now waking up."

"You should have been listening to me," the salesman said. "I been telling you things you ought to know."

II

IF THE BOY had actually trusted his new friend, Meeks, the copper flue salesman, he would have accepted Meeks' offer to take him directly to his uncle's door and let him out. Meeks had turned on the car light and told him to climb over onto the back seat and root around until he found the telephone book and when Tarwater had climbed back with it, he had showed him how to find his uncle's name in the book. Tarwater wrote the address and the telephone number down on the back of one of Meeks' cards. Meeks' telephone number was on the other side and he said any time Tarwater wanted to contact him for a little loan or any assistance, not to be afraid to use it. What Meeks had decided after about a half hour of the boy was that he was just enough off in the head and just ignorant enough to be a very hard worker, and he wanted a very ignorant energetic boy to work for him. But Tarwater was evasive. "I got to contact this uncle of mine, my only blood connection," he said.

Meeks could look at this boy and tell that he was running away from home, that he had left a mother and probably a sot-father and probably four or five brothers and sisters in a two-room shack set in a brush-swept bare-ground clearing just off the highway and that he was hightailing it for the big world, having first, from the way he reeked, fortified himself with stump liquor. He didn't for a minute believe he had any uncle at any such respectable address. He thought the boy had set his finger down on the name, Rayber, by chance and said, "That's him. A schoolteacher. My uncle."

"I'll take you right to his door," Meeks had said, fox-like. "We pass there going through town. We pass right by there."

"No," Tarwater said. He was sitting forward on the seat, looking out the window at a hill covered with old used-car bodies. In the indistinct darkness, they seemed to be drowning into the ground, to be about half-submerged already. The city hung in front of them on the side of the mountain as if it were a larger part of the same pile, not yet buried so deep.

The fire had gone out of it and it appeared settled into its unbreakable parts.

The boy did not intend to go to the schoolteacher's until daylight and when he went he intended to make it plain that he had not come to be beholden or to be studied for a schoolteacher magazine. He began trying to remember the schoolteacher's face so that he could stare him down in his mind before he actually faced him. He felt that the more he could recall about him, the less advantage the new uncle would have over him. The face had not been one that held together in his mind, though he remembered the sloping jaw and the black-rimmed glasses. What he could not picture were the eyes behind the glasses. He had no memory of them and there was every kind of contradiction in the rubble of his great-uncle's descriptions. Sometimes the old man had said the nephew's eyes were black and sometimes brown. The boy kept trying to find eyes that fit mouth, nose that fit chin, but every time he thought he had a face put together, it fell apart and he had to begin on a new one. It was as if the schoolteacher, like the devil, could take on any look that suited him.

Meeks was telling him about the value of work. He said that it had been his personal experience that if you wanted to get ahead, you had to work. He said this was the law of life and it was no way to get around it because it was inscribed on the human heart like love thy neighbor. He said these two laws were the team that worked together to make the world go round and that any individual who wanted to be a success and win the pursuit of happiness, that was all he needed to know.

The boy was beginning to see a consistent image for the schoolteacher's eyes and was not listening to this advice. He saw them dark grey, shadowed with knowledge, and the knowledge moved like tree reflections in a pond where far below the surface shadows a snake may glide and disappear. He had made a habit of catching his great-uncle in contradictions about the schoolteacher's appearance.

"I forget what color eyes he's got," the old man would say, irked. "What difference does the color make when I know the look? I know what's behind it."

"What's behind it?"

"Nothing. He's full of nothing."

"He knows a heap," the boy said. "I don't reckon it's anything he don't know."

"He don't know it's anything he can't know," the old man said. "That's his trouble. He thinks if it's something he can't know then somebody smarter than him can tell him about it and he can know it just the same. And if you were to go there, the first thing he would do would be to test your head and tell you what you were thinking and howcome you were thinking it and what you ought to be thinking instead. And before long you wouldn't belong to your self no more, you would belong to him."

The boy had no intention of allowing this to happen. He knew enough about the schoolteacher to be on his guard. He knew two complete histories, the history of the world, beginning with Adam, and the history of the schoolteacher, beginning with his mother, old Tarwater's own and only sister who had run away from Powderhead when she was eighteen years old and had become—the old man said he would mince no words, even with a child—a whore, until she had found a man by the name of Rayber who was willing to marry one. At least once a week, beginning at the beginning, the old man had reviewed this history through to the end.

His sister and this Rayber had brought two children into the world, one the schoolteacher and one a girl who had turned out to be Tarwater's mother and who, the old man said, had followed in the natural footsteps of her own mother, being already a whore by the time she was eighteen.

The old man had a great deal to say about Tarwater's conception, for the schoolteacher had told him that he himself had got his sister this first (and last) lover because he thought it would contribute to her *self-confidence*. The old man would say this, imitating the schoolteacher's voice and making it sillier than the boy felt it probably was. The old man was thrown into a fury of exasperation that there was not enough scorn in the world to cast upon this idiocy. Finally he would give up trying. The lover had shot himself after the accident, which was a relief to the schoolteacher for he wanted to bring up the baby himself.

The old man said that with the devil having such a heavy

role in his beginning, it was little wonder that he should have an eye on the boy and keep him under close surveillance during his time on earth, in order that the soul he had helped call into being might serve him forever in hell. "You are the kind of boy," the old man said, "that the devil is always going to be offering to assist, to give you a smoke or a drink or a ride, and to ask you your bidnis. You had better mind how you take up with strangers. And keep your bidnis to yourself." It was to foil the devil's plans for him that the Lord had seen to his upbringing.

"What line you going to get into?" Meeks asked.

The boy didn't appear to hear.

Whereas the schoolteacher had led his sister into evil, with success, old Tarwater had made every attempt to lead his own sister to repentance, without success. Through one means or another, he had managed to keep up with her after she ran away from Powderhead; but even after she married, she would not listen to any word that had to do with her salvation. He had twice been thrown out of her house by her husband—each time with the assistance of the police because the husband was a man of no force—but the Lord had prompted him constantly to go back, even in the face of going to jail. When he could not get inside the house, he would stand outside it and shout and then she would let him in lest he attract the attention of the neighbors. The neighborhood children would gather to listen to him and she would have to let him in.

It was not to be wondered at, the old man would say, that the schoolteacher was no better than he was with such a father as he had. The man, an insurance salesman, wore a straw hat on the side of his head and smoked a cigar and when you told him his soul was in danger, he offered to sell you a policy against any contingency. He said he was a prophet too, a prophet of life insurance, for every right-thinking Christian, he said, knew that it was his Christian duty to protect his family and provide for them in the event of the unexpected. There was no use treating with him, the old man said; his brain was as slick as his eyeballs and the truth would no more soak into it than rain would penetrate tin. The schoolteacher, with Tarwater blood in him, at least had his father's strain diluted. "Good blood flows in his veins," the old man said. "And good blood knows the Lord and there ain't a thing he can do about having it. There ain't a way in the world he can get rid of it."

Meeks abruptly poked the boy in the side with his elbow. He said if it was one thing a person needed to learn it was to pay attention to older people than him when they gave him good advice. He said he himself had graduated from the School of Experience with an H.L.L. degree. He asked the boy if he knew what was an H.L.L. degree. Tarwater shook his head. Meeks said the H.L.L. degree was the Hard Lesson from Life degree. He said it was the quickest got and that it stayed learnt the longest.

The boy turned his head to the window.

One day the old man's sister had worked a perfidy on him. He had been in the habit of going on Wednesday afternoon because on that afternoon the husband played a golf game and he could find her alone. On this particular Wednesday, she did not open the door but he knew she was inside because he heard footsteps. He beat on the door a few times to warn her and when she wouldn't open it, he began to shout, for her and for all who would hear.

While he was telling this to Tarwater, he would jump up and begin to shout and prophesy there in the clearing the same way he had done it in front of her door. With no one to hear but the boy, he would flail his arms and roar, "Ignore the Lord Jesus as long as you can! Spit out the bread of life and sicken on honey. Whom work beckons, to work! Whom blood to blood! Whom lust to lust! Make haste, make haste. Fly faster and faster. Spin yourselves in a frenzy, the time is short! The Lord is preparing a prophet. The Lord is preparing a prophet with fire in his hand and eye and the prophet is moving toward the city with his warning. The prophet is coming with the Lord's message. 'Go warn the children of God,' saith the Lord, 'of the terrible speed of justice.' Who will be left? Who will be left when the Lord's mercy strikes?"

He might have been shouting to the silent woods that encircled them. While he was in his frenzy, the boy would take up the shotgun and hold it to his eye and sight along the barrel, but sometimes as his uncle grew more and more wild, he would lift his face from the gun for a moment with a look of uneasy alertness, as if while he had been inattentive, the old man's words had been dropping one by one into him and now, silent, hidden in his bloodstream, were moving secretly toward some goal of their own.

His uncle would prophesy until he exhausted himself and then he would fall with a thud on the swayback step and sometimes it would be five or ten minutes before he could go on and relate how the sister had worked the perfidy on him.

Whenever he came to this part of the story, his breath would at once come short as if he were struggling to run up a hill. His face would get redder and his voice thinner and sometimes it would give out completely and he would sit there on the step, beating the porch floor with his fist while he moved his lips and no sound came out. Finally he would pipe, "They grabbed me. Two. From behind. The door behind. Two."

His sister had had two men and a doctor behind the door, listening, and the papers made out to commit him to the asylum if the doctor thought he was crazy. When he understood what was happening, he had raged through her house like a blinded bull, everything crashing behind him, and it had taken two of them and the doctor and two neighbors to get him down. The doctor had said he was not only crazy but dangerous and they had taken him to the asylum in a strait jacket.

"Ezekiel was in the pit for forty days," he would say, "but I was in it for four years," and he would stop at that point and warn Tarwater that the servants of the Lord Jesus could expect the worse. The boy could see that this was so. But no matter how little they had now, his uncle said, their reward in the end was the Lord Jesus Himself, the bread of life!

The boy would have a hideous vision of himself sitting forever with his great-uncle on a green bank, full and sick, staring at a broken fish and a multiplied loaf.

His uncle had been in the asylum four years because it had taken him four years to understand that the way for him to get out was to stop prophesying on the ward. It had taken him four years to discover what the boy felt he himself would have discovered in no time at all. But at least in the asylum the old man had learned caution and when he got out, he put everything he had learned to the service of his cause. He proceeded about the Lord's business like an experienced crook. He had given the sister up but he intended to help her boy. He planned to kidnap the child and keep him long enough to baptize him and instruct him in the facts of his Redemption and he mapped out his plan to the last detail and carried it out exactly.

Tarwater liked this part best because in spite of himself he had to admire his uncle's craft. The old man had persuaded Buford Munson to send his daughter in to get a job cooking for the sister and with the girl once in the house, he had been able to find out what he needed to know. He learned that there were two children now instead of one and that his sister sat in her nightgown all day drinking whiskey out of a medicine bottle. While Luella Munson washed and cooked and took care of the children, his sister lay on the bed sipping from the bottle and reading books that she had to buy fresh every night from the drugstore. But the principal reason the kidnapping had been so easy was because his great-uncle had had the full cooperation of the schoolteacher himself, a thin boy with a boney pale face and a pair of gold-rimmed spectacles that were always falling down his nose.

The two of them, the old man said, had liked each other from the first. The day he had gone to do the kidnapping, the husband was away on business and the sister, shut up in her room with the bottle, didn't even know the time of day. All the old man had done was to walk in and tell Luella Munson that his nephew was going off to spend a few days with him in the country and then he had gone out to the back yard and spoken to the schoolteacher who had been digging holes and lining them with broken glass.

He and the schoolteacher had taken the train as far as the junction and had walked the rest of the way to Powderhead. The old man had explained to him that he was not taking him on this trip for pleasure but because the Lord had sent him to do it, to see that he was born again and instructed in his Redemption. All these facts were new to the schoolteacher, for his parents had never taught him anything, old Tarwater said, except not to wet the bed.

In four days the old man taught him what was necessary to know and baptized him. He made him understand that his true father was the Lord and not the simpleton in town and that he would have to lead a secret life in Jesus until the day came when he would be able to bring the rest of his family around to repentance. He had made him understand that on the last day it would be his destiny to rise in glory in the Lord Jesus. Since this was the first time anybody had bothered to tell these facts to the schoolteacher, he could not hear too much of them, and as he had never seen woods before or been in a boat or caught a fish or walked on roads that were not paved, they did all those things too and, his uncle said, he even allowed him to plow. His sallow face had become bright in four days. At this point Tarwater would begin to weary of the story.

The schoolteacher had spent four days in the clearing because his mother had not missed him for three days and when Luella Munson had mentioned where he had gone, she had to wait another day before his father came home and she could send him after the child. She would not come herself, the old man said, for fear the wrath of God would strike her at Powderhead and she would not be able to get back to the city again. She had wired the schoolteacher's father and when the simpleton arrived at the clearing, the schoolteacher was in despair at having to leave. The light had left his eyes. He had gone but the old man insisted that he had been able to tell by the look on his face that he would never be the same boy again.

"If he didn't say he didn't want to go, you can't be sure he didn't," Tarwater would say contentiously.

"Then why did he try to come back?" the old man asked. "Answer me that. Why one week later did he run away and try to find his way back and got his picture in the paper when the state patrol found him in the woods? I ask you why. Tell me that if you know so much."

"Because here was less bad than there," Tarwater said. "Less bad don't mean good, it only means better-than."

"He tried to come back," his uncle said slowly, emphasizing each word, "to hear more about God his Father, more about Jesus Christ Who had died to redeem him and more of the Truth I could tell him."

"Well go on," Tarwater would say irritably, "get on with the rest of it." The story always had to be taken to completion. It was like a road that the boy had travelled on so often that half the time he didn't look where they were going, and when at certain points he would become aware where they were, he would be surprised to see that the old man had not got farther on with it. Sometimes his uncle would lag at one point as if he didn't want to face what was coming and then when he finally came to it, he would try to get past it in a rush. At such points, Tarwater plagued him for details. "Tell about when he came when he was fourteen years old and had already decided none of it was true and he give you all that sass."

"Bah," the old man would say. "He was living in confusion. I don't say it was his fault then. They told him I was a crazy man. But I'll tell you one thing: he never believed them neither. They kept him from believing me but I kept him from believing them and he never took on none of their ways though he took on worse ones. And when he got shut of the three of them in that crash, nobody was gladder than he was. Then he turned his mind to raising you. Said he was going to give you every advantage, every advantage." The old man snorted. "You have me to thank for saving you from those advantages."

The boy looked off into the distance as though he were staring blankly at his invisible advantages.

"When he got shut of the three of them in that crash, this was the first place he came. On the very day they were killed he came out here to tell me. Straight out here. Yes sir," the old man said with the greatest satisfaction, "straight out here. He hadn't seen me in years but this is where he came. I was the one he came to. I was the one he wanted to see. Me. I had never left his mind. I had taken my seat in it."

"You skipped all that part about how he came when he was fourteen and give you all that sass," Tarwater said.

"It was sass he had got from them," the old man said. "Just parrot-mouthing all they had ever said about how I was a crazy man. The truth was even if they told him not to believe what I had taught him, he couldn't forget it. He never could forget that there was a chance that that simpleton was not his only father. I planted the seed in him and it was there for good. Whether anybody liked it or not."

"It fell amongst cockles," Tarwater said. "Say the sass."

"It fell in deep," the old man said, "or else after that crash he wouldn't have come out here hunting me."

"He only wanted to see if you were still crazy," the boy offered.

"The day may come," his great-uncle said slowly, "when a pit opens up inside you and you know some things you never known before," and he would give him such a prescient piercing look that the child would turn his face away, scowling fiercely.

His great-uncle had gone to live with the schoolteacher and as soon as he had got there, he had baptized Tarwater, practically under the schoolteacher's nose and the schoolteacher had made a blasphemous joke of it. But the old man could never tell this straight through. He always had to back up and tell why he had gone to live with the schoolteacher in the first place. He had gone for three reasons. One, he said, because he knew the schoolteacher wanted him. He was the only person in the schoolteacher's life who had ever taken two steps out of his way in his behalf. And two, because his nephew was the proper person to bury him and he wanted to have it understood with him how he wanted it done. And three, because the old man meant to see that Tarwater was baptized.

"I know all that," the boy would say, "get on with the rest of it."

"After the three of them perished and the house was his, he cleared it out," old Tarwater said. "He moved every stick of furniture out of it except a table and a chair or two and a bed or two and the crib he bought for you. Taken down all the pictures and all the curtains and taken up all the rugs. Even burned up all his mother's and sister's and the simpleton's clothes, didn't want a thing of theirs around. It wasn't anything left but books and papers that he had collected. Papers everywhere," the old man said. "Every room looked like the inside of a bird's nest. I came a few days after the crash and when he saw me standing there, he was glad to see me. His eyes lit up. He was glad to see me. 'Ha,' he said, 'my house is swept and garnished and here are the seven other devils, all rolled into one!'" The old man slapped his knee with pleasure.

"It don't sound to me like . . ."

"No, he didn't say so," his uncle said, "but I ain't an idiot."

"If he didn't say so you can't be sure."

"I'm as sure," his uncle said, "as I am that this here," and he held up his hand, every short thick finger stretched rigid in front of Tarwater's face, "is my hand and not yours." There was something final in this that always made the boy's impudence subside.

"Well get on with it," he would say. "If you don't make haste, you'll never get to where he blasphemed at."

"He was glad to see me," his uncle said. "He opened the door with all that house full of paper-trash behind him and there I stood and he was glad to see me. It was all underneath his face."

"What did he say?" Tarwater asked.

"He looked at my satchel," the old man said, "and he said, 'Uncle, you can't live with me. I know exactly what you want but I'm going to raise this child my way.'"

These words of the schoolteacher's had always caused a quick charge of excitement to race through Tarwater, an almost sensuous satisfaction. "It might have sounded to you like he was glad to see you," he said. "It don't sound that way to me."

"He wasn't but twenty-four years old," the old man said. "His expression hadn't even set on his face yet. I could still see the seven-year-old boy that had gone off with me, except that now he had a pair of black-rimmed glasses and a nose big enough to hold them up. The size of his eyes had shrunk because his face had grown but it was the same face all right. You could see behind it to what he really wanted to say. When he came out here later to get you back after I had stolen you, it was already set. It was as set then as the outside of a penitentiary but not now when I'm telling you about. Then it wasn't set and I could see he wanted me. Else why had he come out to Powderhead to tell me they were all dead? I ask you that? He could have let me alone."

The boy couldn't answer.

"Anyway," the old man said, "what all he gone on and

done proved he wanted me right then because he took me in. He looked at my satchel and I said, 'I'm on your charity,' and he said, 'I'm sorry, Uncle. You can't live with me and ruin another child's life. This one is going to be brought up to live in the real world. He's going to be brought up to expect exactly what he can do for himself. He's going to be his own saviour. He's going to be free!'" The old man turned his head to the side and spit. "Free," he said. "He was full of such-like phrases. But then I said it. I said what changed his mind."

The boy sighed at this. The old man considered it his master stroke. He had said, "I never come to live with you. I come to die!"

"And you should have seen his face," he said. "He looked like he'd been pushed all of a sudden from behind. He hadn't cared if the other three were wiped out but when he thought of me going, it was like he was losing somebody for the first time. He stood there staring at me." And once, only once, the old man had leaned forward and said to Tarwater, in a voice that could no longer contain the pleasure of its secret, "He loved me like a daddy and he was ashamed of it!"

The boy's face had remained unmoved. "Yes," he said, "and you had told him a bare-face lie. You never had no intention of dying."

"I was sixty-nine years of age," his uncle said. "I could have died the next day as well as not. No man knows the hour of his death. I didn't have my life in front of me. It was not a lie, it was only a speculation. I told him, I said, 'I may live two months or two days.' And I had on my clothes that I bought to be buried in—all new."

"Ain't it that same suit you got on now?" the boy asked indignantly, pointing to the threadbare knee. "Ain't it that one you got on yourself right now?"

"I may live two months or two days, I said to him," his uncle said.

Or ten years or twenty, Tarwater thought.

"Oh it was a shock to him," the old man said.

It might have been a shock, the boy thought, but he wasn't all that sorry about it. The schoolteacher had merely said, "So I'm to put you away, Uncle? All right, I'll put you away. I'll do it with pleasure. I'll put you away for good and all," but the old man insisted that his words were one thing and his actions and the look on his face another.

His great-uncle had not been in the nephew's house ten minutes before he had baptized Tarwater. They had gone into the room where the crib was with Tarwater in it and as the old man looked at him for the first time—a wizened grey-faced scrawny sleeping baby—the voice of the Lord had come to him and said: HERE IS THE PROPHET TO TAKE YOUR PLACE. BAPTIZE HIM.

That? the old man had asked, that wizened grey-faced . . . and then as he wondered how he could baptize him with the nephew standing there, the Lord had sent the paper boy to knock on the door and the schoolteacher had gone to answer it.

When he came back in a few minutes, his uncle was holding Tarwater in one hand and with the other he was pouring water over his head out of the bottle that had been on the table by the crib. He had pulled off the nipple and stuck it in his pocket. He was just finishing the words of baptism as the schoolteacher came back in the door and he had had to laugh when he looked up and saw his nephew's face. It looked hacked, the old man said. Not even angry at first, just hacked.

Old Tarwater had said, "He's been born again and there ain't a thing you can do about it," and then he had seen the rage rise in the nephew's face and had seen him try to conceal it.

"Time has passed you by, Uncle," the nephew said. "That can't even irritate me. That only makes me laugh," and he laughed, a short forced bark, but the old man said his face was mottled. "Just as well you did it now," he said. "If you had got me when I was seven days instead of seven years, you might not have ruined my life."

"If it's ruined," the old man said, "it wasn't me that ruined it."

"Oh yes it was," the nephew said, advancing across the room, his face very red. "You're too blind to see what you did to me. A child can't defend himself. Children are cursed with believing. You pushed me out of the real world and I stayed out of it until I didn't know which was which. You infected me with your idiot hopes, your foolish violence. I'm not always myself, I'm not al . . ." but he stopped. He wouldn't admit what the old man knew. "There's nothing wrong with me," he said. "I've straightened the tangle you made. Straightened it by pure will power. I've made myself straight."

"You see," the old man said, "he admitted himself the seed was still in him."

Old Tarwater had laid the baby back in the crib but the nephew took him out again, a peculiar smile, the old man said, stiffening on his face. "If one baptism is good, two will be better," he said and he had turned Tarwater over and poured what was left in the bottle over his bottom and said the words of baptism again. Old Tarwater had stood there, aghast at this blasphemy. "Now Jesus has a claim on both ends," the nephew said.

The old man had roared, "Blasphemy never changed a plan of the Lord's!"

"And the Lord hasn't changed any of mine either," said the nephew coolly and put the baby back.

"And what did I do?" Tarwater asked.

"You didn't do nothing," the old man said as if what he did or didn't do was of no consequence whatsoever.

"It was me that was the prophet," the boy said sullenly.

"You didn't even know what was going on," his uncle said.

"Oh yes I did," the child said. "I was laying there thinking."

His uncle would ignore this and go on. He had thought for a while that by living with the schoolteacher, he might convince him again of all that he had convinced him of when he had kidnapped him as a child and he had had hope of it up until the time when the schoolteacher showed him the study he had written of him for the magazine. Then the old man had realized at last that there was no hope of his doing anything for the schoolteacher. He had failed the schoolteacher's mother and he had failed the schoolteacher, and now there was nothing to do but try to save Tarwater from being brought up by a fool. In this he had not failed.

The boy felt that the schoolteacher could have made more of an effort to get him back. He had come out and got shot in the leg and the ear but if he had used his head, he might have avoided that and got him back at the same time. "Why didn't he bring the law out here and get me back?" he had asked.

"You want to know why?" his uncle said. "Well I'll tell you why. I'll tell you exactly why. It was because he found you a heap of trouble. He wanted it all in his head. You can't change a child's pants in your head."

The boy would think: but if the schoolteacher hadn't written that piece on him, we might all three be living in town right now.

When the old man had read the piece in the schoolteacher magazine, he had at first not recognized who it was the schoolteacher was writing about, who the type was that was almost extinct. He had sat down to read the piece, full of pride that his nephew had succeeded in having a composition printed in a magazine. He had handed it carelessly to his uncle and said he might want to glance over it and the old man had sat down at once at the kitchen table and commenced to read it. He recalled that the schoolteacher had kept passing by the kitchen door to witness how he was taking the piece.

About the middle of it, old Tarwater had begun to think that he was reading about someone he had once known or at least someone he had dreamed about, for the figure was strangely familiar. "This fixation of being called by the Lord had its origin in insecurity. He needed the assurance of a call and so he called himself," he read. The schoolteacher kept passing by the door, passing and repassing, and finally he came in and sat down quietly on the other side of the small white metal table. When the old man looked up, the schoolteacher smiled. It was a very slight smile, the slightest that would do for any occasion. The old man knew from the smile who it was he had been reading about.

For the length of a minute, he could not move. He felt he was tied hand and foot inside the schoolteacher's head, a space as bare and neat as the cell in the asylum, and was shrinking, drying up to fit it. His eyeballs swerved from side to side as if he were pinned in a strait jacket again. Jonah, Ezekiel, Daniel, he was at that moment all of them—the swallowed, the lowered, the enclosed.

The nephew, his smile still fixed, reached across the table and put his hand on the old man's wrist in a gesture of pity. "You've got to be born again, Uncle," he said, "by your own efforts, back to the real world where there's no saviour but yourself."

The old man's tongue lay in his mouth like a stone but his heart began to swell. His prophet's blood surged in him, surged to floodtide for a miraculous release, though his face remained shocked, expressionless. The nephew patted his huge clenched fist and got up and left the kitchen, bearing away his smile of triumph.

The next morning when he went to the crib to give the baby his bottle, he found nothing in it but the blue magazine with the old man's message scrawled on the back of it: THE PROPHET I RAISE UP OUT OF THIS BOY WILL BURN YOUR EYES CLEAN.

"It was me could act," the old man said, "not him. He could never take action. He could only get everything inside his head and grind it to nothing. But I acted. And because I acted, you sit here in freedom, you sit here a rich man, knowing the Truth, in the freedom of the Lord Jesus Christ."

The boy would move his thin shoulder blades irritably as if he were shifting the burden of Truth like a cross on his back. "He came out here and got shot to get me back," he said obstinately.

"If he had really wanted you back, he could have got you," the old man said. "He could have had the law out here after me or got me put back in the asylum. There was plenty he could have done, but what happened to him was that welfare-woman. She persuaded him to have one of his own and let you go, and he was easy persuaded. And that one," the old man would say, beginning to brood on the schoolteacher's child again, "that one—the Lord gave him one he couldn't corrupt." And then he would grip the boy's shoulder and put a fierce pressure on it. "And if I don't get him baptized, it'll be for you to do," he said. "I enjoin you to do it, boy."

Nothing irritated the boy so much as this. "I take my orders from the Lord," he would say in an ugly voice, trying to pry the fingers out of his shoulder. "Not from you."

"The Lord will give them to you," the old man said, gripping his shoulder tighter.

"He had to change that one's pants and he done it," Tarwater muttered.

"He had the welfare-woman to do it for him," his uncle said. "She had to be good for something, but you can bet she ain't still around there. Bernice Bishop!" he said as if he found this the most idiotic name in the language. "Bernice Bishop!"

The boy had sense enough to know that he had been betrayed by the schoolteacher and he did not mean to go to his house until daylight, when he could see behind and before him. "I ain't going there until daylight," he said suddenly to Meeks. "You needn't to stop there because I ain't getting out there."

Meeks leaned casually against the door of the car, driving with half his attention and giving the other half to Tarwater. "Son," he said, "I'm not going to be a preacher to you. I'm not going to tell you not to lie. I ain't going to tell you nothing impossible. All I'm going to tell you is this: don't lie when you don't have to. Else when you do have to, nobody'll believe you. You don't have to lie to me. I know exactly what you done." A shaft of light plunged through the car window and he looked to the side and saw the white face beside him, staring up with soot-colored eyes.

"How do you know?" the boy asked.

Meeks smiled with pleasure. "Because I done the same thing myself once," he said.

Tarwater caught hold of the sleeve of the salesman's coat and gave it a quick pull. "On the Day of Judgment," he said, "me and you will rise and say we done it!"

Meeks looked at him again with one eyebrow cocked at the same angle he wore his hat. "Will we?" he asked. Then he said, "What line you gonna get into, boy?"

"What line?"

"What you going to do? What kind of *work*?"

"I know everything but the machines," Tarwater said, sitting back again. "My great-uncle learnt me everything but first I have to find out how much of it is true." They were entering the dilapidated outskirts of the city where wooden buildings leaned together and an occasional dim light lit up a faded sign advertising some remedy or other.

"What line was your great-uncle in?" Meeks asked.

"He was a prophet," the boy said.

"Is that right?" Meeks asked and his shoulders jumped several times as if they were going to leap over his head. "Who'd he prophesy to?"

"To me," Tarwater said. "Nobody else would listen to him and there wasn't anybody else for me to listen to. He grabbed me away from this other uncle, my only blood connection now, so as to save me from running to doom."

"You were a captive audience," Meeks said. "And now you're coming to town to run to doom with the rest of us, huh?"

The boy didn't answer at once. Then he said in a guarded tone, "I ain't said what I'm going to do."

"You ain't sure about what all this great-uncle of yours told you, are you?" Meeks asked. "You figure he might have got aholt to some misinformation."

Tarwater looked away, out the window, at the brittle forms of the houses. He was holding both arms close to his sides as if he were cold. "I'll find out," he said.

"Well how now?" Meeks asked.

The dark city was unfolding on either side of them and they were approaching a low circle of light in the distance. "I mean to wait and see what happens," he said after a moment.

"And suppose nothing don't happen?" Meeks asked.

The circle of light became huge and they swung into the center of it and stopped. It was a gaping concrete mouth with two red gas pumps set in front of it and a small glass office toward the back. "I say suppose nothing don't happen?" Meeks repeated.

The boy looked at him darkly, remembering the silence after his great uncle's death.

"Well?" Meeks said.

"Then I'll make it happen," he said. "I can act."

"Attaboy," Meeks said. He opened the car door and put his leg out while he continued to observe his rider. Then he said, "Wait a minute. I got to call my girl."

A man was asleep in a chair tilted against the outside wall of the glass office and Meeks went inside without waking him up. For a minute Tarwater only craned his neck out the window. Then he got out and went to the office door to watch Meeks use the machine. It sat, small and black, in the center of a cluttered desk which Meeks sat down on as if it had been his own. The room was lined with automobile tires and had a concrete and rubber smell. Meeks took the machine in two parts and held one part to his head while he circled with his finger on the other part. Then he sat waiting, swinging his foot, while the horn buzzed in his ear. After a minute an acid smile began to eat at the corners of his mouth and he said, drawing in his breath, "Heythere, Sugar, hyer you?" and Tarwater, from where he stood in the door, heard an actual woman's voice, like one coming from beyond the grave, say, "Why Sugar, is that reely you?" and Meeks said it was him in the same old flesh and made an appointment with her in ten minutes.

Tarwater stood awestruck in the doorway. Meeks put the telephone together and then he said in a sly voice, "Now why don't you call your uncle?" and watched the boy's face change, the eyes swerve suspiciously to the side and the flesh drop around the boney mouth.

"I'll speak with him soon enough," he muttered, but he kept looking at the black coiled machine, fascinated. "How do you use it?" he asked.

"You dial it like I did. Call your uncle," Meeks urged.

"No, that woman is waiting on you," Tarwater said.

"Let 'er wait," Meeks said. "That's what she knows how to do best."

The boy approached it, taking out the card he had written the number on. He put his finger on the dial and began gingerly to turn it.

"Great God," Meeks said and took the receiver off the hook and put it in his hand and thrust his hand to his ear. He dialed the number for him and then pushed him down in the office chair to wait but Tarwater stood up again, slightly crouched, holding the buzzing horn to his head, while his heart began to kick viciously at his chest wall.

"It don't speak," he murmured.

"Give him time," Meeks said, "maybe he don't like to get up in the middle of the night."

The buzzing continued for a minute and then stopped

abruptly. Tarwater stood speechless, holding the earpiece
tight against his head, his face rigid as if he were afraid that
the Lord might be about to speak to him over the machine.
All at once he heard what sounded like heavy breathing in his
ear.

"Ask for your party," Meeks prompted. "How do you expect to get your party if you don't ask for him?"

The boy remained exactly as he was, saying nothing.

"I told you to ask for your party," Meeks said irritably.
"Ain't you got good sense?"

"I want to speak with my uncle," Tarwater whispered.

There was a silence over the telephone but it was not a
silence that seemed to be empty. It was the kind where the
breath is drawn in and held. Suddenly the boy realized that it
was the schoolteacher's child on the other side of the machine. The white-haired, blunted face rose before him. He
said in a furious shaking voice, "I want to speak with my
uncle. Not you!"

The heavy breathing began again as if in answer. It was a
kind of bubbling noise, the kind of noise someone would
make who was struggling to breathe in water. In a second it
faded away. The horn of the machine dropped out of Tarwater's hand. He stood there blankly as if he had received a
revelation he could not yet decipher. He seemed to have been
stunned by some deep internal blow that had not yet made
its way to the surface of his mind.

Meeks picked up the earpiece and listened but there was no
sound. He put it back on the hook and said, "Come on. I
ain't got this kind of time." He gave the stupefied boy a shove
and they left, driving off into the city again. Meeks told him
to learn to work every machine he saw. The greatest invention of man, he said, was the wheel and he asked Tarwater if
he had ever thought how things were before it was a wheel,
but the boy didn't answer him. He didn't even appear to be
listening. He sat slightly forward and from time to time his
lips moved as if he were speaking silently with himself.

"Well, it was terrible," Meeks said sourly. He knew the boy
didn't have any uncle at any such respectable address and to
prove it, he turned down the street the uncle was supposed
to live on and drove slowly past the small shapes of squat

houses until he found the number, visible in phosphorescent letters on a small stick set on the edge of the grass plot. He stopped the car and said, "Okay, kiddo, that's it."

"That's what?" Tarwater mumbled.

"That's your uncle's house," Meeks said.

The boy grabbed the edge of the window with both hands and stared out at what appeared to be only a black shape crouched in a greater darkness a little distance away. "I told you I wasn't going there until daylight," he said angrily, "go on."

"You're going there right now," Meeks said. "Because I ain't getting stuck with you. You can't go with me where I'm going."

"I ain't getting out here," the boy said.

Meeks reached across him and opened the car door. "So long, son," he said, "if you get real hungry by next week, you can contack me from that card and we might make a deal."

The boy gave him one white-faced outraged look and flung himself from the car. He moved up the short concrete walk to the doorstep and sat down abruptly, absorbed into the darkness. Meeks pulled the car door shut. His face hung for a moment watching the barely visible outline of the boy's shape on the step. Then he drew back and drove on. He won't come to no good end, he said to himself.

III

Tarwater sat in the corner of the doorstep, scowling in the dark as the car disappeared down the block. He did not look up at the sky but he was unpleasantly aware of the stars. They seemed to be holes in his skull through which some distant unmoving light was watching him. It was as if he were alone in the presence of an immense silent eye. He had an intense desire to make himself known to the schoolteacher at once, to tell him what he had done and why and to be congratulated by him. At the same time, his deep suspicion of the man continued to work in him. He tried to bring the schoolteacher's face again to mind, but all he could manage was the face of the seven-year-old boy the old man had kidnapped. He stared at it boldly, hardening himself for the encounter.

Then he rose and faced the heavy brass knocker on the door. He touched it and jerked his hand away, burnt by a metallic coldness. He looked quickly over his shoulder. The houses across the street formed a dark jagged wall. The quiet seemed palpable, waiting. It seemed almost to be waiting patiently, biding its time until it should reveal itself and demand to be named. He turned back to the cold knocker and grabbed it and shattered the silence as if it were a personal enemy. The noise filled his head. He was aware of nothing but the racket he was making.

He beat louder and louder, bamming at the same time with his free fist until he felt he was shaking the house. The empty street echoed with his blows. He stopped once to get his breath and then began again, kicking the door frenziedly with the blunt toe of his heavy work shoe. Nothing happened. Finally he stopped and the implacable silence descended around him, immune to his fury. A mysterious dread filled him. His whole body felt hollow as if he had been lifted like Habakkuk by the hair of his head, borne swiftly through the night and set down in the place of his mission. He had a sudden foreboding that he was about to step into a trap laid for him by the old man. He half-turned to run.

At once the glass panels on either side of the door filled

with light. There was a click and the knob turned. Tarwater jerked his hands up automatically as if he were pointing an invisible gun and his uncle, who had opened the door, jumped back at the sight of him.

The image of the seven-year-old boy disappeared forever from Tarwater's mind. His uncle's face was so familiar to him that he might have seen it every day of his life. He steadied himself and shouted, "My great-uncle is dead and burnt, just like you would have burnt him yourself!"

The schoolteacher remained absolutely still as if he thought that by looking long enough his hallucination would disappear. He had been roused by the vibration in the house and had run, half-asleep, to the door. His face was like the face of a sleep-walker who wakes and sees some horror of his dreams take shape before him. After a moment he muttered, "Wait here, deaf," and turned and went quickly out of the hall. He was barefooted and in his pajamas. He came back almost at once, plugging something into his ear. He had thrust on the black-rimmed glasses and he was sticking a metal box into the waist-band of his pajamas. This was joined by a cord to the plug in his ear. For an instant the boy had the thought that his head ran by electricity. He caught Tarwater by the arm and pulled him into the hall under a lantern-shaped light that hung from the ceiling. The boy found himself scrutinized by two small drill-like eyes set in the depths of twin glass caverns. He drew away. Already he felt his privacy imperilled.

"My great-uncle is dead and burnt," he said again. "I was the only one there to do it and I done it. I done your work for you," and as he said the last, a perceptible trace of scorn crossed his face.

"Dead?" the schoolteacher said. "My uncle? The old man's dead?" he asked in a blank unbelieving tone. He caught Tarwater abruptly by the arms and stared into his face. In the depths of his eyes, the boy, shocked, saw an instant's stricken look, plain and awful. It vanished at once. The straight line of the schoolteacher's mouth began turning into a smile. "And how did he go—with his fist in the air?" he asked. "Did the Lord arrive for him in a chariot of fire?"

"He didn't have no warning," Tarwater said, suddenly breathless. "He was eating his breakfast and I never moved him from the table. I set him on fire where he was and the house with him."

The schoolteacher said nothing but the boy read in his look a doubt that this had happened, a suspicion that he dealt with an interesting liar.

"You can go there and see for yourself," Tarwater said. "He was too big to bury. I done it the quickest way."

His uncle's eyes had the look now of being trained on a fascinating problem. "How did you get here? How did you know this was where you belonged?" he asked.

The boy had expended all his energy announcing himself. He was suddenly blank and stunned and he remained stupidly silent. He had never been this tired before. He felt he was about to fall.

The schoolteacher waited, searching his face impatiently. Then his expression changed again. He tightened his grip on Tarwater's arm and his eyes turned, glowering, toward the front door, which was still open. "Is he out there?" he asked in a low enraged voice. "Is this one of his tricks? Is he out there waiting to sneak in a window and baptize Bishop while you're here baiting me? Is that his senile game this time?"

The boy blanched. In his mind's eye he saw the old man, a dark shape standing behind the corner of the house, restraining his wheezing breath while he waited impatiently for him to baptize the dim-witted child. He stared shocked at the schoolteacher's face. There was a wedge-shaped gash in his new uncle's ear. The sight of it brought old Tarwater so close that the boy thought he could hear him laugh. With a terrible clarity he saw that the schoolteacher was no more than a decoy the old man had set up to lure him to the city to do his unfinished business.

His eyes began to burn in his fierce fragile face. A new energy seized him. "He's dead," he said. "You can't be any deader than he is. He's reduced to ashes. He don't even have a cross set up over him. If it's anything left of him, the buzzards wouldn't have it and the bones the dogs'll carry off. That's how dead he is."

The schoolteacher winced, but almost at once he was smiling again. He held Tarwater's arms tightly and peered into his face as if he were beginning to see a solution, one that intrigued him with its symmetry and rightness. "It's a perfect irony," he murmured, "a perfect irony that you should have taken care of the matter in that way. He got what he deserved."

The boy's pride swelled. "I done the needful," he said.

"Everything he touched he warped," the schoolteacher said. "He lived a long and useless life and he did you a great injustice. It's a blessing he's dead at last. You could have had everything and you've had nothing. All that can be changed now. Now you belong to someone who can help you and understand you." His eyes were alight with pleasure. "It's not too late for me to make a man of you!"

The boy's face darkened. His expression hardened until it was a fortress wall to keep his thoughts from being exposed; but the schoolteacher did not notice any change. He gazed through the actual insignificant boy before him to an image of him that he held fully developed in his mind.

"You and I will make up for lost time," he said. "We'll get you started now in the right direction."

Tarwater was not looking at him. His neck had suddenly snapped forward and he was staring straight ahead over the schoolteacher's shoulder. He heard a faint familiar sound of heavy breathing. It was closer to him than the beating of his own heart. His eyes widened and an inner door in them opened in preparation for some inevitable vision.

The small white-haired boy shambled into the back of the hall and stood peering forward at the stranger. He had on the bottoms to a pair of blue pajamas drawn up as high as they would go, the string tied over his chest and then again, harness-like, around his neck to keep them on. His eyes were slightly sunken beneath his forehead and his cheekbones were lower than they should have been. He stood there, dim and ancient, like a child who had been a child for centuries.

Tarwater clenched his fists. He stood like one condemned, waiting at the spot of execution. Then the revelation came, silent, implacable, direct as a bullet. He did not look into the eyes of any fiery beast or see a burning bush. He only knew, with a certainty sunk in despair, that he was expected to baptize the child he saw and begin the life his great-uncle had prepared him for. He knew that he was called to be a prophet and that the ways of his prophecy would not be remarkable. His black pupils, glassy and still, reflected depth on depth his own stricken image of himself, trudging into the distance in the bleeding stinking mad shadow of Jesus, until at last he received his reward, a broken fish, a multiplied loaf. The Lord out of dust had created him, had made him blood and nerve and mind, had made him to bleed and weep and think, and set him in a world of loss and fire all to baptize one idiot child that He need not have created in the first place and to cry out a gospel just as foolish. He tried to shout, "NO!" but it was like trying to shout in his sleep. The sound was saturated in silence, lost.

His uncle put a hand on his shoulder and shook him slightly to penetrate his inattention. "Listen boy," he said, "getting out from under the old man is just like coming out of the darkness into the light. You're going to have a chance now for the first time in your life. A chance to develop into a useful man, a chance to use your talents, to do what you want to do and not what he wanted—whatever idiocy it was."

The boy's eyes were focussed beyond him, the pupils dilated. The schoolteacher turned his head to see what it was that was keeping him from being responsive. His own face tightened. The little boy was creeping forward, grinning.

"That's only Bishop," he said. "He's not all right. Don't mind him. All he can do is stare at you and he's very friendly. He stares at everything that way." His hand tightened on the boy's shoulder and his mouth stretched painfully. "All the things that I would do for him—if it were any use—I'll do for you," he said. "Now do you see why I'm so glad to have you here?"

The boy heard nothing he said. The muscles in his neck stood out like cables. The dim-witted child was not five feet from him and was coming every instant closer with his lopsided smile. Suddenly he knew that the child *recognized* him, that the old man himself had primed him from on high that here was the forced servant of God come to see that he was born again. The little boy was sticking out his hand to touch him.

"Git!" Tarwater screamed. His arm shot out like a whip and knocked the hand away. The child let out a bellow startlingly loud. He clambered up his father's leg, pulling himself up by the schoolteacher's pajama coat until he was almost on his shoulder.

"All right, all right," the schoolteacher said, "there, there, shut up, it's all right, he didn't mean to hit you," and he righted the child on his back and tried to slide him off but the little boy hung on, thrusting his head against his father's neck and never taking his eyes off Tarwater.

The boy had a vision of the schoolteacher and his child as inseparably joined. The schoolteacher's face was red and pained. The child might have been a deformed part of himself that had been accidentally revealed.

"You'll get used to him," he said.

"No!" the boy shouted.

It was like a shout that had been waiting, straining to burst out. "I won't get used to him! I won't have anything to do with him!" He clenched his fist and lifted it. "I won't have anything to do with him!" he shouted and the words were clear and positive and defiant like a challenge hurled in the face of his silent adversary.

TWO

IV

AFTER FOUR DAYS of Tarwater, the schoolteacher's enthusiasm had passed. He would admit no more than that. It had passed the first day and had been succeeded by determination, and while he knew that determination was a less powerful tool, he thought that in this case, it was the one best fitted for the job. It had taken him barely half a day to find out that the old man had made a wreck of the boy and that what was called for was a monumental job of reconstruction. The first day enthusiasm had given him energy but ever since, determination had exhausted him.

Although it was only eight o'clock in the evening, he had put Bishop to bed and had told the boy that he could go to his room and read. He had bought him books, among other things still ignored. Tarwater had gone to his room and had closed the door, not saying whether he intended to read or not, and Rayber was in bed for the night, lying too exhausted to sleep, watching the late evening light fade through the hedge that grew in front of his window. He had left his hearing aid on so that if the boy tried to escape, he would hear and could go after him. For the last two days he had looked poised to leave, and not simply to leave but to be gone, silently and in the night when he would not be followed. This was the fourth night and the schoolteacher lay thinking, with a wry expression on his face, how it differed from the first.

The first night he had sat until daylight by the side of the bed where, still dressed, the boy had fallen. He had sat there, his eyes shining, like a man who sits before a treasure he is not yet convinced is real. His eyes had moved over and over the sprawled thin figure which had appeared lost in an exhaustion so profound that it seemed doubtful it would ever move again. As he followed the outline of the face, he had realized with an intense stab of joy that his nephew looked enough like him to be his son. The heavy work shoes, the worn overalls, the atrocious stained hat filled him with pain and pity. He thought of his poor sister. The only real pleasure she had had in her life was the time she had had the lover who had given her this child, the hollow-cheeked boy who had come from the country to study divinity but whose mind Rayber (a graduate student at the time) had seen at once was too good for that. He had befriended him, had helped him to discover himself and then to discover her. He had engineered their meeting purposely and then had observed to his delight how it prospered and how the relationship developed them both. If there had been no accident, he felt sure the boy would have become completely stable. As it was, after the calamity he had killed himself, a prey to morbid guilt. He had come to Rayber's apartment and had stood confronting him with the gun. He saw again the long brittle face as raw red as if a blast of fire had singed the skin off it and the eyes that had seemed burnt too. He had not felt they were entirely human eyes. They were the eyes of repentance and lacked all dignity. The boy had looked at him for what seemed an age but was perhaps only a second, then he had turned without a word and left and killed himself as soon as he reached his own room.

When Rayber had first opened the door in the middle of the night and had seen Tarwater's face—white, drawn by some unfathomable hunger and pride—he had remained for an instant frozen before what might have been a mirror thrust toward him in a nightmare. The face before him was his own, but the eyes were not his own. They were the student's eyes, singed with guilt. He had left the door hurriedly to get his glasses and his hearing aid.

As he sat that first night by the bed, he had recognized something rigid and recalcitrant about the boy even in repose. He lay with his teeth bared and the hat clenched in his fist like a weapon. Rayber's conscience smote him that all these years he had left him to his fate, that he had not gone back and saved him. His throat had tightened, his eyes had begun to ache. He had vowed to make it up to him now, to lavish on him everything he would have lavished on his own child if he had had one who would have known the difference.

The next morning while Tarwater was still asleep, he had rushed out and bought him a decent suit, a plaid shirt, socks, and a red leather cap. He wanted him to have new clothes to wake up to, new clothes to indicate a new life.

After four days they were still untouched in the box on a chair in the room. The boy had looked at them as if the suggestion he put them on were equal to asking that he appear naked.

It was apparent from everything he did and said exactly who had brought him up. At every turn an almost uncontrollable fury would rise in Rayber at the brand of independence the old man had wrought—not a constructive independence but one that was irrational, backwoods, and ignorant. After Rayber had rushed back with the clothes, he had gone to the bed and put his hand on the still sleeping boy's forehead and decided that he had a fever and should not get up. He had prepared a breakfast on a tray and brought it to the room. When he appeared in the door with it, Bishop at his side, Tarwater was sitting up in the bed, in the act of shaking out his hat and putting it on. Rayber had said, "Don't you want to hang up your hat and stay a while?" and had given him such a smile of welcome and good will as he thought had possibly never been turned on him before.

The boy, with no look of appreciation or even interest, had pulled the hat down farther on his head. His gaze had turned with a peculiar glare of recognition to Bishop. The child had on a black cowboy hat and he was gaping over the top of a trashbasket that he clasped to his stomach. He kept a rock in it. Rayber remembered that Bishop had caused the boy some disturbance the night before and he pushed him back with his free hand so that he could not get in. Then stepping into the room, he closed the door and locked it. Tarwater looked at the closed door darkly as if he continued to see the child through it, still clasping his trashbasket.

Rayber set the tray down across his knees and stood back scrutinizing him. The boy seemed barely aware that he was in the room. "That's your breakfast," his uncle said as if he might not be able to identify it. It was a bowl of dry cereal and a glass of milk. "I thought you'd better stay in bed today," he said. "You don't look too chipper." He pulled up a straight chair and sat down. "Now we can have a real talk," he said, his smile spreading. "It's high time we got to know each other."

No expression of approval or pleasure lightened the boy's

face. He glanced at the breakfast but did not pick up the
spoon. He began to look around the room. The walls were
an insistent pink, the color chosen by Rayber's wife. He used
it now for a store room. There were trunks in the corners
with crates piled on top of them. On the mantel, besides medicine bottles and dead electric lightbulbs and some old match
boxes, was a picture of her. The boy's attention paused there
and the corner of his mouth twitched slightly as if in some
kind of comic recognition. "The welfare woman," he said.

His uncle reddened. The tone he detected under this was
old Tarwater's exactly. Without warning, irritation mounted
in him. The old man might suddenly have obtruded his presence between them. He felt the same familiar fantastic anger,
out of all proportion to its cause, that his uncle had always
been able to stir in him. With an effort, he forced it out of
his way. "That's my wife," he said, "but she doesn't live with
us anymore. This is her old room you're in."

The boy picked up the spoon. "My great-uncle said she
wouldn't hang around long," he said and began to eat rapidly
as if he had established enough independence by this remark
to eat somebody else's food. It was apparent from his expression that he found the quality of it poor.

Rayber sat and watched him, saying to himself in an effort
to calm his irritation: this child hasn't had a chance, remember he hasn't had a chance. "God only knows what the old
fool has told you and taught you!" he said with a sudden
explosive force. "God only knows!"

The boy stopped eating and looked at him sharply. Then
after a second he said, "He ain't had no effect on me," and
returned to his eating.

"He did you a terrible injustice," Rayber said, wishing to
impress this on him as often as he could. "He kept you from
having a normal life, from getting a decent education. He
filled your head with God knows what rot!"

Tarwater continued to eat. Then with a stoney deliberateness, he looked up and his gaze fastened on the gash in his
uncle's ear. Somewhere in the depths of his eyes a glint appeared. "Shot yer, didn't he?" he said.

Rayber took a package of cigarets from his shirt pocket and
lit one, his motions inordinately slow from the effort he was

making to calm himself. He blew the smoke straight into the boy's face. Then he tilted back in the chair and gave him a long hard look. The cigaret hanging from the corner of his mouth trembled. "Yes, he shot me," he said.

The glint in the boy's eyes followed the wires of the hearing aid down to the metal box stuck in his belt. "What you wired for?" he drawled. "Does your head light up?"

Rayber's jaw snapped and then relaxed. After a moment, after extending his arm stiffly and knocking the ash off his cigaret onto the floor, he replied that his head did not light up. "This is a hearing aid," he said patiently. "After the old man shot me I began to lose my hearing. I didn't have a gun when I went to get you back. If I'd stayed he would have killed me and I wouldn't have done you any good dead."

The boy continued to study the machine. His uncle's face might have been only an appendage to it. "You ain't done me no good alive neither," he remarked.

"Do you understand me?" Rayber persisted. "I didn't have a gun. He would have killed me. He was a mad man. The time when I can do you good is beginning now, and I want to help you. I want to make up for all those years."

For an instant the boy's eyes left the hearing aid and rested on his uncle's eyes. "Could have got you a gun and come back terreckly," he said.

Stricken by the distinct sound of betrayal in his voice, Rayber could not say a word. He looked at him helplessly. The boy returned to his eating.

Finally Rayber said, "Listen." He took hold of the fist with the spoon in it and held it. "I want you to understand. He was crazy and if he had killed me, you wouldn't have this place to come to now. I'm no fool. I don't believe in senseless sacrifice. A dead man is not going to do you any good, don't you know that? Now I can do something for you. Now I can make up for all the time we've lost. I can help correct what he's done to you, help you to correct it yourself." He kept hold of the fist all the while it was being drawn insistently back. "This is our problem together," he said, seeing himself so clearly in the face before him that he might have been beseeching his own image.

With a quick yank, Tarwater managed to free his hand.

Then he gave the schoolteacher a long appraising look, tracing the line of his jaw, the two creases on either side of his mouth, the forehead extending into skull until it reached the pie-shaped hairline. He gazed briefly at the pained eyes behind his uncle's glasses, appearing to abandon a search for something that could not possibly be there. The glint in his eye fell on the metal box half-sticking out of Rayber's shirt. "Do you think in the box," he asked, "or do you think in your head?"

His uncle had wanted to tear the machine out of his ear and fling it against the wall. "It's because of you I can't hear!" he said, glaring at the impassive face. "It's because once I tried to help you!"

"You never helped me none."

"I can help you now," he said.

After a second he sank back in his chair. "Perhaps you're right," he said, letting his hands fall in a helpless gesture. "It was my mistake. I should have gone back and killed him or let him kill me. Instead I let something in you be killed."

The boy put down his milk glass. "Nothing in me has been killed," he said in a positive voice, and then he added, "And you needn't to worry. I done your work for you. I tended to him. It was me put him away. I was drunk as a coot and I tended to him." He said it as if he were recalling the most vivid point in his history.

Rayber heard his own heart, magnified by the hearing aid, suddenly begin to pound like the works of a gigantic machine in his chest. The boy's delicate defiant face, his glowering eyes still shocked by some violent memory, brought back instantly to him the vision of himself when he was fourteen and had found his way to Powderhead to shout imprecations at the old man.

An insight came to him that he was not to question until the end. He understood that the boy was held in bondage by his great-uncle, that he suffered a terrible false guilt for burning and not burying him, and he saw that he was engaged in a desperate heroic struggle to free himself from the old man's ghostly grasp. He leaned forward and said in a voice so full of feeling that it was barely balanced, "Listen, listen Frankie," he said, "you're not alone any more. You have a friend. You have more than a friend now." He swallowed. "You have a father."

The boy turned very white. His eyes were blackened by the shadow of some unspeakable outrage. "I ain't ast for no father," he said and the sentence struck like a whip across his uncle's face. "I ain't ast for no father," he repeated. "I'm out of the womb of a whore. I was born in a wreck." He flung this forth as if he were declaring a royal birth. "And my name ain't Frankie. I go by Tarwater and . . ."

"Your mother was not a whore," the schoolteacher said angrily. "That's just some rot he's taught you. She was a good healthy American girl, just beginning to find herself when she was struck down. She was . . ."

"I ain't fixing to hang around here," the boy said, looking about him as if he might throw over the breakfast tray and jump out the window. "I only come to find out a few things and when I find them out, then I'm going."

"What did you come to find out?" the schoolteacher asked evenly. "I can help you. All I want to do is help you any way I can."

"I don't need noner yer help," the boy said, looking away.

His uncle felt something tightening around him like an invisible strait jacket. "How do you mean to find out if you don't have help?"

"I'll wait," he said, "and see what happens."

"And suppose," his uncle asked, "nothing happens?"

An odd smile, like some strange inverted sign of grief, came over the boy's face. "Then I'll make it happen," he said, "like I done before."

In four days nothing had happened and nothing had been made to happen. They had simply covered—the three of them—the entire city, walking and all night Rayber rewalked the same territory backwards in his sleep. It would not have been so tiring if he had not had Bishop. The child dragged backwards on his hand, always attracted by something they had already passed. Every block or so he would squat down to pick up a stick or a piece of trash and have to be pulled up and along. Whereas Tarwater was always slightly in advance of them, pushing forward on the scent of something. In four days they had been to the art gallery and the movies, they had toured department stores, ridden escalators, visited the super-markets, inspected the water works, the post office, the rail-road yards and the city hall. Rayber had explained how the city was run and detailed the duties of a good citizen. He had talked as much as he had walked, and the boy for all the in-terest he showed might have been the one who was deaf. Si-lent, he viewed everything with the same noncommittal eye as if he found nothing here worth holding his attention but must keep moving, must keep searching for whatever it was that appeared just beyond his vision.

Once he had paused at a window where a small red car turned slowly on a revolving platform. Seizing on the display of interest, Rayber had said that perhaps when he was sixteen, he could have a car of his own. It might have been the old man who had replied that he could walk on his two feet for nothing without being beholden. Rayber had never, even when Old Tarwater had lived under his roof, been so con-scious of the old man's presence.

Once the boy had stopped suddenly in front of a tall build-ing and had stood glaring up at it with a peculiar ravaged look of recognition. Puzzled, Rayber said, "You look as if you've been here before."

"I lost my hat there," he muttered.

"Your hat is on your head," Rayber said. He could not look at the object without irritation. He wished to God there were some way to get it off him.

"My first hat," the boy said. "It fell," and he had rushed on, away from the place as if he could not stand to be near it.

Only one other time had he shown a particular interest. He had stopped with a kind of lurch backwards in front of a large grimey garage-like structure with two yellow and blue painted windows in the front of it, and had stood there, pre-cariously balanced as if he were arresting himself in the mid-dle of a fall. Rayber recognized the place for some kind of pentecostal tabernacle. Over the door was a paper banner bearing the words, UNLESS YE BE BORN AGAIN YE SHALL NOT HAVE EVERLASTING LIFE. Beneath it a poster showed a man and woman and child holding hands. "Hear the Car-modys for Christ!" it said. "Thrill to the Music, Message, and Magic of this team!"

Rayber was well enough aware of the boy's trouble to understand the sinister pull such a place would have on his mind. "Does this interest you?" he asked drily. "Does it remind you of something in particular?"

Tarwater was very pale. "Horse manure," he whispered.

Rayber smiled. Then he laughed. "All such people have in life," he said, "is the conviction they'll rise again."

The boy steadied himself, his eyes still on the banner but as if he had reduced it to a small spot a great distance away.

"They won't rise again?" he said. The statement had the lilt of a question and Rayber realized with an intense thrill of pleasure that his opinion, for the first time, was being called for.

"No," he said simply, "they won't rise again." There was a profound finality in his tone. The grimey structure might have been the carcass of a beast he had just brought down. He put his hand experimentally on the boy's shoulder. It was suffered to remain there.

In a voice unsteady with the sudden return of enthusiasm he said, "That's why I want you to learn all you can. I want you to be educated so that you can take your place as an intelligent man in the world. This fall when you start school . . ."

The shoulder was roughly withdrawn and the boy, throwing him one dark look, removed himself to the farthest edge of the sidewalk.

He wore his isolation like a mantle, wrapped it around himself as if it were a garment signifying the elect. Rayber had intended to keep notes on him and write up his most important observations but each night his energy had been too depleted to permit him to do any work. He had dropped off every night into a restless sleep, afraid that he would wake up and find the boy gone. He felt he had hastened his urge to leave by confronting him with the test. He had intended giving him the standard ones, intelligence and aptitude, and then going on to some he had perfected himself dealing with emotional factors. He had thought that in this way he could ferret to the center of the emotional infection. He had laid a simple aptitude test out on the kitchen table—the printed book and a few newly sharpened pencils. "This is a kind of game," he said. "Sit down and see what you can make of it. I'll help you begin."

The expression that came over the boy's face was very peculiar. His eyelids lowered just slightly; his mouth failed a smile by only a fraction; his look was compounded of fury and superiority. "Play with it yourself," he said. "I ain't taking no *test*," and he spit the word out as if it were not fit to pass between his lips.

Rayber sized up the situation. Then he said, "Maybe you don't really know how to read and write. Is that the trouble?"

The boy thrust his head forward. "I'm free," he hissed. "I'm outside your head. I ain't in it. I ain't in it and I ain't about to be."

His uncle laughed. "You don't know what freedom is," he said, "you don't . . ." but the boy turned and strode off.

It was no use. He could no more be reasoned with than a jackal. Nothing gave him pause—except Bishop, and Rayber knew that the reason Bishop gave him pause was because the child reminded him of the old man. Bishop looked like the old man grown backwards to the lowest form of innocence, and Rayber observed that the boy strictly avoided looking him in the eye. Wherever the child happened to be standing or sitting or walking seemed to be for Tarwater a dangerous hole in space that he must keep away from at all costs. Rayber was afraid that Bishop would drive him away with his friendliness. He was always creeping up to touch him and when the boy was aware of his being near, he would draw himself up like a snake ready to strike and hiss, "Git!" and Bishop would scurry off to watch him again from behind the nearest piece of furniture.

The schoolteacher understood this too. Every problem the boy had he had had himself and had conquered, or had for the most part conquered, for he had not conquered the problem of Bishop. He had only learned to live with it and had learned too that he could not live without it.

When he had got rid of his wife, he and the child had begun living together in a quiet automatic fashion like two bachelors whose habits were so smoothly connected that they no longer needed to take notice of each other. In the winter he sent him to a school for exceptional children and he had made great strides. He could wash himself, dress himself, feed himself, go to the toilet by himself and make peanut butter sandwiches though sometimes he put the bread inside. For the most part Rayber lived with him without being painfully aware of his presence but the moments would still come when, rushing from some inexplicable part of himself, he would experience a love for the child so outrageous that he would be left shocked and depressed for days, and trembling for his sanity. It was only a touch of the curse that lay in his blood.

His normal way of looking on Bishop was as an *x* signifying the general hideousness of fate. He did not believe that he himself was formed in the image and likeness of God but that Bishop was he had no doubt. The little boy was part of a simple equation that required no further solution, except at the moments when with little or no warning he would feel himself overwhelmed by the horrifying love. Anything he looked at too long could bring it on. Bishop did not have to be around. It could be a stick or a stone, the line of a shadow, the absurd old man's walk of a starling crossing the sidewalk. If, without thinking, he lent himself to it, he would feel suddenly a morbid surge of the love that terrified him—powerful enough to throw him to the ground in an act of idiot praise. It was completely irrational and abnormal.

He was not afraid of love in general. He knew the value of it and how it could be used. He had seen it transform in cases where nothing else had worked, such as with his poor sister. None of this had the least bearing on his situation. The love that would overcome him was of a different order entirely. It was not the kind that could be used for the child's improvement or his own. It was love without reason, love for something futureless, love that appeared to exist only to be itself, imperious and all demanding, the kind that would cause him to make a fool of himself in an instant. And it only began with Bishop. It began with Bishop and then like an avalanche covered everything his reason hated. He always felt with it a rush of longing to have the old man's eyes—insane, fish-coloured, violent with their impossible vision of a world transfigured—turned on him once again. The longing was like an undertow in his blood dragging him backwards to what he knew to be madness.

The affliction was in the family. It lay hidden in the line of blood that touched them, flowing from some ancient source, some desert prophet or pole-sitter, until, its power unabated, it appeared in the old man and him and, he surmised, in the boy. Those it touched were condemned to fight it constantly or be ruled by it. The old man had been ruled by it. He, at the cost of a full life, staved it off. What the boy would do hung in the balance.

He had kept it from gaining control over him by what amounted to a rigid ascetic discipline. He did not look at anything too long, he denied his senses unnecessary satisfactions. He slept in a narrow iron bed, worked sitting in a straight-backed chair, ate frugally, spoke little, and cultivated the dullest for friends. At his high school he was the expert on testing. All his professional decisions were prefabricated and did not involve his participation. He was not deceived that this was a whole or a full life, he only knew that it was the way his life had to be lived if it were going to have any dignity at all. He knew that he was the stuff of which fanatics and madmen are made and that he had turned his destiny as if with his bare will. He kept himself upright on a very narrow line between madness and emptiness, and when the time came for him to lose his balance, he intended to lurch toward emptiness and fall on the side of his choice. He recognized that in silent ways he lived an heroic life. The boy would go either his way or old Tarwater's and he was determined to save him for the better course. Although Tarwater claimed to believe nothing the old man had taught him, Rayber could see clearly that there was still a backdrag of belief and fear in him keeping his responses locked.

By virtue of kinship and similarity and experience, Rayber was the person to save him, yet something in the boy's very look drained him, something in his very look, something starved in it, seemed to feed on him. With Tarwater's eyes on him, he felt subjected to a pressure that killed his energy before he had a chance to exert it. The eyes were the eyes of the crazy student father, the personality was the old man's, and somewhere between the two, Rayber's own image was struggling to survive and he was not able to reach it. After three days of walking, he was numb with fatigue and plagued with a sense of his own ineffectiveness. All day his sentences had not quite connected with his thought.

That night they had eaten at an Italian restaurant, dark and not crowded, and he had ordered ravioli for them because Bishop liked it. After each meal the boy removed a piece of paper and a stub of pencil from his pocket and wrote down a figure—his estimate of what the meal was worth. In time he would pay back the total sum, he had said, as he did not intend to be beholden. Rayber would have liked to see the figures and learn what his meals were valued at—the boy never asked the price. He was a finicky eater, pushing the food around on his plate before he ate it and putting each forkful in his mouth as if he suspected it was poisoned. He had pushed the ravioli about, his face drawn. He ate a little of it and then put the fork down.

"Don't you like that?" Rayber had asked. "You can have something else if you don't."

"It all come out the same slop bucket," the boy said.

"Bishop is eating his," Rayber said. Bishop had it smeared all over his face. Occasionally he would feed a spoonful into the sugar bowl or touch the tip of his tongue to the dish.

"That's what I said," Tarwater said, and his glance grazed the top of the child's head, "—a hog might like it."

The schoolteacher put his fork down.

Tarwater was glaring at the dark walls of the room. "He's like a hog," he said. "He eats like a hog and he don't think no more than a hog and when he dies, he'll rot like a hog. Me and you too," he said, looking back at the schoolteacher's mottled face, "will rot like hogs. The only difference between me and you and a hog is me and you can calculate, but there ain't any difference between him and one."

Rayber appeared to be gritting his teeth. Finally he said, "Just forget Bishop exists. You haven't been asked to have anything to do with him. He's just a mistake of nature. Try not even to be aware of him."

"He ain't my mistake," the boy muttered. "I ain't having a thing to do with him."

"Forget him," Rayber said in a short harsh voice.

The boy looked at him oddly as if he were beginning to perceive his secret affliction. What he saw or thought he saw seemed grimly to amuse him. "Let's leave out of here," he said, "and get to walking again."

"We are not going to walk tonight," Rayber said. "We are going home and go to bed." He said it with a firmness and finality he had not used before. The boy had only shrugged.

As Rayber lay watching the window darken, he felt that all his nerves were stretched through him like high tension wire. He began trying to relax one muscle at a time as the books recommended, beginning with those in the back of his neck. He emptied his mind of everything but the just visible pattern of the hedge against the screen. Still he was alert for any sound. Long after he lay in complete darkness, he was still alert, unrelaxed, ready to spring up at the least creak of a floor board in the hall. All at once he sat up, wide awake. A door opened and closed. He leapt up and ran across the hall into the opposite room. The boy was gone. He ran back to his own room and pulled his trousers on over his pajamas. Then grabbing his coat, he went out the house by way of the kitchen, barefooted, his jaw set.

V

KEEPING CLOSE to his side of the hedge, he crept through the dark damp grass toward the street. The night was close and very still. A light went on in a window of the next house and revealed, at the end of the hedge, the hat. It turned slightly and Rayber saw the sharp profile beneath it, the set thrust of a jaw very like his own. The boy was stopped still, most likely taking his bearings, deciding which direction to walk in.

He turned again and again Rayber saw only the hat, intransigently ground upon his head, fierce-looking even in the dim light. It had the boy's own defiant quality, as if its shape had been formed over the years by his personality. It had been the first thing that Rayber had seen must go. It suddenly moved out of the light and vanished.

Rayber slipped through the hedge and followed, soundless on his bare feet. Nothing cast a shadow. He could barely make out the boy a quarter of a block in front of him, except when occasionally light from a window outlined him briefly. Since Rayber didn't know whether he thought he was leaving for good or only going for a walk on his own, he decided not to shout and stop him but to follow silently and observe. He turned off his hearing aid and pursued the dim figure as if in a dream. The boy walked even faster at night than in the day time and was always on the verge of vanishing.

Rayber felt the accelerated beat of his heart. He took a handkerchief out of his pocket and wiped his forehead and inside the neck of his pajama top. He walked over something sticky on the sidewalk and shifted hurriedly to the other side, cursing under his breath. Tarwater was heading toward town. Rayber thought it likely he was returning to see something that had secretly interested him. He might discover tonight what he would have found by testing if the boy had not been so pig-headed. He felt the insidious pleasure of revenge and checked it.

A patch of sky blanched, revealing for a moment the outlines of the housetops. Tarwater turned suddenly to the right. Rayber cursed himself for not stopping long enough to get his shoes. They had come into a neighborhood of large ramshackle boarding houses with porches that abutted the sidewalks. On some of them late sitters were rocking and watching the street. He felt eyes in the darkness move on him and he turned on the hearing aid again. On one porch a woman rose and leaned over the banister. She stood with her hands on her hips, looking him over, taking in his bare feet, the striped pajama coat under his seersucker suit. Irritated, he glanced back at her. The thrust of her neck indicated a conclusion formed. He buttoned his coat and hurried on.

The boy stopped on the next corner. His lean shadow made by a street light slanted to the side of him. The hat's shadow, like a knob at the top of it, turned to the right and then the left. He appeared to be considering his direction. Rayber's muscles felt suddenly weighted. He was not conscious of his fatigue until the pace slackened.

Tarwater turned to the left and Rayber began angrily to move again. They went down a street of dilapidated stores. When Rayber turned the next corner, the gaudy cave of a movie house yawned to the side of him. A knot of small boys stood in front of it. "Forgot yer shoes!" one of them chirruped. "Forget yer shirt!"

He began a kind of limping lope.

The chorus followed him down the block. "Hi yo Silverwear, Tonto's lost his underwear! What in the heck do we care?"

He kept his eye wrathfully on Tarwater who was turning to the right. When he reached the corner and turned, he saw the boy stopped in the middle of the block, looking in a store window. He slipped into a narrow entrance a few yards farther on where a flight of steps led upward into darkness. Then he looked out.

Tarwater's face was strangely lit from the window he was standing before. Rayber watched curiously for a few moments. It looked to him like the face of someone starving who sees a meal he can't reach laid out before him. At last, something he *wants*, he thought, and determined that tomorrow he would return and buy it. Tarwater reached out and touched the glass and then drew his hand back slowly. He hung there as if he could not take his eyes off what it was he wanted. A pet shop, perhaps, Rayber thought. Maybe he wanted. A dog might make all the difference. Abruptly the boy broke away and moved on.

Rayber stepped out of the entrance and made for the window he had left. He stopped with a shock of disappointment. The place was only a bakery. The window was empty except for a loaf of bread pushed to the side that must have been overlooked when the shelf was cleaned for the night. He stared, puzzled, at the empty window for a second before he started after the boy again. Everything a false alarm, he thought with disgust. If he had eaten his dinner, he wouldn't be hungry. A man and woman strolling past looked with interest at his bare feet. He glared at them, then glanced to the side and saw his bloodless wired reflection in the glass of a shoe shop. The boy disappeared all at once into an alley. My God, Rayber thought, how long is this going on?

He turned into the alley, which was unpaved and so dark that he could not see Tarwater in it at all. He was certain that any minute he would cut his feet on broken glass. A garbage can materialized in his path. There was a noise like the collapse of a tin house and he found himself sitting up with his hand and one foot in something unidentifiable. He scrambled up and limped on, hearing his own curses like the voice of a stranger broadcast through his hearing aid. At the end of the alley, he saw the lean figure in the middle of the next block, and with a sudden fury he began to run.

The boy turned into another alley. Doggedly Rayber ran on. At the end of the second alley, the boy turned to the left. When Rayber reached the street, Tarwater was standing still in the middle of the next block. With a furtive look around him, he vanished, apparently into the building he had been facing. Rayber dashed forward. As he reached the place, singing burst flatly against his eardrums. Two blue and yellow windows glared at him in the darkness like the eyes of some Biblical beast. He stopped in front of the banner and read the mocking words, UNLESS YE BE BORN AGAIN. . . .

That the boy's corruption was this deep did not surprise him. What unstrung him was the thought that what Tarwater carried into the atrocious temple was his own imprisoned image. Enraged, he started around the building to locate a window he could look through and see the boy's face among the crowd. When he saw him, he would roar at him to come out. The windows near the front were all too high but toward the back, he found a lower one. He pushed through a straggly shrub beneath it and, his chin just above the ledge, looked into what appeared to be a small ante-room. A door on the other side of it opened onto a stage and there a man in a bright blue suit was standing in a spotlight, leading a hymn. Rayber could not see into the main body of the building where the people were. He was about to move away when the man brought the hymn to a close and began to speak.

"Friends," he said, "the time has come. The time we've all been waiting for this evening. Jesus said suffer the little children to come unto Him and forbid them not and maybe it was because He knew that it would be the little children that would call others to Him, maybe He knew, friends, maybe He hadda hunch."

Rayber listened angrily, too exhausted to move away once he had stopped.

"Friends," the preacher said, "Lucette has travelled the world over telling people about Jesus. She's been to India and China. She's spoken to all the rulers of the world. Jesus is wonderful, friends. He teaches us wisdom out of the mouths of babes!"

Another child exploited, Rayber thought furiously. It was the thought of a child's mind warped, of a child led away from reality that always enraged him, bringing back to him his own childhood's seduction. Glaring at the spotlight, he saw the man there as a blur which he looked through, down the length of his life until what confronted him were the old man's fish-coloured eyes. He saw himself taking the offered hand and innocently walking out of his own yard, innocently walking into six or seven years of unreality. Any other child would have thrown off the spell in a week. He could not have. He had analysed his case and closed it. Still, every now and then he would live over the five minutes it had taken his father to snatch him away from Powderhead. Through the blur of the man on the stage, as if he were looking into a transparent nightmare, he had the experience again. He and his uncle sat on the steps of the house at Powderhead watching his father emerge from the woods and sight them across the field. His uncle leaned forward, squinting, his hand cupped over his eyes, and he sat with his hands clenched between his knees, his heart threshing from side to side as his father moved closer and closer.

"Lucette travels with her mother and daddy and I want you to meet them because a mother and daddy have to be unselfish to share their only child with the world," the preacher said. "Here they are, friends—Mr. and Mrs. Carmody!"

While a man and woman moved into the light, Rayber had a clear vision of plowed ground, of the shaded red ridges that separated him from the lean figure approaching. He had let himself imagine that the field had an undertow that would drag his father backwards and suck him under, but he came on inexorably, only stopping every now and then to put a finger in his shoe and push out a clod of dirt.

"He's going to take me back with him," he said.

"Back with him where?" his uncle growled. "He ain't got any place to take you back to."

"He can't take me back with him?"

"Not where you were before."

"He can't take me back to town?"

"I never said nothing about town," his uncle said.

He saw vaguely that the man in the spotlight had sat down but that the woman was still standing. She became a blur and he saw his father again, getting closer and closer and he had one impulse to dart up and run through his uncle's house and tear out the back to the woods. He would have raced along the path, familiar to him then, and sliding and slipping over the waxy pine needles, he would have run down and down until he reached the thicket of bamboo and would have pushed through it and out onto the other side and would have fallen into the stream and lain there, panting and wheezing and safe where he had been born again, where his head had been thrust by his uncle into the water and brought up again into a new life. Sitting on the step, his leg muscles twitched as if they were ready for him to spring up but he remained absolutely still. He could see the line of his father's mouth, the line that had gone past the point of exasperation, past the point of loud wrath to a kind of stoked rage that would feed him for months.

While the woman evangelist, tall and raw-boned, was speaking of the hardships she had endured, he watched his father as he reached the edge of the yard and stepped onto the packed dirt, his face a slick pink from the exertion of crossing a field. He was drawing short hard breaths. For an instant he seemed about to reach forward and snatch him but he remained where he was. His pale eyes moved carefully over the rock-like figure watching him steadily from the steps, at the red hands knotted on the heavy thighs and then at the gun lying on the porch. He said, "His mother wants him back, Mason. I don't know why. For my part you could have him but you know how she is."

"A drunken whore," his uncle growled.

"Your sister, not mine," his father said, and then said, "All right boy, snap it up," and nodded curtly to him.

He explained in a high reedy voice the exact reason he could not go back, "I've been born again."

"Great," his father said, "great." He took a step forward and grabbed his arm and yanked him to his feet. "Glad you got him fixed up, Mason," he said. "One bath more or less won't hurt the bugger."

He had had no chance to see his uncle's face. His father had already lept into the plowed field and was dragging him across the furrows while the pellets pierced the air over their heads. His shoulders, just under the window ledge, jumped. He shook his head to clear it.

"For ten years I was a missionary in China," the woman was saying, "for five years I was a missionary in Africa, and one year I was a missionary in Rome where minds are still chained in priestly darkness; but for the last six years, my husband and I have travelled the world over with our daughter. They have been years of trial and pain, years of hardship and suffering." She had on a long dramatic cape, one side of which was turned backward over her shoulder to reveal a red lining.

His father's face was suddenly very close to his own. "Back to the real world, boy," he was saying, "back to the real world. And that's me and not him, see? Me and not him," and he heard himself screaming, "It's him! Him! Him and not you! And I've been born again and there's not a thing you can do about it!"

"Christ in hell," his father said, "believe it if you want to. Who cares? You'll find out soon enough."

The woman's tone had changed. The sound of something grasping drew his attention again. "We have not had an easy time. We have been a hard-working team for Christ. People have not always been generous to us. Only here are the people really generous. I am from Texas and my husband is from Tennessee but we have travelled the world over. We know," she said in a deepened softened voice, "where the people are really generous."

Rayber forgot himself and listened. He felt a relief from his pain, recognizing that the woman was only after money. He could hear the beginning click of coins falling in a plate.

"Our little girl began to preach when she was six. We saw that she had a mission, that she had been called. We saw that we could not keep her to ourselves and so we have endured many hardships to give her to the world, to bring her to you tonight. To us," she said, "you are as important as the great rulers of the world!" Here she lifted the end of her cape and holding it out as a magician would made a low bow. After a moment she lifted her head, gazed in front of her as if at some grand vista, and disappeared from view. A little girl hobbled into the spotlight.

Rayber cringed. Simply by the sight of her he could tell that she was not a fraud, that she was only exploited. She was eleven or twelve with a small delicate face and a head of black hair that looked too thick and heavy for a frail child to support. A cape like her mother's was turned back over one shoulder and her skirt was short as if better to reveal the thin legs twisted from the knees. She held her arms over her head for a moment. "I want to tell you people the story of the world," she said in a loud high child's voice. "I want to tell you why Jesus came and what happened to Him. I want to tell you how He'll come again. I want to tell you to be ready. Most of all," she said, "I want to tell you to be ready so that on the last day you'll rise in the glory of the Lord."

Rayber's fury encompassed the parents, the preacher, all

the idiots he could not see who were sitting in front of the child, parties to her degradation. She believed it, she was locked tight in it, chained hand and foot, exactly as he had been, exactly as only a child could be. He felt the taste of his own childhood pain laid again on his tongue like a bitter wafer.

"Do you know who Jesus is?" she cried. "Jesus is the Word of God and Jesus is love. The Word of God is love and do you know what love is, you people? If you don't know what love is you won't know Jesus when He comes. You won't be ready. I want to tell you people the story of the world, how it never known when love come, so when love comes again, you'll be ready."

She moved back and forth across the stage, frowning as if she were trying to see the people through the fierce circle of light that followed her. "Listen to me, you people," she said, "God was angry with the world because it always wanted more. It wanted as much as God had and it didn't know what God had but it wanted it and more. It wanted God's own breath, it wanted His very Word and God said, 'I'll make my Word Jesus, I'll give them my Word for a king, I'll give them my very breath for theirs.'

"Listen you people," she said and flung her arms wide, "God told the world He was going to send it a king and the world waited. The world thought, a golden fleece will do for His bed. Silver and gold and peacock tails, a thousand suns in a peacock's tail will do for His sash. His mother will ride on a four-horned white beast and use the sunset for a cape. She'll trail it behind her over the ground and let the world pull it to pieces, a new one every evening."

To Rayber she was like one of those birds blinded to make it sing more sweetly. Her voice had the tone of a glass bell. His pity encompassed all exploited children—himself when he was a child, Tarwater exploited by the old man, this child exploited by parents, Bishop exploited by the very fact he was alive.

"The world said, 'How long, Lord, do we have to wait for this?' And the Lord said, 'My Word is coming, my Word is coming from the house of David, the king.'" She paused and turned her head to the side, away from the fierce light. Her dark gaze moved slowly until it rested on Rayber's head in the window. He stared back at her. Her eyes remained on his face for a moment. A deep shock went through him. He was certain that the child had looked directly into his heart and seen his pity. He felt that some mysterious connection was established between them.

" 'My Word is coming,' " she said, turning back to face the glare, " 'my Word is coming from the house of David, the king.' "

She began again in a dirge-like tone. "Jesus came on cold straw, Jesus was warmed by the breath of an ox. 'Who is this?' the world said, 'who is this blue-cold child and this woman, plain as the winter? Is this the Word of God, this blue-cold child? Is this His will, this plain winter-woman?'

"Listen you people!" she cried, "the world knew in its heart, the same as you know in your hearts and I know in my heart. The world said, 'Love cuts like the cold wind and the will of God is plain as the winter. Where is the summer will of God? Where are the green seasons of God's will? Where is the spring and summer of God's will?'

"They had to flee into Egypt," she said in a low voice and turned her head again and this time her eyes moved directly to Rayber's face in the window and he knew they sought it. He felt himself caught up in her look, held there before the judgment seat of her eyes.

"You and I know," she said turning again, "what the world hoped then. The world hoped old Herod would slay the right child, the world hoped old Herod wouldn't waste those children, but he wasted them. He didn't get the right one. Jesus grew up and raised the dead."

Rayber felt his spirit borne aloft. But not those dead! he cried, not the innocent children, not you, not me when I was a child, not Bishop, not Frank! and he had a vision of himself moving like an avenging angel through the world, gathering up all the children that the Lord, not Herod, had slain.

"Jesus grew up and raised the dead," she cried, "and the world shouted, 'Leave the dead lie. The dead are dead and can stay that way. What do we want with the dead alive?' Oh you people!" she shouted, "they nailed Him to a cross and run a spear through His side and then they said, 'Now we can have some peace, now we can ease our minds.' And they hadn't but only said it when they wanted Him to come again. Their eyes were opened and they saw the glory they had killed.

"Listen world," she cried, flinging up her arms so that the cape flew out behind her, "Jesus is coming again! The mountains are going to lie down like hounds at His feet, the stars are going to perch on His shoulder and when He calls it, the sun is going to fall like a goose for His feast. Will you know the Lord Jesus then? The mountains will know Him and bound forward, the stars will light on His head, the sun will drop down at His feet, but will you know the Lord Jesus then?"

Rayber saw himself fleeing with the child to some enclosed garden where he would teach her the truth, where he would gather all the exploited children of the world and let the sunshine flood their minds.

"If you don't know Him now, you won't know Him then. Listen to me, world, listen to this warning. The Holy Word is in my mouth!

"The Holy Word is in my mouth!" she cried and turned her eyes again on his face in the window. This time there was a lowering concentration in her gaze. He had drawn her attention entirely away from the congregation.

Come away with me! he silently implored, and I'll teach you the truth, I'll save you, beautiful child!

Her eyes still fixed on him, she cried, "I've seen the Lord in a tree of fire! The Word of God is a burning Word to burn you clean!" She was moving in his direction, the people in front of her forgotten. Rayber's heart began to race. He felt some miraculous communication between them. The child alone in the world was meant to understand him. "Burns the whole world, man and child," she cried, her eye on him, "none can escape." She stopped a little distance from the end of the stage and stood silent, her whole attention directed across the small room to his face on the ledge. Her eyes were large and dark and fierce. He felt that in the space between them, their spirits had broken the bonds of age and ignorance and were mingling in some unheard of knowledge of each other. He was transfixed by the child's silence. Suddenly she raised her arm and pointed toward his face. "Listen you people," she shrieked, "I see a damned soul before my eye! I see a dead man Jesus hasn't raised. His head is in the window but his ear is deaf to the Holy Word!"

Rayber's head, as if it had been struck by an invisible bolt, dropped from the ledge. He crouched on the ground, his furious spectacled eyes glittering behind the shrubbery. Inside she continued to shriek, "Are you deaf to the Lord's Word? The Word of God is a burning Word to burn you clean, burns man and child, man and child the same, you people! Be saved in the Lord's fire or perish in your own! Be saved in . . ."

He was groping fiercely about him, slapping at his coat pockets, his head, his chest, not able to find the switch that would cut off the voice. Then his hand touched the button and he snapped it. A silent dark relief enclosed him like shelter after a tormenting wind. For a while he sat limp behind the bush. Then the reason for his being here returned to him and he experienced a moment of loathing for the boy that earlier would have made him shudder. He wanted nothing but to get back home and sink into his own bed, whether the boy returned or not.

He got out of the shrubbery and started toward the front of the building. As he turned onto the sidewalk, the door of the tabernacle flew open and Tarwater flung himself out. Rayber stopped abruptly.

The boy stood confronting him, his face strangely mobile as if successive layers of shock were settling on it to form a new expression. After a moment he raised his arm in an uncertain gesture of greeting. The sight of Rayber seemed to afford him relief amounting to rescue.

Rayber's face had the wooden look it wore when his hearing aid was off. He did not see the boy's expression at all. His rage obliterated all but the general lines of his figure and he saw them moulded in an irreversible shape of defiance. He grabbed him roughly by the arm and started down the block with him. Both of them walked rapidly as if neither could leave the place fast enough. When they were well down the block, Rayber stopped and swung him around and glared into his face. Through his fury he could not discern that for the first time the boy's eyes were submissive. He snapped on his hearing aid and said fiercely, "I hope you enjoyed the show."

Tarwater's lips moved convulsively. Then he murmured, "I only gone to spit on it."

The schoolteacher continued to glare at him. "I'm not so sure of that."

The boy said nothing. He seemed to have suffered some shock inside the building that had permanently slowed his tongue.

Rayber turned and they walked away in silence. At any point along the way, he could have put his hand on the shoulder next to his and it would not have been withdrawn, but he made no gesture. His head was churning with old rages. The afternoon he had learned the full extent of Bishop's future had sprung to his mind. He saw himself rigidly facing the doctor, a man who had made him think of a bull, impassive, insensitive, his brain already on the next case. He had said, "You should be grateful his health is good. In addition to this, I've seen them born blind as well, some without arms and legs, and one with a heart outside."

He had lurched up, almost ready to strike the man. "How can I be grateful," he had hissed, "when one—just one—is born with a heart outside?"

"You'd better try," the doctor had said.

Tarwater walked slightly behind him and Rayber did not cast a glance back at him. His fury seemed to be stirring from buried depths that had lain quiet for years and to be working upward, closer and closer, toward the slender roots of his peace. When they reached the house he went in and straight to his bed without turning to look at the boy's white face which, drained but expectant, lingered a moment at the threshold of his door as if waiting for an invitation to enter.

VI

THE NEXT DAY, too late, he had the sense of opportunity missed. Tarwater's face had hardened again and the steely gleam in his eye was like the glint of a metal door sealed against an intruder. Rayber felt afflicted with a peculiar chilling clarity of mind in which he saw himself divided in two— a violent and a rational self. The violent self inclined him to see the boy as an enemy and he knew that nothing would hinder his progress with the case so much as giving in to such an inclination. He had waked up after a wild dream in which he chased Tarwater through an interminable alley that twisted suddenly back on itself and reversed the roles of pursuer and pursued. The boy had overtaken him, given him a thunderous blow on the head, and then disappeared. And with his disappearance there had come such an overwhelming feeling of release that Rayber had waked up with a pleasant anticipation that his guest would be gone. He was at once ashamed of the feeling. He settled on a rational, tiring plan for the day and by ten o'clock the three of them were on their way to the natural history museum. He intended to stretch the boy's mind by introducing him to his ancestor, the fish, and to all the great wastes of unexplored time.

They passed part of the territory they had walked over the night before but nothing was said about that trip. Except for the circles under Rayber's eyes, there was nothing about either of them to indicate it had been made. Bishop stumped along, squatting every now and then to pick up something off the sidewalk, while Tarwater, to avoid contamination with them, walked a good four feet to the other side and slightly in advance. I must have infinite patience, I must have infinite patience, Rayber kept repeating to himself.

The museum lay on the other side of the city park which they had not crossed before. As they approached it, the boy paled as if he were shocked to find a wood in the middle of the city. Once inside the park, he stopped and stood glaring about him at the huge trees whose ancient rustling branches intermingled overhead. Patches of light sifting through them spattered the concrete walks with sunshine. Rayber observed that something disturbed him. Then he realized that the place reminded him of Powderhead.

"Let's sit down," he said, wanting both to rest and to observe the boy's agitation. He sat down on a bench and stretched his legs in front of him. He suffered Bishop to climb into his lap. The child's shoelaces were untied and he tied them, for the moment ignoring the boy who was standing there, his face furiously impatient. When he finished tying the shoes, he continued to hold the child, sprawled and grinning, in his lap. The little boy's white head fitted under his chin. Above it Rayber looked at nothing in particular. Then he closed his eyes and in the isolating darkness, he forgot Tarwater's presence. Without warning his hated love gripped him and held him in a vise. He should have known better than to let the child onto his lap.

His forehead became beady with sweat; he looked as if he might have been nailed to the bench. He knew that if he could once conquer this pain, face it and with a supreme effort of his will refuse to feel it, he would be a free man. He held Bishop rigidly. Although the child started the pain, he also limited it, contained it. He had learned this one terrible afternoon when he had tried to drown him.

He had taken him to the beach, two hundred miles away, intending to effect the accident as quickly as possible and return bereaved. It had been a beautiful calm day in May. The beach, almost empty, had stretched down into the gradual swell of ocean. There was nothing to be seen but an expanse of sea and sky and sand and an occasional figure, stick-like, in the distance. He had taken him out on his shoulders and when he was chest deep in the water, had lifted him off, swung the delighted child high in the air and then plunged him swiftly below the surface on his back and held him there, not looking down at what he was doing but up, at an imperturbable witnessing sky, not quite blue, not quite white.

A fierce surging pressure had begun upward beneath his hands and grimly he had exerted more and more force downward. In a second, he felt he was trying to hold a giant under. Astonished, he let himself look. The face under the water was wrathfully contorted, twisted by some primeval rage to save itself. Automatically he released his pressure. Then when he realized what he had done, he pushed down again angrily with all his force until the struggle ceased under his hands. He stood sweating in the water, his own mouth as slack as the child's had been. The body, caught by an undertow, almost got away from him but he managed to come to himself and snatch it. Then as he looked at it, he had a moment of complete terror in which he envisioned his life without the child. He began to shout frantically. He plowed his way out of the water with the limp body. The beach which he had thought empty before had become peopled with strangers converging on him from all directions. A bald-headed man in red and blue Roman striped shorts began at once to administer artificial respiration. Three wailing women and a photographer appeared. The next day there had been a picture in the paper, showing the rescuer, striped bottom forward, working over the child. Rayber was beside him on his knees, watching with an agonized expression. The caption said, OVERJOYED FATHER SEES SON REVIVED.

The boy's voice broke in on him harshly. "All you got to do is nurse an idiot!"

The schoolteacher opened his eyes. They were bloodshot and vague. He might have been returning to consciousness after a blow on the head.

Tarwater was glaring to the side of him. "Come on if you're coming," he said, "and if you ain't, I'm going on about my bidnis."

Rayber didn't answer.

"So long," Tarwater said.

"And where would your business be?" Rayber asked sourly. "At another tabernacle?"

The boy reddened. He opened his mouth and said nothing.

"I nurse an idiot that you're afraid to look at," Rayber said. "Look him in the eye."

Tarwater shot a glance at the top of Bishop's head and left it there an instant like a finger on a candle flame. "I'd as soon be afraid to look at a dog," he said and turned his back. After a moment, as if he were continuing the same conversation, he muttered, "I'd as soon baptize a dog as him. It would be as much use."

"Who said anything about baptizing anybody?" Rayber said. "Is that one of your fixations? Have you taken that bug up from the old man?"

The boy whirled around and faced him. "I told you I only gone there to spit on it," he said tensely. "I ain't going to tell you again."

Rayber watched him without saying anything. He felt that his own sour words had helped him recover himself. He pushed Bishop off and stood up. "Let's get going," he said. He had no intention of discussing it further, but as they moved on silently, he thought better of it.

"Listen Frank," he said, "I'll grant that you went to spit on it. I've never for a second doubted your intelligence. Everything you've done, your very presence here proves that you're above your background, that you've broken through the ceiling the old man set for you. After all, you escaped from Powderhead. You had the courage to attend to him the quickest way and then get out of there. And once out, you came directly to the right place."

The boy reached up and picked a leaf from a tree branch and bit it. A wry expression spread over his face. He rolled the leaf into a ball and threw it away. Rayber continued to speak, his voice detached, as if he had no particular interest in the matter, and his were merely the voice of truth, as impersonal as air.

"Say that you went to spit on it," he said, "the point is this: there's no need to spit on it. It's not worth spitting on. It's not that important. You've somehow enlarged the significance of it in your mind. The old man used to enrage me until I learned better. He wasn't worth my hate and he's not worth yours. He's only worth our pity." He wondered if the boy were capable of the steadiness of pity. "You want to avoid extremes. They are for violent people and you don't want . . ." —he broke off abruptly as Bishop let loose his hand and galloped away.

They had come out into the center of the park, a concrete circle with a fountain in the middle of it. Water rushed from the mouth of a stone lion's head into a shallow pool and the little boy was flying toward it, his arms flailing like a windmill. In a second he was over the side and in. "Too late,

goddammit," Rayber muttered, "he's in." He glanced at Tarwater.

The boy stood arrested in the middle of a step. His eyes
were on the child in the pool but they burned as if he beheld
some terrible compelling vision. The sun shone brightly on
Bishop's white head and the little boy stood there with a look
of attention. Tarwater began to move toward him.

He seemed to be drawn toward the child in the water but
to be pulling back, exerting an almost equal pressure away
from what attracted him. Rayber watched, puzzled and suspicious, moving along with him but somewhat to the side. As
he drew closer to the pool, the skin on the boy's face appeared to stretch tighter and tighter. Rayber had the sense
that he was moving blindly, that where Bishop was he saw
only a spot of light. He felt that something was being enacted
before him and that if he could understand it, he would have
the key to the boy's future. His muscles were tensed and he
was prepared somehow to act. Suddenly his sense of danger
was so great that he cried out. In an instant of illumination
he understood. Tarwater was moving toward Bishop to baptize him. Already he had reached the edge of the pool. Rayber
sprang and snatched the child out of the water and set him
down, howling, on the concrete.

His heart was beating furiously. He felt that he had just
saved the boy from committing some enormous indignity. He
saw it all now. The old man *had* transferred his fixation to
the boy, *had* left him with the notion that he must baptize
Bishop or suffer some terrible consequence. Tarwater put his
foot down on the marble edge of the pool. He leaned forward, his elbow on his knee, looking over the side at his broken reflection in the water. His lips moved as if he were
speaking silently to the face forming in the pool. Rayber said
nothing. He realized now the magnitude of the boy's affliction. He knew that there was no way to appeal to him with
reason. There was no hope of discussing it sanely with him,
for it was a compulsion. He saw no way of curing him except
perhaps through some shock, some sudden concrete confrontation with the futility, the ridiculous absurdity of performing
the empty rite.

He squatted down and began to take off Bishop's wet

shoes. The child had stopped howling and was crying quietly, his face red and hideously distorted. Rayber turned his eyes away.

Tarwater was walking off. He was past the pool, his back strangely bent as if he were being driven away with a whip. He was moving off onto one of the narrow tree-shaded paths.

"Wait!" Rayber shouted. "We can't go to the museum now. We'll have to go home and change Bishop's shoes."

Tarwater could not have failed to hear but he kept on walking and in a second was lost to view.

Goddam backwoods imbecile, Rayber said under his breath. He stood looking at the path where the boy had disappeared. He felt no urge to go after him for he knew that he would be back, that he was held by Bishop. His feeling of oppression was caused now by the certain knowledge that there was no way to get rid of him. He would be with them until he had either accomplished what he came for, or until he was cured. The words the old man had scrawled on the back of the journal rose before him: THE PROPHET I RAISE UP OUT OF THIS BOY WILL BURN YOUR EYES CLEAN. The sentence was like a challenge renewed. I will cure him, he said grimly. I will cure him or know the reason why.

VII

THE CHEROKEE LODGE was a two-story converted warehouse, the lower part painted white and the upper green. One end sat on land and the other was set on stilts in a glassy little lake across which were dense woods, green and black farther toward the skyline, grey-blue. The long front side of the building, plastered with beer and cigaret signs, faced the highway, which ran about thirty feet away across a dirt road and beyond a narrow stretch of iron weed. Rayber had passed the place before but had never been tempted to stop.

He had selected it because it was only thirty miles from Powderhead and because it was cheap and he arrived there the next day with the two boys in time for them to take a walk and look around before they ate. The ride up had been oppressively silent, the boy sitting as usual on his side of the car like some foreign dignitary who would not admit speaking the language—the filthy hat, the stinking overalls, worn defiantly like a national costume.

Rayber had hit upon his plan in the night. It was to take him back to Powderhead and make him face what he had done. What he hoped was that if seeing and feeling the place again were a real shock, the boy's trauma might suddenly be revealed. His irrational fears and impulses would burst out and his uncle—sympathetic, knowing, uniquely able to understand—would be there to explain them to him. He had not said they were going to Powderhead. So far as the boy knew, this was to be a fishing trip. He thought that an afternoon of relaxation in a boat before the experiment would help ease the tension, his own as well as Tarwater's.

On the drive up, his thoughts had been interrupted once when he saw Bishop's face rise unorganized into the rearview mirror and then disappear as he attempted to crawl over the top of the front seat and climb into Tarwater's lap. The boy had turned and without looking at him had given the panting child a firm push onto the back seat again. One of Rayber's immediate goals was to make him understand that his urge to baptize the child was a kind of *sickness* and that a sign of returning health would be his ability to begin looking Bishop

in the eye. Rayber felt that once he could look the child in
the eye, he would have confidence in his ability to resist the
morbid impulse to baptize him.

When they got out of the car, he watched the boy closely,
trying to discover his first reaction to being in the country
again. Tarwater stood for a moment, his head lifted sharply
as if he detected some familiar odor moving from the pine
forest across the lake. His long face, depending from the
bulb-shaped hat, made Rayber think of a root jerked suddenly
out of the ground and exposed to the light. The boy's eyes
narrowed so that the lake must have been reduced to the
width of a knife-blade in his sight. He looked at the water
with a peculiar undisguised hostility. Rayber even thought
that as his eye fell on it, he began to tremble. At least he was
certain that his hands clenched. His glare steadied, then with
his usual precipitous gait, he set off around the building without looking back.

Bishop climbed out of the car and thrust his face against
his father's side. Absently Rayber put his hand on the little
boy's ear and rubbed it gingerly, his fingers tingling as if they
touched the sensitive scar of some old wound. Then he
pushed the child aside, picked up the bag and started toward
the screen door of the lodge. As he reached it, Tarwater came
quickly around the side of the building with the distinct look
to Rayber of being pursued. His feeling for the boy alternated
drastically between compassion for his haunted look and fury
at the way he was treated by him. Tarwater acted as if to see
him at all required a special effort. Rayber opened the screen
door and stepped inside, leaving the two boys to come in or
not as they pleased.

The interior was dark. To the left he made out a reception
desk with a heavy plain-looking woman behind it, leaning on
her elbows. He set the bags down and gave her his name. He
had the feeling that though her eyes were on him, they were
looking behind him. He glanced around. Bishop was a few
feet away, gaping at her.

"What's your name, Sugarpie?" she asked.

"His name is Bishop," Rayber said shortly. He was always
irked when the child was stared at.

The woman tilted her head sympathetically. "I reckon

you're taking him off to give his mother a little rest," she said, her eyes full of curiosity and compassion.

"I have him all the time," he said and added before he could stop himself, "his mother abandoned him."

"No!" she breathed. "Well," she said, "it takes all kinds of women. I couldn't leave a child like that."

You can't even take your eyes off him, he thought irritably and began to fill out the card. "Are the boats for rent?" he asked without looking up.

"Free for the guests," she said, "but anybody gets drowned, that's their lookout. How about him? Can he sit still in a boat?"

"Nothing ever happens to him," he murmured, finishing the card and turning it around to her.

She read it, then she glanced up and stared at Tarwater. He was standing a few feet behind Bishop, looking around him suspiciously, his hands in his pockets and his hat pulled down. She began to scowl. "That boy there—is yours too?" she asked, pointing the pen at him as if this were inconceivable.

Rayber realized that she must think he was some one hired for a guide. "Certainly, he's mine too," he said quickly and in a voice the boy could not fail to hear. He made it a point to impress on him that he was wanted, whether he cared to be wanted or not.

Tarwater lifted his head and returned the woman's stare. Then he took a stride forward and thrust his face at her. "What do you mean—is his?" he demanded.

"Is his," she said, drawing back. "You don't look it is all." Then she frowned as if, continuing to study him, she began to see a likeness.

"And I ain't it," he said. He snatched the card from her and read it. Rayber had written, "George F. Rayber, Frank and Bishop Rayber," and their address. The boy put the card down on the desk and picked up the pen, gripping it so hard that his fingers turned red at the tips. He crossed out the name *Frank* and underneath in an old man's meticulous hand he began to write something else.

Rayber looked at the woman helplessly and lifted his shoulders as if to say, "I have more than one problem," and shrug it off, but the gesture ended in a violent tremor. To his horror he felt the side of his mouth give a series of quick jerks. He had an instant's premonition that if he wished to save himself, he should leave at once, that the trip was doomed.

The woman handed him the key and, looking at him suspiciously, said, "Up the steps yonder and four doors down to the right. We don't have anybody to tote the bags."

He took the key and started up a rickety flight of steps to the left. Halfway up, he paused and said in a voice in which there was a remnant of authority, "Bring up that bag when you come, Frank."

The boy was finishing his essay on the card and gave no indication of hearing.

The woman's curious gaze followed Rayber up the stairs until he disappeared. She observed as his feet passed the level of her head that he had on one brown sock and one grey. His shoes were not run-down but he might have slept in his seersucker suit every night. He was in bad need of a haircut and his eyes had a peculiar look—like something human trapped in a switch box. Has come here to have a nervous breakdown, she said to herself. Then she turned her head. Her eyes rested on the two boys, who had not moved. And who wouldn't? she asked herself.

The afflicted child looked as if he must have dressed himself. He had on a black cowboy hat and a pair of short khaki pants that were too tight even for his narrow hips and a yellow t-shirt that had not been washed any time lately. Both his brown hightop shoes were untied. The upper part of him looked like an old man and the lower part like a child. The other, the mean-looking one, had picked up the desk card again and was reading over what he had written on it. He was so taken up with it that he did not see the little boy reaching out to touch him. The instant the child touched him, the country boy's shoulders leapt. He snatched his touched hand up and jammed it in his pocket. "Leave off!" he said in a high voice. "Git away and quit bothering me!"

"Mind how you talk to one of them there, you boy!" the woman hissed.

He looked at her as if it were the first time she had spoken to him. "Them there what?" he murmured.

"That there kind," she said, looking at him fiercely as if he had profaned the holy.

He looked back at the afflicted child and the woman was startled by the expression on his face. He seemed to see the little boy and nothing else, no air around him, no room, no nothing, as if his gaze had slipped and fallen into the center of the child's eyes and was still falling down and down and down. The little boy turned after a second and skipped off toward the steps and the country boy followed, so directly that he might have been attached to him by a tow-line. The child began to scramble up the steps on his hands and knees, kicking his feet up on each one. Then suddenly he flipped himself around and sat down squarely in the country boy's way and stuck his feet out in front of him, apparently wanting his shoes tied. The country boy stopped still. He hung over him like some one bewitched, his long arms bent uncertainly.

The woman watched fascinated. He ain't going to tie them, she said, not him.

He leaned over and began to tie them. Frowning furiously, he tied one and then the other and the child watched, completely absorbed in the operation. When the boy finished tying them, he straightened himself and said in a querulous voice, "Now git on and quit bothering me with them laces," and the child flipped over on his hands and feet and scrambled up the stairs, making a great din.

Confused by this kindness, the woman called, "Hey boy."

She had intended to say, "Whose boy are you?" but she said nothing, her mouth opening on a vanished sentence. His eyes as they turned and looked down at her were the color of the lake just before dark when the last daylight has faded and the moon has not risen yet, and for an instant she thought she saw something fleeing across the surface of them, a lost light that came from nowhere and vanished into nothing. For some moments they stared at each other without issue. Finally, convinced she had not seen it, she muttered, "Whatever devil's work you mean to do, don't do it here."

He continued to look down at her. "You can't just say NO," he said. "You got to do NO. You got to show it. You got to show you mean it by doing it. You got to show you're not going to do one thing by doing another. You got to make an end of it. One way or another."

"Don't you do nothing here," she said, wondering what he would do here.

"I never ast to come here," he said. "I never ast for that lake to be set down in front of me," and he turned and moved on up the stairs.

The woman looked in front of her for some time as if she were seeing her own thoughts before her like unintelligible handwriting on the wall. Then she looked down at the card on the counter and turned it over. "Francis Marion Tarwater," he had written. "Powderhead, Tennessee. NOT HIS SON."

VIII

AFTER THEY had had their lunch, the schoolteacher suggested they get a boat and fish awhile. Tarwater could tell that he was watching him again, his little eyes protected and precise behind his glasses. He had been watching him ever since he came but now he was watching in a different way: he was watching for something that he planned to make happen. The trip was designed to be a trap but the boy had no attention to spare for it. His mind was entirely occupied with saving himself from the larger grander trap that he felt set all about him. Ever since his first night in the city when he had seen once and for all that the schoolteacher was of no significance—nothing but a piece of bait, an insult to his intelligence—his mind had been engaged in a continual struggle with the silence that confronted him, that demanded he baptize the child and begin at once the life the old man had prepared him for.

It was a strange waiting silence. It seemed to lie all around him like an invisible country whose borders he was always on the edge of, always in danger of crossing. From time to time as they had walked in the city, he had looked to the side and seen his own form alongside him in a store window, transparent as a snakeskin. It moved beside him like some violent ghost who had already crossed over and was reproaching him from the other side. If he turned his head the opposite way, there would be the dim-witted boy, hanging onto the schoolteacher's coat, watching him. His mouth hung in a lopsided smile but there was a judging sternness about his forehead. The boy never looked lower than the top of his head except by accident for the silent country appeared to be reflected again in the center of his eyes. It stretched out there, limitless and clear.

Tarwater could have baptized him any one of a hundred times without so much as touching him. Each time the temptation came, he would feel that the silence was about to surround him and he was going to be lost in it forever. He would have fallen but for the wise voice that sustained him—

429

the stranger who had kept him company while he dug his uncle's grave.

Sensations, his friend—no longer a stranger—said. Feelings. What you want is a sign, a real sign, suitable to a prophet. If you are a prophet, it's only right you should be treated like one. When Jonah dallied, he was cast three days in a belly of darkness and vomited up in the place of his mission. That was a sign; it wasn't no sensation.

It takes all my time to set you straight. Look at you, he said—going to that fancy-house of God, sitting there like an ape letting that girl-child bend your ear. What did you expect to see there? What did you expect to hear? The Lord speaks to prophets personally and He's never spoke to you, never lifted a finger, never dropped a gesture. And as for that strangeness in your gut, that comes from you, not the Lord. When you were a child you had worms. As likely as not you have them again.

The first day in the city he had become conscious of the strangeness in his stomach, a peculiar hunger. The city food only weakened him. He and his great-uncle had eaten well. If the old man had done nothing else for him, he had heaped his plate. Never a morning he had not awakened to the smell of fatback frying. The schoolteacher paid scarce attention to what he put inside him. For breakfast, he poured a bowl of shavings out of a cardboard box; in the middle of the day he made sandwiches out of lightbread; and at night he took them to a restaurant, a different one every night run by a different color of foreigner so that he would learn, he said, how other nationalities ate. The boy did not care how other nationalities ate. He had always left the restaurants hungry, conscious of an intrusion in his works. Since the breakfast he had finished sitting in the presence of his uncle's corpse, he had not been satisfied by food, and his hunger had become like an insistent silent force inside him, a silence inside akin to the silence outside, as if the grand trap left him barely an inch to move in, barely an inch in which to keep himself inviolate.

His friend was adamant that he refuse to entertain hunger as a sign. He pointed out that the prophets had been fed. Elijah had lain down under a juniper tree to die and had gone to sleep and an angel of the Lord had come and waked him and fed him a hearth-cake, had done it moreover twice, and Elijah had risen and gone about his business, lasting on the two hearth-cakes forty days and nights. Prophets did not languish in hunger but were fed from the Lord's bounty and the signs given them were unmistakable. His friend suggested he demand an unmistakable sign, not a pang of hunger or a reflection of himself in a store window, but an unmistakable sign, clear and suitable—water bursting forth from a rock, for instance, fire sweeping down at his command and destroying some site he would point to, such as the tabernacle he had gone to spit on.

His fourth night in the city, after he had returned from listening to the child preach, he had sat up in the welfare-woman's bed and raising his folded hat as if he were threatening the silence, he had demanded an unmistakable sign of the Lord.

Now we'll see what class of prophet you are, his friend said. We'll see what the Lord has in mind for you.

The next day the schoolteacher had taken them into a park where trees were fenced together in a kind of island that cars were not allowed in. They had only but entered it when he felt a hush in his blood and a stillness in the atmosphere as if the air were being purged for the approach of revelation. He would have turned and run but the schoolteacher parked himself on a bench and pretended to go to sleep with the dimwit in his lap. The trees rustled thickly and the clearing rose to his mind's eye. He imagined the blackened spot in the center of it between the two chimneys, and saw rising from the ashes the burnt-out frames of his own and his uncle's bed. He opened his mouth to get air and the schoolteacher woke up and began asking questions.

He prided himself that from the first night he had answered his questions with the cunning of a Negro, giving no information, knowing nothing, and each time he was questioned, raising his uncle's fury until it was observable under his skin in patches of pink and white. A few of his ready answers and the schoolteacher was willing to move on.

They had walked deeper into the park and he began to feel again the approach of mystery. He would have turned and run in the opposite direction but it was all on him in an instant. The path widened and they were faced with an open space in the middle of the park, a concrete circle with a fountain in the center of it. Water rushed out of the mouth of a stone lion's head into a shallow pool below and as soon as the dim-witted boy saw the water, he gave a whoop and galloped off toward it, flapping his arms like something released from a cage.

Tarwater saw exactly where he was heading, knew exactly what he was going to do.

"Too late, goddamit," the schoolteacher muttered, "he's in."

The child stood grinning in the pool, lifting his feet slowly up and down as if he liked the feel of the wet seeping into his shoes. The sun, which had been tacking from cloud to cloud, emerged above the fountain. A blinding brightness fell on the lion's tangled marble head and gilded the stream of water rushing from his mouth. Then the light, falling more gently, rested like a hand on the child's white head. His face might have been a mirror where the sun had stopped to watch its reflection.

Tarwater started forward. He felt a distinct tension in the quiet. The old man might have been lurking near, holding his breath, waiting for the baptism. His friend was silent as if in the felt presence, he dared not raise his voice. At each step the boy exerted a force backward but he continued nevertheless to move toward the pool. He reached the rim of it and lifted his foot to swing it over the side. Just as his shoe touched the water, the schoolteacher bounded forward and snatched the dimwit out. The child split the silence with his bellow.

Slowly Tarwater's lifted foot came down on the edge of the pool and he leaned there, looking into the water where a wavering face seemed trying to form itself. Gradually it became distinct and still, gaunt and cross-shaped. He observed, deep in its eyes, a look of starvation. I wasn't going to baptize him, he said, flinging the silent words at the silent face. I'd drown him first.

Drown him then, the face appeared to say.

Tarwater stepped back, shocked. Scowling, he straightened himself and moved away. The sun had gone in and there were black caves in the tree branches. Bishop was lying on his back, roaring from a red distorted face, and the schoolteacher stood above him, staring at nothing in particular as if it were he who had received a revelation.

Well, that's your sign, his friend said—the sun coming out from under a cloud and falling on the head of a dimwit. Something that could happen fifty times a day without no one being the wiser. And it took that schoolteacher to save you and just in time. Left to yourself you would already have done it and been lost forever. Listen, he said, you have to quit confusing a madness with a mission. You can't spend your life fooling yourself this way. You have to take hold and put temptation behind you. If you baptize once, you'll be doing it the rest of your life. If it's an idiot this time, the next time it's liable to be a nigger. Save yourself while the hour of salvation is at hand.

But the boy was shaken. He scarcely heard the voice as he walked off deeper into the park and down a path he scarcely saw. When he finally took note of his surroundings, he was sitting on a bench, looking down at his feet where two pigeons were moving in drunken circles. On the other side of the bench was a man of a generally grey appearance who had been examining a hole in his shoe when Tarwater sat down but who stopped then and devoted himself to a close scrutiny of the boy. Finally he reached over and plucked Tarwater's sleeve. The boy looked up into two pale yellow-rimmed eyes.

"Be like me, young fellow," the stranger said, "don't let no jackasses tell you what to do." He was grinning wisely and his eyes held a malevolent promise of unwanted friendship. His voice sounded familiar but his appearance was as unpleasant as a stain.

The boy got up and left hastily. An interesting coincident, his friend observed, that he should say the same thing as I've been saying. You think there's a trap laid all about you by the Lord. There ain't any trap. There ain't anything except what you've laid for yourself. The Lord is not studying about you, don't know you exist, and wouldn't do a thing about it if He did. You're alone in the world, with only yourself to ask or thank or judge; with only yourself. And me. I'll never desert you.

The first sight that met his eyes when he got out of the car at the Cherokee Lodge was the little lake. It lay there, glass-like, still, reflecting a crown of trees and an infinite overarching sky. It looked so unused that it might only the moment before have been set down by four strapping angels for him to baptize the child in. A weakness working itself up from his knees, reached his stomach and came upward and forced a tremor in his jaw. Steady, his friend said, everywhere you go you'll find water. It wasn't invented yesterday. But remember: water is made for more than one thing. Hasn't the time come? Don't you have to do something at last, one thing to prove you ain't going to do another? Hasn't your hour of dallying passed?

They ate their lunch in the dark other-end of the lobby where the woman who ran the place served meals. Tarwater ate voraciously. With an expression of intense concentration, he ate six buns filled with barbecue and drank three cans of beer. He might have been preparing himself for a long journey or for some action that would take all his strength. Rayber observed his sudden appetite for the poor food and decided that he was eating compulsively. He wondered if the beer might loosen his tongue, but in the boat he was as glum as ever. He sat hunched over, his hat pulled down, and scowled at the spot where his line disappeared in the water.

They had managed to get the boat away from the dock before Bishop came out of the lodge. The woman had drawn him to an icecooler and produced a green popsickle which she held up for him while she gazed fascinated into his mysterious face. They were in the middle of the lake before he came clattering down the dock, the woman running behind. She snatched him just in time to keep him from plunging over the edge.

Rayber made a frantic grabbing motion in the boat and cried out. Then he reddened and scowled. "Don't look," he said, "she'll take care of him. We need a break."

The boy gazed darkly where the accident had been prevented. The child was a black spot in the glare of his vision. The woman turned him around and started leading him back to the lodge. "It wouldn't have been no great loss if he had drowned," he observed.

Rayber had an instant's picture of himself, standing in the ocean, holding the child's limp body in his arms. With a kind of convulsive motion, he cleared his head of the image. Then he saw that Tarwater had observed his discomposure; he was looking at him with a distinct attention, a peculiar prescient look as if he were about to penetrate some secret.

"Nothing ever happens to that kind of child," Rayber said. "In a hundred years people may have learned enough to put them to sleep when they're born."

Something appeared to be working on the boy's face, struggling there, some war between agreement and outrage.

Rayber's blood burned beneath his skin. He tried to restrain the urge to confess. He leaned forward; his mouth opened and closed and then in a dry voice he said, "Once I tried to drown him," and grinned horribly at the boy.

Tarwater's lips parted as if only they had heard, but he said nothing.

"It was a failure of nerve," Rayber said. The glare on the water gave him the sensation of glancing at white fire each time he looked up or out where it was reflected on the water. He turned down the brim of his hat all the way around.

"You didn't have the guts," Tarwater said as if he would put it in a more accurate way. "He always told me you couldn't do nothing, couldn't act."

The schoolteacher leaned forward and said between his teeth, "I've resisted him. I've done that. What have you done? Maybe you attended to him the quickest way but it takes more than that to go against his will for good. Are you quite sure," he said, "are you quite sure you've overcome him? I doubt it. I think you're chained to him right now. I think you're not going to be free of him without my help. I think you've got problems that you're not capable of solving yourself."

The boy scowled and was silent.

The glare pierced Rayber's eyeballs fiercely. He did not think he could stand an afternoon of this. He felt recklessly compelled to pursue the subject. "How do you like being in the country again?" he growled. "Remind you of Powderhead?"

"I come to fish," the boy said disagreeably.

Goddam you, his uncle thought, all I'm trying to do is save you from being a freak. He was holding his line unbaited in the blinding water. He felt a madness on him to talk about the old man. "I remember the first time I ever saw him," he said. "I was six or seven. I was out in the yard playing and all of a sudden I felt something between me and the sun. Him. I looked up and there he was, those mad fish-coloured eyes looking down at me. Do you know what he said to me—a seven year old child?" He tried to make his voice sound like the old man's. " 'Listen boy,' he said, 'the Lord Jesus Christ sent me to find you. You have to be born again.' " He laughed, glaring at the boy with his furious blistered-looking eyes. "The Lord Jesus Christ had my welfare so at heart that he sent a personal representative. Where was the calamity? The calamity was I believed him. For five or six years. I had nothing else but that. I waited on the Lord Jesus. I thought I'd been born again and that everything was going to be different or was different already because the Lord Jesus had a great interest in me."

Tarwater shifted on the seat. He seemed to listen as if behind a wall.

"It was the eyes that got me," Rayber said. "Children may be attracted to mad eyes. A grown person could have resisted. A child couldn't. Children are cursed with believing."

The boy recognized the sentence. "Some ain't," he said.

The schoolteacher smiled thinly. "And some who think they aren't are," he said, feeling that he was back in control. "It's not as easy as you think to throw it off. Do you know," he said, "that there's a part of your mind that works all the time, that you're not aware of yourself. Things go on in it. All sorts of things you don't know about."

Tarwater looked around him as if he were vainly searching for a way to get out of the boat and walk off.

"I think you're basically very bright," his uncle said. "I think you can understand the things that are said to you."

"I never came for no school lesson," the boy said rudely. "I come to fish. I ain't worried what my underhead is doing. I know what I think when I do it and when I get ready to do it, I don't talk no words. I do it." There was a dull anger in his voice. He was becoming aware of how much he had eaten. The food appeared to be sinking like a leaden column inside him and to be pushed back at the same time by the hunger it had intruded upon.

The schoolteacher watched him a moment and then said, "Well anyway, as far as the baptizing went, the old man could have spared himself. I was already baptized. My mother never overcame her upbringing and she had had it done. But the damage to me of having it done at the age of seven was tremendous. It made a lasting scar."

The boy looked up suddenly as if there had been a tug at his line. "Him back there," he said and jerked his head toward the lodge, "he ain't been baptized?"

"No," Rayber said. He looked at him narrowly. He thought that if he could get the right words in now, he might do some good, might give him a painless lesson. "I may not have the guts to drown him," he said, "but I have the guts to maintain my self-respect and not to perform futile rites over him. I have the guts not to become the prey of superstitions. He is what he is and there's nothing for him to be born into. My guts," he finished, "are in my head."

The boy only stared at him, his eyes filmed with a dull cast of nausea.

"The great dignity of man," his uncle said, "is his ability to say: I am born once and no more. What I can see and do for myself and my fellowman in this life is all of my portion and I'm content with it. It's enough to be a man." There was a light ring in his voice. He watched the boy closely to see if he had struck a chord.

Tarwater turned an expressionless face toward the rim of trees that made a paling around the lake. He appeared to stare into emptiness.

Rayber subsided again but he could stand it only a few minutes. He finished the cigaret and lit another. Then he decided to start off on a new tack and leave the morbid alone for a while. "I'll tell you what I've planned for us to do in a couple of weeks," he said in an almost affable tone. "We're going up for a plane ride. How about that?" He had been considering this, holding it in reserve, thinking it would be the greatest marvel he could produce, something that would surely stir the glum child out of himself.

There was no response. The boy's eyes looked glazed.

"Flying is the greatest engineering achievement of man," Rayber said in an irked voice. "Doesn't it stir your imagination even slightly? If it doesn't I'm afraid there's something wrong with you."

"I done flew," Tarwater said and suppressed a belch. He was entirely occupied with his nausea which he could feel minutely rising.

"How could you have flown?" his uncle asked angrily.

"Him and me give a dollar to go up in one at a fair once," he said. "The houses weren't nothing but matchboxes and the people were invisible—like germs. I wouldn't give you nothing for no airplane. A buzzard can fly."

The schoolteacher gripped both sides of the boat and pushed forward. "He's warped your whole life," he said hoarsely. "You're going to grow up to be a freak if you don't let yourself be helped. You still believe all that crap he taught you. You're eaten up with false guilt. I can read you like a book!" The words were out before he could stop them.

The boy did not even look at him. He leaned over the side of the boat and shuddered. The column, released, formed a sweetly sour circle on the water. A wave of dizziness came over him and then his head cleared. A ravenous emptiness raged in his stomach as if it had reestablished its rightful tenure. He washed his mouth out with a handful of the lake and then wiped his face on his sleeve.

Rayber trembled at his recklessness. He felt certain he had produced this by the word *guilt*. He put his hand on the boy's knee and said, "You'll feel better now."

Tarwater said nothing, glaring with his red-lidded wet eyes at the water as if he were glad he had polluted it.

"It's just as much relief," his uncle said, pressing his advantage, "to get something off your mind as off your stomach. When you tell somebody else your troubles, then they don't bother you so much, they don't get in your blood and make you sick. Somebody else shares the weight. God boy," he said, "you need help. You need to be saved right here now from the old man and everything he stands for. And I'm the one who can save you." With his hat turned down all around he looked like a fanatical country preacher. His eyes glistened.

"I know what your problem is," he said. "I know and I can help you. Something's eating you on the inside and I can tell you what it is."

The boy looked at him fiercely. "Why don't you shut your big mouth?" he said. "Why don't you pull that plug out of your ear and turn yourself off? I come to fish. I never came to have no traffic with you."

His uncle snapped the cigaret out of his fingers and it hit the water with a hiss. "Every day," he said coldly, "you remind me more of the old man. You're just like him. You have his future before you."

The boy put down his line. With rigid deliberate movements he lifted his right foot and pulled off his shoe, then his left foot and pulled off that shoe. Then he jerked the straps of his overalls off his shoulders and pulled them down, over his bottom and off. He had on a pair of long thin old man's drawers. He pulled his hat tight down on his head so that it would not possibly come off, then he threw himself out of the boat and swam away, smashing the glassy lake with his cupped fists as if he would like to make it sting and bleed.

My God! Rayber thought, I touched a nerve that time! He kept his eye on the hat in the receding spasm of water. The empty overalls lay at his feet. He grabbed them and felt in the pockets. He took out two stones, a nickel, a box of wooden matches and three nails. He had brought along the new suit and shirt and laid them out on a chair.

Tarwater reached the dock and climbed onto it, the drawers clinging to him, the hat still ground down on his forehead. He turned just in time to see his uncle thrust the bundled overalls below the surface of the water.

Rayber felt as if he had just run across a mined field. At once he was afraid he had made a mistake. The thin rigid figure on the dock did not move. It seemed no more than a wraith-like column of fragile white-hot rage, materialized for an instant, the makings of some pure unfathomable passion. The boy turned and started rapidly toward the lodge and Rayber decided it would be best to linger on the lake a while.

When he came in, he was startled to see Tarwater lying on the far cot in his new clothes and to see Bishop sitting on the other end of it, watching him as if he were mesmerized by the steel-like glint that came from the boy's eyes and was directed into his own. In the plaid shirt and new blue trousers, he looked like a changeling, half his old self and half his new, already half the boy he would be when he was rehabilitated.

Rayber's spirits rose cautiously. He was holding the shoes with the contents of the overall pockets in them. He set them down on the bed and said, "No hard feelings about the clothes, old man. That was just my round."

There was a strange suppressed excitement about the boy's whole figure, as if he had settled on an inevitable course of action. He did not get up, did not acknowledge the shoes, but he acknowledged his uncle's presence by shifting the glint in his eyes slightly, on him and then away. The schoolteacher might have been just enough present to be ignored. Then he looked back at Bishop, triumphantly, boldly, into the very center of his eyes.

Rayber stood puzzled in the doorway. "Who wants to go for a ride?" he asked.

Bishop jumped off the bed and was at his side in an instant. Tarwater started at the little boy's abrupt disappearance from his field of vision, but he did not get up or turn his face toward the schoolteacher in the door.

"Well, we'll leave Frank to his meditations," Rayber said and swung the child around by the shoulder and left with him, hastily. He wanted to escape before the boy changed his mind.

IX

THE HEAT was not as intense on the road as it had been on the lake and he drove with a sense of refreshment he had not felt in the five days Tarwater had been with him. Once out of sight of the boy, he felt a pressure had been lifted from the atmosphere. He eliminated the oppressive presence from his thoughts and retained only those aspects of it that could be abstracted, clean, into the future person he envisioned.

The sky was a cloudless even blue and he drove without destination, though he meant before they returned to the lodge to stop and have the car filled for tomorrow's trip to Powderhead. Bishop was hanging out the window, his mouth open, letting the air dry his tongue. Automatically, Rayber reached over and locked the door and pulled him back in by his shirt. The child sat, solemnly taking his hat off his head and putting it on his feet, then taking it off his feet and putting it on his head. After he had done this a while, he climbed over the seat and disappeared into the back of the car.

Rayber continued to think of Tarwater's future, his thoughts rewarding except when every now and then the boy's actual face would lodge in the path of a plan. The sudden intrusion of the face made him think of his wife. He seldom thought of her anymore. She would not divorce him for fear she would be given custody of the child and she was now as far away as she could get, in Japan, in some welfare capacity. He was aware of his good fortune in getting rid of her. It was she who had prevented his going back and getting Tarwater away from the old man. She would have been glad enough to have had him if she had not seen him that day when they went to Powderhead to face the old man down. The baby had crawled into the door behind old Tarwater and had sat there, unblinking, as the old man raised his gun and shot Rayber in the leg and then in the ear. She had seen him; Rayber had not; but she would not forget the face. It was not simply that the child was dirty, thin, and grey; it was that its expression had no more changed when the gun went off than the old man's had. This had affected her deeply.

If there had not been something repellent in its face, she said, her maternal instinct would have made her rush forward and snatch it. She had even had that in mind before they arrived and she would have had the courage to do it in spite of the old man's gun; but the child's look had frozen her. It was the opposite of everything appealing. She could not express her exact revulsion, for her feeling was not logical. It had, she said, the look of an adult, not of a child, and of an adult with immovable insane convictions. Its face was like the face she had seen in some medieval paintings where the martyr's limbs are being sawed off and his expression says he is being deprived of nothing essential. She had had the sense, seeing the child in the door, that if it had known that at that moment all its future advantages were being stolen from it, its expression would not have altered a jot. The face for her had expressed the depth of human perversity, the deadly sin of rejecting defiantly one's own obvious good. He had thought all this was possibly her imagination but he understood now that it was not imagination but fact. She said she could not have lived with such a face; she would have been bound to destroy the arrogant look on it.

He reflected wryly that she had not been able to live with Bishop's face any better though there was no arrogance on it. The little boy had climbed up from the floor of the back seat and was hanging over breathing into his ear. By temperament and training she was ready to handle an exceptional child, but not one as exceptional as Bishop, not one bearing her own family name and the face of "that horrible old man." She had returned once in the last two years and demanded that he put Bishop in an institution because she said he could not adequately care for him—though it was plain from the look of him that he thrived like an air plant. His own behaviour on that occasion was still a source of satisfaction to him. He had knocked her not quite halfway across the room.

He had known by that time that his own stability depended on the little boy's presence. He could control his terrifying love as long as it had its focus in Bishop, but if anything happened to the child, he would have to face it in itself. Then the whole world would become his idiot child. He had thought what he would have to do if anything happened to

Bishop. He would have with one supreme effort to resist the recognition; with every nerve and muscle and thought, he would have to resist feeling anything at all, thinking anything at all. He would have to anesthetize his life. He shook his head to clear it of these unpleasant thoughts. After it had cleared, they returned one by one. He felt a sinister pull on his consciousness, the familiar undertow of expectation, as if he were still a child waiting on Christ.

The car apparently of its own volition had turned onto a dirt road which without warning pierced his abstraction with its familiarity. He put on his brakes.

It was a narrow corrugated road sunk between deep red embankments. He looked about him angrily. He had not had the least intention of coming here today. His car was on the crest of a hill and the embankments on either side had the look of forming an entrance to a region he would enter at his peril. The road sloped down a quarter of a mile or so within his sight and then turned to disappear behind an edge of the wood. When he had been on this road the first time, he had ridden it backwards. A Negro with a mule and wagon had met him and his uncle at the junction and they had ridden, their feet dangling from the back of the wagon. He had leaned over most of the way, watching the mule's hoofprints in the dust as they rolled over them.

He decided finally that there would be wisdom in looking at the place today so that there would be no surprises for him when he returned tomorrow with the boy, but for some few moments, he did not move on. The road that lay in front of him he remembered as being four or five miles long. Then there was a stretch through the woods that would have to be walked and then the field to be crossed. He thought with distaste of crossing it twice, today and again tomorrow. He thought with distaste of crossing it at all. Then as if to stop his thinking, he put his foot down hard on the accelerator and took the road defiantly. Bishop jumped up and down, squealing and making unintelligible noises of delight.

The road grew narrower as it approached its end and presently he found himself going over what was no more than a rutted wagon path, his speed reduced to nothing. He stopped the car finally in a little clearing grown up in Johnson grass and blackberry bushes where what was left of the road touched the edge of the wood. Bishop jumped out and made for the blackberry bushes, attracted by the wasps that buzzed over them. Rayber leapt out and grabbed him just before he reached for one. Gingerly he picked the child a blackberry and handed it to him. The little boy studied it and then, with his fallen smile, returned it to him as if they were performing a ceremony. Rayber flung it away and turned to find the trail through the woods.

He took the child by the hand and pulled him along on what he thought might shortly become a path. The forest rose about him, mysterious and alien. Descending to speak with the shade of my uncle, he thought irritably and wondered if the old man's charred bones would be lying in the ashes. At the thought he almost stopped but did not. Bishop could barely walk for gaping. He lifted his face to stare open-mouthed above him as if he were in some vast overwhelming edifice. His hat fell off and Rayber picked it up and clamped it on his head again and pulled him on. Somewhere below them out of the silence a bird sounded four crystal notes. The child stopped, his breath held.

Rayber knew suddenly that alone with Bishop he could not go to the bottom and cross the field. Tomorrow with the other boy, with his brain engaged, he would be able to make it. He remembered that somewhere along here there was a point where one could look out between two trees and see the clearing below. When he had first walked through the wood with his uncle, they had stopped at that place and his uncle had pointed down to where, far across the field, a sagging unpainted house stood in a bare hard-packed yard. "Yonder it is," he had said, "and someday it'll be yours—these woods and that field and that fine house." He remembered that his heart had expanded unbelievably.

Suddenly he realized that the place *was* his. In the stress of having the boy return to him, he had never considered the property. He stopped, astounded by the fact that he owned all of this. His trees stood rising above him, majestic and aloof, as if they belonged to an order that had never budged from its first allegiance in the days of creation. His heart began to beat frenetically. Quickly he reduced the whole wood in probable board feet into a college education for the boy. His spirits lifted. He pulled the child along, intending to find the opening where the house could be seen. A few yards below, a sudden patch of sky indicated the spot. He let Bishop go and strode toward it.

The forked tree was familiar to him or seemed so. He put his hand on one trunk, leaned forward and looked out. His gaze moved quickly and unseeing across the field and stopped abruptly where the house had been. Two chimneys stood there, separated by a black space of rubble.

He stood expressionless, his heart strangely wrenched. If the bones were lying in the ashes he could not see them from this distance, but a vision of the old man, farther away in time, rose before him. He saw him standing on the edge of the yard, one hand lifted in an astounded greeting, while he stood a little way off in the field, his fists clenched, trying to shout, trying to make his adolescent fury come out in clear sensible words. He had only stood there shrilling, "You're crazy, you're crazy, you're a liar, you have a head full of crap, you belong in a nut house!" and then had turned and run, carrying away nothing but the registered change in the old man's expression, the sudden drop into some mysterious misery, which afterwards he had never been able to get out of his mind. He saw it as he stared at the two denuded chimneys.

He felt a pressure on his hand and glanced down, continuing to see the same expression and barely noting that it was Bishop he was looking at now. The child wanted to be lifted up to see. Absently he picked him up and held him in the fork of the tree and let him look out. The dull face, the empty grey eyes seemed to Rayber to reflect the ravaged scene across the field. The little boy turned his head after a moment and gazed instead at him. A dreaded sense of loss came over him. He knew that he could not remain here an instant longer. He turned with the child and went quickly back through the woods the way he had come.

On the highway again, he drove gripping the wheel, his face tense, his mind turned on the problem of Tarwater as if his own and not only the boy's salvation depended on his solving it. He had ruined his plan by going to Powderhead too soon. He knew he could not go there again, that he would have to find another way. He went over the afternoon's experience in the boat. There, he thought, he had been on the right track. He had simply not gone far enough. He decided that he would put the whole thing verbally before the boy. He would not argue with him but only tell him, tell him in so many plain words that he had a compulsion and what it was. Whether he answered, whether he cooperated, he would have to listen. He could not escape knowing that there was someone who knew exactly what went on inside him and who understood it for the good reason that it was understandable. He would go the whole way this time and tell him everything. The boy should at least know that he had no secrets. Casually while they ate their supper, he would lift the compulsion from his mind, expose it to the light, and let him have a good look at it. What he did about it would be his own affair. All at once this seemed to him extremely simple, the way he should have proceeded in the first place. Only time simplifies, he thought.

He stopped for gas at a pink stucco filling station where pottery and whirligigs were sold. While the car was being filled, he got out and looked for something to take as a peace offering, for he wanted the encounter to be pleasant if possible. His eye roved over a shelf of false hands, imitation buck teeth, boxes of simulated dog dung to put on the rug, wooden plaques with cynical mottos burnt on them. Finally he saw a combination corkscrew-bottleopener that fit in the palm of the hand. He bought it and left.

When they returned to the room, the boy was still lying on the cot, his face set in a deadly calm as if his eyes had not moved since they left. Again Rayber had a vision of the face his wife must have seen and he experienced a moment's revulsion for the boy that made him tremble. Bishop climbed onto the bottom of the cot and Tarwater returned the child's gaze steadily. He seemed unaware that Rayber was in the room.

"I could eat a horse," the schoolteacher said. "Let's go down."

The boy turned his head and regarded him evenly, with no interest but with no hostility. "It's what you'll get," he said, "if you eat here."

Rayber, unamused, pulled out the corkscrew-bottleopener and dropped it negligently on his chest. "That might come in handy sometime," he said and turned and began to wash his hands at the basin.

In the mirror, he saw him pick it up gingerly and look at it. He pushed the corkscrew out of the circle and then meditatively pushed it back. He studied it back and front and held it in the palm of his hand where it fit like a halfdollar. Presently he said in a grudging voice, "I don't have no use for it but I thank you," and put it in his pocket.

He returned his attention to Bishop as if this were its natural place. He lifted himself on one elbow and fixed the child with a narrow look. "Git up, you," he said slowly. He might have been commanding a small animal he was successfully training. His voice was steady but experimental. The hostility in it seemed contained and directed toward some planned goal. The little boy was watching with complete fascination.

"Git up now, like I tol' you to," Tarwater repeated slowly.

The child obediently climbed down off the bed.

Rayber felt a twinge of ridiculous jealousy. He stood by, his brows working irritably as the boy moved out of the door without a word and Bishop followed him. After a moment he slung his towel into the basin and walked after them.

The lodge was shaking with the stamping of four couples dancing at the other end of the lobby where the woman who ran the place had a nickelodeon. The three of them sat down at the red tin table and Rayber turned off his hearing aid until the racket should stop. He sat glaring around him, disgruntled at this intrusion.

The dancers were about Tarwater's age but they might have belonged to a different species entirely. The girls could be distinguished from the boys only by their tight skirts and bare legs; their faces and heads were alike. They danced with a furious stern concentration. Bishop was entranced. He stood up in his chair, watching them, his head hanging forward as if any moment it might drop off. Tarwater, his eyes dark and distant, stared through them. They might have been insects buzzing across the surface of his vision.

When the music whined to a stop, they clambered back to

their table and sprawled in their chairs. Rayber turned his hearing aid on and winced as Bishop's bellow blared into his head. The child was jumping up and down in his chair, roaring his disappointment. As soon as the dancers saw him, he stopped making the noise and stood still, devouring them with his gape. An angry silence fell over them. Their look was shocked and affronted as if they had been betrayed by a fault in creation, something that should have been corrected before they were allowed to see it. With pleasure Rayber could have dashed across the room and swung his lifted chair in their faces. They got up and pushed each other out sullenly, packed themselves in a topless automobile and roared off, sending an indignant spray of gravel against the side of the lodge. Rayber let out his breath as if it were sharp and might cut him. Then his eyes fell on Tarwater.

The boy was looking directly at him with an omniscient smile, faint but decided. It was a smile that Rayber had seen on his face before. It seemed to mock him from an ever-deepening inner knowledge that grew in indifference as it came nearer and nearer to a secret truth about him. Without warning its meaning pierced Rayber and he felt such a fury that for the moment all his strength left him. Go, he wanted to shout. Get your damn impudent face out of my sight! Go to hell! Go baptize the whole world!

The woman had been standing for some time at his side, waiting to take their order but she could have been invisible for all the notice he paid her. She began tapping the menu on a glass, then she slid it in front of his face. Without reading it, he said, "Three hamburger plates," and thrust it aside.

When she was gone, he said in a dry voice, "I want to lay some cards on the table." He sought the boy's eyes and steadied himself by the hated glint in them.

Tarwater looked at the table as if waiting for the cards to be laid on it.

"That means I want to talk straight to you," Rayber said, rigidly keeping the exasperation out of his voice. He strove to make his gaze, his tone, as indifferent as his listener's. "I have some things to say to you that you'll have to listen to. What you do about what I have to say is your own business. I have no further interest in telling you what to do. I only intend to put the facts before you." His voice was thin and brittle-sounding. He might have been reading from a paper. "I notice that you've begun to be able to look Bishop in the eye. That's good. It means you're making progress but you needn't think that because you can look him in the eye now, you've saved yourself from what's preying on you. You haven't. The old man still has you in his grip. Don't think he hasn't."

The boy continued to give him the same omniscient look. "It's you the seed fell in," he said. "It ain't a thing you can do about it. It fell on bad ground but it fell in deep. With me," he said proudly, "it fell on rock and the wind carried it away."

The schoolteacher grasped the table as if he were going to push it forward into the boy's chest. "Goddam you!" he said in a breathless harsh voice. "It fell in us both alike. The difference is that I know it's in me and I keep it under control. I weed it out but you're too blind to know it's in you. You don't even know what makes you do the things you do."

The boy looked at him angrily but he said nothing.

At least, Rayber thought, I've shocked that look off his face. He did not say anything for a few moments while he thought how to continue.

The woman returned with the three plates. She set them down slowly, giving herself time for observation. The man's face had a sweaty harassed look and so did the boy's. He threw her an ugly glance. The man began to eat at once as if he wanted to get it over with. The little boy took his bun apart and began to lick the mustard off it. The other boy looked at his as if it were probably bad meat and did not touch it. She left and watched indignantly for a few seconds from the kitchen door. The boy finally picked his hamburger up. He raised it half-way to his mouth and then put it down again. He picked it up and put it down twice without biting into it. Then he pulled his hat down and sat there, his arms folded. She had had enough and closed the door.

The schoolteacher leaned forward across the table, his eyes pin-pointed and very bright. "You can't eat," he said, "because something is eating you. And I intend to tell you what it is."

"Worms," the boy hissed as if his disgust could not be contained an instant longer.

"It takes guts to listen," Rayber said.

Tarwater leaned toward him with a kind of blaring attention. "You ain't got nothing to say to me that I don't have the guts to listen to," he said.

The schoolteacher sat back. "All right," he said, "then listen." He folded his arms and looked at him for an instant before he began. Then he started coldly. "The old man told you to baptize Bishop. You have that order lodged in your head like a boulder blocking your path."

The blood drained from the boy's face but his eyes did not swerve. They looked at Rayber furiously, the glint in them gone.

The schoolteacher spoke slowly, picking his words as if he were looking for the steadiest stones to step on across a rushing stream. "Until you get rid of this compulsion to baptize Bishop, you'll never make any progress toward being a normal person. I said in the boat you were going to be a freak. I shouldn't have said that. I only meant you had the choice. I want you to see the choice. I want you to make the choice and not simply be driven by a compulsion you don't understand. What we understand, we can control," he said. "You have to understand what it is that blocks you. I wonder if you're smart enough to take this in. It's not simple."

The boy's face seemed dry and old as if he had taken it in long ago, and now it was part of him like the current of death in his blood. The schoolteacher was touched by this muteness before the facts. His anger left him. The room was silent. A pink cast had fallen from the windows over the table. Tarwater looked away from his uncle at Bishop. The little boy's hair was pink and lighter than his face. He was sucking his spoon; his eyes were drowned in silence.

"I want to put two solutions before you," Rayber said. "What you do is up to you."

Tarwater looked at him again, with no mockery, no glint in his eye, but with no anticipation either, as if his course were irrevocably set.

"Baptism is only an empty act," the schoolteacher said. "If there's any way to be born again, it's a way that you accomplish yourself, an understanding about yourself that you reach after a long time, perhaps a long effort. It's nothing you get from above by spilling a little water and a few words. What you want to do is meaningless, so the easiest solution would be simply to do it. Right here now, with this glass of water. I would permit it in order to get it out of your mind. As far as I'm concerned, you may baptize him at once." He pushed his own glass of water across the table. His look was patient and ironical.

The boy's glance touched the top of the glass and then bounded off. His hand lying by the side of his plate twitched. He jammed it into his pocket and looked the other way, out the window. His whole aspect seemed shaken as if his integrity had been dangerously challenged.

The schoolteacher pulled back the glass of water. "I knew that would be too cheap for you," he said. "I knew you would refuse to do anything so unworthy of the courage you've already shown." He raised the glass and drank the rest of the water. Then he set it down on the table. He looked tired enough to collapse; his aspect was so weary that he might just have attained the top of a mountain he had been climbing for days.

After an interval he said, "The other way is not so simple. It's the way I've chosen for myself. It's the way you take as a result of being born again the natural way—through your own efforts. Your intelligence." His words had a disconnected sound. "The other way is simply to face it and fight it, to cut down the weed every time you see it appear. Do I have to tell you this? An intelligent boy like you?"

"You don't have to tell me nothing," Tarwater murmured.

"I don't have a compulsion to baptize him," Rayber said. "My own is more complicated, but the principle is the same. The way we have to fight it is the same."

"It ain't the same," Tarwater said. He turned toward his uncle. The glint had reappeared. "I can pull it up by the roots, once and for all. I can do something. I ain't like you. All you can do is think what you would have done if you had done it. Not me. I can do it. I can act." He was looking at his uncle now with a completely fresh contempt. "It's nothing about me like you," he said.

"There are certain laws that determine every man's conduct," the schoolteacher said. "You are no exception." He saw with perfect clarity that the only feeling he had for this boy was hate. He loathed the very sight of him.

"Wait and see," Tarwater said as if it needed only a short time to be proved.

"Experience is a terrible teacher," Rayber said.

The boy shrugged and got up. He walked off, across the room to the screen door where he stood looking out. At once Bishop climbed down off his chair and started after him, putting on his hat as he went. Tarwater stiffened when the child approached but he did not move and Rayber watched as the two of them stood there side by side, looking out the door— the two figures, hatted and somehow ancient, bound together by some necessity of nerve that excluded him. He was startled to see the boy put his hand on Bishop's neck just under his hat, open the door and guide him out of it. It occurred to him that what he meant by "doing something" was to make a slave of the child. Bishop would be at his command like a faithful dog. Instead of avoiding him, he planned to control him, to show who was master.

And I will not permit that, he said. If anyone controlled Bishop, it would be himself. He put his money on the table under the salt-shaker and went out after them.

The sky was a bright pink, casting such a weird light that every color was intensified. Each weed that grew out of the gravel looked like a live green nerve. The world might have been shedding its skin. The two were in front of him half way down the dock, walking slowly, Tarwater's hand still resting just under Bishop's hat; but it seemed to Rayber that it was Bishop who was doing the leading, that the child had made the capture. He thought with a grim pleasure that sooner or later the boy's confidence in his own judgment would be brought low.

When they arrived at the end of the dock, they stood looking down into the water. Then to Rayber's chagrin, the boy lifted the child like a sack under the arms and lowered him over the edge of the dock into the boat that was tied there.

"I haven't given you permission to take Bishop out in the boat," Rayber said.

Tarwater may have heard or he may not; he did not answer. He sat down on the edge of the dock and for a few moments looked across the water at the opposite bank. Part of a red globe hung almost motionless in the far side of the lake as if it were the other end of the elongated sun cut through the middle by a swath of forest. Pink and salmon-colored clouds floated in the water at different depths. Suddenly Rayber wanted nothing so much as a half hour to himself, without sight of either of them. "But you may take him," he said, "if you'll be careful."

The boy didn't move. He was leaning forward, his thin shoulders hunched, his hands gripped on the edge of the dock. He seemed poised there waiting to make a momentous move.

He dropped down into the boat with Bishop.

"You'll look after him?" Rayber asked.

Tarwater's face was like a very old mask, colorless and dry. "I'll tend to him," he said.

"Thanks," his uncle said. He experienced a short feeling of warmth for the boy. He strolled back down the dock to the lodge and when he reached the door, he turned and watched the boat move out into view on the lake. He raised his arm and waved but Tarwater showed no sign of seeing him and Bishop's back was turned. The small black-hatted figure sat like a passenger being borne by the surly oarsman across the lake to some mysterious destination.

Back in his room, Rayber lay on the cot trying to feel the release he had felt when he started out in the car in the afternoon. More than anything else, what he experienced in the boy's presence was the feeling of pressure and when it was taken off for a while, he realized how intolerable it was. He lay there thinking with distaste of the moment when the silent mutinous face would appear again in the door. He imagined the rest of the summer spent coping with the boy's cold intractability. He began to consider the possibility of his leaving of his own accord and after a moment he knew that this was actually what he wanted him to do. He no longer felt any challenge to rehabilitate him. All he wanted now was to get rid of him. He thought with horror of being stuck with him for good and began to consider ways that he might hasten his departure. He knew he would never leave as long as Bishop was around. The thought flew through his mind that he might put Bishop in an institution for a few weeks. He was shaken and turned his mind to other things. For a while he dozed and dreamed that he and Bishop were speeding away in the car, escaping safely from a lowering tornado-like cloud. He awoke to find the room growing dim.

He got up and went to the window. The boat with the two of them in it was near the middle of the lake, almost still. They were sitting there facing each other in the isolation of the water, Bishop small and squat, and Tarwater gaunt, lean, bent slightly forward, his whole attention concentrated on the opposite figure. They seemed to be held still in some magnetic field of attraction. The sky was an intense purple as if it were about to explode into darkness.

Rayber left the window and threw himself on the cot again but he was no longer sleepy. He had a peculiar sense of waiting, of marking time. He lay with his eyes closed as if listening to something he could hear only when his hearing aid was off. He had had this sense of waiting, kin in degree but not in kind, when he was a child and expected any moment that the city would blossom into an eternal Powderhead. Now he sensed that he waited for a cataclysm. He waited for all the world to be turned into a burnt spot between two chimneys.

All he would be was an observer. He waited with serenity. Life had never been good enough to him for him to wince at its destruction. He told himself that he was indifferent even to his own dissolution. It seemed to him that this indifference was the most that human dignity could achieve, and for the moment forgetting his lapses, forgetting even his narrow escape of the afternoon, he felt he had achieved it. To feel nothing was peace.

He watched idly as a round red moon rose into the lower corner of his window. It might have been the sun rising on the upsidedown half of the world. He came to a decision. When the boy came back he would say: Bishop and I are returning to town tonight. You may go with us under these conditions: not that you *begin* to cooperate, but that you cooperate, fully and completely, that you change your attitude, that you allow yourself to be tested, that you prepare yourself to enter school in the fall, and that you take that hat off your head right now and throw it out the window into the lake. If you can't meet these requirements, then Bishop and I are leaving by ourselves.

It had taken him five days to reach this state of clarity. He thought of his foolish emotions the night the boy had come, thought of himself sitting by the side of the bed, thinking that at last he had a son with a future. He saw himself again following the boy down back alleys to end finally at a detestable temple, saw the idiot figure of himself standing with his head in the window, listening to the mad child preach. It was unbelievable. Even the plan to take the boy back to Powderhead seemed ridiculous to him now and going to Powderhead this afternoon was the act of an insane person. His indecision, his uncertainty, his eagerness up to now appeared shameful and absurd to him. He felt that he had regained his senses after five days of madness. He could not wait for them to return so that he could deliver his ultimatum.

He closed his eyes and went over the scene in detail, seeing the sullen face at bay, the haughty eyes forced to look down. His power would lie in the fact that he was indifferent now whether the boy stayed or went, or not indifferent for he positively wanted him to leave. He smiled at the thought that his indifference lacked that one perfection. Presently he dozed again, and again he and Bishop were fleeing in the car, the tornado just behind them.

When he awoke again, the moon travelling toward the middle of the window had lost its color. He sat up startled as if it were a face looking in on him, a pale messenger breathlessly arrived.

He got up and went to the window and leaned out. The sky was a hollow black and an empty road of moonlight crossed the lake. He leaned far out, his eyes narrowed, but he could see nothing. The stillness disturbed him. He turned the hearing aid on and at once his head buzzed with the steady drone of crickets and treefrogs. He searched for the boat in the darkness and could see nothing. He waited expectantly. Then an instant before the cataclysm, he grabbed the metal box of the hearing aid as if he were clawing his heart. The quiet was broken by an unmistakable bellow.

He did not move. He remained absolutely still, wooden, expressionless, as the machine picked up the sounds of some fierce sustained struggle in the distance. The bellow stopped and came again, then it began steadily, swelling. The machine made the sounds seem to come from inside him as if something in him were tearing itself free. He clenched his teeth. The muscles in his face contracted and revealed lines of pain beneath harder than bone. He set his jaw. No cry must escape him. The one thing he knew, the one thing he was certain of was that no cry must escape him.

The bellow rose and fell, then it blared out one last time, rising out of its own momentum as if it were escaping finally, after centuries of waiting, into silence. The beady night noises closed in again.

He remained standing woodenly at the window. He knew what had happened. What had happened was as plain to him as if he had been in the water with the boy and the two of them together had taken the child and held him under until he ceased to struggle.

He stared out over the empty still pond to the dark wood that surrounded it. The boy would be moving off through it to meet his appalling destiny. He knew with an instinct as sure as the dull mechanical beat of his heart that he had baptized the child even as he drowned him, that he was headed for everything the old man had prepared him for, that he moved off now through the black forest toward a violent encounter with his fate.

He stood there trying to remember something else before he moved away. It came to him finally as something so distant and vague in his mind that it might already have happened, a long time ago. It was that tomorrow they would drag the pond for Bishop.

He stood waiting for the raging pain, the intolerable hurt that was his due, to begin, so that he could ignore it, but he continued to feel nothing. He stood light-headed at the window and it was not until he realized there would be no pain that he collapsed.

THREE

X

THE HEADLIGHTS revealed the boy at the side of the road, slightly crouched, his head turned expectantly, his eyes for an instant lit red like the eyes of rabbits and deer that streak across the highway at night in the path of speeding cars. His pantslegs were wet up to the knees as if he had been through a swamp. The driver, minute in the glassed cab, brought the looming truck to a halt and left the motor idling while he leaned across the empty seat and opened the door. The boy climbed in.

It was an auto-transit truck, huge and skeletal, carrying four automobiles packed in it like bullets. The driver, a wiry man with a nose sharply twisted down and heavy-lidded eyes, gave the rider a suspicious look and then shifted gears and the truck began to move again, rumbling fiercely. "You got to keep me awake or you don't ride, buddy," he said. "I ain't picking you up to do you a favor." His voice, from some other part of the country, curled at the end of each sentence.

Tarwater opened his mouth as if he expected words to come out of it but none came. He remained, staring at the man, his mouth half-open, his face white.

"I'm not kiddin', kid," the driver said.

The boy kept his elbows gripped into his sides to prevent his frame from shaking. "I only want to go as far as where this road joins 56," he said finally. There were queer ups and downs in his voice as if he were using it for the first time after some momentous failure. He appeared to listen to it himself, to be trying to hear beyond the quaver in it to some solid basis of sound.

"Start talking," the driver said.

The boy wet his lips. After a moment he said in a high voice, entirely out of control, "I never wasted my life talking. I always done something."

"What you done lately?" the man asked. "How come your pantslegs are wet?"

He looked down at his wet pantslegs and kept looking.

They seemed to turn his mind entirely from what he had been going to say, to absorb his attention completely.

"Wake up, buddy," the driver said. "I say how come are your pantslegs wet?"

"Because I never took them off when I done it," he said. "I took off my shoes but I never taken off my pants."

"When you done what?"

"I'm going home," he said. "It's a place I get off at on 56 and then down that road a piece I take a dirt road. It's liable to be morning before I get there."

"How come your pantslegs are wet?" the driver persisted.

"I drowned a boy," Tarwater said.

"Just one?" the driver asked.

"Yes." He reached over and caught hold of the sleeve of the man's shirt. His lips worked a few seconds. They stopped and then started again as if the force of a thought were behind them but no words. He shut his mouth, then tried again but no sound came. Then all at once the sentence rushed out and was gone. "I baptized him."

"Huh?" the man said.

"It was an accident. I didn't mean to," he said breathlessly. Then in a calmer voice he said, "The words just come out of themselves but it don't mean nothing. You can't be born again."

"Make sense," the man said.

"I only meant to drown him," the boy said. "You're only born once. They were just some words that run out of my mouth and spilled in the water." He shook his head violently as if to scatter his thoughts. "There's nothing where I'm going but the stall," he began again, "because the house is burnt up but that's the way I want it. I don't want nothing of his. Now it's all mine."

"Of his whose?" the man muttered.

"Of my great-uncle's," the boy said. "I'm going back there. I ain't going to leave it again. I'm in full charge there. No voice will be uplifted. I shouldn't never have left it except I had to prove I wasn't no prophet and I've proved it." He paused and jerked the man's sleeve. "I proved it by drowning him. Even if I did baptize him that was only an accident. Now all I have to do is mind my own bidnis until I die. I don't have to baptize or prophesy."

The man only looked at him, shortly, and then back at the road.

"It's not going to be any destruction or any fire," the boy said. "There are them that can act and them that can't, and them that are hungry and them that ain't. That's all. I can act. And I ain't hungry." The words crowded out as if they were pushing each other forward. Then he was suddenly silent. He seemed to watch the darkness that the headlights pushed in front of them, always at the same distance. Sudden signs would spring up and vanish at the side of the road.

"That don't make sense but make up some more of it," the driver said. "I gotta stay awake. I ain't riding you just for a good time."

"I don't have no more to say," Tarwater said. His voice was thin, as if many more words would destroy it permanently. It seemed to break off after each sound had found its way out. "I'm hungry," he said.

"You just said you weren't hungry," the driver said.

"I ain't hungry for the bread of life," the boy said. "I'm hungry for something to eat here and now. I threw up my dinner and I didn't eat no supper."

The driver began to feel in his pocket. He pulled out half a bent sandwich wrapped in waxed paper. "You can have this," he said. "It don't have but one bite out of it. I didn't like it."

Tarwater took it and held it wrapped in his hand. He didn't open it.

"Okay, eat it!" the driver said in an exasperated voice. "What's the matter with you?"

"When I come to eat, I ain't hungry," Tarwater said. "It's like being empty is a thing in my stomach and it don't allow nothing else to come down in there. If I ate it, I would throw it up."

"Listen," the driver said, "I don't want you puking in here and if you got something catching, you get out right now."

"I'm not sick," the boy said. "I never been sick in my life except sometimes when I over ate myself. When I baptized him it wasn't nothing but words. Back home," he said, "I'll be in charge. I'll have to sleep in the stall until I get to where I can build me back a house. If I hadn't been a big fool I'd have taken him out and burned him up outside. I wouldn't have burned up the house along with him."

"Live and learn," the driver said.

"My other uncle knows everything," the boy said, "but that don't keep him from being a fool. He can't do nothing. All he can do is figure it out. He's got this wired head. There's an electric cord runs into his ear. He can read your mind. He knows you can't be born again. I know everything he knows, only I can do something about it. I did," he added.

"Can't you talk about something else?" the driver asked. "How many sisters you got at home?"

"I was born in a wreck," the boy said.

He took off his hat and rubbed his head. His hair was flat and thin, dark across his white forehead. He held the hat in his lap like a bowl and looked into it. He took out a box of wooden matches and a white card. "I put all this here in my hat when I drowned him," he said. "I was afraid my pockets would get wet." He held up the card close to his eyes and read it aloud. "T. Fawcett Meeks. Southern Copper Parts. Mobile, Birmingham, Atlanta." He stuck the card in the inside band of his hat and put the hat back on his head. He put the box of matches in his pocket.

The driver's head was beginning to roll. He shook it and said, "Talk, dammit."

The boy reached into his pocket and pulled out the combination corkscrew-bottleopener the schoolteacher had given him. "My uncle give me this," he said. "He ain't so bad. He knows a heap. I speck I'll be able to use this thing some time or other," and he looked at it lying compact in the center of his hand. "I speck it'll come in handy," he said, "to open something."

"Tell me a joke," the driver said.

The boy didn't look as if he knew any joke. He didn't look as if he knew what a joke was. "Do you know what the greatest invention of man is?" he asked finally.

"Naw," the driver said, "what?"

He didn't answer. He was staring ahead again into the darkness and seemed to have forgotten the question.

"What's the greatest invention of man?" the truck driver asked irritably.

The boy turned and looked at him without comprehension. There was a choking sound in his throat and then he said, "What?"

The driver glared at him. "What's the matter with you?"

"Nothing," the boy said. "I feel hungry but I ain't."

"You belong in the booby hatch," the driver muttered. "You ride through these states and you see they all belong in it. I won't see nobody sane again until I get back to Detroit."

For a few miles they rode in silence. The truck moved slower and slower. The driver's lids would fall as if they were weighted with lead and he would shake his head to open them. Almost at once they would close again. The truck began to veer. He shook his head once violently and pulled off the road onto a wide shoulder and leaned back and began to snore without once looking at Tarwater.

The boy sat quietly on his side of the cab. His eyes were open wide without the least look of sleep in them. They seemed not to be able to close but to be open forever on some sight that would never leave them. Presently they closed but his body did not relax. He sat rigidly upright, a still alert expression on his face as if under the closed lids an inner eye were watching, piercing out the truth in the distortion of his dream.

They were sitting facing each other in a boat suspended on a soft bottomless darkness only a little heavier than the black air around them, but the darkness was no hindrance to his sight. He saw through it as if it were day. He looked through the blackness and saw perfectly the light silent eyes of the child across from him. They had lost their diffuseness and were trained on him, fish-colored and fixed. By his side, standing like a guide in the boat, was his faithful friend, lean, shadow-like, who had counseled him in both country and city.

Make haste, he said. Time is like money and money is like blood and time turns blood to dust.

The boy looked up into his friend's eyes, bent upon him, and was startled to see that in the peculiar darkness, they were violet-colored, very close and intense, and fixed on him with a peculiar look of hunger and attraction. He turned his head away, unsettled by their attention.

No finaler act than this, his friend said. In dealing with the dead you have to act. There's no mere word sufficient to say NO.

Bishop took off his hat and threw it over the side where it floated right-side-up, black on the black surface of the lake. The boy turned his head, following the hat with his eyes, and saw suddenly that the bank loomed behind him, not twenty yards away, silent, like the brow of some leviathan lifted just above the surface of the water. He felt bodiless as if he were nothing but a head full of air, about to tackle all the dead.

Be a man, his friend counseled, be a man. It's only one dimwit you have to drown.

The boy edged the boat toward a dark clump of bushes and tied it. Then he removed his shoes, put the contents of his pockets into his hat and put the hat into one shoe, while all the time the grey eyes were fixed on him as if they were waiting serenely for a struggle already determined. The violet eyes, fixed on him also, waited with a barely concealed impatience.

This is no time to dwaddle, his mentor said. Once it's done, it's done forever.

The water slid out from the bank like a broad black tongue. He climbed out of the boat and stood still, feeling the mud between his toes and the wet clinging around his legs. The sky was dotted with fixed tranquil eyes like the spread tail of some celestial night bird. While he stood there gazing, for the moment lost, the child in the boat stood up, caught him around the neck and climbed onto his back. He clung there like a large crab to a twig and the startled boy felt himself sinking backwards into the water as if the whole bank were pulling him down.

Sitting upright and rigid in the cab of the truck, his muscles began to jerk, his arms flailed, his mouth opened to make way for cries that would not come. His pale face twitched and grimaced. He might have been Jonah clinging wildly to the whale's tongue.

The silence in the truck was corrugated with the snores of the driver, whose head rolled from side to side. The boy's jerking arms almost touched him once or twice as he struggled to extricate himself from a monstrous enclosing darkness.

Occasionally a car would pass, illuminating for an instant his contorted face. He grappled with the air as if he had been flung like a fish on the shores of the dead without lungs to breathe there. The night finally began to fade. A plateau of red appeared in the eastern sky just above the treeline and a dun-colored light began to reveal the fields on either side. Suddenly in a high raw voice the defeated boy cried out the words of baptism, shuddered, and opened his eyes. He heard the sibilant oaths of his friend fading away on the darkness.

He sat trembling in the corner of the cab, exhausted, dizzy, holding his arms tight against his sides. The plateau had widened and was broken by the sun which rose through it majestically with a long red wingspread. With his eyes open, his face began to look less alert. Deliberately, forcefully, he closed the inner eye that had witnessed his dream.

In his hand he was clutching the truck driver's sandwich. His fingers had clenched it through. He loosened them and looked at it as if he had no idea what it was; then he put it in his pocket.

After a second he grabbed the driver's shoulder and shook him violently and the man woke up and grabbed the steering wheel convulsively as if the truck were moving at a high rate of speed. Then he perceived that it was not moving at all. He turned and glared at the boy. "What do you think you're doing in here? Where do you think you're going?" he asked in an enraged voice.

Tarwater's face was pale but determined. "I'm going home," he said. "I'm in charge there now."

"Well get out and go then," the driver said. "I don't ride nuts in the day time."

With dignity the boy opened the door and stepped down out of the cab. He stood, scowling but aloof, by the side of the road and waited until the gigantic monster had grated away and disappeared. The highway stretched in front of him, lean and grey, and he began to walk, putting his feet down hard on the ground. His legs and his will were good enough. He set his face toward the clearing. By sundown he would be there, by sundown he would be where he could begin to live his life as he had elected it, and where, for the rest of his days, he would make good his refusal.

XI

A FTER HE had walked about an hour, he took out the truck driver's pierced sandwich which he had stuck, still wrapped, in his pocket. He undid it and let the paper blow behind. The truck driver had bitten off one of the pointed ends. The boy put the unbitten end in his mouth but after a second he took it out again with faint teeth marks in it and put it back in his pocket. His stomach alone rejected it; his face looked violently hungry and disappointed.

The morning had opened up, clear and cloudless and brilliant. He walked on the embankment and did not look over his shoulder as cars came behind him and swiftly passed, but as each one disappeared on the narrowing strip of highway, he felt the distance between himself and his goal grow longer. The ground under him was strange to his feet, as if he were walking on the back of a giant beast which might any moment stretch a muscle and send him rolling into the ditch below. The sky was like a fence of light to keep it in. The glare forced him to lower his lids but on the other side of it, hidden from his daily sight but present to his inner eye that remained rigidly open, there stretched the clear grey borders of the country he had saved himself from crossing into.

He repeated every few yards, to force himself on faster, that he would soon be home, that there was only the rest of the day between him and the clearing. His throat and eyes burned with dryness and his bones felt brittle as if they belonged to a person older than himself and with much experience; and when he considered it—his experience—it was apparent to him that since his great-uncle's death, he had lived the lifetime of a man. It was as no boy that he returned. He returned tried in the fire of his refusal, with all the old man's fancies burnt out of him, with all the old man's madness smothered for good, so that there was never any chance it would break out in him. He had saved himself forever from the fate he had envisioned when, standing in the schoolteacher's hall and looking into the eyes of the dim-witted child, he had seen himself trudging off into the distance in the bleeding stinking mad shadow of Jesus, lost forever to his own inclinations.

The fact that he had actually baptized the child disturbed him only intermittently and each time he thought of it, he reviewed its accidental nature. It was an accident and nothing more. He considered only that the boy was drowned and that he had done it, and that in the order of things, a drowning was a more important act than a few words spilled in the water. He realized that in this small instance the schoolteacher had succeeded where he had failed. The schoolteacher had not baptized him. He recalled his words: "My guts are in my head." My guts are in my head too, the boy thought. Even if by some chance it had not been an accident, what was of no consequence in the first place was of no consequence in the second; and he had succeeded in drowning the child. He had not said NO, he had done it.

The sun, from being only a ball of glare, was becoming distinct like a large pearl, as if sun and moon had fused in a brilliant marriage. The boy's narrowed eyes made a black spot of it. When he was a child he had several times, experimentally, commanded the sun to stand still, and once for as long as he watched it—a few seconds—it had stood still, but when he turned his back, it had moved. Now he would have liked for it to get out of the sky altogether or to be veiled in a cloud. He turned his face enough to rid his vision of it and was aware again of the country which seemed to lie beyond the silence, or in it, stretching off into the distance around him.

Quickly he set his mind again on the clearing. He thought of the burnt spot in the center of it and he imagined with a careful deliberateness how he would pick up any burnt bone that he might find in the ashes of the house and sling it off into the nearest gulley. He envisioned the calm and detached person who would do this, who would clear out the rubble and build back the house. Beyond the glare, he was aware of another figure, a gaunt stranger, the ghost who had been born in the wreck and who had fancied himself destined at that moment to the torture of prophecy. It was apparent to the boy that this person, who paid him no attention, was mad.

As the sun burned brighter, he became more and more thirsty and his hunger and thirst combined in a pain that shot up and down him and across from shoulder to shoulder. He was about to sit down when ahead in a brush-swept space off the side of the road he saw a Negro's shack. A small colored boy stood in the yard, alone except for a razor-backed shoat. His eyes were already fixed on the boy coming down the road. As Tarwater came nearer he saw a cluster of colored children watching him from the shack door. There was a well to the side under a sugarberry tree and he quickened his pace.

"I want me some water," he said, approaching the forward boy. He took the sandwich from his pocket and handed it to him. The child, who was about the size and shape of Bishop, put it to his mouth with the same motion that he took it and never removed his eyes from the boy's face.

"Yonder hit," he said and pointed with the sandwich to the well.

Tarwater went to it and cranked the bucket up level with the rim. There was a dipper but he did not use it. He leaned over and put his face to the water and drank. He drank until he began to feel dizzy. Then he pulled off his hat and thrust his head into the water. As it touched the deeper parts of his face, a shock ran through him, as if he had never been touched by water before. He looked down into a grey clear pool, down and down to where two silent serene eyes were gazing at him. He tore his head away from the bucket and stumbled backwards while the blurred shack, then the hog, then the coloured child, his eyes still fixed on him, came into focus. He slammed his hat down on his wet head and wiped his sleeve across his face and walked hastily away. The little Negroes watched him until he was off the place and had disappeared down the highway.

The vision stuck like a burr in his head and it took him more than a mile to realize he had not seen it. The water had strangely not assuaged his thirst. To take his mind off it, he reached in his pocket and pulled out the schoolteacher's present and began to admire it. It reminded him that he also had a nickel. The first store or filling station he came to, he would buy himself a drink and open it with the opener. The little instrument glittered in the center of his palm as if it promised to open great things for him. He began to realize that he had not adequately appreciated the schoolteacher while he had the opportunity. The lines of his uncle's face had already become less precise in his mind and he began to see again the eyes shadowed with knowledge that he had imagined before he went to the city. He returned the corkscrew-bottleopener to his pocket and held it there in his hand as if henceforth it would be his talisman.

Presently up ahead, he caught sight of the crossroads where 56 joined the highway he was on. The dirt road was not ten miles down from this point. There was a patched-together store and filling station on the far side of the crossroad. He hastened on in anticipation of the drink he was going to buy, his thirst growing by the second. Then as he came closer, he saw the large woman who stood in the door of the place. His thirst increased but his enthusiasm fled. She was leaning against the frame, her arms folded, and she filled almost the whole entrance. She was a black-eyed woman with a granite-like face and a tongue persistent to question. He and his great-uncle had traded at this place on occasion and when the woman was there, the old man had liked to linger and discourse, for he found her as pleasant as a shade tree. The boy had always stood by impatiently, kicking up the gravel, his face dark with boredom.

She spotted him across the highway and although she did not move or raise her hand, he could feel her eyes reeling him in. He crossed the highway and was drawn forward, scowling at a neutral space between her chin and shoulder. After he had arrived and stopped, she did not speak but only looked at him and he was obliged to direct a glance upward at her eyes. They were fixed on him with a black penetration. There was all knowledge in her stony face and the fold of her arms indicated a judgment fixed from the foundations of time. Huge wings might have been folded behind her without seeming strange.

"The niggers told me how you done," she said. "It shames the dead."

The boy pulled himself together to speak. He was conscious that no sass would do, that he was called upon by some force outside them both to answer for his freedom and make bold his acts. A tremor went through him. His soul plunged deep within itself to hear the voice of his mentor at its most profound depths. He opened his mouth to overwhelm the woman and to his horror what rushed from his lips, like the shriek of a bat, was an obscenity he had overheard once at a fair. Shocked, he saw the moment lost.

The woman did not move a muscle. Presently she said, "And now you come back. And who is going to hire out a boy who burns down houses?"

Still aghast at his failure, he said in a shaky voice, "I ain't ast nobody to hire me out."

"And shames the dead?"

"The dead are dead and stay that way," he said, gaining a little strength.

"And scorns the Resurrection and the Life?"

His thirst was like a rough hand clenched in his throat. "Sell me a purple drink," he said hoarsely.

The woman did not move.

He turned and went, his look as dark as hers. There were circles under his eyes and his skin seemed to have shrunk on the frame of his bones from dryness. The obscenity echoed sullenly in his head. The boy's mind was too fierce to brook impurities of such a nature. He was intolerant of unspiritual evils and with those of the flesh he had never truckled. He felt his victory sullied by the remark that had come from his mouth. He thought of turning and going back and flinging the right words at her but he had still not found them. He tried to think of what the schoolteacher would have said to her but no words of his uncle's would rise to his mind.

The sun was behind him now and his thirst had reached the point where it could not get worse. The inside of his throat felt as if it were coated with burning sand. He moved on doggedly. No cars were passing. He made up his mind that he would flag the next car that passed. He hungered now for companionship as much as food and water. He wanted to explain to someone what he had failed to explain to the woman and with the right words to wipe out the obscenity that had stained his thought.

He had gone almost two more miles when a car finally passed him and then slowed down and stopped. He had been trudging absently and had not waved it down but when he saw it stop, he began to run forward. By the time he reached it, the driver had leaned over and opened the door. It was a lavender and cream-colored car. The boy scrambled in without looking at the driver and closed the door and they drove on.

Then he turned and looked at the man and an unpleasant sensation that he could not place came over him. The person who had picked him up was a pale, lean, old-looking young man with deep hollows under his cheekbones. He had on a lavender shirt and a thin black suit and a panama hat. His lips were as white as the cigaret that hung limply from one side of his mouth. His eyes were the same color as his shirt and were ringed with heavy black lashes. A lock of yellow hair fell across his forehead from under his pushed-back hat. He was silent and Tarwater was silent. He drove at a leisurely rate and presently he turned in the seat and gave the boy a long personal look. "Live around here?" he asked.

"Not on this road," Tarwater said. His voice was cracked from dryness.

"Going somewheres?"

"To where I live," the boy croaked. "I'm in charge there now."

The man said nothing else for a few minutes. The window by the boy's side was cracked and patched with a piece of adhesive tape and the handle to lower it had been removed. There was a sweet stale odor in the car and there did not seem enough air to breathe freely. Tarwater could see a pale reflection of himself, eyeing him darkly from the window.

"Don't live on this road, huh?" the man said. "Where do your folks live?"

"No folks," Tarwater said. "It's only me. I take care of myself. Nobody tells me what to do."

"Don't huh?" the man said. "I see it's no flies on you."

"No," the boy said, "there's not."

There was something familiar to him in the look of the stranger but he could not place where he had seen him before. The man put his hand in the pocket of his shirt and brought out a silver case. He snapped it open and passed it over to Tarwater. "Smoke?" he said.

The boy had never smoked anything but rabbit tobacco and he did not want a cigaret. He only looked at them.

"Special," the man said, continuing to hold out the case. "You don't get one of this kind every day, but maybe you ain't had much experience smoking."

Tarwater took the cigaret and hung it in the corner of his mouth, exactly as the man's was hung. Out of another pocket, the man produced a silver lighter and flashed the flame over to him. The cigaret didn't light the first time but the second time he pulled in his breath, it lit and his lungs were unpleasantly filled with smoke. The smoke had a peculiar odor.

"Got no folks, huh?" the man said again. "What road do you live on?"

"It ain't even a road to it," the boy said. "I lived with my great-uncle but he's dead, burnt up, and now it's only me." He began to cough violently.

The man reached across the dashboard and opened the glove compartment. Inside, lying on its side was a flat bottle of whiskey. "Help yourself," he said. "It'll kill that cough."

It was an old-looking stamped bottle without the paper front on it and with a bitten-off cork in the top. "I get that special too," the man said. "If there's flies on you, you can't drink it."

The boy grasped the bottle and began to pull at the cork, and simultaneously there came into his head all his great-uncle's warnings about poisonous liquor, all his idiot restrictions about riding with strangers. The essence of all the old man's foolishness flooded his mind like a rising tide of irritation. He grasped the bottle the more firmly and pulled at the cork, which was too far in, with his fingers. He put the bottle between his knees and took the schoolteacher's corkscrew-bottleopener out of his pocket.

"Say, that's nifty," the man said.

The boy smiled. He pushed the corkscrew in the cork and pulled it out. Never a thought of the old man's but he would change it now. "This here thing will open anything," he said.

The stranger was driving slowly, watching him.

He lifted the bottle to his lips and took a long swallow. The liquid had a deep barely concealed bitterness that he had not expected and it appeared to be thicker than any whiskey he had ever had before. It burned his throat savagely and his thirst raged anew so that he was obliged to take another and fuller swallow. The second was worse than the first and he perceived that the stranger was watching him with what might be a leer.

"Don't like it, huh?" he said.

The boy felt a little dizzy but he thrust his face forward and said, "It's better than the Bread of Life!" and his eyes glittered.

He sat back and took the cork off the opener and put it back on the bottle and returned the bottle to the compartment. Already his motions seemed to be slowing down. It took him some time to get his hand back in his lap. The stranger said nothing and Tarwater turned his face to the window.

The liquor lay like a hot rock in the pit of his stomach, heating his whole body, and he felt himself pleasantly deprived of responsibility or of the need for any effort to justify his actions. His thoughts were heavy as if they had to struggle up through some dense medium to reach the surface of his mind. He was looking into thick unfenced woods. The car moved almost slow enough for him to count the outside trunks and he began to count them, one, one, one, until they began to merge and flow together. He leaned his head against the glass and his heavy lids closed.

After a few minutes the stranger reached over and pushed his shoulder but he did not stir. The man then began to drive faster. He drove about five miles, speeding, before he espied a turnoff into a dirt road. He took the turn and raced along for a mile or two and then pulled his car off the side of the road and drove down into a secluded declivity near the edge of the woods. He was breathing rapidly and sweating. He got out and ran around the car and opened the other door and Tarwater fell out of it like a loosely-filled sack. The man picked him up and carried him into the woods.

Nothing passed on the dirt road and the sun continued to move with a brilliant blandness on its way. The woods were silent except for an occasional trill or caw. The air itself might have been drugged. Now and then a large silent floating bird would glide into the treetops and after a moment rise again.

In about an hour, the stranger emerged alone and looked furtively about him. He was carrying the boy's hat for a souvenir and also the corkscrew-bottleopener. His delicate skin had acquired a faint pink tint as if he had refreshed himself on blood. He got quickly into his car and sped away.

When Tarwater woke up, the sun was directly overhead, very small and silver, sifting down light that seemed to spend itself before it reached him. He saw first his thin white legs stretching in front of him. He was propped up against a log that lay across a small open space between two very tall trees. His hands were loosely tied with a lavender handkerchief which his friend had thought of as an exchange for the hat. His clothes were neatly piled by his side. Only his shoes were on him. He perceived that his hat was gone.

The boy's mouth twisted open and to the side as if it were going to displace itself permanently. In a second it appeared to be only a gap that would never be a mouth again. His eyes looked small and seedlike as if while he was asleep, they had been lifted out, scorched, and dropped back into his head. His expression seemed to contract until it reached some point beyond rage or pain. Then a loud dry cry tore out of him and his mouth fell back into place.

He began to tear savagely at the lavender handkerchief until he had shredded it off. Then he got into his clothes so quickly that when he finished he had half of them on backwards and did not notice. He stood staring down at the spot where the displaced leaves showed him to have lain. His hand was already in his pocket bringing out the box of wooden matches. He kicked the leaves together and set them on fire. Then he tore off a pine branch and set it on fire and began to fire all the bushes around the spot until the fire was eating greedily at the evil ground, burning every spot the stranger could have touched. When it was a roaring blaze, he turned and ran, still holding the pine torch and lighting bushes as he went.

He barely noticed when he ran out of the woods onto the bare red road. It streaked beneath him like fire hardened and only gradually as his breath choked him did he slow down and begin to take his bearings. The sky, the woods on either side, the ground beneath him, came to a halt and the road assumed direction. It swung down between high red embankments and then mounted a flat field plowed to its edges on either side. Off in the distance a shack, sunk a little on one side, seemed to be afloat on the red folds. Down the hill the wooden bridge lay like the skeleton of some prehistoric beast across the stream bed. It was the road home, ground that had been familiar to him since his infancy but now it looked like strange and alien country.

He stood clenching the blackened burnt-out pine bough. Then after a moment he began to move forward again slowly. He knew that he could not turn back now. He knew that his destiny forced him on to a final revelation. His scorched eyes no longer looked hollow or as if they were meant only to guide him forward. They looked as if, touched with a coal like the lips of the prophet, they would never be used for ordinary sights again.

XII

THE BROAD ROAD began to narrow until it was no more than a rutted rain-washed gulley which disappeared finally into a blackberry thicket. The sun, red and mammoth, was about to touch the treeline. Tarwater paused an instant here. His glance passed over the ripening berries, turned sharply and pierced into the wood which lay dark and dense before him. He drew in his breath and held it a second before he plunged forward, blindly following the faint path that led down through the wood to the clearing. The air was laden with the odor of honeysuckle and the sharper scent of pine but he scarcely recognized what they were. His senses were stunned and his thought too seemed suspended. Somewhere deep in the wood a woodthrush called and as if the sound were a key turned in the boy's heart, his throat began to tighten.

A faint evening breeze had begun to stir. He stepped over a tree fallen across his path and plunged on. A thorn vine caught in his shirt and tore it but he didn't stop. Farther away the woodthrush called again. With the same four formal notes it trilled its grief against the silence. He was heading straight for a gap in the wood where, through a forked birch, the clearing could be seen below, down the long hill and across the field. Always when he and his great-uncle were returning from the road, they would stop there. It had given the old man the greatest satisfaction to look out over the field and in the distance see his house settled between its chimneys, his stall, his lot, his corn. He might have been Moses glimpsing the promised land.

As Tarwater approached the tree, his shoulders were set high and tense. He seemed to be preparing himself to sustain a blow. The tree, forked a few feet from the ground, loomed in his way. He stopped and with a hand on either trunk, he leaned forward through the fork and looked out at an expanse of crimson sky. His gaze, like a bird that flies through fire, faltered and dropped. Where it fell, two chimneys stood like grieving figures guarding the blackened ground between them. His face appeared to shrink as he looked.

He remained motionless except for his hands. They

clenched and unclenched. What he saw was what he had expected to see, an empty clearing. The old man's body was no longer there. His dust would not be mingling with the dust of the place, would not be washed by the seeping rains into the field. The wind by now had taken his ashes, dropped them and scattered them and lifted them up again and carried each mote a different way around the curve of the world. The clearing was burned free of all that had ever oppressed him. No cross was there to say that this was ground that the Lord still held. What he looked out upon was the sign of a broken covenant. The place was forsaken and his own. As he looked, his dry lips parted. They seemed to be forced open by a hunger too great to be contained inside him. He stood there open-mouthed, as if he had no further power to move.

He felt a breeze on his neck as light as a breath and he half-turned, sensing that some one stood behind him. A sibilant shifting of air dropped like a sigh into his ear. The boy turned white.

Go down and take it, his friend whispered. It's ours. We've won it. Ever since you first begun to dig the grave, I've stood by you, never left your side, and now we can take it over together, just you and me. You're not ever going to be alone again.

The boy shuddered convulsively. The presence was as pervasive as an odor, a warm sweet body of air encircling him, a violet shadow hanging around his shoulders.

He shook himself free fiercely and grabbed the matches from his pocket and tore off another pine bough. He held the bough under his arm and with a shaking hand struck a match and held it to the needles until he had a burning brand. He plunged this into the lower branches of the forked tree. The flames crackled up, snapping for the drier leaves and rushing into them until an arch of fire blazed upward. He walked backwards from the spot pushing the torch into all the bushes he was moving away from, until he had made a rising wall of fire between him and the grinning presence. He glared through the flames and his spirits rose as he saw that his adversary would soon be consumed in a roaring blaze. He turned and moved on with the burning brand tightly clenched in his fist.

The path twisted downward through reddened tree trunks that gradually grew darker as the sun sank out of sight. From time to time he plunged the torch into a bush or tree and left it blazing behind him. The wood became less dense. Suddenly it opened and he stood at its edge, looking out on the flat cornfield and far across to the two chimneys. Planes of purpling red above the treeline stretched back like stairsteps to reach the dusk. The corn the old man had left planted was up about a foot and moved in wavering lines of green across the field. It had been freshly plowed. The boy stood there, a small rigid, hatless figure, holding the blackened pine bough.

As he looked, his hunger constricted him anew. It appeared to be outside him, surrounding him, almost as if it were visible before him, something he could reach out for and not quite touch. He sensed a strangeness about the place as if there might already be an occupant. Beyond the two chimneys, his eyes moved over the stall, grey and weathered, and crossed the back field and stopped at the far black wall of woods. A deep filled quiet pervaded everything. The encroaching dusk seemed to come softly in deference to some mystery that resided here. He stood, leaning slightly forward. He appeared to be permanently suspended there, unable to go forward or back. He became conscious of the very breath he drew. Even the air seemed to belong to another.

Then near the stall he saw a Negro mounted on a mule. The mule was not moving; the two might have been made out of rock. He started forward across the field boldly, raising his fist in a gesture that was half-greeting and half-threat, but after a second his hand opened. He waved and began to run. It was Buford. He would go home with him and eat.

Instantly at the thought of food, he stopped and his muscles contracted with nausea. He blanched with the shock of a terrible premonition. He stood there and felt a crater opening inside him, and stretching out before him, surrounding him, he saw the clear grey spaces of that country where he had vowed never to set foot. Mechanically he began to move forward. He came out on the hard ground of the yard a few feet from the fig tree, but his eyes took the far circuit to it, lingering above the stall and moving beyond it to the far treeline and back. He knew that the next sight to meet his eyes would be the half-dug gaping grave, almost at his feet.

The Negro was watching him steadily. He began to move forward on the mule. When the boy finally forced his eyes to move again, he saw the mule's hooves first and then Buford's feet hanging at its sides. Above, the brown crinkled face was looking down at him with a scorn that could penetrate any surface.

The grave, freshly mounded, lay between them. Tarwater lowered his eyes to it. At its head, a dark rough cross was set starkly in the bare ground. The boy's hands opened stiffly as if he were dropping something he had been clutching all his life. His gaze rested finally on the ground where the wood entered the grave.

Buford said, "It's owing to me he's resting there. I buried him while you were laid out drunk. It's owing to me his corn has been plowed. It's owing to me the sign of his Saviour is over his head."

Nothing seemed alive about the boy but his eyes and they stared downward at the cross as if they followed below the surface of the earth to where its roots encircled all the dead.

The Negro sat watching his strange spent face and grew uneasy. The skin across it tightened as he watched and the eyes, lifting beyond the grave, appeared to see something coming in the distance. Buford turned his head. The darkening field behind him stretched downward toward the woods. When he looked back again, the boy's vision seemed to pierce the very air. The Negro trembled and felt suddenly a pressure on him too great to bear. He sensed it as a burning in the atmosphere. His nostrils twitched. He muttered something and turned the mule around and moved off, across the back field and down to the woods.

The boy remained standing there, his still eyes reflecting the field the Negro had crossed. It seemed to him no longer empty but peopled with a multitude. Everywhere, he saw dim figures seated on the slope and as he gazed he saw that from a single basket the throng was being fed. His eyes searched the crowd for a long time as if he could not find the one he was looking for. Then he saw him. The old man was lowering himself to the ground. When he was down and his bulk had settled, he leaned forward, his face turned toward the basket, impatiently following its progress toward him. The boy too leaned forward, aware at last of the object of his hunger, aware that it was the same as the old man's and that nothing on earth would fill him. His hunger was so great that he could have eaten all the loaves and fishes after they were multiplied.

He stood there, straining forward, but the scene faded in the gathering darkness. Night descended until there was nothing but a thin streak of red between it and the black line of earth but still he stood there. He felt his hunger no longer as a pain but as a tide. He felt it rising in himself through time and darkness, rising through the centuries, and he knew that it rose in a line of men whose lives were chosen to sustain it, who would wander in the world, strangers from that violent country where the silence is never broken except to shout the truth. He felt it building from the blood of Abel to his own, rising and engulfing him. It seemed in one instant to lift and turn him. He whirled toward the treeline. There, rising and spreading in the night, a red-gold tree of fire ascended as if it would consume the darkness in one tremendous burst of flame. The boy's breath went out to meet it. He knew that this was the fire that had encircled Daniel, that had raised Elijah from the earth, that had spoken to Moses and would in the instant speak to him. He threw himself to the ground and with his face against the dirt of the grave, he heard the command. GO WARN THE CHILDREN OF GOD OF THE TERRIBLE SPEED OF MERCY. The words were as silent as seeds opening one at a time in his blood.

When finally he raised himself, the burning bush had disappeared. A line of fire ate languidly at the treeline and here and there a thin crest of flame rose farther back in the woods where a dull red cloud of smoke had gathered. The boy stooped and picked up a handful of dirt off his great-uncle's grave and smeared it on his forehead. Then after a moment, without looking back he moved across the far field and off the way Buford had gone.

By midnight he had left the road and the burning woods behind him and had come out on the highway once more. The moon, riding low above the field beside him, appeared and disappeared, diamond-bright, between patches of darkness. Intermittently the boy's jagged shadow slanted across the road ahead of him as if it cleared a rough path toward his goal. His singed eyes, black in their deep sockets, seemed already to envision the fate that awaited him but he moved steadily on, his face set toward the dark city, where the children of God lay sleeping.

EVERYTHING THAT RISES
MUST CONVERGE

Contents

Everything That Rises Must Converge

H ER DOCTOR had told Julian's mother that she must lose twenty pounds on account of her blood pressure, so on Wednesday nights Julian had to take her downtown on the bus for a reducing class at the Y. The reducing class was designed for working girls over fifty, who weighed from 165 to 200 pounds. His mother was one of the slimmer ones, but she said ladies did not tell their age or weight. She would not ride the buses by herself at night since they had been integrated, and because the reducing class was one of her few pleasures, necessary for her health, and *free*, she said Julian could at least put himself out to take her, considering all she did for him. Julian did not like to consider all she did for him, but every Wednesday night he braced himself and took her.

She was almost ready to go, standing before the hall mirror, putting on her hat, while he, his hands behind him, appeared pinned to the door frame, waiting like Saint Sebastian for the arrows to begin piercing him. The hat was new and had cost her seven dollars and a half. She kept saying, "Maybe I shouldn't have paid that for it. No, I shouldn't have. I'll take it off and return it tomorrow. I shouldn't have bought it."

Julian raised his eyes to heaven. "Yes, you should have bought it," he said. "Put it on and let's go." It was a hideous hat. A purple velvet flap came down on one side of it and stood up on the other; the rest of it was green and looked like a cushion with the stuffing out. He decided it was less comical than jaunty and pathetic. Everything that gave her pleasure was small and depressed him.

She lifted the hat one more time and set it down slowly on top of her head. Two wings of gray hair protruded on either side of her florid face, but her eyes, sky-blue, were as innocent and untouched by experience as they must have been when she was ten. Were it not that she was a widow who had struggled fiercely to feed and clothe and put him through school and who was supporting him still, "until he got on his feet," she might have been a little girl that he had to take to town.

"It's all right, it's all right," he said. "Let's go." He opened the door himself and started down the walk to get her going.

485

The sky was a dying violet and the houses stood out darkly against it, bulbous liver-colored monstrosities of a uniform ugliness though no two were alike. Since this had been a fashionable neighborhood forty years ago, his mother persisted in thinking they did well to have an apartment in it. Each house had a narrow collar of dirt around it in which sat, usually, a grubby child. Julian walked with his hands in his pockets, his head down and thrust forward and his eyes glazed with the determination to make himself completely numb during the time he would be sacrificed to her pleasure.

The door closed and he turned to find the dumpy figure, surmounted by the atrocious hat, coming toward him. "Well," she said, "you only live once and paying a little more for it, I at least won't meet myself coming and going."

"Some day I'll start making money," Julian said gloomily—he knew he never would—"and you can have one of those jokes whenever you take the fit." But first they would move. He visualized a place where the nearest neighbors would be three miles away on either side.

"I think you're doing fine," she said, drawing on her gloves. "You've only been out of school a year. Rome wasn't built in a day."

She was one of the few members of the Y reducing class who arrived in hat and gloves and who had a son who had been to college. "It takes time," she said, "and the world is in such a mess. This hat looked better on me than any of the others, though when she brought it out I said, 'Take that thing back. I wouldn't have it on my head,' and she said, 'Now wait till you see it on,' and when she put it on me, I said, 'We-ull,' and she said, 'If you ask me, that hat does something for you and you do something for the hat, and besides,' she said, 'with that hat, you won't meet yourself coming and going.'"

Julian thought he could have stood his lot better if she had been selfish, if she had been an old hag who drank and screamed at him. He walked along, saturated in depression, as if in the midst of his martyrdom he had lost his faith. Catching sight of his long, hopeless, irritated face, she stopped suddenly with a grief-stricken look, and pulled back on his arm. "Wait on me," she said. "I'm going back to the house and take this thing off and tomorrow I'm going to return it. I was out of my head. I can pay the gas bill with that seven-fifty."

He caught her arm in a vicious grip. "You are not going to take it back," he said. "I like it."

"Well," she said, "I don't think I ought . . ."

"Shut up and enjoy it," he muttered, more depressed than ever.

"With the world in the mess it's in," she said, "it's a wonder we can enjoy anything. I tell you, the bottom rail is on the top."

Julian sighed.

"Of course," she said, "if you know who you are, you can go anywhere." She said this every time he took her to the reducing class. "Most of them in it are not our kind of people," she said, "but I can be gracious to anybody. I know who I am."

"They don't give a damn for your graciousness," Julian said savagely. "Knowing who you are is good for one generation only. You haven't the foggiest idea where you stand now or who you are."

She stopped and allowed her eyes to flash at him. "I most certainly do know who I am," she said, "and if you don't know who you are, I'm ashamed of you."

"Oh hell," Julian said.

"Your great-grandfather was a former governor of this state," she said. "Your grandfather was a prosperous land-owner. Your grandmother was a Godhigh."

"Will you look around you," he said tensely, "and see where you are now?" and he swept his arm jerkily out to indicate the neighborhood, which the growing darkness at least made less dingy.

"You remain what you are," she said. "Your great-grand-father had a plantation and two hundred slaves."

"There are no more slaves," he said irritably.

"They were better off when they were," she said. He groaned to see that she was off on that topic. She rolled onto it every few days like a train on an open track. He knew every stop, every junction, every swamp along the way, and knew the exact point at which her conclusion would roll majestically into the station: "It's ridiculous. It's simply not realistic. They should rise, yes, but on their own side of the fence."

"Let's skip it," Julian said.

"The ones I feel sorry for," she said, "are the ones that are half white. They're tragic."

"Will you skip it?"

"Suppose we were half white. We would certainly have mixed feelings."

"I have mixed feelings now," he groaned.

"Well let's talk about something pleasant," she said. "I remember going to Grandpa's when I was a little girl. Then the house had double stairways that went up to what was really the second floor—all the cooking was done on the first. I used to like to stay down in the kitchen on account of the way the walls smelled. I would sit with my nose pressed against the plaster and take deep breaths. Actually the place belonged to the Godhighs but your grandfather Chestny paid the mortgage and saved it for them. They were in reduced circumstances," she said, "but reduced or not, they never forgot who they were."

"Doubtless that decayed mansion reminded them," Julian muttered. He never spoke of it without contempt or thought of it without longing. He had seen it once when he was a child before it had been sold. The double stairways had rotted and been torn down. Negroes were living in it. But it remained in his mind as his mother had known it. It appeared in his dreams regularly. He would stand on the wide porch, listening to the rustle of oak leaves, then wander through the high-ceilinged hall into the parlor that opened onto it and gaze at the worn rugs and faded draperies. It occurred to him that it was he, not she, who could have appreciated it. He preferred its threadbare elegance to anything he could name and it was because of it that all the neighborhoods they had lived in had been a torment to him—whereas she had hardly known the difference. She called her insensitivity "being adjustable."

"And I remember the old darky who was my nurse, Caroline. There was no better person in the world. I've always had a great respect for my colored friends," she said. "I'd do anything in the world for them and they'd . . ."

"Will you for God's sake get off that subject?" Julian said. When he got on a bus by himself, he made it a point to sit down beside a Negro, in reparation as it were for his mother's sins.

"You're mighty touchy tonight," she said. "Do you feel all right?"

"Yes I feel all right," he said. "Now lay off."

She pursed her lips. "Well, you certainly are in a vile humor," she observed. "I just won't speak to you at all."

They had reached the bus stop. There was no bus in sight and Julian, his hands still jammed in his pockets and his head thrust forward, scowled down the empty street. The frustration of having to wait on the bus as well as ride on it began to creep up his neck like a hot hand. The presence of his mother was borne in upon him as she gave a pained sigh. He looked at her bleakly. She was holding herself very erect under the preposterous hat, wearing it like a banner of her imaginary dignity. There was in him an evil urge to break her spirit. He suddenly unloosened his tie and pulled it off and put it in his pocket.

She stiffened. "Why must you look like *that* when you take me to town?" she said. "Why must you deliberately embarrass me?"

"If you'll never learn where you are," he said, "you can at least learn where I am."

"You look like a—thug," she said.

"Then I must be one," he murmured.

"I'll just go home," she said. "I will not bother you. If you can't do a little thing like that for me . . ."

Rolling his eyes upward, he put his tie back on. "Restored to my class," he muttered. He thrust his face toward her and hissed, "True culture is in the mind, the *mind*," he said, and tapped his head, "the mind."

"It's in the heart," she said, "and in how you do things and how you do things is because of who you *are*."

"Nobody in the damn bus cares who you are."

"I care who I am," she said icily.

The lighted bus appeared on top of the next hill and as it approached, they moved out into the street to meet it. He put his hand under her elbow and hoisted her up on the creaking step. She entered with a little smile, as if she were going into a drawing room where everyone had been waiting for her. While he put in the tokens, she sat down on one of the broad front seats for three which faced the aisle. A thin woman with protruding teeth and long yellow hair was sitting on the end of it. His mother moved up beside her and left room for Julian beside herself. He sat down and looked at the floor across the aisle where a pair of thin feet in red and white canvas sandals were planted.

His mother immediately began a general conversation meant to attract anyone who felt like talking. "Can it get any hotter?" she said and removed from her purse a folding fan, black with a Japanese scene on it, which she began to flutter before her.

"I reckon it might could," the woman with the protruding teeth said, "but I know for a fact my apartment couldn't get no hotter."

"It must get the afternoon sun," his mother said. She sat forward and looked up and down the bus. It was half filled. Everybody was white. "I see we have the bus to ourselves," she said. Julian cringed.

"For a change," said the woman across the aisle, the owner of the red and white canvas sandals. "I come on one the other day and they were thick as fleas—up front and all through."

"The world is in a mess everywhere," his mother said. "I don't know how we've let it get in this fix."

"What gets my goat is all those boys from good families stealing automobile tires," the woman with the protruding teeth said. "I told my boy, I said you may not be rich but you been raised right and if I ever catch you in any such mess, they can send you on to the reformatory. Be exactly where you belong."

"Training tells," his mother said. "Is your boy in high school?"

"Ninth grade," the woman said.

"My son just finished college last year. He wants to write but he's selling typewriters until he gets started," his mother said.

The woman leaned forward and peered at Julian. He threw her such a malevolent look that she subsided against the seat.

On the floor across the aisle there was an abandoned newspaper. He got up and got it and opened it out in front of him. His mother discreetly continued the conversation in a lower tone but the woman across the aisle said in a loud voice, "Well that's nice. Selling typewriters is close to writing. He can go right from one to the other."

"I tell him," his mother said, "that Rome wasn't built in a day."

Behind the newspaper Julian was withdrawing into the inner compartment of his mind where he spent most of his time. This was a kind of mental bubble in which he established himself when he could not bear to be a part of what was going on around him. From it he could see out and judge but in it he was safe from any kind of penetration from without. It was the only place where he felt free of the general idiocy of his fellows. His mother had never entered it but from it he could see her with absolute clarity.

The old lady was clever enough and he thought that if she had started from any of the right premises, more might have been expected of her. She lived according to the laws of her own fantasy world, outside of which he had never seen her set foot. The law of it was to sacrifice herself for him after she had first created the necessity to do so by making a mess of things. If he had permitted her sacrifices, it was only because her lack of foresight had made them necessary. All of her life had been a struggle to act like a Chestny without the Chestny goods, and to give him everything she thought a Chestny ought to have; but since, said she, it was fun to struggle, why complain? And when you had won, as she had won, what fun to look back on the hard times! He could not forgive her that she had enjoyed the struggle and that she thought *she* had won.

What she meant when she said she had won was that she had brought him up successfully and had sent him to college and that he had turned out so well—good looking (her teeth had gone unfilled so that his could be straightened), intelligent (he realized he was too intelligent to be a success), and with a future ahead of him (there was of course no future ahead of him). She excused his gloominess on the grounds that he was still growing up and his radical ideas on his lack of practical experience. She said he didn't yet know a thing about "life," that he hadn't even entered the real world— when already he was as disenchanted with it as a man of fifty.

The further irony of all this was that in spite of her, he had turned out so well. In spite of going to only a third-rate college, he had, on his own initiative, come out with a first-rate education; in spite of growing up dominated by a small mind, he had ended up with a large one; in spite of all her foolish views, he was free of prejudice and unafraid to face facts. Most miraculous of all, instead of being blinded by love for her as she was for him, he had cut himself emotionally free of her and could see her with complete objectivity. He was not dominated by his mother.

The bus stopped with a sudden jerk and shook him from his meditation. A woman from the back lurched forward with little steps and barely escaped falling in his newspaper as she righted herself. She got off and a large Negro got on. Julian kept his paper lowered to watch. It gave him a certain satisfaction to see injustice in daily operation. It confirmed his view that with a few exceptions there was no one worth knowing within a radius of three hundred miles. The Negro was well dressed and carried a briefcase. He looked around and then sat down on the other end of the seat where the woman with the red and white canvas sandals was sitting. He immediately unfolded a newspaper and obscured himself behind it. Julian's mother's elbow at once prodded insistently into his ribs. "Now you see why I won't ride on these buses by myself," she whispered.

The woman with the red and white canvas sandals had risen at the same time the Negro sat down and had gone further back in the bus and taken the seat of the woman who had got off. His mother leaned forward and cast her an approving look.

Julian rose, crossed the aisle, and sat down in the place of the woman with the canvas sandals. From this position, he looked serenely across at his mother. Her face had turned an angry red. He stared at her, making his eyes the eyes of a stranger. He felt his tension suddenly lift as if he had openly declared war on her.

He would have liked to get in conversation with the Negro

and to talk with him about art or politics or any subject that would be above the comprehension of those around them, but the man remained entrenched behind his paper. He was either ignoring the change of seating or had never noticed it. There was no way for Julian to convey his sympathy.

His mother kept her eyes fixed reproachfully on his face. The woman with the protruding teeth was looking at him avidly as if he were a type of monster new to her.

"Do you have a light?" he asked the Negro.

Without looking away from his paper, the man reached in his pocket and handed him a packet of matches.

"Thanks," Julian said. For a moment he held the matches foolishly. A NO SMOKING sign looked down upon him from over the door. This alone would not have deterred him; he had no cigarettes. He had quit smoking some months before because he could not afford it. "Sorry," he muttered and handed back the matches. The Negro lowered the paper and gave him an annoyed look. He took the matches and raised the paper again.

His mother continued to gaze at him but she did not take advantage of his momentary discomfort. Her eyes retained their battered look. Her face seemed to be unnaturally red, as if her blood pressure had risen. Julian allowed no glimmer of sympathy to show on his face. Having got the advantage, he wanted desperately to keep it and carry it through. He would have liked to teach her a lesson that would last her a while, but there seemed no way to continue the point. The Negro refused to come out from behind his paper.

Julian folded his arms and looked stolidly before him, facing her but as if he did not see her, as if he had ceased to recognize her existence. He visualized a scene in which, the bus having reached their stop, he would remain in his seat and when she said, "Aren't you going to get off?" he would look at her as at a stranger who had rashly addressed him. The corner they got off on was usually deserted, but it was well lighted and it would not hurt her to walk by herself the four blocks to the Y. He decided to wait until the time came and then decide whether or not he would let her get off by herself. He would have to be at the Y at ten to bring her back, but he could leave her wondering if he was going to show up. There was no reason for her to think she could always depend on him.

He retired again into the high-ceilinged room sparsely settled with large pieces of antique furniture. His soul expanded momentarily but then he became aware of his mother across from him and the vision shriveled. He studied her coldly. Her feet in little pumps dangled like a child's and did not quite reach the floor. She was training on him an exaggerated look of reproach. He felt completely detached from her. At that moment he could with pleasure have slapped her as he would have slapped a particularly obnoxious child in his charge.

He began to imagine various unlikely ways by which he could teach her a lesson. He might make friends with some distinguished Negro professor or lawyer and bring him home to spend the evening. He would be entirely justified but her blood pressure would rise to 300. He could not push her to the extent of making her have a stroke, and moreover, he had never been successful at making any Negro friends. He had tried to strike up an acquaintance on the bus with some of the better types, with ones that looked like professors or ministers or lawyers. One morning he had sat down next to a distinguished-looking dark brown man who had answered his questions with a sonorous solemnity but who had turned out to be an undertaker. Another day he had sat down beside a cigar-smoking Negro with a diamond ring on his finger, but after a few stilted pleasantries, the Negro had rung the buzzer and risen, slipping two lottery tickets into Julian's hand as he climbed over him to leave.

He imagined his mother lying desperately ill and his being able to secure only a Negro doctor for her. He toyed with that idea for a few minutes and then dropped it for a momentary vision of himself participating as a sympathizer in a sit-in demonstration. This was possible but he did not linger with it. Instead, he approached the ultimate horror. He brought home a beautiful suspiciously Negroid woman. Prepare yourself, he said. There is nothing you can do about it. This is the woman I've chosen. She's intelligent, dignified, even good, and she's suffered and she hasn't thought it *fun*. Now persecute us, go ahead and persecute us. Drive her out of here, but remember, you're driving me too. His eyes were narrowed and through the indignation he had generated, he saw his mother across the aisle, purple-faced, shrunken to the dwarf-like proportions of her moral nature, sitting like a mummy beneath the ridiculous banner of her hat.

He was tilted out of his fantasy again as the bus stopped. The door opened with a sucking hiss and out of the dark a large, gaily dressed, sullen-looking colored woman got on with a little boy. The child, who might have been four, had on a short plaid suit and a Tyrolean hat with a blue feather in it. Julian hoped that he would sit down beside him and that the woman would push in beside his mother. He could think of no better arrangement.

As she waited for her tokens, the woman was surveying the seating possibilities—he hoped with the idea of sitting where she was least wanted. There was something familiar-looking about her but Julian could not place what it was. She was a giant of a woman. Her face was set not only to meet opposition but to seek it out. The downward tilt of her large lower lip was like a warning sign: DON'T TAMPER WITH ME. Her bulging figure was encased in a green crepe dress and her feet overflowed in red shoes. She had on a hideous hat. A purple velvet flap came down on one side of it and stood up on the other; the rest of it was green and looked like a cushion with the stuffing out. She carried a mammoth red pocketbook that bulged throughout as if it were stuffed with rocks.

To Julian's disappointment, the little boy climbed up on the empty seat beside his mother. His mother lumped all children, black and white, into the common category, "cute," and she thought little Negroes were on the whole cuter than little white children. She smiled at the little boy as he climbed on the seat.

Meanwhile the woman was bearing down upon the empty seat beside Julian. To his annoyance, she squeezed herself into it. He saw his mother's face change as the woman settled herself next to him and he realized with satisfaction that this was more objectionable to her than it was to him. Her face seemed almost gray and there was a look of dull recognition in her eyes, as if suddenly she had sickened at some awful confrontation. Julian saw that it was because she and the woman had, in a sense, swapped sons. Though his mother would not realize the symbolic significance of this, she would feel it. His amusement showed plainly on his face.

The woman next to him muttered something unintelligible to herself. He was conscious of a kind of bristling next to him, a muted growling like that of an angry cat. He could not see anything but the red pocketbook upright on the bulging green thighs. He visualized the woman as she had stood waiting for her tokens—the ponderous figure, rising from the red shoes upward over the solid hips, the mammoth bosom, the haughty face, to the green and purple hat.

His eyes widened.

The vision of the two hats, identical, broke upon him with the radiance of a brilliant sunrise. His face was suddenly lit with joy. He could not believe that Fate had thrust upon his mother such a lesson. He gave a loud chuckle so that she would look at him and see that he saw. She turned her eyes on him slowly. The blue in them seemed to have turned a bruised purple. For a moment he had an uncomfortable sense of her innocence, but it lasted only a second before principle rescued him. Justice entitled him to laugh. His grin hardened until it said to her as plainly as if he were saying aloud: Your punishment exactly fits your pettiness. This should teach you a permanent lesson.

Her eyes shifted to the woman. She seemed unable to bear looking at him and to find the woman preferable. He became conscious again of the bristling presence at his side. The woman was rumbling like a volcano about to become active. His mother's mouth began to twitch slightly at one corner. With a sinking heart, he saw incipient signs of recovery on her face and realized that this was going to strike her suddenly as funny and was going to be no lesson at all. She kept her eyes on the woman and an amused smile came over her face as if the woman were a monkey that had stolen her hat. The little Negro was looking up at her with large fascinated eyes. He had been trying to attract her attention for some time.

"Carver!" the woman said suddenly. "Come heah!"

When he saw that the spotlight was on him at last, Carver drew his feet up and turned himself toward Julian's mother and giggled.

"Carver!" the woman said. "You heah me? Come heah!"

Carver slid down from the seat but remained squatting with his back against the base of it, his head turned slyly around toward Julian's mother, who was smiling at him. The woman reached a hand across the aisle and snatched him to her. He righted himself and hung backwards on her knees, grinning at Julian's mother. "Isn't he cute?" Julian's mother said to the woman with the protruding teeth.

"I reckon he is," the woman said without conviction.

The Negress yanked him upright but he eased out of her grip and shot across the aisle and scrambled, giggling wildly, onto the seat beside his love.

"I think he likes me," Julian's mother said, and smiled at the woman. It was the smile she used when she was being particularly gracious to an inferior. Julian saw everything lost. The lesson had rolled off her like rain on a roof.

The woman stood up and yanked the little boy off the seat as if she were snatching him from contagion. Julian could feel the rage in her at having no weapon like his mother's smile. She gave the child a sharp slap across his leg. He howled once and then thrust his head into her stomach and kicked his feet against her shins. "Be-have," she said vehemently.

The bus stopped and the Negro who had been reading the newspaper got off. The woman moved over and set the little boy down with a thump between herself and Julian. She held him firmly by the knee. In a moment he put his hands in front of his face and peeped at Julian's mother through his fingers.

"I see yoooooooo!" she said and put her hand in front of her face and peeped at him.

The woman slapped his hand down. "Quit yo' foolishness," she said, "before I knock the living Jesus out of you!"

Julian was thankful that the next stop was theirs. He reached up and pulled the cord. The woman reached up and pulled it at the same time. Oh my God, he thought. He had the terrible intuition that when they got off the bus together, his mother would open her purse and give the little boy a nickel. The gesture would be as natural to her as breathing. The bus stopped and the woman got up and lunged to the front, dragging the child, who wished to stay on, after her. Julian and his mother got up and followed. As they neared the door, Julian tried to relieve her of her pocketbook.

"No," she murmured, "I want to give the little boy a nickel."

"No!" Julian hissed. "No!"

She smiled down at the child and opened her bag. The bus door opened and the woman picked him up by the arm and descended with him, hanging at her hip. Once in the street she set him down and shook him.

Julian's mother had to close her purse while she got down the bus step but as soon as her feet were on the ground, she opened it again and began to rummage inside. "I can't find but a penny," she whispered, "but it looks like a new one."

"Don't do it!" Julian said fiercely between his teeth. There was a streetlight on the corner and she hurried to get under it so that she could better see into her pocketbook. The woman was heading off rapidly down the street with the child still hanging backward on her hand.

"Oh little boy!" Julian's mother called and took a few quick steps and caught up with them just beyond the lamppost. "Here's a bright new penny for you," and she held out the coin, which shone bronze in the dim light.

The huge woman turned and for a moment stood, her shoulders lifted and her face frozen with frustrated rage, and stared at Julian's mother. Then all at once she seemed to explode like a piece of machinery that had been given one ounce of pressure too much. Julian saw the black fist swing out with the red pocketbook. He shut his eyes and cringed as he heard the woman shout, "He don't take nobody's pennies!" When he opened his eyes, the woman was disappearing down the street with the little boy staring wide-eyed over her shoulder. Julian's mother was sitting on the sidewalk.

"I told you not to do that," Julian said angrily. "I told you not to do that!"

He stood over her for a minute, gritting his teeth. Her legs were stretched out in front of her and her hat was on her lap. He squatted down and looked her in the face. It was totally expressionless. "You got exactly what you deserved," he said. "Now get up."

He picked up her pocketbook and put what had fallen out back in it. He picked the hat up off her lap. The penny caught his eye on the sidewalk and he picked that up and let it drop before her eyes into the purse. Then he stood up and leaned over and held his hands out to pull her up. She remained immobile. He sighed. Rising above them on either side were black apartment buildings, marked with irregular rectangles of light. At the end of the block a man came out of a door and walked off in the opposite direction. "All right," he said, "suppose somebody happens by and wants to know why you're sitting on the sidewalk?"

She took the hand and, breathing hard, pulled heavily up on it and then stood for a moment, swaying slightly as if the spots of light in the darkness were circling around her. Her eyes, shadowed and confused, finally settled on his face. He did not try to conceal his irritation. "I hope this teaches you a lesson," he said. She leaned forward and her eyes raked his face. She seemed trying to determine his identity. Then, as if she found nothing familiar about him, she started off with a headlong movement in the wrong direction.

"Aren't you going on to the Y?" he asked.

"Home," she muttered.

"Well, are we walking?"

For answer she kept going. Julian followed along, his hands behind him. He saw no reason to let the lesson she had had go without backing it up with an explanation of its meaning. She might as well be made to understand what had happened to her. "Don't think that was just an uppity Negro woman," he said. "That was the whole colored race which will no longer take your condescending pennies. That was your black double. She can wear the same hat as you, and to be sure," he added gratuitously (because he thought it was funny), "it looked better on her than it did on you. What all this means," he said, "is that the old world is gone. The old manners are obsolete and your graciousness is not worth a damn." He thought bitterly of the house that had been lost for him. "You aren't who you think you are," he said.

She continued to plow ahead, paying no attention to him. Her hair had come undone on one side. She dropped her pocketbook and took no notice. He stooped and picked it up and handed it to her but she did not take it.

"You needn't act as if the world had come to an end," he said, "because it hasn't. From now on you've got to live in a new world and face a few realities for a change. Buck up," he said, "it won't kill you."

She was breathing fast.

"Let's wait on the bus," he said.

"Home," she said thickly.

"I hate to see you behave like this," he said. "Just like a child. I should be able to expect more of you." He decided to stop where he was and make her stop and wait for a bus. "I'm not going any farther," he said, stopping. "We're going on the bus."

She continued to go on as if she had not heard him. He took a few steps and caught her arm and stopped her. He looked into her face and caught his breath. He was looking into a face he had never seen before. "Tell Grandpa to come get me," she said.

He stared, stricken.

"Tell Caroline to come get me," she said.

Stunned, he let her go and she lurched forward again, walking as if one leg were shorter than the other. A tide of darkness seemed to be sweeping her from him. "Mother!" he cried. "Darling, sweetheart, wait!" Crumpling, she fell to the pavement. He dashed forward and fell at her side, crying, "Mamma, Mamma!" He turned her over. Her face was fiercely distorted. One eye, large and staring, moved slightly to the left as if it had become unmoored. The other remained fixed on him, raked his face again, found nothing and closed.

"Wait here, wait here!" he cried and jumped up and began to run for help toward a cluster of lights he saw in the distance ahead of him. "Help, help!" he shouted, but his voice was thin, scarcely a thread of sound. The lights drifted farther away the faster he ran and his feet moved numbly as if they carried him nowhere. The tide of darkness seemed to sweep him back to her, postponing from moment to moment his entry into the world of guilt and sorrow.

Greenleaf

MRS. MAY's bedroom window was low and faced on the east and the bull, silvered in the moonlight, stood under it, his head raised as if he listened—like some patient god come down to woo her—for a stir inside the room. The window was dark and the sound of her breathing too light to be carried outside. Clouds crossing the moon blackened him and in the dark he began to tear at the hedge. Presently they passed and he appeared again in the same spot, chewing steadily, with a hedge-wreath that he had ripped loose for himself caught in the tips of his horns. When the moon drifted into retirement again, there was nothing to mark his place but the sound of steady chewing. Then abruptly a pink glow filled the window. Bars of light slid across him as the venetian blind was slit. He took a step backward and lowered his head as if to show the wreath across his horns.

For almost a minute there was no sound from inside, then as he raised his crowned head again, a woman's voice, guttural as if addressed to a dog, said, "Get away from here, Sir!" and in a second muttered, "Some nigger's scrub bull."

The animal pawed the ground and Mrs. May, standing bent forward behind the blind, closed it quickly lest the light make him charge into the shrubbery. For a second she waited, still bent forward, her nightgown hanging loosely from her narrow shoulders. Green rubber curlers sprouted neatly over her forehead and her face beneath them was smooth as concrete with an egg-white paste that drew the wrinkles out while she slept.

She had been conscious in her sleep of a steady rhythmic chewing as if something were eating one wall of the house. She had been aware that whatever it was had been eating as long as she had had the place and had eaten everything from the beginning of her fence line up to the house and now was eating the house and calmly with the same steady rhythm would continue through the house, eating her and the boys, and then on, eating everything but the Greenleafs, on and on, eating everything until nothing was left but the

Greenleafs on a little island all their own in the middle of
what had been her place. When the munching reached her
elbow, she jumped up and found herself, fully awake, standing in the middle of her room. She identified the sound at
once: a cow was tearing at the shrubbery under her window.
Mr. Greenleaf had left the lane gate open and she didn't
doubt that the entire herd was on her lawn. She turned on
the dim pink table lamp and then went to the window and
slit the blind. The bull, gaunt and long-legged, was standing
about four feet from her, chewing calmly like an uncouth
country suitor.

For fifteen years, she thought as she squinted at him
fiercely, she had been having shiftless people's hogs root up
her oats, their mules wallow on her lawn, their scrub bulls
breed her cows. If this one was not put up now, he would be
over the fence, ruining her herd before morning—and Mr.
Greenleaf was soundly sleeping a half mile down the road in
the tenant house. There was no way to get him unless she
dressed and got in her car and rode down there and woke
him up. He would come but his expression, his whole figure,
his every pause, would say: "Hit looks to me like one or both
of them boys would not make their maw ride out in the middle of the night thisaway. If hit was my boys, they would
have got thet bull up theirself."

The bull lowered his head and shook it and the wreath
slipped down to the base of his horns where it looked like a
menacing prickly crown. She had closed the blind then; in a
few seconds she heard him move off heavily.

Mr. Greenleaf would say, "If hit was my boys they would
never have allowed their maw to go after hired help in the
middle of the night. They would have did it theirself."

Weighing it, she decided not to bother Mr. Greenleaf. She
returned to bed thinking that if the Greenleaf boys had risen
in the world it was because she had given their father em-
ployment when no one else would have him. She had had
Mr. Greenleaf fifteen years but no one else would have had
him five minutes. Just the way he approached an object was
enough to tell anybody with eyes what kind of a worker he
was. He walked with a high-shouldered creep and he never
appeared to come directly forward. He walked on the perim-

eter of some invisible circle and if you wanted to look him in
the face, you had to move and get in front of him. She had
not fired him because she had always doubted she could do
better. He was too shiftless to go out and look for another
job; he didn't have the initiative to steal, and after she had
told him three or four times to do a thing, he did it; but he
never told her about a sick cow until it was too late to call
the veterinarian and if her barn had caught on fire, he would
have called his wife to see the flames before he began to put
them out. And of the wife, she didn't even like to think. Beside the wife, Mr. Greenleaf was an aristocrat.

"If it had been my boys," he would have said, "they would
have cut off their right arm before they would have allowed
their maw to . . . ."

"If your boys had any pride, Mr. Greenleaf," she would like
to say to him some day, "there are many things that they
would not *allow* their mother to do."

The next morning as soon as Mr. Greenleaf came to the
back door, she told him there was a stray bull on the place
and that she wanted him penned up at once.

"Done already been here three days," he said, addressing
his right foot which he held forward, turned slightly as if he
were trying to look at the sole. He was standing at the bottom of the three back steps while she leaned out the kitchen
door, a small woman with pale near-sighted eyes and grey
hair that rose on top like the crest of some disturbed bird.

"Three days!" she said in the restrained screech that had
become habitual with her.

Mr. Greenleaf, looking into the distance over the near pasture, removed a package of cigarets from his shirt pocket and
let one fall into his hand. He put the package back and stood for
a while looking at the cigaret. "I put him in the bull pen but
he torn out of there," he said presently. "I didn't see him none
after that." He bent over the cigaret and lit it and then turned
his head briefly in her direction. The upper part of his face
sloped gradually into the lower which was long and narrow,
shaped like a rough chalice. He had deep-set fox-colored eyes
shadowed under a grey felt hat that he wore slanted forward
following the line of his nose. His build was insignificant.

"Mr. Greenleaf," she said, "get that bull up this morning before you do anything else. You know he'll ruin the breeding schedule. Get him up and keep him up and the next time there's a stray bull on this place, tell me at once. Do you understand?"

"Where you want him put at?" Mr. Greenleaf asked.

"I don't care where you put him," she said. "You are supposed to have some sense. Put him where he can't get out. Whose bull is he?"

For a moment Mr. Greenleaf seemed to hesitate between silence and speech. He studied the air to the left of him. "He must be somebody's bull," he said after a while.

"Yes, he must!" she said and shut the door with a precise little slam.

She went into the dining room where the two boys were eating breakfast and sat down on the edge of her chair at the head of the table. She never ate breakfast but she sat with them to see that they had what they wanted. "Honestly!" she said, and began to tell about the bull, aping Mr. Greenleaf saying, "It must be *somebody's* bull."

Wesley continued to read the newspaper folded beside his plate but Scofield interrupted his eating from time to time to look at her and laugh. The two boys never had the same reaction to anything. They were as different, she said, as night and day. The only thing they did have in common was that neither of them cared what happened on the place. Scofield was a business type and Wesley was an intellectual.

Wesley, the younger child, had had rheumatic fever when he was seven and Mrs. May thought that this was what had caused him to be an intellectual. Scofield, who had never had a day's sickness in his life, was an insurance salesman. She would not have minded his selling insurance if he had sold a nicer kind but he sold the kind that only Negroes buy. He was what Negroes call a "policy man." He said there was more money in nigger-insurance than any other kind, and before company, he was very loud about it. He would shout, "Mamma don't like to hear me say it but I'm the best nigger-insurance salesman in this county!"

Scofield was thirty-six and he had a broad pleasant smiling face but he was not married. "Yes," Mrs. May would say, "and if you sold decent insurance, some *nice* girl would be willing to marry you. What nice girl wants to marry a nigger-insurance man? You'll wake up some day and it'll be too late."

And at this Scofield would yodel and say, "Why Mamma, I'm not going to marry until you're dead and gone and then I'm going to marry me some nice fat farm girl that can take over this place!" And once he had added, "—some nice lady like Mrs. Greenleaf." When he had said this, Mrs. May had risen from her chair, her back stiff as a rake handle, and had gone to her room. There she had sat down on the edge of her bed for some time with her small face drawn. Finally she had whispered, "I work and slave, I struggle and sweat to keep this place for them and soon as I'm dead, they'll marry trash and bring it in here and ruin everything. They'll marry trash and ruin everything I've done," and she had made up her mind at that moment to change her will. The next day she had gone to her lawyer and had had the property entailed so that if they married, they could not leave it to their wives.

The idea that one of them might marry a woman even remotely like Mrs. Greenleaf was enough to make her ill. She had put up with Mr. Greenleaf for fifteen years, but the only way she had endured his wife had been by keeping entirely out of her sight. Mrs. Greenleaf was large and loose. The yard around her house looked like a dump and her five girls were always filthy; even the youngest one dipped snuff. Instead of making a garden or washing their clothes, her preoccupation was what she called "prayer healing."

Every day she cut all the morbid stories out of the newspaper—the accounts of women who had been raped and criminals who had escaped and children who had been burned and of train wrecks and plane crashes and the divorces of movie stars. She took these to the woods and dug a hole and buried them and then she fell on the ground over them and mumbled and groaned for an hour or so, moving her huge arms back and forth under her and out again and finally just lying down flat and, Mrs. May suspected, going to sleep in the dirt.

She had not found out about this until the Greenleafs had been with her a few months. One morning she had been out to inspect a field that she had wanted planted in rye but that had come up in clover because Mr. Greenleaf had used the wrong seeds in the grain drill. She was returning through a wooded path that separated two pastures, muttering to herself and hitting the ground methodically with a long stick she carried in case she saw a snake. "Mr. Greenleaf," she was saying in a low voice, "I cannot afford to pay for your mistakes. I am a poor woman and this place is all I have. I have two boys to educate. I cannot . . . ."

Out of nowhere a guttural agonized voice groaned, "Jesus! Jesus!" In a second it came again with a terrible urgency. "Jesus! Jesus!"

Mrs. May stopped still, one hand lifted to her throat. The sound was so piercing that she felt as if some violent unleashed force had broken out of the ground and was charging toward her. Her second thought was more reasonable: somebody had been hurt on the place and would sue her for everything she had. She had no insurance. She rushed forward and turning a bend in the path, she saw Mrs. Greenleaf sprawled on her hands and knees off the side of the road, her head down.

"Mrs. Greenleaf!" she shrilled, "what's happened?"

Mrs. Greenleaf raised her head. Her face was a patchwork of dirt and tears and her small eyes, the color of two field peas, were red-rimmed and swollen, but her expression was as composed as a bulldog's. She swayed back and forth on her hands and knees and groaned. "Jesus, Jesus."

Mrs. May winced. She thought the word, Jesus, should be kept inside the church building like other words inside the bedroom. She was a good Christian woman with a large respect for religion, though she did not, of course, believe any of it was true. "What is the matter with you?" she asked sharply.

"You broken my healing," Mrs. Greenleaf said, waving her aside. "I can't talk to you until I finish."

Mrs. May stood, bent forward, her mouth open and her stick raised off the ground as if she were not sure what she wanted to strike with it.

"Oh Jesus, stab me in the heart!" Mrs. Greenleaf shrieked. "Jesus, stab me in the heart!" and she fell back flat in the dirt, a huge human mound, her legs and arms spread out as if she were trying to wrap them around the earth.

Mrs. May felt as furious and helpless as if she had been insulted by a child. "Jesus," she said, drawing herself back, "would be *ashamed* of you. He would tell you to get up from there this instant and go wash your children's clothes!" and she had turned and walked off as fast as she could.

Whenever she thought of how the Greenleaf boys had advanced in the world, she had only to think of Mrs. Greenleaf sprawled obscenely on the ground, and say to herself, "Well, no matter how far they *go*, they *came* from that."

She would like to have been able to put in her will that when she died, Wesley and Scofield were not to continue to employ Mr. Greenleaf. She was capable of handling Mr. Greenleaf; they were not. Mr. Greenleaf had pointed out to her once that her boys didn't know hay from silage. She had pointed out to him that they had other talents, that Scofield was a successful business man and Wesley a successful intellectual. Mr. Greenleaf did not comment, but he never lost an opportunity of letting her see, by his expression or some simple gesture, that he held the two of them in infinite contempt. As scrub-human as the Greenleafs were, he never hesitated to let her know that in any like circumstance in which his own boys might have been involved, they—O. T. and E. T. Greenleaf—would have acted to better advantage.

The Greenleaf boys were two or three years younger than the May boys. They were twins and you never knew when you spoke to one of them whether you were speaking to O. T. or E. T., and they never had the politeness to enlighten you. They were long-legged and raw-boned and red-skinned, with bright grasping fox-colored eyes like their father's. Mr. Greenleaf's pride in them began with the fact that they were twins. He acted, Mrs. May said, as if this were something smart they had thought of themselves. They were energetic and hard-working and she would admit to anyone that they had come a long way—and that the Second World War was responsible for it.

They had both joined the service and, disguised in their uniforms, they could not be told from other people's children.

You could tell, of course, when they opened their mouths but they did that seldom. The smartest thing they had done was to get sent overseas and there to marry French wives. They hadn't married French trash either. They had married nice girls who naturally couldn't tell that they murdered the king's English or that the Greenleafs were who they were.

Wesley's heart condition had not permitted him to serve his country but Scofield had been in the army for two years. He had not cared for it and at the end of his military service, he was only a Private First Class. The Greenleaf boys were both some kind of sergeants, and Mr. Greenleaf, in those days, had never lost an opportunity of referring to them by their rank. They had both managed to get wounded and now they both had pensions. Further, as soon as they were released from the army, they took advantage of all the benefits and went to the school of agriculture at the university—the taxpayers meanwhile supporting their French wives. The two of them were living now about two miles down the highway on a piece of land that the government had helped them to buy and in a brick duplex bungalow that the government had helped to build and pay for. If the war had made anyone, Mrs. May said, it had made the Greenleaf boys. They each had three little children apiece, who spoke Greenleaf English and French, and who, on account of their mothers' background, would be sent to the convent school and brought up with manners. "And in twenty years," Mrs. May asked Scofield and Wesley, "do you know what those people will be?

"Society," she said blackly.

She had spent fifteen years coping with Mr. Greenleaf and, by now, handling him had become second nature with her. His disposition on any particular day was as much a factor in what she could and couldn't do as the weather was, and she had learned to read his face the way real country people read the sunrise and sunset.

She was a country woman only by persuasion. The late Mr. May, a business man, had bought the place when land was down, and when he died it was all he had to leave her. The boys had not been happy to move to the country to a broken-down farm, but there was nothing else for her to do. She had the timber on the place cut and with the proceeds had set herself up in the dairy business after Mr. Greenleaf had an-swered her ad. "i seen yor add and i will come have 2 boys," was all his letter said, but he arrived the next day in a pieced-together truck, his wife and five daughters sitting on the floor in back, himself and the two boys in the cab.

Over the years they had been on her place, Mr. and Mrs. Greenleaf had aged hardly at all. They had no worries, no responsibilities. They lived like the lilies of the field, off the fat that she struggled to put into the land. When she was dead and gone from overwork and worry, the Greenleafs, healthy and thriving, would be just ready to begin draining Scofield and Wesley.

Wesley said the reason Mrs. Greenleaf had not aged was because she released all her emotions in prayer healing. "You ought to start praying, Sweetheart," he had said in the voice that, poor boy, he could not help making deliberately nasty.

Scofield only exasperated her beyond endurance but Wesley caused her real anxiety. He was thin and nervous and bald and being an intellectual was a terrible strain on his disposi-tion. She doubted if he would marry until she died but she was certain that then the wrong woman would get him. Nice girls didn't like Scofield but Wesley didn't like nice girls. He didn't like anything. He drove twenty miles every day to the university where he taught and twenty miles back every night, but he said he hated the twenty-mile drive and he hated the second-rate university and he hated the morons who attended it. He hated the country and he hated the life he lived; he hated living with his mother and his idiot brother and he hated hearing about the damn dairy and the damn help and the damn broken machinery. But in spite of all he said, he never made any move to leave. He talked about Paris and Rome but he never went even to Atlanta.

"You'd go to those places and you'd get sick," Mrs. May would say. "Who in Paris is going to see that you get a salt-free diet? And do you think if you married one of those odd numbers you take out that *she* would cook a salt-free diet for you? No indeed, she would not!" When she took this line, Wesley would turn himself roughly around in his chair and ignore her. Once when she had kept it up too long, he had snarled, "Well, why don't you do something practical,

Woman? Why don't you pray for me like Mrs. Greenleaf would?"

"I don't like to hear you boys make jokes about religion," she had said. "If you would go to church, you would meet some nice girls."

But it was impossible to tell them anything. When she looked at the two of them now, sitting on either side of the table, neither one caring the least if a stray bull ruined her herd—which was their herd, their future—when she looked at the two of them, one hunched over a paper and the other teetering back in his chair, grinning at her like an idiot, she wanted to jump up and beat her fist on the table and shout, "You'll find out one of these days, you'll find out what *Reality* is when it's too late!"

"Mamma," Scofield said, "don't you get excited now but I'll tell you whose bull that is." He was looking at her wickedly. He let his chair drop forward and he got up. Then with his shoulders bent and his hands held up to cover his head, he tiptoed to the door. He backed into the hall and pulled the door almost to so that it hid all of him but his face. "You want to know, Sugarpie?" he asked.

Mrs. May sat looking at him coldly.

"That's O. T. and E. T.'s bull," he said. "I collected from their nigger yesterday and he told me they were missing it," and he showed her an exaggerated expanse of teeth and disappeared silently.

Wesley looked up and laughed.

Mrs. May turned her head forward again, her expression unaltered. "I am the only *adult* on this place," she said. She leaned across the table and pulled the paper from the side of his plate. "Do you see how it's going to be when I die and you boys have to handle him?" she began. "Do you see why he didn't know whose bull that was? Because it was theirs. Do you see what I have to put up with? Do you see that if I hadn't kept my foot on his neck all these years, you boys might be milking cows every morning at four o'clock?"

Wesley pulled the paper back toward his plate and staring at her full in the face, he murmured, "I wouldn't milk a cow to save your soul from hell."

"I know you wouldn't," she said in a brittle voice. She sat

back and began rapidly turning her knife over at the side of
her plate. "O. T. and E. T. are fine boys," she said. "They
ought to have been my sons." The thought of this was so
horrible that her vision of Wesley was blurred at once by a
wall of tears. All she saw was his dark shape, rising quickly
from the table. "And you two," she cried, "you two should
have belonged to that woman!"

He was heading for the door.

"When I die," she said in a thin voice, "I don't know
what's going to become of you."

"You're always yapping about when-you-die," he growled
as he rushed out, "but you look pretty healthy to me."

For some time she sat where she was, looking straight
ahead through the window across the room into a scene of
indistinct greys and greens. She stretched her face and her
neck muscles and drew in a long breath but the scene in front
of her flowed together anyway into a watery grey mass.
"They needn't think I'm going to die any time soon," she
muttered, and some more defiant voice in her added: I'll die
when I get good and ready.

She wiped her eyes with the table napkin and got up and
went to the window and gazed at the scene in front of her.
The cows were grazing on two pale green pastures across the
road and behind them, fencing them in, was a black wall of
trees with a sharp sawtooth edge that held off the indifferent
sky. The pastures were enough to calm her. When she looked
out any window in her house, she saw the reflection of her
own character. Her city friends said she was the most remarkable woman they knew, to go, practically penniless and with
no experience, out to a rundown farm and make a success of
it. "Everything is against you," she would say, "the weather
is against you and the dirt is against you and the help is
against you. They're all in league against you. There's nothing
for it but an iron hand!"

"Look at Mamma's iron hand!" Scofield would yell and
grab her arm and hold it up so that her delicate blue-veined
little hand would dangle from her wrist like the head of a
broken lily. The company always laughed.

The sun, moving over the black and white grazing cows,
was just a little brighter than the rest of the sky. Looking

down, she saw a darker shape that might have been its shadow cast at an angle, moving among them. She uttered a sharp cry and turned and marched out of the house.

Mr. Greenleaf was in the trench silo, filling a wheelbarrow. She stood on the edge and looked down at him. "I told you to get up that bull. Now he's in with the milk herd."

"You can't do two thangs at oncet," Mr. Greenleaf remarked.

"I told you to do that first."

He wheeled the barrow out of the open end of the trench toward the barn and she followed close behind him. "And you needn't think, Mr. Greenleaf," she said, "that I don't know exactly whose bull that is or why you haven't been in any hurry to notify me he was here. I might as well feed O. T. and E. T.'s bull as long as I'm going to have him here ruining my herd."

Mr. Greenleaf paused with the wheelbarrow and looked behind him. "Is that them boys' bull?" he asked in an incredulous tone.

She did not say a word. She merely looked away with her mouth taut.

"They told me their bull was out but I never known that was him," he said.

"I want that bull put up now," she said, "and I'm going to drive over to O. T. and E. T.'s and tell them they'll have to come get him today. I ought to charge for the time he's been here—then it wouldn't happen again."

"They didn't pay but seventy-five dollars for him," Mr. Greenleaf offered.

"I wouldn't have had him as a gift," she said.

"They was just going to beef him," Mr. Greenleaf went on, "but he got loose and run his head into their pickup truck. He don't like cars and trucks. They had a time getting his horn out the fender and when they finally got him loose, he took off and they was too tired to run after him—but I never known that was him there."

"It wouldn't have paid you to know, Mr. Greenleaf," she said. "But you know now. Get a horse and get him."

In a half hour, from her front window she saw the bull, squirrel-colored, with jutting hips and long light horns, ambling down the dirt road that ran in front of the house. Mr. Greenleaf was behind him on the horse. "That's a Greenleaf bull if I ever saw one," she muttered. She went out on the porch and called, "Put him where he can't get out."

"He likes to bust loose," Mr. Greenleaf said, looking with approval at the bull's rump. "This gentleman is a sport."

"If those boys don't come for him, he's going to be a dead sport," she said. "I'm just warning you."

He heard her but he didn't answer.

"That's the awfullest looking bull I ever saw," she called but he was too far down the road to hear.

It was mid-morning when she turned into O. T. and E. T.'s driveway. The house, a new red-brick, low-to-the-ground building that looked like a warehouse with windows, was on top of a treeless hill. The sun was beating down directly on the white roof of it. It was the kind of house that everybody built now and nothing marked it as belonging to the Greenleafs except three dogs, part hound and part spitz, that rushed out from behind it as soon as she stopped her car. She reminded herself that you could always tell the class of people by the class of dog, and honked her horn. While she sat waiting for someone to come, she continued to study the house. All the windows were down and she wondered if the government could have air-conditioned the thing. No one came and she honked again. Presently a door opened and several children appeared in it and stood looking at her, making no move to come forward. She recognized this as a true Greenleaf trait—they could hang in a door, looking at you for hours.

"Can't one of you children come here?" she called.

After a minute they all began to move forward, slowly. They had on overalls and were barefooted but they were not as dirty as she might have expected. There were two or three that looked distinctly like Greenleafs; the others not so much so. The smallest child was a girl with untidy black hair. They stopped about six feet from the automobile and stood looking at her.

"You're mighty pretty," Mrs. May said, addressing herself to the smallest girl.

There was no answer. They appeared to share one dispassionate expression between them.

"Where's your Mamma?" she asked.

There was no answer to this for some time. Then one of them said something in French. Mrs. May did not speak French.

"Where's your daddy?" she asked.

After a while, one of the boys said, "He ain't hyar neither."

"Ahhhh," Mrs. May said as if something had been proven. "Where's the colored man?"

She waited and decided no one was going to answer. "The cat has six little tongues," she said. "How would you like to come home with me and let me teach you how to talk?" She laughed and her laugh died on the silent air. She felt as if she were on trial for her life, facing a jury of Greenleafs. "I'll go down and see if I can find the colored man," she said.

"You can go if you want to," one of the boys said.

"Well, thank you," she murmured and drove off.

The barn was down the lane from the house. She had not seen it before but Mr. Greenleaf had described it in detail for it had been built according to the latest specifications. It was a milking parlor arrangement where the cows are milked from below. The milk ran in pipes from the machines to the milk house and was never carried in no bucket, Mr. Greenleaf said, by no human hand. "When you gonter get you one?" he had asked.

"Mr. Greenleaf," she had said, "I have to do for myself. I am not assisted hand and foot by the government. It would cost me $20,000 to install a milking parlor. I barely make ends meet as it is."

"My boys done it," Mr. Greenleaf had murmured, and then—"but all boys ain't alike."

"No indeed!" she had said. "I thank God for that!"

"I thank Gawd for ever-thang," Mr. Greenleaf had drawled.

You might as well, she had thought in the fierce silence that followed; you've never done anything for yourself.

She stopped by the side of the barn and honked but no one appeared. For several minutes she sat in the car, observing the various machines parked around, wondering how many of them were paid for. They had a forage harvester and a rotary hay baler. She had those too. She decided that since no one was here, she would get out and have a look at the milking parlor and see if they kept it clean.

She opened the milking room door and stuck her head in and for the first second she felt as if she were going to lose her breath. The spotless white concrete room was filled with sunlight that came from a row of windows head-high along both walls. The metal stanchions gleamed ferociously and she had to squint to be able to look at all. She drew her head out the room quickly and closed the door and leaned against it, frowning. The light outside was not so bright but she was conscious that the sun was directly on top of her head, like a silver bullet ready to drop into her brain.

A Negro carrying a yellow calf-feed bucket appeared from around the corner of the machine shed and came toward her. He was a light yellow boy dressed in the cast-off army clothes of the Greenleaf twins. He stopped at a respectable distance and set the bucket on the ground.

"Where's Mr. O. T. and Mr. E. T.?" she asked.

"Mist O. T. he in town, Mist E. T. he off yonder in the field," the Negro said, pointing first to the left and then to the right as if he were naming the position of two planets.

"Can you remember a message?" she asked, looking as if she thought this doubtful.

"I'll remember it if I don't forget it," he said with a touch of sullenness.

"Well, I'll write it down then," she said. She got in her car and took a stub of pencil from her pocket book and began to write on the back of an empty envelope. The Negro came and stood at the window. "I'm Mrs. May," she said as she wrote. "Their bull is on my place and I want him off *today*. You can tell them I'm furious about it."

"That bull lef here Sareday," the Negro said, "and none of us ain't seen him since. We ain't knowed where he was."

"Well, you know now," she said, "and you can tell Mr. O. T. and Mr. E. T. that if they don't come get him today, I'm going to have their daddy shoot him the first thing in the morning. I can't have that bull ruining my herd." She handed him the note.

"If I knows Mist O. T. and Mist E. T.," he said, taking it, "they goin to say you go ahead on and shoot him. He done busted up one of our trucks already and we be glad to see the last of him."

She pulled her head back and gave him a look from slightly bleared eyes. "Do they expect me to take my time and my worker to shoot their bull?" she asked. "They don't want him so they just let him loose and expect somebody else to kill him? He's eating my oats and ruining my herd and I'm expected to shoot him too?"

"I speck you is," he said softly. "He done busted up . . ."

She gave him a very sharp look and said, "Well, I'm not surprised. That's just the way some people are," and after a second she asked, "Which is boss, Mr. O. T. or Mr. E. T.?" She had always suspected that they fought between themselves secretly.

"They never quarls," the boy said. "They like one man in two skins."

"Hmp. I expect you just never heard them quarrel."

"Nor nobody else heard them neither," he said, looking away as if this insolence were addressed to some one else.

"Well," she said, "I haven't put up with their father for fifteen years not to know a few things about Greenleafs."

The Negro looked at her suddenly with a gleam of recognition. "Is you my policy man's mother?" he asked.

"I don't know who your policy man is," she said sharply. "You give them that note and tell them if they don't come for that bull today, they'll be making their father shoot it tomorrow," and she drove off.

She stayed at home all afternoon waiting for the Greenleaf twins to come for the bull. They did not come. I might as well be working for them, she thought furiously. They are simply going to use me to the limit. At the supper table, she went over it again for the boys' benefit because she wanted them to see exactly what O. T. and E. T. would do. "They don't want that bull," she said, "—pass the butter—so they simply turn him loose and let somebody else worry about getting rid of him for them. How do you like that? I'm the victim. I've always been the victim."

"Pass the butter to the victim," Wesley said. He was in a worse humor than usual because he had had a flat tire on the way home from the university.

Scofield handed her the butter and said, "Why Mamma, ain't you ashamed to shoot an old bull that ain't done nothing but give you a little scrub strain in your herd? I declare," he said, "with the Mamma I got it's a wonder I turned out to be such a nice boy!"

"You ain't her boy, Son," Wesley said.

She eased back in her chair, her fingertips on the edge of the table.

"All I know is," Scofield said, "I done mighty well to be as nice as I am seeing what I come from."

When they teased her they spoke Greenleaf English but Wesley made his own particular tone come through it like a knife edge. "Well lemme tell you one thang, Brother," he said, leaning over the table, "that if you had half a mind you would already know."

"What's that, Brother?" Scofield asked, his broad face grinning into the thin constricted one across from him.

"That is," Wesley said, "that neither you nor me is her boy . . . ," but he stopped abruptly as she gave a kind of hoarse wheeze like an old horse lashed unexpectedly. She reared up and ran from the room.

"Oh, for God's sake," Wesley growled. "What did you start her off for?"

"I never started her off," Scofield said. "You started her off."

"Hah."

"She's not as young as she used to be and she can't take it."

"She can only give it out," Wesley said. "I'm the one that takes it."

His brother's pleasant face had changed so that an ugly family resemblance showed between them. "Nobody feels sorry for a lousy bastard like you," he said and grabbed across the table for the other's shirtfront.

From her room she heard a crash of dishes and she rushed back through the kitchen into the dining room. The hall door was open and Scofield was going out of it. Wesley was lying like a large bug on his back with the edge of the over-turned table cutting him across the middle and broken dishes scattered on top of him. She pulled the table off him and caught his arm to help him rise but he scrambled up and pushed her off with a furious charge of energy and flung himself out of the door after his brother.

She would have collapsed but a knock on the back door stiffened her and she swung around. Across the kitchen and back porch, she could see Mr. Greenleaf peering eagerly through the screenwire. All her resources returned in full strength as if she had only needed to be challenged by the devil himself to regain them. "I heard a thump," he called, "and I thought the plastering might have fell on you."

If he had been wanted someone would have had to go on a horse to find him. She crossed the kitchen and the porch and stood inside the screen and said, "No, nothing happened but the table turned over. One of the legs was weak," and without pausing, "the boys didn't come for the bull so tomorrow you'll have to shoot him."

The sky was crossed with thin red and purple bars and behind them the sun was moving down slowly as if it were descending a ladder. Mr. Greenleaf squatted down on the step, his back to her, the top of his hat on a level with her feet. "Tomorrow I'll drive him home for you," he said.

"Oh no, Mr. Greenleaf," she said in a mocking voice, "you drive him home tomorrow and next week he'll be back here. I know better than that." Then in a mournful tone, she said, "I'm surprised at O. T. and E. T. to treat me this way. I thought they'd have more gratitude. Those boys spent some mighty happy days on this place, didn't they, Mr. Greenleaf?"

Mr. Greenleaf didn't say anything.

"I think they did," she said. "I think they did. But they've forgotten all the nice little things I did for them now. If I recall, they wore my boys' old clothes and played with my boys' old toys and hunted with my boys' old guns. They swam in my pond and shot my birds and fished in my stream and I never forgot their birthday and Christmas seemed to roll around very often if I remember it right. And do they think of any of those things now?" she asked. "NOOOOO," she said.

For a few seconds she looked at the disappearing sun and Mr. Greenleaf examined the palms of his hands. Presently as if it had just occurred to her, she asked, "Do you know the real reason they didn't come for that bull?"

"Naw I don't," Mr. Greenleaf said in a surly voice.

"They didn't come because I'm a woman," she said. "You can get away with anything when you're dealing with a woman. If there were a man running this place . . ."

Quick as a snake striking Mr. Greenleaf said, "You got two boys. They know you got two men on the place."

The sun had disappeared behind the tree line. She looked down at the dark crafty face, upturned now, and at the wary eyes, bright under the shadow of the hatbrim. She waited long enough for him to see that she was hurt and then she said, "Some people learn gratitude too late, Mr. Greenleaf, and some never learn it at all," and she turned and left him sitting on the steps.

Half the night in her sleep she heard a sound as if some large stone were grinding a hole on the outside wall of her brain. She was walking on the inside, over a succession of beautiful rolling hills, planting her stick in front of each step. She became aware after a time that the noise was the sun trying to burn through the tree line and she stopped to watch, safe in the knowledge that it couldn't, that it had to sink the way it always did outside of her property. When she first stopped it was a swollen red ball, but as she stood watching it began to narrow and pale until it looked like a bullet. Then suddenly it burst through the tree line and raced down the hill toward her. She woke up with her hand over her mouth and the same noise, diminished but distinct, in her ear. It was the bull munching under her window. Mr. Greenleaf had let him out.

She got up and made her way to the window in the dark and looked out through the slit blind, but the bull had moved away from the hedge and at first she didn't see him. Then she saw a heavy form some distance away, paused as if observing her. This is the last night I am going to put up with this, she said, and watched until the iron shadow moved away in the darkness.

The next morning she waited until exactly eleven o'clock. Then she got in her car and drove to the barn. Mr. Greenleaf was cleaning milk cans. He had seven of them standing up outside the milk room to get the sun. She had been telling him to do this for two weeks. "All right, Mr. Greenleaf," she said, "go get your gun. We're going to shoot that bull."

"I thought you wanted theseyer cans . . ."

"Go get your gun, Mr. Greenleaf," she said. Her voice and face were expressionless.

"That gentleman torn out of there last night," he murmured in a tone of regret and bent again to the can he had his arm in.

"Go get your gun, Mr. Greenleaf," she said in the same triumphant toneless voice. "The bull is in the pasture with the dry cows. I saw him from my upstairs window. I'm going to drive you up to the field and you can run him into the empty pasture and shoot him there."

He detached himself from the can slowly. "Ain't nobody ever ast me to shoot my boys' own bull!" he said in a high rasping voice. He removed a rag from his back pocket and began to wipe his hands violently, then his nose.

She turned as if she had not heard this and said, "I'll wait for you in the car. Go get your gun."

She sat in the car and watched him stalk off toward the harness room where he kept a gun. After he had entered the room, there was a crash as if he had kicked something out of his way. Presently he emerged again with the gun, circled behind the car, opened the door violently and threw himself onto the seat beside her. He held the gun between his knees and looked straight ahead. He'd like to shoot me instead of the bull, she thought, and turned her face away so that he could not see her smile.

The morning was dry and clear. She drove through the woods for a quarter of a mile and then out into the open where there were fields on either side of the narrow road. The exhilaration of carrying her point had sharpened her senses. Birds were screaming everywhere, the grass was almost too bright to look at, the sky was an even piercing blue. "Spring is here!" she said gaily. Mr. Greenleaf lifted one muscle somewhere near his mouth as if he found this the most asinine remark ever made. When she stopped at the second pasture gate, he flung himself out of the car door and slammed it behind him. Then he opened the gate and she drove through. He closed it and flung himself back in, silently, and she drove around the rim of the pasture until she spotted the bull, almost in the center of it, grazing peacefully among the cows.

"The gentleman is waiting on you," she said and gave Mr. Greenleaf's furious profile a sly look. "Run him into that next pasture and when you get him in, I'll drive in behind you and shut the gate myself."

He flung himself out again, this time deliberately leaving the car door open so that she had to lean across the seat and close it. She sat smiling as she watched him make his way across the pasture toward the opposite gate. He seemed to throw himself forward at each step and then pull back as if he were calling on some power to witness that he was being forced. "Well," she said aloud as if he were still in the car, "it's your own boys who are making you do this, Mr. Greenleaf." O. T. and E. T. were probably splitting their sides laughing at him now. She could hear their identical nasal voices saying, "Made Daddy shoot our bull for us. Daddy don't know no better than to think that's a fine bull he's shooting. Gonna kill Daddy to shoot that bull!"

"If those boys cared a thing about you, Mr. Greenleaf," she said, "they would have come for that bull. I'm surprised at them."

He was circling around to open the gate first. The bull, dark among the spotted cows, had not moved. He kept his head down, eating constantly. Mr. Greenleaf opened the gate and then began circling back to approach him from the rear. When he was about ten feet behind him, he flapped his arms at his sides. The bull lifted his head indolently and then lowered it again and continued to eat. Mr. Greenleaf stooped again and picked up something and threw it at him with a vicious swing. She decided it was a sharp rock for the bull leapt and then began to gallop until he disappeared over the rim of the hill. Mr. Greenleaf followed at his leisure.

"You needn't think you're going to lose him!" she cried and started the car straight across the pasture. She had to drive slowly over the terraces and when she reached the gate, Mr. Greenleaf and the bull were nowhere in sight. This pasture was smaller than the last, a green arena, encircled almost entirely by woods. She got out and closed the gate and stood looking for some sign of Mr. Greenleaf but he had disappeared completely. She knew at once that his plan was to lose the bull in the woods. Eventually, she would see him emerge somewhere from the circle of trees and come limping toward her and when he finally reached her, he would say, "If you can find that gentleman in them woods, you're better than me."

She was going to say, "Mr. Greenleaf, if I have to walk into those woods with you and stay all afternoon, we are going to find that bull and shoot him. You are going to shoot him if I have to pull the trigger for you." When he saw she meant business he would return and shoot the bull quickly himself.

She got back into the car and drove to the center of the pasture where he would not have so far to walk to reach her when he came out of the woods. At this moment she could picture him sitting on a stump, marking lines in the ground with a stick. She decided she would wait exactly ten minutes by her watch. Then she would begin to honk. She got out of the car and walked around a little and then sat down on the front bumper to wait and rest. She was very tired and she lay her head back against the hood and closed her eyes. She did not understand why she should be so tired when it was only mid-morning. Through her closed eyes, she could feel the sun, red-hot overhead. She opened her eyes slightly but the white light forced her to close them again.

For some time she lay back against the hood, wondering drowsily why she was so tired. With her eyes closed, she didn't think of time as divided into days and nights but into past and future. She decided she was tired because she had been working continuously for fifteen years. She decided she had every right to be tired, and to rest for a few minutes before she began working again. Before any kind of judgement seat, she would be able to say: I've worked, I have not wallowed. At this very instant while she was recalling a lifetime of work, Mr. Greenleaf was loitering in the woods and Mrs. Greenleaf was probably flat on the ground, asleep over her holeful of clippings. The woman had got worse over the years and Mrs. May believed that now she was actually demented. "I'm afraid your wife has let religion warp her," she said once tactfully to Mr. Greenleaf. "Everything in moderation, you know."

"She cured a man oncet that half his gut was eat out with worms," Mr. Greenleaf said, and she had turned away, half-sickened. Poor souls, she thought now, so simple. For a few seconds she dozed.

When she sat up and looked at her watch, more than ten minutes had passed. She had not heard any shot. A new thought occurred to her: suppose Mr. Greenleaf had aroused the bull chunking stones at him and the animal had turned on him and run him up against a tree and gored him? The irony of it deepened: O. T. and E. T. would then get a shyster lawyer and sue her. It would be the fitting end to her fifteen years with the Greenleafs. She thought of it almost with pleasure as if she had hit on the perfect ending for a story she was telling her friends. Then she dropped it, for Mr. Greenleaf had a gun with him and she had insurance.

She decided to honk. She got up and reached inside the car window and gave three sustained honks and two or three shorter ones to let him know she was getting impatient. Then she went back and sat down on the bumper again.

In a few minutes something emerged from the tree line, a black heavy shadow that tossed its head several times and then bounded forward. After a second she saw it was the bull. He was crossing the pasture toward her at a slow gallop, a gay almost rocking gait as if he were overjoyed to find her again. She looked beyond him to see if Mr. Greenleaf was coming out of the woods too but he was not. "Here he is, Mr. Greenleaf!" she called and looked on the other side of the pasture to see if he could be coming out there but he was not in sight. She looked back and saw that the bull, his head lowered, was racing toward her. She remained perfectly still, not in fright, but in a freezing unbelief. She stared at the violent black streak bounding toward her as if she had no sense of distance, as if she could not decide at once what his intention was, and the bull had buried his head in her lap, like a wild tormented lover, before her expression changed. One of his horns sank until it pierced her heart and the other curved around her side and held her in an unbreakable grip. She continued to stare straight ahead but the entire scene in front of her had changed—the tree line was a dark wound in a world that was nothing but sky—and she had the look of a person whose sight has been suddenly restored but who finds the light unbearable.

Mr. Greenleaf was running toward her from the side with his gun raised and she saw him coming though she was not looking in his direction. She saw him approaching on the outside of some invisible circle, the tree line gaping behind him and nothing under his feet. He shot the bull four times through the eye. She did not hear the shots but she felt the quake in the huge body as it sank, pulling her forward on its head, so that she seemed, when Mr. Greenleaf reached her, to be bent over whispering some last discovery into the animal's ear.

A View of the Woods

THE WEEK BEFORE, Mary Fortune and the old man had spent every morning watching the machine that lifted out dirt and threw it in a pile. The construction was going on by the new lakeside on one of the lots that the old man had sold to somebody who was going to put up a fishing club. He and Mary Fortune drove down there every morning about ten o'clock and he parked his car, a battered mulberry-colored Cadillac, on the embankment that overlooked the spot where the work was going on. The red corrugated lake eased up to within fifty feet of the construction and was bordered on the other side by a black line of woods which appeared at both ends of the view to walk across the water and continue along the edge of the fields.

He sat on the bumper and Mary Fortune straddled the hood and they watched, sometimes for hours, while the machine systematically ate a square red hole in what had once been a cow pasture. It happened to be the only pasture that Pitts had succeeded in getting the bitterweed off and when the old man had sold it, Pitts had nearly had a stroke; and as far as Mr. Fortune was concerned, he could have gone on and had it.

"Any fool that would let a cow pasture interfere with progress is not on my books," he had said to Mary Fortune several times from his seat on the bumper, but the child did not have eyes for anything but the machine. She sat on the hood, looking down into the red pit, watching the big disembodied gullet gorge itself on the clay, then, with the sound of a deep sustained nausea and a slow mechanical revulsion, turn and spit it up. Her pale eyes behind her spectacles followed the repeated motion of it again and again and her face—a small replica of the old man's—never lost its look of complete absorption.

No one was particularly glad that Mary Fortune looked like her grandfather except the old man himself. He thought it added greatly to her attractiveness. He thought she was the smartest and the prettiest child he had ever seen and he let the rest of them know that if, IF that was, he left anything to anybody, it would be Mary Fortune he left it to. She was now nine, short and broad like himself, with his very light blue eyes, his wide prominent forehead, his steady penetrating scowl and his rich florid complexion; but she was like him on the inside too. She had, to a singular degree, his intelligence, his strong will, and his push and drive. Though there was seventy years' difference in their ages, the spiritual distance between them was slight. She was the only member of the family he had any respect for.

He didn't have any use for her mother, his third or fourth daughter (he could never remember which), though she considered that she took care of him. She considered—being careful not to say it, only to look it—that she was the one putting up with him in his old age and that she was the one he should leave the place to. She had married an idiot named Pitts and had had seven children, all likewise idiots except the youngest, Mary Fortune, who was a throwback to him. Pitts was the kind who couldn't keep his hands on a nickel and Mr. Fortune had allowed them, ten years ago, to move onto his place and farm it. What Pitts made went to Pitts but the land belonged to Fortune and he was careful to keep the fact before them. When the well had gone dry, he had not allowed Pitts to have a deep well drilled but had insisted that they pipe their water from the spring. He did not intend to pay for a drilled well himself and he knew that if he let Pitts pay for it, whenever he had occasion to say to Pitts, "It's my land you're sitting on," Pitts would be able to say to him, "Well, it's my pump that's pumping the water you're drinking."

Being there ten years, the Pittses had got to feel as if they owned the place. The daughter had been born and raised on it but the old man considered that when she married Pitts she showed that she preferred Pitts to home; and when she came back, she came back like any other tenant, though he would not allow them to pay rent for the same reason he would not allow them to drill a well. Anyone over sixty years of age is in an uneasy position unless he controls the greater interest and every now and then he gave the Pittses a practical lesson by selling off a lot. Nothing infuriated Pitts more than to see him sell off a piece of the property to an outsider, because Pitts wanted to buy it himself.

Pitts was a thin, long-jawed, irascible, sullen, sulking individual and his wife was the duty-proud kind: It's my duty to stay here and take care of Papa. Who would do it if I didn't? I do it knowing full well I'll get no reward for it. I do it because it's my duty.

The old man was not taken in by this for a minute. He knew they were waiting impatiently for the day when they could put him in a hole eight feet deep and cover him up with dirt. Then, even if he did not leave the place to them, they figured they would be able to buy it. Secretly he had made his will and left everything in trust to Mary Fortune, naming his lawyer and not Pitts as executor. When he died Mary Fortune could make the rest of them jump; and he didn't doubt for a minute that she would be able to do it.

Ten years ago they had announced that they were going to name the new baby Mark Fortune Pitts, after him, if it were a boy, and he had not delayed in telling them that if they coupled his name with the name Pitts he would put them off the place. When the baby came, a girl, and he had seen that even at the age of one day she bore his unmistakable likeness, he had relented and suggested himself that they name her Mary Fortune, after his beloved mother, who had died seventy years ago, bringing him into the world.

The Fortune place was in the country on a clay road that left the paved road fifteen miles away and he would never have been able to sell off any lots if it had not been for progress, which had always been his ally. He was not one of these old people who fight improvement, who object to everything new and cringe at every change. He wanted to see a paved highway in front of his house with plenty of new-model cars on it, he wanted to see a supermarket store across the road from him, he wanted to see a gas station, a motel, a drive-in picture-show within easy distance. Progress had suddenly set all this in motion. The electric power company had built a dam on the river and flooded great areas of the surrounding country and the lake that resulted touched his land along a half-mile stretch. Every Tom, Dick and Harry, every dog and his brother, wanted a lot on the lake. There was talk of their getting a telephone line. There was talk of paving the road that ran in front of the Fortune place. There was talk of an eventual town. He thought this should be called Fortune, Georgia. He was a man of advanced vision, even if he was seventy-nine years old.

The machine that drew up the dirt had stopped the day before and today they were watching the hole being smoothed out by two huge yellow bulldozers. His property had amounted to eight hundred acres before he began selling lots. He had sold five twenty-acre lots on the back of the place and every time he sold one, Pitts's blood pressure had gone up twenty points. "The Pittses are the kind that would let a cow pasture interfere with the future," he said to Mary Fortune, "but not you and me." The fact that Mary Fortune was a Pitts too was something he ignored, in a gentlemanly fashion, as if it were an affliction the child was not responsible for. He liked to think of her as being thoroughly of his clay. He sat on the bumper and she sat on the hood with her bare feet on his shoulders. One of the bulldozers had moved under them to shave the side of the embankment they were parked on. If he had moved his feet a few inches out, the old man could have dangled them over the edge.

"If you don't watch him," Mary Fortune shouted above the noise of the machine, "he'll cut off some of your dirt!"

"Yonder's the stob," the old man yelled. "He hasn't gone beyond the stob."

"Not YET he hasn't," she roared.

The bulldozer passed beneath them and went on to the far side. "Well you watch," he said. "Keep your eyes open and if he knocks that stob, I'll stop him. The Pittses are the kind that would let a cow pasture or a mule lot or a row of beans interfere with progress," he continued. "The people like you and me with heads on their shoulders know you can't stop the marcher time for a cow. . . ."

"He's shaking the stob on the other side!" she screamed and before he could stop her, she had jumped down from the hood and was running along the edge of the embankment, her little yellow dress billowing out behind.

"Don't run so near the edge," he yelled but she had already reached the stob and was squatting down by it to see how much it had been shaken. She leaned over the embankment and shook her fist at the man on the bulldozer. He waved at her and went on about his business. More sense in her little finger than all the rest of that tribe in their heads put together, the old man said to himself, and watched with pride as she started back to him.

She had a head of thick, very fine, sand-colored hair—the exact kind he had had when he had had any—that grew straight and was cut just above her eyes and down the sides of her cheeks to the tips of her ears so that it formed a kind of door opening onto the central part of her face. Her glasses were silver-rimmed like his and she even walked the way he did, stomach forward, with a careful abrupt gait, something between a rock and a shuffle. She was walking so close to the edge of the embankment that the outside of her right foot was flush with it.

"I said don't walk so close to the edge," he called; "you fall off there and you won't live to see the day this place gets built up." He was always very careful to see that she avoided dangers. He would not allow her to sit in snakey places or put her hands on bushes that might hide hornets.

She didn't move an inch. She had a habit of his of not hearing what she didn't want to hear and since this was a little trick he had taught her himself, he had to admire the way she practiced it. He foresaw that in her own old age it would serve her well. She reached the car and climbed back onto the hood without a word and put her feet back on his shoulders where she had had them before, as if he were no more than a part of the automobile. Her attention returned to the far bulldozer.

"Remember what you won't get if you don't mind," her grandfather remarked.

He was a strict disciplinarian but he had never whipped her. There were some children, like the first six Pittses, whom he thought should be whipped once a week on principle, but there were other ways to control intelligent children and he had never laid a rough hand on Mary Fortune. Furthermore, he had never allowed her mother or her brothers and sisters so much as to slap her. The elder Pitts was a different matter.

He was a man of a nasty temper and of ugly unreasonable resentments. Time and again, Mr. Fortune's heart had pounded to see him rise slowly from his place at the table—

not the head, Mr. Fortune sat there, but from his place at the side—and abruptly, for no reason, with no explanation, jerk his head at Mary Fortune and say, "Come with me," and leave the room, unfastening his belt as he went. A look that was completely foreign to the child's face would appear on it. The old man could not define the look but it infuriated him. It was a look that was part terror and part respect and part something else, something very like cooperation. This look would appear on her face and she would get up and follow Pitts out. They would get in his truck and drive down the road out of earshot, where he would beat her.

Mr. Fortune knew for a fact that he beat her because he had followed them in his car and had seen it happen. He had watched from behind a boulder about a hundred feet away while the child clung to a pine tree and Pitts, as methodically as if he were whacking a bush with a sling blade, beat her around the ankles with his belt. All she had done was jump up and down as if she were standing on a hot stove and make a whimpering noise like a dog that was being peppered. Pitts had kept at it for about three minutes and then he had turned, without a word, and got back in his truck and left her there, and she had slid down under the tree and taken both feet in her hands and rocked back and forth. The old man had crept forward to catch her. Her face was contorted into a puzzle of small red lumps and her nose and eyes were running. He sprang on her and sputtered, "Why didn't you hit him back? Where's your spirit? Do you think I'd a let him beat me?"

She had jumped up and started backing away from him with her jaw stuck out. "Nobody beat me," she said.

"Didn't I see it with my own eyes?" he exploded.

"Nobody is here and nobody beat me," she said. "Nobody's ever beat me in my life and if anybody did, I'd kill him. You can see for yourself nobody is here."

"Do you call me a liar or a blindman!" he shouted. "I saw him with my own two eyes and you never did a thing but let him do it, you never did a thing but hang onto that tree and dance up and down a little and blubber and if it had been me, I'd a swung my fist in his face and . . ."

"Nobody was here and nobody beat me and if anybody did

I'd kill him!" she yelled and then turned and dashed off through the woods.

"And I'm a Poland china pig and black is white!" he had roared after her and he had sat down on a small rock under the tree, disgusted and furious. This was Pitts's revenge on him. It was as if it were *he* that Pitts was driving down the road to beat and it was as if *he* were the one submitting to it. He had thought at first that he could stop him by saying that if he beat her, he would put them off the place but when he had tried that, Pitts had said, "Put me off and you put her off too. Go right ahead. She's mine to whip and I'll whip her every day of the year if it suits me."

Any time he could make Pitts feel his hand he was determined to do it and at present he had a little scheme up his sleeve that was going to be a considerable blow to Pitts. He was thinking of it with relish when he told Mary Fortune to remember what she wouldn't get if she didn't mind, and he added, without waiting for an answer, that he might be selling another lot soon and that if he did, he might give her a bonus but not if she gave him any sass. He had frequent little verbal tilts with her but this was a sport like putting a mirror up in front of a rooster and watching him fight his reflection.

"I don't want no bonus," Mary Fortune said.

"I ain't ever seen you refuse one."

"You ain't ever seen me ask for one neither," she said.

"How much have you laid by?" he asked.

"Noner yer bidnis," she said and stamped his shoulders with her feet. "Don't be buttin into my bidnis."

"I bet you got it sewed up in your mattress," he said, "just like an old nigger woman. You ought to put it in the bank. I'm going to start you an account just as soon as I complete this deal. Won't anybody be able to check on it but me and you."

The bulldozer moved under them again and drowned out the rest of what he wanted to say. He waited and when the noise had passed, he could hold it in no longer. "I'm going to sell the lot right in front of the house for a gas station," he said. "Then we won't have to go down the road to get the car filled up, just step out the front door."

The Fortune house was set back about two hundred feet from the road and it was this two hundred feet that he intended to sell. It was the part that his daughter airily called "the lawn" though it was nothing but a field of weeds.

"You mean," Mary Fortune said after a minute, "the lawn?"

"Yes mam!" he said. "I mean the lawn," and he slapped his knee.

She did not say anything and he turned and looked up at her. There in the little rectangular opening of hair was his face looking back at him, but it was a reflection not of his present expression but of the darker one that indicated his displeasure. "That's where we play," she muttered.

"Well there's plenty of other places you can play," he said, irked by this lack of enthusiasm.

"We won't be able to see the woods across the road," she said.

The old man stared at her. "The woods across the road?" he repeated.

"We won't be able to see the view," she said.

"The view?" he repeated.

"The woods," she said; "we won't be able to see the woods from the porch."

"The woods from the porch?" he repeated.

Then she said, "My daddy grazes his calves on that lot."

The old man's wrath was delayed an instant by shock. Then it exploded in a roar. He jumped up and turned and slammed his fist on the hood of the car. "He can graze them somewheres else!"

"You fall off that embankment and you'll wish you hadn't," she said.

He moved from in front of the car around to the side, keeping his eyes on her all the time. "Do you think I care where he grazes his calves! Do you think I'll let a calf interfere with my bidnis? Do you think I give a damn hoot where that fool grazes his calves?"

She sat, her red face darker than her hair, exactly reflecting his expression now. "He who calls his brother a fool is subject to hell fire," she said.

"Jedge not," he shouted, "lest ye be not jedged!" The tinge of his face was a shade more purple than hers. "You!" he said. "You let him beat you any time he wants to and don't do a thing but blubber a little and jump up and down!"

"He nor nobody else has ever touched me," she said, measuring off each word in a deadly flat tone. "Nobody's ever put a hand on me and if anybody did, I'd kill him."

"And black is white," the old man piped, "and night is day!"

The bulldozer passed below them. With their faces about a foot apart, each held the same expression until the noise had receded. Then the old man said, "Walk home by yourself. I refuse to ride a Jezebel!"

"And I refuse to ride with the Whore of Babylon," she said and slid off the other side of the car and started off through the pasture.

"A whore is a woman!" he roared. "That's how much you know!" But she did not deign to turn around and answer him back, and as he watched the small robust figure stalk across the yellow-dotted field toward the woods, his pride in her, as if it couldn't help itself, returned like the gentle little tide on the new lake—all except that part of it that had to do with her refusal to stand up to Pitts; that pulled back like an undertow. If he could have taught her to stand up to Pitts the way she stood up to him, she would have been a perfect child, as fearless and sturdy-minded as anyone could want; but it was her one failure of character. It was the one point on which she did not resemble him. He turned and looked away over the lake to the woods across it and told himself that in five years, instead of woods, there would be houses and stores and parking places, and that the credit for it could go largely to him.

He meant to teach the child spirit by example and since he had definitely made up his mind, he announced that noon at the dinner table that he was negotiating with a man named Tilman to sell the lot in front of the house for a gas station.

His daughter, sitting with her worn-out air at the foot of the table, let out a moan as if a dull knife were being turned slowly in her chest. "You mean the lawn!" she moaned and fell back in her chair and repeated in an almost inaudible voice, "He means the lawn."

The other six Pitts children began to bawl and pipe, "Where we play!" "Don't let him do that, Pa!" "We won't be able to see the road!" and similar idiocies. Mary Fortune did not say anything. She had a mulish reserved look as if she were planning some business of her own. Pitts had stopped eating and was staring in front of him. His plate was full but his fists sat motionless like two dark quartz stones on either side of it. His eyes began to move from child to child around the table as if he were hunting for one particular one of them. Finally they stopped on Mary Fortune sitting next to her grandfather. "You done this to us," he muttered.

"I didn't," she said but there was no assurance in her voice. It was only a quaver, the voice of a frightened child.

Pitts got up and said, "Come with me," and turned and walked out, loosening his belt as he went, and to the old man's complete despair, she slid away from the table and followed him, almost ran after him, out the door and into the truck behind him, and they drove off.

This cowardice affected Mr. Fortune as if it were his own. It made him physically sick. "He beats an innocent child," he said to his daughter, who was apparently still prostrate at the end of the table, "and not one of you lifts a hand to stop him."

"You ain't lifted yours neither," one of the boys said in an undertone and there was a general mutter from that chorus of frogs.

"I'm an old man with a heart condition," he said. "I can't stop an ox."

"She put you up to it," his daughter murmured in a languid listless tone, her head rolling back and forth on the rim of her chair. "She puts you up to everything."

"No child never put me up to nothing!" he yelled. "You're no kind of a mother! You're a disgrace! That child is an angel! A saint!" he shouted in a voice so high that it broke and he had to scurry out of the room.

The rest of the afternoon he had to lie on his bed. His heart, whenever he knew the child had been beaten, felt as if it were slightly too large for the space that was supposed to hold it. But now he was more determined than ever to see the filling station go up in front of the house, and if it gave Pitts a stroke, so much the better. If it gave him a stroke and paralyzed him, he would be served right and he would never be able to beat her again.

Mary Fortune was never angry with him for long, or seriously, and though he did not see her the rest of that day, when he woke up the next morning, she was sitting astride his chest ordering him to make haste so that they would not miss the concrete mixer.

The workmen were laying the foundation for the fishing club when they arrived and the concrete mixer was already in operation. It was about the size and color of a circus elephant; they stood and watched it churn for a half-hour or so. At eleven-thirty, the old man had an appointment with Tilman to discuss his transaction and they had to leave. He did not tell Mary Fortune where they were going but only that he had to see a man.

Tilman operated a combination country store, filling station, scrap-metal dump, used-car lot and dance hall five miles down the highway that connected with the dirt road that passed in front of the Fortune place. Since the dirt road would soon be paved, he wanted a good location on it for another such enterprise. He was an up-and-coming man—the kind, Mr. Fortune thought, who was never just in line with progress but always a little ahead of it so that he could be there to meet it when it arrived. Signs up and down the highway announced that Tilman's was only five miles away, only four, only three, only two, only one; then "Watch out for Tilman's, Around this bend!" and finally, "Here it is, Friends, TILMAN's!" in dazzling red letters.

Tilman's was bordered on either side by a field of old used-car bodies, a kind of ward for incurable automobiles. He also sold outdoor ornaments, such as stone cranes and chickens, urns, jardinieres, whirligigs, and farther back from the road, so as not to depress his dance-hall customers, a line of tombstones and monuments. Most of his businesses went on out-of-doors, so that his store building itself had not involved excessive expense. It was a one-room wooden structure onto which he had added, behind, a long tin hall equipped for dancing. This was divided into two sections, Colored and White, each with its private nickelodeon. He had a barbecue pit and sold barbecued sandwiches and soft drinks.

As they drove up under the shed of Tilman's place, the old man glanced at the child sitting with her feet drawn up on the seat and her chin resting on her knees. He didn't know if she would remember that it was Tilman he was going to sell the lot to or not.

"What you going in here for?" she asked suddenly, with a sniffing look as if she scented an enemy.

"Noner yer bidnis," he said. "You just sit in the car and when I come out, I'll bring you something."

"Don'tcher bring me nothing," she said darkly, "because I won't be here."

"Haw!" he said. "Now you're here, it's nothing for you to do but wait," and he got out and without paying her any further attention, he entered the dark store where Tilman was waiting for him.

When he came out in half an hour, she was not in the car. Hiding, he decided. He started walking around the store to see if she was in the back. He looked in the doors of the two sections of the dance hall and walked on around by the tombstones. Then his eye roved over the field of sinking automobiles and he realized that she could be in or behind any one of two hundred of them. He came back out in front of the store. A Negro boy, drinking a purple drink, was sitting on the ground with his back against the sweating ice cooler.

"Where did that little girl go to, boy?" he asked.

"I ain't seen nair little girl," the boy said.

The old man irritably fished in his pocket and handed him a nickel and said, "A pretty little girl in a yeller cotton dress."

"If you speakin about a stout chile look lak you," the boy said, "she gone off in a truck with a white man."

"What kind of a truck, what kind of a white man?" he yelled.

"It were a green pick-up truck," the boy said smacking his lips, "and a white man she call 'daddy.' They gone thataway some time ago."

The old man, trembling, got in his car and started home. His feelings raced back and forth between fury and mortification. She had never left him before and certainly never for Pitts. Pitts had ordered her to get in the truck and she was afraid not to. But when he reached this conclusion he was more furious than ever. What was the matter with her that she couldn't stand up to Pitts? Why was there this one flaw in her character when he had trained her so well in everything else? It was an ugly mystery.

When he reached the house and climbed the front steps, there she was sitting in the swing, looking glum-faced in front of her across the field he was going to sell. Her eyes were puffy and pink-rimmed but he didn't see any red marks on her legs. He sat down in the swing beside her. He meant to make his voice severe but instead it came out crushed, as if it belonged to a suitor trying to reinstate himself.

"What did you leave me for? You ain't ever left me before," he said.

"Because I wanted to," she said, looking straight ahead.

"You never wanted to," he said. "He made you."

"I toljer I was going and I went," she said in a slow emphatic voice, not looking at him, "and now you can go on and lemme alone." There was something very final, in the sound of this, a tone that had not come up before in their disputes. She stared across the lot where there was nothing but a profusion of pink and yellow and purple weeds, and on across the red road, to the sullen line of black pine woods fringed on top with green. Behind that line was a narrow gray-blue line of more distant woods and beyond that nothing but the sky, entirely blank except for one or two threadbare clouds. She looked into this scene as if it were a person that she preferred to him.

"It's my lot, ain't it?" he asked. "Why are you so up-in-the-air about me selling my own lot?"

"Because it's the lawn," she said. Her nose and eyes began to run horribly but she held her face rigid and licked the water off as soon as it was in reach of her tongue. "We won't be able to see across the road," she said.

The old man looked across the road to assure himself again that there was nothing over there to see. "I never have seen you act in such a way before," he said in an incredulous voice. "There's not a thing over there but the woods."

"We won't be able to see 'um," she said, "and that's the *lawn* and my daddy grazes his calves on it."

At that the old man stood up. "You act more like a Pitts than a Fortune," he said. He had never made such an ugly remark to her before and he was sorry the instant he had said it. It hurt him more than it did her. He turned and went in the house and upstairs to his room.

*   *   *

Several times during the afternoon, he got up from his bed and looked out the window across the "lawn" to the line of woods she said they wouldn't be able to see any more. Every time he saw the same thing: woods—not a mountain, not a waterfall, not any kind of planted bush or flower, just woods. The sunlight was woven through them at that particular time of the afternoon so that every thin pine trunk stood out in all its nakedness. A pine trunk is a pine trunk, he said to himself, and anybody that wants to see one don't have to go far in this neighborhood. Every time he got up and looked out, he was reconvinced of his wisdom in selling the lot. The dissatisfaction it caused Pitts would be permanent, but he could make it up to Mary Fortune by buying her something. With grown people, a road led either to heaven or hell, but with children there were always stops along the way where their attention could be turned with a trifle.

The third time he got up to look at the woods, it was almost six o'clock and the gaunt trunks appeared to be raised in a pool of red light that gushed from the almost hidden sun setting behind them. The old man stared for some time, as if for a prolonged instant he were caught up out of the rattle of everything that led to the future and were held there in the midst of an uncomfortable mystery that he had not apprehended before. He saw it, in his hallucination, as if someone were wounded behind the woods and the trees were bathed in blood. After a few minutes this unpleasant vision was broken by the presence of Pitts's pick-up truck grinding to a halt below the window. He returned to his bed and shut his eyes and against the closed lids hellish red trunks rose up in a black wood.

At the supper table nobody addressed a word to him, including Mary Fortune. He ate quickly and returned again to his room and spent the evening pointing out to himself the advantages for the future of having an establishment like Tilman's so near. They would not have to go any distance for gas. Anytime they needed a loaf of bread, all they would have to do would be step out their front door into Tilman's back door. They could sell milk to Tilman. Tilman was a likable fellow. Tilman would draw other business. The road would soon be paved. Travelers from all over the country would stop at Tilman's. If his daughter thought she was better than Tilman, it would be well to take her down a little. All men were created free and equal. When this phrase sounded in his head, his patriotic sense triumphed and he realized that it was his duty to sell the lot, that he must insure the future. He looked out the window at the moon shining over the woods across the road and listened for a while to the hum of crickets and treefrogs, and beneath their racket, he could hear the throb of the future town of Fortune.

He went to bed certain that just as usual, he would wake up in the morning looking into a little red mirror framed in a door of fine hair. She would have forgotten all about the sale and after breakfast they would drive into town and get the legal papers from the courthouse. On the way back he would stop at Tilman's and close the deal.

When he opened his eyes in the morning, he opened them on the empty ceiling. He pulled himself up and looked around the room but she was not there. He hung over the edge of the bed and looked beneath it but she was not there either. He got up and dressed and went outside. She was sitting in the swing on the front porch, exactly the way she had been yesterday, looking across the lawn into the woods. The old man was very much irritated. Every morning since she had been able to climb, he had waked up to find her either on his bed or underneath it. It was apparent that this morning she preferred the sight of the woods. He decided to ignore her behavior for the present and then bring it up later when she was over her pique. He sat down in the swing beside her but she continued to look at the woods. "I thought you and me'd go into town and have us a look at the boats in the new boat store," he said.

She didn't turn her head but she asked suspiciously, in a loud voice, "What else are you going for?"

"Nothing else," he said.

After a pause she said, "If that's all, I'll go," but she did not bother to look at him.

"Well put on your shoes," he said. "I ain't going to the city with a barefoot woman." She did not bother to laugh at this joke.

The weather was as indifferent as her disposition. The sky did not look as if it were going to rain or as if it were not going to rain. It was an unpleasant gray and the sun had not troubled to come out. All the way into town, she sat looking at her feet, which stuck out in front of her, encased in heavy brown school shoes. The old man had often sneaked up on her and found her alone in conversation with her feet and he thought she was speaking with them silently now. Every now and then her lips moved but she said nothing to him and let all his remarks pass as if she had not heard them. He decided it was going to cost him considerable to buy her good humor again and that he had better do it with a boat, since he wanted one too. She had been talking boats ever since the water backed up onto his place. They went first to the boat store. "Show us the yachts for po' folks!" he shouted jovially to the clerk as they entered.

"They're all for po' folks!" the clerk said. "You'll be po' when you finish buying one!" He was a stout youth in a yellow shirt and blue pants and he had a ready wit. They exchanged several clever remarks in rapid-fire succession. Mr. Fortune looked at Mary Fortune to see if her face had brightened. She stood staring absently over the side of an outboard motor boat at the opposite wall.

"Ain't the lady innerested in boats?" the clerk asked.

She turned and wandered back out onto the sidewalk and got in the car again. The old man looked after her with amazement. He could not believe that a child of her intelligence could be acting this way over the mere sale of a field. "I think she must be coming down with something," he said. "We'll come back again," and he returned to the car.

"Let's go get us an ice-cream cone," he suggested, looking at her with concern.

"I don't want no ice-cream cone," she said.

His actual destination was the courthouse but he did not want to make this apparent. "How'd you like to visit the ten-cent store while I tend to a little bidnis of mine?" he asked. "You can buy yourself something with a quarter I brought along."

"I ain't got nothing to do in no ten-cent store," she said. "I don't want no quarter of yours."

If a boat was of no interest, he should not have thought a quarter would be and reproved himself for that stupidity. "Well what's the matter, sister?" he asked kindly. "Don't you feel good?"

She turned and looked him straight in the face and said with a slow concentrated ferocity, "It's the lawn. My daddy grazes his calves there. We won't be able to see the woods any more."

The old man had held his fury in as long as he could. "He beats you!" he shouted. "And you worry about where he's going to graze his calves!"

"Nobody's ever beat me in my life," she said, "and if anybody did, I'd kill him."

A man seventy-nine years of age cannot let himself be run over by a child of nine. His face set in a look that was just as determined as hers. "Are you a Fortune," he said, "or are you a Pitts? Make up your mind."

Her voice was loud and positive and belligerent. "I'm Mary—Fortune—Pitts," she said.

"Well I," he shouted, "am PURE Fortune!"

There was nothing she could say to this and she showed it. For an instant she looked completely defeated, and the old man saw with a disturbing clearness that this was the Pitts look. What he saw was the Pitts look, pure and simple, and he felt personally stained by it, as if it had been found on his own face. He turned in disgust and backed the car out and drove straight to the courthouse.

The courthouse was a red and white blaze-faced building set in the center of a square from which most of the grass had been worn off. He parked in front of it and said, "Stay here," in an imperious tone and got out and slammed the car door.

It took him a half-hour to get the deed and have the sale paper drawn up and when he returned to the car, she was sitting on the back seat in the corner. The expression on that part of her face that he could see was foreboding and withdrawn. The sky had darkened also and there was a hot sluggish tide in the air, the kind felt when a tornado is possible.

"We better get on before we get caught in a storm," he said and added emphatically, "because I got one more place to stop at on the way home," but he might have been chauffeuring a small dead body for all the answer he got.

On the way to Tilman's he reviewed once more the many just reasons that were leading him to his present action and he could not locate a flaw in any of them. He decided that while this attitude of hers would not be permanent, he was permanently disappointed in her and that when she came around she would have to apologize; and that there would be no boat. He was coming to realize slowly that his trouble with her had always been that he had not shown enough firmness. He had been too generous. He was so occupied with these thoughts that he did not notice the signs that said how many miles to Tilman's until the last one exploded joyfully in his face: "Here it is, Friends, TILMAN's!" He pulled in under the shed.

He got out without so much as looking at Mary Fortune and entered the dark store where Tilman, leaning on the counter in front of a triple shelf of canned goods, was waiting for him.

Tilman was a man of quick action and few words. He sat habitually with his arms folded on the counter and his insignificant head weaving snake-fashion above them. He had a triangular-shaped face with the point at the bottom and the top of his skull was covered with a cap of freckles. His eyes were green and very narrow and his tongue was always exposed in his partly opened mouth. He had his checkbook handy and they got down to business at once. It did not take him long to look at the deed and sign the bill of sale. Then Mr. Fortune signed it and they grasped hands over the counter.

Mr. Fortune's sense of relief as he grasped Tilman's hand was extreme. What was done, he felt, was done and there could be no more argument, with her or with himself. He felt that he had acted on principle and that the future was assured.

Just as their hands loosened, an instant's change came over Tilman's face and he disappeared completely under the counter as if he had been snatched by the feet from below. A bottle crashed against the line of tinned goods behind where he had been. The old man whirled around. Mary Fortune was in the door, red-faced and wild-looking, with another bottle lifted to hurl. As he ducked, it broke behind him on the counter and she grabbed another from the crate. He sprang at her but she tore to the other side of the store, screaming something unintelligible and throwing everything within her reach. The old man pounced again and this time he caught her by the tail of her dress and pulled her backward out of the store. Then he got a better grip and lifted her, wheezing and whimpering but suddenly limp in his arms, the few feet to the car. He managed to get the door open and dump her inside. Then he ran around to the other side and got in himself and drove away as fast as he could.

His heart felt as if it were the size of the car and was racing forward, carrying him to some inevitable destination faster than he had ever been carried before. For the first five minutes he did not think but only sped forward as if he were being driven inside his own fury. Gradually the power of thought returned to him. Mary Fortune, rolled into a ball in the corner of the seat, was snuffling and heaving.

He had never seen a child behave in such a way in his life. Neither his own children nor anyone else's had ever displayed such temper in his presence, and he had never for an instant imagined that the child he had trained himself, the child who had been his constant companion for nine years, would embarrass him like this. The child he had never lifted a hand to!

Then he saw, with the sudden vision that sometimes comes with delayed recognition, that that had been his mistake.

She respected Pitts because, even with no just cause, he beat her; and if he—with his just cause—did not beat her now, he would have nobody to blame but himself if she turned out a hellion. He saw that the time had come, that he could no longer avoid whipping her, and as he turned off the highway onto the dirt road leading to home, he told himself that when he finished with her, she would never throw another bottle again.

He raced along the clay road until he came to the line where his own property began and then he turned off onto a side path, just wide enough for the automobile and bounced for a half a mile through the woods. He stopped the car at the exact spot where he had seen Pitts take his belt to her. It was a place where the road widened so that two cars could pass or one could turn around, an ugly red bald spot surrounded by long thin pines that appeared to be gathered there to witness anything that would take place in such a clearing. A few stones protruded from the clay.

"Get out," he said and reached across her and opened the door.

She got out without looking at him or asking what they were going to do and he got out on his side and came around the front of the car.

"Now I'm going to whip you!" he said and his voice was extra loud and hollow and had a vibrating quality that appeared to be taken up and passed through the tops of the pines. He did not want to get caught in a downpour while he was whipping her and he said, "Hurry up and get ready against that tree," and began to take off his belt.

What he had in mind to do appeared to come very slowly as if it had to penetrate a fog in her head. She did not move but gradually her confused expression began to clear. Where a few seconds before her face had been red and distorted and unorganized, it drained now of every vague line until nothing was left on it but positiveness, a look that went slowly past determination and reached certainty. "Nobody has ever beat me," she said, "and if anybody tries it, I'll kill him."

"I don't want no sass," he said and started toward her. His knees felt very unsteady, as if they might turn either backward or forward.

She moved exactly one step back and, keeping her eye on him steadily, removed her glasses and dropped them behind a small rock near the tree he had told her to get ready against. "Take off your glasses," she said.

"Don't give me orders!" he said in a high voice and slapped awkwardly at her ankles with his belt.

She was on him so quickly that he could not have recalled which blow he felt first, whether the weight of her whole solid body or the jabs of her feet or the pummeling of her fist on his chest. He flailed the belt in the air, not knowing where to hit but trying to get her off him until he could decide where to get a grip on her.

"Leggo!" he shouted. "Leggo I tell you!" But she seemed to be everywhere, coming at him from all directions at once. It was as if he were being attacked not by one child but by a pack of small demons all with stout brown school shoes and small rocklike fists. His glasses flew to the side.

"I toljer to take them off," she growled without pausing.

He caught his knee and danced on one foot and a rain of blows fell on his stomach. He felt five claws in the flesh of his upper arm where she was hanging from while her feet mechanically battered his knees and her free fist pounded him again and again in the chest. Then with horror he saw her face rise up in front of his, teeth exposed, and he roared like a bull as she bit the side of his jaw. He seemed to see his own face coming to bite him from several sides at once but he could not attend to it for he was being kicked indiscriminately, in the stomach and then in the crotch. Suddenly he threw himself on the ground and began to roll like a man on fire. She was on top of him at once, rolling with him and still kicking, and now with both fists free to batter his chest.

"I'm an old man!" he piped. "Leave me alone!" But she did not stop. She began a fresh assault on his jaw.

"Stop stop!" he wheezed. "I'm your grandfather!"

She paused, her face exactly on top of his. Pale identical eye looked into pale identical eye. "Have you had enough?" she asked.

The old man looked up into his own image. It was triumphant and hostile. "You been whipped," it said, "by me," and then it added, bearing down on each word, "and I'm PURE Pitts."

In the pause she loosened her grip and he got hold of her throat. With a sudden surge of strength, he managed to roll over and reverse their positions so that he was looking down into the face that was his own but had dared to call itself Pitts. With his hands still tight around her neck, he lifted her head and brought it down once hard against the rock that happened to be under it. Then he brought it down twice more. Then looking into the face in which the eyes, slowly rolling back, appeared to pay him not the slightest attention, he said, "There's not an ounce of Pitts in me."

He continued to stare at his conquered image until he perceived that though it was absolutely silent, there was no look of remorse on it. The eyes had rolled back down and were set in a fixed glare that did not take him in. "This ought to teach you a good lesson," he said in a voice that was edged with doubt.

He managed painfully to get up on his unsteady kicked legs and to take two steps, but the enlargement of his heart which had begun in the car was still going on. He turned his head and looked behind him for a long time at the little motionless figure with its head on the rock.

Then he fell on his back and looked up helplessly along the bare trunks into the tops of the pines and his heart expanded once more with a convulsive motion. It expanded so fast that the old man felt as if he were being pulled after it through the woods, felt as if he were running as fast as he could with the ugly pines toward the lake. He perceived that there would be a little opening there, a little place where he could escape and leave the woods behind him. He could see it in the distance already, a little opening where the white sky was reflected in the water. It grew as he ran toward it until suddenly the whole lake opened up before him, riding majestically in little corrugated folds toward his feet. He realized suddenly that he could not swim and that he had not bought the boat. On both sides of him he saw that the gaunt trees had thickened into mysterious dark files that were marching across the water and away into the distance. He looked around desperately for someone to help him but the place was deserted except for one huge yellow monster which sat to the side, as stationary as he was, gorging itself on clay.

The Enduring Chill

ASBURY'S TRAIN stopped so that he would get off exactly where his mother was standing waiting to meet him. Her thin spectacled face below him was bright with a wide smile that disappeared as she caught sight of him bracing himself behind the conductor. The smile vanished so suddenly, the shocked look that replaced it was so complete, that he realized for the first time that he must look as ill as he was. The sky was a chill gray and a startling white-gold sun, like some strange potentate from the east, was rising beyond the black woods that surrounded Timberboro. It cast a strange light over the single block of one-story brick and wooden shacks. Asbury felt that he was about to witness a majestic transformation, that the flat of roofs might at any moment turn into the mounting turrets of some exotic temple for a god he didn't know. The illusion lasted only a moment before his attention was drawn back to his mother.

She had given a little cry; she looked aghast. He was pleased that she should see death in his face at once. His mother, at the age of sixty, was going to be introduced to reality and he supposed that if the experience didn't kill her, it would assist her in the process of growing up. He stepped down and greeted her.

"You don't look very well," she said and gave him a long clinical stare.

"I don't feel like talking," he said at once. "I've had a bad trip."

Mrs. Fox observed that his left eye was bloodshot. He was puffy and pale and his hair had receded tragically for a boy of twenty-five. The thin reddish wedge of it left on top bore down in a point that seemed to lengthen his nose and give him an irritable expression that matched his tone of voice when he spoke to her. "It must have been cold up there," she said. "Why don't you take off your coat? It's not cold down here."

"You don't have to tell me what the temperature is!" he said in a high voice. "I'm old enough to know when I want to take my coat off!" The train glided silently away behind him, leaving a view of the twin blocks of dilapidated stores.

He gazed after the aluminum speck disappearing into the woods. It seemed to him that his last connection with a larger world were vanishing forever. Then he turned and faced his mother grimly, irked that he had allowed himself, even for an instant, to see an imaginary temple in this collapsing country junction. He had become entirely accustomed to the thought of death, but he had not become accustomed to the thought of death *here*.

He had felt the end coming on for nearly four months. Alone in his freezing flat, huddled under his two blankets and his overcoat and with three thicknesses of the New York *Times* between, he had had a chill one night, followed by a violent sweat that left the sheets soaking and removed all doubt from his mind about his true condition. Before this there had been a gradual slackening of his energy and vague inconsistent aches and headaches. He had been absent so many days from his part-time job in the bookstore that he had lost it. Since then he had been living, or just barely so, on his savings and these, diminishing day by day, had been all he had between him and home. Now there was nothing. He was here.

"Where's the car?" he muttered.

"It's over yonder," his mother said. "And your sister is asleep in the back because I don't like to come out this early by myself. There's no need to wake her up."

"No," he said, "let sleeping dogs lie," and he picked up his two bulging suitcases and started across the road with them.

They were too heavy for him and by the time he reached the car, his mother saw that he was exhausted. He had never come home with two suitcases before. Ever since he had first gone away to college, he had come back every time with nothing but the necessities for a two-week stay and with a wooden resigned expression that said he was prepared to endure the visit for exactly fourteen days. "You've brought more than usual," she observed, but he did not answer.

He opened the car door and hoisted the two bags in beside his sister's upturned feet, giving first the feet—in Girl Scout shoes—and then the rest of her a revolted look of recognition. She was packed into a black suit and had a white rag around her head with metal curlers sticking out from under the edges. Her eyes were closed and her mouth was open. He and she had the same features except that hers were bigger. She was eight years older than he was and was principal of the county elementary school. He shut the door softly so she wouldn't wake up and then went around and got in the front seat and closed his eyes. His mother backed the car into the road and in a few minutes he felt it swerve into the highway. Then he opened his eyes. The road stretched between two open fields of yellow bitterweed.

"Do you think Timberboro has improved?" his mother asked. This was her standard question, meant to be taken literally.

"It's still there, isn't it?" he said in an ugly voice.

"Two of the stores have new fronts," she said. Then with a sudden ferocity, she said, "You did well to come home where you can get a good doctor! I'll take you to Doctor Block this afternoon."

"I am not," he said, trying to keep his voice from shaking, "going to Doctor Block. This afternoon or ever. Don't you think if I'd wanted to go to a doctor I'd have gone up there where they have some good ones? Don't you know they have better doctors in New York?"

"He would take a personal interest in you," she said. "None of those doctors up there would take a personal interest in you."

"I don't want him taking a personal interest in me." Then after a minute, staring out across a blurred purple-looking field, he said, "What's wrong with me is way beyond Block," and his voice trailed off into a frayed sound, almost a sob.

He could not, as his friend Goetz had recommended, prepare to see it all as illusion, either what had gone before or the few weeks that were left to him. Goetz was certain that death was nothing at all. Goetz, whose whole face had always been purple-splotched with a million indignations, had returned from six months in Japan as dirty as ever but as bland as the Buddha himself. Goetz took the news of Asbury's approaching end with a calm indifference. Quoting something or other he said, "Although the Bodhisattva leads an infinite number of creatures into nirvana, in reality there are neither any Bodhisattvas to do the leading nor any creatures to be led." However, out of some feeling for his welfare, Goetz had put forth $4.50 to take him to a lecture on Vedanta. It had been a waste of his money. While Goetz had listened enthralled to the dark little man on the platform, Asbury's bored gaze had roved among the audience. It had passed over the heads of several girls in saris, past a Japanese youth, a blue-black man with a fez, and several girls who looked like secretaries. Finally, at the end of the row, it had rested on a lean spectacled figure in black, a priest. The priest's expression was of a polite but strictly reserved interest. Asbury identified his own feelings immediately in the taciturn superior expression. When the lecture was over a few students met in Goetz's flat, the priest among them, but here he was equally reserved. He listened with a marked politeness to the discussion of Asbury's approaching death, but he said little. A girl in a sari remarked that self-fulfillment was out of the question since it meant salvation and the word was meaningless. "Salvation," quoted Goetz, "is the destruction of a simple prejudice, and no one is saved."

"And what do you say to that?" Asbury asked the priest and returned his reserved smile over the heads of the others. The borders of this smile seemed to touch on some icy clarity.

"There is," the priest said, "a real probability of the New Man, assisted, of course," he added brittlely, "by the Third Person of the Trinity."

"Ridiculous!" the girl in the sari said, but the priest only brushed her with his smile, which was slightly amused now.

When he got up to leave, he silently handed Asbury a small card on which he had written his name, Ignatius Vogle, S.J., and an address. Perhaps, Asbury thought now, he should have used it for the priest appealed to him as a man of the world, someone who would have understood the unique tragedy of his death, a death whose meaning had been far beyond the twittering group around them. And how much more beyond Block. "What's wrong with me," he repeated, "is way beyond Block."

His mother knew at once what he meant: he meant he was going to have a nervous breakdown. She did not say a word. She did not say that this was precisely what she could have told him would happen. When people think they are smart—

even when they are smart—there is nothing anybody else can say to make them see things straight, and with Asbury, the trouble was that in addition to being smart, he had an artistic temperament. She did not know where he had got it from because his father, who was a lawyer and businessman and farmer and politician all rolled into one, had certainly had his feet on the ground; and she had certainly always had hers on it. She had managed after he died to get the two of them through college and beyond; but she had observed that the more education they got, the less they could do. Their father had gone to a one-room schoolhouse through the eighth grade and he could do anything.

She could have told Asbury what would help him. She could have said, "If you would get out in the sunshine, or if you would work for a month in the dairy, you'd be a different person!" but she knew exactly how that suggestion would be received. He would be a nuisance in the dairy but she would let him work in there if he wanted to. She had let him work in there last year when he had come home and was writing the play. He had been writing a play about Negroes (why anybody would want to write a play about Negroes was beyond her) and he had said he wanted to work in the dairy with them and find out what their interests were. Their interests were in doing as little as they could get by with, as she could have told him if anybody could have told him anything. The Negroes had put up with him and he had learned to put the milkers on and once he had washed all the cans and she thought that once he had mixed feed. Then a cow had kicked him and he had not gone back to the barn again. She knew that if he would get in there now, or get out and fix fences, or do any kind of work—real work, not writing—that he might avoid this nervous breakdown. "Whatever happened to that play you were writing about the Negroes?" she asked.

"I am not writing plays," he said. "And get this through your head: I am not working in any dairy. I am not getting out in the sunshine. I'm ill. I have fever and chills and I'm dizzy and all I want you to do is leave me alone."

"Then if you are really ill, you should see Doctor Block."

"And I am not seeing Block," he finished and ground himself down in the seat and stared intensely in front of him.

She turned into their driveway, a red road that ran for a quarter of a mile through the two front pastures. The dry cows were on one side and the milk herd on the other. She slowed the car and then stopped altogether, her attention caught by a cow with a bad quarter. "They haven't been attending to her," she said. "Look at that bag!"

Asbury turned his head abruptly in the opposite direction, but there a small, walleyed Guernsey was watching him steadily as if she sensed some bond between them. "Good God!" he cried in an agonized voice, "can't we go on? It's six o'clock in the morning!"

"Yes, yes," his mother said and started the car quickly.

"What's that cry of deadly pain?" his sister drawled from the back seat. "Oh it's you," she said. "Well well, we have the artist with us again. How utterly utterly." She had a decidedly nasal voice.

He didn't answer her or turn his head. He had learned that much. Never answer her.

"Mary George!" his mother said sharply. "Asbury is sick. Leave him alone."

"What's wrong with him?" Mary George asked.

"There's the house!" his mother said as if they were all blind but her. It rose on the crest of the hill—a white two-story farmhouse with a wide porch and pleasant columns. She always approached it with a feeling of pride and she had said more than once to Asbury, "You have a home here that half those people up there would give their eyeteeth for!"

She had been once to the terrible place he lived in New York. They had gone up five flights of dark stone steps, past open garbage cans on every landing, to arrive finally at two damp rooms and a closet with a toilet in it. "You wouldn't live like this at home," she had muttered.

"No!" he'd said with an ecstatic look, "it wouldn't be possible!"

She supposed the truth was that she simply didn't understand how it felt to be sensitive or how peculiar you were when you were an artist. His sister said he was not an artist and that he had no talent and that that was the trouble with him; but Mary George was not a happy girl herself. Asbury said she posed as an intellectual but that her I.Q. couldn't be over seventy-five, that all she was really interested in was getting a man but that no sensible man would finish a first look at her. She had tried to tell him that Mary George could be very attractive when she put her mind to it and he had said that that much strain on her mind would break her down. If she were in any way attractive, he had said, she wouldn't now be principal of a county elementary school, and Mary George had said that if Asbury had had any talent, he would by now have published something. What had he ever published, she wanted to know, and for that matter, what had he ever written?

Mrs. Fox had pointed out that he was only twenty-five years old and Mary George had said that the age most people published something at was twenty-one, which made him exactly four years overdue. Mrs. Fox was not up on things like that but she suggested that he might be writing a very *long* book. Very long book, her eye, Mary George said, he would do well if he came up with so much as a poem. Mrs. Fox hoped it wasn't going to be just a poem.

She pulled the car into the side drive and a scattering of guineas exploded into the air and sailed screaming around the house. "Home again, home again jiggity jig!" she said.

"Oh God," Asbury groaned.

"The artist arrives at the gas chamber," Mary George said in her nasal voice.

He leaned on the door and got out, and forgetting his bags he moved toward the front of the house as if he were in a daze. His sister got out and stood by the car door, squinting at his bent unsteady figure. As she watched him go up the front steps, her mouth fell slack in her astonished face. "Why," she said, "there *is* something the matter with him. He looks a hundred years old."

"Didn't I tell you so?" her mother hissed. "Now you keep your mouth shut and let him alone."

He went into the house, pausing in the hall only long enough to see his pale broken face glare at him for an instant from the pier mirror. Holding onto the banister, he pulled himself up the steep stairs, across the landing and then up the shorter second flight and into his room, a large open airy room with a faded blue rug and white curtains freshly put up for his arrival. He looked at nothing, but fell face down on his own bed. It was a narrow antique bed with a high ornamental headboard on which was carved a garlanded basket overflowing with wooden fruit.

While he was still in New York, he had written a letter to his mother which filled two notebooks. He did not mean it to be read until after his death. It was such a letter as Kafka had addressed to his father. Asbury's father had died twenty years ago and Asbury considered this a great blessing. The old man, he felt sure, had been one of the courthouse gang, a rural worthy with a dirty finger in every pie and he knew he would not have been able to stomach him. He had read some of his correspondence and had been appalled by its stupidity.

He knew, of course, that his mother would not understand the letter at once. Her literal mind would require some time to discover the significance of it, but he thought she would be able to see that he forgave her for all she had done to him. For that matter, he supposed that she would realize what she had done to him only through the letter. He didn't think she was conscious of it at all. Her self-satisfaction itself was barely conscious, but because of the letter, she might experience a painful realization and this would be the only thing of value he had to leave her.

If reading it would be painful to her, writing it had sometimes been unbearable to him—for in order to face her, he had had to face himself. "I came here to escape the slave's atmosphere of home," he had written, "to find freedom, to liberate my imagination, to take it like a hawk from its cage and set it 'whirling off into the widening gyre' (Yeats) and what did I find? It was incapable of flight. It was some bird you had domesticated, sitting huffy in its pen, refusing to come out!" The next words were underscored twice. "I have no imagination. I have no talent. I can't create. I have nothing but the desire for these things. Why didn't you kill that too? Woman, why did you pinion me?"

Writing this, he had reached the pit of despair and he thought that reading it, she would at least begin to sense his tragedy and her part in it. It was not that she had ever forced her way on him. That had never been necessary. Her way had simply been the air he breathed and when at last he had found other air, he couldn't survive in it. He felt that even if she didn't understand at once, the letter would leave her with an enduring chill and perhaps in time lead her to see herself as she was.

He had destroyed everything else he had ever written—his two lifeless novels, his half-dozen stationary plays, his prosy poems, his sketchy short stories—and kept only the two notebooks that contained the letter. They were in the black suitcase that his sister, huffing and blowing, was now dragging up the second flight of stairs. His mother was carrying the smaller bag and came on ahead. He turned over as she entered the room.

"I'll open this and get out your things," she said, "and you can go right to bed and in a few minutes I'll bring your breakfast."

He sat up and said in a fretful voice, "I don't want any breakfast and I can open my own suitcase. Leave that alone."

His sister arrived in the door, her face full of curiosity, and let the black bag fall with a thud over the doorsill. Then she began to push it across the room with her foot until she was close enough to get a good look at him. "If I looked as bad as you do," she said, "I'd go to the hospital."

Her mother cut her eyes sharply at her and she left. Then Mrs. Fox closed the door and came to the bed and sat down on it beside him. "Now this time I want you to make a long visit and rest," she said.

"This visit," he said, "will be permanent."

"Wonderful!" she cried. "You can have a little studio in your room and in the mornings you can write plays and in the afternoons you can help in the dairy!"

He turned a white wooden face to her. "Close the blinds and let me sleep," he said.

When she was gone, he lay for some time staring at the water stains on the gray walls. Descending from the top molding, long icicle shapes had been etched by leaks and, directly over his bed on the ceiling, another leak had made a fierce bird with spread wings. It had an icicle crosswise in its beak and there were smaller icicles depending from its wings and tail. It been there since his childhood and had always irritated him and sometimes had frightened him. He had often had the illusion that it was in motion and about to descend mysteriously and set the icicle on his head. He closed his eyes and thought: I won't have to look at it for many more days. And presently he went to sleep.

When he woke up in the afternoon, there was a pink openmouthed face hanging over him and from two large familiar ears on either side of it the black tubes of Block's stethoscope extended down to his exposed chest. The doctor, seeing he was awake, made a face like a Chinaman, rolled his eyes almost out of his head and cried, "Say AHHHH!"

Block was irresistible to children. For miles around they vomited and went into fevers to have a visit from him. Mrs. Fox was standing behind him, smiling radiantly. "Here's Doctor Block!" she said as if she had captured this angel on the rooftop and brought him in for her little boy.

"Get him out of here," Asbury muttered. He looked at the asinine face from what seemed the bottom of a black hole.

The doctor peered closer, wiggling his ears. Block was bald and had a round face as senseless as a baby's. Nothing about him indicated intelligence except two cold clinical nickel-colored eyes that hung with a motionless curiosity over whatever he looked at. "You sho do look bad, Azzberry," he murmured. He took the stethoscope off and dropped it in his bag. "I don't know when I've seen anybody your age look as sorry as you do. What you been doing to yourself?"

There was a continuous thud in the back of Asbury's head as if his heart had got trapped in it and was fighting to get out. "I didn't send for you," he said.

Block put his hand on the glaring face and pulled the eyelid down and peered into it. "You must have been on the bum up there," he said. He began to press his hand in the small of Asbury's back. "I went up there once myself," he said, "and saw exactly how little they had and came straight on back home. Open your mouth."

Asbury opened it automatically and the drill-like gaze swung over it and bore down. He snapped it shut and in a wheezing breathless voice he said, "If I'd wanted a doctor, I'd have stayed up there where I could have got a good one!"

"Asbury!" his mother said.

"How long you been having the so' throat?" Block asked.

"She sent for you!" Asbury said. "She can answer the questions."

"Asbury!" his mother said.

Block leaned over his bag and pulled out a rubber tube. He pushed Asbury's sleeve up and tied the tube around his upper arm. Then he took out a syringe and prepared to find the vein, humming a hymn as he pressed the needle in. Asbury lay with a rigid outraged stare while the privacy of his blood was invaded by this idiot. "Slowly Lord but sure," Block sang in a murmuring voice, "Oh slowly Lord but sure." When the syringe was full, he withdrew the needle. "Blood don't lie," he said. He poured it in a bottle and stopped it up and put the bottle in his bag. "Azzberry," he started, "how long . . ."

Asbury sat up and thrust his thudding head forward and said, "I didn't send for you. I'm not answering any questions. You're not my doctor. What's wrong with me is way beyond you."

"Most things are beyond me," Block said. "I ain't found anything yet that I thoroughly understood," and he sighed and got up. His eyes seemed to glitter at Asbury as if from a great distance.

"He wouldn't act so ugly," Mrs. Fox explained, "if he weren't really sick. And *I* want you to come back every day until you get him well."

Asbury's eyes were a fierce glaring violet. "What's wrong with me is way beyond you," he repeated and lay back down and closed his eyes until Block and his mother were gone.

In the next few days, though he grew rapidly worse, his mind functioned with a terrible clarity. On the point of death, he found himself existing in a state of illumination that was totally out of keeping with the kind of talk he had to listen to from his mother. This was largely about cows with names like Daisy and Bessie Button and their intimate functions— their mastitis and their screwworms and their abortions. His mother insisted that in the middle of the day he get out and sit on the porch and "enjoy the view" and as resistance was too much of a struggle, he dragged himself out and sat there in a rigid slouch, his feet wrapped in an afghan and his hands gripped on the chair arms as if he were about to spring forward into the glaring china blue sky. The lawn extended for a quarter of an acre down to a barbed-wire fence that divided it from the front pasture. In the middle of the day the dry cows rested there under a line of sweetgum trees. On the other side of the road were two hills with a pond between and his mother could sit on the porch and watch the herd walk across the dam to the hill on the other side. The whole scene was rimmed by a wall of trees which, at the time of day he was forced to sit there, was a washed-out blue that reminded him sadly of the Negroes' faded overalls.

He listened irritably while his mother detailed the faults of the help. "Those two are not stupid," she said. "They know how to look out for themselves."

"They need to," he muttered, but there was no use to argue with her. Last year he had been writing a play about the Negro and he had wanted to be around them for a while to see how they really felt about their condition, but the two who worked for her had lost all their initiative over the years. They didn't talk. The one called Morgan was light brown, part Indian; the other, older one, Randall, was very black and fat. When they said anything to him, it was as if they were speaking to an invisible body located to the right or left of where he actually was, and after two days working side by side with them, he felt he had not established rapport. He decided to try something bolder than talk and one afternoon as he was standing near Randall, watching him adjust a milker, he had quietly taken out his cigarettes and lit one. The Negro had stopped what he was doing and watched him. He waited until Asbury had taken two draws and then he said, "She don't 'low no smoking in here."

The other one approached and stood there, grinning.

"I know it," Asbury said and after a deliberate pause, he shook the package and held it out, first to Randall, who took one, and then to Morgan, who took one. He had then lit the cigarettes for them himself and the three of them had stood there smoking. There were no sounds but the steady click of the two milking machines and the occasional slap of a cow's tail against her side. It was one of those moments of communion when the difference between black and white is absorbed into nothing.

The next day two cans of milk had been returned from the creamery because it had absorbed the odor of tobacco. He took the blame and told his mother that it was he and not the Negroes who had been smoking. "If you were doing it, they were doing it," she had said. "Don't you think I know those two?" She was incapable of thinking them innocent; but the experience had so exhilarated him that he had been determined to repeat it in some other way.

The next afternoon when he and Randall were in the milk house pouring the fresh milk into the cans, he had picked up the jelly glass the Negroes drank out of and, inspired, had poured himself a glassful of the warm milk and drained it down. Randall had stopped pouring and had remained, half-bent, over the can, watching him. "She don't 'low that," he said. "That *the* thing she don't 'low."

Asbury poured out another glassful and handed it to him.

"She don't 'low it," he repeated.

"Listen," Asbury said hoarsely, "the world is changing. There's no reason I shouldn't drink after you or you after me!"

"She don't 'low noner us to drink noner this here milk," Randall said.

Asbury continued to hold the glass out to him. "You took the cigarette," he said. "Take the milk. It's not going to hurt my mother to lose two or three glasses of milk a day. We've got to think free if we want to live free!"

The other one had come up and was standing in the door.

"Don't want noner that milk," Randall said.

Asbury swung around and held the glass out to Morgan. "Here boy, have a drink of this," he said.

Morgan stared at him; then his face took on a decided look of cunning. "I ain't seen you drink none of it yourself," he said.

Asbury despised milk. The first warm glassful had turned his stomach. He drank half of what he was holding and handed the rest to the Negro, who took it and gazed down inside the glass as if it contained some great mystery; then he set it on the floor by the cooler.

"Don't you like milk?" Asbury asked.

"I likes it but I ain't drinking noner that."

"Why?"

"She don't 'low it," Morgan said.

"My God!" Asbury exploded, "she she she!" He had tried the same thing the next day and the next and the next but he could not get them to drink the milk. A few afternoons later when he was standing outside the milk house about to go in, he heard Morgan ask, "Howcome you let him drink all that milk every day?"

"What he do is him," Randall said. "What I do is me."

"Howcome he talks so ugly about his ma?"

"She ain't whup him enough when he was little," Randall said.

The insufferableness of life at home had overcome him and he had returned to New York two days early. So far as he was concerned he had died there, and the question now was how long he could stand to linger here. He could have hastened his end but suicide would not have been a victory. Death was coming to him legitimately, as a justification, as a gift from life. That was his greatest triumph. Then too, to the fine minds of the neighborhood, a suicide son would indicate a mother who had been a failure, and while this was the case, he felt that it was a public embarrassment he could spare her. What she would learn from the letter would be a private revelation. He had sealed the notebooks in a manila envelope and had written on it: "To be opened only after the death of Asbury Porter Fox." He had put the envelope in the desk drawer in his room and locked it and the key was in his pajama pocket until he could decide on a place to leave it.

When they sat on the porch in the morning, his mother felt that some of the time she should talk about subjects that were of interest to him. The third morning she started in on his writing. "When you get well," she said, "I think it would be nice if you wrote a book about down here. We need another good book like *Gone With the Wind*."

He could feel the muscles in his stomach begin to tighten.

"Put the war in it," she advised. "That always makes a long book."

He put his head back gently as if he were afraid it would crack. After a moment he said, "I am not going to write any book."

"Well," she said, "if you don't feel like writing a book, you could just write poems. They're nice." She realized that what he needed was someone intellectual to talk to, but Mary George was the only intellectual she knew and he would not talk to her. She had thought of Mr. Bush, the retired Methodist minister, but she had not brought this up. Now she decided to hazard it. "I think I'll ask Dr. Bush to come to see you," she said, raising Mr. Bush's rank. "You'd enjoy him. He collects rare coins."

She was not prepared for the reaction she got. He began to shake all over and give loud spasmodic laughs. He seemed about to choke. After a minute he subsided into a cough. "If you think I need spiritual aid to die," he said, "you're quite mistaken. And certainly not from that ass Bush. My God!"

"I didn't mean that at all," she said. "He has coins dating from the time of Cleopatra."

"Well if you ask him here, I'll tell him to go to hell," he said. "Bush! That beats all!"

"I'm glad something amuses you," she said acidly.

For a time they sat there in silence. Then his mother looked up. He was sitting forward again and smiling at her. His face was brightening more and more as if he had just had an idea that was brilliant. She stared at him. "I'll tell you who I want to come," he said. For the first time since he had come home, his expression was pleasant; though there was also, she thought, a kind of crafty look about him.

"Who do you want to come?" she asked suspiciously.

"I want a priest," he announced.

"A priest?" his mother said in an uncomprehending voice.

"Preferably a Jesuit," he said, brightening more and more. "Yes, by all means a Jesuit. They have them in the city. You can call up and get me one."

"What is the matter with you?" his mother asked.

"Most of them are very well-educated," he said, "but Jesuits are foolproof. A Jesuit would be able to discuss something besides the weather." Already, remembering Ignatius Vogle, S.J., he could picture the priest. This one would be a trifle more worldly perhaps, a trifle more cynical. Protected by their ancient institution, priests could afford to be cynical, to play both ends against the middle. He would talk to a man of culture before he died—even in this desert! Furthermore, nothing would irritate his mother so much. He could not understand why he had not thought of this sooner.

"You're not a member of that church," Mrs. Fox said shortly. "It's twenty miles away. They wouldn't send one." She hoped that this would end the matter.

He sat back absorbed in the idea, determined to force her to make the call since she always did what he wanted if he kept at her. "I'm dying," he said, "and I haven't asked you to do but one thing and you refuse me that."

"You are NOT dying."

"When you realize it," he said, "it'll be too late."

There was another unpleasant silence. Presently his mother said, "Nowadays doctors don't *let* young people die. They give them some of these new medicines." She began shaking her foot with a nerve-rattling assurance. "People just don't die like they used to," she said.

"Mother," he said, "you ought to be prepared. I think even Block knows and hasn't told you yet." Block, after the first visit, had come in grimly every time, without his jokes and funny faces, and had taken his blood in silence, his nickel-colored eyes unfriendly. He was, by definition, the enemy of death and he looked now as if he knew he was battling the real thing. He had said he wouldn't prescribe until he knew what was wrong and Asbury had laughed in his face. "Mother," he said, "I AM going to die," and he tried to make each word like a hammer blow on top of her head.

She paled slightly but she did not blink. "Do you think for one minute," she said angrily, "that I intend to sit here and let you die?" Her eyes were as hard as two old mountain ranges seen in the distance. He felt the first distinct stroke of doubt.

"Do you?" she asked fiercely.

"I don't think you have anything to do with it," he said in a shaken voice.

"Humph," she said and got up and left the porch as if she could not stand to be around such stupidity an instant longer.

Forgetting the Jesuit, he went rapidly over his symptoms: his fever had increased, interspersed by chills; he barely had the energy to drag himself out on the porch; food was abhorrent to him; and Block had not been able to give her the least satisfaction. Even as he sat there, he felt the beginning of a new chill, as if death were already playfully rattling his bones. He pulled the afghan off his feet and put it around his shoulders and made his way unsteadily up the stairs to bed.

He continued to grow worse. In the next few days he became so much weaker and badgered her so constantly about the Jesuit that finally in desperation she decided to humor his foolishness. She made the call, explaining in a chilly voice that her son was ill, perhaps a little out of his head, and wished to speak to a priest. While she made the call, Asbury hung over the banisters, barefooted, with the afghan around him, and listened. When she hung up he called down to know when the priest was coming.

"Tomorrow sometime," his mother said irritably.

He could tell by the fact that she made the call that her assurance was beginning to shatter. Whenever she let Block in or out, there was much whispering in the downstairs hall. That evening, he heard her and Mary George talking in low voices in the parlor. He thought he heard his name and he got up and tiptoed into the hall and down the first three steps until he could hear the voices distinctly.

"I had to call that priest," his mother was saying. "I'm afraid this is serious. I thought it was just a nervous breakdown but now I think it's something real. Doctor Block thinks it's something real too and whatever it is is worse because he's so run-down."

"Grow up, Mamma," Mary George said, "I've told you and I tell you again: what's wrong with him is purely psychosomatic." There was nothing she was not an expert on.

"No," his mother said, "it's a real disease. The doctor says so." He thought he detected a crack in her voice.

"Block is an idiot," Mary George said. "You've got to face the facts: Asbury can't write so he gets sick. He's going to be an invalid instead of an artist. Do you know what he needs?"

"No," his mother said.

"Two or three shock treatments," Mary George said. "Get that artist business out of his head once and for all."

His mother gave a little cry and he grasped the banister.

"Mark my words," his sister continued, "all he's going to be around here for the next fifty years is a decoration."

He went back to bed. In a sense she was right. He had

failed his god, Art, but he had been a faithful servant and Art was sending him Death. He had seen this from the first with a kind of mystical clarity. He went to sleep thinking of the peaceful spot in the family burying ground where he would soon lie, and after a while he saw that his body was being borne slowly toward it while his mother and Mary George watched without interest from their chairs on the porch. As the bier was carried across the dam, they could look up and see the procession reflected upside down in the pond. A lean dark figure in a Roman collar followed it. He had a mysteriously saturnine face in which there was a subtle blend of asceticism and corruption. Asbury was laid in a shallow grave on the hillside and the indistinct mourners, after standing in silence for a while, spread out over the darkening green. The Jesuit retired to a spot beneath a dead tree to smoke and meditate. The moon came up and Asbury was aware of a presence bending over him and a gentle warmth on his cold face. He knew that this was Art come to wake him and he sat up and opened his eyes. Across the hill all the lights were on in his mother's house. The black pond was speckled with little nickel-colored stars. The Jesuit had disappeared. All around him the cows were spread out grazing in the moonlight and one large white one, violently spotted, was softly licking his head as if it were a block of salt. He awoke with a shudder and discovered that his bed was soaking from a night sweat and as he sat shivering in the dark, he realized that the end was not many days distant. He gazed down into the crater of death and fell back dizzy on his pillow.

The next day his mother noted something almost ethereal about his ravaged face. He looked like one of those dying children who must have Christmas early. He sat up in the bed and directed the rearrangement of several chairs and had her remove a picture of a maiden chained to a rock for he knew it would make the Jesuit smile. He had the comfortable rocker taken away and when he finished, the room with its severe wall stains had a certain cell-like quality. He felt it would be attractive to the visitor.

All morning he waited, looking irritably up at the ceiling where the bird with the icicle in its beak seemed poised and waiting too; but the priest did not arrive until late in the afternoon. As soon as his mother opened the door, a loud unintelligible voice began to boom in the downstairs hall. Asbury's heart beat wildly. In a second there was a heavy creaking on the stairs. Then almost at once his mother, her expression constrained, came in followed by a massive old man who plowed straight across the room, picked up a chair by the side of the bed and put it under himself.

"I'm Fahther Finn—from Purrgatory," he said in a hearty voice. He had a large red face, a stiff brush of gray hair and was blind in one eye, but the good eye, blue and clear, was focussed sharply on Asbury. There was a grease spot on his vest. "So you want to talk to a priest?" he said. "Very wise. None of us knows the hour Our Blessed Lord may call us." Then he cocked his good eye up at Asbury's mother and said, "Thank you, you may leave us now."

Mrs. Fox stiffened and did not budge.

"I'd like to talk to Father Finn alone," Asbury said, feeling suddenly that here he had an ally, although he had not expected a priest like this one. His mother gave him a disgusted look and left the room. He knew she would go no farther than just outside the door.

"It's so nice to have you come," Asbury said. "This place is incredibly dreary. There's no one here an intelligent person can talk to. I wonder what you think of Joyce, Father?"

The priest lifted his chair and pushed closer. "You'll have to shout," he said. "Blind in one eye and deaf in one ear."

"What do you think of Joyce?" Asbury said louder.

"Joyce? Joyce who?" asked the priest.

"James Joyce," Asbury said and laughed.

The priest brushed his huge hand in the air as if he were bothered by gnats. "I haven't met him," he said. "Now. Do you say your morning and night prayers?"

Asbury appeared confused. "Joyce was a great writer," he murmured, forgetting to shout.

"You don't eh?" said the priest. "Well you will never learn to be good unless you pray regularly. You cannot love Jesus unless you speak to Him."

"The myth of the dying god has always fascinated me," Asbury shouted, but the priest did not appear to catch it.

"Do you have trouble with purity?" he demanded, and as

Asbury paled, he went on without waiting for an answer. "We all do but you must pray to the Holy Ghost for it. Mind, heart and body. Nothing is overcome without prayer. Pray with your family. Do you pray with your family?"

"God forbid," Asbury murmured. "My mother doesn't have time to pray and my sister is an atheist," he shouted.

"A shame!" said the priest. "Then you must pray for them."

"The artist prays by creating," Asbury ventured.

"Not enough!" snapped the priest. "If you do not pray daily, you are neglecting your immortal soul. Do you know your catechism?"

"Certainly not," Asbury muttered.

"Who made you?" the priest asked in a martial tone.

"Different people believe different things about that," Asbury said.

"God made you," the priest said shortly. "Who is God?"

"God is an idea created by man," Asbury said, feeling that he was getting into stride, that two could play at this.

"God is a spirit infinitely perfect," the priest said. "You are a very ignorant boy. Why did God make you?"

"God didn't. . . ."

"God made you to know Him, to love Him, to serve Him in this world and to be happy with Him in the next!" the old priest said in a battering voice. "If you don't apply yourself to the catechism how do you expect to know how to save your immortal soul?"

Asbury saw he had made a mistake and that it was time to get rid of the old fool. "Listen," he said, "I'm not a Roman."

"A poor excuse for not saying your prayers!" the old man snorted.

Asbury slumped slightly in the bed. "I'm dying," he shouted.

"But you're not dead yet!" said the priest, "and how do you expect to meet God face to face when you've never spoken to Him? How do you expect to get what you don't ask for? God does not send the Holy Ghost to those who don't ask for Him. Ask Him to send the Holy Ghost."

"The Holy Ghost?" Asbury said.

"Are you so ignorant you've never heard of the Holy Ghost?" the priest asked.

"Certainly I've heard of the Holy Ghost," Asbury said furiously, "and the Holy Ghost is the last thing I'm looking for!"

"And He may be the last thing you get," the priest said, his one fierce eye inflamed. "Do you want your soul to suffer eternal damnation? Do you want to be deprived of God for all eternity? Do you want to suffer the most terrible pain, greater than fire, the pain of loss? Do you want to suffer the pain of loss for all eternity?"

Asbury moved his arms and legs helplessly as if he were pinned to the bed by the terrible eye.

"How can the Holy Ghost fill your soul when it's full of trash?" the priest roared. "The Holy Ghost will not come until you see yourself as you are—a lazy ignorant conceited youth!" he said, pounding his fist on the little bedside table.

Mrs. Fox burst in. "Enough of this!" she cried. "How dare you talk that way to a poor sick boy? You're upsetting him. You'll have to go."

"The poor lad doesn't even know his catechism," the priest said, rising. "I should think you would have taught him to say his daily prayers. You have neglected your duty as his mother." He turned back to the bed and said affably, "I'll give you my blessing and after this you must say your daily prayers without fail," whereupon he put his hand on Asbury's head and rumbled something in Latin. "Call me any time," he said, "and we can have another little chat," and then he followed Mrs. Fox's rigid back out. The last thing Asbury heard him say was, "He's a good lad at heart but very ignorant."

When his mother had got rid of the priest she came rapidly up the steps again to say that she had told him so, but when she saw him, pale and drawn and ravaged, sitting up in his bed, staring in front of him with large childish shocked eyes, she did not have the heart and went rapidly out again.

The next morning he was so weak that she made up her mind he must go to the hospital. "I'm not going to any hospital," he kept repeating, turning his thudding head from side to side as if he wanted to work it loose from his body. "I'm not going to any hospital as long as I'm conscious." He was thinking bitterly that once he lost consciousness, she could drag him off to the hospital and fill him full of blood and prolong his misery for days. He was convinced that the end was approaching, that it would be today, and he was tormented now thinking of his useless life. He felt as if he were a shell that had to be filled with something but he did not know what. He began to take note of everything in the room as if for the last time—the ridiculous antique furniture, the pattern in the rug, the silly picture his mother had replaced. He even looked at the fierce bird with the icicle in its beak and felt that it was there for some purpose that he could not divine.

There was something he was searching for, something that he felt he must have, some last significant culminating experience that he must make for himself before he died—make for himself out of his own intelligence. He had always relied on himself and had never been a sniveler after the ineffable.

Once when Mary George was thirteen and he was five, she had lured him with the promise of an unnamed present into a large tent full of people and had dragged him backwards up to the front where a man in a blue suit and red and white tie was standing. "Here," she said in a loud voice. "I'm already saved but you can save him. He's a real stinker and too big for his britches." He had broken her grip and shot out of there like a small cur and later when he had asked for his present, she had said, "You would have got Salvation if you had waited for it but since you acted the way you did, you get nothing!"

As the day wore on, he grew more and more frantic for fear he would die without making some last meaningful experience for himself. His mother sat anxiously by the side of the bed. She had called Block twice and could not get him. He thought even now she had not realized that he was going to die, much less that the end was only hours off.

The light in the room was beginning to have an odd quality, almost as if it were taking on presence. In a darkened form it entered and seemed to wait. Outside it appeared to move no farther than the edge of the faded treeline, which he could see a few inches over the sill of his window. Suddenly he thought of that experience of communion that he had had in the dairy with the Negroes when they had smoked together, and at once he began to tremble with excitement. They would smoke together one last time.

After a moment, turning his head on the pillow, he said, "Mother, I want to tell the Negroes good-bye."

His mother paled. For an instant her face seemed about to fly apart. Then the line of her mouth hardened; her brows drew together. "Good-bye?" she said in a flat voice. "Where are you going?"

For a few seconds he only looked at her. Then he said, "I think you know. Get them. I don't have long."

"This is absurd," she muttered but she got up and hurried out. He heard her try to reach Block again before she went outside. He thought her clinging to Block at a time like this was touching and pathetic. He waited, preparing himself for the encounter as a religious man might prepare himself for the last sacrament. Presently he heard their steps on the stair.

"Here's Randall and Morgan," his mother said, ushering them in. "They've come to tell you hello."

The two of them came in grinning and shuffled to the side of the bed. They stood there, Randall in front and Morgan behind. "You sho do look well," Randall said. "You looks very well."

"You looks well," the other one said. "Yessuh, you looks fine."

"I ain't ever seen you looking so well before," Randall said.

"Yes, doesn't he look well?" his mother said. "I think he looks just fine."

"Yessuh," Randall said, "I speck you ain't even sick."

"Mother," Asbury said in a forced voice. "I'd like to talk to them alone."

His mother stiffened; then she marched out. She walked across the hall and into the room on the other side and sat down. Through the open doors he could see her begin to rock in little short jerks. The two Negroes looked as if their last protection had dropped away.

Asbury's head was so heavy he could not think what he had been going to do. "I'm dying," he said.

Both their grins became gelid. "You looks fine," Randall said.

"I'm going to die," Asbury repeated. Then with relief he remembered that they were going to smoke together. He reached for the package on the table and held it out to Randall, forgetting to shake out the cigarettes.

The Negro took the package and put it in his pocket. "I thank you," he said. "I certainly do prechate it."

Asbury stared as if he had forgotten again. After a second he became aware that the other Negro's face had turned infinitely sad; then he realized that it was not sad but sullen. He fumbled in the drawer of the table and pulled out an unopened package and thrust it at Morgan.

"I thanks you, Mist Asbury," Morgan said, brightening. "You certly does look well."

"I'm about to die," Asbury said irritably.

"You looks fine," Randall said.

"You be up and around in a few days," Morgan predicted. Neither of them seemed to find a suitable place to rest his gaze. Asbury looked wildly across the hall where his mother had her rocker turned so that her back faced him. It was apparent she had no intention of getting rid of them for him.

"I speck you might have a little cold," Randall said after a time.

"I takes a little turpentine and sugar when I has a cold," Morgan said.

"Shut your mouth," Randall said, turning on him.

"Shut your own mouth," Morgan said. "I know what I takes."

"He don't take what you take," Randall growled.

"Mother!" Asbury called in a shaking voice.

His mother stood up. "Mister Asbury has had company long enough now," she called. "You all can come back tomorrow."

"We be going," Randall said. "You sho do look well."

"You sho does," Morgan said.

They filed out agreeing with each other how well he looked but Asbury's vision became blurred before they reached the hall. For an instant he saw his mother's form as if it were a shadow in the door and then it disappeared after them down the stairs. He heard her call Block again but he heard it without interest. His head was spinning. He knew now there would be no significant experience before he died. There was nothing more to do but give her the key to the drawer where the letter was, and wait for the end.

He sank into a heavy sleep from which he awoke about five o'clock to see her white face, very small, at the end of a well of darkness. He took the key out of his pajama pocket and handed it to her and mumbled that there was a letter in the desk to be opened when he was gone, but she did not seem to understand. She put the key down on the bedside table and left it there and he returned to his dream in which two large boulders were circling each other inside his head.

He awoke a little after six to hear Block's car stop below in the driveway. The sound was like a summons, bringing him rapidly and with a clear head out of his sleep. He had a sudden terrible foreboding that the fate awaiting him was going to be more shattering than any he could have reckoned on. He lay absolutely motionless, as still as an animal the instant before an earthquake.

Block and his mother talked as they came up the stairs but he did not distinguish their words. The doctor came in making faces; his mother was smiling. "Guess what you've got, Sugarpie!" she cried. Her voice broke in on him with the force of a gunshot.

"Found theter ol' bug, did ol' Block," Block said, sinking down into the chair by the bed. He raised his hands over his head in the gesture of a victorious prize fighter and let them collapse in his lap as if the effort had exhausted him. Then he removed a red bandanna handkerchief that he carried to be funny with and wiped his face thoroughly, having a different expression on it every time it appeared from behind the rag.

"I think you're just as smart as you can be!" Mrs. Fox said. "Asbury," she said, "you have undulant fever. It'll keep coming back but it won't kill you!" Her smile was as bright and intense as a lightbulb without a shade. "I'm so relieved," she said.

Asbury sat up slowly, his face expressionless; then he fell back down again.

Block leaned over him and smiled. "You ain't going to die," he said, with deep satisfaction.

Nothing about Asbury stirred except his eyes. They did not appear to move on the surface but somewhere in their blurred depths there was an almost imperceptible motion as if something were struggling feebly. Block's gaze seemed to reach down like a steel pin and hold whatever it was until the life was out of it. "Undulant fever ain't so bad, Azzberry," he murmured. "It's the same as Bang's in a cow."

The boy gave a low moan and then was quiet.

"He must have drunk some unpasteurized milk up there," his mother said softly and then the two of them tiptoed out as if they thought he were about to go to sleep.

When the sound of their footsteps had faded on the stairs, Asbury sat up again. He turned his head, almost surreptitiously, to the side where the key he had given his mother was lying on the bedside table. His hand shot out and closed over it and returned it to his pocket. He glanced across the room into the small oval-framed dresser mirror. The eyes that stared back at him were the same that had returned his gaze every day from that mirror but it seemed to him that they were paler. They looked shocked clean as if they had been prepared for some awful vision about to come down on him. He shuddered and turned his head quickly the other way and stared out the window. A blinding red-gold sun moved serenely from under a purple cloud. Below it the treeline was black against the crimson sky. It formed a brittle wall, standing as if it were the frail defense he had set up in his mind to protect him from what was coming. The boy fell back on his pillow and stared at the ceiling. His limbs that had been racked for so many weeks by fever and chill were numb now. The old life in him was exhausted. He awaited the coming of new. It was then that he felt the beginning of a chill, a chill so peculiar, so light, that it was like a warm ripple across a deeper sea of cold. His breath came short. The fierce bird which through the years of his childhood and the days of his illness had been poised over his head, waiting mysteriously, appeared all at once to be in motion. Asbury blanched and the last film of illusion was torn as if by a whirlwind from his eyes. He saw that for the rest of his days, frail, racked, but enduring, he would live in the face of a purifying terror. A feeble cry, a last impossible protest escaped him. But the Holy Ghost, emblazoned in ice instead of fire, continued, implacable, to descend.

The Comforts of Home

THOMAS WITHDREW to the side of the window and with his head between the wall and the curtain he looked down on the driveway where the car had stopped. His mother and the little slut were getting out of it. His mother emerged slowly, stolid and awkward, and then the little slut's long slightly bowed legs slid out, the dress pulled above the knees. With a shriek of laughter she ran to meet the dog, who bounded, overjoyed, shaking with pleasure, to welcome her. Rage gathered throughout Thomas's large frame with a silent ominous intensity, like a mob assembling.

It was now up to him to pack a suitcase, go to the hotel, and stay there until the house should be cleared.

He did not know where a suitcase was, he disliked to pack, he needed his books, his typewriter was not portable, he was used to an electric blanket, he could not bear to eat in restaurants. His mother, with her daredevil charity, was about to wreck the peace of the house.

The back door slammed and the girl's laugh shot up from the kitchen, through the back hall, up the stairwell and into his room, making for him like a bolt of electricity. He jumped to the side and stood glaring about him. His words of the morning had been unequivocal: "If you bring that girl back into this house, I leave. You can choose—her or me."

She had made her choice. An intense pain gripped his throat. It was the first time in his thirty-five years . . . He felt a sudden burning moisture behind his eyes. Then he steadied himself, overcome by rage. On the contrary: she had not made any choice. She was counting on his attachment to his electric blanket. She would have to be shown.

The girl's laughter rang upward a second time and Thomas winced. He saw again her look of the night before. She had invaded his room. He had waked to find his door open and her in it. There was enough light from the hall to make her visible as she turned toward him. The face was like a comedienne's in a musical comedy—a pointed chin, wide apple cheeks and feline empty eyes. He had sprung out of his bed and snatched a straight chair and then he had backed her out the door, holding the chair in front of him like an animal trainer driving out a dangerous cat. He had driven her silently down the hall, pausing when he reached it to beat on his mother's door. The girl, with a gasp, turned and fled into the guest room.

In a moment his mother had opened her door and peered out apprehensively. Her face, greasy with whatever she put on it at night, was framed in pink rubber curlers. She looked down the hall where the girl had disappeared. Thomas stood before her, the chair still lifted in front of him as if he were about to quell another beast. "She tried to get in my room," he hissed, pushing in. "I woke up and she was trying to get in my room." He closed the door behind him and his voice rose in outrage. "I won't put up with this! I won't put up with it another day!"

His mother, backed by him to her bed, sat down on the edge of it. She had a heavy body on which sat a thin, mysteriously gaunt and incongruous head.

"I'm telling you for the last time," Thomas said, "I won't put up with this another day." There was an observable tendency in all of her actions. This was, with the best intentions in the world, to make a mockery of virtue, to pursue it with such a mindless intensity that everyone involved was made a fool of and virtue itself became ridiculous. "Not another day," he repeated.

His mother shook her head emphatically, her eyes still on the door.

Thomas put the chair on the floor in front of her and sat down on it. He leaned forward as if he were about to explain something to a defective child.

"That's just another way she's unfortunate," his mother said. "So awful, so awful. She told me the name of it but I forget what it is but it's something she can't help. Something she was born with. Thomas," she said and put her hand to her jaw, "suppose it were you?"

Exasperation blocked his windpipe. "Can't I make you see," he croaked, "that if she can't help herself you can't help her?"

His mother's eyes, intimate but untouchable, were the blue of great distances after sunset. "Nimpermaniac," she murmured.

"Nymphomaniac," he said fiercely. "She doesn't need to supply you with any fancy names. She's a moral moron. That's all you need to know. Born without the moral faculty—like somebody else would be born without a kidney or a leg. Do you understand?"

"I keep thinking it might be you," she said, her hand still on her jaw. "If it were you, how do you think I'd feel if nobody took you in? What if you were a nimpermaniac and not a brilliant smart person and you did what you couldn't help and . . ."

Thomas felt a deep unbearable loathing for himself as if he were turning slowly into the girl.

"What did she have on?" she asked abruptly, her eyes narrowing.

"Nothing!" he roared. "Now will you get her out of here!"

"How can I turn her out in the cold?" she said. "This morning she was threatening to kill herself again."

"Send her back to jail," Thomas said.

"I would not send *you* back to jail, Thomas," she said.

He got up and snatched the chair and fled the room while he was still able to control himself.

Thomas loved his mother. He loved her because it was his nature to do so, but there were times when he could not endure her love for him. There were times when it became nothing but pure idiot mystery and he sensed about him forces, invisible currents entirely out of his control. She proceeded always from the tritest of considerations—it was the *nice thing to do*—into the most foolhardy engagements with the devil, whom, of course, she never recognized.

The devil for Thomas was only a manner of speaking, but it was a manner appropriate to the situations his mother got into. Had she been in any degree intellectual, he could have proved to her from early Christian history that no excess of virtue is justified, that a moderation of good produces likewise a moderation in evil, that if Antony of Egypt had stayed at home and attended to his sister, no devils would have plagued him.

Thomas was not cynical and so far from being opposed to virtue, he saw it as the principle of order and the only thing that makes life bearable. His own life was made bearable by the fruits of his mother's saner virtues—by the well-regulated house she kept and the excellent meals she served. But when virtue got out of hand with her, as now, a sense of devils grew upon him, and these were not mental quirks in himself or the old lady, they were denizens with personalities, present though not visible, who might any moment be expected to shriek or rattle a pot.

The girl had landed in the county jail a month ago on a bad check charge and his mother had seen her picture in the paper. At the breakfast table she had gazed at it for a long time and then had passed it over the coffee pot to him. "Imagine," she said, "only nineteen years old and in that filthy jail. And she doesn't look like a bad girl."

Thomas glanced at the picture. It showed the face of a shrewd ragamuffin. He observed that the average age for criminality was steadily lowering.

"She looks like a wholesome girl," his mother said.

"Wholesome people don't pass bad checks," Thomas said.

"You don't know what you'd do in a pinch."

"I wouldn't pass a bad check," Thomas said.

"I think," his mother said, "I'll take her a little box of candy."

If then and there he had put his foot down, nothing else would have happened. His father, had he been living, would have put his foot down at that point. Taking a box of candy was her favorite nice thing to do. When anyone within her social station moved to town, she called and took a box of candy; when any of her friend's children had babies or won a scholarship, she called and took a box of candy; when an old person broke his hip, she was at his bedside with a box of candy. He had been amused at the idea of her taking a box of candy to the jail.

He stood now in his room with the girl's laugh rocketing away in his head and cursed his amusement.

When his mother returned from the visit to the jail, she had burst into his study without knocking and had collapsed full-length on his couch, lifting her small swollen feet up on the arm of it. After a moment, she recovered herself enough to sit up and put a newspaper under them. Then she fell back again. "We don't know how the other half lives," she said.

Thomas knew that though her conversation moved from cliché to cliché there were real experiences behind them. He was less sorry for the girl's being in jail than for his mother having to see her there. He would have spared her all unpleasant sights. "Well," he said and put away his journal, "you had better forget it now. The girl has ample reason to be in jail."

"You can't imagine what all she's been through," she said, sitting up again, "listen." The poor girl, Star, had been brought up by a stepmother with three children of her own, one an almost grown boy who had taken advantage of her in such dreadful ways that she had been forced to run away and find her real mother. Once found, her real mother had sent her to various boarding schools to get rid of her. At each of these she had been forced to run away by the presence of perverts and sadists so monstrous that their acts defied description. Thomas could tell that his mother had not been spared the details that she was sparing him. Now and again when she spoke vaguely, her voice shook and he could tell that she was remembering some horror that had been put to her graphically. He had hoped that in a few days the memory of all this would wear off, but it did not. The next day she returned to the jail with Kleenex and cold-cream and a few days later, she announced that she had consulted a lawyer.

It was at these times that Thomas truly mourned the death of his father though he had not been able to endure him in life. The old man would have had none of this foolishness. Untouched by useless compassion, he would (behind her back) have pulled the necessary strings with his crony, the sheriff, and the girl would have been packed off to the state penitentiary to serve her time. He had always been engaged in some enraged action until one morning when (with an angry glance at his wife as if she alone were responsible) he had dropped dead at the breakfast table. Thomas had inherited his father's reason without his ruthlessness and his mother's love of good without her tendency to pursue it. His plan for all practical action was to wait and see what developed.

The lawyer found that the story of the repeated atrocities was for the most part untrue, but when he explained to her that the girl was a psychopathic personality, not insane enough for the asylum, not criminal enough for the jail, not stable enough for society, Thomas's mother was more deeply affected than ever. The girl readily admitted that her story was untrue on account of her being a congenital liar; she lied, she said, because she was insecure. She had passed through the hands of several psychiatrists who had put the finishing touches to her education. She knew there was no hope for her. In the presence of such an affliction as this, his mother seemed bowed down by some painful mystery that nothing would make endurable but a redoubling of effort. To his annoyance, she appeared to look on *him* with compassion, as if her hazy charity no longer made distinctions.

A few days later she burst in and said that the lawyer had got the girl paroled—to her.

Thomas rose from his Morris chair, dropping the review he had been reading. His large bland face contracted in anticipated pain. "You are not," he said, "going to bring that girl here!"

"No, no," she said, "calm yourself, Thomas." She had managed with difficulty to get the girl a job in a pet shop in town and a place to board with a crotchety old lady of her acquaintance. People were not kind. They did not put themselves in the place of someone like Star who had everything against her.

Thomas sat down again and retrieved his review. He seemed just to have escaped some danger which he did not care to make clear to himself. "Nobody can tell you anything," he said, "but in a few days that girl will have left town, having got what she could out of you. You'll never hear from her again."

Two nights later he came home and opened the parlor door and was speared by a shrill depthless laugh. His mother and the girl sat close to the fireplace where the gas logs were lit. The girl gave the immediate impression of being physically crooked. Her hair was cut like a dog's or an elf's and she was dressed in the latest fashion. She was training on him a long familiar sparkling stare that turned after a second into an intimate grin.

"Thomas!" his mother said, her voice firm with the injunction not to bolt, "this is Star you've heard so much about. Star is going to have supper with us."

The girl called herself Star Drake. The lawyer had found that her real name was Sarah Ham.

Thomas neither moved nor spoke but hung in the door in what seemed a savage perplexity. Finally he said, "How do you do, Sarah," in a tone of such loathing that he was shocked at the sound of it. He reddened, feeling it beneath him to show contempt for any creature so pathetic. He advanced into the room, determined at least on a decent politeness and sat down heavily in a straight chair.

"Thomas writes history," his mother said with a threatening look at him. "He's president of the local Historical Society this year."

The girl leaned forward and gave Thomas an even more pointed attention. "Fabulous!" she said in a throaty voice.

"Right now Thomas is writing about the first settlers in this county," his mother said.

"Fabulous!" the girl repeated.

Thomas by an effort of will managed to look as if he were alone in the room.

"Say, you know who he looks like?" Star asked, her head on one side, taking him in at an angle.

"Oh some one very distinguished!" his mother said archly.

"This cop I saw in the movie I went to last night," Star said.

"Star," his mother said, "I think you ought to be careful about the kind of movies you go to. I think you ought to see only the best ones. I don't think crime stories would be good for you."

"Oh this was a crime-does-not-pay," Star said, "and I swear this cop looked exactly like him. They were always putting something over on the guy. He would look like he couldn't stand it a minute longer or he would blow up. He was a riot. And not bad looking," she added with an appreciative leer at Thomas.

"Star," his mother said, "I think it would be grand if you developed a taste for music."

Thomas sighed. His mother rattled on and the girl, paying no attention to her, let her eyes play over him. The quality of her look was such that it might have been her hands, resting now on his knees, now on his neck. Her eyes had a mocking glitter and he knew that she was well aware he could not stand the sight of her. He needed nothing to tell him he was in the presence of the very stuff of corruption, but blameless corruption because there was no responsible faculty behind it. He was looking at the most unendurable form of innocence. Absently he asked himself what the attitude of God was to this, meaning if possible to adopt it.

His mother's behavior throughout the meal was so idiotic that he could barely stand to look at her and since he could less stand to look at Sarah Ham, he fixed on the sideboard across the room a continuous gaze of disapproval and disgust. Every remark of the girl's his mother met as if it deserved serious attention. She advanced several plans for the wholesome use of Star's spare time. Sarah Ham paid no more attention to this advice than if it came from a parrot. Once when Thomas inadvertently looked in her direction, she winked. As soon as he had swallowed the last spoonful of dessert, he rose and muttered, "I have to go, I have a meeting."

"Thomas," his mother said, "I want you to take Star home on your way. I don't want her riding in taxis by herself at night."

For a moment Thomas remained furiously silent. Then he turned and left the room. Presently he came back with a look of obscure determination on his face. The girl was ready, meekly waiting at the parlor door. She cast up at him a great look of admiration and confidence. Thomas did not offer his arm but she took it anyway and moved out of the house and down the steps, attached to what might have been a miraculously moving monument.

"Be good!" his mother called.

Sarah Ham snickered and poked him in the ribs.

While getting his coat he had decided that this would be his opportunity to tell the girl that unless she ceased to be a parasite on his mother, he would see to it, personally, that she was returned to jail. He would let her know that he understood what she was up to, that he was not an innocent and that there were certain things he would not put up with. At his desk, pen in hand, none was more articulate than Thomas. As soon as he found himself shut into the car with Sarah Ham, terror seized his tongue.

She curled her feet up under her and said, "Alone at last," and giggled.

Thomas swerved the car away from the house and drove fast toward the gate. Once on the highway, he shot forward as if he were being pursued.

"Jesus!" Sarah Ham said, swinging her feet off the seat, "where's the fire?"

Thomas did not answer. In a few seconds he could feel her edging closer. She stretched, eased nearer, and finally hung her hand limply over his shoulder. "Tomsee doesn't like me," she said, "but I think he's fabulously cute."

Thomas covered the three and a half miles into town in a little over four minutes. The light at the first intersection was red but he ignored it. The old woman lived three blocks beyond. When the car screeched to a halt at the place, he jumped out and ran around to the girl's door and opened it. She did not move from the car and Thomas was obliged to wait. After a moment one leg emerged, then her small white crooked face appeared and stared up at him. There was something about the look of it that suggested blindness but it was the blindness of those who don't know that they cannot see. Thomas was curiously sickened. The empty eyes moved over him. "Nobody likes me," she said in a sullen tone. "What if you were me and I couldn't stand to ride you three miles?"

"My mother likes you," he muttered.

"Her!" the girl said. "She's just about seventy-five years behind the times!"

Breathlessly Thomas said, "If I find you bothering her again, I'll have you put back in jail." There was a dull force behind his voice though it came out barely above a whisper.

"You and who else?" she said and drew back in the car as if now she did not intend to get out at all. Thomas reached into it, blindly grasped the front of her coat, pulled her out by it and released her. Then he lunged back to the car and sped off. The other door was still hanging open and her laugh, bodiless but real, bounded up the street as if it were about to jump in the open side of the car and ride away with him. He reached over and slammed the door and then drove toward home, too angry to attend his meeting. He intended to make his mother well-aware of his displeasure. He intended to leave no doubt in her mind. The voice of his father rasped in his head.

Numbskull, the old man said, put your foot down now. Show her who's boss before she shows you.

But when Thomas reached home, his mother, wisely, had gone to bed.

The next morning he appeared at the breakfast table, his brow lowered and the thrust of his jaw indicating that he was in a dangerous humor. When he intended to be determined, Thomas began like a bull that, before charging, backs with his head lowered and paws the ground. "All right now listen," he began, yanking out his chair and sitting down, "I have something to say to you about that girl and I don't intend to say it but once." He drew breath. "She's nothing but a little slut. She makes fun of you behind your back. She means to get everything she can out of you and you are nothing to her."

His mother looked as if she too had spent a restless night. She did not dress in the morning but wore her bathrobe and a grey turban around her head, which gave her face a disconcerting omniscient look. He might have been breakfasting with a sibyl.

"You'll have to use canned cream this morning," she said, pouring his coffee. "I forgot the other."

"All right, did you hear me?" Thomas growled.

"I'm not deaf," his mother said and put the pot back on the trivet. "I know I'm nothing but an old bag of wind to her."

"Then why do you persist in this foolhardy . . ."

"Thomas," she said, and put her hand to the side of her face, "it might be . . ."

"It is not me!" Thomas said, grasping the table leg at his knee.

She continued to hold her face, shaking her head slightly. "Think of all you have," she began. "All the comforts of home. And morals, Thomas. No bad inclinations, nothing bad you were born with."

Thomas began to breathe like some one who feels the onset of asthma. "You are not logical," he said in a limp voice. "*He* would have put his foot down."

The old lady stiffened. "You," she said, "are not like him."

Thomas opened his mouth silently.

"However," his mother said, in a tone of such subtle accusation that she might have been taking back the compliment, "I won't invite her back again since you're so dead set against her."

"I am not set against her," Thomas said. "I am set against your making a fool of yourself."

As soon as he left the table and closed the door of his study on himself, his father took up a squatting position in his mind. The old man had had the countryman's ability to converse squatting, though he was no countryman but had been born and brought up in the city and only moved to a smaller place later to exploit his talents. With steady skill he had made them think him one of them. In the midst of a conversation on the courthouse lawn, he would squat and his two or three companions would squat with him with no break in the surface of the talk. By gesture he had lived his lie; he had never deigned to tell one.

Let her run over you, he said. You ain't like me. Not enough to be a man.

Thomas began vigorously to read and presently the image faded. The girl had caused a disturbance in the depths of his being, somewhere out of the reach of his power of analysis. He felt as if he had seen a tornado pass a hundred yards away and had an intimation that it would turn again and head directly for him. He did not get his mind firmly on his work until mid-morning.

Two nights later, his mother and he were sitting in the den after their supper, each reading a section of the evening paper, when the telephone began to ring with the brassy intensity of a fire alarm. Thomas reached for it. As soon as the receiver was in his hand, a shrill female voice screamed into the room, "Come get this girl! Come get her! Drunk! Drunk in my parlor and I won't have it! Lost her job and come back here drunk! I won't have it!"

His mother leapt up and snatched the receiver.

The ghost of Thomas's father rose before him. Call the sheriff, the old man prompted. "Call the sheriff," Thomas said in a loud voice. "Call the sheriff to go there and pick her up."

"We'll be right there," his mother was saying. "We'll come and get her right away. Tell her to get her things together."

"She ain't in no condition to get nothing together," the voice screamed. "You shouldn't have put something like her off on me! My house is respectable!"

"Tell her to call the sheriff," Thomas shouted.

His mother put the receiver down and looked at him. "I wouldn't turn a dog over to that man," she said.

Thomas sat in the chair with his arms folded and looked fixedly at the wall.

"Think of the poor girl, Thomas," his mother said, "with nothing. Nothing. And we have everything."

When they arrived, Sarah Ham was slumped spraddle-legged against the banister on the boarding house front-steps. Her tam was down on her forehead where the old woman had slammed it and her clothes were bulging out of her suit-case where the old woman had thrown them in. She was carrying on a drunken conversation with herself in a low personal tone. A streak of lipstick ran up one side of her face. She allowed herself to be guided by his mother to the car and put in the back seat without seeming to know who the res-cuer was. "Nothing to talk to all day but a pack of god-damned parakeets," she said in a furious whisper.

Thomas, who had not got out of the car at all, or looked at her after the first revolted glance, said, "I'm telling you once and for all, the place to take her is the jail."

His mother, sitting on the back seat, holding the girl's hand, did not answer.

"All right, take her to the hotel," he said.

"I cannot take a drunk girl to a hotel, Thomas," she said. "You know that."

"Then take her to a hospital."

"She doesn't need a jail or a hotel or a hospital," his mother said, "she needs a home."

"She does not need mine," Thomas said.

"Only for tonight, Thomas," the old lady sighed. "Only for tonight."

Since then eight days had passed. The little slut was estab-lished in the guest room. Every day his mother set out to find her a job and a place to board, and failed, for the old woman had broadcast a warning. Thomas kept to his room or the den. His home was to him home, workshop, church, as personal as the shell of a turtle and as necessary. He could not believe that it could be violated in this way. His flushed face had a constant look of stunned outrage.

As soon as the girl was up in the morning, her voice throbbed out in a blues song that would rise and waver, then plunge low with insinuations of passion about to be satisfied and Thomas, at his desk, would lunge up and begin frantically stuffing his ears with Kleenex. Each time he started from one room to another, one floor to another, she would be certain to appear. Each time he was half way up or down the stairs, she would either meet him and pass, cringing coyly, or go up or down behind him, breathing small tragic spearmint-flavored sighs. She appeared to adore Thomas's repugnance to her and to draw it out of him every chance she got as if it added delectably to her martyrdom.

The old man—small, wasp-like, in his yellowed panama hat, his seersucker suit, his pink carefully-soiled shirt, his small string tie—appeared to have taken up his station in Thomas's mind and from there, usually squatting, he shot out the same rasping suggestion every time the boy paused from his forced studies. Put your foot down. Go to see the sheriff.

The sheriff was another edition of Thomas's father except that he wore a checkered shirt and a Texas type hat and was ten years younger. He was as easily dishonest, and he had genuinely admired the old man. Thomas, like his mother, would have gone far out of his way to avoid his glassy pale blue gaze. He kept hoping for another solution, for a miracle.

With Sarah Ham in the house, meals were unbearable.

"Tomsee doesn't like me," she said the third or fourth night at the supper table and cast her pouting gaze across at the large rigid figure of Thomas, whose face was set with the look of a man trapped by insufferable odors. "He doesn't want me here. Nobody wants me anywhere."

"Thomas's name is Thomas," his mother interrupted. "Not Tomsee."

"I made Tomsee up," she said. "I think it's cute. He hates me."

"Thomas does not hate you," his mother said. "We are not

the kind of people who hate," she added, as if this were an imperfection that had been bred out of them generations ago.

"Oh, I know when I'm not wanted," Sarah Ham continued. "They didn't even want me in jail. If I killed myself I wonder would God want me?"

"Try it and see," Thomas muttered.

The girl screamed with laughter. Then she stopped abruptly, her face puckered and she began to shake. "The best thing to do," she said, her teeth clattering, "is to kill myself. Then I'll be out of everybody's way. I'll go to hell and be out of God's way. And even the devil won't want me. He'll kick me out of hell, not even in hell . . ." she wailed.

Thomas rose, picked up his plate and knife and fork and carried them to the den to finish his supper. After that, he had not eaten another meal at the table but had had his mother serve him at his desk. At these meals, the old man was intensely present to him. He appeared to be tipping backwards in his chair, his thumbs beneath his galluses, while he said such things as, She never ran me away from my own table.

A few nights later, Sarah Ham slashed her wrists with a paring knife and had hysterics. From the den where he was closeted after supper, Thomas heard a shriek, then a series of screams, then his mother's scurrying footsteps through the house. He did not move. His first instant of hope that the girl had cut her throat faded as he realized she could not have done it and continue to scream the way she was doing. He returned to his journal and presently the screams subsided. In a moment his mother burst in with his coat and hat. "We have to take her to the hospital," she said. "She tried to do away with herself. I have a tourniquet on her arm. Oh Lord, Thomas," she said, "imagine being so low you'd do a thing like that!"

Thomas rose woodenly and put on his hat and coat. "We will take her to the hospital," he said, "and we will leave her there."

"And drive her to despair again?" the old lady cried. "Thomas!"

Standing in the center of his room now, realizing that he had reached the point where action was inevitable, that he must pack, that he must leave, that he must go, Thomas remained immovable.

His fury was directed not at the little slut but at his mother. Even though the doctor had found that she had barely damaged herself and had raised the girl's wrath by laughing at the tourniquet and putting only a streak of iodine on the cut, his mother could not get over the incident. Some new weight of sorrow seemed to have been thrown across her shoulders, and not only Thomas, but Sarah Ham was infuriated by this, for it appeared to be a general sorrow that would have found another object no matter what good fortune came to either of them. The experience of Sarah Ham had plunged the old lady into mourning for the world.

The morning after the attempted suicide, she had gone through the house and collected all the knives and scissors and locked them in a drawer. She emptied a bottle of rat poison down the toilet and took up the roach tablets from the kitchen floor. Then she came to Thomas's study and said in a whisper, "Where is that gun of his? I want you to lock it up."

"The gun is in my drawer," Thomas roared, "and I will not lock it up. If she shoots herself, so much the better!"

"Thomas," his mother said, "she'll hear you!"

"Let her hear me!" Thomas yelled. "Don't you know she has no intention of killing herself? Don't you know her kind never kill themselves? Don't you . . ."

His mother slipped out the door and closed it to silence him and Sarah Ham's laugh, quite close in the hall, came rattling into his room. "Tomsee'll find out. I'll kill myself and then he'll be sorry he wasn't nice to me. I'll use his own lil gun, his own lil ol' pearl-handled revol-lervuh!" she shouted and let out a loud tormented-sounding laugh in imitation of a movie monster.

Thomas ground his teeth. He pulled out his desk drawer and felt for the pistol. It was an inheritance from the old man, whose opinion it had been that every house should contain a loaded gun. He had discharged two bullets one night into the side of a prowler, but Thomas had never shot anything. He had no fear that the girl would use the gun on herself and he closed the drawer. Her kind clung tenaciously to life and were able to wrest some histrionic advantage from every moment.

Several ideas for getting rid of her had entered his head but each of these had been suggestions whose moral tone indicated that they had come from a mind akin to his father's, and Thomas had rejected them. He could not get the girl locked up again until she did something illegal. The old man would have been able with no qualms at all to get her drunk and send her out on the highway in his car, meanwhile notifying the highway patrol of her presence on the road, but Thomas considered this below his moral stature. Suggestions continued to come to him, each more outrageous than the last.

He had not the vaguest hope that the girl would get the gun and shoot herself, but that afternoon when he looked in the drawer, the gun was gone. His study locked from the inside, not the out. He cared nothing about the gun, but the thought of Sarah Ham's hands sliding among his papers infuriated him. Now even his study was contaminated. The only place left untouched by her was his bedroom.

That night she entered it.

In the morning at breakfast, he did not eat and did not sit down. He stood beside his chair and delivered his ultimatum while his mother sipped her coffee as if she were both alone in the room and in great pain. "I have stood this," he said, "for as long as I am able. Since I see plainly that you care nothing about me, about my peace or comfort or working conditions, I am about to take the only step open to me. I will give you one more day. If you bring the girl back into this house this afternoon, I leave. You can choose—her or me." He had more to say but at that point his voice cracked and he left.

At ten o'clock his mother and Sarah Ham left the house.

At four he heard the car wheels on the gravel and rushed to the window. As the car stopped, the dog stood up, alert, shaking.

He seemed unable to take the first step that would set him walking to the closet in the hall to look for the suitcase. He was like a man handed a knife and told to operate on himself if he wished to live. His huge hands clenched helplessly. His expression was a turmoil of indecision and outrage. His pale blue eyes seemed to sweat in his broiling face. He closed them for a moment and on the back of his lids, his father's image leered at him. Idiot! the old man hissed, idiot! The criminal slut stole your gun! See the sheriff! See the sheriff!

It was a moment before Thomas opened his eyes. He seemed newly stunned. He stood where he was for at least three minutes, then he turned slowly like a large vessel reversing its direction and faced the door. He stood there a moment longer, then he left, his face set to see the ordeal through.

He did not know where he would find the sheriff. The man made his own rules and kept his own hours. Thomas stopped first at the jail where his office was, but he was not in it. He went to the courthouse and was told by a clerk that the sheriff had gone to barber-shop across the street. "Yonder's the deppity," the clerk said and pointed out the window to the large figure of a man in a checkered shirt, who was leaning against the side of a police car, looking into space.

"It has to be the sheriff," Thomas said and left for the barber-shop. As little as he wanted anything to do with the sheriff, he realized that the man was at least intelligent and not simply a mound of sweating flesh.

The barber said the sheriff had just left. Thomas started back to the courthouse and as he stepped on to the sidewalk from the street, he saw a lean, slightly stooped figure gesticulating angrily at the deputy.

Thomas approached with an aggressiveness brought on by nervous agitation. He stopped abruptly three feet away and said in an over-loud voice, "Can I have a word with you?" without adding the sheriff's name, which was Farebrother.

Farebrother turned his sharp creased face just enough to take Thomas in, and the deputy did likewise, but neither spoke. The sheriff removed a very small piece of cigaret from his lip and dropped it at his feet. "I told you what to do," he said to the deputy. Then he moved off with a slight nod that indicated Thomas could follow him if he wanted to see him. The deputy slunk around the front of the police car and got inside.

Farebrother, with Thomas following, headed across the courthouse square and stopped beneath a tree that shaded a quarter of the front lawn. He waited, leaning slightly forward, and lit another cigaret.

Thomas began to blurt out his business. As he had not had

time to prepare his words, he was barely coherent. By repeating the same thing over several times, he managed at length to get out what he wanted to say. When he finished, the sheriff was still leaning slightly forward, at an angle to him, his eyes on nothing in particular. He remained that way without speaking.

Thomas began again, slower and in a lamer voice, and Farebrother let him continue for some time before he said, "We had her oncet." He then allowed himself a slow, creased, all-knowing, quarter smile.

"I had nothing to do with that," Thomas said. "That was my mother."

Farebrother squatted.

"She was trying to help the girl," Thomas said. "She didn't know she couldn't be helped."

"Bit off more than she could chew, I reckon," the voice below him mused.

"She has nothing to do with this," Thomas said. "She doesn't know I'm here. The girl is dangerous with that gun."

"He," the sheriff said, "never let anything grow under his feet. Particularly nothing a woman planted."

"She might kill somebody with that gun," Thomas said weakly, looking down at the round top of the Texas type hat.

There was a long time of silence.

"Where's she got it?" Farebrother asked.

"I don't know. She sleeps in the guest room. It must be in there, in her suitcase probably," Thomas said.

Farebrother lapsed into silence again.

"You could come search the guest room," Thomas said in a strained voice. "I can go home and leave the latch off the front door and you can come in quietly and go upstairs and search her room."

Farebrother turned his head so that his eyes looked boldly at Thomas's knees. "You seem to know how it ought to be done," he said. "Want to swap jobs?"

Thomas said nothing because he could not think of anything to say, but he waited doggedly. Farebrother removed the cigaret butt from his lips and dropped it on the grass. Beyond him on the courthouse porch a group of loiterers who had been leaning at the left of the door moved over to the right where a patch of sunlight had settled. From one of the upper windows a crumpled piece of paper blew out and drifted down.

"I'll come along about six," Farebrother said. "Leave the latch off the door and keep out of my way—yourself and them two women too."

Thomas let out a rasping sound of relief meant to be "Thanks," and struck off across the grass like some one released. The phrase, "them two women," stuck like a burr in his brain—the subtlety of the insult to his mother hurting him more than any of Farebrother's references to his own incompetence. As he got into his car, his face suddenly flushed. Had he delivered his mother over to the sheriff—to be a butt for the man's tongue? Was he betraying her to get rid of the little slut? He saw at once that this was not the case. He was doing what he was doing for her own good, to rid her of a parasite that would ruin their peace. He started his car and drove quickly home but once he had turned in the driveway, he decided it would be better to park some distance from the house and go quietly in by the back door. He parked on the grass and on the grass walked in a circle toward the rear of the house. The sky was lined with mustard-colored streaks. The dog was asleep on the back doormat. At the approach of his master's step, he opened one yellow eye, took him in, and closed it again.

Thomas let himself into the kitchen. It was empty and the house was quiet enough for him to be aware of the loud ticking of the kitchen clock. It was a quarter to six. He tiptoed hurriedly through the hall to the front door and took the latch off it. Then he stood for a moment listening. From behind the closed parlor door, he heard his mother snoring softly and presumed that she had gone to sleep while reading. On the other side of the hall, not three feet from his study, the little slut's black coat and red pocketbook were slung on a chair. He heard water running upstairs and decided she was taking a bath.

He went into his study and sat down at his desk to wait, noting with distaste that every few moments a tremor ran through him. He sat for a minute or two doing nothing. Then he picked up a pen and began to draw squares on the back of an envelope that lay before him. He looked at his watch. It was eleven minutes to six. After a moment he idly drew the center drawer of the desk out over his lap. For a moment he stared at the gun without recognition. Then he gave a yelp and leaped up. She had put it back!

Idiot! his father hissed, idiot! Go plant it in her pocketbook. Don't just stand there. Go plant it in her pocketbook!

Thomas stood staring at the drawer.

Moron! the old man fumed. Quick while there's time! Go plant it in her pocketbook.

Thomas did not move.

Imbecile! his father cried.

Thomas picked up the gun.

Make haste, the old man ordered.

Thomas started forward, holding the gun away from him. He opened the door and looked at the chair. The black coat and red pocketbook were lying on it almost within reach.

Hurry up, you fool, his father said.

From behind the parlor door the almost inaudible snores of his mother rose and fell. They seemed to mark an order of time that had nothing to do with the instants left to Thomas. There was no other sound.

Quick, you imbecile, before she wakes up, the old man said.

The snores stopped and Thomas heard the sofa springs groan. He grabbed the red pocketbook. It had a skin-like feel to his touch and as it opened, he caught an unmistakable odor of the girl. Wincing, he thrust in the gun and then drew back. His face burned an ugly dull red.

"What is Tomsee putting in my purse?" she called and her pleased laugh bounced down the staircase. Thomas whirled.

She was at the top of the stair, coming down in the manner of a fashion model, one bare leg and then the other thrusting out the front of her kimona in a definite rhythm. "Tomsee is being naughty," she said in a throaty voice. She reached the bottom and cast a possessive leer at Thomas whose face was now more grey than red. She reached out, pulled the bag open with her finger and peered at the gun.

His mother opened the parlor door and looked out.

"Tomsee put his pistol in my bag!" the girl shrieked.

"Ridiculous," his mother said, yawning. "What would Thomas want to put his pistol in your bag for?"

Thomas stood slightly hunched, his hands hanging helplessly at the wrists as if he had just pulled them up out of a pool of blood.

"I don't know what for," the girl said, "but he sure did it," and she proceeded to walk around Thomas, her hands on her hips, her neck thrust forward and her intimate grin fixed on him fiercely. All at once her expression seemed to open as the purse had opened when Thomas touched it. She stood with her head cocked on one side in an attitude of disbelief. "Oh boy," she said slowly, "is he a case."

At that instant Thomas damned not only the girl but the entire order of the universe that made her possible.

"Thomas wouldn't put a gun in your bag," his mother said. "Thomas is a gentleman."

The girl made a chortling noise. "You can see it in there," she said and pointed to the open purse.

You *found* it in her bag, you dimwit! the old man hissed.

"I found it in her bag!" Thomas shouted. "The dirty criminal slut stole my gun!"

His mother gasped at the sound of the other presence in his voice. The old lady's sybil-like face turned pale.

"Found it my eye!" Sarah Ham shrieked and started for the pocketbook, but Thomas, as if his arm were guided by his father, caught it first and snatched the gun. The girl in a frenzy lunged at Thomas's throat and would actually have caught him around the neck had not his mother thrown herself forward to protect her.

Fire! the old man yelled.

Thomas fired. The blast was like a sound meant to bring an end to evil in the world. Thomas heard it as a sound that would shatter the laughter of sluts until all shrieks were stilled and nothing was left to disturb the peace of perfect order.

The echo died away in waves. Before the last one had faded, Farebrother opened the door and put his head inside the hall. His nose wrinkled. His expression for some few seconds was that of a man unwilling to admit surprise. His eyes were clear as glass, reflecting the scene. The old lady lay on the floor between the girl and Thomas.

The sheriff's brain worked instantly like a calculating machine. He saw the facts as if they were already in print: the fellow had intended all along to kill his mother and pin it on the girl. But Farebrother had been too quick for him. They were not yet aware of his head in the door. As he scrutinized the scene, further insights were flashed to him. Over her body, the killer and the slut were about to collapse into each other's arms. The sheriff knew a nasty bit when he saw it. He was accustomed to enter upon scenes that were not as bad as he had hoped to find them, but this one met his expectations.

The Lame Shall Enter First

SHEPPARD SAT on a stool at the bar that divided the kitchen in half, eating his cereal out of the individual pasteboard box it came in. He ate mechanically, his eyes on the child, who was wandering from cabinet to cabinet in the panelled kitchen, collecting the ingredients for his breakfast. He was a stocky blond boy of ten. Sheppard kept his intense blue eyes fixed on him. The boy's future was written in his face. He would be a banker. No, worse. He would operate a small loan company. All he wanted for the child was that he be good and unselfish and neither seemed likely. Sheppard was a young man whose hair was already white. It stood up like a narrow brush halo over his pink sensitive face.

The boy approached the bar with the jar of peanut butter under his arm, a plate with a quarter of a small chocolate cake on it in one hand and the ketchup bottle in the other. He did not appear to notice his father. He climbed up on the stool and began to spread peanut butter on the cake. He had very large round ears that leaned away from his head and seemed to pull his eyes slightly too far apart. His shirt was green but so faded that the cowboy charging across the front of it was only a shadow.

"Norton," Sheppard said, "I saw Rufus Johnson yesterday. Do you know what he was doing?"

The child looked at him with a kind of half attention, his eyes forward but not yet engaged. They were a paler blue than his father's as if they might have faded like the shirt; one of them listed, almost imperceptibly, toward the outer rim.

"He was in an alley," Sheppard said, "and he had his hand in a garbage can. He was trying to get something to eat out of it." He paused to let this soak in. "He was hungry," he finished, and tried to pierce the child's conscience with his gaze.

The boy picked up the piece of chocolate cake and began to gnaw it from one corner.

"Norton," Sheppard said, "do you have any idea what it means to share?"

A flicker of attention. "Some of it's yours," Norton said.

"Some of it's *his*," Sheppard said heavily. It was hopeless. Almost any fault would have been preferable to selfishness—a violent temper, even a tendency to lie.

The child turned the bottle of ketchup upside-down and began thumping ketchup onto the cake.

Sheppard's look of pain increased. "You are ten and Rufus Johnson is fourteen," he said. "Yet I'm sure your shirts would fit Rufus." Rufus Johnson was a boy he had been trying to help at the reformatory for the past year. He had been released two months ago. "When he was in the reformatory, he looked pretty good, but when I saw him yesterday, he was skin and bones. He hasn't been eating cake with peanut butter on it for breakfast."

The child paused. "It's stale," he said. "That's why I have to put stuff on it."

Sheppard turned his face to the window at the end of the bar. The side lawn, green and even, sloped fifty feet or so down to a small suburban wood. When his wife was living, they had often eaten outside, even breakfast, on the grass. He had never noticed then that the child was selfish. "Listen to me," he said, turning back to him, "look at me and listen."

The boy looked at him. At least his eyes were forward.

"I gave Rufus a key to this house when he left the reformatory—to show my confidence in him and so he would have a place he could come to and feel welcome any time. He didn't use it, but I think he'll use it now because he's seen me and he's hungry. And if he doesn't use it, I'm going out and find him and bring him here. I can't see a child eating out of garbage cans."

The boy frowned. It was dawning upon him that something of his was threatened.

Sheppard's mouth stretched in disgust. "Rufus's father died before he was born," he said. "His mother is in the state penitentiary. He was raised by his grandfather in a shack without water or electricity and the old man beat him every day. How would you like to belong to a family like that?"

"I don't know," the child said lamely.

"Well, you might think about it sometime," Sheppard said.

Sheppard was City Recreational Director. On Saturdays he worked at the reformatory as a counselor, receiving nothing for it but the satisfaction of knowing he was helping boys no one else cared about. Johnson was the most intelligent boy he had worked with and the most deprived.

Norton turned what was left of the cake over as if he no longer wanted it.

"You started that, now finish it," Sheppard said.

"Maybe he won't come," the child said and his eyes brightened slightly.

"Think of everything you have that he doesn't!" Sheppard said. "Suppose you had to root in garbage cans for food? Suppose you had a huge swollen foot and one side of you dropped lower than the other when you walked?"

The boy looked blank, obviously unable to imagine such a thing.

"You have a healthy body," Sheppard said, "a good home. You've never been taught anything but the truth. Your daddy gives you everything you need and want. You don't have a grandfather who beats you. And your mother is not in the state penitentiary."

The child pushed his plate away. Sheppard groaned aloud.

A knot of flesh appeared below the boy's suddenly distorted mouth. His face became a mass of lumps with slits for eyes. "If she was in the penitentiary," he began in a kind of racking bellow, "I could go to seeeeee her." Tears rolled down his face and the ketchup dribbled on his chin. He looked as if he had been hit in the mouth. He abandoned himself and howled.

Sheppard sat helpless and miserable, like a man lashed by some elemental force of nature. This was not a normal grief. It was all part of his selfishness. She had been dead for over a year and a child's grief should not last so long. "You're going on eleven years old," he said reproachfully.

The child began an agonizing high-pitched heaving noise.

"If you stop thinking about yourself and think what you can do for somebody else," Sheppard said, "then you'll stop missing your mother."

The boy was silent but his shoulders continued to shake. Then his face collapsed and he began to howl again.

"Don't you think I'm lonely without her too?" Sheppard said. "Don't you think I miss her at all? I do, but I'm not sitting around moping. I'm busy helping other people. When do you see me just sitting around thinking about my troubles?"

The boy slumped as if he were exhausted but fresh tears streaked his face.

"What are you going to do today?" Sheppard asked, to get his mind on something else.

The child ran his arm across his eyes. "Sell seeds," he mumbled.

Always selling something. He had four quart jars full of nickels and dimes he had saved and he took them out of his closet every few days and counted them. "What are you selling seeds for?"

"To win a prize."

"What's the prize?"

"A thousand dollars."

"And what would you do if you had a thousand dollars?"

"Keep it," the child said and wiped his nose on his shoulder.

"I feel sure you would," Sheppard said. "Listen," he said and lowered his voice to an almost pleading tone, "suppose by some chance you did win a thousand dollars. Wouldn't you like to spend it on children less fortunate than yourself? Wouldn't you like to give some swings and trapezes to the orphanage? Wouldn't you like to buy poor Rufus Johnson a new shoe?"

The boy began to back away from the bar. Then suddenly he leaned forward and hung with his mouth open over his plate. Sheppard groaned again. Everything came up, the cake, the peanut butter, the ketchup—a limp sweet batter. He hung over it gagging, more came, and he waited with his mouth open over the plate as if he expected his heart to come up next.

"It's all right," Sheppard said, "it's all right. You couldn't help it. Wipe your mouth and go lie down."

The child hung there a moment longer. Then he raised his face and looked blindly at his father.

"Go on," Sheppard said. "Go on and lie down."

The boy pulled up the end of his t-shirt and smeared his mouth with it. Then he climbed down off the stool and wandered out of the kitchen.

Sheppard sat there staring at the puddle of half-digested food. The sour odor reached him and he drew back. His gorge rose. He got up and carried the plate to the sink and turned the water on it and watched grimly as the mess ran down the drain. Johnson's sad thin hand rooted in garbage cans for food while his own child, selfish, unresponsive, greedy, had so much that he threw it up. He cut off the faucet with a thrust of his fist. Johnson had a capacity for real response and had been deprived of everything from birth; Norton was average or below and had had every advantage.

He went back to the bar to finish his breakfast. The cereal was soggy in the cardboard box but he paid no attention to what he was eating. Johnson was worth any amount of effort because he had the potential. He had seen it from the time the boy had limped in for his first interview.

Sheppard's office at the reformatory was a narrow closet with one window and a small table and two chairs in it. He had never been inside a confessional but he thought it must be the same kind of operation he had here, except that he explained, he did not absolve. His credentials were less dubious than a priest's; he had been trained for what he was doing.

When Johnson came in for his first interview, he had been reading over the boy's record—senseless destruction, windows smashed, city trash boxes set afire, tires slashed—the kind of thing he found where boys had been transplanted abruptly from the country to the city as this one had. He came to Johnson's I. Q. score. It was 140. He raised his eyes eagerly.

The boy sat slumped on the edge of his chair, his arms hanging between his thighs. The light from the window fell on his face. His eyes, steel-colored and very still, were trained narrowly forward. His thin dark hair hung in a flat forelock across the side of his forehead, not carelessly like a boy's, but fiercely like an old man's. A kind of fanatic intelligence was palpable in his face.

Sheppard smiled to diminish the distance between them.

The boy's expression did not soften. He leaned back in his chair and lifted a monstrous club foot to his knee. The foot was in a heavy black battered shoe with a sole four or five inches thick. The leather parted from it in one place and the end of an empty sock protruded like a grey tongue from a severed head. The case was clear to Sheppard instantly. His mischief was compensation for the foot.

"Well Rufus," he said, "I see by the record here that you don't have but a year to serve. What do you plan to do when you get out?"

"I don't make no plans," the boy said. His eyes shifted indifferently to something outside the window behind Sheppard in the far distance.

"Maybe you ought to," Sheppard said and smiled.

Johnson continued to gaze beyond him.

"I want to see you make the most of your intelligence," Sheppard said. "What's important to you? Let's talk about what's important to *you*." His eyes dropped involuntarily to the foot.

"Study it and git your fill," the boy drawled.

Sheppard reddened. The black deformed mass swelled before his eyes. He ignored the remark and the leer the boy was giving him. "Rufus," he said, "you've got into a lot of senseless trouble but I think when you understand why you do these things, you'll be less inclined to do them." He smiled. They had so few friends, saw so few pleasant faces, that half his effectiveness came from nothing more than smiling at them. "There are a lot of things about yourself that I think I can explain to you," he said.

Johnson looked at him stonily. "I ain't asked for no explanation," he said. "I already know why I do what I do."

"Well good!" Sheppard said. "Suppose you tell me what's made you do the things you've done?"

A black sheen appeared in the boy's eyes. "Satan," he said. "He has me in his power."

Sheppard looked at him steadily. There was no indication on the boy's face that he had said this to be funny. The line of his thin mouth was set with pride. Sheppard's eyes hardened. He felt a momentary dull despair as if he were faced with some elemental warping of nature that had happened too long ago to be corrected now. This boy's questions about life had been answered by signs nailed on pine trees: DOES SATAN HAVE YOU IN HIS POWER? REPENT OR BURN IN

HELL. JESUS SAVES. He would know the Bible with or without reading it. His despair gave way to outrage. "Rubbish!" he snorted. "We're living in the space age! You're too smart to give me an answer like that."

Johnson's mouth twisted slightly. His look was contemptuous but amused. There was a glint of challenge in his eyes.

Sheppard scrutinized his face. Where there was intelligence anything was possible. He smiled again, a smile that was like an invitation to the boy to come into a school room with all its windows thrown open to the light. "Rufus," he said, "I'm going to arrange for you to have a conference with me once a week. Maybe there's an explanation for your explanation. Maybe I can explain your devil to you."

After that he had talked to Johnson every Saturday for the rest of the year. He talked at random, the kind of talk the boy would never have heard before. He talked a little above him to give him something to reach for. He roamed from simple psychology and the dodges of the human mind to astronomy and the space capsules that were whirling around the earth faster than the speed of sound and would soon encircle the stars. Instinctively he concentrated on the stars. He wanted to give the boy something to reach for besides his neighbor's goods. He wanted to stretch his horizons. He wanted him to *see* the universe, to see that the darkest parts of it could be penetrated. He would have given anything to be able to put a telescope in Johnson's hands.

Johnson said little and what he did say, for the sake of his pride, was in dissent or senseless contradiction, with the club-foot raised always to his knee like a weapon ready for use, but Sheppard was not deceived. He watched his eyes and every week he saw something in them crumble. From the boy's face, hard but shocked, braced against the light that was ravaging him, he could see that he was hitting dead center.

Johnson was free now to live out of garbage cans and rediscover his old ignorance. The injustice of it was infuriating. He had been sent back to the grandfather; the old man's imbecility could only be imagined. Perhaps the boy had by now run away from him. The idea of getting custody of Johnson had occurred to Sheppard before, but the fact of the grandfather had stood in the way. Nothing excited him so much as thinking what he could do for such a boy. First he would have him fitted for a new orthopedic shoe. His back was thrown out of line every time he took a step. Then he would encourage him in some particular intellectual interest. He thought of the telescope. He could buy a second-hand one and they could set it up in the attic window. He sat for almost ten minutes thinking what he could do if he had Johnson here with him. What was wasted on Norton would cause Johnson to flourish. Yesterday when he had seen him with his hand in the garbage can, he had waved and started forward. Johnson had seen him, paused a split-second, then vanished with the swiftness of a rat, but not before Sheppard had seen his expression change. Something had kindled in the boy's eyes, he was sure of it, some memory of the lost light.

He got up and threw the cereal box in the garbage. Before he left the house, he looked into Norton's room to be sure he was not still sick. The child was sitting cross-legged on his bed. He had emptied the quart jars of change into one large pile in front of him, and was sorting it out by nickels and dimes and quarters.

That afternoon Norton was alone in the house, squatting on the floor of his room arranging packages of flower seeds in rows around himself. Rain slashed against the window panes and rattled in the gutters. The room had grown dark but every few minutes it was lit by silent lightning and the seed packages showed up gaily on the floor. He squatted motionless like a large pale frog in the midst of this potential garden. All at once his eyes became alert. Without warning the rain had stopped. The silence was heavy as if the downpour had been hushed by violence. He remained motionless, only his eyes turning.

Into the silence came the distinct click of a key turning in the front door lock. The sound was a very deliberate one. It drew attention to itself and held it as if it were controlled more by a mind than by a hand. The child leapt up and got into the closet.

The footsteps began to move in the hall. They were deliberate and irregular, a light and then a heavy one, then a silence as if the visitor had paused to listen himself or to examine something. In a minute the kitchen door screeked. The footsteps crossed the kitchen to the refrigerator. The closet wall and the kitchen wall were the same. Norton stood with his ear pressed against it. The refrigerator door opened. There was a prolonged silence.

He took off his shoes and then tiptoed out of the closet and stepped over the seed packages. In the middle of the room, he stopped and remained where he was, rigid. A thin bony-faced boy in a wet black suit stood in his door, blocking his escape. His hair was flattened to his skull by the rain. He stood there like an irate drenched crow. His look went through the child like a pin and paralyzed him. Then his eyes began to move over everything in the room—the unmade bed, the dirty curtains on the one large window, a photograph of a wide-faced young woman that stood up in the clutter on top of the dresser.

The child's tongue suddenly went wild. "He's been expecting you, he's going to give you a new shoe because you have to eat out of garbage cans!" he said in a kind of mouse-like shriek.

"I eat out of garbage cans," the boy said slowly with a beady stare, "because I like to eat out of garbage cans. See?"

The child nodded.

"And I got ways of getting my own shoe. See?"

The child nodded, mesmerized.

The boy limped in and sat down on the bed. He arranged a pillow behind him and stretched his short leg out so that the big black shoe rested conspicuously on a fold of the sheet.

Norton's gaze settled on it and remained immobile. The sole was as thick as a brick.

Johnson wiggled it slightly and smiled. "If I kick somebody *once* with this," he said, "it learns them not to mess with me."

The child nodded.

"Go in the kitchen," Johnson said, "and make me a sandwich with some of that rye bread and ham and bring me a glass of milk."

Norton went off like a mechanical toy, pushed in the right direction. He made a large greasy sandwich with ham hanging out the sides of it and poured out a glass of milk. Then he returned to the room with the glass of milk in one hand and the sandwich in the other.

Johnson was leaning back regally against the pillow. "Thanks, waiter," he said and took the sandwich.

Norton stood by the side of the bed, holding the glass.

The boy tore into the sandwich and ate steadily until he finished it. Then he took the glass of milk. He held it with both hands like a child and when he lowered it for breath, there was a rim of milk around his mouth. He handed Norton the empty glass. "Go get me one of them oranges in there, waiter," he said hoarsely.

Norton went to the kitchen and returned with the orange. Johnson peeled it with his fingers and let the peeling drop in the bed. He ate it slowly, spitting the seeds out in front of him. When he finished, he wiped his hands on the sheet and gave Norton a long appraising stare. He appeared to have been softened by the service. "You're his kid all right," he said. "You got the same stupid face."

The child stood there stolidly as if he had not heard.

"He don't know his left hand from his right," Johnson said with a hoarse pleasure in his voice.

The child cast his eyes a little to the side of the boy's face and looked fixedly at the wall.

"Yaketty yaketty yak," Johnson said, "and never says a thing."

The child's upper lip lifted slightly but he didn't say anything.

"Gas," Johnson said. "Gas."

The child's face began to have a wary look of belligerence. He backed away slightly as if he were prepared to retreat instantly. "He's good," he mumbled. "He helps people."

"Good!" Johnson said savagely. He thrust his head forward. "Listen here," he hissed, "I don't care if he's good or not. He ain't *right*!"

Norton looked stunned.

The screen door in the kitchen banged and some one entered. Johnson sat forward instantly. "Is that him?" he said.

"It's the cook," Norton said. "She comes in the afternoon."

Johnson got up and limped into the hall and stood in the kitchen door and Norton followed him.

The colored girl was at the closet taking off a bright red raincoat. She was a tall light-yellow girl with a mouth like a large rose that had darkened and wilted. Her hair was dressed in tiers on top of her head and leaned to the side like the Tower of Pisa.

Johnson made a noise through his teeth. "Well look at Aunt Jemima," he said.

The girl paused and trained an insolent gaze on them. They might have been dust on the floor.

"Come on," Johnson said, "let's see what all you got besides a nigger." He opened the first door to his right in the hall and looked into a pink-tiled bathroom. "A pink can!" he murmured.

He turned a comical face to the child. "Does he sit on that?"

"It's for company," Norton said, "but he sits on it sometimes."

"He ought to empty his head in it," Johnson said.

The door was open to the next room. It was the room Sheppard had slept in since his wife died. An ascetic-looking iron bed stood on the bare floor. A heap of Little League baseball uniforms was piled in one corner. Papers were scattered over a large roll-top desk and held down in various places by his pipes. Johnson stood looking into the room silently. He wrinkled his nose. "Guess who?" he said.

The door to the next room was closed but Johnson opened it and thrust his head into the semi-darkness within. The shades were down and the air was close with a faint scent of perfume in it. There was a wide antique bed and a mammoth dresser whose mirror glinted in the half light. Johnson snapped the light switch by the door and crossed the room to the mirror and peered into it. A silver comb and brush lay on the linen runner. He picked up the comb and began to run it through his hair. He combed it straight down on his forehead. Then he swept it to the side, Hitler fashion.

"Leave her comb alone!" the child said. He stood in the door, pale and breathing heavily as if he were watching sacrilege in a holy place.

Johnson put the comb down and picked up the brush and gave his hair a swipe with it.

"She's dead," the child said.

"I ain't afraid of dead people's things," Johnson said. He opened the top drawer and slid his hand in.

"Take your big fat dirty hands off my mother's clothes!" the child said in a high suffocated voice.

"Keep your shirt on, sweetheart," Johnson murmured. He pulled up a wrinkled red polka dot blouse and dropped it back. Then he pulled out a green silk kerchief and whirled it over his head and let it float to the floor. His hand continued to plow deep into the drawer. After a moment it came up gripping a faded corset with four dangling metal supporters. "Thisyer must be her saddle," he observed.

He lifted it gingerly and shook it. Then he fastened it around his waist and jumped up and down, making the metal supporters dance. He began to snap his fingers and turn his hips from side to side. "Gonter rock, rattle and roll," he sang. "Gonter rock, rattle and roll. Can't please that woman, to save my doggone soul." He began to move around, stamping the good foot down and slinging the heavy one to the side. He danced out the door, past the stricken child and down the hall toward the kitchen.

A half hour later Sheppard came home. He dropped his raincoat on a chair in the hall and came as far as the parlor door and stopped. His face was suddenly transformed. It shone with pleasure. Johnson sat, a dark figure, in a high-backed pink upholstered chair. The wall behind him was lined with books from floor to ceiling. He was reading one. Sheppard's eyes narrowed. It was a volume of the Encyclopedia Britannica. He was so engrossed in it that he did not look up. Sheppard held his breath. This was the perfect setting for the boy. He had to keep him here. He had to manage it somehow.

"Rufus!" he said, "it's good to see you boy!" and he bounded forward with his arm outstretched.

Johnson looked up, his face blank. "Oh hello," he said. He ignored the hand as long as he was able but when Sheppard did not withdraw it, he grudgingly shook it.

Sheppard was prepared for this kind of reaction. It was part of Johnson's make-up never to show enthusiasm.

"How are things?" he said. "How's your grandfather treating you?" He sat down on the edge of the sofa.

"He dropped dead," the boy said indifferently.

"You don't mean it!" Sheppard cried. He got up and sat down on the coffee table nearer the boy.

"Naw," Johnson said, "he ain't dropped dead. I wisht he had."

"Well where is he?" Sheppard muttered.

"He's gone with a remnant to the hills," Johnson said. "Him and some others. They're going to bury some Bibles in a cave and take two of different kinds of animals and all like that. Like Noah. Only this time it's going to be fire, not flood."

Sheppard's mouth stretched wryly. "I see," he said. Then he said, "In other words the old fool has abandoned you?"

"He ain't no fool," the boy said in an indignant tone.

"Has he abandoned you or not?" Sheppard asked impatiently.

The boy shrugged.

"Where's your probation officer?"

"I ain't supposed to keep up with him," Johnson said. "He's supposed to keep up with me."

Sheppard laughed. "Wait a minute," he said. He got up and went into the hall and got his raincoat off the chair and took it to the hall closet to hang it up. He had to give himself time to think, to decide how he could ask the boy so that he would stay. He couldn't force him to stay. It would have to be voluntary. Johnson pretended not to like him. That was only to uphold his pride, but he would have to ask him in such a way that his pride could still be upheld. He opened the closet door and took out a hanger. An old grey winter coat of his wife's still hung there. He pushed it aside but it didn't move. He pulled it open roughly and winced as if he had seen the larva inside a cocoon. Norton stood in it, his face swollen and pale, with a drugged look of misery on it. Sheppard stared at him. Suddenly he was confronted with a possibility. "Get out of there," he said. He caught him by the shoulder and propelled him firmly into the parlor and over to the pink chair where Johnson was sitting with the encyclopedia in his lap. He was going to risk everything in one blow.

"Rufus," he said, "I've got a problem. I need your help."

Johnson looked up suspiciously.

"Listen," Sheppard said, "we need another boy in the house." There was a genuine desperation in his voice. "Norton here has never had to divide anything in his life. He doesn't know what it means to share. And I need somebody to teach him. How about helping me out? Stay here for a while with us, Rufus. I need your help." The excitement in his voice made it thin.

The child suddenly came to life. His face swelled with fury. "He went in her room and used her comb!" he screamed, yanking Sheppard's arm. "He put on her corset and danced with Leola, he . . ."

"Stop this!" Sheppard said sharply. "Is tattling all you're capable of? I'm not asking you for a report on Rufus's conduct. I'm asking you to make him welcome here. Do you understand?

"You see how it is?" he asked, turning to Johnson.

Norton kicked the leg of the pink chair viciously, just missing Johnson's swollen foot. Sheppard yanked him back.

"He said you weren't nothing but gas!" the child shrieked.

A sly look of pleasure crossed Johnson's face.

Sheppard was not put back. These insults were part of the boy's defensive mechanism. "What about it, Rufus?" he said. "Will you stay with us for a while?"

Johnson looked straight in front of him and said nothing. He smiled slightly and appeared to gaze upon some vision of the future that pleased him.

"I don't care," he said and turned a page of the encyclopedia. "I can stand anywhere."

"Wonderful." Sheppard said. "Wonderful."

"He said," the child said in a throaty whisper, "you didn't know your left hand from your right."

There was a silence.

Johnson wet his finger and turned another page of the encyclopedia.

"I have something to say to both of you," Sheppard said in a voice without inflection. His eyes moved from one to the other of them and he spoke slowly as if what he was saying he would say only once and it behooved them to listen. "If it made any difference to me what Rufus thinks of me," he said, "then I wouldn't be asking him here. Rufus is going to help me out and I'm going to help him out and we're both going to help you out. I'd simply be selfish if I let what Rufus thinks of me interfere with what I can do for Rufus. If I can help a person, all I want is to do it. I'm above and beyond simple pettiness."

Neither of them made a sound. Norton stared at the chair cushion. Johnson peered closer at some fine print in the encyclopedia. Sheppard was looking at the tops of their heads. He smiled. After all, he had won. The boy was staying. He reached out and ruffled Norton's hair and slapped Johnson on the shoulder. "Now you fellows sit here and get acquainted," he said gaily and started toward the door. "I'm going to see what Leola left us for supper."

When he was gone, Johnson raised his head and looked at Norton. The child looked back at him bleakly. "God, kid," Johnson said in a cracked voice, "how do you stand it?" His face was stiff with outrage. "He thinks he's Jesus Christ!"

II

Sheppard's attic was a large unfinished room with exposed beams and no electric light. They had set the telescope up on a tripod in one of the dormer windows. It pointed now toward the dark sky where a sliver of moon, as fragile as an egg shell, had just emerged from behind a cloud with a brilliant silver edge. Inside, a kerosene lantern set on a trunk cast their shadows upward and tangled them, wavering slightly, in the joists overhead. Sheppard was sitting on a packing box, looking through the telescope, and Johnson was at his elbow, waiting to get at it. Sheppard had bought it for fifteen dollars two days before at a pawn shop.

"Quit hoggin it," Johnson said.

Sheppard got up and Johnson slid onto the box and put his eye to the instrument.

Sheppard sat down on a straight chair a few feet away. His face was flushed with pleasure. This much of his dream was a reality. Within a week he had made it possible for this boy's vision to pass through a slender channel to the stars. He looked at Johnson's bent back with complete satisfaction. The boy had on one of Norton's plaid shirts and some new khaki trousers he had bought him. The shoe would be ready next week. He had taken him to the brace shop the day after he came and had him fitted for a new shoe. Johnson was as touchy about the foot as if it were a sacred object. His face had been glum while the clerk, a young man with a bright pink bald head, measured the foot with his profane hands. The shoe was going to make the greatest difference in the boy's attitude. Even a child with normal feet was in love with the world after he had got a new pair of shoes. When Norton got a new pair, he walked around for days with his eyes on his feet.

Sheppard glanced across the room at the child. He was sitting on the floor against a trunk, trussed up in a rope he had found and wound around his legs from his ankles to his knees. He appeared so far away that Sheppard might have been looking at him through the wrong end of the telescope. He had had to whip him only once since Johnson had been with them—the first night when Norton had realized that Johnson was going to sleep in his mother's bed. He did not believe in whipping children, particularly in anger. In this case, he had done both and with good results. He had had no more trouble with Norton.

The child hadn't shown any positive generosity toward Johnson but what he couldn't help, he appeared to be resigned to. In the mornings Sheppard sent the two of them to the Y swimming pool, gave them money to get their lunch at the cafeteria and instructed them to meet him in the park in the afternoon to watch his Little League baseball practice. Every afternoon they had arrived at the park, shambling, silent, their faces closed each on his own thoughts as if neither were aware of the other's existence. At least he could be thankful there were no fights.

Norton showed no interest in the telescope. "Don't you want to get up and look through the telescope, Norton?" he said. It irritated him that the child showed no intellectual curiosity whatsoever. "Rufus is going to be way ahead of you."

Norton leaned forward absently and looked at Johnson's back.

Johnson turned around from the instrument. His face had begun to fill out again. The look of outrage had retreated from his hollow cheeks and was shored up now in the caves of his eyes, like a fugitive from Sheppard's kindness. "Don't waste your valuable time, kid," he said. "You seen the moon once, you seen it."

Sheppard was amused by these sudden turns of perversity. The boy resisted whatever he suspected was meant for his improvement and contrived when he was vitally interested in something to leave the impression he was bored. Sheppard was not deceived. Secretly Johnson was learning what he wanted him to learn—that his benefactor was impervious to insult and that there were no cracks in his armor of kindness and patience where a successful shaft could be driven. "Some day you may go to the moon," he said. "In ten years men will probably be making round trips there on schedule. Why you boys may be spacemen. Astronauts!"

"Astro-nuts," Johnson said.

"Nuts or nauts," Sheppard said, "it's perfectly possible that you, Rufus Johnson, will go to the moon."

Something in the depths of Johnson's eyes stirred. All day his humor had been glum. "I ain't going to the moon and get there alive," he said, "and when I die I'm going to hell."

"It's at least possible to get to the moon," Sheppard said dryly. The best way to handle this kind of thing was with gentle ridicule. "We can see it. We know it's there. Nobody has given any reliable evidence there's a hell."

"The Bible has give the evidence," Johnson said darkly, "and if you die and go there you burn forever."

The child leaned forward.

"Whoever says it ain't a hell," Johnson said, "is contradicting Jesus. The dead are judged and the wicked are damned. They weep and gnash their teeth while they burn," he continued, "and it's everlasting darkness."

The child's mouth opened. His eyes appeared to grow hollow.

"Satan runs it," Johnson said.

Norton lurched up and took a hobbled step toward Sheppard. "Is she there?" he said in a loud voice. "Is she there burning up?" He kicked the rope off his feet. "Is she on fire?"

"Oh my God," Sheppard muttered. "No no," he said, "of course she isn't. Rufus is mistaken. Your mother isn't anywhere. She's not unhappy. She just isn't." His lot would have been easier if when his wife died he had told Norton she had gone to heaven and that some day he would see her again, but he could not allow himself to bring him up on a lie.

Norton's face began to twist. A knot formed in his chin.

"Listen," Sheppard said quickly and pulled the child to him, "your mother's spirit lives on in other people and it'll live on in you if you're good and generous like she was."

The child's pale eyes hardened in disbelief.

Sheppard's pity turned to revulsion. The boy would rather she be in hell than nowhere. "Do you understand?" he said. "She doesn't exist." He put his hand on the child's shoulder. "That's all I have to give you," he said in a softer, exasperated tone, "the truth."

Instead of howling, the boy wrenched himself away and caught Johnson by the sleeve. "Is she there, Rufus?" he said. "Is she there, burning up?"

Johnson's eyes glittered. "Well," he said, "she is if she was evil. Was she a whore?"

"Your mother was not a whore," Sheppard said sharply. He had the sensation of driving a car without brakes. "Now let's have no more of this foolishness. We were talking about the moon."

"Did she believe in Jesus?" Johnson asked.

Norton looked blank. After a second he said, "Yes," as if he saw that this was necessary. "She did," he said. "All the time."

"She did not," Sheppard muttered.

"She did all the time," Norton said. "I heard her say she did all the time."

"She's saved," Johnson said.

The child still looked puzzled. "Where?" he said. "Where is she at?"

"On high," Johnson said.

"Where's that?" Norton gasped.

"It's in the sky somewhere," Johnson said, "but you got to be dead to get there. You can't go in no space ship." There was a narrow gleam in his eyes now like a beam holding steady on its target.

"Man's going to the moon," Sheppard said grimly, "is very much like the first fish crawling out of the water onto land billions and billions of years ago. He didn't have an earth suit. He had to grow his adjustments inside. He developed lungs."

"When I'm dead will I go to hell or where she is?" Norton asked.

"Right now you'd go where she is," Johnson said, "but if you live long enough, you'll go to hell."

Sheppard rose abruptly and picked up the lantern. "Close the window, Rufus," he said. "It's time we went to bed."

On the way down the attic stairs he heard Johnson say in a loud whisper behind him, "I'll tell you all about it tomorrow, kid, when Himself has cleared out."

The next day when the boys came to the ball park, he watched them as they came from behind the bleachers and around the edge of the field. Johnson's hand was on Norton's shoulder, his head bent toward the younger boy's ear, and on the child's face there was a look of complete confidence, of dawning light. Sheppard's grimace hardened. This would be Johnson's way of trying to annoy him. But he would not be annoyed. Norton was not bright enough to be damaged much. He gazed at the child's dull absorbed little face. Why try to make him superior? Heaven and hell were for the mediocre, and he was that if he was anything.

The two boys came into the bleachers and sat down about ten feet away, facing him, but neither gave him any sign of recognition. He cast a glance behind him where the Little Leaguers were spread out in the field. Then he started for the bleachers. The hiss of Johnson's voice stopped as he approached.

"What have you fellows been doing today?" he asked genially.

"He's been telling me . . ." Norton started.

Johnson pushed the child in the ribs with his elbow. "We ain't been doing nothing," he said. His face appeared to be covered with a blank glaze but through it a look of complicity was blazoned forth insolently.

Sheppard felt his face grow warm, but he said nothing. A child in a Little League uniform had followed him and was nudging him in the back of the leg with a bat. He turned and put his arm around the boy's neck and went with him back to the game.

That night when he went to the attic to join the boys at the telescope, he found Norton there alone. He was sitting on the packing box, hunched over, looking intently through the instrument. Johnson was not there.

"Where's Rufus?" Sheppard asked.

"I said where's Rufus?" he said louder.

"Gone somewhere," the child said without turning around.

"Gone where?" Sheppard asked.

"He just said he was going somewhere. He said he was fed up looking at stars."

"I see," Sheppard said glumly. He turned and went back down the stairs. He searched the house without finding Johnson. Then he went to the living room and sat down. Yesterday he had been convinced of his success with the boy. Today he faced the possibility that he was failing with him. He had been over-lenient, too concerned to have Johnson like him. He felt a twinge of guilt. What difference did it make if Johnson liked him or not? What was that to him? When the boy came in, they would have a few things understood. As long as you stay here there'll be no going out at night by yourself, do you understand?

I don't have to stay here. It ain't nothing to me staying here.

Oh my God, he thought. He could not bring it to that. He would have to be firm but not make an issue of it. He picked up the evening paper. Kindness and patience were always called for but he had not been firm enough. He sat holding the paper but not reading it. The boy would not respect him unless he showed firmness. The doorbell rang and he went to answer it. He opened it and stepped back, with a pained disappointed face.

A large dour policeman stood on the stoop, holding Johnson by the elbow. At the curb a patrolcar waited. Johnson looked very white. His jaw was thrust forward as if to keep from trembling.

"We brought him here first because he raised such a fit," the policeman said, "but now that you've seen him, we're going to take him to the station and ask him a few questions."

"What happened?" Sheppard muttered.

"A house around the corner from here," the policeman said. "A real smash job, dishes broken all over the floor, furniture turned upside-down . . ."

"I didn't have a thing to do with it!" Johnson said. "I was walking along minding my own bidnis when this cop came up and grabbed me."

Sheppard looked at the boy grimly. He made no effort to soften his expression.

Johnson flushed. "I was just walking along," he muttered, but with no conviction in his voice.

"Come on, bud," the policeman said.

"You ain't going to let him take me, are you?" Johnson said. "You believe me, don't you?" There was an appeal in his voice that Sheppard had not heard there before.

This was crucial. The boy would have to learn that he could not be protected when he was guilty. "You'll have to go with him, Rufus," he said.

"You're going to let him take me and I tell you I ain't done a thing?" Johnson said shrilly.

Sheppard's face became harder as his sense of injury grew. The boy had failed him even before he had had a chance to give him the shoe. They were to have got it tomorrow. All his regret turned suddenly on the shoe; his irritation at the sight of Johnson doubled.

"You made out like you had all this confidence in me," the boy mumbled.

"I did have," Sheppard said. His face was wooden.

Johnson turned away with the policeman but before he moved, a gleam of pure hatred flashed toward Sheppard from the pits of his eyes.

Sheppard stood in the door and watched them get into the patrolcar and drive away. He summoned his compassion. He would go to the station tomorrow and see what he could do about getting him out of trouble. The night in jail would not hurt him and the experience would teach him that he could not treat with impunity someone who had shown him nothing but kindness. Then they would go get the shoe and perhaps after a night in jail it would mean even more to the boy.

The next morning at eight o'clock the police sergeant called and told him he could come pick Johnson up. "We booked a nigger on that charge," he said. "Your boy didn't have nothing to do with it."

Sheppard was at the station in ten minutes, his face hot with shame. Johnson sat slouched on a bench in a drab outer office, reading a police magazine. There was no one else in the room. Sheppard sat down beside him and put his hand tentatively on his shoulder.

The boy glanced up—his lip curled—and back to the magazine.

Sheppard felt physically sick. The ugliness of what he had done bore in upon him with a sudden dull intensity. He had failed him at just the point where he might have turned him once and for all in the right direction. "Rufus," he said, "I apologize. I was wrong and you were right. I misjudged you."

The boy continued to read.

"I'm sorry."

The boy wet his finger and turned a page.

Sheppard braced himself. "I was a fool, Rufus," he said.

Johnson's mouth slid slightly to the side. He shrugged without raising his head from the magazine.

"Will you forget it, this time?" Sheppard said. "It won't happen again."

The boy looked up. His eyes were bright and unfriendly. "I'll forget it," he said, "but you better remember it." He got up and stalked toward the door. In the middle of the room, he turned and jerked his arm at Sheppard and Sheppard jumped up and followed him as if the boy had yanked an invisible leash.

"Your shoe," he said eagerly, "today is the day to get your shoe!" Thank God for the shoe!

But when they went to the brace shop, they found that the shoe had been made two sizes too small and a new one would not be ready for another ten days. Johnson's temper improved at once. The clerk had obviously made a mistake in the measurements but the boy insisted the foot had grown. He left the shop with a pleased expression, as if, in expanding, the foot had acted on some inspiration of its own. Sheppard's face was haggard.

After this he redoubled his efforts. Since Johnson had lost interest in the telescope, he bought a microscope and a box of prepared slides. If he couldn't impress the boy with immensity, he would try the infinitesimal. For two nights Johnson appeared absorbed in the new instrument, then he abruptly lost interest in it, but he seemed content to sit in the living room in the evening and read the encyclopedia. He devoured the encyclopedia as he devoured his dinner, steadily and without dint to his appetite. Each subject appeared to enter his head, be ravaged, and thrown out. Nothing pleased Sheppard more than to see the boy slouched on the sofa, his mouth shut, reading. After they had spent two or three evenings like this, he began to recover his vision. His confidence returned. He knew that some day he would be proud of Johnson.

On Thursday night Sheppard attended a city council meeting. He dropped the boys off at a movie on his way and picked them up on his way back. When they reached home, an automobile with a single red eye above its windshield was waiting in front of the house. Sheppard's lights as he turned into the driveway illuminated two dour faces in the car.

"The cops!" Johnson said. "Some nigger has broke in somewhere and they've come for me again."

"We'll see about that," Sheppard muttered. He stopped the car in the driveway and switched off the lights. "You boys go in the house and go to bed," he said. "I'll handle this."

He got out and strode toward the squad car. He thrust his head in the window. The two policemen were looking at him with silent knowledgeable faces. "A house on the corner of Shelton and Mills," the one in the driver's seat said. "It looks like a train run through it."

"He was in the picture show down town," Sheppard said. "My boy was with him. He had nothing to do with the other one and he had nothing to do with this one. I'll be responsible."

"If I was you," the one nearest him said, "I wouldn't be responsible for any little bastard like him."

"I said I'd be responsible," Sheppard repeated coldly. "You people made a mistake the last time. Don't make another."

The policemen looked at each other. "It ain't our funeral,"

the one in the driver's seat said, and turned the key in the ignition.

Sheppard went in the house and sat down in the living room in the dark. He did not suspect Johnson and he did not want the boy to think he did. If Johnson thought he suspected him again, he would lose everything. But he wanted to know if his alibi was airtight. He thought of going to Norton's room and asking him if Johnson had left the movie. But that would be worse. Johnson would know what he was doing and would be incensed. He decided to ask Johnson himself. He would be direct. He went over in his mind what he was going to say and then he got up and went to the boy's door.

It was open as if he had been expected but Johnson was in bed. Just enough light came in from the hall for Sheppard to see his shape under the sheet. He came in and stood at the foot of the bed. "They've gone," he said. "I told them you had nothing to do with it and that I'd be responsible."

There was a muttered "Yeah," from the pillow.

Sheppard hesitated. "Rufus," he said, "you didn't leave the movie for anything at all, did you?"

"You make out like you got all this confidence in me!" a sudden outraged voice cried, "and you ain't got any! You don't trust me no more now than you did then!" The voice, disembodied, seemed to come more surely from the depths of Johnson than when his face was visible. It was a cry of reproach, edged slightly with contempt.

"I do have confidence in you," Sheppard said intensely. "I have every confidence in you. I believe in you and I trust you completely."

"You got your eye on me all the time," the voice said sullenly. "When you get through asking me a bunch of questions, you're going across the hall and ask Norton a bunch of them."

"I have no intention of asking Norton anything and never did," Sheppard said gently. "And I don't suspect you at all. You could hardly have got from the picture show down town and out here to break in a house and back to the picture show in the time you had."

"That's why you believe me!" the boy cried, "—because you think I couldn't have done it."

"No, no!" Sheppard said. "I believe you because I believe you've got the brains and the guts not to get in trouble again. I believe you know yourself well enough now to know that you don't have to do such things. I believe that you can make anything of yourself that you set your mind to."

Johnson sat up. A faint light shone on his forehead but the rest of his face was invisible. "And I could have broke in there if I'd wanted to in the time I had," he said.

"But I know you didn't," Sheppard said. "There's not the least trace of doubt in my mind."

There was a silence. Johnson lay back down. Then the voice, low and hoarse, as if it were being forced out with difficulty, said, "You don't want to steal and smash up things when you've got everything you want already."

Sheppard caught his breath. The boy was thanking him! He was thanking him! There was gratitude in his voice. There was appreciation. He stood there, smiling foolishly in the dark, trying to hold the moment in suspension. Involuntarily he took a step toward the pillow and stretched out his hand and touched Johnson's forehead. It was cold and dry like rusty iron.

"I understand. Good night, son," he said and turned quickly and left the room. He closed the door behind him and stood there, overcome with emotion.

Across the hall Norton's door was open. The child lay on the bed on his side, looking into the light from the hall.

After this, the road with Johnson would be smooth.

Norton sat up and beckoned to him.

He saw the child but after the first instant, he did not let his eyes focus directly on him. He could not go in and talk to Norton without breaking Johnson's trust. He hesitated, but remained where he was a moment as if he saw nothing. Tomorrow was the day they were to go back for the shoe. It would be a climax to the good feeling between them. He turned quickly and went back into his own room.

The child sat for some time looking at the spot where his father had stood. Finally his gaze became aimless and he lay back down.

The next day Johnson was glum and silent as if he were ashamed that he had revealed himself. His eyes had a hooded look. He seemed to have retired within himself and there to be going through some crisis of determination. Sheppard could not get to the brace shop quickly enough. He left Norton at home because he did not want his attention divided. He wanted to be free to observe Johnson's reaction minutely. The boy did not seem pleased or even interested in the prospect of the shoe, but when it became an actuality, certainly then he would be moved.

The brace shop was a small concrete warehouse lined and stacked with the equipment of affliction. Wheel chairs and walkers covered most of the floor. The walls were hung with every kind of crutch and brace. Artificial limbs were stacked on the shelves, legs and arms and hands, claws and hooks, straps and human harnesses and unidentifiable instruments for unnamed deformities. In a small clearing in the middle of the room there was a row of yellow plastic-cushioned chairs and a shoe fitting stool. Johnson slouched down in one of the chairs and set his foot up on the stool and sat with his eyes on it moodily. What was roughly the toe had broken open again and he had patched it with a piece of canvas; another place he had patched with what appeared to be the tongue of the original shoe. The two sides were laced with twine.

There was an excited flush on Sheppard's face; his heart was beating unnaturally fast.

The clerk appeared from the back of the shop with the new shoe under his arm. "Got her right this time!" he said. He straddled the shoe-fitting stool and held the shoe up, smiling as if he had produced it by magic.

It was a black slick shapeless object, shining hideously. It looked like a blunt weapon, highly polished.

Johnson gazed at it darkly.

"With this shoe," the clerk said, "you won't know you're walking. You'll think you're riding!" He bent his bright pink bald head and began gingerly to unlace the twine. He removed the old shoe as if he were skinning an animal still half alive. His expression was strained. The unsheathed mass of foot in the dirty sock made Sheppard feel queasy. He turned his eyes away until the new shoe was on. The clerk laced it up rapidly. "Now stand up and walk around," he said, "and see if that ain't power glide." He winked at Sheppard. "In that shoe," he said, "he won't know he don't have a normal foot."

Sheppard's face was bright with pleasure.

Johnson stood up and walked a few yards away. He walked stiffly with almost no dip in his short side. He stood for a moment, rigid, with his back to them.

"Wonderful!" Sheppard said. "Wonderful." It was as if he had given the boy a new spine.

Johnson turned around. His mouth was set in a thin icy line. He came back to the seat and removed the shoe. He put his foot in the old one and began lacing it up.

"You want to take it home and see if it suits you first?" the clerk murmured.

"No," Johnson said. "I ain't going to wear it at all."

"What's wrong with it?" Sheppard said, his voice rising.

"I don't need no new shoe," Johnson said. "And when I do, I got ways of getting my own." His face was stony but there was a glint of triumph in his eyes.

"Boy," the clerk said, "is your trouble in your foot or in your head?"

"Go soak your skull," Johnson said. "Your brains are on fire."

The clerk rose glumly but with dignity and asked Sheppard what he wanted done with the shoe, which he dangled dispiritedly by the lace.

Sheppard's face was a dark angry red. He was staring straight in front of him at a leather corset with an artificial arm attached.

The clerk asked him again.

"Wrap it up," Sheppard muttered. He turned his eyes to Johnson. "He's not mature enough for it yet," he said. "I had thought he was less of a child."

The boy leered. "You been wrong before," he said.

That night they sat in the living room and read as usual. Sheppard kept himself glumly entrenched behind the Sunday New York *Times*. He wanted to recover his good humor, but every time he thought of the rejected shoe, he felt a new charge of irritation. He did not trust himself even to look at Johnson. He realized that the boy had refused the shoe because he was insecure. Johnson had been frightened by his own gratitude. He didn't know what to make of the new self he was becoming conscious of. He understood that something he had been was threatened and he was facing himself and his possibilities for the first time. He was questioning his identity. Grudgingly, Sheppard felt a slight return of sympathy for the boy. In a few minutes, he lowered his paper and looked at him.

Johnson was sitting on the sofa, gazing over the top of the encyclopedia. His expression was trancelike. He might have been listening to something far away. Sheppard watched him intently but the boy continued to listen, and did not turn his head. The poor kid is lost, Sheppard thought. Here he had sat all evening, sullenly reading the paper, and had not said a word to break the tension. "Rufus," he said.

Johnson continued to sit, stock-still, listening.

"Rufus," Sheppard said in a slow hypnotic voice, "you can be anything in the world you want to be. You can be a scientist or an architect or an engineer or whatever you set your mind to, and whatever you set your mind to be, you can be the best of its kind." He imagined his voice penetrating to the boy in the black caverns of his psyche. Johnson leaned forward but his eyes did not turn. On the street a car door closed. There was a silence. Then a sudden blast from the door bell.

Sheppard jumped up and went to the door and opened it. The same policeman who had come before stood there. The patrolcar waited at the curb.

"Lemme see that boy," he said.

Sheppard scowled and stood aside. "He's been here all evening," he said. "I can vouch for it."

The policeman walked into the living room. Johnson appeared engrossed in his book. After a second he looked up with an annoyed expression, like a great man interrupted at his work.

"What was that you were looking at in that kitchen window over on Winter Avenue about a half hour ago, bud?" the policeman asked.

"Stop persecuting this boy!" Sheppard said. "I'll vouch for the fact he was here. I was here with him."

"You heard him," Johnson said. "I been here all the time."

"It ain't everybody makes tracks like you," the policeman said and eyed the clubfoot.

"They couldn't be his tracks," Sheppard growled, infuriated. "He's been here all the time. You're wasting your own time and you're wasting ours." He felt the *ours* seal his solidarity with the boy. "I'm sick of this," he said. "You people are too damn lazy to go out and find whoever is doing these things. You come here automatically."

The policeman ignored this and continued looking through Johnson. His eyes were small and alert in his fleshy face. Finally he turned toward the door. "We'll get him sooner or later," he said, "with his head in a window and his tail out."

Sheppard followed him to the door and slammed it behind him. His spirits were soaring. This was exactly what he had needed. He returned with an expectant face.

Johnson had put the book down and was sitting there, looking at him slyly. "Thanks," he said.

Sheppard stopped. The boy's expression was predatory. He was openly leering.

"You ain't such a bad liar yourself," he said.

"Liar?" Sheppard murmured. Could the boy have left and come back? He felt himself sicken. Then a rush of anger sent him forward. "Did you leave?" he said furiously. "I didn't see you leave."

The boy only smiled.

"You went up in the attic to see Norton," Sheppard said.

"Naw," Johnson said, "that kid is crazy. He don't want to do nothing but look through that stinking telescope."

"I don't want to hear about Norton," Sheppard said harshly. "Where were you?"

"I was sitting on that pink can by my ownself," Johnson said. "There wasn't no witnesses."

Sheppard took out his handkerchief and wiped his forehead. He managed to smile.

Johnson rolled his eyes. "You don't believe in me," he said. His voice was cracked the way it had been in the dark room two nights before. "You make out like you got all this confidence in me but you ain't got any. When things get hot, you'll fade like the rest of them." The crack became exaggerated, comic. The mockery in it was blatant. "You don't believe in me. You ain't got no confidence," he wailed. "And you ain't any smarter than that cop. All that about tracks—that was a trap. There wasn't any tracks. That whole place is concreted in the back and my feet were dry."

Sheppard slowly put the handkerchief back in his pocket. He dropped down on the sofa and gazed at the rug beneath his feet. The boy's clubfoot was set within the circle of his vision. The pieced-together shoe appeared to grin at him with Johnson's own face. He caught hold of the edge of the sofa cushion and his knuckles turned white. A chill of hatred shook him. He hated the shoe, hated the foot, hated the boy. His face paled. Hatred choked him. He was aghast at himself.

He caught the boy's shoulder and gripped it fiercely as if to keep himself from falling. "Listen," he said, "you looked in that window to embarrass me. That was all you wanted—to shake my resolve to help you, but my resolve isn't shaken. I'm stronger than you are. I'm stronger than you are and I'm going to save you. The good will triumph."

"Not when it ain't true," the boy said. "Not when it ain't right."

"My resolve isn't shaken," Sheppard repeated. "I'm going to save you."

Johnson's look became sly again. "You ain't going to save me," he said. "You're going to tell me to leave this house. I did those other two jobs too—the first one as well as the one I done when I was supposed to be in the picture show."

"I'm not going to tell you to leave," Sheppard said. His voice was toneless, mechanical. "I'm going to save you."

Johnson thrust his head forward. "Save yourself," he hissed. "Nobody can save me but Jesus."

Sheppard laughed curtly. "You don't deceive me," he said. "I flushed that out of your head in the reformatory. I saved you from that, at least."

The muscles in Johnson's face stiffened. A look of such repulsion hardened on his face that Sheppard drew back. The boy's eyes were like distorting mirrors in which he saw himself made hideous and grotesque. "I'll show you," Johnson whispered. He rose abruptly and started headlong for the door as if he could not get out of Sheppard's sight quick enough, but it was the door to the back hall he went through, not the front door. Sheppard turned on the sofa and looked behind him where the boy had disappeared. He heard the door to his room slam. He was not leaving. The intensity had gone out of Sheppard's eyes. They looked flat and lifeless as if the shock of the boy's revelation were only now reaching the center of his consciousness. "If he would only leave," he murmured. "If he would only leave now of his own accord."

The next morning Johnson appeared at the breakfast table in the grandfather's suit he had come in. Sheppard pretended not to notice but one look told him what he already knew, that he was trapped, that there could be nothing now but a battle of nerves and that Johnson would win it. He wished he had never laid eyes on the boy. The failure of his compassion numbed him. He got out of the house as soon as he could and all day he dreaded to go home in the evening. He had a faint hope that the boy might be gone when he returned. The grandfather's suit might have meant he was leaving. The hope grew in the afternoon. When he came home and opened the front door, his heart was pounding.

He stopped in the hall and looked silently into the living room. His expectant expression faded. His face seemed suddenly as old as his white hair. The two boys were sitting close together on the sofa, reading the same book. Norton's cheek rested against the sleeve of Johnson's black suit. Johnson's finger moved under the lines they were reading. The elder brother and the younger. Sheppard looked woodenly at this scene for almost a minute. Then he walked into the room and took off his coat and dropped it on a chair. Neither boy noticed him. He went on to the kitchen.

Leola left the supper on the stove every afternoon before she left and he put it on the table. His head ached and his nerves were taut. He sat down on the kitchen stool and remained there, sunk in his depression. He wondered if he could infuriate Johnson enough to make him leave of his own accord. Last night what had enraged him was the Jesus business. It might enrage Johnson, but it depressed him. Why not simply tell the boy to go? Admit defeat. The thought of facing Johnson again sickened him. The boy looked at him as if he were the guilty one, as if he were a moral leper. He knew without conceit that he was a good man, that he had nothing to reproach himself with. His feelings about Johnson now were involuntary. He would like to feel compassion for him. He would like to be able to help him. He longed for the time when there would be no one but himself and Norton in the house, when the child's simple selfishness would be all he had to contend with, and his own loneliness.

He got up and took three serving dishes off the shelf and took them to the stove. Absently he began pouring the butterbeans and the hash into the dishes. When the food was on the table, he called them in.

They brought the book with them. Norton pushed his place setting around to the same side of the table as Johnson's and moved his chair next to Johnson's chair. They sat down and put the book between them. It was a black book with red edges.

"What's that you're reading?" Sheppard asked, sitting down.

"The Holy Bible," Johnson said.

God give me strength, Sheppard said under his breath.

"We lifted it from a ten cent store," Johnson said.

"We?" Sheppard muttered. He turned and glared at Norton. The child's face was bright and there was an excited sheen to his eyes. The change that had come over the boy struck him for the first time. He looked alert. He had on a blue plaid shirt and his eyes were a brighter blue than he had ever seen them before. There was a strange new life in him, the sign of new and more rugged vices. "So now you steal?" he said, glowering. "You haven't learned to be generous but you have learned to steal."

"No he ain't," Johnson said. "I was the one lifted it. He only watched. He can't sully himself. It don't make any difference about me. I'm going to hell anyway."

Sheppard held his tongue.

"Unless," Johnson said, "I repent."

"Repent, Rufus," Norton said in a pleading voice. "Repent, hear? You don't want to go to hell."

"Stop talking this nonsense," Sheppard said, looking sharply at the child.

"If I do repent, I'll be a preacher," Johnson said. "If you're going to do it, it's no sense in doing it half way."

"What are you going to be, Norton," Sheppard asked in a brittle voice, "a preacher too?"

There was a glitter of wild pleasure in the child's eyes. "A space man!" he shouted.

"Wonderful," Sheppard said bitterly.

"Those space ships ain't going to do you any good unless you believe in Jesus," Johnson said. He wet his finger and began to leaf through the pages of the Bible. "I'll read you where it says so," he said.

Sheppard leaned forward and said in a low furious voice, "Put that Bible up, Rufus, and eat your dinner."

Johnson continued searching for the passage.

"Put that Bible up!" Sheppard shouted.

The boy stopped and looked up. His expression was startled but pleased.

"That book is something for you to hide behind," Sheppard said. "It's for cowards, people who are afraid to stand on their own feet and figure things out for themselves."

Johnson's eyes snapped. He backed his chair a little way from the table. "Satan has you in his power," he said. "Not only me. You too."

Sheppard reached across the table to grab the book but Johnson snatched it and put it in his lap.

Sheppard laughed. "You don't believe in that book and you know you don't believe in it!"

"I believe it!" Johnson said. "You don't know what I believe and what I don't."

Sheppard shook his head. "You don't believe it. You're too intelligent."

"I ain't too intelligent," the boy muttered. "You don't know nothing about me. Even if I didn't believe it, it would still be true."

"You don't believe it!" Sheppard said. His face was a taunt.

"I believe it!" Johnson said breathlessly. "I'll show you I believe it!" He opened the book in his lap and tore out a page of it and thrust it into his mouth. He fixed his eyes on Sheppard. His jaws worked furiously and the paper crackled as he chewed it.

"Stop this," Sheppard said in a dry, burnt-out voice. "Stop it."

The boy raised the Bible and tore out a page with his teeth and began grinding it in his mouth, his eyes burning.

Sheppard reached across the table and knocked the book out of his hand. "Leave the table," he said coldly.

Johnson swallowed what was in his mouth. His eyes widened as if a vision of splendor were opening up before him. "I've eaten it!" he breathed. "I've eaten it like Ezekiel and it was honey to my mouth!"

"Leave this table," Sheppard said. His hands were clenched beside his plate.

"I've eaten it!" the boy cried. Wonder transformed his face. "I've eaten it like Ezekiel and I don't want none of your food after it nor no more ever."

"Go then," Sheppard said softly. "Go. Go."

The boy rose and picked up the Bible and started toward the hall with it. At the door he paused, a small black figure on the threshold of some dark apocalypse. "The devil has you in his power," he said in a jubilant voice and disappeared.

After supper Sheppard sat in the living room alone. Johnson had left the house but he could not believe that the boy had simply gone. The first feeling of release had passed. He felt dull and cold as at the onset of an illness and dread had settled in him like a fog. Just to leave would be too anticlimactic an end for Johnson's taste; he would return and try to prove something. He might come back a week later and set fire to the place. Nothing seemed too outrageous now.

He picked up the paper and tried to read. In a moment he threw it down and got up and went into the hall and listened. He might be hiding in the attic. He went to the attic door and opened it.

The lantern was lit, casting a dim light on the stairs. He didn't hear anything. "Norton," he called, "are you up there?" There was no answer. He mounted the narrow stairs to see.

Amid the strange vine-like shadows cast by the lantern, Norton sat with his eye to the telescope. "Norton," Sheppard said, "do you know where Rufus went?"

The child's back was to him. He was sitting hunched, intent, his large ears directly above his shoulders. Suddenly he waved his hand and crouched closer to the telescope as if he could not get near enough to what he saw.

"Norton!" Sheppard said in a loud voice.

The child didn't move.

"Norton!" Sheppard shouted.

Norton started. He turned around. There was an unnatural brightness about his eyes. After a moment he seemed to see that it was Sheppard. "I've found her!" he said breathlessly.

"Found who?" Sheppard said.

"Mamma!"

Sheppard steadied himself in the door way. The jungle of shadows around the child thickened.

"Come and look!" he cried. He wiped his sweaty face on the tail of his plaid shirt and then put his eye back to the telescope. His back became fixed in a rigid intensity. All at once he waved again.

"Norton," Sheppard said, "you don't see anything in the telescope but star clusters. Now you've had enough of that for one night. You'd better go to bed. Do you know where Rufus is?"

"She's there!" he cried, not turning around from the telescope. "She waved at me!"

"I want you in bed in fifteen minutes," Sheppard said. After a moment he said, "Do you hear me, Norton?"

The child began to wave frantically.

"I mean what I say," Sheppard said. "I'm going to call in fifteen minutes and see if you're in bed."

He went down the steps again and returned to the parlor. He went to the front door and cast a cursory glance out. The sky was crowded with the stars he had been fool enough to think Johnson could reach. Somewhere in the small wood behind the house, a bull frog sounded a low hollow note. He went back to his chair and sat a few minutes. He decided to go to bed. He put his hands on the arms of the chair and leaned forward and heard, like the first shrill note of a disaster warning, the siren of a police car, moving slowly into the neighborhood and nearer until it subsided with a moan outside the house.

He felt a cold weight on his shoulders as if an icy cloak had been thrown about him. He went to the door and opened it.

Two policemen were coming up the walk with a dark snarling Johnson between them, handcuffed to each. A reporter jogged alongside and another policeman waited in the patrol car.

"Here's your boy," the dourest of the policemen said. "Didn't I tell you we'd get him?"

Johnson jerked his arm down savagely. "I was waitin for you!" he said. "You wouldn't have got me if I hadn't of wanted to get caught. It was my idea." He was addressing the policemen but leering at Sheppard.

Sheppard looked at him coldly.

"Why did you want to get caught?" the reporter asked, running around to get beside Johnson. "Why did you deliberately want to get caught?"

The question and the sight of Sheppard seemed to throw the boy into a fury. "To show up that big tin Jesus!" he hissed and kicked his leg out at Sheppard. "He thinks he's God. I'd rather be in the reformatory than in his house, I'd rather be in the pen! The Devil has him in his power. He don't know his left hand from his right, he don't have as much sense as his crazy kid!" He paused and then swept on to his fantastic conclusion. "He made suggestions to me!"

Sheppard's face blanched. He caught hold of the door facing.

"Suggestions?" the reporter said eagerly, "what kind of suggestions?"

"Immor'l suggestions!" Johnson said. "What kind of suggestions do you think? But I ain't having none of it, I'm a Christian, I'm . . ."

Sheppard's face was tight with pain. "He knows that's not true," he said in a shaken voice. "He knows he's lying. I did everything I knew how for him. I did more for him than I did for my own child. I hoped to save him and I failed, but it was an honorable failure. I have nothing to reproach myself with. I made no suggestions to him."

"Do you remember the suggestions?" the reporter asked. "Can you tell us exactly what he said?"

"He's a dirty atheist," Johnson said. "He said there wasn't no hell."

"Well, they seen each other now," one of the policemen said with a knowing sigh. "Let's us go."

"Wait," Sheppard said. He came down one step and fixed his eyes on Johnson's eyes in a last desperate effort to save himself. "Tell the truth, Rufus," he said. "You don't want to perpetrate this lie. You're not evil, you're mortally confused. You don't have to make up for that foot, you don't have to . . ."

Johnson hurled himself forward. "Listen at him!" he screamed. "I lie and steal because I'm good at it! My foot don't have a thing to do with it! The lame shall enter first! The halt'll be gathered together. When I get ready to be saved, Jesus'll save me, not that lying stinking atheist, not that . . ."

"That'll be enough out of you," the policeman said and yanked him back. "We just wanted you to see we got him," he said to Sheppard, and the two of them turned around and dragged Johnson away, half turned and screaming back at Sheppard.

"The lame'll carry off the prey!" he screeched, but his voice was muffled inside the car. The reporter scrambled into the front seat with the driver and slammed the door and the siren wailed into the darkness.

Sheppard remained there, bent slightly like a man who has been shot but continues to stand. After a minute he turned and went back in the house and sat down in the chair he had left. He closed his eyes on a picture of Johnson in a circle of reporters at the police station, elaborating his lies. "I have nothing to reproach myself with," he murmured. His every action had been selfless, his one aim had been to save Johnson for some decent kind of service, he had not spared himself, he had sacrificed his reputation, he had done more for Johnson than he had done for his own child. Foulness hung about him like an odor in the air, so close that it seemed to come from his own breath. "I have nothing to reproach myself with," he repeated. His voice sounded dry and harsh. "I did more for him than I did for my own child." He was swept with a sudden panic. He heard the boy's jubilant voice. Satan has you in his power.

"I have nothing to reproach myself with," he began again. "I did more for him than I did for my own child." He heard his voice as if it were the voice of his accuser. He repeated the sentence silently.

Slowly his face drained of color. It became almost grey beneath the white halo of his hair. The sentence echoed in his mind, each syllable like a dull blow. His mouth twisted and he closed his eyes against the revelation. Norton's face rose before him, empty, forlorn, his left eye listing almost imperceptibly toward the outer rim as if it could not bear a full view of grief. His heart constricted with a repulsion for himself so clear and intense that he gasped for breath. He had stuffed his own emptiness with good works like a glutton. He had ignored his own child to feed his vision of himself. He saw the clear-eyed Devil, the sounder of hearts, leering at him from the eyes of Johnson. His image of himself shrivelled until everything was black before him. He sat there paralyzed, aghast.

He saw Norton at the telescope, all back and ears, saw his arm shoot up and wave frantically. A rush of agonizing love for the child rushed over him like a transfusion of life. The little boy's face appeared to him transformed; the image of his salvation; all light. He groaned with joy. He would make everything up to him. He would never let him suffer again. He would be mother and father. He jumped up and ran to his room, to kiss him, to tell him that he loved him, that he would never fail him again.

The light was on in Norton's room but the bed was empty. He turned and dashed up the attic stairs and at the top reeled back like a man on the edge of a pit. The tripod had fallen and the telescope lay on the floor. A few feet over it, the child hung in the jungle of shadows, just below the beam from which he had launched his flight into space.

Revelation

THE DOCTOR'S waiting room, which was very small, was almost full when the Turpins entered and Mrs. Turpin, who was very large, made it look even smaller by her presence. She stood looming at the head of the magazine table set in the center of it, a living demonstration that the room was inadequate and ridiculous. Her little bright black eyes took in all the patients as she sized up the seating situation. There was one vacant chair and a place on the sofa occupied by a blond child in a dirty blue romper who should have been told to move over and make room for the lady. He was five or six, but Mrs. Turpin saw at once that no one was going to tell him to move over. He was slumped down in the seat, his arms idle at his sides and his eyes idle in his head; his nose ran unchecked.

Mrs. Turpin put a firm hand on Claud's shoulder and said in a voice that included anyone who wanted to listen, "Claud, you sit in that chair there," and gave him a push down into the vacant one. Claud was florid and bald and sturdy, somewhat shorter than Mrs. Turpin, but he sat down as if he were accustomed to doing what she told him to.

Mrs. Turpin remained standing. The only man in the room besides Claud was a lean stringy old fellow with a rusty hand spread out on each knee, whose eyes were closed as if he were asleep or dead or pretending to be so as not to get up and offer her his seat. Her gaze settled agreeably on a well-dressed grey-haired lady whose eyes met hers and whose expression said: if that child belonged to me, he would have some manners and move over—there's plenty of room there for you and him too.

Claud looked up with a sigh and made as if to rise.

"Sit down," Mrs. Turpin said. "You know you're not supposed to stand on that leg. He has an ulcer on his leg," she explained.

Claud lifted his foot onto the magazine table and rolled his trouser leg up to reveal a purple swelling on a plump marble-white calf.

"My!" the pleasant lady said. "How did you do that?"

"A cow kicked him," Mrs. Turpin said.

"Goodness!" said the lady.

Claud rolled his trouser leg down.

"Maybe the little boy would move over," the lady suggested, but the child did not stir.

"Somebody will be leaving in a minute," Mrs. Turpin said. She could not understand why a doctor—with as much money as they made charging five dollars a day to just stick their head in the hospital door and look at you—couldn't afford a decent-sized waiting room. This one was hardly bigger than a garage. The table was cluttered with limp-looking magazines and at one end of it there was a big green glass ash tray full of cigaret butts and cotton wads with little blood spots on them. If she had had anything to do with the running of the place, that would have been emptied every so often. There were no chairs against the wall at the head of the room. It had a rectangular-shaped panel in it that permitted a view of the office where the nurse came and went and the secretary listened to the radio. A plastic fern in a gold pot sat in the opening and trailed its fronds down almost to the floor. The radio was softly playing gospel music.

Just then the inner door opened and a nurse with the highest stack of yellow hair Mrs. Turpin had ever seen put her face in the crack and called for the next patient. The woman sitting beside Claud grasped the two arms of her chair and hoisted herself up; she pulled her dress free from her legs and lumbered through the door where the nurse had disappeared.

Mrs. Turpin eased into the vacant chair, which held her tight as a corset. "I wish I could reduce," she said, and rolled her eyes and gave a comic sigh.

"Oh, *you* aren't fat," the stylish lady said.

"Ooooo I am too," Mrs. Turpin said. "Claud he eats all he wants to and never weighs over one hundred and seventy-five pounds, but me I just look at something good to eat and I gain some weight," and her stomach and shoulders shook with laughter. "You can eat all you want to, can't you, Claud?" she asked, turning to him.

Claud only grinned.

"Well, as long as you have such a good disposition," the stylish lady said, "I don't think it makes a bit of difference what size you are. You just can't beat a good disposition."

Next to her was a fat girl of eighteen or nineteen, scowling into a thick blue book which Mrs. Turpin saw was entitled *Human Development*. The girl raised her head and directed her scowl at Mrs. Turpin as if she did not like her looks. She appeared annoyed that anyone should speak while she tried to read. The poor girl's face was blue with acne and Mrs. Turpin thought how pitiful it was to have a face like that at that age. She gave the girl a friendly smile but the girl only scowled the harder. Mrs. Turpin herself was fat but she had always had good skin, and, though she was forty-seven years old, there was not a wrinkle in her face except around her eyes from laughing too much.

Next to the ugly girl was the child, still in exactly the same position, and next to him was a thin leathery old woman in a cotton print dress. She and Claud had three sacks of chicken feed in their pump house that was in the same print. She had seen from the first that the child belonged with the old woman. She could tell by the way they sat—kind of vacant and white-trashy, as if they would sit there until Doomsday if nobody called and told them to get up. And at right angles but next to the well-dressed pleasant lady was a lank-faced woman who was certainly the child's mother. She had on a yellow sweat shirt and wine-colored slacks, both gritty-looking, and the rims of her lips were stained with snuff. Her dirty yellow hair was tied behind with a little piece of red paper ribbon. Worse than niggers any day, Mrs. Turpin thought.

The gospel hymn playing was, "When I looked up and He looked down," and Mrs. Turpin, who knew it, supplied the last line mentally, "And wona these days I know I'll we-eara crown."

Without appearing to, Mrs. Turpin always noticed people's feet. The well-dressed lady had on red and grey suede shoes to match her dress. Mrs. Turpin had on her good black patent leather pumps. The ugly girl had on Girl Scout shoes and heavy socks. The old woman had on tennis shoes and the white-trashy mother had on what appeared to be bedroom slippers, black straw with gold braid threaded through them—exactly what you would have expected her to have on.

Sometimes at night when she couldn't go to sleep, Mrs. Turpin would occupy herself with the question of who she would have chosen to be if she couldn't have been herself. If Jesus had said to her before he made her, "There's only two places available for you. You can either be a nigger or white-trash," what would she have said? "Please, Jesus, please," she would have said, "just let me wait until there's another place available," and he would have said, "No, you have to go right now and I have only those two places so make up your mind." She would have wiggled and squirmed and begged and pleaded but it would have been no use and finally she would have said, "All right, make me a nigger then—but that don't mean a trashy one." And he would have made her a neat clean respectable Negro woman, herself but black.

Next to the child's mother was a red-headed youngish woman, reading one of the magazines and working a piece of chewing gum, hell for leather, as Claud would say. Mrs. Turpin could not see the woman's feet. She was not white-trash, just common. Sometimes Mrs. Turpin occupied herself at night naming the classes of people. On the bottom of the heap were most colored people, not the kind she would have been if she had been one, but most of them; then next to them—not above, just away from—were the white-trash; then above them were the home-owners, and above them the home-and-land owners, to which she and Claud belonged. Above she and Claud were people with a lot of money and much bigger houses and much more land. But here the complexity of it would begin to bear in on her, for some of the people with a lot of money were common and ought to be below she and Claud and some of the people who had good blood had lost their money and had to rent and then there were colored people who owned their homes and land as well. There was a colored dentist in town who had two red Lincolns and a swimming pool and a farm with registered white-face cattle on it. Usually by the time she had fallen asleep all the classes of people were moiling and roiling around in her head, and she would dream they were all crammed in together in a box car, being ridden off to be put in a gas oven.

"That's a beautiful clock," she said and nodded to her right. It was a big wall clock, the face encased in a brass sunburst.

"Yes, it's very pretty," the stylish lady said agreeably. "And right on the dot too," she added, glancing at her watch.

The ugly girl beside her cast an eye upward at the clock, smirked, then looked directly at Mrs. Turpin and smirked again. Then she returned her eyes to her book. She was obviously the lady's daughter because, although they didn't look anything alike as to disposition, they both had the same shape of face and the same blue eyes. On the lady they sparkled pleasantly but in the girl's seared face they appeared alternately to smolder and to blaze.

What if Jesus had said, "All right, you can be white-trash or a nigger or ugly"!

Mrs. Turpin felt an awful pity for the girl, though she thought it was one thing to be ugly and another to act ugly.

The woman with the snuff-stained lips turned around in her chair and looked up at the clock. Then she turned back and appeared to look a little to the side of Mrs. Turpin. There was a cast in one of her eyes. "You want to know wher you can get you one of themther clocks?" she asked in a loud voice.

"No, I already have a nice clock," Mrs. Turpin said. Once somebody like her got a leg in the conversation, she would be all over it.

"You can get you one with green stamps," the woman said. "That's most likely wher he got hisn. Save you up enough, you can get you most anything. I got me some joo'ry."

Ought to have got you a wash rag and some soap, Mrs. Turpin thought.

"I get contour sheets with mine," the pleasant lady said.

The daughter slammed her book shut. She looked straight in front of her, directly through Mrs. Turpin and on through the yellow curtain and the plate glass window which made the wall behind her. The girl's eyes seemed lit all of a sudden with a peculiar light, an unnatural light like night road signs give. Mrs. Turpin turned her head to see if there was anything going on outside that she should see, but she could not see anything. Figures passing cast only a pale shadow through the curtain. There was no reason the girl should single her out for her ugly looks.

"Miss Finley," the nurse said, cracking the door. The gum-chewing woman got up and passed in front of her and Claud and went into the office. She had on red high-heeled shoes.

Directly across the table, the ugly girl's eyes were fixed on Mrs. Turpin as if she had some very special reason for disliking her.

"This is wonderful weather, isn't it?" the girl's mother said.

"It's good weather for cotton if you can get the niggers to pick it," Mrs. Turpin said, "but niggers don't want to pick cotton any more. You can't get the white folks to pick it and now you can't get the niggers—because they got to be right up there with the white folks."

"They gonna *try* anyways," the white-trash woman said, leaning forward.

"Do you have one of those cotton-picking machines?" the pleasant lady asked.

"No," Mrs. Turpin said, "they leave half the cotton in the field. We don't have much cotton anyway. If you want to make it farming now, you have to have a little of everything. We got a couple of acres of cotton and a few hogs and chickens and just enough white-face that Claud can look after them himself."

"One thang I don't want," the white-trash woman said, wiping her mouth with the back of her hand. "Hogs. Nasty stinking things, a-gruntin and a-rootin all over the place."

Mrs. Turpin gave her the merest edge of her attention. "Our hogs are not dirty and they don't stink," she said. "They're cleaner than some children I've seen. Their feet never touch the ground. We have a pig-parlor—that's where you raise them on concrete," she explained to the pleasant lady, "and Claud scoots them down with the hose every afternoon and washes off the floor." Cleaner by far than that child right there, she thought. Poor nasty little thing. He had not moved except to put the thumb of his dirty hand into his mouth.

The woman turned her face away from Mrs. Turpin. "I know I wouldn't scoot down no hog with no hose," she said to the wall.

You wouldn't have no hog to scoot down, Mrs. Turpin said to herself.

"A-gruntin and a-rootin and a-groanin," the woman muttered.

"We got a little of everything," Mrs. Turpin said to the

pleasant lady. "It's no use in having more than you can handle yourself with help like it is. We found enough niggers to pick our cotton this year but Claud he has to go after them and take them home again in the evening. They can't walk that half a mile. No they can't. I tell you," she said and laughed merrily, "I sure am tired of buttering up niggers, but you got to love em if you want em to work for you. When they come in the morning, I run out and I say, 'Hi yawl this morning?' and when Claud drives them off to the field I just wave to beat the band and they just wave back." And she waved her hand rapidly to illustrate.

"Like you read out of the same book," the lady said, showing she understood perfectly.

"Child, yes," Mrs. Turpin said. "And when they come in from the field, I run out with a bucket of icewater. That's the way it's going to be from now on," she said. "You may as well face it."

"One thang I know," the white-trash woman said. "Two thangs I ain't going to do: love no niggers or scoot down no hog with no hose." And she let out a bark of contempt.

The look that Mrs. Turpin and the pleasant lady exchanged indicated they both understood that you had to *have* certain things before you could *know* certain things. But every time Mrs. Turpin exchanged a look with the lady, she was aware that the ugly girl's peculiar eyes were still on her, and she had trouble bringing her attention back to the conversation.

"When you got something," she said, "you got to look after it." And when you ain't got a thing but breath and britches, she added to herself, you can afford to come to town every morning and just sit on the Court House coping and spit.

A grotesque revolving shadow passed across the curtain behind her and was thrown palely on the opposite wall. Then a bicycle clattered down against the outside of the building. The door opened and a colored boy glided in with a tray from the drug store. It had two large red and white paper cups on it with tops on them. He was a tall, very black boy in discolored white pants and a green nylon shirt. He was chewing gum slowly, as if to music. He set the tray down in the office opening next to the fern and stuck his head through to look for the secretary. She was not in there. He rested his arms on the ledge and waited, his narrow bottom stuck out, swaying slowly to the left and right. He raised a hand over his head and scratched the base of his skull.

"You see that button there, boy?" Mrs. Turpin said. "You can punch that and she'll come. She's probably in the back somewhere."

"Is thas right?" the boy said agreeably, as if he had never seen the button before. He leaned to the right and put his finger on it. "She sometime out," he said and twisted around to face his audience, his elbows behind him on the counter. The nurse appeared and he twisted back again. She handed him a dollar and he rooted in his pocket and made the change and counted it out to her. She gave him fifteen cents for a tip and he went out with the empty tray. The heavy door swung to slowly and closed at length with the sound of suction. For a moment no one spoke.

"They ought to send all them niggers back to Africa," the white-trash woman said. "That's wher they come from in the first place."

"Oh, I couldn't do without my good colored friends," the pleasant lady said.

"There's a heap of things worse than a nigger," Mrs. Turpin agreed. "It's all kinds of them just like it's all kinds of us."

"Yes, and it takes all kinds to make the world go round," the lady said in her musical voice.

As she said it, the raw-complexioned girl snapped her teeth together. Her lower lip turned downwards and inside out, revealing the pale pink inside of her mouth. After a second it rolled back up. It was the ugliest face Mrs. Turpin had ever seen anyone make and for a moment she was certain that the girl had made it at her. She was looking at her as if she had known and disliked her all her life—all of Mrs. Turpin's life, it seemed too, not just all the girl's life. Why, girl, I don't even know you, Mrs. Turpin said silently.

She forced her attention back to the discussion. "It wouldn't be practical to send them back to Africa," she said. "They wouldn't want to go. They got it too good here."

"Wouldn't be what they wanted—if I had anythang to do with it," the woman said.

"It wouldn't be a way in the world you could get all the niggers back over there," Mrs. Turpin said. "They'd be hiding out and lying down and turning sick on you and wailing and hollering and raring and pitching. It wouldn't be a way in the world to get them over there."

"They got over here," the trashy woman said. "Get back like they got over."

"It wasn't so many of them then," Mrs. Turpin explained.

The woman looked at Mrs. Turpin as if here was an idiot indeed but Mrs. Turpin was not bothered by the look, considering where it came from.

"Nooo," she said, "they're going to stay here where they can go to New York and marry white folks and improve their color. That's what they all want to do, every one of them, improve their color."

"You know what comes of that, don't you?" Claud asked.

"No, Claud, what?" Mrs. Turpin said.

Claud's eyes twinkled. "White-faced niggers," he said with never a smile.

Everybody in the office laughed except the white-trash and the ugly girl. The girl gripped the book in her lap with white fingers. The trashy woman looked around her from face to face as if she thought they were all idiots. The old woman in the feed sack dress continued to gaze expressionless across the floor at the high-top shoes of the man opposite her, the one who had been pretending to be asleep when the Turpins came in. He was laughing heartily, his hands still spread out on his knees. The child had fallen to the side and was lying now almost face down in the old woman's lap.

While they recovered from their laughter, the nasal chorus on the radio kept the room from silence.

> "You go to blank blank
> And I'll go to mine
> But we'll all blank along
> To-geth-ther,
> And all along the blank
> We'll hep eachother out
> Smile-ling in any kind of
> Weath-ther!"

Mrs. Turpin didn't catch every word but she caught enough to agree with the spirit of the song and it turned her thoughts sober. To help anybody out that needed it was her philosophy of life. She never spared herself when she found somebody in need, whether they were white or black, trash or decent. And of all she had to be thankful for, she was most thankful that this was so. If Jesus had said, "You can be high society and have all the money you want and be thin and svelte-like, but you can't be a good woman with it," she would have had to say, "Well don't make me that then. Make me a good woman and it don't matter what else, how fat or how ugly or how poor!" Her heart rose. He had not made her a nigger or white-trash or ugly! He had made her herself and given her a little of everything. Jesus, thank you! she said. Thank you thank you thank you! Whenever she counted her blessings she felt as buoyant as if she weighed one hundred and twenty-five pounds instead of one hundred and eighty.

"What's wrong with your little boy?" the pleasant lady asked the white-trashy woman.

"He has a ulcer," the woman said proudly. "He ain't give me a minute's peace since he was born. Him and her are just alike," she said, nodding at the old woman, who was running her leathery fingers through the child's pale hair. "Look like I can't get nothing down them two but Co' Cola and candy."

That's all you try to get down em, Mrs. Turpin said to herself. Too lazy to light the fire. There was nothing you could tell her about people like them that she didn't know already. And it was not just that they didn't have anything. Because if you gave them everything, in two weeks it would all be broken or filthy or they would have chopped it up for lightwood. She knew all this from her own experience. Help them you must, but help them you couldn't.

All at once the ugly girl turned her lips inside out again. Her eyes were fixed like two drills on Mrs. Turpin. This time there was no mistaking that there was something urgent behind them.

Girl, Mrs. Turpin exclaimed silently, I haven't done a thing to you! The girl might be confusing her with somebody else. There was no need to sit by and let herself be intimidated.

"You must be in college," she said boldly, looking directly at the girl. "I see you reading a book there."

The girl continued to stare and pointedly did not answer.

Her mother blushed at this rudeness. "The lady asked you a question, Mary Grace," she said under her breath.

"I have ears," Mary Grace said.

The poor mother blushed again. "Mary Grace goes to Wellesley College," she explained. She twisted one of the buttons on her dress. "In Massachusetts," she added with a grimace. "And in the summer she just keeps right on studying. Just reads all the time, a real book worm. She's done real well at Wellesley; she's taking English and Math and History and Psychology and Social Studies," she rattled on, "and I think it's too much. I think she ought to get out and have fun."

The girl looked as if she would like to hurl them all through the plate glass window.

"Way up north," Mrs. Turpin murmured and thought, well, it hasn't done much for her manners.

"I'd almost rather to have him sick," the white-trash woman said, wrenching the attention back to herself. "He's so mean when he ain't. Look like some children just take natural to meanness. It's some gets bad when they get sick but he was the opposite. Took sick and turned good. He don't give me no trouble now. It's me waitin to see the doctor," she said.

If I was going to send anybody back to Africa, Mrs. Turpin thought, it would be your kind, woman. "Yes, indeed," she said aloud, but looking up at the ceiling, "it's a heap of things worse than a nigger." And dirtier than a hog, she added to herself.

"I think people with bad dispositions are more to be pitied than anyone on earth," the pleasant lady said in a voice that was decidedly thin.

"I thank the Lord he has blessed me with a good one," Mrs. Turpin said. "The day has never dawned that I couldn't find something to laugh at."

"Not since she married me anyways," Claud said with a comical straight face.

Everybody laughed except the girl and the white-trash.

Mrs. Turpin's stomach shook. "He's such a caution," she said, "that I can't help but laugh at him."

The girl made a loud ugly noise through her teeth.

Her mother's mouth grew thin and tight. "I think the worst thing in the world," she said, "is an ungrateful person. To have everything and not appreciate it. I know a girl," she said, "who has parents who would give her anything, a little brother who loves her dearly, who is getting a good education, who wears the best clothes, but who can never say a kind word to anyone, who never smiles, who just criticizes and complains all day long."

"Is she too old to paddle?" Claud asked.

The girl's face was almost purple.

"Yes," the lady said, "I'm afraid there's nothing to do but leave her to her folly. Some day she'll wake up and it'll be too late."

"It never hurt anyone to smile," Mrs. Turpin said. "It just makes you feel better all over."

"Of course," the lady said sadly, "but there are just some people you can't tell anything to. They can't take criticism."

"If it's one thing I am," Mrs. Turpin said with feeling, "it's grateful. When I think who all I could have been besides myself and what all I got, a little of everything, and a good disposition besides, I just feel like shouting, 'Thank you, Jesus, for making everything the way it is!' It could have been different!" For one thing, somebody else could have got Claud. At the thought of this, she was flooded with gratitude and a terrible pang of joy ran through her. "Oh thank you, Jesus, Jesus, thank you!" she cried aloud.

The book struck her directly over her left eye. It struck almost at the same instant that she realized the girl was about to hurl it. Before she could utter a sound, the raw face came crashing across the table toward her, howling. The girl's fingers sank like clamps into the soft flesh of her neck. She heard the mother cry out and Claud shout, "Whoa!" There was an instant when she was certain that she was about to be in an earthquake.

All at once her vision narrowed and she saw everything as if it were happening in a small room far away, or as if she were looking at it through the wrong end of a telescope.

Claud's face crumpled and fell out of sight. The nurse ran in, then out, then in again. Then the gangling figure of the doctor rushed out of the inner door. Magazines flew this way and that as the table turned over. The girl fell with a thud and Mrs. Turpin's vision suddenly reversed itself and she saw everything large instead of small. The eyes of the white-trashy woman were staring hugely at the floor. There the girl, held down on one side by the nurse and on the other by her mother, was wrenching and turning in their grasp. The doctor was kneeling astride her, trying to hold her arm down. He managed after a second to sink a long needle into it.

Mrs. Turpin felt entirely hollow except for her heart which swung from side to side as if it were agitated in a great empty drum of flesh.

"Somebody that's not busy call for the ambulance," the doctor said in the off-hand voice young doctors adopt for terrible occasions.

Mrs. Turpin could not have moved a finger. The old man who had been sitting next to her skipped nimbly into the office and made the call, for the secretary still seemed to be gone.

"Claud!" Mrs. Turpin called.

He was not in his chair. She knew she must jump up and find him but she felt like some one trying to catch a train in a dream, when everything moves in slow motion and the faster you try to run the slower you go.

"Here I am," a suffocated voice, very unlike Claud's, said.

He was doubled up in the corner on the floor, pale as paper, holding his leg. She wanted to get up and go to him but she could not move. Instead, her gaze was drawn slowly downward to the churning face on the floor, which she could see over the doctor's shoulder.

The girl's eyes stopped rolling and focused on her. They seemed a much lighter blue than before, as if a door that had been tightly closed behind them was now open to admit light and air.

Mrs. Turpin's head cleared and her power of motion returned. She leaned forward until she was looking directly into the fierce brilliant eyes. There was no doubt in her mind that the girl did know her, knew her in some intense and personal way, beyond time and place and condition. "What you got to say to me?" she asked hoarsely and held her breath, waiting, as for a revelation.

The girl raised her head. Her gaze locked with Mrs. Turpin's. "Go back to hell where you came from, you old wart hog," she whispered. Her voice was low but clear. Her eyes burned for a moment as if she saw with pleasure that her message had struck its target.

Mrs. Turpin sank back in her chair.

After a moment the girl's eyes closed and she turned her head wearily to the side.

The doctor rose and handed the nurse the empty syringe. He leaned over and put both hands for a moment on the mother's shoulders, which were shaking. She was sitting on the floor, her lips pressed together, holding Mary Grace's hand in her lap. The girl's fingers were gripped like a baby's around her thumb. "Go on to the hospital," he said. "I'll call and make the arrangements."

"Now let's see that neck," he said in a jovial voice to Mrs. Turpin. He began to inspect her neck with his first two fingers. Two little moon-shaped lines like pink fish bones were indented over her windpipe. There was the beginning of an angry red swelling above her eye. His fingers passed over this also.

"Lea' me be," she said thickly and shook him off. "See about Claud. She kicked him."

"I'll see about him in a minute," he said and felt her pulse. He was a thin grey-haired man, given to pleasantries. "Go home and have yourself a vacation the rest of the day," he said and patted her on the shoulder.

Quit your pattin me, Mrs. Turpin growled to herself.

"And put an ice pack over that eye," he said. Then he went and squatted down beside Claud and looked at his leg. After a moment he pulled him up and Claud limped after him into the office.

Until the ambulance came, the only sounds in the room were the tremulous moans of the girl's mother, who continued to sit on the floor. The white-trash woman did not take her eyes off the girl. Mrs. Turpin looked straight ahead at nothing. Presently the ambulance drew up, a long dark shadow, behind the curtain. The attendants came in and set the stretcher down beside the girl and lifted her expertly onto it and carried her out. The nurse helped the mother gather up her things. The shadow of the ambulance moved silently away and the nurse came back in the office.

"That there girl is going to be a lunatic, ain't she?" the white-trash woman asked the nurse, but the nurse kept on to the back and never answered her.

"Yes, she's going to be a lunatic," the white-trash woman said to the rest of them.

"Po' critter," the old woman murmured. The child's face was still in her lap. His eyes looked idly out over her knees. He had not moved during the disturbance except to draw one leg up under him.

"I thank Gawd," the white-trash woman said fervently, "I ain't a lunatic."

Claud came limping out and the Turpins went home.

As their pick-up truck turned into their own dirt road and made the crest of the hill, Mrs. Turpin gripped the window ledge and looked out suspiciously. The land sloped gracefully down through a field dotted with lavender weeds and at the start of the rise their small yellow frame house, with its little flower beds spread out around it like a fancy apron, sat primly in its accustomed place between two giant hickory trees. She would not have been startled to see a burnt wound between two blackened chimneys.

Neither of them felt like eating so they put on their house clothes and lowered the shade in the bedroom and lay down, Claud with his leg on a pillow and herself with a damp washcloth over her eye. The instant she was flat on her back, the image of a razor-backed hog with warts on its face and horns coming out behind its ears snorted into her head. She moaned, a low quiet moan.

"I am not," she said tearfully, "a wart hog. From hell." But the denial had no force. The girl's eyes and her words, even the tone of her voice, low but clear, directed only to her, brooked no repudiation. She had been singled out for the message, though there was trash in the room to whom it might justly have been applied. The full force of this fact struck her only now. There was a woman there who was neglecting her own child but she had been overlooked. The message had been given to Ruby Turpin, a respectable, hard-working, church-going woman. The tears dried. Her eyes began to burn instead with wrath.

She rose on her elbow and the washcloth fell into her hand. Claud was lying on his back, snoring. She wanted to tell him what the girl had said. At the same time, she did not wish to put the image of herself as a wart hog from hell into his mind.

"Hey, Claud," she muttered and pushed his shoulder.

Claud opened one pale baby blue eye.

She looked into it warily. He did not think about anything. He just went his way.

"Wha, whasit?" he said and closed the eye again.

"Nothing," she said. "Does your leg pain you?"

"Hurts like hell," Claud said.

"It'll quit terreckly," she said and lay back down. In a moment Claud was snoring again. For the rest of the afternoon they lay there. Claud slept. She scowled at the ceiling. Occasionally she raised her fist and made a small stabbing motion over her chest as if she was defending her innocence to invisible guests who were like the comforters of Job, reasonable-seeming but wrong.

About five-thirty Claud stirred. "Got to go after those niggers," he sighed, not moving.

She was looking straight up as if there were unintelligible handwriting on the ceiling. The protuberance over her eye had turned a greenish-blue. "Listen here," she said.

"What?"

"Kiss me."

Claud leaned over and kissed her loudly on the mouth. He pinched her side and their hands interlocked. Her expression of ferocious concentration did not change. Claud got up, groaning and growling, and limped off. She continued to study the ceiling.

She did not get up until she heard the pick-up truck coming back with the Negroes. Then she rose and thrust her feet in her brown oxfords, which she did not bother to lace, and stumped out onto the back porch and got her red plastic bucket. She emptied a tray of ice cubes into it and filled it half full of water and went out into the back yard.

Every afternoon after Claud brought the hands in, one of the boys helped him put out hay and the rest waited in the back of the truck until he was ready to take them home. The truck was parked in the shade under one of the hickory trees.

"Hi yawl this evening?" Mrs. Turpin asked grimly, appearing with the bucket and the dipper. There were three women and a boy in the truck.

"Us doin nicely," the oldest woman said. "Hi you doin?" and her gaze stuck immediately on the dark lump on Mrs. Turpin's forehead. "You done fell down, ain't you?" she asked in a solicitous voice. The old woman was dark and almost toothless. She had on an old felt hat of Claud's set back on her head. The other two women were younger and lighter and they both had new bright green sun hats. One of them had hers on her head; the other had taken hers off and the boy was grinning beneath it.

Mrs. Turpin set the bucket down on the floor of the truck. "Yawl hep yourselves," she said. She looked around to make sure Claud had gone. "No. I didn't fall down," she said, folding her arms. "It was something worse than that."

"Ain't nothing bad happen to you!" the old woman said. She said it as if they all knew that Mrs. Turpin was protected in some special way by Divine Providence. "You just had you a little fall."

"We were in town at the doctor's office for where the cow kicked Mr. Turpin," Mrs. Turpin said in a flat tone that indicated they could leave off their foolishness. "And there was this girl there. A big fat girl with her face all broke out. I could look at that girl and tell she was peculiar but I couldn't tell how. And me and her mama were just talking and going along and all of a sudden WHAM! She throws this big book she was reading at me and . . ."

"Naw!" the old woman cried out.

"And then she jumps over the table and commences to choke me."

"Naw!" they all exclaimed, "naw!"

"Hi come she do that?" the old woman asked. "What ail her?"

Mrs. Turpin only glared in front of her.

"Somethin ail her," the old woman said.

"They carried her off in an ambulance," Mrs. Turpin continued, "but before she went she was rolling on the floor and they were trying to hold her down to give her a shot and she said something to me." She paused. "You know what she said to me?"

"What she say?" they asked.

"She said," Mrs. Turpin began, and stopped, her face very dark and heavy. The sun was getting whiter and whiter, blanching the sky overhead so that the leaves of the hickory tree were black in the face of it. She could not bring forth the words. "Something real ugly," she muttered.

"She sho shouldn't said nothin ugly to you," the old woman said. "You so sweet. You the sweetest lady I know."

"She pretty too," the one with the hat on said.

"And stout," the other one said. "I never knowed no sweeter white lady."

"That's the truth befo' Jesus," the old woman said. "Amen! You des as sweet and pretty as you can be."

Mrs. Turpin knew just exactly how much Negro flattery was worth and it added to her rage. "She said," she began again and finished this time with a fierce rush of breath, "that I was an old wart hog from hell."

There was an astounded silence.

"Where she at?" the youngest woman cried in a piercing voice.

"Lemme see her. I'll kill her!"

"I'll kill her with you!" the other one cried.

"She b'long in the sylum," the old woman said emphatically. "You the sweetest white lady I know."

"She pretty too," the other two said. "Stout as she can be and sweet. Jesus satisfied with her!"

"Deed he is," the old woman declared.

Idiots! Mrs. Turpin growled to herself. You could never say anything intelligent to a nigger. You could talk at them but not with them. "Yawl ain't drunk your water," she said shortly. "Leave the bucket in the truck when you're finished with it. I got more to do than just stand around and pass the time of day," and she moved off and into the house.

She stood for a moment in the middle of the kitchen. The

dark protuberance over her eye looked like a miniature tornado cloud which might any moment sweep across the horizon of her brow. Her lower lip protruded dangerously. She squared her massive shoulders. Then she marched into the front of the house and out the side door and started down the road to the pig parlor. She had the look of a woman going single-handed, weaponless, into battle.

The sun was a deep yellow now like a harvest moon and was riding westward very fast over the far tree line as if it meant to reach the hogs before she did. The road was rutted and she kicked several good-sized stones out of her path as she strode along. The pig parlor was on a little knoll at the end of a lane that ran off from the side of the barn. It was a square of concrete as large as a small room, with a board fence about four feet high around it. The concrete floor sloped slightly so that the hog wash could drain off into a trench where it was carried to the field for fertilizer. Claud was standing on the outside, on the edge of the concrete, hanging onto the top board, hosing down the floor inside. The hose was connected to the faucet of a water trough nearby.

Mrs. Turpin climbed up beside him and glowered down at the hogs inside. There were seven long-snouted bristly shoats in it—tan with liver-colored spots—and an old sow a few weeks off from farrowing. She was lying on her side grunting. The shoats were running about shaking themselves like idiot children, their little slit pig eyes searching the floor for anything left. She had read that pigs were the most intelligent animal. She doubted it. They were supposed to be smarter than dogs. There had even been a pig astronaut. He had performed his assignment perfectly but died of a heart attack afterwards because they left him in his electric suit, sitting upright throughout his examination when naturally a hog should be on all fours.

A-gruntin and a-rootin and a-groanin.

"Gimme that hose," she said, yanking it away from Claud. "Go on and carry them niggers home and then get off that leg."

"You look like you might have swallowed a mad dog," Claud observed, but he got down and limped off. He paid no attention to her humors.

Until he was out of earshot, Mrs. Turpin stood on the side of the pen, holding the hose and pointing the stream of water at the hind quarters of any shoat that looked as if it might try to lie down. When he had had time to get over the hill, she turned her head slightly and her wrathful eyes scanned the path. He was nowhere in sight. She turned back again and seemed to gather herself up. Her shoulders rose and she drew in her breath.

"What do you send me a message like that for?" she said in a low fierce voice, barely above a whisper but with the force of a shout in its concentrated fury. "How am I a hog and me both? How am I saved and from hell too?" Her free fist was knotted and with the other she gripped the hose, blindly pointing the stream of water in and out of the eye of the old sow whose outraged squeal she did not hear.

The pig parlor commanded a view of the back pasture where their twenty beef cows were gathered around the hay-bales Claud and the boy had put out. The freshly cut pasture sloped down to the highway. Across it was their cotton field and beyond that a dark green dusty wood which they owned as well. The sun was behind the wood, very red, looking over the paling of trees like a farmer inspecting his own hogs.

"Why me?" she rumbled. "It's no trash around here, black or white, that I haven't given to. And break my back to the bone every day working. And do for the church."

She appeared to be the right size woman to command the arena before her. "How am I a hog?" she demanded. "Exactly how am I like them?" and she jabbed the stream of water at the shoats. "There was plenty of trash there. It didn't have to be me.

"If you like trash better, go get yourself some trash then," she railed. "You could have made me trash. Or a nigger. If trash is what you wanted why didn't you make me trash?" She shook her fist with the hose in it and a watery snake appeared momentarily in the air. "I could quit working and take it easy and be filthy," she growled. "Lounge about the sidewalks all day drinking root beer. Dip snuff and spit in every puddle and have it all over my face. I could be nasty.

"Or you could have made me a nigger. It's too late for me

to be a nigger," she said with deep sarcasm, "but I could act like one. Lay down in the middle of the road and stop traffic. Roll on the ground."

In the deepening light everything was taking on a mysterious hue. The pasture was growing a peculiar glassy green and the streak of highway had turned lavender. She braced herself for a final assault and this time her voice rolled out over the pasture. "Go on," she yelled, "call me a hog! Call me a hog again. From hell. Call me a wart hog from hell. Put that bottom rail on top. There'll still be a top and bottom!"

A garbled echo returned to her.

A final surge of fury shook her and she roared, "Who do you think you are?"

The color of everything, field and crimson sky, burned for a moment with a transparent intensity. The question carried over the pasture and across the highway and the cotton field and returned to her clearly like an answer from beyond the wood.

She opened her mouth but no sound came out of it.

A tiny truck, Claud's, appeared on the highway, heading rapidly out of sight. Its gears scraped thinly. It looked like a child's toy. At any moment a bigger truck might smash into it and scatter Claud's and the niggers' brains all over the road.

Mrs. Turpin stood there, her gaze fixed on the highway, all her muscles rigid, until in five or six minutes the truck reappeared, returning. She waited until it had had time to turn into their own road. Then like a monumental statue coming to life, she bent her head slowly and gazed, as if through the very heart of mystery, down into the pig parlor at the hogs. They had settled all in one corner around the old sow who was grunting softly. A red glow suffused them. They appeared to pant with a secret life.

Until the sun slipped finally behind the tree line, Mrs. Turpin remained there with her gaze bent to them as if she were absorbing some abysmal life-giving knowledge. At last she lifted her head. There was only a purple streak in the sky, cutting through a field of crimson and leading, like an extension of the highway, into the descending dusk. She raised her hands from the side of the pen in a gesture hieratic and profound. A visionary light settled in her eyes. She saw the streak as a vast swinging bridge extending upward from the earth through a field of living fire. Upon it a vast horde of souls were rumbling toward heaven. There were whole companies of white-trash, clean for the first time in their lives, and bands of black niggers in white robes, and battalions of freaks and lunatics shouting and clapping and leaping like frogs. And bringing up the end of the procession was a tribe of people whom she recognized at once as those who, like herself and Claud, had always had a little of everything and the God-given wit to use it right. She leaned forward to observe them closer. They were marching behind the others with great dignity, accountable as they had always been for good order and common sense and respectable behavior. They alone were on key. Yet she could see by their shocked and altered faces that even their virtues were being burned away. She lowered her hands and gripped the rail of the hog pen, her eyes small but fixed unblinkingly on what lay ahead. In a moment the vision faded but she remained where she was, immobile.

At length she got down and turned off the faucet and made her slow way on the darkening path to the house. In the woods around her the invisible cricket choruses had struck up, but what she heard were the voices of the souls climbing upward into the starry field and shouting hallelujah.

Parker's Back

PARKER'S WIFE was sitting on the front porch floor, snapping beans. Parker was sitting on the step, some distance away, watching her sullenly. She was plain, plain. The skin on her face was thin and drawn as tight as the skin on an onion and her eyes were grey and sharp like the points of two ice-picks. Parker understood why he had married her—he couldn't have got her any other way—but he couldn't understand why he stayed with her now. She was pregnant and pregnant women were not his favorite kind. Nevertheless, he stayed as if she had him conjured. He was puzzled and ashamed of himself.

The house they rented sat alone save for a single tall pecan tree on a high embankment overlooking a highway. At intervals a car would shoot past below and his wife's eyes would swerve suspiciously after the sound of it and then come back to rest on the newspaper full of beans in her lap. One of the things she did not approve of was automobiles. In addition to her other bad qualities, she was forever sniffing up sin. She did not smoke or dip, drink whiskey, use bad language or paint her face, and God knew some paint would have improved it, Parker thought. Her being against color, it was the more remarkable she had married him. Sometimes he supposed that she had married him because she meant to save him. At other times he had a suspicion that she actually liked everything she said she didn't. He could account for her one way or another; it was himself he could not understand.

She turned her head in his direction and said, "It's no reason you can't work for a man. It don't have to be a woman."

"Aw shut your mouth for a change," Parker muttered.

If he had been certain she was jealous of the woman he worked for he would have been pleased but more likely she was concerned with the sin that would result if he and the woman took a liking to each other. He had told her that the woman was a hefty young blonde; in fact she was nearly seventy years old and too dried up to have an interest in anything except getting as much work out of him as she could.

Not that an old woman didn't sometimes get an interest in a young man, particularly if he was as attractive as Parker felt he was, but this old woman looked at him the same way she looked at her old tractor—as if she had to put up with it because it was all she had. The tractor had broken down the second day Parker was on it and she had set him at once to cutting bushes, saying out of the side of her mouth to the nigger, "Everything he touches, he breaks." She also asked him to wear his shirt when he worked; Parker had removed it even though the day was not sultry; he put it back on reluctantly.

This ugly woman Parker married was his first wife. He had had other women but he had planned never to get himself tied up legally. He had first seen her one morning when his truck broke down on the highway. He had managed to pull it off the road into a neatly swept yard on which sat a peeling two-room house. He got out and opened the hood of the truck and began to study the motor. Parker had an extra sense that told him when there was a woman nearby watching him. After he had leaned over the motor a few minutes, his neck began to prickle. He cast his eye over the empty yard and porch of the house. A woman he could not see was either nearby beyond a clump of honeysuckle or in the house, watching him out the window.

Suddenly Parker began to jump up and down and fling his hand about as if he had mashed it in the machinery. He doubled over and held his hand close to his chest. "God dammit!" he hollered, "Jesus Christ in hell! Jesus God Almighty damm! God dammit to hell!" he went on, flinging out the same few oaths over and over as loud as he could.

Without warning a terrible bristly claw slammed the side of his face and he fell backwards on the hood of the truck. "You don't talk no filth here!" a voice close to him shrilled.

Parker's vision was so blurred that for an instant he thought he had been attacked by some creature from above, a giant hawk-eyed angel wielding a hoary weapon. As his sight cleared, he saw before him a tall raw-boned girl with a broom.

"I hurt my hand," he said. "I HURT my hand." He was so incensed that he forgot that he hadn't hurt his hand. "My hand may be broke," he growled although his voice was still unsteady.

"Lemme see it," the girl demanded.

Parker stuck out his hand and she came closer and looked at it. There was no mark on the palm and she took the hand and turned it over. Her own hand was dry and hot and rough and Parker felt himself jolted back to life by her touch. He looked more closely at her. I don't want nothing to do with this one, he thought.

The girl's sharp eyes peered at the back of the stubby red-dish hand she held. There emblazoned in red and blue was a tattooed eagle perched on a cannon. Parker's sleeve was rolled to the elbow. Above the eagle a serpent was coiled about a shield and in the spaces between the eagle and the serpent there were hearts, some with arrows through them. Above the serpent there was a spread hand of cards. Every space on the skin of Parker's arm, from wrist to elbow, was covered in some loud design. The girl gazed at this with an almost stupe-fied smile of shock, as if she had accidentally grasped a poisonous snake; she dropped the hand.

"I got most of my other ones in foreign parts," Parker said. "These here I mostly got in the United States. I got my first one when I was only fifteen year old."

"Don't tell me," the girl said, "I don't like it. I ain't got any use for it."

"You ought to see the ones you can't see," Parker said and winked.

Two circles of red appeared like apples on the girl's cheeks and softened her appearance. Parker was intrigued. He did not for a minute think that she didn't like the tattoos. He had never yet met a woman who was not attracted to them.

Parker was fourteen when he saw a man in a fair, tattooed from head to foot. Except for his loins which were girded with a panther hide, the man's skin was patterned in what seemed from Parker's distance—he was near the back of the tent, standing on a bench—a single intricate design of brilliant color. The man, who was small and sturdy, moved about on the platform, flexing his muscles so that the arabesque of men and beasts and flowers on his skin appeared to have a subtle motion of its own. Parker was filled with emotion, lifted up as some people are when the flag passes. He was a boy whose mouth habitually hung open. He was heavy and earnest, as ordinary as a loaf of bread. When the show was over, he had remained standing on the bench, staring where the tattooed man had been, until the tent was almost empty.

Parker had never before felt the least motion of wonder in himself. Until he saw the man at the fair, it did not enter his head that there was anything out of the ordinary about the fact that he existed. Even then it did not enter his head, but a peculiar unease settled in him. It was as if a blind boy had been turned so gently in a different direction that he did not know his destination had been changed.

He had his first tattoo some time after—the eagle perched on the cannon. It was done by a local artist. It hurt very little, just enough to make it appear to Parker to be worth doing. This was peculiar too for before he had thought that only what did not hurt was worth doing. The next year he quit school because he was sixteen and could. He went to the trade school for a while, then he quit the trade school and worked for six months in a garage. The only reason he worked at all was to pay for more tattoos. His mother worked in a laundry and could support him, but she would not pay for any tattoo except her name on a heart, which he had put on, grumbling. However, her name was Betty Jean and nobody had to know it was his mother. He found out that the tattoos were attractive to the kind of girls he liked but who had never liked him before. He began to drink beer and get in fights. His mother wept over what was becoming of him. One night she dragged him off to a revival with her, not telling him where they were going. When he saw the big lighted church, he jerked out of her grasp and ran. The next day he lied about his age and joined the navy.

Parker was large for the tight sailor's pants but the silly white cap, sitting low on his forehead, made his face by contrast look thoughtful and almost intense. After a month or two in the navy, his mouth ceased to hang open. His features hardened into the features of a man. He stayed in the navy five years and seemed a natural part of the grey mechanical ship, except for his eyes, which were the same pale slate-color as the ocean and reflected the immense spaces around him as if they were a microcosm of the mysterious sea. In port Parker wandered about comparing the run-down places he was in to Birmingham, Alabama. Everywhere he went he picked up more tattoos.

He had stopped having lifeless ones like anchors and crossed rifles. He had a tiger and a panther on each shoulder, a cobra coiled about a torch on his chest, hawks on his thighs, Elizabeth II and Philip over where his stomach and liver were respectively. He did not care much what the subject was so long as it was colorful; on his abdomen he had a few obscenities but only because that seemed the proper place for them. Parker would be satisfied with each tattoo about a month, then something about it that had attracted him would wear off. Whenever a decent-sized mirror was available, he would get in front of it and study his overall look. The effect was not of one intricate arabesque of colors but of something haphazard and botched. A huge dissatisfaction would come over him and he would go off and find another tattooist and have another space filled up. The front of Parker was almost completely covered but there were no tattoos on his back. He had no desire for one anywhere he could not readily see it himself. As the space on the front of him for tattoos decreased, his dissatisfaction grew and became general.

After one of his furloughs, he didn't go back to the navy but remained away without official leave, drunk, in a rooming house in a city he did not know. His dissatisfaction, from being chronic and latent, had suddenly become acute and raged in him. It was as if the panther and the lion and the serpents and the eagles and the hawks had penetrated his skin and lived inside him in a raging warfare. The navy caught up with him, put him in the brig for nine months and then gave him a dishonorable discharge.

After that Parker decided that country air was the only kind fit to breathe. He rented the shack on the embankment and bought the old truck and took various jobs which he kept as long as it suited him. At the time he met his future wife, he was buying apples by the bushel and selling them for the same price by the pound to isolated homesteaders on back country roads.

"All that there," the woman said, pointing to his arm, "is

no better than what a fool Indian would do. It's a heap of vanity." She seemed to have found the word she wanted. "Vanity of vanities," she said.

Well what the hell do I care what she thinks of it? Parker asked himself, but he was plainly bewildered. "I reckon you like one of these better than another anyway," he said, dallying until he thought of something that would impress her. He thrust the arm back at her. "Which you like best?"

"None of them," she said, "but the chicken is not as bad as the rest."

"What chicken?" Parker almost yelled.

She pointed to the eagle.

"That's an eagle," Parker said. "What fool would waste their time having a chicken put on themselves?"

"What fool would have any of it?" the girl said and turned away. She went slowly back to the house and left him there to get going. Parker remained for almost five minutes, looking agape at the dark door she had entered.

The next day he returned with a bushel of apples. He was not one to be outdone by anything that looked like her. He liked women with meat on them, so you didn't feel their muscles, much less their old bones. When he arrived, she was sitting on the top step and the yard was full of children, all as thin and poor as herself; Parker remembered it was Saturday. He hated to be making up to a woman when there were children around, but it was fortunate he had brought the bushel of apples off the truck. As the children approached him to see what he carried, he gave each child an apple and told it to get lost; in that way he cleared out the whole crowd.

The girl did nothing to acknowledge his presence. He might have been a stray pig or goat that had wandered into the yard and she too tired to take up the broom and send it off. He set the bushel of apples down next to her on the step. He sat down on a lower step.

"Hep yourself," he said, nodding at the basket; then he lapsed into silence.

She took an apple quickly as if the basket might disappear if she didn't make haste. Hungry people made Parker nervous. He had always had plenty to eat himself. He grew very uncomfortable. He reasoned he had nothing to say so why should he say it? He could not think now why he had come or why he didn't go before he wasted another bushel of apples on the crowd of children. He supposed they were her brothers and sisters.

She chewed the apple slowly but with a kind of relish of concentration, bent slightly but looking out ahead. The view from the porch stretched off across a long incline studded with iron weed and across the highway to a vast vista of hills and one small mountain. Long views depressed Parker. You look out into space like that and you begin to feel as if someone were after you, the navy or the government or religion.

"Who them children belong to, you?" he said at length.

"I ain't married yet," she said. "They belong to momma." She said it as if it were only a matter of time before she would be married.

Who in God's name would marry her? Parker thought.

A large barefooted woman with a wide gap-toothed face appeared in the door behind Parker. She had apparently been there for several minutes.

"Good evening," Parker said.

The woman crossed the porch and picked up what was left of the bushel of apples. "We thank you," she said and returned with it into the house.

"That your old woman?" Parker muttered.

The girl nodded. Parker knew a lot of sharp things he could have said like "You got my sympathy," but he was gloomily silent. He just sat there, looking at the view. He thought he must be coming down with something.

"If I pick up some peaches tomorrow I'll bring you some," he said.

"I'll be much obliged to you," the girl said.

Parker had no intention of taking any basket of peaches back there but the next day he found himself doing it. He and the girl had almost nothing to say to each other. One thing he did say was, "I ain't got any tattoo on my back."

"What you got on it?" the girl said.

"My shirt," Parker said. "Haw."

"Haw, haw," the girl said politely.

Parker thought he was losing his mind. He could not believe for a minute that he was attracted to a woman like this.

She showed not the least interest in anything but what he brought until he appeared the third time with two canta-loups. "What's your name?" she asked.

"O. E. Parker," he said.

"What does the O.E. stand for?"

"You can just call me O.E.," Parker said. "Or Parker. Don't nobody call me by my name."

"What's it stand for?" she persisted.

"Never mind," Parker said. "What's yours?"

"I'll tell you when you tell me what them letters are the short of," she said. There was just a hint of flirtatiousness in her tone and it went rapidly to Parker's head. He had never revealed the name to any man or woman, only to the files of the navy and the government, and it was on his baptismal record which he got at the age of a month; his mother was a Methodist. When the name leaked out of the navy files, Parker narrowly missed killing the man who used it.

"You'll go blab it around," he said.

"I'll swear I'll never tell nobody," she said. "On God's holy word I swear it."

Parker sat for a few minutes in silence. Then he reached for the girl's neck, drew her ear close to his mouth and revealed the name in a low voice.

"Obadiah," she whispered. Her face slowly brightened as if the name came as a sign to her. "Obadiah," she said.

The name still stank in Parker's estimation.

"Obadiah Elihue," she said in a reverent voice.

"If you call me that aloud, I'll bust your head open," Parker said. "What's yours?"

"Sarah Ruth Cates," she said.

"Glad to meet you, Sarah Ruth," Parker said.

Sarah Ruth's father was a Straight Gospel preacher but he was away, spreading it in Florida. Her mother did not seem to mind his attention to the girl so long as he brought a bas-ket of something with him when he came. As for Sarah Ruth herself, it was plain to Parker after he had visited three times that she was crazy about him. She liked him even though she insisted that pictures on the skin were vanity of vanities and even after hearing him curse, and even after she had asked him if he was saved and he had replied that he didn't see it

was anything in particular to save him from. After that, inspired, Parker had said, "I'd be saved enough if you was to
kiss me."

She scowled. "That ain't being saved," she said.

Not long after that she agreed to take a ride in his truck.
Parker parked it on a deserted road and suggested to her that
they lie down together in the back of it.

"Not until after we're married," she said—just like that.

"Oh, that ain't necessary," Parker said and as he reached for
her, she thrust him away with such force that the door of the
truck came off and he found himself flat on his back on the
ground. He made up his mind then and there to have nothing
further to do with her.

They were married in the County Ordinary's office because
Sarah Ruth thought churches were idolatrous. Parker had
no opinion about that one way or the other. The Ordinary's
office was lined with cardboard file boxes and record books
with dusty yellow slips of paper hanging on out of them. The
Ordinary was an old woman with red hair who had held
office for forty years and looked as dusty as her books. She
married them from behind the iron-grill of a stand-up desk
and when she finished, she said with a flourish, "Three dollars
and fifty cents and till death do you part!" and yanked some
forms out of a machine.

Marriage did not change Sarah Ruth a jot and it made
Parker gloomier than ever. Every morning he decided he had
had enough and would not return that night; every night he
returned. Whenever Parker couldn't stand the way he felt, he
would have another tattoo, but the only surface left on him
now was his back. To see a tattoo on his own back he would
have to get two mirrors and stand between them in just the
correct position and this seemed to Parker a good way to
make an idiot of himself. Sarah Ruth who, if she had had
better sense, could have enjoyed a tattoo on his back, would
not even look at the ones he had elsewhere. When he attempted to point out especial details of them, she would shut
her eyes tight and turn her back as well. Except in total darkness, she preferred Parker dressed and with his sleeves rolled
down.

"At the judgement seat of God, Jesus is going to say to

you, 'What you been doing all your life besides have pictures drawn all over you?' " she said.

"You don't fool me none," Parker said, "you're just afraid that hefty girl I work for'll like me so much she'll say, 'Come on, Mr. Parker, let's you and me . . .' "

"You're tempting sin," she said, "and at the judgement seat of God you'll have to answer for that too. You ought to go back to selling the fruits of the earth."

Parker did nothing much when he was at home but listen to what the judgement seat of God would be like for him if he didn't change his ways. When he could, he broke in with tales of the hefty girl he worked for. " 'Mr. Parker,' " he said she said, 'I hired you for your brains.' " (She had added, "So why don't you use them?")

"And you should have seen her face the first time she saw me without my shirt," he said. " 'Mr. Parker,' she said, 'you're a walking panner-rammer!' " This had, in fact, been her remark but it had been delivered out of one side of her mouth.

Dissatisfaction began to grow so great in Parker that there was no containing it outside of a tattoo. It had to be his back. There was no help for it. A dim half-formed inspiration began to work in his mind. He visualized having a tattoo put there that Sarah Ruth would not be able to resist—a religious subject. He thought of an open book with HOLY BIBLE tattooed under it and an actual verse printed on the page. This seemed just the thing for a while; then he began to hear her say, "Ain't I already got a real Bible? What you think I want to read the same verse over and over for when I can read it all?" He needed something better even than the Bible! He thought about it so much that he began to lose sleep. He was already losing flesh—Sarah Ruth just threw food in the pot and let it boil. Not knowing for certain why he continued to stay with a woman who was both ugly and pregnant and no cook made him generally nervous and irritable, and he developed a little tic in the side of his face.

Once or twice he found himself turning around abruptly as if someone were trailing him. He had had a granddaddy who had ended in the state mental hospital, although not until he was seventy-five, but as urgent as it might be for him to get a tattoo, it was just as urgent that he get exactly the right one to bring Sarah Ruth to heel. As he continued to worry over it, his eyes took on a hollow preoccupied expression. The old woman he worked for told him that if he couldn't keep his mind on what he was doing, she knew where she could find a fourteen-year-old colored boy who could. Parker was too preoccupied even to be offended. At any time previous, he would have left her then and there, saying drily, "Well, you go ahead on and get him then."

Two or three mornings later he was baling hay with the old woman's sorry baler and her broken down tractor in a large field, cleared save for one enormous old tree standing in the middle of it. The old woman was the kind who would not cut down a large old tree because it was a large old tree. She had pointed it out to Parker as if he didn't have eyes and told him to be careful not to hit it as the machine picked up hay near it. Parker began at the outside of the field and made circles inward toward it. He had to get off the tractor every now and then and untangle the baling cord or kick a rock out of the way. The old woman had told him to carry the rocks to the edge of the field, which he did when she was there watching. When he thought he could make it, he ran over them. As he circled the field his mind was on a suitable design for his back. The sun, the size of a golf ball, began to switch regularly from in front to behind him, but he appeared to see it both places as if he had eyes in the back of his head. All at once he saw the tree reaching out to grasp him. A ferocious thud propelled him into the air, and he heard himself yelling in an unbelievably loud voice, "GOD ABOVE!"

He landed on his back while the tractor crashed upside-down into the tree and burst into flame. The first thing Parker saw were his shoes, quickly being eaten by the fire; one was caught under the tractor, the other was some distance away, burning by itself. He was not in them. He could feel the hot breath of the burning tree on his face. He scrambled backwards, still sitting, his eyes cavernous, and if he had known how to cross himself he would have done it.

His truck was on a dirt road at the edge of the field. He moved toward it, still sitting, still backwards, but faster and faster; halfway to it he got up and began a kind of forward-bent run from which he collapsed on his knees twice. His legs felt like two old rusted rain gutters. He reached the truck finally and took off in it, zigzagging up the road. He drove past his house on the embankment and straight for the city, fifty miles distant.

Parker did not allow himself to think on the way to the city. He only knew that there had been a great change in his life, a leap forward into a worse unknown, and that there was nothing he could do about it. It was for all intents accomplished.

The artist had two large cluttered rooms over a chiropodist's office on a back street. Parker, still barefooted, burst silently in on him at a little after three in the afternoon. The artist, who was about Parker's own age—twenty-eight—but thin and bald, was behind a small drawing table, tracing a design in green ink. He looked up with an annoyed glance and did not seem to recognize Parker in the hollow-eyed creature before him.

"Let me see the book you got with all the pictures of God in it," Parker said breathlessly. "The religious one."

The artist continued to look at him with his intellectual, superior stare. "I don't put tattoos on drunks," he said.

"You know me!" Parker cried indignantly. "I'm O. E. Parker! You done work for me before and I always paid!"

The artist looked at him another moment as if he were not altogether sure. "You've fallen off some," he said. "You must have been in jail."

"Married," Parker said.

"Oh," said the artist. With the aid of mirrors the artist had tattooed on the top of his head a miniature owl, perfect in every detail. It was about the size of a half-dollar and served him as a show piece. There were cheaper artists in town but Parker had never wanted anything but the best. The artist went over to a cabinet at the back of the room and began to look over some art books. "Who are you interested in?" he said, "saints, angels, Christs or what?"

"God," Parker said.

"Father, Son or Spirit?"

"Just God," Parker said impatiently. "Christ. I don't care. Just so it's God."

The artist returned with a book. He moved some papers

off another table and put the book down on it and told
Parker to sit down and see what he liked. "The up-to-date
ones are in the back," he said.

Parker sat down with the book and wet his thumb. He
began to go through it, beginning at the back where the up-
to-date pictures were. Some of them he recognized—The
Good Shepherd, Forbid Them Not, The Smiling Jesus, Jesus
the Physician's Friend, but he kept turning rapidly backwards
and the pictures became less and less reassuring. One showed
a gaunt green dead face streaked with blood. One was yellow
with sagging purple eyes. Parker's heart began to beat faster
and faster until it appeared to be roaring inside him like a
great generator. He flipped the pages quickly, feeling that
when he reached the one ordained, a sign would come. He
continued to flip through until he had almost reached the
front of the book. On one of the pages a pair of eyes glanced
at him swiftly. Parker sped on, then stopped. His heart too
appeared to cut off; there was absolute silence. It said as
plainly as if silence were a language itself, GO BACK.

Parker returned to the picture—the haloed head of a flat
stern Byzantine Christ with all-demanding eyes. He sat there
trembling; his heart began slowly to beat again as if it were
being brought to life by a subtle power.

"You found what you want?" the artist asked.

Parker's throat was too dry to speak. He got up and thrust
the book at the artist, opened at the picture.

"That'll cost you plenty," the artist said. "You don't want
all those little blocks though, just the outline and some better
features."

"Just like it is," Parker said, "just like it is or nothing."

"It's your funeral," the artist said, "but I don't do that kind
of work for nothing."

"How much?" Parker asked.

"It'll take maybe two days work."

"How much?" Parker said.

"On time or cash?" the artist asked. Parker's other jobs had
been on time, but he had paid.

"Ten down and ten for every day it takes," the artist said.

Parker drew ten dollar bills out of his wallet; he had three
left in.

"You come back in the morning," the artist said, putting the money in his own pocket. "First I'll have to trace that out of the book."

"No no!" Parker said. "Trace it now or gimme my money back," and his eyes blared as if he were ready for a fight.

The artist agreed. Any one stupid enough to want a Christ on his back, he reasoned, would be just as likely as not to change his mind the next minute, but once the work was begun he could hardly do so.

While he worked on the tracing, he told Parker to go wash his back at the sink with the special soap he used there. Parker did it and returned to pace back and forth across the room, nervously flexing his shoulders. He wanted to go look at the picture again but at the same time he did not want to. The artist got up finally and had Parker lie down on the table. He swabbed his back with ethyl chloride and then began to outline the head on it with his iodine pencil. Another hour passed before he took up his electric instrument. Parker felt no particular pain. In Japan he had had a tattoo of the Buddha done on his upper arm with ivory needles; in Burma, a little brown root of a man had made a peacock on each of his knees using thin pointed sticks, two feet long; amateurs had worked on him with pins and soot. Parker was usually so relaxed and easy under the hand of the artist that he often went to sleep, but this time he remained awake, every muscle taut.

At midnight the artist said he was ready to quit. He propped one mirror, four feet square, on a table by the wall and took a smaller mirror off the lavatory wall and put it in Parker's hands. Parker stood with his back to the one on the table and moved the other until he saw a flashing burst of color reflected from his back. It was almost completely covered with little red and blue and ivory and saffron squares; from them he made out the lineaments of the face—a mouth, the beginning of heavy brows, a straight nose, but the face was empty; the eyes had not yet been put in. The impression for the moment was almost as if the artist had tricked him and done the Physician's Friend.

"It don't have eyes," Parker cried out.

"That'll come," the artist said, "in due time. We have another day to go on it yet."

Parker spent the night on a cot at the Haven of Light Christian Mission. He found these the best places to stay in the city because they were free and included a meal of sorts. He got the last available cot and because he was still barefooted, he accepted a pair of second-hand shoes which, in his confusion, he put on to go to bed; he was still shocked from all that had happened to him. All night he lay awake in the long dormitory of cots with lumpy figures on them. The only light was from a phosphorescent cross glowing at the end of the room. The tree reached out to grasp him again, then burst into flame; the shoe burned quietly by itself; the eyes in the book said to him distinctly GO BACK and at the same time did not utter a sound. He wished that he were not in this city, not in this Haven of Light Mission, not in a bed by himself. He longed miserably for Sarah Ruth. Her sharp tongue and icepick eyes were the only comfort he could bring to mind. He decided he was losing it. Her eyes appeared soft and dilatory compared with the eyes in the book, for even though he could not summon up the exact look of those eyes, he could still feel their penetration. He felt as though, under their gaze, he was as transparent as the wing of a fly.

The tattooist had told him not to come until ten in the morning, but when he arrived at that hour, Parker was sitting in the dark hallway on the floor, waiting for him. He had decided upon getting up that, once the tattoo was on him, he would not look at it, that all his sensations of the day and night before were those of a crazy man and that he would return to doing things according to his own sound judgement.

The artist began where he left off. "One thing I want to know," he said presently as he worked over Parker's back, "why do you want this on you? Have you gone and got religion? Are you saved?" he asked in a mocking voice.

Parker's throat felt salty and dry. "Naw," he said, "I ain't got no use for none of that. A man can't save his self from whatever it is he don't deserve none of my sympathy." These words seemed to leave his mouth like wraiths and to evaporate at once as if he had never uttered them.

"Then why . . ."

"I married this woman that's saved," Parker said. "I never

should have done it. I ought to leave her. She's done gone and got pregnant."

"That's too bad," the artist said. "Then it's her making you have this tattoo."

"Naw," Parker said, "she don't know nothing about it. It's a surprise for her."

"You think she'll like it and lay off you a while?"

"She can't hep herself," Parker said. "She can't say she don't like the looks of God." He decided he had told the artist enough of his business. Artists were all right in their place but he didn't like them poking their noses into the affairs of regular people. "I didn't get no sleep last night," he said. "I think I'll get some now."

That closed the mouth of the artist but it did not bring him any sleep. He lay there, imagining how Sarah Ruth would be struck speechless by the face on his back and every now and then this would be interrupted by a vision of the tree of fire and his empty shoe burning beneath it.

The artist worked steadily until nearly four o'clock, not stopping to have lunch, hardly pausing with the electric instrument except to wipe the dripping dye off Parker's back as he went along. Finally he finished. "You can get up and look at it now," he said.

Parker sat up but he remained on the edge of the table.

The artist was pleased with his work and wanted Parker to look at it at once. Instead Parker continued to sit on the edge of the table, bent forward slightly but with a vacant look. "What ails you?" the artist said. "Go look at it."

"Ain't nothing ail me," Parker said in a sudden belligerent voice. "That tattoo ain't going nowhere. It'll be there when I get there." He reached for his shirt and began gingerly to put it on.

The artist took him roughly by the arm and propelled him between the two mirrors. "Now *look*," he said, angry at having his work ignored.

Parker looked, turned white and moved away. The eyes in the reflected face continued to look at him—still, straight, all-demanding, enclosed in silence.

"It was your idea, remember," the artist said. "I would have advised something else."

Parker said nothing. He put on his shirt and went out the door while the artist shouted, "I'll expect all of my money!"

Parker headed toward a package shop on the corner. He bought a pint of whiskey and took it into a nearby alley and drank it all in five minutes. Then he moved on to a pool hall nearby which he frequented when he came to the city. It was a well-lighted barn-like place with a bar up one side and gambling machines on the other and pool tables in the back. As soon as Parker entered, a large man in a red and black checkered shirt hailed him by slapping him on the back and yelling, "Yeyyyyyy boy! O. E. Parker!"

Parker was not yet ready to be struck on the back. "Lay off," he said, "I got a fresh tattoo there."

"What you got this time?" the man asked and then yelled to a few at the machines. "O.E.'s got him another tattoo."

"Nothing special this time," Parker said and slunk over to a machine that was not being used.

"Come on," the big man said, "let's have a look at O.E.'s tattoo," and while Parker squirmed in their hands, they pulled up his shirt. Parker felt all the hands drop away instantly and his shirt fell again like a veil over the face. There was a silence in the pool room which seemed to Parker to grow from the circle around him until it extended to the foundations under the building and upward through the beams in the roof.

Finally some one said, "Christ!" Then they all broke into noise at once. Parker turned around, an uncertain grin on his face.

"Leave it to O.E.!" the man in the checkered shirt said, "That boy's a real card!"

"Maybe he's gone and got religion," some one yelled.

"Not on your life," Parker said.

"O.E.'s got religion and is witnessing for Jesus, ain't you, O.E.?" a little man with a piece of cigar in his mouth said wryly. "An o-riginal way to do it if I ever saw one."

"Leave it to Parker to think of a new one!" the fat man said.

"Yyeeeeeeyyyyyyy boy!" someone yelled and they all began to whistle and curse in compliment until Parker said, "Aaa shut up."

"What'd you do it for?" somebody asked.

"For laughs," Parker said. "What's it to you?"

"Why ain't you laughing then?" somebody yelled. Parker lunged into the midst of them and like a whirlwind on a summer's day there began a fight that raged amid overturned tables and swinging fists until two of them grabbed him and ran to the door with him and threw him out. Then a calm descended on the pool hall as nerve shattering as if the long barn-like room were the ship from which Jonah had been cast into the sea.

Parker sat for a long time on the ground in the alley behind the pool hall, examining his soul. He saw it as a spider web of facts and lies that was not at all important to him but which appeared to be necessary in spite of his opinion. The eyes that were now forever on his back were eyes to be obeyed. He was as certain of it as he had ever been of anything. Throughout his life, grumbling and sometimes cursing, often afraid, once in rapture, Parker had obeyed whatever instinct of this kind had come to him—in rapture when his spirit had lifted at the sight of the tattooed man at the fair, afraid when he had joined the navy, grumbling when he had married Sarah Ruth.

The thought of her brought him slowly to his feet. She would know what he had to do. She would clear up the rest of it, and she would at least be pleased. It seemed to him that, all along, that was what he wanted, to please her. His truck was still parked in front of the building where the artist had his place, but it was not far away. He got in it and drove out of the city and into the country night. His head was almost clear of liquor and he observed that his dissatisfaction was gone, but he felt not quite like himself. It was as if he were himself but a stranger to himself, driving into a new country though everything he saw was familiar to him, even at night.

He arrived finally at the house on the embankment, pulled the truck under the pecan tree and got out. He made as much noise as possible to assert that he was still in charge here, that his leaving her for a night without word meant nothing except it was the way he did things. He slammed the car door, stamped up the two steps and across the porch and rattled the door knob. It did not respond to his touch. "Sarah Ruth!" he yelled, "let me in."

There was no lock on the door and she had evidently placed the back of a chair against the knob. He began to beat on the door and rattle the knob at the same time.

He heard the bed springs screak and bent down and put his head to the keyhole, but it was stopped up with paper. "Let me in!" he hollered, bamming on the door again. "What you got me locked out for?"

A sharp voice close to the door said, "Who's there?"

"Me," Parker said, "O.E."

He waited a moment.

"Me," he said impatiently, "O.E."

Still no sound from inside.

He tried once more. "O.E.," he said, bamming the door two or three more times. "O. E. Parker. You know me."

There was a silence. Then the voice said slowly, "I don't know no O.E."

"Quit fooling," Parker pleaded. "You ain't got any business doing me this way. It's me, old O.E., I'm back. You ain't afraid of me."

"Who's there?" the same unfeeling voice said.

Parker turned his head as if he expected someone behind him to give him the answer. The sky had lightened slightly and there were two or three streaks of yellow floating above the horizon. Then as he stood there, a tree of light burst over the skyline.

Parker fell back against the door as if he had been pinned there by a lance.

"Who's there?" the voice from inside said and there was a quality about it now that seemed final. The knob rattled and the voice said peremptorily, "Who's there, I ast you?"

Parker bent down and put his mouth near the stuffed keyhole. "Obadiah," he whispered and all at once he felt the light pouring through him, turning his spider web soul into a perfect arabesque of colors, a garden of trees and birds and beasts.

"Obadiah Elihue!" he whispered.

The door opened and he stumbled in. Sarah Ruth loomed there, hands on her hips. She began at once, "That was no hefty blonde woman you was working for and you'll have to pay her every penny on her tractor you busted up. She don't keep insurance on it. She came here and her and me had us a long talk and I . . ."

Trembling, Parker set about lighting the kerosene lamp.

"What's the matter with you, wasting that keresene this near daylight?" she demanded. "I ain't got to look at you."

A yellow glow enveloped them. Parker put the match down and began to unbutton his shirt.

"And you ain't going to have none of me this near morning," she said.

"Shut your mouth," he said quietly. "Look at this and then I don't want to hear no more out of you." He removed the shirt and turned his back to her.

"Another picture," Sarah Ruth growled. "I might have known you was off after putting some more trash on yourself."

Parker's knees went hollow under him. He wheeled around and cried, "Look at it! Don't just say that! *Look* at it!"

"I done looked," she said.

"Don't you know who it is?" he cried in anguish.

"No, who is it?" Sarah Ruth said. "It ain't anybody I know."

"It's him," Parker said.

"Him who?"

"God!" Parker cried.

"God? God don't look like that!"

"What do you know how he looks?" Parker moaned. "You ain't seen him."

"He don't *look*," Sarah Ruth said. "He's a spirit. No man shall see his face."

"Aw listen," Parker groaned, "this is just a picture of him."

"Idolatry!" Sarah Ruth screamed. "Idolatry! Enflaming yourself with idols under every green tree! I can put up with lies and vanity but I don't want no idolator in this house!" and she grabbed up the broom and began to thrash him across the shoulders with it.

Parker was too stunned to resist. He sat there and let her beat him until she had nearly knocked him senseless and large welts had formed on the face of the tattooed Christ. Then he staggered up and made for the door.

She stamped the broom two or three times on the floor

and went to the window and shook it out to get the taint of him off it. Still gripping it, she looked toward the pecan tree and her eyes hardened still more. There he was—who called himself Obadiah Elihue—leaning against the tree, crying like a baby.

Judgment Day

TANNER WAS CONSERVING all his strength for the trip home. He meant to walk as far as he could get and trust to the Almighty to get him the rest of the way. That morning and the morning before, he had allowed his daughter to dress him and had conserved that much more energy. Now he sat in the chair by the window—his blue shirt buttoned at the collar, his coat on the back of the chair, and his hat on his head—waiting for her to leave. He couldn't leave until she got out of the way. The window looked out on a brick wall and down into an alley full of New York air, the kind fit for cats and garbage. A few snow flakes drifted past the window but they were too thin and scattered for his failing vision.

The daughter was in the kitchen washing dishes. She dwaddled over everything, talking to herself. When he had first come, he had answered her, but that had not been wanted. She glowered at him as if, old fool that he was, he should still have had sense enough not to answer a woman talking to herself. She questioned herself in one voice and answered herself in another. With the energy he had conserved yesterday letting her dress him, he had written a note and pinned it in his pocket. IF FOUND DEAD SHIP EXPRESS COLLECT TO COLEMAN PARRUM, CORINTH, GEORGIA. Under this he had continued: COLEMAN SELL MY BELONGINGS AND PAY THE FREIGHT ON ME & THE UNDERTAKER. ANYTHING LEFT OVER YOU CAN KEEP. YOURS TRULY T.C. TANNER. P.S. STAY WHERE YOU ARE. DON'T LET THEM TALK YOU INTO COMING UP HERE. ITS NO KIND OF PLACE. It had taken him the better part of thirty minutes to write the paper; the script was wavery but decipherable with patience. He controlled one hand by holding the other on top of it. By the time he had got it written, she was back in the apartment from getting her groceries.

Today he was ready. All he had to do was push one foot in front of the other until he got to the door and down the steps. Once down the steps, he would get out of the neighborhood. Once out of it, he would hail a taxi cab and go to the freight yards. Some bum would help him onto a car. Once he got in the freight car, he would lie down and rest.

During the night the train would start South, and the next day or the morning after, dead or alive, he would be home.

If he had had good sense he would have gone the day after he arrived; better sense and he would not have arrived. He had not got desperate until two days ago when he had heard his daughter and son-in-law taking leave of each other after breakfast. They were standing in the front door, she seeing him off for a three-day trip. He drove a long distance moving van. She must have handed him his leather head-gear. "You ought to get you a hat," he heard her say, "a real one."

"And sit all day in it," the son-in-law said, "like him in there. All he does is sit all day with that hat on. Sits all day with that damm black hat on his head. Inside!"

"Well you don't even have you a hat," she said. "Nothing but that leather cap with flaps. People that are somebody wear hats. Other kinds wear those leather caps like you got on."

"People that are somebody!" he cried. "People that are somebody! That kills me! That really kills me!" The son-in-law had a stupid muscular face and a yankee voice to go with it.

"My daddy is here to stay," his daughter said. "He ain't going to last long. He was somebody when he was somebody. He never worked for nobody in his life but himself, and he had people—other people—working for him."

"Niggers is what he had working for him," the son-in-law said. "That's all. I've worked a nigger or two myself."

"Those were just nawthun niggers you worked," she said, her voice suddenly going lower so that Tanner had to lean forward to catch the words. "It takes brains to work a real nigger. You got to know how to handle them."

"Yah so I don't have brains," the son-in-law said.

"You got them," she said. "You don't always use them."

One of the sudden, very occasional, feelings of warmth for the daughter came over Tanner. Every now and then she said something that might make you think she had a little sense stored away somewhere for safe keeping.

"He didn't have the brains to hang on to what he did have," the son-in-law said. "He has a stroke when he sees a nigger in the building, and she tells me he can handle a . . ."

"Shut up talking so loud," she said. "That's not why he had the stroke."

There was a silence. "Where you going to bury him?" the son-in-law asked, taking a different tack.

"Right here in New York," she said. "Where do you think? We got a lot. I'm not taking that trip down there again with anybody."

"You stick to your guns," he said. "I just wanted to make sure."

When she returned to the room, Tanner had had both hands gripped on the chair arms. His eyes were trained on her like the eyes of an angry corpse. "You promised you'd bury me there," he said. "Your promise ain't any good. Your promise ain't any good. Your promise ain't any good." His voice was so dry it was barely audible. He began to shake, his hands, his head, his feet. "Bury me here and burn in hell!" he cried and fell back into his chair.

The daughter shuddered to attention. "You ain't dead yet!" She threw out a ponderous sigh. "You got a long time to be worrying about that." She turned and began to pick up parts of the newspaper scattered on the floor. She had grey hair that hung to her shoulders and a round face, beginning to wear. "I do every last living thing for you," she muttered, "and this is the way you carry on." She stuck the papers under her arm and said, "And don't throw hell at me. I don't believe in it. That's a lot of hardshell Baptist hooey." Then she went into the kitchen.

He kept his mouth stretched taut, his top plate gripped between his tongue and the roof of his mouth. Still the tears ran down his cheeks; he wiped each one furtively on his shoulder.

Her voice rose from the kitchen. "As bad as having a child. He wanted to come and now he's here, he don't like it."

He had not wanted to come.

"Pretended he didn't but I could tell. I said if you don't want to come I can't make you. If you don't want to live like decent people there's nothing I can do about it."

"As for me," her higher voice said, "when I die that ain't the time I'm going to start getting choosey. They can lay me in the nearest spot. When I pass from this world I'll be considerate of them that stay in it. I won't be thinking of just myself."

"Certainly not," the other voice said, "you never been that selfish. You're the kind that looks out for other people."

"Well I try," she said, "I try."

He laid his head on the back of the chair for a moment and the hat tilted down over his eyes. He had raised three boys and her. The three boys were gone, two in the war and one to the devil and there was nobody left who felt a duty toward him but her, married and childless, and living in New York City like Mrs. Big. After he lost the place, she had come down in person to offer him a home with her. The son-in-law brought her and leaned against a tree with a cigaret hanging out of his mouth. He never said a word but hello. She had put her face in the door of the shack and had stared, expressionless, for a second. Then all at once she had screamed and jumped back.

"What's that on the floor?"

"Coleman," he said.

The old negro was curled up on a pallet asleep at the foot of Tanner's bed, a stinking skin full of bones, arranged in what seemed vaguely human form. When Coleman was young, he had looked like a bear; now that he was old he looked like a monkey. With Tanner it was the opposite: when he was young he had looked like a monkey but when he got old, he looked like a bear.

The daughter stepped back onto the ground. The bottoms of two cane chairs were tilted against the side of the shack but she declined to take a seat. She stepped out about ten feet as if it took that much space to clear the odor. Then she spoke her piece.

"If you don't have any pride I have and I know my duty and I was raised to do it. My mother raised me to do it. She was from plain people but not the kind that likes to settle in with niggers."

At that point Coleman roused up and slid out the door, a doubled-up shadow which Tanner just caught sight of gliding away.

He shouted so both she and Coleman could hear. "Who you think cooks? Who you think cuts my firewood and empties my slops? He's paroled to me. That scoundrel has been on my hands for thirty years. He ain't a bad nigger."

She was unimpressed. "Whose shack is this anyway?" she had asked. "Yours or his? It looks like him and you built it. Whose land is it on?"

"Him and me built it," he said. "You go on back up there. I wouldn't come with you for no million dollars or no sack of salt."

"Whose land is it?" she persisted.

"Some people that live in Florida," he said evasively. He had known then that it was land up for sale but he thought it was too sorry for anyone to buy. He should have known different.

Later in the summer when he saw the brown porpoise-shaped figure striding across the field, he knew at once what had happened; no one had to tell him. If that nigger had owned the whole world except for one runty rutted pea-field and he acquired it, he would walk across it that way, beating the weeds aside, his thick neck swelled, his stomach a throne for his gold watch and chain. Doctor Foley. He was only part black. The rest was Indian and white.

He was everything to the niggers—druggist and under-taker and general counsel and real estate man and sometimes he got the evil eye off them and sometimes he put it on. Be prepared, he said to himself, watching him approach, to take something off him, nigger though he be. Be prepared, be-cause you ain't got a thing to hold up to him but the skin you come in, and that's no more use to you now than what a snake would shed. You don't have a chance with the government against you.

He was sitting on the porch in the piece of straight chair tilted against the shack. "Good evening, Foley," he said and nodded as the doctor came up and stopped short at the edge of the clearing, as if he had only just that minute seen him though it was plain he had sighted him as he crossed the field.

"I be out here to look at my property," the doctor said. "Good evening." His voice was quick and high.

Ain't been your property long, Tanner said to himself. "I seen you coming," he said.

"I acquired this here recently," the doctor said and

proceeded without looking at him again to walk around to one side of the shack. In a moment he came back and stopped in front of him. Then he stepped boldly to the door of the shack and put his head in. Coleman was in there that time too, asleep. He looked for a moment and then turned aside. "I know that nigger," he said. "Coleman Parrum—how long does it take him to sleep off that stump liquor you all make?"

Tanner took hold of the knobs on the chair bottom and held them hard. "This shack ain't in your property. Only on it, by mistake," he said.

The Doctor removed his cigar momentarily from his mouth. "It ain't my mistake," he said and smiled.

He had only sat there, looking ahead.

"It don't pay to make this kind of mis-take," the doctor said.

"I never found nothing that payed yet," Tanner muttered.

"Everything pays," the negro said, "if you knows how to make it," and he remained there smiling, looking the squatter up and down. Then he turned and went around the other side of the shack. There was a silence. He was looking for the still.

Then would have been the time to kill him. There was a gun inside the shack and he could have done it as easy as not, but, from childhood, he had been weakened for that kind of violence by the fear of hell. He had never killed one, he had always handled them with his wits and with luck. He was known to have a way with niggers. There was an art to handling them. The secret of handling a nigger was to show him his brains didn't have a chance against yours; then he would jump on your back and know he had a good thing there for life. He had had Coleman on his back for thirty years.

Tanner had first seen Coleman when he was working six of them at a saw mill in the middle of a pine forest fifteen miles from nowhere. They were as sorry a crew as he had worked, the kind that on Monday they didn't show up. What was in the air had reached them. They thought there was a new Lincoln elected who was going to abolish work. He managed them with a very sharp penknife. He had had something wrong with his kidney then that made his hands shake and he had taken to whittling to force that waste motion out of sight. He did not intend them to see that his hands shook of their own accord and he did not intend to see it himself or to countenance it. The knife had moved constantly, violently, in his quaking hands and here and there small crude figures—that he never looked at again and could not have said what they were if he had—dropped to the ground. The negroes picked them up and took them home; there was not much time between them and darkest Africa. The knife glittered constantly in his hands. More than once he had stopped short and said in an off-hand voice to some half-reclining, head-averted negro, "Nigger, this knife is in my hand now but if you don't quit wasting my time and money, it'll be in your gut shortly." And the negro would begin to rise—slowly, but he would be in the act—before the sentence was completed.

A large black loose-jointed negro, twice his own size, had begun hanging around the edge of the saw mill, watching the others work and when he was not watching, sleeping, in full view of them, sprawled like a gigantic bear on his back. "Who is that?" he had asked. "If he wants to work, tell him to come here. If he don't, tell him to go. No idlers are going to hang around here."

None of them knew who he was. They knew he didn't want to work. They knew nothing else, not where he had come from, nor why, though he was probably brother to one, cousin to all of them. Tanner had ignored him for a day; against the six of them he was one yellow-faced scrawny white man with shaky hands. He was willing to wait for trouble, but not forever. The next day the stranger came again. After the six Tanner worked had seen the idler there for half the morning, they quit and began to eat, a full thirty minutes before noon. He had not risked ordering them up. He had gone to the source of the trouble.

The stranger was leaning against a tree on the edge of the clearing, watching with half-closed eyes. The insolence on his face barely covered the wariness behind it. His look said, this ain't much of a white man so why he come on so big, what he fixing to do?

He had meant to say, "Nigger, this knife is in my hand now but if you ain't out of my sight . . ." but as he drew closer he changed his mind. The negro's eyes were small and bloodshot. Tanner supposed there was a knife on him some-where that he would as soon use as not. His own penknife moved, directed solely by some intruding intelligence that worked in his hands. He had no idea what he was carving, but when he reached the negro, he had already made two holes the size of half dollars in the piece of bark.

The negro's gaze fell on his hands and was held. His jaw slackened. His eyes did not move from the knife tearing reck-lessly around the bark. He watched as if he saw an invisible power working on the wood.

He looked himself then and, astonished, saw the connected rims of a pair of spectacles.

He held them away from him and looked through the holes past a pile of shavings and on into the woods to the edge of the pen where they kept their mules.

"You can't see so good, can you, boy?" he said and began scraping the ground with his foot to turn up a piece of wire. He picked up a small piece of haywire; in a minute he found another shorter piece and picked that up. He began to attach these to the bark. He was in no hurry now that he knew what he was doing. When the spectacles were finished, he handed them to the negro. "Put these on," he said. "I hate to see anybody can't see good."

There was an instant when the negro might have done one thing or another, might have taken the glasses and crushed them in his hand or grabbed the knife and turned it on him. He saw the exact instant in the muddy liquor-swollen eyes when the pleasure of having a knife in this white man's gut was balanced against something else, he could not tell what.

The negro reached for the glasses. He attached the bows carefully behind his ears and looked forth. He peered this way and that with exaggerated solemnity. And then he looked di-rectly at Tanner and grinned, or grimaced, Tanner could not tell which, but he had an instant's sensation of seeing before him a negative image of himself, as if clownishness and cap-tivity had been their common lot. The vision failed him be-fore he could decipher it.

"Preacher," he said, "what you hanging around here for?" He picked up another piece of bark and began, without look-ing at it, to carve again. "This ain't Sunday."

"This here ain't Sunday?" the negro said.

"This is Friday," he said. "That's the way it is with you preachers—drunk all week so you don't know when Sunday is. What you see through those glasses?"

"See a man."

"What kind of a man?"

"See the man make theseyer glasses."

"Is he white or black?"

"He white!" the negro said as if only at that moment was his vision sufficiently improved to detect it. "Yessuh, he white!" he said.

"Well, you treat him like he was white," Tanner said. "What's your name?"

"Name Coleman," the negro said.

And he had not got rid of Coleman since. You make a monkey out of one of them and he jumps on your back and stays there for life, but let one make a monkey out of you and all you can do is kill him or disappear. And he was not going to hell for killing a nigger. Behind the shack he heard the doctor kick over a bucket. He sat and waited.

In a moment the doctor appeared again, beating his way around the other side of the house, whacking at scattered clumps of Johnson grass with his cane. He stopped in the middle of the yard.

"You don't belong here," he began. "I could have you prosecuted."

Tanner remained there, dumb, staring across the field.

"Where's your still?" the doctor asked.

"If it's a still around here, it don't belong to me," he said and shut his mouth tight.

The negro laughed softly. "Down on your luck, ain't you?" he murmured. "Didn't you used to own a little piece of land over acrost the river and lost it?"

He had continued to study the woods ahead.

"If you want to run the still for me, that's one thing," the doctor said. "If you don't, you might as well be packing up."

"The governmint ain't got around yet to forcing the white folks to work for the colored," Tanner said.

The doctor polished the stone in his ring with the ball of his thumb. "I don't like the governmint no bettern you," he said. "Where you going instead? You going to the city and get you a soot of rooms at the Biltmo' Hotel?"

Tanner said nothing.

"The day coming," the doctor said, "when the white folks IS going to be working for the colored and you might's well to git ahead of the crowd."

"That day ain't coming for me," Tanner said shortly.

"Done come for you," the doctor said. "Ain't come for the rest of them."

Tanner's gaze drove on past the farthest blue edge of the treeline into the pale afternoon sky. "I got a daughter in the north," he said. "I don't have to work for you."

The doctor took his watch from his watch pocket and looked at it and put it back. He gazed for a moment at the back of his hands. He appeared to have measured and to know secretly the time it would take the world to turn upsidedown. "She don't want no old daddy like you," he said. "Maybe she say she do, but that ain't likely. Even if you rich," he said, "they don't want you. They got they own ideas. The black ones they rears and they pitches. I made mine," he said, "and I ain't done none of that." He looked again at Tanner. "I be back here next week," he said, "and if you still here, I know you going to work that still for me." He remained there a moment, rocking on his heels, waiting for some answer. Finally he turned and started beating his way back through the overgrown path.

Tanner had continued to look across the field as if his spirit had been sucked out of him into the woods and nothing was left on the chair but a shell. If he had known it was a question of this—sitting here looking out of this window all day in this no-place, or just running a still for a nigger, he would have run the still for the nigger. He would have been a nigger's white nigger any day. Behind him he heard the daughter come in from the kitchen. His heart beat faster. He heard her plump herself down on the sofa. She was not yet ready to go. He did not turn and look at her.

She sat there silently a few moments. Then she began. "The trouble with you is," she said, "you sit in front of that window all the time where there's nothing to look out at. You need some inspiration and an out-let. If you would let me pull your chair around to look at the TV, you would quit thinking about morbid stuff, death and hell and judgment. My Lord."

"The Judgment is coming," he muttered. "The sheep'll be separated from the goats. Them that kept their promises from them that didn't. Them that did the best they could with what they had from them that didn't. Them that honored their father and their mother from them that cursed them. Them that . . ."

She heaved a mammoth sigh that all but drowned him out. "What's the use in me wasting my good breath?" she asked. She rose and went back in the kitchen and began knocking things about.

She was so high and mighty! At home he had been living in a shack but there was at least air around it. He could put his feet on the ground. Here she didn't even live in a house. She lived in a pigeon-hutch of a building, with all stripes of foreigner, all of them twisted in the tongue. It was no place for a sane man. The first morning here she had taken him sightseeing and he had seen in fifteen minutes exactly how it was. He had not been out of the apartment since. He never wanted to set foot again on the underground railroad or the steps that moved under you while you stood still or any elevator to the thirty-fourth floor. When he was safely back in the apartment again, he had imagined going over it with Coleman. He had to turn his head every few seconds to make sure Coleman was behind him. Keep to the inside or these people'll knock you down, keep right behind me or you'll get left, keep your hat on, you damm idiot, he had said, and Coleman had come on with his bent running shamble, panting and muttering, What we doing here? Where you get this fool idea coming here?

I come to show you it was no kind of place. Now you know you were well off where you were.

I knowed it before, Coleman said. Was you didn't know it.

When he had been here a week, he had got a post card from Coleman that had been written for him by Hooten at the railroad station. It was written in green ink and said, "This is Coleman—X—howyou boss." Under it Hooten had written from himself, "Quit frequenting all those nitespots

and come on home, you scoundrel, yours truly, WT Hooten."
He had sent Coleman a card in return, care of Hooten, that
said, "This place is alrite if you like it. Yours truly, T.C. Tanner." Since the daughter had to mail the card, he had not put
on it that he was returning as soon as his pension check came.
He had not intended to tell her but to leave her a note. When
the check came, he would hire himself a taxi to the bus station
and be on his way. And it would have made her as happy as
it made him. She had found his company dour and her duty
irksome. If he had sneaked out, she would have had the pleasure of having tried to do it and to top that off, the pleasure
of his ingratitude.

As for him, he would have returned to squat on the doctor's land and to take his orders from a nigger who chewed
ten-cent cigars. And to think less about it than formerly. Instead he had been done in by a nigger actor, or one who
called himself an actor. He didn't believe the nigger was any
actor.

There were two apartments on each floor of the building.
He had been with the daughter three weeks when the people
in the next hutch moved out. He had stood in the hall and
watched the moving-out and the next day he had watched a
moving-in. The hall was narrow and dark and he stood in the
corner out of the way, offering only a suggestion every now
and then to the movers that would have made work easier for
them if they had paid any attention. The furniture was new
and cheap so he decided the people moving in might be a
newly married couple and he would just wait around until
they came and wish them well. After a while a large negro in
a light blue suit came lunging up the stairs, carrying four
bulging canvas suitcases, his head lowered against the strain.
Behind him stepped a young tan-skinned woman with bright
copper-colored hair. The negro dropped the suitcases with a
thud in front of the door of the next apartment.

"Be careful, Sweetie," the woman said. "My make-up is in
there."

It broke upon him then just what was happening.

The negro was grinning. He took a swipe at one of her
hips.

"Quit it," she said, "there's an old guy watching."

They both turned and looked at him.

"Had-do," he said and nodded. Then he turned quickly into his own door.

His daughter was in the kitchen. "Who you think's rented that apartment over there?" he asked, his face alight.

She looked at him suspiciously. "Who?" she muttered.

"A nigger!" he said in a gleeful voice. "A South Alabama nigger if I ever saw one. And got him this high-yeller, high-stepping woman with a red wig and they two are going to live next door to you!" He slapped his knee. "Yes siree!" he said. "Damm if they ain't!" It was the first time since coming up here that he had had occasion to laugh.

Her face squared up instantly. "All right now you listen to me," she said. "You keep away from them. Don't you go over there trying to get friendly with him. They ain't the same around here and I don't want any trouble with niggers, you hear me? If you have to live next to them, just you mind your business and they'll mind theirs. That's the way people were meant to get along in this world. Everybody can get along if they just mind their business. Live and let live." She began to wrinkle her nose like a rabbit, a stupid way she had. "Up here everybody minds their own business and everybody gets along. That's all you have to do."

"I was getting along with niggers before you were born," he said. He went back out into the hall and waited. He was willing to bet the nigger would like to talk to someone who understood him. Twice while he waited, he forgot and in his excitement, spit his tobacco juice against the baseboard. In about twenty minutes, the door of the apartment opened again and the negro came out. He had put on a tie and a pair of horn-rimmed spectacles and Tanner noticed for the first time that he had a small almost invisible goatee. A real swell. The negro came on without appearing to see there was any-one else in the hall.

"Haddy, John," Tanner said and nodded, but the negro brushed past without hearing and went rattling rapidly down the stairs.

Could be deaf and dumb, Tanner thought. He went back into the apartment and sat down but each time he heard a noise in the hall, he got up and went to the door and stuck his head out to see if it might be the negro. Once in the middle of the afternoon, he caught the negro's eye, or thought he did, just as he was rounding the bend of the stairs again but before he could get out a word, the man was in his own apartment and had slammed the door. He had never known one to move that fast unless the police were after him.

He was standing in the hall early the next morning when the woman came out of her door alone, walking on high gold-painted heels. He wished to bid her good morning or simply to nod but instinct told him to beware. She didn't look like any kind of woman, black or white, he had ever seen before and he remained pressed against the wall, frightened more than anything else, and feigning invisibility.

The woman gave him a flat stare, then turned her head away and stepped wide of him as if she were skirting an open garbage can. He held his breath until she was out of sight. Then he waited patiently for the man.

The negro came out about ten o'clock.

This time Tanner advanced squarely in his path. "Good morning, Preacher," he said. It had been his experience that if a negro tended to be sullen, this title usually cleared up his expression.

The negro stopped abruptly.

"I seen you move in," Tanner said. "I ain't been up here long myself. It ain't much of a place if you ask me. I reckon you wish you were back in South Alabama."

The negro did not take a step or answer. His eyes began to move. They moved from the top of the black hat, down to the collarless blue shirt, neatly buttoned at the neck, down the faded galluses to the grey trousers and the high-top shoes and up again, very slowly, while some unfathomable dead-cold rage seemed to stiffen and shrink him.

"I thought you might know somewhere around here we could find us a pond and fish, Preacher," Tanner said in a voice growing thinner but still with considerable hope in it.

A seething noise came out of the negro before he spoke. "I'm not from South Alabama," he said in a breathless wheezing voice. "I'm from New York City. And I'm not a preacher! I'm an actor."

Tanner chortled. "It's a little actor in most preachers, ain't it?" he said and winked. "I reckon you just preach on the side."

"I don't preach!" the negro cried and rushed past him as if a swarm of bees had suddenly come down on him out of nowhere. He dashed down the stairs and was gone.

Tanner stood there for some time before he went back in the apartment. The rest of the day he sat in his chair and debated whether he would have one more try at making friends with him. Every time he heard a noise on the stairs he went to the door and looked out, but the negro did not return until late in the afternoon. Tanner was standing in the hall waiting for him when he reached the top of the stairs. "Good evening, Preacher," he said.

The negro stopped and gripped the banister rail. A tremor racked him from his head to his crotch. Then he began to come forward slowly. When he was close enough he lunged and grasped Tanner by both shoulders. "I don't take no crap," he whispered, "off no wool-hat red-neck son-of-a-bitch peckerwood old bastard like you." He caught his breath. And then his voice came out in the sound of an exasperation so profound that it rocked on the verge of a laugh. It was high and piercing and weak. "And I'm not a preacher! I'm not a Christian. I don't believe in that crap. There ain't no Jesus and there ain't no God."

The old man felt his heart inside him hard and tough as an oak knot. "And you ain't black," he said. "And I ain't white!"

The negro slammed him against the wall. He yanked the black hat down over his eyes. Then he grabbed his shirt front and shoved him backwards to his open door and knocked him through it. From the kitchen the daughter saw him blindly hit the edge of the inside hall door and fall reeling into the living room.

Hard as his head was, the fall cracked it and when he got over the concussion he had a little stroke.

For days his tongue appeared to be frozen in his mouth. When it unthawed it was twice its normal size and he could not make her understand him. What he wanted to know was if the government check had come. He meant to buy a bus ticket with it and go home. After a few weeks, he made her understand. "It came," she said, "and it'll just pay the first two weeks doctor-bill and please tell me how you're going home when you can't talk or walk or think straight and you got one eye crossed yet? Just please tell me that?"

It had come to him then slowly just what his present situation was. He would never see Corinth again. At least he would have to make her understand that he must be sent home to be buried. They could have him shipped back in a refrigerated car so that he would keep for the trip. He didn't want any undertaker up here messing with him. Let them get him off at once and he would come in on the early morning train and they could wire Hooten to get Coleman and Coleman would do the rest. I'm not letting no nigger bury you, she said, but quit talking morbid. You'll be up and around in a while. After a lot of argument, he wrung the promise from her. She would ship him back. It had only been, he saw now, to shut him up.

After that he slept peacefully and improved a little. In his waking dreams he could feel the cold early morning air of home coming in through the cracks of the pine box. He saw Coleman waiting, red-eyed, on the station platform and Hooten standing there with his green eyeshade and black alpaca sleeves, waiting for the train to stop. Hooten would be thinking: if the old fool had stayed at home where he belonged, he wouldn't be arriving on the 6:03 in no box. Coleman would turn the borrowed mule and cart so that they could slide the box off the platform onto the open end of the wagon. When the coffin was off the train the two of them, shut-mouthed, would inch the loaded coffin toward the wagon. From inside he would begin to scratch on the wood. They would drop the box as if it had caught fire.

They stood looking at each other, then at the box.

"That him," Coleman would say. "He in there his self."

"Naw," Hooten would say, "must be a rat got in there with him."

"That him. This here one of his tricks."

"If it's a rat he might as well stay."

"That him. Git a crowbar."

Hooten would go grumbling off and get the crowbar and come back and begin to pry open the lid. Even before he had the upper end pried open, Coleman would be jumping up and down, wheezing and panting from excitement. Tanner would give a thrust upward with both hands and spring up in the box. "Judgment Day! Judgment Day!" he would cry. "Don't you two fools know it's Judgment Day?"

Now that he knew exactly what her promises were worth, he would do as well to trust to the note pinned in his coat and to any stranger who found him dead in the street or in the boxcar or wherever. There was nothing to be looked for from her except that she would do things her way. She came out of the kitchen again, holding her hat and coat and rubber boots.

"Now listen," she said, "I have to go to the store. Don't you try to get up and walk around while I'm gone. You've been to the bathroom and you shouldn't have to go again. I don't want to find you on the floor when I get back."

You won't find me atall when you get back, he said to himself. This was the last time he would see her flat dumb face. Then he felt guilty. She had been good to him and he had been nothing but a nuisance to her.

"Do you want you a glass of milk before I go?" she asked.

"No," he said. Then he drew breath and said, "You got a nice place here. It's a nice part of the country. I'm sorry if I've give you a lot of trouble getting sick. It was my fault trying to be friendly with that city nigger." And I'm a dammed liar besides, he said to himself to kill the taste such a statement made in his mouth.

For a moment she stared as if he were losing his mind. Then she seemed to think better of it. "Now don't saying something pleasant like that once in a while make you feel better?" she asked and sat down on the sofa.

His knees itched to unbend. Git on, git on, he fumed silently. Make haste and go.

"It's great to have you here," she said in return. "I wouldn't have you any other place. My own daddy." She gave him a big smile and hoisted her right leg up and began to pull on her boot. "I wouldn't wish a dog out on a day like this," she said, "but I got to go. You can sit here and hope I don't slip and break my neck." She stamped the booted foot on the floor and then began to tackle the other one.

He turned his eyes to the window. The snow was beginning to stick and freeze to the outside pane. When he looked at her again, she was standing there like a big doll stuffed into its hat and coat. She drew on a pair of green knitted gloves. "Okay," she said, "I'm gone. You sure you don't want anything?"

"No," he said, "go ahead on."

"Well so long then," she said.

He raised the hat enough to reveal a bald palely speckled head. The hall door closed behind her. He began to tremble with excitement. He reached behind him and drew the coat into his lap. When he got it on, he waited until he had stopped panting, then he gripped the arms of the chair and pulled himself up. His body felt like a great heavy bell whose clapper swung from side to side but made no noise. Once up, he remained standing a moment, swaying until he got his balance. A sensation of terror and defeat swept over him. He would never make it. He would never get there dead or alive. He pushed one foot forward and did not fall and his confidence returned. "The Lord is my shepherd," he muttered, "I shall not want." He began moving toward the sofa where he would have support. He reached it! He was on his way.

By the time he got to the door, she would be down the four flights of steps and out of the building. He got past the sofa and crept along by the wall, keeping his hand on it for support. Nobody was going to bury him here. He was as confident as if the woods of home lay at the bottom of the stairs. He reached the front door of the apartment and opened it and peered into the hall. This was the first time he had looked into it since the actor had knocked him down. It was dank-smelling and empty. The thin piece of linoleum stretched its moldy length to the door of the other apartment, which was closed. "Nigger actor," he said.

The head of the stairs was ten or twelve feet from where he stood and he bent his attention to getting there without creeping around the long way with a hand on the wall. He held his arms a little way out from his sides and pushed forward directly. He was half way there when all at once his legs disappeared, or felt as if they had. He looked down, bewildered, for they were still there. He fell forward and grasped the banister post with both hands. Hanging there, he gazed for what seemed the longest time he had ever looked at anything down the steep unlighted steps; then he closed his eyes and pitched forward. He landed upsidedown in the middle of the flight.

He felt presently the tilt of the box as they took it off the train and got it on the baggage wagon. He made no noise yet. The train jarred and slid away. In a moment the baggage wagon was rumbling under him, carrying him back to the station side. He heard footsteps rattling closer and closer to him and he supposed that a crowd was gathering. Wait until they see this, he thought.

"He in there," Coleman said, "one of his tricks."

"It's a damm rat in there," Hooten said.

"It's him. Git the crowbar."

In a moment a shaft of greenish light fell on him. He pushed through it and cried in a weak voice, "Judgment Day! Judgment Day. You idiots didn't know it was Judgment Day, did you?"

"Coleman?" he murmured.

The negro bending over him had a large surly mouth and sullen eyes.

This must be the wrong station, Tanner thought. Those fools put me off too soon. Who is this nigger? It ain't even daylight here.

At the negro's side was another face, a woman's, pale, topped with a pile of copper-glinting hair and twisted as if she had just stepped in a pile of dung.

"Oh," Tanner murmured, "it's you."

The actor leaned closer and grasped him by the front of his shirt. "Judgment day," he said in a mocking voice. "There's not any judgment day, old man. Except this. Maybe this here is judgment day for you."

Tanner tried to catch hold of a banister spoke to raise himself but his hand grasped air. The two faces, the black one and the pale one, appeared to be wavering. By an effort of will he kept them focussed before him while he lifted his hand, as light as a breath, and said in his jauntiest voice, "Hep me up, Preacher. I'm on my way home!"

His daughter found him when she came in from the

grocery store. His hat had been pulled down over his face and his head and arms thrust between the spokes of the banister; his feet dangled over the stairwell like those of a man in the stocks. She tugged at him frantically and then flew for the police. They cut him out with a saw and said he had been dead about an hour.

She buried him in New York City, but after she had done it she could not sleep at night. Night after night she turned and tossed and very definite lines began to appear in her face, so she had him dug up and shipped the body to Corinth. Now she rests well at night and her good looks have mostly returned.

STORIES AND
OCCASIONAL PROSE

Contents

STORIES

THE GERANIUM
A Collection of Short Stories

The Geranium

Old Dudley folded into the chair he was gradually molding to his own shape and looked out the window fifteen feet away into another window framed by blackened red brick. He was waiting for the geranium. They put it out every morning about ten and they took it in at five-thirty. Mrs. Carson back home had a geranium in her window. There were plenty of geraniums at home, better looking geraniums. Ours are sho nuff geraniums, Old Dudley thought, not any er this pale pink business with green, paper bows. The geranium they would put in the window reminded him of the Grisby boy at home who had polio and had to be wheeled out every morning and left in the sun to blink. Lutisha could have taken that geranium and stuck it in the ground and had something worth looking at in a few weeks. Those people across the alley had no business with one. They set it out and let the hot sun bake it all day and they put it so near the ledge the wind could almost knock it over. They had no business with it, no business with it. It shouldn't have been there. Old Dudley felt his throat knotting up. Lutish could root anything. Rabie too. His throat was drawn taut. He laid his head back and tried to clear his mind. There wasn't much he could think of to think about that didn't do his throat that way.

His daughter came in. "Don't you want to go out for a walk?" she asked. She looked provoked.

He didn't answer her.

"Well?"

"No." He wondered how long she was going to stand there. She made his eyes feel like his throat. They'd get watery and she'd see. She had seen before and had looked sorry for him. She'd looked sorry for herself too; but she could er saved herself, Old Dudley thought, if she'd just have let him alone—let him stay where he was back home and not be so taken up with her damn duty. She moved out of the room leaving an audible sigh to crawl over him and remind him again of that one minute—that wasn't her fault at all— when suddenly he had wanted to go to New York to live with her.

He could have got out of going. He could have been stubborn and told her he'd spend his life where he'd always spent it, send him or not send him the money every month, he'd get along with his pension and odd jobs. Keep her damn money—she needed it worse than he did. She would have been glad to have had her duty disposed of like that. Then she could have said if he died without his children near him, it was his own fault; if he got sick and there wasn't anybody to take care of him, well, he'd asked for it, she could have said. But there was that thing inside him that had wanted to see New York. He had been to Atlanta once when he was a boy and he had seen New York in a picture show. "Big Town Rhythm" it was. Big towns were important places. The thing inside him had sneaked up on him for just one instant. The place like he'd seen in the picture show had room for him! It was an important place and it had room for him! He'd said, yes, he'd go.

He must have been sick when he said it. He couldn't have been well and said it. He had been sick and she had been so taken up with her damn duty, she had wangled it out of him. Why did she have to come down there in the first place to pester him? He had been doing all right. There was his pension that could feed him and odd jobs that kept him his room in the boarding house.

The window in that room showed him the river—thick and red as it struggled over rocks and around curves. He tried to think how it was besides red and slow. He added green blotches for trees on either side of it and a brown spot for trash somewhere upstream. He and Rabie had fished it in a flat-bottom boat every Wednesday. Rabie knew the river up and down for twenty miles. There wasn't another nigger in Coa County that knew it like he did. He loved the river, but it hadn't meant anything to Old Dudley. The fish were what he was after. He liked to come in at night with a long string of them and slap them down in the sink. "Few fish I got," he'd say. It took a man to get those fish, the old girls at the

boarding house always said. He and Rabie would start out
early Wednesday morning and fish all day. Rabie would find
the spots and row; Old Dudley always caught them. Rabie
didn't care much about catching them—he just loved the
river. "Ain't no use settin' yo' line down dere, boss," he'd say,
"ain't no fish dere. Dis ol' riber ain't hidin' none nowhere
'round hyar, nawsuh," and he would giggle and shift the boat
downstream. That was Rabie. He could steal cleaner than a
weasel but he knew where the fish were. Old Dudley always
gave him the little ones.

Old Dudley had lived upstairs in the corner room of the
boarding house ever since his wife died in '22. He protected
the old ladies. He was the man in the house and he did the
things a man in the house was supposed to do. It was a dull
occupation at night when the old girls crabbed and crocheted
in the parlor and the man in the house had to listen and judge
the sparrow-like wars that rasped and twittered intermittently.
But in the daytime there was Rabie. Rabie and Lutisha lived
down in the basement. Lutish cooked and Rabie took care of
the cleaning and the vegetable garden; but he was sharp at
sneaking off with half his work done and going to help Old
Dudley with some current project—building a hen house or
painting a door. He liked to listen, he liked to hear about
Atlanta when Old Dudley had been there and about how
guns were put together on the inside and all the other things
the old man knew.

Sometimes at night they would go 'possum hunting. They
never got a 'possum but Old Dudley liked to get away from
the ladies once in a while and hunting was a good excuse.
Rabie didn't like 'possum hunting. They never got a 'possum; they never even treed one; and besides, he was mostly
a water nigger. "We ain't gonna go huntin' no 'possum tonight, is we, boss? I got a lil' business I wants tuh tend tuh,"
he'd say when Old Dudley would start talking about hounds
and guns. "Whose chickens you gonna steal tonight?" Dudley would grin. "I reckon I be huntin' 'possum tonight,"
Rabie'd sigh.

Old Dudley would get out his gun and take it apart and,
as Rabie cleaned the pieces, would explain the mechanism to
him. Then he'd put it together again. Rabie always marveled

at the way he could put it together again. Old Dudley would have liked to have explained New York to Rabie. If he could have showed it to Rabie, it wouldn't have been so big—he wouldn't have felt pressed down every time he went out in it. "It ain't so big," he would have said. "Don't let it get you down, Rabie. It's just like any other city and cities ain't all that complicated."

But they were. New York was swishing and jamming one minute and dirty and dead the next. His daughter didn't even live in a house. She lived in a building—the middle in a row of buildings all alike, all blackened-red and gray with rasp-mouthed people hanging out their windows looking at other windows and other people just like them looking back. Inside you could go up and you could go down and there were just halls that reminded you of tape measures strung out with a door every inch. He remembered he'd been dazed by the building the first week. He'd wake up expecting the halls to have changed in the night and he'd look out the door and there they stretched like dog runs. The streets were the same way. He wondered where he'd be if he walked to the end of one of them. One night he dreamed he did and ended at the end of the building—nowhere.

The next week he had become more conscious of the daughter and son-in-law and their boy—no place to be out of their way. The son-in-law was a queer one. He drove a truck and came in only on the weekends. He said "nah" for "no" and he'd never heard of a 'possum. Old Dudley slept in the room with the boy who was sixteen and couldn't be talked to. But sometimes when the daughter and Old Dudley were alone in the apartment, she would sit down and talk to him. First she had to think of something to say. Usually it gave out before what she considered was the proper time to get up and do something else, so he would have to say something. He always tried to think of something he hadn't said before. She never listened the second time. She was seeing that her father spent his last years with his own family and not in a decayed boarding house full of old women whose heads jiggled. She was doing her duty. She had brothers and sisters who were not.

Once she took him shopping with her but he was too slow.

They went in a "subway"—a railroad underneath the ground like a big cave. People boiled out of trains and up steps and over into the streets. They rolled off the street and down steps and into trains—black and white and yellow all mixed up like vegetables in soup. Everything was boiling. The trains swished in from tunnels, up canals, and all of a sudden stopped. The people coming out pushed through the people coming in and a noise rang and the train swooped off again. Old Dudley and the daughter had to go in three different ones before they got where they were going. He wondered why people ever went out of their houses. He felt like his tongue had slipped down in his stomach. She held him by the coat sleeve and pulled him through the people.

They went on an overhead train too. She called it an "El." They had to go up on a high platform to catch it. Old Dudley looked over the rail and could see the people rushing and the automobiles rushing under him. He felt sick. He put one hand on the rail and sank down on the wooden floor of the platform. The daughter screamed and pulled him over from the edge. "Do you want to fall off and kill yourself?" she shouted.

Through a crack in the boards he could see the cars swimming in the street. "I don't care," he murmured, "I don't care if I do or not."

"Come on," she said, "you'll feel better when we get home."

"Home?" he repeated. The cars moved in a rhythm below him.

"Come on," she said, "here it comes; we've just got time to make it." They'd just had time to make all of them.

They made that one. They came back to the building and the apartment. The apartment was too tight. There was no place to be where there wasn't somebody else. The kitchen opened into the bathroom and the bathroom opened into everything else and you were always where you started from. At home there was upstairs and the basement and the river and down town in front of Fraziers . . . damn his throat.

The geranium was late today. It was ten-thirty. They usually had it out by ten-fifteen.

Somewhere down the hall a woman shrilled something

unintelligible out to the street; a radio was bleating the worn music to a soap serial; and a garbage can crashed down a fire-escape. The door to the next apartment slammed and a sharp footstep clipped down the hall. "That would be the nigger," Old Dudley muttered. "The nigger with the shiny shoes." He had been there a week when the nigger moved in. That Thursday he was looking out the door at the dog run halls when this nigger went into the next apartment. He had on a grey, pin-stripe suit and a tan tie. His collar was stiff and white and made a clear-cut line next to his neck. His shoes were shiny tan—they matched his tie and his skin. Old Dudley scratched his head. He hadn't known the kind of people that would live thick in a building could afford servants. He chuckled. Lot of good a nigger in a Sunday suit would do them. Maybe this nigger would know the country around here—or maybe how to get to it. They might could hunt. They might could find them a stream somewhere. He shut the door and went to the daughter's room. "Hey!" he shouted, "the folks next door got 'em a nigger. Must be gonna clean for them. You reckon they gonna keep him every day?"

She looked up from making the bed. "What are you talking about?"

"I say they got 'em a servant next door—a nigger—all dressed up in a Sunday suit."

She walked to the other side of the bed. "You must be crazy," she said. "The next apartment is vacant and besides, nobody around here can afford any servant."

"I tell you I saw him," Old Dudley snickered. "Going right in there with a tie and a white collar on—and sharp-toed shoes."

"If he went in there, he's looking at it for himself," she muttered. She went to the dresser and started fidgeting with things.

Old Dudley laughed. She could be right funny when she wanted to. "Well," he said, "I think I'll go over and see what day he gets off. Maybe I can convince him he likes to fish," and he'd slapped his pocket to make the two quarters jingle. Before he got out in the hall good, she came tearing behind him and pulled him in. "Can't you hear?" she'd yelled. "I meant what I said. He's renting that himself if he went in there. Don't you go asking him any questions or saying anything to him. I don't want any trouble with niggers."

"You mean," Old Dudley murmured, "he's gonna live next door to you?"

She shrugged. "I suppose he is. And you tend to your own business," she added. "Don't have anything to do with him."

That's just the way she'd said it. Like he didn't have any sense at all. But he'd told her off then. He'd stated his say and she knew what he meant. "You ain't been raised that way!" he'd said thundery-like. "You ain't been raised to live tight with niggers that think they're just as good as you, and you think I'd go messin' around with one er that kind! If you think I want anything to do with them, you're crazy." He had had to slow down then because his throat was tightening. She'd stood stiff up and said they lived where they could afford to live and made the best of it. Preaching to him! Then she'd walked stiff off without a word more. That was her. Trying to be holy with her shoulders curved around and her neck in the air. Like he was a fool. He knew yankees let niggers in their front doors and let them set on their sofas but he didn't know his own daughter that was raised proper would stay next door to them—and then think he didn't have no more sense than to want to mix with them. Him!

He got up and took a paper off another chair. He might as well appear to be reading when she came through again. No use having her standing there staring at him, believing she had to think up something for him to do. He looked over the paper at the window across the alley. The geranium wasn't there yet. It had never been this late before. The first day he'd seen it, he had been sitting there looking out the window at the other window and he had looked at his watch to see how long it had been since breakfast. When he looked up, it was there. It startled him. He didn't like flowers, but the geranium didn't look like a flower. It looked like the sick Grisby boy at home and it was the color of the drapes the old ladies had in the parlor and the paper bow on it looked like the one behind Lutish's uniform she wore on Sundays. Lutish had a fondness for sashes. Most niggers did, Old Dudley thought.

The daughter came through again. He had meant to be looking at the paper when she came through. "Do me a favor, will you?" she asked as if she had just thought up a favor he could do.

He hoped she didn't want him to go to the grocery again. He got lost the time before. All the blooming buildings looked alike. He nodded.

"Go down to the third floor and ask Mrs. Schmitt to lend me the shirt pattern she uses for Jake."

Why couldn't she just let him sit? She didn't need the shirt pattern. "All right," he said. "What number is it?"

"Number 10—just like this. Right below us three floors down."

Old Dudley was always afraid that when he went out in the dog runs, a door would suddenly open and one of the snipe-nosed men that hung off the window ledges in his undershirt would growl, "What are you doing here?" The door to the nigger's apartment was open and he could see a woman sitting in a chair by the window. "Yankee niggers," he muttered. She had on rimless glasses and there was a book in her lap. Niggers don't think they're dressed up till they got on glasses, Old Dudley thought. He remembered Lutish's glasses. She had saved up thirteen dollars to buy them. Then she went to the doctor and asked him to look at her eyes and tell her how thick to get the glasses. He made her look at animals' pictures through a mirror and he stuck a light through her eyes and looked in her head. Then he said she didn't need any glasses. She was so mad she burned the corn bread three days in a row, but she bought her some glasses anyway at the ten cent store. They didn't cost her but $1.98 and she wore them every Saddey. "That was niggers," Old Dudley chuckled. He realized he had made a noise, and covered his mouth with his hand. Somebody might hear him in one of the apartments.

He turned down the first flight of stairs. Down the second he heard footsteps coming up. He looked over the banisters and saw it was a woman—a fat woman with an apron on. From the top, she looked kind er like Mrs. Benson at home. He wondered if she would speak to him. When they were four steps from each other, he darted a glance at her but she wasn't looking at him. When there were no steps between them, his eyes fluttered up for an instant and she was looking at him cold in the face. Then she was past him. She hadn't said a word. He felt heavy in his stomach.

He went down four flights instead of three. Then he went back up one and found number 10. Mrs. Schmitt said O. K., wait a minute and she'd get the pattern. She sent one of the children back to the door with it. The child didn't say anything.

Old Dudley started back up the stairs. He had to take it more slowly. It tired him going up. Everything tired him, looked like. Not like having Rabie to do his running for him. Rabie was a light-footed nigger. He could sneak in a henhouse 'thout even the hens knowing it and get him the fattest fryer in there and not a squawk. Fast too. Dudley had always been slow on his feet. It went that way with fat people. He remembered one time him and Rabie was hunting quail over near Molton. They had 'em a hound dog that could find a covey quickern any fancy pointer going. He wasn't no good at bringing them back but he could find them every time and then set like a dead stump while you aimed at the birds. This one time the hound stopped cold-still. "Dat gonna be a big 'un," Rabie whispered, "I feels it." Old Dudley raised the gun slowly as they walked along. He had to be careful of the pine needles. They covered the ground and made it slick. Rabie shifted his weight from side to side, lifting and setting his feet on the waxen needles with unconscious care. He looked straight ahead and moved forward swiftly. Old Dudley kept one eye ahead and one on the ground. It would slope and he would be sliding forward dangerously or in pulling himself up an incline, he would slide back down.

"Ain't I better get dem birds dis time, boss?" Rabie suggested. "You ain't never easy on yo' feets on Monday. If you falls in one dem slopes, you gonna scatter dem birds fo' you gits dat gun up."

Old Dudley wanted to get the covey. He could er knocked four out it easy. "I'll get 'em," he muttered. He lifted the gun to his eye and leaned forward. Something slipped beneath him and he slid backward on his heels. The gun went off and the covey sprayed into the air.

"Dem was some mighty fine birds we let get away from us," Rabie sighed.

"We'll find another covey," Old Dudley said, "now get me out of this damn hole."

He could er got five er those birds if he hadn't fallen. He could er shot 'em off like cans on a fence. He drew one hand back to his ear and extended the other forward. He could er knocked 'em out like clay pigeons. Bang! A squeak on the staircase made him wheel around—his arms still holding the invisible gun. The nigger was clipping up the steps toward him, an amused smile stretching his trimmed mustache. Old Dudley's mouth dropped open. The nigger's lips were pulled down like he was trying to keep from laughing. Old Dudley couldn't move. He stared at the clear-cut line the nigger's collar made against his skin.

"What are you hunting, old timer?" the negro asked in a voice that sounded like a nigger's laugh and a white man's sneer.

Old Dudley felt like a child with a pop-pistol. His mouth was open and his tongue was rigid in the middle of it. Right below his knees felt hollow. His feet slipped and he slid three steps and landed sitting down.

"You better be careful," the negro said. "You could easily hurt yourself on these steps," and he held out his hand for Old Dudley to pull up on. It was a long narrow hand and the tips of the fingernails were clean and cut squarely. They looked like they might have been filed. Old Dudley's hands hung between his knees. The nigger took him by the arm and pulled up. "Whew!" he gasped, "you're heavy. Give a little help here." Old Dudley's knees unbended and he staggered up. The nigger had him by the arm. "I'm going up anyway," he said. "I'll help you." Old Dudley looked frantically around. The steps behind him seemed to close up. He was walking with the nigger up the stairs. The nigger was waiting for him on each step. "So you hunt?" the nigger was saying. "Well, let's see. I went deer hunting once. I believe we used a Dodson 38 to get those deer. What do you use?"

Old Dudley was staring through the shiny tan shoes. "I use a gun," he mumbled.

"I like to fool with guns better than hunting," the nigger was saying. "Never was much at killing anything. Seems kind of a shame to deplete the game reserve. I'd collect guns if I had the time and the money, though." He was waiting on every step till Old Dudley got on it. He was explaining guns and makes. He had on grey socks with a black fleck in them. They finished the stairs. The nigger walked down the hall with him, holding him by the arm. It probably looked like he had his arm locked in the nigger's.

They went right up to Old Dudley's door. Then the nigger asked, "You from around here?"

Old Dudley shook his head looking at the door. He hadn't looked at the nigger yet. All the way up the stairs, he hadn't looked at the nigger. "Well," the nigger said, "it's a swell place—once you get used to it." He patted Old Dudley on the back and went into his own apartment. Old Dudley went into his. The pain in his throat was all over his face now, leaking out his eyes.

He shuffled to the chair by the window and sank down in it. His throat was going to pop. His throat was going to pop on account of a nigger—a damn nigger that patted him on the back and called him "old timer." Him that knew such as that couldn't be. Him that had come from a good place. A good place. A place where such as that couldn't be. His eyes felt strange in their sockets. They were swelling in them and in a minute there wouldn't be any room left for them there. He was trapped in this place where niggers could call you "old timer." He wouldn't be trapped. He wouldn't be. He rolled his head on the back of the chair to stretch his neck that was too full.

A man was looking at him. A man was in the window across the alley looking straight at him. The man was watching him cry. That was where the geranium was supposed to be and it was a man in his undershirt, watching him cry, waiting to watch his throat pop. Old Dudley looked back at the man. It was supposed to be the geranium. The geranium belonged there, not the man. "Where is the geranium?" he called out of his tight throat.

"What you cryin' for?" the man asked. "I ain't never seen a man cry like that."

"Where is the geranium?" Old Dudley quavered. "It ought to be there. Not you."

"This is my window," the man said. "I got a right to set here if I want to."

"Where is it?" Old Dudley shrilled. There was just a little room left in his throat.

"It fell off if it's any of your business," the man said.

Old Dudley got up and peered over the window ledge. Down in the alley, way six floors down, he could see a cracked flower pot scattered over a spray of dirt and something pink sticking out of a green paper bow. It was down six floors. Smashed down six floors.

Old Dudley looked at the man who was chewing gum and waiting to see the throat pop. "You shouldn't have put it so near the ledge," he murmured. "Why don't you pick it up?"

"Why don't you, pop?"

Old Dudley stared at the man who was where the geranium should have been.

He would. He'd go down and pick it up. He'd put it in his own window and look at it all day if he wanted to. He turned from the window and left the room. He walked slowly down the dog run and got to the steps. The steps dropped down like a deep wound in the floor. They opened up through a gap like a cavern and went down and down. And he had gone up them a little behind the nigger. And the nigger had pulled him up on his feet and kept his arm in his and gone up the steps with him and said he hunted deer, "old timer," and seen him holding a gun that wasn't there and sitting on the steps like a child. He had shiny tan shoes and he was trying not to laugh and the whole business was laughing. There'd probably be niggers with black flecks in their socks on every step, pulling down their mouths so as not to laugh. The steps dropped down and down. He wouldn't go down and have niggers pattin' him on the back. He went back to the room and the window and looked down at the geranium.

The man was sitting over where it should have been. "I ain't seen you pickin' it up," he said.

Old Dudley stared at the man.

"I seen you before," the man said. "I seen you settin' in that old chair every day, starin' out the window, looking in my apartment. What I do in my apartment is my business, see? I don't like people looking at what I do."

It was at the bottom of the alley with its roots in the air.

"I only tell people once," the man said and left the window.

The Barber

IT IS TRYING on liberals in Dilton.

After the Democratic White Primary, Rayber changed his barber. Three weeks before it, while he was shaving him, the barber asked, "Who you gonna vote for?"

"Darmon," Rayber said.

"You a nigger-lover?"

Rayber started in the chair. He had not expected to be approached so brutally. "No," he said. If he had not been taken off balance, he would have said, "I am neither a negro- nor a white-lover." He had said that before to Jacobs, the philosophy man, and—to show you how trying it is for liberals in Dilton—Jacobs—a man of his education—had muttered, "That's a poor way to be."

"Why?" Rayber had asked bluntly. He knew he could argue Jacobs down.

Jacobs had said, "Skip it." He had a class. His classes frequently occurred, Rayber noticed, when Rayber was about to get him in an argument.

"I am neither a negro- nor a white-lover," Rayber would have said to the barber.

The barber drew a clean path through the lather and then pointed the razor at Rayber. "I'm tellin' you," he said, "there ain't but two sides now, white and black. Anybody can see that from this campaign. You know what Hawk said? Said a hunnert and fifty years ago, they was runnin' each other down eatin' each other—throwin' jewel rocks at birds—skinnin' horses with their teeth. A nigger come in a white barber shop in Atlanta and says, 'Gimme a haircut.' They throwed him out but it just goes to show you. Why listen, three black hyenas over in Mulford last month shot a white man and took half of what was in his house and you know where they are now? Settin' in their county jail eatin' like the President of the United States—they might get dirty in the chain gang; or some damn nigger-lover might come by and be heart-broke to see 'em pickin' rock. Why, lemme tell you this—ain't nothin' gonna be good again until we get rid of them Mother

Hubbards and get us a man can put these niggers in their places. Shuh."

"You hear that, George?" he shouted to the colored boy wiping up the floor around the basins.

"Sho do," George said.

It was time for Rayber to say something but nothing appropriate would come. He wanted to say something that George would understand. He was startled that George had been brought into the conversation. He remembered Jacobs telling about lecturing at a negro college for a week. They couldn't say negro—nigger—colored—black. Jacobs said he had come home every night and shouted, "NIGGER NIGGER NIGGER" out the back window. Rayber wondered what George's leanings were. He was a trim looking boy.

"If a nigger come in my shop with any of that haircut sass, he'd get it cut all right." The barber made a noise between his teeth. "You a Mother Hubbard?" he asked.

"I'm voting for Darmon if that's what you mean," Rayber said.

"You ever heard Hawkson talk?"

"I've had that pleasure," Rayber said.

"You heard his last one?"

"No, I understand his remarks don't alter from speech to speech," Rayber said curtly.

"Yeah?" the barber said. "Well, this last speech was a killeroo! Ol' Hawk let them Mother Hubbards have it."

"A good many people," Rayber said, "consider Hawkson a demagog." He wondered if George knew what demagog meant. Should have said, "lying politician."

"Demagog!" The barber slapped his knee and whooped. "That's what Hawk said!" he howled. "Ain't that a shot! 'Folks,' he says, 'them Mother Hubbards says I'm a demagog.' Then he rears back and says sort of soft-like, 'Am I a demagog, you people?' And they yells, 'Naw, Hawk, you ain't no demagog!' And he comes forward shouting, 'Oh yeah I am, I'm the best damn demagog in this state!' And you should hear them people roar! Whew!"

"Quite a show," Rayber said, "but what is it but a. . . ."

"Mother Hubbard," the barber muttered. "You been taken

in by 'em all right. Lemme tell you somethin'. . . ." He reviewed Hawkson's Fourth of July speech. It had been another killeroo, ending with poetry. Who was Darmon? Hawk wanted to know. Yeah, who was Darmon? the crowd had roared. Why, didn't they know? Why, he was Little Boy Blue, blowin' his horn. Yeah. Babies in the meadow and niggers in the corn. Man! Rayber should have heard that one. No Mother Hubbard could have stood up under it.

Rayber thought that if the barber would read a few. . . .

Listen, he didn't have to read nothin'. All he had to do was think. That was the trouble with people these days—they didn't think, they didn't use their horse sense. Why wasn't Rayber thinkin'? Where was his horse sense?

Why am I straining myself? Rayber thought irritably.

"Nossir!" the barber said, "big words don't do nobody no good. They don't take the place of thinkin'."

"Thinking!" Rayber shouted. "You call yourself thinking?"

"Listen," the barber said, "do you know what Hawk told them people at Tilford?" At Tilford Hawk had told them that he liked niggers fine in their place and if they didn't stay in that place, he had a place to put 'em. How about that?

Rayber wanted to know what that had to do with thinking.

The barber thought it was plain as a pig on a sofa what that had to do with thinking. He thought a good many other things too, which he told Rayber. He said Rayber should have heard the Hawkson speeches at Mullin's Oak, Bedford, and Chickerville.

Rayber settled down in his chair again and reminded the barber that he had come in for a shave.

The barber started back shaving him. He said Rayber should have heard the one at Spartasville. "There wasn't a Mother Hubbard left standin', and all the Boy Blues got their horns broke. Hawk said," he said, "that the time had come when you had to sit on the lid with. . . ."

"I have an appointment," Rayber said. "I'm in a hurry." Why should he stay and listen to that tripe?

As much rot as it was, the whole asinine conversation stuck with him the rest of the day and went through his mind in persistent detail after he was in bed that night. To his disgust, he found that he was going through it, putting in what he would have said if he'd had an opportunity to prepare himself. He wondered how Jacobs would have handled it. Jacobs had a way about him that made people think he knew more than Rayber thought he knew. It was not a bad trick in his profession. Rayber often amused himself analyzing it. Jacobs would have handled the barber calmly enough. Rayber started through the conversation again, thinking how Jacobs would have done it. He ended doing it himself.

The next time he went to the barber's, he had forgotten about the argument. The barber seemed to have forgotten it too. He disposed of the weather and stopped talking. Rayber was wondering what was going to be for supper. Oh. It was Tuesday. On Tuesday his wife had canned meat. Took canned meat and baked it with cheese—slice of meat and a slice of cheese—turned out striped—why do we have to have this stuff every Tuesday?—if you don't like it you don't have to—

"You still a Mother Hubbard?"

Rayber's head jerked. "What?"

"You still for Darmon?"

"Yes," Rayber said and his brain darted to its store of preparations.

"Well, look-a-here, you teachers, you know, looks like, well. . . ." He was confused. Rayber could see that he was not so sure of himself as he'd been the last time. He probably thought he had a new point to stress. "Looks like you fellows would vote for Hawk on account of you know what he said about teachers' salaries. Seems like you would now. Why not? Don't you want more money?"

"More money!" Rayber laughed. "Don't you know that with a rotten governor I'd lose more money than he'd give me?" He realized that he was finally on the barber's level. "Why, he dislikes too many different kinds of people," he said. "He'd cost me twice as much as Darmon."

"So what if he would?" the barber said. "I ain't one to pinch money when it does some good. I'll pay for quality any day."

"That's not what I meant!" Rayber began, "that's not. . . ."

"That raise Hawk's promised don't apply to teachers like him anyway," somebody said from the back of the room. A fat man with an air of executive assurance came over near Rayber. "He's a college teacher, ain't he?"

"Yeah," the barber said, "that's right. He wouldn't get Hawk's raise; but say, he wouldn't get one if Darmon was elected neither."

"Ahh, he'd get something. All the schools are supporting Darmon. They stand to get their cut—free text books or new desks or something. That's the rules of the game."

"Better schools," Rayber sputtered, "benefit everybody."

"Seems like I been hearin' that a long time," the barber said.

"You see," the man explained, "you can't put nothing over on the schools. That's the way they throw it off—benefits everybody."

The barber laughed.

"If you ever thought. . . ." Rayber began.

"Maybe there'd be a new desk at the head of the room for you," the man chortled. "How about that, Joe?" He nudged the barber.

Rayber wanted to lift his foot under the man's chin. "You ever heard about reasoning?" he muttered.

"Listen," the man said, "you can talk all you want. What you don't realize is, we've got an issue here. How'd you like a couple of black faces looking at you from the back of your class room?"

Rayber had a blind moment when he felt as if something that wasn't there was bashing him to the ground. George came in and began washing basins. "Willing to teach any person willing to learn—black or white," Rayber said. He wondered if George had looked up.

"All right," the barber agreed, "but not mixed up together, huh? How'd you like to go to a white school, George?" he shouted.

"Wouldn't like that," George said. "We needs sommo powders. These here the las' in this box." He dusted them out into the basin.

"Go get some then," the barber said.

"The time has come," the executive went on, "just like

Hawkson said, when we got to sit on the lid with both feet and a mule." He went on to review Hawkson's Fourth of July speech.

Rayber would like to have pushed him into the basin. The day was hot and full enough of flies without having to spend it listening to a fat fool. He could see the courthouse square, blue-green cool, through the tinted glass window. He wished to hell the barber would hurry. He fixed his attention on the square outside, feeling himself there where, he could tell from the trees, the air was moving slightly. A group of men sauntered up the courthouse walk. Rayber looked more closely and thought he recognized Jacobs. But Jacobs had a late afternoon class. It was Jacobs, though. Or was it. If it were, who was he talking to? Blakeley? Or was that Blakeley. He squinted. Three colored boys in zoot suits strolled by on the sidewalk. One dropped down on the pavement so that only his head was visible to Rayber, and the other two lounged over him, leaning against the barber shop window and making a hole in the view. Why the hell can't they park somewhere else? Rayber thought fiercely. "Hurry up," he said to the barber, "I have an appointment."

"What's your hurry?" the fat man said. "You better stay and stick up for Boy Blue."

"You know you never told us why you're gonna vote for him," the barber chuckled, taking the cloth from around Rayber's neck.

"Yeah," the fat man said, "see can you tell us without sayin', goodgovermint."

"I have an appointment," Rayber said. "I can't stay."

"You just know Darmon is so sorry you won't be able to say a good word for him," the fat man howled.

"Listen," Rayber said, "I'll be back in here next week and I'll give you as many reasons for voting for Darmon as you want—better reasons than you've given me for voting for Hawkson."

"I'd like to see you do that," the barber said. "Because I'm telling you, it can't be done."

"All right, we'll see," Rayber said.

"Remember," the fat man carped, "you ain't gonna say, goodgovermint."

"I won't say anything you can't understand," Rayber muttered and then felt foolish for showing his irritation. The fat man and the barber were grinning. "I'll see you Tuesday," Rayber said and left. He was disgusted with himself for saying he would give them reasons. Reasons would have to be worked out—systematically. He couldn't open his head in a second like they did. He wished to hell he could. He wished to hell "Mother Hubbard" weren't so accurate. He wished to hell Darmon spit tobacco juice. The reasons would have to be worked out—time and trouble. What was the matter with him? Why not work them out? He could make everything in that shop squirm if he put his mind to it.

By the time he got home, he had the beginnings of an outline for an argument. It would be filled in with no waste words, no big words—no easy job, he could see.

He got right to work on it. He worked on it until supper time and had four sentences—all crossed out. He got up once in the middle of the meal to go to his desk and change one. After supper he crossed the correction out.

"What is the matter with you?" his wife wanted to know.

"Not a thing," Rayber said, "not a thing. I just have to work."

"I'm not stopping you," she said.

When she went out, he kicked the board loose on the bottom of the desk. By eleven o'clock he had one page. The next morning it came easier, and he finished it by noon. He thought it was blunt enough. It began, "For two reasons, men elect other men to power," and it ended, "Men who use ideas without measuring them are walking on wind." He thought the last sentence was pretty effective. He thought the whole thing was effective enough.

In the afternoon he took it around to Jacobs' office. Blakeley was there but he left. Rayber read the paper to Jacobs.

"Well," Jacobs said, "so what? What do you call yourself doing?" He had been jotting figures down on a record sheet all the time Rayber was reading.

Rayber wondered if he were busy. "Defending myself against barbers," he said. "You ever tried to argue with a barber?"

"I never argue," Jacobs said.

"That's because you don't know this kind of ignorance," Rayber explained. "You've never experienced it."

Jacobs snorted. "Oh, yes I have," he said.

"What happened?"

"I never argue."

"But you know you're right," Rayber persisted.

"I never argue."

"Well, I'm going to argue," Rayber said. "I'm going to say the right thing as fast as they can say the wrong. It'll be a question of speed. Understand," he went on, "this is no mission of conversion; I'm defending myself."

"I understand that," Jacobs said. "I hope you're able to do it."

"I've already done it! You read the paper. There it is." Rayber wondered if Jacobs were dense or preoccupied.

"Okay, then leave it there. Don't spoil your complexion arguing with barbers."

"It's got to be done," Rayber said.

Jacobs shrugged.

Rayber had counted on discussing it with him at length. "Well, I'll see you," he said.

"Okay," Jacobs said.

Rayber wondered why he had ever read the paper to him in the first place.

Before he left for the barber's Tuesday afternoon, Rayber was nervous and he thought that by way of practice, he'd try the paper out on his wife. He didn't know but what she was for Hawkson herself. Whenever he mentioned the election, she made it a point to say, "Just because you teach doesn't mean you know everything." Did he ever say he knew anything at all? Maybe he wouldn't call her. But he wanted to hear how the thing was actually going to sound said casually. It wasn't long; wouldn't take up much of her time. She would probably dislike being called. Still, she might possibly be affected by what he said. Possibly. He called her.

She said all right, but he'd just have to wait until she got through what she was doing; it looked like every time she got her hands in something, she had to leave and go do something else.

He said he didn't have all day to wait—it was only forty-five minutes until the shop closed—and would she please hurry up?

She came in wiping her hands and said all right; all right, she was there, wasn't she? Go ahead.

He began saying it very easily and casually, looking over her head. The sound of his voice playing over the words was not bad. He wondered if it were the words themselves or his tones that made them sound the way they did. He paused in the middle of a sentence and glanced at his wife to see if her face would give him any clue. Her head was turned slightly toward the table by her chair where an open magazine was lying. As he paused, she got up. "That was very nice," she said and went back to the kitchen. Rayber left for the barber's.

He walked slowly, thinking what he was going to say in the shop and now and then stopping to look absently at a store window. Block's Feed Company had a display of automatic chicken-killers—"So Timid Persons Can Kill Their Own Fowl" the sign over them read. Rayber wondered if many timid persons used them. As he neared the barber's, he could see obliquely through the door the man with the executive assurance was sitting in the corner reading a newspaper. Rayber went in and hung up his hat.

"Howdy," the barber said; "ain't this the hottest day in the year, though!"

"It's hot enough," Rayber said.

"Hunting season soon be over," the barber commented.

All right, Rayber wanted to say, let's get this thing going. He thought he would work into his argument from their remarks. The fat man hadn't noticed him.

"You should have seen the covey this dog of mine flushed the other day," the barber went on as Rayber got in the chair. "The birds spread once and we got four and they spread again and we got two. That ain't bad."

"Never hunted quail," Rayber said hoarsely.

"There ain't nothing like taking a nigger and a hound dog and a gun and going after quail," the barber said. "You missed a lot out of life if you ain't had that."

Rayber cleared his throat and the barber went on working.

The fat man in the corner turned a page. What do they think I came in here for? Rayber thought. They couldn't have forgotten. He waited, hearing the noises flies make and the mumble of the men talking in the back. The fat man turned another page. Rayber could hear George's broom slowly stroking the floor somewhere in the shop, then stop, then scrape, then. . . . "You er, still a Hawkson man?" Rayber asked the barber.

"Yeah!" the barber laughed. "Yeah! You know I had forgot. You was gonna tell us why you are voting for Darmon. Hey Roy!" he yelled to the fat man, "come over here. We gonna hear why we should vote for Boy Blue."

Roy grunted and turned another page. "Be there when I finish this piece," he mumbled.

"What you got there, Joe?" one of the men in the back called, "one of them goodgovermint boys?"

"Yeah," the barber said. "He's gonna make a speech."

"I've heard too many of that kind already," the man said.

"You ain't heard one by Rayber," the barber said. "Rayber's all right. He don't know how to vote, but he's all right."

Rayber reddened. Two of the men strolled up. "This is no speech," Rayber said. "I only want to discuss it with you—sanely."

"Come on over here, Roy," the barber yelled.

"What are you trying to make of this?" Rayber muttered; then he said suddenly, "if you're calling everybody else, why don't you call your boy, George. You afraid to have him listen?"

The barber looked at Rayber for a second without saying anything.

Rayber felt as if he had made himself too much at home.

"He can hear," the barber said. "He can hear back where he is."

"I just thought he might be interested," Rayber said.

"He can hear," the barber repeated. "He can hear what he hears and he can hear two times that much. He can hear what you don't say as well as what you do."

Roy came over folding his newspaper. "Howdy boy," he said, putting his hand on Rayber's head, "let's get on with this speech."

Rayber felt as if he were fighting his way out of a net. They were over him with their red faces grinning. He heard the words drag out—"Well, the way I see it, men elect. . . ." He felt them pull out of his mouth like freight cars, jangling, backing up on each other, grating to a halt, sliding, clinching back, jarring, and then suddenly stopping as roughly as they had begun. It was over. Rayber was jarred that it was over so soon. For a second—as if they were expecting him to go on—no one said anything.

Then, "How many yawl gonna vote for Boy Blue!" the barber yelled.

Some of the men turned around and snickered. One doubled over.

"Me," Roy said. "I'm gonna run right down there now so I'll be first to vote for Boy Blue tomorrow morning."

"Listen!" Rayber shouted, "I'm not trying. . . ."

"George," the barber yelled, "you heard that speech?"

"Yessir," George said.

"Who you gonna vote for, George?"

"I'm not trying to. . . ." Rayber yelled.

"I don't know is they gonna let me vote," George said. "Do, I gonna vote for Mr. Hawkson."

"Listen!" Rayber yelled, "do you think I'm trying to change your fat minds? What do you think I am?" He jerked the barber around by the shoulder. "Do you think I'd tamper with your damn fool ignorance?"

The barber shook Rayber's grip off his shoulder. "Don't get excited," he said, "we all thought it was a fine speech. That's what I been saying all along—you got to think, you got to. . . ." He lurched backward when Rayber hit him, and landed sitting on the foot rest of the next chair. "Thought it was fine," he finished, looking steadily at Rayber's white, half-lathered face glaring down at him. "It's what I been saying all along."

The blood began pounding up Rayber's neck just under his skin. He turned and pushed quickly through the men around him to the door. Outside, the sun was suspending everything in a pool of heat and before he had turned the first corner, almost running, lather began to drip inside his collar and down the barber's bib, dangling to his knees.

Wildcat

OLD GABRIEL shuffled across the room waving his stick slowly sideways in front of him.

"Who that?" he whispered appearing in the doorway. "I smells fo' niggers."

Their soft, minor-toned laughter rose above the frog's hum and blended into voices.

"Cain't you do no bettern that, Gabe?"

"Is you goin' with us, Granpaw?"

"You oughter be able to smell good enough to git our names."

Old Gabriel moved out on the porch a little way. "That Matthew an' George an' Willie Myrick. An' who that other?"

"This Boon Williams, Granpaw."

Gabriel felt for the edge of the porch with his stick. "What yawl doin'? Set down a spell."

"We waitin' on Mose an' Luke."

"We goin' huntin' that cat."

"What yawl huntin' him with?" old Gabriel muttered. "Yawl ain't got nothin' fit to kill a wildcat with." He sat down on the edge of the porch and hung his feet over the side. "I done tol' Mose an' Luke that."

"How many wildcats you killed, Gabrul?" Their voices, rising to him through the darkness, were full of gentle mockery.

"When I was a boy, there was a cat once," Gabriel started. "It come 'round here huntin' blood. Come in through the winder of a cabin one night an' sprung in bed with a nigger an' tore that nigger's throat open befo' he could holler good."

"This cat in the woods, Granpaw. It jus' come out to git cows. Jupe Williams seen it when he gone through to the sawmill."

"What he done about it?"

"Started runnin'." Their laughter broke over the night sounds again. "He thought it was after him."

"It was," old Gabriel murmured.

"It after cows."

Gabriel sniffed. "It comin' out the woods for mo' than cows. It gonna git itssef some folkes blood. You watch. An' yawl goin' off huntin' it ain't gonna do no good. It goin' huntin' itssef. I been smellin' it."

"How you know that it you smellin'?"

"Ain't no mistakin' a wildcat. Ain't been one 'round here since I was a boy. Why don't yawl set a spell?" he added.

"You ain't afraid to stay here by yosef, is you, Granpaw?"

Old Gabriel stiffened. He felt for the post to pull himself up on. "Ef you waitin' on Mose an' Luke," he said, "you better git goin'. They started over to yawl's place an hour ago."

II

"Come in here, I say! Come in here right now!"

The blind boy sat alone on the steps, staring ahead. "All the men gone?" he called.

"All gone but ol' Hezuh. Come in."

He hated to go in—among the women.

"I smells it," he said.

"You come in here, Gabriel."

He went in and walked to where the window was. The women were muttering at him.

"You stay in here, boy."

"You be 'tractin' that cat right in this room, settin' out there."

No air was coming through the window, and he scratched at the shutter latch to open it.

"Don't open that winder, boy. Us don't want no wildcat jumpin' in here."

"I could er gone wit 'em," he said sullenly. "I could er smelled it out. I ain't afraid." Shut up wit these women like he one too.

"Reba say she kin smell it herself."

He heard the old woman groan in the corner. "They ain't gonna do no good out huntin' it," she whined. "It here. It right around here. Ef it jump in this room it gonna git me fust, then it gonna git that boy, then it gonna git. . . ."

"Hush yo' mouth, Reba," he heard his mother say. "I look after my boy."

He could look after hissef. He warn't afraid. He could

smell it—him an' Reba could. It'd jump on them fust; fust Reba an' then him. It was the shape of a reg'lar cat only bigger, his mother said. An' where you felt the sharp points on a house cat's foot, you felt big knife-claws in a wildcat's, an' knife teeth, too; an' it breathed heat an' spit wet lime. Gabriel could feel its claws in his shoulders and its teeth in his throat. But he wouldn't let 'em stay there. He'd lock his arms 'round its body an' feel up for its neck an' jerk its head back an' go down wit it on the floor until its claws dropped away from his shoulders. Beat, beat, beat its head, beat, beat beat . . .

"Who wit ol' Hezuh?" one of the women asked.

"Jus' Nancy."

"Oughter be somebody else down there," his mother said softly.

Reba moaned. "Anybody go out gonna git sprung on befo' they gits there. It around here, I say. It gittin' closer an' closer. It gonna git me sho'."

He could smell it strong.

"How it gonna git in here? Yawl jus' frettin' for nothin'."

That was Thin Minnie. Nothin' could git her. She'd had a spell on her since when she was small—put there by a conjer woman.

"It come in easy ef it wanter," Reba snorted. "It tear up that cat-hole an' come through."

"We could be down to Nancy's by then," Minnie sniffed.

"Yawl could," the old woman muttered.

Him an' her couldn't, he knew. But he'd stay an' fight it. You see that blin' boy there? He the one kill the wildcat!

Reba started groaning.

"Hush that!" his mother ordered.

The groaning turned into singing—low in her throat.

> "Lord, Lord,
> Gonna see yo' pilgrim today.
> Lord, Lord,
> Gonna see yo' . . ."

"Hush!" his mother hissed. "What that I hear?"

Gabriel leaned forward in the silence; stiff, ready.

It was a thump, thump and maybe a snarl, away, muffled, and then a shriek, far away, then louder and louder, closer and closer, over the edge of the hill into the yard and up on the porch. The cabin was shaking with the weight of a body against the door. There was the feel of a rush inside the room and the scream was let in. Nancy!

"It got him!" she screamed. "Got him, sprung in through the winder, got him in the throat. Hezuh," she wailed, "ol' Hezuh."

Later in the night the men returned, carrying a rabbit and two squirrels.

III

Old Gabriel crept back through the darkness to his bed. He could sit in the chair a while or he could lie down. He eased down in the bed and pushed his nose into the feel and smell of the quilt. They won't no use to do that. He could smell the other jus' the same. He had been smellin' it, been smellin' it ever since they started talkin' about it. There it was one evenin'—different from all the smells around, different from niggers' and cows' an' ground smells. Wildcat. Tull Williams seen it jump on a bull.

Gabriel sat up suddenly. It was nearer. He got out the bed and pushed to the door. He had bolted that one; the other must be open. A breeze was coming in and he walked in it until he felt the night air full in his face. This one was open. He slammed it shut and pushed the bolt in. What was the use to do that? Ef the cat aimed on comin' in, it could git there. He went back to the chair and sat down. It come in easy ef it wanta. There were little draughts all around him. By the door there was a hole the hound could git under; that cat could gnaw it through an' be in befo' he got out. Maybe ef he sat by the back do', he could git away quicker. He got up and dragged his chair after him across the room. The smell was near. Maybe he'd count. He could count to a thousand. Won't no nigger for five miles could count that fur. He started counting.

Mose an' Luke wouldn't be back for six hours yet. Tomorrow night they wouldn't go; but the cat was gonna git him tonight. Lemme go wit you boys an' smell him out for you. I the onliest one kin smell 'round here.

They'd lose him in the woods, they'd said. Huntin' wild-cats won't no business for him.

I ain't afraid er no wildcat er no woods neither. Lemme go wit you boys, lemme go.

Ain't no reason to be 'fraid to stay here by yosef, they'd laughed. Ain't nothin' gonna git you. We take you up the road to Mattie's ef you scaird.

Mattie's! Take him to Mattie's! Settin' wit the women. What yawl think I is? I ain't afraid er no wildcat. But it comin', boys; an' it ain't gonna be in no woods—it gonna be here. Yawl wastin' yo' time in the woods. Stay here an' you ketch it.

He suppose to be countin'. Where he lef' off at? Five hunnert an' five, five hunnert an' six . . . Mattie's! What they think he is? Five hunnert an' two, five hunnert an'. . . .

He sat stiff in the chair with his hands gripped tight to the stick across his knees. It won't gonna git him like he was a woman. His shirt was stuck wet to him, making him smell higher. The men had come back later in the night with a rabbit and two squirrels. He began to remember the other wildcat and he remembered as if he had been in Hezuh's cabin instead of with the women. He wondered was he Hezuh. He was Gabrul. It won't gonna git him like Hezuh. He was gonna hit it. He was gonna pull it off. He was gonna . . . how he gonna do all that? He hadn't been able to wring a chicken's neck for fo' years. It was gonna git him. Won't nothin' to do but wait. The smell was near. Won't nothin' for old people to do but wait. It was gonna git him tonight. The teeth would be hot an' the claws cold. The claws would sink in soft, an' the teeth would cut sharp an' scrape his bones inside.

Gabriel felt the sweat on himself. It kin smell me good's I kin smell it, he thought. I settin' here smellin' an' it comin' here smellin'. Two hunnert an' fo'; where he lef' off at? Fo' hunnert an' five. . . .

There was a sudden scratching by the chimney. He sat forward, tense, tight-throated. "Come on," he whispered, "I here. I waitin'." He couldn't move. He couldn't make himself move. There was another scratching. It was the pain he didn't want. But he didn't want the waiting either. "I here," he—

there was another, just a small noise and then a flutter. Bats. His grip on the stick loosened. He should have known that won't it. It won't no farther than the barn yet. What ail his nose? What ail him? Won't no nigger for hunnert miles could smell like he could. He heard the scratching again, coming differently, coming from the corner of the house where the cat hole was. Pick . . pick . . pick. That was a bat. He knowd that was a bat. Pick . . . pick. "Here I is," he whispered. Won't no bat. He braced his feet to get up. Pick. "Lord waitin' on me," he whispered. "He don't want me with my face tore open. Why don't you go on, Wildcat, why you want me?" He was on his feet now. "Lord don't want me with no wildcat marks." He was moving toward the cat hole. Across on the river bank the Lord was waiting on him with a troup of angels and golden vestments for him to put on and when he came, he'd put on the vestments and stand there with the Lord and the angels, judging life. Won't no nigger for fifty miles fitter to judge than him. Pick. He stopped. He smelled it right outside, nosing the hole. He had to climb onto something! What he going toward it for? He had to get on something high! There was a shelf nailed over the chimney and he turned wildly and fell against a chair and shoved it up to the fire place. He caught hold of the shelf and pulled himself onto the chair and sprang up and backwards and felt the narrow shelf board under him for an instant and then felt it sag and jerked his feet up and felt it crack somewhere from the wall. His stomach flew inside him and stopped hard and the shelf board fell across his feet and the rung of the chair hit against his head and then, after a second of stillness, he heard a low, gasping animal cry wail over two hills and fade past him; then snarls, tearing short, furious, through the pain wails. Gabriel sat stiff on the floor.

"Cow," he breathed finally. "Cow."

Gradually he felt his muscles loosen. It got to her befo' him. It would go on off now, but it would be back tomorrer night. He rose shaking from the chair and stumbled to his bed. The cat had been a half mile away. He won't sharp like he used to be. They shouldn't leave old people by theyselves. He done tole 'em they won't gonna ketch nothin' off in no woods. Tomorrer night it would come back. Tomorrer night they would stay here an' kill it. Now he want to sleep. He done tole 'em they couldn't get no wildcat in no woods. He the one tole 'em where it gonna be. They'd a listened to him, they'd done had it by now. When he die he want to be sleepin' in a bed; didn't want to be on no floor with a wildcat stuck in his face. Lord waitin'.

When he woke up, the darkness was full of morning things. He heard Mose and Luke at the stove and smelled the side meat in the skillet. He reached for his snuff and filled his lip. "What yawl ketch?" he asked trenchantly.

"Ain't caught nothin' las' night." Luke put the plate in his hands. "Here yo' side meat. How you bust that shelf?"

"Ain't busted no shelf," old Gabriel muttered. "Wind to' it down and waked me up in the middle of the night. It been due to fall. You ain't never built nothin' yet stayed together."

"We sot a trap," Mose said. "We git that cat tonight."

"Yawl sho will, boys," Gabriel said. "It'll be right here to-night. Ain't it done kill a cow a half a mile from here las' night?"

"That don't mean it comin' this way," Luke said.

"It comin' this way," Gabriel said.

"How many wildcats you killed, Granpaw?"

Gabriel stopped; the plate of side meat tremored in his hand. "I knows what I knows, boy."

"We git it soon. We sot a trap over in Ford's Woods. It been around there. We goin' up in a tree over the trap every night an' wait 'til we gits it."

Their forks were scraping back and forth over their tin plates like knife-teeth against stone.

"You wants sommo' side meat, Granpaw?"

Gabriel put his fork down on the quilt. "No, boy," he said, "no mo' side meat." The darkness was hollow around him and through its depth, animal cries wailed and mingled with the beats pounding in his throat.

The Crop

Miss Willerton always crumbed the table. It was her particular household accomplishment and she did it with great thoroughness. Lucia and Bertha did the dishes and Garner went into the parlor and did the Morning Press crossword puzzle. That left Miss Willerton in the dining room by herself and that was all right with Miss Willerton. Whew! Breakfast in that house was always an ordeal. Lucia insisted that they have a regular hour for breakfast just like they did for other meals. Lucia said a regular breakfast made for other regular habits, and with Garner's tendency to upsets, it was imperative that they establish some system in their eating. This way she could also see that he put the Agar-Agar on his Cream-of-Wheat. As if, Miss Willerton thought, after having done it for fifty years, he'd be capable of doing anything else. The breakfast dispute always started with Garner's Cream-of-Wheat and ended with her three spoonfuls of pineapple crush. "You know your acid, Willie," Miss Lucia would always say, "you know your acid;" and then Garner would roll his eyes and make some sickening remark and Bertha would jump and Lucia would look distressed and Miss Willerton would taste the pineapple crush she had already swallowed.

It was a relief to crumb the table. Crumbing the table gave one time to think and if Miss Willerton were going to write a story, she had to think about it first. She could usually think best sitting in front of her typewriter, but this would do for the time being. First, she had to think of a subject to write a story about. There were so many subjects to write stories about that Miss Willerton never could think of one. That was always the hardest part of writing a story she always said. She spent more time thinking of something to write about than she did writing. Sometimes she discarded subject after subject and it usually took her a week or two to decide finally on something. Miss Willerton got out the silver crumber and the crumb-catcher and started stroking the table. I wonder, she mused, if a baker would make a good subject? Foreign bakers were very picturesque, she thought. Aunt Myrtile Filmer had left her four color-tints of French bakers in mushroom-looking hats. They were great tall fellows—blond and. . . .

"Willie!" Miss Lucia screamed, entering the dining room with the salt-cellars. "For heaven's sake, hold the catcher under the crumber or you'll have those crumbs on the rug. I've Bisseled it four times in the last week and I am not going to do it again."

"You have not Bisseled it on account of any crumbs I have spilled," Miss Willerton said tersely. "I always pick up the crumbs I drop," and she added, "I drop relatively few."

"And wash the crumber before you put it up this time," Miss Lucia returned.

Miss Willerton drained the crumbs into her hand and threw them out the window. She took the catcher and crumber to the kitchen and ran them under the cold-water faucet. She dried them and stuck them back in the drawer. That was over. Now she could get to the typewriter. She could stay there until dinner time.

Miss Willerton sat down at her typewriter and let out her breath. Now! What had she been thinking about? Oh. Bakers. Hmmm. Bakers. No, bakers wouldn't do. Hardly colorful enough. No social tension connected with bakers. Miss Willerton sat staring through her typewriter. A S D F G—her eyes wandered over the keys. Hmmm. Teachers? Miss Willerton wondered. No. Heavens no. Teachers always made Miss Willerton feel peculiar. Her teachers at Willowpool Seminary had been all right but they were women. Willowpool Female Seminary, Miss Willerton remembered. She didn't like the phrase, Willowpool Female Seminary—it sounded biological. She always just said she was a graduate of Willowpool. Men teachers made Miss Willerton feel as if she were going to mispronounce something. Teachers weren't timely anyhow. They weren't even a social problem.

Social problem. Social problem. Hmmm. Sharecroppers! Miss Willerton had never been intimately connected with sharecroppers but, she reflected, they would make as arty a subject as any, and they would give her that air of social concern which was so valuable to have in the circles she was hoping to travel! "I can always capitalize," she muttered, "on the hookworm." It was coming to her now! Certainly! Her fingers plinked excitedly over the keys, never touching them. Then suddenly she began typing at great speed.

"Lot Motun," the typewriter registered, "called his dog." "Dog" was followed by an abrupt pause. Miss Willerton always did her best work on the first sentence. "First sentences," she always said, "came to her—like a flash! Just like a flash!" she would say and snap her fingers, "like a flash!" And she built her story up from them. "Lot Motun called his dog" had been automatic with Miss Willerton, and reading the sentence over, she decided that not only was "Lot Motun" a good name for a sharecropper, but also that having him call his dog was an excellent thing to have a sharecropper do. "The dog pricked up its ears and slunk over to Lot." Miss Willerton had the sentence down before she realized her error—two "Lots" in one paragraph. That was displeasing to the ear. The typewriter grated back and Miss Willerton applied three x's to "Lot." Over it she wrote in pencil, "him." Now she was ready to go again. "Lot Motun called his dog. The dog pricked up its ears and slunk over to him." Two dogs, too, Miss Willerton thought. Ummm. But that didn't affect the ears like two "Lots," she decided.

Miss Willerton was a great believer in what she called, "phonetic art." She maintained that the ear was as much a reader as the eye. She liked to express it that way. "The eye forms a picture," she had told a group at the United Daughters of the Colonies, "that can be painted in the abstract, and the success of a literary venture (Miss Willerton liked the phrase, "literary venture") depends on the abstract created in the mind and the tonal quality (Miss Willerton also liked, "tonal quality") registered in the ear." There was something biting and sharp about "Lot Motun called his dog," followed by, "the dog pricked up its ears and slunk over to him," it gave the paragraph just the send-off it needed.

"He pulled the animal's short, scraggy ears and rolled over with it in the mud." Perhaps, Miss Willerton mused, that would be overdoing it. But a sharecropper, she knew, might reasonably be expected to roll over in the mud. Once she had read a novel dealing with that kind of people in which they had done just as bad and, throughout three-fourths of the narrative, much worse. Lucia found it in cleaning out one of Miss Willerton's bureau drawers and after glancing at a few random pages, took it between thumb and index finger to the furnace and threw it in. "When I was cleaning your bureau out this morning, Willie, I found a book that Garner must have put there for a joke," Miss Lucia told her later. "It was awful, but you know how Garner is. I burned it." And then tittering she added, "I was sure it couldn't be yours." Miss Willerton was sure it could be none other's than hers but she hesitated in claiming the distinction. She had ordered it from the publisher because she didn't want to ask for it at the library. It had cost her $3.75 with the postage and she had not finished the last four chapters. At least, she had got enough from it, though, to be able to say that Lot Motun might reasonably roll over in the mud with his dog. Having him do that would give more point to the hookworm, too, she decided. "Lot Motun called his dog. The dog pricked up its ears and slunk over to him. He pulled the animal's short, scraggy ears and rolled over with it in the mud."

Miss Willerton settled back. That was a good beginning. Now she would plan her action. There had to be a woman, of course. Perhaps Lot could kill her. That type of woman always started trouble. She might even goad him on to kill her because of her wantonness and then he would be pursued by his conscience maybe.

He would have to have principles if that were going to be the case, but it would be fairly easy to give him those. Now how was she going to work that in with all the love interest there'd have to be, she wondered. There would have to be some quite violent, naturalistic scenes, the sadistic sort of thing one read of in connection with that class. It was a problem. However, Miss Willerton enjoyed such problems. She liked to plan passionate scenes best of all but when she came to write them, she always began to feel peculiar and to wonder what the family would say when they read them. Garner would snap his fingers and wink at her at every opportunity; Bertha would think she was terrible; and Lucia would say in that silly voice of hers, "What have you been keeping from us, Willie? What have you been keeping from us?" and titter like she always did. But Miss Willerton couldn't think about that now; she had to plan her characters.

Lot would be tall, stooped, and shaggy but with sad eyes that made him look like a gentleman in spite of his red neck and big fumbling hands. He'd have straight teeth and, to indicate that he had some spirit, red hair. His clothes would hang on him but he'd wear them nonchalantly like they were part of his skin; maybe, she mused, he'd better not roll over with the dog after all. The woman would be more or less pretty—yellow hair, fat ankles, muddy-colored eyes.

She would get supper for him in the cabin and he'd sit there eating the lumpy grits she hadn't bothered to put salt in and thinking about something big something way off— another cow, a painted house, a clean well, a farm of his own even. The woman would yowl at him for not cutting enough wood for her stove and would whine about the pain in her back. She'd sit and stare at him eating the sour grits and say he didn't have nerve enough to steal food. "You're just a damn beggar!" she'd sneer. Then he'd tell her to keep quiet. "Shut your mouth!" he'd shout, "I've taken all I'm gonna." She'd roll her eyes mocking him and laugh—"I ain't afraid er nothin' that looks like you." Then he'd push his chair behind him and head toward her. She'd snatch a knife off the table— Miss Willerton wondered what kind of a fool the woman was—and back away holding it in front of her. He'd lunge forward but she'd dart from him like a wild horse. Then they'd face each other again—their eyes brimming with hate—and sway back and forth. Miss Willerton could hear the seconds dropping on the tin roof outside. He'd dart at her again but she'd have the knife ready and would plunge it into him in an instant—Miss Willerton could stand it no longer. She struck the woman a terrific blow on the head from behind. The knife dropped out of her hands and a mist swept her from the room. Miss Willerton turned to Lot. "Let me get you some hot grits," she said. She went over to the stove and got a clean plate of smooth white grits and a piece of butter.

"Gee, thanks," Lot said and smiled at her with his nice

teeth. "You always fix 'em just right. You know," he said, "I been thinkin'—we could get out of this tenant farm. We could have a decent place. If we made anything this year over, we could put it in a cow an' start buildin' things up. Think what it would mean, Willie. Just think."

She sat down beside him and put her hand on his shoulder. "We'll do it," she said. "We'll make better than we've made any year and by spring, we should have us that cow."

"You always know how I feel, Willie," he said. "You always have known."

They sat there for a long time thinking of how well they understood each other. "Finish your food," she said finally.

After he had eaten, he helped her take the ashes out the stove and then, in the hot July evening, they walked down the pasture toward the creek and talked about the place they were going to have some day.

When late March came and the rainy season was almost there, they had accomplished almost more than was believable. For the past month, Lot had been up every morning at five, and Willie an hour earlier to get in all the work they could while the weather was clear. Next week, Lot said, the rain would probably start and if they didn't get the crop in by then, they would lose it—and all they had gained in the past months. They knew what that meant—another year of getting along with no more than they'd had the last. Then too, there'd be a baby next year instead of a cow. Lot had wanted the cow anyway. "Children don't cost all that much to feed," he'd argued, "an' the cow would help feed him," but Willie had been firm—the cow could come later—the child must have a good start. "Maybe," Lot had said finally, "we'll have enough for both," and he had gone out to look at the new-plowed ground as if he could count the harvest from the furrows.

Even with as little as they'd had, it had been a good year. Willie had cleaned the shack, and Lot had fixed the chimney. There was a profusion of petunias by the doorstep and a colony of snap-dragons under the window. It had been a peaceful year. But now they were becoming anxious over the crop. They must gather it before the rain. "We need another week,"

Lot muttered when he came in that night. "One more week an' we can do it. Do you feel like gatherin'? It isn't right that you should have to," he sighed, "but I can't hire any help."

"I'm all right," she said, hiding her trembling hands behind her. "I'll gather."

"It's cloudy tonight," Lot said darkly.

The next day they worked until nightfall—worked until they could work no longer and then stumbled back to the cabin and fell into bed.

Willie woke in the night conscious of a pain. It was a soft, green pain with purple lights running through it. She wondered if she were awake. Her head rolled from side to side and there were droning shapes grinding boulders in it.

Lot sat up. "Are you bad off?" he asked trembling.

She raised herself on her elbow and then sank down again. "Get Anna up by the creek," she gasped.

The droning became louder and the shapes grayer. The pain intermingled with them for seconds first, then interminably. It came again and again. The sound of the droning grew more distinct and toward morning, she realized that it was rain. Later she asked hoarsely, "How long has it been raining?"

"Most two days, now," Lot answered.

"Then we lost." Willie looked listlessly out at the dripping trees. "It's over."

"It isn't over," he said softly. "We got a daughter."

"You wanted a son."

"No, I got what I wanted—two Willies instead of one— that's better than a cow, even," he grinned. "What can I do to deserve all I got, Willie?" He bent over and kissed her forehead.

"What can I?" she asked slowly. "And what can I do to help you more?"

"How about your going to the grocery, Willie?"

Miss Willerton shoved Lot away from her. "W-what did you say, Lucia?" she stuttered.

"I said how about your going to the grocery this time? I've been every morning this week and I'm busy now."

Miss Willerton pushed back from the typewriter. "Very well," she said sharply. "What do you want there?"

"A dozen eggs and two pounds of tomatoes—ripe tomatoes—and you'd better start doctoring that cold right now. Your eyes are already watering and you're hoarse. There's empirin in the bathroom. Write a check on the house for the groceries. And wear your coat. It's cold."

Miss Willerton rolled her eyes upward. "I am forty-four years old," she announced, "and able to take care of myself."

"And get ripe tomatoes," Miss Lucia returned.

Miss Willerton, her coat buttoned unevenly, tramped up Broad Street and into the Super Market. "What was it now?" she muttered. "Two dozen eggs and a pound of tomatoes, yes." She passed the lines of canned vegetables and the crackers and headed for the box where the eggs were kept. But there were no eggs. "Where are the eggs?" she asked a boy weighing snapbeans.

"We ain't got nothin' but pullet eggs," he said fishing up another handful of beans.

"Well where are they and what is the difference?" Miss Willerton demanded.

He threw several beans back into the bin, slouched over to the egg box and handed her a carton. "There ain't no difference really," he said pushing his gum over his front teeth, "a teen-age chicken or somethin', I don't know. You want 'em?"

"Yes, and two pounds of tomatoes. Ripe tomatoes," Miss Willerton added. She did not like to do the shopping. There was no reason those clerks should be so condescending. That boy wouldn't have dwaddled with Lucia. She paid for the eggs and tomatoes and left hurriedly. The place depressed her somehow.

Silly that a grocery should depress one—nothing in it but trifling domestic doings—women buying beans—riding children in those grocery go-carts—higgling about an eighth of a pound more or less of squash—what did they get out of it? Miss Willerton wondered. Where was there any chance for self-expression, for creation, for art? All around her it was the same—sidewalks full of people scurrying about with their hands full of little packages and their minds full of little packages—that woman there with the child on the leash, pulling him, jerking him, dragging him away from a window with a jack-o-lantern in it; she would probably be pulling and jerking him the rest of her life. And there was another, dropping a shopping bag all over the street, and another wiping a child's nose, and up the street an old woman was coming with three grandchildren jumping all over her, and behind them was a couple walking too close for refinement.

Miss Willerton looked at the couple sharply as they came nearer and passed. The woman was plump with yellow hair and fat ankles and muddy-colored eyes. She had on high-heel pumps and blue anklets, a too-short cotton dress, and a plaid jacket. Her skin was mottled and her neck thrust forward as if she were sticking it out to smell something that was always being drawn away. Her face was set in an inane grin. The man was long and wasted and shaggy. His shoulders were stooped and there were yellow knots along the side of his large, red neck. His hands fumbled stupidly with the girl's as they slumped along, and once or twice he smiled sickly at her and Miss Willerton could see that he had straight teeth and sad eyes and a rash over his forehead.

"Ugh," she shuddered.

Miss Willerton laid the groceries on the kitchen table and went back to her typewriter. She looked at the paper in it. "Lot Motun called his dog," it read. "The dog pricked up its ears and slunk over to him. He pulled the animal's short, scraggy ears and rolled over with it in the mud."

"That sounds awful!" Miss Willerton muttered. "It's not a good subject anyway," she decided. She needed something more colorful—more arty. Miss Willerton looked at her typewriter for a long time. Then of a sudden her fist hit the desk in several ecstatic little bounces. "The Irish!" she squealed, "the Irish!" Miss Willerton had always admired the Irish. Their brogue, she thought, was full of music; and their history—splendid! And the people, she mused, the Irish people! They were full of spirit—red-haired, with broad shoulders and great, drooping mustaches.

The Turkey

H<small>IS GUNS GLINTED</small> sun steel in the ribs of the tree and, half-aloud through a crack in his mouth, he growled, "All right, Mason, this is as far as you go. The jig's up." The six-shooters in Mason's belt stuck out like waiting rattlers but he flipped them into the air and when they fell at his feet, kicked them behind him like so many dried steer skulls. "You varmit," he muttered, drawing his rope tight around the captured man's ankles, "this is the last rustlin' you'll do." He took three steps backward and leveled one gun to his eye. "Okay," he said with cold, slow precision, "This is. . . ." And then he saw it, just moving slightly through the bushes farther over, a touch of bronze and a rustle and then, through another gap in the leaves, the eye, set in red folds that covered the head and hung down along the neck, trembling slightly. He stood perfectly still and the turkey took another step, then stopped, with one foot lifted, and listened.

If he only had a gun, if he only had a gun! He could level aim and shoot it right where it was. In a second, it would slide through the bushes and be up in a tree before he could tell which direction it had gone in. Without moving his head, he strained his eyes to the ground to see if there were a stone near, but the ground looked as if it might just have been swept. The turkey moved again. The foot that had been poised half way up went down and the wing dropped over it, spreading so that Ruller could see the long single feathers, pointed at the end. He wondered if he dived into the bush on top of it. . . . It moved again and the wing came up, again and it went down.

It's limping, he thought quickly. He moved a little nearer, trying to make his motion imperceptible. Suddenly its head pierced out of the bush—he was about ten feet from it—and drew back and then abruptly back into the bush. He began edging nearer with his arms rigid and his fingers ready to clutch. It was lame he could tell. It might not be able to fly. It shot its head out once more and saw him and shuttled back into the bushes and out again on the other side. Its motion was half-lopsided and the left wing was dragging. He was going to get it. He was going to get it if he had to chase it out of the county. He crawled through the brush and saw it about twenty feet away, watching him warily, moving its neck up and down. It stooped and tried to spread its wings and stooped again and went a little way to the side and stooped again, trying to make itself go up; but, he could tell, it couldn't fly. He was going to have it. He was going to have it if he had to run it out of the state. He saw himself going in the front door with it slung over his shoulder, and them all screaming, "Look at Ruller with that wild turkey! Ruller! where did you get that wild turkey!"

Oh, he had caught it in the woods; he had thought they might like to have him catch them one.

"You crazy bird," he muttered, "you can't fly. I've already got you." He was walking in a wide circle, trying to get behind it. For a second, he almost thought he could go pick it up. It had dropped down and one foot was sprawled, but when he got near enough to pounce, it shot off in a heavy speed that made him start. He tore after it, straight out in the open for a half acre of dead cotton; then it went under a fence and into some woods again and he had to get on his hands and knees to get under the fence but still keep his eye on the turkey but not tear his shirt; and then dash after it again with his head a little dizzy, but faster to catch up with it. If he lost it in the woods, it would be lost for good; it was going for the bushes on the other side. It would go on out in the road. He was going to have it. He saw it dart through a thicket and he headed for the thicket and when he got there it darted out again and in a second disappeared under a hedge. He went through the hedge fast and heard his shirt rip and felt cool streaks on his arms where they were getting scratched. He stopped a second and looked down at his torn shirt sleeves but the turkey was only a little ahead of him and he could see it go over the edge of the hill and down again into an open space and he darted on. If he came in with the turkey, they wouldn't pay any attention to his shirt. Hane hadn't ever got a turkey. Hane hadn't ever caught anything. He guessed they'd be knocked out when they saw him; he guessed they'd talk about it in bed. That's what they did about him and Hane. Hane didn't know; he never woke up.

Ruller woke up every night exactly at the time they started talking. He and Hane slept in one room and their mother and father in the next and the door was left open between and every night Ruller listened. His father would say finally, "How are the boys doing?" and their mother would say, Lord, they were wearing her to a frazzle, Lord, she guessed she shouldn't worry but how could she help worrying about Hane, the way he was now? Hane had always been an unusual boy, she said. She said he would grow up to be an unusual man too; and their father said, yes if he didn't get put in the penitentiary first, and their mother said how could he talk that way? and they argued just like Ruller and Hane and sometimes Ruller couldn't get back to sleep for thinking. He always felt tired when he got through listening but he woke up every night and listened just the same and whenever they started talking about him, he sat up in bed so he could hear better. Once his father asked why Ruller played by himself so much and his mother said how was she to know? if he wanted to play by himself, she didn't see any reason he shouldn't; and his father said that worried him and she said well, if that was all he had to worry about, he'd do well to stop; someone told her, she said, that they had seen Hane at the Ever-Ready; hadn't they told him he couldn't go there?

His father asked Ruller the next day what he had been doing lately and Ruller said, "playing by himself," and walked off sort of like he had a limp. He guessed his father had looked pretty worried. He guessed he'd think it was something when he came home with the turkey slung over his shoulder. The turkey was heading out into a road and for a gutter along the side of it. It ran along the gutter and Ruller was gaining on it all the time until he fell over a root sticking up and spilled the things out his pockets and had to snatch them up. When he got up, it was out of sight.

"Bill, you take a posse and go down South Canyon; Joe, you cut around by the gorge and head him off," he shouted to his men. "I'll follow him this way." And he dashed off again along the ditch.

The turkey was in the ditch, not thirty feet from him, lying almost on its neck panting, and he was nearly a yard from it before it darted off again. He chased it straight until the ditch ended and then it went out in the road and slid under a hedge on the other side. He had to stop at the hedge and catch his breath and he could see the turkey on the other side through the leaves, lying on its neck, its whole body moving up and down with the panting. He could see the tip of its tongue going up and down in its opened bill. If he could stick his arm through, he might could get it while it was still too tired to move. He pushed up closer to the hedge and eased his hand through and then gripped it quickly around the turkey's tail. There was no movement from the other side. Maybe the turkey had dropped dead. He put his face close to the leaves to look through. He pushed the twigs aside with one hand but they would not stay. He let go the turkey and pulled his other hand through to hold them. Through the hole he had made, he saw the bird wobbling off drunkenly. He ran back to where the hedge began and got on the other side. He'd get it yet. It needn't think it was so smart, he muttered.

It zigged across the middle of the field and toward the woods again. It couldn't go into the woods! He'd never get it! He dashed behind it, keeping his eyes sharp on it until suddenly something hit his chest and knocked the breath black out of him. He fell back on the ground and forgot the turkey for the cutting in his chest. He lay there for a while with things rocking on either side of him. Finally he sat up. He was facing the tree he had run into. He rubbed his hands over his face and arms and the long scratches began to sting. He would have taken it in slung over his shoulder and they would have jumped up and yelled, "Good Lord look at Ruller! Ruller! Where did you get that wild turkey!" and his father would have said, "Man! That's a bird if I ever saw one!" He kicked a stone away from his foot. He'd never see the turkey now. He wondered why he had seen it in the first place if he wasn't going to be able to get it.

It was like somebody had played a dirty trick on him.

All that running for nothing. He sat there looking sullenly at his white ankles sticking out of his trouser legs and into his shoes. "Nuts," he muttered. He turned over on his stomach and let his cheek rest right on the ground dirty or not. He had torn his shirt and scratched his arms and got a knot on his forehead—he could feel it rising just a little, it was going to be a big one all right—all for nothing. The ground was cool to his face, but the grit bruised it and he had to turn over. Oh hell, he thought.

"Oh hell," he said cautiously.

Then in a minute he said just, "hell."

Then he said it like Hane said it, pulling the e-ull out and trying to get the look in his eye that Hane got. Once Hane said, "God!" and his mother stomped after him and said, "I don't want to hear you say that again. Thou shalt not take the name of the Lord, Thy God, in vain. Do you hear me?" and he guessed that shut Hane up. Ha! He guessed she dressed him off that time.

"God," he said.

He looked studiedly at the ground, making circles in the dust with his finger. "God!" he repeated.

"God dammit," he said softly. He could feel his face getting hot and his chest thumping all of a sudden inside. "God dammit to hell," he said almost inaudibly. He looked over his shoulder but no one was there.

"God dammit to hell, good Lord from Jerusalem," he said. His uncle said, "good Lord from Jerusalem."

"Good Father, good God, sweep the chickens out the yard," he said and began to giggle. His face was very red. He sat up and looked at his white ankles sticking out of his pants legs into his shoes. They looked like they didn't belong to him. He gripped a hand around each ankle and bent his knees up and rested his chin on a knee. "Our Father Who art in heaven, shoot 'em six and roll 'em seven," he said, giggling again. Boy, she'd smack his head in if she could hear him. God dammit, she'd smack his goddam head in. He rolled over in a fit of laughter. God dammit, she'd dress him off and wring his goddam neck like a goddam chicken. The laughing cut his side and he tried to hold it in but every time he thought of his goddam neck, he shook again. He lay back on the ground, red and weak with laughter, not able not to think of her smacking his goddam head in. He said the words over and over to himself and after a while he stopped laughing. He said them again but the laughing had gone out. He said them again but it wouldn't start back up. All that chasing for nothing, he thought again. He might as well go home. What did he want to be sitting around here for? He felt suddenly like he would if people had been laughing at him. Aw, go to hell, he told them. He got up and kicked his foot sharply into somebody's leg and said, "take that, sucker," and turned into the woods to take the short trail home.

And as soon as he got in the door, they would holler, "How did you tear your clothes and where did you get that knot on your forehead?" He was going to say he fell in a hole. What difference would it make? Yeah, God, what difference would it make?

He almost stopped. He had never heard himself think that tone before. He wondered should he take the thought back. He guessed it was pretty bad; but heck, it was the way he felt. He couldn't help feeling that way. Heck . . . hell, it was the way he felt. He guessed he couldn't help that. He walked on a little way, thinking about it. He wondered suddenly if he were going "bad." That's what Hane had done. Hane played pool and smoked cigarets and sneaked in at twelve-thirty and boy he thought he was something. "There's nothing you can do about it," their grandmother had told their father, "he's at that age." What age? Ruller wondered. I'm eleven, he thought. That's pretty young. Hane hadn't started until he was fifteen. I guess it's worse in me, he thought. He wondered would he fight it. Their grandmother had talked to Hane and told him the only way to conquer the devil was to fight him—if he didn't, he couldn't be her boy anymore—Ruller sat down on a stump—and she said she'd give him one more chance, did he want it? and he yelled at her, no! and would she leave him alone? and she told him, well, she loved him even if he didn't love her and he was her boy anyway and so was Ruller. Oh no I ain't Ruller thought quickly. Oh no. She's not pinning any of that stuff on me.

Boy, he could shock the pants off her. He could make her teeth fall in her soup. He started giggling. The next time she asked him if he wanted to play a game of Parcheesi, he'd say, hellno, goddammit, didn't she know any good games? Get out her goddam cards and he'd show her a few. He rolled over on the ground, choking with laughter. "Let's have some booze, kid," he'd say. "Let's get stinky." Boy, he'd knock her out of her socks! He sat on the ground, red and grinning to himself, bursting every now and then into a fresh spasm of giggles. He remembered the minister had said young men were going to the devil by the dozens this day and age; forsaking gentle ways; walking in the tracks of Satan. They would rue the day, he said. There would be weeping and gnashing of teeth. "Weeping," Ruller muttered. Men didn't weep.

How do you gnash your teeth? he wondered. He grated his jaws together and made an ugly face. He did it several times.

He bet he could steal.

He thought about chasing the turkey for nothing. It was a dirty trick. He bet he could be a jewel thief. They were smart. He bet he could have all Scotland Yard on his tail. Hell.

He got up. God could go around sticking things in your face and making you chase them all afternoon for nothing.

You shouldn't think that way about God though.

But that was the way he felt. If that was the way he felt, could he help it? He looked around quickly as if someone might be hiding in the bushes; then suddenly he started.

It was rolled over at the edge of a thicket—a pile of ruffled bronze with a red head lying limp along the ground. Ruller stared at it, unable to think; then he leaned forward suspiciously. He wasn't going to touch it. Why was it there now for him to take? He wasn't going to touch it. It could just lie there. The picture of himself walking in the room with it slung over his shoulder came back to him. Look at Ruller with that turkey! Lord look at Ruller! He squatted down beside it and looked without touching it. He wondered what had been wrong with its wing. He lifted it up by the tip and looked under. The feathers were blood-soaked. It had been shot. It must weigh ten pounds, he figured.

Lord, Ruller! It's a huge turkey! He wondered how it would feel slung over his shoulder. Maybe, he considered, he was supposed to take it.

Ruller gets our turkeys for us. Ruller got it in the woods, chased it dead. Yes, he's a very unusual child.

Ruller wondered suddenly if he were an unusual child.

It came down on him in an instant: he was . . an . . unusual . . . child.

He reckoned he was more unusual than Hane.

He had to worry more than Hane because he knew more how things were.

Sometimes when he was listening at night, he heard them arguing like they were going to kill each other; and the next day his father would go out early and his mother would have the blue veins out on her forehead and look like she was expecting a snake to jump from the ceiling any minute. He guessed he was one of the most unusual children ever. Maybe that was why the turkey was there. He rubbed his hand along the neck. Maybe it was to keep him from going bad. Maybe God wanted to keep him from that.

Maybe God had knocked it out right there where he'd see it when he got up.

Maybe God was in the bush now, waiting for him to make up his mind. Ruller blushed. He wondered if God could think he was a very unusual child. He must. He found himself suddenly blushing and grinning and he rubbed his hand over his face quick to make himself stop. If You want me to take it, he said, I'll be glad to. Maybe finding the turkey was a sign. Maybe God wanted him to be a preacher. He thought of Bing Crosby and Spencer Tracy. He might found a place to stay for boys who were going bad. He lifted the turkey up—it was heavy all right—and fitted it over his shoulder. He wished he could see how he looked with it slung over like that. It occurred to him that he might as well go home the long way—through town. He had plenty of time. He started off slowly, shifting the turkey until it fit comfortably over his shoulder. He remembered the things he had thought before he found the turkey. They were pretty bad, he guessed.

He guessed God had stopped him before it was too late. He should be very thankful. Thank You, he said.

Come on, boys, he said, we will take this turkey back for our dinner. We certainly are much obliged to You, he said to God. This turkey weighs ten pounds. You were mighty generous.

That's okay, God said. And listen, we ought to have a talk about these boys. They're entirely in your hands, see? I'm leaving the job strictly up to you. I have confidence in you, McFarney.

You can trust me, Ruller said. I'll come through with the goods.

He went into town with the turkey over his shoulder. He wanted to do something for God but he didn't know what he could do. If anybody was playing the accordian on the street today, he'd give them his dime. He only had one dime, but he'd give it to them. Maybe he could think of something better, though. He had been going to keep the dime for something. He might could get another one from his grandmother. How about a goddam dime, kid? He pulled his mouth piously out of the grin. He wasn't going to think that way anymore. He couldn't get a dime from her anyway. His mother was going to whip him if he asked his grandmother for money again. Maybe something would turn up that he could do. If God wanted him to do something, he'd turn something up.

He was getting into the business block and through the corner of his eye he noticed people looking at him. There were eight thousand people in Mulrose County and on Saturday every one of them was in Tilford on the business block. They turned as Ruller passed and looked at him. He glanced at himself reflected in a store window, shifted the turkey slightly, and walked quickly ahead. He heard someone call, but he walked on, pretending he was deaf. It was his mother's friend, Alice Gilhard, and if she wanted him, let her catch up with him.

"Ruller!" she cried, "my goodness, where did you get that turkey?" She came up behind him fast and put her hand on his shoulder. "That's some bird," she said. "You must be a good shot."

"I didn't shoot it," Ruller said coldly. "I captured it. I chased it dead."

"Heavens," she said. "You wouldn't capture me one sometime would you?"

"I might if I ever have time," Ruller said. She thought she was so cute.

Two men came over and whistled at the turkey. They yelled at some other men on the corner to look. Another of his mother's friends stopped and some country boys who had been sitting on the curb got up and tried to see the turkey without showing they were interested. A man with a hunting suit and gun stopped and looked at Ruller and walked around behind him and looked at the turkey.

"How much do you think it weighs?" a lady asked.

"At least ten pounds," Ruller said.

"How long did you chase it?"

"About an hour," Ruller said.

"The goddam imp," the man in the hunting suit muttered.

"That's really amazing," a lady commented.

"About that long," Ruller said.

"You must be very tired."

"No," Ruller said. "I have to go. I'm in a hurry." He worked his face to look as if he were thinking something out and hurried down the street until he was out of their view. He felt warm all over and nice as if something very fine were going to be or had been. He looked back once and saw that the country boys were following him. He hoped they would come up and ask to look at the turkey. God must be wonderful, he felt suddenly. He wanted to do something for God. He hadn't seen anyone playing the accordian though or selling pencils and he was past the business block. He might see one before he really got to the streets where people lived at. If he did, he'd give away the dime—even while he knew he couldn't get another one any time soon. He began to wish he would see somebody begging.

Those country kids were still trailing along behind him. He thought he might stop and ask them did they want to see the turkey; but they might just stare at him. They were tenants' children and sometimes tenant's children just stared at you. He might found a home for tenant's children. He thought about going back through town to see if he had passed a beggar without seeing him, but he decided people might think he was showing off with the turkey.

Lord, send me a beggar, he prayed suddenly. Send me one before I get home. He had never thought before of praying on his own, but it was a good idea. God had put the turkey there. He'd send him a beggar. He knew for a fact God would send him one. He was on Hill Street now and there were nothing but houses on Hill Street. It would be strange to find a beggar here. The sidewalks were empty except for a few children and some tricycles. Ruller looked back; the country boys were still following him. He decided to slow down. It might make them catch up with him and it might give a beggar more time to get to him. If one were coming. He wondered if one were coming. If one came, it would mean God had gone out of His way to get one. It would mean God was really interested. He had a sudden fear one wouldn't come; it was a whole fear quick.

One will come, he told himself. God was interested in him because he was a very unusual child. He went on. The streets were deserted now. He guessed one wouldn't come. Maybe God didn't have confidence in—no, God did. Lord, please send me a beggar! he implored. He squinched his face rigid and strained his muscles in a knot and said, "please! one right now;" and the minute he said it—the minute—Hetty Gilman turned around the corner before him, heading straight to where he was.

He felt almost like he had when he ran into the tree.

She was walking down the street right toward him. It was just like the turkey lying there. It was just as if she had been hiding behind a house until he came by. She was an old woman whom everybody said had more money than anybody in town because she had been begging for twenty years. She sneaked into people's houses and sat until they gave her something. If they didn't, she cursed them. Nevertheless, she was a beggar. Ruller walked faster. He took the dime out of his pocket so it would be ready. His heart was stomping up and down in his chest. He made a noise to see if he could talk. As they neared each other, he stuck out his hand. "Here!" he shouted. "Here!"

She was a tall, longfaced old woman in an antique black cloak. Her face was the color of a dead chicken's skin. When she saw him, she looked as if she suddenly smelled something bad. He darted at her and thrust the dime into her hand and dashed on without looking back.

Slowly his heart calmed and he began to feel full of a new feeling—like being happy and embarrassed at the same time. Maybe, he thought, blushing, he would give all his money to her. He felt as if the ground did not need to be under him any longer. He noticed suddenly that the country boys' feet were shuffling just behind him and almost without thinking, he turned and asked graciously, "You all wanta see this turkey?"

They stopped where they were and stared at him. One in front spit. Ruller looked down at it quickly. There was real tobacco juice in it! "Wheered you git that turkey?" the spitter asked.

"I found it in the woods," Ruller said. "I chased it dead. See, it's been shot under the wing." He took the turkey off his shoulder and held it down where they could see. "I think it was shot twice," he went on excitedly, pulling the wing up.

"Lemme see it here," the spitter said.

Ruller handed him the turkey. "You see down there where the bullet hole is?" he asked. "Well, I think it was shot twice in the same hole, I think it was. . . ." The turkey's head flew in his face as the spitter slung it up in the air and over his own shoulder and turned. The others turned with him and together, they sauntered off in the direction they had come, the turkey sticking stiff out on the spitter's back and its head swinging slowly in a circle as he walked away.

They were in the next block before Ruller moved. Finally, he realized that he could not even see them any longer they were so far away. He turned toward home, almost creeping. He walked four blocks and then suddenly, noticing that it was dark, he began to run. He ran faster and faster, and as he turned up the road to his house, his heart was running as fast as his legs and he was certain that Something Awful was tearing behind him with its arms rigid and its fingers ready to clutch.

The Train

THINKING ABOUT the porter, he had almost forgotten the berth. He had an upper one. The man in the station had said he could give him a lower and Haze had asked didn't he have no upper ones; the man said sure if that was what he wanted, and gave him an upper one. Leaning back on the seat, Haze had seen how the ceiling was rounded over him. It was in there. They pulled the ceiling down and it was in there, and you climbed up to it on a ladder. He hadn't seen any ladders around; he reckoned they kept them in the closet. The closet was up where you came in. When he first got on the train, he had seen the porter standing in front of the closet, putting on his porter's jacket. Haze had stopped right then—right where he was.

The turn of his head was like and the back of his neck was like and the short reach of his arm. He turned away from the closet and looked at Haze and Haze saw his eyes and they were like; they were the same—same as old Cash's for the first instant, and then different. They turned different while he was looking at them; hardened flat. "Whu . . what time do you pull down the beds?" Haze mumbled.

"Long time yet," the porter said, reaching into the closet again.

Haze didn't know what else to say to him. He went on to his section.

Now the train was greyflying past instants of trees and quick spaces of field and a motionless sky that sped darkening away in the opposite direction. Haze leaned his head back on the seat and looked out the window, the yellow light of the train lukewarm on him. The porter had passed twice, twice back and twice forward, and the second time forward he had looked sharply at Haze for an instant and passed on without saying anything; Haze had turned and stared after him as he had done the time before. Even his walk was like. All them gulch niggers resembled. They looked like their own kind of nigger—heavy and bald, rock all through. Old Cash in his day had been two hundred pounds heavy—no fat on him—and five feet high with not more than two inches over. Haze wanted to talk to the porter. What would the porter say when he told him: I'm from Eastrod? What would he say?

The train had come to Evansville. A lady got on and sat opposite Haze. That meant she would have the berth under him. She said she thought it was going to snow. She said her husband had driven her down to the station and he said if it didn't snow before he got home, he'd be surprised. He had ten miles to go; they lived in the suburbs. She was going to Florida to visit her daughter. She had never had time to take a trip that far off. The way things happened, one thing right after another, it seemed like time went by so fast you couldn't tell if you were old or young. She looked as if it had been cheating her, going double quick when she was asleep and couldn't watch it. Haze was glad to have someone there talking.

He remembered when he was a little boy, him and his mother and the other children would go into Chattanooga on the Tennessee Railroad. His mother had always started up a conversation with the other people on the train. She was like an old bird dog just unpenned that raced, sniffing up every rock and stick and sucking in the air around everything she stopped at. There wasn't a person she hadn't spoken to by the time they were ready to get off. She remembered them too. Long years after, she would say she wondered where the lady was who was going to Fort West, or she wondered if the man who was selling Bibles had ever got his wife out the hospital. She had a hankering for people—as if what happened to the ones she talked to happened to her then. She was a Jackson. Annie Lou Jackson.

My mother was a Jackson, Haze said to himself. He had stopped listening to the lady although he was still looking at her and she thought he was listening. My name is Hazel Wickers, he said. I'm nineteen. My mother was a Jackson. I was raised in Eastrod, Eastrod, Tennessee; he thought about the porter again. He was going to ask the porter. It struck him suddenly that the porter might even be Cash's son. Cash had a son run away. It happened before Haze's time. Even so, the porter would know Eastrod.

Haze glanced out the window at the shapes black-spinning past him. He could shut his eyes and make Eastrod at night out of any of them—he could find the two houses with the road between and the store and the nigger houses and the one barn and the piece of fence that started off into the pasture, grey-white when the moon was on it. He could put the mule face, solid, over the fence and let it hang there, feeling how the night was. He felt it himself. He felt it light-touching around him. He seen his ma coming up the path, wiping her hands on an apron she had taken off, looking like the night change was on her, and then standing in the doorway: Haaazzzzeeeee, Haazzzeee, come in here. The train said it for him. He wanted to get up and go find the porter.

"Are you going home?" Mrs. Hosen asked him. Her name was Mrs. Wallace Ben Hosen; she had been a Miss Hitchcock before she married.

"Oh!" Haze said, startled— "I get off at, I get off at Taulkinham."

Mrs. Hosen knew some people in Evansville who had a cousin in Taulkinham—a Mr. Henrys, she thought. Being from Taulkinham Haze might know him. Had he ever heard the. . . .

"Taulkinham ain't where I'm from," Haze muttered. "I don't know nothin' about Taulkinham." He didn't look at Mrs. Hosen. He knew what she was going to ask next and he felt it coming and it came, "Well, where do you live?"

He wanted to get away from her. "It was there," he mumbled, squirming in the seat. Then he said, "I don't rightly know, I was there but . . . this is just the third time I been at Taulkinham," he said quickly—her face had crawled out and was staring at him—"I ain't been since I went when I was six. I don't know nothin' about it. Once I seen a circus there but not. . . ." He heard a clanking at the end of the car and looked to see where it was coming from. The porter was pulling the walls of the sections farther out. "I got to see the porter a minute," he said and escaped down the aisle. He didn't know what he'd say to the porter. He got to him and he still didn't know what he'd say. "I reckon you're fixing to make them up now," he said.

"That's right," the porter said.

"How long does it take you to make one up?" Haze asked.

"Seven minutes," the porter said.

"I'm from Eastrod," Haze said. "I'm from Eastrod, Tennessee."

"That isn't on this line," the porter said. "You on the wrong train if you counting on going to any such place as that."

"I'm going to Taulkinham," Haze said. "I was raised in Eastrod."

"You want your berth made up now?" the porter asked.

"Huh?" Haze said. "Eastrod, Tennessee; ain't you ever heard of Eastrod?"

The porter wrenched one side of the seat flat. "I'm from Chicago," he said. He jerked the shades down on either window and wrenched the other seat down. Even the back of his neck was like. When he bent over, it came out in three bulges. He was from Chicago. "You standing in the middle of the aisle. Somebody gonna want to get past you," he said, suddenly turning on Haze.

"I reckon I'll go sit down some," Haze said, blushing.

He knew people were staring at him as he went back to his section. Mrs. Hosen was looking out the window. She turned and eyed him suspiciously; then she said it hadn't snowed yet, had it? and relaxed into a stream of talk. She guessed her husband was getting his own supper tonight. She was paying a girl to come cook his dinner but he was having to get his own supper. She didn't think that hurt a man once in a while. She thought it did him good. Wallace wasn't lazy but he didn't think what it took to keep going with housework all day. She didn't know how it would feel to be in Florida with somebody waiting on her.

He was from Chicago.

This was her first vacation in five years. Five years ago she had gone to visit her sister in Grand Rapids. Time flies. Her sister had left Grand Rapids and moved to Waterloo. She didn't suppose she'd recognize her sister's children if she saw them now. Her sister wrote they were as big as their father. Things changed fast, she said. Her sister's husband had worked with the city water supply in Grand Rapids—he had a good place—but in Waterloo, he . . .

"I went back there last time," Haze said. "I wouldn't be getting off at Taulkinham if it was there; it went apart like, you know, it . . ."

Mrs. Hosen frowned. "You must be thinking of another Grand Rapids," she said. "The Grand Rapids I'm talking about is a large city and it's always where it's always been." She stared at him for a moment and then went on: when they were in Grand Rapids they got along fine, but in Waterloo he suddenly took to liquor. Her sister had to support the house and educate the children. It beat Mrs. Hosen how he could sit there year after year.

Haze's mother had never talked much on the train; she mostly listened. She was a Jackson.

After a while Mrs. Hosen said she was hungry and asked him if he wanted to go into the diner. He did.

The dining car was full and people were waiting to get in it. Haze and Mrs. Hosen stood in line for a half hour, rocking in the narrow passageway and every few minutes flattening themselves against the side to let a trickle of people through. Mrs. Hosen began talking to the lady on the side of her. Haze stared stupidly at the wall. He would never have had the courage to come to the diner by himself; it was fine he had met Mrs. Hosen. If she hadn't been talking, he would have told her intelligently that he had gone there the last time and that the porter was not from there but that he looked near enough like a gulch nigger to be one, near enough like old Cash to be his child. He'd tell her while they were eating. He couldn't see inside the diner from where he was; he wondered what it would be like in there. Like a restaurant, he reckoned. He thought of the berth. By the time they got through eating, the berth would probably be made up and he could get in it. What would his ma say if she seen him having a berth in a train! He bet she never reckoned that would happen. As they got nearer the entrance to the diner he could see in. It was like a city restaurant! He bet she never reckoned it was like that.

The head man was beckoning to the people at the first of the line every time someone left—sometimes for one person, sometimes for more. He motioned for two people and the line moved up so that Haze and Mrs. Hosen and the lady she was talking to were standing at the end of the diner, looking in. In a minute, two more people left. The man beckoned and Mrs. Hosen and the lady walked in, and Haze followed them.

The man stopped Haze and said, "only two," and pushed him back to the doorway. Haze's face went an ugly red. He tried to get behind the next person and then he tried to get through the line to go back to the car he had come from, but there were too many people bunched in the opening. He had to stand there while everyone around looked at him. No one left for a while and he had to stand there. Mrs. Hosen did not look at him again. Finally a lady up at the far end got up and the head man jerked his hand and Haze hesitated and saw the hand jerk again and then lurched up the aisle, falling against two tables on the way and getting his hand wet with somebody's coffee. He didn't look at the people he sat down with. He ordered the first thing on the menu and when it came, ate it without thinking what it might be. The people he was sitting with had finished and, he could tell, were waiting, watching him eat.

When he got out the diner he was weak and his hands were making small jittery movements by themselves. It seemed a year ago that he had seen the head man beckon to him to sit down. He stopped between two cars and breathed in the cold air to clear his head. It helped. When he got back to his car all the berths were made up and the aisles were dark and sinister, hung in heavy green. He realized again that he had a berth, an upper one, and that he could get in it now. He could lie down and raise the shade just enough to look out from and watch—what he had planned to do—and see how everything went by a train at night. He could look right into the night, moving.

He got his sack and went to the men's room and put on his night clothes. A sign said to get the porter to let you into the upper berths. The porter might be a cousin of some of them gulch niggers, he thought suddenly; he might ask him if he had any cousins around Eastrod, or maybe just in Tennessee. He went down the aisle, looking for him. They might have a little conversation before he got in the berth. The porter was not at that end of the car and he went back to look at the other end. Going around the corner he ran into something heavily pink; it gasped and muttered, "clumsy!" It was Mrs. Hosen in a pink wrapper with her hair in knots around her head. He had forgotten about her. She was terrifying with her hair slicked back and the knobs like dark toad stools framing her face. She tried to get past him and he tried to let her but they were both moving the same way each time. Her face became purplish except for little white marks over it that didn't heat up. She drew herself stiff and stopped still and said, "What IS the matter with you?" He slipped past her and dashed down the aisle and ran suddenly into the porter so that the porter slipped and he fell on top of him and the porter's face was right under his and it was old Cash Simmons. For a minute he couldn't move off the porter for thinking it was Cash and he breathed, "Cash," and the porter pushed him off and got up and went down the aisle quick and Haze scrambled off the floor and went after him saying he wanted to get in the berth and thinking, this is Cash's kin, and then suddenly, like something thrown at him when he wasn't looking: this is Cash's son run away; and then: he knows about Eastrod and doesn't want it, he doesn't want to talk about it, he doesn't want to talk about Cash.

He stood staring while the porter put the ladder up to the berth and then he started up it, still looking at the porter, seeing Cash there only different, not in the eyes, and half way up the ladder he said, still looking at the porter, "Cash is dead. He got the cholera from a pig." The porter's mouth jerked down and he muttered, looking at Haze with his eyes thin, "I'm from Chicago. My father was a railroad man," and Haze stared at him and then laughed: a nigger being a railroad "man": and laughed again, and the porter jerked the ladder off suddenly with a wrench of his arm that sent Haze clutching at the blanket into the berth.

He lay on his stomach in the berth, trembling from the way he had got in. Cash's son. From Eastrod. But not wanting Eastrod; hating it. He lay there for a while on his stomach, not moving. It seemed a year since he had fallen over the porter in the aisle.

After a while he remembered that he was actually in the berth and he turned and found the light and looked around him. There was no window.

The side wall did not have a window in it. It didn't push up to be a window. There was no window concealed in it.

There was a fish net thing stretched across the side wall; but no windows. For a second it flashed through his mind that the porter had done this—given him this berth that there were no windows to and had just a fish net strung the length of—because he hated him. But they must all be like this.

The top of the berth was low and curved over. He lay down. The curved top looked like it was not quite closed; it looked like it was closing. He lay there for a while not moving. There was something in his throat like a sponge with an egg taste. He had eggs for supper. They were in the sponge in his throat. They were right in his throat. He didn't want to turn over for fear they would move; he wanted the light off; he wanted it dark. He reached up without turning and felt for the button and snapped it and the darkness sank down on him and then faded a little with light from the aisle that came in through the foot of space not closed. He wanted it all dark, he didn't want it diluted. He heard the porter's footsteps coming down the aisle, soft into the rug, coming steadily down, brushing against the green curtains and fading up the other way out of hearing. He was from Eastrod. From Eastrod but he hated it. Cash wouldn't have put any claim on him. He wouldn't have wanted him. He wouldn't have wanted anything that wore a monkey white coat and toted a whiskbroom in his pocket. Cash's clothes had looked like they'd set a while under a rock; and they smelled like nigger. He thought how Cash smelled, but he smelled the train. No more gulch niggers in Eastrod. In Eastrod. Turning in the road, he saw in the dark, half-dark, the store boarded and the barn open with the dark free in it, and the smaller house half carted away, the porch gone and no floor in the hall. He had been supposed to go to his sister's in Taulkinham on his last furlough when he came up from the camp in Georgia but he didn't want to go to Taulkinham and he had gone back to Eastrod even though he knew how it was: the two families scattered in towns and even the niggers from up and down the road gone into Memphis and Murfreesboro and other places. He had gone back and slept in the house on the floor in the kitchen and a board had fallen on his head out of the roof and cut his face. He jumped, feeling the board, and the train jolted and unjolted and went again. He went looking through the house to see they hadn't left nothing in it ought to been taken.

His ma always slept in the kitchen and had her walnut shifferrobe in there. Wasn't another shifferrobe nowhere around. She was a Jackson. She had paid thirty dollars for it and hadn't bought herself nothing else big again. And they had left it. He reckoned they hadn't had room on the truck for it. He opened all the drawers. There were two lengths of wrapping cord in the top one and nothing in the others. He was surprised nobody had come and stolen a shifferrobe like that. He took the wrapping cord and tied the legs through the floor boards and left a piece of paper in each of the drawers: THIS SHIFFERROBE BELONGS TO HAZEL WICKERS. DO NOT STEAL IT OR YOU WILL BE HUNTED DOWN AND KILLED.

She could rest easier knowing it was guarded some. If she come looking any time at night, she would see. He wondered if she walked at night and came there ever—came with that look on her face, unrested and looking, going up the path and through the barn open all around and stopping in the shadow by the store boarded up, coming on unrested with that look on her face like he had seen through the crack going down. He seen her face through the crack when they were shutting the top on her, seen the shadow that came down over her face and pulled her mouth down like she wasn't satisfied with resting, like she was going to spring up and shove the lid back and fly out like a spirit going to be satisfied: but they shut it on down. She might have been going to fly out of there, she might have been going to spring—he saw her terrible like a huge bat darting from the closing—fly out of there but it was falling dark on top of her, closing down all the time, closing down; from inside he saw it closing, coming closer, closer down and cutting off the light and the room and the trees seen through the window through the crack faster and darker closing down. He opened his eyes and saw it closing down and he sprang up between the crack and wedged his body through it and hung there moving, dizzy, with the dim light of the train slowly showing the rug below, moving, dizzy. He hung there wet and cold and saw the porter at the other end of the car, a white shape in the darkness, standing there, watching him and not moving. The tracks curved and he fell back sick into the rushing stillness of the train.

An Afternoon in the Woods

H IS GUNS GLINTED in the side of the tree and half aloud,
through a crack in his mouth, he growled, "All right,
Mason, this is as far as you go," and then for lack of any
prepared sequel, he squatted down and began to pick a length
of thorn vine out of the sleeve of his white coat. He was
dressed, except for the guns, for the child's party he had escaped. She had seen him off at the door with the present and
had watched him turn the corner. He had waited there, behind a truck, and when he saw her drive off in the car, he had
returned for the holster and guns, getting in and out through
a back window. Then he had gone to the woods to spend the
afternoon. He was a fat white-haired boy of ten with pale
blue eyes that watered constantly behind a thick pair of silver-
rimmed spectacles.

The present had been wrapped in pink paper with a silver
bow on it. When he had got far enough into the woods, he
had torn off the paper and ribbon. The thing was a heart-
shaped bottle of perfume for a little girl with the words,
"Hearts and Flowers," printed on it—the selection of his
mother and grandmother. He took a good-sized rock and
crushed the bottle and buried it with the paper and ribbon in
a ditch. This gave him such an exquisite pleasure that he
walked on, noticing almost for the first time the brilliance of
the leaves, which were turning. He often came to the woods,
but not to see them, only to get out of doing something else.
Walking in the woods he continued to be part of what was
always passing on the television screen, and now when he saw
the great splashes of living red and yellow over his head, he
felt disturbed and withdrew into the role of the Lone Ranger
for five or ten minutes. It was when he stopped to pick the
thorn vine out that he became conscious again of the wild
color all around him. The trees sprang up and met like leaping arches of fire over his head. There was a peculiar life all
through the woods, a kind of watching presence. He felt suddenly as if he had wandered onto strange property and was
about to be ambushed. His skin prickled. In the bushes not

five feet from him, he saw a dark wine-colored eye watching him with a fierce tranquillity.

He squatted there, trembling as if he were waiting for an ax to strike the back of his neck. The eye that held him closed softly and he made out a large bronze breast and part of a drooping wing. He released his breath. It was a wild turkey. It took a lurching step and stopped, with one foot lifted, and listened.

He saw it was limping and his fright left him. He moved a little nearer on his hands and knees and it took another step. Then he began edging forward quickly on his knees, regardless of the white pants. His arms were rigid and his fingers ready to clutch when it gave a high broken-bugle sound and crashed out the other side and off down a sparsely wooded hillside. He jumped up and ran around the line of brush and down the hillside after it. Near the bottom it squatted and tried to spread its wings and could not; it sat heavily on the ground panting while he came down fast on top of it, already seeing himself walking in the door with it slung over his shoulder and them all screaming, "Look at Manley with that wild turkey! Manley! where in the world did YOU get that turkey!" All he would say was that he had gone to the woods to catch him one and had caught him one. His hand was almost on it when it shot up and lumbered off again. "You can't fly, Mason, you haven't got a chance," he shouted and tore after it, out through a dead cotton field and then under a fence and into another section of woods. Its nub-like head had turned from blue to a violent red and from his distance it looked like a small bloody fist hurtling through the underbrush. He saw it dart into a thicket but when he got there, it shot out again and disappeared under a wild hedge. He went through the hedge and heard something rip and without stopping, he put his finger in a split that ran from his elbow to the end of the sleeve. He kept on running. If he came in with the turkey, they would forget about his clothes. Whenever Roy Jr. came in with something he had killed, they forgot whatever was the last thing he had done wrong. The time Roy Jr. killed the bobcat, they forgot that he had backed the car into an icetruck the day before.

The turkey was running in a drunken zigzag, not thirty feet

away, along the edge of a ditch. When the ditch ended, it slid under a hedge and fell forward on its neck. For a minute or two he and the bird rested on either side of the bush, panting. He could see the tail through the leaves; very cautiously, he reached forward and closed his hand around it. There was no movement from the turkey. He put his face close to the leaves to look through and an eye, like a black diamond clenched in a bloody fist, gazed into his shallow eyes. With a gasp he let go the tail and the turkey wheeled off.

After a second he jumped up, furious, and scrambled over the hedge and ran in the direction he thought it had gone. He went up and down two small steep hills without catching sight of it and then just as he thought he saw a streak of red far away, he tripped over a root and fell spraddled on the ground. He did not get up. His glasses were about three feet off, broken against the side of a rock.

He looked at them languidly. He should have known all along that HE wouldn't catch it. He had never in his life won a prize or a fight or killed anything to make them proud of him. If they were proud of him, it was because he belonged to them. Roy Jr. did plenty to make them proud of him but even if he hadn't, they would have been proud of him anyway because he was Roy Jr. They were proud now that he was going bad. Their grandmother said, "Roy Jr. is going bad!" and looked as if she could hardly hold herself in for pride because it was Roy Jr. that was doing it. His father said, "Oh, he'll snap out of that and make us proud of him yet!" but he already looked too proud for another nickel's worth to get in. Then when they had finished saying how proud they were going to be of Roy Jr., his mother would say, pushing an extra charge in her voice like a tired cheerleader, "And we're all going to be proud of old Manley someday too!" and his father would say, "Sure we are," like he could convince himself of anything, and his grandmother would say, "Particularly when he learns to scrape his feet on the mat before he comes in the hall!" He would have taken the turkey in slung over his shoulder and they would all have jumped up and yelled, "Look at Manley! Manley! Where did YOU get that wild turkey?"

He sat up and began kicking his heels into the dirt with a

kind of methodic viciousness while his watery eyes squinted into the blurred woods. The glasses would cost twenty-two dollars, the suit would cost plenty, and they would ask where he had been. If he said he'd been hit by a truck, they would have to see the truck. He reflected that every time he did something even a little wrong, he got punished for it fifty times over. He wondered why he had seen the turkey in the first place if he wasn't going to be able to catch it. It was like God had played a dirty trick on him. He checked himself here, always being careful what he let himself think about God. He sat for a few minutes looking disgustedly at his fat white ankles sticking out of his trouser legs into his socks. Then he turned over on his stomach and let his cheek rest on the ground but the grit cut him and he sat up again. Oh hell, he thought.

"Oh hell," he said cautiously.

Then in a second he said just, "Hell," in a louder experimental voice as if he might be calling someone.

Then he said it like Roy Jr. said it, with authority. Once Roy Jr. said, "God!" and his grandmother had stomped after him and said, "I don't want to hear you say that again! Thou shalt not take the name of the Lord thy God in vain do you hear me!" but when Roy Jr. was out of the way she had looked proud and said, "He's going through that stage!" as if nothing could be better.

"God," Manley said.

He looked studiedly at the diamond-shaped piece of ground that his legs closed in. "God," he repeated.

"God dammit," he said softly. He could feel his face getting hot and his heart beginning to thump aloud. "God dammit to hell," he said almost inaudibly. He looked over his shoulder, keeping his head rather low and turning his eyes around slowly.

"Good Father, Good God, back the truck in-to the yard," he said and began to giggle. His face was getting very red. "Our Father Who art in heaven, shoot em six and roll em seven," he improvised, giggling helplessly. Boy, the old lady would smack his head in if she could hear him. God dammit, she'd smack his goddam head in. He rolled over in a fit of laughter that shook him all over. Goddammit she'd wring his neck, she'd wring his goddam neck, she'd goddam his god-dam, she'd. . . . The laughing cut his side and he tried to hold it in but everytime he thought of his goddam neck, he shook again. He lay back on the ground, red and weak, and after a while he stopped laughing almost as suddenly as he had started.

He repeated the words but he couldn't make himself laugh again. He thought of his broken glasses and his torn suit and of all the chasing for nothing. As soon as he got in the door, they would holler, "How did you tear your clothes? Where are your glasses? Who beat you up this time?"

He picked up the broken glasses and held them for a min-ute, a little out from him as if he were presenting them as evidence and then he put them in his pocket and got up. He had ceased entirely to notice the colors of the woods. He was weighing the crime and punishment in terms of dollars and cents: against about two dollars for the smashed present, there were twenty-two dollars for the glasses and fifteen or so for the suit. The injustice of it was there for anybody to see in the figures. The only way you could beat it would be by doing something that was so bad that being killed dead for it wouldn't be as bad as what you had done. He tried for a while to think what this would be. He couldn't think of a crime against anybody else that wouldn't be as great an in-convenience to himself. Then he did think of one and the thought was so startling that he stopped where he was and stood with his mouth slack and his hands held half-opened in front of him as if he had just let something fall on the ground.

What he had thought of was blasphemy, a sin open to chil-dren as well as adults—though he had never thought before how accessible it was to him. His mouth turned up slightly and then down again, one corner at a time, like a scale bal-ancing his fat cheeks. He looked as if he were undecided whether to giggle or cry.

The feeling of this evil was murky but cold. It was not like the feeling of his secret sins or the more open kind like smash-ing the bottle. Those made him tingle with a hot absence of thought. This was something entirely of the mind. He put his hands in his pockets, close to his sides.

"Goddam God," he said in a quick treble voice that sounded like a young bird hitting a new note for the first time.

After a second he began to move forward mechanically, conscious that the colors were raised over his head like a canopy. There was a quiet breeze and all the small bushes seemed to bow before him. The late afternoon sun slanted a ray of light along his path and pushed into the thickets and before he had gone a hundred feet, it lit the breast of the dead turkey with a sudden spark of bronze. The bird was rolled over against a large white quartz rock, the blue head and neck lying limp along the ground and the terrible eye closed. For a full minute he stared and did not move; then he began to creep toward it.

He was not going to touch it. He was certain that this was a trap. Why was it here now for him to take? He squatted down by it. The feathers on one side were bloodsoaked and he lifted the wing and saw the bullet hole just over the leg. The picture of himself walking in with it slung over his shoulder came back to him. He decided that it must weigh twenty pounds. It did not seem to be a trap. It was the same turkey and it was dead and still warm.

He began trying to decide what motive God could have if this were not a trap. He recalled the lost sheep and the prodigal son, and then an illuminating flash lit his dark brain: he had been going bad! Without knowing it, he had been going bad all the time and this was a warning. This was God's way of saying that He wanted him on His side. It was not a trap; it was a bribe, but he didn't allow the word *bribe* to enter his mind. It's a present, he thought, to keep me straight!

He had the sense that God was waiting for him to make up his mind whether he would take it or not. God must certainly feel that he was worth saving. He found himself suddenly blushing and grinning and he rubbed his hand over his large mouth and pushed his glasses higher on his nose. He let out a wild giggle and quickly checked himself. A very distinct and ugly voice inside him said, "He must not be so hot if He has to bribe a jerk like you with a lousy turkey."

He could look at the turkey and see that it was not a lousy one.

"There would be more in it for you if you went bad," the voice continued.

He picked the turkey up by the feet and decided it must weigh thirty or forty pounds. He bent and slung it over his shoulder. Its head swung at the level of his bottom and he started off with it through the gorgeous violent woods that were reflected in prisms and bronze lights in its feathers. He stopped, realizing suddenly that what had happened was a clear call to the ministry.

"Yaaa," the voice said, "now you have to be a preacher, wise guy."

He shifted the turkey slightly on his shoulder. Like Billy Ghrame, he thought, flying to Europe all the time.

"Naaa, like the fat old glick at the Methodist church in town," said the voice.

No, like that priest that founded Boys' Town, he said. I'll found a town for boys that are going bad. The appropriateness of this struck him with force and he began to imagine a line of boys that he had reformed, walking after him through the woods. Come on, boys, he said, God has given us a turkey.

You gave us a good bird, he said to God.

Only the best for a valuable man, God said. Glad to have you on my side, Mason.

He decided to go home the long way, through town. Once, on the way, he heard the voice say, "Oh well, you can go bad later," but he covered it at once with a good thought. He tried to think of something he could do to show his appreciation to God and he decided that if he saw a blind man or a beggar, he would drop the ten cents he had in his pocket into the cup. Beggars were very rare on the street but they were a possibility and he thought that if God really wanted him to give up the dime, He would have a beggar show up.

When he got into the business block, he attracted general attention. Two men came over to him and whistled and called over some other men who had been lounging on the corner. Manley stopped and allowed a group to gather around him. A man in a hunting suit came up and looked at the turkey a long time, cursing softly. A lady asked how much he thought it weighed and a man said there were not many more wild turkeys left in the woods around here. The man in the hunting suit kept muttering, "The goddam imp, the goddam imp."

"You must be tired out," the lady said.

"No," Manley said, "but I have to go now. I have some business to attend to." He worked his face to look as if he were thinking something out and hurried down the street with the bird bumping slightly on his back.

"God must be a real sucker to let you get away with this," the familiar voice said, but he paid no attention to it. Three country boys who had been sitting on the curb got up and tried to see the turkey without showing they were interested. He imagined himself in a roman collar, leading these three reformed boys down the street. They would have been crooks if he had not got them in time. He felt very warm and kindly. He glanced back and saw that the three boys were actually following him. He hoped they would come up and ask to look at the turkey closer. He felt an urgency to do something for God. He had not seen a beggar and he was already out of the business block. He might see one before he got to the streets where people lived at, and if he did, he would give away the dime—even though they were hard to get.

The country boys were still trailing along behind him. He thought he might stop and ask them if they wanted to see the turkey but they were tenant's children and sometimes tenant's children only stared at you. He thought he might found a town for tenant's children. He thought about going back through the business block to see if he might pass a beggar. Then he thought of praying that one show up.

Lord, let a beggar show up, he prayed suddenly. Let one show up before I get home.

"Testing Him out, huh?" the voice asked.

He had reached the streets where the houses began and where a beggar would not be likely found. The sidewalks were empty except for a few tricycles that had not been taken in. The country boys were still following him. He decided to slow down. It might give them a chance to catch up with him and it would give God more time to produce a beggar. He had a sinking fear that God had lost interest since no beggar could possibly be on these streets.

He guessed one wouldn't come. Maybe God didn't have confidence in him anymore. No. God did! Lord, please send me a beggar, he implored. He squinted his face rigid and strained every muscle and said, Please have one show up fast! Their preacher said knock and it would be opened to you, ask and you would receive! But he was afraid to open his eyes because he knew it wouldn't be that way. He knew there wouldn't be any beggar. He opened his eyes and saw Hetty Gilman turning the corner, heading in his direction.

This was, so far, the greatest shock of his afternoon.

She was walking rapidly toward him with her lop-sided gait. She was an old woman who, people said, had more money than any one else in town because she had been begging for twenty years. She sneaked into houses and would not leave until she got something and she left with curses if she didn't get as much as she thought she ought. Manley walked faster. He took the dime out of his pocket so that he would have it ready as they passed. His heart was stomping up and down in his chest. She came on, a tall long-faced old woman in a black coat and black pulled-down hat. Her face was the color of a dead chicken's skin. As they neared each other, he stuck out his hand with the dime glinting on it and her arm shot forward and she snatched it off his palm with a razor-like scrape. Then her mouth cracked and she gave him a voracious leer that said: all the brat can spare is a thin dime! He hurried on, only conscious that a miracle had been performed for his sake.

Slowly his heart calmed down and he began to feel as if the ground did not need to be under him any longer. He felt he could have walked on the water. Maybe, he thought, he would give all his money to beggars. He would devote his life to helping people like Hetty Gilman. He noticed that the country boys' feet were shuffling just behind him and almost without thinking, he turned and asked graciously, "You all want to see this turkey?"

They stopped where they were and stared at him. They were pale and composed looking with colorless hair and thin transparent eyes. The tallest one turned his head slightly and spit. Manley looked down at it. There was real tobacco juice in it!

"Wheer'd you git thet turkey?" the spitter asked.

"I found it in the woods," Manley said. "I chased it dead. See, it's been shot under the wing." He eased the turkey off his shoulder and held it so the wing hung open. "I think it was shot twice," he said excitedly. "I chased it about twenty-five min. . . ."

"Lemme see it here," the spitter said.

Manley handed him the turkey. "You see there where the bullet hole is?" he asked; "well, I think it was shot twice in the same hole, I think it. . . ."

The turkey's head flew in his face as the spitter slung it up in the air and over his own shoulder and turned. The others turned with him and together they sauntered off in the direction they had come, the turkey sticking stiffly out on the spitter's back and its head swinging in a slow circle as he walked away.

They were in the next block before Manley moved. Finally he realized he could not even see them any longer they were so far away. He turned toward home, almost creeping. He walked four blocks and then suddenly, noticing that it was dark, he began to run. He ran faster and faster and as he turned up the road to his house, his heart was running as fast as his legs and he was certain that Something Awful was tearing behind him with its arms rigid and its fingers ready to clutch.

The Partridge Festival

CALHOUN PARKED his small pod-shaped car in the driveway to his great-aunts' house and got out cautiously, looking to the right and left as if he expected the profusion of azalea blossoms to have a lethal effect upon him. Instead of a decent lawn, the old ladies had three terraces crammed with red and white azaleas, beginning at the sidewalk and running backwards to the very edge of their imposing unpainted house. The two of them were on the front porch, one sitting, the other standing.

"Here's our baby!" his Aunt Bessie intoned in a voice meant to reach the other one, two feet away but deaf. It turned the head of a girl in the next yard, who sat cross-legged under a tree, reading. She raised her spectacled face, stared at Calhoun, and then returned her attention—with what he saw plainly was a smirk—to the book. Scowling, he passed stolidly on to the porch to get over the preliminaries with his aunts. They would take his voluntary presence in Partridge at Azalea Festival time to be a sign that his character was improving.

They were box-jawed old ladies who looked like George Washington with his wooden teeth in. They wore black suits with large ruffled jabots and had dead-white hair pulled back. After each had embraced him, he dropped limply into a rocker and gave them a sheepish smile. He was here only because Singleton had captured his imagination, but he had told his Aunt Bessie over the telephone that he was coming to enjoy the festival.

The deaf one, Aunt Mattie, shouted, "Your great-grandfather would have been delighted to see you taking an interest in the festival, Calhoun. He initiated it himself, you know."

"Well," the boy yelled back, "what about the little extra excitement you've had this time?"

Ten days before the festival began, a man named Singleton had been tried by a mock court on the courthouse lawn for not buying an Azalea Festival Badge. During the trial he had been imprisoned in a pair of stocks and when convicted, he had been locked in the "jail" together with a goat that had been tried and convicted previously for the same offense. The "jail" was an outdoor privy borrowed for the occasion by the Jaycees. Ten days later, Singleton had appeared in a side door on the courthouse porch and with a silent automatic pistol, had shot five of the dignitaries seated there and by mistake one person in the crowd. The innocent man received the bullet intended for the mayor who at that moment had reached down to pull up the tongue of his shoe.

"An unfortunate incident," his Aunt Mattie said. "It mars the festive spirit."

He heard the girl on the other lawn slam her book. The top of her rose into view above the hedge—a sloping-forward neck and a small face with a fierce expression, which she trained briefly on them before she disappeared. "It doesn't seem to have marred anything," he said. "As I passed through town I saw more people than ever before and all the flags were up. Partridge," he shouted, "will bury its dead but will not lose a nickel." The girl's front door slammed in the middle of the sentence.

His Aunt Bessie had gone into the house and come out again with a small leather box. "You look very like Father," she said and pulled up her chair beside him.

Without enthusiasm Calhoun opened the box, which shed a rust-colored dust over his knees, and removed the miniature of his great-grandfather. He was shown this every time he came. The old man—round-faced, bald, altogether unremarkable-looking—sat with his hands knotted on the head of a black stick. His expression was all innocence and determination. The master merchant, the boy thought, and flinched. "And what would this stalwart worthy think of Partridge today," he asked wryly, "with its festival in full swing after six citizens have been shot?"

"Father was progressive," his Aunt Bessie said, "—the most forward-looking merchant Partridge ever had. He would either have been one of the prominent men shot or he would have been the one to subdue the maniac."

The boy did not know how much of this he could stand. In the paper there had been pictures of the six "victims" and one of Singleton. Singleton's was the only distinctive face in the lot. It was broad but boney and bleak. One eye was more nearly round than the other and in the more nearly round one Calhoun had recognized the composure of the man who knows he will and who is willing to suffer for the right to be himself. A calculating contempt lurked in the regular eye but in the general expression there was the tortured look of the man who becomes maddened finally by the madness around him. The other six faces were of the same general stamp as his great-grandfather's.

"As you get older, you'll look more and more like Father," his Aunt Mattie prophesied. "You have his ruddy complexion and much the same expression."

"I'm a different type entirely," he said stiffly.

"Peaches and cream," his Aunt Bessie guffawed. "You're getting a little pot-tummy too," she said and took a lunge at his middle with her fist. "How old is our baby now?"

"Twenty-three," he muttered, thinking that it could not go on like this for the whole visit, that once they had roughed him up a bit, they would leave off.

"And do you have a girl?" his Aunt Mattie asked.

"No," he said wearily. "I take it," he went on, "that around here Singleton is considered nothing but a mental case?"

"Yes," his Aunt Bessie said, "—peculiar. He never conformed. He was not like the rest of us here."

"A terrible drawback," the boy said. Though his eyes were not mismatched, the shape of his face was broad like Singleton's; but the real likeness between them was interior.

"Since he is insane, he is not responsible," his Aunt Bessie said.

The boy's eyes brightened. He sat forward and fixed the old lady with a narrow gaze. "And where then," he asked, "does the real guilt lie?"

"Father's head was as smooth as an infant's by the time he was thirty," she said. "You had better hurry and get you a girl. Ha ha. What are you going to do with yourself now?"

He reached into his pocket and withdrew his pipe and a sack of tobacco. You could not ask them questions in depth. They were both good low-church Episcopalians but they had amoral imaginations. "I think I shall write," he said and began to load the bowl.

"Well," his Aunt Bessie said, "that's fine. Maybe you'll be another Margaret Mitchell."

"I hope you'll do us justice," his Aunt Mattie shouted. "Few do."

"I'll do you justice all right," he said grimly. "I'm writing an expos. . . ." He stopped and put the pipe in his mouth and sat back. It would be ridiculous to tell *them*. He removed the pipe and said, "Well, that's too much to go into. It wouldn't interest you ladies."

His Aunt Bessie inclined her head significantly. "Calhoun," she said, "we wouldn't want to be disappointed in you." They eyed him as if it had just occurred to them that the pet snake they had been fondling might after all be poisonous.

"Know the truth," the boy said with his fiercest look, "and the truth shall make you free."

They appeared reassured at his quoting Scripture. "Isn't he sweet," his Aunt Mattie asked, "with his little pipe?"

"Better get you a girl, boy," his Aunt Bessie said.

He escaped them in a few minutes and took his bag upstairs and then came down again, ready to go out and immerse himself in his material. His intention was to spend the afternoon interviewing people about Singleton. He expected to write something that would vindicate the madman and he expected the writing of it to mitigate his own guilt, for his doubleness, his shadow, was cast before him more darkly than usual in the light of Singleton's purity.

For the three summer months of the year, he lived with his parents and sold air-conditioners, boats, and refrigerators so that for the other nine months he could afford to meet life naturally and bring his real self—the rebel-artist-mystic—to birth. During these other months he lived on the opposite side of the city in an unheated walk-up with two other boys who also did nothing. But guilt for the summer pursued him into the winter; the fact was, he could have fared without the orgy of selling he cast himself into in the summer.

When he had explained to them that he despised their values, his parents had looked at each other with a gleam of recognition as if this were what they had been expecting from what they had read, and his father had offered to give him a small allowance to finance the flat. He had refused it for the sake of his independence, but in the depths of himself, he knew it was not for his independence but because he *enjoyed* selling. In the face of a customer, he was carried outside himself; his face began to beam and sweat and all complexity left him; he was in the grip of a drive as strong as the drive of some men for liquor or a woman; and he was horribly good at it. He was so good at it that the company had given him an achievement scroll. He had put quotation marks around the word *achievement* and he and his friends used the scroll as a target for darts.

As soon as he had seen Singleton's picture in the paper, the face began to burn in his imagination like a dark reproachful liberating star. The next morning he had telephoned his aunts to expect him and he had driven the hundred and fifty miles to Partridge in a little short of four hours.

On his way out of the house, his Aunt Bessie halted him and said, "Be back by six, Baby Lamb, and we'll have a sweet surprise for you."

"Rice pudding?" he asked. They were terrible cooks.

"Sweeter by far!" the old lady said and rolled her eyes. He hastened away.

The girl next door had returned with her book to the lawn. He suspected that he might be supposed to know her. When he came for visits as a child, his aunts had always produced one of the neighbor's freak children to play with him—once a fat moron in a Girl Scout suit, another time a near-sighted boy who recited Bible verses, and another an almost square girl who had blackened his eye and left. He thanked God he was now grown and they would no longer dare to fill his time for him. The girl did not look up as he passed and he did not speak.

Once on the sidewalk, he was affected by the profusion of azaleas. They seemed to wash in tides of color across the lawns until they surged against the white house-fronts, crests of pink and crimson, crests of white and a mysterious shade that was not yet lavender, wild crests of yellow-red. The profusion of color almost stopped his breath with insidious pleasure. Moss hung from the old trees. The houses were the most picturesque types of run-down ante-bellum. The taint of

the place was expressed in his great-grandfather's words
which had survived as the town's motto: Beauty is Our
Money Crop.

His aunts lived five blocks from the business section. He
walked them quickly and came after a few minutes to the edge
of the bare commercial scene, which had the ramshackle
courthouse for its center. The sun beat down fiercely on the
tops of cars parked in every available space. Flags, national,
state and confederate, flapped on every corner street light.
People milled about. On the quiet shaded street where his
aunts lived and the azaleas were best, he had not passed three
people, but here they all were, staring avidly at the pathetic
store displays and moving with languid reverence past the
courthouse porch, the spot where blood had been spilled.

He wondered if any of them might think he was here for
the same reason they were. He would have liked to start, in
Socratic fashion, a street discussion about where the real guilt
for the six deaths lay, but as he surveyed the scene, he saw no
one who looked capable of any genuine interest in meaning.
Without set purpose, he entered a drugstore. The place was
dark and smelled of sour vanilla.

He sat down on the high stool at the counter and ordered
a limeade. The boy preparing the drink had elaborate red sideburns and wore on his shirtfront an Azalea Festival Badge—
the emblem which Singleton had refused to buy. Calhoun's
eye fell on it at once. "I see you've paid your tribute to the
god," he said.

The boy did not seem to get the significance of this.

"The badge," Calhoun said, "the badge."

The boy looked down at it and then back at Calhoun. He
put the drink on the counter and continued to look at him as
if he were serving someone with an interesting deformity.

"Are you enjoying the festive spirit?" Calhoun asked.

"All these doings?" the boy said.

"These grand events," Calhoun said, "commencing with, I
believe, six deaths."

"Yessir," the boy said, "six in cold blood. And I knew four
of them myself."

"You too have had your share of the glory then," Calhoun
said. He felt suddenly a distinct hush fall on the street out-

side. He turned his eyes to the door just in time to see a hearse pass, followed by a line of slowly moving cars.

"That's the man that's having his funeral to himself," the boy said reverently. "The five that were supposed to get shot had theirs yesterday. One big one. But he didn't die in time for it."

"They have innocent as well as guilty blood on their hands," Calhoun said and glared at the boy.

"It wasn't no *they*," the boy said. "One man done it all. A man named Singleton. He was bats."

"Singleton was only the instrument," Calhoun said. "Partridge itself is guilty." He finished his drink in a gulp and put down the glass.

The boy was looking at him as if he were mad. "Partridge can't shoot nobody," he said in a high exasperated voice.

Calhoun put his dime on the counter and left. The last car had turned at the end of the block. He thought he observed less activity. People had obviously hastened away at the sight of the hearse. Two doors from him an old man leaned out of a hardware store and glared up the street where the procession had disappeared. Calhoun's need to communicate was urgent. He approached diffidently. "I understand that was the last funeral," he said.

The old man put a hand behind his ear.

"The funeral of the innocent man," Calhoun shouted and nodded up the street.

The old man cleared his nostrils loudly. His expression was not affable. "The only bullet that went right," he said in a rasping voice. "Biller was a wastrel. Drunk at the time."

The boy scowled. "I suppose the other five were heroes?" he suggested archly.

"Fine men," the old man said. "Perished in the line of duty. We givem a hero's fu'nel—all five in one big service. Biller's folks tried to rush up the undertaker so they could get Biller in on it but we saw to it Biller didn't make it. Would have been a disgrace."

My God, the boy thought.

"The only thing Singleton ever did good was to rid us of Biller," the old man continued. "Now somebody ought to rid us of Singleton. There he is at Quincy, living in the laper luxury, laying in a cool bed at no expense, eating up your taxes and mine. They should have shot him on the spot."

This was so appalling that Calhoun was speechless.

"Going to keep him there, they ought to charge him board," the old man said.

With a contemptuous glance, the boy walked off. He crossed the street to the courthouse square, moving at an odd angle in order to put as much distance between himself and the old fool as quickly as possible. Here benches were scattered beneath the trees. He found an unoccupied one and sat down. To the side of the courthouse steps, several viewers stood admiring the "jail" where Singleton had been locked with the goat. The pathos of his friend's situation was borne in on him with a rush of empathy. He felt himself flung in the privy, the padlock clicked, he glared between the rotting planks at the fools howling and cavorting outside. The goat made an obscene noise; he saw that he was confined with the spirit of the community.

"Six men was shot here," an odd muffled voice close by said.

The boy jumped.

A small white girl whose tongue was curled in the mouth of a Coca Cola bottle was sitting in a patch of sand at his feet, watching him with a detached gaze. Her eyes were the same green as the bottle. She was barefooted and had straight white hair. She withdrew her tongue from the bottle with an explosive sound. "A bad man did it," she said.

The boy felt the kind of frustration that accompanies contact with the certainty of children. "No," he said, "he was not a bad man."

The child put her tongue back in the bottle and withdrew it silently, her eyes on him.

"People were not good to him," he explained. "They were mean to him. They were cruel. What would you do if someone were cruel to you?"

"Shoot them," she said.

"Well, that's what he did," Calhoun said, frowning.

She continued to sit there and did not take her eyes off him. Her gaze might have been the depthless gaze of Partridge itself.

"You people persecuted him and finally drove him mad," the boy said. "He wouldn't buy a badge. Was that a crime? He was the Outsider here and you couldn't stand that. One of the fundamental rights of man," he said, glaring through the child's transparent stare, "is the right not to behave like a fool. The right to be different," he said hoarsely. "My God. The right to be yourself."

Without taking her eyes off him, she lifted one of her feet and set it on her knee.

"He was a bad bad bad man," she said.

Calhoun got up and walked off, glaring in front of him. His indignation swathed his vision in a kind of haze. He saw none of the activity around him distinctly. Two high-school girls in bright skirts and jackets swung into his path and shrilled, "Buy a ticket for the beauty contest tonight. See who'll be Miss Partridge Azalea!" He swerved sharply to the side and did not throw them so much as a glance. Their giggles followed him until he was past the courthouse and onto the block behind it. He stood there a moment, undecided what he would do next. He faced a barber shop which looked empty and cool. After a moment he entered it.

The barber, alone in the shop, raised his head from behind the paper he was reading. Calhoun asked for a haircut and sat down gratefully in the chair.

The barber was a tall emaciated fellow with eyes that might have faded from some deeper color. He looked to be a man who had suffered himself. He put the bib on the boy and stood staring at his round head as if it were a pumpkin he was wondering how to slice. Then he twirled the chair so that Calhoun faced the mirror. He was confronted with an image that was round-faced, unremarkable-looking and innocent. The boy's expression turned fierce. "Are you eating up this slop like the rest of them?" he asked belligerently.

"Come again?" the barber said.

"Do the tribal rites going on here improve the barber trade? All these doings, all these doings," he said impatiently.

"Well," the barber said, "last year it was a thousand extra people here and this year it looks to be more—on account," he said, "of the tragedy."

"The tragedy," the boy repeated and stretched his mouth.

"The six that was shot," the barber said.

"That tragedy," the boy said. "And what about the other tragedy—the man who was persecuted by these idiots until he shot six of them?"

"Oh him," the barber said.

"Singleton," the boy said. "Did he patronize your place?"

The barber began clipping his hair. A peculiar expression of disdain had come over his face at the mention of the name. "Tonight it's a beauty contest," he said, "tomorrow night it's a band concert, Thursday afternoon it's a big parade with Miss. . . ."

"Did you or didn't you know Singleton?" Calhoun interrupted.

"Known him well," the barber said and shut his mouth.

A tremor went through the boy as he realized that Singleton had probably sat in the chair he himself was now sitting in. He searched his face in the mirror desperately for its hidden likeness to the man. Slowly he saw it appear, a secret message brought to light by the heat of his feelings. "Did he patronize your shop?" he asked and held his breath for the answer.

"Him and me was related by marriage," the barber said indignantly, "but he never come in here. He was too big a skinflint to have his hair cut. He cut his own."

"An unpardonable crime," Calhoun said in a high voice.

"His second cousin married my sister-in-law," the barber said, "but he never known me on the street. Pass him as close as I am to you and he'd keep going. Kept his eyes on the ground all the time like he was following a bug."

"Preoccupied," the boy muttered. "He doubtless didn't know you were on the street."

"He known it," the barber said and his mouth curled unpleasantly. "He known it. I clip hair and he clipped coupons and that was that. I clip hair," he repeated as if this sentence had a particularly satisfying ring to his ears, "and he clipped coupons."

The typical have-not psychology, Calhoun thought. "Was the Singleton family once wealthy?" he asked.

"It wasn't but half of him Singleton," the barber said, "and the Singletons claimed there wasn't none of him Singleton. One of the Singleton girls gone off on a nine-months vacation and come back with him. Then they all died off and left him their money. It's no telling what the other half of him is. Something foreign I would judge." His tone insinuated more.

"I begin to get the picture," Calhoun said.

"He ain't clipping no coupons now," said the barber.

"No," Calhoun said and his voice rose, "now he's suffering. He's the scapegoat. He's laden with the sins of the community. Sacrificed for the guilt of others."

The barber paused, his mouth partway open. After a moment he said in a more respectful voice, "Reverend, you got him wrong. He wasn't a church-going man."

The boy reddened. "I'm not a church-going man myself," he said.

The barber seemed stopped again. He stood holding the scissors uncertainly.

"He was an individualist," Calhoun said. "A man who would not allow himself to be pressed into the mold of his inferiors. A non-conformist. He was a man of depth living among caricatures and they finally drove him mad, unleashed all his violence on themselves. Observe," he continued, "that they didn't try him. They simply had him committed at once to Quincy. Why? Because," he said, "a trial would have brought out his essential innocence and the real guilt of the community."

The barber's face lightened. "You're a lawyer, ain't you?" he asked.

"No," the boy said sullenly. "I'm a writer."

"Ohhh," the barber murmured. "I known it must be something like that." After a moment he said, "What you written?"

"He never married?" Calhoun went on rudely. "He lived alone in the Singleton place in the country?"

"What there was of it," the barber said. "He wouldn't have spent a nickel to keep it from falling down and no woman wouldn't have had him. That was the one thing he always had to pay for," he said and made a vulgar noise in his cheek.

"You know because you were always there," the boy said, barely able to control his disgust for this bigot.

"Naw," the barber said, "it was just common knowledge. I

clip hair," he said, "but I don't live like a hog. I got plumbing in my house and a refrigerator that spits ice cubes into my wife's hand."

"He was not a materialist," Calhoun said. "There were things that meant more to him than plumbing. Independence, for instance."

"Ha," the barber snorted. "He wasn't so independent. Once lightning almost struck him and those that saw it said you should have seen him run. Took off like bees were swarming in his pants. They liked to died laughing," and he gave a hyena-like laugh himself and slapped his knee.

"Loathsome," the boy murmured.

"Another time," the barber continued, "somebody went out there and put a dead cat in his well. Somebody was always doing something to see if they could make him turn loose a little money. Another time . . ."

Calhoun began fighting his way out of the bib as if it were a net he was caught in. When he was free of it, he thrust his hand in his pocket and brought out a dollar which he flung on the startled barber's shelf. Then he made for the door, letting it slam behind him in judgment on the place.

The walk back to his aunts' did not calm him. The colors of the azaleas had deepened with the approach of sundown and the trees rustled protectively over the old houses. No one here had a thought for Singleton, who lay on a cot in a filthy ward at Quincy. The boy felt now in a concrete way the force of his innocence, and he thought that to do justice to all the man had suffered, he would have to write more than a simple article. He would have to write a novel; he would have to show, not say, how primary injustice operated. Preoccupied with this, he went four doors past his aunts' house and had to turn and go back.

His Aunt Bessie met him at the door and drew him into the hall. "Told you we'd have a sweet surprise for you!" she said, pulling him by the arm into the parlor.

On the sofa sat a rangy-looking girl in a lime-green dress. "You remember Mary Elizabeth," his Aunt Mattie said, "—the cute little trick you took to the picture show once when you were here." Through his rage he recognized the girl who had been reading under the tree. "Mary Elizabeth is home for her spring holidays," his Aunt Mattie said. "Mary Elizabeth is a real scholar, aren't you, Mary Elizabeth?"

Mary Elizabeth scowled, indicating she was indifferent to whether she was a real scholar or not. She gave him a look which told him plainly she expected to enjoy this no more than he did.

His Aunt Mattie gripped the knob of her cane and began to lift herself from her chair. "We're going to have supper early," the other one said, "because Mary Elizabeth is going to take you to the beauty contest and it begins at seven."

"Great," the boy said in a tone that would be lost on them but he hoped not on Mary Elizabeth.

Throughout the meal he ignored the girl completely. His repartee with his aunts was markedly cynical but they did not have sense enough to understand his allusions and laughed like idiots at everything he said. Twice they called him "Baby Lamb" and the girl smirked. Otherwise she did nothing to suggest she was enjoying herself. Her round face was still childish behind her glasses. Retarded, Calhoun thought.

When the meal was over and they were on the way to the beauty contest, they continued to say nothing to each other. The girl, who was several inches taller than he, walked slightly in advance of him as if she would like to lose him on the way, but after two blocks she stopped abruptly and began to rummage in a large grass bag she carried. She took out a pencil and held it between her teeth while she continued to rummage. After a minute she brought up from the bottom of the bag two tickets and a stenographer's note pad. With these out, she closed the pocketbook and walked on.

"Are you going to take notes?" Calhoun inquired in a tone heavy with irony.

The girl looked around as if trying to identify the speaker. "Yes," she said, "I'm going to take notes."

"You appreciate this sort of thing?" Calhoun asked in the same tone. "You enjoy it?"

"It makes me vomit," she said. "I'm going to finish it off with one swift literary kick."

The boy looked at her blankly.

"Don't let me interfere with your pleasure in it," she said, "but this whole place is false and rotten to the core." Her voice came with a hiss of indignation. "They prostitute azaleas!"

Calhoun was astounded. After a moment he recovered himself. "It takes no great mind to come to that conclusion," he said haughtily. "What requires insight is finding a way to transcend it."

"You mean a form to express it in."

"It comes to the same thing," he said.

They walked the next two blocks in silence but both appeared shaken. When the courthouse was in view they crossed the street to it and Mary Elizabeth stuck the tickets at a boy who stood beside an entrance that had been formed by roping in the rest of the square. People were beginning to assemble on the grass inside.

"And do we stand here while you take notes?" Calhoun asked.

The girl stopped and faced him. "Look, Baby Lamb," she said, "you can do what you please. I'm going up to my father's office in the building where I can work. You can stay down here and help select Miss Partridge Azalea if you want to."

"I shall come," he said, controlling himself, "I'd like to observe a great female writer taking notes."

"Suit yourself," she said.

He followed her up the courthouse steps and through a side door. His irritation was so extreme that he did not realize he had passed through the very door where Singleton had stood to shoot. They walked through an empty barnlike hall and silently up a flight of tobacco-stained steps into another barnlike hall. Mary Elizabeth rooted in the grass bag for a key and then unlocked the door to her father's office. They entered a large threadbare room lined with lawbooks. As if he were an incompetent, the girl dragged two straight chairs from one wall to a window that overlooked the porch. Then she sat down and stared out, apparently absorbed at once in the scene below.

Calhoun sat down in the other chair. To annoy her he began to look her over thoroughly. For what seemed at least five minutes, he did not take his eyes off her as she leaned with her elbows in the window. He stared at her so long that he was afraid her image would be etched forever on his retina. Finally he could stand the silence no longer. "What is your opinion of Singleton?" he asked abruptly.

She raised her head and appeared to look through him. "A Christ-figure," she said.

The boy was stunned.

"I mean as myth," she said scowling. "I'm not a Christian." She returned her attention to the scene outside. Below a bugle sounded. "Sixteen girls in bathing suits are about to appear," she drawled. "Surely this will be of interest to you?"

"Listen," Calhoun said fiercely, "get this through your head. I'm not interested in the damm festival or the damm azalea queen. I'm here only because of my sympathy for Singleton. I'm going to write about him. Possibly a novel."

"I intend to write a non-fiction study," the girl said in a tone that made it evident fiction was beneath her.

They looked at each other with open and intense dislike. Calhoun felt that if he probed sufficiently he would expose her essential shallowness. "Since our forms are different," he said, again with his ironical smile, "we might compare findings."

"It's quite simple," the girl said. "He was the scapegoat. While Partridge flings itself about selecting Miss Partridge Azalea, Singleton suffers at Quincy. He expiates . . ."

"I don't mean your abstract findings," the boy said. "I mean your concrete findings. Have you ever seen him? What did he look like? The novelist is not interested in narrow abstractions—particularly when they're obvious. He's . . ."

"How many novels have you written?" she asked.

"This will be my first," he said coldly. "Have you ever seen him?"

"No," she said, "that isn't necessary for me. What he looks like makes no difference—whether he has brown eyes or blue—that's nothing to a thinker."

"You are probably," he said, "afraid to look at him. The novelist is never afraid to look at the real object."

"I would not be afraid to look at him," the girl said angrily, "if it were at all necessary. Whether he has brown eyes or blue is nothing to me."

"There is more to it," Calhoun said, "than whether he has brown eyes or blue. You might find your theories enriched by the sight of him. And I don't mean by finding out the color of his eyes. I mean your existential encounter with his personality. The mystery of personality," he said, "is what interests the artist. Life does not abide in abstractions."

"Then what's keeping you from going and having a look at him?" she said. "What are you asking me what he looks like for? Go see for yourself."

The words fell on his head like a sack of rocks. After a moment he said, "Go see for yourself? Go see where?"

"At Quincy," the girl said. "Where do you think?"

"They wouldn't let me see him," he said. The suggestion was appalling to him; for some reason he could not at the moment understand, it struck him as unthinkable.

"They would if you said you were kin to him," she said. "It's only twenty miles from here. What's to stop you?"

He was about to say, "I'm not kin to him," but he stopped and reddened furiously on the edge of the betrayal. They were spiritual kin.

"Go see whether his eyes are brown or blue and have yourself a little old exis . . ."

"I take it," he said, "that if I go you would like to go along? Since you aren't afraid to see him."

The girl paled. "You won't go," she said. "You're not up to the old exis . . ."

"I will go," he said, seeing his opportunity to shut her up. "And if you care to go with me, you can be at my aunts' at nine in the morning. But I doubt," he added, "that I'll see you there."

She thrust forward her long neck and glared at him. "Oh yes you will," she said. "You'll see me there."

She returned her attention to the window and Calhoun looked at nothing. Each seemed sunk suddenly in some mammoth private problem. Raucous cheers came intermittently from outside. Every few minutes there was music and clapping but neither took any notice of it, or of each other. Finally the girl pulled away from the window and said, "If you've got the general idea, we can leave. I prefer to go home and read."

"I had the general idea before I came," Calhoun said.

✳   ✳   ✳

He saw her to her door and when he had left her, his spirits lifted dizzily for an instant and then collapsed. He knew that the idea of going to see Singleton would never have occurred to him alone. It would be a torturing experience, but it might be his salvation. The sight of Singleton in his misery might cause him suffering sufficient to raise him once and for all from his commercial instincts. Selling was the only thing he had proved himself good at; yet it was impossible for him to believe that every man was not created equally an artist if he could but suffer and achieve it. As for the girl, he doubted if the sight of Singleton would do anything for her. She had that particular repulsive fanaticism peculiar to smart children —all brain and no emotion.

He spent a restless night, dreaming in snatches of Singleton. At one point he dreamed he was driving to Quincy to sell Singleton a refrigerator. When he awoke in the morning, a slow rain was descending indifferently. He turned his head to the grey window pane. He could not remember what he had dreamed but he sensed it had been unpleasant. A vision of the girl's flat face came to him. He thought of Quincy and saw rows and rows of low red buildings with rough heads sticking out of barred windows. He tried to concentrate on Singleton but his mind shied from the thought. He did not wish to go to Quincy. He remembered that it was a novel he was going to write. His desire to write a novel had gone down overnight like a defective tire.

While he lay in bed, the drizzle turned into a steady downpour. The rain might keep the girl from coming, or at least she might think she could use it as an excuse. He decided to wait until exactly nine o'clock and if she had not shown up by then to be off. He would not go to Quincy but would go home. It would be better to see Singleton at a later date when he would perhaps have responded to treatment. He got up and wrote the girl a note to be left with his aunts, saying he presumed she had decided, upon consideration, that she was not equal to the experience. It was a very concise note and he ended it, "Cordially yours."

She arrived at five minutes to nine and stood dripping in his aunts' hall, a tubular bundle of baby-blue plastic from which nothing showed but her face. She was holding a damp paper sack and her large mouth was twisted in an uncertain smile. Overnight she had apparently lost some of her self-assurance.

Calhoun was barely able to be polite. His aunts, who thought this was a romantic outing in the rain, kissed him out the door and stood on the porch idiotically waving their handkerchiefs until he and Mary Elizabeth were in the car and gone.

The girl was much too big for the small car. She kept shifting about and twisting inside her raincoat. "The rain has beat the azaleas down," she observed in a neutral tone.

Calhoun rudely kept silent. He was trying to obliterate her from his consciousness so that he could reestablish Singleton there. He had lost Singleton completely. The rain was coming down in grey swaths. When they reached the highway, they could barely see across the fields to a faint line of woods. The girl kept leaning forward, squinting into the opaque windshield. "If a truck were to come out of that," she said with a gawkish laugh, "that would be the end of us."

Calhoun stopped the car. "I'll be glad to take you back and go on by myself," he said.

"I have to go," she said hoarsely, staring at him. "I have to see him." Behind her spectacles, her eyes appeared larger than they should have been and suspiciously liquid. "I have to face this," she said.

Roughly, he started the car again.

"You have to prove to yourself that you can stand there and watch a man be crucified," she said. "You have to go through it with him. I thought about it all night."

"It may give you," Calhoun muttered, "a more balanced view of life."

"This is personal," she said. "You wouldn't understand," and she turned her head to the window.

Calhoun tried to concentrate on Singleton. Feature by feature, he brought the face together in his mind and each time he had it almost constructed, it fell apart and he was left with nothing. He drove in silence, at a reckless speed as if he would like to hit a hole in the road and see the girl go through the windshield. Every now and then she blew her nose weakly. After fifteen miles or so the rain slackened and stopped. The treeline on either side of them became black and clear and the fields intensely green. They would have an unmistakable view of the hospital grounds as soon as these should come in sight.

"Christ only had to take it three hours," the girl said all at once in a high voice, "but he'll be in this place the rest of his life!"

Calhoun cut his eyes toward her. There was a fresh wet line down the side of her face. He turned his eyes away, awed and furious. "If you can't stand this," he said, "I can still take you home and come back by myself."

"You wouldn't come back by yourself," she said, "and we're almost there." She blew her nose. "I want him to know that somebody takes his side. I want to say that to him no matter what it does to me."

Through his rage, the terrible thought occurred to the boy that he would have to *say* something to Singleton. What could he say to him in the presence of this woman? She had shattered the communion between them. "We've come to listen I hope you understand," he burst out. "I haven't driven all this way to hear you startle Singleton with your wisdom. I've come to listen to *him*."

"We should have brought a tape recorder!" she cried, "then we'd have what he says all our lives!"

"You don't have elementary understanding," Calhoun said, "if you think you approach a man like this with a tape recorder."

"Stop!" she shrieked, leaning toward the windshield, "that's it!"

Calhoun slammed on his brakes and looked forward wildly.

A cluster of low buildings, hardly noticeable, rose like a rich growth of warts on the hill to their right.

The boy sat helpless while the car, as if of its own volition, turned and headed toward the entrance. The letters QUINCY STATE HOSPITAL were cut in a concrete arch which it rolled effortlessly through.

"Abandon hope all ye who enter here," the girl murmured.

They had to stop within a hundred yards of the gate while a fat white-capped nurse led a line of patients, straggling like elderly schoolchildren, across the road in front of them. A snaggle-toothed woman in a candy-striped dress and black wool hat shook her fist at them, and a baldheaded man waved energetically. A few threw malevolent looks as the line shuffled off across the green to another building.

After a moment the car rolled forward again. "Park in front of that center building," Mary Elizabeth directed.

"They won't let us see him," he mumbled.

"Not if you have anything to do with it," she said. "Park and let me out. I'll handle this." Her cheek had dried and her voice was businesslike. He parked and she got out. He watched her disappear into the building, thinking with grim satisfaction that she would soon turn into a full-grown ogre—false intellect, false emotions, maximum efficiency, all operating to produce the dominant hair-splitting Ph.D. Another line of patients passed in the road and several of them pointed at the small car. Calhoun did not look but he sensed he was being watched. "Hup up there," he heard the nurse say.

He looked again and gave a little cry. A gentle face, wrapped around with a green hand towel, was in his window, smiling toothlessly but with an agonizing tenderness.

"Get a move on, sweetie," the nurse said and the face retreated.

The boy rolled his window up rapidly but his heart was wrenched. He saw again the agonized face in the stocks—the slightly mismatched eyes, the wide mouth parted in a stifled useless cry. The vision lasted only a moment but when it passed, he was certain that the sight of Singleton was going to effect a change in him, that after this visit, some strange tranquility he had not before conceived of would be his. He sat for ten minutes with his eyes closed, knowing that a revelation was near and trying to prepare himself for it.

All at once the car door opened and the girl folded herself, panting, in beside him. Her face was pale. She held up two green permission slips and pointed to the names written on them: Calhoun Singleton on one, Mary Elizabeth Singleton on the other. For a moment they stared at the slips, then at each other. Both appeared to recognize that in their common kinship with him, a kinship with each other was unavoidable. Generously, Calhoun held out his hand. She shook it. "He's in the fifth building to the left," she said.

They drove to the fifth building and parked. It was a low red brick structure with barred windows, like all the others except that the outside of it was streaked with black stains. In one window two hands hung out, palms downward. Mary Elizabeth opened the paper sack she had brought and began to take out presents for Singleton. She had brought a box of candy, a carton of cigarets and three books—a Modern Library *Thus Spake Zarathustra*, a paper-back *Revolt of the Masses*, and a thin decorated volume of Housman. She handed the cigarets and the candy to Calhoun and got out of the car with the books herself. She started forward, but halfway to the door she stopped and put her hand to her mouth. "I can't take it," she murmured.

"Now now," Calhoun said kindly. He put his hand on her back and gave her a slight push and she began to move forward again.

They entered a stained linoleum-covered hall where a peculiar odor met them at once like an invisible official. There was a desk facing the door, behind which sat a frail harassed-looking nurse whose eyes darted to right and left as if she expected ultimately to be hit from behind. Mary Elizabeth handed her the two green permits. The woman looked at them and groaned. "Go in yonder and wait," she said in a weary insult-bearing voice. "He'll have to be got ready. They shouldn't have give you these slips over there. What do they know about what goes on over here over there and what do them doctors care anyhow? If it was up to me the ones that don't cooperate wouldn't see nobody."

"We're his kin," Calhoun said. "We have every right to see him."

The nurse threw her head back in a soundless laugh and went off muttering.

Calhoun put his hand on the girl's back again and guided her into the waiting room where they sat down close together on a mammoth black leather sofa which faced an identical piece of furniture five feet away. There was nothing else in the room but a rickety table in one corner with an empty white vase on it. A barred window cast squares of damp light on the floor at their feet. There seemed an intense stillness about them although the place was anything but quiet. From one end of the building came a continuous mourning sound as delicate as the fluttering wail of owls; at the other end they heard rocketing peals of laughter. Closer at hand, a steady monotonous cursing broke the silence around it with a machine-like regularity. Each noise seemed to exist isolated from every other.

The two sat together as if they were waiting for some momentous event in their lives—a marriage or instantaneous deaths. They seemed already joined in a predestined convergence. At the same instant each made an involuntary motion as if to run but it was too late. Heavy footsteps were almost at the door and the machine-like curses were bearing down.

Two burly attendants entered with Singleton spider-like between them. He was holding his feet high up off the floor so that the attendants had to carry him. It was from him the curses were coming. He had on a hospital gown of the type that opens and ties up the back and his feet were stuck in black shoes from which the laces had been removed. On his head was a black hat, not the kind countrymen wear, but a black derby hat such as might be worn by a gunman in the movies. The two attendants came up to the empty sofa from behind and swung him over the back of it, then still holding him, each passed around the sofa arms and sat down beside him, grinning. They might have been twins for though one was blond and the other bald, they had identical looks of good-natured stupidity.

As for Singleton, he fixed Calhoun with his green slightly mismatched eyes. "Whadaya want with me?" he shrilled. "Speak up! My time is valuable." They were almost exactly the eyes that Calhoun had seen in the paper, except that the penetrating gleam in them had a slight reptilian quality.

The boy sat mesmerized.

After a moment, Mary Elizabeth said in a slow, hoarse, barely audible voice, "We came to say we understand."

The old man's glare shifted to her and for one instant his eyes remained absolutely still like the eyes of a treetoad that has sighted its prey. His throat appeared to swell. "Ahhh," he said as if he had just swallowed something pleasant, "eeeee."

"Mind out now, dad," one of the attendants said.

"Lemme sit with her," Singleton said and jerked his arm

away from the attendant, who caught it again at once. "She knows what she wants."

"Let him sit with her," the blond attendant said, "she's his niece."

"No," the bald one said, "keep aholt to him. He's liable to pull off his frock. You know *him*."

But the other one had already let one of his wrists loose and Singleton was leaning outward toward Mary Elizabeth, straining away from the attendant who held him. The girl's eyes were glazed. The old man began to make suggestive noises through his teeth.

"Now now, dad," the idle attendant said.

"It's not every girl gets a chance at me," Singleton said. "Listen here, sister, I'm well-fixed. There's nobody in Partridge I can't skin. I own the place—as well as this hotel." His hand grasped toward her knee.

The girl gave a small stifled cry.

"And I got others elsewhere," he panted. "You and me are two of a kind. We ain't in their class. You're a queen. I'll put you on a float!" and at that moment he got his wrist free and lunged toward her but both attendants sprang after him instantly. As Mary Elizabeth crouched against Calhoun, the old man jumped nimbly over the sofa and began to speed around the room. The attendants, their arms and legs held wide apart to catch him, tried to close in on him from either side. They almost had him when he kicked off his shoes and leaped between them onto the table, sending the empty vase shattering to the floor. "Look girl!" he shrilled and began to pull the hospital gown over his head.

Mary Elizabeth was already dashing out the room and Calhoun ran behind her and thrust open the door just in time to prevent her crashing into it. They scrambled into the car and the boy drove it away as if his heart were the motor and would never go fast enough. The sky was bone-white and the slick highway stretched before them like a piece of the earth's exposed nerve. After five miles Calhoun pulled the car to the side of the road and stopped from exhaustion. They sat silently, looking at nothing until finally they turned and looked at each other. There each saw at once the likeness of their kinsman and flinched. They looked away and then back, as if with concentration they might find a more tolerable image. To Calhoun, the girl's face seemed to mirror the nakedness of the sky. In despair he leaned closer until he was stopped by a miniature visage which rose incorrigibly in her spectacles and fixed him where he was. Round, innocent, undistinguished as an iron link, it was the face whose gift of life had pushed straight forward to the future to raise festival after festival. Like a master salesman, it seemed to have been waiting there from all time to claim him.

Why Do the Heathen Rage?

Tilman had had his stroke in the state capital where he had gone on business, and he had stayed two weeks in the hospital there. He did not remember his arrival home by ambulance but his wife did. She had sat for two hours on the jump seat at his feet, gazing fixedly at his face. Only his left eye, twisted inward, seemed to harbor his former personality. It burned with rage. The rest of his face was prepared for death. Justice was grim and she took satisfaction in it when she found it. It might take just this ruin to wake Walter up.

By accident both children had been at home when they arrived. Mary Maud had driven in from school, not realizing that the ambulance was behind her. She got out—a large woman of thirty with a round, childish face and a pile of carrot-colored hair that seeped about in an invisible net on top of her head—kissed her mother, glanced at Tilman and gasped; then, grim-faced but flustered, marched behind the rear attendant, giving him high-pitched instructions on how to get the stretcher around the curve of the front steps. Exactly like a schoolteacher, her mother thought. Schoolteacher all over. As the forward attendant reached the porch, Mary Maud said sharply in a voice used to controlling children, "Get up, Walter, and open the door!"

Walter was sitting on the edge of his chair, absorbed in the proceedings, his finger folded in the book he had been reading before the ambulance came. He got up and held open the door and while the attendants carried the stretcher across the porch, he gazed, obviously fascinated, at his father's face. "Glad to see you back, capt'n," he said and raised his hand in a sloppy salute.

Tilman's enraged left eye appeared to include him in its vision but he gave him no sign of recognition.

Roosevelt, who from now on would be nurse instead of yard man, stood inside the door, waiting. He had put on the white coat that he was supposed to wear for occasions. He peered forward at what was on the stretcher. The bloodshot veins in his eyes swelled. Then, all at once, tears glazed them and glistened on his black cheeks like sweat. Tilman made a

797

weak rough motion with his good arm. It was the only
gesture of affection he had given any of them. The Negro
followed the stretcher to the back bedroom, snuffling as if
someone had hit him.

Mary Maud went in to direct the stretcher bearers. Walter
and his mother remained on the porch. "Close the door," she
said, "you're letting flies in."

She had been watching him all along, searching for some
sign in his big, bland face that some sense of urgency had
touched him, some sense that now he had to take hold, that
now he had to do something, anything—she would have
been glad to see him make a mistake, even make a mess of
things if it meant that he was doing something—but she saw
that nothing had happened. His eyes were on her, glittering
just slightly behind his glasses. He had taken in every detail
of Tilman's face, he had registered Roosevelt's tears, Mary
Maud's confusion, and now he was studying her to see how
she was taking it. She yanked her hat straight, seeing by his
eyes that it had slipped toward the back of her head.

"You ought to wear it that way," he said. "It makes you
look sort of relaxed-by-mistake."

She made her face hard, as hard as she could make it. "The
responsibility is yours now," she said in a harsh, final voice.

He stood there with his half smile and said nothing. Like
an absorbent lump, she thought, taking everything in, giving
nothing out. She might have been looking at a stranger using
the family face. He had the same noncommittal lawyer's smile
as her father and grandfather, set in the same heavy jaw, under the same Roman nose; he had the same eyes that were
neither blue nor green nor gray; his skull would soon be bald
like theirs. Her face became even harder. "You'll have to take
over and manage this place," she said, "if you want to stay
here."

The smile left him. He looked at her once hard, his expression empty, and then beyond her out across the meadow, beyond the four oaks and the black distant tree line into the
vacant afternoon sky. "I thought it was home," he said, "but
it don't do to presume."

Her heart constricted. She had an instant's revelation that
he was homeless. Homeless here and homeless anywhere. "Of

course it's home," she said, "but somebody has to take over. Somebody has to make these Negroes work."

"I can't make Negroes work. That's about the last thing I'm capable of."

"I'll tell you everything to do," she said.

"Ha!" he said. "That you would." His half smile returned. "Lady," he said, "you're coming into your own. You were born to take over. If the old man had had his stroke ten years ago, we'd all be better off. You could have run a wagon train through the Badlands. You could stop a mob. You're the last of the nineteenth century, you're . . ."

"Walter, you're a man. I'm only a woman."

"A woman of your generation," Walter said, "is better than a man of mine."

Her mouth drew into a tight line of outrage and her head trembled almost imperceptibly. "I would be ashamed to say it!" she whispered.

Walter dropped into the chair he had been sitting in and opened his book. A sluggish-looking flush settled on his face. "The only virtue of my generation," he said, "is that it ain't ashamed to tell the truth about itself." He was already reading. Her interview was at an end.

She remained standing there, rigid, her eyes on him in stunned disgust. Her son. Her only son. His eyes and his skull and his smile belonged to the family face, but underneath them was a different kind of man from any she had ever known. There was no innocence in him, no rectitude, no conviction either of sin or election. The man she saw courted good and evil impartially and saw so many sides of every question that he could not move, he could not work, he could not even make niggers work. Any evil could enter that vacuum. God knows, she thought, and caught her breath, God knows what he might do!

He had not done anything. He was twenty-eight now and, so far as she could see, nothing occupied him but trivia. He had the air of a person who is waiting for some big event and can't start any work because it would only be interrupted. Since he was always idle, she had thought that perhaps he wanted to be an artist or a philosopher or something, but this was not the case. He did not want to write anything with a name. He amused himself writing letters to people he did not know and to the newspapers. Under different names and using different personalities, he wrote to strangers. It was a peculiar, small, contemptible vice. Her father and her grandfather had been moral men, but they would have scorned small vices more than great ones. They knew who they were and what they owed to themselves. It was impossible to tell what Walter knew or what his views were on anything. He read books that had nothing to do with anything that mattered now. Often she came behind him and found some strange underlined passage in a book he had left lying somewhere and she would puzzle over it for days. One passage she found in a book he had left lying on the upstairs bathroom floor stayed with her ominously.

"Love should be full of anger," it began, and she thought, well mine is. She was furious all the time. It went on, "Since you have already spurned my request, perhaps you will listen to admonishment. What business have you in your father's house, O you effeminate soldier? Where are your ramparts and trenches, where is the winter spent at the front lines? Listen! the battle trumpet blares from heaven and see how our General marches fully armed, coming amid the clouds to conquer the whole world. Out of the mouth of our King emerges a double-edged sword that cuts down everything in the way. Arising finally from your nap, do you come to the battlefield! Abandon the shade and seek the sun."

She turned back in the book to see what she was reading. It was a letter from a St. Jerome to a Heliodorus, scolding him for having abandoned the desert. A footnote said that Heliodorus was one of the famous group that had centered around Jerome at Aquileia in 370. He had accompanied Jerome to the Near East with the intention of cultivating a hermitic life. They had separated when Heliodorus continued on to Jerusalem. Eventually he returned to Italy, and in later years he became a distinguished churchman as the bishop of Altinum.

This was the kind of thing he read—something that made no sense for now. Then it came to her, with an unpleasant jolt, that the General with the sword in his mouth, marching to do violence, was Jesus.

The Fiction Writer and His Country

Among the many complaints made about the modern American novelist, the loudest, if not the most intelligent, has been the charge that he is not speaking for his country. A few seasons back an editorial in *Life* magazine asked grandly, "Who speaks for America today?" and was not able to conclude that our novelists, or at least our most gifted ones, did.

The gist of the editorial was that in the last ten years this country had enjoyed an unparalleled prosperity, that it had come nearer to producing a classless society than any other nation and that it was the most powerful country in the world, but that our novelists were writing as if they lived in packing boxes on the edge of the dump while they awaited admission to the poorhouse. Instead of this, the editorial requested that they give us something that really represented this country, and it ended with a very smooth and slick shift into a higher key and demanded further that the novelist show us the redeeming quality of spiritual purpose, for it said that "what is most missing from our hot-house literature" is "the joy of life itself."

This was irritating enough to provoke answers from many novelists and critics, but I do not know that any of those who answered considered the question specifically from the standpoint of the novelist with Christian concerns, who, presumably, would have an interest at least equal to the editors of *Life* in "the redeeming quality of spiritual purpose."

What is such a writer going to take his "country" to be? The word usually used by literary folk in this connection would be "world," but the word "country" will do; in fact, being homely, it will do better, for it suggests more. It suggests everything from the actual countryside that the novelist describes, on, to, and through the peculiar characteristics of his region and his nation, and on, through, and under all of these to his true country, which the writer with Christian convictions will consider to be what is eternal and absolute. This covers considerable territory, and if one were talking of any other kind of writing than the writing of fiction, one

would perhaps have to say "countries," but it is the peculiar
burden of the fiction writer that he has to make one country
do for all and that he has to evoke that one country through
the concrete particulars of a life that he can make believable.

This is first of all a matter of vocation, and a vocation is a
limiting factor which extends even to the kind of material that
the writer is able to apprehend imaginatively. The writer can
choose what he writes about but he cannot choose what he is
able to make live, and so far as he is concerned a living deformed character is acceptable and a dead whole one is not.
The Christian writer particularly will feel that whatever his
initial gift is, it comes from God; and no matter how minor
a gift it is, he will not be willing to destroy it by trying to use
it outside its proper limits.

The country that the writer is concerned with in the most
objective way is, of course, the region that most immediately
surrounds him, or simply the country, with its body of manners, that he knows well enough to employ. It's generally
suggested that the Southern writer has some advantage here.
Most readers these days must be sufficiently sick of hearing
about Southern writers and Southern writing and what so
many reviewers insist upon calling the "Southern school." No
one has ever made plain just what the Southern school is or
which writers belong to it. Sometimes, when it is most respectable, it seems to mean the little group of Agrarians that
flourished at Vanderbilt in the twenties; but more often the
term conjures up an image of Gothic monstrosities and the
idea of a preoccupation with everything deformed and grotesque. Most of us are considered, I believe, to be unhappy
combinations of Poe and Erskine Caldwell.

At least, however, we are all known to be anguished. The
writers of the editorial in question suggest that our anguish
is a result of our isolation from the rest of the country. I feel
that this would be news to most Southern writers. The anguish that most of us have observed for some time now has
been caused not by the fact that the South is alienated from
the rest of the country, but by the fact that it is not alienated
enough, that every day we are getting more and more like the
rest of the country, that we are being forced out, not only of

our many sins but of our few virtues. This may be unholy anguish but it is anguish nevertheless.

Manners are of such great consequence to the novelist that any kind will do. Bad manners are better than no manners at all, and because we are losing our customary manners we are probably overly conscious of them; this seems to be a condition that produces writers. In the South there are more amateur authors than there are rivers and streams. In almost every hamlet you'll find at least one lady writing epics in Negro dialect and probably two or three old gentlemen who have impossible historical novels on the way. The woods are full of regional writers, and it is the great horror of every serious Southern writer that he will become one of them.

The writer himself will probably feel that the only way for him to keep from becoming one of them is to examine his conscience and to observe our fierce but fading manners in the light of an ultimate concern; others would say that the way to escape being a regional writer is to widen the region. Don't be a Southern writer; be an American writer. Express this great country—which is enjoying an unparalleled prosperity, which is the strongest nation in the world, and which has almost produced a classless society. How, with all this prosperity and strength and classlessness staring you in the face, can you honestly produce a literature which doesn't make plain the joy of life?

The writer whose position is Christian, and probably also the writer whose position is not, will begin to wonder at this point if there could not be some ugly correlation between our unparalleled prosperity and the stridency of these demands for a literature that shows us the joy of life. He may at least be permitted to ask if these screams for joy would be quite so piercing if joy were really more abundant in our prosperous society.

The Christian writer will feel that in the greatest depth of vision, moral judgment will be implicit and that when we are invited to represent the country according to survey, what we are asked to do is to separate mystery from manners and judgment from vision, in order to produce something a little more palatable to the modern temper. We are asked to form our consciences in the light of statistics, which is to establish the relative as absolute. For many this may be a convenience, since we don't live in an age of settled belief; but it cannot be a convenience, it cannot even be possible, for the writer who is a Catholic. He will feel that any long-continued service to it will produce a soggy, formless, and sentimental literature, one that will provide a sense of spiritual purpose for those who connect the spirit with romanticism and a sense of joy for those who confuse that virtue with satisfaction. The storyteller is concerned with what is; but if what is, is what can be determined by survey, then the disciples of Dr. Kinsey and Dr. Gallup are sufficient for the day thereof.

In the greatest fiction, the writer's moral sense coincides with his dramatic sense, and I see no way for it to do this unless his moral judgment is part of the very act of seeing, and he is free to use it. I have heard it said that belief in Christian dogma is a hindrance to the writer, but I myself have found nothing further from the truth. Actually, it frees the storyteller to observe. It is not a set of rules which fixes what he sees in the world. It affects his writing primarily by guaranteeing his respect for mystery.

In the introduction to a collection of his stories called *Rotting Hill*, Wyndham Lewis has written, "If I write about a hill that is rotting, it is because I despise rot." The general accusation passed against writers now is that they write about rot because they love it. Some do, and their works may betray them, but it is impossible not to believe that some write about rot because they see it and recognize it for what it is.

It may well be asked, however, why so much of our literature is apparently lacking in a sense of spiritual purpose and in the joy of life, and if stories lacking such are actually credible. The only conscience I have to examine in this matter is my own, and when I look at stories I have written I find that they are, for the most part, about people who are poor, who are afflicted in both mind and body, who have little—or at best a distorted—sense of spiritual purpose, and whose actions do not apparently give the reader a great assurance of the joy of life.

Yet how is this? For I am no disbeliever in spiritual purpose and no vague believer. I see from the standpoint of Christian orthodoxy. This means that for me the meaning of life is centered in our Redemption by Christ and that what I see in the world I see in its relation to that. I don't think that this is a position that can be taken halfway or one that is particularly easy in these times to make transparent in fiction.

Some may blame preoccupation with the grotesque on the fact that here we have a Southern writer and that this is just the type of imagination that Southern life fosters. I have written several stories which did not seem to me to have any grotesque characters in them at all, but which have immediately been labeled grotesque by non-Southern readers. I find it hard to believe that what is observable behavior in one section can be entirely without parallel in another. At least, of late, Southern writers have had the opportunity of pointing out that none of us invented Elvis Presley and that that youth is himself probably less an occasion for concern than his popularity, which is not restricted to the Southern part of the country. The problem may well become one of finding something that is *not* grotesque and of deciding what standards we would use in looking.

My own feeling is that writers who see by the light of their Christian faith will have, in these times, the sharpest eyes for the grotesque, for the perverse, and for the unacceptable. In some cases, these writers may be unconsciously infected with the Manichaean spirit of the times and suffer the much discussed disjunction between sensibility and belief, but I think that more often the reason for this attention to the perverse is the difference between their beliefs and the beliefs of their audience. Redemption is meaningless unless there is cause for it in the actual life we live, and for the last few centuries there has been operating in our culture the secular belief that there is no such cause.

The novelist with Christian concerns will find in modern life distortions which are repugnant to him, and his problem will be to make these appear as distortions to an audience which is used to seeing them as natural; and he may well be forced to take ever more violent means to get his vision across to this hostile audience. When you can assume that your audience holds the same beliefs you do, you can relax a little and use more normal ways of talking to it; when you have to assume that it does not, then you have to make your vision apparent by shock—to the hard of hearing you shout, and for the almost blind you draw large and startling figures.

Unless we are willing to accept our artists as they are, the answer to the question, "Who speaks for America today?" will have to be: the advertising agencies. They are entirely capable of showing us our unparalleled prosperity and our almost classless society, and no one has ever accused them of not being affirmative. Where the artist is still trusted, he will not be looked to for assurance. Those who believe that art proceeds from a healthy, and not from a diseased, faculty of the mind will take what he shows them as a revelation, not of what we ought to be but of what we are at a given time and under given circumstances; that is, as a limited revelation but a revelation nevertheless.

When we talk about the writer's country we are liable to forget that no matter what particular country it is, it is inside as well as outside him. Art requires a delicate adjustment of the outer and inner worlds in such a way that, without changing their nature, they can be seen through each other. To know oneself is to know one's region. It is also to know the world, and it is also, paradoxically, a form of exile from that world. The writer's value is lost, both to himself and to his country, as soon as he ceases to see that country as a part of himself, and to know oneself is, above all, to know what one lacks. It is to measure oneself against Truth, and not the other way around. The first product of self-knowledge is humility, and this is not a virtue conspicuous in any national character.

St. Cyril of Jerusalem, in instructing catechumens, wrote: "The dragon sits by the side of the road, watching those who pass. Beware lest he devour you. We go to the Father of Souls, but it is necessary to pass by the dragon." No matter what form the dragon may take, it is of this mysterious passage past him, or into his jaws, that stories of any depth will always be concerned to tell, and this being the case, it requires considerable courage at any time, in any country, not to turn away from the storyteller.

The Church and the Fiction Writer

THE QUESTION of what effect the Church has on the fiction writer who is a Catholic cannot always be answered by pointing to the presence of Graham Greene among us. One has to think not only of gifts that have ended in art or near it, but of gifts-gone-astray and of those never developed. In 1955, the editors of FOUR QUARTERS, a quarterly magazine published by the faculty of La Salle College in Philadelphia, printed a Symposium on the subject of the dearth of Catholic writers among the graduates of Catholic colleges and in subsequent issues published letters from writers and critics, Catholic and non-Catholic, in response to the Symposium. These ranged from the statement of Mr. Philip Wylie that "A Catholic, if he is devout, i.e., sold on the authority of his Church, is also brain-washed, whether he realizes it or not," (and consequently does not have the freedom necessary to be a first-rate creative writer) to the often-repeated explanation that the Catholic in this country suffers from a parochial aesthetic and a cultural insularity. A few held the situation no worse among Catholics than among other groups, creative minds always being hard to find; a few held the times responsible.

The faculty of a college must consider this as an educational problem; the writer who is a Catholic will consider it a personal one. Whether he is a graduate of a Catholic college or not, if he takes the Church for what She takes Herself, he must decide what She demands of him and if and how his freedom is restricted by Her. The material and method of fiction being what they are, the problem may seem greater for the fiction writer than for any other.

For the writer of fiction everything has its testing point in the eye, an organ which eventually involves the whole personality and as much of the world as can be got into it. Msgr. Guardini has written that the roots of the eye are in the heart. In any case, for the Catholic they stretch far and away into those depths of mystery which the modern world is divided about—part of it trying to eliminate mystery while another part tries to rediscover it in disciplines less personally demanding than religion. What Mr. Wylie contends is that the Catholic writer, because he believes in certain defined mysteries, cannot, by the nature of things, see straight; and this contention, in effect, is not very different from that made by Catholics who declare that whatever the Catholic writer *can* see, there are certain things that he should not see, straight or otherwise. These are the Catholics who are victims of the parochial aesthetic and the cultural insularity and it is interesting to find them sharing, even for a split second, the intellectual bed of Mr. Wylie.

It is generally supposed, and not least by Catholics, that the Catholic who writes fiction is out to use fiction to prove the truth of the Faith, or at the least, to prove the existence of the supernatural. He may be. No one certainly can be sure of his low motives except as they suggest themselves in his finished work, but when the finished work suggests that pertinent actions have been fraudulently manipulated or overlooked or smothered, whatever purposes the writer started out with have already been defeated. What the fiction writer will discover, if he discovers anything at all, is that he himself cannot move or mold reality in the interests of abstract truth. The writer learns, perhaps more quickly than the reader, to be humble in the face of what-is. What-is is all he has to do with; the concrete is his medium; and he will realize eventually that fiction can transcend its limitations only by staying within them.

Henry James said that the morality of a piece of fiction depended on the amount of "felt life" that was in it. The Catholic writer, in so far as he has the mind of the Church, will feel life from the standpoint of the central Christian mystery: that it has, for all its horror, been found by God to be worth dying for. But this should enlarge not narrow his field of vision. To the modern mind, as represented by Mr. Wylie, this is warped vision which "bears little or no relation to the truth as it is known today." The Catholic who does not write for a limited circle of fellow Catholics will in all probability consider that, since this is his vision, he is writing for a hostile audience, and he will be more than ever concerned to have his work stand on its own feet and be complete and self-sufficient and impregnable in its own right. When people have told me that because I am a Catholic, I cannot be an artist, I have had to reply, ruefully, that because I am a Catholic I cannot afford to be less than an artist.

The limitations that any writer imposes on his work will grow out of the necessities that lie in the material itself and these will generally be more rigorous than any that religion could impose. Part of the complexity of the problem for the Catholic fiction writer will be the presence of grace as it appears in nature, and what matters for him here is that his faith not become detached from his dramatic sense and from his vision of what-is. No one in these days, however, would seem more anxious to have it become detached than those Catholics who demand that the writer limit, on the natural level, what he allows himself to see.

If the average Catholic reader could be tracked down through the swamps of letters-to-the-editor and other places where he momentarily reveals himself, he would be found to be more of a Manichean than the Church permits. By separating nature and grace as much as possible, he has reduced his conception of the supernatural to pious cliche and has become able to recognize nature in literature in only two forms, the sentimental and the obscene. He would seem to prefer the former, while being more of an authority on the latter, but the similarity between the two generally escapes him. He forgets that sentimentality is an excess, a distortion of sentiment usually in the direction of an overemphasis on innocence and that innocence whenever it is overemphasized in the ordinary human condition, tends by some natural law to become its opposite. We lost our innocence in the Fall and our return to it is through the Redemption which was brought about by Christ's death and by our slow participation in it. Sentimentality is a skipping of this process in its concrete reality and an early arrival at a mock state of innocence, which strongly suggests its opposite. Pornography, on the other hand, is essentially sentimental, for it leaves out the connection of sex with its hard purposes and so far disconnects it from its meaning in life as to make it simply an experience for its own sake.

Many well-grounded complaints have been made about religious literature on the score that it tends to minimize the

importance and dignity of life here and now in favor of life
in the next world or in favor of the miraculous manifestations
of grace. When fiction is made according to its nature, it
should reinforce our sense of the supernatural by grounding
it in concrete observable reality. If the writer uses his eyes in
the real security of his Faith, he will be obliged to use them
honestly and his sense of mystery and his acceptance of it will
be increased. To look at the worst will be for him no more
than an act of trust in God; but what is one thing for the
writer may be another for the reader. What leads the writer
to his salvation may lead the reader into sin, and the Catholic
writer who looks at this possibility directly looks the Medusa
in the face and is turned to stone.

By now anyone who has had the problem is equipped with
Mauriac's advice: "purify the source." And along with it has
become aware that while he is attempting to do that, he has
to keep on writing. He becomes aware too of sources that,
relatively speaking, seem amply pure but from which come
works that scandalize. He may feel that it is as sinful to scandalize the learned as the ignorant. In the end, he will either
have to stop writing or limit himself to the concerns proper
to what he is creating. It is the person who can follow neither
of these courses who becomes the victim, not of the Church,
but of a false conception of Her demands.

The business of protecting souls from dangerous literature
belongs properly to the Church. All fiction, even when it sat-
isfies the requirements of art, will not turn out to be suitable
for everyone's consumption, and if in some instance, the
Church sees fit to forbid the faithful to read a work without
permission, the author, if he is a Catholic, will be thankful
that the Church is willing to perform this service for him. It
means that he can limit himself to the demands of art.

The fact would seem to be that for many writers it is easier
to assume universal responsibility for souls than it is to produce a work of art, and it is considered better to save the
world than to save the work. This view probably owes as
much to romanticism as to piety but the writer will not be
liable to entertain it unless it has been foisted on him by a
sorry education or unless writing is not his vocation in the
first place. That it is foisted on him by the general atmosphere

of Catholic piety in this country is hard to deny, and even if this atmosphere cannot be held responsible for every talent killed along the way, it is at least general enough to give an air of credibility to Mr. Wylie's conception of what belief in Christian Dogma does to the creative mind.

A belief in fixed dogma cannot fix what goes on in life or blind the believer to it. It will, of course, add a dimension to the writer's observation which many cannot, in conscience, acknowlege exists, but as long as what they can acknowlege, is present in the work, they cannot claim that any freedom has been denied the artist. A dimension taken away is one thing; a dimension added is another, and what the Catholic writer and reader will have to remember is that the reality of the added dimension will be judged in a work of fiction by the truthfulness and wholeness of the natural events presented. If the Catholic writer hopes to reveal mysteries, he will have to do it by describing truthfully what he sees from where he is. An affirmative vision cannot be demanded of him without limiting his freedom to observe what man has done with the things of God.

If we intend to encourage Catholic fiction writers, we must convince those coming along that the Church does not restrict their freedom to be artists but insures it (the restrictions of art are another matter), and to convince them of this requires, perhaps more than anything else, a body of Catholic readers who are equipped to recognize something in fiction besides passages that they consider obscene. It is popular to suppose that anyone who can read the telephone book can read a short story or a novel, and it is more than usual to find the attitude among Catholics that since we possess the Truth in the Church, we can use this Truth directly as an instrument of judgment on any discipline at any time without regard for the nature of that discipline itself. Catholic readers are constantly being offended and scandalized by novels that they don't have the fundamental equipment to read in the first place, and often these are works that are permeated with a Christian spirit.

It is when the individual's faith is weak, not when it is strong, that he will be afraid of an honest fictional representation of life, and when there is a tendency to compartmentalize the spiritual and make it resident in a certain type of life only, the sense of the supernatural is apt gradually to be lost. Fiction, made according to its own laws, is an antidote to such a tendency, for it renews our knowlege that we live in the mystery from which we draw our abstractions. The Catholic fiction writer, as fiction writer, will look for the will of God first in the laws and limitations of his art and will hope that if he obeys these, other blessings will be added to his work. The happiest of these, and the one he may presently least expect, will be the satisfied Catholic reader.

Some Aspects of the Grotesque
in Southern Fiction

I THINK THAT if there is any value in hearing writers talk, it will be in hearing what they can witness to and not what they can theorize about. My own approach to literary problems is very like the one Dr. Johnson's blind housekeeper used when she poured tea—she put her finger inside the cup.

These are not times when writers in this country can very well speak for one another. In the twenties there were those at Vanderbilt University who felt enough kinship with eachother's ideas to issue a pamphlet called, I'LL TAKE MY STAND, and in the thirties there were writers whose social consciousness set them all going in more or less the same direction; but today, there are no good writers, bound even loosely together, who would be so bold as to say that they speak for a generation or for eachother. Today each writer speaks for himself, even though he may not be sure that his work is important enough to justify his doing so.

I think that every writer when he speaks of his own approach to fiction hopes to show that, in some crucial and deep sense, he is a realist; and for some of us, for whom the ordinary aspects of daily-life prove to be of no great fictional interest, this is very difficult. I have found that if one's young hero can't be identified with the average American boy, or even with the average American delinquent, then his perpetrator will have a good deal of explaining to do.

The first necessity confronting him will be to say what he is not doing; for even if there are no genuine schools in American letters today, there is always some critic who has just invented one and who is ready to put you into it. If you are a Southern writer, that label, and all the misconceptions that go with it, is pasted on you at once, and you are left to get it off as best you can. I have found that no matter for what purpose peculiar to your special dramatic needs, you use the Southern scene, you are still thought by the general reader to be writing about the South and are judged by the fidelity your fiction has to typical Southern life.

I am always having it pointed out to me that life in Georgia is not at all the way I picture it, that escaped criminals do not roam the roads exterminating families, nor Bible salesmen prowl about looking for girls with wooden legs.

The social sciences have cast a dreary blight on the public approach to fiction. When I first began to write, my own particular bête noire was that mythical entity, The School of Southern Degeneracy. Every time I heard about the School of Southern Degeneracy, I felt like Brer Rabbit stuck on the tar-baby. There was a time when the average reader read a novel simply for the moral he could get out of it, and however naive that may have been, it was a good deal less naive than some of the more limited objectives he now has. Today novels are considered to be entirely concerned with the social or economic or psychological forces that they will by necessity exhibit, or with those details of daily life that are for the good novelist only means to some deeper end.

Hawthorne knew his own problem and perhaps anticipated ours when he said he did not write novels, he wrote romances. Today many readers and critics have set up for the novel a kind of orthodoxy. They demand a realism of fact which may, in the end, limit rather than broaden the novel's scope. They associate the only legitimate material for long fiction with the movement of social forces, with the typical, with fidelity to the way things look and happen in normal life. Along with this usually goes a great interest in and a thorough treatment of the sexual aspects of their characters' existence. It has been only within the last five or six decades that writers have won the right to treat this last subject exhaustively. This was a right that opened up many possibilities for fiction, but it is always a bad day for culture when any liberty of this kind is assumed to be general. The writer has no rights at all except those he forges for himself inside his own work. We have become so flooded with sorry fiction based on unearned liberties, or on the notion that fiction must represent the typical, that in the public mind the deeper kinds of realism are less and less understandable.

The writer who writes within what might be called the modern romance tradition may not be writing novels which in all respects partake of a novelistic orthodoxy; but as long as these works have vitality, as long as they present something that is alive, however eccentric its life may seem to the general reader, then they have to be dealt with; and they have to be dealt with on their own terms.

When we look at a good deal of serious modern fiction, and particularly Southern fiction, we find this quality about it that is generally described, in a pejorative sense, as grotesque. Of course, I have found that anything that comes out of the South is going to be called grotesque by the Northern reader, unless it is grotesque, in which case it is going to be called realistic. But for this occasion, we may leave such misapplications aside and consider the kind of fiction that may be called grotesque with good reason, because of a directed intention that way on the part of the author.

In these grotesque works, we find that the writer has made alive some experience which we are not accustomed to observe everyday, or which the ordinary man may never experience in his ordinary life. We find that connections which we would expect in the customary kind of realism have been ignored, that there are strange skips and gaps which anyone trying to describe manners and customs would certainly not have left. Yet the characters in these novels are alive in spite of these things. They have an inner coherence, if not always a coherence to their social framework. Their fictional qualities lean away from typical social patterns, toward mystery and the unexpected. It is this kind of realism that I want to consider.

All novelists are fundamentally seekers and describers of the real, but the realism of each novelist will depend on his view of the ultimate reaches of reality. Since the 18th century, the popular spirit of each succeeding age has tended more and more to the view that the ills and mysteries of life will eventually fall before the scientific advances of man. If the novelist is in tune with this spirit, if he believes that actions are predetermined by psychic make-up or the economic situation or some other determinable factor, then he will be concerned above all with an accurate reproduction of the things that most immediately concern man, with the natural forces that he feels control his destiny. Such a writer may produce a great tragic naturalism, for by his responsibility to the things he sees, he may transcend the limitations of his narrow vision.

On the other hand, if the writer believes that our life is and will remain essentially mysterious, if he looks upon us as beings existing in a created order to whose laws we freely respond, then what he sees on the surface will be of interest to him only as he can go through it into an experience of mystery itself. His kind of fiction will always be pushing its own limits outward toward the limits of mystery, because for this kind of writer, the meaning of a story does not begin except at a depth where the adequate motivation and the adequate psychology and the various determinations have been exhausted. Such a writer will be interested in what we don't understand rather than in what we do. He will be interested in possibility rather than in probability. He will be interested in characters who are forced out to meet evil and grace and who act on a trust beyond themselves—whether they know very clearly what it is they act upon or not. To the modern mind, this kind of character, and his creator, are typical Don Quixotes, tilting at what is not there.

I would not like to suggest that this kind of writer, because his interest is predominantly in mystery, is able in any sense to slight the concrete. Fiction begins where human knowlege begins—with the senses—and every fiction writer is bound by this fundamental aspect of his medium. I do believe, however, that the kind of writer I am describing will use the concrete in a more drastic way. His way will much more obviously be the way of distortion.

Henry James said that in his fiction, he did things in the way that took the most doing. I think the writer of grotesque fiction does them in the way that takes the least, because in his work distances are so great. He's looking for one image that will connect or combine or embody two points; one is a point in the concrete and the other is a point not visible to the naked eye, but believed in by him firmly, just as real to him, really, as the one that everybody sees.

It's not necessary to point out that the look of this fiction is going to be wild, that it is almost of necessity going to be violent and comic, because of the discrepancies that it seeks to combine.

Even though the writer who produces grotesque fiction may not consider his characters any more freakish than ordinary fallen man usually is, his audience is going to; and it is going to ask him, or more often tell him, why he has chosen to bring such maimed souls alive. Thomas Mann has said that the grotesque is the true anti-bourgeoise style, but I believe that in this country, the general reader has managed to connect the grotesque with the sentimental, for whenever he speaks of it favorably, he seems to associate it with the writer's compassion.

It's considered an absolute necessity these days for writers to have compassion. Compassion is a word that sounds good in anybody's mouth and which no book jacket can do without. It is a quality which no one can put his finger on in any exact critical sense, so it is always safe for anybody to use. Usually I think what is meant by it is that the writer excuses all human weakness because human weakness is human. The kind of hazy compassion demanded of the writer now makes it difficult for him to be anti-anything. Certainly when the grotesque is used in a legitimate way, the intellectual and moral judgments implicit in it will have the ascendency over feeling.

In 19th century American writing, there was a good deal of grotesque literature which came from the frontier and was supposed to be funny; but our present grotesque characters, comic though they may be, are at least not primarily so. They seem to carry an invisible burden; their fanaticism is a reproach, not merely an eccentricity. I believe that they come about from the prophetic vision peculiar to any novelist, but particularly and, in these times, deliberately peculiar to the novelist whose concerns I have been describing. In the novelist's case, prophecy is a matter of seeing near things with their extensions of meaning and thus of seeing far things close up. The prophet is a realist of distances, and it is this kind of realism that you find in the best modern instances of the grotesque.

Whenever I'm asked why Southern writers particularly have a penchant for writing about freaks, I say it is because we are still able to recognize one. To be able to recognize a freak, you have to have some conception of the whole man, and in the South the general conception of man is still, in the main, theological. That is a large statement, and it is dangerous to make it, for almost anything you say about Southern belief can be denied in the next breath with equal propriety. But approaching the subject from the standpoint of the writer, I think it is safe to say that while the South is hardly Christ-centered, it is most certainly Christ-haunted. The Southerner who isn't convinced of it, is very much afraid that he may have been formed in the image and likeness of God. Ghosts can be very fierce and instructive. They cast strange shadows, particularly in our literature. In any case, it is when the freak can be sensed as a figure for our essential displacement that he attains some depth in literature.

There is another reason in the Southern situation that makes for a tendency toward the grotesque and this is the prevalence of good Southern writers. I think the writer is initially set going by literature more than by life. When there are many writers all employing the same idiom, all looking out on more or less the same social scene, the individual writer will have to be more than ever careful that he isn't just doing badly what has already been done to completion. The presence alone of Faulkner in our midst makes a great difference in what the writer can and cannot permit himself to do. Nobody wants his mule and wagon stalled on the same track the Dixie Limited is roaring down.

The Southern writer is forced from all sides to make his gaze extend beyond the surface, beyond mere problems, until it touches that realm which is the concern of prophets and poets. When Hawthorne said that he wrote romances, he was attempting, in effect, to keep for fiction some of its freedom from social determinisms and to steer it in the direction of poetry. I think this tradition of the dark and divisive romance-novel has combined with the comic grotesque tradition and with the lessons all writers have learned from the naturalists, to preserve our Southern literature for at least a little while from becoming the kind of thing Mr. Van Wyck Brooks desired when he said he hoped that our next literary phase would restore that central literature which combines the great subject matter of the middlebrow writers with the technical expertness bequeathed by the new critics and which would thereby restore literature as a mirror and guide for society.

For the kind of writer I have been describing, a literature which mirrors society would be no fit guide for it, and one which did manage, by sheer art, to do both these things would have to have recourse to more violent means than middlebrow subject matter and mere technical expertness.

We are not living in times when the realist of distances is understood or well thought of, even though he may be in the dominant tradition of American letters. Whenever the public is heard from, it is heard demanding a literature which is balanced and which will somehow heal the ravages of our times. In the name of social order, liberal thought, and sometimes even Christianity, the novelist is asked to be the handmaid of his age.

I have come to think of this handmaid as being very like the Negro porter who set Henry James' dressing case down in a puddle when James was leaving the hotel in Charleston. James was then obliged to sit in the crowded carriage with the satchel on his knees. All through the South the poor man was ignobly served and he afterwards wrote that our domestic servants were the last people in the world who should be employed in the way they were, for they were by nature unfitted for it. The case is the same with the novelist. When he is given the function of domestic, he is going to set the public's luggage down in puddle after puddle.

The novelist must be characterized not by his function but by his vision and we must remember that his vision has to be transmitted and that the limitations and blind spots of his audience will very definitely affect the way he is able to show what he sees. This is another thing, which in these times, increases the tendency toward the grotesque in fiction.

Those writers who speak for and with their age are able to do so with a great deal more ease and grace than those who speak counter to prevailing attitudes. I once received a letter from an old lady in California who informed me that when the tired reader comes home at night, he wishes to read something that will lift up his heart. And it seems her heart had not been lifted up by anything of mine she had read. I think that if her heart had been in the right place, it would have been lifted up.

You may say that the serious writer doesn't have to bother about the tired reader, but he does, because they are all tired. One old lady who wants her heart lifted up wouldn't be so bad, but you multiply her two hundred and fifty thousand times and what you get is a book club. I used to think it should be possible to write for some supposed elite, for the people who attend the universities and sometimes know how to read, but I have since found that though you may publish your stories in *Botteghe Oscure*, if they are any good at all, you are eventually going to get a letter from some old lady in California, or some inmate of the Federal Penitentiary or the state insane asylum or the local poorhouse, telling you where you have failed to meet his needs.

And his need, of course, is to be lifted up. There is something in us, as story-tellers and as listeners to stories, that demands the redemptive act, that demands that what falls at least be offered the chance to be restored. The reader of today looks for this motion, and rightly so, but what he has forgotten is the cost of it. His sense of evil is diluted or lacking altogether and so he has forgotten the price of restoration. When he reads a novel, he wants either his senses tormented or his spirits raised. He wants to be transported, instantly, either to a mock damnation or a mock innocence.

I am often told that the model of balance for the novelist should be Dante, who divided his territory up pretty evenly between hell, purgatory and paradise. There can be no objection to this, but also there can be no reason to assume that the result of doing it in these times will give us the balanced picture that it gave in Dante's. Dante lived in the 13th century when that balance was achieved in the faith of his age. We live now in an age which doubts both fact and value, which is swept this way and that by momentary convictions. Instead of reflecting a balance from the world around him, the novelist now has to achieve one from a felt balance inside himself. There are ages when it is possible to woo the reader; there are others when something more drastic is necessary.

There is no literary orthodoxy that can be prescribed as settled for the fiction writer, not even that of Henry James who balanced the elements of traditional realism and romance so admirably within each of his novels. But this much can be said. The great novels we get in the future are not going to be those that the public thinks it wants, or those that critics demand. They are going to be the kind of novels that interest the novelist. And the novels that interest the novelist are those that have not already been written. They are those that put the greatest demands on him, that require him to operate at the maximum of his intelligence and his talents, and to be true to the particularities of his own vocation. The direction of many of us will be toward concentration and the distortion that is necessary to get our vision across; it will be more toward poetry than toward the traditional novel.

The problem for such a novelist will be to know how far he can distort without destroying, and in order not to destroy, he will have to descend far enough into himself to reach those underground springs that give life to his work. This descent into himself will, at the same time, be a descent into his region. It will be a descent through the darkness of the familiar into a world where, like the blind man cured in the gospels, he sees men as if they were trees, but walking. This is the beginning of vision, and I feel it is a vision which we in the South must at least try to understand if we want to participate in the continuance of a vital Southern literature. I hate to think that in twenty years Southern writers too may be writing about men in grey flannel suits and may have lost their ability to see that these gentlemen are even greater freaks than what we are writing about now. I hate to think of the day when the Southern writer will satisfy the tired reader.

When that day comes, the Dorothy Blunt Lamar lectures will have to be concerned exclusively with the literature of the past.

Introduction to
A Memoir of Mary Ann

S TORIES OF pious children tend to be false. This may be
because they are told by adults, who see virtue where
their subjects would see only a practical course of action; or
it may be because such stories are written to edify and what
is written to edify usually ends by amusing. For my part, I
have never cared to read about little boys who build altars
and play they are priests, or about little girls who dress up as
nuns, or about those pious Protestant children who lack this
equipment but brighten the corners where they are.

Last spring I received a letter from Sister Evangelist, the
Sister Superior of Our Lady of Perpetual Help Free Cancer
Home in Atlanta. "This is a strange request," the letter read,
"but we will try to tell our story as briefly as possible. In 1949,
a little three-year-old girl, Mary Ann, was admitted to our
Home as a patient. She proved to be a remarkable child and
lived until she was twelve. Of those nine years, much is to be
told. Patients, visitors, Sisters, all were influenced in some
way by this afflicted child. Yet one never thought of her as
afflicted. True she had been born with a tumor on the side of
her face; one eye had been removed, but the other eye sparkled, twinkled, danced mischievously, and after one meeting
one never was conscious of her physical defect but recognized
only the beautiful brave spirit and felt the joy of such contact.
Now Mary Ann's story should be written but who to write it?"

Not me, I said to myself.

"We have had offers from nuns and others but we don't
want a pious little recital. We want a story with a real impact
on other lives just as Mary Ann herself had that impact on
each life she touched . . . This wouldn't have to be a factual
story. It could be a novel with many other characters but the
outstanding character, Mary Ann."

A novel, I thought. Horrors.

Sister Evangelist ended by inviting me to write Mary Ann's
story and to come up and spend a few days at the Home in
Atlanta and "imbibe the atmosphere" where the little girl had
lived for nine years.

It is always difficult to get across to people who are not professional writers that a talent to write does not mean a talent to write anything at all. I did not wish to imbibe Mary Ann's atmosphere. I was not capable of writing her story. Sister Evangelist had enclosed a picture of the child. I had glanced at it when I first opened the letter, and had put it quickly aside. Now I picked it up to give it a last cursory look before returning it to the Sisters. It showed a little girl in her first Communion dress and veil. She was sitting on a bench, holding something I could not make out. Her small face was straight and bright on one side. The other side was protuberant, the eye was bandaged, the nose and mouth crowded slightly out of place. The child looked out at her observer with an obvious happiness and composure. I continued to gaze at the picture long after I had thought to be finished with it.

After a while I got up and went to the book case and took out a volume of Nathaniel Hawthorne's stories. The Dominican Congregation to which the nuns belong who had taken care of Mary Ann had been founded by Hawthorne's daughter, Rose. The child's picture had brought to mind his story, *The Birthmark*. I found the story and opened it at that wonderful section of dialogue where Alymer first mentions his wife's defect to her.

One day Alymer sat gazing at his wife with a trouble in his countenance that grew stronger until he spoke.

"Georgiana," said he, "has it never occurred to you that the mark upon your cheek might be removed?"

"No, indeed," said she, smiling; but perceiving the seriousness of his manner, she blushed deeply. "To tell you the truth it has been so often called a charm that I was simple enough to imagine it might be so."

"Ah, upon another face perhaps it might," replied her husband, "but never on yours. No, dearest Georgiana, you came so nearly perfect from the hand of Nature that this slightest defect, which we hesitate whether to term a defect or a beauty, shocks me, as being the visible mark of earthly imperfection."

"Shocks you, my husband!" cried Georgiana, deeply

hurt, at first reddening with momentary anger, but then bursting into tears. "Then why did you take me from my mother's side? You cannot love what shocks you!"

The defect on Mary Ann's cheek could not have been mistaken for a charm. It was plainly grotesque. She belonged to fact and not to fancy. I conceived it my duty to write Sister Evangelist that if anything were written about this child, it should indeed be a "factual story," and I went on to say that if anyone should write these facts, it should be the Sisters themselves, who had known and nursed her. I felt this strongly. At the same time I wanted to make it plain that I was not the one to write the factual story, and there is no quicker way to get out of a job than to prescribe it for those who have prescribed it for you. I added that should they decide to take my advice, I would be glad to help them with the preparation of their manuscript and do any small editing that proved necessary. I had no doubt that this was safe generosity. I did not expect to hear from them again.

In *Our Old Home*, Hawthorne tells about a fastidious gentleman who, while going through a Liverpool workhouse, was followed by a wretched and rheumy child, so awful-looking that he could not decide what sex it was. The child followed him about until it decided to put itself in front of him in a mute appeal to be held. The fastidious gentleman, after a pause that was significant for himself, picked it up and held it. Hawthorne comments upon this:

> Nevertheless, it could be no easy thing for him to do, he being a person burdened with more than an Englishman's customary reserve, shy of actual contact with human beings, afflicted with a peculiar distaste for whatever was ugly, and, furthermore, accustomed to that habit of observation from an insulated standpoint which is said (but I hope erroneously) to have the tendency of putting ice into the blood.
>
> So I watched the struggle in his mind with a good deal of interest, and am seriously of the opinion that he did a heroic act and effected more than he dreamed of toward his

final salvation when he took up the loathsome child and caressed it as tenderly as if he had been its father.

What Hawthorne neglected to add is that he was the gentleman who did this. His wife, after his death, published his notebooks in which there was this account of the incident:

> After this, we went to the ward where the children were kept, and, on entering this, we saw, in the first place, two or three unlovely and unwholesome little imps, who were lazily playing together. One of them (a child about six years old, but I know not whether girl or boy) immediately took the strangest fancy for me. It was a wretched, pale, half-torpid little thing, with a humor in its eye which the Governor said was the scurvy. I never saw, till a few moments afterward, a child that I should feel less inclined to fondle. But this little sickly, humor-eaten fright prowled around me, taking hold of my skirts, following at my heels, and at last held up its hands, smiled in my face, and standing directly before me, insisted on my taking it up! Not that it said a word, for I rather think it was underwitted, and could not talk; but its face expressed such perfect confidence that it was going to be taken up and made much of, that it was impossible not to do it. It was as if God had promised the child this favor on my behalf, and that I must needs fulfill the contract. I held my undesirable burden a little while, and after setting the child down, it still followed me, holding two of my fingers and playing with them, just as if it were a child of my own. It was a foundling, and out of all human kind it chose me to be its father! We went upstairs into another ward; and on coming down again there was this same child waiting for me, with a sickly smile around its defaced mouth, and in its dim-red eyes . . . I should never have forgiven myself if I had repelled its advances.

Rose Hawthorne, Mother Alphonsa in religious life, later wrote that the account of this incident in the Liverpool workhouse seemed to her to contain the greatest words her father ever wrote.

The work of Hawthorne's daughter is perhaps known by

few in this country where it should be known by all. She
discovered much that he sought, and fulfilled in a practical
way the hidden desires of his life. The ice in the blood which
he feared, and which this very fear preserved him from, was
turned by her into a warmth which initiated action. If he observed, fearfully but truthfully; if he acted, reluctantly but
firmly, she charged ahead, secure in the path his truthfulness
had outlined for her.

Toward the end of the nineteenth century, she became
aware of the plight of the cancerous poor in New York and
was stricken by it. Charity patients with incurable cancer were
not kept in the city hospitals but were sent to Blackwell's Island or left to find their own place to die. In either case, it
was a matter of being left to rot. Rose Hawthorne Lathrop
was a woman of great force and energy. A few years earlier
she had become a Catholic and had since been seeking the
kind of occupation that would be a practical fulfillment of her
conversion. With almost no money of her own, she moved
into a tenement in the worst section of New York and began
to take in incurable cancer patients. She was joined later by a
young portrait painter, Alice Huber, whose steady and patient qualities complemented her own forceful and exuberant
ones. With their concerted effort, the grueling work prospered. Eventually other women came to help them and they
became a congregation of nuns in the Dominican Order—
the Servants of Relief for Incurable Cancer. There are now
seven of their free cancer homes over the country.

Mother Alphonsa inherited a fair share of her father's literary gift. Her account of the grandson of her first patient
makes fine reading. He was a lad who, for reasons unprevent-
able, had been brought to live for a while in the tenement
apartment with his ailing grandmother and the few other patients there at the time.

> The boy was brought by an officer of the institution, to
> remain for a visit. My first glance at his rosy, healthy, clever
> face struck a warning shiver through my soul. He was a
> flourishing slip from criminal roots. His eyes had the sturdy
> gaze of satanic vigor . . . I began to teach him the cate-
> chism. With the utmost good nature he sat in front of me

as long as I would sit, giving correct answers. "He likes to study it better than to be idle," said his grandmother; "and I taught it to him myself, long ago." His eyes took on a mystic vagueness during these lessons, and I felt certain he would tell the truth in future and be gentle instead of barbaric.

Food was hidden away in dark corners for the cherubic, overfed pet, and his pranks and thefts were shielded and denied, and the nice clothing which I provided him with, out of our stores, with a new suit for Sundays, strangely disappeared when Willie went to call upon his mother . . . In a few weeks Willie had become famous in the neighborhood as the worst boy it had ever experienced, although it was lined with little scoundrels. The inmates of the house and adjacent shanties feared him, the scoundrels made circles around him as he flew from one escapade to another on the diabolical street which was never free from some sort of outrages perpetrated by young or old. Willie built fires upon the shed roofs, threw bricks that guardian angels alone averted from our heads, and actually hit several little boys at sundry times, whom we mended in the Relief Room. He uttered exclamations that hideously rang in the ears of the profane themselves . . . He delighted in the pictures of the saints which I gave him, stole those I did not give, and sold them all. I preached affectionately, and he listened tenderly, and promised to "remember," and was very sorry for his sins when he had been forced by an iron grasp to accept their revelation. He made a very favorable impression upon an experienced priest who was summoned to rescue his soul; and he built a particularly large bonfire on our woodshed when let go. The poor grandmother began to have severe hemorrhages, because of the shocks she received and the scoldings she gave. Before he came she used to call him "that little angel." Now she wisely declared that he was good-hearted.

Bad children are harder to endure than good ones, but they are easier to read about, and I congratulated myself on having minimized the possibility of a book about Mary Ann by suggesting that the Sisters do it themselves. Although I heard from Sister Evangelist that they were about it, I felt that a few attempts to capture Mary Ann in writing would lead them to think better of the project. It was doubtful that any of them had the literary gifts of their foundress. Moreover, they were busy nurses and had their hands full following a strenuous vocation.

Their manuscript arrived the first of August. After I had gathered myself together, I sat down and began to read it. There was everything about the writing to make the professional writer groan. Most of it was reported, very little was rendered; at the dramatic moment—where there was one—the observer seemed to fade away, and where an exact word or phrase was needed, a vague one was usually supplied. Yet when I had finished reading, I remained for some time, the imperfections of the writing forgotten, thinking about the mystery of Mary Ann. They had managed to convey it.

The story was as unfinished as the child's face. Both seemed to have been left, like creation on the seventh day, to be finished by others. The reader would have to make something of the story as Mary Ann had made something of her face.

She and the Sisters who had taught her had fashioned from her unfinished face the material of her death. The creative action of the Christian's life is to prepare his death in Christ. It is a continuous action in which this world's goods are utilized to the fullest, both positive gifts and what Père Teilhard de Chardin calls "passive diminishments." Mary Ann's diminishment was extreme, but she was equipped by natural intelligence and by a suitable education, not simply to endure it, but to build upon it. She was an extraordinarily rich little girl.

Death is the theme of much modern literature. There is *Death in Venice, Death of a Salesman, Death in the Afternoon, Death of a Man*. Mary Ann's was the death of a child. It was simpler than any of these, yet infinitely more knowing. When she entered the door of Our Lady of Perpetual Help Home in Atlanta, she fell into the hands of women who are shocked at nothing and who love life so much that they spend their own lives making comfortable those who have been pronounced incurable of cancer. Her own prognosis was six

months, but she lived twelve years, long enough for the Sisters to teach her what alone could have been of importance
to her. Hers was an education for death, but not one carried
on obtrusively. Her days were full of dogs and party dresses,
of Sisters and sisters, of Coca Colas and Dagwood sandwiches, and of her many and varied friends—from Mr. Slack
and Mr. Connolly to Lucius, the yard man; from patients afflicted the way she was to children who were brought to the
Home to visit her and were perhaps told when they left to
think how thankful they should be that God had made their
faces straight. It is doubtful if any of them were as fortunate
as Mary Ann.

The Sisters had set all this down artlessly and had devoted
a good deal of their space to detailing Mary Ann's many pious
deeds. I was tempted to edit away a good many of these.
They had willingly given me the right to cut and I could have
laid about me with satisfaction but for the fact that there was
nothing with which to fill in any gaps I created. I felt too that
while their style had been affected by traditional hagiography
and even a little by Parson Weems, what they had set down
was what had happened and there was no way to get around
it. This was a child brought up by seventeen nuns; she was
what she was, and the itchy hand of the fiction writer would
have to be stayed. I was only capable of dealing with another
Willie.

I later suggested to Sister Evangelist, on an occasion when
some of the Sisters came down to spend the afternoon with
me to discuss the manuscript, that Mary Ann could not have
been much *but* good, considering her environment. Sister
Evangelist leaned over the arm of her chair and gave me a
look. Her eyes were blue and unpredictable behind spectacles
that unmoored them slightly. "We've had some demons!" she
said, and a gesture of her hand dismissed my ignorance.

After an afternoon with them, I decided that they had had
about everything and flinched before nothing, even though
one of them asked me during the course of the visit why I
wrote about such grotesque characters, why the grotesque (of
all things) was my vocation. They had in the meantime inspected some of my writing. I was struggling to get off the
hook she had me on when another of our guests supplied the

one answer that would make it immediately plain to all of them. "It's your vocation too," he said to her.

This opened up for me also a new perspective on the grotesque. Most of us have learned to be dispassionate about evil, to look it in the face and find, as often as not, our own grinning reflections with which we do not argue, but good is another matter. Few have stared at that long enough to accept the fact that its face too is grotesque, that in us the good is something under construction. The modes of evil usually receive worthy expression. The modes of good have to be satisfied with a cliché or a smoothing down that will soften their real look. When we look into the face of good, we are liable to see a face like Mary Ann's, full of promise.

Bishop Hyland preached Mary Ann's funeral sermon. He said that the world would ask why Mary Ann should die. He was thinking undoubtedly of those who had known her and knew that she loved life, knew that her grip on a hamburger had once been so strong that she had fallen through the back of a chair without dropping it, or that some months before her death, she and Sister Loretta had got a real baby to nurse. The Bishop was speaking to her family and friends. He could not have been thinking of that world, much farther removed yet everywhere, which would not ask why Mary Ann should die, but why she should be born in the first place.

One of the tendencies of our age is to use the suffering of children to discredit the goodness of God, and once you have discredited His goodness, you are done with Him. The Alymers whom Hawthorne saw as a menace have multiplied. Busy cutting down human imperfection, they are making headway also on the raw material of good. Ivan Karamazov cannot believe, as long as one child is in torment; Camus' hero cannot accept the divinity of Christ, because of the massacre of the innocents. In this popular pity, we mark our gain in sensibility and our loss in vision. If other ages felt less, they saw more, even though they saw with the blind, prophetical, unsentimental eye of acceptance, which is to say, of faith. In the absence of this faith now, we govern by tenderness. It is a tenderness which, long since cut off from the person of Christ, is wrapped in theory. When tenderness is detached from the source of tenderness, its logical outcome is terror.

It ends in forced labor camps and in the fumes of the gas chamber.

These reflections seem a long way from the simplicity and innocence of Mary Ann; but they are not so far removed. Hawthorne could have put them in a fable and shown us what to fear. In the end, I cannot think of Mary Ann without thinking also of that fastidious, sceptical New Englander who feared the ice in his blood. There is a direct line between the incident in the Liverpool workhouse, the work of Hawthorne's daughter, and Mary Ann—who stands not only for herself but for all the other examples of human imperfection and grotesquerie which the Sisters of Rose Hawthorne's order spend their lives caring for. Their work is the tree sprung from Hawthorne's small act of Christlikeness and Mary Ann is its flower. By reason of the fear, the search, and the charity that marked his life and influenced his daughter's, Mary Ann inherited, a century later, the wealth of Catholic wisdom that taught her what to make of her death. Hawthorne gave what he did not have himself.

This action by which charity grows invisibly among us, entwining the living and the dead, is called by the Church the Communion of Saints. It is a communion created upon human imperfection, created from what we make of our grotesque state. Of hers Mary Ann made what, like all good things, would have escaped notice had not the Sisters and many others been affected by it and wished it written down. The Sisters who composed the memoir have told me that they feel they have failed to create her as she was, that she was more lively than they managed to make her, more gay, more gracious, but I think that they have done enough and done it well. I think that for the reader this story will illuminate the lines that join the most diverse lives and that hold us fast in Christ.

Milledgeville,
Georgia
December 8, 1960

The King of the Birds

WHEN I WAS five, I had an experience that marked me for life. Pathé News sent a photographer from New York to Savannah to take a picture of a chicken of mine. This chicken, a buff Cochin Bantam, had the distinction of being able to walk either forward or backward. Her fame had spread through the press and by the time she reached the attention of Pathé News, I suppose there was nowhere left for her to go—forward or backward. Shortly after that she died, as now seems fitting.

If I put this information in the beginning of an article on peacocks, it is because I am always being asked why I raise them, and I have no short or reasonable answer.

From that day with the Pathé man I began to collect chickens. What had been only a mild interest became a passion, a quest. I had to have more and more chickens. I favored those with one green eye and one orange or with over-long necks and crooked combs. I wanted one with three legs or three wings but nothing in that line turned up. I pondered over the picture in Robert Ripley's book, *Believe It Or Not*, of a rooster that had survived for thirty days without his head; but I did not have a scientific temperament. I could sew in a fashion and I began to make clothes for chickens. A gray bantam named Colonel Eggbert wore a white piqué coat with a lace collar and two buttons in the back. Apparently Pathé News never heard of any of these other chickens of mine; it never sent another photographer.

My quest, whatever it was actually for, ended with peacocks. Instinct, not knowledge, led me to them. I had never seen or heard one. Although I had a pen of pheasants and a pen of quail, a flock of turkeys, seventeen geese, a tribe of mallard ducks, three Japanese silky bantams, two Polish Crested ones, and several chickens of a cross between these last and the Rhode Island Red, I felt a lack. I knew that the peacock had been the bird of Hera, the wife of Zeus, but since that time it had probably come down in the world—the Florida *Market Bulletin* advertised three-year-old peafowl at sixty-five dollars a pair. I had been quietly reading these ads for some years when one day, seized, I circled an ad in the *Bulletin* and passed it to my mother. The ad was for a peacock and hen with four seven-week-old peabiddies. "I'm going to order me those," I said.

My mother read the ad. "Don't those things eat flowers?" she asked.

"They'll eat Startena like the rest of them," I said.

The peafowl arrived by railway express from Eustis, Florida, on a mild day in October. When my mother and I arrived at the station, the crate was on the platform and from one end of it protruded a long royal-blue neck and crested head. A white line above and below each eye gave the investigating head an expression of alert composure. I wondered if this bird, accustomed to parade about in a Florida orange grove, would readily adjust himself to a Georgia dairy farm. I jumped out of the car and bounded forward. The head withdrew.

At home we uncrated the party in a pen with a top on it. The man who sold me the birds had written that I should keep them penned up for a week or ten days and then let them out at dusk at the spot where I wanted them to roost; thereafter, they would return every night to the same roosting place. He had also warned me that the cock would not have his full complement of tail feathers when he arrived; the peacock sheds his tail in late summer and does not regain it fully until after Christmas.

As soon as the birds were out of the crate, I sat down on it and began to look at them. I have been looking at them ever since, from one station or another, and always with the same awe as on that first occasion; though I have always, I feel, been able to keep a balanced view and an impartial attitude. The peacock I had bought had nothing whatsoever in the way of a tail, but he carried himself as if he not only had a train behind him but a retinue to attend it. On that first occasion, my problem was so greatly what to look at first that my gaze moved constantly from the cock to the hen to the four young peachickens, while they, except that they gave me as wide a berth as possible, did nothing to indicate they knew I was in the pen.

Over the years their attitude toward me has not grown more generous. If I appear with food, they condescend, when no other way can be found, to eat it from my hand; if I appear without food, I am just another object. If I refer to them as "my" peafowl, the pronoun is legal, nothing more. I am the menial, at the beck and squawk of any feathered worthy who wants service. When I first uncrated these birds, in my frenzy I said, "I want so many of them that every time I go out the door, I'll run into one." Now every time I go out the door, four or five run into me—and give me only the faintest recognition. Nine years have passed since my first peafowl arrived. I have forty beaks to feed. Necessity is the mother of several other things besides invention.

For a chicken that grows up to have such exceptional good looks, the peacock starts life with an inauspicious appearance. The peabiddy is the color of those large objectionable moths that flutter about light bulbs on summer nights. Its only distinguished features are its eyes, a luminous gray, and a brown crest which begins to sprout from the back of its head when it is ten days old. This looks at first like a bug's antennae and later like the head feathers of an Indian. In six weeks green flecks appear in its neck, and in a few more weeks a cock can be distinguished from a hen by the speckles on his back. The hen's back gradually fades to an even gray and her appearance becomes shortly what it will always be. I have never thought the peahen unattractive, even though she lacks a long tail and any significant decoration. I have even once or twice thought her more attractive than the cock, more subtle and refined; but these moments of boldness pass.

The cock's plumage requires two years to attain its pattern, and for the rest of his life this chicken will act as though he designed it himself. For his first two years he might have been put together out of a rag bag by an unimaginative hand. During his first year he has a buff breast, a speckled back, a green neck like his mother's and a short gray tail. During his second year he has a black breast, his sire's blue neck, a back which is slowly turning the green and gold it will remain; but still no long tail. In his third year he reaches his majority and acquires his tail. For the rest of his life—and a peachicken may live to be thirty-five—he will have nothing better to do than manicure it, furl and unfurl it, dance forward *and backward* with it spread, scream when it is stepped upon and arch it carefully when he steps through a puddle.

Not every part of the peacock is striking to look at, even when he is full-grown. His upper wing feathers are a striated black and white and might have been borrowed from a Barred Rock Fryer; his end wing feathers are the color of clay; his legs are long, thin and iron-colored; his feet are big; and he appears to be wearing the short pants now so much in favor with playboys in the summer. These extend downward, buff-colored and sleek, from what might be a blue-black waistcoat. One would not be disturbed to find a watch chain hanging from this, but none does. Analyzing the appearance of the peacock as he stands with his tail folded, I find the parts incommensurate with the whole. The fact is that with his tail folded, nothing but his bearing saves this bird from being a laughingstock. With his tail spread, he inspires a range of emotions, but I have yet to hear laughter.

The usual reaction is silence, at least for a time. The cock opens his tail by shaking himself violently until it is gradually lifted in an arch around him. Then, before anyone has had a chance to see it, he swings around so that his back faces the spectator. This has been taken by some to be insult and by others whimsey. I suggest it means only that the peacock is equally well satisfied with either view of himself. Since I have been keeping peafowl, I have been visited at least once a year by first-grade school children, who learn by living. I am used to hearing this group chorus as the peacock swings around, "Oh, look at his underwear!" This "underwear" is a stiff gray tail, raised to support the larger one, and beneath it a puff of black feathers that would be suitable for some really regal woman—a Cleopatra or a Clytemnestra—to use to powder her nose.

When the peacock has presented his back, the spectator will usually begin to walk around him to get a front view; but the peacock will continue to turn so that no front view is possible. The thing to do then is to stand still and wait until it pleases him to turn. When it suits him, the peacock will face you. Then you will see in a green-bronze arch around him a galaxy of gazing haloed suns. This is the moment when most people are silent.

"Amen! Amen!" an old Negro woman once cried when this happened and I have heard many similar remarks at this moment that show the inadequacy of human speech. Some people whistle; a few, for once, are silent. A truck driver who was driving up with a load of hay and found a peacock turning before him in the middle of our road shouted, "Get a load of that bastard!" and braked his truck to a shattering halt. I have never known a strutting peacock to budge a fraction of an inch for truck or tractor or automobile. It is up to the vehicle to get out of the way. No peafowl of mine has ever been run over, though one year one of them lost a foot in the mowing machine.

Many people, I have found, are congenitally unable to appreciate the sight of a peacock. Once or twice I have been asked what the peacock is "good for"—a question which gets no answer from me because it deserves none. The telephone company sent a lineman out one day to repair our telephone. After the job was finished, the man, a large fellow with a suspicious expression half hidden by a yellow helmet, continued to idle about, trying to coax a cock that had been watching him to strut. He wished to add this experience to a large number of others he had apparently had. "Come on now, bud," he said, "get the show on the road, upsy-daisy, come on now, snap it up, snap it up."

The peacock, of course, paid no attention to this.

"What ails him?" the man asked.

"Nothing ails him," I said. "He'll put it up terreckly. All you have to do is wait."

The man trailed about after the cock for another fifteen minutes or so; then, in disgust, he got back in his truck and started off. The bird shook himself and his tail rose around him.

"He's doing it!" I screamed. "Hey, wait! He's doing it!"

The man swerved the truck back around again just as the cock turned and faced him with the spread tail. The display was perfect. The bird turned slightly to the right and the little planets above him were hung in bronze, then he turned slightly to the left and they were hung in green. I went up to the truck to see how the man was affected by the sight.

He was staring at the peacock with rigid concentration, as if he were trying to read fine print at a distance. In a second the cock lowered his tail and stalked off.

"Well, what did you think of that?" I asked.

"Never saw such long ugly legs," the man said. "I bet that rascal could outrun a bus."

Some people are genuinely affected by the sight of a peacock, even with his tail lowered, but do not care to admit it; others appear to be incensed by it. Perhaps they have the suspicion that the bird has formed some unfavorable opinion of them. The peacock himself is a careful and dignified investigator. Visitors to our place, instead of being barked at by dogs rushing from under the porch, are squalled at by peacocks whose blue necks and crested heads pop up from behind tufts of grass, peer out of bushes and crane downward from the roof of the house, where the bird has flown, perhaps for the view. One of mine stepped from under the shrubbery one day and came forward to inspect a carful of people who had driven up to buy a calf. An old man and five or six white-haired, barefooted children were piling out the back of the automobile as the bird approached. Catching sight of him, the children stopped in their tracks and stared, plainly hacked to find this superior figure blocking their path. There was silence as the bird regarded them, his head drawn back at its most majestic angle, his folded train glittering behind him in the sunlight.

"Whut is thet thang?" one of the small boys asked finally in a sullen voice.

The old man had got out of the car and was gazing at the peacock with an astounded look of recognition. "I ain't seen one of them since my granddaddy's day," he said, respectfully removing his hat. "Folks used to have 'em, but they don't no more."

"Whut is it?" the child asked again in the same tone he had used before.

"Churren," the old man said, "that's the king of the birds!"

The children received this information in silence. After a

minute they climbed back into the car and continued from there to stare at the peacock, their expressions annoyed, as if they disliked catching the old man in the truth.

The peacock does most of his serious strutting in the spring and summer when he has a full tail to do it with. Usually he begins shortly after breakfast, struts for several hours, desists in the heat of the day and begins again in the late afternoon. Each cock has a favorite station where he performs every day in the hope of attracting some passing hen; but if I have found anyone indifferent to the peacock's display, besides the telephone lineman, it is the peahen. She seldom casts an eye at it. The cock, his tail raised in a shimmering arch around him, will turn this way and that, and with his clay-colored wing feathers touching the ground, will dance forward and backward, his neck curved, his beak parted, his eyes glittering. Meanwhile the hen goes about her business, diligently searching the ground as if any bug in the grass were of more importance than the unfurled map of the universe which floats nearby.

Some people have the notion that only the cock spreads his tail and that he does it only when the hen is present. This is not so. A peafowl only a few hours hatched will raise what tail he has—it will be about the size of a thumbnail—and will strut and turn and back and bow exactly as if he were three years old and had some reason to be doing it. The hens will raise their tails when they see an object on the ground which alarms them, or sometimes when they have nothing better to do and the air is brisk. Brisk air goes at once to the peafowl's head and inclines him to be sportive. A group of birds will dance together or four or five will chase one another around a bush or tree. Sometimes one will chase himself, end his frenzy with a spirited leap into the air and then stalk off as if he had never been involved in the spectacle.

Frequently the cock combines the lifting of his tail with the raising of his voice. He appears to receive through his feet some shock from the center of the earth, which travels upward through him and is released: *Eee-ooo-ii! Eee-ooo-ii!* To the melancholy this sound is melancholy and to the hysterical it is hysterical. To me it has always sounded like a cheer for an invisible parade.

The hen is not given to these outbursts. She makes a noise like a mule's bray—*hehaw, heehaaw, aa-aaww-w*—and makes it only when necessary. In the fall and winter, peafowl are usually silent unless some racket disturbs them; but in the spring and summer, at short intervals during the day and night, the cock, lowering his neck and throwing back his head, will give out with seven or eight screams in succession as if this message were the one on earth which needed most urgently to be heard.

At night these calls take on a minor key and the air for miles around is charged with them. It has been a long time since I let my first peafowl out at dusk to roost in the cedar trees behind the house. Now fifteen or twenty still roost there; but the original old cock from Eustis, Florida, stations himself on top of the barn, the bird who lost his foot in the mowing machine sits on a flat shed near the horse stall, there are others in the trees by the pond, several in the oaks at the side of the house and one that cannot be dissuaded from roosting on the water tower. From all these stations calls and answers echo through the night. The peacock perhaps has violent dreams. Often he wakes and screams, "Help! Help!" and then from the pond and the barn and the trees around the house a chorus of adjuration begins:

> *Lee-yon lee-yon,*
> *Mee-yon mee-yon!*
> *Eee-e-yoy eee-e-yoy,*
> *Eee-e-yoy eee-e-yoy!*

The restless sleeper may wonder if he wakes or dreams.

It is hard to tell the truth about this bird. The habits of any peachicken left to himself would hardly be noticeable, but multiplied by forty, they become a situation. I was correct that my peachickens would all eat Startena; they also eat everything else. Particularly they eat flowers. My mother's fears were all borne out. Peacocks not only eat flowers, they eat them systematically, beginning at the head of a row and going down it. If they are not hungry, they will pick the flower anyway, if it is attractive, and let it drop. For general eating they prefer chrysanthemums and roses. When they are not eating flowers, they enjoy sitting on top of them, and where the peacock sits he will eventually fashion a dusting hole. Any chicken's dusting hole is out of place in a flower bed, but the peafowl's hole, being the size of a small crater, is more so. When he dusts he all but obliterates the sight of himself with sand. Usually when someone arrives at full gallop with the leveled broom, he can see nothing through the cloud of dirt and flying flowers but a few green feathers and a beady, pleasure-taking eye.

From the beginning, relations between these birds and my mother were strained. She was forced, at first, to get up early in the morning and go out with her clippers to reach the Lady Bankshire and the Herbert Hoover roses before some peafowl had breakfasted upon them; now she has halfway solved her problem by erecting hundreds of feet of twenty-four-inch-high wire to fence the flower beds. She contends that peachickens do not have sense enough to jump over a low fence. "If it were a high wire," she says, "they would jump onto it and over, but they don't have sense enough to jump over a low wire."

It is useless to argue with her on this matter. "It's not a challenge," I say to her; but she has made up her mind.

In addition to eating flowers, peafowl also eat fruit, a habit which has created a lack of cordiality toward them on the part of my uncle, who had the fig trees planted about the place because he has an appetite for figs himself. "Get that scoundrel out of that fig bush!" he will roar, rising from his chair at the sound of a limb breaking, and someone will have to be dispatched with a broom to the fig trees.

Peafowl also enjoy flying into barn lofts and eating peanuts off peanut hay; this has not endeared them to our dairyman. And as they have a taste for fresh garden vegetables, they have often run afoul of the dairyman's wife.

The peacock likes to sit on gates or fence posts and allow his tail to hang down. A peacock on a fence post is a superb sight. Six or seven peacocks on a gate are beyond description; but it is not very good for the gate. Our fence posts tend to lean in one direction or another and all our gates open diagonally.

In short, I am the only person on the place who is willing to underwrite, with something more than tolerance, the presence of peafowl. In return, I am blessed with their rapid multiplication. The population figure I give out is forty, but for some time now I have not felt it wise to take a census. I had been told before I bought my birds that peafowl are difficult to raise. It is not so, alas. In May the peahen finds a nest in some fence corner and lays five or six large buff-colored eggs. Once a day, thereafter, she gives an abrupt *hee-haa-awww!* and shoots like a rocket from her nest. Then for half an hour, her neck ruffled and stretched forward, she parades around the premises, announcing what she is about. I listen with mixed emotions.

In twenty-eight days the hen comes off with five or six mothlike murmuring peachicks. The cock ignores these unless one gets under his feet (then he pecks it over the head until it gets elsewhere), but the hen is a watchful mother and every year a good many of the young survive. Those that withstand illnesses and predators (the hawk, the fox and the opossum) over the winter seem impossible to destroy, except by violence.

A man selling fence posts tarried at our place one day and told me that he had once had eighty peafowl on his farm. He cast a nervous eye at two of mine standing nearby. "In the spring, we couldn't hear ourselves think," he said. "As soon as you lifted your voice, they lifted their'n, if not before. All our fence posts wobbled. In the summer they ate all the tomatoes off the vines. Scuppernongs went the same way. My wife said she raised her flowers for herself and she was not going to have them eat up by a chicken no matter how long his tail was. And in the fall they shed them feathers all over the place anyway and it was a job to clean up. My old grandmother was living with us then and she was eighty-five. She said, 'Either they go, or I go.' "

"Who went?" I asked.

"We still got twenty of them in the freezer," he said.

"And how," I asked, looking significantly at the two standing nearby, "did they taste?"

"No better than any other chicken," he said, "but I'd a heap rather eat them than hear them."

I have tried imagining that the single peacock I see before me is the only one I have, but then one comes to join him; another flies off the roof, four or five crash out of the crêpe-myrtle hedge; from the pond one screams and from the barn I hear the dairyman denouncing another that has got into the cow-feed. My kin are given to such phrases as, "Let's face it."

I do not like to let my thoughts linger in morbid channels but there are times when such facts as the price of wire fencing and the price of Startena and the yearly gain in peafowl all run uncontrolled through my head. Lately I have had a recurrent dream: I am five years old and a peacock. A photographer has been sent from New York and a long table is laid in celebration. The meal is to be an exceptional one: myself. I scream, "Help! Help!" and awaken. Then from the pond and the barn and the trees around the house, I hear that chorus of jubilation begin:

> *Lee-yon lee-yon,*
> *Mee-yon mee-yon!*
> *Eee-e-yoy eee-e-yoy!*
> *Eee-e-yoy eee-e-yoy!*

I intend to stand firm and let the peacocks multiply, for I am sure that, in the end, the last word will be theirs.

The Regional Writer

I'M DELIGHTED to have this scroll. In fact, I'm delighted just to know that some one remembers my book two years after it was published and can get the name of it straight. I've had a hard time all along with the title of that book. It's been called THE VALIANT BEAR IT ALWAYS and THE VIOLETS BLOOM AWAY, and recently a friend of mine went into a book store looking for a copy of my stories and he claims that the clerk said, "We don't have those but we have another book by that person. It's called THE BEAR THAT RAN AWAY WITH IT."

Anyway, the bear is glad to get away with one of these scrolls. I believe that for purely human reasons, and for some important literary ones too, awards are valuable in direct ratio to how near they come from home.

I remember that the last time I spoke to the Georgia Writers Association, the jist of my talk was that being a Georgia Author is a rather specious dignity, on the same order as, for the pig, being a Talmadge ham. I still think that that approach has merit, particularly where there is any danger of the Georgia part of the equation over-balancing the writer part. The moral of my talk on that occasion was that a pig is a pig, no matter who puts him up. But I don't like to say the same thing twice to the same audience, and I have found, over the years, that on subjects like this, a slight shift in emphasis may produce an entirely different vision, without endangering the truth of the previous one.

Fortunately, the Georgia writer's work often belongs in that larger and more meaningful category, Southern Literature, and it is really about that that I have a word to say. There is one myth about writers that I have always felt was particularly pernicious and untruthful—the myth of the "lonely writer," the myth that writing is a lonely occupation, involving much suffering because, supposedly, the writer exists in a state of sensitivity which cuts him off, or raises him above, or casts him below the community around him. This is a common cliché, a hangover probably from the romantic period and the idea of the artist as Sufferer and Rebel.

Probably any of the arts that are not performed in chorus line are going to come in for a certain amount of romanticizing, but it seems to me particularly bad to do this to writers and especially fiction writers, because fiction writers engage in the homeliest, and most concrete, and most unromanticizable of all arts. I suppose there have been enough genuinely lonely suffering novelists to make this seem a reasonable myth, but there is every reason to suppose that such cases are the result of less admirable qualities in these writers, qualities which have nothing to do with the vocation of writing itself.

Unless the novelist has gone utterly out of his mind, his aim is still communication and communication suggests talking inside a community. One of the reasons Southern fiction thrives is that our best writers are able to do this. They are not alienated, they are not lonely suffering artists gasping for purer air. The Southern writer apparently feels the need of expatriation less than other writers in this country. Moreover, when he does leave and stay gone, he does so at great peril to that balance between principle and fact, between judgment and observation, which is so necessary to maintain if fiction is to be true. The isolated imagination is easily corrupted by theory, but the writer inside his community seldom has such a problem.

To call yourself a Georgia writer is certainly to declare a limitation, but one which, like all limitations, is a gateway to reality. It is a great blessing, perhaps the greatest blessing a writer can have, to find at home what others have to go elsewhere seeking. Faulkner was at home in Oxford; Miss Welty is usually "locally underfoot," as she puts it, in Jackson; Mr. Montgomery, your poetry man here, is a member of the Crawford Voluntary Fire Department, and most of you and myself, and many others are sustained in our writing by the local and the particular and the familiar without loss to our principles or our reason.

I wouldn't want to suggest that the Georgia writer has the unanimous collective ear of his community, but only that his true audience, the audience he checks himself by, is at home. There's a story about Faulkner that I like. It may be apocryphal but it's nice anyway. A local lady is supposed to have rushed up to him in a drugstore in Oxford and said, "Oh Mr. Faulkner, Mr. Faulkner, I've just bought your book! But before I read it, I want you to tell me something: do you think I'll like it?" and Faulkner is supposed to have said, "Yes, I think you'll like that book. It's trash."

It wasn't trash and she probably didn't like it, but there were others who did, and you may be sure that if there were two or three in Oxford who liked it, two or three of an honest and unpretentious bent, who relished it as they would relish a good meal, that they were an audience more desirable to Faulkner than all the critics in New York City. For no matter how favorable all the critics in New York City may be, they are an unreliable lot, as incapable as the day they were born of interpreting Southern literature to the world.

Fortunately for the Southern writer, the Southern audience is becoming larger and more responsive to Southern writing. In the 19th century, Southern writers complained bitterly about the lack of attention they got at home, and in a good part of this century, they complained bitterly about the quality of it, for the better Southern writers were for a long time unheard of by the average Southerner. When I went to college twenty years ago, nobody mentioned any good Southern writers to me later than Joel Chandler Harris, and the ones mentioned before Harris, with the exception of Poe, were not widely known outside the region. As far as I knew, the heroes of Hawthorne and Melville and James and Crane and Hemingway were balanced on the Southern side by Brer Rabbit— an animal who can always hold up his end of the stick, in equal company, but here too much was being expected of him.

Today, every self-respecting Southern college has itself an arts festival where Southern writers can be heard and where they are actually read and commented upon, and people in general see now that the type of serious Southern writer is no longer some one who leaves and can't come home again, or some one who stays and is not quite appreciated, but some one who is a part of what he writes about and is recognized as such.

All this sounds fine, but while it has been happening, other ground has been shifting under our feet. I read some stories at one of the colleges not long ago—all by Southerners—but with the exception of one story, they might all have originated in some synthetic place that could have been anywhere or nowhere. These stories hadn't been influenced by the outside world at all, only by the television. It was a grim view of the future. And the story that was different was phony-Southern which is just as bad, if not worse, than the other, and an indication of the same basic problem.

I have a friend from Wisconsin who moved to Atlanta recently and was sold a house in the suburbs. The man who sold it to her was himself from Massachusetts and he recommended the property by saying, "You'll like this neighborhood. There's not a Southerner for two miles." At least we can still be identified when we do occur.

The present state of the South is one wherein nothing can be taken for granted, one in which our identity is obscured and in doubt. In the past, the things that have seemed to many to make us ourselves have been very obvious things, but now no amount of nostalgia can make us believe they will characterize us much longer. Prophets have already been heard to say that in twenty years there'll be no such thing as Southern literature. It will be ironical indeed if the Southern writer has discovered he can live in the South and the Southern audience has become aware of its literature just in time to discover that being Southern is relatively meaningless, and that soon there is going to be precious little difference in the end product whether you are a writer from Georgia or a writer from Hollywood, California.

It's in these terms that the Georgia part of being a Georgia writer has some positive significance.

It is not a matter of so-called local color, it is not a matter of losing our peculiar quaintness. Southern identity is not really connected with mocking birds and beaten biscuits and white columns any more than it is with hookworm and bare feet and muddy clay roads. Nor is it necessarily shown forth in the antics of our politicians, for the development of power obeys strange laws of its own. An identity is not to be found on the surface; it is not accessible to the poll-taker; it is not something that *can* become a cliché. It is not made from the mean average or the typical, but from the hidden and often the most extreme. It is not made from what passes, but from those qualities that endure, regardless of what passes, because they are related to truth. It lies very deep. In its entirety, it is known only to God, but of those who look for it, none gets so close as the artist.

The best American fiction has always been regional. The ascendancy passed roughly from New England to the Midwest to the South; it has passed to and stayed longest wherever there has been a shared past, a sense of alikeness, and the possibility of reading a small history in a universal light. In these things the South still has a degree of advantage. It is a slight degree and getting slighter, but it is a degree of kind as well as of intensity, and it is enough to feed great literature if our people—whether they be newcomers or have roots here—are enough aware of it to foster its growth in themselves.

Every serious writer will put his finger on it as a slightly different spot but in the same region of sensitivity. When Walker Percy won the National Book Award, newsmen asked him why there were so many good Southern writers and he said, "Because we lost the War." He didn't mean by that simply that a lost war makes good subject matter. What he was saying was that we have had our Fall. We have gone into the modern world with an inburnt knowledge of human limitations and with a sense of mystery which could not have developed in our first state of innocence—as it has not sufficiently developed in the rest of our country.

Not every lost war would have this effect on every society but we were doubly blessed, not only in our Fall, but in having a means to interpret it. Behind our own history, deepening it at every point, has been another history. Mencken called the South the Bible Belt, in scorn and thus in incredible innocence.

In the South we have, in however attenuated a form, a vision of Moses' face as he pulverized our idols. This knowledge is what makes the Georgia writer different from the writer from Hollywood or New York. It is the knowledge that the novelist finds in his community. When he ceases to find it there, he will cease to write, or at least he will cease to write anything enduring. The writer operates at a peculiar crossroads where time and place and eternity somehow meet. His problem is to find that location.

Fiction Is a Subject with a History
—It Should Be Taught That Way

IN TWO recent instances in Georgia, parents have objected to their eighth and ninth grade children's reading assignments in modern fiction. This seems to happen with some regularity in cases throughout the country. The unwitting parent picks up his child's book, glances through it, comes upon passages of erotic detail or profanity and takes off at once to complain to the school board. Sometimes, as in one of the Georgia cases, the teacher is dismissed and hackles rise in liberal circles everywhere.

The two cases in Georgia, which involved Steinbeck's, EAST OF EDEN, and John Hersey's, A BELL FOR ADANO, provoked considerable newspaper comment. One columnist, in commending the enterprise of the teachers, announced that students do not like to read the fusty works of the 19th century, that their attention can best be held by novels dealing with the realities of our own time, and that the Bible too is full of racy stories.

Mr. Hersey himself addressed a letter to the State School Superintendent in behalf of the teacher who had been dismissed. He pointed out that his book is not scandalous, that it attempts to convey an earnest message about the nature of democracy, and that it falls well within the limits of the principle of "total effect," that principle followed in legal cases by which a book is judged not for isolated parts but by the final effect of the whole book upon the general reader.

I do not want to comment on the merits of these particular cases. What concerns me is what novels ought to be assigned in the eighth and ninth grades as a matter of course, for if these cases indicate anything, they indicate the haphazard way in which fiction is approached in our high schools. Presumably there is a state reading list which contains "safe" books for teachers to assign; after that it is up to the teacher.

English teachers come in Good, Bad and Indifferent, but too frequently in high schools anyone who can speak English is allowed to teach it. Since several novels can't easily be gathered into one text book, the fiction that students are assigned depends upon their teacher's knowledge, ability and taste, variable factors at best. More often than not, the teacher assigns what he thinks will hold the attention and interest of the students. Modern fiction will certainly hold it.

Ours is the first age in history which has asked the child what he would tolerate learning, but that is a part of the problem with which I am not equipped to deal. The devil of Educationism that possesses us is the kind that can be cast out only by prayer and fasting. No one has yet come along strong enough to do it. In other ages the attention of children was held by Homer and Virgil, among others, but by the reverse evolutionary process, that is no longer possible; our children are too stupid now to enter the past imaginatively. No one asks the student if algebra pleases him or if he finds it satisfactory that some French verbs are irregular, but if he prefers Hersey to Hawthorne, his taste must prevail.

I would like to put forward the proposition, repugnant to most English teachers, that fiction, if it is going to be taught in the high schools, should be taught as a subject and as a subject with a history. The total effect of a novel depends not only on its innate impact, but upon the experience, literary and otherwise, with which it is approached. No child needs to be assigned Hersey or Steinbeck until he is familiar with a certain amount of the best work of Cooper, Hawthorne, Melville, the early James and Crane, and he does not need to be assigned these until he has been introduced to some of the better English novelists of the 18th and 19th centuries.

The fact that these works do not present him with the realities of his own time is all to the good. He is surrounded by the realities of his own time and he has no perspective whatever from which to view them. Like the college student who wrote in her paper on Lincoln that he went to the movies and got shot, many students go to college unaware that the world was not made yesterday; their studies began with the present and dipped backward occasionally when that seemed necessary or unavoidable.

There is much to be enjoyed in the great British novels of the 19th century, much that a good teacher can open up in them for the young student. There is no reason why these novels should be either too simple or too difficult for the eighth grade. For the simple they offer simple pleasures, for the more precocious they can be made to yield subtler ones if the teacher is up to it. Let the student discover, after reading the 19th century British novel, that the 19th century American novel is quite different as to its literary characteristics, and he will thereby learn something not only about these individual works but about the sea-change which a new historical situation can effect in a literary form. Let him come to modern fiction with this experience behind him and he will be better able to see and to deal with the more complicated demands of the best 20th century fiction.

Modern fiction often looks simpler than the fiction which preceded it, but in reality it is more complex. A natural evolution has taken place. The author has for the most part absented himself from direct participation in the work and has left the reader to make his own way amid experience dramatically rendered and symbolically ordered. The modern novelist merges the reader in the experience; he tends to raise the passions he touches upon. If he is a good novelist, he raises them to effect by their order and clarity a new experience—the total effect—which is not in itself sensuous or simply of the moment. Unless the child has had some literary experience before, he is not going to be able to resolve the immediate passions the book arouses into any true total picture.

It is here the moral problem will arise. It is one thing for a child to read about adultery in the Bible or in ANNA KARENINA and quite another for him to read about it in most modern fiction. This is not only because in both the former instances adultery is considered a sin, and in the latter, at most, an inconvenience, but because modern writing involves the reader in the action with a new degree of intensity, and literary mores now permit him to be involved in any action a human being can perform.

In our fractured culture, we cannot agree on morals, we cannot even agree that moral matters should come before literary ones when there is a conflict between them. All this is another reason why the high-schools would do well to return to their proper business of preparing foundations. Whether in the senior year students should be assigned modern novelists should depend both on their parent's consent and on what they have already read and understood.

The high school English teacher will be fulfilling his responsibility if he furnishes the student a guided opportunity, through the best writing of the past, to come, in time, to an understanding of the best writing of the present. He will teach literature, not social studies or little lessons in democracy or the customs of many lands.

And if the student finds that this is not to his taste? Well, that is regrettable. Most regrettable. His taste should not be consulted; it is being formed.

The Catholic Novelist in the Protestant South

I T'S A GREAT pleasure to speak here at Georgetown tonight. But for someone like myself who is not a teacher, and not even a literary person in the accepted sense of the phrase, it's always difficult to throw off the habits of the story-teller and to come up with some abstract statement instead. I'd much prefer to be reading you one of my stories tonight, but these are times when stories are considered not quite as satisfying as statements and statements are considered not quite as satisfying as statistics. Most novelists these days are English teachers. Their talk about fiction is designed to fill the heads of students, and their approach is consequently microscopic. I'm frequently appalled at the questions students ask me about my stories and at the very learned and literary interpretations they come up with.

I was recently at a college where a student asked me, in a voice loaded with cunning: "Miss O'Connor, what is the significance of the Misfit's hat?" Of course, I had no idea the Misfit's hat was significant, but finally I managed to say, "Its significance is to cover his head." Those students went away thinking that here was real innocence, a writer who didn't know what she was doing!

My own approach to fiction, at least when I have to talk about it, is very like the one Dr. Johnson's blind housekeeper used when she poured tea. She put her finger inside the cup. I think that if there is any value in hearing writers talk, it would be in hearing what they can witness to, and not what they can theorize about. I think it would be in hearing what some of their larger concerns are—the really important things that make details fall into place without too much sinister calculation on the writer's part. And so I'm talking tonight about "The Catholic Novelist in the Protestant South."

I have experienced his situation, and I think his situation has particular lessons both for Catholics anywhere who write or read fiction and for those Southerners who feel that the quality of future Southern literature will not hold up unless the best traditions of the South have reinforcement from some stable source of truth. I find frequently among Catholics a certain impatience with Southern literature—sometimes a fascinated impatience—but usually a definite feeling that with all the violence and grotesquery and religious enthusiasm reflected in its fiction, the South is a little beyond the pale of Catholic respect and that certainly it would be ridiculous to expect the emergence in such soil of anything like a literature inspired by Catholic belief. But for my part I don't think that this is at all unlikely. There are certain conditions necessary for the emergence of Catholic literature which are found nowhere else in this country in such abundance as in the South, and I look forward with considerable relish to the day when we are going to have to enlarge our notions about the Catholic novel to include some pretty odd Southern specimens.

The American Catholic trusts the fictional imagination about as little as he trusts anything. Before it's well on its feet, he's busy looking for heresy in it. The Catholic press is constantly broken out in a rash of articles on the failure of the Catholic novelist. The Catholic novelist is failing to reflect the virtue of hope, failing to show the Church's interest in social justice, failing to show life as a positive good, failing to portray our beliefs in a light that will make them desirable to others. He occasionally writes well, but he always writes wrong. Now if in the next twenty years we find ourselves with a batch of wild Southern Catholic novelists who fail in all these things and, in addition, have certain positive obnoxious qualities—such as a penchant for violence and grotesquery and religious enthusiasm—we are doubtless going to wonder how these strange birds got hatched in our nest. Catholic discussions of the Catholic novel are frequently ridiculous because every given circumstance of the writer is ignored except his faith. No one taking part in these discussions seems to remember that the eye sees what it has been given to see by concrete circumstances, and that the imagination reproduces what by some related gift it is able to make live.

I collect articles from the Catholic press on the failure of the Catholic novelist. And in one of them I find this typical sentence: "Why not a positive novel based on the Church's fight for social justice, or the liturgical revival, or life in the seminary?" I take it that if seminarians began to write novels about life in the seminary, there would soon be several less seminarians. But we are to assume that anybody who can write at all and who has the energy to do some research can give us a novel on this or any needed topic and can make it *positive*. A lot of novels do get written in this way, but they are not the ones that concern us as literature usually. In this same article the writer asks this: "Would it not seem in order now for some of our younger men to explore the possibilities inherent in certain positive factors which make Catholic life and the Catholic position in this country increasingly challenging?" This whole attitude, which proceeds from the standpoint of what it would be good to do or have to supply a general need, is totally opposite from the novelist's own approach. No serious novelist "explores possibilities inherent in factors." Some schoolteacher wrote that. Conrad wrote that the artist descends within himself and in that region of stress and strife—if he be deserving and fortunate—he finds the terms of his appeal. Where you find the terms of your appeal may have little or nothing to do with what is challenging in the life of the Church at the moment. And this is particularly apparent to the Southern Catholic writer whose imagination has been cast by life in a region which is traditionally Protestant.

The things we see, hear, smell and touch affect us long before we believe anything at all. The South impresses its image on the Southern writer from the moment he is able to distinguish one sound from another. He takes it in through his ears and hears it again in his own voice, and, by the time he is able to use his imagination for fiction, he finds that his senses respond irrevocably to a certain reality, and particularly to the sound of a certain reality. The Southern writer's greatest tie with the South is through his ear, which is usually sharp but not too versatile outside his own idiom. With a few exceptions, such as Miss Katherine Anne Porter, he is not too often successfully cosmopolitan in fiction, but the fact is that he doesn't need to be. A distinctive idiom is a powerful instrument for keeping fiction social. When one Southern character speaks, regardless of his station in life, an echo of all Southern life is heard. This helps to keep Southern fiction from being a fiction of purely private experience.

Unless the novelist has gone entirely out of his mind, his

aim is still communication, and communication suggests, at least to some of us, talking inside a community of which one is a part. One of the reasons Southern fiction thrives is that today a significant number of our best writers are able to do this. They are not alienated from their society. They are not lonely, suffering artists gasping for purer air. Although there are a few always who run from the South as from the plague, in general the Southern writer feels the need of expatriation less than other writers in this country. Moreover, when he does leave and stay gone out of choice and continues to write about the South, he does so at great peril to that violence between principle and fact, between judgment and observation which is so necessary to maintain if fiction is to be true. The isolated imagination is easily corrupted by theory. Alienation was once a diagnosis, but in much of the fiction of our time it has become an ideal. The modern hero is the outsider. His experience is rootless. He can go anywhere. He belongs nowhere. Being alien to nothing, he ends up being alienated from any kind of community based on common tastes and interests. The borders of his country are the sides of his skull.

The South is traditionally hostile to outsiders, except on her own terms. She is traditionally against intruders, foreigners from Chicago or New Jersey, all those who come from afar with moral energy that increases in direct proportion to their distance from home. It is difficult to separate the virtues of this quality from the narrowness which accompanies and colors it for the outside world. It is more difficult still to reconcile the South's instinct to preserve her identity with her equal instinct to fall eager victim to every poisonous breath from Hollywood or Madison Avenue. But good and evil appear to be joined in every culture at the spine, and, as far as the creation of a body of fiction is concerned, the social is superior to the purely personal. Somewhere is better than anywhere. And traditional manners, however unbalanced, are better than no manners at all. The discovery of having his senses respond to a particular society and a particular history, to particular sounds and a particular idiom, is for the Southern writer the beginning of a recognition that first puts his work in real human perspective for him. He discovers that the imagination is *not* free, but bound. The energy of the

South is so strong in him that it is a force which has to be encountered and engaged, and it is when this is a true engagement that its meaning will lead outward to universal human interest.

The Catholic novel that fails is usually one in which this kind of engagement is absent. It is a novel which doesn't grapple with any particular culture. It may try to make a culture out of the Church, but this is always a mistake because the Church is not a culture. The Catholic novel that fails is one in which there is no genuine sense of place and in which feeling is by that much diminished. Its action occurs in an abstracted setting. It could be anywhere or nowhere. This reduces its dimensions drastically and cuts down on those tensions that keep it from being facile and slick. Where the Catholic writer does have a place, such as the Midwestern parishes which serve as J. F. Powers' region or South Boston which belongs to Edwin O'Connor, he fares considerably better. But these places have very definite limitations that have to be compensated for by a considerable talent on the part of the writer. Whereas in the South some fairly modest talents can come up with some fairly respectable fiction simply because society and history come more than half-way to meet them. What I am suggesting is that Catholic fiction can come easy from the sturdiest natural stock, and that in this country now that is to be found in the South. But there are reasons other than merely literary ones why the South is good ground for Catholic fiction. The writer whose themes are religious particularly needs a region where these themes find a response in the life of the people, and this condition is met in the South as nowhere else. A secular society understands the religious mind less and less. It becomes more and more difficult in America to make belief believable, which is what the novelist has to do. It takes less and less belief acted upon to make one appear a fanatic. When you create a character who believes vigorously in Christ, you have to explain his aberration. Here the Southern writer has the greatest possible advantage; he lives in the Bible Belt, where such people, though not as numerous as they used to be, are taken for granted. It was about 1919 that Mencken called the South the "Bible Belt" and said that it was "the Sahara of the *beaux arts.*" That was

only a few years before the emergence in the South of a literature to reckon with. Today Southern literature is known
around the world, and the South is still the Bible Belt. Sam
Jones' grandma read the Bible thirty-seven times on her knees.
And the rural and small town, and even a certain level of
the city South, is made up of the descendants of old ladies
like her. You don't shake off their influence in even several
generations.

It has been suggested, apparently with a straight face, that
the Biblical flavor of the South is a hindrance to the Catholic
writer because Catholic readers are not accustomed to seeing
religion Biblically. It is true that if your readers are not well
acquainted with the Bible, you don't have the instrument to
plumb meaning—and specifically Christian meaning—that
you would have if the Biblical background conditioned everyone's response to life. Some of the writer's instruments have,
unfortunately, to be shared with his reader. But the fact that
Catholics are not accustomed to seeing religion Biblically is a
deficiency on the part of Catholics, and, if the Catholic writer
tries to accommodate himself to such deficiency, our literature
will always be going downhill and ourselves behind it. This
is, after all, a correctable deficiency, not invincible ignorance.
Nothing, I think, will insure the future of Catholic literature
in this country so much as the Biblical revival. Unfortunately,
that revival is still the pursuit of the educated, and it is the
good which the poor and the ignorant hold in common that
is most valuable to the fiction writer. When the poor hold
sacred history in common, they have concrete ties to the universal and the holy which allow the meaning of their every
action to be heightened and seen under the aspect of eternity.
To be great story-tellers, we need something to measure ourselves against, and this is what we conspicuously lack in this
age. Men judge themselves now by what they find themselves
doing. The Catholic has the teachings of the Church to serve
him in this regard. But for the writing of fiction something
more is necessary. For the purposes of fiction, these guides
have to exist in the form of stories which affect our image
and our judgment of ourselves. Abstractions, formulas, laws
will not do here. We have to have stories. It takes a story to
make a story. It takes a story of mythic dimensions; one

which belongs to everybody; one in which everybody is able to recognize the hand of God and imagine its descent upon himself. In the Protestant South the Scriptures fill this role. The ancient Hebrew genius for making the absolute concrete has conditioned the Southerner's way of looking at things. That is one of the big reasons why the South is a story-telling section at all. Our response to life is different if we have been taught only a definition of faith than it is if we have trembled with Abraham as he held the knife over Isaac. Both of these kinds of knowledge are necessary, but in the last four or five centuries we in the Church have over-emphasized the abstract and consequently impoverished our imagination and our capacity for prophetic insight. The circumstance of being a Southerner, of living in a non-Catholic but religiously inclined society, furnishes the Catholic novelist with some very fine antidotes to his own worst tendencies.

I once read a review of two books by a Catholic on the subject of the Catholic novel. One writer said that in order for a novel to be a Catholic one, it would have to be about a saint. The other one said it would have to be *by* a saint. We enjoy indulging ourselves in the logic that kills, in making categories smaller and smaller, in prescribing subjects and proscribing attitudes. The Catholic novelist in the South is forced to follow the spirit into strange places and to recognize it in many forms not totally congenial to him. His interests and sympathies may very well go, as I find my own do, directly to those aspects of Southern life where the religious feeling is most intense and where its outward forms are farthest from the Catholic and most revealing of a need that only the Church can fill. The Catholic novelist in the South will see many distorted images of Christ, but he will certainly feel that a distorted image of Christ is better than no image at all. I think he will feel a good deal more kinship with backwoods prophets and shouting fundamentalists than he will with those politer elements for whom the supernatural is an embarrassment and for whom religion has become a department of sociology or culture or personality development.

A few years ago a preacher in Tennessee attracted considerable attention when he sacrificed a live lamb chained to a cross at his Lenten revival service. It is possible that this was simple showmanship, but I doubt it. I presume that this was as close to the Mass as that man could come. The Catholic writer may at first feel that the kind of religious enthusiasm that has influenced Southern life has run hand in hand with extreme individualism for so long that there is nothing left of it that he can recognize. But when he penetrates to the human aspiration beneath it, he sees not only what has been lost to the life he observes, but more the terrible loss to us in the Church of human faith and passion. The result of these underground religious affinities will be a strange and, to many, perverse fiction—one which serves no felt need, which gives us no picture of Catholic life or the religious experiences that are usual with us. But I believe it will be Catholic fiction. There is only one Holy Spirit, and He is no respecter of persons. These people in the invisible Church make discoveries that have meaning for us who are better protected from the vicissitudes of our own natures and who are often too dead to the world to make any discoveries at all. These people in the invisible Church may be grotesque, but their grotesqueness has a significance and a value which the Catholic should be in a better position than the others to assess.

I find that any fiction that comes out of the South is going to be called "grotesque" by the Northern reader, unless it is grotesque, in which case it is going to be called "photographic realism." The word "grotesque" should not necessarily be used as a pejorative term. There is the grotesque of the animated cartoon. But there is also that grotesque which is a constant in literature when any considerable depth of reality has been penetrated. In Southern fiction there is a growing tradition of the grotesque. In nineteenth century American writing there was a good deal of grotesque literature which came from the frontier and was supposed to be funny—such as *Sut Lovingood*. But our present grotesque heroes are not comic, or at least not primarily so. They seem to carry an invisible burden and to fix us with eyes that remind us that we all bear some heavy responsibility whose nature we have forgotten. They are prophetic figures. In the novelist's case prophecy is a matter of seeing near things with their extensions of meaning and thus of seeing far things close up. The prophet is a realist of distances, distances in the qualitative sense, and it is this kind of realism that you find in the modern instances of the grotesque. But to the eye of the general reader, these prophet-heroes are freaks. The public invariably approaches them from the standpoint of abnormal psychology.

Whenever I am asked why Southern writers particularly have this penchant for writing about freaks, I say it is because we are still able to recognize one. To be able to recognize a freak, you have to have some conception of the whole man. And in the South, the general conception of man is still, in the main, theological. Of course, the South is changing so rapidly that almost anything you say about Southern belief can be denied in the next breath with equal propriety. But approaching the subject from the standpoint of the writer, I think it is safe to say that while the South is hardly Christ-centered, it is most certainly Christ-haunted. It is interesting that as belief in the divinity of Christ decreases, there seems to be a preoccupation with Christ-figures in our fiction. What is pushed to the back of the mind makes its way forward somehow. Ghosts can be very fierce and instructive. They cast strange shadows, particularly in our literature, for it is the business of the artist to reveal what haunts us. We in the South may be in the process of exorcising this ghost which has given us our vision of perfection. Robert Penn Warren has said that in twenty years there may be no such thing as Southern literature. By that time the writer from the South may be writing about men in grey flannel suits and may have lost his ability to see that these gentlemen are even greater freaks than what we are writing about now.

The South is struggling mightily to retain her identity against great odds and without knowing always, I believe, quite in what her identity lies. An identity is not made from what passes, from slavery or from segregation, but from those qualities that endure because they are related to truth. It is not made from the mean average or the typical but often from the hidden and most extreme. I think that Catholic novelists in the future will be able to reinforce the vital strength of Southern literature, for they will know that what has given the South her identity are those beliefs and qualities which she has absorbed from the Scriptures and from her own history of defeat and violation: a distrust of the abstract, a sense of human dependence on the grace of God, and a knowledge that evil is not simply a problem to be solved, but a mystery to be endured. It is to be hoped that Catholics will look deeper into Southern literature and the subject of the grotesque and learn to see there more than what appears on the surface. Thomas Mann has said that the grotesque is a true anti-bourgeois style. Certainly Catholicism is opposed to the bourgeois mind. But in the dealings of Catholics with fiction you usually find a good deal of what is basically un-Catholic.

Or perhaps what you find is a misunderstanding of what the operation of grace *can* look like in fiction. The reader wants his grace warm and binding, not dark and disruptive. He is very busy always looking for some new Doctor Pangloss who will assure him that this is the best of all possible worlds. The word that occurs again and again in his demands of the novel is the word "positive." He seems to assume that what the writer writes about will follow a broad general attitude he has about the goodness of creation and our redemption and resurrection in Christ. There may be writers whose genuine vocation it is to do this. But it is not a vocation that can be demanded of every Catholic writer. These truths may serve for others simply as a light in which evil is seen more closely. We cannot demand centrality of the writer. We cannot even advise him, as so many do, to let evil be balanced by good. Dante divided up his territory pretty evenly between hell, purgatory and paradise. But then Dante lived in the thirteenth century when that balance was achieved in the faith of his age. We live now in an age which doubts both fact and value, which is moved this way and that by momentary convictions, which regards religion as a purely private matter. Instead of reflecting a balance from the world around him, the novelist now has to *achieve* one by being a counterweight to the prevailing heresy. People will differ as to what this heresy is, but the particular writer's view of it will have to come from looking at what he sees from where he is. Most of the people who want this positive literature are not able to recognize it when they get it.

Not long ago I received a letter from an old lady in California who informed me that when the tired reader comes home at night, he wishes to read something that will "lift up his heart." And it seems that her heart had not been lifted up by anything of mine she had read. I wrote her back that if her heart had been in the right place, it would have been lifted up. You may say that the serious writer doesn't have to bother about the tired reader, but he does, because they are all tired. One old lady who wants her heart lifted up wouldn't be so bad, but you multiply her 250,000 times and what you get is a book club.

The writer, without softening his vision, is obliged to capture or conjure readers. And this means any kind of reader. It means whatever is there. I used to think that it should be possible to write for some supposed elite, for the people who attend the universities and sometimes know how to read, but I have since found that, though you may publish your stories in the *Yale Review*, if they are any good at all you are eventually going to get a letter from some old lady in California, or some inmate of the Federal penitentiary, or the state insane asylum, or the local poorhouse, telling you where you have failed to meet his needs. And his need of course is to be lifted up. There is something in us as story-tellers, and as listeners to stories, that demands the redemptive act, that demands that what falls at least be offered the chance of restoration. The reader of today looks for this motion, and rightly so, but he has forgotten the cost of it. His sense of evil is deluded or lacking altogether, and so he has forgotten the *price* of restoration. He has forgotten the cost of truth, even in fiction.

I don't believe that you can impose orthodoxy on fiction. I do believe that you can deepen your own orthodoxy by reading if you are not afraid of strange visions. Our sense of what is contained in our faith is deepened less by abstractions than by an encounter with mystery in what is human and often perverse. We Catholics are much given to the instant answer. Fiction doesn't have any. Saint Gregory wrote that every time the sacred text describes a fact, it reveals a mystery. And this is what the fiction writer, on his lower level, attempts to do also.

The danger for the writer who is spurred by the religious

view of the world is that he will consider this two operations instead of one. He will lift up the old lady's heart without cost to himself or to her. He will forget that the devil is still at his task of winning souls and that grace cuts with the sword Christ said he came to bring. He will try to enshrine the mystery without the fact, and there will follow a further set of separations which are inimical to art. Judgment will be separated from vision; nature from grace; and reason from the imagination. These are separations which are very apparent today in American life and in American writing. I believe they are less true of the South, in spite of her well-publicized sins, than of any other section of the country, and in this I believe that the South is the place where a Catholic literature can thrive. The Catholic novelist in the South will bolster the South's best traditions, for they are the same as his own. And the South will perhaps lead him to be less timid as a novelist, more respectful of the concrete, more trustful of the blind imagination.

The poet is traditionally a blind man. But the Christian poet, and the story-teller as well, is like the blind man Christ touched, who looked then and saw men as if they were trees—but walking. Christ touched him again, and he saw clearly. We will not see clearly until Christ touches us in death, but this first touch is the beginning of vision, and it is an invitation to deeper and stranger visions that we shall have to accept if we want to realize a Catholic literature.

LETTERS

Contents

To Elizabeth McKee

Yaddo
Saratoga Springs
New York

Dear Miss McKee,   June 19, 1948

I am looking for an agent. Paul Moor suggested I write you.

I am at present working on a novel for which I received the Rinehart-Iowa Fiction Award ($750) last year. This award gives Rinehart an option but nothing else. I have been on the novel a year and a half and will probably be two more years finishing it. The first chapter appeared as a short story, "The Train," in the Spring 1948 issue of THE SEWANEE REVIEW. The fourth chapter will be printed in a new quarterly to appear in the fall, AMERICAN LETTERS. I have another chapter which I have sent to PARTISAN REVIEW and which I expect to be returned. A short story of mine will be in MADEMOISELLE sometime in the fall.

The novel, except for isolated chapters, is in no condition to be sent to you at this point. My main concern right now is to get the first draft of it done; however as soon as PARTISAN REVIEW returns the chapter I sent them, I would like to send it to you, and probably also a short story which I expect to get back from a quarterly in a few days.

I am writing you in my vague and slack season and mainly because I am being impressed just now with the money I am not making by having stories in such places as AMERICAN LETTERS. I am a very slow worker and it is possible that I won't write another story until I finish this novel and that no other chapters of the novel will prove salable. I have never had an agent so I have no idea what your disposition might be toward my type of writer. Please consider this letter an introduction to me and let me know if you would like to look at what I can get together when I get it together. I expect to be in New York a day or two in early August, and if you are interested, I would like to talk to you then.

Yours sincerely,

To Elizabeth McKee

Yaddo
Saratoga Springs
New York
Dear Elizabeth: February 17, 1949

I received Selby's letter today. Please tell me what is under this Sears-Roebuck Straight Shooter approach. I presume Selby says either that Rinehart will not take the novel as it will be if left to my fiendish care (it will be essentially as it is), or that Rinehart would like to rescue it at this point and train it into a conventional novel.

The criticism is vague and really tells me nothing except that they don't like it. I feel the objections they raise are connected with its virtues, and the thought of working with them specifically to correct these lacks they mention is repulsive to me. The letter is addressed to a slightly dim-witted Camp-fire Girl, and I cannot look with composure on getting a lifetime of others like them. I have not yet answered it and won't until I hear further from you, but if I were certain that Harcourt would take the novel, I would write Selby immediately that I prefer to be elsewhere.

Would it be possible for you to get the manuscript back now and show it to Harcourt, or does Rinehart hang onto it until we break relations? Please advise me what the next step is to be, or take it yourself. I'll probably come down week after next if you think it advisable. I am anxious to have this settled and off my mind so that I can get to work.

Thank you for sending the carbons of my stories. They and the carbon of the novel have been sent to Mr. Moe.

Sincerely,

To John Selby

Yaddo
Saratoga Springs
New York
Dear Mr. Selby: February 18, 1949

Thank you for your letter of the 16th. I plan to come down next week and I have asked Elizabeth McKee to make an appointment with you for me on Thursday. I think, however, that before I talk to you my position on the novel and on your criticism in the letter should be made plain.

I can only hope that in the finished novel the direction will be clearer, but I can tell you that I would not like at all to work with you as do other writers on your list. I feel that whatever virtues the novel may have are very much connected with the limitations you mention. I am not writing a conventional novel, and I think that the quality of the novel I write will derive precisely from the peculiarity or aloneness, if you will, of the experience I write from. I do not think there is any lack of objectivity in the writing, however, if this is what your criticism implies; and also I do not feel that rewriting has obscured the direction. I feel it has given whatever direction is now present.

In short, I am amenable to criticism but only within the sphere of what I am trying to do; I will not be persuaded to do otherwise. The finished book, though I hope less angular, will be just as odd if not odder than the nine chapters you have now. The question is: is Rinehart interested in publishing this kind of novel?

I'll hope to see you Thursday and hear further what you think.

Sincerely,

To Paul Engle

Milledgeville

Dear Paul: April 7, 1949

I am in the process of moving. I left Yaddo March 1 and have since been in transit and am now getting ready to go back to New York City where I have a room and where I hope to keep on working on the novel as long as my money holds out, which is not due to be long. Therefore, being in a swivit, I am writing you in brief what I take the situation with Rinehart to be but when I get to New York in ten days I will write you further and send back the letter Rinehart sent you. Thank you for sending it to me.

When I was in New York in September, my agent and I asked Selby how much of the novel they wanted to see before we asked for contract and an advance. The answer was—about six chapters. So in February I sent them nine chapters (108 pages and all I've done) and my agent asked for an advance and for their editorial opinion.

Their editorial opinion was a long time in coming because obviously they didn't think much of the 108 pages and didn't know what to say. When it did come, it was *very* vague and I thought totally missed the point of what kind of a novel I am writing. My impression was that they want a conventional novel. However, rather than trust my own judgment entirely I showed the letter to Lowell who had already read the 108 pages. He too thought that the faults Rinehart had mentioned were not the faults of the novel (some of which he had previously pointed out to me). I tell you this to let you know I am not, as Selby implied to me, working in a vacuum.

In answer to the editorial opinion, I wrote Selby that I would have to work on the novel without direction from Rinehart, that I was amenable to criticism but only within the sphere of what I was trying to do.

In New York a few weeks later, I learned indirectly that nobody at Rinehart liked the 108 pages but Raney (and whether he likes it or not I couldn't really say), that the ladies there particularly had thought it unpleasant (which pleased me). I told Selby that I was willing enough to listen to Rinehart criticism but that if it didn't suit me, I would disregard it. That is the impasse.

Any summary I might try to write for the rest of the novel would be worthless and I don't choose to waste my time at it. I don't write that way. I can't write much more without money and they won't give me any money because they can't see what the finished book will be. That is Part Two of the impasse.

To develope at all as a writer I have to develope in my own way. The 108 pages are very angular and awkward but a great deal of that can be corrected when I have finished the rest of it—and only then. I will not be hurried or directed by Rinehart. I think they are interested in the conventional and I have had no indication that they are very bright. I feel the heart of the matter is they don't care to lose $750 (or as they put it, Seven Hundred and Fifty Dollars.)

If they don't feel I am worth giving more money to and leaving alone, then they should let me go. Other publishers, who have read the two printed chapters, are interested. Selby and I came to the conclusion that I was "prematurely arrogant." I supplied him with the phrase.

Now I am sure that no one will understand my need to work this novel out in my own way better than you; although you may feel that I should work faster. Believe me, I work ALL the time, but I cannot work fast. No one can convince me I shouldn't rewrite as much as I do. I only hope that in a few years I won't have to so much.

I didn't get any Guggenheim.

If you see Robie tell him to write me.

Yours,

To Betty Boyd

255 W 108 NYC
After Sept 1–:
Care of Fitzgerald
RD 4
Ridgefield, Conn.

Dear B—

I am wondering about you & Los Alamos?

Me & novel are going to move to the rural parts of Connecticut. I have some friends named Fitzgerald who have bought a house on top of a ridge, miles from anything you could name. An exaggeration. The nearest neighbor is a mile & a half and is Mrs. Alger Hisses first husband. I can't decide whether he should be a bad neighbor for having selected her or a good one for having discarded her, but I suppose it is no matter. I have no particular desire to leave New York except that I will save a good deal of money this way &, my publishing connections still being in a snarl, that is a great consideration. I am on a tightrope somewhere between Rinehart & Harcourt-Brace. There should be some kind of insurance to take care of such cases.

I learned by the Alumna Junkal that B——B——M—— is not ten blocks from me, filling her noddle full of Lord knows what at the Columbia trough. Fancy the mental champaine (SP?) that will be brought back, brimming & bristling, to be dispensed in Parks basement. Also fancy it mingling there with the vinegar, the pop, & the hogwash.

Isn't Los Alamos in California? I would be obliged for your impressions of California if you go there. It puzzles me about like the thinking machine.

Yours,

To Mavis McIntosh

70 Acre Rd., RD 4
Ridgefield, Conn.
Dear Mavis: October 31, 1949

I have been pondering Selby's statement of release for some days now. I think it is insulting and shows very clearly that I could not work with him. However, since they still feel that they have an option and that I am being dishonest, it seems to me that I should present them with more of the manuscript one more time.

Now since if I sign the contract with Harcourt, I won't get any money until next fall anyway, and that providing they take the book, it seems to me that it would be better all around to try to arrange something like this with Rinehart: that next March, I show them what I have done up to that date. This will be considerably more than what they saw last year at the same time and the direction of the book will be more apparent. If they are not able by that time to know if they want it, then they will never know. Now it seems that if I do this, they should agree IN WRITING to release me without condition or any such malicious statement as accompanied the present release if they don't want the book. It should also be made clear that I will not work with them or sign any contract which includes an option on the next book or any such thing as that. I feel certain that they will not want the book if they see it in the spring or at any time later, for that matter.

This would simply be an attempt on my part to be fair with them and to give them a chance to be fair with me. As you said, they owe me something. The announcement of the contest was so worded that I am held to a "moral" obligation and they are not. Further, I understood last spring that they would make up their minds on six chapters. Selby told Elizabeth and me that at lunch. It wasn't in writing and apparently dealings with them should be.

Perhaps after all your trouble this seems unnecessarily scrupulous to you or anyway, a late-in-the-day scrupulosity. It may well be, but the fact remains that the statement of release was not much of a release; if Harcourt doesn't take the book, we are back where we started from. If Rinehart will make this agreement with me, in writing, we might get the thing settled by summer and I would be free to work with an open mind; which I am certainly not now.

I am going to try to be in town Thursday and Friday of this week. I will call you and hope to see you, but I am writing this before hand so that you will know what is on my mind. I wrote Elizabeth that I thought it would be best to go ahead and sign the contract with Harcourt, but this letter is the fruit of more thought.

Thank you for bothering with such unrewarding people.

Sincerely,

To Robie Macauley

70 Acre Rd., RD 4

Dear Robie,   Ridgefield, Conn.

I wrote Dilly to find out where you and Ann were this year and she said at Iowa. I congratulate you on your endurance. I had a letter from Paul Engle and he intimated that everything out there was filthy rich and florishing and said they would be in LIFE in December. This must be the end. There must be going to be a picture of Engle surrounded by foreign students and looking like the Dean of American Letters, and one of Paul Griffith surrounded by natives and trying to look as if he were in Paris, and one of Martin surrounded by bottles and looking as if he didn't know he wasn't in Paris. What about you? I hope you manage to escape.

Me and Enoch are living in the woods in Connecticut with the Robert Fitzgeralds. Enoch didn't care so much for New York. He said there wasn't no privetcy there. Every time he went to sit in the bushes there was already somebody sitting there ahead of him. He was very nervous before we left and somebody at the Partisan Review told him to go to an analyst. He went and the analyst said what was wrong with him was his daddy's fault and Enoch was so mad that anybody should defame his daddy that he pushed the analyst out the window. You can see why we would never last in New York. Enoch is going to be in the Partisan Review again in December or January but he don't like it at all and is mad with me because I didn't get him in Click, which has pictures.

This summer I chanced on a copy of FURIOSO and I liked that story of yours in it very much and was glad they didn't waste their $250. I haven't seen the other stories as I have largely given up reading polite magazines since I have given up trying to be a gracious lady. Mrs. Ames was too much for me. I am going back to raising mandrils. How is Austin Warren?

The Brothers Rinehart and I have parted company to our mutual satisfaction and I have a contract with Harcourt-Brace, but I am largely worried about wingless chickens. I feel this is the time for me to fulfill myself by stepping in and saving the chicken but I don't know exactly how since I am not bold. I only know I believe in the *complete* chicken. You think about the complete *chicken* for a while.

The best to you and Ann.

To Elizabeth Hardwick and Robert Lowell

Dear Elizabeth and Cal   Milledgeville
    I won't see you again as I have to go to the hospital Friday and have a kidney hung on a rib. I will be there a month and at home a month. This was none of my plan.

I hope if you go to Iowa you won't make the mistake of trusting —— ——. I said I liked him but I don't.

Please write me a card while I am in the hospital. I won't be able to do anything there but dislike the nurses.

To Elizabeth McKee

Box 246
Milledgeville
Georgia
Dear Elizabeth: February 13, 1950

Thank you for your note. I am out of the hospital and don't expect to be ill again any time soon after such a radical cure. I hope to be back in Connecticut by March 20th.

Your office (in January) forwarded a letter to me at 255 West 108th. I received it by the grace of Miss Fenwick who at that time lived next door but has now moved, so I wish you would ask your secretary to scratch that address off her books. Either the Connecticut address or this one will always eventually get me.

I'm anxious to be on with the book but don't have any strength yet.

Remember me to Miss McIntosh.

Sincerely,

To Betty Boyd Love

Baldwin Memorial Horspital as usuel
Dear B.   12.23.50

Thanks yr cd. I am languishing on my bed of semi affliction, this time with *AWRTHRITUS* or, to give it all it has, *the* acute rheumatoid arthritis, what leaves you always willing to sit down, lie down, lie flatter, etc. But I am taking cortisone so I will have to get up again. These days you caint even have you a good psychosomatic ailment to get yourself a rest. I will be in Milledgeville Ga a birdsanctuary for a few months,

waiting to see how much of an invalid I am going to get to
be. At Christmas the horsepital is full of old rain crows &
tree frogs only—& accident victims—& me, but I don't believe in time no more much so its all one to me. And hope
you are the same & have some chuldrun by now. I always
want to hear.

I have been reading *Murder in the Cathedral* & the nurses
thus conclude I am a mystery fan. Its a marvelous play if you
dont know it, better if you do.

Write me a letter of sympathy.

Yours

To Elizabeth McKee

Emery University Hosp.
Dear Elizabeth   Atlanta Georgia

Thank you for your letter that I received after Christmas. I
am in Atlanta right now at the Emery University Hospital,
much improved and expect to go home next week.

During the cortisone period I managed to finish the first
draft of the novel and send it to Mr. Fitzgerald in Conn. He
is satisfied that it is good and so am I. I think I have found
somebody here in Atlanta to make me some copies. Any way
I am trying to get you a copy & one to Harcourt.

When I get home I plan to add an extra chapter and make
some changes on a few others.

It will all just take some time.

Regards to Miss McI.

To Robert Giroux

311 Wst Green Street
Milledgeville, Georgia
Dear Bob: March 10, 1951

Thank you for your letter. Enclosed is the manuscript of
the book and I hope you'll like it and decide to publish it.

I'm still open to suggestion about improving it and will welcome any you have; however, I'm anxious to be done with it and if it could be out in the Fall that would suit me fine.

Miss McKee or Miss McIntosh will probably see you about it. Miss McKee has the notion that some more of the chapters will be salable, but I don't.

I am up and around again now but won't be well enough to go back to Connecticut for some time.

Thank you for Dr. Stern's book. I've wanted to read it.

Sincerely,

To Mavis McIntosh

Milledgeville,
Georgia

Dear Mavis: September 1, 1951

Bob Giroux and Mrs. Tate made some suggestions for improving my book and I have been working on these and have by now about come up with another draft of it, of which I will have one copy—readable but with a good many inked-in corrections—I hope in a few weeks.

I'm not familiar with the necessities or the niceties of sending a final draft to the publisher. Is it alright for me to send this copy? Or is their deadline for the spring already up anyhow? If so, there's no need for me to hurry myself. I have been in and out of the hospital this summer and am too decrepit to type a hundred and fifty pages under a month.

Will you need a copy? I hate to think of that other draft batting around at British publishing houses when this improved version exists. There is not much chance of its being bought there, however, I would think.

Giroux sent me the other ms. back and I have been inserting the additions and corrections, etc., into it and that is the copy I'll have in a few weeks. He said they would like to have it as soon as possible; but that is nothing definite.

I'd be much obliged for what information you can give me. Regards to Elizabeth.

Sincerely,

To Sally and Robert Fitzgerald

Dear S&R   9-20-51

I reckon you all are under way with the academic year '51–'52 and No. 5. I hope this one will be a girl & have a fierce Old Testament name and cut off a lot of heads. You had better stay down and take care of yourself. Your children sound big enough to do all the work. By beating them moderately & moderately often you should be able to get them in the habit of doing domestic chores.

Me & maw are still at the farm and are like to be, I perceive, through the winter. She is nuts about it out here, surrounded by the lowing herd and other details, and considers it beneficial to my health. The same has improved. I am down to two moderate shots a day from four large ones when we first got to the farm. The large doses of ACTH send you off in a rocket and are scarcely less disagreeable than the disease so I am happy to be shut of them.

I am working on the end of the book while a lady around here types the first part of it. I think its a lot better but I may be mistaken and will have to be told.

I got as far in Cal's book as the quotation in the front from Dr. Williams. The local librarian brought me *Dominations & Powers*, what I have been reading for the style, not being able to take in the thought; and one of my English-teacher friends was so good as to leave with me *twenty old* Saturday Reviews—only a loan—they like to save them. The face of Malcolm Cowley shines out in every issue.

I have twenty one brown ducks with blue wing bars. They walk everywhere they go in single-file.

Let us hear how you do; and steel yourselfs to read the changed parts of that manuscript again.

We pray for your mother's wavering; I would put it in the miracle class should she waver all the way. I am reading Dr. Johnson's Life of Dryden. Dryden "embraced Popery" but Dr. Johnson is very lenient with him about it and says the measure of his sincerety was, he taught it [Popery] to his children. You'll be more than a genius if you can teach it to your parents.

To Sally and Robert Fitzgerald

Dear S&R   Tuesday

Enclosed is Opus Nauseous No. 1. I had to read it over after it came from the typist's and that was like spending the day eating a horse blanket. It seems mighty sorry to me but better than it was before. My mother said she wanted to read it again so she went off with it and I found her a half hour later on page 9 and sound asleep. I sent it on to Giroux and said if he thought it was alright to go on with it but I doubt if the poor man puts himself to reading it again. Do you think Mrs. Tate would? All the changes are efforts after what she suggested in that letter and I am much obliged to her. If you think she wouldn't mind, would you send this copy on to her after you read it as I don't have another copy or her address? I would like to thank her for reading it the first time so if you would send me her address I would be obliged for that too. I am also obliged, while I am at this, for your reading it again. My vocabulary don't touch such a service.

Note that I changed the Car to Bee. If you are possessed of an Aunt Bee, let me know and I will change it to Flea. If you have an Aunt Flea . . .

I hope you got the pickle recipe. Regina had never made any such but got the recipe out of a very dirty old cookbook so it should be alright.

Regina says I should invite you to visit us on this farm. I tell her you have 5 or 6 children and couldn't hardly do such a thing but she says I should anyway that it would be the *nice thing to do.*

I have read about that book Catcher in the Rye and will be glad to see it when it comes.

I have just discovered that my mother's dairyman calls all the cows *he*: he ain't give but two gallons, he ain't come in yet,—also he changes the name endings: if its Maxine, he calls it Maxima. I reckon he doesn't like to feel surrounded by females or something.

To Sally and Robert Fitzgerald

Dear S&R,   Saturday

I certainly enjoyed the Catcher in the Rye. Read it up the same day it came. Regina said I was going to RUIN MY EYES reading all that in one afternoon. I reckon that man owes a lot to Ring Lardner. Anyway he is very good. Regina said would she like to read it and I said, well it was very fine. She said yes but would *she* like to read it, so I said she would have to try it and see. She hasn't tried it yet. She likes books with Frank Buck and a lot of wild animals.

Thank you for sending the ms to Caroline. She sent it back to me with some nine pages of comments and she certainly increased my education thereby. So I am doing some more things to it and then I mean to send it off for the LAST time.

I enclose the enclosed on acct. of the liberal mention of Sary Larence. Old Budenz is in the black books but what I don't see is why Wallace's word is now the gospel. What's he done to redeem himself besides going back to raising them hogs?

You ought to hear all the Baptists down here hollering about the Separation of Church & State. They are having conventions all over the place and making resolutions and having the time of their lives. You'd think the Pope was about to annex the Sovereign State of Georgia.

What ever happened to Maritain? Is he still at Princeton or did Frank the Spell man get him a job in some Catholic institution?

Regina is glad you liked the cake and will send you the recipe when she finds it. I think she just throws the stuff in. She likes em dry and Sister likes em wet. That was Sister's recipe.

I am glad you have come to favor chickens. You won't favor them so much when you have to clean up their apartment but the eggs are certainly worth it. I have got me five geese. We also have turkeys. They all have the sorehead and the cure for that is liquid black shoe polish—so we have about fifteen turkeys running around in blackface. They look like domesticated vultures.

Yours,

To Robert Giroux

Milledgeville
Georgia

Dear Bob: December 3, 1951

I am enclosing the changes and I will be much obliged to you if you can get them substituted at the printers. I think they make a lot of difference. I had a good many more for the first chapter but I presume it is too late for that. Caroline thought that some places went too fast for anybody to get them; also that I needed some preparation for the title. About how much can I mess around on the proofs without costing myself a lot of money? Fifteen percent of the cost of composition doesn't mean anything to me. What I want to know is: how many paragraphs (approximately) could I insert?

The biographical statement: Born, Savannah, Georgia, March 1925. Attended Georgia State College for Women, A.B. degree; State University of Iowa, M.F.A. degree. Published stories in *Accent*, *The Sewanee Review*, *Partisan Review*, *Mademoiselle*, and *Tomorrow*. No prizes except the Rinehart money which shouldn't be mentioned. (Doubtless Miss McIntosh didn't show you their letter of release. It said I was "stiff-necked, uncooperative, and unethical.") I have lived in Connecticut and am at present living in Milledgeville, Georgia, raising ducks and game birds, and writing. (This is the way all those things sound to me. If you need any more, I will have to make it up.)

I'll have to have the picture taken and will send it to you but I doubt if they give it to me by the 10th.

Please send me the proofs here.

Thank you for all this trouble I am putting you to about the changes.

Sincerely,

To Sally and Robert Fitzgerald

Dear S&R   Thursday

A very noisy Christmas to you all and assorted blessings for the new year. My mamma is getting ready for what she hopes will be one of her blessings: a D. P. family to arrive here Christmas night. She has to fix up and furnish a house for them, don't know how many there will be or what nationality or occupation or nothing. She and Mrs. S——, the dairy-man's wife, have been making curtains for the windows out of flowered chicken feed sacks. Regina was complaining that the green sacks wouldn't look so good in the same room where the pink ones were and Mrs. S—— (who has no teeth on one side of her mouth) says in a very superior voice, "Do you think they'll know what colors even is?" Usually the fam-ilies that have been got around here for dairy work have turned out to be Polish shoe makers and have headed for Chi-cago just as soon as they could save the money. For which they can't be blamed. However, we are waiting to see how this comes out.

What I forgot to say the last time I wrote was dont send me any two weeks rent that you may think you owe me. If the Lord is with me this next year I aim to visit you, at which time I will be glad to eat it out. I am only a little stiff in the heels so far this winter and am taking a new kind of ACTH, put up in glue, and I am on a pretty low maintenance dose. I only hope I can keep it that way.

My momma sends hers for the season.

To Sally and Robert Fitzgerald

Dear S&R   Thursday

I certainly am enjoying the Reformation in England. I feel like I was at it. I showed it to the college librarian so she would get it for them. Sometimes the students check out a good book by mistake; not often, according to her. They are very careful. She says they all go in for sociology and case studies. Case studies are the big thing.

My mamma's D. P.s haven't come yet; she don't know why. She is very anxious to get them here and have the difficulties begin. She says I ought to be able to teach them English (educ!) and I say well I ain't able to and she says well *she* could if she wanted to and I say how and she says CAT:

C- A- T. and you draw a picture of one. I don't doubt but what she could do it.

The Macauleys have asked me to come to Greensboro in March for an Arts Forum thing that Catherin Anne Porter is to be the phenomenon at. I may try this to see how my travelling legs are. I think I could do with out Catherin Anne.

I had to go have my picture taken for the purposes of Harcourt Brace. They were all bad. (The pictures.) The one I sent looked as if I had just bitten my grandmother and that this was one of my few pleasures, but all the rest were worse.

We liked your Christmas card very much and recognized yer assorted children.

Yours,

To Sally and Robert Fitzgerald

Dear S&R,   Wednesday
I thank you for the information about the Ford book. I don't have anything good enough right now to send to high class places and it's also necessary for me to convert everything I can into ACTH, so I'll spare old Blackmur the pleasure of using my return envelope. Do they use reprints? I could ask Giroux to send them a book. One reprint has been bought by the New American Library for something called New World Writing—the part about Enoch and the gorilla. Then my agent wrote me that the New Am. Lib. had bought the whole thing for $4,000, and that I would get $2,000. Then she writes that that ain't actually the case yet but is going to be. I never believe nothing until I got the money. However, they advanced me $500 against the garantee of $4,000, but I still suspicion the whole thing, as my mama's dairyman's wife says.

Have you seen the book? They haven't sent me any copy but they sent one to the lady here who is going to sell it and she kindly showed it to me. The book itself is very pretty but the jacket is lousy with me blown up on the back of it, looking like a refugee from deep thought. It has Caroline's imprimatur on it so that ought to help. My current literary asignment (from Regina) is to write an introduction for

Cousin Katie "so she won't be shocked," to be *pasted* on the inside of her book. This piece has to be in the tone of the Sacred Heart Messenger and carry the burden of contemporary critical thought. I keep putting it off.

Regina is getting very literary. "Who is this Kafka?" she says. "People ask me." A German Jew, I says, I think. He wrote a book about a man that turns into a roach. "Well I can't tell people *that*," she says. "Who is this Evalin Wow?"

I am having a terrible time getting out of parties. An old dame that I abide with gritted teeth is having a luncheon for me on the 10th—only because she got to Regina before she got to me. Two others got to me before Regina and I squashed their plans into a pulp. I have to be very stealthy, all eyes and ears. You will see me very early in June.

Did that book I sent you come? If not I write them as I ordered it from a place in Chicago.

I have eleven enfant geese.

Yours,

—They just sent me a copy. I will ast them to send you one.

To Robert Lowell

Milledgeville, Ga.

Dear Cal,   May 2

I was powerful glad to hear from you and I am pleased that you liked the gorilla. I hope you'll like the whole thing. I asked Bob Giroux to send you one.

I've been in Georgia with the buzzards for the last year and a half on acct. of arthritis but I am going to Conn. in June to see the Fitzgeralds. They have about a million children, all with terrific names and all beautiful. I'm living with my mother in the country. She raises cows and I raise ducks and pheasants. The pheasant cock has horns and looks like some of those devilish people and dogs in Russeau's paintings. I have been taking painting myself, painting mostly chickens and guinneas and pheasants. My poor mother thinks they're great stuff. She prefers me painting to me writing. She hasn't learned to love Mrs. Watts. Harcourt sent my book to Waugh and his comment was: "If this is really the unaided work of a young lady, it is a remarkable product." My mother was vastly insulted. She put the emphasis on *if* and *lady*. Does he suppose you're not a lady? she says. WHO is he?

I'm all with Elizabeth on the sightseeing and will take mine sitting down or not at all. I like food with mine instead of politics, though.

If you ever see Omar give him my regards. I met a doctor recently who had been at St. Elizabeth's and knew Mr. and Mrs. Pound, and liked them very much. He said a lot of people came out to see Pound and one who came insistently had sprouted a beard and French collar.

The best to you both.

To Helen Greene

                                                Milledgeville
Dear Helen,   May 23, 1952

I was distressed yesterday to have some of your students tell me that I was a follower of Kafka and exhibited that pessimism that had been going around with European intellectuals for the last fifty years but was just getting to the young people of this country. Perhaps they misquoted you as they are often apt to do; but since my beliefs are a long way from Kafka I thought I had better write you and see if I couldn't clear it up.

Kafka was mentioned in connection with the book in the matter of technique—a kind of fantasy rooted in the specific that I seem to have got in common with him. But that is all.

My philosophical notions don't derive from Kierkegard (I can't even spell it) but from St. Thomas Aquinas. And I don't intend the tone of the book to be pessimistic. It is after all a story about redemption and if you admit redemption, you are no pessimist. The gist of the story is that H. Motes couldn't really believe that he hadn't been redeemed. Maybe this is what R. Neibur (can't spell that one either) calls Christian pessimism, but if so, it too is a long way from Kafka and Kierkegaard.

We really wish you would come out to see us some time. I never seem to see the people I would really like to see.

Yours sincerely,

To Robert Fitzgerald

Milledgeville
Dear Robert,   Tuesday

I hated to leave Sally there with only Maria when she was sick, but as I seemed to be getting sick myself, I thought I had better. Also I was able to take M. Loretta back to New York with me and leave her in the lap of the welfare woman. I felt that when she was gone, Sally would be better. Loretta would perhaps have been controllable if there had been a Federal Marshall in the house, though I have my doubts. She had to stay in the room with Sally and she was full of wise sass and argument and there was no rest for Sally with her there.

I went over to Elsie Hill's Sunday afternoon and told her that Sally was there and not supposed to get out of bed. She immediately came over. She drives and she speaks Italian and I think she likes to take charge. Also Albert Levitt was going away Monday so she wouldn't have much to do but mind Sally's business. She took all the telephone numbers and was very nice. Nicer by far than her daughter, who didn't even come up. Mr. Latham said he would stay up there Monday and Tuesday nights. Teddy didn't want him staying any longer lest he overdo himself. In my opinion the old man likes it better at the Fitzgeralds than at the Lathams. Anybody that wants Teddy can have him.

I tried to call you Sunday night but the operator never could get you. S. was debating if she should call her mother but she couldn't make up her mind about it. I was afraid myself that Mrs. Morgan might not add to the quiet and I thought quiet was what was needed most, but Mr. Latham was prepared to call her if Sally decided she wanted her to come. I also suggested calling Eileen Berryman but S. was afraid that would upset Maria, who had already been upset by Loretta Washington. She was allergic to Loretta on first sight.

I saw my doctor as soon as I got to Atlanta. He said I had had a virus infection and it had reacted on my complaint (I now know that is lupus and am very glad to so know) and he increased my dose but doesn't think I will have any trouble. It was a great boon to me to be able to spend a month in Connecticut and the Lord knows I appreciate your hospitality. I only wish I could have done more for Sally before I left. Please keep me informed on how she does. I think with food and rest she will be all right.

Yours,

Mr. Isaac Rosenfeld unburdened himself on the subject of Wise Blood in the New Republic. He found it completely bogus, at length.

To Caroline Gordon Tate

Milledgeville
9/11/52

Dear Caroline,

Last night I happened on this picture of your connection here. Since I had sent him two bucks in memory of Mark Twain (before I asked you about him), I figure I must have at least paid for the license. He's mighty well preserved.

I am up again now and looking forward to a recessive period of my come-and-go ailment. It's very good working again. I am just writing a story to see if I can get away from the freaks for a while.

This summer while I was at the Fitzgeralds, I read "The Strange Children." I thought it was a beautiful book, part one probably in the development of Grace in these people. Of the characters I noticed that the Catholic, Mr. Reardon, was the least filled in. Was that because he would have taken the book over if he had been? It was not his story of course but it takes some doing to put a Catholic in a novel.

I have just read "Victory." Everything I read of Conrad's I like better than the last thing. I've also just read the "Turn of

the Screw" again and to me it fairly shouts that it's about
expiation.

Have you seen the Fitzgeralds? Sally seems to be having a
bad time still. I had to leave in a hurry on account of my
fever a few days before she lost the baby. Benedict has had
the chicken pox but they say it has only given him more
zest—which he didn't particularly need. The day before I left,
he climbed in the car, drove it twelve feet over a chair and
into a pile of rocks, climbed out the window, looking exactly
like Charles Lindburg, and received a whipping from me
(Sally was in bed sick) as if it were a great honor.

I suspect you are getting ready for Minnesota.

                                                    Yours,

To Robie Macauley

                                              Milledgeville
Dear Robie,   10/28/52

I've read your book with great delight and I wish I had
some reasons to tell you why I think it's so fine. However, I
merely enjoys, I does not analyze. Doubtless as soon as it
comes out officially all the jokers will turn up and tell the
folks exactly what you haven't said and exactly how you
haven't said it. I particularly liked Gordon and the parties—
I've seen the winner and the jockey. It's a book that's alive all
the way through and that is as close as I can come to saying
anything intelligent about it.

Also I was very pleased to get a free copy. I'm developing
a Scrooge-like character and collecting things (anything)
against the coming Republican depression. I'm in a new business too. I've bought a hen and rooster peafowl from Eustis,
Florida and four peachickens. You get $65 dollars for a pair
of three-year-old peafowl, so you see where I'll be in a couple
of years. The man I bought them from in Eustis assures me
that the demand always exceeds the supply.

I had a letter from Paul Engle this summer about my book. He didn't like the title or think the end was clear but otherwise he thought it was fine etc etc and he would permit himself "only one note of harshness," to wit: from the jacket nobody would have known I had ever been at Iowa WHEREAS my book had really been "shaped" there and this was a "simple honorable fact that I should have thought of myself." I was sick at the time so I didn't answer it, but I got around to it recently and told him that in the information I had sent Harcourt I had of course put in that I had been to Iowa and studied under him but that I hadn't had anything to do with the jacket and didn't know how it would look until I saw it, but I told him I'd fix it up on the drugstore reprint that has been sold to the New American Library. I told him that would really be a jacket, with Mrs. Watts on the front cover, wearing the least common denominator, and I would certainly see that everything about Iowa etc etc was on that one. He's in New York now on a Ford Fellowship; he said he intended to get out a book of poetry and a book of prose during the year.

Where are the Lowells these days? There were some wonderful letters in the last issue of The Commonweal that Santayanna had written Cyril Clemens, in which he mentioned his interest in Cal and told about some visits from him. When your book is out, you'll probably get a fancy scroll from Clemens saying you have been elected an Honorary Member of the Mark Twain Society (along with Winston Churchill, Lord Smuts, TSEliot, Dorothy Canfield Fisher & Several of The Living & The Dead) and that contributions are gratefully accepted. He is apparently in on this with an old bird named Meriwether, a cousin of Caroline's, who is filthy rich and, she says, pure goat. Before I was talking to her about it, I sent them two dollars in memory of Mark Twain and "to Unite the Whole World in Bonds of Cultured Peace."

Regards to Anne. I hope to hear from you one of these days.

I am going to write the lady that sent the book how much I liked it.

To Sally Fitzgerald

Dear S. M.   The Sabbath

I have just read the review in the Commonweal and I think you have nailed the lid on his box. He makes me sick just to read about and I don't see how you got through his book. Also the S. M. is very impressive. I would suspect it stood for something like Smernkchs Maupasuntanti if I wasn't so up on the literary WORLD. I never have read Aiken or Henry Miller or that dope that wrote the Jurgen things but from what I have read about them they all sound like steps on the same ladder—with old Aiken the high rung. There is a very funny piece on Henry Miller in the second New World Writing.

I thank you extremely for sending the coat and camera, and enclose the postage for same. Parent has taken passionate dislike of coat and waits for colder weather when I won't have to wear it. She is composing you a fruit cake but I don't know if it will be composed in time for Thanksgiving or not. I don't know when Thanksgiving is. Anyway it'll be along.

I had a note from John Crowe Ransom, saying there was such a thing as a Kenyon Review Fellowship in Fiction that they got from Rockerfeller money and would I like to apply, that Robt. Fitzgrld & Peter Taylor had mentioned me to him. I applied before the envelope was opened good but I reckon there are a lot of others as would like to come off with it too. Anyway, I thank Robt. for the mentioning. He said he had read my book and had been impressed so that is a help. I am wondering did he also see George's piece. George has been violently writing letters to the Atlanta Constitution about the election—he always calls Stalin Uncle Joe in the letters; they sound mad and sporty too with just a dash of art and a dash of philosophy. I am going to try to force a loan of Art & Scholasticism on him when I see him.

I hear tell the Lowells are in Rome. I thought those were good pieces on Santayana in the Commonweal.

To Sally and Robert Fitzgerald

Dear S&R—   Tuesday
I would certly be obliged for some word on this. I have
been working on it two months & its cold as a fish to me.
I don't know the front from the back & I don't want to
send it around if its not good & I can, some way, make it
better.

I got to have another transfusion but I am doing all right
& work every day. The J——s & P——s have moved out
but I learned a lot while they were here. I am sending you a
copy of Robie Macauleys novel as Random House sent me
one & he sent me another. I think its a good book. My
mamma & I are on the way to the polls to cancel out each
other's vote.

Many thanks for this great service you render me.

To Sally and Robert Fitzgerald

Dear S&R   Thursday
I am much obliged for both letters and think I have fixed
up the story much better now on acct of same. I had to
send some stuff to the Kenyon Review in applying for that
fellowship so I sent that one and the first chapter of what
proposes itself to be a novel—the one with the hero named
Tarwater.

We hope the cake got there in time for Thanksgiving.
There was also one enclosed for Maria to take to her room
and eat with her secret beer. I never got to send her that
screw driver I was going to on acct of being sick and what-
not.

We are real glad there will be a fifth small devil in June. I
reccoment turnip green potliquor with cornbread broke up
in it, and hope you will continue to be well.

I agree with you about the Macauley book. I thought it
was very funny but as the guy in the Commonweal said "no

theological dimension" a fact of which Bro. Macauley is unfortunately proud I am afraid. He has to justify a lapsed Catholic wife among other things. The news about Cal is fine and
I'm not surprised that Elizabeth is willing. I imagine after a few
years of that you'd be so weak you'd be willing to turn him
over to the salvation army. I enclose a letter from Mrs. ——
that tells about her husband. I don't know if that poor man
will ever get there or not. The Holy Ghost will have to operate a bulldozer to push —— a fraction of an inch. Of
course, He does, but.

My parent is out chasing two visiting mules off the premises. She runs the car after them for about thirty feet. Then
they stop, turn around and stand there looking at the car.
Then she gets out and says SHOO and throws up her arms.
Then they run about twenty feet. Then she gets in the car and
looks as if she is going to run smack over them. They stand
there and look at the car, she gets out again and says SHOO
and throws up her hands. It goes on that way all down to the
entrance of the place. She will chase them out and then I
suspect they will follow the car back, and be where they were
when she arives. We finally got shut of the P——-J——s but
last week we hear the Klan burned a cross on our place, up
the road in front of a house that we rent to some people
named L——. They are very peaceable people so we suspicion that the Klan maybe mistook them for the P——-J——s,
but we only suspicion it. They also deliver Thanksgiving bas-
kets at this time of the year and have themselves a general big
time. Imagine your Thanksgiving basket delivered with a
burning cross. When the Grand Dragon comes, they have an
electric cross.

Mrs. S—— has been telling about how her new preacher
sings his sermons. He puts a chair out on the platform and
then calls up various Biblical characters to testify. "Paul," he
says, "will you come up and testify?" They imagine the Apostle Paul getting up and taking a seat in the chair I suppose.
Then the preacher sings Rock of Ages. Then he says, "Peter,
will you come up and testify?" and sings something for Peter
to testify. Mrs. S—— thinks it's wonderful. "Evy eye is on
him," she says. "Not a breath stirs."

Yours,

To Sally and Robert Fitzgerald

Dear S&R   12/20/52

Merry Christmas to you all from Grimrack. I got the Kenyon Fellowship, thanks being no doubt to your saying to him this summer that I was an existing writer. My mamma is getting a big bang out of notifying all the kin who didn't like the book that the Rockerfeller Foundation, etc, etc,—this very casual like on the back of Christmas cards. Money talks, she says, and the name of Rockerfeller don't hurt a bit. It don't, except that all they'll think is that the Foundation is going to pot. I reckon most of this money will go to blood and ACTH and books, with a few sideline researches into the ways of the vulgar. I would like to go to California for about two minutes to further these researches, though at times I feel that a feeling for the vulgar is my natural talent and don't need any particular encouragement. Did you see the picture of Roy Roger's horse attending a church service in Pasadena? I forget whether his name was Tex or Trigger but he was dressed fit to kill and looked like he was having a good time. He doubled the usual attendance.

I think George is going to think he was solely responsible for my getting the Fellowship. They finally came out and the first thing he said was he was reading Ushant. So I pull out SMFitzgerald's review and set him to reading it and he said it was right. He didn't seem to think much of Aiken though he liked some of the puns and named a few which made me cringe. I told him SM was the wife of Robt and he says oh the translator and knows all about that because he uses the first two; he hadn't seen the Edipus but I think now he will order it for the library.

We found out the Klan was only initiating three new members. The L——s said they sat on their porch and had "the grandest time," watching them. They were all over the highway and across the road and "put out the cross real good" when they finished. Lights went on and off in the woods. The J——s are excused.

Mrs. S—— met Mrs. J—— wandering around down town yesterday. They didn't take to each other a tall but Mrs. S—— never loses an opportunity to get any information about any-

thing whatsoever so she stopped her and asked if Mr. J——
was working *yet*. Well, says Mrs. J—— (whine), dairy work
is so reglar, we decided he better just had get him a job where
he could work when he wanted to. Mrs. S—— has not got
over this yet. She never will. She manages to repeat it every
day in Mrs. J——'s tone of voice.

I don't think the ——'s difficulties would have anything to
do with ——'s former marriage but with his. He has another
wife and child somewhere. I imagine however he just hasn't
made up his mind.

Would you mind sending me the address of the place where
I write to subscribe to The Month? I am going to let old
Rockerfeller furnish me with that journal for a while. Incidentally I see where Miss Gertrude Himmelfarb has come forth
with her treatise on Acton. I am going to read Acton and
leaver lay.

                                                    Yours

Mr Ransom said he would take either "The River," or "The
Life You Save May Be Your Own," for the Kenyon Review
(the one with Mr. Shiftlet—your title) so I hope to give him
the latter. It's been very generously rejected by now. I think
Mr. Shiftlet will look just fine in the Kenyon Review.

To Sally and Robert Fitzgerald

Dear S&R,   1/25/53
My first issue of Kenyon Review came yestiddy and I felt
very learned sitting down reading it. There was a chapter of
a novel by Randal Jarrell in it. I suppose you would say it was
good Randal Jarrell but it wasn't good fiction. It was of the
School of Mary (McCarthy). The Kenyon Review sent me a
thoouusand bucks the other day, no note, no nothing; just the
dough. My kin folks think I am a commercial writer now and
really they are very proud of me. My uncle Louis is always bringing a message from somebody at the King Hdw. Co. who
has read Wise Blood. The last was: ask her why she don't write
about some nice people. Louis says, I told them you wrote
what *paid*. There was another message from "the brains of

the King Hdw. Co." He said, yeah it was a good book well written and all that but tell her the next time to write about some rich folks I'm mighty tired of reading about poor folks.

My mamma says what do I think is funny about the enclosed clipping? It kills me.

She has been dickering (negotiating) with the C—— B——s to take the J——s place. Old man J—— looked like he might have had an ancestor back a couple of centuries ago who was at least a decayed gentleman (he wouldn't wear overalls; only khaki) but these C—— B——s look like they've been joined up with the human race for only a couple of months now. Mrs. B—— says she went to school for one day and didn't loin nothin and ain't went back. She has four children and I thought she was one of them. The oldest girl is 14 with a mouth full of snuff. The first time I saw her she had long yellow hair and the next time it was short in an all-over good-for-life permanent and Regina says—they were standing outside the car and we were in—"I see you have a new permanent." "Got it Sad-day," she says and then another pair of hands and eyes pulls up on the window of the car and says, "I'm gonter git me mine next Sad-day." Mamma has one too. I was all set for the B——s but he traded with the saw-mill man instead of Regina. I hope he gets tired of it and quits though.

The Notre Dame business sounds very good to me. I had some friends who were there and were crazy about it. I visited them but I didn't get to see the university. If sometime next summer proves convenient for you to have me visit you, I would like to come if I am well; but I imagine you will have a crowded schedule as your prospective chilren don't always travel by the doctor's clock. If my presence would be convenient at any particular time, I would be pleased to try to manage to have it on hand. My mamma is none too favorable toward any kind of travel for me or at least nothing longer than two weeks she says because you know who has to do the nursing when you get sick; and I do. However, I think I will go to New York anyways sometime next summer if it ain't but to spend the week. I am doing fairly well these days, though I am practically bald-headed on top and have a water-melon face. I think that this is going to be permanent. There is another lady in town now with lupus. She went to the hospital a couple of weeks ago and couldn't open her hands but now she is full of ACTH and up cooking her dinner. Now that I know I have the stuff I can take care of myself a lot better. I stay strictly out of the sun and strictly do not take any exercise. No great hardship.   Yours,

To Sally and Robert Fitzgerald

Dear S&R,   2/1/53

The Maple Oats really send me. I mean they are a heap of improvement over saltless oatmeal, horse biscuit, stewed kleenex, and the other delicacies that I have been eating. They send Regina too but I think it is because they smell like what the cows here eat. We are going to get Louis to see if he can get them in Atlanta for us. I also like the O'Faolin book but I like all he writes that I have seen.

The enclosed is a poem. I tell you this. The Poetry Society of Georgia (a social outfit) is offering 50 bucks for one and I thought I would bite but I would like to know first if it works as they say. Beinst as your occupation is properly poetry, please let me know. This is my first and last. I think it is a filthy habit for a fiction writer to get into. The novel seems to be doing very well. I have a nice gangster of 14 in it named Rufus Florida Johnson. Much more in my line.

My mamma and I have interesting literary discussions like the following which took place over some Modern Library books that I had just ordered:

SHE: "Mobby Dick. I've always heard about that."
ME: "Mow-by Dick."
SHE: "MOW-by Dick. The Idiot. You would get something called The Idiot. What's it about?"
ME: "An idiot."

I am sending you a subscription to something called the Shenandoah that is put out at Washington and Lee University. I told them to begin it with the Autumn issue that has a review in it of my book by a man named Brainard Cheney. It also has a review of The Old Man & the Sea by Wm.

Faulkner, the review I mean, that is nice. He says that Hemmingway discovered God the Creator in this one. What part I liked in that was where the fishes eye was like a saint in a procession; it sounded to me like he was discovering something new maybe for him.

THE PEACOCK ROOSTS

The clown-faced peacock
Dragging sixty suns
Barely looks west where
The single one
Goes down in fire.

Bluer than moon-side sky
The trigger head
Circles and backs.
The folded forest squats and flies
The ancient design is raised.

Gripped oak cannot be moved.
This bird looks down
And settles, ready.
Now the leaves can start the wind
That combs these suns

Hung all night in the gold-green silk wood
Or blown straight back until
The single one
Mounting the grey light
Will see the flying forest
Leave the tree and run.

To Elizabeth Hardwick and Robert Lowell

March 17, 1953
Dear Cal & Elizabeth,   Milledgeville

I'm glad you liked the story. That is my contribution to Mother's Day throughout the land. I felt I ought to do something like Senator Pappy O'Daniels. He conducted the Light Crust Dough Boys over the radio every Mother's Day and recited an original poem. One went: "I had an old mother. I had to have. I lover whether she's good or bad. I lover whether she's alive or dead. Whether she's a angel or a old dope head." You poets express yourselves so well in so little space.

I suppose Iowa City is very restful after Europe, it being naturally blank. I always liked it inspite of those sooty tubercular-looking houses. When I was there there was a zoo with two indifferent bears in it and a sign over them that said: These lions donated by the Iowa City Elks Club. But they had a good collection of game bantams that I used to go and admire and I admired that electric railroad car that ran to Cedar Rapids.

I am making out fine inspite of any conflicting stories. I have a disease called lupus and I take a medicine called ACTH and I manage well enough to live with both. Lupus is one of those things in the rheumatic department; it comes and goes, when it comes I retire and when it goes, I venture forth. My father had it some twelve or fifteen years ago but at that time there was nothing for it but the undertaker; now it can be controlled with the ACTH. I have enough energy to write with and as that is all I have any business doing anyhow, I can with one eye squinted take it all as a blessing. What you have to measure out, you come to observe closer or so I tell myself.

Last summer I went to Connecticut to visit the Fitzgeralds and smuggled three live ducks over Eastern Airlines for their children, but I have been inactive criminally since then. My mother and I live on a large place and I have bought me some peafowl and sit on the back steps a good deal studying them. I am going to be the World Authority on Peafowl, and I hope to be offered a chair some day at the Chicken College.

Yours,

To Ashley Brown

Milledgeville, Ga.

Dear Mr. Brown,   May 22, 1953

Thank you for writing me about my book. It is always good to get some reaction to what you've written and I don't get much.

I'm no Georgia Kafka. I emerged from college with the requirements but I never heard of Kafka until I got to graduate school. I didn't persevere to the end of The Castle and have never read The Trial and a story like The Hunter Gracchus leaves me a little blank. I can see that it's beautifully visualized but to me it's like a ladder with the bottom rungs missing. You only need to read a little Kafka to become a bolder writer and I am sure reading the little bit I have has done that for me. I think I have the Gift of Low Taste that Kafka lacks and that I have been influenced by less fashionable people that nobody mentions—Max Beerbohm and Richard Hughs and maybe, since this is all in the family below the MDixon line, by some of the walled-in monsters of Mr. Poe. I have a book called The Humerous Tales of E.A. Poe that I used to read before the age of reason. They were anything but funny. And for Mr. Davis' information I haven't read Raymond Chandler. I suppose the point is you don't have to.

I didn't like the first half of Warren's poem. I have always heard people say he tried to do too much, but those were people who hadn't done *as* much. I don't know much about poetry. I know a very good poem from a very bad one; that's about all.

When I read Henry James, I feel something is happening to me. I'm not always sure if I like it but it is something happening. Perhaps I feel it's "the deep deep sea," keeping me up. Anyhow you see I read Conrad. I don't think there is any writer I like so much as Conrad.

I was surprised to learn from Robie Macauley that the Shenandoah existed and surprised when I saw it that it should be so good.

Yours sincerely,

To Sally and Robert Fitzgerald

Dear S&R,   Friday

I did like the Shakespeare poem and thank you for sending it. My mamma asked me the other day if I knew Shakespeare was an Irishman. I said no I didn't. She said well its right

there in the Savannah paper; and sure enough some gent
from the University of Chicago had made a speech somewhere saying Shakespeare was an Irishman. I said well it's just
him that says it, you better not go around saying it and she
said listen SHE didn't care whether he was an Irishman or a
Chinaman. She is getting ready to build herself a pond for
the cows to lie down in and cool off in the summer time. The
government says it has to go down two feet straight to keep
from breeding mosquitoes but she don't want it that way for
fear the cows will break their legs getting in.

The Tates sent me the piece in the New Republic about
orthodoxy & the standard of literature. I wrote Caroline that
I liked the piece but that my line about the Cardinal was: if
we must have trash this is the kind of trash we ought to have.
Of course this was the wrong thing to say to them and I got
a letter back saying Allen said we shouldn't have trash in the
first place and the Cardinal was the last person who ought to
write it in the second. Caroline also said you had written
Allen a letter of reprimand about the piece. Well I thought
the piece was all right but that it shouldn't have been in the
New Republic of all places. I also shudder to think what
would happen if Francis Cardinal acquainted himself with the
masters of the novel in the 19th century. Caroline said Allen
wasn't allowed to contribute to THOUGHT. That piece
would have been all right expanded in a Catholic publication.
She said it was originally a talk to a Newman Club around
there somewhere.

Today I had a letter from Cal who said he was thirty-six
years old and feeling very elderstatesmanish and peaceful to
be in Iowa City again. He had just been to Kenyon to visit
Peter Taylor. I gather from Caroline that he is not back in or
near it, in spite of the rumors.

I sold the story about the child that got baptized to the
Sewanee Review.

I am taking painting again but none of my paintings go
over very big in this house although mamma puts them up
and is loth to take them down again. Sister used to teach
painting classes in her youth and she says she doesn't like this
modern art because it's not "smoothed down." My mamma
says its *not* modern art (insulted), its very true to nature and

there's no use spending five hours on a painting you can do in two. This refers to the fact that I have been painting with a palette knife because I don't like to wash the brushes.

My eighty-five year old cousin has had two heart attacks and so is having an elevator installed in her house.

Yours,

To Robie Macauley

Milledgeville

Dear Robie,　　　　　　　　　　　　　　13 October 53

I have just recently been reading your story in the Partisan 35¢ thing and feel called upon to tell you how much I like it and what your stories remind me of. Of course I offer all my critical opinions on long sticks that can be jerked back at once because I really seldom know what I'm talking about but I'm willing to defend this one like a fox terrier. Conrad. They remind me of Conrads (I mean like in the Secret Agent or UWEyes etc) and I have read just about everything he wrote by now. I don't have one perception about the novels, but I keep reading them hoping they'll affect my writing without my being bothered knowing how. Anyway I have thought this about several of your stories that I have seen and I asked that woman that sent me your book why they didn't publish your stories and she said she wouldn't be surprised or some such politeness. I never pay any attention to what they say.

I have recently been to Connecticut to visit the Fitzgeralds and stopped on the way back to have an accounting with Harcourt Brace and a lovely time I had. You see, he says, 208 returned before the first statement but only 200 before the second, now that is a difference of *eight*, you see that is much better, etc. etc.

Some time during the summer a young man named Lane appeared who had been to a party where you and Anne were. He seemed to have a very vague idea about that, but he was investigating one of our local killings and visiting everybody in town who could speak understandable English. He was very severe about the Tates whom he considered faddists. I have never seen him since and wouldn't know about him but my opinion is that the Southern Young Man of Parts is busy building himself up to be Quentin. I think they all want to go to Harvard or Princeton so they can sit in a window and say I hate it I hate it but I have to go back. Or maybe they only learn to say it after they get up there.

Also this summer I went to Nashville to see the Cheneys who had stopped by previously to see me on their way to St. Simons. They had Ashley at the same time. I heard a lot of Tennessee politics and more literary talk, most of it over my head, than since I left Iowa. Ashley managed to board his dog, Tiejens, with a family named Ford when he went to Europe. The last I heard from him he had stumbled over Swift's birthplace in Dublin.

The college here is crowning a president on the 30th and I, if you please, am going to represent Virgil M. Hancher—in full academic regalia, walk up and shake the President's hand. I feel just like Enoch and am trying desperately to think of something horrible to say, such as I represent Verge Hancher of the Iowa Barber College. I will probably not do the occasion any justice.

I hope that you and Anne are well and that I'll hear from you sometime.

To Sally and Robert Fitzgerald

Dear S&R   11/11/53

If you have a cook, a gardener, and a nurse I suppose we will never see you again. My mother was not impressed by the 16½ hours. In fact there was no comment at all from her. She wants to send you a fruit cake; however it actually takes her about two months to bring one into being. It's like building a nest. First she thinks about it, then she begins to gather the material, then she begins to put it together. Right now she has hinted that I may pick out the nuts. I ain't sure my health permits this. Anyway, sometime or other it will arrive.

Caroline sent me your address on the back of a letter of hers a few days ago but didn't say if she had seen you. I have been sending poor Caroline stories by the dozen it seems to me. I have written three in a row, all in the interest of excusing myself from writing on the novel. But now I have seven good stories and two lousy ones for my collection.

I had a letter from the Cheneys and they were very pleased to have seen you, and thought everything very attractive, particularly the children.

Mamma has a new silage cutter and Mrs. S—— has a new set of teeth. Otherwise nothing that I know of has happened in the United States since you left.

I hope you are keeping the whip hand on all your help and learning to act like a tyrant. Regina says she has broken Shot of the habit of borrowing money from Louis. However, Shot is doing well by his insurance these days. He is always cutting his hand and having to go to the doctor. Regina has a policy which takes care of all his accidents but he has one too and never fails to collect on it at the same time. He made four dollars on his last cut. She says these niggers are smart as tacks when it comes to looking out for No. 1.

Regards to children.

To Sally and Robert Fitzgerald

Dear S&R   Jan. 4.

We are distressed that that cake hasn't arrived as we sent it before Thanksgiving, complete with all the govermint stickers and stamps and other paraphernalia. Doubtless some official along the way ate it. I was going to ask you how you fared for peanut butter and if you needed it was going to send you some, but I won't if things don't get there any better than that. I hate to think of your suffering for want of peanut butter though and I doubt if they have advanced to the state of culture where they have it over there. If you ever do get the cake it should be good and stale.

I got word the other day that I had been reappointed a Kenyon Fellow so that means the Rockerfellers will see to my blood and ACTH for another year and I will have to keep on praying for the repose of John D.'s soul. Also I sold a story to Kenyon and another to Harper's Bazaar. I don't know if I ought to buy AT&T or go in for colored rental property. I am wondering if I own colored houses with outdoor privies that drain into the water supply if my burden of social guilt will be so great it offsets the little income? Maybe I'll write a book called "Prudence and Low Finance."

About a month ago I went to spend the weekend with the Cheneys. They had the Spears up—Spears is the editor of the Sewanee Review—and so I caught up on literary and ecclesiastical discussions.

Today I got a letter from *Jimmie Crum* of Los Angeles, California who has just read Wise Blood and wants to know what happened to the guy in the ape suit. He would also like an autographed picture of me for his office. He has a rare stamp and coin shop and is a notary public and has had an article accepted in a technical magazine; I feel that since I have now reached the lunatic fringe there is no place left for me to go. I am also corresponding with the Secretary of The Chefs' National Magazine, The Culinary Review. This lady has written me five letters and sent me a sonnet since September. I had a note from Cal who says next year they are going to live in the house in Duxbury and that Elizabeth has at last learned to cook.

I would certainly like to think of coming come Spring but I doubt if it will get out of the stage of thought. Where would I be coming should I come and what airline should I write for information? I wouldn't even know how to get a passport.

I am glad to hear the Odyssey is ahead of schedule and that we'll see you again. I hope you don't get mobbed like Allen.

Yours,

To Elizabeth Fenwick

Milledgeville
2/12/54

Dear E.

I am at a loss where to send this as the Birches doesn't sound like a winter residence. I forget now that people do have to live in the North in the winter time—it seems a pity. I am becoming mighty unreconstructed. I have been wondering about you since about a month ago when I saw Bob

Giroux in Atlanta. He was on tour seeing various people, and I went up and had lunch with him and consulted about the story collection; anyway when I asked about you, he said they had decided not to use your book. He seemed distressed about it himself. I gathered that he had liked the one called People From Detroit better than this last one. However all this has set me to inquire about you & hope that you are in a state of well-being, and perhaps back at Stonington—which sounds to me more appropriate for a Yankee winter than the Birches. No offense to the Birches but I HAVE BEEN TO STONINGTON. I hope the novel proves to be retrievable. I enjoy retrieving mine better than I do writing them. Perhaps you finished it under a strain. Try rearranging it backwards and see what you see. I thought this stunt up from my art classes, where we always turn the picture upside down, on its two sides, to see what lines need to be added. A lot of excess stuff will drop off this way.

I have developed a decided limp but I am told it has nothing to do with the lupus but is rheumatism in the hip, and I trust them to be telling me this straight as otherwise they would increase my dose of ACTH. However it galls me to have supported the lupus for four years and then to be crippled with rheumatism (a vulgar disease at best) of the hip. I am not able enough to walk straight but not crippled enough to walk with a cane so that I give the appearance of merely being a little drunk all the time. No spots or butterfly wings.

My peachicken has turned out to be a cock which means that in three years if he survives dogs, foxes, weasels, mink, and internal worms, he will have a tail-spread of four feet. He has one trick: he runs up to anyone holding a cigaret and snatches it away and eats it. He has eaten two hot cigarets so far.

Regards and let me hear how you do.

To Ben Griffith

Dear Mr. Griffith,

Milledgeville, Georgia
13 February 54

Thank you so very much for your kind letter. I am much more like Enoch than like the gorilla and I always answer any letter I get, at once and at length. This may be because I don't get many.

I don't know how to cure the source-itis except to tell you that I can discover a good many possible sources myself for Wise Blood but I am often embarrassed to find that I read the sources after I had written the book. I have been exposed to Wordsworth's Intimation Ode but that is all I can say about it. I have one of those food-chopper brains that nothing comes out of the way it went in. The Oedipus business comes nearer home. Of course Hazel Motes is not an Oedipus figure but there are the obvious resemblences. At the time I was writing the last of the book, I was living in Connecticut with the Robert Fitzgeralds. Robert Fitzgerald translated the Theban cycle with Dudley Fitts, and their translation of the Oedipus Rex had just come out and I was much taken with it. Do you know that translation? I am not an authority on such things but I think it must be the best, and it is certainly very beautiful. Anyway, all I can say is, I did a lot of thinking about Oedipus.

My background and my inclinations are both Catholic and I think this is very apparent in the book. Something is usually said about Kafka in connection with WB but I have never succeeded in making my way through The Castle or The Trial and wouldn't pretend to know anything about Kafka. I think reading a little of him perhaps makes you a bolder writer. My reading is botchy. I have what passes for an education in this day and time, but I am not deceived by it. I read Henry James, thinking this may affect my writing for the better without my knowing how. A touching faith, and I have others.

Right now I am working on another novel and a collection of short stories. I was five years writing WB and will perhaps be that many on the one I am working on now. The effort to maintain a tone is a considerable strain, particularly as I never know exactly what tone I am maintaining.

Since you show an interest in the book I presume you are a foreigner, as nobody in Georgia shows much interest. Southern people don't know anything about the literature of the South unless they have gone to Northern colleges or to some of the conscious places like Vanderbilt or Sewanee or W&L. At least this is my theory.

I have heard of Bessie Tift but never saw one they put out. What is it—adulterated Methodist or militant genteel? We have a girls' college here too but the lacy atmosphere is fortunately destroyed by a reformatory, an insane asylum, and a military school.

It was the section about Enoch shaking the gorilla's hand that was in the Mentor book.

Yours sincerely,

To Carl Hartman

Dear Mr. Hartman,

Milledgeville
2 March 54

I would like so much to be able to answer all these questions and I will really try but it is always a great struggle to be honest and a great deal of this is "after the fact;"—as you must know I wrote the book just like Enoch would have, not knowing too well why I did what but knowing it was right. I think everything in the book is right and I am astounded by it.

My view of your view of the book is that it (your view) is too narrow and I suppose this will make you laugh.

I don't think you can be a good Catholic without being catholic. Wise Blood is about a Protestant saint, written from the point of view of a Catholic. Of course I don't mean to imply a direct connection between Catholic with a large C and the simple fact of Haze's having declared there was no fall and no sin, but first you must accept the fact that the book is written by some one who believes that there was a fall, has been a Redemption, and will be a judgment. This is what I believe as a Catholic and this is what I imply that Haze could not get away from (though in his terms, not in mine) so I suppose that if you want to say (you don't have to say it) that the irony is directed against Haze for having decided there was no fall you are correct (Great Heavens!) but you are only halfway correct for if there were no more to it than this, it would be of no account.

The book is about somebody whose insistance on what he would like to think is the truth leads him to what he most does not want. As I see Haze, he most does not want to have been redeemed. He most wants man to be shut of God. Enoch, with his wise blood, unerringly lights on what man looks like without God and obligingly brings it for Haze to have a look at.

Now you are right that Haze himself is without any specific sin in the catalogue sense. But he has a great sense of sin, because he has been taught to believe in the Redemption. If he hadn't believed in it, he wouldn't have had to reject it so vigorously (the society* was not forcing it on him). He walks a mile with rocks in his shoes to make up for looking at the woman in the sideshow coffin. The Redemption creates a debt that has to be paid. (This is a fact to anybody who believes he has been redeemed by Christ.) The Redemption simply changes everything. The fact is that try as he will Haze cannot get rid of his sense of debt and his inner vision of Christ. Mrs. Watts sees this at once. (I never see why when Mrs. Watts saw it nobody else seems to.) Even the taxi driver sees it.

From my point of view Haze does not come into his absolute integrity until he blinds himself. While he is preaching the Church Without Christ he is going counter actually to his own wise blood. Haze and Enoch both have wise blood, which is something that enables you to go in the right direction after what you want. Enoch's gets him inside an ape suit and Haze's gets him further & further inside himself where one may be supposed to find the answer. When I say he negates his way back to the cross I only mean that complete nihilism has led him the long way (or maybe it's really the short way) around to the Redemption again.

I sense this is repugnant to you. I wish we could have it both ways. However, I don't think anything I have said contradicts the feeling of the book which is certainly that human beings do have free choice. I as a Catholic look on H. Motes

*of Taulkinham

as the only right kind of man, in his circumstances. If the irony is directed against him, this is because he is the only one in the book who can stand it. My Lord, how could you direct any irony at Enoch? Of course he finds that being an animal is no fun either but this is just funny. It's not full dress irony to my way of thinking.

When Haze blinds himself he turns entirely to an inner vision. Now one irony is that where he started out preaching the Church Without Christ he ends up with Christ without a church. A Catholic can't write about a Catholic world because none exists so he has to write about a Protestant one and you are right I have directed the irony against this Protestant world or against the society that reads the Bible and the Sears Roebuck catalogue wrong, but Haze himself is in it and of it, he is the ultimate Protestant; he transcends it though. Its not either/or, it's both and one through the other. To my mind, you are right, you just arn't right enough.

I don't mean to suggest that Haze is Christ but I believe that everybody, through suffering, takes part in the Redemption, and I believe they suffer most who live closest to all the possibilities of disbelief. Kierkegaard perhaps throws some light on this but I had not read Kierkegaard when I wrote the book.

Choosing between trifles is not free choice, it has to be between heaven and hell, as far as you can approximate the shades of either in a grey world. But, the book certainly says that in the end the man himself must choose what is sin and what isn't, i. e., conscience is the ultimate sanction. But, paradox or not, and apart from this book, I myself believe this because the Holy Roman Catholic & Apostolic Church teaches it, c.f., Fr. Feeney's excommunication in Boston for preaching that there is no salvation outside the Catholic Church.

The penances are certainly acts of assertion even though they are instinctive. Haze is here asserting his wise blood in the ultimate way. When he says he does it to pay, he means to pay his part of the debt of Redemption.

If you feel a mild horror that I should believe these Christian mysteries understand that my belief in them survives the strain of approaching the whole problem (in this book) from your point of view—which is Haze's when he declares they don't exist. I presume. You probably have not imagined what it is to write as a Catholic, knowing that most of the people who read you will think what you believe is utter rubbish. (This explains one reason my book is grotesque and that you were afraid that on sight I might bite. I don't bite.) I have read people (Orwell) who say Catholics can't write novels on acct. of being Catholics.

You must excuse the tone of this letter which so far sounds like a First Epistle to the Heathen. I am not really so sanctimonious as I sound. I just unfortunately have Haze's vision and Enoch's disposition. But I count on hearing from you again whether any of this makes sense to you.

About the talks (incidentally I wasn't being snide when I said I had no learning. I have not been helped or hurt by my education, only kind of haunted) well I have made two. One to a ladies club. The heart of my message to them was that they would all fry in hell if they didn't quit reading trash. I pretended I was Billy Ghrame. The other one was to the local college on The Novel—400 girls who don't know a novel from a hole in the head and were very impressed with everything I said and would have been if I had said the opposite. I do fine talking to people who don't know anything but I couldn't say anything at Cornell that they hadn't already heard before. What I do do is read my stories rather well, at least people tell me so, and I am sure that even when I don't read them well, they enjoy listening to the barbarous Georgia accent. What I mean to say is that while I don't go for this sort of thing, I go for leaving town occasionally and need almost no persuasion to do so.

I had been debating whether to include that story you mentioned. I am not entirely sure the curse is really off it, but I reckon you persuade me.

I see I did not send enough money for a proper subscription but if you will let me know when I have got two dollars worth of Epoch, I will renew the subscription, provided I am still being supported by the dole. I already have one of them Bibles.

Yours,

To Ben Griffith

Milledgeville
Dear Mr. Griffith,   3 March 54

I am amused by the "tare" in his throat. I had to look it up in the dictionary. The truth is, it was my error; not the printer's. I meant it in the sense of "split" in his voice. I have always been a very innocent speller. I never sense that I am spelling something incorrectly and so don't look up the words. The simpler the word, the more liable I am to come up with a rare spelling. If anybody else asks me about this, I am certainly going to say I meant it in the sense of first principle, a seed of evil, and thus pass myself off for a scholar. "Tear in his throat" must be a colloquial expression as it comes very naturally to me (whereas someone else might think it mannered). However, the omniscient narrator is not properly supposed to use colloquial expressions. I send a good many of my things to Caroline Gordon (Tate) for her criticism and she is always writing me that I mustn't say such things, that the om. nar. never speaks like anyone but Dr. Johnson. Of course, it is a great strain for me to speak like Dr. Johnson. Most of the images I make up when the need arises but I suppose some of them are to be found in the local idiom.

Vaguely I remember passing Java's Oasis but I am not liable to get there to make their acquaintance as I don't drive and no one else I know would be interested in such a place. It sounds very interesting to me, however.

Let me assure you that no one but a Catholic could have written Wise Blood even though it is a book about a kind of Protestant saint. It reduces Protestantism to the twin ultimate absurdities of The Church Without Christ or The Holy Church of Christ Without Christ, which no pious Protestant would do. And of course no unbeliever or agnostic could have written it because it is entirely Redemption-centered in thought. Not too many people are willing to see this, and perhaps it is hard to see because H. Motes is such an admirable nihilist. His nihilism leads him back to the fact of his Redemption, however, which is what he would have liked so much to get away from.

When you start describing the significance of a symbol like the tunnel which recurs in the book, you immediately begin to limit it and a symbol should go on deepening. Everything should have a wider significance—but I am a novelist not a critic and I can excuse myself from explication de texts on that ground. The real reason of course is laziness.

I don't know anything about the Peabody sisters so your children's biography will be just the thing for me. I do seem to have in mind that one of them married Hawthorne and my opinion of Hawthorne is that he was a very great writer indeed.

I think H. M. McLuhan's piece in the Southern Vanguard is one good one. It possibly takes a Canadian to throw a sharper light on things here. I notice I have marked in my copy the sentence "Formality becomes a condition of survival." That apparently struck me when I first read it and it strikes me now, out of context, as true. The formality that is left in the South now is quite dead and done for of course.

Regards,

To Robert Lowell

Dear Cal,   26 March 54

Your news is neither this nor that; however, Elizabeth is perhaps to be congratulated. All the people I know are getting separated, even the stupid ones.

That you are not in the Church is a grief to me and always has been and will be and I know no more to say about it. I severely doubt that you will do any good to anybody "outside" as you call it, but it is probably true that you will do good for yourself in as much as you will be the only one in a position to. But the good you can do for yourself, in or out, is very limited. The sacraments give grace. But I am not St. Bernard and this bores me as much as it does you.

Don't pray for everybody else and leave me out. Your good wishes are not valuable to anybody who loves you.

To Beverly Brunson

Milledgeville
Dear Beverely,   13 September 54

I am sorry that the point of The Temple of the Holy Ghost escaped you and also that you think our letters revolve around the subject of the It in the story; which I am sure in the first place has a very different meaning for me than what you apparently read into it. The hermaphrodite here is no invention of mine, it having appeared at a fair here last summer where our dairyman's daughter attended its performance. She came back and told me about it and my account in the story is substantially hers. The freak told them that God had made it this way and that therefore it was making the best of it. Any freak so inspired could say the same and I could have used any freak but there is certainly a more poignant element of suffering in this than in anything else one could find at a fair. The point is of course in the resignation to suffering, which is one of the fruits of the Holy Ghost; not to any element of sex or sexlessness. As for the child in the story, I find your interpretation of her only rather silly—there is no concern or question here of any kind of inversion. The child is still innocent and here you needed an innocent observer.

As for lesbianism I regard that as any other form of uncleanness. Purity is the twentieth centuries dirty word but it is the most mysterious of the virtues and not to be discussed in a light fashion even with ones own and surely not with strangers. Heidegger writes a great deal about the poet's business being to name what is holy. His essays on Holderlin are very rich.

Thank you for the view of you and your mother which I return lest you hold it sacred. It is very funny. You look like the serpent after having just successfully tempted Eve and your mother makes a very pensive Eve—as if she has not quite realized yet that Paradise is really lost.

Best regards,

To Caroline Gordon Tate

Milledgeville

Dear Caroline,   14 November 54

I am being very piggish with your time sending you The Displaced Person again but I have made a novella out of it or maybe I only think I have. Anyway, the business of the peacock and the priest etc etc was not done to my satisfaction before and I think this is better. I am not sure it works though, and if it doesn't I don't want to use it for the collection. Mr. Ransom took the Artificial Nigger for the Kenyon but I think without enthusiasm. He complained it was very flat and had no beautiful sentences in it. I rewrote it but there still ain't any beautiful sentences. It may be too long.

The first freeze came and carried off my frizzly chicken (she was molting and didn't have but ten feathers (and they turned the wrong way)) and my youngest peachicken.

I suppose you have heard from the Fitzgeralds that Sally and Barnaby are coming back at the end of this month to see her father who is apparently dying in Houston. She plans to stop here and I hope she will stay a couple of days and rest. My mother is afraid she won't be able to walk up the steps, being pregnant, but I tell my mother it is a state Mrs. Fitzgerald takes lightly.

It must be very fine to look at your family and see it becoming Catholic. We look at ours and I am afraid see the Catholicity washing away. The grandchildren get married outside the Church, etc. etc. Part is from poor instruction and part from that awful jell the Irish manage to set their religion in. They pass it on from generation to generation. We all prefer comfort to joy.

I am doing very well these days except for a limp which I am informed is rheumatism. Colored people call it "the misery." Anyway I walk like I have one foot in the gutter but it's not an inconvenience and I get out of doing a great many things I don't want to do.

You are mighty nice to ask me to come to see you next summer when you get in your house and I entertain the idea with great pleasure. And you are mighty nice to read this stuff. I don't know who else would.

Yours,

To Sally Fitzgerald

Dear S— 26 Dec 54

We are sorry you missed us but it sounds like a ghastly trip and I think you did well to get home. Regina and I are having a mass said for your father and will continue to pray for him. I hope Mrs. Morgan improves.

I have finally got off the ms for my collection and it is scheduled to appear in May. Without yr kind permission I have taken the liberty of dedicating (grand verb) it to you and Robert. This is because you all are my adopted kin and if I dedicated it to any of my blood kin they would think they had to go into hiding. Nine stories about original sin, with my compliments.

I have been invited to go to Greensboro to the Women's College in March to be on an arts panel. That is where Brother Randall Jarrell holds forth. I accepted but I am not looking forward to it. Can you fancy me hung in conversation with the likes of him?

When I had lunch with Giroux in Atlanta he told me about Cal's escapade in Cincinnati. It seems he convinced everybody it was Elizabeth who was going crazy. Apparently he almost convinced Elizabeth. Toward the end he gave a lecture at the university that was almost pure gibberish. I guess nobody noticed, thinking it was the new criticism. Anyhow I gather they are both all right now. Caroline says she would like to wrap him up and send him to a first class Jungian practitioner.

I just got a check for $200 for the 2nd prize in the O. Henry book this year. My ex-mentor Paul Engle does the selecting. Jean Stafford got the first one.

I am walking with a cane these days which gives me a great air of distinction. The scientist tells me this has nothing to do with the lupus but is rheumatism. I would not believe it except that the dose of ACTH has not been increased. Besides which I now feel it makes very little difference what you call it. As the niggers say, I have the misery.

I am reading everything I can of Romano Guardini's. Have you become acquainted with his work? A book called *The Lord* of his is very fine.

Regards to children.

To Beverly Brunson

Milledgeville
1/1/55

Dear Beverly

The angels were sent to redeem me, as before Christmas when I was looking through some papers I came across a copy of the last letter I wrote you (I keep copies to keep myself from writing the same thing twice & for other conventional reasons) and I was astonished by the tone. I seemed to have surpassed my usual rudeness and achieved an air of superiority out of all proportion to my character. What I said is true but I did not mean to imply any moral judgment on you; that would be neither my right nor my business. Actually what I think is that you don't have the information (not quite the right word) to be either clean or unclean. Compared with you I think Hazel Motes is an enlightened man. This is not rudeness, this is just my point of view. You may put me in your zoo, along with the Indian and his wife—a hyena in apostolic robes—but just remember that the absurdity is in me, not in what I stand for.

You are quite right that it is easier to be a Catholic than something else. It is easier than anything else and if any Catholic should tell you otherwise, you can tell him to go to the devil. The Church does not demand any sacrifice out of proportion to what she gives.

Naw, I don't think life is a tragedy. Tragedy is something that can be explained by the professors. Life is the will of God and this cannot be defined by the professors; for which all thanksgiving. I think it is impossible to live and not to grieve but I am always suspicious of my own grief lest it be self-pity in sheeps clothing. And the worst thing is to grieve for the wrong reason, for the wrong loss. Altogether it is better to pray than to grieve; and it is greater to be joyful than to grieve. But it takes more grace to be joyful than any but the greatest have.

I know about violence only from hearsay. I come from very careful people who lock their doors at night and look under all the beds and never find anything. I suspect that what protects us from it is 50% charity and 50% good business sense. This is a combination that lets in rot but seldom any kind of terror that moves in a hurry. I have not seen the last New Writing. Milledgeville doesn't boast of a book store.

Regards and do not be offended by me again; I take you as seriously as I take myself.

To Robert Giroux

Milledgeville
Georgia
Dear Bob: 26 February 55

I have just written a story called GOOD COUNTRY PEOPLE that Allen and Caroline both say is the best thing I have written and should be in this collection. I told them I thought it was too late, but anyhow I am writing now to ask if it is. It is really a story that would set the whole collection on its feet. It is 27 pages and if you can eliminate the one called "A Stroke of Good Fortune," and the other called "An Afternoon in the Woods," this one would fit the available space nicely. Also I remember you said it would be good to have one that had never been published before. I could send it to you at once on *being wired*. Please let me know.

Yours,

To Thomas Mabry

Milledgeville
Dear Mr. Mabry, 1 March 55

You have done me a favor writing me about that story. It had been worrying me for the longest time. I felt it was wrong but I didn't know why and like you I have so much respect for what he does that I didn't have the courage to think it was so bad; but I have always felt the lack of a belief in anything vital in his work. Of course, the others don't believe anything either but you don't miss it in their general slush. He is the kind of a writer who could stand to be a fanatic.

I am glad you see the belief in mine because it is there. The truth is my stories have been watered and fed by Dogma. I am a Catholic (not because it's advantageous to my writing but because I was born and brought up one) and at some point in my life I realized that not only was I a Catholic but that this was all I was, that I was a Catholic not like someone else would be a Baptist or a Methodist but like someone else would be an atheist. If my stories are complete it is because I see everything as beginning with original sin, taking in the Redemption, and reckoning on a final judgment. I have heard people say that all this stifles a writer, but that is foolishness; it only preserves your sense of mystery. Caroline has experienced this both ways and knows more about it. She said she was so glad to be able finally to stop creating a new universe for each novel and to accept the one we have. As for me, I have always been free to do nothing but look, though I haven't always had sense enough to.

I read the story called Joshua of Shirley Ann Grou's in the O. Henry collection. It was highly praised in every review I read and they must have had some reason for selecting it, so I am wondering what is wrong with me that I didn't like it. It was too long but it seems to me that it was also sentimental, in as much as the writer's attitude seems to be applause for the little boy who steals a coat off a dead man—which means that the writer is not showing much awareness. But I may just be intolerant. It may be fine writing. Anyway I have an aversion to fine writing. I know how your wife must feel about undertaking the whole book.

I have delayed my collection a little by writing a story two weeks ago called "Good Country People." It is the best thing I have done and they will include it if doing so doesn't cost them too much money. If they don't include it, I am going to send you a copy of it because it is one of those examples of the will and the imagination fusing and it is so rare an experience for me that I am a little unhinged by it.

Yours sincerely,

To Ben Griffith

Milledgeville

Dear Mr. Griffith: 4 May 1955

I have gotten one other letter about The Artificial Nigger and in that one I was asked if Mr. Head didn't represent Peter and Nelson the Christ-Child. I had to say that Mr. Head's behaviour certainly resembled Peter's a little but that I found it harder to gin up Nelson's character so he could suitably represent the Christ-Child. What I had in mind to suggest with the artificial nigger was the redemptive quality of the Negro's suffering for us all. You may be right that Nelson's reaction to the colored woman is too pronounced, but I meant for her in an almost physical way to suggest the mystery of existence to him—he not only has never seen a nigger but he didn't know any women and I felt that such a black mountain of maternity would give him the required shock to start those black forms moving up from his unconscious. I wrote that story a good many times, having a lot of trouble with the end. I frequently send my stories to Mrs. Tate and she is always telling me that the endings are too flat and that at the end I must gain some altitude and get a larger view. Well the end of The Artificial Nigger was a very definite attempt to do that and in those last two paragraphs I have practically gone from the Garden of Eden to the Gates of Paradise. I am not sure it is successful but I mean to keep trying with other things.

I am writing Harcourt, Brace to send you an advance copy of "A Good Man Is Hard to Find," which is my collection of short stories (ten) due to be published June 6. There is one very long story in it, 60 pages, that I would like you to see, and another called Good Country People that pleases me to no end. You will observe that I admire my own work as much if not more than anybody else does. I have read The Artificial Nigger several times since it was printed, enjoying it each time as if I had had nothing to do with it. I feel that this is not quite delicate of me but it may be balanced by the fact that I write a great deal that is not fit to read which I properly destroy.

The people on our place always say, "we gone to see it," or "we gone and done it," when the action is past—never "went" when "went" would be correct. I had Nelson say "I'm glad I've went once," because I couldn't resist the "went once."

I am at home every afternoon but Monday and would be most happy to have you come over. We live 4 miles from Milledgeville on the road to Eatonton in a two-story white farm house. The place is called Andalusia. Any time in the afternoon would be fine but if you drop me a card when you plan to come, I will make it a point to be here.

Occasionally I see the Georgia Review but not often; however, it would be very agreeable to me to see something written about my work for local consumption by somebody who knows something. Recently I talked in Macon (nobody had ever heard tell of me, of course) and it was announced in the paper the next day that I was a "writer of the realistic school." I presume the lady came to this conclusion from looking at the cover of the drugstore edition of Wise Blood. In a few weeks I am going to talk to some more ladies in Macon and I am going to clear up that detail. I am interested in making up a good case for distortion, as I am coming to believe it is the only way to make people see.

Yours sincerely,

To Sally and Robert Fitzgerald

Dear S&R,   8 May 1955

We were certainly glad to get our notice about CMT's arrival and then the letter. I reckon my mother is now convinced that a child can be born in Europe. I think she thought forin children could but not regular children—and then to have it's blood changed too! My my. Well, as she says, showing that she can add correctly, this makes six, three boys and three girls. She approves of this one's being a girl.

I have been discovered by the Club ladies of middle Georgia. Last month the Macon Writer's Club had a breakfast IN MY HONOR and allowed me to address them for 25 minutes. I tell you it was a great success. One old lady told me that it was a very important day, "April 23, the birthdays of William Shakespear, Harry Stillwell Edwards, and Shirley Temple." I have been wasting my time all these years writing—my talent lies in a kind of intellectual vaudeville. I leave them not knowing exactly what I have said but feeling that they have been inspired. On the 20th I am to address the Book Review Group of the Macon Women's Club on Southern Letters and the fact that I have never read any Sothern Letters ain't holding me back none. My mother thinks this is very fine and likely to *broaden* me; she finds me very narrow in my outlook.

Harcourt is supposed to send you a copy of the book but I reckon it will take some time to get there. Old Giroux took himself off and is now Vice President of Farrar, Straus and Cudahy as I reckon you have been informed. There is a Catharine Carver there who is also fiction editor of Partisan Review, a friend of the Lowells and she is taking care of me in so far as I have to be taken care of. Your friend Denver Lindley is in charge and was recently in the South and inquired could he come to see me. So I gave him explicit instructions how to get here, making it seem as if I lived in the middle of the Okefenokee Swamp, and he didn't come. I don't think I would have known exactly what to do with him if he had. Some Very Peculiar Types have beat a path to my door these last few years and it is always interesting to see my mother hostessing-it-up on these occasions.

Today is The Great Commercial Feast but we were spared a sermon on mothers and merely asked to give generously to the special collection.

Regards to Oddyssie.

Yours,

To Robie Macauley

Milledgeville
Dear Robie,   18 May 55

I certainly am glad you like the stories because now I feel it's not bad that I like them so much. The truth is I like them better than anybody and I read them over and over and laugh and laugh, then get embarrassed when I remember I was the one wrote them. Unlike Wise Blood, they were all relatively painless to me; but now I have to quit enjoying life and get on with the second novel. The first chapter of it is going to be published in the fall in the New World Writing thing and is to be called YOU CAN'T BE ANY POORER THAN DEAD —which is the way I feel every time I get to work on it.

Nobody has given me any gold even in a medal but you are right about the television. I am going to New York on the 30th to be, if you please, interviewed by Mr Harvey Breit (on the 31st) on a program he is starting up over NBC-TV. They are also going to dramatize the opening scene from The Life You Save etc. Do you reckon this is going to corrupt me? I already feel like a combination of Msgr. Sheen and Gorgeous George. Everybody who has read Wise Blood thinks I'm a hillbilly nihilist, whereas I would like to create the impression over the television that I'm a hillbilly Thomist, but I will probably not be able to think of anything to say to Mr. Harvey Breit but "Huh?" and "Ah dunno." When I come back I'll probably have to spend three months day and night in the chicken pen to counteract these evil influences.

Although I am a prominent Georgia Author I have never went to Washington but I have went over it and shall this time at an altitude of 14,000 feet compliments Eastern Airlines.

Greensboro was moderately gastly, the more so than it would have been if you and Anne had come down. The panel was the worst as I never can think of anything to say about a story and the conferences were high comedy. I had one with a bearded intellectual delinquent from Kenyon who wouldn't be convinced he hadn't written a story, and the rest with girls writing about life in the dormitory.

A couple of weeks ago Ashley came down of a Sunday

afternoon with Fred Bornhauser and they took in the architecture and had supper with me. Ashley was telling me that you are an admirer of Dr. Frank Crane, my favorite Protestant theologian (salvation by the compliment club). I was glad to hear this because I think the doctor ought to be more widely appreciated. He is really a combination minister and masseur, don't you think? He appears in the Atlanta Constitution on the same page as the funnies. I like to hear him tell Alma A. that she can keep her husband by losing 75 pounds and just the other day he told a girl who was terrified of toads how not to let this ruin her life—know the truth & the truth shall make you free. However, his best column was where he told about getting the letter from the convict who had joined the compliment club. I hope you saw that one.

Please thank Mr. W. P. Southard for liking my stories. I am always glad to know I have a reader of quality because I have so many who aren't. I get some letters from people I might have created myself—one from a Mr. Jimmie Crum of Hollywood, Calif., who said he ran an old coin and stamp shop and his mother came from Tennessee and he wondered would I send him a picture of myself for his office. I guess he thought I would fit in with the old stamps. I also got one from a young man in California who was starting a magazine to be called HEARSE—"a vehicle to convey stories and poems to the great cemetery of the American intellect." Then I got a message from two theological students at Alexandria who said they had read Wise Blood and that I was their pin-up girl—the grimmest distinction to date. I got a real ugly letter from a Boston lady about that story called A Temple of the Holy Ghost. She said she was a Catholic and so she couldn't understand how anybody could even HAVE such thoughts. I wrote her a letter that could have been signed by the bishop and now she is my fast friend and recently wrote me that her husband had run for attorney general but hadn't been elected. I wish somebody real intelligent would write me sometime but I seem to attract the lunatic fringe mainly.

I will be real glad when this television thing is over with. I keep having a mental picture of my glacial glare being sent out over the nation onto millions of children who are waiting impatiently for The Batman to come on.

Best to you and Anne and write me again before my next
book comes out because that may be in 1984.

Yours,

To Erik Langkjaer

23 May 55

Dear Erik,   Milledgeville

When I told my mother this time what you were now
going to do, she said, "I told you that boy wouldn't enjoy
being a ragpicker." Moral: you can't get ahead of mother. In
any case you know you have my best wishes, affection and
prayers in this new venture and I hope it will be the beginning for you of always finding what you want. As for the
Abbe, I presume he prefers those with a criminal background
and that he is not out a very energetic hand for the hammer
anyway. We are glad that you plan to return South and we
want you to let us help you make your wife at home in this
part of the country. Consider us your people here because
that is what we consider ourselves.

My own course these days is not so edifying as yours. I am
on my way to New York on the 30th for a television interview
with Harvey Breit; also the opening section of The Life You
Save is going to be dramatized on this same program and as
no New Yorker has any insight into what comes out of the
South, I know it will be a mess—actors without shoes, New
Jersey hillbilly voices, etc. etc. And then I have a mental picture of my glacial glare being sent out over the nation onto
millions of children who are impatiently waiting for The Batman to come on. I am fast getting a reputation out of all
proportion to my desire for one and this largely because I am
now competing with The Lone Ranger. Everybody here
shakes my hand but nobody reads my stories. Which is just
as well. After New York I am going to do some visiting in
Connecticut and Boston and then go to Nashville. In August
I am invited to Princeton but it is doubtful there will be
enough of me left to get there.

The State of Georgia recently banned two text books for
sale in the schools here, one that said Negroes learned as fast

as white folks and another, a song book, that changed the word "darkies" to the word "brothers," in one of Stephen Forster's songs. With the latter I am wholly in sympathy (with the banning that is) as I am afraid the next thing to go will be "Ol Black Joe." "Old Neutral-colored Joe." It is good you will have an opportunity to further observe the Southern character. I have been hearing a good deal about some aspects of it lately from my Kentucky friend who now lives in Tenn. He was telling me that the Gov. of Tenn., who is a great pal of Billy Ghrame's and thinks that he has been called by God to be Governor, recently appointed his own daddy to be head of the Tenn. Supreme Court and when criticized for this, replied, "We all like to honor our parents but few, like myself, are in a position to do so." Billy recently had a crusade in New Orleans and the Gov. hired a train of hymn-singing politicians and travelled down to cash in on the crowd.

Your reflections on the Church are painful, as usual. The merit of the Church doesn't lie in what she does but what she is. The day is going to come when the Church is so hemmed in & nailed down that she won't be doing anything but being, which will be enough.

All the best and don't neglect to let us know what you are doing etc.

To Ben Griffith

Milledgeville
Dear Ben,   6/8/55

Thanks so much for the review and the Plunkett Rainbow prayers and the story. Too bad we both can't write like Plunkett—tears would roll down everybody's cheeks. The review I naturally liked very much. It was much more perceptive than the one in Time and the horrible one in the Atlanta Journal. I read them all and shudder. You brought out a lot of points I wanted to see brought out.

As soon as I read your story I thought of two other stories that I felt you should read before you start rewriting this one. One of these is *The Lament* by Checkhov, the other *War* by Luigi Pirandello. Both of these stories are in a book called

Understanding Fiction by Cleanth Brooks and R. P. Warren, which you may know but should if you don't. It is a book that has been of invaluable help to me and I think would be to you.

Your story, like these other two, is essentially the presenting of a pathetic situation, and when you present a pathetic situation, you have to let it speak entirely for itself. I mean you have to present it and leave it alone. You have to let the things in the story do the talking. I mean that, as author, you can't force it and I think you tend to force it in your story, every now and then. The first thing is to see the people at every minute. You get into the old man's mind before you let us know exactly what he looks like. You have got to learn to paint with words. Have the old man there first so that the reader can't escape him. This is something that it has taken me a long time to learn. Ford Madox Ford said you couldn't have somebody sell a newspaper in a story unless you said what he looked like. You have to learn to do this unobtrusively of course. The old man thinks of the daughter-in-law and son talking and recalls their conversation—well he should see them, the reader should see them, should feel from seeing them what their conversation is going to be almost before he hears it.

Let the old man go through his motions without any comment from you as author and let the things he sees make the pathetic effects. Do you know Joyce's story *The Dead*? See how he makes the snow work in that story. Checkhov makes everything work—the air, the light, the cold, the dirt, etc. Show these things and you don't have to say them. I think what the colored man says in your story is very good. But you don't have to say the colored man is about 45—instead paint him there so the reader will know he's a fat middle-aged insolent Negro and as hurt by the old man as the old man will shortly be by him.

The deaf and dumb child should be seen better—it does no good just to tell us she is seraphically beautiful. She has to move around and make some kind of show of herself so we'll know she's there all the time.

Also in a story like this you don't want to rely on local effects, such as calling the paper he picks up the Macon Telegraph. This is not the kind of story that gets its effects from local things, but from the universal feeling of grief that old age and unwantedness call up. I think it could be made into a very fine story if you have the time to work on it. I am a great hand at rewriting myself. It takes a long time to make a thing like this work. Looks simple but is not.

If you do rewrite it, I hope you will let me see it again. This is just the repressed school-teacher in me cropping out.

Please do bring your wife and children over any time you get ready. Merrill, Lynch, Pierce, Fenner and Bean are slated for the deep freeze in August but Clair Booth Loose Goose is going to live a natural life until she dies a natural death. My mother is head of the horse department, so I will have to ask her about an Oveta. I hope you enjoy North Carolina.

Regards,

The television was mildly ghastly and I am very glad to be back with the chickens who don't know I have just published a book.

To Sally and Robert Fitzgerald

Milledgeville
Dear S&R, 10 June 55
Gladjer got the book. You are right about A Stroke of Good Fortune. It don't appeal to me either and I really didn't want it there but Giroux thought it ought to be. It is, in its way, Catholic, being about the rejection of life at the source, but too much of a farce to bear the weight. As to the Pole's looking for a Catholic, I'm afraid he would not. There are no Catholic girls in the country in the South and these European Catholics anyway are not like Irish Catholics—a great many of them are going to the Baptist church three months after they get here. The Methodists might have got ours, in fact, by social strategies, if my mother had not raised her big guns and laid down the law.

I have just got back from a week in New York at the expense of Harcourt Brace, being, if you please, on a television program with Harvey Breit. They dramatized The Life You

Save up to the point where the old woman says she'll give 17.50 if Mr. Shiftlet will marry the idiot daughter. Harvey Breit narrated the story and they had three live actors and then he interviewed me. It was all mildly ghastly as you may well imagine. I had interviews with this one and that one, ate with this one and that one, drank with this one and that one, and generally managed to conduct myself as if this were all very well but I had business at home. This book is getting much more attention than Wise Blood and may even sell a few copies.

The atmosphere at Harcourt Brace, at least in regard to meself, has changed to one of eager enthusiasm. I had tea with Giroux and he told me all about it. He looks better than when I saw him in the Fall. He advised me to (q. t.) have a clause in my contract saying that my editor had to be a certain Miss Carver whom I like or the contract would be void so this has been done. If she leaves I can escape the textbook people if they prove to be too much. I liked Denver Lindley fine and am satisfied at Harcourt Brace as long as he and Miss Carver are there.

I spent the weekend in Conn. with Caroline and Sue Jenkens. They had a party at which the chief guests were dear old Malcolm Cowley and dear old Van Wyke Brooks. Dear old Van Wyke insisted that I read a story at which horror-striken looks appeared on the faces of both Caroline and Sue. "Read the shortest one!" they both screamed. I read a Good Man Is Hard to Find and Mr. Brooks later remarked to Miss Jenkens that it was a shame someone with so much talent should look upon life as a horror story. Malcolm was very polite and asked me if I had a wooden leg.

Congratulations on the Shelly Memorial Award which certainly sounds elegant. I am going to apply for a Guggenheim, hoping that now that my need is not so great they may see fit to reward me.

The Macon Women's Club was highly pleased with my performance. I leave them with the impression that something has been said though they don't know exactly what.

I have never read the Golden Bowl but I guess that condition will have to be corrected.

To Ben Griffith

Milledgeville
Dear Ben: 9 July 55

Thanks for lending my books around to the scholars. I relish the idea of being read by scholars. I have been getting some very funny fan mail—a lot of it from gentlemen who have got no farther than the title—"Do you really think a good man is hard to find? I am 31 years old, single, work like a dog . . ." etc. etc. etc. One wants to write a novel with me—"With your know-how and my experiences, we could write a novel together as good as Gone With The Wind." One from a West Virginia mountaineer whose favorite word is "literature" which he spells "litatur."

I agreed about the similarity of other characters to Haze Motes (Motes, not Moates); in fact, Mrs. Tate wrote me that she thought the Bible salesman was a super Haze Motes, one with all his evil potentialities realized. Of course, I think of Haze Motes as a kind of saint. His overwhelming virtue is integrity. I also liked what you said about some of the stories being about children who meet theological truths beyond their understanding.

My editor wrote me that the book was selling better than anything on their list except Thomas Merton—which doesn't say much for their list, I guess. However, they have ordered a second printing. The review in Time was terrible, nearly gave me apoplexy. The one in the Atlanta Journal was so stupid it was painful. It was written I understand by the lady who writes about gardening. They shouldn't have taken her away from the petunias.

I have never read Kraft-Ebbing or Memoirs of Hecate County. A little self-knowlege goes a long way.

I sort of doubt if the Western Review would take anything on me, but I seldom see that.

I passed Plunkett on to a friend in Nashville. Plunkett is really real modern when you come down to it—"pray and your food will taste better" is just another version of "Grace before meals is an aid to digestion" which is what religion is coming to in some parts.

Best regards,

To A.

Milledgeville
Dear Miss A.,   20 July 55

I am very pleased to have your letter. Perhaps it is even more startling to me to find someone who recognizes my work for what I try to make it than it is for you to find a God-conscious writer near at hand. The distance is 87 miles but I feel the spiritual distance is shorter.

I write the way I do because (not though) I am a Catholic. This is a fact and nothing covers it like the bald statement. However, I am a Catholic peculiarly possessed of the modern consciousness, that thing Jung describes as unhistorical, solitary, and guilty. To possess this *within* the Church is to bear a burden, the necessary burden for the conscious Catholic. It's to feel the contemporary situation at the ultimate level. I think that the Church is the only thing that is going to make the terrible world we are coming to endurable; the only thing that makes the Church endurable is that it is somehow the body of Christ and that on this we are fed. It seems to be a fact that you have to suffer as much from the Church as for it but if you believe in the divinity of Christ, you have to cherish the world at the same time that you struggle to endure it. This may explain the lack of bitterness in the stories.

The notice in the New Yorker was not only moronic, it was unsigned. It was a case in which it is easy to see that the moral sense has been bred out of certain sections of the population, like the wings have been bred off certain chickens to produce more white meat on them. This is a generation of wingless chickens, which I suppose is what Nietzsche meant when he said God was dead.

I am mighty tired of reading reviews that call "A Good Man" brutal and sarcastic. The stories are hard but they are hard because there is nothing harder or less sentimental than Christian realism. I believe that there are many rough beasts now slouching toward Bethlehem to be born and that I have reported the progress of a few of them, and when I see these stories described as horror stories I am always amused because the reviewer always has hold of the wrong horror.

You were very kind to write me and the measure of my appreciation must be to ask you to write me again. I would like to know who this is who understands my stories.

Yours sincerely,

To A.

Milledgeville
Dear Miss A.,   2 August 55

Thank you for writing me again. I feel I should apologize for answering so promptly because I may seem to force on you a correspondence that you don't have time for or that will become a burden. I myself am afflicted with time, as I do not work out on account of an energy-depriving ailment and my work in, being creative, can go on only a few hours a day. I live on a farm and don't see many people. My avocation is raising peacocks, something that requires everything of the peacock and nothing of me, so time is always at hand.

I believe too that there is only one Reality and that that is the end of it, but the term, "Christian Realism," has become necessary for me, perhaps in a purely academic way, because I find myself in a world where everybody has his compartment, puts you in yours, shuts the door and departs. One of the awful things about writing when you are a Christian is that for you the ultimate reality is the Incarnation, the present reality is the Incarnation, the whole reality is the Incarnation, and nobody believes in the Incarnation; that is, nobody in your audience. My audience are the people who think God is dead. At least these are the people I am conscious of writing for.

As for Jesus' being a realist: if He was not God, He was no realist, only a liar, and the crucifixtion an act of justice.

Dogma can in no way limit a limitless God. The person outside the Church attaches a different meaning to it than the person in. For me a dogma is only a gateway to contemplation and is an instrument of freedom and not of restriction. It preserves mystery for the human mind. Henry James said the young woman of the future would know nothing of mystery or manners. He had no business to limit it to one sex.

You are right that I won't ever be able entirely to understand my own work or even my own motivations. It is first of all a gift, but the direction it has taken has been because of the Church in me or the effect of the Churches teaching, not because of a personal perception or love of God. For you to think this would be possible because of your ignorance of me; for me to think it would be sinful in a high degree. I am not a mystic and I do not lead a holy life. Not that I can claim any interesting or pleasurable sins (my sense of the devil is strong) but I know all about the garden variety, pride, gluttony, envy and sloth, and what is more to the point, my virtues are as timid as my vices. I think sin occasionally brings one closer to God, but not habitual sin and not this petty kind that blocks every small good. A working knowledge of the devil can be very well had from resisting him.

However, the individual in the Church is, no matter how worthless himself, a part of the Body of Christ and a participator in the Redemption. There is no blueprint that the Church gives for understanding this. It is a matter of faith and the Church can force no one to believe it. When I ask myself how I know I believe, I have no satisfactory answer at all, no assurance at all, no feeling at all. I can only say with Peter, Lord I believe, help my unbelief. And all I can say about my love of God, is, Lord help me in my lack of it. I distrust pious phrases, particularly when they issue from my mouth. I try militantly never to be affected by the pious language of the faithful but it is always coming out when you least expect it. In contrast to the pious language of the faithful, the liturgy is beautifully flat.

I am wondering if you have read Simone Weil. I never have and doubt if I would understand her if I did; but from what I have read about her, I think she must have been a very great person. She and Edith Stein are the two 20th century women who interest me most.

Whether you are a Christian or not, we both worship the God Who Is. St. Thomas on his death bed said of the Summa, "it's all straw,"—this was in the vision of that God.

Yours sincerely,

To A.

Milledgeville
Dear Miss A., 9 August 55

I have thought of Simone Weil in connection with you almost from the first and I got out this piece I enclose and reread it and the impression was not lessened. In the face of anyone's experience, someone like myself who has had almost no experience, must be humble. I will never have the experience of the convert, or of the one who fails to be converted, or even in all probability of the formidable sinner; but your effort not to be seduced by the Church moves me greatly. God permits it for some reason though it is the devil's greatest work of hallucination. Fr. de Menacse told somebody not to come into the Church until he felt it would be an enlargement of his freedom. This is what you are doing and you are right, but do not make your feeling of the voluptuous seductive powers of the Church into a hardshell to protect yourself from her. I suppose it is like marriage, that when you get into it, you find it is the beginning, not the end, of the struggle to make love work.

I think most people come to the Church by means the Church does not allow, else there would be no need their getting to her at all. However, this is true inside as well as the operation of the Church is entirely set up for the sinner; which creates much misunderstanding among the smug.

I suppose I read Aristotle in college but not to know I was doing it; the same with Plato. I don't have the kind of mind that can carry such beyond the actual reading, i. e., total non-retention has kept my education from being a burden to me. So I couldn't make any judgment on the Summa, except to say this: I read it for about twenty minutes every night before I go to bed. If my mother were to come in during this process and say, "Turn off that light. It's late," I with lifted finger and broad bland beatific expression, would reply, "On the contrary, I answer that the light, being external and limitless, cannot be turned off. Shut your eyes," or some such thing. In any case, I feel I can personally guarantee that St. Thomas loved God because for the life of me I cannot help loving St. Thomas. His brothers didn't want him to waste himself being a Dominican and so locked him up in a tower and introduced a prostitute into his apartment; her he ran out with a red-hot poker. It would be fashionable today to be in sympathy with the woman, but I am in sympathy with St. Thomas.

I don't know Byron Reece well, but he came out here one evening and had desert with us. I have a friend who is very fond of him and so I hear a lot about him and his troubles, of which he seems to be so well supplied that it's a miracle he's still alive. My impression was that he was a very fine and a very proud man. When he was sick about a year ago, I sent him a copy of St. Bernard's letters and in thanking me, he said he was an agnostic. You are right that he's an anachronism, I guess, strangely cut-off anyway. I wrote to my friend who is so fond of him that perhaps he might be sent something to read that would at least set him thinking in a wider direction, but I am afraid this filled the poor girl with apprehension, she thinking I would probably produce Cardinal Newman or somebody. I had had in mind Gabriel Marcel whose Gifford Lectures I had just read. This girl is a staunch and excellent Presbyterian with a polite horror of anything Romish.

I am highly pleased you noticed the shirts though it hadn't occurred to me that they suggested the lack of hairshirts. I am chiefly exercised by the hero rampant on the shirt and the always somewhat-less occupying it. This is funny to me. The only embossed one I ever had had a fierce-looking bulldog on it with the word GEORGIA over him. I wore it all the time, it being my policy at that point in life to create an unfavorable impression. My urge for such has to be repressed as my mother does not approve of making a spectacle of oneself when over thirty.

I have some long and tall thoughts on the subject of God's working through nature but I will not inflict them on you now. I find I have a habit of announcing the obvious in pompous and dogmatic periods. I like to forget that I'm only a story-teller. Right now I am trying to write a lecture that I have been invited to deliver next spring in Lansing, Mich. to a wholesale gathering of the AAUW. I am trying to write this thing on the justification of distortion in fiction, call it something like The Freak in Modern Fiction. Anyway, I have it born in on me that my business is to write fiction and not talk about it. I have ten months to write the lecture in and it is going to take every bit of it. I don't read much modern fiction. I have never read Nelson Algren that you mention. I feel lumpish.

Yours,

To A.

Milledgeville
Dear Miss A.,   21 August 55

I am really much obliged to you for sending me this book of Algren's to read, as it is something I ought to be familiar with. I have read almost 200 pages so far. I don't think he is a good writer. This may be a hasty judgment and I suspect the book as a whole has an impact, but I have the impression page by page of a talent wasted by sentimentalism and a certain over-indulgence in the writing. In any fiction where the omnicient narrator uses the same language as the characters, there is a loss of tension and a lowering of tone. This is something that it has taken me a long time to learn myself; Mrs. Tate is my mentor in matters of this kind and she has drummed it into me on every occasion so I am very conscious of it.

It may be that a writer can sentimentalize certain segments of the population and get away with it but he cannot sentimentalize the poor and get away with it. I don't have much to compare Nelson Algren with in this country as I have never read JT Farrel or Steinbeck or any of the people who deal with the afflicted (econimically afflicted that is). I have read Celine, though (Journey to the End of the Night) and there is no comparison. Nelson Algren doesn't look like a serious writer beside Celine. It may be that no American can write about the poor the way a European can.

It may also be that poverty in this country is not a matter of physical want anyway, except in certain particular areas. In any case, when you write about the poor, you have to be writing about yourself first, everybody else second, and the actual poor third. The particular appeal of the poor for the fiction writer is existential not economic, but a great deal of the writing about them since and during the 30s seems to consist in numbering their lice (not that I think Algren particularly guilty of that). I have been reading an essay of Wyndam Lewis' (Percy, not D. B.) on George Orwell. It seems Orwell felt he had to force himself to get used to the poor physically; he was repulsed by the way the lower classes smelled. Lewis says that the Orwells had only one servant whereas he, Lewis, came up in a family with a cook, two chamber maids and a nurse, and "being exposed to four stinkers instead of one," felt no necessity of making a special effort to get used to their odor.

All of which is a little beside the point of Algren. I think my particular objection is as a writer—that this is sloppy writing. I write that way myself all the time, and tear it up. I hope.

The enclosed compliments of my peacock.

Yours,

To A.

Milledgeville

Dear Miss A., 28 August 55

I wish St. Thomas were handy to consult about the fascist business. Of course this word doesn't really exist uncapitalized so in making it that way you have the advantage of using a word with a private meaning and a public odor; which you must not do. But if it does mean a doubt of the efficacy of love and if this is to be observed in my fiction, then it has to be explained or partly explained by what happens to conviction (I believe love to be efficacious in the loooong run) when it is translated into fiction designed for a public with a predisposition to believe the opposite. This along with the limitations of the writer could account for the negative appearance. But find another word than fascist, for me and St. Thomas too. And totalitarian won't do either. Both St.

Thomas and St. John of the Cross, dissimilar as they were, were entirely united by the same belief. The more I read St. Thomas the more flexible he appears to me. Incidentally, St. John would have been able to sit down with the prostitute and said, "Daughter, let us consider this," but St. Thomas doubtless knew his own nature and knew that he had to get rid of her with a poker or she would overcome him. I am not only for St. Thomas here but am in accord with his use of the poker. I call this being tolerantly realistic, not being a fascist.

Another reason for the negative appearance: if you live today you breathe in nihilism. In or out of the Church, it's the gas you breathe. If I hadn't had the Church to fight it with or to tell me the necessity of fighting it, I would be the stinkingest logical positivist you ever saw right now. With such a current to write against it (the result) almost has to be negative. It does well just to be.

Then another thing, what one has as a born Catholic is something given and accepted before it is experienced. I am only slowly coming to experience things that I have all along accepted. I suppose the fullest writing comes from what has been accepted and experienced both and that I have just not got that far yet all the time. Conviction without experience makes for harshness.

The magazine that had the piece on Simon Weil is called The Third Hour and is put out spasmodically* by a Russian lady named Helene Iswolsky who teaches at Fordham. I used to go with her nephew so I heard considerable about it and ordered some back issues. The old lady is a Catholic of the Eastern Rite persuasion and sort of a one-man Catholic ecumenical movement. The enclosed of Edith Stein came out of there too. I've never read anything E. Stein wrote. None of it that I know of has been translated. There is a new biography by Hilda Graef but I have not seen it. My interest in both of them comes only from what they have done, which overshadows anything they may have written. But I would very much like you to lend me the books of Simon Weil's when you get through with them. There's no decent public

*when she can get the money

library here and I have to use the college one through the librarians, who are very nice about letting me get books; however, the library is very 19th century in choice of what it buys. I am sure they haven't heard of Simon Weil.

Mrs. Tate is Caroline Gordon Tate, the wife of Allen Tate. She writes fiction as good as anybody, though I have not read much of it myself. They, with John Crowe Ransom and R. P. Warren were prominent in the 20s in that group at Vanderbilt that called itself the Fugitives. The Fugitives are now here there and yonder. Any way Mrs. Tate has taught me a lot about writing.

Which brings me to the embarrassing subject of what I have not read and been influenced by. I hope nobody ever asks me in public. If so I intend to look dark and mutter "Henry James Henry James"—which will be the veriest lie, but no matter. I have not been influenced by the best people. The only good things I read when I was a child were the Greek and Roman myths which I got out of a set of a child's encyclopedia called The Book of Knowlege. The rest of what I read was Slop with a capital S. The Slop period was followed by the Edgar Allan Poe period which lasted for years and consisted chiefly in a volume called The Humerous Tales of EAPoe. These were mighty humerous—one about a young man who was too vain to wear his glasses and consequently married his grandmother by accident; another about a fine figure of a man who in his room removed wooden arms, wooden legs, hair piece, artificial teeth, voice box, etc etc; another about the inmates of a lunatic asylum who take over the establishment and run it to suit themselves. This is an influence I would rather not think about. I went to a progressive highschool where one did not read if one did not wish to; I did not wish to (except the Humerous Tales etc.). In college I read works of social-science, so-called. The only thing that kept me from being a social-scientist was the grace of God and the fact that I couldn't remember the stuff but a few days after reading it.

I didn't really start to read until I went to Graduate School and then I began to read and write at the same time. When I went to Iowa I had never heard of Faulkner, Kafka, Joyce, much less read them. Then I began to read everything at once, so much so that I didn't have time I suppose to be influenced by any one writer. I read all the Catholic novelists, Mauriac, Bernanos, Bloy, Green, Waugh; I read all the nuts like Djuna Barnes and Dorothy Richardson and Va. Woolfe (unfair to the dear lady of course); I read the best Southern writers like Faulkner and the Tates, K. A. Porter, Eudora Welty and Peter Taylor; read the Russians, not Tolstoi so much but Dostoievski, Turgenev, Checkov and Gogol. I became a great admirer of Conrad and have read almost all of his fiction. I have totally skipped such people as Dreiser, Anderson (except for a few stories) and Thomas Woolf. I have learned something from Hawthorne, Flaubert, Balzac and something from Kafka, though I have never been able to finish one of his novels. I've read almost all of Henry James— from a sense of High Duty and because when I read James I feel something is happening to me, in slow motion but happening nevertheless. I admire Dr. Johnson's Lives of the Poets. But always the largest thing that looms up is The Humerous Tales of Edgar Allan Poe. I am sure he wrote them all while drunk too.

I have more to say about the figure of Christ as merely human but this has gone on long enough and I will save it. Have you read Romano Guardini? A German of Italian descent. His master work is something called *The Lord* which in my opinion there is nothing like anywhere, certainly not in this country. I can lend it to you if you would like to see it.

Yours,

To A.

Milledgeville

Dear Miss A.,   6 September 55

I looked in my Webster's and see it is 1948 so you are five years ahead of me in your vocabulary and I'll have to concede you the word. But I can't concede that I'm a fascist. The thought is probably more repugnant to me than to you, as I see it as an offense against the body of Christ. I am wondering why you convict me of believing in the use of force? It must be because you connect the Church with a belief in the use of force; but the Church is a mystical body which cannot, does not, believe in the use of force (in the sense of forcing conscience, denying the rights of conscience, etc.). I know all her hair-raising history, of course, but principle must be separated from policy. Policy and politics generally go contrary to principle. I in principle do not believe in the use of force, but I might well find myself using it, in which case I would have to convict myself of sin. I believe and the Church teaches that God is as present in the idiot boy as in the genius.

Of course I do not connect the Church exclusively with the Patriarchal Ideal. The death of such would not be the death of the Church, which is only now a seed and a Divine one. The things that you think she will be added to, will be added to her. In the end we visualize the same thing but I see it as happening through Christ and His Church.

But I can never agree with you that the Incarnation, or any truth, has to satisfy emotionally to be right (and I would not agree that for the natural man the Incarnation does not satisfy emotionally). It does not satisfy emotionally for the person brought up under many forms of false intellectual disipline such as 19th century mechanism, for instance. Leaving the Incarnation aside, the very notion of God's existence is not emotionally satisfactory anymore for great numbers of people, which does not mean that God ceases to exist. M. Sartre finds God emotionally unsatisfactory in the extreme, as do most of my friends of less stature than he. The truth does not change according to our ability to stomach it emotionally. A higher paradox confounds emotion as well as reason and there are long periods in the lives of all of us, and of the saints, when the truth as revealed by faith is hideous, emotionally disturbing, downright repulsive. Witness the dark night of the soul in individual saints. Right now the whole world seems to be going through a dark night of the soul.

There is a question whether faith can or is supposed to be emotionally satisfying. I must say that the thought of everyone lolling about in an emotionally satisfying faith is repugnant to me. I believe that we are ultimately directed Godward but that this journey is often impeded by emotion. I don't think you are a jellyfish. But I suspect you of being a

Romantic. Which is not such an opprobrious thing as being a fascist. I do hope you will reconsider and relieve me of the burden of being a fascist. The only force I believe in is prayer, and it is a force I apply with more doggedness than attention.

To see Christ as God and man is probably no more difficult today than it has always been, even if today there seem to be more reasons to doubt. For you it may be a matter of not being able to accept what you call a suspension of the laws of the flesh and the physical, but for my part I think that when I know what the laws of the flesh and the physical really are, then I will know what God is. We know them as we see them, not as God sees them. For me it is the virgin birth, the Incarnation, the resurrection which are the true laws of the flesh and the physical. Death, decay, destruction are the suspension of these laws. I am always astonished at the emphasis the Church puts on the body. It is not the soul she says that will rise but the body, glorified. I have always thought that purity was the most mysterious of the virtues, but it occurs to me that it would never have entered the human consciousness to conceive of purity if we were not to look forward to a resurrection of the body, which will be flesh and spirit united in peace, in the way they were in Christ. The resurrection of Christ seems the high point in the law of nature.

If Msgr. Sheen would conceive of wanting to be what Msgr. Guardini is, then that prelate would go up in my estimation. Not that I am one of his detractors. I think his supreme external attribute is vulgarity and that the vulgar must be saved and that generally this is to be accomplished by the vulgar, or the vulgarer than they. Who may be closer to God even than the Idiot Boy.

You are right about a Stroke of Good Fortune. In fact I didn't want it in the collection but was prevailed upon by my editor. It is much too farcical to support anything. Actually it was intended as a part of Wise Blood but I had the good sense to take it out of there. I suppose The Artificial Nigger is my favorite. I have often had the experience of finding myself not as adequate to the situation as I thought I would be, but there turned out to be a great deal more to that story than just that. And there is nothing that screams out the tragedy of the South like what my uncle calls "nigger statuary." And then there's Peter's denial. They all got together in that one.

You are also right about this negativity being in large degree personal. My disposition is a combination of Nelson's and Hulga's. Or perhaps I only flatter myself.

Yours,

To A.

Milledgeville

Dear Miss A.,   15 September 55

I didn't mean to suggest that science is unreliable but only that we can't judge God by the limits of our knowledge of natural things. This is a fundamental difference in your belief and mine: I see God as all perfect, all complete, all powerful. God is Love and I would not believe Love efficacious if I believed there were negative stages or imperfections in it.

Also I don't think as you seem to suppose that to be a true Christian you believe that mutual interdependence is a conceit. This is far from Catholic doctrine; in fact it strikes me as highly Protestant, a sort of justification by faith. God became not only a man, but Man. This is the mystery of the Redemption and our salvation is worked out on earth according as we love one another, see Christ in one another, etc., by works. This is one reason I am chary of using the word, love, loosely. I prefer to use it in its practical forms, such as prayer, almsgiving, visiting the sick and burying the dead and so forth.

I don't think LaCroix is reconciled to atheists as "useful lost." He makes no judgment about the "lost," but leaves that to the providence of God. I read recently somewhere about a priest up for canonization. It was reported in the findings about him that he had said of a man on the scaffold who had been blasphemous up to the last that this man would surely go to hell; on the basis of this remark he was denied canonization.

I guess by emotion you mean something like our deepest

psychological needs. I have recently been reading some depth psychologists, mainly Jung, Neumann, and a Dominican, Victor White (God and the Unconscious). All this throws light momentarily on some of the dark places in my brain but only momentarily. I have also read a book which is fairly elementary I suppose but certainly profound in spots, by Karl Stern, called The Third Revolution. His remarks on the subject of guilt are very interesting and parallel yours to some extent—an interesting contrast of the Greek idea of guilt (the Furies) and the Christian.

About the fascist business: don't consider calling me that out of order as I would rather know what you are thinking than not and it is proper to let me defend myself against such if it can occur to you. Your writing me forces me to clarify what I think on various subjects or at least to think on various subjects and is all to my good and to my pleasure.

About the vacuum my writing seems to create as to (I suppose) a love of people—I won't say the poor, because I don't like to distinguish them. Everybody, as far as I am concerned, is The Poor. Anyway, it occurs to me to put forward that fiction writing is not an exercise in charity, except of course as one is expected to give the devil his due—something I have at least been scrupulous about. I suppose it is true, however, that one's personal affection for people or lack of it carries over and colors the work. Henry James (actually) could write better about vulgar people than any writer I can think of, and this I take it was because there was very little vulgarity in him and he must have hated it thoroughly. James said the morality of a work of fiction depended on the *felt life* that was in it; and St. Thomas said that art didn't require rectitude of the appetite. When you start thinking of a phrase like *felt life*, you can get beyond your depth in a minute. But St. Thomases remark is plain enough: you don't have to be good to write well. Much to be thankful for.

Which brings me to Mr. Byron Reece and his novel. Have you read it? I have not but from the favorable reviews in the Atlanta and Savannah papers last Sunday I would judge that it is not very good. I hope I am wrong.

When I call myself a Catholic with a modern consciousness I don't mean what might be implied in the phrase "modern

Catholic," which doesn't make sense. If you're a Catholic you believe what the Church teaches and the climate makes no difference. What I mean is that I am conscious in a general way of the world's present historical position, which according to Jung is un-historical. I am afraid I got this concept from his book, Modern Man in Search of a Soul—and am applying it in a different way.

Yours,

To A.

Milledgeville

Dear Miss A.,   24 September 55

I am learning to walk on crutches and I feel like a large stiff anthropoid ape who has no cause to be thinking of St. Thomas or Aristotle; however, you are making me more of a Thomist than I ever was before and an Aristotelian where I never was before. I am one, of course, who believes that man is created in the image and likeness of God. I believe that all creation is good but that what has free choice is more completely God's image than what does not have it; also I define humility differently from you. Msgr. Guardini can explain that. I think it is good to have these differences defined. I really don't think *folly* is a wise word to use in connection with these orthodox beliefs or that you should call Aristotle "foolish and self-idolizing." At least, not until you have coped with all the intricacies of his thought. These things may look tortuous to you because they take in more psychological and metaphysical realities than you are accounting for. Of course, I couldn't say about that, but in any case I don't think it's good critical language. However, my crutches are my complete obsession right now. I have never used such before and I am to be on them for a year or two. They change the whole tempo of everything. I no longer am going to cross the room without making a major decision to do it.

I hope I have not left you with the impression that I tote any flags for Celine. All I can say for him is that from what I have read (Journey to the End of the Night) I find him superior as a writer to N. Algren. I can't take Algren seriously inspite of his good intentions whereas I can take the other seriously inspite of his bad ones. He is, I think, a REAL Fascist. I believe he was even tried as a collaborator of the Germans though I may be wrong here. Mauriac recently made the statement that "Bonjour Tristesse" was written by the devil, so I read it. Well it was a very stupid remark for Mauriac to make because the devil writes better than Mademoiselle Saigon. Your comments on how much of oneself one reveals in the work are a little too sweeping for me. Now I understand that something of oneself gets through and often something that one is not conscious of. Also to have sympathy for any character you have to put a good deal of yourself in him. But to say that any complete denudation of the writer occurs in the successful work is, according to me, a romantic exaggeration. A great part of the art of it is precisely in seeing that this does not happen. Maritain says that to produce a work of art requires the "constant attention of the purified mind," and the business of the purified mind in this case is to see that those elements of the personality that don't bear on the subject at hand are excluded. Stories don't lie when left to themselves. Everything has to be subordinated to a whole which is not you. Any story I reveal myself completely in will be a bad story.

I am reading the Weil books now, having finished the Letters to A Priest and got onto the other one and I am very much obliged to you and will keep these books until you want them. I am struck by the coincidence (?) of title of "Waiting for God," and "Waiting for Godot"—have you read that play, by an Irishman named Beckett? The life of this remarkable woman still intrigues me while much of what she writes, naturally, is ridiculous to me. Her life is almost a perfect blending of the Comic and the Terrible, which two things may be opposite sides of the same coin. In my own experience, everything funny I have written is more terrible than it is funny, or only funny because it is terrible, or only terrible because it is funny. Well Simone Weil's life is the most comical life I have ever read about and the most truely tragic and terrible. If I were to live long enough and develope as an artist to the proper extent, I would like to write a comic novel about a woman—and what is more comic and terrible than the angular intellectual proud woman approaching God inch by inch with ground teeth?

I must be off on my two aluminum legs.

Yours,

To A.

Milledgeville

Dear Miss A., 30 September 55

I can't imagine either who would think the Lord would need defending on the score of romanticizing sin. It seems more or less like a crutch Guardini is using to get to the next thought on; or possibly he has come across some such notion in the German youth he instructs. Such is possible. Somewhere lately I read about some child who asked his mother why he should take Jesus' word for anything and she replied, "Because He was a gentleman." This was announced with much approval by the columnist. I wish I could remember where I saw it. I should have cut it out. It might have been Billy Graham or Dr. Crane but I wouldn't accuse them as I'm not sure. Do you read Dr. Crane? I never miss him. He is an odd mixture of fundamentalism (against the grape), psychology, business administration and Dale Carnegie. The originator of The Compliment Club. He appears in the Atlanta Constitution on the same page as the comic strips. He is always telling Alma A. how to keep her husband by losing 75 pounds.

By saying Simone Weil's life was both comic and terrible, I am not trying to reduce it, but mean to be paying her the highest tribute I can, short of calling her a saint, which I don't believe she was. Possibly I have a higher opinion of the comic and terrible than you do. To my way of thinking it includes her great courage and to call her anything less would be to see her as merely ordinary. She was certainly not ordinary. Of course, I can only say, as you point out, this is what I see, not, this is what she is—which only God knows. But I didn't mean that my heroine would be a hypothetical Miss Weil. My heroine already is, and is Hulga. Miss Weil's existence only parallels what I have in mind, and it strikes me especially hard because I had it in mind before I knew as much as I do now about Simone Weil. Hulga in this case would be a projection of myself into this kind of tragic-comic action—presumably only a projection, because if I could not stop short of it myself, I could not write it. Stop short or go beyond it, I should say. You have to be able to dominate the existence that you characterize. That is why I write about people who are more or less primitive. I couldn't dominate a Miss Weil because she is more intelligent and better than I am but I can project a Hulga. However, writing this wouldn't be a thing I would see as a duty. I write what I can and accept what I write; after I have given it all I can. This is loose language and doesn't say what I am after saying exactly but you might piece it out.

I have forgotten Guardini's definition of Romanticism. There are so many definitions of it that I suppose it is a meaningless word to use unless you throw in another definition of your own. I think it was only suggested to me to think you Romantic by ideas you express that would perhaps more properly be seen as pantheistic or something of that sort. As to jelly fish, I read in a filler the other day that there were jelly fish so diaphonous that you could be next to them in the water and you wouldn't know they were there. This does not seem to fit you and it is all I know about jelly fish. If you are going to read 1500 pages of St. Thomas and 650 pages of Aristotle, you will at least be an ossified jelly fish when you get through—if such is possible. I am currently reading Etienne Gilson's History of Christian Philosophy in the Middle Ages and I am surprised to come across various answers to Simone Weil's questions to Fr. Perrin. St. Justin Martyr anticipated her in the 2nd century on the question of the Logos enlightening every man who comes into the world. This is really one of her central questions and St. Justin answered it in what I am sure would have been her own way. Gilson* is a vigorous writer, more so than Maritain; the other thing I have read of his is The Unity of Philosophical Experience, which I am an admirer of.

My being on the crutches is not an accident or the energy-depriving ailment either but something that has been coming

*Etienne Gilson.

on in the top of the leg bone, a softening of it on acct. of a failure of circulation to the hip. They say if I keep the weight off it entirely for a year or two, it may harden up again; otherwise in my old age I will be charging people from my wheel chair or have to have a steel plate put on it. Anyway, it is not as great an inconvenience for me as it would be for somebody else, as I am not the sporty type. I don't run around or play games. My greatest exertion and pleasure these last years has been throwing the garbage to the chickens and I can still do this, though I am in danger of going with it.

You are very good to offer to get me books from the Atlanta library and if there is something I especially need and can't get here, I will not hesitate to ask you. The enclosed article is about a woman I have never heard of before. I wrote the place in New York where I buy books and asked them if they could get her books for me but that was a month ago and they haven't even answered the letter. I don't think there is the remotest chance any of them would be in the Atlanta library but if you would ask the next time you have time there, I would be very glad to know. I am going to write to Fordham and try to get the back issues of Thought that have the Graham Green thing and the Death of the Imagination. She sounds interesting to me. I think she contends that in spite of Green's Catholic convictions, he writes from the standpoint of "neo-Romantic decadence." This much I got from a review of my own stories, a review by a priest who said that while my convictions might be Catholic, my sensibility appeared to be Lutheran. This after I announce to you in grand terms that I write the way I do because I am a Catholic. Anyhow, I do not agree with the reverend Father but no matter. I just read another review from a Kansas City paper that ended with the sentence: "These stories are technically excellent; spiritually empty."

My friend in Atlanta who is so fond of Byron Reece wrote me that she was sending me his book. What she wants is an opinion and it will have to be a pleasant one for the sake of her feelings, so I am glad to hear that it is not so bad. I would like to be able to write him too and say I like it, so I hope I will. Few poets have any business to write novels.

Yours,

P.S. I have an interesting article on St. Thomas and Freud—
if you think you could stand it.

To Sally and Robert Fitzgerald

Milledgeville
Dear S&R,   30 September 55
This would be a fine time for me to come to Italy if it were
not for the fact that I have just been put on crutches. It requires some decision for me at this point to cross the room,
much less the ocean. This has nothing to do with the lupus,
which is fine and all but controlled with the Meticorten. This
is something NEW. Or at least it has been coming on and
has only just got here. A softening of the top of the leg bone
due to a failure of the circulation to the hip.* They say if I
take the weight off the hip for a year or two, I may be able
to save it, otherwise a wheelchair or an operation where they
put in a steel cap or something. So I am swinging around on
two aluminum legs. It's good I'm not the sporty type. I can
still throw the garbage to the chickens, so life is still beautiful,
(though I am in danger of going with it** if I lunge the
wrong way.) I am real awkward and there is always a crash
going on behind me, but I am learning. I hope by next spring
I will be able to make it to Michigan but I am not so enthusiastic about the thought of that anymore. You had better set
your praying children on the subject of my leg bone. I will be
much obliged. Crutches make a big difference in the tempo
you live at. Mine always was slow, but now!
   Wise Blood came out in England this summer and I have
seen three reviews, all respectful but not very perceptive.
   Mamma sends hers. Regards to children.

*I got this *straight*, having seen the Xrays and spoken with
the scientist *before* the parental conference with him.
**the garbage

To A.

Milledgeville
Dear A., 20 October 55

I go from bad to worse in your imagination—first a fascist and now Cupid. I can defend myself on the first score but the Lord only knows what line I'm to take against this other. I'd rather be the Minataur or the Gorgon or that three-headed dog at the river Styx, or ANYBODY. Just reconsider. The enclosed should help you. I don't want it back. I am the one on the left; the one on the right is the Muse. This is a copy of a self-portrait I painted three years ago. Nobody admires my painting much but me. Of course this is not exactly the way I look but it's the way I feel. It's better looked at from a distance.

I have adjusted my image of you to five three, one thirty. This was less trouble than I thought as I also am five three and in the neighborhood of one thirty. It is a neighborhood I would like to get out of as I have to pick it up on my two wrists now. Anyway, I now distinguish you with thick hornrimmed spectacles, a Roman nose, and ash blonde hair.

The reason your packages go quicker than mine is that they look more respectable; consequently I got me some scotch tape and some of those stickers and the two books I returned today do not look like that Mentor package, as if mailed by one of the great unwashed. I used the same paper you used. Now if you send me another book, just reverse this paper and use your old sticker already licked and addressed and when I return it I will reverse it again and use mine. I envision this going on for several years, same paper, same stickers, at a saving to us both of 15 or 20¢ over the annual period. Frugality is next to cleanliness which is next to Godliness. The next time you are at the library will you see if they have Percy Wyndam Lewis' novel, *Tarr*? I can't get it here and WL is much worth my study.

I have put Nelson Algren on the respected shelf of Books Given, Not Paid For, where it looks excellent. Many thanks.

What translation of the Theban cycle are you reading? A Good Man is dedicated to Robert Fitzgerald (and his wife) who translated the plays with Dudley Fitts. I think their translation is the best going from the standpoint of poetry. I have it in a paperback Harcourt book that I'll send you if you don't have it. I lived with the Fitzgeralds for several years in Connecticut.

I am glad you read the stories aloud as I like to do it myself and I think most of them gain in the reading. I do it everytime I go to Nashville or anytime anybody asks me, which is not often. Usually it works very well; however, the funnier the story, the straighter the face it should be read with and I am the kind who laughs heartily at my own jokes. This weekend I read the first story in the book and disgraced myself in this fashion.

There is a story in the Mentor thing called "We're All Guests," by George Clay. I don't know him but he has written me some letters about my stuff, the first one being about Good Country People which he thought very successful. I asked him to read the rest and recently he has written me about that. He said WB bored and exasperated him because H. Motes was not human enough to sustain his interest and he thought A Good Man, A Temple of the Holy Ghost and A Circle in the Fire were substantially marred by the "religious reference that didn't fit in." About WB I think he is in a sense correct but of course he doesn't know what he's talking about about the others. However, his interesting comment was that the best of my work sounded like the Old Testament would sound if it were being written today—in as much (partly) as the character's relation is directly with God rather than with other people. He points out, correctly, that it is hard to sustain the reader's interest in a character like that unless he is very human. I am trying to make this new novel more human, less farcial. A great strain for me.

I didn't hear Russell Kirk lecture as that turned out to be on Mon. instead of Sat. as I had thought; however, he and I were visiting the same people for the weekend so I saw a plenty of him. He is about 37, looks like Humpty Dumpty (intact) with constant cigar and (outside) porkpie hat. He is non-conversational and so am I, and the times we were left alone together our attempts to make talk were like the efforts of two midgits to cut down a California redwood. However, at one point we burst forth into the following spurt of successful uncharitable conversation:

ME: I read old William Heard Kilpatrick died recently.
         John Dewey's dead too, isn't he?
KIRK: Yes, thank God. Gone to his reward. Ha ha.
ME: I hope there're children crawling all over him.
KIRK: Yes, I hope he's with the unbaptized enfants.
ME: No, they would be too innocent.
KIRK: Yes. Ha ha. With the baptized enfants.
ME: Yes.

Curtain

He is starting a bi-monthly magazine to be called The Conservative Review which will be out in two weeks. It should be very good.

The business of the broken sleep is interesting but the business of sleep generally is interesting. I once did without it almost all the time for several weeks. I had high fever and was taking cortisone in big doses, which prevents your sleeping. I was starving to go to sleep. Since then I have come to think of sleep as metaphorically connected with the mother of God. Hopkins said she was the air we breathe, but I have come to realize her most in the gift of going to sleep. Life without her would be equivalent to me to life without sleep and as she contained Christ for a time, she seems to contain our life in sleep for a time so that we are able to wake up in peace.

On the purely spiritual side, I refer you to Atl. Const. Tues. Oct 18, pp 18, Dr. Crane: who reccomends that pastors get their congregations to contribute tangible gifts to the Church like water coolers, kitchen stoves, typewriters, folding steel chairs, because Jesus stated (sic): "Where your treasure is, there will your heart be also."

Hi yo silver.

To A.

Dear A.,   30 October 55

I think Mlle. Weil was a far piece from the Church too but
considering where she started from, the distance she came toward it seems remarkable. And jackass is your word. She was
obviously no pantheist. I accept that a saint is a soul in heaven
but then I am a strong believer in Purgatory. I already have a
berth there reserved for myself. Have you ever read St. Catherine of Genoa's Treatese (not the way to spell Treatiss, eze,
aeze????) on Purgatory? I got interested in St. Catherine of
Genoa when I saw her picture—a most beautiful woman. I
have the T. with her picture in it if you'd like to see it.

The enclosed is more of my articles. These two are re the
question of false mysticism. There's only one answer to that,
which I'll refrain from forcing on you. It can be found in St.
Theresa, St. John of the Cross, St. Catherine of Siena or
whomever you will. Should I say it, it would smack of the
too apt. I have recently been reading one of Mr. Sheed's collection called Born Catholics (which the too apt makes me
think of). This was forced on me by the nun from whom I
took piano lessons (I dispise the piano and all its works and
pomps but this is a way of supporting the good Sisters who
teach the bad children). Anyway I found it more interesting
than I had thought as there are many and diverse degrees of
experience in it (some very dull) and I think more should be
written about conversion within the Church. It is a more difficult subject than conversion without.

I am only too glad to swap all my images of you for the
ginger beer bottle with the head of Socrates. Being dammed
by a faint prettiness turned a mite sour, I wish I looked like
that but as I don't I'm at least glad I can write somebody who
does. I first sent Harper's Bazaar my self portrait and can you
imagine, they said: this is not exactly what we want, a little
stiff, couldn't you send us a snapshot? I also sent it to Harcourt Brace to use on the jacket of my book. They said: this
is a little odd, we don't think it would increase the sale of the
stories, etc.

I take it you are propelled by great energy if you stay up reading until 1. All my mental lights are out by 9.

A study should be made of Dr. Crane's face. (The lower class form, "puss" might be more adequate here.) He lately reported that C-students who make a practice of delivering *sincere* compliments will be found, over a ten year period, to earn more money in their professions than A-students who preserve a close-mouthed and sour demeanor. Blessed are the smilers; their teeth shall show.

Yours,

To John Lynch

Milledgeville
Georgia
Dear Mr. Lynch,　　　　　　　　　　　6 November 55

I am extremely obliged to you for sending me the copy of the review and very much surprised and pleased that a Catholic magazine would want it and would get somebody intelligent to do it. The silence of the Catholic critic is so often preferable to his attention. I always look in the Catholic magazines my mother reads, to see if my book has been reviewed and when I find it hasn't, I say an act of thanksgiving. This should not be the case but it is, and for me, the ironical part of my silent reception by Catholics is the fact that I write the way I do because and only because I am a Catholic. I feel that if I were not a Catholic, I would have no reason to write, no reason to see, no reason ever to feel horrified or even to enjoy anything. I am a born Catholic, went to Catholic schools in my early years, and have never left or wanted to leave the Church. I have never had the sense that being a Catholic is a limit to the freedom of the writer, but just the reverse. Mrs. Tate told me that after she became a Catholic, she felt she could use her eyes and accept what she saw for the first time, she didn't have to make a new universe for each book but could take the one she found. I feel myself that being a Catholic has saved me a couple of thousand years in learning to write. I don't want to bother you but I would like to know if this has been your experience, since you write fiction. I have never talked to another Catholic writer of fiction, except converts, and the experience there is different. They have been formed by other things, I have been formed by the Church, and perhaps you have also.

I am wondering too if you teach writing at Notre Dame and if they go about it there any differently from what they do at Stanford or Iowa—if they go on about "reflecting Christian values," etc. I am not very sure that I think the business of the Catholic writer is to reflect anything but what he sees the most of; but the subject of what is and what isn't a Catholic novel is one I give a wide berth to. Ultimately, you write what you *can*, what God gives you.

I have not read any of your fiction but I am familiar with your name from, I presume, the Commonweal, which I read. However, I'll get the 1947 O. Henry and read your story in there. My first story was published along about that time (Accent, 1946) but was not very good.

Thank you again for the review and your special kindness in sending it to me.

Sincerely,

To A.

Milledgeville
Dear A., 10 November 55

I thought you might like to see the enclosed before it finds its natural place in the Hell of my filing system. I didn't answer it as I thought the lady's temper should not be further disturbed. She didn't sign her name as I guess she was afraid I would try to forge it.

I have looked at the Messenier. It's nothing I would like to form a hasty judgment about. I think that if I saw it framed and in a place proper to it after considerable time, I might grow to have some feeling for it; but I don't know enough about art to appreciate the purely formal qualities. I think I approve of distortion but not of abstraction. There is at least enough I can recognize in this that I would be willing to stand around and let it have its way with me. Actually I know nothing about it. I am in the unenviable state where the plastic arts are concerned of knowing what is bad but not knowing what is good. What do you think of it? I am always prepared for a violent opinion from you. It must have struck you forcibly one way or the other.

About Clay—I don't agree with you that he has no talent. I just think that is all he has. He can create a believable character and set him about his business with some grace; but there it ends. We're All Guests wasn't related to anything larger than itself. He has written me that he believes that the highest thing the writer can do is to explain the reasonable man to himself. He then explained that the reasonable man was a legal concept (he studied law a year)—juries try to decide if the reasonable man would act thus and so, etc. He went on to admit that H. Motes might ultimately be found to be more reasonable than the legal reasonable man, but nevertheless . . . his reasonable man is the legal one.

Mine is certainly something else—God's reasonable man, the prototype of whom must be Abraham, willing to sacrifice his son and thereby show that he is in the image of God Who sacrifices His Son. All H. Motes had to sacrifice was his sight but then (you are right) he was a mystic and he did it. The failure of the novel seems to be that he is not believable enough as a human being to make his blinding himself believable for the reasons that he did it. For the things that I want them to do, my characters apparently will have to seem twice as human as humans. Well, it's a problem not solved by the will; if I am able to do anything about it, it will simply be something given. I never understand how writers can succumb to vanity—what you work the hardest on is usually the worst. Tell me what you mean by a limitation of categories. What's categories? This is too abstract to do me any good. Do you mean feeling or experience or some social range or what? There is an interesting review of the stories in the Fall Kenyon Review that if you ever see, I would like to know what you think of.

About Dante—the Church leaves the judgment of art and artists up to the individual. Of course if the work is a danger to faith or morals it may be put on the Index but this is not a judgment of its artistic value or of the character of the artist,

e. g., Gide may have produced works of art and may now be resting in peace but his works are on the Index as a warning to the Catholic that they are dangerous. For my money Dante is about as great as you can get.

About yclept Pseudo-Dionysius—he was Somebody who wrote between 475 and 525 and ascribed his works to Dionysius the Areopagite who was a friend of St. Pauls. He addressed certain letters on mysticism to Timothy, St. Pauls fellow-worker. He was probably, according to Evelyn Underhill (from the back of whose book this learning comes) a Syrian monk and he wrote treatises on the Angelic Hierarchies and on the Names of God which were very influential for medieval mysticism. You would enjoy this book, *Mysticism*, by Evelyn Underhill, a paperbound Meridian book. I read it last spring is howcome I know all this. It's a mine of information. I would like to read Baron von Hugel's book, The Mystical Element in Religion. Do you reckon the Atlanta PL would have that?

I have decided I must be a pretty pathetic sight with these crutches. I was in Atlanta the other day in Davisons. An old lady got on the elevator behind me and as soon as I turned around she fixed me with a moist gleaming eye and said in a loud voice, "Bless you, darling!" I felt exactly like the Misfit and I gave her a weakly lethal look, whereupon greatly encouraged, she grabbed my arm and whispered (very loud) in my ear, "Remember what they said to John at the gate, darling!" It was not my floor but I got off and I suppose the old lady was astounded at how quick I could get away on crutches. I have a one-legged friend and I asked her what they said to John at the gate. She said she reckoned they said, "The lame shall enter first." This may be because the lame will be able to knock everybody else aside with their crutches.

Yours,

To A.

Milledgeville
Dear A.,   25 November 55
You are in many ways an uncanny girl and very right about the lacking category, which reminds me that Checkov said

"he and she is the machine that makes fiction work," or something near that. Of course I think it is too exclusive a view. You are right that this is the category lacking but wrong that I don't associate it with the virtuous emotions. I associate it a good deal beyond the simply virtuous emotions; I identify it plainly with the sacred. My inability to handle it so far in fiction may be purely personal, as my up-bringing has smacked a little of Jansenism even if my convictions do not. But there is also the fact that it being for me the center of life and most holy, I should keep my hands off it until I feel that what I can do with it will be right, which is to say, given. Purity strikes me as the most mysterious of the virtues and the more I think about it the less I know about it. A Temple of the Holy Ghost all revolves around what is purity. The enclosed is a correspondence I had on the subject with a Boston lady, whose wrath I managed to turn away. I doubt if the same would work with my California friend. As to Brother Elder, he probably don't admit that this kind of a virtue exists so he couldn't be expected to make much out of that story. I never have anything balanced in my mind when I set out; if I did I'd resign this profession from boredom and operate a hatchery.

I suppose what you work hardest on is what you know least, but listen, I never had a moment's thought over Enoch but I struggled over Haze. Everything Enoch said and did was as plain to me as my hand. I was five years writing that book and up to the last I was sure it was a failure and didn't work. When it was almost finished I came down with my energy-depriving ailment and began to take cortesone in large doses and cortesone makes you think night and day until I suppose the mind dies of exhaustion if you are not rescued. I was, but during this time I was more or less living my life and H. Mote's too and as my disease affected the joints, I conceived the notion that I would eventually become paralized and was going blind and that in the book I had spelled out my own course, or that in the illness I had spelled out the book. Well, God rescues us from ourselves if we want Him to.

The displaced person did accomplish a kind of redemption in that he destroyed the place, which was evil, and set Mrs. McIntyre on the road to a new kind of suffering, not Purgatory as St. Catherine would conceive it (realization) but Purgatory at least as a beginning of suffering. None of this was adequately shown and to make the story complete it would have had to be—so I did fail myself. Understatement was not enough. However, there is certainly no reason why the effects of redemption must be plain to us and I think they usually are not. This is where we share Christ's agony when he was about to die and cried out, "My God, why have You forsaken Me?" I needed some instrument to get this across that I didn't have. As to the peacock, he was there because peacocks might be found properly on such a place but you can't have a peacock anywhere without having a map of the universe. The priest sees the peacock as standing for the Transfiguration, for which it is certainly a most beautiful symbol. It also stands in medieval symbology for the Church—the eyes are the eyes of the Church. All this would be lost to Mr. Elder and I suppose all priests are addled to him because they are priests—those who arn't addled will be sinister. Anyway, he was not addled and nothing survived but him and the peacock and Mrs. McIntyre suffering. Isn't her position, entirely helpless to herself, very like that of the souls in Purgatory? I missed making this clear but how are you going to make such things clear to people who don't believe in God, much less in Purgatory?

The scholar known to you as Benjaman is one Ben C Griffith who until last year taught at Bessie Tift (poor man). He now teaches at Mercer but anyhow two years ago, finding Wise Blood in the drugstore he read and favored it and wrote me a very intelligent letter about it and after that kept up with my stories. Last spring he came over to see me as he proposed to write a piece for the Ga. Review about my stuff. I think the Ga. Review gave him to understand they weren't terribly interested in a piece about my stuff. They took one from him on James Jones, his other critical interest! I have not read James Jones so I'm not judging myself by the company I keep. But Mr. Griffith is a nice man anyway, with a slight stutter. I have never met anybody with a stutter who was not nice. He remarked that in these stories there was usually a strong kind of sex potential that was always turned aside and that this gave the stories some of their tension—as for instance in A

Circle in the Fire where there is a strong possibility that the child in the woods with the boys may be attacked—but the attack takes another form. I really hadn't thought of it until he pointed it out but I believe it is a very perceptive comment.

I am sending you along the issue of Thought with the Sewell piece on Graham Green in it. I admire her but all through the piece, my sympathy goes out to Mr. Green, or his carcus, which has to suffer this lady-like vulture dining off him. What I feel I suppose is that she is right without much effort but that he is the one sweating to bring something to birth.* A much better piece is the one following by Fr. Lynch, one of the most learned priests in this country I think. I haven't read Green lately enough to know what I think of him. I don't know whether pity is the beginning of love or the corruption of it, or whether it is harder to love something perfect or something feeble.

I read Kristin Lavrensdatter long years ago and remember being much gripped with that love and that writing, although in those days I wasn't thinking of it as writing. Do you think she could have done it without returning to the 13th century?

I'll pass up the biographies of the Baron von Hugel. I intend to order off after his Letters to a Neice which has recently been put out by Regnery. The other books came—don't feel you have to hurry with these things. A man wrote me yesterday, never heard of him, and said he had enjoyed Wise Blood more than any book to come out of the South since Newman's HBV. Well I racked my brain as to who Newman was and I finally remembered Frances Newman, an Atlanta woman, who wrote in the 20s. I had read one story of hers but she did write a novel called The Hard Boiled Virgin I find, which now I must read. I am going to see if they have it in the GSCW library—the title may keep it out of there, a natural inconsistincy since half the teachers at that place are surely such; but if they don't have it, I will ask you to get it for me at the Atl PL.

                                        Yours,

*bother the metaphor

To A.

Milledgeville
Dear A.,   8 December 55

I'm sure it isn't uncanny to you but I am unaccustomed to a reader who relates her findings back to me, that is, findings more subtle than Mrs. Naomi Myers', so that it must necessarily seem to me at least startling. I would react violently only if I didn't know that what you find you find in charity. Charity is hard to come by and I value you more for your charity than your perception. Nevertheless, you are mighty perceptive. But on the matter of the possible attack on the child in A Circle in the Fire, I think you are off because you assume I think that would be an act of passion, that the boys, if they attacked her, would do it because there was an attraction. No. There couldn't be any attraction or any dependence. They would do it because they would be sharp enough to know that it would be their best revenge on Mrs. Cope; they would do it to humiliate the child and the mother, not to enjoy themselves. And children, particularly in numbers, are quite capable of using themselves in this way, of committing the most monstrous crimes out of the urge to destroy and humiliate. They might well have done this if they had seen the child behind the tree. I didn't let them see the child behind the tree. I couldn't have gone through that myself.

It has always seemed necessary to me to throw the weight of circumstance against the character I favor. The friends of God suffer, etc. The priest is right, therefore he can carry the burden of a certain social stupidity. This may be something I learned from Graham Green and that whiskey priest of his, or it may just be instinct. Anyhow, it seems to me proper.

I have read two of the Grau stories—one about a small colored boy who steals a coat off a dead man and the other about the colored convict who goes home and his children throw bottles at him. They didn't seem to me to have any moral focus, which made them tedious, but I daresay there is considerable talent there and that she is too young yet to make any judgment about. The ugly truth is that of young people writing fiction now, besides meself, I don't like any of it but Peter Taylor's (A long Fourth) some of J. F. Powers' (Prince of Darkness and one that will be out soon called The Presence of Grace) some, mostly early, of Eudora Welty's. Mr. Truman Capote makes me plumb sick, as does Mr. Tenn. Williams. Of foreigners living I like Frank O'Connor. I keep waiting for some club lady to ask me if I am kin to Frank O'Connor. At which I hope to reply, "I am his mother." So far no opportunity.

Your friend was generous in the report about my talk, but the truth is these clubs seldom have anybody to talk to them who thinks they are worth being serious with. Everybody tells them how to write and sell, which is what they think they want to know, but they are always grateful to hear something else, or so they always appear to be to me. I always come away with a lot of faces without names and a lot of names without faces and it is very frustrating. When it was over, one lady said to me, "That was such a nice dispensation you gave us, honey." Another said, "What's wrong with your leg, sugar?" I will be powerful glad when they leave off sugaring me. The lady who officiates at these things does it in a sweet dying voice as if over the casket of a late beloved. They pray, then eat, then introduce everybody but the waiters and the cat, then get around to the speaker. I always read mine off the paper so it is not much strain. In this one I managed to quote both St. Thomas and Dr. Crane so you see the range was remarkable. I sat next to the lady who runs the Atl. PL, a Miss Coston. She asked me if I had seen the library and I wanted to say no but I have read me some books out of it but I desisted as I thought she might not favor her books going through the mail to Milledgeville.

I asked the librarian at the college if she had the HBV and she said she would see but informed me it wasn't any good though it had made a big racket in Atl. in the 20s. Librarians are the last people you can trust about the inside of books. She hasn't produced it yet but if you send me yours, she will, so don't yet anyway.

The enclosed will amuse you. It is part of a letter I had from a young boy I helped get into the University of Iowa. He now writes me about what goes on in his writing class. This Miss Young referred to is Marguerite Young, a convinced Freudian. Mr. Bowen is a lapsed Catholic who according to this boy talks about myth all the time. The other, Calvin Kentfield, he says is the Tough Guy type. These three run what is called a Writers Workshop under the direction of Paul Engle.

About the woman who is the Realist: this is a complicated subject but the only light I have to throw on it is that Poetry is always dependent on Realism, that you have to be a realist or you can't be a poet. Mrs. Hopewell is a realist but not a poet, whereas Hulga has tried to be a poet without being a realist. Where the poet and the realist are truely combined you have . . . St. Catherine of Genoa maybe. I do not think of the realist anyhow as the ogre.

What I was thinking about Undset was that she did write a couple of novels set in the 20th century that were not so successful as the others. I take this on what I have vaguely read. I haven't read the novels so I don't really know.

Yours,

To A.

Milledgeville
Dear A.,   16 December 55
The subject of the moral basis of fiction is one of the most complicated and I don't doubt that I contradict myself on it, for I have no foolproof aesthetic theory. However, I think we are talking about different things or mean different things here by moral basis. I continue to think that art doesn't require rectitude of the appetite but this is not to say that it does not have (fiction anyway) a moral basis. I identify this with James' *felt life* and not with any particular moral system and I believe that the fiction writer's moral sense must coincide with his dramatic sense. I don't like Nelson Algren because his moral sense sticks out, is not one with his dramatic sense. With the Grau stories, I can't discover that life is felt at a moral depth at all. As I remember Celine, I felt that he did feel life at a moral depth—or rather that his work made

me feel life at a moral depth; what he feels I can't care about. Focus is a bad word anyway.

When I said that the devil was a better writer than Mlle. Saigon, I meant to indicate that the devil's moral sense coincides at all points with his dramatic sense.

As I understand it, the Church teaches that our resurrected bodies will be intact as to personality, that is, intact with all the contradictions beautiful to you, except the contradiction of sin; sin is the contradiction, the interference, of a greater good by a lesser good. I look for all variety in that unity but not for a choice: for when all you see will be God, all you will want will be God.

About its being cowardly to accept only the nun's embrace: remember that when the nun hugged the child, the crucifix on her belt was mashed into the side of the child's face, so that that one accepted embrace was marked with the ultimate all-inclusive symbol of love, and that when the child saw the sun again, it was a red ball, like an elevated Host drenched in blood and it left a line like a red clay road in the sky. Now here the martyrdom that she had thought about in a childish way (which turned into a happy sleeping with the lions) is shown in the final way that it has to be for us all—an acceptance of the Crucifixtion, Christ's and our own. As near as I get to saying what purity is in this story is saying that it is an acceptance of what God wills for us, an acceptance of our individual circumstances. Now to accept renunciation, when those are your circumstances, is not cowardly but of course I am reading you short here too. I understand that you don't mean that renunciation is cowardly. What you do mean, I don't in so many words know. Understand though, that, like the child, I believe the Host is actually the body and blood of Christ, not a symbol. If the story grows for you it is because of the mystery of the Eucharist in it.

I was once, five or six years ago, taken by some friends to have dinner with Mary McCarthy and her husband, Mr. Broadwater. (She just wrote that book, A Charmed Life, reviewed in Time.) She departed the Church at the age of 15 and is a Big Intellectual. We went at eight and at one, I hadn't opened my mouth once, there being nothing for me in such company to say. The people who took me were Robert

Lowell and his now wife, Elizabeth Hardwick. Having me there was like having a dog present who had been trained to say a few words but overcome with inadequacy had forgotten them. Well, toward morning the conversation turned on the Eucharist, which I, being the Catholic, was obviously supposed to defend. Mrs. Broadwater said when she was a child and received the Host, she thought of it as the Holy Ghost, He being the "most portable" person of the Trinity; now she thought of it as a symbol and implied that it was a pretty good one. I then said, in a very shaky voice, "Well, if it's a symbol, to hell with it." That was all the defense I was capable of but I realize now that this is all I will ever be able to say about it, outside of a story, except that it is the center of existence for me; all the rest of life is expendable.

Why didn't the lady say I identified myself with St. Thomas? I was recommending to these innocents self-knowledge as the way to overcome regionalism—to know oneself is to know one's region, it is also to know the world, and it is also, paradoxically, a form of exile from that world, to know oneself is above all to know what one lacks, etc etc etc. I then went on to say that St. Catherine of Siena had called self-knowledge a "cell," and that she, an unlettered woman, had remained in it literally for three years and had emerged to change the politics of Italy. The first product of self-knowledge was humility, I said, and added that this was not a virtue conspicuous in the Southern character. Well, betwixt us two, I do not identify myself with St. Catherine. What's furthermore, I never quoted St. Augustine. Anyway, I'm real pleased to have impressed with my attire. Nothing shocks like conventionality and this will remind me when attending the fire sales where I buy my clothes not to get anything the Duchesser Windsor wouldn't eat with the Duke in.

Tuesday I attended another one of these things—the Penwomen. The average age of a Penwoman is 75; however, there were one or two under 50 there. There are always one or two that I would like to see again although I never can remember the names or am not given them. I reported on the characteristics of the short story and afterwards they asked questions, such as, "What do you think of the frame-within-a-frame short story?" They know all the "frames." Most of them live in a world God never made. There is one of them who attends all these things who reminds you of Stone Mountain on the move. She's a large grey mass, near-sighted, pious, and talks about "messages" all the time. I haven't got her name yet but she is going to pursue me in dreams I feel.

If the fact that I am a "celebrity" makes you feel silly, what dear girl do you think it makes me feel? It's a comic distinction shared with Roy Roger's horse and Miss Watermelon of 1955. In a great many ways it makes things difficult for the only friends you can have are old friends or new ones who are willing to ignore it. I am very thankful that you are willing to ignore it.

Yours,

To A.

Milledgeville

Dear A.,   1 January 56

The enclosed says where my thought heads on the subject of all things working toward becoming a woman—a phrase I am made suspicious of naturally when you go on to mention the artistic sterility "that a woman is." I guess you mean "can be." Also what I call a moral basis is a good deal more than a masculine drive—it is, in part, the accurate naming of the things of God (in fiction and poetry, that is). Remember that I am not a pantheist and do not think of the creation as God, but as made and sustained by God.

I don't assume that renunciation goes with submission, or even that renunciation is good in itself. Always you renounce a lesser good for a greater; the opposite is what sin is. And along this line, I think the phrase "naive purity" is a contradiction in terms. I don't think purity is mere innocence; I don't think babies and idiots possess it. I take it to be something that comes either with experience or with Grace so that it can never be naieve. On the matter of purity we can never judge ourselves, much less anybody else. Anyone who thinks he's pure is surely not.

I sent you the other Sewell piece and the one on St. Thomas & Freud. This latter has the answer in it to what you call my struggle to submit, which is not struggle to submit but a struggle to accept and with passion. I mean, possibly, with joy. Picture me with my ground teeth stalking joy—fully armed too as it's a highly dangerous quest. The other day I ran up on a wonderful quotation: "The dragon is at the side of the road watching those who pass. Take care lest he devour you! You are going to the Father of souls, but it is necessary to pass by the dragon." That is Cyril of Jerusalem instructing catechumens.

There is a new Sewell thing in the latest Thought on Chesterton but I haven't read it. Would you be interested in reading Guardini's monograph on the Grand Inquisitor section of the Brother's Karamozov? The librarian never came through with the HBV; she must have disapproved of it too strongly. I'd like to see it if the time on it isn't up but if so I can do without it all right. I am interested in seeing something called The Bridge, edited by John M. Oesterreicher. This hasn't been out long so they may not have it. It has a piece in it on Simone Weil that was criticized in the Commonweal recently and one on the Finaly case and one on the growth of human conscience by Raissa Maritain that I would like to see.

My novel is at an impasse. In fact it has been at one for as long as I can remember. Before Christmas I couldn't stand it any longer so I began a short story. It's like escaping from the penitentiary. It may well be that I'll have another book of stories before I have a novel. I work from such a basis of poverty that everything I do is a miracle to me. However, don't think I write for purgation. I write because I write well.

As for the crutches, I am used to them and I might as well be as I think I will be on them for considerable time. He didn't look for any improvement under a year and then he said, what's a year or two or three off your life? Truely not much, as I was inactive anyway. I get around about as much as I ever did.

I got two beautiful things for Christmas. Robert Fitzgerald sent me a manuscript copy of the first seven books of the Odyssey which he is translating (for an Anchor book) and somebody sent me a pointsetta (sp) without any name on it.

I never got anything before without any name on it and I was much touched with it.

Russell Kirk's magazine has been delayed. I have the feeling it will be delayed many times and be short-lived when it gets here but we shall see. A friend of mine who teaches at Vanderbilt is supposed to have a review of my book in it and he promises to send me a copy of the magazine if it ever appears.

My current problem is: are Northern ladies more intelligent than Southern ladies? I have to write this talk for the AAUW in Michigan and I see it is going to drive me nuts. The subject is supposed to be "Some Aspects of Modern Fiction." It revolts me to think of it.

Yours,

To A.

Milledgeville
13 January 56

Dear A.,

The two Weils and the HBV and the magazines all received and with thanks. I haven't started these two Weil ones but I have read fifty or so pages in the HBV—dear Lord, it's all reported; the most undramatic fifty pages I have been exposed to since Marius the Epicurean. She must have been a very intelligent miserable woman—but no fiction writer. After a while the eye merely glides over all that cleverness, there's nothing to stop it (the eye not the cleverness).

I enclose the Guardini and another section of a report from Iowa that I just got. It will make you even gladder that you didn't get a degree. I can see Bowen and Mrs. de Luna chained together by mutual hate on one of the less important circles of the inferno, eternally arguing if church steeples are phallic symbols. My days there were not like this boy's I must say. I did pretty much nothing, which seems to be a better thing to do than he's doing.

I suppose when I say that the moral basis of Poetry is the accurate naming of the things of God, I mean about the same thing that Conrad meant when he said that his aim as an artist was to render the highest possible justice to the visible universe. For me the visible universe is a reflection of the invisible universe. Somewhere St. Augustine says that the things of the world poured forth from God in a double way: intellectually into the minds of the angels and physically into the world of things. (I am sure that an angelic world is no part of your belief but of course it is very much a part of mine). Since you believe that the world itself is God, that all is God, this can hardly meet with your sympathy. No more than Ong. About him, let me say that his position would be the same if Freud had never been alive and that it is certainly no part of his concern whether one sex is superior to another. He's off on an entirely different track, and whether the male or female is the superior sex ain't going to ruffle his orthodoxy any; or mine. You may be right that a man is an incomplete woman. It don't change anybody's external destination however, or the observable facts of the sexes uses (a nice phrase). Anyway, we can be thankful we arn't between the crossfire of Bowen and Madam de Luna. She fascinates me, though.

The Church it should be said is no less a Gospel reader than the separated brethren. Beginning in the 16th century it was less emphasized for obvious reasons—anyhow an acquaintance with the liturgy is enough to show it without the commentaries of the Church Fathers. While Christ sometimes seemed impatient of his mother, he performed his first miracle at her request, and on the cross he gave her to John and John to her.

To get back to the accurate naming of the things of God I am wondering if what worries you about that, what may seem THE contradiction for me to say such a thing is the fact that I write about good men being hard to find. The only way I can explain that is by repeating that I think evil is the defective use of good. Perhaps you do too.

I am sending back the stamps because I must owe them to you or if I don't I will shortly. They will even theirselfs out. Do not trouble to send me any more.

I am very happy right now writing a story in which I plan

for the heroine, aged 63, to be gored by a bull. I am not convinced yet that this is purgation or whether I identify myself with her or the bull. In any case, it is going to take some doing to do it and it may be the risk that is making me happy.

Yours,

To A.

Milledgeville
Dear A.,   17 January 56

I'm never prepared for anything. I felt sure you were 7 ft. tall and ash blonde and you turn out to be dark and shaped like a ginger beer bottle and I have been equally positive that you were a Pantheist in good standing with whatever they're in good standing with and now you allow you're as orthodox as I am if not more. More, I suppose, as baptism is something you choose and I had it thrust upon me. To my credit it can be said anyway that I never considered you unbaptized. There are the three kinds, of water, blood, and desire, and with the last I thought you as baptized as I am. So that may be the reason I have nothing to say about this when I ought to say something. All voluntary baptisms are a miracle to me and stop my mouth as much as if I had just seen Lazarus walk out of the tomb. I suppose it's because I know that it had to be given me before the age of reason, or I wouldn't have used any reason to find it.

In any case I can't climb down off the high powered defence reflex whateveritis. The fleas come with the dog as Mr. McG. says. If you were Pius XII, my communications would still sound as if they came from a beseiged defender of the faith. I know well enough that it is not a defense of the faith, which don't need it, but a defense of myself who does. The Church becomes a part of your ego and gets messed in with your own impurity. It's a situation I can't handle myself so I wait for purgatory to do it for me. Anyway, I know it exists.

I frequently disagree with priests who get themselves printed in various places but generally it's not with the contents but the tone. My mind is usually at ease, but my sensibilities seldom so. Smugness is the Great Catholic Sin. I find it in myself and don't dislike it any less. One reason Guardini is a relief to read is that he has nothing of it. With a few exceptions the American clergy, when it takes to the pen, brings this particular sin with it in full force. One reason I favor Cross Currents is the frequency of articles without the american-clerical tone. Thought seldom has it either. I blame it all on the Irish.

It's a very pompous phrase—the accurate naming of the things of God—I'll grant you. Suitable for a Thomist with that ox-like look. But then I said it was a basis. What I suppose I mean is an aim. Anyway, I don't mean it's an accomplishment. It's only trying to see straight and it's the least you can set yourself to do, the least you can ask for. You ask God to let you see straight and write straight. I read somewhere that the more you asked God, the more impossible what you asked, the greater glory you were giving Him. This is something I don't fail to practice, although not with the right motives.

I don't want to be any angel but my relations with them have improved over a period of time. They weren't always even speakable. I went to the Sisters to school for the first 6 years or so. They administer the True Faith with large doses of Pious Crap and at their hands I developed something the Freudians have not named—anti-angel aggression, call it. From 8 to 12 years it was my habit to seclude myself in a locked room every so often and with a fierce (and evil) face, whirl around in a circle with my fists knotted, socking the angel. This was the guardian angel with which the Sisters assured us we were all equipped. He never left you. My dislike of him was poisonous. I'm sure I even kicked at him and landed on the floor. You couldn't hurt an angel but I would have been happy to know I had dirtied his feathers—I conceived him in feathers. Anyway, the Lord removed this fixation from me by His Merciful Kindness and I have not been troubled by it since. In fact I forgot that angels existed until a couple of years ago the Catholic Worker sent me a card on which was printed a prayer to St. Raphael. It was sometime before it dawned on me Raphael was an arch angel, the guide of Tobias. The prayer had some imagery in it that I took over and put in The Displaced Person—the business about Mrs. Shortley looking on the frontiers of her true country. The prayer askes St. Raphael to guide us to the province of joy so that we may not be ignorant of the concerns of our true country. All this led me to find out eventually what angels were, or anyway what they were not. And what they are not is a big comfort to me.

I read 50 more pages of the HBV and couldn't finish it. The librarian was right, probably for the wrong reasons. I will send it back in time for some other member of the Atl. PL to have the benefit of it.

I have just sold Wise Blood to a French publisher, Gallimard. I can't feature H. Motes in French, and my own French is too sorry to be able to tell if the translation will be any good or not. Which may be a blessing. I read a book called The American novel in France. The French think Erskine Caldwell is just about the best thing since Shakespeare, or that is the impression I got.

The bull, yes. He is the pleasantest character in the story.

Yours,

To Sally and Robert Fitzgerald

Dear S&R—   2/6/56

The voice of sanity enclosed. My friend in Nashville tells me that Dr. Giovanini wears a beard and dresses like Pound.

These Jesuits work fast. Ten days after I had the visit from the one in Macon, I receive a communication from Harold C. Gardiner, S.J. asking me to contribute to America. Fancy me contributing to America?

Caroline's book was to be dedicated to Dorothy Day, but Miss Day on inspecting the page proofs declared she would burn every copy she could get her hands on if she had her way. So the dedication has been withdrawn at the request of both author and dedicatee and now with that tree off the road, Miss D. begins to like the book better.

Blessings and cheers.

To A.

Dear A.,   11 February 56

What you say about there being two now brings it home
to me. I've always believed there were two but generally acted
as if there were only one. I guess meditation and contemplation and all the ways of prayer boil down to keeping it firmly
in sight that there are two. I've never spent much time over
the bride-bride groom analogy. For me, perhaps because it
began for me in the beginning, it's been more father and
child. The things you have said about my being surprised to
be over twelve, etc., have struck me as being quite comically
accurate. When I was twelve I made up my mind absolutely
that I would not get any older. I don't remember how I
meant to stop it. There was something about "teen" attached
to anything that was repulsive to me. I certainly didn't approve of what I saw of people that age. I was a very ancient
twelve; my views at that age would have done credit to a Civil
War veteran. Anyway. I went through the years 13 to 20 in a
very surly way * * * I am much younger now than I was at
twelve or anyway, less burdened. The weight of centuries lies
on children, I'm sure of it.

According to a recent communication from Steele, Mrs.
De Luna's thought for the week is: "nobody would have paid
any attention to Jesus if he hadn't been a martyr but had died
at the age of eighty of athletes foot." I told Steele that
Mrs. De Luna's trouble was she was orthodox and didn't
know it. Steele, incidentally, is a youth I have never seen. He
wrote me last summer and sent a story he had written and
asked me to recommend him at Iowa. The story was not
good but it showed some talent so I did. He had a long history of being in mental institutions but now he takes one of
those new drugs. Last summer he would write me twice a
week letters of from 30 to 50 typewritten pages—full of violence and all kinds of foolishness. He's highly anti-Catholic. I
finally wrote him that I couldn't read the things and not ever
to write me a letter over two pages—which is a terrible
cramping of his spirit. He says he's now on Bowen's side as
Bowen has started treating him like a human being, every-

body in fact has, even Miss Young. When he first went to Iowa he once opened the door for Miss Young and she swept through like Queen Elizabeth I but the other day she smiled at him. He has written a story which he is convinced is shocking and he's terribly pleased with himself.

I have put the bull aside for further thought on it. It's finished but I'm not sure it works yet. Meanwhile I occupy myself with busy-work—a talk to the Council of Teachers of English in March and this ordeal in Michigan and a book review for The Bulletin. This latter being my first emergence into the Catholic Press. The other week a white Cadillac drove up into the yard and out jumped an unknown priest. He turned out to be one of the Jesuits from Macon, come over to tell me that he had read and liked my stories. This almost knocked me out, as no priest has ever said turkey-dog to me about liking anything I wrote. In he came and we had a lively discussion. Ten days later I had a letter from the literary editor of America asking me to contribute to their columns—this was the result of the other visit. The one from Macon called again a few days ago, this time in a black and white Cadillac. I asked him where he got his Cadillacs and he said they belonged to a liquor dealer he is bringing into the Church. I sent him off with the Sewell article on Greene and with a 25¢ edition of Wise Blood for Mr. Ridley, the liquor dealer, as he said Mr. Ridley was much impressed that I had a book out in a drug store edition and said that was really where you made the money. Mr. Ridley said a book had to have a good many trashy spots for him to be able to appreciate it. I am waiting for his comment on Wise Blood.

Keep me posted on that elevator girl.

Yours,

On the subject of my guile I will preserve the ominous silence. The ominous silence is preserved best when I can't think of anything to say.

To Eileen Hall

Milledgeville
Dear Mrs. Hall,   10 March 56

I'm enclosing a copy of an essay that has answered some of my questions and may answer some of yours, but I'd be much obliged if you'd send it back when you're through with it, because I don't have but this one copy.

About scandalizing the "little ones." When I first began to write I was much worried about this thing of scandalizing people, as I fancied that what I wrote was highly inflammatory. I was wrong—it wouldn't even have kept anybody awake, but anyway, thinking this was my problem, I talked to a priest about it. The first thing he said to me was, "You don't have to write for fifteen year old girls." Of course, the mind of a fifteen year old girl lurks in many a head that is seventy-five and people are every day being scandalized not only by what is scandalous of its nature but by what is not. If a novelist wrote a book about Abraham passing his wife Sarah off as his sister—which he did—and allowing her to be taken over by those who wanted her for their lustful purposes—which he did to save his skin—how many Catholics would not be scandalized at the behavior of Abraham? The fact is that in order not to be scandalized, one has to have a whole view of things, which not many of us have.

This is a problem that has concerned Mauriac very much and he wrote a book about it called, "God and Mammon." His conclusion was that all the novelist could do was "purify the source"—his mind. A young man had written Mauriac a letter saying that as a result of reading one of his novels, he had almost committed suicide. It almost paralyzed Mauriac. At the same time, he was not responsible for the lack of maturity in the boy's mind and there were doubtless other souls who were profiting from his books. When you write a novel, if you have been honest about it and if your conscience is clear, then it seems to me that you have to leave the rest in God's hands. When the book leaves your hands, it belongs to God. He may use it to save a few souls or to try a few others, but I think that for the writer to worry about this is to take over God's business.

I'm not one to pit myself against St. Paul but when he said "let it not so much as be named among you," I presume he was talking about society and what goes on there and not about art. Art is not anything that goes on "among" people, not the art of the novel anyway. It is something that one experiences alone and for the purpose of realizing in a fresh way, through the senses, the mystery of existence. Part of the mystery of existence is sin. When we think about the Crucifixion, we miss the point of it if we don't think about sin.

About bad taste, I don't know, because taste is a relative matter. There are some who will find almost everything in bad taste, from spitting in the street to Christ's association with Mary Magdalen. Fiction is supposed to represent life, and the fiction writer has to use as many aspects of life as are necessary to make his total picture convincing. The fiction writer doesn't state, he shows, renders. It's the nature of fiction and it can't be helped. If you're writing about the vulgar, you have to prove they're vulgar by showing them at it. The two worst sins of bad taste in fiction are pornography and sentimentality. One is too much sex and the other too much sentiment. You have to have enough of either to prove your point but no more. Of course there are some fiction writers who feel they have to retire to the bathroom or the bed with every character every time he takes himself to either place. Unless such a trip is used to further the story, I feel it is in bad taste. In the second chapter of my novel, I have such a scene but I felt it was vital to the meaning. I don't think you have to worry much about bad taste with a competent writer, because he uses everything for a reason. The reader may not always see the reason. But it's when sex or scurrility are used for their own sakes, that they are in bad taste.

What offends my taste in fiction is when right is held up as wrong, or wrong as right. Fiction is the concrete expression of mystery—mystery that is lived. Catholics believe that all creation is good and that evil is the wrong use of good and that without Grace we use it wrong most of the time. It's almost impossible to write about supernatural Grace in fiction. We almost have to approach it negatively. As to natural Grace, we have to take that the way it comes—through nature. In any case, it operates surrounded by evil.

I haven't so much been asked these questions as I have asked them of myself. People don't often even have the courtesy to ask them—they merely tell you where you have failed. I don't take the questions lightly and my answers are certainly not complete, but they're the best I can do to date.

Don't feel you have to review the Gordon book if you think it would cause the Bulletin embarrassment or trouble. I will certainly understand. Most of your readers wouldn't like The Malefactors if it were favorably reviewed by Pius XII.

Have you read "Art and Scholasticism" by Jaques Maritain? This "God and Mammon" is published by Sheed & Ward. Maybe that should be reviewed in the Bulletin! About twenty years late, but better late than never.

Yours with all best wishes,

To A.

Milledgeville
Dear A., 24 March 56

Isn't the enclosed your old lady? I wrote her back at once and now I am a member of NDBSLL.

So the fender is not the thing that goes across the front? It was my conviction that the fender went across the front and the bumper went across the back. This still seems eminently logical to me but I am willing to take your word for it because a similar embarrassment happened to me before. In the Kenyon Review Mr. Shiftlet started his car by stepping on the clutch. I was afterwards told that this was against the nature of the automobile and I changed it before it got in the book. I will attend to this other on the page proofs and also change faught to fought. Mrs. Tate had to tell me once that there was no such thing as bob-wire. It is barbed wire. Isn't that silly? My mother says, "You talk just like a nigger and someday you are going to be away from home and do it and people are going to wonder WHERE YOU CAME FROM."

I thought Mrs. Greenleaf was a sympathetic character. She and the sun and the bull were connected and sympathetic. At one point Mrs. May sees the bull as the sun's shadow cast at an oblique angle moving among the cows, and of course he's a Greenleaf bull! What personal problems are worked out in stories must be unconscious. My preoccupations are technical. My preoccupation is how I am going to get this bulls horns into this womans ribs. Of course why his horns belong in her ribs is something more fundamental but I can't say I give it much thought. Perhaps you are able to see things in these stories that I can't see because if I did see I would be too frightened to write them. I have always insisted that there is a fine grain of stupidity required in the fiction writer.

Well you should read my latest interpreter for a real chill —this is a young lady from Texas State College for Women who is entering a Mademoiselle contest with a feature story on my work. She is twenty-one and SUCH SOPHISTICA-TION—of a sort. She sent me a copy of the feature, not for my approval as she had already sent it to Mademoiselle; possibly for my edification. It is called "Flannery O'Connor: The Pattern in the Fire," and contains such statements as "Her message is immoralistic, in the Gidean sense." "She merely states that it is probably impossible to know how to be one (a good man)." Of course I don't know what the Gidean sense of "immoralistic message" is. What she has done is to disinfect the word "message" with the word "immoralistic." I wrote her a long gentle epistle (I hope she'll take it that way) pointing out that the message, if she wished to use the word, was a highly moral one, and that I was quite simply of a Christian conviction with a belief in all the Christian dogmas and that there was nothing more repulsive to me than the thought of myself setting up my own universe and propounding my own immoralistic message, and further that I found it thoroughly possible to know how to be one, only hard to be one without the assistance of grace. I think she is a nice little girl and that this is going to be something of a blow to her. I had to tell her I had no idea what the Gidean sense was so maybe that will make her feel better. Now they latch onto Gide when they are twenty-one.

The Tates were great friends of Hart Crane. Last summer I spent a weekend with Caroline in Connecticut near the place where they and Crane lived one winter. There was a lot of his stuff piled up in a corner, a pair of snow shoes and some other things. Allen has written a piece about him that is in

The Man of Letters in the Modern World—a Meridian book worth reading—that I think is very fine. You are right about her not being timid. She lays about her right and left and has considerable erudition to back herself up with. She says my trouble is I don't have a classical education, I don't know what Sophocles "middle diction" is. (I do now as she has told me). Nobody my age, says she, has an education—which is true. She is currently at the University of Kansas teaching a course in contemporary writers. She says she is going to *make* them see the difference in Wise Blood and the works of Truman Capote if she has to use the word "religion." According to her, the two words not allowed to be used at the U. of K. are "whiskey" and "religion." She takes great pains and is very generous with her criticism. Is highly energetic and violently enthusiastic. When I am around her, I feel like her illiterate grandmother.

I am making progress with The Bridge. The piece on Simone Weil is very good I think. When you get ready for it let me know and also The Malefactors.

I want to do something celebrative when you come into the Church, which desire brings me sharply up against the idiocy of all human gestures. You can imagine me holding some kind of figurative candle and croaking the proper responses. But what I will do is go to Communion for you and your intention Easter morning, and since we will then share the same actual food, you will know that your being where you are increases me and the other way around. I have a sentence in mind to end some story that I am going to write. The character all through it will have been hungry and at the end, he is so hungry that "he could have eaten all the loaves and fishes, after they were multiplied."

Yours,

To A.

Milledgeville
Dear A.,   21 April 56
   St. Catherine in hand. I have never got beyond page 87 in that book myself. I located the spot with difficulty. It's very

interesting. All my books are spotted with Ovaltine which has put me and little Orphan Annie to sleep these many years. I sent you The Malefactors and when you get through with it, keep it or leave it in a basket on somebody's doorstep. One copy is sufficient for me. I put in the sentence about Jung because, according to Caroline, this is the first Jungian novel— as distinguished from Freudian. I think Jung is probably just as dangerous as Freud. I see Scury T. has latched onto Freud this week. Last week I guess you observed they latched onto yer friend Walter Ong, S.J. This time I will have to be the one to disagree with Walter, S.J. This may be a better age for the Faith, but this is certainly not an age of Faith.

I agree with you that nothing in this present collection of Powers equals the best in the first. However, who am I to be saying that in public? These are the only reviews I have ever written and I make the discovery that they are not the place for that kind of absolute honesty. In the first place you can be so absolutely honest and so absolutely wrong at the same time that I think it is better to be a combination of cautious and polite. I prefer the good manners of an idiot to his honesty and while I am not an idiot in these matters, I have found myself mighty far wrong mighty often. Well, Mauriac says *only* fiction does not lie and I believe him.

You ask about Cal Lowell. I feel almost too much about him to be able to get to the heart of it. He is a kind of grief to me. I first knew him at Yaddo (a place in Saratoga Springs, NY, where writers and painters and musicians are invited to go live and work). We were both there one fall and winter. At that time he had left his first wife, Jean Stafford, and the Church. To make a long story short, I watched him that winter come back into the Church. I had nothing to do with it but of course it was a great joy to me. I was only 23 and didn't have much sense. He was terribly excited about it and got more and more excited and in about two weeks had a complete mental breakdown. That second conversion went with it, of course. He had shock treatments and all that, and when he came out, he was well for a time, married again a very nice girl named Elizabeth Hardwick, and since then has been off and on, in and out, of institutions. Now he is doing very well on one of these drugs—but the Church is out of it, though I don't believe he has been able to convince himself that he doesn't believe. What I pray is that one day it will be easy for him to come back into the Church. He is one of the people I love and there is a part of me that won't be at peace until he is at peace in the Church. Pray for him because the Lord knows he is in a hard position. The last thing he wrote was called The Mills of the Kavanaughs. Right now he is writing an autobiography. This is part of some kind of analytical therapy.

I have no letter-writing duties except that every Tuesday come fire pestilence or plague I write to my 86 year old cousin in Savannah. This is one of those how are you—I am fine—it's cold here—I hope it's hot there affairs, done at white hot speed, but she has been very good to me and writing to her is less a duty than a support to my character. Anyway, be it understood that my writing to you is a free act, unconnected with character, duty, or compulsion. I am afraid that if I tell you your writing to me is a kindness, you will lay this to some more of my guile or feel obliged to write me when YOU don't feel like it. Don't do that, but do be assured that these letters from you are something in my life. I have the sense that they are too much concerned with me and my works but I don't know how to avoid that, as the works do interest me.

I think the lady from Forsyth thought the story merely funny. She went on to say that she didn't allow quite so much freedom to her college age sons. What's funny about it is that it represents so well an illogical position, represents it in the concrete. I have a friend, a man in his fifties, who claims he quit going to the Methodist sunday school because he attended one Mother's Day and listened to a discussion in favor of birth control. Now he's a follower of Robert Graves and the white goddess or something so it's frequently a matter of out-of-the-frying-pan.

Monday I departs for Lansing, Friday, d. v., I returns. After that I will shut up about it. I am to stay with one Mrs. Rumsey Haynes and her spouse, she being a mogul in the AAUW there. Rumsey, says she, will help me up and down the stairs; but I am just going to tell Rumsey to stand by at the bottom as there is nothing more dangerous to the safety

of those on crutches than a gentleman's assistance. She allows
there are many interesting young writers and intellectuals
there that I will enjoy meeting. Anything I can't stand it's a
young writer or intellectual. Well, I brought this on myself.
May the Lord have mercy on my soul.

Yours,

To A.

Milledgeville
Dear A.,   5 May 56
   I'll be real pleased to be your sponsor for Confirmation—
that is, if I read that right and am not just inviting myself.
Once I was godmother for a child in California by proxy and
I had to send a statement saying I was willing. I don't know
if that's necessary for sponsors but if it is, drop me a card and
I will send it on. I never have been anybody's sponsor before.
What's it mean? I am supposed to come and ask you what
the fruits of the Holy Ghost are once a year or something?
Anyway, I am highly pleased to be asked and to do it and as
for your horrible history, that has nothing to do with it. I'm
interested in the history because it's you but not for this or
any other occasion.
   We have got crossed up on our book intentions all around
as I had already got rid of The Malefactors when I got your
instructions to take it to the grocery store. What I done with
it, I sent it to Mrs. Rumsey Marshall Haynes who had expressed an interest. To which subject, let me get. The steps
were gradual and carpeted with a about-two-inch-thick Ori-
ental rug. Rumsey's granddaddy invented the cure for foot-
rot in sheep (he told me this story at the breakfast table) and
made a pile. Rumsey is retired and clips cupons and draws
interest. Rumsey is his name and I didn't have a thing to do
with it. Mrs. Rumsey is the same size as Rumsey, 6 ft., 2 in.,
and weighs about the same, two-fifty, I would judge. They
were really very nice people and I enjoyed them. Rumsey collects postcards and gave me a bunch of them to send out. I
have discussed the weather with every clubwoman in Lansing
and the thirty minutes when I did the talking were among the

most enjoyable for me. An exaggeration. You always like these people better than you had expected to and perhaps the dreary part is that you will never see them again.

As for the Catholic function—one is always paid for ones sins. They decided against both the tea and the talk to the Newman Club and instead, decreed that I should be invited to a huge convention luncheon of the Nat. Asso. of Cat. Women. If ever there has been devised something suitable for the remission of temporal punishment due to sin, this is it. It lasted three hours, included a talk by a priest and one by a bishop, the introduction of sixteen guests (I was the sixteenth like Gen. Tennessee Flintrock Sash), pledges, resolutions, welcomes, responses, and dedications. There were about five hundred attending. I sat at a table with 8 ladies I had never seen before and an ancient deaf priest named Fr. Murphy—next to him. Said he to me:

> And wharre are you from?
> Milledgeville, Georgia, Father.
> Eh?
> Milledgeville, Georgia.
> I didn't get that.
> MILLEDGEVILLE GEORGIA
> What city is that near?
> M A C O N (great volume)
> Mi-kun? I never heard of that.
> Where are you from, Father?
> (Pause—waiting to get ladies' attention.) Purrrgatory.
> (Laughter)

During the priest's and bishop's addresses he took out his breviary and read it under the table. I wished I had had one.

Mr. Billy has been invited down here to visit Dr. Rosa Lee Walston, the head of the English Department and twice I have had notes from him saying he would be around at such and such a time, but every note contradicted the last one, and now it is that he may come next Thursday when their president is getting some kind of award. So it may well be I will get to see Billy in person but I doubt it. I haven't heard about the Alabama college business. I guess that is Spring Hill, a Jesuit school. I had an uncle expelled from it.

I think, or anyway, hope, that I have heard the last of Steele. The two letters I sent you were sane. The last couple I have had have not been. They have been full of abuse, obscenity, real hate. The first one I didn't answer. Then there was another one waiting on me when I got back from Michigan so I wrote him that since there was nothing I could do for him, I saw no reason to keep up the correspondence. The letters were filthy but terribly pathetic as well. There's nothing you can do for such people but pray for them. The boy is homosexual and apparently scizophrenic (sp?) to boot and he tries to make you feel personally responsible for both conditions in him.

What do you think of The Malefactors or did you think anything? I frequently think nothing, and I feel inadequate to that particular book. Would you be interested in reading Baron von Hugel's letters to his neice? I've just reviewed it for The Bulletin and according to me it is absolutely finer than anything I've seen in a long long time. You can read one letter a night without straining yourself much. I'll send it if you'd be interested. No hurry to return any of these books.

What building do you work in? The next time I am in Atlanta I think I will come ride in your elevators and converse with some of those girls that run them.

Oh. My TSCW prodigy has been chosen as one of the twenty guest editors for the month of June at Mademoiselle. She wrote me a very nice, and intelligent letter, explaining what she meant about Gide. I still don't exactly understand what but I'm pleased she is going to get this reward, since she wants it. I once visited the Mlle. offices—full of girls in peasant skirts and horn-rimmed spectacles and ballet shoes.

Yours,

Oh. Jean Stafford. She's the one you think. The first book was Boston Adventure, then The Mountain Lion, and then something called The Catherine Wheel. Also a lot of stories. She came into the Church and left it later, married a photographer after Cal, left him and I don't know what she does now. She must be a very nice person who has had a hard time, from all I can hear. I never met her.

To A.

Milledgeville
28 June 56
Dear A.,

You always make of me what I would like to be but if I took your notion of me for present reality, I'd be in the devil's hands right now; however, I only take your idea of what I am as an indication of what I should become and the Lord has never instructed me in such a pleasant way before.

I had the impression that all the time you were here you were poised for flight—a lark with a jet engine—and that if I had turned my back, you would have been gone. The next time I'll know better and will use the commanding tone since I am capable of it, at least through the mail. In person I lack command.

Nobody attains reality for my mother until he eats. Therefore she is not quite convinced that you exist on the plane with the rest of us, but when you come again, you can correct that by staying long enough to take in some of your meals. She is wondering if you eat on the 7th day, in the middle of it, that is. I approve of the iron will but it should be used only on what resists with an equal force. To meander further, you don't look anything like I expected you to as I always take people at their word and I was prepared for white hair, horn-rimmed spectacles, nose of eagle and shape of gingerbeer bottle. Seek the truth and pursue it: you ain't even passably ugly.

You are wrong that it was long ago I gave up thinking anything could be worked out on the surface. I have found it out, like everybody else, the hard way and only in the last years as a result of I think two things, sickness and success. One of them alone wouldn't have done it for me but the combination was guaranteed. I have never been anywhere but sick. In a sense sickness is a place, more instructive than a long trip to Europe, and it's always a place where there's no company, where nobody can follow. Sickness before death is a very appropriate thing and I think those who don't have it miss one of God's mercies. Success is almost as isolating and nothing points out vanity as well. But the surface hereabouts has always been very flat. I come from a family where the only emotion respectable to show is irritation. In some this tendency produces hives, in others literature, in me both.

According to Nancy the only way you can help a person on crutches is going down the steps to hold on to her belt in the back. Then if she falls, you got her. But she says if anybody takes your arm or your crutch, he'll throw you every time. After which she describes all the occasions on which she has been thrown and the resulting fractures. For my part I am always glad to have the door held open but that's all that's necessary. I don't want any of those apple-eyed old boys helping me on any busses. Did you have to sit with any of those boys? The delegation from Cornelia? To get back to the crutches, the truth about them is that they worry the onlooker more than the user.

Well the Bulletin got around to the Baron so I withdraw all my ugly thoughts. I will expect to see A. in there next issue though I would prefer M. E.—highly businesslike. Oh. W—— may get to be 14 but not much older. I predict her absorption into the convent at an early age. Or maybe I mean her osmosis.

Well I am off for the city of Nashville. Caroline may be there but more than likely not, in which case the weekend should be more peaceful. I always feel like Caroline's old grandmother.

Oh I meant to ask you. Do you read The National Geographic or do you smell it? I smell it. A cousin gave me a subscription when I was a child as she noted I always made for it at her house, but it wasn't a literary or even a geographical interest. It has a distinct unforgettable trancendent apotheotic (?) and very grave odor. Like no other mere magazine. If Time smelled like the Nat'l. Geo. there would be some excuse for its being printed.

Yours,

To A.

Milledgeville
24 August 56

Dear A.,

Well don't throw the Bulletin over on acct. of Mrs. Hall. She should certainly not correct your review but should send it to you with her suggestions and let you decide what you want to do. This is what she did with me on one occasion and as I thought she was right, I corrected it. Be firm with her but don't give up the Bulletin. What you do on the Bulletin you do for God and not Mrs. Hall and just because it can't be made over is no reason it can't be made a little better here and there. Let the holy angels take Mrs. Hall. I find that everything that is done in this world is done through sob-sisters like her. The people who are willing to do the work don't have the imagination and the people with the imagination arn't willing to do the work. The Bulletin may get worse instead of better but I intend to hang onto it until she absolutely refuses to send me another book. Billy asked me to write her to get him Daniel Rops "Jesus and His Times," to review. A Catholic translation says he is to be out this fall. That's all he knows. So if you see her again I'd be obliged if you'd ask her to get it for him, and if you don't see her, I'll risk writing her at her house * * *

You can consign the rabid magazine to yr trashcan. CH is a young man named Carl Hartman who reviewed Wise Blood and found it dandy and a kind of manifestoe for all us athe-ists. In time I got into correspondence with him and with a number of Bulls and Enclycals set him straight as to my intentions if not as to my accomplishments. So if he knew it was affirmative, he knew it owing to my having told him so. But he's a nice man.

Sent you one of my favorite books to look at in your lei-sure. This book is not as jazzy as it sounds on first reading. I have read it three times.

The enclosed talk is aimed merely at the common preju-dices of my amiable audience and I trust the common prob-lems and not mine specifically. I'm afraid it won't even keep them awake.

About GCP let me say that you are not reading the story itself. Where do you get the idea that Hulga's need to wor-ship "comes to flower" in GCP? or that she had never had any faith at any time? or never loved anybody before? None of these things are said in the story. She is full of contempt for the Bible salesman until she finds he is full of contempt for her. Nothing "comes to flower" here except her realization in the end that she ain't so smart. It's not said that she has never had any faith but it is implied that her fine education has got rid of it for her, that purity has been over-ridden by pride of intellect through her fine education. Further it's not said that she's never loved anybody, only that she's never been kissed by anybody—a very different thing. And of course I have thrown you off myself by informing you that Hulga is like me. So is Nelson, so is Haze, so is Enoch, but you cannot read a story from what you get out of a letter. Nor I repeat, can you, inspite of anything Sister Sewell may say, read the author by the story.* That my stories scream to you that I have never consented to be in love with anybody is merely to prove that they are screaming an historical inaccuracy. I have God help me consented to this frequently.

Now that Hulga is repugnant to you only makes her more believable. I had a letter from a man who said Allen Tate was wrong about the story that Hulga was not a "maimed soul" she was just like us all. He ended the letter by saying he was in love with Hulga and he hoped some day she would learn to love him. Quaint. But I stick neither with you nor with that gent here but with Mr. Allen T. A maimed soul is a maimed soul.

I have also led you astray by talking of technique as if it were something that could be separated from the rest of the story. Technique can't operate at all, of course, except on believable material. But there was less conscious technical control in GCP than in any story I've ever written. Technique works best when it is unconscious, and it was unconscious there.

What Fr. Simons was talking about saying "Lutheran sensibility" he explained this way: Luther said a man was like a horse, ridden either by Christ or the devil. My characters are ridden either, said he, by Christ or the devil and therefore lack any self-determination, hence Lutheran sensibility. ????????

What you say about your experience last August and since all rings true to me though I have never experienced anything

*You may but you shouldn't—See T. S. Eliot

like that myself. When you are born in it I suppose that is gift enough without asking for anything else. In any case you now have the Church and don't need anything else. And that about Edith Stein rings true too. I have been reading about eternity in a book of Jean Guitton's called The Virgin Mary —one that Billy left here—and have had considerable light thrown on the subject for me. He says that eternity begins in time and that we must stop thinking of it as something that follows time. It's all very instructive and I recommend it.

Sunday I am to entertain a man who wants to make a movie out of The River. He has never made a movie before but is convinced The River is the dish for him—"a kind of documentary" he said over the telephone. It is sort of disconcerting to think of somebody getting hold of your story and doing something else to it and I doubt if I will be able to see my way through him. But we shall see. How to document the sacrament of Baptism?????

                                                              Yours,

To A.

                                        Milledgeville
Dear A.,   8 September 56

So the old girl wants 200 words only? Well, the difference between 200 words and one page (the original stipulation) is 50 words so all you have to do is leave out the conjunctions. She has not told me this new ruling yet; in fact, she has ignored me entirely lately and I haven't got a book in two months anyway. I am afraid I cooked my goose with her by asking for that Metamorphic Tradition in Modern Poetry. She's never printed the review. Anyway, I sympathise with her about the 200 words. 200 words is enough. These arn't reviews, just notices and what you need to develope for them is something I call Church Prose (from Church Mouse)— lean spare poor and hungry. It's no great question of art here though you can say one or two pertinent things with 200 words. Me, I have had a hard time making some of my reviews even that long. But this is something that has apparently plagued her all along as she told me when she first started writing me that most of the reviews were too long. She said Mrs. Zsuffa's were always good but too long. I guess she was giving me fair warning.

The lecture for the ladies I redone. It was not abtruse but it was too abtruse for them and so I redid it along the lines of "What Is A Wholesome Novel?" which, according to the Jesuit is all they will be interested in anyway. Incidentally, this Jesuit, the one who comes over with the liquor dealer, is a friend of your friend, Walter J. Ong, S. J. He says Walter J. is fine. I found that out on his last visit when he brought along another Jesuit who teaches at the Catholic University—English to freshmen. I asked him what he thought about The Malefactors and he said he thought it was "pious pap."

My objection to the Luce thesis about writers goes farther than I was able to say in that paper. I believe they are wrong in general as well as in particular. I don't believe that you can ask an artist to be affirmative, any more than you can ask him to be negative. The human condition includes both states in truth and "art," according to Msgr. Guardini, "fastens on one aspect of the world, works through to its essence, to some essential thing in it, and presents it in the unreal arena of the performance." I mortally and strongly defend the right of the artist to select a negative aspect of the world to portray and as the world gets more materialistic there will be more such to select from. Of course you are only enabled to see what is black by having light to see it by—but that is no part of the Luce contention. Furthermore, the light you see by may be altogether outside of the work itself. The question is not is this negative or positive but is it believable. The Luces say the negativeness of our novels is not believable because statistics tell us that we are rich and strong and democratic. In which case Dr. Kinsey and Dr. Gallop are sufficient for the day thereof. I don't believe that in all this you can be so cavalier about particulars. When the particulars are wrong, the general is usually wrong too. If you are too cavalier about particulars you will find yourself a Manichean without knowing how it happened.

Sent you a piece out of the Catholic Worker that I thought was about Edith Stein until I read it but maybe in the next issue he will get back to the subject of her. If she is ever canonized, she will be one saint that I don't think they can sweeten up on holy cards and write a lot of "pious pap" about. Do you see the Catholic Worker? It irritates me considerably because I don't go for the pacifist-anarchist business but every now and then you will find something fine in it— it is where I first came across the name of Miss Sewell. It also has the distinction of costing 25¢ a year—the ideal subscription rate.

The enclosed was sent me recently by a friend of mine who lives in South Bend and used to be the editor of something called Ave Maria, which he claimed was the worst magazine in the Catholic Press. He was recently fired from there to the satisfaction of all concerned I think and now writes for an aircraft corporation. Anyway, this is interesting for the symposium. I immediately wrote off for a subscription.

When I saw The Mechanical Bride before it had fairly arrived, I said to myself—hate at first sight, no doubt. Then later I wondered how you could tell it wasn't your kind of thing on such a quick perusal. Then when I saw you had decided it was comic, I began to understand. No mam, it isn't comic or meant to be and it isn't sociology or written by a sociologist. To be understood, it has to be read completely and slowly, as McLuhan has a packed style. I will admit that occasionally he says something crudely funny—as when he calls the hero of the ad "Big Barnsmell"—this seems just right to me I must admit but it's not why I appreciate the book. Also you can omit the little captions by the pictures. The meat is in the text and has to be read carefully. McLuhan teaches English at some Canadian Catholic college or used to the last I heard. A friend of mine was telling me that there is a fictional portrait of him in Wyndham Lewis' novel, Self-Condemmed. Apparently McLuhan was very kind to Lewis when Lewis was in Canada during the war. I first came across McLuhan in an article on Southern writers in the Southern Vanguard and was taken by it. I see he occasionally has an article in Thought but I will be looking around for something shorter of his that may make a better impression on you.

The fellow who wants to make the movie arrived. He's never made a movie before but he envisions The River as just the thing for a low cost movie made by him. My agent is opposed to the whole idea but I rather liked the man. He stuttered. But we shall see. Anyway, I have just sold the television rights to the Life You Save May Be Your Own to what I understand is called The General Electric Playhouse. All I know about television is hearsay but somebody told me that this was a production conducted by Ronald Regan (?). I don't know if this means RR will be Mr. Shiflet or not. A staggering thought. Mr. Shiflet and the idiot daughter will no doubt go off in a Chrisler and live happily ever after. Anyway, on account of this, I am buying my mother a new refrigerator. While they make hash out of my story, she and me will make ice in the new refrigerator.

Yours,

To A.

Milledgeville

Dear A.,   17 November 56

What you say about Self-Condemned and the last paragraph seems very true. His mother said early in the book, "Don't be a fool, son," and in spite of his sympathy with Rene, Lewis was with her all the way; but he's a rationalist through and through I guess. According to Ashley, McKenzie is a portrait of your friend McLuhan, Herbert Marshall, who was very good to Lewis when he was in Canada. I'm more interested in the way Lewis writes than what he has to say. Sometimes as you say it's very tedious but when he moves, he moves. Have you seen the collection of stories, Rotting Hill? I liked it.

The scrollgiving was very funny though it was not intended to be. I sat next to Byron and drug a few words out of him. He is about the size of a telephone pole split lengthwise and I noticed for the first time what a peculiar *color* he is. When he visited us in the evening, he looked more or less white. At this dinner, he was a kind of dark dead red, as if he had been burnt out from the inside, maybe the effect of the TB or maybe just the lights. The audience was mostly old ladies. First they ate and then they gave out the prize money—450 bucks given out by tens, twenties and fifties. Every winner comes up and gets her envelope. Applause for each. This takes about an hour. Then there is an incredible musical interlude, put on by "composer" A—— —— ——, an ancient in an electric blue quilted-looking wrapper. She has set two poems to music, one by the great Sidney Lanier, the other by our great poet laureate of Georgia, Ollie Reeves. A—— makes a little speech comparing Ollie to Sidney and Ollie says, oh no A——, I'm not in his class at all. You are, she says emphatically, *you are*; now you read your poem before I play it and Joe Holmes sings it for us. The poem is called "That Inner Glow," and he reads it for us, looking quite ashamed of himself. Then A—— seats herself at the grand and Joe (a girl of about 55) sings it for us in a piercing tenor. Then Ollie is told to read Sidney's poem aloud, which he does. Then Sidney's poem gets the same treatment from A—— and Joe. Then the musical interlude is over and we get down to the business of the award winners. Dying Voice is a master of dragging things out. Instead of giving each his scroll and then letting him speak his piece, she has each of us speak our piece, then each is awarded the scroll, then each scroll is read by the person who wrote it, i. e., backwards in slowmotion.

First to speak her piece was Elizabeth Stevenson. She appears to me to be a very nice intelligent scholarly awkward nearsighted girl and I would like to have got to talk to her but I only saw her for a minute afterwards. She had her piece written down on little cards or scraps of paper and she mostly read it from them, looking up and down in an uncomfortable fashion. It was some advice for writers, short and to the point, and she said it in a great hurry as if to get to sit down as quickly as possible. Then came the old lady who wrote the book about Sea Island. She was a handsome old girl, was used to talking and enjoyed herself hugely and I am sure if she hadn't been told to make it brief, she would have been standing there at it now. Then came Byron who, said Dying Voice, was being honored with his fourth scroll. Lucky Boy. He read four poems; if I recall one was about poverty, one was about death, one about old age and the last about general decay. It was quite a relief after That Inner Glow.

Then me. I enjoyed myself as much as the old lady from Sea Island but was much briefer. Each of us, of course, was preceded by a flowery introduction by Dying Voice. Then the scrolls were actually awarded, that is they were read by the person who wrote them. The old lady from Sea Island embraced the old lady who read hers, kissed her on the cheek and wiped away a tear. Finally it was over, but when these things are over, they are just beginning as each and every one comes up and says a politeness to you and you shake more hands than Estes Kefauver. I must say I'm very good at it though—I expose every tooth in my head and insist that they all come to see me down on the farm. The next morning we got out of Atlanta immediately after breakfast with great thanksgiving to be departing. The only time I enjoy Atlanta is when I'm leaving it.

At this thing I also met the Atl. girl who has just written the book—Blue River. She's pleasant and unpretentious and last Friday as she was at Wesleyan, she came over here and we had lunch together. She sent me the book and told me that it is NOT a good book and that if I told her it was, she wouldn't believe me and that if I told her the truth it would kill her. The book seems to me to be an example of a talent that hasn't found itself and probably won't, though there are three or four of the stories that I consider successful. A great many of them are an unfortunate combination of the bizarre and the trite rather well reported. However, I wrote her which I like and why and didn't say much about the rest of it. If you're interested, I'll send it to you. It's short.

There was great excitement here yesterday. A Holstein cow elected to leap into the water trough—which is concrete, about five feet deep and three feet wide and four feet high. She was found apparently several hours after she came to this decision. She was on her side more or less with one or two feet sticking out and she was swollen tight in there. The wrecker was called and a rope somehow got under her and she was hauled out. My mother tells this story better than I.

You are right of course about not understanding the ordinary emotions any better than the extraordinary ones. But the writer doesn't have to understand, only reproduce. And what makes him reproduce is not having the experience but contemplating the experience and contemplating it don't mean understanding it so much as understanding that he doesn't understand it. Where conservatism comes into this I haven't decided. I certainly have no idea how I have written about some of the things I have, as they are things I am not conscious of having thought about one way or the other. Experiences must have some parallel relationship. This must have some connection with the analogical way of seeing. The enclosed is what I am going to say at Wesleyan in December and I touch on this here and there. I manage to be dogmatic about it, in fact. I am sending you this speech without even reading it over I am so sick of it. I don't seem to get out of one before I am into another. Now it is Emory. They are having some courses in their winter quarter—a different writer every week—Byron, Harnet Kane(!), Paul Boles, Lillian Smith (!) and me and Lord knows who else but in other words a zoo, featuring a different animal every week. I wrote the man that as far as I was concerned this was entertainment and not education. However, the people at Emory have been rather nice to me and if I use old stuff, it shouldn't be much of a pain.

I have other things to say but they can wait and you will have had enough of this incoherence.

Yours,

Post Scriptum 11/18/56

I wish you could come but I respect your reasons. Perhaps what I should have said is that you are more than your history. I don't believe the fundamental nature changes but that it's put to a different use when a conversion occurs and of course it requires vigilance to put it to the proper use. What will happen to Billy remains to be seen. I can't decide whether he is supported by faith or excitement or a mixture of both but I gather that those two stories you saw are now on the way to me. He has an awed respect for what he calls "your belligerent honesty," so I suppose you went pretty deep into it with him, and maybe I am just suppose to lick the wounds. However, I aim to stay strictly within the confines of the story and I pray to the good Lord that there will be something good about them. I am loath to see all of Thanksgiving day spent discussing these stories so I have invited the Jesuit who rides with Ridley and a Mr. Cheney who is a great talker and his wife who is also a great talker. This is going to be a case of four conversational bulldozers grinding eachother to a halt maybe. We shall see.

Look in your last Commonweal and see a poem by a girl named Carol Johnson. She is the only writer I ever initiated a correspondence with. Caroline put me onto her poems which have appeared from time to time in the Sewanee Review. She was not a Catholic but was a student at St. Catherine's College in Minnesota, run by the Sisters of St. Joseph of Corondelet, and according to Caroline she was the only girl they ever graduated and told never to come back. She was "difficult." I don't know how. Anyway, the year after she graduated from there, back she came, a Catholic and wanting to join the order. She had been a great reader of Rimbaud and announced that she had followed Rimbaud as far as he went and had found herself, much against her will, at the Church. She therefore entered, with I presume, love and a profound distaste. When I first wrote her about a year ago, she was Sister Marya. I wrote her that I had read her poems and thought they were real poetry though I didn't know anything about poetry and I sent her a copy of A Good Man. I liked her letters very much. They didn't sound like any Sister of St. Joseph I had ever heard from before. We only exchanged a letter or two and then I didn't hear from her again but last week I did and she is out of the convent—"having followed my vocation where it seemed to lead and out again"—but still a Catholic and doing graduate work and teaching at Marquette. Anyway, I think hers is the poetry to watch.

Last year Ashley told me there was a very funny piece in The Chicago Review by a young man who had been an inmate of the Handy Institution for a while, as long as he could stand it. Ashley's description was just about like what appeared in Time so I presume that they lifted it from the boy without troubling to mention his name. I read three pages of FHTE and decided I could live a useful life without it.

To Sally and Robert Fitzgerald

Milledgeville
Georgia

Dear S&R,   10 December 56

We were real glad to hear from you and get the picture of the large and sturdy brood. They look like a formidable crew and I hope you have gained a few pounds. I think you should each weigh about a hundred and eighty so your mere presence will scare hell out of them and you never have to resort to violence of word or deed. This is my theoretical contribution to child care and development.

I enclose a little morality play of mine for your Christmas cheer but as it is not very cheerful, I'd advise you to leave off reading it until after the season. It's sold to the Partisan Review but any criticism would be appreciated because I can still make corrections before they get around to using it. I'm looking forward to getting my year's batch of Telemacus.

My mama is thinking about getting a Hungarian family. We still have the Poles but they are mighty trying and trifling at this point. She will not let them go but they do very little. The question will be how many mixtures can you add to the broth without its exploding.

I have just learned via one of those gossip columns that the story I sold for a TV play is going to be put on in the spring and that a *tap-dancer* by the name of Gene Kelly is going to make his tellyvision debut in it. The punishment always fits the crime. They must be going to make a musical out of it. This is the story about Mr. Shiftlet who marries the old woman's idiot daughter.

Lon Cheney spent last weekend with us and he said the Tates had decided again not to live together. Caroline is in Princeton. This is a simpliste explanation but I insist on thinking that a lot of their troubles would be lessened if they both took to drinking *only* unfermented beverages.

I am fine but still on the crutches, of course. However, after the last x-rays the scientist has definitely decided that it is not lupus of the bone but just a roughening of the bone, about which nothing can be done except to continue on the crutches. Which don't bother me none.

Merry Christmas from us both.

To A.

                                                    Milledgeville
Dear A.,   12/11/56
This Chicago magazine (sent it separate) is being lent me by Ben Griffith, the man who admires the respective works of me and James Jones, but I can't resist sending it to you as I'm sure he won't mind. G. wrote an article on Jones in the Georgia Review. I didn't see it but I think it was called "A Backwoods Robin Hood," or something like that, though *backwoods* don't sound right. Should you ever run across it in your researches, do gimme a report. Griffith is a nice little man but he has his head full of myth and symbol. This article on the Handy Institute is by the same boy Ashley read, though not the same article, probably a condensation. Anyway it's hard to see why Mrs. Handy and her boys shouldn't stay dead and buried after what he's done to them here.

Also enclosed are the four letters I've had from CJ. I can't see an escape from *that* order for *her* as a defeat. I bet she was like a hyena in a cage full of doves there. Either she would have gone plumb slap nuts or she would have just dried up and blown away. But doubtless she learned something there that will do her in good stead for whatever she has to face outside. Of the books she mentions, the only one I have is the New Tower of Babel if you'd be interested.

* * *

It remains to be seen whether we see me in America or not. It seems that Fr. McCown sent a copy of my talk to the Macon girls to Harold C. SJ. I had sent it to Fr. McCown before I gave it to make sure it was theologically correct, as I wanted to be on firm ground with these old biddies. After considerable time Harold C. writes me that he would like to condense it (himself) for America. Well, I can see where it would have to be condensed, but I can't see me letting Harold C condense it. If my name is going to be attached to it, I am the one that is going to do the condensing. The which, in politer terms, I wrote him; and have not heard again. So we shall see. I showed Fr. McCown the letter I wrote him and asked if he thought it might hurt Fr. Gardiner's feelings, if they were delicate. He said no, you ought to just tell him to keep his dirty red pencil off your manuscript. That was about three weeks ago and no reply.

Your letter about The Forest of the South immediately put my sins before me: I had never read The Forest of the South. Only Old Red in an anthology. So I called the college librarian and asked her if she had it and she did and I went and got it, and so I am now up with you enough to be able to say that I have read Summer Dust. The first thing that hit me in the face was the child's quoting the Bible verse—"He who calls his brother a fool is subject to hell's fire." Mary Fortune quoted the exact verse in A View of the Woods. Now I am in a quandary as to whether I should change that in A View of the Woods. What do you think? I find it effective there and I hate the thought of having to take it out. Caroline has read the story and didn't mention it. She probably never dreams that Old Red is all of her stories I had read. Some prediction of hell for the old man is essential to my story. This has never come up before. What do you think?

But to get on to Summer Dust—it's a good example I guess of what you would call an impressionistic short story. You read it and then you have to sit back and let your mind blend it together—like those pictures that you have to get so far away from before they come together. She is a great student of Flaubert and is great on getting things there so concretely that they can't possibly escape—note how that horse goes through that gate, the sun on the neck and then on the girl's leg and then she turns and watches it slide off his rump. That is real masterly doing, and nobody does it any better than Caroline. You walk through her stories like you are walking in a complete real world. And watch how the meaning comes from the things themselves and not from her imposing anything. Right when you finish reading that story, you don't think you've read anything but the more you think about it the more it grows.

I haven't read enough to know much what she does with her men but I would think from Old Red that she makes a contrast between the kind of man her father was, the Aleck Maury, and the kind of man Allen is—the kind who has to come to the surface when he's spoken to. She is saying the Aleck M. kind is the more complete certainly and I don't doubt but what she's right.

Last weekend Lon Cheney spent here. He is a contemporary of the Tates and he told me about their present deciding not to live together. He says Allen is a spoiled brat and there is not much for it, one side of his character is the man-of-genius and the other side the spoiled brat. But from my own observation I deduce another culprit, namely liquor. I guess they just don't see anything wrong with drinking (both of them) as much as they do, but the Lord knows it creates a terrible waste, waste of time, waste of talent, waste of spiritual energy, waste of existence. It must come from some misunderstanding about the nearness of God. You get drunk when you aren't conscious that God is immediately present. I mean that is the only time it would seem possible to get drunk. According to Lon Cheney, the best of Caroline's novels is None Shall Look Back. I haven't read it, but he says the unnamed adversary is Death in it and it is all understatement which is Caroline's specialty.

Last spring a quarterly by the name of Critique published an entire issue on Caroline. I had a copy and lent it to Billy and he made three trips here expressly to return it, forgetting it on each one. So I wrote him last week to put it in an envelope and mail it to you. There are some things in it you may enjoy. Of course Billy has probably lost it but it won't hurt him to look it up. I am in no hurry for it whatsoever if he does send it to you. Never lend a book to a man as you will have to set a stick of dynamite under him before you get it back. I'll probably get a frantic letter saying he has misplaced it.

I am very handy with my advice and then when anybody appears to be following it, I get frantic. Anyway, the thought of your writing something—anything—as a kind of exercise has got me down. It may just be the word exercise. Experiment but for heaven sakes don't go writing exercises. You will never be interested in anything that is just an exercise and there is no reason you should. Don't do anything that you are not interested in and that don't have a promise of being whole. This doesn't mean you have to have a plot in mind. You would probably do just as well to get that plot business out of your head and start simply with a character or anything that you can make come alive, when you have a character he will create his own situation and his situation will suggest some kind of resolution as you get into it. Wouldn't it be better for you to discover a meaning in what you write than to impose one? Nothing you write will lack meaning because the meaning is in you.

Once you have done a first draft then read it and see what it says and then see how you can bring out better what it says. If I don't shut up I will get to sounding like Lowney Handy.

I have taken out the whole last paragraph of A View of the Woods and changed the ending so that the old man has more time to realize what he has done, and I've left it on an image of the trees walking across the water and on. When I get it copied again, I will send it to you for a Christmas card but let me know if you think this ending is an improvement. There is still time for me to mess with it yet—and I may have to take out the Bible quotation.

The talk in Macon went over very well, at least with those who were interested enough in the first place to listen. You are right that I can't do too much of this kind of thing but when you refuse you always feel bad about it. Last month I declined to talk to the Rotarians. I just couldn't face the Rotarians. It would have taken me twice as long to prepare something suitable for the Rotarians as for Wesleyan or Emory; but nevertheless my conscience hurt me and my mother would have liked for me to do it etc etc.

The man who lives with the family of bears reminds me of Cal Lowell who has an imaginary friend named Arms, a policeman, kind of half man and half bear. Arms of the Law, he calls him, and Arms says all the outrageous things that Cal is too polite to say. That man sounds very nice.

I am writing my agent to make haste and sell all my stories for musical comedies. There ought to be enough tap dancers around to take care of them, and there's always Elvis Presley.

Momento mori.

To A.

Milledgeville
Dear A.,   28 December 56

The Lord knows I never expected to own the Notebooks of Simone Weil. This is almost something to live up to; anyway, reading them is one way to try to understand the age. I intend to find that Time with her picture (some weeks ago) and cut out the picture and stick it in the front. That face gives a kind of reality to the notes. I am more than a little obliged to you. These are books that I can't begin to exhaust, and Simone Weil is a mystery that should keep us all humble, and I need it more than most. Also she's the example of the religious consciousness without a religion which maybe sooner or later I will be able to write about.

You were good to read AVOTW again and if you are like me you are now thoroughly sick of it; however, it ain't over until it is finished and I am always long in finishing anything. The first point is whether Pitts is or can be a Christ symbol. I had that role cut out for the woods. Pitts is a pathetic figure by virtue of the fact that he beats his child to ease his feelings about Mr. Fortune. He is a Christian and a sinner, pathetic by virtue of his sin. And I don't feel that a Christ figure can be pathetic by virtue of his sins. Pitts and Mary Fortune realize the value of the woods, and the woods, if anything, are the Christ symbol. They walk across the water, they are bathed in a red light, and they in the end escape the old man's vision and march off over the hills. The name of the story is a view of the woods and the woods alone are pure enough to be a Christ symbol if anything is. Part of the tension of the story is created by Mary Fortune and the old man being images of each other but opposite in the end. One is saved and the other is dammed and there is no way out of it, it must be pointed out and underlined. Their fates are different. One has to die first because one kills the other, but you have read it wrong if you think they die in different places. The old man dies by her side; he only thinks he runs to the edge of the lake, that is his vision. I changed the verb to the conditional which makes that clearer now. He runs in imagination. I have thought that since the old last-paragraph was only an appendage anyhow, that it might be added to the new ending, but I don't really think it does anything for it. You can see what you think. I also changed the sentence that was confusing. And spelled them words right. I don't see how you can tell about the words. Dain looks just as good to me as deign. In fact better.

I ought to defend poor Powers. I don't take him as meaning it was a mistake to kill Mrs. May for a short story, but only that I should have left her alive so that I could write a novel about her. Powers' instincts are too good on what to do with short stories for him to mean anything else; besides, he was only giving half a mind to it and being pleasant. And I ought to defend myself against the charge of producing in this second ending something "slick." I only worry in these things about serving my own artistic conscience, not a mythical set of admirers who expect a certain thing. God and posterity are only served with well-made articles.

Apropos of the Christ image business, the fall issue of Cross Currents has an essay on The Idiot as a Christ symbol by Msgr. Guardini. I ordered you a subscription to it and told them to make it retro what you call it to the fall issue. Yesterday I get an extra copy of the fall issue, I don't know if they just made a mistake or not. Anyway, if you don't get a fall issue of it before long, let me know. They are a very slipshod organization and it takes months for them to do anything and then like as not they do it backwards.

In my novel I have a child—the school teacher's boy— whom I aim to have a kind of Christ image, though a better way to think of it is probably just as a kind of redemptive figure. None of this may work however; but I have made some progress these last three months or think I have.

I am still reading Caroline's stories. I see where Mr. Maury gets a mite irritating, a mite cute at times. Too much of Mr. Maury.

You are probably right about the liquor, but I don't mean they stay drunk, I mean they just have to step down one step to reach the ground all the time.

You had better send the Chicago magazine back to me as I didn't inform him I was going to send it to anybody else. I guess the author suffers from youth and the University of Chicago but obviously it is Illinois that saves them—and Harry or whatever his name was. I would like to visualize Harry, after years of not knowing what ails him, suddenly being possessed with the idea of hurling a bomb into the colony one day. He does and feels fine ever after.

Harold C. Gardiner SJ has not seen fit to answer my communication of November 22.

I have just refused to address the Southern Speech Association at their anyul April 4.

I have never heard from O. Henry.

A letter from my agent today announces that The Life You Save will be presented February 1 on the Schlitz Playhouse at 9:30 New York Time. My eager beaver friend in NY keeps sending me clippings of gossip columns, one announcing that Kelly will star in Flannery O'Connor's "backwoods love story." Another saying Kelly says "it's a kind of hillbilly thing in which I play a guy who *befriends* a deaf mute girl in the hills of Kentucky. It gives me a great chance to do some straight acting, something I really have no opportunity to do in movies." See? He ain't had the opportunity before. There'll be no singing & dancing, Kelly says. I think it's chanel 5 and people tell me you can't get it very good here, so I hope you will absolutely be in front of your set this time at the correct hour, as I must have some representative there to give Kelly a good leer every now and then for me. I don't know who his leading lady will be, but doubtless my NY friend will be providing that information before long. She thinks this is all hilariously funny and keeps writing me, "Has dignity no value for you?" etc. It will probably be appropriate to smoke a corn cob pipe while watching this. All my kin folks are going to think that it is a great improvement over the original story.

29 December

Correction: O. Henry sent me the money this morning. Now we will see what Greenleaf is subjected to by the people who review the book.

I am glad you are working on the long thing. I like that length myself but it is never wise to decide before hand what length a thing will be. It will be as long as it takes to do it. Oh. I found out in the course of Billy's conversation that the version of his dance story that I saw was shown to me after he had corrected it by your strictures. This may be why I didn't think it was as bad as you did.

I will keep in the Bible quotation in AVOTW. All I needed was the strong voice of encouragement. I sometimes suffer from literary scruples.

I have two books that I think would help you in your writing—not immediately perhaps but in the long run—but I won't send them unless you want me to. One is a book by Percy Lubbock called, The Craft of Fiction. This sounds like a how-to-do-it book but it is not: a very profound study of point of view. Lubbock is a Jamesian. The other is a text book I used at Iowa. It is pure textbook and very uninviting and part of the value of it for me was that I had it in conjunction with Paul Engle who was able to breathe some life into it; but even without him, it might help you some—called Understanding Fiction, Brooks&Warren.

Well, a happy new year and more thanks than I can tell you for the many things you have done for me, for Baron von Hugel and Simone Weil but even more for your own letters.

Yours,

To Sally and Robert Fitzgerald

Milledgeville
Georgia

Dear S&R,   1 January 56

The sweater, the like of which I have never seen before, arrived yesterday and I assure you that no day from now until the hot weather will see me outside of it. It's the answer to an uninsolated house and I have told my mother she needn't bother to chink up the cracks around in the windows in here with newspaper this year. Do all the I-talians go about in these garments or is it a new invention? It couldn't be better for my needs and purposes and I do thank you no end.

I was also much taken with the poem and if it hasn't appeared before over here, it ought to. The Commonweal has an occasional poem of John Logan's and of that girl that the Tates were interested in—Carol Johnson. She was Sister Marya but last year she got out of the convent and now she has an assistanceship at Marquette. She is a correspondent of mine—occasionally—and I imagine that in that convent the poor girl felt like a hyena in a cageful of doves. Anyway, it would be nice to see something of yours gracing the Commonweal as it could frequently stand a little gracing. Their reviews are getting worser and worser, though there's an occasional good one.

That lay committee to advise Cardinal Spellman on how to keep his feet out of his mouth should certainly reorganize. He is at it again, this time over a movie called "Baby Doll," a dirty little piece of trash by Tennessee Williams, which he is on good ground in condemning but not the way he did it. The rector of the Episcopal Cathedral (Pike) immediately answered him in a sermon, pointing out that Baby Doll was no more obscene than "The Ten Commandments" which the Cardinal had recommended highly.

I have got the O.Henry prize this year—$300—for the thing that was in the Kenyon this summer. I keep hearing that Mr. Ransom is going to retire and go back to Nashville but I don't believe it.

I was not satisfied with the ending of that story I sent you for Christmas and have redone the last paragraph, which I enclose just for the record.

We haven't got the Hungarians. She keeps dragging along with the Matysiaks. She gave the old man a pair of glasses this Christmas that cost her $19 but as she said, he never said Thank you or Merry Christmas or kiss-my-foot. She also gave him a shirt and he came over with it on and, she said, stood there grinning at her. So after a while she says, "Well how do you like your shirt?" He pulls at the collar and says, "Leetle bit too beeg." "Well," she says, "you just grow to it." I think she sometimes feels for the Russians.

Our best for the new year and my awed thanks for the sweater.

Cheers,

To Maryat Lee

Milledgeville
A Bird Sanctuary
Dear Maryat,   9 January 57

A few days after you left, my mother and I saw Emmet rolling down the street. He looked as if he were in the state of euphoria that follows being psychodramatized, and I decided that you had had them at that all the way to Atlanta. I find it mighty hard to imagine any conversation that might have taken place in that car. When you left, my mother said to me, "Don't you tell a soul that she is going in *Emmet's* car. Don't you even tell Sister. If that got out, it would ruin Dr. Lee." A few days ago, Dr. Lee called Sister to find out something and Sister asked him if you got there all right with Emmet. "Oh," he said, "she went with friends." Sister later told us that you hadn't gone with Emmet after all, that you had gone with *friends* and that SHE thought that was much better. I think Dr. Lee will last a long time here; in fact as long as he cares to last.

It is often so funny that you forget it is also terrible. Once about ten years ago while Dr. Wells was president, there was an education meeting held here at which two Negro teachers or superintendents or something attended. The story goes that every thing was as separate and equal as possible, even down to two Coca Cola machines, white and colored; but that night a cross was burned on Dr. Wells' side lawn. And those times weren't as troubled as these. The people who burned the cross couldn't have gone past the fourth grade but for the time, they were mighty interested in education.

Our "contact"—on the strength I guess of having done me one favor by seeing that I got introduced to you—forthwith sent me four more poems to criticize. The next time you come we will get you out here before you are ready to leave. Incidentally, neither my mother nor I was conscious of any rudeness. However, the parental presence never contributes to my articulateness, and I might have done better at answering some of your questions had I entertained you in the hen house. That's a place I would like to keep two cane-bottomed chairs in if there were any way to keep the chickens from sitting on them in my absence. My ambition is to have a private office out there complete with refrigerator. My mother's contention would be that my own room looks enough like a chicken pen that I ought to be satisfied.

I'm glad you liked the stories of mine you read and felt that they weren't a dead-end taken. Many's the dead-end I have taken, however, but the results of those trips are I hope in the trashcan. I suppose you come to know yourself as much by what you throw away as what you keep and at times it is appalling. I wonder if you can have thought the dead-end a likely possibility for me because of the orthodoxy, which I remember you said was a ceiling you had come through? I take it that what you have come through is some expression of orthodoxy. I have come through several of those myself, always with a deepened sense of mystery and always several degrees more orthodox.

Meanwhile, I'll be looking forward to reading the play and to hearing from you when you are inclined to write me and to seeing you out here again under more lesurely (sp?) circumstances.

Yours,

I hope you go to see that Godot with the all Negro cast!

To Elizabeth Bishop

Andalusia
Milledgeville, Ga.
13 January 57

Dear Miss Bishop,

You were very kind to write me and it means considerable to me to know that you have read and liked my stories. The stories are, by now, much better travelled than I am, as I have never been out of the United States and have been few places in it. Every now and then I get some perception of how they might be taken by someone out of the country and it is a revelation that enlarges my own view. I hadn't realized that life in Brazil might resemble life here in the South but I guess there are many similarities. We have a lot of students who come here from South America. A friend of mine who taught a special course designed for them and their problems with English told me he found them much disgruntled at having to read the short stories he assigned. "Why do we have to read stories like these?" one of them asked him. "Nobody gets married in them." Which is an attitude I am right familiar with from hearing my connections estimate my own work.

You were good to mention them to the editor of Revista Contemporanea and I would like to see some of them used. There is a French translation in the making but that is the only one. They have received a little critical attention in Italy; at least, Robert Fitzgerald, who is now living in Genova, sent me a translation of an essay on Miss Eudora Welty's stories and mine, done by Mario Praz, the Romantic Agony man. He described the story called "A Circle in the Fire" in such a way that I barely recognized it but otherwise he appeared to know what they were about and to approve. He had apparently once visited Savannah which he described as "a city of decayed 19th century elegance, negro shacks, suffocating heat, lugubrious large trees draped with 'Spanish moss' and innumerable mosquitoes."

Once Cal Lowell showed me a picture of you (I am supposing the same Miss Bishop) sitting on a porch in Florida; he left me with the vague notion (how much owing to him and how much to my imagination I don't know) that you travelled up and down the coast, sort of with the seasons. If that is the case and you ever pass by here or near us, my mother and I would be so pleased to have you stop and visit us. She and I live in the country a few miles outside of Milledgeville. The place is a dairy farm and I am glad to say that most of the violences carried to their logical conclusions in the stories manage to be warded off in fact here—though most of them exist in potentiality. We have a Polish displaced family and are now dickering to get a Hungarian family as well. We have two sets of colored people and up until a year ago we had some good country people too, but they couldn't stand the Poles and so decamped. Off and on we find ourselves with some not so good country people but they are the type always on the move and we never have them for long.

Thank you again for writing me. I have a great respect for your own work though I am almost too ignorant ever to know why I like what I like. I used to live with the Fitzgeralds in Connecticut and I remember that Robert always spoke of you with great admiration.

Sincerely,

To Maryat Lee

Milledgeville
24 February 57

Dear Maryat,

Your brother was not only there, he introduced me—as one who had been on and off the best seller lists. I decided this was an innocent calumniation and ignored it.

I tried to decide if any of your agents could be mine— Mavis McIntosh and Elizabeth McKee. Miss McIntosh is an old lady who sits at her desk with her hat on and Miss McKee is a youngish lady who speaks out of the side of her mouth like a refined dead-end kid. Should you run onto them give them my regards.

Thanks for the Atkinson review. How weird to think that he would consider the cliche about the room from which faith had gone being like the marriage from which love had gone as sensitive! My my. What I would like to know is what did Walter Kerr say about Potting Shed?

If you have Voices you'd better listen to them and let the form take care of itself. What does this appear to be heading up to—fiction you mean? I was startled at first when you asked me here something about how or where I got my material. At Emory they had a list of questions for me to answer and the first one was: Do you write from imagination or experience? My inclination at such a point is always to get deathly stupid and say, "Ah jus writes." This has anyway never occurred to me except as a theoretical consideration, of no concern to anybody seriously engaged in the act of writing. I draw the line at any kind of research and even object to looking up words in the dictionary. I think you probably collect most of your experience as a child—when you really had nothing else to do—and then transfer it to other situations when you write. The first story I wrote and sold was about an old man who went to live in a New York slum—no experience of mine as far as old men and slums went, but I did know what it meant to be homesick. I couldn't though have written a story about *my* being homesick.

I wish I had Voices anyway, or anyway distinct voices. I have something that might be a continuing muttering snarl like cats courting under the house, but no clear Voice in years.

If you ever get in front of the television and you wish to see one of my stories rouged for an elegant interment, be in front of some set on Friday, March 1, 9:30 PM NY time for the Schlitz Playhouse of Stars. Channel 5

At Emory they had a little dinner party before I talked, a table full of College Liberals. One gent said, "I'm working with a group on interpersonal relations." Somebody asked what interpersonal relations were and one of the novelists said, "He means niggers and whitefolks."

Cheers,

To George Haslam

Milledgeville

Dear George: 2 March 57

Well I have seen the production and I thought it was slop of the third water. I aver that everybody connected in any way with it, except me, had a stinking pole cat for both mother and father.

It was *well* received here in the Bird Sanctuary and everybody thinks that I have now arrived.

Cheers anyway and regards to May.

Best,

To A.

Milledgeville
Dear A.,   9 March 57
This new ending is right. Just right. And as I stack the whole thing up in my head it seems to me that the whole thing must be just right now. I suggested sending two out at a time but reconsidering it I don't much see why you don't go on and send this one out by itself. I am not so sure that anyplace will take it because I think the Mass scene might scare them off; however, the purpose of sending it around would be to show various people that you CAN write stories. After reading this, they will remember you and be interested to see the next one. Somebody might even take it. If I were doing it, I would first send it to Mrs. Arabel J. Porter, New World Writing, 501 Madison Avenue, New York City. If you will, I'll write her that it is coming so she will look at it herself. When she sends it back to you, I would send it to Epoch or Accent or the University of Kansas City Review, addresses of which I will furnish you, if you want them. This process of sending things out and getting them back depresses some people but it is necessary for a certain length of time. Don't send any letter with the manuscript, just a stamped self-addressed return envelope, and always when you get it back, send it back out again the same day or the next. Practical advice from Practical Annie, the Writer's Friend.

Well, how did you like THAT picture in the bulletin? They will all think that if my face is habitually that dirty I should not be writing for a Cathlick paper. This I will say for Eileen: when she doesn't know what to say for herself, she quotes somebody who does.

Yours truly is speaking at Notre Dame University on April 15 and those Jesuits are paying me a hundred bucks and my plane fare; also I will get to see Robert who will meet me in Chicago. And that so help me will be the last talking I am going to do this season.

Yes I saw the television play. The college librarian who is a great friend had a supper party—me and six local old ladies and my mamma—and then we repaired to Sister's to see the play. All the old ladies were entranced. They thought it was the sweetest thing they had ever seen. All over town old ladies were gathered to witness it. And other groups too. Immediately it was over, the telephone rang and a friend of the family said, "Three generations of S——s have just watched your television play and we were all spellbound!" My mother has been collecting congratulations all week like eggs in a basket. Several children have stopped me on the street and complimented me. Dogs who live in houses with television have paused to sniff me. The local city fathers think I am a credit now to the community. One old lady said, "That was a play that really made me think!" I didn't ask her what. As for me I stood the play a good deal better than I am standing the congratulations.

Sent you the book on Fenelon and the Edith Stein. Never any hurry about these and don't feel you have to read them just because they are sent. Also have a copy of PR with Cal Lowell's first chapter of his autobiography in it to send.

Mr. Matysiack is gone and one Mr. P—— is installed. Mr. P——'s family consists of himself, wife, two babies, mother and daddy, whose name is Buster. According to Mr. P——, "There ain't a thang wrong with daddy but two thangs, heart trouble and asmer." And Mr. P—— says he has heart trouble hisself, that sometimes he gets down and don't have the heart to get up. Mr. P—— is twenty-four years of age but looks older. His wife is probably about eighteen. She dips and he chews. His mother is separated from Buster but also separated from her second husband so she has returned to Mr. P——'s hearth. According to Mr. P—— her second husband hit her in the stomach so hard that she had to be carried to the hospital. Mr. P—— went to see him about this and told him that if he did it again that he would get two or three others and they would come and lynch him. My mother said she reckoned Mr. P—— didn't really mean that but Mr. P—— said yesm he did. He said he figured it that no matter how strong a woman was, she wasn't no match for a man and any man that come picking on any woman, Mr. P—— wouldn't care if he lynched him or not. Therefore we are expecting to be adequately protected if nothing else. English is flowing freely now for the first time in three years. Mr. P—— talks every minute that he is not spitting or that my

mother is not talking. He also gets along very well with Jack
and Shot. My mother told him that she wasn't going to hire
anybody who would hit her negroes in the head and Mr.
P—— said he didn't believe in doing nothing to nobody else
that he wouldn't want done to him. The other morning Mr.
P——'s wife would not get up and cook his breakfast and
Mr. P—— told her she could get up and cook it or she could
get up and get the hell out of there. My mother told him she
didn't want any fussing and feuding going on on our place
and Mr. P—— said wouldn't be none go on. Mr. P—— has
been on "public works" and so he hasn't been eating too regularly and is very glad to have the job. And we are very glad
to have Mr. P——.

Billy is absolved for the false impression and I will take it
on myself. He is going to talk in Macon on the 15th and the
next day come to dinner, bringing Fr. McCown. Fr. McCown
called Billy up to call off the talk but Billy persuaded him not
to call it off.

My agent's seccetary has just written me that she saw the
tv play and thought it "was as close to the original story as
it could possibly have been"—which must mean she hasn't
read the original. Anyway, she allowed that they were going
to query Rogers and Hammerstein and see if they would
like to do a musical adaptation. I can't decide if this was supposed to be a joke or not. I rather think not. I would rather
see it a musical than what it was on that tv program.

> The life you save may be your own
> Hand me that there tellyphone
> Hideho and hip hooray
> I am in this thang for pay.

I will submit same to Rogers and Hammerstein.

Cheers,

To Maryat Lee

Milledgeville
Dear Maryat,   10 March 57
The enclosed is for you to read on the Japanese freighter. I
have heard about these freighters—you eat eleven times a day

and all is elegance. Your companions according to my speculations will be wealthy widows and widowers and retired school teachers and there will be parlor games. Let me know if I am right.

The following is good Georgia advice: don't marry no foreigner. Even if his face is white, his heart is black.

Thanks for offering to let me use your apartment but I don't think on crutches I am up to the city alone and I intend this summer to try to force this novel somewhat. I am going to Notre Dame to talk on April 15, and so I have stopped to write that talk, but when that is over, I aim to get at it, and stay at it (two hours a day that is).

For the last ten days I have been sustaining congratulations on "my" television play. Old ladies all over town have told me they thought it was the sweetest play they ever saw. One old lady said it really made her think! I didn't ask her what. Children now point to me on the street. The city fathers think that I have arrived finally. Most think it a great improvement on the original but forbear to say so openly. My agent's secretary wrote me that they were querying Rogers and Hammerstein to see if they would like to do a musical adaptation. I can't decide if she was joking or not. When I think they're joking, they're usually in dead earnest and when I think they're in earnest, they're joking. Anyhow, I thought the production stunk.

Well I'm glad you liked the rest of the stories. The Artificial Nigger is my favorite and probably the best thing I'll ever write. All I seem to be doing these days is writing these stinking talks.

Let me hear about this Japanese freighter, and be sure you book your return passage as there is nothing but cannibals, savages, heathen Chinese and opium parlors in those parts, and we expect you to visit again in Milledgeville, a Bird Sanctuary, where all is culture, graciousness, refinement and bidnis-like common sense.

Meanwhile yours affectionately,

To A.

Milledgeville
Dear A.,   6 April 56

What his Reverence corrected was the paragraph about the responsibility of the artist (I had Mauriac's name to purify the source all right). He changed it to read that the artist would realize that he as well as the Church had a responsibility for souls. I had said that the responsibility for souls was the business of the Church and that the responsibility of the artist was to his art. Now it seems to me that he is correct but that some explanation should be given of how the artist's responsibility for souls operates. Is it, for instance, the same in kind as the responsibility of the Church, is it to children, to idiots, to old ladies, to fifteen year old girls, to unbalanced people? If I had been consulted about this I would have changed the paragraph to suit him, but I would have tried to clarify the other as much as possible. The paragraph seems to slide over the problem to me, and to contradict itself. Just in the paragraph before I had said that this kind of responsibility would turn the artist to stone. He left that as it was. I don't by any means think he is a small or mean man, I think he just sees this as an abstract theoretical problem and from a great distance. Whereas the writer himself is traveling the rocky road, and feels every individual bump.

You needn't worry, I ain't going to perform for the Rotarians & Elks but when something comes up where I am actually asked to do something for the Church, then it is right for me to do it even when it is a drop in the bucket. As for the Bulletin, I've gotten more out of that than I've given and probably will out of this America thing too. Doing these things is doing the only corporal work of mercy open to me. My mother takes care of all the visiting the sick and burying the dead that goes on around here. I can't fast on acct. of what I've got. I can't even kneel down to say my prayers. Every opportunity for performing any kind of charity is something to be snatched at. I have no notion that the artist should be above the common people; the question is who are the common people right now? I confess I don't know. I don't think the Rotarians and Elks are—they look down on the artist. I even dislike the concept *artist* when it sets you above, all it is is working in a certain kind of medium to make something right. The material is no more exalted than any other kind of material and the idea of making it right is what should be applied to all making. St. Thomas said the artist is concerned with the good of that which is made, that art is a good-in-itself. Are you familiar with Art & Scholasticism? I'll send you my copy if you want it. About the only good thing Dr. Johnson had to say about Milton was that he didn't scorn teaching Latin to school boys.

Well I'd like to hear Fr. Ossteriecher but we are always out here at that time on Sunday morning. Let me know how he goes.

Agnes Scott was rather dreary. They had it in a long basement room and set me in the middle of it with the inconsiderable audience strung out the length so that you couldn't possibly make them all hear at once. Then half of them came when I was half through the talk, bang bang and scrape scrape. I don't think the man who introduced me had ever read a word I'd written, but he averred they were very fortunate to have me there. I now await my check for $50.

Now I am sure that I didn't call your story a "study of pride." A story is never a study if it is any good and I took that one to be good. But any story can be looked at in the light of any quality and pride being the most fundamental to human nature, I generally look at characters in the light of it. Further to judge the character is not to judge the story. You think too much of interpreting and analyzing and all that. Learn to write a story and then learn some more from the story you have written. I wrote Arabel and I hope she gets her hands on it. There's no guarantee she will even with my having written her but it more likely.

With forty others, the Confirmation should be got over without undue strain. I am glad I got all my ceremonies over at a numb(er) age.

Mr. P——'s 16 month old son had a recent intestinal spell and my mother asked Mr. P—— what the little boy might have eaten. Mr. P—— allowed that he hadn't eaten nothing out of the way, the night before he had had sausage. Sausage! says my mother. It wasn't the sausage, Mr. P—— said, he's

been eating sausage since he was 6 month old. Mr. P——
said that with some of his paycheck he was going to buy a
second-hand git-tar although he owes money to almost everybody in town. My mother gave him a lecture entitled "A
good name is better than a large bank account," so he agreed
that he would pay his grocery bill first.

All the books have arrived though the packages are so neat
I cannot bring myself to open them.

Mary Sallee sent me the enclosed review which I pass on to
you as you will admire what Belloc said to his electors. Throw
it away when you get through.

I will report on Notre Dame. I don't feel up to the trip but
I have to go. I would like to be there without having to get
there, but I am afraid it can't be arranged.

Yrs,

To A.

Milledgeville

Dear A.,   20 April 57
Enclose you the Notre Dame speech, though there ain't
much new in it. Also Madame Fitzgerald on Gardiner. You
would like Madame FitzG I am sure. The trip was entirely
successful. I escaped the snow by exactly one day and made
all the necessary connections, which was what had me worried. I had thought the speech was to be in the afternoon and
for students, but when I arrived Robt. announced it was to
be 8 PM Monday and a Public Lecture. The room was full
and they had to go out for more chairs. It appeared I was an
object of considerable curiosity, being a writer about "Southern degeneracy" and a Catholic at oncet and the same time.
The audience was not ominously clerical though there was a
sprinkling of baby faces under heavy black berettas. During
the talk I trained my gaze on one of them and he trained his
back on me as if he didn't believe a damm word of it; nevertheless they appeared impressed, though they didn't laugh in
all the right places. After it a girl came up to me and said,
"I'm not a Catholic, I'm a Lutheran but you've given me

some hope for the first time that Catholic writers may do something." I said, "Well please pray that we will." And she said, "I will, I will in Christ." And she meant it and she will and it is that kind of thing that makes these trips worth the effort. I also saw a godchild of mine for the first time who lives in South Bend and a few other people that I am glad to have met.

Naw you didn't say the artist is above the common people, that was just my digression on the subject, but you do seem to exalt him above his place in the scheme of things though it is hard to put my finger on just how. The word "dreams" which you did use, always terrifies me. The artist dreams no dreams. That is precisely what he does not do, as you very well know. Every dream is an obstruction to his work. I have sent you Art & Scholasticism. It's the book I cut my aesthetic teeth on, though I think even some of the things he says get soft at times. He is a philosopher and not an artist but he does have great understanding of the nature of art, which he gets from St. Thomas.

Billy sent his story, which I liked. The truth is that Billy just has a natural gift for imitation and he has considerable technical competence and with the Church, he also has some purpose and point to use these things for. It may however be almost *too* easy a gift, too facile, I don't know but time will tell. I objected to his use of the word "majic" in the paragraph toward the end about confession. I also thought that their sexy talk would have been more effective if there had been less of it but I didn't tell him that as I think I might have thrown him off the track. It don't do to carp about trifles.

A friend of mine in Virginia is going to send me an extra copy he has of THE RED PRIEST. He says Peter Russell (a British bookseller) wrote him that Lewis was dictating a novel before he died, that he would dictate a while, then lapse into a coma, then pick up when he came out of it at exactly where he had left it, but Russell said it was too confused to publish.

Yrs. truly has declined to talk to the Ga. Liberry Association in November.

You are right about the exhaustion but now that I don't have to think about any trip I hope to pick up. I am getting some stinking award from GSCW that I have to say two pages of thanksgiving for but that should be no terrible burden, except that I also have to go to a coffee and a tea for it and shake innumerable paws. These things are fine for the people that like them and the people that don't, as my mother tells me, are just peculiar.

Last Saturday Mary Sallee was in town and we had Mary and Nancy to supper at the same time—these two representing the two opposite poles of human social contrariness. Nancy doggedly kept the conversation in the barnyard but Mary referred to even barnyard affairs with the broad A.

Mrs. Hall is going to the Ga. State Collidge of Bidnis Administration and taking English. Do you suppose we shall soon see a litry influence in the Bulletin? Do not give up reading it now. I look forward to gret things.

Cheers,

To Maryat Lee

Milledgeville

Dear Maryat,   19 May 57

Greetings from historic Milledgeville where the ladies and gents wash in separate tubs. Are you sure you haven't caught anything; what I mean is, the blood disease and all, what I mean is there are certain advantages to being stiff-necked? Unadaptability is often a virtue. If I were in Japan, I would be pretty high by the time I left out of there as I wouldn't have washed during the trip. My standard is: when in Rome, do as you done in Milledgeville.

Last Friday week I stood in a receiving line with your brother and sister-in-law for a good hour, pressing the soggy paws of citizens from all over the state who have daughters in college. Your sister-in-law is a whiz bang at it. The guests had their names pinned on them and she never failed to see the name and say it. As for me, my eye was as glazed as the one on the fish served to Mr. Kawara by the Shinnahon Lines.

Last Sunday the Wesleyan student who wrote me about

you appeared bringing a Miss Wynn and a Miss Stewart, the last I gather being your friend from there. I entertained them by describing your meals on the freighter. By the time you come back, you will be eating nothing but lizards I presume.

Well, you have a decision in front of you if you have to decide whether you will live your whole life with a man. I am sure it requires a metamorphosis for anybody and cannot be done without grace. My prayers are unfeeling but habitual, not to say dogged, and I do include you in them.

I hope you understand that it is not the tooth of the sabor-toothed tiger I want, it is the *tiger*. I don't care if it's a old toothless tiger or not, just so its alive. I intend to start a zoo.

Cheers & affection,

To Cecil Dawkins

Milledgeville
Georgia

Dear Miss Dawkins,   19 May 57

Thank you for writing me—and for mailing the letter. It is fine to know that freshmen are being introduced to contemporary literature somewhere. I had never heard of K. A. Porter or Faulkner or Eudora Welty until I got to graduate school, which may have been time enough for me in as much as I got to graduate school, but so many do not; they leave college thinking that literature is anything written before 1900 and that contemporary literature is anything found on the best-seller list.

I wondered where on that list of writers you introduce them to was Caroline Gordon. Do you know her collection of stories, "The Forest of the South"? I think she is a very fine writer, probably as good as K. A. Porter and a lot better than some of the others.

Of course I hear the complaint over and over that there is no sense in writing about people who disgust you. I think there is; but the fact is that the people I write about certainly don't disgust me entirely though I see them from a standard of judgment from which they fall short. Your freshman who said there was something religious here was correct. I take the Dogmas of the Church literally and this, I think, is what creates what you call the "missing link." The only concern, so far as I see it, is what Tillich calls the "ultimate concern." It is what makes the stories spare and what gives them any permanent quality they may have.

There is really only one answer to the people who complain about one's writing about "unpleasant" people—and that is that one writes what one can. Vocation implies limitation but few people realize it who don't actually practice an art. Your freshman might be improved by a look at Maritain's "Art and Scholasticism." He dwells on St. Thomas' definition of art as a virtue of the practical intellect, etc.

The girl you knew who was from Milledgeville was probably Mary Sallee—a would-be writer friend of mine who went to the University of Alabama to study under Hudson Strode. Milledgeville is a Bird Sanctuary, population 12,000 (people, not birds). I live four miles outside of it on a dairy farm. If you are ever in this direction, stop and see me, and thank you again for writing.

Sincerely,

To Cecil Dawkins

Milledgeville
19 June 57

Dear Cecil, if the Miss can go:

Mary Sallee had supper with us the other night (she lives in Atlanta now but visits periodically) and the subsequent bread and butter letter appears to be more to you than to me so I enclose it.

I had a friend who once applied for a teaching job at Sarah Lawrence and was interviewed and asked what novels she would teach and she named The Portrait of a Lady and suchlike but at everything she named, they said, "That's too hard for the kids." Around here Stevens is thought of as a place where they teach how to behave on dates but I gather from what you say that this must not be entirely so.

I don't really think the standard of judgment, the missing

link, you spoke of that you find in my stories emerges from any religion but Christianity, because it concerns specifically Christ and the Incarnation, the fact that there has been a unique intervention in history. It's not a matter in these stories of Do Unto Others. That can be found in any ethical culture series. It is the fact of the Word made flesh. As the Misfit said, "He thrown everything off balance and it's nothing for you to do but follow Him or find some meanness." That is the fulcrum that lifts my particular stories. I'm a Catholic but this is in orthodox Protestantism also, though out of context—which makes it grow into grotesque forms. The Catholic, using his own eyes and the eyes of the Church (when he is inclined to open them) is in a most favorable position to recognize the grotesque.

If you get to Atlanta, by all means come down. We are two houses from the road on Hwy. 441, four miles before you get to Milledgeville. We have a telephone—2-5335.

Best,

To Maryat Lee

Milledgeville
Dear Maryat,   28 June 57

No I haven't heard anything from the Mansion. The other day I saw yr brother on the sidewalk and he gave me a modified military handwave and said "Hello Flannery," in an impressive voice. I met Dean in the hall of a local eatery and asked her to come to see us but I doubt if she does. Somebody said she was going off July 8.

Well however you work it out, you will continue to have my limp, obfuscating and airless prayers. You are of course entirely right that the reply was inadequate and cliche-ridden. It always will be. These are mysteries that I can in no way approach—except with the coin of the realm which has the face worn off it. I doubtless hate pious language worse than you because I believe the realities it hides. Nevertheless, you do misinterpret me if you think I mean that it all ends in tatattatum and a tragic little pie. I believe in the resurrection of the body. I also believe in it before it gets that way, dear girl, so don't put me down in yr Associate Reformed Presbyterian black books. It's my own & your own but also the Essential.

Anyway, what I said in the letter, I also said in The Artificial Nigger, and that is the way I should keep on saying it, it being my vocation to say it that way.

What I want to know is, you mean you're going to produce this play in New York? Off-Broadway or something? I thought it took about a million dollars. Lord, I'm glad I'm a hermit novelist.

What did Ritchie write that impressed you on the boat? I am having to go to Athens at the end of the month to conduct a workshop. Senator Pappy O'Daniels used to conduct the Light Crust Dough Boys every Mother's Day over the radio and I feel this is the same bill of goods—haddeyer get an agent? etc. The last time, one old lady said, "Will you give me the technique for the frame-within-a-frame shortstory?"

Let me know if you make it legal, though I can't think it would make the foggiest difference (as I only believe in making it sacramental) whether you did or not. But we won't hear about it around here I reckon until you do make it legal. About Aunt Attie. She won't kick off over the telegram. I had an 83 yr old cousin that I was certain my first novel was going to kill, but it gave her a new lease. Her strength is as the strength of ten. You are just keeping that money from the Presbyterian Home.

Love & Cheers & the Rattle of ETC ETC

To Cecil Dawkins

Milledgeville
Dear Cecil,   16 July 57
    You certainly are nice to want to give me that dog but I'll have to take the thought for the dog. I didn't tell you what I raise: I raise peacocks—and you can't keep dogs and peacocks on the same place. When people come to see us with a dog, we have to ask them to keep the dog in the car—else the

peachickens will take to the trees and have nervous prostrations. I have 27 right now. This place sounds like the jungle at night as they yell and scream at the slightest atmospheric disturbance or mechanical noise. In addition to the peafowl I have ducks and geese and several different kinds of chickens but the peafowl are the main interest. I spend a good deal of my time sitting on the back steps with them. They have no proper sense of place; we have a very nice lawn that they could decorate to advantage but they prefer to sit on the tractors or the top of the chicken house or the garbage can lid. So I adjust myself to their tastes, including being anti-dog. But I do appreciate your wanting to give it to me.

I am always vastly irritated by these people (I guess like Stegner) who know as much about the South as I do about lower Hobokin and on the strength of it advise Southern writers to leave it and forget the myth. Which myth? If you're a writer and the South is what you know, then it's what you'll write about and how you judge it will depend on how you judge yourself. It's perhaps good and necessary to get away from it physically for a while, but this is by no means to escape it. I stayed away from the time I was 20 until I was 25 with the notion that the life of my writing depended on my staying away. I would certainly have persisted in that delusion had I not got very ill and had to come home. The best of my writing has been done here.

This is not to say that what the South gives is enough, or that it is even significant in any but a practical way—as in providing the texture and the idiom and so forth. But these things have to be provided. So much depends on what you have an ear for. And I don't think you can have much of an ear for what you hear when you're over 20—that is, for a new kind of talk and life. The advantages and disadvantages of being a Southern writer can be endlessly debated but the fact remains that if you are, you are.

Catholicity has given me my perspective on the South and probably gives you yours. I know what you mean about being repulsed by the Church when you have only the Jansenist-Mechanical Catholic to judge it by. I think that the reason such Catholics are so repulsive is that they don't really have faith but a kind of false certainty. They operate by the slide rule and the Church for them is not the body of Christ but the poor man's insurance system. It's never hard for them to believe because actually they never think about it. Faith has to take in all the other possibilities it can. Anyhow, I don't think it's a matter of wanting miracles. The miracles seem in fact to be the great embarrassment for the modern man, a kind of scandal. If the miracles could be argued away and Christ reduced to the status of a teacher, domesticated and fallible, then there'd be no problem. Anyway, to discover the Church you have to set out by yourself. The French Catholic novelists were a help to me in this—Bloy, Bernanos, Mauriac. In philosophy, Gilson, Maritain and Gabriel Marcel, an existentialist. They all seemed to be French for a while and then I discovered the Germans—Max Picard, Romano Guardini and Karl Adam. The Americans seem just to be producing pamphlets for the back of the Church (to be avoided at all costs) and installing heating systems—though there are a few good sources like THOUGHT, a quarterly published at Fordham. This spring I went to lecture at Notre Dame and met some very intelligent people. In any case, discovering the Church is apt to be a slow procedure but it can only take place if you have a free mind and no vested interest in disbelief.

I have read two collections of stories lately that you might find something in for your course—though they are uneven collections. One called The Strangers Were There by a man called John Bell Clayton, a Virginian, who died two years ago. One of his stories got the O. Henry prize one year. They are very respectably done stories. The other is The End of Pity by Robie Macauley, a friend of mine. This one won't be out until early fall.

Since you hadn't read Caroline Gordon, I'm sending you a copy of a quarterly that came out last year and was entirely devoted to her. You might find something in it that would be of use.

Regards and thanks for the dog I can't have.

To A.

Dear A.,

I haven't seen Modern Age yet but I am trying to get hold of it and will send it along to you if I do. This is what was going to be The Conservative Review. I say Russell's articles will have to have permanent value as they will all be at least three years old before they appear. He had gotten a review from Ashley of A Good Man is Hard to Find but that being no longer a new book, he asked him to expand it into a short piece for the second issue. A. said he was going to if he had time, but I don't think he has much faith in the appearance of a second issue. Russell had also got one of John Lynch's poems. I don't know but what Lynch has asked for it back before now. When anybody wants to get hold of Russell he is always in Scotland.

I am sure they weren't referring to The Malefactors but to that book about Dylan Thomas, can't think who wrote it, but a friend of his (John Malcom Brinnin??); I think it was called Dylan Thomas in America, or something like that, and now his wife Caitlin has written one. It's awful the way they pick on the dead; feast on the dead.

Sent you Robie's stories. I recommend them on the jacket. I was asked to comment by McDowell his editor and frankly I couldn't think of anything to say. I think Robie's best stories are as good as any being written and his worst as bad as any and there are some of both in this collection. Robie himself I am very fond of. I'll send you his novel if you'd like to read it.

Also sent you Brother Waugh's remarks, some of which are very sensible.

The jamboree in Athens was a real farce. Penwomen! Nothing but penwomen and believe me they are a tribe apart; they are mostly over sixty, blood-thirsty to sell, they will take any amount of encouragement and their works are heavily inspirational. There were forty or fifty in the room and three men, the man who was running the thing, Frazier Moore (he had to be there), a youth with the name of Mr. Phinizy Spalding, and an old man named Mr. Meadows who came from Louvail, Ga., sent I am sure by the Lord to be a plague to the penwomen. This old boy was a poet and he had his poems in a paper bag from the tencent store; he attended every session he could and tried whenever possible to get the floor away from the ladies. After I had made my talk, we had read the best (the least awful) of the seven stories. This job fell to Mr. Phinizy Spalding as the author was not supposed to be known. Then when it was read, the old girls discussed it. Their comments were of this kind: "I just thought that man was awful!" "I just loved him!" "I thought SHE was just right!" etc etc etc. This discussion went on for half an hour, Mr. Meadows sitting quietly but his eyes getting glittery. Mrs. P—— who had heard how he liked to get the floor continued to ignore him until the last minute. Then she let him talk. She should have let him talk sooner. He said he thought the problem should be looked at *historically*, and then he launched into a long account of what Jesus had said to the woman taken in adultery. There was nothing about adultery in the story but he seemed to be having a good time. After he had told that, he said he had discussed this passage from the Bible with a genteel and reefined Georgia lady, cutting his eyes around at the audience, and she said, "What do you think He meant by that?" "I think He meant some of them folks might be saved before you and me," said Mr. Meadows. "You *know* he didn't!" she said. "I reckon I know He did," Mr. Meadows said. Then I kind of saw the point: he hoped they might all be dammed, all penwomen. His eyes were glittering with a secret wisdom. The women were growling under their breaths for him to sit down, but he held on until the bell rang. He was worth my trip.

Mr. Phinizy Spalding must have been a graduate student. When he got home he wrote me a letter saying that as an undergraduate he had written a term paper entitled "Children in the Stories of Flannery O'Connor," and that he liked my stories. I intend to invite him to drop in if he is ever in this direction. Anybody with a name like that could not but be welcome.

It's a little hard to imagine that Petry story in a straight version but I'll be anxious to look—at any number of versions. Thinking about your writing in general and what might be your "authentic" material, I suspect that the best story you have done is the one about the fellow who butts the plane and gets himself court-martialed, the one the NWW said the narrator kept from being dramatic. That story was the least strained as far as the characters were concerned and there was an authenticity about it that Uncle Petry lacks— because they were people and he is a two-dimensional illustration. I have been reading your friend Uncle Henry James' essay on de Maupassant and inspired by same have written off for the Modern Library de Maupassant. To get back on course: you may ultimately be right that what you have to handle is your own neurosis (don't like that word though) but there are plenty of people who can handle their neurosises and can't write and plenty can write but can't handle etc. In any case, I would not be hasty to make two problems one and when I thought about the story I would forget about myself and when I thought about myself I would forget about the story.

Eileen sent s.o.s. saying her file was empty and could I send a review of anything—anything! So I promptly sent a review of Baron Von Hugel's Essays and Addresses, omitting to mention that they were first published in 1921. The Petrine Claims incidentally are the claims of the Pope to be supreme head of the Church, as opposed to you, me, Haze, and Hoover Shoats being supreme head. You want to see it, I'll send it.

We have got the bull, this one from Perry, the Mulachee Farms. He is 17 months old and my mother has named him Banjo. I couldn't say why. I always thought that if she had a dog she'd name him Spot—without irony. If I had a dog, I'd name him Spot, with irony. But for all practical purposes nobody would know the difference.

LATER

I liked most of Waugh's answers but he has too narrow a definition of what would be a Catholic novel. He says a novel that deals with the problem of the faith; I'd rather say a Catholic mind looking at anything, making the category generous enough to include myself.

I managed to be in good health throughout the visit of Mr. Ashley though I daresay he contributed to my subsequent decline by his ability to sit up until 1 o'clock and not know the difference. I go to bed at nine and am always glad to get there. Don't however refer to him as "your" A.; there are no claims there and none desired. He is very dry and very intelligent and it is always good to have somebody like that to talk to.

An old soul who heard the Catholic Hour last Sunday— seems it comes on at 6:30 AM of all ungodly hours. Anyways, my statement or such of it as was used was apparently read by Paul Horgan who referred to me as an old Iowa friend of his. Of course at Iowa, I was only a student and Horgan never even knew I was in the room, I am sure—though once he noted forty things wrong with a story of mine and I thought him a fine teacher. Anyways, the old lady is going to write off for a transcript of the program, which it seems you can get for the asking, so I intend to read what I did not hear.

The Sign is not much of a magazine though occasionally they have something good in it like that interview. Their reviews are lousy and I pass their fiction in haste. My 87 year old cousin sends it to my mother as a Christmas present.

Cheers,

To Cecil Dawkins

Milledgeville

Dear Cecil,   22 September 57

I'm a full-time believer in writing habits, pedestrian as it all may sound. You may be able to do without them if you have genius but most of us only have talent and this is simply something that has to be assisted all the time by physical and mental habits or it dries up and blows away. I see it happen all the time. Of course you have to make your habits in this conform to what you *can* do. I write only about two hours every day because that's all the energy I have, but I don't let anything interfere with those two hours, at the same time and the same place. This doesn't mean I produce much out of the two hours. Sometimes I work for months and have to throw everything away, but I don't think any of that was time wasted. Something goes on that makes it easier when it does come well. And the fact is if you don't sit there every day, the day it would come well, you won't be sitting there.

Everybody has a different problem about finding a set time to do it, but you should do it while you have a fresh mind anyway. After you've taught all day, you must be too tired and what creative energy you have must have gone to the little ladies of Stevens. If I had to teach I think I'd rather teach the Peter Bells (what they call the unteachable ones at the local college) which end of the sentence you put the period on rather than teach the bright ones Literature. You can't be creative in all directions at once. Freshman English would suit me fine. I'd make them diagram sentences.

Guardini has a number of things on Dostoyevsky and I like the one I enclose and here is also a thing Caroline wrote on her debt to the Greeks. This is one of Caroline's favorite themes which in part I take with several grains of salt; anyway, I wrote her that I was still after mastering me English and would doubtless not be getting onto no Greek. Most of Caroline's friends say they knew her *after* her Greek period.

Mr. Schneider of Wilton Junction has a nice face. I think I remember Wilton Junction, also East Liberty and West Liberty. Is Missouri more like the South or more like the West? I was in St. Louis once for a few days but not taking any notes.

Regards,

To William Sessions

Milledgeville
27 September 57

Dear Billy,

We were cheered to hear via your letter to A. My mother says we must save your letters and present them to you when you come back so you will have a record of all this. I say well I reckon old Billy is taking him some notes, etc. I sent your letter to me to Fr. McCown with instructions for him to return it, which he did, saying to send him some more as he certainly had enjoyed it and liked to travel even if vicariously.

I think he is having a sad time at that retreat house. He said seagulls got to be tiresome and he felt as if his words bounced on the walls. Do write him if you have time. Address: Xavier Hall, Pass Christian, Miss.

I was much taken with the card that had the picture of the ivory piece on it. Have to get my culture vicariously too.

We were wondering if there is anything you can't get there that we could send you. I send Madame Fitzgerald the home permanent wave and the gingerbread mix, both inappropriate for you, but there might be something else. Could you use some Instant Tea or Coffee? Supersuds, corn plasters, or Hadacol? Let us know.

There was a picture of a very anemic little man named W—— in the paper the other day—head of the Humanities Division at West Ga. He don't look like he'll last a year.

The Ga. Literature Commission has just declared God's Little Acre to be obscene. They have been debating about whether a book called The Dice of God by an Alabama author is obscene or not. A group of gentlemen from Macon brought it to their attention, demanding that it be declared obscene. There was a hearing and it turned out the gentlemen had read only the obscene parts; asked when something was obcene they said it was obsene when it couldn't be read before a lady.

Are you going to see Heidegger on his mountain top? Are you going to see Msgr. Guardini, Karl Adam, or Max Picard, or is Max Picard still living? What about Marcel and what about that lady critic that is so good—Claude Edmond Magny? I wrote the Fitzgeralds that you would likely show up and etc. I suggest that you write them a note to their present address and find out when they are going to move. Now it is Presso Bordone, Levanto (La Spezia). They said they'd look forward to seeing you and you might be near this summer place.

The Bell House is now down and nothing left but two beechtrees on either side of the lot so it is going to be called The Beechtree Parking Lot. Time Marches On. We have inherited their old birdbath, which is giving an antique look to the west side of the house.

Excelsior,

To Maryat Lee

Milledgeville

Dear Maryat, 8 October 57

I was much cheered and relieved to hear from you though the vein was mysterious. I haven't received any crusty note. Maybe you didn't put enough postage on it and it's simmering on the high seas; anyway, if you sent it, I reckon I provoked it. I scrounged around in my trash system trying to find if I had a carbon of my last to you. I had, and reading it over, found it in part disagreeable, vain, and unclear. I take it at this point to have been one of my attempts to be funny. It was not, but was as I saw with horror open to many possible interpretations of a vulgar nature. None of these was intended so put it down to my native idiocy. I just don't have a highly developed sensibility and I don't know when I've hurt people until they tell me. To have caused you any pain is very painful to me and is the last thing I would have wanted to do, or to have seemed to doubt for an instant that you ever act in any way not according to your conscience.

The only thing that irked me about the last letter I did get from you was your use of the word eternity in the plural, with airless in front of it. I don't mind being a pathetic quaver but eternity means the beatific vision to me and my quaver, or anybody elses, has nothing to do with it. Anyway, it would be impossible for me not to want you as a friend. A ridiculous notion. I am not to be got rid of by crusty letters. I'm as insult-proof as my buff orpington hen and if the letter ever does show up, I doubtless won't know the difference.

Miss E. Wynn wrote me a card from NYC and said she had had an announcement of your marriage and I was glad to hear it as I had begun to think you might have drowned in a Japanese tub or been eaten by the sabor toothed tiger. I hope you made yourself a play in Hongkong. I read in the paper that Carson McCullars is going to have a play shortly to be called "The Square Root of Wonderful"—a title that makes me cringe.

The local institution is open again but I have not seen your brother or sister-in-law and I am wondering if he faces an inauguration this year. They inaugurated the last one within an inch of his life, only to have him depart within two years. This cured them of making haste and your brother's hair may be allowed to turn white in office before they make his position formally official; but when the occasion occurs, hit will be great and you should plan to be here. You must get your visit in anyhow before we secede from the Union. The Russian moon is just light diversion for us. The latest thing is the American Resettlement Association, whose object is to resettle Georgia colored families in refined northern residential areas (only the best areas), lots in which will be bought up by the ARA with state funds. This is not quite as permanent as sending them all back to Africa but it has a lot of supporters.

I am keeping my mind on the important things, like peachickens. The season here has been terrifyingly productive. I used to say I wanted so many of them that every time I went out the door I stepped on one. Now every time I go out the door, one steps on me.

Cheers, love, & make haste to come South.

To Cecil Dawkins

Milledgeville
Dear Cecil,   27 October 57
Thanks so much for the picture. One of these days I'll send you one of me and two of my friends but my friends are not very cooperative about having their pictures struck—don't like to be seen with me or something.

I have heard that Katherine Anne Porter writes her stories in her head before she puts them down but I always tend to think such reports are exaggerated, perhaps just because they don't fit in with what I find I can do. I always have an idea of what I want to do when I write a story, but whether I'll be able to remains always to be seen. I am writing a story now and have proceded at a regular rate of two pages a day, following my nose more or less. They have to work out some way or other, and I think you discover a good deal more in the process when you don't have too definite ideas about what you want to do. That is interesting about your reading some Shakespeare to limber up your language before you start; though I think that anything that makes you overly conscious of the language is bad for the story usually.

Your schedule sounds horrible and I suppose the worst of such a job is that something extra is always coming up. I find girls of that age awfully hard to talk to. I lectured at Wesleyan College in Macon last year and as a result some of their students who have a vague urge to "express themselves" began to come regularly to see me. When they appear, they do all the talking and they have fantastic but very positive ideas about how everything is and ought to be; and they are mighty sophisticated on the outside. The visits leave me exhausted and yearning to go sit with the chickens.

Anything having to do with this "learning for life" stuff turns my stomach permanently. I had to attend a "progressive" high-school here, one of those connected with a teacher's college. In the summer all the teachers went to T. C. and sat at the feet of an old boy named William Heard Kilpatrick and those who couldn't afford that went to Peabody and sat at the feet of somebody who had sat at the feet of William Heard Kilpatrick. In the winter they returned and asked us what, as mature children, we thought we ought to study. At that school we were always "planning." They would as soon have given us arsenic in the drinking fountains as let us study Greek. I know no history whatsoever. We studied that hindside foremost, beginning with the daily paper and tracing problems from it backward.

I hope you are avoiding the Asian and other flus.

Cheers,

To Sally and Robert Fitzgerald

Dear S&R,

Milledgeville
4 November 1957

A letter from Lynch at Notre Dame requests your address—I don't reckon this will be it for long so I will wait until I hear from you. An illegible letter from Brother Sessions seems to say that he is calling on you today. Maybe I will get to call on you in the spring; or more likely, maybe you can call on me in Rome. My 88 year old cousin has decided that my mother and I must go on a pilgrimage to Lourds and Rome that one Msgr. McNamara is conducting this spring out of the Diocese of Savannah. She not only insists upon it but aims to give us the trip. My mother is all for it. I think I may be able to stand it if I just cut my motor off and allow myself to be towed behind the old lady. It is a 17 day pilgrimage—Ireland (I bet that'll be real sickening), London, Paris, Lourds, Rome and Lisbon. I foresee a battalion of fortress-footed Catholic females herded from holy place to holy place by the Rev. McNamara to the point of holy exhaustion. In fact, I can feel that holy exhaustion right now; but anyhow, this is likely to be the only way I'll ever get there and my cousin is certainly very good to give us this trip. I don't know whether I am expected to wash my bones in the waters of Lourds or not; that don't interest me in the least; I think the crutches preferable to having to do it.

A few weeks back Elizabeth Bishop called me up from Savannah. She was on her way back to Rio de Janiero (sp??) and her boat docked in Savannah unexpectedly so she called me; I have never met her or talked to her before but she sounds very nice. She said Cal had been ill this summer but was all right now. I didn't ask if it was the usual thing. Then the other day, I had a letter from him, enclosing some pictures of the baby. It was about my last story which he said he liked but had one complaint to make: I was too much of a moralist. Recently I had a visit from a Harvard student who went to the Episcopal Church in Cambridge where he said Lowell attended "mass" every morning.

I relished the Indian's letter but these Indians are a caution apparently. I receive a regular letter addressed to Honorable Flannery O'Connor, MFA, from an Indian priest who tells me about his arthritis and how bad he needs money. I send something to him every Christmas and Easter. I thought he was a very old man. The last letter he sends me a picture of himself—the picture of health and about 25 years old.

My book of stories has just come out in England. The publisher changed the title to The Artificial Nigger and there is a big black granit African on the cover being tortured or something.

Cheers and let me know your new address and be prepared to visit the dowdy pilgrums in Rome. I'll probably need artificial respiration by that time.

Regards to children,

Enclosed find triplets. Too bad you couldn't have thought of some good names like these.

To A.

Milledgeville
Dear A.,   16 November 57

Another travelog from William. On page three he gets around to what I wanted to hear which was about the Fitzgeralds. He says maybe show this letter to the Bockmans and then seems to think better of it. I certainly would not show it to the Bockmans, whoever they are. I don't know them and you probably don't either. If he wants to write the Bockmans, they should have the full and private treatment. If you don't object I'll send it to Fr. McCown, as he poor man seems to get a big bang out of them. He says he knows he'll never get to Europe.

Your visit was thoroughly enjoyed by us and is always good for me though I may look tired. The truth is I am tired every afternoon and there's nothing to be done about it. It's the nature of the disease. A lot of people decide I am bored or indifferent or uppity but at a certain hour of the day my motor cuts off automatically. I am really wondering if either my mother or I will be able to stand this trip. She is used to going all the time, but not that kind of going, and I don't think it would be worth any strain on her. However, it appears we are going. I guess I will advise her to cut off her motor too and the two of us will be towed by the Rev. McN.

She is reading the Lourds book and every now and then announces a fact, such as, "It doesn't make any difference how much you beg and plead, they won't let you in." "Won't let you in where?" "In Lourds with a short sleeved dress on or low cut." "I ain't got any low cut dress." I am going to read it when she gets through.

Enclosed very good review of the McCarthy book out of the Catholic Worker.

It appears I may get to behold Madam Holzhauer after all. I had an invitation to give something they call a Matrix lecture to the something with Greek letters women's journalism fraternity at Marquette in Milwaukee in April. They don't know what the date is to be but I said that if it were early in April, I'd come. I can use practically the same thing I used at Notre Dame and they pay my way and gimme a hundred dollars and I get to see the horrors of Milwaukee; also I get to see Carol Johnson; also Madam H., as it seems it was she and no other who recommended me for this high honor. Well, we shall see.

I am glad Eileen is sending you something decent to review instead of Sister Potluck and the Gravediggers Grandmother. You have exactly the right idea of how such a heavy tome should be handled. You are not expected in 200 words to give any judgement. Just tellum it's Theology and who wrote it and why and then settle down to enjoy it yourself.

I see I should ride the bus more often. I used to when I went to school in Iowa, as I rode the train from Atl. and the bus from M'ville, but no more. Once I heard the driver say to the rear occupants, "All right, all you stove-pipe blonds, git on back ther." At which moment I became an integrationist.

I announce with wild pleasure that I have finished the story once through as of today and that when I go over it about three more times, I think I will have done it; another month, I guess. Right now I am highly satisfied with all its possibilities and all that's already in it. This can be a delusion. Monday it may appear hopeless to me, but I doubt it. Nobody appreciates my work the way I do.

Thursday morning we had a short sharp wind which Jack came and announced as a "twister." My mother didn't pay too much attention though he said it had hurt the barn roof and taken the washing machine off their porch and set it down in the woodpile. When she went down there, she found there practically wasn't any roof. The insurance people estimate about $800 or so damage. Henry lost his front porch. Later in the day, Pussonalities in the Noos, called up and my mother announced the damage and so forth and at 12:35, we listened to her over the radio. She declared it was *not* her voice, that she didn't sound like that, but that she wasn't going to criticise anybody elses voice over the radio again. Having had the little experience myself, I sympathised. I am glad you got to hear the rural radio.

                                                            Excelsior,

To A.

                                                Milledgeville
Dear A.,   30 November 57
    I enclose the Plunketts because I am struck with a strong facial resemblence between Eldridge and our friend ———. Ruth looks a little like Mrs. Roosevelt as would be expected for anyone who has this intimacy with God. There are several things in their pursuits that interest me, that seem to be logical perversions of doctrines of the Church. I looked up Acts 19:11−12 and see that what they are talking about originated in things that had touched St. Paul. Your handkerchief, if you order one, will have touched Eldridge, who is backed up with one quarter of a million hours of prayer since 1943. The awful thing about the Plunketts is that they may not be crooks. However, they both look pretty crooked to me.

    I think Herr is very funny too. The old soul knows him apparently as she is always mentioning him. Once she wrote me that she didn't see how Dan Herr could have been so wrong about my book, Wise Blood. I didn't enquire but I gather that he must have somewhere been funny about that. I don't think he has too much literary judgment but a wonderful eye for Actual Absurdities etc. Did you see that some incompetent reviewed the Battista book in the Bulletin? Said something about the *great scientist*, Dr. Battista and averred the book would be a great help to those wishing to live a fuller life, or something. I read it with a hot eye, feeling pain.

Ye old soule has just sent me an article out of The Ave Maria, one of her favorites, about Camus. You reckon she spends her idle hours reading Camus? I doubt it. Anyway, she allowed she had met my friend Miss A. at the library and they had both said how much they enjoyed knowing me. Tanks. I'm glad to hear she thinks I'm a person of influence. She doesn't know about all those delinquent youth.

If you intend to throw Allen Tate out as a poet, you are going to have to get you some better aesthetic grounds than that there is no color in his poems or none of the things that have color. This will not do. This is a confusion of one thing with another and a sentimental, or close to it, approach to poetry. If he goes on your grounds, so do almost all the Metaphysical poets. You take Ode to the Confederate Dead—as I remember it there is only one color used in that and it is really *used*—green—the insane grass and the green of the serpent in the last stanza. That is a poem in which any color but the greys and seres and drabs would be inappropriate. That is a masterly poem; read it, forgetting who wrote it. Color is not necessary to all poetry. That depends entirely on the nature of the poem and what the poet is trying to do and what he manages to do. Your method tends to be to read the poem and judge the poet—because I reckon you are more interested in people than in art, which is as it should be, but when you read a poem you are only entitled to comment on the poem as a poem. What you seem to do is read the poem, judge the poet, and then judge the poem from your judgement of the poet.

Yrs. tr. will not be going to Milwaukee after all as they couldn't arrange the date. Also had to turn down a chance to go to the University of Chicago. I don't fancy myself amongst those toughs, cutting much of a figure that is, but I would have gone, for the fee was ample.

The scientist says I may take the shots, so that is the next thing on the agenda. My mamma has finished the Lourdes book. I am almost afraid to read it.

Caroline has sent me her latest called How To Read a Novel. I had asked Eileen to get it for me to review for the Bulletin. You want to see it? I think you would find it valuable, it's really more for writers than readers, and it is uneven

I think, but you would still find it valuable. Will send it if you want it. Also will send if you want it something called The Living Novel, a symposium, edited by Granville Hicks. He is a friend of mine and I am in the book (a thing of mine that you've already read anyhow), but there are nine others in it of varying degrees of sense. As Ashley says, they have to have one colored man and one Catholic.

I have a few things to do to the story yet but you will see it shortly. I go from liking it to not liking it. When I am in the liking-it stage I am tempted to send it to you, but when I am in the not-liking it stage I decide to keep it a while longer.

Cheers,

To Sally and Robert Fitzgerald

Milledgeville
Dear S&R,   1 December 57

We were highly pleased to know you could use a fruit cake and sent you off one Friday. The gent at the P.O. said it would take it 20 days to get there so you can be watchful on the 18th or thereabouts. I would hate for some Eye-talian to getaholt to it before you.

Billy wrote me an ecstatic letter, praising yr establishment and its fingerbowls. I hope they are cast iron. Incidentally he don't work on my mother or me at anytime except to our extreme irritation. You have to know him in the Light of the Lord to put up with him, but I appreciate your being so nice to him. He has his points.

It appears that the pilgrumidge is from April 22 to May 7. I had to write the monsignor to find out as I had an invitation to go to some kind of Catholic Thing in Milwaukee and talk in April but won't be able to now. Also could have gone to the University of Chicago for two classes and 500 bucks onccount of Holy Tour had to turn that down too. Not that I fancy myself amongst them toughs at the U. of C., but I am subject to the lure of filthy lucre. My parent is currently worried about where you can drink water and where you can't over there. All the ladies who have "been" tell her something different. If you haven't been to Lourdes yet, howcome you don't meet us there? The geography is beyond me, of course.

Do you know what the undertakers are doing with the ashes of the folks they cremate? Well, they are sending them to the cannibals to make Instant People out of. My mother came home with that the other day. She circulates among all and sundry.

Our colored man, Jack, has had all his teeth pulled and is about ready now to get his new teeth. The dentist asked him what kind he wanted and he said he wanted "pearly white teeth." The dentist asked what kind of pearly white teeth and he said, "you know, like on the handle of a gun." He also wants some gold ones scattered through the plate. Regina has been trying to talk him out of this but he says he ain't going to spend his money for no ordinary looking teeth.

Cheers,

Enclosed find items to induce homesickness.

To Caroline Gordon Tate

Milledgeville
Georgia
Dear Caroline,   10 December 57

I'm busy with The Holy Ghost. He is going to be a water-stain—very obvious but the only thing possible. I also have a fine visitor for Asbury to liven him up slightly. I'm highly obliged for your thoughts on this and I am making the most of them. When I get this finished I'd like you to see it again because it is already much improved—but I notice my stories get longer and longer and I'm afraid this one may be too long. If I'm finished with it, I'd like to send it to the Cheneys for a Christmas card and will hope that you might have time to look at it there. If not, I'll send it to you after Christmas.

I had counted on getting to the Cheneys for the weekend of the 20th, but I have lately been getting dizzy because I am taking a new medicine and have got an overdose of it. So I figure I'll do my staggering around at home. It takes some time for the dose to get regulated. Every time something new is invented I get in on the ground floor with it. There have been five improvements in the medicine in the 7 years I've had the lupus, and they are all great improvements.

A friend of mine at Wesleyan, a Dr. Gossett, wrote me that he and his wife had just come from the Modern Language Asso. convention in Knoxville or somewhere and had heard Willard Thorpe read a paper on the grotesque in Southern literature. He (Thorpe) allowed as how the roots of it were in anti-bellam Southern writings but that the grotesque you met with in Southern writing today was something else and has serious implications which the other didn't approach. He said he had no satisfactory explanation for the change. The Gossetts decided the reason he didn't was because he doesn't know enough theology. I seem to remember that he wrote one of the better reviews of The Malefactors, but I may be mixed up on the name.

You are more sanguine about this pilgrimage than I am. It's not that I'd rather be a tourist; I'd rather stay at home. You are good to ask us to stop by Princeton, but knowing the difficulties of getting anywhere, I doubt we could engineer it. I envy you that energy you have. I wish you would come to see us. We have a lovely place—as evidenced by my reluctance to leave it for 17 days of Holy Culture & Pious Exhaustion. Pray that the Lord will (gently) improve my attitude so I can at least endure it.

Cheers, thanks, love and Merry Christmas to you & Allen.

To A.

Milledgeville

Dear A.,   14 December 57

Wal, I can't argue with you or Caroline either about The Golden Bowl because haw haw I haven't read it. She probably exalts James overmuch out of admiration for his technical achievements, and you sell him short for never having had temptations. Now I think it is a great grace not to be tempted. I used to have a Swedenborgian friend who was very critical of the Lord's Prayer. "Imagine," said she, "asking not to be led into temptation! We should ask to be led into temptations so that we could grow strong and overcome them!" Which might be logical enough if we hadn't been instructed otherwise by Christ Himself. Apparently after a while in his life, St. Thomas was relieved of all temptations of the flesh and certainly this was necessary if he was to write a Summa. James apparently knew nothing of any real religion. Ghrame Green has an essay on this subject in The Lost Childhood but I forget exactly what his view of it was.

Tom Gossett sent me back A Path Through Genesis and the Two-edged Sword and I sent them on to you without even opening the package so I presume they are in the wrapper. I was expecting Eileen to send me a copy of How to Read a Novel so I gave my copy away; now she writes me that Viking has given out all their review copies; so I won't be sending that.

About the Lourdes business. I am going as a pilgrim, not a patient. I will not be taking any bath. I am one of those people who could die for his religion easier than take a bath for it. The one thing in France I have a real desire to see is Matisses chapel in Vince; but of course they won't be going near any suchlike as that. The Msgr. wrote me there would be four days in Rome and he knew I'd like that. What I can't figure is: we are going 7 places in 17 days, 7 into 17 is 2 and a fraction and if four days are devoted to Rome, I figure them other places will not see much of us. By my calculations we should see more airports than shrines, and I suspect that if you've seen one shrine you've seen them all. Aside from penance being a good thing for us, I'm sure religion can be served as well at home. I'll be glad when the 17 days are over. Also I am afraid I may miss the geese hatching. But back to the baths. If there were any danger of my having to take one, I would not go. I don't think I'd mind washing in somebody elses blood and pus, but the lack of privacy would be what I couldn't stand. This is neither right nor holy of me but it is what is.

The time interfered with Chicago. It also interfered with an invitation to an Arts Festival in Colorado, where I'd like to go because I've never been there. I would have got 500 bucks for those two classes in Chicago, so even if I ain't taking a bath, I figure I am making a financial sacrifice. On second thought, what a lousy conclusion!

I have torn the story up and am doing it over or at least a good deal of it over. It bids fair to be very long. Parts of it are very funny and it contains a memorable Jesuit, but I haven't got it right yet. But I am anxious to send it to you & trust it will get there before Christmas.

Also I am sending you a little book for Christmas but after I got it, it occurred to me that you might already have it as it is standard. Now if you do already have it, send it back to me and I will send you one you don't already have.

We are anxiously awaiting Jack's teeth. He told the dentist that he wanted "pearly white teeth." The dentist said what do you mean pearly white? Jack said he meant pearly like the pearl on the handle of a pistol; also he wanted one gold crown. He said he wasn't going to pay his money for any ordinary looking teeth. Regina has tried to talk him out of it but to no avail. We wait.

Yrs,

To Father James H. McCown

Dear Fr. McCown,

29 December 57
Milledgeville

Two or three things have come up on which I need some expert SOS spiritual advice. Not long ago the local Episcopal minister came out and wanted me to get up a group with him of people who were interested in talking about theology in modern literature. This suited me all right so about six or seven of them are coming out here every Monday night—a couple of Presbyterians, the rest Episcopalians of one stripe or another (scratch an Episcopalian and you're liable to find most anything) and me as the repersentative of the Holy

Roman Catholic & Apostolic Church. The strain is telling on me. Anyway this minister is equipped with a list of what he would like us to read and upon the list is naturally, Gide, also listed on the Index. I dispise Gide but if they read him I want to be able to put in my two cents worth. I don't think there is any way to ask the local reverend father for permission. Some women in the parish, college graduates & pillars of the church, asked him if they could read some Jehova Witness pamphlets. They wanted to see what the Witnesses believed. He told them flatly no. He is a letter of the law man, no ifs, ands or buts, and very hard to approach anyway. You said once you would see if you had the faculties to give me permission to read such as this. Do you and will you? All these Protestants will be shocked if I say I can't get permission to read Gide.

The other thing concerns a girl I am writing to who is a lapsed Catholic. She says she found that instead of "make straight the way," it was "make tight the straight jacket," and that her family was very strict about trifles and treated the negroes terrible, etc etc. A typical Catholic family, I gather. Anyway, apparently the straw that broke the camel's back with her was when a priest told her that it was a mortal sin to eat meat on Friday. She is real confused and I am trying to give her suggestions about reading some people like Maritain as she has obviously never read anything but the Do-Nots. Anyway, would eating meat on Friday be a mortal sin if she didn't understand it as an act of rebellion; I was afraid to make any pronouncement on this to her? You can't tell her to see a priest because she wouldn't but I could help her if I knew myself. Thanks & Happy New Year.

To A.

Milledgeville

Dear A.,   11 January 58

We are having a big funeral here tomorrow as Henry died last Saturday night—eight days between these events. He had been having trouble getting his breath and Regina went over there last Saturday and said she wanted to take him to the doctor but he said he would go Monday. She went back in the afternoon and tried to make him go but he said no, Paul said you must be swaded by your pinion and his pinion was that he would wait until Monday. He was sitting by the fire eating an apple. He died that night still sitting in the chair. Shot said that when he died, he grabbed aholt of him Shot and he like to have never got away. He has a daughter in Macon and she has a policy on him. A niece arrived from Philadelphia yesterday and another daughter arrives from Detroit Sunday. The undertaker offered to send out chairs but Louise said not to send no chairs out she didn't have time to be sitting around talking to all those niggers. We'll miss him around here as he was kind of an institution. The pearly white teeth are appropriately in for the occasion. They seem to be satisfactory. Louise says Jack ain't got any business with those teeth, he can eat just as well without them.

Naw those two pieces of paper I sent you—the beginning and end—were no good and I have done them over a different way. Caroline said that was not subtle enough and she is right. Allen says I am too flat-footed. This time I have really improved it. I'll send you a copy when I get it done. You are doubtless as sick of it as I am but this is what you get for agreeing to see something before its published.

My opinion of the Irish has gone up. We had a visitor, one of the Irish delegates to the UN. The Gossetts brought her over and we had supper with them. This girl is about 35, a lawyer, and a poet (in Irish). I asked her what they had in Ireland to correspond with the angry young men in England. She said they had some angry young men but that they didn't have the class business to be angry over. Anti-clerical? I asked her. Yes and anti-religious too. Most of them go the way of Joyce, she said, but it is very painful to them because when they cut themselves off from the religion they cut themselves off from what they have grown up with—as the religion is so bound in with the rest of life. She has an uncle who is Master General of the Dominicans in Rome and she wants us to go see him. She said that when it was learned that the Irish delegation was going to vote with the Communist bloc on whether or not to debate the admission of Red China, they immediately had a call from Cardinal Spellman telling them not to do it. That, said she, confirmed them in their resolution. Of course they had their orders from home, and they voted with the Communist bloc as they had planned. She seems properly anti-clerical but not particularly anti-religious.

The chief result of the Monday night affairs is that we have to air the damm room all of the next day to get the stinking cigaret smell out of it. I like two or three of the people and of course nothing very strenuous goes on and they are all very polite and theology is seldom mentioned because I don't think any body knows anything about it, including the Episky minister. I have bought an airwick and I aim to set it in a conspicuous spot. Mary's accent gets worse by the day. By next year I expect her to be completely unintelligible. There are some words I had thought couldn't possibly be pronounced but one way, but they don't faze her. She could squeeze some artificial culture into the word stone.

Poor Mrs. Slayden. She had better stick to the lepers.

The Red Priest is a novel by Wyndham-Lewis. Very funny. Will send iffen you like.

Cheers,

To Father James H. McCown

Milledgeville
Dear Fr. McCown,   12 January 58
I enclose you my latest published work lest you fall behind in your pursuit of Modern Literature. I have just completed one as I said with a one-eyed Jesuit in it but that has not been published yet.

I am very much obliged for your taking the time to find out about the permissions etc. I will use the epikia and also invoke that word, which is very fancy. I have for the time being led them away from Gide, with the good reason that he is to be had in no 35cent edition and we are all in the 35¢ class. I am afraid though that they are headed for Sartre—

also on the Index. So if you can include him in with Gide, I'd be obliged. These meetings are marked by such excessive politeness that not much gets said; also nobody knows anything about theology, including the Episcopal preacher.

For the other information I am also obliged. It sounds better on paper than it works out in fact, however, as you can never so well decide if a thing is deliberate or not, or if the delectation is morose or not. Then you begin to wonder if your confessions have been adequate and if you are compounding sin on sin. This probably all comes from faulty training and being taught by the sisters to measure your sins with a slide rule. It drives some folks nuts and some folks to the Baptists. I feel sure it will drive me nuts and not to the Baptists.

That girl wrote me the other day that she had not gone home for Christmas because she did not want her mother to know she had left the Church as her mother was subject to heart attacks. They live in Alabama (the family) but the girl teaches at Stevens. I sent her a book by Mauriac called The Stumbling Block. She is one of those you have to go at obliquely, because I think she is much relieved to think that she has, with a good conscience, got rid of her faith. She'd never read a book called Rebuilding a Lost Faith for fear that would happen and she be stuck with it again.

The Gossetts were recently over and said they met a Fr. Murray from Spring Hill (at a convent) and they asked him about you, feeling very sorry for you stuck off in that retreat house, and Fr. Murray said, "Oh we see him in Mobile every weekend." They like to have killed themselves laughing. They brought over a lady who was talking there & is an Irish delegate to the UN. After seeing her, my opinion of the Irish has to be lifted, grudgingly. I asked her about modern Irish writers and she said most of them were anti-religious, went the way of Joyce. Her uncle is Master General of the Dominicans at Santa Sabina in Rome and she wants us to meet him when we go there.

That doctor cousin who was in New Orleans has moved to Shreveport.

Much obliged again.

To Elizabeth Bishop

Milledgeville
Georgia
Dear Elizabeth, 6 February 58

Thank you so much for sending me "The Diary of Helena Morley." We've all enjoyed it. My mother got hold of it first and could not help reading it aloud every now and then so I feel I have read it twice already. It reminds me a little of a diary written by a young New York woman who came to live in Georgia before the War Between the States (designation preferred by the UDC). It took her considerable time to get used to living with "the black shadows" everywhere. I suppose the two races can live together more agreeably in a Catholic country.

It was awfully nice of you to call me up on your way to South America. Of course I misinformed you about the night Mae Sarton was to be in Savannah. It was the next night so I hope you didn't seek out the performance. Two of the college teachers here attended. One reported it was over her head—she teaches sociology; the other said it was a great waste of time to take poetry that seriously when there are so many important *present-day* problems to be discussed—she was a Doctor of Education and was only slumming that night.

Caroline Tate wrote me last week that Cal had recently had another spell; "seizure" she called it. This was reported to her by Madame Claude Edmond-Magny who is at Princeton.

We certainly hope that you will be able to stop over with us on your way north next time. My mother and I may go on a pilgrimage to Rome this spring (April 22–May 7). I am not in favor of the trip myself as it is too much going, too fast, and I judge we'll see more airports than anything else.

Yours,

To Maryat Lee

Milledgeville

Dear Maryat,   11 February 58

Here I am misinforming my dear friends a mile a minute. No I am not going to Rome nor nowhere else (except Missouri). The doctor as of yesterday says I can't go. You didn't know I had a DREAD DISEASE didja? Well I got one. My father died of the same stuff at the age of 44 but the scientists hope to keep me here until I am 96. I owe my existence and cheerful countenance to the pituitary glands of thousands of pigs butchered daily in Chicago Illinois at the Armour packing plant. If pigs wore garments I wouldn't be worthy to kiss the hems of them. They have been supporting my presence in this world for the last seven years. What you met here was a product of Artificial Energy. The name of my dread disease is Lupus Erethematosis, or as we litterary people prefer to call it, Red Wolf. Anyway, no Europe. I am bearing this with my usual magnificent fortitude.

I would be plumb charmed to get to read the play. We are having tornados and hurricanes here and if the roof blows off and the play blows all over Baldwin County, I seek not to be responsible. Don't send it unless you have another legible copy. One blow a few months ago took the roof off the barn, or did I inform you of that?

I understand your friend Mr. Tillich is going to be at Wesleyan this year, also Miss Katherine Anne Porter. Wesleyan is filthy rich and can pay the price for the best people.

My Chinese goose has now laid five eggs but they all froze so I shall eatum.

Only a half a page but afterall, this ain't New York City. I don't get to go to no Shakespeer productions. I don't even have a television.

Well, love from the dear old dirty Southland,

To Sally and Robert Fitzgerald

Milledgeville

Dear S&R,   26 February 58

This seems to be one of those on again off again trips. Cousin Katie was so disappointed that she says we must go anyway and not stay with the tour. I don't know if this can be arranged or not but what we thought we would like to do, if it can be arranged, is to go with the tour to Ireland and skip all the England and Paris stuff and fly from Ireland to Milan and stay with you the week while they are doing those other things. I want you to say if this will be an inconvenience to you to have the two of us for a week. I mean sho nuf feel free to say so because if you don't have the room, we can get a room somewhere near you. You said Levanto was on the train line to Lourdes so I thought you might would go to Lourdes with us, and on to Rome with the tour. They stay in Rome three days and then go on to Lisbon. I don't know if this will work out but would it suit you if it would? Could you meet us in Milan? Left for two minutes alone in foreign parts, Regina and I would probably end up behind the Iron Curtain asking the way to Lourdes in sign language. I cannot bear to contemplate it. Cousin Katie has a will of iron. My will is apparently made out of a feather duster.

The Monsigneur God help him wants me to "write up" the Lourdes part of the pilgrimage. I don't think he has thought this through.

Regina and I have just got out of the hospital where we spent a week in a double room with identical colds and sore throats, taking identical red mycins. She after being cured of the disease had to be cured of the medicine. No medicines affect me anymore. The colored orderly was named Ulysses and all day we heard over the loud speaker, "Ulysses to X-ray," "Ulysses to emergency," "Ulysses to surgery." Ulysses brought us our dinner once and came and took away the trays when we were finished. He was light yellow and had a pea green cotton hospital cap on his head and his only words were, "Yawl sho ain't et much."

Thanks for asking me to come in May and stay a while but I will be doing good if I get there for this week in April. I have to go to the University of Missouri in May. I'd like to see Praz fine. The other one is in the U S according to the Sewanee Review. Let me know what you think of all this and if you'll go with us to Lourdes.

Cheers,

To Sally and Robert Fitzgerald

Dear S&R, 11 March 58

We were cheered to hear you can have us and meet us but that is horrifying news about Lourdes. It is Cousin Katie's end-all and be-all that I get to Lourdes and if I am dead upon arrival that's too bad but I still have to get there. A 22 hour train trip would be the end of me, so I have written the travel agent to route us to Lourdes some way by plane, even if we have to fly from Milan back to Paris and join the tour there on the 28th. We would love you to do this with us but if you can't I can understand. I had no notion all these distances were so great. I am in the hands of this travel agent woman whom I imagine as the same sort of character that unloaded the garbadine stockings on Robt. Her letters to me get less and less cordial and I get the idea that by now she is convinced I am a moron. I am convinced of it too so she ain't by herself. As soon as she sends me the itinerary I will let you know what it is—if she don't throw up the whole idea of having us as customers. I suppose they get a rake-off in the deal somewhere and I should quit worrying about her. If you can't go to Paris with us and down to Lourdes, you can meet us in Rome we hope.

The stockings are on order and I am glad to know there is something we can bring. I wanted to get Louis to get me some pocket knives to bring your boys and Regina said you'd kill me, that you wouldn't want boys that size to have knives. I don't want to cause bloodshed in your clan but are they too young to have knives? Is there anything else you need or want?

Last Sunday I was visited by a poet named James Dickey who is an admirer of Robert.

I haven't been able to turn up that recipe though I remember it. We will keep looking. I found one of yours for lemmon chiffon pie.

I am glad to hear its not so cold. I told my mother that that long sweater you gave me plus a raincoat which is lined would be sufficient but I was making no headway with her until your letter. She is afraid my poor white trash look will disgrace you.

I will get out of my head seeing that Matisse chapel at Vince as I will be doing well if I get alive to Lourdes.

Excelsior,

To A.

Milledgeville
Dear A., 4 April 58

I have been holding the fort alone since Sunday night. In the middle of the night my mother had a severe pain in her back, so bad that she went to the hospital in the middle of the night. It proves—or so they think—to be a bruised kidney. She hit her back on the edge of the sink somehow Saturday when the telephone rang. She appears to be better and hopes to come home tomorrow. I don't know what this will lead to for her; pray that this will be the end of it. A blow on the kidney could cause permanent trouble. The doctor thinks she will be all right and able to go on the trip. She wants to go. Since I've never much wanted to go anyhow, I am more than willing to call it off, but we will just have to wait and see how she gets on when she gets home. This has convinced me of one thing: that I must learn to drive. Louise stays with me at night but as to getting in town I am dependent on Sister—who can drive me nuts in about two minutes. Incidentally I had intended to ask you down one Saturday before we go if we go, but now I won't until I am sure she is all right.

I haven't read None Shall Look Back but I have heard Lon Cheney expound on it. He says that the antagonist in NSLB is Death—the foe we don't know but all care about. You will see I really haven't ever read Caroline, just a few things here and there. I agree that Tom and his dreams don't work—it's really abstract, too much like an equation.

About the novel of religious conversion. You can't have a stable character being converted, you are right, but I think you are wrong that heros have to be stable. If they were stable there wouldn't be any story. It seems to me that all good stories are about conversion, about a character's changing. If it is the Church he's converted to, the Church remains stable and he has to change as you say—so why do you also say the character has to remain stable? The action of grace changes a character. Grace can't be experienced in itself. An example: when you go to Communion, you receive grace but you experience nothing; or if you do experience something, what you experience is not the grace but an emotion caused by it. Therefore in a story all you can do with grace is to show that it is changing the character. Mr. Head is changed by his experience even though he remains Mr. Head. He is stable but not the same man at the end of the story. Stable in the sense that he bears his same physical contours and peculiarities but they are all ordered to a new vision. Part of the difficulty of all this is that you write for an audience who doesn't know what grace is and don't recognize it when they see it. All my stories are about the action of grace on a character who is not very willing to support it, but most people think of these stories as hard, hopeless, brutal, etc.

Katherine Anne Porter read in Macon on the 27th and the next day the Gossetts brought her over to have lunch with us. She was very pleasant. Caroline had written me that a couple of years ago she had pneumonia and came back into the Church but that when she got shut of the pneumonia, she also got shut of the Church again, but that it was apparently much on her mind. When she asked me where we were going in Europe and I said Lourdes, a very strange expression came over her face, just a slight shock as if some sensitive spot had been touched. She said that she had always wanted to go to Lourdes, perhaps she would get there some day and make a novena that she would finish her novel—she's been on it 27 years. After that the conversation somehow got on the subject of death—there were two professors from North Carolina and the Gossetts and us and her—in the way that death is discussed at dinner tables—as if it were a funny subject. She said she thought it was very nice to believe that we would all meet in heaven and she rather hoped we would but she didn't really know. She wished she knew who exactly was in charge of this universe, and where she was going. She would be glad to go where she was expected to if she knew. All this accompanied by much banter from the gentlemen. It was a little coy and a little wistful but there was a terrible need evident underneath it. She's about 65.

The Thought was located exactly where I put it after you handed it to me—on top of the piano. Revolting.

I am glad you have got yr. Faulkner straight. Merry Joe Christmas.

To Cecil Dawkins

Milledgeville
Dear Cecil,   14 April 58

Thanks so much for the picture book about Rome. I'll probably see more Rome in the picture book than I do in Rome. Anyhow, we are about ready to go, have our tickets and other paraphernalia, and are prepared to endure—more or less. I'll probably be a beady-eyed specter by the time I get to Missouri.

A letter from Mr. Peden the other day announced they would meet me in St. Louis, as otherwise I would have a seven hour wait. There's a train but I can't ride them on account of the crutches. Come on Monday and go on Wednesday. This is to be a public lecture I gather so I presume anybody from anywhere can come. He hasn't told me whether it is to be at night or in the day time—although I asked him. If you see it listed somewhere, I wish you'd let me know.

Miss Katherine Anne was very nice indeed. Very pleasant and agreeable, crazy about my peacocks; plowed all over the yard behind me in her spike-heeled shoes to see my various kinds of chickens. I didn't hear her read but most of the people I talked to who did thought she read well. They say she had on a black halter type dress sans back, & long black gloves which interfered with her turning the pages. After each story, she made a kind of curtsy, which someone described as "wobbly." She's about sixty-five. She's been on her novel 27 years and says all her friends call it "you-know-what." I hope I won't be on mine 27 years from now.

I'm not going to judge any literary contest that I've heard of. I hate to do things like that. I'll have a hard enough time talking to their students. Students always know more than I do.

Cheers. I'll be back here May 8, Lord willing.

To Sally and Robert Fitzgerald

Dear S&R,   11 May 58

I enjoyed most you all and the Pope, and we are certainly more than grateful to you for the days we spent with you and for your coming with us the rest of the way. It would have been an awful trip if you hadn't. As for me, my capacity for staying at home has been greatly increased. It is doubtful if after this trip to Missouri I will ever depart from Baldwin County again. The plane ride back home about finished me. Regina revived as soon as she hit the cow country.

The plane ride from Rome to Lisbon was on the Argentine Airways in which we set facing eachother, me and Regina facing Slowburn and one of the little boys, with Margaret and Mrs. Stoddard and the Monsignor and Fr. Burke facing eachother across. Slowburn took out his needle and thread and began to patch his pocket; then he put that up and put a monocle in his eye and took out a dime novel in Spanish called "Solo tu, Veronica," and began to read that, then finally he went to sleep with his mouth open and the little boy had a great time making as if to insert a coin in it.

We didn't go to Fatima as it was an all-day trip and R. had a bad cold. Shrines to the Virgin do not seem to increase my devotion to her and I was glad not to go. They left at eight in the morning and came back at eight at night, all beat except the Bennet sisters who declared they felt much better at the end of the pilgrimage than they had at the beginning. We left them in new York waiting to get on an Eastern Airlines plane for Charlotte where they were to change for Augusta. The next day I read that an Eastern plane with a broken landing gear had circled the field at Charlotte for three hours to use up fuel, then had crash-landed but nobody was hurt. I think it was the one they were on, which was fortunate as I am sure they could take it.

Fr. Burke bid me goodby with the information that he had read my stories and that when I wrote one about the pilgrimage he hoped I would be kind to them—he preserved a kind of wary cordiallity toward me.

Everybody thought you were a great addition to the pilgrimage and Margaret took your address so she could thank you for helping her get the bolt of cloth. We left her in Atlanta, lugging the can of Lourdes water. The little boys amused themselves all the way to Lisbon telling her that if she would go out on the back of the plane she would find a little balcony where she could look out, that we were about to crash, that if she gave Mr. Slowburn a commission he would find her a husband, etc etc. She kept telling Slowburn she wanted to take him home with her. Nell Green bought three pairs of shoes in Rome. Mr. Brennan spilled his liquor in his TWA bag and it went all over his clothes.

You can't know how much we appreciate all you did for us and all the trouble you took. Enclose some more Weigel. Excelsior to you and children.

To William Sessions

Milledgeville
Dear Billy,   15 May 58
It was a treat to see you in Lourdes and my mother intends to get off a note to your mother to tell her that you look healthy etc. We have put up the Nativity plaque in the front room and it has attracted considerable comment. My mother has managed to learn to operate her pin and it now stays on

successfully. Thanks for it all and also for getting us the water from the spring. I wrote Caroline that she owed her thanks for it to you, who went in in your drip-dry pants to get it.

Sally discovered that her bill at the Hotel Grotto was 42 dollars for two and a half days. This had included meals but they hadn't told her that. She made a minor scene and got it reduced to 37 but we were doubtless in a clip joint. Our American Express guide in Paris had told us that everybody at Lourdes intended to be a millionaire within the year.

I was sick on the rest of the trip and didn't see much but we did in Rome sit on the first seats at the general audience because we were with the Arch-Bishop and when it was over the Pope came down and spoke to us. He is very gracious and very much alive. Never seen anybody quite so alive.

Haven't gotten the things to A. but I expect to ask her down and will let her take them back herself.

All middle Georgia is agog over a Mrs. Lyles from Macon who has just been discovered to have lost her two husbands (successive) mother-in-law and daughter by putting ant poison in their food. It appears she has been a Voodoo practicer for the last number of years but everyone in Macon thought she was "lovely." Well, back to normal.

Let us hear of your further adventures.

Cheers,

To Ashley Brown

Milledgeville
Dear Ashley,   26 May 58

I hope you got a card from me saying I had endured. I could have added, "only but just." Anyway, my capacity for staying at home is now 100%. I will probably never be seen outside of Baldwin County again. Of course, I'm glad I've went once. I suspect that in an offish way I enjoyed it. The first cold germ I met on the other side moved in and stayed for the 17 days so most everything I saw was through a fog. Seeing the Fitzgeralds was fine. They have got a place there for Peter and another for Randall Jarrell for the summer. We stayed there about four days and then went to Paris. My cold kept me in the hotel room but I was visited by a girl named Gabrielle Rolin who has written a couple of books that haven't been translated yet but probably will. Instead of seeing Paris I saw her. Lourdes is a beautiful little village pockmarked with religious junk shops. The heavy hand of the prelate smacks down on this free enterprise at the gates of the grotto however. This is always full of peasants milling around and of the sick being wheeled on stretchers. Mauriac wrote somewhere that the religious goods stores were the devil's answer there to the Virgin Mary. Anyway, it's apparent that the devil has a good deal to answer to. We batted around Rome for a couple of days and stayed in Lisbon a day. When the reality has somewhat subsided I may be able to do something with it. At present, I am just relishing being at home, and getting back to the Opus Nauseous.

Miss Katherine Anne wrote somebody in Macon last week that she had finished her novel. I saw Caroline in New York and Caroline said that in her opinion, KA had finished it ten years ago, that it was good but nothing extra. Caroline speaking.

Robie has invited me to do a piece for the Kenyon to be called "Conflict in Crane." This is conflict in Dr. George Crane. Unfortunately my paper doesn't carry him anymore.

Do you mean Edgar Bogardus is *dead* from the faulty flue? That is too much.

I have just read Kingley Amis's three novels. Lucky Jim I liked but the other two you can have. Too many too fast. At the Fitzgeralds I read the Nabokov thing, Pnin, which I thought was wonderful. I took their children a copy of Uncle Remus but the children it appears speak only Italian, so I read it myself. It's really very fine.

I wish I were going to be able to get to Nashville but the negro who used to drive us to Atlanta has the highblood so I am reduced to staying at home. When you come back from Serbo-Croatia or wherever it is you are taking yourself, you will have to come to see us. Let me hear from you from there. I am sure you could live in Portugal for about 25¢ a day.

Cheers,

To Elizabeth Bishop

Milledgeville
Georgia
1 June 58

Dear Elizabeth,

We went to Europe and I lived through it but my capacity for staying at home has now been perfected, sealed & is going to last me the rest of my life. The crowds weren't so bad but it was too much too fast. I found that the crutches were a great asset. Never a plane I wasn't let on first. My crutches are aluminum; apparently nobody over there has aluminum crutches. Everybody stared and took his time about it, particularly the Italians.

Lourdes was not as bad as I expected it to be. It is a beautiful village or would be if it weren't pockmarked with religious junk shops—one right after the other in an unbroken chain right up to the entrance of the grotto. Here the heavy hand of the prelate smacks down on free enterprise and its a pity the whole town can't be controlled the way the grotto is. Somebody in Paris told me the miracle at Lourdes is that there are no epidemics and I found this to be the truth. Apparently nobody catches anything. The water in the baths is changed once a day, regardless of how many people with running sores get into it. I went early in the morning and it was clean; sat in a long line of peasants to wait for my turn. They passed around a thermos bottle of Lourdes water and everybody had a drink out of the top. I had a nasty cold so I figured I left more germs than I took away. The sack you take the bath in is the same one the person before you took off, regardless of what ailed him. At least there are no society trappings along with the medieval hygiene. I saw nothing but peasants and was very conscious of the distinct odor of the crowd. The supernatural is a fact there but it displaces nothing natural; except maybe those germs.

I am sure the ceremonies at the convent would get me down. I am a long standing avoider of May processions and such-like nun-inspired doings. I am always thankful the Church doesn't teach these things are necessary. I read somewhere about some South American old lady who was entering the convent; perhaps it was the same one you know.

There is a rich school thirty miles from here that is always having visiting poets. It's a Methodist girls college and every time a wealthy Methodist old lady dies, she leaves a big endowment. Anyway, the fellow who invites the visiting poets wants to have you so I gave him your address, hoping you might pay us a visit if they made it worth your time to come there. They want to have Eliot next year. Tom Gossett, the one who does the inviting, told me he had to explain to the President very tactfully who Eliot is before he would consent to paying him $1000, which is the fee for Eliot.

Anyway, we hope that sooner or later we'll have sight of you here.

Yours,

To Father James H. McCown

Milledgeville
Georgia
June 29, 1958

Dear Fr. McCown,

Your mother sounds just like my mother. You should bring her down some time as I feel sure there is nothing they wouldn't agree about.

There are two Jesuits here at the language school this summer and Fr. Al whom you knew last year came back and spent a few days but we didn't see him. All the Protestants around here like the Spanish priests, which is a good thing as his reverence, the local pastor, is diligent to win himself as many enemies as possible. He is so Irish that on St. Patrick's day, he orders green carnations for the altar, his sermons are full of such locutions as, "as the Irishman said," and he has lately caused a big stew at the college by declaring that the students couldn't attend the baccalaureate sermon. They always have in the past. The president wrote the Bishop and the boys were allowed to go, but not before much unnecessary ill feeling was stirred up. His latest threat is to paint the church flamingo with a sandal-wood ceiling.

I have been taking driving lessons and last week I went to take the test to get the license. To prove that I ain't adjusted to the modern world, I failed the driving test. Now in two weeks I have to go take it again. I barely brought the patrolman back alive so I don't know if he'll relish taking me around the block again.

If you ever get to read a book these days, read one called "The Magic Barrel" by a Bernard Malamud. The stories deal with Jews and they are the real thing. Really spiritual and very funny. Somebody was telling me yesterday that the reason Jews are ahead of Catholics in every intellectual pursuit is very simple: they have more brains. I believe it.

My story with the one-eyed Jesuits in it is going to be in the August issue of Harper's Bazaar, which you shouldn't be seen buying, but your mother could.

Best to you both. I certainly enjoyed the telephone conversation.

To John Hawkes

Milledgeville
Dear John,   27 July 58

I haven't written and thanked you for the books because I have been reading them. I braved the Faulkner, without tragic results. Probably the real reason I don't read him is because he makes me feel that with my one-cylander syntax I should quit writing and raise chickens altogether.

I am very much taken with your books and their wonderful imaginative energy. The more fantastic the action the more precise the writing and this is the way it ought to be. I have a friend, James Dickey, a poet, who was down here recently to show his little boy the ponies. I told him I was reading your books and it turned out that he has read all of them, including ones called The Owl and The Goose on the Grave. He described a passage in one of them where a man flies— he was lost in admiration. It appears he reads your books as they come out. You may state without fear of contradiction that you now have two fans in Georgia.

Your student's story is amusing and shows a wonderful imagination at work. However, I think she makes a mistake to set it in Georgia. That seems to me to detract from the fantasy. A fantasy attached to Georgia ought to have something of Georgia about it, and of course this doesn't.

I am more than pleased that you stopped to see me and that I've been introduced to your writing. Remember me to your wife and please stop again when you are down this way.

Yours,

To Dr. T. R. Spivey

                                                    Milledgeville
Dear Dr. Spivey,   19 October 58

You may be right about Marcel but I would have to reread him to know. I've read three of his books and I remember a great deal being said in them about the "broken world," etc. I can't think of anybody really apocalyptic to offer you though. It's in the nature of the Church to survive all crises — in however battered a fashion. The Church can't be identified with Western culture and I suppose the wreck of it doesn't cause her much of a sense of crisis. We certainly have no crisis theologians but in the Eastern countries there are many martyrs, whose blood counts for more in the mystical order of things.

What you say about the story interests me. It's not so much a story of conversion as of self-knowlege, which I suppose has to be the first step in conversion. You can't tell about conversion until you live with it a while. I can take all you have to say about it except that about the "sudden switch to undulant fever." That's no sudden switch. He contracts the undulant fever when he drinks the raw milk in the dairy and it's the knowlege that he has no high and tragic mortal illness but only a cow's disease that brings the shock of self-knowlege that clears the way for the Holy Ghost. I couldn't have written the story at all without the undulant fever. Everything has to operate first on the literal level. I've thought that maybe there is enough in these characters to make a novel out of them sometime but it would be a novel with this story as the first chapter and the rest of it would be concerned with the boy's effort to live with the Holy Ghost, which is a subject for a comic novel of no mean proportions.

I suppose what bothers us so much about writing about the return of modern people to a sense of the Holy Spirit is that the religious sense seems to be bred out of them in the kind of society we've lived in since the 18th century. And it's bred out of them double quick now by the religious substitutes for religion. There's no where to latch on to, in the characters or the audience. If there were in the public just a slight sense of ordinary theology, (much less crisis theology), if they only believed at least that God has the power to do certain things. There is no sense of the power of God that could produce the Incarnation and the Resurrection. They are all so busy explaining away the virgin birth and such things, reducing everything to human proportions that in time they lose even the sense of the human itself, what they were aiming to reduce everything to. As for fiction, the meaning of a piece of fiction only begins where everything psychological and sociological has been explained.

All this is underlining the obvious but I am unaccustomed to finding anyone else interested in it.

Regards,

To A.

Milledgeville
Dear A.,   8 November 58

The almanac has already come in very handy. I had an invitation to talk at the College of St. Teresa in Winona, Minnesota so I forthwith looked it up. The good sisters wanted me to lecture at four or five Catholic colleges in Minn., the which I have no intention of doing. I have also been through the book collecting odd facts. I thank you very much. This is a contribution that will continue to be useful.

Caroline is an old lady. I can't point out any more of her errors to her. Maybe the people who publish it will. Anyway, its not up to me. As for any comparison between the Malfactors and Lucky Jim, it isn't in order. Amis was writing with great success from the top of his head. Caroline with less success from much farther in. Amis is not burdened with a belief in God. Mrs. Tate is. Amis had no problem. Lucky Jim is his only good novel. I've read them all and they get progressively worse. This Iris Murdoch is very good. Have you tried her?

Six or seven years ago I read three of Cary's novels and I must have liked them or I wouldn't have read three but I don't remember too much about them now. Herself Surprised, The Horses Mouth, and To Be A Pilgrim. The latter I keep racking my head to try to remember because it must have been the most interesting one. He has gusto. The pictures of him working at the end when he was all but paralysed were very touching.

Harrassed I am but if it weren't Tarwater it would be another one. This is the condition of man. And I am heading toward the end of Tarwater. The greatest gift of the writer is patience.

I think you ought to include the idiot story because the conception is wonderful but it will have to be dramatized so it works more normal-like. Anyway, you have got something in the lot.

The article in the Commonweal on the Japanese was right in line with what you say—some kind of spiritual void there. I have never read any Japanese writers myself. Right now I am reading the Pasternak. It is really something. Also a travel book on Greece by Henry Miller. Never read Henry Miller before but this book is very fine. Also reading a book called The Eclipse of God by Martin Buber that Dr. Spivey sent me. I have introduced him to Bernanos whom he likes. Do you know any Catholic crisis theologians? Only crisis theologians seem to excite him. He has a very fine mind inspite of the apocalyptic tastes.

Yesterday I went to a lunch for Claire Huchet Bishop whom you have probably read in the Commonweal. She's here lecturing giving three or four lectures all on different subjects. A very versatile woman. European education makes ours look sick.

Cheers,

To Dr. T. R. Spivey

Milledgeville

Dear Ted,   16 November 58

I think this book you sent me is wonderful and I am so very much obliged to you. Buber is a good antidote to the prevailing tenor of Catholic philosophy which, as this Fr. Murchland points out in the enclosed review, is too often apologetic rather than dialogic. Buber is an artist. That is one thing. Thomism usually comes in a hideous wrapper, but Buber's thought is cast in a form that is always readable. Just from reading the Eclipse of God, I didn't realize that Buber doesn't believe that man can participate in the Divine life. There is for him the Encounter with the Other, but no interpenetration, no "I live now not I but Christ in me." Although I knew Jewish theology wouldn't countenance God made man, I thought that the Holy Spirit might be considered to enter in, or something. In this it is very far from Catholic theology (also from Tillich) but closer at other points.

You are right about Guardini needing to take in the corrupt organization. If he were writing about the Inquisition he would agree with you as far as that goes. But in the Legend, Dost. is using the Inquisition as a figure for the whole Church. To him the Church was one grand corrupt organization. For Guardini it is the mystical body of Christ, inspite of its spots of corruption like the Inquisition. I presume this is why he didn't consider the Inquisition itself. He doubtless should have.

I have started reading the Diary of a Country Priest to see what I make of it after all these years. I must have read it ten or twelve years ago, once and not since. So far it seems to be only a slight framework of novel to hang Bernanos' religious reflections on. The diary form gives him leave to do this otherwise he would have a hard time. I am wondering if this is not something you have had to cope with in your own novel. It is futile to speculate from the not-well-known-to-you person to the probable work, but nevertheless tempting, and I should just imagine from some of the things you have said that your novel is more reflective than externalized. You said something about my stories dipping into life—as if this were commendable but a trifle unusual; from which I get the notion that you may dip largely into your head. This would be in line with the Protestant temper—approaching the spiritual directly instead of through matter. This is something Buber is opposed to and it is one of the points on which he is close to Catholic theology.

Bernanos stands very high with Catholics, at least with the ones who read. As for the Church itself, it takes no official notice of writers unless the work is contrary to faith & morals, upon which it is put on the Index.

I like Pascal but I don't think the Jansenist influence is healthy in the Church. The Irish are notably infected with it because all the Jansenist priests were chased out of France at the time of the Revolution and ended up in Ireland. It was a bad day if you ask me. I read a novel by Sean O'Faillon about the demise of the Irish novel. Apparently someone had suggested that there wasn't enough sin in Ireland to supply the need. O'Faillon said no, the Irish sinned constantly but with no great emotion except fear. Jansenism doesn't seem to breed so much a love of God as a love of asceticism.

I am reading the Pasternak book and it is something of what you are looking for. I was suspicious of all the praise given it; I thought it was just because Pasternak was a "good" Russian. But not so. It is a great book. At one point he has Dr. Zhivago say that "art has two constant, two unending concerns: it always meditates on death and thus creates life. All great, genuine art resembles and continues the Revelation of St. John." Perhaps it is right that this should have been wrung out of Russia. I can't fancy its being wrung out of America right now.

Very glad to get rid of the Miss-Dr. business. I felt as if I were writing to Dr. Johnson; and Miss O'Connor sounds like the Last Librarian. I shudder to think that might have gone on and on.

Regards,

To Caroline Gordon Tate

Milledgeville
Dear Caroline.   16 November 58

I guess they sent you a copy of CRITIQUE. It helped to have you say something good about the novel since Brother Louis D. Rubin didn't exactly get it. On reading it over, I have discovered what is wrong in the name of the Church as you have it. I knew something was wrong but I have only just realized what it is. Haze's church is always called simply The Church Without Christ, never the Church of Christ Without Christ. That one comes in with Hoover Shoates and is further lengthened to the Holy Church of Christ Without Christ by Onnie Jay Holy. This doesn't make any difference in the CRITIQUE but you will want to correct it in the introduction or the book will contradict what you say. Also another detail I noted is that Haze reads the sign about Leora Watts' friendly bed in the train station, not on the train. M. Coindreu probably isn't through with the translation. I mean to write him and ask him to visit us when he comes South.

I gather Lon is very disappointed over the reception his book has met with. McDowell didn't get the review copies out in time; also they surely didn't proofread the book. And this is a shame because it is a good book.

Big news for me. The doctor says my hip bone is recalcifying. He is letting me walk around the room and for short spaces without the crutches. If it continues to improve, I may be off of them in a year or so. Maybe this is Lourdes. Anyway, it's something to be thankful to the same Source for.

Cheers,

To A.

Milledgeville
Dear A.,   22 November 58

I would as soon break into an armored car as unwrap one of these books you send. You must single-handed support the scotch tape industry. Dear girl, wrap it up once and tie a

string around it. It will get here and should it go astray, I can
sustain the loss.

I am surprised you don't know anything about the Crisis
theologians; in any case don't make a virtue of this ignorance
for it is not. They are the greatest of the Protestant theologians writing today and it is to our misfortune that they are
much more alert and creative than their Catholic counter-
parts. We have very few thinkers to equal Barth and Tillich,
perhaps none. This is not an age of great Catholic theology.
We are living on our capital and it is past time for a new
synthesis. What St. Thomas did for the new learning of the
13th century we are in bad need of someone to do for the
20th. Crisis means something different of course for the Catholic than for the Protestant. For them it is the dissolution of
their churches; for us it is losing the world. We have produced artists that might be thought of as crisis artists, for
instance Bernanos and Peguy. One American Catholic writer
who has the sense of crisis is Fr. Murchland whom you have
read in the Commonweal. Fortunately, some of the best commentaries on the Protestant theologians, and some of the
most appreciative, have been written by Catholics, e.g., Fr.
Weigle on Tillich.

Called you up Thursday a week ago whilst I was in Atlanta
attending the Southern Baptist Convention but you were not
yet in.

The CRITIQUE as you have seen is a well-meant but not
highly successful effort to do me a favor. Powers came out
better in the people he had to write about his stuff. Caroline
is wildly mixed up, Rubin is mainly interested in sitting on
the neck of Aldrige. Sr. Bernetta is obviously a careful woman
with very good sense.

The harshness with which you speak of Caroline is not justified. She may be basically irreligious but we are not judged
by what we are basically. We are judged by how hard we use
what we have been given. Success means nothing to the Lord,
nor gracefulness. She tries and tries violently and has a great
deal to struggle against and to overcome. The violent bear it
away. She is much to be admired for not repeating Penhally.
It is better to be young in your failures than old in your
successes.

Our cousin who gave us the trip to Lourdes is dying in Savannah but before she lost consciousness she had the happiness of knowing that the trip to Lourdes has effected some improvement in my bones. Before we went they told me I would never be off the crutches. Since last week I am being allowed to walk around the house without them as the bone is beginning to recalcify.

Will be on lookout for story.

Cheers,

To Cecil Dawkins

Milledgeville

Dear Cecil,   9 December 58

Thanks for the clippings. No one there sent them to me so I wouldn't have seen them otherwise. I don't exactly remember telling the lady the writer didn't need inspiration. At interviews I always feel like a dry cow being milked. There is no telling what they will get out of you. She asked me who my favorite author was and I said I liked James and Conrad mighty well and in a minute she said, "And you said your favorite author was James Conrad, now . . ." If you do manage to say anything that makes sense, they put down the opposite.

Never read the fiction in the quarterlies expecting to see anything first-rate. Yours is better. Ignore the rejection slips and concentrate on what you are writing.

I am strapped up with a broken rib, of all things. I broke it coughing. I never knew such was possible but I warn you: if you get a cough, buy yourself some cough syrup, don't just sit around coughing.

Glibness is the great danger in answering people's questions about religion. I won't answer yours because you can answer them as well yourself but I will give you, for what it's worth, my own perspective on them. All your dissatisfaction with the Church seems to me to come from an incomplete understanding of sin. This will perhaps surprise you because you are very conscious of the sins of Catholics; however what

you seem actually to demand is that the Church put the kingdom of heaven on earth right here now, that the Holy Ghost
be translated at once into all flesh. The Holy Spirit very rarely
shows Himself on the surface of anything. You are asking that
man return at once to the state God created him in, you are
leaving out the terrible radical human pride that causes death.
Christ was crucified on earth and the Church is crucified in
time, and the Church is crucified by all of us, by her members
most particularly because she is a Church of sinners. Christ
never said that the Church would be operated in a sinless or
intelligent way, but that it would not teach error. This does
not mean that each and every priest won't teach error but that
the whole Church speaking through the Pope will not teach
error in matters of faith. The Church is founded on Peter who
denied Christ three times and couldn't walk on the water by
himself. You are expecting his successors to walk on the
water. All human nature vigorously resists grace because grace
changes us and the change is painful. Priests resist it as well
as others. To have the Church be what you want it to be
would require the continuous miraculous meddling of God in
human affairs, whereas it is our dignity that we are allowed
more or less to get on with those graces that come through
faith and the sacraments and which work through our human
nature. God has chosen to operate in this manner. We can't
understand this but we can't reject it without rejecting life.

Human nature is so faulty that it can resist any amount of
grace and most of the time it does. The Church does well to
hold her own; you are asking that she show a profit. When
she shows a profit you have a saint, not necessarily a canonized one. I agree with you that you shouldn't have to go back
centuries to find Catholic thought, and to be sure, you don't.
But you are not going to find the highest principles of Catholicism exemplified on the surface of life nor the highest
Protestant principles either. It is easy for any child to pick out
the faults in the sermon on his way home from Church every
Sunday. It is impossible for him to find out the hidden love
that makes a man inspite of his intellectual limitations, his
neuroticism, his own lack of strength, give up his life to the
service of God's people, however bumblingly he may go
about it.

Your own family with the aid of a few priests have helped to make a mess of your cousin and have obscured your own view of everything holy in the Church. (I don't count as anything an appreciation of the music and the liturgy. Mass could be said out of a suitcase in a furnace room and the same sacrifice would take place.) You and your cousin are the "little ones" who have been scandalized and perhaps somewhere along the line the millstone has been hung around the appropriate neck, but it may be a neck you never saw. Your family have probably been impelled by a love that is quite ignorant and mute. It is what is invisible that God sees and that the Christian must look for. Because he knows the consequences of sin, he knows how deep in you have to go to find love. We have our own responsibility for not being "little ones" too long, for not being scandalized. By being scandalized too long, you will scandalize others and the guilt for that will belong to you.

It's our business to try to change the external faults of the Church—the vulgarity, the lack of scholarship, the lack of intellectual honesty—wherever we find them and however we can. In the past ten years there has been a regular rash of Catholic self-criticism. It has generally come from high sources and been reviled by low. If the same knowlege could be shared uniformly in the Church we would live in a miraculous world or belong to a monolithic organization. Just in the last few years have sisters teaching in parochial schools begun to get AB degrees. Doubtless the good soul who didn't know papal history would never believe it if she read it anyway, but there are plenty of Catholic sources, all with the Nihil Obstat, that she could pick it up in. The Church in America is largely an immigrant Church. Culturally it is not on its feet. But it will get there. In the meantime, the culture of the whole Church is ours and it is our business to see that it is disseminated through out the Church in America. You don't serve God by saying: the Church is ineffective, I'll have none of it. Your pain at its lack of effectiveness is a sign of your nearness to God. We help overcome this lack of effectiveness simply by suffering on account of it.

To expect too much is to have a sentimental view of life and this is a softness that ends in bitterness. Charity is hard and endures. I don't want to discourage you from reading St. Thomas but don't read him with the notion that he is going to clear anything up for you. That is done by study but more by prayer. What you want, you have to be not above asking for. But homiletics isn't in my line, particularly with a broken rib. Are you going to stay there for Christmas?

Cheers,

To Robert Lowell

Milledgeville
Dear Cal,   25 December 58

It is mighty unseemly of you to enshrine me in your memory falling up the steps with a bottle of gin. I recollect the incident. It was not gin but rum (unopened) and the steps were slick. The moral is: there are some as have no business with liquor either inside or out. I don't get any these days anyhow. In our house the liquor is kept in the bathroom closet between the Draino and the plunger, and you don't get any unless you are about dead. The last time I had any was when I dropped the side of the chicken brooder on my foot and broke my toe.

This spring we spent four days with the Fitzgeralds in Levanto and then Sally went with us to Paris and Lourdes and then to Rome. Europe didn't affect me none, but since coming back my bone has begun to recalcify, an improvement that was not expected.

My other accomplishment is that I have learned to drive the car. I flunked the driving test the first time, barely bringing the patrolman back alive. When he could pull himself together, he said, "You need sommo practice, young lady," and told me to come back in two weeks. The next time I didn't shake him up so bad. I don't drive very good yet.

I would like to think I will finish my book this year but this may be just what I would like to think. I will hope to read yours.

My love to you and Elizabeth and Harriet. That Harriet is going to take over if you don't watch out. You ought to raise her in the South and then she wouldn't have to go to school. I am really looking forward to the next generation being uneducated.

Cheers,

To A.

Dear A.,   3 January 59

Quote from Caroline's latest: "Your admirer Miss Somebody or other, feels that anybody who makes as many mistakes as I did is not capable of grasping your work. I am keeping her letter—to show anybody who is ever fool enough to ask me to write another preface. Show em I can't do it." It seems she is having more introduction trouble than just mine. I didn't ask her to write me an introduction but Tom Mabry and Ward Dorrence, friends of hers who are going to have a volume of stories out together by the University of Missouri Press, did ask her to write one. She wrote it and it appears Tommy Mabry has just written her a violent letter saying he doesn't like what she has written. I gather he wasn't even polite about it. Poor Caroline. Their volume is going to be called "The White Mule." Mabry is very good. I don't know about the other one.

She was agreeable to my knock-down of the introduction but as I haven't heard anything from the translator, I will just wait a while to see what I am going to do.

Billy arrived with a purple shirt and tyrolian hat on the 30th and had to be entertained the better part of the afternoon. He had a gallon jar of Horry County bootleg wine which he offered us a drink out of. As it tasted like gasoline we did not avail ourselves of the offer to keep any of it. It seemed to me that the conversation dealt exclusively with his mother.

Kazantzakis is all blood and guts. Somebody was telling me he wrote a movie but I forget what it was.

I think Spivey meant Eileen was old compared with the rest of the youth who overrun the place. He was telling me that

Betsy Locheridge teaches a writing class one night a week. I
was thinking the blind leading the blind, but I guess one is as
good as another with what she is liable to get.

I read Man's Fate but never have read anything else
of Malraux's. I have just finished the second volume of
Voegelin. I don't think you would like it because it is more
full of technical stuff than the other one. Parts of it were very
exciting but for the most part you need to be a Greek scholar
to read it.

I am very near the end of my opus. Three or four more
pages and I'll have a first draft. This is a very good feeling I
can tell you after so many years. Of course now I have to go
back to the beginning. I'm by no means finished but at least
I know that it's possible. I must say I attribute this to
Lourdes more than the recalcifying bone. Anyway it means
more to me.

Cheers,

To A.

Milledgeville

Dear A.,   28 February 59

Thanks for getting me sent the Commonweal. It would
have done your heart good to see all the marks on the copy,
everything commented upon, doodles, exclamation points,
cheers, growls. You can know that really she enjoys reading it
and reads every word and reacts to every one she reads. Also
she sent a paper she had written and a couple of other things
for me to remark on.

If Eileen goes I'm afraid that will be the last of the book
page. I wish you could do it, that is be the brains, and have
a flunky to do the mailing. Old Eileen has her virtues which
will go unappreciated until they cease.

Mr. William Ready gives me the creeps. Have you read his
book, The Poor Hater? All these moralists who condemm
Lolita give me the creeps. Have you read Lolita yet? I go by
the notion that a comic novel has its own criteria.

Little Locheridge as you call her has the misfortune of

having too much of an opportunity to hear herself talk. I daresay she has already begun to believe everything she writes. It'll be the ruination of her. ✳ ✳ ✳

If I were you I would just write Elizabeth Stevenson a letter and tell her you liked her book and would like to talk about it. I just met her that once at the Writers' Thing, her and her mother, and they looked to me like real nice people and no foolishness. I don't know her address but they must be in the book. I imagine the people she would have any interest in talking to in Atlanta are few and far between and you would be one of them, but I judged her to be on the reserved side.

Haven't seen the new poems of Cal. Ashley wrote they were weird, like sections of a free-form memoir. Farrer, Straus is going to bring out a book of his this year. I hear Miss K. A. Porter's is to be out in September. At the rate I am going, mine won't be out until January. I am again very dissatisfied with it, inspite of Caroline and her enthusiasm.

Rebarbative is not in my dictionary but it reminds me of something between regurgitate and vituperative. My novel must be rebarbative. If you find it, let me know.

My Chinese goose has laid two eggs. Things are beginning to pick up. Consider what Sareday you can come down and pick you up some country air.

Cheers,

To Sally and Robert Fitzgerald

Milledgeville

Dear S&R,   24 March 59
This is it and I will be much obliged for your considered comments and consider that I want to know the worst before publication and not after. I can work on this a good while longer if need be but I am 100% pure sick of it. I cannot see it any longer and the only thing I can determine about it is that nobody else would have wanted to write it but me.

People are very respectful of me these days, thinking that $150,000 of Mr. Ford's money has been divided eleven ways. I even got an advertisement from an investment broker this morning.

As for Caroline, I don't think it's money she needs, or anyway that she needs most. Maybe Allen's liver will give out before he disgraces himself completely. She has mentioned the state of his liver several times. I picture it in shreds. The young thing ought to have her head examined.

I hope you are accustoming yourself to the pressure of the grant. I feel it myself.

Regards to children and let me
hear about this novel, yours,

To Catharine Carver

Milledgeville
Dear Catharine, 27 March 59

I've rewritten the last pages so I'll enclose them as I think they're an improvement. When the grim reaper comes to get me, he'll have to give me a few extra hours to revise my last words. No end to this.

Cheers & thanks,

To Thomas Stritch

Milledgeville
Georgia
Dear Tom, 28 March 59

No, I am not going away and eat up my money. I have bought me a comfortable chair and I am being tempted by an electric typewriter; for the rest I am seriously considering usury. They don't want me to work for two years but I don't *ever* want to work so it's up to me to multiply the talent. I had some Rockefeller money a few years back and it is still contributing to my upkeep because I bought a five room house on the way to the water-works. The house is subject to termite and poor white trash but I get $55 a month for it. I'm pretty sure Henry Ford would commend this course.

The Fitzgeralds will never come home now.

I have finished my novel for all practical purposes but am still tinkering with it. Pretty soon I'll have to send it to the publisher. The name of it is *The Violent Bear It Away*. Matthew 11:12 as the Protestants say.

I am going to Nashville in a few weeks for a symposium at Vanderbilt and stay with the Cheneys. Lon is going to write a trilogy. He went to New York to try to meet some Negroes socially (Research) but wasn't able to meet a one. I reckon he don't know the right people.

Do come to see us. We'll absolutely expect you and the Wests to appear this summer.

Yours,

To Louise Abbot

Milledgeville

Dear Louise,   30 March 59

Much as we would like to have you for a neighbor, I am glad you managed to avoid the local institution. We have a new local institution here called "Green Acres" for "Elders." They had a formal opening two Sundays ago and my mother must go; so we went. The place is divided into two sections—Magnolia Hall for rich elders, and Camelia Hall for poor elders. When I foresaw my future in Camelia Hall I decided at once that I would rather go to the State Hospital.

Chicago was all right except that my plane was grounded in Louisville, Ky., and I had a nine hour bus ride from there to Chicago, arriving in the middle of the night. After that, I could have taken anything. Their writing students were pretty sorry. I read twelve or fifteen manuscripts, all bad but two. At the public reading there was no public.

I don't have to go anywhere with the Ford grant. I am thinking about buying an electric typewriter. I hear tell it cuts the work in two, and I have just finished typing my novel through twice, and that puts me even more in the mind to do it.

Your friend Spivey breezed through here the other day and gave me a very cheerful view on the school situation. He says it will follow this course: the issue will come to a head and the Governor will close all the schools. Then in a few days the people will realize that this means the end of collegiate football and force him to open them again. He awaits Armageddon in an excellent humor.

Maybe you all can drive over some Sunday afternoon when you won't have to do the driving?

Meanwhile cheers,

To Elizabeth Bishop

Milledgeville

Dear Elizabeth,   9 April 59

I'll be cheered to have you review the book. It appears to be out of print but I have written Mrs. Porter at the Signet place to see if they can provide me with some. If so, I'll send you one myself. As for the music it's all one to me. I am a complete musical ignoramus, don't know Mozart from Spike Jones. I never hear any music and don't seek it out. I don't know whether I feel guilty or cynical about this cultural deficiency, but anyhow, I do nothing about it.

I've finished my novel and am trying to decide if it's any good or not before I send it to the publisher. It has the virtue of being very short and it has a good title—THE VIOLENT BEAR IT AWAY (the kingdom of heaven, that is) but apart from those things, I'm doubtful about it. I've sent it to Catharine Carver who agrees to tell me what she thinks. The action of it, incidentally, is built around a baptism.

Last month I went to the University of Chicago to "assist" at two writing classes and give a public reading and live in the dormitory for five days. Some old lady left them money to have a woman-writer or some other female character live in the dormitory a week and be asked questions. The last one they had was a sculptor and she brought a piece of marble and hacked at it for them and this was apparently most entertaining, but I was less of a success. The girls were mostly freshmen and sophomores and their questions gave out long before my patience. I had to sit with them drinking tea every afternoon while they tried to think of something to ask me. The low point was reached when—after a good ten minute silence—one little girl said, "Miss O'Connor, what are the Christmas customs in Georgia?" I was mighty glad to leave after five days. They didn't have much in the way of writing students and at the public reading there was no public. And the weather was revolting.

My friend at the Methodist college who was going to ask you there to read has been asked to leave (too good for them) but you must stop here anyway if you come in October. The only visitor we've had lately is Maurice Coindreau. He has been translating Wise Blood into French and brought the translation down for me to see before he takes it to Paris next month. We had no idea what we'd do with an elderly Frenchman for three days but he was quite a nice guest and amused himself taking pictures of the peafowl with a movie camera. We'd certainly love to have you come. Anyway, if you have a different address next fall, let me know because I'll want to send you a copy of my novel.

                                                              Best,

To Catharine Carver

                                                      Milledgeville
                                                      Georgia
Dear Catharine,   18 April 59
    Everything you say makes wonderful sense to me; in fact, your first note made sense and I started at once rewriting Part II, doing about what you suggested in your second letter. Rayber has been the difficulty all along. I'll never manage to get him as alive as Tarwater and the old man but I can certainly improve on him. I sent the ms. to the Fitzgeralds in Italy and yesterday I heard from Robert. He said essentially the same thing you have, so that corroborates it. He put it

this way: be sure you haven't made too much of a parody of Rayber, as if you do, you take away from the point and significance of what Tarwater sees.

I would probably never have got the end written if I hadn't telescoped the middle and got on with it, because I dallied with them in the city for about two years and got nowhere. But now that I have the end, I think I can get the middle, anyway get it better.

You have not seen the last of this. As soon as I get a new middle in it, I must send it to you again. I want Denver to read it but ask him to wait until I send you the new middle as there is no use his reading what isn't going to be like that. Keep the manuscript and you can add the middle to it when I send it to you and then show it to him. I am glad you haven't told anyone else you have it. It occurred to me that the people at FS&C might take it amiss that I have sent it to some one at Viking, even though it was to a friend and nobody's bidnis but mine.

You have done me an immense favor that nobody else could have or would have done. Caroline read it but her strictures always run to matters of style. She swallows a good many camels while she is swatting the flies—though what she has taught me has been invaluable and I can never thank her enough. Or you.

Be prepared to undergo this again in a couple of months.

Gratefully,

I am sending this to you at Viking because I sent you a note to 146 E. 89th telling you not to hurry with the criticism and got it back—no such person at this address. Are you sure you are getting all your mail there?

To Maryat Lee

Milledgeville
Dear Maryat,   25 April 59
No I can't see James Baldwin in Georgia. It would cause the greatest trouble and disturbance and disunion. In New York it would be nice to meet him; here it would not. I

observe the traditions of the society I feed on—it's only fair. Might as well expect a mule to fly as me to see James Baldwin in Georgia. I have read one of his stories and it was a good one.

I am just back from Vanderbilt and have had enough of writers for a while, black or white. Whoever invented the cocktail party should have been drawn and quartered. It was a good symposium for the most part but one a year is anuf for me.

Thanks for asking your broker but it don't look like I am going to have any money any time soon to invest. My cousin left me a house in Savannah and I am now learning whatall it needs; among the items is a new roof. When you clip your cool cupons, think of me coping with my hot renter. I just had to buy a $129 hot water heater for the other tenant who, bless his heart, isn't but two months behind in his rent.

You forgot to enclose the review of the Georgia boy's play. I don't know him, this is just interest in the products of the native state.

No'm I don't know who Audrey Wood is. I never heard of her. I guess this is some kind of disgrace. Enlighten me.

Incidentally, I have a friend in Tennessee who would like to meet James Baldwin I am sure. His name is Brainard Cheney and he is writing a novel set in inter-racial circles in New York. So last month he took a trip to New York where he has a lot of liberal abolishionist friends to get them to introduce him to some inter-racial society. He stayed two weeks and pulled all his strings and wasn't able to meet one negro socially. Well, at least down here we are benighted over the table not under it. If he comes to New York again, I'll get him to call you and maybe you could scout up a few. But don't worry, he's not coming. I think he's decided to rely on his imagination.

I am fixing to add a chapter or two in the middle of my novel, so I am not as finished as I thought I was.

Cheers anyway—I have 25 enfant geese.

To A.

Milledgeville

Dear A.,   16 May 59

Let me hear what Berg thinks of the novel and what you think of Berg. I hope this is to be a pussonal interview.

James has no preoccupation about avoiding vulgarity. James is a master of vulgarity. A good part of all his books and the whole of many of his stories are studies in vulgarity. Certainly he recognized it in himself, but he *recognized* it, he was able to define it in the concrete, and being able to define it and to see it where it was only adds to his greatness. And as for James physical infirmity, that is negligible in the Christian order of things and it is not good to carry it over and make a criticism of his work. James said he had the "imagination of disaster." Read his books and look for it and you will carp about him less, or to more effect. Have you read What Maisie Knew? Several processes of parents and their successive divorces and lovers seen through the consciousness of a child. You sometimes think the child must have a bald head and a swallow tail coat; nevertheless it is a very moving book.

My good editor came down weekend before last and stopped in Atlanta and went out to the monastery where who should he meet but guess who Sessions. In a half hour Billy had given him his (Billy's) life history, driven him into town, eaten dinner with him (on Farrar Straus), instructed him to look for him (Billy) an apartment in New York this summer, and I suppose given him various incidental information relative to the place he was shortly to visit. We met him the next day at the gate. He had seen Fr. Paul. Everybody says to see Fr. Paul. Tom Gossett says he will take us up there so perhaps I will see him myself.

I suppose I will work on Tarwater the rest of the summer. It is too good a book not to be a better one. It'll never be the way it ought to be but it will have to stand up straighter than it is now before I let it go.

Positive charity as opposed to flagellation and the hairshirt. It's harder and more wearing on the nerves and availeth more. I presume. But you don't need to read it. I am reading a corker called The Image Industries by William Lynch S.J. I have four piled up to review but they will have to wait for me to finish the Big Thing, namely: The Mystical Element of Religion. Mrs. Cheney checked it out of the Vanderbilt theological library for me, two volumes. I have read it in too big a hurry but at least I am reading it. Also I have persuaded my editor to read Von Hugel and I have an eye to trying to persuade him further to bring out a collection of the essays. This would be a great contribution to the tone of American Catholicism.

Chrs,

To Dr. T. R. Spivey

Milledgeville
Dear Ted,   25 May 59

On the surface of it it doesn't seem appropriate sending you letters designed for the baron's neice; however it may be appropriate after all as you are interested in the education of women and this is the way he thought a woman should be educated. But anyhow, don't judge him as to his real work by this. All the "darling Gwen-childs" have to be ignored.

Next month there is going to be a book out from the Helicon Press on Chardin—his thought. My editor from Farrer, Straus was down here to visit me last week and I was asking him about Chardin and it turned out he knew him for about a month in New York before he died. He said he was very impressive.

I am reading a book I like called "The Disinherited Mind," by Erich Heller—essays on Goethe, Nietzche, Rilke, Spengler, Kafka, and a few others. I know practically nothing about German literature.

Week before last I went to Wesleyan and read A Good Man Is Hard to Find. After it I went to one of the classes where I was asked questions. There were a couple of young teachers there and one of them, an ernest type, started asking the questions. "Miss O'Connor," he said, "why was the Misfit's hat *black*?" I said most countrymen in Georgia wore black hats. He looked pretty disappointed. Then he said, "Miss O'Connor, the Misfit represents Christ, does he not?" "He does not," I said. He looked crushed. "Well, Miss O'Connor," he said, "what is the significance of the Misfit's hat?" I said it was to cover his head; and after that he left me alone. Anyway, that's what's happening to the teaching of literature.

To Dr. T. R. Spivey

Milledgeville

Dear Ted,   21 June 59

I haven't read the article in PR or the beat writers themselves. That seems about the most appalling thing you could set yourself to do—read them. But reading about them and reading what they have to say about themselves makes me think that there is a lot of ill-directed good in them. Certainly some revolt against our exagerrated materialism is long overdue. They seem to know a good many of the right things to run away from, but to lack any necessary discipline. They call themselves holy but holiness costs and so far as I can see they pay nothing. It's true that grace is the free gift of God but in order to put yourself in the way of being receptive to it you have to practice self-denial. I observe that Baron von Hugel's most used words are derivatives of the word *cost*. As long as the beat people abandon themselves to all sensual satisfactions, on principle, you can't take them for anything but false mystics. A good look at St. John of the Cross makes them all look sick.

You can't trust them as poets either because they are too busy acting like poets. The true poet is anonymous, as to his habits, but these boys have to look, act, and apparently smell like poets.

I am reviewing a book for Mrs. Hall on Zen and Japanese Culture. I took it up as a burden but I find it very interesting and it's easy to see what attracts the beat people to Zen and where it leads them astray. If you took Christ, the Church, law and dogma out of Christianity, you would have something like Zen left. The beat people's need for it witnesses to their need for the contemplative life. Do you think it would be possible for Protestantism ever to come up with a form of monasticism? I asked a divine from Mercer that and he said No. In any case if there could be such a thing in Protestantism, a lot of these people could be salvaged from Zen.

I don't believe that if God intends for the world to be spared He'll have to lead a few select people into the wilderness to start things over again. I think that what He began when Moses and the children of Israel left Egypt continues today in the Church and is meant to continue that way. And I believe all this is accomplished in the patience of Christ in history and not with select people but with very ordinary ones—as ordinary as the vacillating children of Israel and the fishermen apostles. This comes from a different conception of the Church than yours. For us the Church is the body of Christ, Christ continuing in time, and as such a divine institution. The Protestant considers this idolatry. If the Church is not a divine institution it will turn into an Elks Club by and by & can be dispensed with & you will find yourself going into the wilderness to establish other future Elks Clubs.

Yours,

To Catharine Carver

Milledgeville
1 July 59

Dear Catharine,

This is what I think is better. I may be wrong but it seems better mechanically, and I have added sentences here and there that seem to bring out things that needed to be brought out, such as your suggestion about Rayber's looking at the burnt house, etc. Typing it over I have been very pleased with almost every sentence and have been grinning constantly while I worked. Nothing like appreciating your own efforts. And you just don't know how much I appreciate yours.

To Cecil Dawkins

Milledgeville

Dear Cecil,   17 July 59

Well my novel is finished and on its way courtesy the US Postal Service to the publisher. Catharine Carver's final verdict was that it is the best thing I've done. The most I am willing to say is that it has taken more doing than anything else I've done. I dread all the reviews, all the misunderstanding of my intentions, etc etc. Sometimes the most you can ask is to be ignored.

The current ordeal is that my mother is now in the process of reading it. She reads about two pages, gets up and goes to the back door for a conference with Shot, comes back, reads two more pages, gets up and goes to the barn. Yesterday she read a whole chapter. There are twelve chapters. All the time she is reading, I know she would like to be in the yard digging. I think the reason I am a short story writer is so my mother can read my work in one sitting.

Well I don't envy your having to talk three hours a day. Did I tell you that one of the teachers around here asked her class to define "classicism?" One answer: work in class.

I have been sent a copy of John Updike's short stories from Knopf—to be published in August. I liked the novel right much and I like some of the stories but a great many of them seem too slight to be included. Anyway, I am sending you the book for the good ones.

If you all get to drive balls into the dean of women I see why you like to play golf. I can't imagine any other advantages to it.

Cheers,

To A.

Milledgeville

Dear A.,   25 July 59

The first will be fine and we will meetcha at the entrance to this estate.

Thank you for what you say about the novel. Your appreciation always adds something to my own. I will shore it up against the day when I am faced with the misunderstanding reviews. I expect this one to be pounced on and torn limb from limb. Nevertheless, I am pleased with it myself, everything in it seems to me to be inevitable in the economy of the situation.

Now about Tarwater's future. He must of course not live to realize his mission, but die to realize it. The children of God I daresay will despatch him pretty quick. Nor am I saying that he has a great mission or that God's solution for the problems of our particular world are prophets like Tarwater. Tarwater's mission might only be to baptize a few more idiots. The prophets in the Bible are only the great ones but there is doubtless unwritten sacred history like uncanonized saints. Someday if I get up enough courage I may write a story or a novella about Tarwater in the city. There would be no reformatory I assure you. That murder is forgotten by God and of no interest to society, and I would proceed quickly to show what the children of God do to him. I am much more interested in the nobility of unnaturalness than in the nobility of naturalness. As Robert says, it is the business of the artist to uncover the strangeness of truth. The violent are not natural. St. Thomas's gloss on this verse is that the violent Christ is here talking about represent those ascetics who strain against mere nature. St. Augustine concurrs.

I will take just as much naturalness as I need to accomplish my purposes, no more but a Freudian could read this novel and explain it all on the basis of Freud. Many will think that the author shares Rayber's point of view and praise the book on account of it. This book is less grotesque than WB and as you say less funny. But if it had been funny, the tone would have been destroyed at once. In some places I may have gone too near the edge already. As you say, one distraction, one look aside or up or down, and the jig is up.

I will not be doing any more after the book is published than at any other time. I do not attend book parties.

My mother has read it but of course I couldn't tell what she thought of it. She has got the idea that "literary" writing is distinguished from what normal people enjoy and therefore cannot be judged by her feeling about it. She said, "Does it

have symbolisms in it? You know when I was coming along,
they didn't have symbolisms."

P.S. You neednt return the ms. but if I should lose my copy
or something I might have to borrow it back from you.
    We await yr arrival.

                                                    Chers,

To Dr. T. R. Spivey

                                                    Milledgeville
Dear Ted,   19 August 59
    I'll try to answer your questions but as they are not doc-
trinal questions, you must remember that this is just my opinion about these things.
    The good Catholic acts upon the beliefs (assumptions if
you want to call them that) that he receives from the Church
and he does this in accordance with his degree of intelligence,
his knowlege of what the Church teaches, and the grace, natural & supernatural, that he's been given. You seem to have
met nothing but sorry or dissatisfied Catholics and abrupt
priests with no understanding of what you want to find out.
Any Catholic or Protestant either is defenceless before those
who judge his religion by how well its members live up to it
or are able to explain it. These things depend on too many
entirely human elements. If you want to know what Catholic
belief is you will have to study what the Church teaches in
matters of faith and morals. And I feel that if you do, you
will find that the doctrinal differences between Catholics and
Protestants are a great deal more important than you think
they are. I am not so naieve as to think such an investigation
would make a Catholic of you; it might even make you a
better Protestant; but as you say, whatever way God leads
you will be good. You speak of the Eucharist as if it were not
important, as if it could wait until you are better able to practice the two great commandments. Christ gave us the sacraments in order that we might better keep the two great

commandments. You will learn about Catholic belief by studying the sacramental life of the Church. The center of this is the Eucharist.

To get back to all the sorry Catholics. Sin is sin whether it is committed by Pope, bishops, priests, or lay people. The Pope goes to confession like the rest of us. I think of the Protestant churches as being composed of people who are good, and I don't mean this ironically. Most of the Protestants I know are good, if narrow sometimes. But the Catholic Church is composed of those who accept what she teaches, whether they are good or bad, and there is a constant struggle through the help of the sacraments to be good. For instance when we commit sin, we receive the sacrament of penance (there is an obligation to receive it once a year but the recommendation is every three weeks). This doesn't make it easier to commit sin as some Protestants think; it makes it harder. The things that we are obliged to do, such as hear Mass on Sunday, fast and abstain on the days appointed, etc. can become mechanical and merely habit. But it is better to be held to the Church by habit than not to be held at all. The Church is mighty realistic about human nature. Further it is not at all possible to tell what's going on inside the person who appears to be going about his obligations mechanically. We don't believe that grace is something you have to feel. The Catholic always distrusts his emotional reaction to the sacraments. Your friend is very far afield if she presumes to judge that most of the Catholics she knows go about their religion mechanically. This is something only God knows.

At the age of 15 one would come into the Church with possibly many expectations of perfections and little real knowlege of human nature, and from 15 to 18 is an age at which one is very sensitive to the sins of others, as I know from recollections of myself. At that age you don't look for what is hidden. It is a sign of maturity not to be scandalized and to try to find explanations in charity. I doubt that she has seen any "lying" nuns. What she is probably talking about is "intellectual honesty" and she is forgetting that in order to be intellectually honest, you have to have an intellect in the first place. Most nuns go into the convent right out of highschool, they have no knowlege of the world, their ways of loving the

Church are frequently unwise, they are unbelievably innocent, most usually ignorant, and victims of the edifying tendency; a lot of them who are teaching are competent at most to wash dishes; but I have been in the Church for 34 years and I know many nuns, have gone to school to them, correspond with a few, and I have never found one who deliberately lied. At the other end of the scale I know some who are both educated and intelligent and whom it would be a privilege to have for teachers.

As for the neurotic priests, neurosis is an illness and no one should be condemmed for it. It takes a strong person to meet the responsibilities of the priesthood. They take vows for life of poverty, chastity, and obedience, and there are very few defections. Most of the priests I know are not neurotic but most are unimaginative and overworked. Also the education they get at the seminaries leaves much to be desired.

About the Churches political actions. God never promised her political infallibility or wisdom and sometimes she doesn't appear to have even elementary good sense. She seems always to be either on the wrong side politically or simply a couple of hundred years behind the world in her political thinking. She tries to get along with any form of government that does not set itself up as a religion. Communism is a religion of the state, committed to the extinction of the Church. Mussolini was only a gangster. The Church has been consorting with gangsters since the time of Constantine or before, sometimes wisely, sometimes not. She condemms Communism because it is a false religion, not because of the form of gvt. it is. The Spanish clergy seems to be shortsighted in much the same way that the French clergy was shortsighted in the 19th century, but you may be sure that the Pope is not going to issue a bull condemming the Spanish Churches support of Franco and destroy the Churches right to exist in Spain. The Spanish clergy has good and bad in it like any other. If Catholics in Hungary fight for freedom and Catholics in Spain don't, all I can tell you is that Catholics in Hungary have more sense or are more courageous or perhaps have their backs to the wall more than those in Spain. A Protestant habit is to condemm the Church for being authoritarian and then blame her for not being authoritarian enough. They object that politically

all Catholics do not think alike but that religiously they all
hold the same beliefs.

You are good to ask these questions and in such a charitable spirit & I hope I can answer them in the same spirit.

Yours,

To Maryat Lee

Milledgeville

Dear Maryat,   21 August 59

Well you're the doctor and you may be right.

Did I understand you right that you are writing from 5000
to 7000 words of bad prose a day? By my calculations this is
about 20 pages. Girl, it couldn't be anything else but bad.
That is too much prose to write in one day. It must be automatic writing. Slow down for pity sake. Practice your mouth
organ, do anything, but don't write 20 pages of prose a day.
At that rate you would write a novel in two weeks.

Mine is in, yes, and scheduled for February. The reaction
is favorable though some of the comments seem a little non-
plussed, of the "yes, but" variety. I don't think there will be
any cheers from reviewers as it is just not the kind of thing
they go for, but I myself am entranced with how well it is
put-together. It will have one genuine appreciator.

Nothing doing hereabouts. When do you remove again to
the city?

Love,

To Maryat Lee

Milledgeville

Dear Maryat,   6 September 59

Well thanks for the offer of yr. apartment but I ain't coming to New York unless somebody pays me to and nobody is
liable to pay me to. I do not attend autograph parties etc.

Once only was I roped into any such as that and now I would rather be drawn and quartered.

Been working on that book for seven years with time off occasionally to write a story. The relief of finishing it was extreme but I haven't spit up or anything. I am now writing a story that seems very light weight indeed and don't seem anyhow much of a challenge. Next I intend to write me a lecture to deliver at yr brother's institution this fall and anywhere else I am asked, that is, paid, to deliver it.

I read about 80 pages of Dr. Pasternak but I am so slow that the book had to go back ere I had fairly begun. There were a lot of wonderful things in those 80 pages but I don't think I could have stood that much formlessness for however many hundred pages there were. A friend of mine reviewed it and said it was like a huge shipwreck with a lot of beautiful things floating in it. You are not supposed to feel at home or at ease in any of the forms you see around you. Create your own form out of what you've got, let it take care of itself.

I cut out the Pfeifer cartoon about the Eisenhower speech and show it to everybody that comes. I also enjoyed the interview with the Hansberry girl; and there are such things as the information of Mr. Ginsberg that the way to reach God is through mariuana. They are revoltingly sentimental about their own bohemianism sometimes.

The thing for you to do is write something with a delayed reaction like those capsules that take an hour to melt in your stomach. In this way, it could be performed in Milledgeville on Monday and not make them vomit until Wednesday, by which time they would not be sure who was to blame. This is the principle I operate under and I find it works very well.

Love & cheers,

To John Hawkes

Milledgeville
Dear Jack,   13 September 59
Your letter made me want you to read my novel now, so much so that I was tempted to send it to you (carbon) but I

think this *would* be an infringement on your time and friendship, so I am sparing you. If FS&C have bound half-galleys I'll get them to send you a set. Sometimes publishers send these to me and they are very easy to read. Anyway, I would like to tell you something about this novel (much of which you have rightly anticipated) and its kinship to WB.

I don't think you should write something as long as a novel around anything that is not of the gravest concern to you and everybody else and for me this is always the conflict between an attraction for the Holy and the disbelief in it that we breathe in with the air of the times. It's hard to believe always but more so in the world we live in now. There are some of us who have to pay for our faith every step of the way and who have to work out dramatically what it would be like without it and if being without it would be ultimately possible or not. I can't allow any of my characters, in a novel anyway, to stop in some halfway position. This doubtless comes of a Catholic education and a Catholic sense of history—everything works toward its true end or away from it, everything is ultimately saved or lost. Haze is saved by virtue of having wise blood; it's too wise for him ultimately to deny Christ. Wise blood has to be these people's means of grace—they have no sacraments. The religion of the South is a do-it-yourself religion, something which I as a Catholic find painful and touching and grimly comic. It's full of unconscious pride that lands them in all sorts of ridiculous religious predicaments. They have nothing to correct their practical heresies and so they work them out dramatically. If this were merely comic to me, it would be no good, but I accept the same fundamental doctrines of sin and redemption and judgment that they do.

Now in the new book, all this is still there but it is a more ambitious undertaking. The great-uncle is not a puritan here, as you saw. He is a prophet. And the boy doesn't just get himself saved by the skin of his teeth, he in the end prepares to be a prophet himself and to accept what prophets can expect from their earthly lives (the worst.) That was a shortened version of the first chapter. In the real first chapter it is brought out that the old man considers himself a prophet and that he has stolen the boy away from the school teacher

in order to raise him up to take his place as a prophet when
he dies. As soon as the old man dies, the boy is left alone
with the threat of the Lord's call. He heads for the school
teacher and the burden of the book is taken up with the
struggle for the boy's soul between the dead uncle and the
school teacher.

The modern reader will identify himself with the school
teacher, but it is the old man who speaks for me.

I hadn't thought about the cross shaped face as meaning
anything but that he was marked out for the Lord—or at
least marked out as one who will have the struggle, who will
know what the choice is. Haze knows what the choice is and
the Misfit knows what the choice is—either throw away
everything and follow Him or enjoy yourself by doing some
meanness to somebody, and in the end there's no real pleasure in life, not even in meanness. I can fancy a character like
the Misfit being redeemable, but a character like Mr. Shiftlet
as being unredeemable. Mr. Head's redemption is all laid out
inside the story.

This is too much about me and my works. I read The Velvet Horn and I was entirely taken with it. I didn't follow all
the intricasies of the symbolism but it had its effect without
working it all out. I also thought that since I was recommending A Name for Evil right and left, I had better read it
myself. And do you know that I couldn't? After the other
one, it seemed mannered, unconvincing, entirely unmoving. I
didn't finish it.

I'll be waiting for The Lime Twig and will prepare the
other two members of the Georgia Hawkes Appreciation Society. And I do appreciate your interest in this book of mine.
It's not every book that gets itself understood before it has
been read.

My best,

To John Hawkes

Milledgeville
Dear Jack,   6 October 59

You were awfully good to write me such a long and detailed letter about the book. The proofs came early and seeing

the thing in print very nearly made me sick. It all seemed awful to me. There seemed too much to correct to make correcting anything feasible. I did what I could or could stand to and sent them back this morning and my mother brought your letter in after they were mailed. It may be that on the page proofs I can get rid of some more of the as-if and seems. I was terribly conscious of them seeing it for the first time in print. This is what I have to *learn*, to keep the level of the prose up. Caroline Tate, who has taught me considerable, says I can't even write a complex sentence, but I do think that the first sentence and the last sentence in that book are mighty fine sentences and I cheer myself meditating on them.

Rayber, of course, was always the stumbling block. I had a version of this book about a year ago in which Rayber was really no more than a caricature. He may have been better that way but the book as a whole was not. It may just be a matter of giving the devil his due. As you say, your vision, though it doesn't come by way of theology, is the same as mine. You arrive at it by your own perception and sensitivity, but I have had it given me whole by faith because I couldn't possibly have arrived at it by my own powers. This perhaps creates a gap that I have to get over some how or other. Anyway I am usually out of my depth, and I don't really know Rayber or have the ear for him.

It is strange that in both these novels, what makes them possible as novels, I mean what makes them work, is the same thing that detracts or lowers the interest. I couldn't have written WB without Enoch. It would have been impossible mechanically. I was five years on WB and seven on this one, and in that time you turn and twist and try it every possible way and only one thing works. What you are really twisting about in is your limitations, of course. I had no trouble writing the first chapter and the last thirty pages; I spent most of the seven years on Rayber.

Send me back the chapter you have marked and keep the rest if you like until you have finished your Brandeis talk.

People are always asking me if I am a Catholic writer and I am afraid that I sometimes say no and sometimes say yes, depending entirely on who the visitor is. Actually, the question seems so remote from what I am doing when I am doing it, that it doesn't bother me at all.

Very very many thanks.

To Louise Abbot

Milledgeville
Dear Louise,   Sat.

I think there is no suffering greater than what is caused by the doubts of those who want to believe. I know what torment this is, but I can only see it, in myself anyway, as the process by which faith is deepened. A faith that just accepts is a child's faith and all right for children, but eventually you have to grow religiously as every other way, though some never do.

What people don't realize is how much religion costs. They think faith is a big electric blanket, when of course it is the cross. It is much harder to believe than not to believe. If you feel you can't believe, you must at least do this: keep an open mind. Keep it open toward faith, keep wanting it, keep asking for it, and leave the rest to God.

Penance rightly considered is not acts performed in order to attract God's attention or get credit for oneself. It is something natural that follows sorrow. If I were you, I'd forget about penance until I felt called to perform it. Don't anticipate too much. I have the feeling that you irritate your soul with a lot of things that it isn't time to irritate it with.

My reading of the priest's article on hell was that hell is what God's love becomes to those who reject it. Now no one has to reject it. God made us to love Him. It takes two to love. It takes liberty. It takes the right to reject. If there were no hell, we would be like the animals. No hell, no dignity. And remember the mercy of God. It is easy to put this down as a formula and hard to believe it, but try believing the opposite, and you will find it too easy. Life has no meaning that way.

Intellectual questions like Christ's belief in the end of the world have been tackled by a lot of Christian thinkers, Biblical scholars, etc. I am going to send you a book with one such discussion in it, which may not satisfy you but should at least let you know what good minds grapple with the same problem you do.

As for unbelievers being saved, the Church teaches that those who live according to the light they have received will be saved—this goes for sincere pagans, jews, etc. At least this is what the Catholic church teaches and I would presume some of the Protestant churches do too, though probably not the extreme ones.

I too think Fr. Weigle does not give credit where it is due on the matter of receiving and constructing doctrine. I think most Protestants believe they receive it. However, the more modern and liberal they get the less they receive it. The health nurse must have had terrible instructions. Most Catholics know better than that.

Whatever you do anyway, remember that these things are mysteries and that if they were such that we could understand them, they wouldn't be worth understanding. A God you understood would be less than yourself.

This letter is full of non-sequiturs (sp?). I don't set myself up to give spiritual advice but all I would like you to know is that I sympathize and I suffer this way myself. When we get our spiritual house in order, we'll be dead. This goes on. You arrive at enough certainty to be able to make your way, but it is making it in darkness. Don't expect faith to clear things up for you. It is trust, not certainty.

—— ——'s gift is for finding money, not literature. I wouldn't pay a great deal of attention to her advice on how your story ought to be. If I could look at it for you any time and offer any word, I'd be glad to.

My novel will come out in February and I am now correcting the proof which is an awful job. The novel seems dull and half-done to me. It makes me sick. I can barely make myself read the proof.

Come to see us whenever you can. We are building two extra rooms and a bath onto the house—a back parlor. We will let you set in it.

Cheers,

P.S.—From time to time when I find anything I think interesting on some of these subjects that affect you, I am going to send them to you. I hesitate to do this sometimes because what I see is usually from a Catholic point of view and I do not want to force this on you.

To Maryat Lee

Milledgeville
Dear Gargantua,   Eisenhower's Birthday

Anybody else would just bake a loaf of bread but old Maryat she bakes corn bread, banana bread, nut bread and I-talian bread. Who eats it? If I lived near you I would beg my bread at your back door. And then there is the practising 9 hours and the painting 9 hours and all the pages and pages. You should have a special length of day to fit you.

I always tell people I paint because it helps my writing but I am not sure that this is true or only something to say. I think I only paint because occasionally we need something to put on the wall and I like to make my own mark on my own house. Right now we are building on an extra sitting room and bed room and I have a big canvas that cost $4 that I got about five years ago and never have painted up because I have never painted on anything so big before. It still intimidates me but I intend to paint it up now because we need it for the new room. I did caricatures when I was in college too, not of individuals but of the types found around the place and I enjoyed that greatly, there is something immediate about it, it either is successful or it isn't, there are never any doubts, such as you feel over a piece of fiction, that you can't see all at once.

I looked over my words on the short story but they are all addressed to innocents or creeps and would do you no good whatsoever. The only way I could do you any good would be to look at the thing itself, and then it wouldn't be anything but impressions I would have to offer. The impressions of my novel so far have been very different, all depending on what was brought to it not what is necessarily in it.

I have just corrected the proofs and that is very depressing. You see everything that is wrong and believe me I saw plenty but it was too much to correct. At least you recognize again your limitations and accept them. I know that this is the best in seven years I can do. So be it. It is now time to do something else. I'm at another story. Did I tell you I finished the other one and then realized that I couldn't publish it because it would hurt some people around here? They all read my stuff. We once had a centenniel here and some people got shot, the most melodramatic event in the history of the bird sanctuary, and I should have let it alone. In about twenty years I ought to be able to publish it, if I am still about.

Where will I find the Twain essay on Cooper? Thanks for the enclosed. The next I hear from you I expect you to have 12 tons of granite in your room & to be carving a monu-ment.

Excelsior,

To Dr. T. R. Spivey

Milledgeville

Dear Ted,   30 November 59

I was rather horrified to see that I had put the word *merely* before the word *spiritual*. This was inexcusably sloppy writing as, of cource, I did not intend to delegate the spiritual to an inferior status. I mean the spiritual by itself alone or the spiritual not embodied in matter. God is pure Spirit but our salvation was accomplished when the Spirit was made flesh. I meant to imply no more than the traditional teaching of the Incarnation as Catholics see it in the Church. When the Spirit and the flesh are separated in theological thinking, the result is some form of Manicheism. The Catholic's end in worship is always God Who is Pure Spirit.

If your vision of the future is Manichean, or even if it is purely Protestant, I'm not ready for it on principle. I am also not ready to say that literature and knowlege have come to an end for all practical purposes. These things are good in themselves. They reflect the Creator. Mauriac says God does not care anything about what we write, He uses it. So much the more reason I think that we have to give Him the best we've got for His use and leave the uses to Him. I do not know from what you say whether you have departed from, or never considered worthy in the first place, a Christian humanism. The times do seem a bit apocalyptic for anything so sane. Anyway, regardless of the specifics of your vision of the future, I should think that in so far as it is the desire for the Kingdom to come, anyone who has been given the grace of hope could share in it. In this sense I am still with you.

About hiding in the Church. I suppose you mean by this that I am hiding in the Church from, not in, Christ. This is to accuse me of some pretty repulsive qualities and I hope you are wrong. It is certainly possible to hide from spiritual reality in the Church. I know a few who succeed at it, but for me to do so would at least be against the currents of all I feel and hope for. Anyway, it is something to be alert against.

About trying to be a type of saint I can't be, you don't say what type this is. I believe there are as many types of saints as there are souls to be saved. I am quite interested in saving my soul but I see this as a long developmental evolutionary process, extending into Purgatory, and the only moment of it that concerns me in the least is the instant I am living in.

I haven't read Pere Teilhard yet so I don't know whether I agree with you or not on The Phenomenon of Man. In any case, I doubt very much if his researches are a product of the "Jesuit mind." Some of the severest criticism I have read about it has come from other Jesuits.

I hope to be around in the middle of December and will look forward to seeing you. That is if I dont freeze in the meantime. It is so cold here I can barely work the typewriter.

                                                        Best,

To Cecil Dawkins

                                            Milledgeville
Dear Cecil,   23 December 59
    In my day at Yaddo the maids were all well over forty, large, grim and granit-jawed or shrivelled and shrunk. This

man's remark sounds as if it were made by someone who feels dutybound to show that he has been about. Of course I was there in 1948 and this is 1960 almost. Things may now have changed but in my day the help was morally superior to the guests by all I could judge of.

Liquor was not served by the management but of course you could get your own and in any collection of so-called artists you will find a good percentage alcoholic in one degree or another. There were a good many parties at which everybody contributed something for the liquor. I went to one or two of these but always left before they began to break things. In such a place you have to expect them all to sleep around. This is not sin but Experience, and if you do not sleep with the opposite sex, it is assumed that you sleep with your own. This was in pre-beatnik days but I presume it is all about the same. At the breakfast table they talked about seconol and barbiturates and now maybe it's marujana. You survive in this atmosphere by minding your own business and by having plenty of your own business to mind; and by not being afraid to be different from the rest of them.

I don't recall specifically that passage in Dom Aelred Graham's book; however, I read the whole thing and was not shocked by anything in it nor did I find anything in it I hadn't heard before. It has an imprimatur. I gather from what you say that you don't understand that doctrine *develops*. "Innovation" seems a bad word to me for it implies that this teaching was not implicit in the deposit of faith, but I would have to see the passage again to find out. In any case, you may not understand from this that Dom Aelred does not believe in the real presence or that a Catholic has a choice in this matter. The Mass is a memorial but it is a memorial in which Christ is "really, truly, and substantially" present under the forms of bread and wine.

From what you ask me I see that you do not have any real imaginative vision of what the Church is. I don't take this to be your fault—Catholic education being what it is—but it is time you were learning what it is that you are rejecting. Besides not knowing what the Church is in the large sense, you don't know what she teaches. For example, where on earth did you get the notion that the Imaculate Conception means

that the Virgin Mary was conceived sexlessly? You must be
confusing this with the Virgin Birth which is not the birth of
the Virgin but Christ's birth. The Imaculate Conception
means that Mary was preserved free from Original Sin. Original Sin has nothing to do with sex. This is a spiritual doctrine. Her preservation from Original Sin was something God
effected in her soul: it had nothing to do with the way she
was conceived. The Assumption means that after her physical
death, her body was not allowed to remain on earth and corrupt, but was assumed, or like Christ's body after the resurrection, was caused by God to come into its transfigured and
glorified state. Now neither of these doctrines can be measured with a slide rule. You don't have to think of the Assumption as the artist has to paint it—with the Virgin rising
on an invisible elevator into the clouds. We don't know how
the Assumption or the Imaculate Conception were brought
about nor is this a matter for science in any way. Dogma is
the guardian of mystery. The doctrines are spiritually significant in ways that we cannot fathom. According to St.
Thomas, prophetic vision is not a matter of seeing clearly, but
of seeing what is distant, hidden. The Church's vision is
prophetic vision; it is always widening the view. The ordinary
person does not have prophetic vision but he can accept it on
faith. St. Thomas also says that prophetic vision is a quality
of the imagination, that it does not have anything to do
with the moral life of the prophet. It is the imaginative vision
itself that endorses morality. The Church stands for and
preserves always what is larger than human understanding.
If you think of these doctrines in this sense, you will find
them less arbitrary.

I think that what you want is not a Church that can be
"liberalized" but one that can be "naturalized." If there were
a scientific explanation or even suggestion for these supernatural doctrines, you could accept them. If you could fit
them into what man can know by his own resources, you
could accept them; if this were not religion but knowlege, or
even hypothesis, you could accept it. All around you today
you will find people accepting "religion" that has been rid of
its religious elements. This is what you are asking: if you can
be a Catholic and find a natural explanation for mysteries we

can never comprehend, you are asking if you can be a Catholic and substitute something for faith. The answer is no.

What the Church has decided definitively on matters of faith and morals, all Catholics must accept. On what has not been decided definitively, you may follow what theologian seems most reasonable to you. On matters of policy you may disagree, or on matters of opinion. You do not have to accept everything your particular pastor says unless it is something that is accepted by the whole Church, i.e., defined or canon law. We are all bound by the Friday abstinence. This does not mean that the sin is in eating meat but that the sin is in refusing the penance; the sin is in disobedience to Christ who speaks to us through the Church; the same with missing Mass on Sunday. Catholicism is full of such inconveniences and you will not accept these until you have that larger imaginative view of what the Church is, or until you are more alive to spiritual reality and how it affects us in the flesh.

The Church has always been mindful of the relation between spirit and flesh; this has shown up in her definitions of the double nature of Christ, as well as in her care for what may seem to us to have nothing to do with religion—such as contraception. The Church is all of a piece. Her prohibition against the frustration of the marriage act has its true center perhaps in the doctrine of the resurrection of the body. This again is a *spiritual* doctrine, and beyond our comprehension. The Church doesn't say what this body will look like, but the doctrine proclaims the value of what is least about us, our flesh. We are told that it will be transfigured in Christ, that what is human will flower when it is united with the Spirit.

The Catholic can't think of birth control in relation to expediency but in relation to the nature of man under God. He has to find another solution to the population problem. Not long ago a lady wrote a letter to Time and said the reason the Puerto Ricans were causing so much trouble in New York was on account of the Church's stand on birth control. This is a typical "liberal" view, but the Church is more liberal still.

Your thinking about the Church is from the standpoint of a kind of ethical sociology. You judge it by your own dimensions, want it to conform to what you can know and see and above all you want it to let you alone in your personal life. Also you judge it strictly by its human element, by unimaginative and half-dead Catholics who would be startled to know the nature of what they defend by formula. The miracle is that the Church's doctrine is kept pure both by and from such people. Nature is not prodigal of genius and the Church makes do with what nature gives her. At the age of 11, you encounter some old priest who calls you a heretic for inquiring about evolution; at about the same time Pere Pierre Teilhard de Chardin, S. J. is in China discovering Pekin man.

I am going to send you some books along that may clear up one thing or another. This is one part apostolic zeal and two parts horror at some of your misconceptions about what is taught. I probably have a lot of misconceptions myself and what I say to you is subject to correction by anybody more in command of the subject than I am; I mean by any competent Catholic theologian. I'm no theologian, but all this is vital to me, and I feel it's vital to you.

> Cheers and a happy new year,

To John Hawkes

Dear Jack,

Milledgeville
26 December 59

I certainly do mean Tarwater's friend to be the Devil. If I could have treated Rayber in the same way I treat Tarwater, then it would have been possible to show to what extent Rayber, like Tarw., accepts and resists the Devil; but I couldn't do this because the Devil who prompts Rayber speaks a language I can't get down, an idiom I just can't reproduce—maybe because it's so dull I can't sustain any interest in it. The Devil that prompts Rayber would never say, "How about all those drowned at sea that the fish have et . . . ?" etc.

Several years ago a friend of mine in a writing class at Iowa wrote me that his workshop had read and discussed the first chapter of this novel (it was in New World Writing) and the discussion revolved around who the voice was. Only one thought it was the Devil. The rest of them thought it was a voice of light, there to liberate Tarwater from that "horrible old man."

I share your present sense of outrage about English publishers. Longman's is going to bring out mine, and the other day I had a letter from them. The ms. had reached them and they had read it "several" times and wanted to know what the significance was of Tarwater's violation in the woods by the man in the motor car. I wrote a polite letter and said the man in the motor car was an actualization of Tarwater's friend and mentor, the Devil, and that if they thought there was any doubt about their readers understanding this, they had better put the information on the jacket. This is all very depressing. The general reader is going to think that violation is a piece of arbitrary grotesquery. I was once mentioned in an article as belonging to the "School of the Gratuitous Grotesque" (along with Paul Bowles). You must be classed in this brotherhood yourself.

Meeks is one of those comic characters but, like Mr. Shiftlet, of the Devil because nothing in him resists the Devil. There's not much use to distinguish between them. In general the Devil can always be a subject for my kind of comedy one way or another. I suppose this is because he is always accomplishing ends other than his own. More than in the Devil I am interested in the indication of Grace, the moment when you know that Grace has been offered and accepted—such as the moment when the Grandmother realizes the Misfit is one of her own children. These moments are prepared for (by me anyway) by the intensity of the evil circumstances. It is the violation in the woods that brings home to Tarwater the real nature of his rejection. I couldn't have brought off the final vision without it.

This is too much talk about my own book. You should be getting an advance copy shortly as I think they are to be sent out some time after Jan. 1 and I hope you will see some improvement in the prose of middle section, thanks to your advice. I'll be waiting on those chapters of yours with real anticipation and a feeling of kinship. And my best to you and Sophie for the new year.

To Katherine Anne Porter

Milledgeville
Dear Miss Porter,   22 January 1960

Thank you so much for your note and for wanting me to sign the card. Now that the book is in print, I see all the things that could have, should have, been done to it. Still it is a great relief to have it out of the way.

I wish you were about, to see my Chinese geese. I don't think I had them when you were here. They have knobs at the top of their bills and a very handsome shape on them and terrible voices (?), and they are mortal enemies to the peacocks. The racket is sometimes unbelievable. Geese fight on the ground and peacocks about four feet above. So they have not managed to kill eachother yet.

My very best to you and many thanks again for your kind note.

Yours,

To Robert Lowell

Milledgeville
Dear Cal,   2 February 60

I'll keep your letter about the book nearby when the trouncing begins. After working on it so long, I lose sense and confidence and forget what my own struggle is about. I am not through with prophets, though. I think the next one will be about how the children of God finish off Tarwater in the city; and that one may finish me off. Prophecy is a matter of seeing, not saying, and is certainly the most terrible vocation. My prophet will be inarticulate and burnt by his own visions. He'll have to explode somewhere.

You at least ought to bring your daughter on a visit here, at which I would present her with a peacock and a Chinese goose—both very imperious birds themselves.

This is Ground Hog day.

My love to you all,

To Andrew Lytle

Milledgeville
Dear Andrew,   4 February 60

I feel better about the book, knowing you think it works. I expect it to get trounced but that won't make any difference if it really does work. There are not many people whose opinion on this I set store by.

I have got to the point now where I keep thinking more and more about the presentation of love and charity, or better call it grace, as love suggests tenderness, whereas grace can be violent or would have to be to compete with the kind of evil I can make concrete. At the same time, I keep seeing Elias in that cave, waiting to hear the voice of the Lord in the thunder and lightning and wind, and only hearing it finally in the gentle breeze, and I feel I'll have to be able to do that sooner or later, or anyway keep trying.

There is a moment of grace in most of the stories, or a moment where it is offered, and is usually rejected. Like when the Grandmother recognizes the Misfit as one of her own children and reaches out to touch him. It's the moment of grace for her anyway—a silly old woman—but it leads him to shoot her. This moment of grace excites the devil to frenzy.

The book is going to be published by Longman's, Green in England. After they read the manuscript, they wrote to inquire what the significance was of Tarwater's violation in the woods by the man in the motor car. Besides the fact that nobody knows about the devil now, I have to reckon on the fact that baptism is just another idiocy to the general reader. A lady-librarian reviewing it in the Library Journal said that there was not "enough convincing action to bring this macabre tale to a successful conclusion." She also noted that Tarwater added to my "band of poor God-driven Southern whites." God-driven means underprivileged.

Well anyway, I am most grateful to you and steadied by you. If you get up this way, please stop with us. Ashley enjoyed his visit with you all. That boy is on the road more than Kerouac, though in a more elegant manner.

Yours,

To Maryat Lee

Milledgeville
Dear Maryat,   Thurs.

I have the feeling that the synopsis is ill-advised. It suggests that you don't have enough faith in the play itself coming across, or else in the reader getting it. Furthermore, I think it will suggest to them even more strongly that this is the stuff of a novel.

If I were going to use the quote at bottom of page 3, I would use the longer one. You can get by with that "nigh" in the whole play, but you can't get by with it out of context like that.

Also your prose is awfully cluttered. If you are going to write a synopsis, you will have to think a little about syntax and such pedestrian matters.

I was wondering—and this is just idle wondering of the non-theatre mind—why, instead of a synopsis, you don't write this play without any of the monkey business, without any of the heightening of language or parallel talking or that kind of stuff. This doesn't mean that you should just write it without their emotions coming through, but it means that you would make their emotions come through their language and not yours—no "nighs" and such stuff. Then you could present both plays to be read and the reader could see which one he liked best, and anyway get a better idea of the heightened one from reading the other. Also you might find after you had done it that the other was the better play. I ain't saying you would, I'm saying you might.

We have no water, no electricity, all the trees are broken with ice and the peacock's tails are frozen. My innocent face has not been washed in twenty-four hours.

Bob has just sent me a jazzy review from the San Francisco Chronicle which says my book is like a superior hillbilly concert. The fellow obviously adores hillbilly concerts and advises everybody to read the book.

Blessings from yr aunt Fannie.

To A.

Milledgeville
Georgia
Dear A.,   5 March 60
I enclose the latest in idiot reviews. I think this is the fun-
niest to date. Return.

If you don't want it, I'd like to have the Comforts of
Home back as I would like to send it to the Fitzgeralds who
haven't seen it. I disagree entirely with your comments on
both the sheriff's deputy and the piece of paper. I hope you
are not developing these kinds of rigidities about stories,
about mine anyway. The piece of paper floating down is there
to dramatize one of the sheriff's silences. While he is saying
nothing the sun changes from one side of the porch and the
loiterers move into it and a piece of paper floats down. That
this paper should be expected to have any meaning other than
its simple function is not to be countenanced. As for the deputy, he is part of the sheriff's world and he slinks into the car
because the sheriff has apparently been telling him what to
do. The sheriff controls this amount of fat by a mere look.
The deputy dramatizes the sheriff's power. You ought to read
Dubliners again. These things have their functions but they
are not functions leading to action, nor do they have to be.

Well I am glad they've sent you the book. I never read any
of her 27 books. Isn't she an English woman?

I am sure Billy is highly delighted to have at last met Dr.
Spivey because that gentleman has held his curiosity for some
time. They might do each other some good, but I don't
know.

Your review in the Bulletin looked good to me. Cecilia is
either meditating on writing me her criticisms at length or
she has the flu or her tongue is stopped by indecision, which
seems unlikely; but I have not heard from her.

During this past spell of weather, we had no water or lights
and the peacocks came down from the tree in the morning
with their tails frozen stiff and went limping about until the
middle of the day looking very miserable.

I am wondering where you got the idea that my childhood
was full of "endless illnesses." Besides the usual measles,

chickenpox and mumps, I was never sick. You say there is love between man and God in the stories, but never between people—yet the grandmother is not in the least concerned with God but reaches out to touch the Misfit. As you say, there is very much the business of the characters not wishing to be swallowed up in another's will. Rayber's love for Bishop is the purest love I have ever dealt with. It is because of its terrifying purity that Rayber has to destroy it. Very interesting.

                                             Cheers,

To Elizabeth Fenwick Way

                                          Milledgeville
Dear E,   April 13, 1960

Thanks for the loveletter from the New Yorker and the Japanese book. We are enjoying the Japanese book and will return it before too long, but if you want it before I get through with it, send an SOS. As for the New Yorker, it goes true to form, except for the word "majestic"—how did that get in there?

Yesterday and today I have been broken out in an interesting rash. I foresee a little spell. I also have one finger which has the feeling of being dead at the bottom, at the tip, I mean. I remember you had trouble with your fingers. Was it like that? Sort of as if the finger were packed in dry-ice or had novacaine in it?

In spite of your "bursitis" and them supersonic sound waves, I still give you credit for having Lupus with a capital L. The LE cells don't have to show up in the tests for you to have it. I hope some time you will go to Dr. Sofer there at Mt. Sinai. I get told from several sources that he is the lupus authority.

I itch so I shall leave you. Write me about the fingers.

To John Hawkes

Milledgeville
Dear Jack,   14 April 60

Thanks for your letter of some time back. I have been busy keeping my blood pressure down while reading various reviews of my book. Some of the favorable ones are as bad as the unfavorable; most reviewers seem to have read the book in fifteen minutes and written the review in ten. The funniest to date was in the Savannah paper—Savannah, where I have innumerable kin. It was highly favorable, called the hero "Tarbutton" throughout and said he was nine years old. I hope that when yours comes out you'll fare better.

It's interesting to me that your students naturally work their way to the idea that the Grandmother in "A Good Man" is not pure evil and may be a medium for Grace. If they were Southern students I would say this was because they all had grandmothers like her at home. These old ladies exactly reflect the banalities of the society and the effect is of the comical rather than the seriously evil. But Andrew insists that she is a witch, even down to the cat. These children, yr students, know their grandmothers aren't witches.

Perhaps it is a difference in theology, or rather the difference that an ingrained theology makes in the sensibility. Grace, to the Catholic way of thinking, can and does use as its medium the imperfect, purely human, and even hypocritical. Cutting yourself off from Grace is a very decided matter, requiring a real choice, act of will, and affecting the very ground of the soul. The Misfit is touched by the Grace that comes through the old lady when she recognizes him as her child, as she has been touched by the Grace that comes through him in his particular suffering. His shooting her is a recoil, a horror at her humanness, but after he has done it and cleaned his glasses, the Grace has worked in him and he pronounces his judgment: she would have been a good woman if *he* had been there every moment of her life. True enough. In the Protestant view, I think Grace and nature don't have much to do with each other. The old lady, because of her hypocracy and humanness and banality couldn't be a medium for Grace. In the sense that I see things the other way, I'm a Catholic writer.

I hope you are writing and that "The Lime Twig" is on the way. Also that you all may be going to Florida this year and will stop for a longer visit with us.

My best for the season to you and Sophie,

To Elizabeth Bishop

Milledgeville
Georgia
23 April 60

Dear Elizabeth,

The pictures are wonderful and I am glad to know you got back from looking at the Amazon and were not leaned upon by one of the tame buffalos and pushed over. I kept having that mental picture, sort of in snapshot form—"one of the rare photographs of the poet, Miss Bishop," and the tame buffalo, smiling, leaning you down. My notion of the jungle is all out of Frank Buck so tame buffalos seem very funny to me. Maybe it wasn't even jungle where you were. I would love to come to see you but I guess I will have to let the jets get it down to a fine point before I undertake a trip. Already they go from New York to Miami in 2 hrs & 40 min. We were going to take a trip to Europe again but instead we added a wing onto the house and my mother says we are sitting in our trip to Europe. I would just as soon sit in it, though I feel guilty about my attachment to comfort over culture.

My book has received considerable attention, most all of it simple-minded—a revolting review in Time, worse from Orville Prescott, the usual snide paragraph in the New Yorker & some very funny items from newspapers. The funniest to date was in the Savannah paper, Savannah where I was brought up & have lots of kin. It was highly favorable, called the hero "Tarbutton" throughout and said he was nine years old.

Caroline's comment on the back had really been written about Wise Blood and the stories. In the piece they took it from she went on to quote Blake's thing about oft in midnight streets I hear, about the harlot's curse blighting with plagues the marriage hearse etc; so I suppose what she had in mind was Blake's vision of evil. Anyway, I would just as soon they had used a variety of quotes on the back, some from other points of view. Although I am a Catholic writer, I don't care to get labeled as such in the popular sense of it, as it is then assumed that you have some religious axe to grind. However, since the review in Time, my mail has been full of attempts to save me from the Church—a set of tracts marked "personal" but with no return address arrived from Ossining New York, all about "how a priest was saved by Grace," "the Pope's blessing," etc. etc.; that professional atheist who advertises in the NYTimes book section sent me his book, "Jonah: Fact or Myth?" and I have received an anonymous message in a shaky hand to the effect that my religion is phoney. I suppose a book like mine attracts all the lunatics. I had one letter telling me that people such as I write about do not exist and in the same mail a friend sent me a clipping about a Rev. Mr. Pike of Lebanon, Tenn. who has got himself in the news for immolating a lamb, wired to a cross, at his "special" revival services; also one about a boy named Jimmy Sneed, a 13 year old evangelist, who hung himself because his mother spanked him for sassing her. A neighbor was quoted as saying, "He was a good boy. He had been preaching around here some lately and was doing fine."

You asked about Catharine Carver. She saw the book when the middle section was composed of three instead of six chapters. She told me it wasn't long enough and that it broke apart in the middle and that Rayber didn't come through— all of which was true. So I added all the business about the child evangelist and the chase through the city at night and that helped it no end. After that, she thought it was fine. I value her opinion and she will tell me when something is bad. I have a horror of somebody publishing something of mine when it isn't fit to publish.

A few weeks ago she came down here from Philadelphia (she works for Lippincott there now) and spent the weekend with me. She said it was the first time she had gone anywhere in ten years; she seems to have nobody and to exist in a kind of desert, but I think she liked it here and I hope to get her down here from time to time. The day she came I was to talk in Atlanta at something called The Georgia Council of Teachers of English—an unctious order of highschool English teachers. Their project for the last two years has been getting up a "map of Georgia Authors." So after two years of hard labor, they had the thing ready to unveil at their annual luncheon meeting; I was the speaker. I got them to let me bring Catharine and this was her introduction to the South. They had the menu all worked in with Georgia literature—Tara Prime Ribs, Ransy Sniffle Potatoes, Tarwater Baby String Beans, Uncle Remus pecan pie, etc. There was a long eulogy of Georgia literature written by John Donald Wade and read for him by an old gentleman with a trembling voice; the program went on for about two hours until finally they unveiled the map, a hideous modernistic thing with twenty ugly little faces completely covering it; the rest of the Georgia writers were listed around the margin, a hundred or so. My talk was the last thing on the bill but it was a real anti-climax because they were all sleepy by then. But she was amused by the whole thing and I was delighted to have such a silly occasion to entertain her with.

I see Cal has got a Ford grant to observe the opera; and also the Natl. Book Award, which must amuse him.

If there is any chance of your getting this way this summer, please don't fail to let me know. We could probably meet you in Savannah or Atlanta and bring you on here. We are just about in the center of the state.

Best,

To Elizabeth Fenwick Way

Milledgeville
Dear E,   22 May 60

Thanks for the clipping and if you run up on the horrifying one, don't fail to send it. I don't horrify easily. They say my bones aren't leaking calcium; there is some kind of blood test they gimme to determine that, but they believe that the lupus has affected those blood vessels that feed the top of the thigh bones, or anyway that is the likeliest possibility. But I will go along with you on that aspirin any day—the World's Finest Medicine. Last summer my jaw was popping out of the socket every time I opened my mouth and I couldn't chew good red meat for the pain. I took eight aspirin a day for a month and haven't had any more jaw trouble.

A lady I know said a lady she knew said a doctor who knew Dr. Sofer said Dr. Sofer said lupus sometimes just went away and stayed away for as long as ten years or so. One of these days I may yet take myself to be inspected by Dr. Sofer.

The japan book is in good hands but if you want it immediately let me know.

Await litry communication.

Cheers,

To A.

Milledgeville
Dear A.,   23 July 60

I sent Last Session a card and suggested he and you come on July 30 and he sent me one back saying unless you balked, he and you would do so. So kindly do not balk.

We had quite a gathering here Monday—six sisters from the Cancer Home, the Trappist Abbot, and a Msgr. Dodwell. I was greatly impressed with the Sister Superior. She is one of the funniest women I have ever encountered and has all the rock-like qualities that you would have to have to do what they do. She brought two old sisters, one of whom was Mary Ann's nurse, and three younger sisters, one of whom draws (very badly) and the other two write (very very badly). However, the Sister Superior is the one doing the writing on the book and she writes better than the others. She don't write like Shakespeare but she does well enough for this. What will come of the book, I wouldn't know but I am convinced that the child had an outsize cross and bore it with what most of us don't have and couldn't muster. The founder of their order was Hawthorne's daughter. I have just read a biography of her—very interesting if you'd like to see it.

I sure hope the Critic don't buy Calhoun. Think of all the awful letters they would get in the letters column; however, they might like the controversy.

That Haze rejects that mummy suggests everything. What he has been looking for with body and soul throughout the book is suddenly presented to him and he sees it has to be rejected, he sees it ain't really what he's looking for. I don't regard it in any abstracted sense at all.

According to Eileen, Mr. Zuber has written offering himself for the book column, so I reckon we will plug along. A man probably won't have the time or patience to fool with it long, but we shall see.

Five or six places is not enough places to send Miss Nancy. If you get tired of sending it around, just send it down here and I will send it around for you.

This is a new edition of The House of Fiction and also of Understanding Fiction, and includes a good many new stories. I have looked at some of the comentaries in the H of F and while some are good, some seem rather poor excuses. I haven't looked over the Understanding Fiction yet.

Well poor old Jack. I hope he gets it. I think King Kong would be better than Nixon. We didn't see any of it, having no television but one night I listend for a spell on the radio when we had company who must hear it. Fortunately the company soon left to seek out a television so we went to bed.

                                        Chrs until Sat. 30

To William Sessions

                                        Milledgeville
Dear Billy,   13 September 60
    I'm sorry the book didn't come off for you but I think it is no wonder it didn't since you see everything in terms of sex symbols, and in a way that would not enter my head—the

lifted bough, the fork of the tree, the corkscrew. It doesn't seem to be conceivable to you that such things merely have a natural place in the story, a natural use. Your criticism sounds to me as if you have read too many critical books and are too smart in an artificial, destructive, and very limited way.

The lack of realism would be crucial if this were a realistic novel or if the novel demanded the kind of realism you demand. I don't believe it does. The old man is very obviously not a Southern Baptist, but an independent, a prophet in the true sense. The true prophet is inspired by the Holy Ghost, not necessarily by the dominant religion of his region. Further, the traditional Protestant bodies of the South are evaporating into secularism and respectability and are being replaced on the grass roots level by all sorts of strange sects that bear not much resemblance to traditional Protestantism—Jehovah's Witnesses, snake-handlers, Free Thinking Christians, Independent Prophets, the swindlers, the mad, and sometimes the genuinely inspired. A character has to be true to his own nature and I think the old man is that. He was a prophet, not a church-member. As a prophet, he has to be a natural Catholic. Hawthorne said he didn't write novels, he wrote romances; I am one of his descendants.

In any case, your critique is too far from the spirit of the book to make me want to go into it with you in detail. I do hope, however, that you will get over the kind of thinking that sees in every door handle a phallic symbol and that ascribes such intentions to those who have other fish to fry. The Freudian technique can be applied to anything at all with equally ridiculous results. The fork of the tree! My Lord, Billy, recover your simplicity. You ain't in Manhattan. Don't inflict that stuff on the poor students there; they deserve better.

We'll look for you for Thanksgiving day and bring A. with you if you come that way. Her address is 2795 Peachtree Rd. NE.

Best,

To Robert Giroux

Milledgeville
Georgia
29 September 60

Dear Bob:

Thank you for sending the ad. I have received my six copies of the Longman's edition of the book. The jacket appears to belong on a good Western; however, I passed on it myself in a rough stage so I have no one to blame. The rough stage was so rough that it didn't look so bad.

I am engaged in an odd project right now which I would like to solicit your professional advice about sooner or later. In Atlanta there is a home for incurable cancer patients run by the Dominican congregation of nuns that was founded by Hawthorne's daughter. In the early part of the summer, the Sister Superior there wrote me about a child with a face cancer whom they had kept for nine years. She came when she was three, died when she was twelve. Many people in Atlanta heard about her and became friends of the home through her. She apparently had considerable charm in addition to this outsize cross. The Sister Superior is determined that something must be written about her. She had written a man named Hugh Cave (because he had published a book about a little girl) and asked him to write about this child. He told her a Catholic ought to do it (I suppose to get her off his hands). Through the monastery she heard about me, so she wrote and asked me to write a story about a child like this one. Just my kind of thing.

I wrote her that this was not the sort of thing that made fiction and that if it had to be written, the Sisters should write it themselves and it should just be a factual account* of the child's life and death in the Home. I told her if they did happen to write it, I'd be glad to go over the manuscript and would supply a little introduction if that would help. I thought that would be the last I'd hear of her. Never underestimate them. They forthwith sat down and wrote it and they are hell bent to see it through. The Abbot is interested in it and so is the Bishop who wants it to have the imprimatur. I hear he thinks the child was a saint.

*non fiction

The manuscript is not very good, of course. I set about to get the obnoxious pieties out of it and that proved almost impossible. I'm still working on it, and they are expecting me not only to turn it into a decent manuscript but to get them a publisher. Would you read it when I get it edited? I know I can't make it into the kind of thing you would publish but you might be able to tell me who might or if you think it's publishable at all.

Fr. Paul thinks it's quite comic that they have lit on me to do this. He asked them which of my murder stories gave them the idea I should help them with it.

The Abbot is so interested in this that he brought six of the sisters down here to spend the afternoon.

If you are making any of your journeys in this direction, we hope you will come down and see us. I am going to be in Minnesota October 17–21, talking at two Catholic colleges.

Best,

To John Hawkes

Milledgeville
Georgia
9 October 60

Dear Jack,

This is about how much I like THE LIME TWIG. It came last Sunday and I read it that afternoon and evening in a sitting that was unwillingly interrupted once or twice. The action seems to take place at that point where dreams are lightest (and fastest?), just before you wake up. It seems to me that you have retained all the virtues of the other books in this one, but added something that will hold the reader to the reading. I can't make any intelligent comments about this book any more than I could about the others; but I can register my sensations.

You suffer this like a dream. It seems to be something that is happening to you, that you want to escape from but can't. It's quite remarkable. Your other books I could leave when I wanted to, but this one I might have been dreaming myself. The reader even has that slight feeling of suffocation that you have when you can't wake up and some evil is being worked on you. I don't know if you intended any of this but it's the feeling I had when the book was happening to me.

I want to read it again in a month or so and see if the second time I can take it as observer and not victim. Meanwhile my admiration is 90% awe and wonder.

I am about to take off for Minnesota where I am going to talk at two Catholic colleges and read at the University—a Good Man is Hard to Find. I think when I read this story aloud I get over my interpretation of it—as against yours and Andrew's—fairly well, but I have an unfair advantage, since I sound pretty much like the old lady. After Minnesota, I am going to an Arts Festival thirty miles from here where Katherine Anne Porter, Caroline Gordon, Madison Jones and me are going to be paid (well) to swap cliches about Southern culture. An old lady left her sizable fortune for an Arts Festival every year at this college with the stipulation that the guests had to be Southernors and discuss Southern culture. The money goes on whether the culture does or not. I think it's programs like this that are going to hasten the end of it.

I understand that Andrew's wife has recently been operated on for lung cancer but I haven't heard how she is getting along.

Again my admiration. Nobody else writes like you do.

Yours,

To A.

Dear A.,   Tuesday
I wondered if you would let me send your letter to Hawkes? I wouldn't do it without your permission but I am tempted to. I think it would mean a lot to him to know that somebody really reads him. I don't think it would make any difference to him whether you have interpreted it right or wrong, just to know that someone he has never heard of has read it with this attention and intelligence and pleasure. It must be an experience he doesn't have often.

Lemme hear if you'll let me.

Boy are we sick of Great Lady Guests!

Cheers,

To Cecil Dawkins

Milledgeville
Dear Cecil,   8 November 60

I have been recuperating from Minnesota and then an Arts Festival at Wesleyan attended also by Caroline and Miss K. A. Porter. Caroline spent the weekend here after it and she is a strenuous woman and one night of it, we had the lot of them to supper. Katherine Anne remembered to inquire about a chicken of mine that she had met here two years before. I call that really having a talent for winning friends and influencing people when you remember to inquire for a chicken that you met two years before. She was so sorry that it was night and she wouldn't get to see him again as she had particularly wanted to. I call that social grace.

I liked the two schools I visited in Minnesota very much. Nuns like neither you nor I saw the likes of in our days in the parochial school.

A. writes that you have broken with the ranks of investment peddlers but gives no details. I was just about to write and congratulate you and ask for some financial advice. The trouble with writing is you make all your money at once and then don't get any for years. I have my two houses on the way to the waterworks but think I would like me some intangible investments; I keep wondering if Coca Cola will be good for eternity, etc. All the rich widows in M'ville are voting for Nixon, fearing lest Kennedy give their money to the niggers.

I have seen the MVSEVM in St. Louis but it was too big to impress me. Last year when Catharine Carver visited me, we met her in Atlanta and took her to the cyclorama in the mvsevm where Enoch got the mummy. Catharine wanted to see the mummy herself, so she and Regina went upstairs to look for it and I waited down stairs. After a while they came back but hadn't found it. On the way out, Catharine asked the girl at the ticket place if there had used to be one and the girl said yes there had, but she didn't know what had happened to it. Catharine was satisfied then that Enoch had taken it.

Cheers to you & Betty and keep me posted as to your writing and other occupations.

To Robert Giroux

Milledgeville
Dear Bob: 12 November 60

Thank you so much for sending me THE NEPHEW and THE CHRISTENING PARTY. I've already read THE NEPHEW and I think it is very fine; I haven't got around to the other one yet but am expecting to shortly.

I'm obliged for the clipping from TLS. The only British review I have seen that you haven't sent me was one by Kingsley Amis in the Observer. It was extremely unfavorable but he ended up saying that I had convinced him that this is the way people were in Georgia. (Horrors!) Longmans has boldly quoted this in their ads, ignoring the fact that the review was unfavorable. I would send it but I can't lay hands on it at the moment. Did I tell you that Longmans wrote me they were disappointed in the way the book was selling— after a month it had only sold 1500 copies. That was about 1500 more than I would have expected.

Would you send a copy of THE VIOLENT BEAR IT AWAY to M. Maritain in Princeton? Last spring, M. Coindreau took his French translation of WISE BLOOD over to Maritain and according to him, Maritain was so much taken with it that he asked M. Coindreau to come over to talk about it. I would like him to be sent this last novel.

We are all highly pleased with the results of the election. All the Baptist ministers in Georgia are having to find a new subject.

Best,

To A.

Milledgeville
Dear A.,   25 November 60

I was distressed you wouldn't come and have been worrying about what could be the matter. I started to call you up and try to persuade you to change your mind and then I decided I had better mind my own business and didn't do it. Now I am sorry I didn't because I think too many people and especially me mind their own business when their real business is somebody else's business. I feel very strongly that your business is my business, even if I don't always act quick enough on the feeling. I asked Billy what he thought might be the matter and he said he thought you might be depressed because you had shown something you had written to some young man who had made a lot of criticisms of it that you thought were just. Then I doubly wished that I had called up and insisted that you come and I also wished I were up there so that in the spirit of Christian charity I could knock you in the head with the nearest stick of wood.

Of course Billy may be wrong and I hope he was but assuming for the moment he wasn't, I have this to say. No matter how just the criticism, any criticism at all which depresses you to the extent that you feel you cannot ever write anything worth anything is from the devil and to subject yourself to it is for you an occasion of sin. In you, the talent is there and you are expected to use it. Whether the work itself is completely successful, or whether you ever get any worldly success out of it, is a matter of no concern to you. It is like the Japanese swordsmen who are indifferent to getting slain in the duel. I feel that you are distracted, particularly when you say, for instance, that it is Billy's writing that interests you considerably more than he does. This is certainly not so, no matter how good a writer he gets to be, or how silly he gets to be himself. The human comes before art. You do not write the best you can for the sake of art but for the sake of returning your talent increased to the invisible God to use or not use as he sees fit. Resignation to the will of God does not mean that you stop resisting evil or obstacles, it means that you leave the outcome out of your personal considerations. It is the most concern coupled with the least concern. This sermon is now ended. It may be as wide of the mark as Pittypat's, in which case ignore it. But you owe me a visit.

Didn't pay all that much attention to the pastoral. Like the good Puerto Ricans. I thought some kind of statement was in order, but you just wouldn't expect him to write a very

good one. It should never have appeared as a paid political
ad in the Sunday papers. I thought that was the worst of it.

My mother thought Billy tremendously improved; I
thought he might be a trifle more subdued than usual. My
cousin —— and her husband and boy had dinner with us.
Her husband is a rather officious type from —— who calls
Regina Eeunt Reegeena and me Meyuhry Flaynerry, but the
day went off well enough. Billy announced that he will be
returning Christmas and in January so I'll have further opportunity to decide whether he has improved.

I didn't know that copy of the introduction had that bad
place in it. I guess that should teach me to look at the carbons. The Sisters were very pleased with it and even Regina
liked it which means something as she is usually bored by my
productions I am afraid. I enclose Caroline's comments. I
have no intention of changing the opening, but I will do the
smaller things she suggests. I feel that the opening is all right.
I think she is right about putting myself in too much. This is
supposed to be about Mary Ann, but correcting that is mostly
a matter of taking out the I-thinks and I-feels.

We liked the Zubers very much. Madame Z is as thin as he
is partridge-like. He is full of ideas. He was much taken with
you. I wish he were editing the whole paper.

                                                        Cheers,

I thought a bloody semicolon was for a long pause. What is
it for?

To Robert Giroux

                                              Milledgeville
Dear Bob: 8 December 60

The enclosed jolly treat is the Sister's manuscript. If you
think there is any possibility at all of its getting published
anywhere, I might be able to get them to improve it. After I
had got the thing all typed for them, they decided there were
"a few other little things" they had forgot to mention. So I
told them to write them down and I would insert them. Today they sent me the insertions, three of them. Two I have

inserted and the other I am sparing you. It had to do with Mary Ann eating some applesauce.

Caroline proclaimed that this should be called DEATH OF A CHILD. I presented this to the Sisters but they did not take to it at all. They then got together to think of titles and came up with some that would curl your hair: THE BRIDE-GROOM COMETH, SONG WITHOUT END, THE CROOKED SMILE. The Abbot, who is in on this too, came up with the worst: SCARRED ANGEL. I informed them that none of these would do, and suggested the title I have put on it. They accept this reluctantly but think it is very "flat."

Now that they have produced a book, Sister Evangelist thinks a movie should be made about Mary Ann. They are serious. I have declined to take part in the production (for their postulants) of the movie.

I am entering the hospital in Atlanta Tuesday to have my bones inspected as they are not doing well, but I am sure I'll be spared at least until I find a publisher for the Sisters as they are all praying for it.

I hope you will have a Merry Christmas and thank you very much for reading this. I think there is a great deal in this child and wish her book were written better but I don't know anybody who would write it.

Best,

Jubilee is going to look at the introduction and some pictures of Mary Ann.

To Maryat Lee

hospital

Dear Maryatwater   Thursday PM

I was cheered by the sound of that familiar voice of yourn & today your letter came & tonight I may be chased through impassable white banks by a silent bus. Big Sister don't speak through the walls at night and I sleep very well. One of the Sisters at the cancer home has brought me a box of cresants, an aunt has brought me six egg custards, & my Florida friend sent me an artificial spider to put in the bed to frighten the nurses. It does not look like I will get home Friday. The old man says lets leave it on a day to day basis. My mother says when we leave, Piedmont will have my money, the doctors will have a lot more information and I will be about where I was when I came in. You can't get ahead of Mother.

All they do is draw my blood and xray my bones but they are learning. Another friend today brought me "A la recherche de temps perdue" in 2 volumes but I hope I won't be here long enough to read it. The food is lousy didn't you find?

When I came in & gave the information about myself at the admitting place, the woman, who had carrot-colored hair & eyeglasses to match, asked me by whom was I employed. "Self-employed," says I. "Whats your bidnis?" she says. "I'm a writer," I says. She stopped typing & after a second said, "What?"

"Writer," I says.

She looked at me for a while, then she says, "How do you spell that?"

Maybe I told you that over the telephone. I forget what I say like the old ladies.

I must leave you to eat an egg custard & a cresant as I have to stop eating & drinking by 12.

Yours,
O'authwarter

To A.

Milledgeville
24 December 60

Dear A.,

I read 50 pages of Proust in the hospital and was surprised how much I enjoyed it. We got home to find all my furniture piled in the middle of the room, newspapers and sheets all over every thing. Louise and Walter had had four days on the room and were about half finished. Also we had frozen pipes and all week we have been in a mess so I ain't got to any more of M. Proust, but I am going to enjoy it all next year and I trust by next Christmas to have it finished. I am still enjoying those Greek plays you gave me. From time to time I read one I haven't read yet.

What they found out at the hospital is that my bone disintegration is being caused by the steroid drugs which I have been taking for ten years to keep the lupus under control. So they are going to try to withdraw the steroids and see if I can get along without them. If I cant, as Dr. Merrill says, it is better to be alive with joint trouble than dead without it. Amen.

Monday or Tuesday I will send you Billy's play which arrived the other day, half coming out of the envelope, with dollar bill still miraculously attached. I am very much afraid that this play is a good deal worse than the last one; at least it seems so to me, and I am beginning to think that this verse drama exaggerates Billy's worst tendencies. He has a fictional talent that is largely lost here in pomposity. The characters are quite out of Billy's experience, they are always making motions at each other preparatory to rape, and saying things like There Is No Escape, etc. Billy is just not Claudel, T. S. Eliot, or anybody in fact but Billy. I think he is easily deflated in some respects and I don't want to say these things to him. But I think I am going to say that this is not his authentic material. I think the first one of them was the best.

I had a card from Cecilia and she said to write her and give her courage for her journey. So I wrote her but I doubt if I gave her courage for the journey.

I think that is dandy your taking over the GBD if you do. If you don't nobody else will and something will be lost.

Jubilee accepted the introduction. I was surprised. They will run it in February or March. The sisters are tickled pink and maybe if the book don't get published, this will be something for them anyway.

Me, I am working on that story I told you about and having the best time I have had in a spell of working. If I can work it out, I'll have something here.

I think your friend is ready for the psychiatrist. I don't think Betty is reading for HB and if she is, she wouldn't be the one to reject the book.

Chrs

To Elizabeth McKee

Dear Elizabeth,   1/3/61

Thanks for your note before Christmas and for calling Harcourt, Brace. As for those Germans, they can omit "A Stroke of Good Fortune" and "A Temple of the Holy Ghost" but not "The Displaced Person" or as they call it, "Misplaced Persons."

I am out of the hospital but not at full capacity yet.

To Robert Giroux

                                            Milledgeville
Dear Bob: 23 January 61

The Sisters are dancing jigs all over the place. I bet them a pair of peafowl nobody would ever buy the book so I am out a pair of peafowl.

Sister Evangelist called up the Bishop at once and he was delighted. However, he wanted one thing in the manuscript out before he can give the imprimatur. The scene where Mary Ann goes to confession and the Sisters hear her say, "Fife times, Monsignor." The Bishop says that can't be in there as you are not supposed to hear what goes on in the confessional. Bishops will be Bishops. Then there is one thing he wants added, which I think is a good idea and will improve the book. It seems that before she died, the Sisters allowed Mary Ann to become a tertiary and she was buried in the Dominican habit. The Sisters had thought it better to suppress that as no one under fifteen is supposed to be a tertiary and they were afraid they would get in trouble with headquarters. But the Bishop thinks it ought to be in and that this was a case of *in extremis* so it would have been permissable. I told the Sisters to write it up and indicate where it should come and send it to me. I will send it on in a few days.

Sister Evangelist wanted to know what "a free editorial hand" meant and I told her it meant you all would improve the book some, so she is all for a free editorial hand.

She is the one you should write to. Sister M. Evangelist,

O.P., Our Lady of Perpetual Help Free Cancer Home, 760 Washington Street, Atlanta, Georgia. She is being transferred in February sometime and will not be Superior after that, so if you could get the contract to her as soon as you can so that she can sign it herself, that will be best. She has written to the Head in Hawthorne to find out if it will be all right for her to sign it. She wants it fixed so the money will go to the Atlanta home, but has to get that okayed at Hawthorne. Hawthorne breaths for all houses.

Suggest to her whatever you think is right for my share in it. My share will have to go through Elizabeth, but not theirs. I'll write to Elizabeth about it.

Would you like a picture of Mary Ann to go in the front of the book? They have plenty of them at *Jubilee* that you can see. I enclose one for you. There are a million others because they were always taking pictures of her.

I like the idea of the brochure on my book because all the good reviews are stuck off where nobody will ever see them. If you do get it up, I wish you would include Richard Gilman's remarks on it in the Christmas book issue of Commonweal.

I'd also like to talk to you sometime about getting WISE BLOOD back in print. I get letters from college libraries asking where it can be found. You said once that you all might be willing to put it in print if Harcourt wouldn't.

Yours,

P.S. I think the galleys on the Mary Ann book should be sent to me as the Sisters don't even know what they are. If you would like to have their original manuscript for the person who is going to edit this, I can send it to you.

To A.

Milledgeville
Dear A., 4 February 61
I don't think the dead are held to any vow of obedience. As long as he lived he was faithful to his Jesuit superiors but

I think he must have figured that in death he would be a citizen of some other sphere and that the fate of his books with the Church would rest with the Lord. After reading both books, I doubt that his work will be put on the Index, though I think some of the people who latch upon his thought and distort it may cause certain propositions in it to be condemned. I think myself he was a great mystic. The second volume complements the first and makes you see that even if there were errors in his thought, there were none in his heart.

In the matter of conversion, I think you are thinking about the initial conversion. I am thinking possibly about the deepening of conversion. I don't think of conversion as being once and for all and that's that. I think once the process is begun and continues that you are continually turning inward toward God and away from your own egocentricity and that you have to see this selfish side of yourself in order to turn away from it. I measure God by everything that I am not. I begin with that. Maybe this depends on the person and is different for different people.

I can't get over the Mary Ann business. I told the Sisters that if that child was a saint, her first miracle would be getting a publisher for their book. And now the more I think about the way that book is written, the more convinced I am that it is a genuine miracle. Giroux wrote, "I read the story with a few misgivings which somehow are not important." And I guess that about sums it up. They have asked for a free editorial hand, so I am hoping this will improve the book a little.

I have been reading Mauriac's MEMOIRES INTE-RIEURS, which when I finish it I am going to send to you to read what he says about Emily Bronte. He sounds so much like you he might be you. He also has some good things to say about Hawthorne. I shall claim to be the only living person who doesn't have a theory about Emily Bronte. I don't know anything about her except she lived on the moor. I don't know what a moor is but I should guess a piece of land that was desolate and damp. I read Wuthering Heights once but I am going to have to read it again to see why it fascinates you so.

The only thing for apostate priests to do is to be violently anti-Catholic and write books against the Church or go on the sawdust trail with "I was a Catholic priest but I was saved by the Bible," etc. Perhaps this man's heart couldn't be in that.

The pageant was such a success, they are thinking of putting it on every year. There is no wound, my girl; this is merely a gorgeous way to make money.

Chrs,

To Ashley Brown

Milledgeville

Dear Ashley, 13 February 61

This is the story that came out of that potato festival clipping. I am a receptive depository for clippings. The latest I have got to add to my collection is one of a man who has just had Christ tattooed on his back. This is obviously for artistic and not religious purposes as he also has tiger and panther heads and an eagle perched on a cannon.

I have just got through reading "I Choose to Die," by B. Cheney based on Sam Davis, boy hero of the Confederacy. It has several places in it for choreography by Joy Zibart. I like it all but the song and dance.

We have been vigorously celebrating Secession here—parade, pageant, pilgrimages, etc. I sat over the hole in the upholstery in the living room sofa and shook the hands of all and sundry. About 500 people showed up. Lance Phillips (the Englishman whose house we went to for tea) wrote the pageant and oddly enough it was a great success. Everybody is falling around now trying to get the copyright out of him, so they can make this thing like the Paul Green business in North Carolina. He is holding out for a rising percentage of the net profits, which is certainly what he should get. They spent $1000 for fireworks and $600 for floats, and would not pay him but $200 for the pageant.

I have a friend in the divinity school at Princeton who goes to see Caroline and digs in her yard for her. He says she is a "lonesome old lady."

Louise recently stuck an icepick in Shot but otherwise we go on our peaceful way around here.

Cheers,

Item: I got Rememberance of Things Past for Christmas and have read 998 pages in it. Old age.

To John Hawkes

Milledgeville
Georgia
3 March 61

Dear Jack,

The enclosed is some Southern hot air to help melt the snow up there. This is the kind of silly business that ensues when Southern writers get together before an audience. Also enclosed is a story of mine, lighter than I usually write, but which will provide a view of some more metamorphoses.

Thanks so much for your article on Edwin Honig's poetry, which I enjoyed, without knowing the poetry, for the way it was written. A. is reading it now and will doubtless have something intelligent to say about it. It made me want to read the poetry it described. Elizabeth Way wrote me that David and Edwin Honig were going to start a poetry magazine. Maybe I can subscribe and read some of it.

A. says she sent you her last novel. I think you will see from it how much talent she has and how much it needs direction so that it won't blow itself out in violence.

From what I gather, Andrew has been quite influenced by Caroline. He wrote a fine essay on her work, which appeared in the issue of *Critique* (U. of Minn.) devoted to her. She is death on technique; too death on it to my way of thinking, but as I have learned a great deal from her, I preserve more or less a respectful silence.

The sheriff's vision is not meant to be taken literally, but to be the devil's eye view. And nobody is "redeemed." I am afraid that one of the great disadvantages of being known as a Catholic writer is that no one thinks you can lift the pen without trying to show somebody redeemed. To me, the old lady is the character whose position is right and the one who is right is usually the victim. If there is any question of a symbolic redemption, it would be through the old lady who brings Thomas face to face with his own evil—which is that of putting his comfort before charity (however foolish.) His doing that destroys the one person his comfort depended on, his mother. The sheriff's view is as the world will see it, not as it is. Sarah Ham is like Enoch and Bishop—the innocent character, always unpredictable and for whom the intelligent characters are in some measure responsible for, (responsible in the sense of looking after them). I am much interested in this sort of innocent person who sets the havoc in motion.

The Lime Twig has just arrived and I like the looks of it.

Best to you both,

To Maryat Lee

Milledgeville
Dear Maribennyfactor,   25 March 61

Yesterday was my birthday and in the midst of it arrived a Waring Blender. I am bowled over and under. You only can be the donor of this instrument which makes me speechless. Ah, now my jaw can rot at its leisure. I am at once attracted in the book by something called burbon balls and if I succeed in producing any, I will send you a sample. Are you coming here for Easter? If so, you can hold some demonstrations. My parent is equally took with it. Mary Jo and Miss White, who do not have one, are coming out this afternoon to see it. Incidentally, did you know it was my birthday?

No story has showed up so I presume you are typing it. I have just written one and sold it to NWW that will be out in October. It is called EVERYTHING THAT RISES MUST CONVERGE and touches on a certain topical issue in these parts and takes place on a bus. When I get an extra copy, I will send it to you. I am highly pleased with it.

The Sisters that I got their book published came down week before last and picked up the two peafowl they won from me on the bet. They wanted to give me something to remember them by; they said, what did I want, and I said I didn't want anything; that I would have no difficulty remembering them. They don't have any money of their own. The Superior called up and said, We've found what we're going to send you. In fact we've already got it. My brother gave it to me to give you—a portable television. So now we have a portable television. One of the first things I saw on it was your brother. We get the University station and he was on it telling the folks about the needs of women's colleges, etc. The television didn't do much for him. His face looked like it had been slicked down the middle and not put together right.

I am about to get onto those liquor balls, having bought the stuff to do it with. Be on lookout for small reeking box.

> Innumberable thanks.
> Tarblender

To Mr. ——

Milledgeville
Georgia
28 March 61

Dear Mr. ——,

The interpretation of your ninety students and three teachers is fantastic and about as far from my intentions as it could get to be. If it were a legitimate interpretation, the story would be little more than a trick and its interest would be simply for abnormal psychology. I am not interested in abnormal psychology.

There is a change of tension from the first part of the story to the second where the Misfit enters, but this is no lessening of reality. This story is, of course, not meant to be realistic in the sense that it portrays the everyday doings of people in Georgia. It is stylized and its conventions are comic even though its meaning is serious.

Bailey's only importance is as the Grandmother's boy and the driver of the car. It is the Grandmother who first recognizes the Misfit and who is most concerned with him throughout. The story is a dual of sorts between the Grandmother and her superficial beliefs and the Misfit's more profoundly felt involvement with Christ's action which set the world off balance for him.

The meaning of a story should go on expanding for the reader the more he thinks about it, but meaning cannot be captured in an interpretation. If teachers are in the habit of approaching a story as if it were a research problem for which any answer is believable so long as it is not obvious, then I think students will never learn to enjoy fiction. Too much interpretation is certainly worse than too little, and where feeling for a story is absent, theory will not supply it.

My tone is not meant to be obnoxious. I am in a state of shock.

Yours,

To John Hawkes

Milledgeville
Georgia
Dear Jack,   20 April 61

I was terribly pleased to know that Lillian Hellman likes my stories. I had never thought of her even remotely as a person who would read them. It is always a revelation to find out the people who like and dislike them. It is another way of reading the stories.

The enclosed is a horrible little piece of correspondence which please return to me as I feel it deserves a place in my files, possibly just as a lesson to me. I am conscience-stricken that I answered the man in such a harsh fashion. At the time, the thought of this interpretation multiplied by 93 was too much for me, but there was no excuse for this rudeness. I hope that before I die I either mend my manners or have less occasion to employ them.

The divine is probably the sum of what Singleton lacks and thereby suggests, but as he stands I look on him as another comic instance of the diabolical. I think that perhaps for you the diabolical is the divine, but I am a Thomist three times removed and live amongst many distinctions. (A Thomist three times removed is one who doesn't read Latin or St. Thomas but gets it by osmosis.) Fallen spirits are of course still spirits, and I suppose the devil teaches most of the lessons that lead to self-knowlege.

A. does seem to kill off her energy when she writes fiction, but it pains me to see this much intelligence with nothing to do with itself. She says what she is writing now has to do with her own self so maybe her true voice will be liberated.

I hope maybe the summer will bring you all to Florida. You can stop and see me on Hwy. 441, and the goat man on Hwy. 80.

Best,

To Maryat Lee

Dear Marywitchywater, 21 April 61

I have not yet tried a whole egg in the blender as my parent seems to have a prejudice about it. However she is all for making some more liquor balls. The way we make them is she does the work and I turn the blender on and off. I am very good at it. We saw Len Hart at the Sanford House and he inquired as to your doings and I told him you were eating egg shells & taking a reading course.

I am going to Atlanta Monday to have some cortesone injected into both hips in the hope that this eases my sitting down and my getting up. Its an office job; I don't have to go to Piedmont.

It is very decent weather here you should come to see us & renew your ties with the dear old dirty Southland.

Blessings
Tarsot

To John Hawkes

Milledgeville
Dear Jack, 22 June 61

About that grandmother and the Misfit: it is the fact that the old lady's gesture is the result of grace that makes it right that the Misfit shoot her. Grace is never received warmly. Always a recoil, or so I think.

I don't think much of the traditional association of insanity with the Divine. That's for romantics. Quincy State Hospital is actually two miles out of Milledgeville, the same only bigger. A five minute stroll through the grounds would dampen any enthusiasm you might have for the traditional association. I think you think I'm my own Mr. Parish, but actually I don't think we read Singleton so differently. I use Divine in the traditional Christian sense of the Holy and you don't. From that standpoint the old man is not divine. He's a lecherous old nut and stands for his own reality against the young people's absurd notions of him, and like you, I am all for Singleton in this, devil though I rightly consider him to be. He's one of those devils who go about piercing pretensions, not the devil who goes about like a roaring lion seeking whom he may devour. There is a hierarchy of devils surely.

My Tennessee friends tell me that Andrew is probably going to take over the Sewanee Review. I hope this is so. Edna seems to be fine and they are now in Mont Eagle.

Farrar, Straus & Cudahy have bought Wise Blood and are going to bring it out again and I am trying, unsuccessfully, to make myself write a foreword or note to the second edition or something like that, but I find I have nothing whatsoever to say about it. Then I think of the Parishes who will and decide I had better.

A good summer to you all,

To Thomas Stritch

Milledgeville
Dear Tom,   14 September 61

You ought to see my swans. They are as moth-eaten a pair as you ever laid eyes on, but I am well pleased and expect them to improve under my supervision. They snort and hiss but are very slow on their feet and don't attempt to go anywhere but from the feed bucket to the water trough. This reminds me to tell you that if you do manage to cook up anything at Notre Dame, please also cook up a way to get me there from Chicago short of the airplane. I am sufficiently decrepit now to have retired myself from any but the simplest ways of getting anywhere. But the way it looks to me, nobody will be travelling in May. We talk about the shelter and put it in a different place every day and haven't put it anywhere yet. And at night I dream of radiated bulls and peacocks and swans. But then, the Lord spared Nineve where there were over a hundred and twenty thousand persons who didn't know their left hand from their right, and many beasts, so maybe there is a precedent for us to be spared too.

I don't know any new German theologians. All I know is Guardini and Adam and I reckon you know them—could hardly have escaped it. I'm much taken, though, with Pere Teilhard. I don't understand the scientific end of it or the philosophical but even when you don't know those things, the man comes through. He was alive to everything there is to be alive to and in the right way. I've even taken a title from him—"Everything That Rises Must Converge" and am going to put it on my next collection of stories.

I hope you are finding the essays you need for the volume you mentioned. I had wanted to ask you about it when you were here but there was too much going on. Probably those people who run Cross Currents could help you find them. They must know everything in that order that has been printed in the last fifteen years.

It was awfully good to see you and always is.

Love,

PS—If Robt. honors you with his address in rural Italy, please pass it on to me.

To A.

Milledgeville
Dear A.,   28 October 61

I don't know anything that could grieve us here like this news. I know that what you do you do because you think it is right, and I don't think any the less of you outside the Church than in it, but what is painful is the realization that this means a narrowing of life for you and a lessening of the desire for life. Faith is a gift, but the will has a great deal to do with it. The loss of it is basicly a failure of appetite, assisted by sterile intellect. Some people when they lose their faith in Christ, substitute a swollen faith in themselves. I think you are too honest for that, that you never had much faith in yourself in the first place and that now that you don't believe in Christ, you will believe even less in yourself; which in itself is regretable. But let me tell you this: faith comes and goes. It rises and falls like the tides of an invisible ocean. If it is presumptuous to think that faith will stay with you forever, it is just as presumptuous to think that unbelief will. Leaving the Church is not the solution, but since you think it is, all I can suggest to you, as your one-time sponsor, is that if you find in yourself the least return of a desire for faith, to go back to the Church with a light heart and without the conscience raking to which you are probably subject. Subtlety is the curse of man. It is not found in the deity.

Now about the Mary Ann book—of course I want you to review it if Leo asks you to and if you can still say the same things about Mary Ann and the Sisters. But do not mention the introduction. The introduction is about the things that hold us fast in Christ when Christ is taken to be divine. It is worthless if it is not true.

We hear, via the grapevine, that Shot is going to sue us. Jack says, "I ain't so dumb, Miss, some nigger is putting him up to that." Shot hasn't said anything about it himself but he avoids us; sleeps all day and prowls all night. Regina consulted the insurance man and he said Shot couldn't sue because he had accepted the compensation insurance. However I have a drama all worked out in my head in which the NAACP is called in to defend Shot in his struggle against injustice.

Cecil was going to try to meet me at Marillac but a letter from the Sister says the place is not open for the public because they are all nuns. So I reckon I won't see her. She can't make herself write, but the girl she lives with, who has no particular interest in it, sat down last summer and completed a novel in two months, and according to Cecil, it is a good one.

Yours,

To A.

Milledgeville

Dear A.,   25 November 61

Oh dear. However I expressed it, it had not occurred to me that you didn't feel for people. I wasn't thinking of feeling. I was thinking of something a good deal more radical. I don't really think it's too important what your feelings are. I doubt if even Miss Nancy and her strings deserves the feeling you lavish on her. People's suffering tears us up now in a way that in a healthier age it did not. And of course everybody weeps over loneliness. It is practically a disease. The kind of concern I mean is a doing, not a feeling, and it is the result of a grace which neither you nor I nor Elizabeth Bishop in the remotest sense possesses, but which Sister Evangelist, for example, does. It doesn't have to be associated with religious; I am just trying to isolate this kind of abandonment of self which is the result of sanctifying grace.

I see that I was wrong in my speculation that you would now have even less confidence in yourself. You have more, of course. Faith is blindness and now you can see. Faith is an over-reaching; now what you reach for is within your grasp. I think you are right to take off six months and I think that you will be able now to do anything you want to—the novel or criticism or whatever you set your hand to, and believe me, nobody will rejoice in this like I will—not the heresy but in the success. Send me the Murdoch thing. I don't know anything about her but I can at least tell you what I think about how it is written.

This has been one hellish week here. Thanksgiving began to be celebrated by the staff on Sat. 18th. On Monday Louise's neice, Shirley, turned up with a baby, which meant that Louise's mamma, Camilla, age 100, had to be sent out here to stay with Louise. The old woman and Shirley slept in the same bed and there wasn't but one so the baby had to have Camilla's half. The old woman is mindless, wets the bed at night, has to be watched every minute to be kept out of the fire, and according to Louise is mean and hateful. The only way Louise can stand it is to be thoroughly soused. When drunk Louise raises her hand high and bows low with it and says, "The goverment is suppose to take care of my mamma. If they sends me a check every month, then I'll take care of her, but if they don't, they needn't be expecting me to fool with her." When sober, she just wrings her hands and says, "What I going to do with that ole woman—mean and hateful as she can be." Regina asked her how Shirley liked the baby and she said, "She's just crazy about it—big ole black ugly thing."

I don't know what Andrew means by concrete in Jack's case but probably not what you are thinking because he admires The Turn of the Screw. He would probably be interested in your piece on Jack.

Chrs,

To John Hawkes

Milledgeville
Georgia
28 November 61

Dear Jack,

I have been fixing to write you ever since last summer when we saw the goat man. We went up to north Georgia to buy a bull and when we were somewhere above Conyers we saw up ahead a pile of rubble some eight feet high on the side of the road. When we got about fifty feet from it, we could begin to make out that some of the rubble was distributed around something like a cart and that some of it was alive. Then we began to make out the goats. We stopped in front of it and looked back. About half the goats were asleep, venerable and exhausted, in a kind of heap. I didn't see Chess. Then my mother located an arm around the neck of one of the goats. We also saw a knee. The old man was lying on the road, asleep amongst them, but we never located his face.

That is wonderful about the new baby. I can't equal that but I do have some new additions to my menage. For the last few years I have been hunting a pair of swans that I could afford. Swans cost $250 a pair and that was beyond me. My friend in Florida, the one I wrote you about once, took upon herself to comb Florida for cheap swans. What she sets out to do, she does. She found a rare bird farm going out of business where everything was half price. $125 was still too much for me. Then she found out that the man had one pair of swans that he would sell for $65 because the female was blind in one eye. So now I am the owner of a one-eyed swan and her consort. They are Polish, or immutable, swans and very tractable and I radiate satisfaction every time I look at them.

I've had brief notes from Andrew a couple of times lately. In fact he has a story of mine but I haven't heard from him whether he's going to use it or not. He said he had asked you to write an article about my fiction and that if he used my story I might want to send it to you. If he does take it and you write an article and want to see the story, I'll send it. It's about one of Tarwater's terrible cousins, a lad named Rufus Johnson, and it will add fuel to your theory though not legitimately I think.

You haven't convinced me that I write with the devil's will or belong in the romantic tradition and I'm prepared to argue some more with you on this if I can remember where we left off at. I think the reason we can't agree on this is because there is a difference in our two devils. My devil has a name, a history and a definite plan. His name is Lucifer, he's a fallen angel, his sin is pride, and his aim is the destruction of the Divine plan. Now I judge that your devil is co-equal to God, not his creature; that pride is his virtue, not his sin; and that his aim is not to destroy the Divine plan because there isn't any Divine plan to destroy. My devil is objective and yours is subjective. You say one becomes "evil" when one leaves the herd. I say that depends entirely on what the herd is doing.

The herd has been known to be right, in which case the one who leaves it is doing evil. When the herd is wrong, the one who leaves it is not doing evil but the right thing. If I remember rightly, you put that word, evil, in quotation marks which means the standards you judge it by there are relative; in fact you would be looking at it there with the eyes of the herd.

I think I would admit to writing what Hawthorne called "romances," but I don't think that has anything to do with the romantic mentality. Hawthorne interests me considerably. I feel more of a kinship with him than with any other American, though some of what he wrote I can't make myself read through to the end.

I didn't write the note to WISE BLOOD. I just let it go as is. I thought here I am wasting my time saying what I've written when I've already written it and I could be writing something else. I couldn't hope to convince anybody anyway. A friend of mine wrote me that he had read a review in one of the university magazines of the VIOLENT BEAR ETC that said that since the seeds that had opened one at a time in Tarwater's blood were put there in the first place by the great uncle that the book was about homosexual incest. When you have a generation of students who are being taught to think like that, there's nothing to do but wait for another generation to come along and hope it won't be worse.

I have heard one funny story about the book that restores my cheer somewhat. A lady in Texas wrote me that a friend of hers went to look for a paperback copy of A GOOD MAN. The clerk said, "We don't have that one but we have another one by that writer. It's called THE BEAR THAT RAN AWAY WITH IT."

I've introduced THE LIME TWIG to several people and they're all enthusiastic. Somebody has gone off with my copy now. I hope you are at another one.

                                                                   Cheers,

To John Hawkes

                                                         Milledgeville
Dear Jack,   6 Feb 62
    Here finally is the story that will be in *Sewanee*. I've had the flu and ended up with less than my usual amount of energy, but I may make some minor changes here and there eventually. In this one, I'll admit that the devil's voice is my own.

    I'm cheered to be one of the "wild talents." Right now I feel something less.

                                                                   Yours,

To A.

Dear A.,   24 February 62

We have really had it this week. Last weekend Louise didn't
come out of her house at all. Jack said she was "down in the
back," which we took for a euphemism for "dead drunk."
Monday he came over and said she couldn't get out the bed,
so Regina went over there and sure enough, she was moaning
and groaning and said she couldn't get up. Regina called the
doctor and he said giver some aspirin. Regina made her take
the aspirin and then went on in to town. When she came back
at dinner time, Jack said she wasn't no better and she'd have
to go to the doctor so Regina called the doctor and made
arrangements for her to come while he was still in his office,
then went down to pick up Louise and Louise wouldn't
come. Scared to death. Going to die. Fifty six years old and
never had been to no doctor. Regina couldn't do anything
with her, so we went to town and got some Absorbine Jr.
and Regina came back and rubbed her back. Didn't do any
good, but Regina couldn't get her to the doctor. So finally
we went up to Eatonton and got Shot's mama to come down
and see what she could do. Her name is Ida. She talks in a
high voice, constantly, and has a very high opinion of herself.
On the way back she diagnosed the case as a "wranch back"
and said she would make a poltice of mud and salt and that
would take care of everything. She did this and administered
a dose of Black Draught and then came over and said she had
decided Louise would have to go to the doctor because she
couldn't pass her water. So for about the fourth time that day
Regina called the doctor and he said bring her in. All the way
in she weeped and wailed and said she never had been to the
doctor and to call Lucy Mae and she was fifty six years old
and had never been sick, never been to no doctor. "You on
your way now," Ida says. They stayed in the doctor's office
about an hour, and came out in high spirits. "How do you
feel?" I said. "Feels better," she said, "I feel a heap better."
"She didn't even know what a specimen was," Ida said and
the rest of the way home Ida entertained us with how ignorant Louise was and how she had had to take charge and tell

the doctor what was wrong with her etc. Ida said Louise's people were dropsical on her mother's side and on her father's side they went crazy. Anyway, what was wrong with her was the flu and the doctor had given her a shot of penicillin, and all week she has been recuperating. Regina says next year she is going to see she gets a flu shot.

Fr. Mayhew turned up the next day, thank the Lord not the one before. He is about to be transferred to LaGrange and Fr. Mulroy to Athens. I guess you know Fr. Boyce died—33 years old.

The Sessions heir is to arrive in August, Regina is to be the godmother. Billy says the money is going to run out just when the baby comes, but he is still going to Columbia and try to get a job on the side. All this I think is going to bring Billy up to his potential stature.

Chrs,

To Walker Percy

Milledgeville
Georgia

Dear Mr. Percy,   29 March 62

I'm glad we lost the War and you won the Nat'l Book Award. I didn't think the judges would have that much sense but they surprized me.

Regards,

To John Hawkes

Milledgeville

Dear Jack,   5 April 62

I like the piece very very much and I hope Andrew takes it or if not him somebody else. This is not to say that you have convinced me at all what you say is perverse is perverse. But you are very fine in pointing out where I disagree with you so I don't feel this does any damage to my views and the quality of the just plain textual insights is so wonderful that of course I hope this will be read. It doesn't seem stuffy to me.

I think what you do is to reduce the good and give what you take from it to the diabolical. Isn't it arbitrary to call these images such as the cat-faced baby and the old woman that looked like a cedar fence post and the grandfather who went around with Jesus hidden in his head like a stinger—perverse? They are right, accurate, so why perverse? I think you call them perverse because you like them. They may be perverse to the bourgeoise mind. Thomas Mann has said the grotesque is the true anti-bourgeoise style. But you don't have a bourgeoise mind and for you perverse means good. Nobody with a religious consciousness is going to call these images perverse and mean that they are really perverse. What I mean to say is that when you call them perverse, you are departing from that word's traditional meaning.

This is a sloppy and hasty letter, but I want to send it right away because you seem to be in some doubt over the piece and I don't think you ought to be. Also I am fixing to take off on some bread-winning expeditions and don't have the time to sit down and write better, but I will later. I am going to Raleigh to talk at North Carolina State College next week, then the week after I am going to the Southern Literary Festival in Spartanburg. Andrew is going too so I'll ask him what he thought of your piece. Eudora Welty and Cleanth Brooks will be there as the other two guests. The week after that I am going to a Catholic college in Chicago and then down to Notre Dame and then home with my tongue hanging out and a firm resolve not to go anywhere else for as long as possible.

Do you want this copy back? I would like to send it to A. as she reads everything of yours she can come by. She has been having a hard time lately (depression) but I think she is coming out of it.

I hope Sophie is all right and you too. More later. I just wanted you to know that I appreciate what has gone into the piece and what has come out and I am touched and honored that you did it.

Yours,

To Cecil Dawkins

Milledgeville
Dear Cecil,   25 April 62

My editor has written me that he must have a note to the new edition of WB as this will enable him to change the copyrite so I have had to do it. What do you think of the enclosed? It is as much as I can get out of myself.

The Hickses spent a week here recently and were asking about you and if you had got your acceptance yet. I hope you meet them when you go up there. I have a friend in Schenectady—the one the Hickses came down with—an ex-liberrian, rather stary on first sight, but really very nice, and I am going to ask her to ask you over or something when you are there.

I have just got back from Converse & the Southern Litry Festival where there was Eudora Welty, Cleanth Brooks, Andrew Lytle and me. I really liked Eudora Welty—no pretence whatsoever, just a real nice woman. She read a paper on Place in Fiction. It was very beautifully written but a little hard to listen to as anything like that is that is written to be read. These affairs are powerful social. There was a coffee in the morning, a tea in the afternoon and a reception with a receiving line in the evening. She told a story about a beauty parlor operator in Jackson who writes novels about the North West Mounted Police. She sent one of her love scenes to Faulkner through the mail for criticism and when she didn't hear from him she called him up and said, "Mr. Faulkner, what did you think of that little love scene of mine?" He said, "Honey, it isn't the way I would do it, but you go right ahead, you go right ahead."

The week before Converse I went to North Carolina State. That is strictly a technical school, they don't give an AB or have any English majors, nevertheless have thirty people on the English faculty and the students are sharp.

Next week I go to Rosary College in Chicago and then to Notre Dame. Then the next week I have to go to Emory and talk to a Methodist Student congregation on "The South." Their choice of topic. Of course I don't know any more about the South than they do, but I hopes to pull it off. The first of June I go back to Notre Dame because I am being given a degree by St. Mary's College. Then after that boy, I am going to stay at home and write me some fiction. A little of this honored guest bidnis goes a long way, but it sure does help my finances.

Everything is hatching around here in the goose line but no peafowl or swan eggs yet. I hope those swans don't disappoint me.

Cheers to you and Betty.

To A.

Notre Dame

Dear A.,   5/5/62

I am about at the tail end of my present travels—first the Sisters at Rosary College outside of Chicago for two days & now here. The good Sisters really know how to get it out of you. I had 5 classes, a public lecture, read two mss. and underwent a tea in which each student was determined to ask me an intelligent question.* Notre Dame is entirely opposite—much liquor and male companionship, both of which I could stand more of more often. My friend Tom Stritch is my host here and it would be worth it to come just for him as I have an inordinate affection for him.

I agree with you about the two sentences and will probably drop them, though I am less sure of dropping the one about students being professional readers of too much into everything. It is something they badly need to be warned against and most of my readers will be students.

Well, cheers,

*400 students

To Thomas Stritch

Milledgeville

Dear Tom,   7 May 62

I enjoyed it an awful lot, particularly talking to you, but as I can't thank you enough I won't thank you at all. I'll just cherish what the dwarf said.

I have instructions from my mamma to find out when I come back in June whether the nails in your plyboard walls are countersunk and filled with putty—which is what her carpenter tells her will have to be done here. (She is full of construction terms like "countersunk.")

She was on hand to meet me with, I regret to say, a wheelchair, so I was rolled to the main concourse, feeling at least 102 years old. And you complain about being 49.

When I finish dickering with the airlines, I'll let you know when to meet me on the 1st.

Much love,

To Alfred Corn

Milledgeville
Dear Mr. Corn,   30 May 62

I think that this experience you are having of losing your faith, or as you think, of having lost it, is an experience that in the long run belongs to faith; or at least it can belong to faith if faith is still valuable to you, and it must be or you would not have written me about this.

I don't know how the kind of faith required of a Christian living in the 20th century can be at all if it is not grounded on this experience that you are having right now of unbelief. This may be the case always and not just in the 20th century. Peter said, "Lord, I believe. Help my unbelief." It is the most natural and most human and most agonizing prayer in the gospels, and I think it is the foundation prayer of faith.

As a freshman in college you are bombarded with new ideas, or rather pieces of ideas, new frames of reference, an activation of the intellectual life which is only beginning, but which is already running ahead of your lived experience. After a year of this, you think you cannot believe. You are just beginning to realize how difficult it is to have faith and the measure of a commitment to it, but you are too young to decide you don't have faith just because you feel you can't believe. About the only way we know whether we believe or not is by what we do, and I think from your letter that you will not take the path of least resistance in this matter and simply decide that you have lost your faith and that there is nothing you can do about it.

One result of the stimulation of your intellectual life that takes place in college is usually a shrinking of the imaginative life. This sounds like a paradox, but I have often found it to be true. Students get so bound up with difficulties such as reconciling the clashing of so many different faiths such as Buddhism, Mohamedanism, etc., that they cease to look for God in other ways. Bridges once wrote Gerard Manley Hopkins and asked him to tell him how he, Bridges, could believe. Bridges was an agnostic. He must have expected from Hopkins a long philosophical answer. Hopkins wrote back, "Give alms." He was trying to say to Bridges that God is to be experienced in Charity (in the sense of love for the divine image in human beings). Don't get so entangled with intellectual difficulties that you fail to look for God in this way.

The intellectual difficulties have to be met, however, and you will be meeting them for the rest of your life. When you get a reasonable hold on one, another will come to take its place. At one time, the clash of the different world religions was a difficulty for me. Where you have absolute solutions, however, you have no need of faith. Faith is what you have in the absence of knowledge. The reason this clash doesn't bother me any longer is because I have got, over the years, a sense of the immense sweep of creation, of the evolutionary process in everything, of how incomprehensible God must necessarily be to be the God of heaven and earth. You can't fit the Almighty into your intellectual categories. I might suggest that you look into some of the works of Pierre Teilhard de Chardin (THE PHENOMENON OF MAN et al.). He was a paleontologist—helped to discover Pekin man—and also a man of God. I don't suggest you go to him for answers but for different questions, for that stretching of the imagination that you need to make you a sceptic in the face of much that you are learning, much of which is new and shocking but which when boiled down becomes less so and takes its place in the general scheme of things. What kept me a sceptic in college was precisely my Christian faith. It always said: wait, don't bite on this, get a wider picture, continue to read.

If you want your faith, you have to work for it. It is a gift, but for very few is it a gift given without any demand for equal time devoted to its cultivation. For every book you read that is anti-Christian, make it your business to read one that presents the other side of the picture; if one isn't satisfactory read others. Don't think that you have to abandon reason to be a Christian. A book that might help you is THE UNITY OF PHILOSOPHICAL EXPERIENCE by Etienne Gilson. Another is Newman's THE GRAMMAR OF ASSENT. To find out about faith, you have to go to the people who have it and you have to go to the most intelligent ones if you are going to stand up intellectually to agnostics and the general run of pagans that you are going to find in the majority of people around you. Much of the criticism of belief that you find today comes from people who are judging it from the standpoint of another and narrower discipline. The Biblical criticism of the 19th century, for instance, was the product of historical disciplines. It has been entirely revamped in the 20th century by applying broader criteria to it, and those people who lost their faith in the 19th century because of it, could better have hung on in blind trust.

Even in the life of a Christian, faith rises and falls like the tides of an invisible sea. It's there, even when he can't see it or feel it, if he wants it to be there. You realize, I think, that it is more valuable, more mysterious, altogether more immense than anything you can learn or decide upon in college. Learn what you can, but cultivate Christian scepticism. It will keep you free—not free to do anything you please, but free to be formed by something larger than your own intellect or the intellects of those around you.

I don't know if this is the kind of answer that can help you, but any time you care to write me, I can try to do better.

Yours,

To Alfred Corn

Milledgeville
Georgia
Dear Mr. Corn,   16 June 62

I certainly don't think that the death required that "ye be born again," is the death of reason. If what the Church teaches is not true, then the security and emotional release and sense of purpose it gives you are of no value and you are right to reject it. One of the effects of modern liberal Protestantism has been gradually to turn religion into poetry and therapy, to make truth vaguer and vaguer and more and more relative, to banish intellectual distinctions, to depend on feeling instead of thought, and gradually to come to believe that God has no power, that he cannot communicate with us, cannot reveal himself to us, indeed has not done so, and that religion is our own sweet invention. This seems to be about where you find yourself now.

Of course, I am a Catholic and I believe the opposite of all this. I believe what the Church teaches—that God has given us reason to use and that it can lead us toward a knowlege of him, through analogy; that he has revealed himself in history and continues to do so through the Church, and that he is present (not just symbolically) in the Eucharist on our altars. To believe all this I don't take any leap into the absurd. I find it reasonable to believe, even though these beliefs are beyond reason.

If you are interested, the enclosed book will give you one general line of reasoning about why I do. I'm not equipped to talk philosophically; this man is. I want it back sometime, but I am in no hurry for it. It shouldn't be read rapidly.

Satisfy your demand for reason always but remember that charity is beyond reason, and that God can be known through charity.

Regards,

To Sister Julie

Dear Sister Julie,   17 June 62

My head peacock sends you the tip of this feather which he regrets to say he lost in battle. I have too many cocks for the number of hens I have and they do nothing but fight all day. They scream all night but I don't hear them anymore.

I have been reading a book called "Word of God in Words of Men"—about the trials of Biblical scholars since about 1880. Very enlightening to me. It's certainly easier to be a Bible reader in 1962 than in 1904.

I am writing every day but I don't know what as the brew has not begun to thicken yet. Please pray it will. Sometimes it doesn't.

A man who runs a zoo in Florida has informed me through a friend that swans nest according to the weather, so I still have some hope that these two of mine will get with it before the summer is out.

                    Affectionately,

To A.

Milledgeville
Dear A.,   23 June 62

I was sorry I didn't get in on the conversation last night. I don't envy Jenny having to spend six weeks with Momma in Conway. Did you meet the famous Eleanor? Report. This morning I sent you four Simone Weil books. There are two more, but I thought four made a big enough package for one trip, and I will send the other two (The Notebooks) next week along with The Fox in the Attic.

Cecil didn't seem to think much of the Fox in the Attic, said it was not as good as A High Wind in Jamaica. I can't agree with her. I think A High Wind is small enough to be perfect, but this other thing is part of something much larger and can't be judged by such standards. Regina is now reading Ship of Fools and she says they sure are fools all right. She says don't read it before you eat. She read the part about the bull dog being seasick just before we went to the Sanford House to eat. Then she read another such part before she ate another time. Her timing has been bad. I'll admit Katherine Anne don't have the grace to see around the corner. What she does have aplenty is the ability to make things actual. The old girl can create the sweating stinking life out of anything, the purely animal.

This week I signed a contract with Mr. Jiras to make his movie. So after five years he has gotten this far. I don't know when the shooting will begin or what obstacles he'll now encounter, but he has some money from somewhere. I am supposed to get a thousand dollars now, and two thousand when the picture is over, and then 7½% of the profit after about a million things have been taken out. I also have no control over the script. The Lord knows what will issue forth.

All I can tell you about that dream is that the nigger is The Instincts, according to Dr. Spivey. Whether he is anybody in particular's instincts I am not learned enough to say. Too bad I had to be entertaining an air plant though. Did I tell you the original air plant is on his way to Africa?

What would you call The Violent Bear It Away if you couldn't call it that? Apparently that doesn't mean anything in German and they have written me for a new title. All they have come up with is The Bursting Sun, which they are not happy with, nor me neither. I am thinking of Food for the Violent or The Prophet's Country. I don't like either.

The Florida Hoods visited us this week. They got up early in the morning, made their coffee and took it to the pond with them in two mugs, which they set on the bank while they fished. Deen heard slurping. Earnest was drinking her coffee.

                                                    Cheers,

To Thomas Stritch

                                                    Milledgeville
Dear Tom,   3 July 62
   I hope you are having a good time and are not becoming converted to culture or anything. Dr. Crane, with whom I

am in daily telepathic communication, says to tell you that the American traveler abroad is a salesman of the USA and that in Europe the Sincere Compliment is an important part of our foreign policy. Don't hesitate, he says, to use the same sincere compliment any number of times as sincerity is always fresh and useful.

My degree hasn't done a thing for me so far, hasn't increased my self-confidence or improved my personality or anything I expected it to do. The local wags have already got tired of calling me "Doctor." Regina wrapped the hood up in newspaper and put it away and unless I wear it Halloween, I guess it'll stay there. I had a letter from Sr. Maria Renata. She don't write at the length she speaks. They sent me a copy of their school paper in which my book was reviewed. The girl who reviewed it said that Tarwater's great uncle was buried by a negro *slave*. Gave me pause about the school.

You might be interested in this: in the last batch of books Leo sent me to review for the Bulletin was something called "The Cardinal Stritch Story" by a Maria Buerle, put out by Bruce. Anyway it was a very clap-trap pasted-together second-hand job.

The Emory student who once wanted to be a Christian minister is still writing me. His unlikely name is A. D. Corn III and if he weren't so typical I'd say he had invented the name and himself too. I can't talk philosophical so I sent him a book of Tresmontant's called "Toward the Knowledge of God" which is all in favor of reason.

I forgot to tell R&S I had signed a paper with the USIA to have that last book of mine translated into Greek. Tell them that and cheers to them and children.

Love and thanks for your recent fortitude. Try to add a day or so onto your Ga. trip for us here, so we can go to the monastery.

PS—The Archbishop is laying about him. Already integrated the schools for September, and has us saying some Latin aloud at Mass.

To Alfred Corn

Milledgeville
Georgia
Dear Mr. Corn,   25 July 62

What you ask about Rayber loving Bishop is interesting. He did love him, but throughout the book he was fighting his inherited tendency to mystical love. He had the idea that his love could be contained in Bishop but that if Bishop were gone, there would be nothing to contain it and he would then love everything and specifically Christ. The point where Tarwater is drowning Bishop is the point where he has to choose. He makes the Satanic choice, and the inability to feel the pain of his loss is the immediate result. His collapse then may indicate that he is not going to be able to sustain his choice—but that is another book maybe. Rayber and Tarwater are really fighting the same current in themselves. Rayber wins out against it and Tarwater loses; Rayber achieves his own will, and Tarwater submits to his vocation. Here if you like are two interpretations. There is still an authority to say which interpretation is right.

I hope you'll find the experience you need to make the leap toward Christianity seem the only one to you. Pascal had a good deal to say about this. Sometimes it may be as simple as asking for it, sometimes not; but don't neglect to ask for it.

Sometime when you are going to Emory, stop by here and pay me a visit. I would like to fit your face to your search. I don't remember which one of those students you were.

Best,

To Roslyn Barnes

Milledgeville
Dear Roslyn,   4 Aug 62

I was very glad to hear this account of what Msgr. Illych is trying to do and I can see why he sends home half. He won't send you home I don't think. That is a school for sanctity and he must know that he can't create saints in 4 months though he has to try. This is surely what it means to bear away the kingdom of heaven with violence: the violence is directed inward.

The monitum on Teilhard was depressing at first but not after you considered it. Some say this method will replace the Index which would be a great thing. A warning on T. is necessary since his work is incomplete and unclear on the subject of grace—the idea may be inferred from it apparently that grace comes up from the bottom instead of down from the top. I don't think for a moment this was T.'s idea of course.

Enclose clipping. These people kill me talking about your being Davenport's contribution when you are plainly and irrevocably from the sovereign State of Georgia.

Cheers & keep me posted.

To A.

Milledgeville
4 August 62

Dear A.,

We were real sorry not to get to see Billy, but I am not about to expose myself to mononucleosis or Regina either. I called up the doctor to be sure I knew what I was doing and he said that even three months after you were apparently over the stuff, you could be carrying the virus—so I am worried that he might give it to Jenny. He *would* get something like that just at the wrong time. A pure-Billy event.

Yes that was a good review of Franny & Zooey. I ask myself what you could expect a book called Franny and Zooey to be anyhow. I read two of them in the New Yorker. Dick Gilman had an even better review of it in Jubilee. That Jewish mind of his made short work of it.

The Hickes got Cecil and took her down to dinner at the Pollers—my friends in Schenectady—and she appeared to enjoy it—as I think she would because they are less arty people than what she is finding at Yaddo. The Pollers are insurance salesman and ex-librarian respectively and after a few weeks at Yaddo, you long to talk to an insurance salesman, dog-catcher, bricklayer—anybody who isn't talking about Form or sleeping pills. Hortense Calisher and her husband seem to be the biggest cheezes there. Cecil was going down last weekend and look at the city.

Last Saturday two of the Sisters came down and brought the L—— family, all except —— ——, who has had a couple of tumors removed already and couldn't take any more riding. The father is dying of cancer and looked it. They brought Mary Ann very close. The mother has huge black eyes and the father has an over-large elongated head, the face covered with warts. I was much impressed with them. You hear of The Poor, but you seldom see them. I don't mean just poor folks, I mean people whose vocation it is to be poor and to have God touch them in just that way.

Odd about The Temple of the Holy Ghost. Nobody notices it. It is never anthologized, never commented upon. A few nuns have mentioned it with pleasure, but nobody else besides you.

A letter from the Airplant who has been holed up in Exeter, writing a critical piece. He attended the theatre several times in London with Miss Carol Johnson before she took off for the continent. He reports that Caroline is going to teach in California next year, 9 months for $15,000, a course of Emily Dickenson, Stephen Crane and HJ—and that she has already discovered a streak of diabolism in Emily—I guess in preparation for the course.

Cheers,

To Alfred Corn

Milledgeville

Dear Mr. Corn,   12 August 62

I think the strongest of Rayber's psychological pulls are in the direction that he does not ultimately choose, so I don't believe he exhibits in any sense a lack of free will. You might make out a case of sorts for Tarwater being determined since his great uncle has expressly trained him to be a prophet and to expect the Lord's call, but actually neither of them exhibits a lack of free will. An absence of free will in these characters would mean an absence of conflict in them, whereas they spend all their time fighting within themselves, drive against drive. Tarwater wrestles with the Lord and Rayber wins. Both examples of free will in action.

Free will has to be understood within its limits; possibly we all have some hinderances to free action but not enough to be able to call the world determined. In some people (psychotics) hinderances to free action may be so strong as to preclude free will in them, but the Church (Catholic) teaches that God does not judge those acts that are not free, and that he does not predestine any soul to hell—for his glory or any other reason. This doctrine of double predestination is strictly a Protestant phenomenon. Until Luther and Calvin, it was not countenanced. The Catholic Church has always condemned it. Romans IX is held by the Church to refer not to eternal reward or punishment but to our actual lives on earth, where one is given talent, wealth, education, made a "vessel of honor," and another is given the short end of the horn, so to speak—the "vessel of wrath."

This brings us naturally to the second question about priests and laity. It is the Bishops, not priests, who decide religious questions in the Catholic Church. Their job is to guard the deposit of faith. The coming Vatican Council is an example of how this works. The Bishop of Rome is the final authority. Catholics believe that Christ left the Church with a teaching authority and that this teaching authority is protected by the Holy Ghost; in other words that in matters of faith and morals the Church cannot err, that in these matters she is Christ speaking in time. So you can see that I don't find it an infringement of my independence to have the Church tell me what is true and what is not in regard to faith and what is right and what is wrong in regard to morals. Certainly I am no fit judge. If left to myself, I certainly wouldn't know how to interpret Romans IX. I don't believe Christ left us to chaos.

But to go back to determinism. I don't think literature would be possible in a determined world. We might go through the motions but the heart would be out of it. Nobody then could "smile darkly and ignore the howls." Even if there were no Church to teach me this, writing two novels would do it. I think the more you write, the less inclined you will be to rely on theories like determinism. Mystery isn't something that is gradually evaporating. It grows along with knowlege.

Best,

To Cecil Dawkins

Milledgeville
Dear Cecil,   6 September 62

I'm glad you're going to stay there for a while longer as it is beautiful in the fall and winter and most of the creepy characters take off at the end of the summer.

About the story I certainly agree that it don't work and have never felt that it did, but in heaven's name where do you get the idea that Sheppard represents Freud? Freud never entered my mind and looking back over it, I can't make him fit now. The story is about a man who thought he was good and thought he was doing good when he wasn't. Freud was a great one, wasn't he, for bringing home to people the fact that they weren't what they thought they were, so if Freud were in this, which he is not, he would certainly be on the other side of the fence from Shepp. The story doesn't work because I don't know, don't sympathize, don't like Mr. Sheppard in the way that I know and like most of my other characters. This is a story, not a statement. I think you ought to look for simpler explanations of why things don't work and not mess around with philosophical ideas where they haven't been intended or don't apply. There's nothing *in* the story that could possibly suggest that Sheppard represents Freud. This is some theory of which you are possessed. I am wondering if this kind of theorizing could be what is interfering with your getting going on some writing. Don't mix up thought-knowlege with felt-knowlege. If Sheppard represents anything here, it is, as he realizes at the end of the story, the empty man who fills up his emptiness with good works. I just don't know such a man, don't have any felt-knowlege of him. I don't want to go on to higher mathematics, but to people I do know.

Elizabeth McKee wrote me that she had seen you and she seemed pleased with the visit. I'm cheered that the book is going to be published and if I can say anywhere that these shore are good stories, tell Mr. Haydn to let me know.

I have just read a review in the Chicago Sun about Wise Blood in which I am congratulated for producing a *Lolita* five or six years before Nabokov—so Freud is dogging my tracks all the way. I really have quite a respect for Freud when he isn't made into a philosopher. If I can lay hands on it, I will send you an article about him and St. Thomas in which they are rowing in the same boat. You probably hear a lot about Freud at Yaddo. To religion I think he is much less dangerous than Jung.

The army worms have eaten up my mamma's coastal bermuda.

Cheers,

To Sister Julie

Milledgeville
Dear Sister Julie,   12 Dec 62

Thank you for the poem of Br. Antoninus. It's the only one I've read but I like it. If they were all like this, I'd be most enthusiastic. I haven't seen the Atlantic with the prize essay in it. Do you know I've never read anything of L. Hellman's? I don't even know what kind of a writer she is—I mean as to quality. I know she writes plays.

I wouldn't believe anything the Atlantic prints about the South. The radical right wing exists in pockets. There is much diversity of opinion in the South. I have just been to Texas and Southern Louisiana and I witnessed some radical conservatism and some radical liberalism too.

The swan has taken up with three Moscovy ducks. They are the only birds around here he's not scared of. He goes to the pond with them & he acts like a large nurse maid trying to keep up with three lively children. When they feel like it, they fly away and leave him.

We are having a bad freeze here. All our pipes are frozen and we have no water. I'm just limber enough to wish you a Merry Christmas.

Yours,

To Sally and Robert Fitzgerald

Milledgeville
Georgia

Dear S&R,   1 January 63

I sure do like the head scarf and I will appear in it and my long sweater together. Regina has Cultivated Illiteracy and wants me to thank you for the handkerchief. She really uses them. I reckon it's the generation. Anyway, we both thank you.

Of late several visitors have come by here who knew you. The first was Claudio Gorlier. He spent the afternoon with us and stayed to supper. He is spending six months at Vanderbilt and six at Berkeley. He told us about being the gendarme for routing Michael from his room. He also said you were disappointed in his position as regarded the Church. I gather his "position" is strictly political. We had grits and sausages for supper. He didn't appear to go for the grits but he ate many sausages and when there was only one left on the dish, I passed it to him and asked him to have it. A stricken look crossed his face and he said, "Oh no. I could not take the responsibility." We liked him.

The other was the younger sister of John Clark. She is attending the University of Georgia and my cousin who attends likewise brought her down. She appeared much taken with all the children, particularly Michael. Everybody appears much taken with the children, particularly Michael. This was the case with Tom Stritch.

I am about to get me a car that you drive without using your feet. Mine just don't work quick enough any more for me not to be afraid I'd kill somebody. I hate to drive but if R. got sick or something, we'd be stuck out here, so I guess it's the thing to do.

Cheers to you all for the new year and if any of you get in this direction, let us know.

To J. F. Powers

Milledgeville
Georgia
Dear Jim: 14 January 63
I wrote a review of your book for the diocesan paper but it has just got a new editor whose first act was to eliminate the book page, so the review never got printed and so I cant send it to you. I can't even find a copy of it. But it was so favorable some one might have thought I was in your employ. I chiefly said that it was a novel and all the people who said otherwise were nuts. I thought it really hung together as a whole piece and that it was worth holding onto for ten years or however long you held onto it. I sent a copy to the Fitzgeralds for Christmas. They are in Italy. They too were much taken with it and Robert said he didn't see how "anyone can ever again get windy about the Church in America without faltering at least once in tribute to Powers' work."

I don't have any proper address for you so I'll try this through the CRITIC. I just wanted to set down my vote of appreciation before the year starts piling up.

Yours,

To A.

Milledgeville
Dear A.,   2 February 63
This is Ground Hog Day and I salute you. I think you ought to go on full speed ahead on this idea that has got you. Out of the head and onto the paper. That is the only way you can cope with its intricasies or discover what you are doing.

I have just read the autobiography of a lady named Katharine Trevelyan of that British Trevelyan family. It is subtitled, "the autobiography of a natural mystic." It was interesting from the standpoint of your theory, but I couldn't decide whether the woman was just batty at times or whether she was advanced on the evolutionary ladder above the average of us. Anyway, this thing was sent me in bound galleys if you would like to look it over. It reminded me a little of Roslyn too—these people who are always lying in the grass feeling God.

Mr. Sherry was to come down to see me yesterday but called and said he didn't relish driving back after dark in the fog, so we have reset the apintment for next Thursday. I have it round-about that he plans some kind of supplement once a month on the arts, but I have not heard this from him.

This has been one of our weeks of complications with Louise. The Negro's method of escape is fool-proof. She can effect complete mental absence when she wants to—she's there, grinning, agreeing, but gone gone. No white person can cope with this, not even my parent. Least of all my parent.

Elizabeth N——, the lady who don't believe in tything because they didn't have the income tax in Jesus' time met us at the Sanford House yesterday and screamed, "Well, they're going to operate on Miss L—— tomorrow and me and M—— are taking turns keeping her cook and if she don't pull through, we'll get her. Of course I hope she pulls through but she's nearly ninety and you know we might as well have her cook as anybody else etc etc etc."

Cheers,

To Janet McKane

Dear Miss McKane,   25 February 63

I am very happy to have both these books you sent me and your letter. I had not read either book strange to say, but I had tried to get hold of the C. S. Lewis one without success.

We have no book store here. I order books from Brentano's and they come, if at all, in six months. Anyway you couldn't have sent me two books that I would have appreciated more.

Pere Teilhard talks about "passive diminishments" in THE DIVINE MILIEU. He means those afflictions that you can't get rid of and have to bear. Those that you can get rid of he believes you must bend every effort *to* get rid of. I think he was a very great man.

I've been to Lourdes once, as a patient not as a helper. I felt that being only on crutches I was probably the healthiest person there. I prayed there for the novel I was working on, not for my bones, which I care about less, but I guess my prayers were answered about the novel, in as much as I finished it.

I would like to send you THE DIVINE MILIEU but I lent my copy to somebody who didn't return it, so I'll send you instead a genuine work of the Lord, a feather from the tail of one of my peacocks. The peacock is a great comic bird with five different screaming squawks. The eyes in the tail stand for the eyes of the Church. I have a flock of about thirty so I am surrounded.

My best to you always and please continue to keep me and my work in your prayers.

To Sally and Robert Fitzgerald

Milledgeville
Dear S&R,   15 March 63
    I should have given you Caroline's address. It is 436 University Avenue, Davis, Calif.
    I have just got back from the Symposium on Religion & Art at Sweet Briar and boy do I have a stomach full of liberal religion! The devil had his day there. It began with Boaz talking about Art & Magic. I don't know what he meant to say but he left the impression that religion was good because it was art and magic. Nothing behind it but it's good for you. Then they had the Dean of Theological School at Drew. He

was a Methodist-Universalist. I gather this means you don't drink but about theology you are as vague as possible and talk a lot about how the symbology has played out in Christianity and how it's up to artists to make up a new symbology. At these things you are considered great in direct proportion to how often you can repeat the word symbology. They wedged me and James Johnson Sweeney in there somewhere. He was above the fray as he confined himself to Art, but I waded in and gave them a nasty dose of orthodoxy, which I am sure they thought was pretty quaint. It ended with John Chiardi who told them why religion was no good—or so I hear, I didn't go to his lecture.

James Johnson Sweeney asked most especially for you when he found out I knew you. I didn't get a chance to say much to him as everywhere they sat me I was next to the Methodist-Universalist. He left in the middle of my talk. I don't think it was a protest gesture, I just think he thought he could live a useful life without it. I told them that when Emerson decided in 1832 that he could no longer celebrate the Lord's supper unless the bread and wine were removed that an important step in the vaporization of religion in America had taken place. It was somewhere after that I think that he left.

Let us know your plans when the madwoman sends them. Could this be Alma Savage? If you can, stop by here and take yourself a rest between labors.

I haven't seen it in print but somebody told me he thought you got the Bollingen Prize. I congratulate you. You should have got it if you didn't. I guess you saw that Powers got the National Book Award. I was much cheered at that. I got the O. Henry this year. Walker Percy got the N'tl Book Award last year. Katherine Anne will probably get the Pulitzer prize. I think you ought to judge the prize by the book but even so these hold up and all these people are Catlicks so this should be some kind of answer to the people who are saying we don't contribute to the arts.

Cheers to you all,

P.S. Have you read about the lady who is having a chapel built in the shape of John Glen's capsule?

To A.

Dear A.,

I meant you to keep the book but if you want it you can get it sometime. I read it and it held my attention about two-thirds of the way and then I began to feel I was reading a connundrum about some philosophical problem and not about folks and I got most weary. I thought the allegory was thin and rather oppressive in this one. This is a purely physical reaction of course.

I got shut of my last lecture this week and was feeling like somebody let out of the penitentiary when Regina gets a letter from her colored friend Annie that I am to write her a piece for Mother's Day at Flag Chapel (A.M.E.) entitled "Woman's Day." Last year I was summoned to write her one on "The Value of Sunday School," a subject much more to my liking. An invite to the White House I could decline, but not this, unsuited as the subject is to my taste. A friend of mine from Louisville who works on the paper there was telling me about one of the discussion topics that was sent in for a colored Baptist church anniversary church news—"Who Have the Soul of the World—Adam or Noah?" But I got to write her a paper on "Woman's Day."

No mam, Elizabeth does not yet have the cook. Every time we see her she screams something like, "There's a heap worse things than death let me tell you. Poor Miss L——, just laying up there. Now she thinks there's people in the room playing cards." A peculiarly horrible fantasy if you ask me. Elizabeth has been somewhat deflected from that topic though because another lady here in town ran into her car.

Regina got her hand closed in somebody's car door week before last so she has been somewhat curbed. Only somewhat though.

I have a copy of MAN ON A DONKEY but I've never read it. I don't see how you read all you do. It seems to me I don't have much time to read. I intend to read Dostoievski this summer.

There haven't been any moths here, believe me. If they're

students they come because they have to usually, and the rest all bring more than they take away.

Cheers. I must get to work on "Woman's Day."

To Sister Mariella Gable

Milledgeville

Dear Sister Mariella,   4 May 63

Thank you so very much for your letter. I remember that at Marillac, you and I said we were easily defeated when it came to defending what we thought were necessary judgments about fiction in the face of people who didn't see them. I still am, and I'm much more liable to try to get out of the way as fast as possible than to struggle to make my views plain. I think though that it's the people and not the questions that defeat us.

When they ask you to make Christianity look desirable, they are asking you to describe its essence, not what you see. Ideal Christianity doesn't exist, because anything the human being touches, even Christian truth, he deforms slightly in his own image. Even the saints do this. I take it to be the effects of Original Sin and I notice that Catholics often act as if that doctrine is always perverted and always an indication of Calvinism. They read a little corruption as total corruption. The writer has to make the corruption believable before he can make the grace meaningful.

The tendency of people who ask questions like this is always towards the abstract and therefore toward allegory, thinness, and ultimately what they are looking for is an apologetic fiction. The best of them think: make it look desirable because it is desirable. And the rest of them think: make it look desirable so I won't look like a fool for holding it. In a really Christian culture of real believers this wouldn't come up.

I know that the writer does call up the general and maybe the essential through the particular, but this general and essential is still deeply embedded in mystery. It is not answerable to any of our formulas. It doesn't rest finally in a statable kind of solution. It ought to throw you back on the living God. Our Catholic mentality is great on paraphrase, logic, formula, instant and correct answers. We judge before we experience and never trust our faith to be subjected to reality, because it is not strong enough. And maybe in this we are wise. I think this spirit is changing on account of the council but the changes will take a long time to soak through.

About the fanatics. People make a judgment of fanaticism by what they are themselves. To a lot of Protestants I know, monks and nuns are fanatics, none greater. And to a lot of the monks and nuns I know, my Protestant prophets are fanatics. For my part, I think the only difference between them is that if you are a Catholic and have this intensity of belief you join the convent and are heard from no more; whereas if you are a Protestant and have it, there is no convent for you to join and you go about in the world, getting into all sorts of trouble and drawing the wrath of people who don't believe anything much at all down on your head.

This is one reason why I can write about Protestant believers better than Catholic believers—because they express their belief in diverse kinds of dramatic action which is obvious enough for me to catch. I can't write about anything subtle. Another thing, the prophet is a man apart. He is not typical of a group. Old Tarwater is not typical of the Southern Baptist or the Southern Methodist. Essentially, he's a crypto-Catholic. When you leave a man alone with his Bible and the Holy Ghost inspires him, he's going to be a Catholic one way or another, even though he knows nothing about the visible church. His kind of Christianity may not be socially desirable, but it will be real in the sight of God. If I set myself to write about a socially desirable Christianity, all the life would go out of what I do. And if I set myself to write about the essence of Christianity, I would have to quit writing fiction, or either become another person.

I'll be glad when Catholic critics start looking at what they've got to criticize for what it is itself, for its sort of "inscape" as Hopkins would have had it. Instead they look for some ideal intention, and criticize you for not having it.

In the gospels it was the devils who first recognized Christ and the evangelists didn't censor this information. They apparently thought it was pretty good witness. It scandalizes us when we see the same thing in modern dress only because we have this defensive attitude toward the faith.

I probably have enough stories for a collection but I want to wait and see what this turns out to be that I am writing on now. Then perhaps if it turns out to be a long story, I'll put them all together in a collection. I'm not in much of a hurry about publishing. I hate the racket that's made over a book and all the reviews. The praise as well as the blame— its all bad for your writing.

I appreciate and need your prayers. I've been writing eighteen years and I've reached the point where I can't do again what I know I can do well, and the larger things that I need to do now, I doubt my capacity for doing.

I'm glad your paper is going to be on the ecumenic side of my writing. I am more and more impressed with the amount of Catholicism that fundamentalist Protestants have been able to retain. Theologically our differences with them are on the nature of the Church, not on the nature of God or our obligation to him.

Sincerely and with much gratitude,

To Thomas Stritch

Milledgeville
Dear Thos.   14 June 63

I'm glad you observed the holiday in a creditable way since you missed the race anyhow. I would love to see that crowd but I guess the nearest I'll get is on television. I watch the stock-car races sometimes but you don't see anything but cars. I know about Fireball Roberts though and I watched an interview with Tiny Lunn. He is a huge dead-serious innocent-faced boy who must have made it big, he had just won the one in Jacksonville when I saw him but he never smiled once. This is the kind I'd like to write a story about, like him. I have to write about the dumb ones as well as I'd have to teach that kind if I knew anything to teach, which I don't. When I was at Southwestern La. last fall my host was somebody named Jack Ward who did his undergraduate work at N.D. I asked him if he knew you. He said he wasn't in your dept but he audited your course because he wanted to be there. He said "It was a grab-bag but it was wonderful." I watch the sports cast everyday. A man named Savage interviews all the local athletes and others not so local when he can get them. He's kind of smirkey but they seldom smile. Last week there was a model railroaders convention in Macon and he interviewed some of them, all rich retired business men. One old boy said, "People think this is a child's game (scowl) well it isn't, it takes great skill and is *very* expensive."

Robert looked kind of bad and tired to me but I guess by the time he got around to Smith he had a right to be. To take a month or so of being the honored guest you've got to be somebody like Chiardi. Anyway they were powerful pleased with me at Smith for bringing them Robt. I also brought them about a dozen kinfolks, including Regina. We went to Boston first where she has a sister & neices and they all came over to Smith. R. says yankees never have anything to do social and they will go anywhere. They all went all right, even down to the children and it looked like a family reunion. I bore up passible. The people were nice. The citation had a few words in it like "inexorable" and something (fishy) about "man's inhumanity to man" which means whoever wrote it hadn't read me, but of course that's not something I require. Five other old ladies got one and they even gave away an honorary masters. Bargain day. What did you think of McGill? I think he's a good man, but sentimental. I much prefer him to Sherry because he's at least not far from where he came from and he belongs where he's at. Sherry belongs in a baloon.

I have some advice for you about the Cardinal's portrait. My advice is free, excellent, unsought after but given without stint. If you have only written it three times, it is still supposed to be no good. You have a defect of patience, not a defect of energy. But even if you have both you ought to keep on with it. He is not in the back of my missal that I don't take a proprietary interest in him. I have a defect of energy

myself but not a defect of patience. I can wait on myself in-
definitely.

We are real cheered you're coming to see us & suit yourself
about the time. We'll take you when we can get you. Love,

P.S. I gave my cousin a card to mail you from Bos. but he
may not have.

                                                      15 June
Your note asking about Caroline just came. I don't know if
she's still in Calif. or not. If she is the address is 436 University Ave., Davis, Calif. If she's not there she's probably in
Princeton, 145 Ewing St. *Or* she may even now be descending
on her Southern kin & connections in which case I had
better be preparing my parent for the ordeal.

To Louise Abbot

Dear Louise,   15 June 63
No, I hadn't got any of this out of the Hans Kung book.
It may be that you have to be a Jew to be this sensitive to
things of this kind. I imagine all this was far from Kung's
mind when he wrote the book but I hope this will get to him
and he can clarify his views on it. I'll hold onto it until you
come. Let us know when. We've got nothing to do any time
soon and are looking forward to seeing you. Don't make it
Wednesday, make it a Thursday or Friday.

I gather the Spiveys are letting the world see them. I had a
letter from him not long ago detailing several of his dreams
in which I figured. In one the Spiveys, the Abbots & I were
all in the same bed. This means, says he, that we are all very
close. He said that if I cared to comment I might answer the
letter, but I figured comment would be superfluous.

Drop us a card when to expect you.

                                                      Cheers,

To Janet McKane

19 June 63
Milledgeville

Dear Janet McK,

The prints of the two pieces of sculpture are beautiful and I do appreciate them. They came yesterday along with the Cath. World. Someone had mentioned in a letter that an article on G. Fielding said something about me, but I hadn't seen it. I used to take the Cath. Wld. but it was a case of the issues piling up unread so I dropped that one. I take the Critic, incidentally; I just forgot about it. There's another interview in that and another of those silly pictures. I hate like sin to have my picture taken and most of them don't look much like me, or maybe they look like I'll look after I've been dead a couple of days. Those in Jubilee were taken in winter by a very arty photographer whose favorite types of pictures were migrant fruit-pickers and the interiors of flophouses. We have a beautiful place here but he made it look like Oklahoma after the duststorm. I look like one of the Oakies with the burden of world peace on my shoulders. The picture in the Critic is a little more like me but the interview is not very good. I hate to deliver opinions. On most things I don't deserve an opinion and on a lot of things I simply don't have an opinion.

In the self portrait that is not a peacock. That's a pheasant cock. I used to raise pheasants but they got too much for me as they require attention and have to be caged. The peacocks take care of themselves. But I like very much the look of the pheasant cock. He has horns and a face like the devil. The self-portrait was made ten years ago, after a very acute seige of lupus. I was taking cortisone which gives you what they call a moon-face and my hair had fallen out to a large extent from the high fever, so I looked pretty much like the portrait. When I painted it I didn't look either at myself in the mirror or at the bird. I knew what we both looked like.

I enjoyed the interview with H. Kung in the Cath. Wld. Only the day before a Protestant friend sent me the May 29 issue of the Christian Century in which there is an attack on Kung accusing him of being anti-semitic in "The Council, Reform & Reunion." I guess you've read it. I thought it was wonderful and didn't observe any anti-semitism in it, but this piece was by a Jew who had apparently been grievously offended by Kung's references to things Jewish. My friend who is an A.R.P. (Associate Reformed Presbyterian) with strong Catholic leanings was much upset by it. I sent her off the Freedom speech in Commonweal and I'll also show her this. I don't think Kung intended any anti-semitism.

I never read all the articles in THOUGHT but there are always one or two I'm interested in. I am sending you a representative issue. Fr. Wm. Lynch was editor for many years and much of Christ & Apollo appeared there in essays.

I've got all of Muriel Spark but strangely I've never read G. Fielding. I'll have to get around to it sooner or later. Right now I have Barth staring me in the face, plus a book of Pastor Lackmann's on the Augsburg Confession, one on Biblical studies and another on Biblical research and another by an Episcopalian on Teilhard. I like to read them but I loathe to write the reviews. I'll look forward to reading the Episode of Sparrows when I get some of this behind me.

I didn't see much of the city when I stayed in New York. I didn't realize Hunter and Fordham were all out that way near the Cloisters. I had a notion Fordham was down town, maybe a part of it was at that time. I didn't go to a single play or even to the Frick museum. I went to the natural history museum but didn't do anything the least cultural. The public library was much too much for me. I did well to get out and get a meal or two a day. I finally ended up eating at the Columbia University student cafeteria. I looked enough like a student to get by with it, and it was one of the few places I suspected the food of being clean.

The peacocks are beginning slowly to shed so when I get a good bunch of fresh feathers, I'll send them to you and you can put them in a vase.

Cheers to you and much thanks for your thought of me.

To Thomas Stritch

Milledgeville

Dear Tom,   4 July 63

I have this temptation to write you on the 4th of July though I usually don't celebrate it. However, don't be alarmed. You don't have to answer these things. I like it when you do but I know you have other bidnis to occupy yourself with. So do I and ought to be at it but I get weary writing, everyday, what don't exist for who don't exist. We don't celebrate the 4th but the help does. Shot was at the back door early this morning to say he had a cousin who died last Friday and he must be off for the funeral today. He'll spend it riding up and down the road with a bad crowd that lives across the way and we also heard that they are going to barbecue a goat over there. R. let him go after giving a Jonathan Edwards type sermon and letting him know she didn't accept the cousin story. He does love bad company.

The creep-feeder is a total bust. She got it up and they took it off down in the field and filled it up. The calves wouldn't have anything to do with it but the man at the feedstore said when they got hungry they'd go for it. So last week she went down to look at it and the peachickens were lined up at it like patrons at a diner. She claims they have eaten seventeen dollars and fifty cents worth of calf feed in the last month. It seems the geese have been at it too. I've got to pay for half the calf-feed now.

No credit to Sherry for making that interview sound authentic. He sent the questions through the mail and I answered them likewise. So it wasn't really authentic talk, it was all thought out because when I do talk I stammer and stutter and beat around the bush. Anyway I didn't want it sounding like him. He has been down here twice but he did most of the talking those times himself. I am sick to death of all these interviews. All they want to know about is the race business and that's the last thing I feel like talking about. Jubilee sent a horrid arty photographer down here, man with one yellow eyebrow and one black one and a likewise two-toned mustache. He sat around the whole afternoon talking about his "art" and showing photographs he had taken, most of migrant fruit-pickers and the insides of flop-houses. Finally he said, "I can't take your picture. Your resistance is too great." It must have been the truth because in the pictures he took I look like one of the Oakey women about to murder a reve-nuer. Jubilee sent me the proofs and I wrote and asked them not to use the pictures but they said it was too late. They'll never get anything else out of me.

I'm glad you liked McGill. The citation was probably very pleasing to him if it was properly portentous. His taste in literature runs to Carl Sanburg, Steven Vincent Benet & Thomas Woolf. (sp?) His theology seems to be kind of Uni-versalist with vestments.

A slew of my Athens kin were here yesterday for a funeral and one of them had seen Conn the day before and said she was fine and "her husband was coming along behind her in that sports car." A nice picture. I mean to ask them down now that the rains have let up. Love,

PS Katherine Anne sent me a review out of L'Express of Les Braves Gens Ne Whateveritis. It seems to be favorable but not sensible except it says I live on a *vast* estate among many beasts.

To Janet McKane

Milledgeville
Georgia
27 August 63

Dear Janet,

Thanks so much for the museum bulletins with devilish dogs etc. The dog I like in painting is one in a painting of Rousseau. I don't know the name of it but the family is in a wagon, all looking ahead and there is one dog in the wagon and one underneath, kind of prim diabolical dogs. It's very funny. It used to hang in the Fitzgerald's kitchen (the people I lived with in Connecticut) but I have never seen it anywhere else.

I don't much agree with you and your friend, the nun,

about suffering teaching you much about the redemption. You learn about the redemption simply from listening to what the Church teaches about it and then following this to its logical conclusion. People are depressed by the ending of the VBIA because they think: poor Tarwater, his mind has been warped by that old man and he's off to make a fool or a martyr of himself. They forget that the old man has taught him the truth and that now he's doing what is right, however crazy. I haven't suffered to speak of in my life and I don't know any more about the redemption than anybody else. All I do is follow it through literally in the lives of my characters. You understand this so the ending didn't depress you. People who are depressed by it believe that it would have been better if the school teacher had civilized Tarwater and sent him to college where he could have got an engineering degree or some such. A good many Catholics are put off because they think the old man, being a Protestant prophet, so to speak, has no hold on the truth. They look at everything in a confessional way.

I'm glad you saw the statue. I didn't know they shifted them around like that.

I've been reading Shakespeare myself lately because I have found that the Marboro book stores are offering various volumes of the Arden Shakespeare for $1 a piece, which I think is a good bargain. I've got King Lear, Richard II, Anthony & Cleopatra and The Tempest and I'm hoping they'll eventually put them all on the list. I get that Marboro sales sheet every month. A good deal of it is junk (Sex in the South Sea Islands) but occasionally you find something worth having.

I like cartoons. I used to try to do them myself, sent a batch every week to the New Yorker, all rejected of course. I just couldn't draw very well. I like the ones that are drawn well better than the situations.

I haven't had time to look for it but I have the suspicion that that almond tree verse may be in one of the minor prophets???

Yours,

To Maryat Lee

Milledgeville
Dear Rayworker,   10 September 63

Lord bless us, what next? Here I have been commiserating with my image of you that was so po and energyless it couldn't go to Washington to march for freedom with all its natural cousins and you all the time were fixing to hire yourself out as a Super char to a super Catholic family. I can think of a lot of things I'd prefer your services at than housekeeping. No wonder she got another girl. You probably blended their garbage and baked it. The next book would have been THE DAY WE WERE POISONED BY THE HOUSEKEEPER. I never saw any of his columns and didn't know he wrote one. They don't penetrate down here I reckon. And I never read any of his books but them I have heard of. And they never heard of mine at all I would suppose, though they might have seen the Sisters' book about Mary Ann. If you would like a copy of that to give the 8 and 10 year olds at your departure, I will send you one. Children read that in Catholic schools and apparently like it.

I'm glad he's making you write about the natural cousins. Seems to me that's all to the good. He might know exactly what to do with it after you had written it. It should be very good if you keep it objective and don't go rummaging around in people's heads, including your own.

We were in the car going around the corner the other day and a car was coming opposite in which was the Lee jaw. I thought for a minute it was you for sure but it was your brother.

I visited the bone doctor yesterday and he allowed after looking at my x-rays that my bones are sounder than of yore, last year to be exact. The heads are still flat and that won't change, but I can put a little more pressure on them. I'm glad I don't have no steel in me.

Next month I go to Hollins, Notre Dame of Maryland and Georgetown and hope to return with the bacon.

Shot killed an owl this morning and they intend to eat him

for supper. Thank the Lord there are one or two left who are not ready to march on Washington.

Cheers,
Unreconstructed Tarbutter

To A.

Milledgeville
14 September 63

Dear A.,

A letter from Jack Hawkes says they are back from their paradise and back in Providence where the wind is already fierce. He is having another novel out in January called Second Skin, a good Hawkesian title if I ever heard one.

Mr. Jiras is no sooner down than he is up again, on the trail of other money. He has sent me the script again and I find it much improved. The part that is strictly his own—about the boy's existence in the city—is the best part of it. He's much better with the city than the country. They all lack the right touch there. Either they make it tobacco road or they make it an extension of Mrs. Wiggs of the Cabage Patches back yard. I have another one of these gentlemen of the movies on my trail, this one after The Life You Save. He sent me his script. About the only change he had made was to have Mr. Shiftlet say he wouldn't marry Elizabeth Taylor unless he could take her to a restaurant and buy her something good to eat. Instead of the Duchesser Windser, which is naturally much better, but I guess he is not of the Duchesser Windser's generation. Only the use of an elegant tramp there would be funny though. Elizabeth Taylor, lacking it, is useless for style.

I am reading Eichmann in Jerusalem, which Tom sent me. Anything is credible after such a period of history. I've always been haunted by the boxcars, but they were actually the least of it. And old Hannah is as sharp as they come.

Cheers,

To Janet McKane

Milledgeville
Dear Janet,   20 September 63

I'm glad the feathers got there. If they bent it in half I hope they didn't break the stems. If you put some sand in the vase you put them in you can make them do the way you want; without it they mostly turn their faces to the wall. The birds are very ratty right now. The new tails are out about three inches and there are a few long feathers left from last year still in. Day before yesterday they made a big racket early in the morning. An owl had got into a pen where I have the muscovy duck and her hatch and had taken a swipe at one of the ducks. Shot (the colored man who works for us) heard the commotion and came with his gun and shot the owl, a large hoot owl. It had a face very much like a cats only the eyes were bigger. It had eye-lashes. The colored folks ate it for supper. I asked Louise (the colored woman who works here) what it tasted like and she said "About like hawk." Which left me where I started at as I haven't eaten any hawk. These colored people are country negroes and very primitive.

What do you think of that business of hawling children out of their neighborhood so that they can attend a "racially balanced" school? I should think it would be hard on all concerned, children and teachers, and do nothing to help the race situation.

I have been reading Hannah Arendts book "Eichmann in Jerusalem," the one they made a fuss about in the Time Book Review. I'm on her side. I think she's a wonderful writer, Jewish but without that sensitiveness we were talking about.

Thanks for the copy of America. I'm always a little behind but I'll enjoy it when I get to it.

Too bad I can't send you a burro but if the baby one gets here I'll try to send you a picture of it, though I'm no good at taking pictures.

I hope your energy is holding up. Cheers and thanks.

To Janet McKane

Milledgeville
Dear Janet,   28 November 63

Well happy Thanksgiving, somewhat after the fact when you get this. Nan Kleinman's Equinox is much appreciated and also the clippings you've sent. I was interested in the reviews of the Carson McCullar's adaptation. I dislike intensely the work of Carson McCullars but it is interesting to see what is made of it in the theatre, and by Edward Allbee at that.

We spent most of the weekend looking at the sad events on television. It made me wonder if children draw any line between history and fiction. Murder in the living room. We saw Oswald killed three times, twice in slow motion. What do they make of it?

I'll be interested in the symposium on The Jew in American culture. The declaration on the Jews and on religious liberty seems to have got sidetracked at the council. I hope they manage to get it going again.

I was much amused at your lyrics for the ladies and gents of PS 86 Br and marginal comments. It's real good to be able to do something like this; it fills a real social need. I used to do it when I was young but I guess now I have the cares that go with professionalism and the black heart as well.

Equinox has been invited to be in the Hardwick Christian Churches Christmas crib. We think we will send his papa, Ernest, instead, as Ernest is more liable to enter into the spirit of it. Regina says he will eat all the hay out of the manger, but anyway he is easier to handle at this point. In fact demands all the attention he can get. I gave Ernest to my mother for a mother's day present two years ago. Somebody said that was for the mother who had everything.

Sometime in the next few weeks—as soon as I can manage to get them off—I am sending you a little box of pecans—product of the family home in town—in honor of the season.

Cheers,

To Maryat Lee

Milledgeville
Dear Maryrightofway,   18 Jan 64

I been sick. Fainted a few days before Christmas and was in bed about 10 days and not up to much thereafter. Blood count had gone down to 8 & you can't operate on that. It's up now & so am I but aint operating yet on normal load. Ma has been in bed with intestinal flu this last week so if it hasn't been one thing its been another. I'll try to get them nuts off before they get rancid.

Dont know which is worse, CORE or Young Republicans for Goldwater but I reckon it is inevitable that they fall into the hands of one or the other. I guess this will get laid at your door though it is only nature taking its cose.

Glad you're picking up. Old doctor Greenleaf must not be a quack after all. I see where your friend J. Bishop has written a novel. Probably shouldn't have.

Cheers,
Tarpot

To Thomas Stritch

Milledgeville
Dear Tom,   22 Jan 64

I think the Nashville banner could have left out one of those pictures of the bride and put in one of the ushers—as a more curious and note-worthy group. I would have liked it better anyway. I'm fine now and blundering around, as Louise says, as usual. "I hears you blunderin around in there," she says. But I had only just got up good when Regina came down with the current virus. She don't ever like to admit she's sick but it was fairly obvious and she stayed in bed a week and had to suffer my ministrations—which I thought were efficient enough and she was too sick to take note of. Louise was sick at her house and the weather was froze up but we made out. I'd rather suffer the cold than Savannah or Tampa. I guess we feel it more than you do. The wind comes through the cracks and howls and moans generally and there is this business about water pipes that you have to cut off and drain and then cut on again in the morning, only it don't always work that way. Well, if it wouldn't be scandalous and a bad example to youth I would surely come and live in your house. You could get rid of Opal. But today its in the 60s and the peacocks are hollering and as Caroline tells me Isaac Walton said about Donne, "I shall see it reanimated." Meaning me, though he meant him.

I had from Caroline a six page account of her Christmas vacation which was from Lafayette to Chattanooga to Princeton to Lafayette, all on broken down railroads and misconnected busses and planes that didn't fly. She may look old but that woman has Vitality; or maybe its just recklessness. I sent her a story I wrote before Christmas, a real good one too, better than I have pulled off in a long time, and she wrote me another six page letter about that, or rather all about grammar which I ain't got the principles of besides not being able to spell anything. She was crazy about the story. I was just thinking if you have any boys that are halfway good at stories you ought to shove them under her nose when she goes to St. Marys for those lectures because that's what she's good at—helping individuals. I improved that story from her letter, good as it already was. I don't always carry on so over my own stories but in this last one I got confidence, as you can see. She said she had a real good time at N. D. thanks to your skill and engineering ability. She seemed appreciative of you and what you did. She didn't mention the lecture.

We finally rented the little house across the pond—to an 18 yr old couple named Kennedy, no kin to the late President and not Episcopalians either, strictly C. of G. which is what we need. They turn the gas up full tilt and Regina says it will be fine if they don't burn down the house. They announced several days after moving in that both his mama and hers had got burned out oncet each. The boy got bit once by a mad cat and he says he don't like cats and he don't like niggers. However, every time you look out the window he's racing up and down the road with Shot or Jack in the front seat of his car.

Relations with Shot for the last month have been just like

with Panama. He got fired and simultaneously quit before Christmas and has just been taken back. He wouldn't leave the place. I told R. that since she *will* be obeyed, and he was going to stay, she had better issue him permission to stay, which she did through Louise—which is like dealing with Panama through the Russian embassy.

I wish you would send me a couple of those record reviews you write in Ave Maria. I never bought the record player. I saved up the money and then I thought this is a lot of money to spend for something you don't already appreciate and no guarantee that you ever will so I ordered me a pair of swans instead. My old one died. Then after Christmas the Sisters in Atlanta called up and said somebody had given them a new record player for Christmas and they were sending their old one down for me by Louis, which they did. They said the automatic didn't work on the somethingorother but I don't see anything wrong with it. It makes a noise like popcorn is popping in it somewhere and Mary Jo says that is dust but I don't see any. Anyway, now that I've got it, I'm going to educate my self if possible.

Ashley shouldn't send that thing but to one place at a time, no.

The secretary of the Review of Politics sent me a note saying they had received Roslyn's piece and I haven't heard any more about it but don't inquire; it might well rest there as anywhere. She is presently lost in the wilds of Chile, the last letter she was somewhere for Christmas that was just like Nazereth, no water no lights no nothing but holy Indians and mud houses and she was eating it up. I guess I'm just old. What piety I got is totally dependent on water, plumbing and electricity.

I reckon you read where Red Wally Butts had to settle for just $460,000. I don't think that's a proper lesson to those New York journalists to quit picking on Southern higher edcation, do you? But that's the way it goes. I had a card from Robert that said he was leaving in a few days for North Hadley.

Love,

P.S. The Archbishop is in the hospital with hepatitis contracted, say the papers, "at the Second Vatican Council."

To A.

Milledgeville
Georgia
Dear A., 25 Jan 64

General conditions hereabouts have improved. I am fully restored, Louise is prowling about as usual. I don't think Regina is all right yet but her policy is never to admit anything but perfect health. My aunt Julia who was near death in the hospital last week has rallied this and appears to be going to make it. I have hopes of everybody's survival.

Caroline was crazy about my story. She read it to her class and they laughed until they cried or so she reported and Lord knows who she's reading it to now because she hasn't sent it back to me yet. This did not keep her from writing me six pages on the principles of grammar and on how to spell such words as horde which I spelled hoard but which means something else. She saw my second version which is really better and she understood it perfectly and thought it was probably the profoundest so far. So my mind is settled on that score. I also sent it to Ward Dorrance, an old friend of mine in Washington of whom I am very fond and he allowed the same. So I hope in the next few weeks to get it typed up and send it on to the Sewanee Review. I could get $1500 for it from Esquire but I emulate my better characters and feel like Mr. Shiftlet that there should be some folks that some things mean more to them than money.

My friend Ward Dorrance incidentally is dying from emphesema—that's one of the main things you get from smoking—which he has done all his life. We all gotta go, but not by slow drowning in our own juices.

Very glad you are putting aside metaphisics if that's what you call what you're putting aside. Babies are no doubt healthier, for women. Even chickens are healthier as a matter of fact.

I had a letter from Jack Hawkes said he hoped I would give you the galleys of the novel because he really wasn't sure about that novel and he would like to have some of your impassioned analysis. So I really should have sent it to you and if I can jam it in a book box I will so don't groan when you see it. It would be a good deed to read it and write him about it. I just pure didn't know what to say about it myself.

I have the Original Tin Ear, that is to say, the First and Prime Tin Ear. So I like music that is guaranteed good because I have no way of finding out for myself. Old stuff like Haydn that there is positively no doubt about. On my own I wouldn't know it from Music to Clean Up By.

Cheers,

To Thomas Stritch

Milledgeville

Dear Tom,   11 February 64

Leroy Bates is more efficient than you think. Those records came Friday and we've been playing them ever since and haven't got to the bottom of the pack yet. It's a real gift to us even if not from your point of view. If I had known R. would enjoy this thing so much I would have done something about getting one before now. I think she just likes some noise in the background, I don't know if she listens or not. Every now and then she says, that's pretty. This is the first time I've listened to music except once when I was at Yaddo so I don't have any preference yet though I think I like the kind that is straight up and down better than what slides around, if you know what I mean. I would like to see some of those reviews because I would like to see how knowledgeable folks talk about it. If you don't send me any I'll be obliged to subscribe to Ave Marie, from which I had hoped the Lord would preserve this Christian home.

The swans came too, week before last but it has done nothing but rain and howl here so I haven't got to be out there with them any. I found out about the man where I could get these swans from from Fr. Ginder of all people. He called me up from somewhere in Pennsylvania one Sunday last fall to know how he could get his peafowl down out of the trees. He had bought a pair from the Mother Superior and they had got out of the patio and been in the trees for three days. He was very genial and talked for twenty or twenty five minutes on the long distance telephone, which my parent said is just like them, no sense about money. I don't like his politics but I like him fine. I got the swans from the same place he got his peafowl. I couldn't tell him how to get them down out the trees so he says—to prove R.'s point—"well, I think I'll just let them stay up there then and get her two new ones."

One of my ——— uncles and his wife were through here last week and spent the afternoon with us. They live in ——— and he's retired recently so they move around and take it easy. The ———s are always having run-ins with the clergy which they relate at length and with relish. He was telling about some set-to he had with a Msgr Carney (I think it was) who told one of my cousins that it was the same as murder not to go to the parochial school and the child came dashing home with this afraid he was going to hell and my uncle gets on the phone at once and takes on Msgr. Carney etc etc and they went on about that kind of priest. Then my aunt said, "But our pastor is not that kind, we're very fortunate" and she goes on to say what a good pastor they have. It turns out he is your brother. They said he was a very holy man and had no fault to find with him except he preached too long. Occupational hazard, I reckon.

I hope Caroline left St. Mary's in good shape. Did I tell you that on her last visit to Princeton she went over to the Carmelite convent to see about ending her days in their establishment. I don't imagine they took too eagerly to the idea. I guess if they've survived since the time of Elias she's no real threat, but still, they must have a sense of self-preservation.

This day began for us with the voices of Louise and Shot on their porch but easily heard over here. Shot came over and said Louise wouldn't give him any breakfast. Regina went over there after a while and Louise said she couldn't feed him for no dollar a day. They go through this every six weeks or so. Regina said, well you know he can't afford to pay you any more than a dollar a day and you know you're going to feed him whether he pays you or not so why don't you just take the dollar and hush? Louise says well I can't feed him for no dollar a day as much as he eats. Then she says, well, I'll feed him but I'll just feed him scarce.

Thank you for those records. To look at us putting them on the machine you'd think we'd been at it a long time.

Love,

To Louise Abbot

Milledgeville
Dear Louise,   21 Feb. 64

Well it looks as though I am going to arrive at the cutting table before you. Dr. ——'s stuff is still doing fine but I have a large tumor and if they dont make haste and get rid of it, they will have to remove me and leave it. So this operation is going to take place this Tuesday. (the 25th) Pray for me.

I will miss another visit from the Spiveys, (this is not why I am having the operation) who are scheduled to be through on the 14th. He sent me a paper on my stuff which he read recently at Georgia State. I liked it very much, much more than the last one. It seemed better put together, maybe because it had to be spoken.

When I get back on my four feet, we must definitely have that visit.

Cheers,

To A.

14 March 64
Dear A.,   Milledgeville

I think the most classic thing you could do with Jack's galleys would be to hang them out of your fourth story windows and let the birds tear them into strips for their nests. If you have a better idea do anything you think appropriate. Just so I never lay eyes on them again. I hate galleys. The Monday before I was operated on on Tuesday here come galleys from the Sewanee Review for Revelation and I had to correct them there in the hospital. The story didn't seem so hot.

One of my nurses was a dead ringer for Mrs. Turpin. Her Claud was named Otis. She told me all the time about what a good nurse she was. Her favorite grammatical construction was "it were." She said she treated everybody alike whether it were a person with money or a black nigger. She told me all about the low life in Wilkinson County. I seldom know in any given circumstance whether the Lord is giving me a reward or a punishment. She didn't know she was funny and it was agony to laugh and I reckon she increased my pain about 100%. She was an LPN; (licenced practical nurse) the other two were R.N.s. There's great rivalry between the two. The RNs get more money. The night RN told me everything that had happened to Lassie for the last 3 Sundays. The day RN was the wife of the chief of police. So it was not an uneventful stay in the hospital. Nor unprofitable, I trust. But I aint up to much yet & if you don't hear from me, you'll know the old energy just aint there yet.

Cheers,

To Dr. T. R. Spivey

Milledgeville
Georgia

Dear Ted, 17 March 64

Thank you for the invitation to talk at Georgia State. I appreciate it but I canceled all my talks for April and May and therefore couldn't accept another; also I'm not strong enough yet to undertake it. If I ever did talk or read there, it would have to be in the day time. My idea about Atlanta is get in, get it over with and get out before dark.

I'd surely prefer to see you and Julia both here than just you, but lest I leave the wrong impression, let me tell you again that I have no interest whatsoever in all the dream business and don't want to hear about any dreams you all have had about me or my mother. Into that I can't go with you and there's an end to it.

Also I take a dim view of remnants, and such, though from a good distance I wouldn't mind seeing one in action.

Best to you both for the seasons.

Yours,

To Father James H. McCown

21 March 64

Dear Fr. McCown,   Milledgeville

I am back at home but more or less still in bed, entertaining all the little infections that follow an operation. I'm not really up to your request but you could tell them that anybody who wants to be introduced to Catholic fiction will have to start with the French—Mauriac and Bernanos. You can't dispose of a writer with a paragraph about his significance. I couldn't even compose such. You'd just better read them if you aim to say anything about them. The English are Waugh & Greene and Spark (Muriel) & the Americans: Powers, Percy (our friend Walker) Wilfred Sheed *The Hack*, and some would include Edwin O'Connor. I dont know as I've never read him.

The most important non-fiction writer is Pere Pierre Teilhard de Chardin S.J. who died in 1955 and has so far escaped the Index, although a Monition has been issued on him. If they are good, they are dangerous. I wish I could be of more help but I am not very good at this even when well and right now I'm full of bugs. I do appreciate your prayers. I won't be out of the woods for a few months—until we are sure that all this stress is not going to reactivate the lupus.

I much appreciated your mother's note. Please tell her.

Cheers

Shot & Louise want to know when Preacher is coming back to fish?

To A.

Dear A.,   28 Mar 64

I can scratch you out this kind of a note anyway but if you are like me when I see one of your hand-written communications, you will just wish it would go away. As far as the operation goes it was a howling success; but the patient still languishes. I suspect it has kicked up the lupus again. Anyway I am full of kidney pus and am back on the steroids. Possibly I will end up at Piedmont. I hope not. Piedmont is a little more antiseptic socially than this country hospital here. You dont, as I recollect, hear what groans are being groaned in other rooms. Here there was an old lady across the hall from me who had been in the hospital since last November. She was about 92. Whenever they touched her, she roared LORD LORD LORD in the voice of a stevedore. At night when she coughed a nurse came in and also in a voice you could hear anywhere said "Pit that old stuff out, Sugar. Pit it out. Pit that old stuff out. Pit it out, Sugar," etc.

Yesterday we went to the doctor's office—same scene as in Revelation but nobody in there but us and two old countrymen—about 6 ft tall & skin and bones in overalls. They just had to talk. The first one said, "Six months from now this here room will be half full of niggers. I'd like to git me a machine gun and line em up by sixes and just shoot em down." And he holds his hands up like guns and illustrates. "Aw," says the other one, "it aint the niggers so much. It's them high officials. Jest take the money away from them high officials & you won't have no trouble. All it is is money." Cassius Clay says he don't like all this talk about hate. Says, a tiger come in the room with you you gonna either run or shoot him. That dont mean you hate that tiger. It just means you know you and him cant make out. Did you see Cassius interviewed by Eric Severeid on CBS? Worth seeing.

                                                            Cheers,

To Richard Stern

Milledgeville
Lincoln Assassinated Day
1964

Dear Richard,

I'm cheered my Chicago agent is keeping up with his duty to keep you informed on my state of being. It ain't much but I'm able to take nourishmint and participate in a few Klan rallies. You're that much better off than me, scrapping Tuesday what you wrote Monday. All I've written this year have been a few letters. I have a little contribution to human understanding in the Spring Sewanee but I wrote that last year. You might read something called GOGOL'S WIFE if you haven't already—by one of those Eyetalians, I forget which. As for me I don't read anything but the newspaper and the Bible. Everybody else did that it would be a better world.

Our springs done come and gone. It is summer here. My muscovy duck is setting under the back steps. I have two new swans who sit on the grass and converse with eachother in low tones while the peacocks scream and holler. You just ought to leave that place you teach at and come teach in one of our excellent military colleges or female academies where you could get something good to eat. One of these days you will see the light and I'll be the first to shake your hand.

Keep me posted what you publish. Since you've slowed down, I might be able to keep up with you. I'm only one book behind now and if my head clears this year, I'm going to read it first thing.

Cheers and thanks for thinking of me. I think of you often in that cold place among them interleckchuls.

To Louise and Tom Gossett

Milledgeville
12 May 64

Dear Louise & Tom,

Well our state has changed considerably since you last heard from me. I have been in the hospital again and now am in bed full time. That operation started up the old trouble (disseminated lupus) and I am back on the cortesone and doing none too well—though I feel no pain, only weakness. Yesterday I had a blood transfusion [you get up and go after hit] so today I got the energy to write some letters. In addition to me here, we have my aunt Mary. She grandly survived her heart attack and is out here with us. So my parent is running the Creaking Hill Nursing Home instead of the Andalusia Cow Plantation. Or rather she is running both.

If my trouble runs its predictable course, I reckon I will be in bed all summer. I havent had it active since 1951 and it is something renewing acquaintance with it. I am not supposed to have company or go anywhere but to the doctor, which I do once a week. Maybe you all will be coming back this way in the Fall. I sure hope for better things then. It's a good thing I cancelled that trip to Texas in May. Let us hear from you anyhow.

                                                          Yours,

To Maryat Lee

                                                    Milledgeville
Dear Raybucket,   15 May 64
     Sure you are right. She gets the vision. Wouldn't have been any point in that story if she hadnt. I like Mrs. Turpin as well as Mary Grace. You got to be a very big woman to shout at the Lord across a hog pen. She's a country female Jacob. And that vision is purgatorial. Purrrgatory—and I don't reckon Deanies Presbyterian instincts operate on middling planes of glory. Anyhow the young are a trial to listen to. I'm very intolerant of them.

     I had a blood transfusion Tuesday so I am feeling sommut better and for the last two days I have worked one hour each day and my my I do like to work. I et up that one hour like it was filet mignon.

     Is your hemoglobin low? Mine was down to 8 is why the transfusion. I just wish, if the rest at Chester don't do something for you, you would go to Dr. Sofer. Dr. Burrell says I

have declared a moratorium on making blood—something
that apparently happens in lupus. In '51 I had about 10 transfusions. This time is not as bad as the last—because I know
what's wrong with me. When I first came home May 1 from
the hospital I was hearing the celestial chorus—Clementine is
what it renders when I am weak enough to hear it. Over &
over. "Wooden boxes without topses, They were shoes for
Clementine." The transfusion cut that out. Must come from
not enough blood getting to the head.

Cheers,
Tarbutter

To Maryat Lee

Dear Grace Bug,   21 May 64
   That about Griffin was that Billy Sessions (you met him)
was at the Monastery when Griffin in his black face hove in
& Billy was on his way down here & was going to bring
Griffin but I forget what happened, they didn't get here—if
I had been one of them white ladies Griffin sat down by on
the bus, I would have got up PDQ preferring to sit by a
genuine Negro. I read his other 2 books, one called The Devil
Rides Outside (hysterical) (I dont mean hysterical ha ha but
hystericaleeeek) and another called Nuni about some primitive tribe he fell in with. An interesting man but I wouldn't
have liked him.
   About the Negroes, the kind I don't like is the philosophis-
ing prophesying pontificating kind, the James Baldwin kind.
Very ignorant but never silent. Baldwin can tell us what it
feels like to be a Negro in Harlam but he tries to tell us everything else too. M. L. King I dont think is the ages great saint
but he's at least doing what he can do & has to do. Don't
know anything about Ossie Davis except you like him but
you probably like them all. My question is usually would this
person be endurable if white. If Baldwin were white nobody
would stand him a minute. I prefer Cassius Clay. "If a tiger
move into the room with you," says Cassius, "and you leave,
that dont mean you hate the tiger. Just means you know you

and him can't make out. Too much talk about hate." Cassius is too good for the Moslems.

You can have half interest in Mary Grace.

I think I'll have a book of stories out in the fall. I can't do the work on it, they'll have to print it up from the published stories, but I want to get it out of the way so I can use my limited energy for something new.

Glad she gave you some new stuff. You have to be half dead to impress doctors.

Cheers,
Tarbug

To Maryat Lee

Dear Grrrrrr,   21 May 64
Going to Piedmont tomorrow to let Arthur J. Merrill take over. F. & B. give up, more or less, for the present anyways.
Cheers,
Mrs. Turpin

To Louise Abbot

28 May 64
Piedmont Hosp.
Dear Louise,   Atlanta
I'm in stir as the criminals say. That operation or its aftermath kicked up the lupus for me. I was in the hospital at home 10 days last month & it looks like I'll be in this one 10 days or so. I've been here since last Saturday. But when I get back home and on my feet, we'll set us a day for a visit.

I wouldn't spend much time worrying about dryness. It's hard to steer a path between indifference and presumption and a kind of constant spiritual temperature-taking that don't do any good or tell you anything either. There's a passage in Mark's gospel about the seed planted & growing in its own time. I'll have to look it up.

This evening I had a visit from the Abbot, bubbling over as usual. Regina (she's up here staying with my aunt) met him on his way in & told him he could stay 3 minutes. (I got the high blood) He was here a full 30 I am sure.

Cheers,

P.S. Prayers requested. I am sick of being sick.

To Catharine Carver

Piedmont Hospital
Atlanta, Ga.

Dear Catharin,   17 June 64

I'm still stuck up here in the hospital. I thought I was coming for a week or ten days and I'll have been here a month Saturday. I wrote Giroux and asked him to hold off the publication date of the stories until spring. In that way I thought I could probably manage another story. I've got one that I'm not satisfied with that I finished about the same time as *Revelation* and when I get home I'm going to send it to you, as is, and ask you to let me know what you think of it.

I have another in the making that I scratch on in longhand here at the hospital at night but that's not my idea of writing. How do those French ladies such as Madame Mallet-Joris write in cafes, for pitys sake? Anybody can write in a cafe is made different. No word from Giroux on making it Spring.

I think when they finally let me out of here I'll be able to work—if they ever let me out.

Cheers,

To Janet McKane

Piedmont Hosp

Dear Janet,   19 June 64

I found your note in the Newman book last night but hadn't before. I'm glad your sister is with you. I had wondered if anybody was. I do hope you are better. Keep your feet on the coffee table or better, keep yourself in bed.

I go home tomorrow, praise the Lord. I'll have to stay in bed, even eat in bed for a while, but home is home. I got another transfusion last night and will get another today and they ought to hold me for a while.

My doctor once told me that if I were ever in new york & needed to go to a doctor to go to a Dr. Sofer at Mt. Sinai—the best up there. Fortunately I didn't need one up there, or when I did I got on the plane & came home.

The mail-lady just arrived (call them Pink Ladies here—they wear pink smock & work 2 days a week voluntarily in hospitals—mostly society women with not enough to do at home—good souls really) with 3 letters from you which I was cheered to get. I do enjoy your letters. They are much more interesting than anything I have the energy to cook up in return. I realize I dont even answer half your questions. It is not lack of interest but lack of energy—mental & physical right now. I have always been a terrible conversationalist. I like to be around people who talk all the time because when somebody else is doing it, I dont have to.

I like Hopkins (to answer one) particularly a sonnet beginning

> "Margaret, are you grieving
> Over Goldengrove unleaving—."

Cheers

To Maryat Lee

Dear Marybat,   23 June 64

I must have left something out or else you just aint sectionally small-minded enough to get it. I think it is hilarious. Sen. Everett (from Mass. 1800 & something) and Sen. Davy Crockett are watching a herd of cattle go down Constitution Ave. in Wash. D.C. Everett says, "There are Sen. Crockett's constituents. Where are they going, Sen. Crockett?" "They're a-going to Massachusetts, sir," says Crockett, "to teach school." That kills me, girl. You must be trying to give hit a fancy interpitation.

Dr. Fulghum is back in the driver's seat & Dr. M. has

checked out. I'll see F about Monday. Meantime, he says send him that story so he can see if he's going to sue me. Word of it has got around. Its your office, I said, but its been thoroughly pickled before using.

Our phone is being worked on to give us a new straight line is why I reckon you couldnt get us.

Haven't heard yet about intergration at WC except what I done wrote you. Stories will drift in, I dare say.

I'm much cheered you can take a sup of beer.

                                                        Tarroot

To Thomas Stritch

                                                  Milledgeville
Dear Tom,   28 June 64

Here I am yours truly on the electric typewriter and I feel more or less like folks. An old lady here wrote me that anyone who could survive a month at Piedmont had a strong constitution and need have no fears for his health; she was there a week. I do what amounts to two hours of work a day and that is about as good as I ever did anyway. I asked the doctor if I could sit up at the electric typewriter and work. You can work, says he, but you can't exert yourself. I haven't quite figured this out yet; anyway I am confined to these two rooms and the porch so far and ain't allowed to wash the dishes. I guess that is exerting yourself where writing is officially not. When I was worst off I signed a contract for a book of stories and told FS&C they could get it out themselves; I didn't want Regina to have to fool with it. As soon as I got better I repented of that rash act and I've now told them that I'll have to rewrite some of the stories so the collection won't be until Spring, & I have the work to do.

When we left here to go to Piedmont we left in a hurry and Regina said to Louise, "Take care of everything." It wasn't quite specific enough. When we came back everything was exactly the way we left it, the dirty breakfast dishes were still in the sink and the refrigerator was full of rotten food.

The hay was ready to be cut but Mr. Shot was keeping 11–4 hours. This afternoon he is in the county jail for hitting somebody in a borrowed car while drunk and leaving the scene of the accident. The sheriff says "I'd leave him in there at least until tomorrow." Regina says, "I'm going to leave him in there until the hay dries."

I forget if I told you that the Archbishop came to see me when I was in Piedmont. He is still in St. Josephs but they let him out a couple of afternoons a week and I hear he is writing a book about the council. He won't get back to the 3rd session.

The records are a real boon and when I am not working, I'm listening to them which is in between times. There's no use fooling myself I know what's being worked out anywhere or what's dramatic. Of the ones you sent I think I like the 4-hand piano Chopin thing best; there is a point in it where the peafowls join in.

I hope you have managed to dry up that sister's tears. My dealings with them are mostly through the mail but they shed a lot of verbal ones thataway. One of my favorites at the Cancer Home in Atlanta is trying to have a nervous breakdown or something. They lay it to her age but I lay it to their brand of hot-house piety. They thought she needed a change so they sent her to Boston to attend an ordination, if you please. She also saw her family which she hadn't laid eyes on in 16 years. Came back prostrate.

Thanks for the prayers and the pushing. It must be doing some good. I look like a bull frog but I can work. Give me Robert's news.

Love,

To Janet McKane

Milledgeville Ga
Dear Janet,   7/1/64
Thanks for the Mauriac book. I know its fine and I hope I'll get to it sooner or later but right now I am rather cut in half by the drop in the dose of prednisone and want to use

my little bit of energy on my work. It seems to be doing remarkably well & I know your prayers must be pushing it along. Do you know anything about St. Raphael besides his being an archangel? He leads you to the people you are supposed to meet and in the prayer to him composed I think by Ernest Hello, the words Light & Joy are found. It's a prayer I've said every day for many years. Will send you a copy if you dont know it.

Cheers,

To Janet McKane

Milledgeville

Dear Janet,   8 July 64

Somebody sent me this fancy paper and as it is near at hand I will use it. I've got my share of cards with chickens and Bugs Bunnies and the "funny" kind that say "Get the hell out of that bed" & all the rest of them. Also much soap and such like. People mean well. I put the cards in the trash forth with together with a prayer for the soul of the sender, but the paper I use no matter.

I'm glad you have the children with you for their sakes but I hope its not too much on you.

I have been right weak since my dose was cut in half but now we are going back to smaller doses 4 times a day so I hope for some increase in energy. Yesterday the priest brought me Communion as it looks like it'll be a long time before I'm afoot. I also had him give me the now-called Sacrament of the Sick. Once known as Extreme Unction.

We passed a peaceful 4th of July, with most local restaurants either integrated peacefully or not tested, I'm cheered that bombshell is past. The local college also took in two colored students this summer and is expecting more in the fall. Did I thank you for the Mauriac book? If not I do. I havent got to it yet but I will in time.

Cheers,

To Maryat Lee

Milledgeville
Dear Raycheek,   10 July 64

Somebody gave me this paper—as being, I suppose, a reflection of my personality. Little stickers come with it as says such like as "Hi There!" "Just a Note . . ." and you spit on them and stick them anywhere you please. I have decided to use it all up on you.

That grass hopper you left in the cage for me reminded me so much of the poor colored people in the jails that I let him out and fed him to a duck. I'm sure you'll understand. I'm enjoying old Gunter Grass and the Japanese pillow. That Grass is really something. I'll be all year reading it.

We've changed my dose back to smaller broken doses, same amount of prednisone really but taken in a different way. And I feel better with it. Look better than when you left and feel the same.

Miss Regina got Shot off with the lightest fine ($100) and paroled for a year to the court. She went with him. Otherwise he'd be at the prison farm tonight.

Cheers,

VOTE FOR BARRY GOLDWATER

To Marcus Smith

Milledgeville
Georgia
Dear Mr. Smith: 12 July 64

West may have had some influence on me stylistically. I read him when I was in my early twenties and everything was an influence one way or another. I read him again a few years ago and was disappointed; it was not as good as I had thought, Miss Lonely Hearts seemed a sentimental Christ figure which is a contradiction in terms.

The South anyway has much more to do with it; also Catholicism.

Thanks for your interest. I wish I could be of more help but I doubt if most writers have much idea where their greatest influence came from. For me, I wouldn't say West.

Yours sincerely,

To Catharine Carver

Dear Catharine,

15 July
Milledgeville

I do thank you and I'll get to work on this one you sent back. I can see the point about the daughter's coming being too close to his encounter with the doctor. As for the "on his back" business—thats a cherished Southern white asertion—that the negro *is* on his back and in a way it's quite true. But you have to be born below the M.D. line to appreciate it fully.

I have drug another out of myself and I enclose it. I think it's much better than the last, but I want to know what you think. I think with these two new stories, I'll just leave it at 9 and forget about "You Cant Be Poorer Than Dead." I never thought much of including it anyway.

Have you read over the one called "The Enduring Chill?" I dont much like it but I am afraid once I get to messing with it, I'll make it worse than it is.

About the stroke right after the actor hits him: I have to immobilize him at once or he'd start walking home that minute. The old man in A View of the Woods was Mr. Fortune so I'm alright on Tanner.

This is certainly a great favor you're doing me reading these things. I'm still in bed but I climb out of it into the typewriter about 2 hours every morning.

Cheers,

To A.

Dear A.,   17 July 64

I agree with all you got to say about this and enclose a better barroom scene. You sound like Caroline to the teeth. I

sent it to her same time as I sent it to you and got a telegram
back saying some mechanical details would follow but she
thought it unique, that I had succeeded in dramatizing a heresy. Well not in those terms did I set out but only thinking
that the spirit moveth where it listest. I found out about tattooing from a book I found in the Marboro list called "Memoirs of a Tattooist." The old man that wrote it took tattooing
as a high art and a great profession. No nonsense. Picture of
his wife in it—very demure Victorian lady in off shoulder
gown. Everything you can see except her face & hands is tattooed. Looks like fabric. *He did it.*

Its the other story that was published but this one is so
different I aim to sell it again. I'll send that when I get up the
steam to copy it. I can sit up at the typewriter about an hour
at a time and I reckon I put in two and a half hours a day but
you can't do much that way.

I'm cheered you got that raise. The Republican convention
wasn't much. I look forward to the Democratic one as they
are better at the corn.

There's a right interesting review of Richard Hughes Fox
in the Attic by Walker Percy in the summer 64 Sewanee. Hate
to subject you to this writing (hand) (mine). Its almost as bad
as yours.

> Cheers and much thanks

To Maryat Lee

> Milledgeville
> 21 July 64

Dear Raybat,

I seemed to be doing all right and then I got another spell
of kidney pus & tomorrow I'm going to the Baldwin County
to spend the day and have a blood transfusion as the haema-
globin has dropped to below eight again. I'll take The Tin
Drum along.

The racial front appears to have switched momentarily to
Harlem. Are you participating? Do you ride the subways at
night by yourself? NY sounds to me like a lousy place to live
now.

I'm still puttering on my story that I thought I'd finished but not long at a time. I go across the room & I'm exhausted.

Cheers
Tarweary

To A.

Milledgeville
Dear A.,   25 July 64

No Caroline didnt mean the tattoos were the heresy. Sarah Ruth was the heretic—the notion that you can worship in pure spirit. Caroline gave me a lot of advice about the story but most of it I'm ignoring. She thinks every story must be built according to the pattern of the Roman arch and she would enlarge the beginning and the end, but I'm letting it lay. I did well to write it at all. I had another transfusion Wednesday but it don't seem to have done much good.

We can worry about the interpitations of Revelation but not its fortunes. I had a letter from the O. Henry prize people & it got first.

Cheers,

To Janet McKane

Dear Janet,   26 July 64

Thanks for the cards. I'll use up these before I start on the others. I like them all. I had better correct your barnyard-ology. There is no goose in that picture. That is a muscovy duck name Sister. No religious significance. Sister sets about four times a year & hatches more than any of the others. The creature with the wattles is a guinea. The ones strolling on the steps are peahens (female of peafowl). If I were you I'd throw away The Art of Plain Talk and keep at your Milton & Shakespeare. Sometime at your library you might see if you could find "The Ethics of Rhetoric" by R. M. Weaver. I once had a copy but I gave it to somebody for a graduation present and now I'm sorry I did.

Cheers,

To Maryat Lee

Milledgeville
Dear Raybutter,   26 July 64

As far as me and Senator Russell are concerned those riots couldn't be located in a better place than Harlem, not to mention Rochester and Brooklyn. And you seem to be having the heat too. It aint even hot here, very delightful. It don't do much but rain but its very delightful.

I got a pint of blood or so last Wednesday and now I'm taking a double dose of anti biotic for the kidney pus & they are withdrawing the cortesone. Its six of one and a half dozen of the other. I feel lousy but I dont have much idea how I really am.

That letter head knocked me out boy that's some letter head—so many folks theres almost no room for the letter. I hope those farm agents don't give you any trouble.

Cheers

To Janet McKane

Dear Janet,   27 July 64

The books & the burro came today and I do appreciate them. I'm not up to the books yet but I will be let us hope later on. I'm up to the burro. Equinox inside & out.

Today I went to the doctor and that always wears me out. He has had three coronaries and so his patients have to go to him.

Cheers,

To Maryat Lee

Milledgeville
Dear Raybat,   28 July 64

Cowards can be just as vicious as those who declare themselves—more so. Dont take any romantic attitude toward
that call. Be properly scared and go on doing what you have
to do, but take the necessary precautions. And call the police.
That might be a lead for them.

Dont know when I'll send those stories. I've felt too bad to
type them.

Cheers
Tarfunk

Index to Letters

Index of Stories and Occasional Prose

Chronology

ville, house once used as interim governor's mansion when town was state capital. Becomes familiar with numerous aunts, great-aunts, uncles, and cousins who live in or visit Cline household.

1931   Enters first grade at St. Vincent's Grammar School at the Cathedral, taught by Sisters of Mercy from Ireland. Enjoys drawing and writing at home and school. Develops fondness for domestic fowl and delights in unusual examples. Trains "frizzled" chicken (so-called because its feathers grow backward) to walk backward. Feat attracts attention of Pathé News, New York newsreel company, which sends cameraman to record O'Connor and her chicken in action.

1932–35   Makes First Communion in the Cathedral on May 8, 1932, and is confirmed there May 20, 1934. Father encounters increasing business difficulties as Depression worsens.

1936–37   Transfers to Sacred Heart School on Bull Street, taught by Sisters of St. Joseph of Corondolet. Joins Girl Scout troop but does not enjoy hikes. Draws and writes verses, notes, and stories for her parents (later tells friends that she never minded being an only child). Makes comments on flyleaves of books, including Lewis Carroll's *Alice in Wonderland* ("Awful. I wouldn't read this book"), Shirley Watkin's *Georgia Finds Herself* ("This is the worst book I ever read next to 'Pinnochio'"), and Louisa May Alcott's *Little Men* ("first rate. Splendid"). Father is elected State Commander of American Legion and travels frequently on Legion affairs until declining health forces him to resign position. (Illness, initially thought to be arthritis, later diagnosed as lupus erythematosus, incurable collagen disease in which the body's immune system attacks its own vital tissues.) Father's business difficulties continue, and at end of year he seeks position with the Federal Housing Administration.

1938   Father is appointed zone real estate appraiser for the FHA and in March family moves to Atlanta, taking house at 2525 Potomac Street, N.E. O'Connor enters parochial school of St. Joseph's Church in mid-term. Adjustment to life in new city is difficult for family, and at beginning of fall school term O'Connor moves with mother to Cline family home in Milledgeville; father remains in Atlanta, living in Bell House (rooming house where mother's brothers Dr. Bernard and Louis Cline have resided for many years) and spending weekends in Milledgeville. In absence of parochial schools in mainly Protestant town, O'Connor enters freshman class of Peabody High School, experimental school run by Education Department of Georgia State College for Women (now Georgia College).

1939–40   Draws cartoons and writes for the *Peabody Palladium*, school newspaper. Sets up attic studio at home as her workspace. Father's health continues to deteriorate until he is forced to resign from the FHA and retire to Milledgeville.

1941   Father dies of lupus on February 1. O'Connor feels loss deeply (afterwards speaks of him only rarely). Works hard in school and continues to contribute cartoons, book reviews, and occasional verse to school newspaper. Attempts to learn to play accordion (liking "the flash and glitter of it"), clarinet, and bass fiddle, but does not persist. Designs and makes lapel pins for sale in local shop. Attracts notice at school by sewing clothes for bantam hen in home economics course. Writes and illustrates "books," usually about geese, described by her as "too old for children and too young for grown-ups." Reading at experimental school is unsystematic; develops taste on her own for Poe, especially *The Narrative of Arthur Gordon Pym* and collection of "humorous" tales that includes "The Man That Was Used Up," "The Spectacles," and "The System of Doctor Tarr and Professor Fether." During summer visits maternal aunt and cousins in Arlington, Massachusetts.

1942   Graduates from Peabody High School and enters summer school freshman class of Georgia State College for Women, a block from her home in Milledgeville, following accelerated three-year wartime course. Takes active part in student life, except for dances and sports, when official academic year opens in September. Majors in sociology and English. Begins to sign academic work as Flannery O'Connor (family and friends continue to address her as Mary Flannery). Greene Street household (where she will live throughout college) now consists of O'Connor, her mother, two unmarried aunts, lodger from college faculty, and uncles who visit on weekends. Writes and illustrates comic depictions of family members and their vagaries ("My Relitives" and "Why I Chose Heart Trouble" among them).

1943 Writes stories and poems for college literary magazine *The Corinthian*. Studies English literature and writes comic pieces about writers ("The Domestic Bliss of Samuel Taylor Coleridge," "The Bookkeeper's Chaucer") for class assignments. Forms lifelong friendship with mathematician Betty Boyd (later Betty Boyd Love). Meets Marine Sergeant John Sullivan, stationed at the college naval base, who becomes close friend and frequent visitor to Greene Street household.

1944 Assumes extra course work, intent on winning scholarship for further study. Serves as art editor of college yearbook *The Spectrum* and contributes linoleum-block cartoons satirizing undergraduate life and college's wartime women's auxiliary naval training program. Sends cartoons to *The New Yorker* in April, but magazine shows no interest. Poems and stories appear regularly in *The Corinthian* but are rejected by commercial magazines. Corresponds regularly with John Sullivan after his transfer to another base and then to the Pacific, carefully drafting and reworking her letters. Favorably impresses George Beiswanger, new member of college faculty, who encourages her to apply to the State University of Iowa graduate writing program.

1945 Applies to graduate schools of State University of Iowa and Duke University. Accepts scholarship in journalism from Iowa providing tuition plus stipend of $65 per term. Receives AB degree in June. Goes with mother to Iowa City in September and moves into Currier House, graduate dormitory at 32 E. Bloomington Street. Begins to introduce herself as Flannery O'Connor. Gains admission to Writers' Workshop and submits cartoons and drawings to art department. Takes courses in literature, advanced drawing, American political cartooning, advertising, and magazine writing. Begins attending Mass daily at St. Mary's Church. Becomes part of dormitory community and forms friendships with roommate Louise Trovato and fellow student Ruth Sullivan. Writes to mother daily (will continue to do so whenever she is away from Milledgeville) and reads Milledgeville newspaper regularly. Allows Workshop director Paul Engle, who thinks her Georgia accent will not be understood, to read her work aloud for her in class. November, on Engle's advice sends stories to literary magazines. Decides to submit collection of short stories as master's thesis. Hoping to augment income, submits cartoons to trade journals, where she considers competition to be weaker, but without success. Encouraged when John Crowe Ransom, editor of *Kenyon Review*, chooses one of her stories to read aloud during classroom visit and comments favorably upon it (later will have her stories chosen for discussion by Robert Penn Warren and novelist Andrew Lytle). Returns home by train for Christmas.

1946   On return to Iowa City in January learns that *Sewanee Review* has rejected two of her stories. Discovers that she has grown more than an inch during first semester. Begins reading program under Engle's direction and encounters work of Joyce, Kafka, Faulkner, and other modern writers for first time. On advice of Paul Horgan, new director of Workshop's fiction program, begins to write set number of hours each day at the same time and without interruption (will follow practice throughout career). Story "The Geranium" is accepted by *Accent* in March (appears in Summer issue). Awarded English Department fellowship for the following year, with stipend increased to $20 a month. Flies home in late May. "Wildcat" and "The Coat" are rejected by *The Southwest Review* during summer. When *American Courier* accepts "The Coat," refuses to let it be printed without payment (story remains unpublished). Told by descendant of previous owners that Grey Quail Farm, property four miles outside of Milledgeville now owned by uncle Bernard Cline, was once called Andalusia (later persuades family to adopt earlier name). Returns to Iowa City in September and moves back into Currier House. Enrolls in Writers' Workshop and takes courses in imaginative writing, aesthetics, and seminar in literary criticism taught by Austin Warren (O'Connor chooses Joyce's *Dubliners* and Cleanth Brooks and Robert Penn Warren's *Understanding Fiction* as supplementary texts for criticism course). John Sullivan, now demobilized, writes that he is entering seminary to study for priesthood; correspondence gradually ends. Seeks

solitude for writing and is pleased by roommate's frequent
weekend travel. Engle sends two of her stories to John
Selby, editor-in-chief of Rinehart & Company. Begins
work on novel in December before going to Milledgeville
for Christmas.

1947 Returns to Iowa City. Applies for several college teaching
positions. Story "The Barber" is accepted by anthology of
student writing, *New Signatures*. Uncle Bernard Cline dies
suddenly in late January, leaving Andalusia farm, comprising 500 acres of fields and 1,000 acres of woods, to her
mother and uncle Louis Cline. Works on novel through
spring term and submits first four chapters (all later revised extensively) to Rinehart-Iowa Fiction Award competition for first novel. Awarded the $750 prize in late
May, with Rinehart holding option to publish upon satisfactory completion. With Engle's backing, obtains fellowship for following year that will permit her to work in
Iowa City. Submits thesis, *The Geranium: A Collection of
Short Stories* (includes "The Geranium," "The Barber,"
"Wildcat," "The Crop," "The Turkey," and "The Train"),
and receives Master of Fine Arts degree on June 1. Works
on novel in Georgia during summer. Returns to Iowa
City in September and rents single room in boarding
house at 115 E. Bloomington Street. Enrolls as post-grad-
uate student in Writers' Workshop and takes course in European literature. Sells "The Turkey" to *Mademoiselle* for
$300 (appears as "The Capture" in November 1948). "The
Train," opening chapter of novel, sold to *Sewanee Review*
for $105 (appears April 1948). Impressed by visiting poet
Robert Lowell at dinner and public reading. Enjoys company of novelists and Workshop instructors Robie Macauley and Paul Griffith, and student writers Jean Williams
(later Jean Wylder) and Clyde McLeod (later Clyde Hoff-
man). Visits Milledgeville for Christmas.

1948 Novelist and Workshop teacher Andrew Lytle begins to
oversee O'Connor's work on novel. Accepts invitation
from Yaddo Foundation to spend June and July at its artists' colony near Saratoga Springs, New York, and tells
family that she will not visit until August. Becomes friends
at Yaddo with writers Edward Maisel and Elizabeth Fenwick and painter Clifford Wright. Attends Mass with

colony's domestic staff. Receives offer from Engle of modest fellowship at Iowa for following academic year. Engages Elizabeth McKee as literary agent. Philip Rahv, editor of *Partisan Review*, accepts "The Heart of the Park," story taken from novel (appears February 1949). Elizabeth Ames, director of Yaddo, invites O'Connor to return in mid-September and remain through end of the year. O'Connor accepts and declines Iowa fellowship (decision does not please her mother). Visits Milledgeville, then returns to Yaddo in September, where she joins group of fifteen guests, including Robert Lowell, who offers advice on novel, and critic Malcolm Cowley. Learns in mid-October that she may stay through March of following year. Guests leave during autumn until only O'Connor, Lowell, Maisel, Wright, and writer James Ross remain. Applies for Guggenheim fellowship in November, with recommendations from Lowell, Rahv, and Robert Penn Warren. Remains at Yaddo for the Christmas holidays to economize.

1949   Learns in early January that she will be able to stay at Yaddo beyond March. Ross and Wright leave colony and writer Elizabeth Hardwick arrives. Sends nine draft chapters of novel to agent Elizabeth McKee with request that she forward them to John Selby at Rinehart and negotiate advance with him. Angered by letter from Selby in early February criticizing novel (writes McKee that Selby's comments are "addressed to a slightly dim-witted Camp Fire Girl . . ."). Replies to Selby that she is not writing a "conventional" novel and will accept criticism "only within the sphere of what I am trying to do." Becomes involved in political controversy when the press reports allegations that radical journalist Agnes Smedley, a Yaddo resident 1943–48, had served as Soviet intelligence agent and guests learn that colony and Elizabeth Ames have been under FBI investigation for several years. Joins other guests in choosing Robert Lowell as spokesman and attends private meeting with Yaddo's board of directors where Lowell charges Ames with endangering colony by politically motivated favoritism toward Smedley and demands her dismissal. Leaves Yaddo at end of February and goes to New York with Lowell and Hardwick. (When supporter of Ames on board gives transcript of meeting to the press, over fifty writers publicly defend Ames,

attacking Lowell and his supporters. Yaddo board decides
at second meeting in March to retain Ames as director,
but establishes committee to determine length of guests'
residencies.) Stays briefly with Hardwick in her apartment
at 28 East 10th Street before finding room "that smelled
like an unopened Bible" in YWCA residence at East 38th
Street and Lexington Avenue. Introduced by Lowell to
editor Robert Giroux at Harcourt, Brace and Company.
Meets and begins lifelong friendship with poet and translator Robert Fitzgerald and his wife, Sally. Rinehart refuses advance for novel unless she reworks it under Selby's
direction; O'Connor refuses. Application for Guggenheim
fellowship is rejected. Story "Woman on the Stairs" (written as fourth chapter of novel but then cut out) accepted
for August issue of *Tomorrow*. Distressed by news that
Lowell has suffered severe mental collapse. Visits Milledgeville in late March and returns to New York in April.
With help of Elizabeth Fenwick, finds furnished room in
apartment at 255 West 108th Street. Accepts invitation from
Fitzgeralds to live with them in Ridgefield, Connecticut,
as paying guest while she finishes novel. Moves September
1 into room over attached garage at Fitzgeralds' house on
70 Acre Road. Writes four hours every morning, baby-sits
with eldest Fitzgerald child for hour in afternoon, and
joins Fitzgeralds for meals and long conversations in evening. October, receives provisional contract from Harcourt, Brace for publication of novel. Angered by release
from Rinehart agreement, written by Selby, that describes
her as "stiff-necked, uncooperative, and unethical," offers
to submit additional chapters to Rinehart in six months'
time with understanding that she will be granted uncon-
ditional release if Rinehart still considers manuscript unsatisfactory. "The Peeler," story taken from novel, appears
in December *Partisan Review*. Recommends Faulkner's *As
I Lay Dying* and Nathanael West's *Miss Lonelyhearts* to
Fitzgeralds. Goes to Milledgeville for Christmas and learns
that she must undergo operation.

1950   Spends January in hospital after surgery. Convalesces at
            home before returning to Ridgefield in early March.
            Works through spring and summer to mid-autumn with-
            out interruption. Decides on resolution of novel after
            reading Robert Fitzgerald's translations of Sophocles'
            Oedipus Rex and *Oedipus at Colonus*. Completes prelimi-

nary draft, considers using title *Wise Blood and Simple*, then shortens it to *Wise Blood*. Signs contract in October with Harcourt, Brace after Rinehart gives her final release. Begins to suffer pains and heaviness in arms and shoulder joints shortly before departure for Christmas visit to Milledgeville. Without time for laboratory tests, Fitzgerald family physician makes provisional diagnosis of arthritis, but advises thorough examination when O'Connor reaches home. Becomes dangerously ill with high fever while on train to Georgia and is taken to Baldwin County Hospital in Milledgeville on arrival, where she is diagnosed as having acute rheumatoid arthritis and treated with cortisone.

1951 Atlanta internist Dr. Arthur J. Merrill diagnoses disseminated lupus erythematosus in telephone consultation with Milledgeville physician. Transferred in February to Emory University Hospital in Atlanta, where she receives blood transfusions and massive injections of adrenocorticotropic hormone (ACTH), recently developed cortisone derivative. Blood tests confirm illness is lupus; when family is told, they decide to withhold information from O'Connor, fearing that diagnosis of incurable disease would cause physical setback. Temporarily loses hair from fevers and suffers facial swelling from cortisone. Dr. Merrill warns mother that O'Connor may die. Works on novel by hand while in hospital and sends revised draft to Fitzgeralds. Leaves hospital in March, learns to give herself daily ACTH injections, and goes on rigorous salt-free diet. Moves with mother to Andalusia and takes room on ground floor (is too weak to climb stairs), but hopes eventually to live in Connecticut again. Sends novel to Giroux and McKee in early March, expecting quick reply, but does not receive news of its acceptance until June. Readmitted to Emory University Hospital several times during summer when condition worsens. Following Robert Fitzgerald's suggestion, asks writer and critic Caroline Gordon to read novel. Makes extensive revisions based on Gordon's detailed comments, beginning lifelong friendship and practice of sending manuscripts to Gordon for criticism. Submits revised manuscript to Giroux in October and sends further changes in early December. Finds increasing pleasure in Andalusia, operated by her mother (with hired labor) as dairy farm.

1952   Returns corrected and revised galleys of *Wise Blood* in Jan-
        uary. "Enoch and the Gorilla," story drawn from two
        chapters of novel, sold to anthology *New World Writing* in
        February (appears in April). Corrects proofs of novel
        while visiting Mrs. Semmes in Savannah. Earns $2,000
        from sale of paperback rights to New American Library
        (edition appears in 1953). *Wise Blood* published by Har-
        court, Brace on May 15. Receives mixed reviews and pro-
        vokes outrage among some Milledgeville residents. Begins
        new story "The World Is Almost Rotten." Takes up paint-
        ing, using scenes of farm life as subjects. Goes to Ridge-
        field in early June, smuggling three live ducklings on
        board plane as gifts for Fitzgerald children. Stays for five
        weeks before viral infection reactivates lupus and forces
        her return to Georgia. Receives two transfusions, in-
        creased dosage of ACTH, and spends six weeks in bed.
        Sends for clothing and books left with Fitzgeralds in 1950,
        having learned during summer that she has lupus. Orders
        first pair of peafowl and four peachicks. Writes story "A
        Late Encounter with the Enemy" and sells it to *Harper's
        Bazaar* in August (appears September 1953). Finishes "The
        World Is Almost Rotten" in the fall, retitling it "The Life
        You Save May Be Your Own." Writes "The River," and
        begins new novel, Receives letter from John Crowe Ran-
        som in November praising *Wise Blood* and inviting her to
        apply for new *Kenyon Review* fellowship. Learns shortly
        before Christmas that she has won the $2,000 grant (will
        use it to pay for blood transfusions, ACTH, and books).

1953   Begins correspondence with writer Brainard Cheney in
        February by responding to his review of *Wise Blood* in
        Shenandoah. Paints self-portrait depicting herself holding
        pheasant. Visited at Andalusia by Danish-born Harcourt,
        Brace textbook representative Erik Langkjaer, who be-
        comes friend and frequent guest; O'Connor falls in love
        with him during following months. "Woman on the
        Stairs" appears under new title "A Stroke of Good For-
        tune" in Spring issue of *Shenandoah*, "The Life You Save
        May Be Your Own" in Spring issue of *Kenyon Review*, and
        "The River" in Summer issue of *Sewanee Review*. Resumes
        work on novel. Meets Brainard Cheney and his wife,
        Frances, teacher at George Peabody College Library
        School in Nashville, when they visit Andalusia in June.
        Told by Dr. Merrill that her health is stable enough to

permit limited travel. Pays first visit to Cheneys at Cold Chimneys, their home in Smyrna, Tennessee, where she meets teacher and critic Ashley Brown, who becomes valued friend. "A Good Man Is Hard to Find" appears in anthology *Modern Writing I*, edited by William Phillips and Philip Rahv, and "The Life You Save May Be Your Own" wins second prize in O. Henry Awards. Family of Polish refugees arrives in August to live and work at Andalusia. O'Connor spends three weeks in Ridgefield (her last visit before Fitzgeralds move to Italy). December, reads draft of "The Displaced Person" aloud to hosts and guests while staying with Cheneys in Smyrna. Returns home and finishes "A Circle in the Fire." Plans collection of short stories, *A Good Man Is Hard to Find*.

1954   Reappointed *Kenyon Review* fellow in January. Submits "A Temple of the Holy Ghost" to *Harper's Bazaar* (appears in May) and "The Displaced Person" to *Atlantic Monthly*. Begins to limp from persistent hip pain, thought to be caused by incipient rheumatism. "A Circle in the Fire" appears in Spring issue of *Kenyon Review*. "The Displaced Person" is rejected by *Atlantic Monthly* and accepted by *Sewanee Review* in late March (appears Autumn 1954). Distressed by Erik Langkjaer's decision to return to Denmark. After several British publishers reject *Wise Blood*, O'Connor signs contract for its publication with Neville Spearman Ltd., giving company option on her future work. Three of her stories are nominated for O. Henry Awards and "A Circle in the Fire" wins second prize. Earns $1.35 net in royalties from *Wise Blood* in first six months of year and $62.16 from sale of English serial rights to "A Temple of the Holy Ghost." Ransom accepts story "The Artificial Nigger" for *Kenyon Review* (appears Spring 1955) after briefly objecting to title. Sends manuscript of short-story collection, including expanded version of "The Displaced Person," to Giroux in November. Rewrites "The Artificial Nigger" after Caroline Gordon reads it; submits new version, along with revised opening of "The Displaced Person," in December. Suggests omitting "An Afternoon in the Woods," rewritten version of "The Capture," and "A Stroke of Good Fortune" when Giroux writes that book now exceeds its planned length. By year's end is forced to use cane when walking.

1955   Offers self-portrait with pheasant for jacket cover of story
collection, but publishers decline. Writes "Good Country
People" in February in "about four days" and, encouraged
by Gordon and her husband, poet and critic Allen Tate,
tries to have it included in the book. Giroux agrees and
omits "An Afternoon in the Woods" and "An Exile in the
East" (rewritten version of "The Geranium") to make
room. Attends arts forum in March at Women's College
of the University of North Carolina, Greensboro, where
she meets Peter Taylor and Randall Jarrell. Robert Giroux
resigns from Harcourt, Brace in April but O'Connor remains with company, reassured by his regard for her new
editor, Catharine Carver. Receives announcement of Erik
Langkjaer's impending marriage in Denmark. Gives talks
to Macon Writers' Club and Macon Women's Club. Goes
to New York for appearance on television program *Galley
Proof*, May 31, where she is interviewed by Harvey Breit of
The New York Times and watches dramatization of opening
scene of "The Life You Save May Be Your Own." Stays in
New York for week of further interviews and meetings,
and is taken to see Tennessee Williams' *Cat on a Hot Tin
Roof*, her only experience of Broadway theater; does not
like play. Spends weekend near Sherman, Connecticut,
with Caroline Gordon and Sue Jenkins Brown and is visited by Malcolm Cowley and Van Wyck Brooks. *A Good
Man Is Hard to Find and Other Stories* is published by Harcourt, Brace on June 6, receives critical praise, and sells
unexpectedly well (4,000 copies in three printings by September). Signs contract with Harcourt, Brace for new
novel, giving her option to cancel if Catharine Carver
ceases to be her editor. Receives $1,250 advance, with
book to be delivered within five years. "Good Country
People" appears in June *Harper's Bazaar*. Writes of family
and neighbors' reaction to collection and its public reception: "Everybody here shakes my hand but nobody reads
my stories. Which is just as well." Receives letter in July
from young Atlanta woman she has never met (referred
to as "A." in *The Habit of Being*, posthumously published
edition of O'Connor's letters), beginning lifelong correspondence. *Wise Blood* is published in England by Neville
Spearman Ltd. and receives respectful reviews; O'Connor
is unhappy with poor quality of printing and cover art.
Visits Cheneys in July. Begins taking new Meticorten cap-

sules in place of ACTH injections. Applies for Guggenheim fellowship (is again rejected). Hip condition worsens and in September begins to use crutches "for a year or two" to avoid future operation. "You Can't Be Any Poorer Than Dead," first chapter of novel in progress, appears in *New World Writing* in October. Learns in December that French rights to *Wise Blood* have been sold to Gallimard.

1956   Signs revised Harcourt, Brace contract in January after Carver leaves company, naming Denver Lindley as her new editor and retaining option to cancel if he resigns. Learns that Maurice-Edgar Coindreau, Faulkner's French translator, will translate *Wise Blood* for Gallimard. Begins to write short book reviews for Atlanta diocesan weekly *The Bulletin* (will write 120 reviews, mostly for Georgia diocesan papers, through 1964). Receives unexpected visit from Jesuit James McCown, who has read her stories, beginning sustained friendship; McCown recommends her to literary editor of Jesuit weekly *America*. Signs agreement with Neville Spearman for English publication of *A Good Man Is Hard to Find*, with proviso releasing her from future obligations if work is altered in any way. X-ray examination reveals that hip bone is progressively degenerating and that use of crutches will have to be permanent. Refuses to allow sale of her work to Polish and Czech publishers, fearing that it will be used for anti-American propaganda. Addresses Lansing, Michigan, chapter of the American Association of University Women in late April, and continues to speak at local club and literary meetings in Milledgeville, Macon, and Atlanta. "Greenleaf" appears in Summer issue of *Kenyon Review*. Visited in late June by "A.", first meeting after year of exchanging letters fortnightly ("A." will continue to visit Andalusia occasionally). Meets writer and teacher William Sessions in early July, beginning lasting friendship. First telephone is installed at Andalusia in late July. "The Life You Save May Be Your Own" is sold to television production company, earning O'Connor $800, which she uses to buy her mother new refrigerator (continues to decline occasional offers of screenwriting work). Completes "A View of the Woods" in early September and sells it to *Partisan Review* (appears Fall 1957) after it is rejected by *Harper's Bazaar*. October, New American Library issues *A Good Man Is*

Hard to Find in paperback. Meets playwright Maryat Lee, sister of president of Georgia State College for Women, in late December, beginning long friendship. "Greenleaf" wins first prize of $300 in O. Henry Awards.

1957   Replies to appreciative letter from poet Elizabeth Bishop, beginning correspondence (they never meet). Works slowly through winter on novel, setting it aside to write article "The Church and the Fiction Writer" for Jesuit journal *America* (appears March 30) and to give talk at Emory University (continues to speak at southern colleges, usually receiving $50 fee). Visited by writer Louise Abbot, from nearby Louisville, Georgia, who becomes close friend. Intensely dislikes television production of "The Life You Save May Be Your Own" broadcast on CBS March 1, with Gene Kelly playing Mr. Shiftlet, which is widely praised in Milledgeville ("They feel that I have arrived at last"). Writes essay "The Fiction Writer and His Country" for *The Living Novel: A Symposium* edited by Granville Hicks. April, lectures at University of Notre Dame in South Bend, Indiana, to receptive audience of 250. Enjoys reunions with Robert Fitzgerald and Ruth Sullivan Finnegan, Iowa friend now married to professor at university. Meets Thomas Stritch, professor of communications, who becomes close friend. Receives $1,000 grant from National Institute of Arts and Letters. Writer Cecil Dawkins initiates continuing correspondence. X-ray in mid-June shows no further deterioration in hip. Buys inexpensive house in Milledgeville with savings from literary grants and earnings (will be let for $55 a month). Works on novel through summer and fall and considers using *The Violent Bear It Away* as title. October, *A Good Man Is Hard to Find* published in England by Neville Spearman as *The Artificial Nigger and Other Tales*. Change of title without O'Connor's permission breaches contract and frees her to seek new English publisher. Meets weekly at Andalusia with group of local readers to discuss literature and theology (meetings continue until fall 1960). Sets novel aside in November and begins story "The Enduring Chill." Despite misgivings, accepts offer from Mrs. Semmes to send her and mother on seventeen-day pilgrimage to Ireland, London, Paris, Lourdes, Rome, and Lisbon in following spring. December, sends draft of new story to Caroline Gordon and Allen Tate for criticism.

1958   Revised version of "The Enduring Chill" sold to *Harper's Bazaar* (appears July). Resumes work on novel. Declines invitation from Elizabeth Ames to re-apply to Yaddo. Dr. Merrill advises that planned trip is too strenuous and O'Connor arranges to stay and rest with Fitzgeralds in Italy. Katherine Anne Porter visits Andalusia in late March after reading in Macon. Denver Lindley resigns from Harcourt, Brace in early April and O'Connor signs new contract with Farrar, Straus and Cudahy, naming Robert Giroux as her editor. Flies with mother to Milan on April 24 and spends four days with Fitzgeralds in Ligurian coastal town of Levanto before rejoining pilgrimage in Paris with Sally Fitzgerald, who accompanies them for remainder of trip. Visited in Paris hotel by Gabrielle Rolin, Belgian novelist with whom she will correspond. Joined at Lourdes by William Sessions, who is in Europe on fellowship. Moved by suppliants crowding shrine but repelled by souvenir shops in the town; compares village to "a beautiful child with smallpox." Reluctantly bathes in waters from spring (later writes that she "prayed for my book, not my bones"). Tired and worried about health, tries unsuccessfully to find flight home from Barcelona before continuing on pilgrimage to Rome. Attends general audience in St. Peter's and afterwards is personally greeted and blessed by Pius XII (writes of Pope, "Whatever the special superaliveness that holiness is, it is very apparent in him"). Returns home May 9 and quickly makes progress on novel. Takes driving lessons and passes test in July on second try, but drives only when necessary. Visited by novelist John Hawkes and by Theodore Spivey, professor of English at Georgia State University in Atlanta; both become correspondents. X-rays in mid-November show hip to be unexpectedly improving. Allowed to walk around house without crutches, expresses belief that Lourdes pilgrimage may be responsible; is able to tell news to Mrs. Semmes before her death in late November. Inherits childhood home on Liberty Square in Savannah from Mrs. Semmes (will let it).

1959   Completes first draft of novel, now titled *The Violent Bear It Away*, in early January and sends copy to Gordon for criticism. Spends five days at University of Chicago in February, substituting for Eudora Welty as guest instructor in writing program. Conducts two workshops and gives sparsely attended public reading; receives $700. Becomes friends with Richard Stern, director of program. Meets Cecil Dawkins for first time. Awarded $8,000 grant from the Ford Foundation, meant to assist her for two years, but which she intends to "stretch into ten." Signs with Longmans, Green for English publication of *The Violent Bear It Away*. Sends manuscript to Carver (now editor at Viking and trusted literary adviser) and Fitzgeralds in late March. Maurice-Edgar Coindreau visits in early April and O'Connor supplies him with material for article on itinerant American preachers he is writing to help French readers understand background of *Wise Blood*. Begins expanding and rewriting middle section of *The Violent Bear It Away* in April in response to comments of Carver and Fitzgeralds. Visits Holy Ghost Monastery, Trappist community at Conyers, Georgia, in late May, and becomes friends with Abbot Augustine Moore and Father Paul Bourne. Sends rewritten middle section of novel to Carver, then makes further changes after receiving telegraphed praise of new version. Submits manuscript to Giroux in mid-July after Fitzgeralds respond favorably to latest revisions. Suffers necrosis in jaws, making eating difficult until large doses of aspirin bring relief from pain. Begins writing "The Azalea Festival" in September. Corrects proofs of novel and anticipates unfavorable reviews, considering it "dull and half-done." Writes new story, "The Comforts of Home," and then rewrites it after Carver criticizes it as undramatic. Addition to farmhouse, comprising sitting room, bedroom, and bath, is completed in December.

1960   "The Comforts of Home" is sold to *Kenyon Review* in January (appears in Fall issue). *The Violent Bear It Away* published by Farrar, Straus and Cudahy on February 8 and receives mixed reviews. O'Connor considers her intentions to have been misunderstood by both favorable and unfavorable critics, and is angered by review in *Time* mentioning lupus in relation to her work. Encouraged by letters from Robert Lowell, Andrew Lytle, Thomas Stritch, and Robert Penn Warren praising book. In April receives letter from Sister Evangelist, Superior of Our Lady of Perpetual Help Cancer Home in Atlanta, asking her to write book about child with disfiguring facial tumor whom the Sisters had cared for during last nine years of her twelve-year life-

time. Replies that Sisters should write it themselves, but
offers editorial assistance and introduction. Jaw pains return, again affecting ability to bite and chew. Coindreau
visits in June, bringing favorable reviews of *La Sagesse dans
le Sang*, French edition of *Wise Blood*. "The Partridge Festival," rewritten and retitled version of "The Azalea Festival," is sold to Catholic magazine *The Critic* (appears
August). Meets with Sister Evangelist and five other nuns
from cancer home in July to discuss their book. Accepts
offer from *Holiday* magazine to write article on peafowl
(appears September 1961, with her title "The King of the
Birds" changed to "Living with a Peacock") and receives
$750, most she has ever been paid by a magazine. *The Vi-
olent Bear It Away* published in England by Longmans,
Green in September. Travels to Minnesota for week in
October, speaking at St. Teresa's and St. Catherine's colleges and to Newman Club of the University of Minnesota in Minneapolis. Returns to take part in arts festival at
Wesleyan College in Macon, delivering lecture "Some Aspects of the Grotesque in Southern Fiction" and participating in panel with Caroline Gordon, Katherine Anne
Porter, novelist Madison Jones, and critic Louis Rubin.
Writes introduction to Sisters' book and persuades them
to use plain title, *A Memoir of Mary Ann*. Sends manuscript to Giroux for his opinion in early December. Noting increase in bone symptoms, enters Piedmont Hospital
in Atlanta for tests. Results establish that disintegration in
hips and jaws is caused by steroid drugs necessary to control lupus; doctors try reduced dosage. Introduction to *A
Memoir of Mary Ann* is accepted by *Jubilee* magazine (appears May 1961). Begins story "Parker's Back."

1961   Allows publishers of West German edition of story collection to omit "A Stroke of Good Fortune" and "A Temple
of the Holy Ghost" but insists that "The Displaced Person" be retained. Learns from Giroux on January 23 that
Farrar, Straus will publish *A Memoir of Mary Ann*. Loses
pair of peacocks to Sister Evangelist on bet that book
would not be published, and receives as gift from Sisters
a television set, which she unexpectedly enjoys. Reads
proofs and handles other publication details for the nuns.
Completes story "Everything That Rises Must Converge,"
which appears in *New World Writing* in October. Hip
joints are injected with novocaine and cortisone in April,

but relief from pain lasts only two weeks. Proposes operation to insert steel hip joints, but Dr. Merrill forbids it as dangerous to stability of lupus. Resolves to stop writing nonfiction after Gordon criticizes draft of story "The Lame Shall Enter First" as undramatic and tells her that writing essays has adversely affected her style. November, addresses Benedictine nuns at Marillac College in St. Louis. *A Memoir of Mary Ann* published by Farrar, Straus and Cudahy December 7 and is well received (appears in England as *Death of a Child* in 1962). Continues working on "The Lame Shall Enter First" after it is accepted by *Sewanee Review*.

1962   Investigates new bone-graft surgery for hips, but operation is again ruled out by Dr. Merrill. Weakened by winter influenza. Story collection appears in Germany as *Ein Kreis im Feuer* to favorable reviews. To help finances, speaks at four colleges in late April and early May, including Converse College, Spartanburg, South Carolina, where she meets Eudora Welty and Cleanth Brooks, and Notre Dame, where she sees Thomas Stritch. Writes short preface to Farrar, Straus reprinting of *Wise Blood* when Giroux informs her it is needed for copyright purposes (book is published later in year). Granville Hicks and his wife visit Andalusia. Receives honorary Doctor of Letters degree from Saint Mary's, women's college of University of Notre Dame. Works on new short novel, tentatively titled *Why Do the Heathen Rage?* "The Lame Shall Enter First" appears in Summer issue of *Sewanee Review* along with several critical essays on her fiction. September, visited by Thomas Stritch. Follows first session of Second Vatican Council with enthusiasm. Obtains temporary relief from hip pain with new injection in October. Speaks at four colleges in Texas and Louisiana during six-day trip in mid-November. Tours New Orleans with friend Richard Allen, curator of Tulane University jazz museum (writes that city is "both Southern and Catholic and with indications that the Devil's existence is freely recognized"). Buys electric typewriter to conserve energy, but finds she cannot compose on it. "Everything That Rises Must Converge" wins first prize in O. Henry Awards.

1963   *A Good Man Is Hard to Find*, translated by Henri Morisset, published in France by Gallimard. Enjoys films of

W. C. Fields on television ("I think I might have written a picture that would be good for him"). Receives honorary degree from Smith College in Northampton, Massachusetts, where she sees Robert Fitzgerald. Counts fourteen of her forty peacocks in simultaneous full tail spread at Andalusia in early June. "Why Do the Heathen Rage?", opening chapter of novel in progress, appears in July *Esquire*. With her mother, buys new Chevrolet with power brakes adapted to her needs, but still does not like driving. August, cause of increased fatigue is diagnosed as severe anemia; begins iron treatment. Visited by Thomas Stritch for week at end of summer. New X-rays show improvement in hip bones. Speaks in October at Hollins College in Virginia, Notre Dame of Maryland in Baltimore, and Georgetown University in Washington, D.C., where she becomes friends with novelist Ward Dorrance. New American Library issues both novels and *A Good Man Is Hard to Find* under one cover as *Three by Flannery O'Connor*. November, gives Cecil Dawkins permission to adapt several of her stories for stage (play, *The Displaced Person*, is first produced in 1966). Sets aside *Why Do the Heathen Rage?* to work on "Revelation." Finishes draft in eight weeks and sends it to Carver. Faints shortly before Christmas and spends more than a week in bed.

1964 Rewrites "Revelation" and sells it to *Sewanee Review* (appears in spring). Receives used record player from Sisters at cancer home and begins listening to records sent by Thomas Stritch ("all classical music sounds alike to me and all the rest of it sounds like the Beatles"). Plans new collection of stories with Giroux for fall publication and hopes to deliver manuscript, with revisions, in May. Examination in early February reveals fibroid tumor to be cause of anemia. Operation is scheduled despite high risk that surgery will reactivate lupus. Takes large doses of cortisone as preventive measure. Insists that surgery be done at Baldwin County Hospital in Milledgeville so that mother can continue to care for aunt Mary Cline, who had suffered heart attack. Corrects proofs of "Revelation" in hospital on day before operation. Tumor is successfully removed, February 25. Returns home in early March and is treated with antibiotics for post-operative kidney infection. Distressed by threat of lawsuit by Mary Ann's parents (later learns that suit has been prevented by prepublication release obtained by nuns). Grows weaker from infections and reactivated lupus, returns to hospital in late March, and is confined to bed after release in early April. Writes McKee in early May after further hospital stay that she is too ill to revise stories for collection and suggests using published magazine versions, then decides to try completing two unfinished stories, "Judgment Day" (reworking of earlier "The Geranium" and "An Exile in the East") and "Parker's Back," for inclusion in book. Receives transfusions and cortisone but is unable to regain strength. Signs contract for collection on May 21 before leaving for Piedmont Hospital in Atlanta, choosing *Everything That Rises Must Converge* as title. Hides unfinished stories under pillow lest she be forbidden to work on them. Develops dangerously high blood pressure; visitors are severely restricted. Returns home on June 20 and on June 27 sends "Judgment Day" to Carver for comment. Asks Giroux to postpone publication of collection to following spring. Works at typewriter for two hours a day. Requests and receives Sacrament of the Sick (formerly known as Extreme Unction) from parish priest on July 7. Receives "Judgment Day" back from Carver in mid-July and makes suggested changes. Continues to revise "Parker's Back" until exhaustion in late July prevents further work on collection. (*Everything That Rises Must Converge* is published by Farrar, Straus and Giroux in 1965.) Learns that "Revelation" has won first prize in O. Henry Awards. Enters Baldwin County Hospital at end of July. Slips into coma on August 2 and dies of kidney failure shortly after midnight on August 3. Buried beside father in Memory Hill cemetery on August 4 following low Requiem Mass at the Sacred Heart Church in Milledgeville.

Note on the Texts

Flannery O'Connor began her first novel, *Wise Blood*, while a student in the School for Writers at the State University of Iowa and worked on it until its publication by Harcourt, Brace and Company, May 15, 1952. One of the six stories she submitted as her Master of Fine Arts thesis in 1947, "The Train," was developed and expanded into chapter 1 of *Wise Blood*. The thesis version of "The Train," only slightly revised, had appeared earlier in *Sewanee Review*, April 1948. Other chapters of the work in progress were also published separately: "The Peeler" (chapter 3) and "The Heart of the Park" (chapter 5) were published in reverse order in *Partisan Review*, February and December 1949; and "Enoch and the Gorilla" (forming parts of chapters 11 and 12) was published in *New World Writing 1*, April 1952. (These versions are included in *The Complete Stories*, Farrar, Straus and Giroux, 1971.) O'Connor made revisions in *Wise Blood* through the proof stage but made no changes in the text after the book was published in 1952. In 1961, when *Wise Blood* was out of print and the rights reverted to the author, O'Connor was asked by Robert Giroux, her editor, if she had any corrections for the Farrar, Straus reprinting of the work, but she had none. Her letter of October 14, 1961, to A. makes this clear: ". . . are there any corrections I would like to make. I can't even make myself read the thing again." When the novel was reprinted in 1962, she supplied a short preface, "Author's Note to the Second Edition," but no changes were made in the text of the novel. The text printed here is that of the first edition, first printing. Her preface is included in the notes to this volume.

In June 1955, Harcourt, Brace and Company published O'Connor's first collection of short stories, *A Good Man Is Hard to Find and Other Stories*. Nine of the ten stories had appeared elsewhere before their inclusion in the collection. "A Good Man Is Hard to Find" was published in 1953 in *Avon Book of Modern Writing*, edited by William Phillips and Philip Rahv; "The River" in *Sewanee Review*, Summer 1953; "The Life You Save May Be Your Own" in *Kenyon Review*, Spring 1953; "A Stroke of Good Fortune" in *Shenandoah*, Spring 1953 (the first of these stories to be written, it originally appeared in *Tomorrow*, August 1949, under the title "Woman on the Stairs"); "A Temple of the Holy Ghost" in *Harper's Bazaar*, May 1954; "The Artificial Nigger" in *Kenyon Review*, Spring 1955; "A Circle in the Fire" in *Kenyon Review*, Spring 1954; "A Late Encounter with the Enemy" in *Harper's Bazaar*, September 1953; "The Displaced Person" in *Sewanee Review*, Fall 1954. All of the stories—except "Good Country People," which appeared in *Harper's Bazaar*, June 1955, the month the book was published—were revised for publication in the collection. Especially heavily revised were "A Stroke of Good Fortune," which had once been intended as a chapter in *Wise Blood*, and "A Good Man Is Hard to Find." "The Displaced Person" was more than doubled in length for the collection; O'Connor added two sections to the story and made many changes in the first part. Following her usual practice, O'Connor revised until the last phase of the proofreading, but she made no further revisions once the stories were published in the collection. The texts printed here are from the first edition, first printing of *A Good Man Is Hard to Find*.

In January 1960, Farrar, Straus and Cudahy (now Farrar, Straus and Giroux) published O'Connor's second novel, *The Violent Bear It Away*. O'Connor had worked on the novel for many years: a version of the first chapter appeared in *New World Writing 8*, October 1955, under the title "You Can't Be Any Poorer Than Dead." In the novel this chapter contains some revisions, as well as new material. As usual, O'Connor revised the book through page proofs but made no further changes once it was published. The text used in this volume is that of the first printing, first edition.

Flannery O'Connor's last collection of short stories, *Everything That Rises Must Converge*, was published posthumously by Farrar, Straus and Giroux in the spring of 1965. O'Connor had long before chosen the title. On March 26, 1961, she wrote her literary agent, Elizabeth McKee, about a story she had just finished: "The story is called EVERYTHING THAT RISES MUST CONVERGE and this is the title I want to put on my next collection." By spring of 1964, when plans for the collection's publication were being made, O'Connor's health was failing rapidly. Seven of the nine stories in the volume had been published in journals: "Everything That Rises Must Converge" in *New World Writing 19*, 1961; "Greenleaf" in *Kenyon Review*, Summer 1956; "A View of the Woods" in *Partisan Review*, Fall 1957; "The Enduring Chill" in *Harper's Bazaar*, July 1958; "The Comforts of Home" in *Kenyon Review*, Fall 1960; "The Lame Shall Enter First" in *Sewanee Review*, Summer 1962; and "Revelation" in *Sewanee Review*, Spring 1964.

In a letter of May 7, 1964, to Elizabeth McKee, O'Connor wrote: "I was wondering if you have copies of the magazines the stories have been published in, if FS&G couldn't just print up the book from those? If I were well there is a lot of rewriting and polishing I could do, but in my present state of health I see no reason for me to spend my energies on old stories that are essentially all right as they are." Instead, she used her energies to complete two other stories for the collection: "Parker's Back" and "Judgment Day." She had begun writing "Parker's Back" in December 1960 but had put it aside and worked on other stories. On July 15, 1964, less than three weeks before her death, O'Connor wrote her friend and former editor, Catharine Carver, "I have drug another out of myself and enclose it." ("Parker's Back" was published posthumously in *Esquire*, April 1965.)

"Judgment Day," the ninth story in the collection, was the final form of a story Flannery O'Connor had worked on since her days at the University of Iowa. The earliest known version is "The Geranium," the opening story of her M.F.A. thesis. The second known version is "An Exile in the East" (published posthumously in *South Carolina Review*, November 1978). "An Exile in the East" was considered for inclusion in *A Good Man Is Hard to Find* but was dropped in favor of other stories. O'Connor was still revising "Judgment Day" at the time of her death. In her July 15, 1964, letter to Catharine Carver (page 1216 in this volume) she wrote, "I do thank you and I'll get to work on this one you sent back." A carbon copy of the typescript of this story, marked by both Carver and O'Connor, shows that the author did make a number of changes suggested by Carver as well as many more of her own, including changing the spelling of "judgement" to "judgment." (The importance of the carbon typescript was recognized and is described by Karl-Heinz Westarp in *The Flannery O'Connor Bulletin*, volume II, 1982, pp. 108–22.) Unfortunately, as O'Connor's strength waned she was apparently unable to get these changes to her editor, Robert Giroux. This volume prints "Judgment Day" from the marked carbon typescript version of the story which incorporates these last revisions.

O'Connor made few changes in the other stories between the publication of the periodical versions and the printing of *Everything That Rises Must Converge*; these changes appear in the collection. Therefore, except for "Judgment Day," the text used here is that of the first edition, first printing of *Everything That Rises Must Converge*.

The Geranium: A Collection of Short Stories is the title of Flannery O'Connor's 1947 Master of Fine Arts thesis. Four of the six stories in this collection were published separately during her lifetime: "The Geranium" in *Accent*, Summer 1946; "The Barber" in *New Signatures*, 1947, an anthology of student writing; "The Turkey" in *Mademoiselle*, November 1948, as "The Capture"; and "The Train" in *Sewanee Review*, April 1948. The published versions of "The Geranium" and "The Train" vary slightly from the thesis versions. However, "The Turkey" was considerably revised when it appeared as "The Capture" in *Mademoiselle*. The other two stories—"Wildcat" and "The Crop," which O'Connor had noted on the typescript was "unpublishable"—were published posthumously. (*The Complete Stories*, Farrar, Straus and Giroux, 1971, contains all six stories.) *The Geranium: A Collection of Short Stories* is printed here from the M.F.A. thesis typescript.

The three remaining fiction pieces contained in this volume did not appear in any collected form during O'Connor's lifetime. "An Afternoon in the Woods" is the final version of "The Turkey" (and therefore of "The Capture") and in this form has not been printed before. Like "An Exile in the East" (the intermediate version between "The Geranium" and "Judgment Day"), it was originally meant to be included in *A Good Man Is Hard to Find* but was omitted to make room for "Good Country People." "An Afternoon in the Woods" is printed here from O'Connor's own typescript. "The Partridge Festival" was published in *The Critic*, March 1961. When

O'Connor selected the contents of *Everything That Rises Must Converge* in the spring of 1964, she originally intended to include this story, but after rereading it decided to omit it. "Why Do the Heathen Rage?," a portion of a larger work that was never completed, was published in *Esquire*, July 1963. Both "The Partridge Festival" and "Why Do the Heathen Rage?" are printed in this volume from these published texts.

Eight of O'Connor's occasional essays are also included in this volume. Although O'Connor did write some nonfiction expressly for publication, she wrote other pieces for lectures that she presented with various modifications on more than one occasion. (*Mystery and Manners,* occasional prose, selected and edited by Sally and Robert Fitzgerald, Farrar, Straus and Giroux, 1969, gives examples of some of these variations.) "A Fiction Writer and His Country" was written as a lecture to be given at the University of Notre Dame in April 1957, and for publication in *The Living Novel: A Symposium*, edited by Granville Hicks (Macmillan Company, 1957). This publication is the text of the essay printed here. "The Church and the Fiction Writer" was originally published in *America*, March 30, 1957, but the editor of the journal, Father Harold C. Gardiner, made a change in one paragraph which disturbed O'Connor because she felt that it seriously distorted what she had wanted to say. The text of "The Church and the Fiction Writer" printed in this volume is taken from her typescript and presents the paragraph in its original form. (The edited paragraph is included in the notes to this volume.) "Some Aspects of the Grotesque in Southern Fiction" was a talk given in the Dorothy Lamar Blount Lecture Series at Wesleyan College in Macon, Georgia, on October 28, 1960. Never published during O'Connor's lifetime, it is printed in this volume from her typescript. The "Introduction" to *A Memoir of Mary Ann* (Farrar, Straus and Cudahy, 1961) is taken from the first edition, first printing of the book. "The King of the Birds," with one paragraph deleted, appeared in *Holiday*, September 1961, under the title "Living with a Peacock." O'Connor was particularly unhappy about the change in title, writing to her friend Maryat Lee in August 1961, "They changed the title to something stupid & cut out a necessary paragraph but otherwise it is unmauled." Since the completed typescript is not available, this volume prints the *Holiday* version, but restores the original title and reprints in the notes the missing paragraph, taken from a typescript draft. "The Regional Writer" was a talk given by O'Connor in the fall of 1962 when she accepted from the Georgia Writers' Association a scroll awarded for *The Violent Bear It Away*. The talk was published in *Esprit*, Winter 1963, and that text is printed in this volume. "Fiction Is a Subject with a History— It Should Be Taught That Way" was published in the *Georgia Bulletin*, March 21, 1963, and that text is printed here. The last essay included in this volume, "The Catholic Novelist in the Protestant South," was originally given as a lecture at Georgetown University on October 18, 1963, on the occasion of the university's 175th anniversary celebration. The text of that lecture published in *Viewpoint*, Spring 1966, is printed in this volume.

The final section of this volume contains a selection of 259 letters written by O'Connor between June 1948 and the week before her death on August 3, 1964. Most of these letters were printed previously (in *The Habit of Being*, a larger collection edited by Sally Fitzgerald, Farrar, Straus and Giroux, 1979). However, twenty-one of the letters are published here for the first time: To Helen Greene, May 23, 1952; Caroline Gordon Tate, September 11, 1952; Ashley Brown, May 22, 1953; Carl Hartman, March 2, 1954; Robert Lowell, March 26, 1954; Beverly Brunson, September 13, 1954; Caroline Gordon Tate, November 14, 1954; Beverly Brunson, January 1, 1955; Thomas Mabry, March 1, 1955; Erik Langkjaer, May 23, 1955; George Haslam, March 2, 1957; Sally and Robert Fitzgerald, November 4, 1957; William Sessions, May 15, 1958; Catharine Carver, July 1, 1959; Maryat Lee, August 21, 1959; Maryat Lee, October 14, 1959; A., November (?) 1960; Maryat Lee, April 21, 1961; A., May 5, 1962; Louise Abbot, June 15, 1963; Marcus Smith, July 12, 1964. In those cases where it was necessary to delete a name, long dashes have been inserted instead, or an initial followed by a long dash; the only exception to this rule are the letters to "A.," where the single initial is used throughout (as established in *The Habit of Being*). In the very few instances where the omission of part of a sentence or part of a paragraph was required, three asterisks (* * *) are inserted in the paragraph; in the case of a paragraph deletion, the three asterisks are on a line by themselves. All the letters in this volume are transcribed from the original typescript and manuscript sources by the editor and preserve O'Connor's own spellings.

This volume presents the texts of the original editions and typescripts chosen for inclusion here. It does not attempt to reproduce features of their typographic design, such as the display capitalization of chapter openings. The texts are reproduced without change, except for the correction of typographical errors. Spelling, punctuation, and capitalization are often expressive features, and they are not altered, even when inconsistent or irregular. The following is a list of typographical errors corrected, cited by page and line number: 58.37, again.; 67.26, warf; 158.39, life; 220.20, you; 228.15, tyring; 235.25, now; 252.33, teacher's; 300.25, poured; 314.35, yourself,; 324.16, out; 346.14, lawyers; 353.15, schoolteacher; 362.13, customer's; 370.19, principle; 374.4, he uncle; 392.16, repentence; 403.1, inffectiveness; 404.5, finaltiy; 444.26, btween; 447.20, obediantly; 448.37, Listener's; 461.4, a him; 478.27, to command; 488.25, it it; 507.30, E. T,; 517.22, growled,; 533.39, Don't; 560.2, God!'; 567.1, Ghost"; 568.31, than; 584.3, repectable; 616.6, no else; 620.23, a; 648.39, into in; 667.2, up-t-date; 676.29, scrip; 677.37, some where; 682.27, shakey; 686.10, mammouth; 686.13, aboot; 687.3, W.T.; 688.22, get; 688.29, apaprtment; 688.31, firtst; 689.30, gallusses; 694.2, even; 694.29, It's; 707.32, this; 711.12, "Old; 714.20, negro; 714.29, "Gimme a haircut."; 715.34, people?"; 716.34, "Hawk; 720.33, Jacob's; 722.13, nice."; 722.32, covy; 723.11, Raoy; 727.10, Beat, Beat; 727.32, Lord; 728.26, east; 730.25, fet; 735.10, others; 735.31, come; 736.21, I've; 739.32, co-carts; 740.20, graceries; 741.7, sculls; 745.22, Jerusalem.; 746.17, thinking thinking; 746.21, about,"; 755.22, Taulkinham"; 765.28, nickle's; 766.1, visciousness; 768.1, trebble; 771.4, on; 788.33, Raucus; 793.19, harrassed; 794.4, montonous; 797.1, *Heathens*; 807.13, Phillip; 813.25, delinquint; 813.35, to by; 815.7, perjorative; 815.36, of of; 818.5, Southernor; 818.34, Van Wyke; 819.15, James; 820.26, prugatory; 832.6, has; 849.14, ADONO; 849.24, democrary; 849.24, if falls; 851.14, preceeded; 853.6, intsead; 853.9–10, satifying; 853.19, It's; 856.24, proportion from; 856.31, appears;

856.40, in *not*; 857.16, Power's; 858.20, accomodate; 859.35–36, embarassment; 859.37, develpment; 860.33, *Sutt*; 863.19, penetentiary; 863.20, haveZ; 886.18, C lick; 890.3, yer; 892.25, Princton; 899.34, Everthing; 901.28, Snuts; 904.27, havethemselves; 904.36, "Peter,"; 906.11, adress; 923.32, Prostestant; 926.16, ((and; 927.19, Rnadall; 934.34, nevr; 970.26, II; 981.38, do; 1001.24, conjuctions; 1006.22, togehter; 1016.27, Kentuckl; 1019.14–15, mighthave; 1028.14, ladies; 1031.38, Novemeber; 1042.14, prgram; 1052.18, seers; 1057.1, interferred; 1059.14, instituion; 1066.31, donw; 1069.23, inwhich; 1072.20, Coraline; 1076.27–28, contracticts; 1077.18, everthing; 1078.30, sont; 1089.30–31, beefore; 1095.32, myabe; 1100.19, yourhaving; 1104.36, Hungry; 1109.5, broght; 1113.10, eventin; 1113.22, spirtual; 1113.23–24, spirtual; 1118.13, of about; 1118.24, samw; 1141.4, Waht; 1141.38, Bettys; 1156.7, immuatable; 1176.11, usues; 1180.1, Mthodist-Universalist; 1183.31, teh; 1187.13, I8ve; 1189, 31, Anywya; 1192.37, and; 1206.7, I8m; 1214.1, to be to be.

Notes

In the notes below, the reference numbers denote page and line of the present volume (the line count includes chapter headings). No note is made for material included in a standard desk-reference book. Notes at the foot of the page in the text are O'Connor's own. For more detailed notes, references to other studies, and further biographical background, see Flannery O'Connor, *The Habit of Being*, letters edited and with an introduction by Sally Fitzgerald (New York: Farrar, Straus & Giroux, 1979); Flannery O'Connor, *Mystery and Manners*, occasional prose, selected and edited by Sally and Robert Fitzgerald (New York: Farrar, Straus & Giroux, 1969); Flannery O'Connor, *Everything That Rises Must Converge*, introduction by Robert Fitzgerald (New York: Farrar, Straus & Giroux, 1965); Flannery O'Connor, *The Complete Stories*, introduction by Robert Giroux (New York: Farrar, Straus & Giroux, 1971); and *Three by Flannery O'Connor*, introduction by Sally Fitzgerald (New York: New American Library, 1983). Many full names and titles of books and articles referred to in the letters are identified in the Index to Letters, pages 1221–34, and the Chronology, pages 1237–56, in this volume.

WISE BLOOD

1.1   WISE BLOOD] The "Author's Note to the Second Edition," written for the book's printing in 1962: "WISE BLOOD has reached the age of ten and is still alive. My critical powers are just sufficient to determine this, and I am gratified to be able to say it. The book was written with zest and, if possible, it should be read that way. It is a comic novel about a Christian *malgré lui*, and as such, very serious, for all comic novels that are any good must be about matters of life and death. *Wise Blood* was written by an author congenitally innocent of theory, but one with certain preoccupations. That belief in Christ is to some a matter of life and death has been a stumbling block for readers who would prefer to think it a matter of no great consequence. For them Hazel Motes' integrity lies in his trying with such vigor to get rid of the ragged figure who moves from tree to tree in the back of his mind. For the author Hazel's integrity lies in his not being able to. Does one's integrity ever lie in what he is not able to do? I think that usually it does, for free will does not mean one will, but many wills conflicting in one man. Freedom cannot be conceived simply. It is a mystery and one which a novel, even a comic novel, can only be asked to deepen."

11.26–27   walking . . . drown.] "And Peter going down out of the boat, walked upon the water to come to Jesus. But seeing the wind strong, he was afraid: and when he began to sink, he cried out, saying: Lord, save me." (Matthew 14:29–30, Douay Rheims Version)

30.5   eyes . . . not]   "Hear, O foolish people, and without understanding: who have eyes, and see not; and ears, and hear not." (Jeremiah 5:21; also Ezekiel 12:2, Matthew 13:14–15, Mark 8:18, Douay Rheims Version)

80.38   tare]   See letter to Ben Griffith, March 3, 1954 (page 923 in this volume).

117.6   666]   The mystical number associated with the beast of Revelation 14:18.

A GOOD MAN IS HARD TO FIND

137.1   *A Good . . . Find*]   The title, drawn from a blues song made famous by Bessie Smith, caught O'Connor's attention in a newspaper caption to a photograph of a seven-year-old girl in a tutu, who had sung the song in a talent contest and won first prize. See letter to Sally and Robert Fitzgerald, January 25, 1953 (page 907.4–5 in this volume).

138.15–16   eight . . . 55890]   Device used by Ring Lardner in "The Golden Honeymoon," a favorite story of O'Connor's.

142.36   Toombsboro]   Toomsboro, Georgia, is a town about twenty-five miles from Milledgeville.

172.1   *The Life . . . Own*]   Cautionary highway sign in the early 1950s.

197.1   *A Temple . . . Ghost*]   I Corinthians 6:19.

200.7   Wendell and Cory]   After film actor Wendell Cory.

201.25–33   "I've . . . near!"]   "The Lily of the Valley," Protestant hymn; see The Song of Solomon 2:1.

201.37–38   "The Old Rugged Cross"]   Protestant hymn by George Bennard (1913).

202.4–21   *"Tantum . . . Amen."*]   *Tantum Ergo*, hymn to the Eucharist composed by St. Thomas Aquinas and part of Roman Catholic liturgy since the thirteenth century. "Lowly bending, deep adoring, / Lo! the Sacrament we hail: / Types and shadows have their ending, / Newer rites of grace prevail: / Faith for all defects supplying / Where the feeble senses fail. / To the everlasting Father, / And the Son who reigns on high / With the Holy Ghost proceeding / Forth from each eternally, / Be salvation, honor, blessing, / Might and endless majesty. / Amen."

202.27   dumb ox]   Dumb (mute) ox, the nickname of St. Thomas Aquinas as a seminarian.

210.1   *The Artificial Nigger*]   O'Connor first heard this term when she accompanied her mother to a cattle auction near Milledgeville.

218.25   "Firstoppppmry,"]   I.e., "First stop Emory," referring to former northeast Atlanta suburban stop, near Emory University.

251.7   prophets . . . furnace] See Daniel 3:13–30.

254.3   preemy . . . Atlanta] The premiere of *Gone With the Wind*, held in Atlanta in 1939.

255.16   UDC] The United Daughters of the Confederacy, an organization composed of the descendants of Confederate soldiers.

260.33   Chickamauga, Shiloh] Civil War battles.

260.33   Johnston, Lee] Confederate generals Joseph Eggleston Johnston and Robert E. Lee.

261.28   Marthasville] Former name of Atlanta.

268.40–269.6   "Science . . . Nothing."] From Martin Heidegger's "What Is Metaphysics?" in *Existence and Being* (1927, trans. 1949).

277.3   Vapex] Trade name of a mentholated salve used in treating head and chest colds.

287.21   "Time marches on!"] Closing intonation from "The March of Time," a popular radio and movie news feature of the 1940s and 1950s.

301.2   Whore of Babylon] Opprobrious term applied to the Roman Catholic Church by anti-Catholic Protestants. The reference is to Revelation 17:1–6.

326.14–15   slipping . . . mouth] A Communion wafer, as part of the last rites of the Roman Catholic Church.

THE VIOLENT BEAR IT AWAY

329.4   Matthew 11:12] In a letter to Janet McKane, July 25, 1963, O'Connor wrote: "The Violent Bear It Away is from the Douay, also Confraternity versions. In a lot of instances the new ones are no improvement."

343.13–16   name . . . creation.] Cf. Adam's naming of the animals in Genesis 2:19–20.

343.16–17   voice . . . trumpet] Cf. Revelation 1:10 and 4:1.

343.19   wheels . . . beasts.] Cf. Ezekiel, chapter 1.

344.34–36   Lord's . . . prophet!] Cf. I Kings, chapter 13.

355.22–23   Jezebel . . . there,] Cf. II Kings 9:30–37.

355.38   bush . . . flame.] Cf. Exodus 3:2–3.

356.13   Elijah and Elisha] II Kings, chapter 2.

361.35   whirling chariot] Cf. II Kings 2:11, and also Ezekiel 10:13.

369.27   Ezekiel . . . days,]   Cf. Ezekiel 4:6.

378.38—40   Jonah . . . enclosed]   Cf. Jonah 1:17, Ezekiel 37:1, and Daniel 6:16—17.

385.34—35   Habakkuk . . . mission]   Daniel 14:32—38 (Douay Rheims Version; the Apocryphal book of Bel and the Dragon).

398.36—37   UNLESS . . . LIFE.]   John 3:3.

402.3   pole-sitter]   Christian ascetics and hermits, such as St. Simeon Stylites, who lived atop pillars.

430.39—431.3   Elijah . . . nights.]   I Kings 19:5—8.

453.24—25   oarsman . . . destination.]   An allusion to Charon, ferryman of the river Styx, who carried souls across to the underworld in classical mythology.

474.27—28   Moses . . . land.]   Deuteronomy 34:1—4.

475.35—36   wall of fire]   Cf. page 201.25—33 and note.

478.6—7   loaves . . . multiplied.]   Matthew 15:32—38.

478.17   blood of Abel]   Genesis 4:8—12.

478.23—25   fire . . . Moses]   Daniel 3, II Kings 2:11, and Exodus 3:2.

478.27—28   GO . . . MERCY.]   Cf. Ezekiel 3:17—21 and 33:7—20.

EVERYTHING THAT RISES MUST CONVERGE

485.1   *Everything . . . Converge*]   In a letter to Roslyn Barnes, March 29, 1961, O'Connor wrote: "I have also written & sold to New World Writing a story called Everything That Rises Must Converge, which is a physical proposition that I found in Pere Teilhard and am applying to a certain situation in Southern states & indeed in all the world."

501.3   bull]   In Greek mythology, Zeus took the form of a bull to ravish a mortal woman, Europa (mother of Minos).

532.35—36   "He . . . fire,"]   Matthew 5:22.

532.37   "Jedge . . . jedged!"]   Matthew 7:1.

533.10   Whore of Babylon]   See note to 301.2.

554.29   'whirling . . . gyre']   From William Butler Yeats' "The Second Coming."

564.15—16   Jesuit . . . meditate.]   Allusion to a joke about Jesuits. Jesuit to his superior: "May I smoke while I meditate?" Superior: "Certainly not." Jesuit: "May I meditate while I smoke?" Superior: "Of course, my son."

566.13 "Who made you?"] First question in the *Baltimore Catechism*.

566.16 "Who is God?"] Second question in the *Baltimore Catechism*.

566.20 Why . . . you?"] Third question in the *Baltimore Catechism*. The priest's answers to all three questions are from this catechism.

575.35 Antony of Egypt] St. Antony of Egypt (251–356), abbot and desert ascetic, was subject to extravagant temptations and diabolic visitations. His life was a favorite subject of artists, including Brueghel, Bosch, and Grünewald, and writers, including Flaubert.

628.9–10 Ezekiel . . . mouth!"] Ezekiel 3:1–3.

630.20–21 know . . . right] "And shall I not spare Nineveh, that great city, in which there are more than a hundred and twenty thousand persons that know not how to distinguish between their right hand and their left, and many beasts." (Jonah 4:11, Douay Rheims Version)

660.3 "Vanity of vanities,"] Ecclesiastes 1:2.

665.31–34 shoes . . . tree] "Come not nigh hither, put off the shoes from thy feet: for the place whereon thou standest is holy ground." (Exodus 3:5, Douay Rheims Version)

672.8–9 Jonah . . . sea.] Jonah 1:15.

674.31–32 "Idolatry! . . . tree!] ". . . enflaming yourself with idols under every green tree." (Jeremiah 2:20, King James Version)

676.1 *Judgment Day*] Following are examples of some of the changes made in the carbon typescript that were not included in the first edition of *Everything That Rises Must Converge*.

677.2 home.] In the earlier version, the paragraph continues: "Dead or alive. It was being there that mattered; the dead or alive did not."

679.11–14 Big . . . She] ". . . Big and ready when she came back and found him living the way he was to take him back with her. She . . ."

680.13–14 different . . . when] ". . . different. He had found out in time to go back with her. If he had found out a day later, he might still be there, squatting on the doctor's land. [¶] When . . ."

690.33–34 Hard . . . stroke.] This paragraph was not in the earlier version.

691.15–16 It . . . up.] This sentence was added in the final version.

693.20–21 "The Lord . . . want."] Psalms 23:1.

694.31–32 "There's . . . this.] Dialect was changed to standard English. The earlier version read: "Ain't no judgement day, old man. Cept this."

STORIES AND OCCASIONAL PROSE

701.1   THE GERANIUM]   The title page of the collection included: "A thesis submitted in partial fulfillment of the requirements for the degree of Master of Fine Arts, in the Department of English, in the Graduate College of the State University of Iowa/June, 1947." The thesis carried the following dedication: "To Paul Engle/whose interest and criticism have made these stories better than they would otherwise have been."

810.25–32   The business . . . art.]   This paragraph was altered by the editor of *America* to read as follows: "The author must, of course, realize that it is his function, no less than it is the function of the Church, to protect souls from dangerous literature. But in striving to live up to the legitimate requirements of his art, he will know that not all fiction will turn out to be suitable for everyone's consumption. If in some instances the Church sees fit to forbid the faithful to read a work without permission, the Catholic author will be thankful that he has been recalled to a sense of responsibility."

832.13–15   answer. . . . interest]   When this piece appeared in *Holiday*, September 1961, as "Living With a Peacock," a paragraph (following 832.13) was deleted (it is supplied here from an earlier manuscript), and the opening of the subsequent paragraph was altered, as follows:

"I think I was in the picture with the chicken, though that Pathe newsreel didn't come to any of the Savannah theatres and I never had the pleasure of seeing myself. I know I did what I could to get in it and that I was dressed for the part. I had on my best clothes and an expression of dignified ferocity which I wore when I felt I was being observed. The picture-taking did not go too well. The chicken, after scratching normally about the yard for half a day while the New Yorker waited with an unpleasant expression on his face, began without warning to back. The man plunged his head under the tent on his camera, there was a grinding noise, and I leaped to the hen's side and backed too. It was over almost at once; the star hit a bush and sat down. The photographer left quickly, refusing even to come in and enjoy a dish of icecream.

"From that day I began to collect chickens. What had been a mild interest . . ."

LETTERS

879.6   Paul Moor]   A client of Elizabeth McKee's and a guest at Yaddo at the time.

880.29   Mr. Moe]   Henry Allen Moe, director of the John Simon Guggenheim Foundation.

883.24   Los Alamos]   Boyd, a mathematician, was considering a job offer there.

885.32   Dilly]   Wife of critic and poet John Thompson.

885.32   Ann]   Anne Macauley.

886.6   Enoch]   Character in *Wise Blood*.

887.23   *Betty Boyd Love*]   Betty Boyd had married James Love and was living in California.

889.9   Dr. Stern's book]   *Pillar of Fire* (1951), an account of his conversion to Roman Catholicism, by Jewish psychiatrist Karl Stern.

890.21   Cal's book]   *The Mills of the Kavanaughs*, by Robert Lowell, who was first called "Cal"—for Caligula—by friends in his youth.

890.22   Dr. Williams]   William Carlos Williams.

891.20   Car to Bee]   O'Connor had planned to use the nickname "Car," which amused her, after one of Sally Fitzgerald's aunts who was called "Aunt Car" because she was the only one of several sisters who could drive.

892.16   Sary Larence]   Sarah Lawrence College, where Robert Fitzgerald was then teaching.

892.16–17   Old . . . Wallace]   That October, Louis Budenz, economics professor at Fordham University and a former American Communist Party member, had charged that Henry A. Wallace's 1944 mission to China had "helped the Communists"; Wallace responded that his recommendations, if followed, would have aided Chiang Kai-shek. Wallace was vice president (1941–45) and ran for president on the Progressive Party ticket.

892.26   Frank the Spell man]   Cardinal Francis Spellman, archbishop of New York.

892.30   Sister]   Mary Cline, O'Connor's aunt, eldest sister of Regina O'Connor.

895.16   the Ford book]   A projected collection, never completed, of writings by young American authors, to be edited by R. P. Blackmur and funded by the Ford Foundation.

896.1   Cousin Katie]   Mrs. Raphael Semmes, elderly second cousin in Savannah.

897.9   Omar]   Omar Pound, son of Dorothy and Ezra Pound.

897.15   *Helen Greene*]   O'Connor's sociology teacher at Georgia State College for Women.

898.9   Maria]   Maria Ivancic, a displaced person from Yugoslavia sponsored by the Fitzgeralds.

898.11   M. Loretta]   Mary Loretta Washington, a child on a two-week Fresh Air Fund holiday with the Fitzgeralds.

898.18   Elsie Hill's]   Suffragette and feminist who had built the house owned by the Fitzgeralds and kept a summer cottage nearby.

898.21 Albert Levitt] Husband of Elsie Hill.

898.25 Mr. Latham] Edward M. Latham, Sr., father of neighbor "Teddy" Latham, son-in-law of Elsie Hill and Albert Levitt.

898.33 Mrs. Morgan] Sally Fitzgerald's mother.

898.36 Eileen Berryman] Author Eileen Simpson, then wife of poet John Berryman.

899.19 your connection] Gordon's cousin Lee Meriwether, a member of the Mark Twain Society, wrote for the *Mark Twain Journal*. See also page 901.25–31.

902.9 the Jurgen things] *Jurgen*, by James Branch Cabell.

902.28 George] Dr. George Beiswanger, friend and former faculty member at Georgia State College for Women.

903.3 this] "The Life You Save May Be Your Own."

906.12 The Month] English Jesuit magazine.

906.27–29 novel . . . (McCarthy).] *Pictures from an Institution*, a novel about academic life, comparing it to Mary McCarthy's *The Groves of Academe*.

907.5 clipping] See note to 137.1.

909.31 the story] "A Stroke of Good Fortune."

910.32 *Ashley Brown*] Instructor of English at Washington and Lee University and advisory editor to literary magazine *Shenandoah*.

911.35 Shakespeare poem] "W.S. Life & Times" by Robert Fitzgerald: "The actor's shame, the sonnetteer's despair, / The candlelighting and the passing bell, / The song, a wandering angel of the air— / Sweet bee of London; and the hum of hell; / The sun with his great glances, and his power / That burned upon the fair cheek of the hour, / Before death's snowy ravishment came by; / The April of the heart, and summer's range / In grief contracted, heavy petals curled, / As time grew tempest and the paws of change / Came lionish upon the golden world: / All carelessly the fresh quatorzains keep / In dreams beyond his dustiness asleep."

912.13 the Cardinal] Cardinal Spellman had written a best-selling novel, *The Foundling* (1951).

913.4 eighty-five . . . cousin] See note to 896.1.

914.3 Quentin] Quentin Compson, character in William Faulkner's *The Sound and the Fury* and *Absalom, Absalom!*

914.12 dog . . . Ford] Tietjens is the protagonist in Ford Madox Ford's *Parade's End*.

914.16 Virgil M. Hancher] President of the State University of Iowa.

915.11   Shot]   Farm hand at Andalusia.

915.12   Louis]   O'Connor's uncle, Louis Cline.

916.16–17   Secretary . . . Review]   Beverly Brunson.

916.28   mobbed like Allen]   Allen Tate's small automobile had been surrounded by students when he happened into a university protest in Rome; he was rescued by a passerby.

917.26   spots . . . wings]   The acute phase of lupus is characterized by rashes, especially in the shape of butterfly wings over the bridge of the nose.

919.1   Sewanee]   University of the South.

919.2   W&L]   Washington and Lee University.

919.11   *Carl Hartman*]   Editor of *Epoch*, a literary review.

923.24   Java's Oasis]   A roadside café recommended by Griffith.

924.12   McLuhan . . . Vanguard]   "The Southern Quality," in *A Southern Vanguard* (1947), edited by Allen Tate.

929.32   that story]   "Bad Dreams" by Peter Taylor.

932.33–34   CMT's arrival]   The new Fitzgerald child, Caterina Maria Teresa.

935.1   Fred Bornhauser]   Teacher of English at the University of Virginia.

936.4   *To Erik Langkjaer*]   This is in answer to his letter telling O'Connor of his engagement to be married.

936.9   ragpicker]   Langkjaer earlier had written O'Connor of his tentative plan to spend the summer in charitable works with Abbé Pierre, French priest and social worker.

937.27   Plunkett]   Ruth and Eldridge Plunkett, newspaper evangelists and optimists.

940.21–22   Sue Jenkens]   Sue Jenkins Brown. In a letter to Maryat Lee dated March 29, 1959, O'Connor said about her: "She was in the Provincetown Players beginnings and has connections. Her first husband was somebody named James Light who was O'Neill's first director. All this I am told." Jenkins had also been a friend of Hart Crane's.

940.31   Shelly Memorial Award]   Shelley award from the Poetry Society of America.

945.13   Fr. de Menacse]   Jean de Menasce, O.P., scholar and Jewish convert to Roman Catholicism.

946.5   Byron Reece]   Georgia poet of some renown; he died a suicide in 1958.

949.28   her nephew]   Erik Langkjaer, longtime family friend of Helene Iswolsky; a courtesy title, he was not her actual nephew.

949.32   I've . . . wrote.]   O'Connor was to review two books by Stein, translated by Hilda Graef, for *The Bulletin*: *Writings of Edith Stein* (1956), also edited by Graef, a selection of "spiritual, mystical, educational and philosophical writings, but in each case not a large enough sample to do more than tantalize the reader who has a real interest in the subject she is writing about"; the spiritual writings she found "very impressive, being the type of spirituality based on thought rather than emotion" (March 2, 1957); and *The Science of the Cross: A Study of St. John of the Cross* (1960), which she called "a moving book but less for what is in it than for Edith Stein's own background—for the modern crucifixion that the reader knows was waiting for her as she wrote the book" (Oct. 1, 1960). See also note to 1003.1–2.

955.35   Mr. . . . novel]   *The Hawk and the Sun* (1955).

957.5   "Bonjour Tristesse"]   Published in Paris in 1954, the prize-winning first novel of Françoise Sagan (pseudonym for Françoise Quoirez, 1935–) was remarkable for its cynical amoralism.

959.29   Fr. Perrin]   J. M. Perrin, O.P., close friend and confidante of Weil in Marseilles, with whom she discussed the church, religion, and Christ, but whom he was unable to convince to be baptized (Weil was Jewish by birth). See Weil's letters to Perrin in *Waiting for God*, translated by Emma Craufurd (1951).

960.14   a woman]   Elizabeth Sewell, English Roman Catholic poet and critic.

963.35   the same people]   Frances and Brainard (Lon) Cheney.

972.12   Fr. Lynch]   William J. Lynch, S.J., editor of Jesuit magazine *Thought*.

973.6   Mrs. Naomi Myers']   Naomi Meier had written O'Connor a letter violently attacking her fiction.

973.30   whiskey priest]   The unnamed Mexican priest who is the protaganist of *The Power and the Glory*.

974.38   young boy]   Poet Paul Curry Steele.

979.19   John M. Oesterreicher]   In New York in 1942, Weil and Oesterreicher, a priest, had engaged in heated theological discussions.

980.28   Mrs. de Luna]   Member of class at Writers' Workshop in Iowa.

981.11   Ong]   Walter J. Ong, S.J., then assistant professor of English at St. Louis University, contributed articles and chapters of work-in-progress to journals; his *Frontiers of American Catholicism* was published in 1957.

982.26−27   Mr. McG.]   Ralph McGill, editor and publisher of *Atlanta Journal* and *Constitution* and an admirer of O'Connor's work.

983.38   prayer . . . Raphael]   See note to 1214.5−7.

983.40   Tobias]   Old Testament figure, from the Book of Tobit in the Apocrypha (Septuagint and Vulgate Bibles).

984.24   Dr. Giovanini]   Dr. Giovannini, an admirer of Ezra Pound, regularly visited the poet at St. Elizabeth's Hospital, Washington, D.C.

984.26   one in Macon]   James H. McCown, S.J.

984.26−27   Harold . . . S.J.]   Literary editor of *America*, Jesuit newspaper featuring essays on church and religion, published in New York.

984.29   Caroline's book]   *The Malefactors*.

987.1   *Eileen Hall*]   Book page editor of *The Bulletin*.

989.19   NDBSLL]   Notre Dame Book Store Lending Library.

990.11   young . . . Women]   Shirley Abbott.

998.3   Nancy]   Nancy Smith, a Milledgeville friend who had lost a leg.

1001.10−11   man . . . River]   Robert Jiras.

1002.15   Luce]   Henry Luce, publisher and editor-in-chief of *Time* magazine.

1003.1−2   If . . . canonized]   Edith Stein (Teresa Benedicta of the Cross), a Jewish Carmelite nun who died in the gas chambers at Auschwitz in 1942, was beatified in 1987.

1003.30   some . . . college]   St. Michael's College of the University of Toronto.

1004.30   Byron]   Byron Reece.

1005.26   Elizabeth Stevenson]   Critic and biographer, faculty member at Emory University.

1007.19   Harnet Kane]   Harnett Thomas Kane, a Southern writer popular in the 1940s and 1950s, author of *Louisiana Hayride* (1941).

1008.38   Handy Institution]   Handy Colony, an "institute" for aspiring writers in Marshall, Illinois, founded and directed by Lowney Handy with the support and financial backing of James Jones.

1009.2   FHTE]   *From Here to Eternity* (1951) by James Jones.

1009.20   Telemacus]   Copies of the year's work on Robert Fitzgerald's translation of the *Odyssey* (hence Telemachus) were sent to O'Connor every Christmas.

1017.34   sweater . . . before] The sweater was full-length.

1018.32   have . . . paragraph] The rewritten paragraph appears in the story as published. The first version read: "Pitts, by accident, found them that evening. He was walking home through the woods about sunset. The rain had stopped but the polished trees were hung with clear drops of water that turned red where the sun touched them; the air was saturated with dampness. He came on them suddenly and shied backward, his foot not a yard from where they lay. For almost a minute he stood still and then, his knees buckling, he squatted down by their sides and stared into their eyes, into the pale blue pools of rainwater that the sky had filled."

1019.10   Emmet] Emmet Jones, black gardener in Milledgeville.

1019.26   Dr. Wells] Guy Herbert Wells, Sr., president of Georgia State College for Women from July 1934 to May 1953.

1020.30   Godot] *Waiting for Godot* (1952), by Samuel Beckett.

1022.25–29   Atkinson . . . Kerr] Theater critics Brooks Atkinson of *The New York Times* and Walter Kerr of the New York *Herald Tribune*.

1023.26   *George Haslam*] Friend and former sociology teacher at Georgia State College for Women, then working for King Features in Atlanta.

1023.29   the production] In addition to Gene Kelly, it starred Agnes Moorehead and Janice Rule.

1028.4–10   What . . . art.] See page 810.25–32 and note.

1030.9   Mary Sallee] Girlhood friend in Milledgeville.

1033.14   *Cecil Dawkins*] Alabama-born writer, then teaching at Stephens College in Columbia, Missouri.

1036.14   Senator Pappy O'Daniels] W. Lee O'Daniel, former governor and senator from Texas.

1039.24   McDowell] David McDowell of McDowell, Obolensky, publishers.

1039.38   Mr. Phinizy Spalding] Later historian and biographer of General James Oglethorpe.

1043.21   Mr. Schneider] Subject of newspaper clipping sent by Dawkins.

1049.7–8   Enclosed . . . these.] A newspaper clipping announcing the birth of Wanda Darline, Rhonda Garline, and Songa Malene.

1051.26   Herr] Dan Herr, journalist, publisher (1948–81) of *The Critic: A Catholic Review of Books and the Arts*.

1056.25   Matisses . . . Vince] Dominican nuns' Chapelle du Rosaire, in

Vence, France; renowned example of modern ecclesiastical design, it is the work of Henri Matisse.

1057.7   the story]   "The Enduring Chill."

1058.34   Henry]   Elderly farm worker living at Andalusia.

1060.19   Mrs. Slayden]   An Atlanta woman who proposed to found a literary magazine.

1068.24   Mr. Peden]   William Peden, professor of English at the University of Missouri, who had arranged O'Connor's prospective visit.

1072.1   Peter]   Peter Taylor.

1074.29   the college]   Georgia Military College, boys' preparatory school in Milledgeville.

1087.15   Ward Dorrence]   Dorrance later became a friend and correspondent.

1087.21   "The . . . Mule."]   The actual title was *The White Hound* (1959).

1087.33   Kazantzakis . . . guts.]   The Greek novelist's *The Odyssey, a Modern Sequel* (1938; translated 1958) was A.'s Christmas gift to O'Connor.

1088.5–6   second . . . Voegelin]   *The World of the Polis* (1957), the second of a proposed six-volume study, *Order and History*, by Eric Voegelin, German historian and philosopher who taught at Louisiana State University in Baton Rouge and the University of Munich. O'Connor's review of the first volume, *Israel and Revelation* (1956), appeared in *The Bulletin* on November 15, 1958.

1091.14–15 the Wests]   Conn and Robert West, friends of Stritch's in Athens, Georgia.

1096.4   Berg]   Norman Berg, Macmillan Publishing Company's editorial representative in Atlanta.

1102.33   two great commandments]   "Thou shalt love the Lord thy God with thy whole heart, and with thy whole soul, and with thy whole mind. This is the greatest and the first commandment. And the second is like to this: Thou shalt love thy neighbor as thyself." (Matthew 22:37–39, Douay Rheims version)

1106.22   Hansberry girl]   Lorraine Hansberry's *A Raisin in the Sun*, the first work by a black playwright to be produced on Broadway, opened in New York that year.

1110.26   priest's . . . hell]   "Hell: An Apology," by Robert W. Gleason, appeared in *Thought*, Summer 1958.

1115.21–22 Dom Aelred Graham]   Benedictine scholar, prior of the Portsmouth Priory (now Abbey) in Portsmouth, Rhode Island, author of *Chris-*

tian Thought and Action and *Zen Catholicism: A Suggestion* (1963), which O'Connor also would read.

1123.30   Cecilia]   Cecilia Lopez Hines, another reviewer for *The Bulletin*.

1128.13   John Donald Wade]   Georgia writer.

1129.28–29   Mary . . . nurse]   Sister Loretta, O.P.

1130.11   Mr. Zuber]   Leo Zuber, who later replaced Eileen Hall as editor of the book page for *The Bulletin*.

1135.18–19   the . . . peddlers]   Dawkins had taken a job in a brokerage office.

1136.1   Betty]   Betty Littleton, dean at Stephens College.

1137.37   Pittypat's]   O'Connor's sobriquet for Atlanta Archbishop Paul J. Hallinan.

1140.6   You . . . Mother.]   A direct quotation from one of O'Connor's favorite stories, "The Golden Honeymoon," by Ring Lardner. See also page 138.16 and note.

1140.8   Another friend]   A.

1141.28   GBD]   *Georgia Diocesan Bulletin*.

1141.34   that . . . about]   An early attempt at "Parker's Back." On January 21, 1961, O'Connor again wrote A., "Parker's Back is not coming along too well. It is too funny to be as serious as it ought. I have a lot of trouble with getting the right tone."

1141.38   Betty]   Betty Littleton.

1142.4   those Germans]   Claasen Verlag, a Hamburg publishing company.

1143.35   he]   Pierre Teilhard de Chardin, S.J.

1145.12–13   the story . . . clipping.]   "The Partridge Festival."

1146.13   a story of mine]   "The Partridge Festival."

1148.16   *Mr. ——*]   A professor of English.

1150.8   the goat man]   "Chess," an eccentric nomad who traveled the state of Georgia in a cart drawn—and surrounded—by goats.

1151.6   Mr. Parish]   A reader and correspondent.

1152.22   people . . . Currents]   Sally and Joseph Cunneen.

1154.8   Miss Nancy]   Character in a story by A.

1154.26   Murdoch thing]   An article by A. on the work of Iris Murdoch.

1156.7   Polish . . . swans] In a letter to Caroline Gordon, November 16, 1961, O'Connor had written: "We have decided that my swans are Polish swans because they have such even dispositions. I will be able to tell when they hatch. If they are Polish, they will be white; if mute, grey."

1157.30   story . . . *Sewanee*] "The Lame Shall Enter First."

1159.7–9   Fr. Mayhew . . . Boyce] Priests from Christ the King, Cathedral Church of Atlanta diocese.

1159.21–22   Nat'l . . . Award] Percy had just received this award for *The Moviegoer* (1961).

1162.34   what . . . said] Stritch had told O'Connor that the motto of a New York edition of the works of Joseph Conrad was taken from Grimm: " 'No,' said the dwarf. 'Something human is dearer to me than all the gold in the world.' "

1163.12   *Alfred Corn*] See page 1169.22–27. Later a poet and teacher.

1166.27   enclosed book] *Toward the Knowledge of God* by Claude Tresmontant, translated by Robert J. Olsen (1961).

1167.1   *Sister Julie*] One of the nuns at Rosary College in Lake Forest, Illinois.

1167.8–9   "Word . . . Men"] *The Bible: Word of God in Words of Men* by Jean Levie, translated by S. H. Treman (1962).

1167.24   Jenny] Zenobia Sessions, William Sessions' wife.

1168.20   original air plant] Ashley Brown.

1168.27   Florida Hoods] Devene (Deen) Harrold and her husband, Robert Hood. Devene, who corresponded with O'Connor, had lupus.

1168.30   Earnest] In a letter to Maryat Lee, May 21, 1962, O'Connor had written: "For Mother's Day I gave Regina a jackass named Earnest. It was what she wanted. We hope to raise little spotted mules."

1169.19   "The Cardinal . . . Story"] Stritch, too, was engaged in writing about the cardinal, his uncle.

1169.28   USIA] The United States Information Agency.

1170.30   Roslyn Barnes] Formerly a student at Georgia State College for Women, a Roman Catholic convert who had sought out O'Connor. She was at this time studying with Msgr. Ivan Illych in Mexico, before going to teach chemistry in a mission school in South America.

1171.31   Hickes] Granville Hicks, editor of *Saturday Review of Literature*, and his wife.

1175.4–5   the book . . . published] *The Quiet Enemy*, a collection of stories published by Atheneum (1963).

1175.6   Mr. Haydn] Hiram Haydn, Dawkins' editor at Atheneum and editor of *American Scholar*.

1175.16−17   coastal bermuda] A kind of grass for grazing animals.

1176.15   Claudio Gorlier] Italian poet and critic.

1178.11   Mr. Sherry] Gerard E. Sherry, new editor of *The Bulletin*, was not a Southerner. He eliminated the book page as a regular feature.

1178.31   *Janet McKane*] Primary school teacher in New York City who first wrote to O'Connor in January 1963.

1180.7   James Johnson Sweeny] Sweeney, an art critic and museum curator.

1180.23   the madwoman] Agent who was arranging readings for Robert Fitzgerald.

1185.31   Sherry] See note to 1178.11

1185.34   Cardinal's portrait] See see note to 1169.19.

1186.16   Hans Kung] Hans Küng, Swiss priest and theologian, adviser to the Second Vatican Council.

1187.7   G. Fielding] Gabriel Fielding, English Roman Catholic poet and novelist.

1190.14   Conn] Conn West; see note to 1091.14−15.

1190.27−28   painting of Rousseau] "Old Juniet's Cariole."

1191.20   the statue] A standing Madonna and Child, at the Cloisters.

1192.8   Super . . . family] Maryat Lee had taken a job with journalist and author Jim Bishop, whose books then included *The Day Lincoln Was Shot*, *The Day Christ Died*, and *The Day Christ Was Born*.

1195.7−9   Carson . . . Allbee] *Ballad of the Sad Café*, dramatized by Edward Albee.

1197.15   a story] "Revelation."

1198.32   Red Wally Butts] Wallace Butts, head football coach (1939−60) and athletic director (1939−63) at the University of Georgia. In a letter to A., March 30, 1963, O'Connor had written: "Last Wednesday I went to the University of Georgia and read that night A Good Man Is Hard To Find. It was a perfect audience because they caught everything, it all being familiar to them. When I reached the point where Red Sammy Butts comes in, there was an appreciable titter of another order that rolled through the audience. (That case interests me greatly). Later somebody told me that the character of Red Sammy was not unlike the character of Wally."

1198.36−37   North Hadley]   South Hadley, Massachusetts, where Fitz-gerald was teaching at Mt. Holyoke College.

1208.14   Griffin]   John Howard Griffin traveled the country disguised as a black man and wrote a book based on his experiences, *Black Like Me* (1961).

1210.15   I've got one]   "Judgment Day."

1210.19   I have another]   "Parker's Back."

1211.22−23   "Margaret, . . . unleaving—."]   From "Spring and Fall" by Gerard Manley Hopkins.

1214.5−7   prayer . . . copy]   O'Connor included the prayer in a letter to McKane, July 14, 1964:

PRAYER TO SAINT RAPHAEL

O Raphael, lead us toward those we are waiting for, those who are waiting for us; Raphael, Angel of happy meeting, lead us by the hand toward those we are looking for. May all our movements be guided by your Light and transfigured with your joy.

Angel, guide of Tobias, lay the request we now address to you at the feet of Him on whose unveiled Face you are privileged to gaze. Lonely and tired, crushed by the separations and sorrows of life, we feel the need of calling you and of pleading for the protection of your wings, so that we may not be as strangers in the province of joy, all ignorant of the concerns of our country. Remember the weak, you who are strong, you whose home lies beyond the region of thunder, in a land that is always peaceful, always serene and bright with the resplendent glory of God.

1215.23   *Marcus Smith*]   A reader who had written to O'Connor.

1216.8   this one]   "Judgment Day."

1216.15   I . . . myself]   "Parker's Back."

1219.8   Senator Russell]   Senator Richard Russell of Georgia.

CATALOGING INFORMATION

O'Connor, Flannery, 1925–1964.
    Collected works.
    Ed. by Sally Fitzgerald

    (The Library of America ; 39)
I. Title: Wise blood. II. Title: A good man is hard to find.
III. Title: The violent bear it away. IV. Title: Everything that
rises must converge. V. Title: The geranium. VI. Title: Essays.
VII. Title: Letters. VIII. Series.
PS3565.C57   1988   813'.54   87–37829
ISBN 0–940450–37–2 (alk. paper)

For a list of titles in The Library of America, write to:
The Library of America
14 East 60th Street
New York, NY 10022

This book is set in 10 point Linotron Galliard,
a face designed for photocomposition by Matthew Carter
and based on the sixteenth-century face Granjon. The paper
is acid-free Ecusta Nyalite and meets the requirements for perma-
nence of the American National Standards Institute. The binding
material is Brillianta, a 100% woven rayon cloth made by
Van Heek-Scholco Textielfabrieken, Holland. The com-
position is by Haddon Craftsmen, Inc., and The
Clarinda Company. Printing and binding
by R. R. Donnelley & Sons Company.
Designed by Bruce Campbell.